INVIDICUM

OTHER WORKS BY MICHAEL BRODSKY

NOVELS

Detour, 1977 (revised 2003)
Circuits, 1985
Xman, 1987
Dyad, 1989
*** (Three Asterisks), 1994
We Can Report Them, 1999
Lurianics, 2013

FICTION COLLECTIONS

Wedding Feast and Two Novellas, 1981
Project and Other Short Pieces, 1982
X in Paris, 1988
Three Goat Songs, 1991
Southernmost and Other Stories, 1996
Limit Point, 2007

PLAYS

Terrible Sunlight, 1980
Dose Center, 1990
Night of the Chair, 1991
Six Scenes: A Barracks Brawl, 1994
The Anti-Muse, 2000

TRANSLATION

Eleuthéria, by Samuel Beckett, 1995

ESSAYS

"Svevo: The Artist as Analyzand," *Review of Existential Psychology and
      Psychiatry,* vol. 15, No. 2 and 3 (1977), pp. 112–133
"Toward the Plane of the Sacred: Hafftka's Great Chain of Being," in
      Michael Hafftka: A Retrospective—Large Oils, 1985–2003 (Bridgeport,
      Connecticut, Housatonic Museum of Art, 2004)

TRANSLATED WORKS

Der Tatbestand und seine Hülle, translation by Jürg Laederach of the
      story "The Envelope of the Given" in *Project and Other Short Pieces*
      (Frankfurt, Suhrkamp, 1982)

INVIDICUM
a novel by
MICHAEL BRODSKY

Cover art and illustrations
by Michael Hafftka

TOUGH POETS PRESS
ARLINGTON, MASSACHUSETTS

In memoriam:

Charles Sanders Peirce, Emily Dickinson, Thomas Eakins

"Don't you ever stop with your thinking long enough ever to have any feeling Jeff Campbell," said Melanctha a little sadly. "I don't know," said Jeff Campbell slowly, "I don't know Miss Melanctha much about that. No, I don't stop thinking much Miss Melanctha and if I can't ever feel without stopping thinking, I certainly am very much afraid Miss Melanctha that I never will do much with that kind of feeling."

Gertrude Stein, *Three Lives*

"I'll never stoop to onion soup,
And pork and beans are taboo . . ."

Cole Porter, "I'm Gettin' Myself Ready for You"

"The doors are broke."

Hamlet, act IV, sc. V

HAFFTKA   2023

CHAPTER ONE

For Trial Subject One (Martin Eden), a far from perfect day for walking over the Bridge, from Middagh Street to the Amygdala Institute. The silvery rash below mirrors expertly the lability of his own forever-adolescent skin. Adding insult to injury, premature ejaculation of the toothpaste down the drain, with not enough remaining to kill the after-stench of dream-free sleep. Could be taken for an omen but why be lashed to the mainmast of mumbo-jumbo? Such a malevolently sunny morning's been created specifically for men, like One's bullying father, with an obscene zest for life. Yet, like a true snake, it has elected to give its unjustifiable all to somebody like him—purely to taunt said somebody's inhering inability to savor. An injustice, this, very much on the order of, say, Bush-Cheney-RUMPsfeld's toddling off to die entwined in the same bed of roses after having regretlessly sent thousands of kids to their death—in what was once called Mesopotamia, of all places. Beautiful-souled Eden is obliged to concede that the scum is managing yet again to inherit the earth. He tries to saunter up summer-smouldering Essex Street—more of a Grand Boulevard, if you ask me—while at the same time dodging the flip-floppers with their tattooed fedoras and remaining hyper-alert to the one psychotic out of a thousand who might just decide to stab him in the neck simply for staring cross-eyed or refusing to. And with this thought in tow, he is suddenly too weighed down even to limp, much less saunter.

Sits down for a minute in Seward Park—why not? People—people he decrees to be unintentionally sad—deploying their essence no matter what they do whether it's walking, eating breakfast out of aluminum troughlets, talking convincingly to themselves. One office-bound *gal* digging into her tote, looking for what she already knows all too well is there—her selves. A beauty in their aimless walking under the acacias—a certain defensive unawareness of equally aimless prying eyes out to catch essence—haecceity—idiosyncrasy—all right then, mortality (might as well call a spade a spade)—in the act. Here I am—the steps proclaim (all the more beautiful for their graceless plodding)—sure to die and proud of going on in spite of the fact.

He checks the address in his little brown notebook—picked up in Jackson Heights during one of too many self-edificatory jaunts through a city no longer brand new to him—though he knows it by heart. No hope of getting lost and thereby delaying one of too many Moments of Untruth. The shadows pissed by lampposts, parking meters, working stiffs, ginkgo tentacles have an axiomatic clarity. Such would be their shape in a world free of sandbagging contingency. And, hey, isn't that some homeless guy's piss trail migrating toward a sunpatch? And while we're at it isn't *that* a curved-mast post, its sputtering but stalwart bulb coaching (like any press agent worth his salt)—goading—prodding—a plane to parlay the sublime shadow of its trunk into an off-off-off Broadway contract good for, say, two or three chamber plays. But Mr. Trunk clearly has other fish to fry, his vocation of the moment being to defer, compliments of as many as boughs-crippling twists and turns as can be mismanaged, his shameful (because roots-forswearing) ascent into the sky.

Enough, Eden finally barks at whoever—or whatever—is feeding him these conceits, i.e., rebuking him for not coming up with them on his own steam. Who's responsible—the lady rummaging in her tote?

Subject Two (Melanctha Herbert aka Fredi Washington) wonders why it is always the straphangers with already enough trouble making ends meet who must be assaulted by the manhandling panhandlers—while the self-designated rare birds of a feather caged on, say, Upper Fifth, are mercilessly spared. One of them has taken a shine to this particular subway line at this particular time of the morning. Every day he's at his battle station flaunting the three missing fingers of his right hand and every day the sport he professes to coach despite such an affliction changes names, all of which (to make a short story shorter) entitles him to enjoin—that's right, bub, *enjoin,* you heard me right the first time—those lucky enough to be employed, to hurry up and show their gratitude by forking over a little cash or—if there's none, supposedly, to burn—by brandishing a big fat gums-packed smile. Little does he know that for the Melancthas of the world, to smile on demand is an order far too tall to scale.

At Sheridan Square, with which she isn't as familiar as she should be (but didn't Willa write one of her books right around the corner or was it Katherine Anne or Edith or Dreiser?), Melanctha is tempted despite all her hard-won disbeliefs to kneel down in the nearest church and entreat forgiveness for having been the abjectest of parents barring none. But then she remembers to be advised that—that—that—well, that prayers are always answered in the order in which they were received. Hold on for the next available operator.

Tossing his cigarette to inject a little street theater into the hailing of a taxi on Park, Subject Three (John Gabriel Borkman, or MacGabe, as he is known to his victims) wonders whether it is the worst thing of all that may in fact happen: he'll come back cured, but with no prospects to come back *to,* a sorry business at his ripe old middle age. Having himself perpetrated so much outsourcing, maybe his partners will have seen fit to play that good old white-shoe game of Outsource the Outsourcer—to Saturn's rings, say, or some planetesimal yet to be catalogued. He wouldn't put it past them. But they must know he's irreplaceable—the very first of his kind—but what kind is that?—to have recognized that what the super-rich currently crave are nothing less than once-in-a-lifetime experiences (which leave no taxable trace)—not Dark Age tangibles (which have a bad habit of doing the opposite).

Subject Four (Moira Shearer née Allegra Cohen) stretches her legs (once beautiful for what they could invoke) at 110th and Broadway, of all places, just before she boards the M104. A few feet from the kiosk, against the backdrop of Riverside's sylphides looking to all the unseeing world like elms, a low-impact drug deal is being concluded with exemplary tact. She is reminded preposterously hence all too plausibly of the wedding divertissement pas de deux in Mr. B.'s *Midsummer Night's Dream*—specifically the moment (don't make like you don't know the one: there's a fine line, my good man, between the otherworldliness connoted by not knowing a damn thing about the things of the world and dumb-ass brute ignorance) when the ballerina's left hand—Shearer's hand!—is, as if effortlessly, extended backward under her right arm (twice in the piece!) suavely sure of its retrieval by her cavalier. Smiling radiantly (onstage habits die harder than any others) into the stonefaced bus-driver's blue eyes, she inserts her MetroCard in the slot, a little brutally for an ex-prima. Astonishedly (or is it astonishingly) he smiles back, his ticlike overblinking all at once high-priestly and then some, since it reminds her of Balanchine's.

From her window seat, she studies the driver. Look, he's still smiling. Has he recognized her? Is he by any chance a fan of the sanguinic Shearer of *Concerto Barocco, Liebeslieder Waltzes, Apollo, Serenade, Divertimento No.15, Bugaku, Mozartiana, The Four Temperaments* and best of all *La Sonnambula*? Fans are a poison/antidote—a pharmakon!—to which she's still addicted even if, in confirming her talent, they establish its limits and the breadth of its mis-use. They seduce her, the little devils, into surrendering posthumous valida-tion without bound for a fatefully minuscule niche as a "dancer's dancer"—no designation more smarmily detestable—in the overrated here and now. And nothing—or almost nothing—more exhausting than this hunger for the more, more and still more which such encounters leave in their wide wake. Though maybe he's just a guy who, without knowing it, goes for the superannuated gamine type and wants to fuck her—imagine!—its supreme incarnation.

Borkman's soon-to-be ex- has of course been his severest critic: too much merger-and-acquisitions mania and too many morning-after spinoffs. Every new acquisition utilized to narcotize him, or so she insists, to the pain—no, the excruciation—of having to child-rear its predecessor. Until it, too, became a dead weight, his mirror image qua grim reaper. According to the missus, working from inside a core of corporate coherence is self-coincidence and for him, self-coincidence is death—a cancer of unknown origin. Only during the dealmaking process did the teratoma of selfhood go vociferously into remis-sion, and not a minute too soon. Or was it somebody else who'd made that diagnosis?

Subject Five (just Cantor, if you please, maestro: he loathes his first name and the middle one is even worse, or at least no better), thirty-seven-year-old mathematician and HIV-positivist since the mid-nineties, is wary of letting himself in for yet another bout of *rehabilitation*—the word being an especial target of his loathing. A lifer in that department and by no means proud of the fact, he much prefers, to *therapist*, the exquisitely crude *angekok* (Eskimo for *shaman*), so much more manly, primal, enigmatic—in a word, monop-olar—don't you think? Besides, an angekok's body is all eyes. Given his mix of feelings, mostly shades of dread, he decides it would be a good—all right then, a therapeutic—idea to bicycle down to the clinic, or whatever it was, and thereby work off some prejudicial, premonitory steam.

All the way down deeply mournful West End, the air is crisp, even a wee bit chilly—what his father in lighter moments used to call (but what *did* he call it?: they'd always been too much at loggerheads to resort to banter)—though it's far too early for a foretaste of autumn—of . . . of . . . of . . . *Mother nature's fall collection.* Oops! there he goes again, succumbing to the old unstraightness, crookedness, i.e., *gayness* (detestable designation!)—to what that arch busybody cum know-it-all J.P. Sartre, referring to Genet, his favorite JO buddy, called, at least in translation, homosexual archness. He doesn't mind—as long as the foretaste doesn't last too long. But is he as affected by sights and smells—things outside thought—as he would have rumor have it? Is he porous to the world, and therefore real? He never feels real. Not even the diagnosis of Envy disease can quite . . . *realize* him. Yet suddenly the thrill of outpacing everybody around him (and at his age)—no matter what the mode of locomotion—does what several lifetimes' rehab couldn't—it makes the question of realness irrelevant. All that matters is his life's work—proving Hilbert's lemma. Thing is, the exaltation makes him want to laugh (before everybody else starts laughing at his abject failure to do so)—retch—lose his balance. Exaltation always makes him think . . . stupidly. He'll never learn. So what if he has his life's work—his . . . *making* to come home to (just stick it in the mentalist microwave and *voilà!*). No need to get all mock-epical about it. Everybody, after all, is a maker—even if the only thing she ends up making is a big stink or a molehill out of a mountain or a pass or a faux pas or a scene in the men's room.

Thing is, his life's work smells vastly different from everybody else's. For it is competing not just with the work of this or that more productive (because devoutly heterosexual?) colleague, or with his own work (after all, he's already chalked up a few feathers to his untenured cap) or with unrelated activities (like that bereavement trip to San Diego) but with everything else under the sun. Everything under the sun—and the sun itself—contests its primacy. His work, aka his very being, is competing with the Work of one infinitely prolific success-ridden Rival. And to give the lie to whoever insists said Rival gets everything the easy way He has a horde of imbecile detractors all ready and willing to demonstrate that His lucky-stardom is the bruised fruit of titanic struggle. All bases are covered by—for—said Rival. And as if things aren't invidious enough, Cantor's very making is being bludgeoned by the ghost of the process as it would—should—be unfolding, under the baton not of some tone-deaf hack like him but of a bona fide maestro like the Rival, so as to issue, way way ahead of schedule and well under budget, in a pluperfection unscarred by the vulgarity of drafts and redactions and extruded incorrigible and full-blown as from the unwrinkled brow of Zeus. And what about all the things bought in the name of psychic enrichment—like a ballet ticket or a rollerball pen? Acquired, they immediately dwarf the Work—sorry, the work—out of existence. Eat him out of house and home, so to speak. Buying—consuming—he signs the warrant of his own self-deletion.

Thing is, he has this most unMarxist bad habit of wanting to convert— no, transmogrify—doings into things before (long before) they *are* doings. End products are what his kind mightily covets—end products to spare him the wear-and-tear of a beginning. Since when he pretends to be at work he can't quite locate, much less capture himself. He eludes himself. Is he making anything—more to the point, is he himself anything—while in process, with nothing full-blown and incorrigible to show? But isn't having nothing to show, fly-blown or otherwise, precisely the thew and sinew—the very gist—of the making. Isn't all that nothingness what makes doing so much worth doing?

Yet he has the funny feeling that such thoughts are at this very moment being had or are about to be had by somebody else, to whom they belong by much more divine right. And that the somebody else—rather, the Some Body Else—has the very same feeling. Some Body with whose path his is slowly converging . . .

So is there any point in joining this trial? After all, Five's envy (like magic as practiced by Evans-Pritchard's Azande) is so organically woven into the texture of his being (make that the fabric of his tripes) as to be inextricable. Most of all, he envies people who make no bones about harboring stark preferences—A, say, rather than B and C—without feeling in any way disqualified—eroded—ablated—minimized by the severed connection with B and C. But disqualified for what precisely? He likes nothing better than to stew around in the juices of everyday routine as lusciously described by average joes and josephines. What compares with overhearing on public buses—and aren't such revelations (far more obscene than confessions, say, of how shit feels when extruded from the anus with an all-too-rare effortlessness or the penis when penetrating some orifice just a wee bit too deeply) *made* to be overheard? It is the eavesdropper—Cantor—who gives them life. They have no existence otherwise (*but does he really believe they have no existence otherwise or is the wordflow doing the believing for him? or is there a somebody feeding him the wordflow's believing and if so shouldn't that somebody be feeding the wordflow to a more worthy—a more relevant—opponent—somebody else in the trial, say?*). But by the same token, some of those josephines tend to so overstate their case—or rather, so overshriek it—as to put all ambient eavesdroppers, whatever their level of mastery, out of business and make their vocation a thing of the remote past. He likes to hear about what kind of sandwiches they pack for the beach, and where there was a sale on thongs and how many times they intend to see that new film with Meryl Schwartz—why, he positively swills, Sturges style, in the ale of their mediocrity (a term he'd never dream of using pejoratively: how could he when he is not just daunted but intimidated out of his skin by its force?—and this is not—he repeats, is *not*—a populist pose). Their preferences—rather, the depiction of their preferences—is almost edible—no, it *is* edible and knowing a tasty dish when he smelled one, Five invariably helps himself to seconds and—depending on where and when he or they get off—even to thirds and fourths. *His* (oddball) likes, on the other hand—wandering in multistoried shopping malls, watching Lifetime Movie Network soapers—engender disidentity.

Here and now, riding his bike en route to overhaul is giving him the courage to own his preferences. Preferences far more shameful-shameless than the preference for men. The preference for Horton Mall in San Diego, for example. Precepting one summer, he took the bus in from Imperial Beach simply to stand at the highest level and listen to the piped-in "classical" music eternalize the moment. How? By laying bare the non-hearing of each and every bargain hunter. So that filet of Chopin lite, though very much of the mall, became otherworldly by virtue of resolute consumer indifference, hence more poignant than it had any right to be.

On those wonderful, unavowable mall afternoons, the piped-in soundtrack, unheard by everybody else, consumed all other noises. The music embodied the *blindness* of all those buyers and sellers and gawkers for it was music meant to be unheard, and by remaining unheard it became the embodiment of time passing, of lives passing, never to be retrieved. The meaning of the music was its unheeded warning—that all bargain hunters should stop dead in their tracks and take a good hard look at themselves in the mirror of the moment before it was too late for crocodile tears. Just as the meaning of a shot in a Hitchcock movie always lay (*always*?!) not in what was in the frame but in the fact that what was in the frame had been missed by somebody who was looking but not seeing what his professional duty required him to see.

But enough about making and envying, getting and spending. What better time to *take in* the spectacle of men modeling, on runways of sparkling asphalt, the latest crazes? And here's the catch, he thinks: each specimen the least bit desirable seems to be inventing this season's look, on his very own . . . recognizance (wrong word, but just too irresistibly neoclassical to ignore), from scratch, without outside influence—seems to be erecting his very own version of the temple of virility—virility so dour—even dire—as to become a kind of ethical stance. The effect of discounting the obvious—that fashion's just mimicry run wild—is laceration pure and simple. Each time a specimen proclaims his independent invention of The Look, he inflicts a fresh wound. Wasn't it Auden, that prideful old fruit, who said Homosexuality is Envy? Shrugging, and in shrugging almost colliding with a Mack, Cantor decides to let the dictum stand, as he cuts across Fifty-Ninth Street to Third Avenue under the girdership—the tutelage—of the Queensborough Bridge, as a subject for further research.

Borkman sinks into the back seat, the taxi smelling of sweat laced with cat piss—or what he imagines cat piss must smell like after a few days in Midtown. The wife, in the way of wives, holds him responsible for the struggles of the older boy. He tries to establish a special friendship with the cabby (possibly an Arab), because the older boy has been one, and maybe still is. And calling him an Arab makes short work of him—rolls him away on a gurney of diminishment—of obliteration. How useful labels are for cutting everything—especially everybody—down to size—forestalling comprehension until the crack of doom. Is Borkman thinking all this? Are you kidding? He tries to joke about Bush's lordly and heroic assumption of full responsibility for his latest Katrina (abominable conditions at Walter Reed's outpatient outhouses), as if all the blame weren't in fact layable on Boy George's bloodstained doorstep and his alone. The driver doesn't react. This stance, if stance it is, reminds him of the older boy's when Borkman decides to go savagely ironical about his success as a parent (the savagery costs him little since failure at run-of-the-mill things like fatherhood is exalting: proves he's a great man with a great man's flaws). At such times, his son routinely refuses to honor the "brutal honesty" behind the words, professing to take them at face value.

And he, in turn, takes his son's enthusiasm about bartending in a Greenpoint bistro as sheer provocation played for all it's worth and simulated solely to get his goat, since the boy surely knows by now that he's incapable of cheering him on. Correct him if he's wrong, but haven't its victims already deemed Borkman's failure as a father unmodifiable—definitively irrevocable—*once and for all.* It doesn't matter in the least whether he's forgiven or condemned—just as long as that failure can be archived away "for the duration" as a bad joke. But the older boy won't let him off so easy. No matter how roundly the father embraces failure, the son resolutely refuses to play by the rules of disability qua fait accompli. His refusal—his failure!—to give up on Borkman becomes the deadliest provocation of all. How can the boy expect anything from a father who's many a time proclaimed that his real children are his start-ups—his spinoffs—his . . . inversions? Haven't his crimes against nature earned him the right to consider himself horrifically beyond redemption?

Is mockery of his own inadequacy no longer an acceptable bad-joke substitute for fatherly competence? In any case, he's way too old to have to handle a kid who insists on perpetrating, deadpan, the unspeakable good deed of giving him yet another chance. His self-made failure must remain fluid, facultative, reversible—as long, that is, as such charitable leeway has the capacity to enrage the recipient. Borkman is loathsome, true, but not loathsome enough, alas, to have the right to consider himself dishonorably exempted from any hands-on effort—i.e., the pretense thereof—to vacate his suspended sentence.

It has been over a year since the death of Subject Two's only son. True, she's been in pain but maybe not enough to merit that *formal feeling* Amherst's favorite son warbled about so morbid-merrily. Or maybe it's the wrong kind of pain. The boy is dead yet Bush and his gang are very much alive and kicking, each anticipating quite a bidding war for his veteran's guide to waging war by proxy. Stuff happens—but not to the RUMPsfelds of the world. And while we're at it, How could she have ever believed in Kerry who made such wretchedly inept—worse, *cowardly*—use of his hero's credentials? apologizing for his post-combat anti-war stance thirty years before as "over the top"! How could outrage, honestly earned on the battlefield, not be? How forgive such a spineless concession where none was required?

At the corner of Greenwich Avenue and Jane, already stinking of lunchtime garlic, Melanctha looks at her watch and realizes there's plenty of time for a quick takeout from the emporium on what must be Hudson. She rips her number out of the dispenser and, while waiting to be called, admires the steaming delicacies. Her son would have been about the age of the handsome, even noble-looking Hispanic behind the counter, a quiver of fun-loving insolence around the full mouth and flared nostrils.

Amputation of the right arm, including the shoulder, simply because the vest's ceramic plates didn't cover him there. Too little money for armor, while unaccounted-for billions are being handed over to Halliburton and vile Blackwater's Erik the Prince. Followed by amputation of his right leg below the knee compliments of a bomb that exploded in a dead dog. She's pleased there's been a drop in the number of black enlistees. But she must avoid haranguing anybody who'll listen the way she did in the beginning. She'll save her rage for the next Military Families Speak Out meeting, two weeks from tomorrow. Most of all, she has to stop thinking—worse, thinking she has to be thinking—about Building 18.

Come to think of it, she's about the same age as the woman just before her on line who, though she sports a very expensive blouse and a wedding ring as (discreetly) big as Fitzgerald's Ritz, is chatting with the counterman un-class-consciously—even maternally. Things are going along swimmingly in other words, as, per her tactful directions, he packs one container with paella and another with Cajun shrimp and still another with steamed asparagus. And particularly noteworthy is the fact that she trusts him so implicitly that all the while he's busy provisioning she doesn't interrupt his talk about wife and daughter and the upcoming trip to the Dominican Republic. She isn't even watching what he's doing. If you please, the great lady's gaze is on Him the Person as he goes about expertly satisfying the needs of a genial regular. Jorge, she calls him, pronouncing the name correctly. Fact is, Two is quite entranced by their camaraderie. She is already burrowing deep inside its labyrinth. Yet from a subliminal drop in the lady's attention, suddenly she knows the camaderie's a fragile creature, and doesn't want anything to destroy it. After all, it's partly her creation. For a second, she panics on behalf of this Jorge, her son. She dreads the lady's impatience and is convinced if only he had seen fit to allow it, she could have related all the information about the wife and the daughter and Santo Domingo and the stopover in Albuquerque, or is it Santa Fe, long before Milady's boredom, or, worse, her irritation at this menial's presumption, set in. Yet Milady seems to have recaptured her motherliness. It is only when, immediately upgraded to countess, She asks, whimsically, for some of the chicken meatballs parmesan that things start going downhill and the spell is broken—so abruptly that for a moment Two believes it is she herself who, through her intrusive eavesdropping, has broken it. Fact of the matter is he hasn't been packing them quite the way the Countess explicitly indicated or meant to. "I told you," she complains: "a few meatballs then some sauce, then a little garnish, then a few more meatballs, then some more sauce." Clearly, she is no longer interested in Santa Fe, much less in wife and daughter. And so cogent is her irritation, compared with the previous solicitude, that it immediately relegates Jorge and his entire clan, even the family dog (Pepe?), back to the sub-sub-basement of being from which it was most unwise of her to let them emerge unchaperoned. He has lese-majestically soiled her produce, which is now the whole show.

So, Two, whatever she *lavished* (Milady's word) on Jorge turns out to have had nothing to do with genuine interest—she simply enjoyed ladling out a little convivial small talk to one of the otherwise—and rightly—invisible. Will she ever find it in her heart to forgive his half-humanity for leading her astray? Attention eavesdroppers: The only commerce that mattered after all was not that between him and her but the commerce between her and the meatballs, with Jorge the expendable middleman.

The customer has immigrated in medium-to-high dudgeon to the baked-goods section, giving Two the opportunity to say, "That woman was impossible, just impossible." But Jorge, mute, looks unappreciative. He's not ready to stand with her on the wrong side of the tracks, i.e., the right side of the barricades. He forces himself to smile but his flaring nostrils are thinking very different thoughts, at least as far as she's concerned. Does he believe it's useless to try to make her understand that the countess was operating in heuristic "as if" mode? What Two witnessed was how the countess would behave if she were a bitch, which clearly couldn't be further from the truth, since who in her right mind would want to be so straitjacketed beyond appeal? Instead, what she'd given was a master class in odiousness to enable others to learn from her example (heuristic, remember) and refrain. It was all cautionary—designed to inoculate victims and perpetrators alike against outbreaks of the real thing. It was all about Eve and the serpent, poison as remedy, remedy as poison, poison never more poisonous than as remedy, remedy never more remedial than as poison. It was, this little actor's studio presentation (Off-off was already expressing interest), the countess's vehicle for establishing that she was the exact opposite of a bitch—for demonstrating that she knew firsthand, from the gut, the extent of the irreparable injury such bitchery could inflict. Since, pursuant to Bayes' theorem, there was always somebody bound to *turn bitch* in circumstances where meatballs were ladled out and compacted, it might as well be her or somebody like her, who could enact the bitchery as something devoutly to be shunned. To wit, there was no more reliable curator of the unspeakable than the Countess Pharmakon.

Minutes later, Two finds herself out on the pavement, without being able to remember quite how she got there. Simple: excruciation hustled her out of danger—was her mode of locomotion. She's carrying a paper bag with what looks like a bill neatly stapled to its lips, so she must have paid. She needs to get her bearings before ascending the stoop of the Amygdala Institute. She stares: at a bare stuccoed wall. She wants at least one of the pigeons flapping above to mar the whiteness with its shadow. But as the shadow doesn't intervene, she experiences sadness. Yet, with sadness comes the inevitable sensation that the non-intervention has achieved an even bigger, and better, marring.

Subject One, Eden, Envy-free, isn't sure what he feels about being the sole subject entering the trial under false pretenses. He didn't expect to meet up with Mabuse so soon, even if it has already been three years since the old man was laid to rest. Must he remember: When his father, a much-decorated Korean War veteran, was diagnosed with stomach cancer he was chosen to participate in an experimental-drug trial at the Veterans Affairs Medical Center in Carlsbad, north of San Diego (who is providing this circumstantial information, and to whom? he wonders). His stark ineligibility, due to a lymphoma in remission and poor bladder function, was brushed aside as a mere inconvenience. Florid and flatulent, Fritz Mabuse made it clear he was a strong—no, the perfect—candidate—pumping him full of that most toxic of all experimental drugs, hope. Like Eden's father, Mabuse had gotten in through the cracks (which the VA system made as large as possible), inventing medical credentials, conveniently irretrievable, all down the line. *It had all come out in the trial.* As each pencil-pushing stooge obviously assumed he'd been thoroughly vetted at the previous checkpoint, the worm was able to make it through them all without let. And toward the end Pop was hospitalized not because the cancer warranted it but because unbeknownst to anybody Mabuse had enrolled him in another trial, where he ended up receiving, in the six days before his death, no less than seventy-three infusions of Pispordal, a microniche drug for a very rare scrotal malignancy, all compliments of Pharmakon, Inc., the doctor's patron, which was hoping to cash in, following approval, on its off-label use for a much more widespread and potentially profitable condition, iatrogenic depression.

On just another beautiful summer day in downtown San Diego—the kind of day when Martin felt it was nothing less than his civic duty to not just gawk at the deep blue sky but prove worthy of it—Mabuse pleaded guilty to doctoring his father's medical data and to criminally negligent homicide. Eleven months later (same courthouse, different courtroom), he was let off with—what was it?—three years of community service because he'd dutifully blown or promised to blow the whistle on Pharmakon's top crooks. Intent on murder, One followed Mabuse into a bar in Little Italy, maybe (now that he'd seen New York) the world's Littlest Italy, then followed him out, ultimately losing him on India Street. And here he is, Eden thinks, back in the trials business and, armed with a new nose, jaw, hairline, and name: Straynge, once again subsidized by the most respected companies—or, as Pop would have said, *outfits*—in the business.

So, Mabuse MacStraynge has resurfaced and Eden has succeeded in finding him. At long last, he is a smashing success—and at something monumental, if only to him. Though he feels no envy for successes bigger than his. And what success story isn't? Yet he is suddenly very much afraid, here in New York, the city of winners, of being cured of his . . . failure, *armament* and *scepter*—permanently. Who is putting words like armament and scepter in my mouth? Eden wonders. That is, if he could wonder. But take heart, one success does not a Winner make. After all, didn't he vow, many a time (without exactly thinking it—much less, *thinking it through*), under the skirts of the eucalypti on the Coronado public golf course, and anywhere else he could shadily lay his rangy carcass, that even if he managed to do Mabuse in royally, he'd never abandon his arduously earned stance as Failure, as Loser? He will maintain an unrelentingly grateful grip on that stance and if his new stance, of master bounty hunter, refuses to civilly cohabit with the old Eden, then it will simply have to learn, and fast, how to do so. No matter how much in demand he becomes, his allegiance will always be to the failure years. He will never jilt failure at the first delusive sign of success. You have his wordless word on that.

He'll resolutely refuse, blandishments notwithstanding, to look back on those years as constituting nothing more than a now-irrelevant interim. Failure is the best and biggest wonder drug, better than any Mabuse brazenly pumped unmonitored into his father pre-corpse: it has allowed him to make the condescenders, the patronizers, cower. In pretending to chitchat with the better off, a demographic that comprises just about everybody, he in fact compels them to bear witness to a wicked self-dialogue through which he declaims past them to the point where they can't be sure whether it is he or they who are target of a frenzied abasement. They always know, these stooges, that when Eden's around, homicidal hostility can't be far behind only they can't quite locate it or fix its target. As his best teacher (Eden himself!) once said—high above the Pacific in the Santa Barbara cemetery, a few feet from his father's well-tended grave—failure certainly had—has—its privileges. But by getting closer to Straynge he is losing his authority. Things are falling into place too easily, he feels too well-disposed even toward the women whose breasts are tumbling out of their blouses at every streetcorner but who manage nonetheless to look primly affronted at every chops-licking leer, etc. He is becoming too much at home in this, the Boobozoic Era.

Borkman alights in front of the Flatiron Building, even if it has too many unpleasant associations: once upon a time he had a disastrously protracted affair with a blowsily neurotic medical editor whose corner office on the penultimate floor served as site of their trysts. But what neighborhood doesn't have its ghosts clamoring for attention? He needs to walk because he can't help thinking about the older boy's attempt to strangle his mother—or rather, his mother's anxiety—a little over a month ago and he can do so only in the open air. How explain that its rancid upsurge was in the best interest of the victim? With his arms around her tiny throat, he demanded she admit she'd forced him to play tennis in high school, when all he cared about was football, and consequently ruined his life. Both their psychopharmacologist and their lawyer concurred: the boy was dangerous. He was therefore ordered—no, directed—to lie in wait for his son, then call 911. The police would arrive, and forcibly restrained, he'd be taken to the nearest hospital for transfer to Payne Whitney in White Plains.

So Borkman did as he was told for a change: for a master serial acquirer he could be surprisingly passive. He was to wait up for the boy, all night if necessary, so as to catch him in the act of being post-matricidal. Pity for his big blond blue-eyed bounty was strictly optional. He tried the *Journal* but the thought of being caught in the act of shameless absorption in something other than the boy's fate made him toss it aside. On the other hand, he couldn't just sit there making a great show of being gaplessly alert.

He made sure the lighting wasn't too ominous, and that the front door was unlocked. But now that he'd proved to the experts he could set an expert trap, wasn't that enough? He couldn't help feeling that all of this preparation was a mere test of his competence in the abstract. There was to be no exercise of that competence out in the world of troubled sons and hyperanxious mothers. Able to stand it no longer, he went upstairs and called the boy's partner/boss (far more boss than partner), asking if he knew what his employee/co-partner had tried to do to his own mother that very morning. Surprisingly, the partner/boss said yes: he not only knew but had taken the time to extract a promise that such hijinks would never repeat themselves. And the words sounded immune to refutation, not just now but for all time. Though he knew in his old bones that any solid guarantee of the boy's never laying a hand on his mother again, however authoritative, could easily be abrogated. In fact, the guarantee positively cried out for a reprise. And it was deep inside the guarantee's gut that the reprise would get its start. He knew from his own experience in the business world where untarnishable reputations were wiped out in a minute that guarantees came across as airtight only this side of perpetration. Once the deed was done, their futility would prove not only self-evident but, according to tabloid protocol, absolutely necessary. If *Never again!* had become mere genocide-unfriendly boilerplate, what did his little chamber calamity have to hope for? The only convincing calamities were those that had been decreed unplayable by well-informed bystanders.

He'll never forget the self-disgust at his *Invasion of the Body Snatchers*-style betrayal of his son for everybody's greater good which overcame him when he went for the phone as the unsuspecting felon lay sweatily sprawled on his lower bunk bed—exhausted not just from the morning's horror but from his subsequent fourteen-hour stretch on the bistro's wheel of fortune. Fortunately (a tribute to the inability of both doctor and lawyer to get their facts straight), the voice at the other end informed him that if his son was to be apprehended, he would have to be committing an act of violence *while they spoke* (the straitjacket squad didn't just show up at the drop of an incoherent phone call). So the boy will never know what was planned at the behest of the professionally ill-informed. In any case, Borkman can't be accused of envying other parents. He's proud of his boys. His affliction has other fish to fry.

Shearer lets the ever-more-seductive bus driver lift and carry her off, as Sanguinic, into the musty wings of the not-distant-enough past. But it's chilly in the wings so she fast-forwards to the young man (at least he sounded young) of the day before who called up out of the blue to tell her, with a smiling sob in his voice, that she was simply the purest living exponent of the Balanchine aesthetic. She'd just come back after a long walk, ending up as she always did at the marina. She was expecting to hear from her nieces as she sat skimming through her (figurative) scrapbook by the (implied) fire. But it was the Fan she heard from instead. The fact that she didn't know the call awaited her—faithfully expected nothing—and was *as a result* rewarded—dividended—for her resignation moves her to tears of admiration. She looks around. Nobody is interested enough to be mindreading. Irradiated by The Fan's faith she is emboldened to look back on the walk (even if she was unable to live it) without flinching. Because, now, it is not any old walk, but a walk reverentially choreographed on her by Him. If only, wielding the orb of this unexpected validation, she can irradiate everything else in a life ravished by so much self-doubt.

The problem with such calls, as with all drugs, is that they generate a hunger for more. They goose the brain's reward circuits and won't let up (where did she read or hear this?), becoming harbinger and handsel of great things that have been so long withheld. So to hell, I say, with these out-of-the-woodwork specters whose breathless enthusiasm only further disables *the much-martyred limbs of her soul*, to quote somebody's favorite poet. Yet, she not-so-simply cannot control her envy of yesterday's self.

What a lump in the armpit her vocation has been. How vulnerable it has made her, this tumor of striving—how conspicuous, especially now, as a has-been. How public, like a frog. Especially to her nieces, whose professed adoration is by no means incompatible with—in fact comprises pretty much only—excoriation and (the relief of) abandonment. She's come to detest them mightily. The older is kept handsomely by a married corporate lawyer yet, not to be intimidated by self-contradiction, has no trouble thinking of herself as a *radical*—even a radical thinker. There is no self-contradiction here, Shearer suddenly realizes, as she's suddenly realized billions of times before, because in the case of niece No. 1 (call her Annie-Fannie) being kept is purely an experiment—infiltration behind enemy lines to determine what it is the fatcats are intending to seize next. For only somebody who knows how to lay a siege to the fortresses of the super-rich can defend poor innocents against them. Doing exactly the opposite of what she preaches constitutes Annie-Fannie's particular brand of piety. Which makes her even more of a radical. And the truth of the matter is that Shearer, although roundly hating herself for it, has fallen hook, line and sinker for Annie-Fannie's self-contradiction as *the* steppingstone to greatness, or at least contentment, unachievable otherwise, at least not by herself, much less by the almost-anorexic gazelles into whom she inculcates, Tuesdays, Fridays and Saturdays, the ethics of the Balanchine body, the badge of its austerity being the chignon.

As Melanctha Herbert ascends the stairs of the Institute she proclaims: The individual counts for nothing but his anguish encompasses worlds. Will she be required to speak before all the other guinea pigs—of motherhood's impact on Envy, say? But what if Amygdala's unwanted empathizers end up determining her anguish to be very much wanting. This is precisely why she prefers to live her grief in isolation—because she fears that what she undergoes is the furthest thing from grief. Only in isolation, when she is not forced to live by the world's rules, does she begin to feel she is not only grieving but grieving far beyond the call of duty. So whether or not anybody's looking she tries to be, or at least look, *excessively* sad and sorrowful. There is always the hope, through a dutiful disconnection from life as others, and not just white folks, live it, that the response will turn out to be disproportionate to the stimulus. And so for her surplus tears and blood she will be amply dividended—but in terms of what sort of financial instrument? In what sort of currency will her points be redeemed: resurrection of the dead or . . . or . . . vocational triumph? So through all this grieving beyond the call of duty is she (she is!) simply trying to seal a deal with fate?

Borkman stares hard at the skywalk connecting two monoliths: the Metropolitan Life Insurance Company's North Building and the Home Office. Nothing left, however, in the very heart of Borkmanland—where mergers are simply spinoffs waiting in the wings—to connect him and the wife. This morning, as usual, she looked down the too-long dining table past her husband, exalted, also as usual, by the unenviable lucidity of her take on Borkman's trademark self-sabotage (though wasn't self-sabotage double-edged?) and as she dipped the obligatory cracker in her tea (exertion, however minimal, was needed to lend weight to the verdict, don't ask me why—yet), convinced by the tone of his slurp that he heartily agreed to all the terms of that take. And who's to say he didn't? If only she could invoke some meaty defect of her own to reassure herself that he, too, forbore in the face of exploitation and that the glories of unabating martyrdom were not all hers.

Oh, to be able to regress to his first instar, whose hallmark was revelment in the creation of a single company, not purchasing platform after purchasing platform. When did focusing on any one company become unbearable—too much of a straitjacket? As an extension of himself it wasn't worth much because he felt he wasn't worth much, at least that's what his last girlfriend deduced, or was she merely passing on the fortune-cookie wisdom of her rehab man? How did he manage to go from endosurgical and consumer health products (his specialty) to a fatras of boutique hotel chains, electric stun guns, the bad debt of the just-paroled, steel mills, last wills and testaments, etc. Not so suddenly, it turns out to be only in the moment of inversion or takeover or spinoff that he can tolerate the excruciation of living in his own skin. Work on any deal past the very first stage is boondogglery, temporizing, an impediment to frantic pursuit of the next, although he manages to convince himself en route that frantic pursuit is in fact conscientious bywork in the service of the present deal, the apple of his eye. Hey, he never has as many brainstorms about the deal as when he is far from the site of its making, i.e., the site of self-coincidence—in fact the minute he has one he must get as far away as possible to rhapsodize his way out of getting on with the task at hand. In other words, brainstorms are never about the deal at hand: they're already sketching the contours of a new one, to be abandoned in its turn.

One of his mentors always reminded him how you had to live inside the deal as inside an old shoe until it hurt. But it isn't his fault, he wants to cry out, if once a deal is in the works, it automatically turns off all the spigots of receptivity, refuses to accommodate second thoughts, amendments, better ideas. On the way to being done, a deal takes on a life of its own and carried away by its own self-sufficiency, gets too big for its britches, too picky. The deal alienates him and he it, refuses to stretch its sinews—the very sinews he himself has loaned it—so as to let in a little of the fresh air of improvisation. Thereby condemning him, its mastermind, to other deals, future deals, where his new brainstorms, roundly rejected by the deal now itself calling all the shots, might—must—find a home. Any deal is a rejecting spouse, driving him into the arms of another.

Thing is, the rejected elements may very well not be suited to the new deal—or any deal. Maybe it is only exclusion from the domain of the current deal that gives them a certain tragic luster. Hence, he can never rid himself of a sense of burning responsibility for finding these rejects a home. What we have here is The Art of the Deal.

The wife's growing bold in the shadow of his decline. It vouchsafes her a grossly inflated view of the slenderness of the odds against her. But why be appalled? All this misery, old as the matrimonial hills, stems from the fact that the Stranger's pure Otherness always exhilarates, at least at first. The greater the differentness, the more precious the object. To think that one so Other should choose a schmuck like me, etc., etc! The trick, however, is to get enhanced by that differentness faster than it can annihilate—to get complemented by the Other before It can overpower.

Each has fallen short of what the other wanted or, more to the point, thought she/he wanted, which is as it should be—if only out of respect for the divorce lawyers. What he's gotten and what she's gotten is the very disappointment—frustration of their ostensible hopes—they were hoping for since disappointment and the reproach that brings up its rear are what is familiar—disappointment and frustration are all they're equipped for. But don't take their word for it . . .

They're smart enough to know, without knowing they know (*who is speaking for him? he wonders*), that in the marriage maze, you must never get too far away from the very thing you're convinced you don't want to be caught dead with. Because that is the only thing you knew how to *deal* with (*see above*), that is, inveigh against for all you're worth. And if you don't have something to inveigh against, you might as well be dead. He started off wanting a muse for all his mighty mergers. But for him, or rather somebody like him, an anti-muse like the wife is the only conceivable muse: calling her an anti-muse is in fact the highest tribute his kind can pay. Over and over, he craves the nearness of somebody who holds out the promise of a bloody transformation so he can resist that transformation and excoriate the transformer with every faculty and fiber and that has been what he's gotten—in spades.

The wife is the husband's remedy—and vice versa—to the extent that each rejects the other as a poison. Rejection of the remedy is itself the cure. The remedy is a remedy only if it doesn't work—if it isn't dutifully metabolized. If it works then it is a poison which cures the patient by savaging his identity. It's a tricky, a sticky business, this being forever on the verge of ingesting the very pharmakon one wants to spit back into the dispenser's face. He wants, though he doesn't admit it, to be his own muse—his own Phaedrus—a Nero who is both fiddle and flames.

He can only guffaw when he reviews their disingenuous gall in affecting disappointment with each other. After all, they've had their cake and choked on it, too. How many pairs have had as much to show for their failings? For a partner, if you're savvy, you pick somebody who embodies a stance secretly, that is, not-so-secretly, antithetical to your own, who promises rehab—transformation into a better—an ideal—you. Not that he ever had any real intention of going through with rehab: he just needed her near, always near, so he didn't have to feel as if he were abandoning the good—the wholesome—idea of metamorphosing into what he was not: he could have it—the dream of being what he was not—comfortably near. Needed her near to be able to dare her to rehabilitate him faster than he, the terminal patient, could stymie the process through a justified fear of identity rape.

Yes, one day there will be a commodities market for marital dysfunction as there is for gold, grain, water and asteroidal platinum—a futures exchange where bets on whether a marriage dissolves or not, based on the shadow play of its particular dysfunctions, will be lightning-traded like cash—or bitcoin. An authentic futures market replete with shorts, longs, puts, indexes of indexes, shadow derivatives—with credit default swaps indexed to dysfunctions. A market where futures contracts will derive from assessment of dearths, overabundances, absences.

So they went on tormenting each other for refusing to be refashioned, not that he would know what to do with a bedmate who suddenly took into her head to come up to his expectations, or vice versa. Who decided to have the temerity to accept him as he was.

Yet here on West Fourteenth Street (and maybe just because it *was* Fourteenth Street and not, say, East Thirty-fourth or the hefty slice of Houston between Sullivan and Lafayette), he suddenly feels for the soon-to-be ex-something he never dreamed he'd feel. Though without knowing it he distrusts himself for playing the hyperlative card, succumbs to the temptation of saying to that self, Oh, come now! Stop using phrases like *something he'd never felt!* *Only he wasn't talking to his self* but to the being—the maestro—the Thamus (or was it the Theuth)—who's taken it upon himself to dispense his wordflow. But—no matter who was talking to whom—here it was, the real McCoy, the feeling never felt, namely, pity. Maybe he hewed to the path of self-sabotage not because his essence—the Deal—demanded it but out of sheer perversity. Who knows how many steeps of normality—good clean family fun—he could (still?) scale if he only put his mind to it? *Wife:* You mean to tell me that all these years he's been suppressing an appetite—an instinctive talent—for normality out of mere spite? *Prison chaplain:* No, missus, he's simply had a bad habit of being himself.

So why did she pick him? She hadn't marketed her cunt too astutely but never mind about that. Her project was in fact to get her hooks into somebody to whom she could sell the Norm, purged of the unwarranted bad press. Since she knew *in some part of him* he wanted to be just like she wanted the two of them to be. And selling it to him would make her worthy of the product. Since once upon a time, normal men terrified her. They might find her wanting. But she and he would grow normal *together*, building their impregnable dream house, card by card. But they didn't and now here she is getting ready to wed a psychiatrist, all the more normal—super-normal, in fact—to the extent that he loftily withholds judgment on the so many deviations from the norm with which he's confronted daily, bemoaning only in private the triumph of freaks and mutants. Or is this exercise of mock forbearance an exercise *against*—in this case, against those of his colleagues who have taken to riding roughshod over the compassionate conceptualizations of psychic silliness (for lack of a better term) to which he pretends to subscribe? All in the name of busily burnishing their credentials by resurrecting (in a move so *arrière-garde* as to be avant-) the I-call-a-freak-a-freak approach to conversion therapeutics after its undeservedly long exile.

Subject Five, now lord of the West Village, plies the sidestreets in search of the dead, distracted only by the wasps' nest sizzle of the already burned out oak leaves. He crosses the highway and props up his bike against a bollard on the Christopher Street pier, scaring off a seagull by either his proximity, however slender, or the fixity of his gaze. For its pains, the gull is obliterated by the sun, warmer than it should be this time of the morning.

He suddenly catches himself in the act of being so distracted he's actually missed a beat of his usual alertness to any sign of interest, which has certainly made him much more interesting to the two men who, squatting widely apart, are giving him the surprisingly eager eye. Such lapses introduce him to a new Cantor, one he doesn't but would very much like to know, a Cantor buddhistically beyond any ignoble lust-driven eagerness to please.

Should he look away in virile outrage and thereby convince them, and by extension himself, if only for a millisecond, that he is no queer on the midmorning make? Should he allow himself to wallow in the unmitigated triumph of that millisecond's masquerade? He is still playing such games with himself, and after all these years! emboldened, no doubt, by the smell of the pilings. When he turns back—which makes him realize he *did* look away—

both have already lost interest. The dead man, whose code name was Berry Sundae, resembled neither but all of a sudden through untamable fusion they have become his spitting image.

Charles Lane on a sultry July morning, a little like this one, sky clear except for a few off-white dirigibles above the expanding Hoboken skyline. They are lying in bed, but apart, listening to the joyous schoolyard shrieks. It is now Berry Sundae who, nearing death, can't bear to be touched: belated revenge on Subject Five's frequent recoils, on grounds of Creative Despair, during their too few years together. Pain has given him license to be stridently sick of Cantor's all-consuming Envy of anything and everything that is, as logicians so inclined might put it, Not-Cantor. He's been worn down by Cantor's gluttonous goings for his own jugular (Berry Sundae and Sundae's jugular simply don't matter). He's tired of standing helplessly by while Cantor goes about creating a one-to-one correspondence between his own misery and that of the accursed models he has no choice but to revere, in the hope that the effort will yield up a registrable identity.

Cantor has tried many a time to explain the facts of his case to Berry Sundae's body (particularly to the blond hair on the inside of the thighs, surprisingly thick for one with such a smooth chest and belly, and to the oaty bristle accentuating the fullness of the mouth)—a body that gives him no choice but to acknowledge—still reluctantly after all these decades—Despair is my country and the male body is my home town. He agrees with his lover (but what good does that do?) that, mistakenly, he takes his supposed resemblance to one who suffered as he is suffering in life and work and who ultimately triumphed, as a confirmation of his own uniqueness and its ultimate triumph. But similarity automatically bodes abasement: the model in question, call him Ishmael, didn't need a model. He was content to suffer without guarantees. He didn't need a pre-Ishmael to cast the Technicolor shadow of a happy ending over his plight. Cantor, feckless as usual, is trading in his risk-incurring uniqueness for the false security of resemblance to a model. Doesn't he understand it's only in living the irreducible tension of not knowing how he and his misery, to wit, his mission, will turn out, that there lies any hope of indemnification precisely because the tension promises nothing (*or is this just wordflow imposed on him by . . . by . . .?*). Rather, the excruciation of living his uniqueness is so great it drowns out the unquenchable murmur of the promise buried at its heart thereby allowing the promise to do its work undeterred.

He was told to be careful. Testily, he asked about what (his lover was expected to accept this testiness as a sign, i.e., of vulnerability, and the sign as a gift). After he world-famously solved his conjecture or theorem or whatever it was or wasn't, he must ensure that *his* struggle didn't become a paradigm . . . for some disciple. Or some academic blowhard might invoke *his* trek through the continuum as the only one in town, merely because praising it was the fastest way to squash the aspirations of that disciple.

All at once, Subject One knows it is no accident that he now finds himself between Tenth and Eleventh Avenues, in front of her building, a completely revamped tenement. A plaque directly above the griffins-grimy lintel advertises, with the obligatory British accent, 1-2-3 bedroom "condominium residences." Does he have time and if he does is it still too early to drop off her accessories? Suddenly he doesn't want to have them in his possession. He can't decide. Only he knows it's never a question of deciding. The deciding comes after, in the wake of having already decided. But here he is dutifully keeping up the fiction—heart pounding, entrails grinding, bowels loosening—of being still deep in the process of deciding whether or not to surrender.

His addiction, like all addictions worth their salt, is so structured as to make it impossible to *decide* whether or not to give in. This is what vice is all about. Or is it? Where has this mighty pronouncement come from? From within? Or are the words doing the thinking for the two of them, without so much as a curtsy to reality, as he thinks he knows it, lives it? But what body or thing is making the words do the thinking for the two of them? And who is asking this very question? Eden? the body or thing aforementioned? what- or whoever is pulling the strings of that body or thing? And so on in an infinite regression. *Eden thinks (without knowing he thinks it): Oh, let's call the aforementioned body or thing the Master and have done with the matter.* If he could think on the go, Eden would think something along the lines of: An aphorism is the epitaph on an emotion just as an orgasm is the epitaph on an image. My aphorism decrees that addiction is only about the impossibility of deciding whether or not to give in. It's fearless, even in the face of a thousand counterexamples. But shouldn't I know by now that aphorisms grow fat on the carcass of counterexamples—the more cogent the juicier? Shouldn't I know by now that what an aphorism is really all about is making the mountain of a universal truth out of nothing more than the molehill of a local itch? In fact, it's a vengeance on the itch for being local. Or is it? But if Eden could think all this, he wouldn't be Eden. But remember: being unable to think all this doesn't stem from a lack of intelligence. There's more intelligence in such an inability than in all the scribblings of Plato not to mention all the footnotes to Plato excreted by the too many deep thinkers who came after.

After all these years on the boards of addiction he is still prone to stage fright. After so many surrenders (some of them life-threatening), his capacity for shame hasn't lost the youthful bloom of its virulence. His credulity (about the unspeakableness of these vicious surrenders, etc.) still operates at fever pitch. But maybe after the Mabuse job is all said and done, the addiction will vanish. Yet he can't imagine himself addictionless. For the poison of addiction is the only remedy for a despair deeper than addiction, even if at the same time the addiction serves to intensify the despair. How many times hasn't he felt the only thing keeping him from vanquishing it is addiction? He has his father to thank for the despair.

He suddenly discovers that he has been propelled back toward Eighth Avenue (so he can think on the run, after all), away from the lady of the month, and closer to Mabuseland. Although he is still saddled with the guilty accessories—special effects, she calls them (will they ask him to open his burlap messenger bag?)—there is a momentary feeling of having outsmarted his self. He's let that self lead him right up to the doorstep of the tenement but at the very moment it imagined they would enter together, like soused buddies on furlough, he's quick enough on the trigger to ditch his demon (doubled over on the just-swept doorstep in full view of the poker-faced doorman) and disappear into the morning crowd, each figure incised by a burin of light. He is immediately curious about just what he'll do now that he's unshackled, no longer himself, stronger than himself.

Merely by resisting the impulse to dump the special effects in the lady's lap, he is transformed from drudge into man of leisure *à la Veblen*, into a predatory dandy *à la Carlyle* (do those names by any chance ring a bell, Eden?) who isn't afraid to sport incriminating evidence in his buttonhole. He is a man who, repudiating nothing about himself, however disgusting, allows that evidence to remain in his messenger bag—the sort of man who does not flush immediately but allows himself to savor the stench. It's all good clean masturbatory fun.

But then he remembers having awakened with a pimple on his jaw. Under even the very best of circumstances he keeps his distance—and is even more distant at those times when his skin plum forgets he's an adolescent no longer. When he feels *this* disfigured, it's a matter of honor never to commit the most disfiguring gaffe of all, which is to overestimate somebody else's tolerance for disfigurement. Except in the arena of his addiction, where the body's shameless imperfection is aphrodisiac. He has learned only too well—being a superfast learner where humiliation is the teacher—to carefully titrate the level of presumability against the magnitude of his deformity.

So there's a dialectical tension between deformity and self-presentation. Ultimately, deformity is lodged not on his skin but in his gaze, which must always be one step ahead of the Other's inspection, judgment, verdict, repudiation. His gaze, in its lowering penetration, must ensure that the Other's does not have any opportunity to catch him in the act of forgetting he's deformed: his gaze must dare the Other's to catch him in the act of forgetting even for a millisecond that he is disfigured beyond redemption. His gaze must convey at any given moment the fact that he's *already* not only taken into account both the disfigurement and the Other's recoil from its unsightliness but chewed 'em up and spit 'em out in record time. The strategy works! and he ends up feeling far more attractive than when utterly unmarred. Envy of the flawless turns out to be unnecessary.

But talk about shamelessness. Directly above Seventh Avenue, a pair of cumuli, all thighs and buttocks, are engaged in the sort of unspeakable acts that would give pause even to the most seasoned sex-show performers. Fortunately, there are few children in sight and those that are look like they're safely entranced by the pretty shadows roiling the pavement.

So he's not a loser after all. And what's "loser" anyway but just another label affixed to somebody by a somebody else afflicted with an unbearable intimation of his own bad smell? To be handled with punctuational pincers (quotation marks or italics). Being quicker than the next guy on the mudslinging trigger—that's all it took to be a winner. And, by the way, wasn't it Abraham Lincoln (someone is asking him) who insisted that a man's integrity was proportionate to his capacity to italicize labels out of existence?

With shoulders straightened in her very best Joan Crawford manner, Subject Six (Jean Rhys) walks into the coffee shop near the corner of Twenty-

Fourth and Second, of whose fat- and taste-free cranberry walnut muffins she's become frankly fond, and sits down at the unwiped—and probably unwipeable—counter. Her sister's estranged husband insisted on giving her a lift to the Institute on this, the first day of the trial. It's his clout as a consultant that has enabled her to secure the very last slot. She still isn't quite clear about what a consultant does (and maybe he isn't either) but what *is* clear is that he was to the manner born (though no Prince Hamlet, nor was he meant to be). Even if *consultant* appears more and more to be a ship without a rudder—worse, a signifier without a referent. In any case, his self-importance no longer irritates her, or rather she transposes every irritant into the key of desire, which absorbs *her every waking moment* (she likes the urgency of the phrase) but is certain to fade for that very reason. It is already fading, she knows all the signs.

He's assured her over and over that nobody need know she, unlike her fellow probands,[1] will be taking the drug not for Envy disease (from which she suffers only subclinically) but for another disorder. He concedes that Envy provides an easy adit to Food and Drug Administration approval but why, he asks, should Warner-Metro be content, once Invidicum *is* approved, with serving a mere niche market of Envy sufferers, when its potentially biggest star could be used to treat a full range of far more prevalent conditions, albeit off label? She's grateful that he never refers to her condition by name. Thanks to untapped—unsuspected—stores of tact.

So, as the only guinea pig wriggling her way in under false pretenses—inasmuch as, unlike the others, she suffers, according to her consultant, from what is referred to in the industry as an orphan disease (i.e., affecting fewer than 200,000 and incurable)—she's something of a star herself. But at least as far as movies go, isn't it the often nameless peripherals who move her most, drifting into the frame every now and then to give a stir to the lard-laden soup of the protagonist's self-absorption?

He sees her before she sees him, drumming on the table. Problem is, at this moment, consultant or not, he needs to be noticed—to see her face light up with the pleasure of, or at least register, recognition, pleasurable or not. He asks her why she pretended not to see him. She points to her immersion in deep forebodings about being the only impostor on the team. But somehow an immersion that leaves no room for his visibility is as bad as—or worse than—intentional avoidance. He is about to say as much when she reminds him they are going to be late for orientation. "Why Amygdala?" she asks, on their way to his car. "I already told you." "You've told me hundreds of times. But I like hearing you say it." "It's a part of the brain associated with pangs of anxiety."

En route, taking him to task for using his connections at Voracicom, the advertising conglomerate which is handling all the PR for Warner-Metro, to

---

[1]Hereinafter, from time to time, for variety's sake, and for the purpose of giving a ring of authenticity to the goings-on, the term *proband* or maybe even *propositus* will be standing in, probably incorrectly, for "trial subject," "guinea pig" and the like.

get her said last slot, he replies as he's already done, also hundreds of times, that if she thinks he's somehow fleecing the company then he must agree. But as far as he's concerned every company man has an ethical obligation to fleece the hand that feeds him. This shows he takes the company seriously—that he's an ideal worker, since his private life, kept alive by perks, belongs more to the company than to him. If he isn't interested in everything the company has to offer, why should anybody else be? He remembers her hand around the coffee cup: hadn't the instruction sheet said something about avoiding caffeine for at least twelve hours or so before check-in? She didn't take a single sip, she assures him. She is holding the cup at a rakish angle for effect.

"And by the way," he adds, incited by the surprising tenderness in her tone, "if things go according to plan and why shouldn't they? we're thinking of building an entire cable TV show around Invidicum, starting off with a dozen or so mini-episodes on the Web. It will be all about a suburban haus-frau completely immobilized by Envy of her beautiful and excessively compe-tent neighbor a couple of doors down the drive. But don't breathe a word of this" (she shrugs: whom is she likely to breathe a word to?). "Yes, I know what you must be thinking but, let's face it, profitability is no longer a contingency external to any product's core." She thinks of protesting. Then she remembers that for him—or rather, the likes of him—the world's poor, for example, are but a well-deserved pox on themselves and reducible to nothing more than a category of thought teeming with self-serving paradoxes.

Straynge, né Mabuse, examines himself in the mirror. Post-middle age has never looked so good, so . . . dashing. The maid, an illegal, but (hence?) deferential and hardworking to a fault, is wielding the vacuum cleaner down the hall, not quite drowning out the birds or his wife's last-minute instructions about which parts of the house are, under no circumstances, to be overlooked. Another trial: another feather in the fakir's cap: another horde of hopefuls in various stages of advanced psychic distress. Understandably, because Envy, as everybody knows, is a killer syndrome—currently assuming pandemic pro-portions—its victims worthy of moat-encircled quarantine.

He now prepares to do what he always does after a hearty breakfast, which is to log on to the Internet (user name: Straynger than Fiction; pass-word: POSTERITY2020) and google himself silly. But his wife looms, as is often the case, very much in the way. From the sound of her voice it's clear she's once again having second thoughts about leaving the maid unsupervised and it's all he can do to keep from wrapping that unwieldy python around both their necks and the neck of anybody else who dares to stand between him and his remedial poison.

If she doesn't leave with that shopping cart of hers this very minute, so help me God I'll kill her, he self-says through gritted teeth. Still he knows that somewhere deep inside him slumbers the strength to perceive this tug of war between his need and her delay from an angle that, albeit only slightly differ-ent, will render the whole state of affairs uproarious. Just a slight shift in the position of his chair and all the pent-up comic potential will be unleashed—a promised land of smiles is just a parallactic hop, skip and a jump away. Eyeing the vacuum cleaner (going full blast) on the landing through his half-open study door, he wonders whether moving a little more to its right will do the trick. Thing is, in his present state of duress, the required shift will be equivalent to swimming the Channel. So he is doomed to go on seeing things from one humorless angle only, that of his strangled thirst for an update on his virtual status.

Yet strange to say, when, finally, from behind the curtain of the big bow window, he sees the wife, descending at last the steep slope down to the village, cart in tow, he undergoes a what-do-I-do-now sort of conversion. He is realizing what any addict worth his grain of salt comes to realize—namely, that the essence of addiction is form, not content (content is ex post facto) and all addictions have the same form. Addiction is practiced not for the prize at the end of the tunnel but for the tunneling itself—shamelessly clandestine and thrilled by the dread of exposure—which transforms everything that is not the tunneling into an obstacle. Or is this just the wordflow taking him where thinking doesn't necessarily want to tread?

And to think that this morning the googling was to be different—an inspection from afar of a foreign country—home to the googler he no longer was. Cured of the need to assess his status online (cure coinciding magically with the start of the trial)—or so he believed while dressing—he intended today's self-googling to be different—to constitute research on behalf of the addicts he'd soon be treating—he was out to discover what in the world could have led a normal healthy healthily aging red-blooded American male to engage in such a life-or-death pastime.

He hits "Enter." Typically, far more references to him than to his namesakes, a brigadier general and a balletmaster: good. But still not enough. So how can he be sure his authorized hack hagiographer will have enough documentation to make a case for him? But isn't it precisely loose ends that hacks pray for as they go about refining their warts-are-all approach? The sloppiest of archivists, life—his life—by virtue of her very sloppiness creates a future for the hacks. The hectic speculation generated by conflicting or, better yet, by a total absence of testimony will only serve to exalt him.

And why shouldn't he be exalted since he's already well on his way to proving that Envy is not a botched soufflé whipped up to justify the marketing of a new drug but a bona fide on the order of, say, Creutzfeldt-Jakob or Huntington's disease and as such, it deserves a place in the *Diagnostic and Statistical Manual of Mental Disorders*—but, heaven forbid, not in the Not Otherwise Specified or Provisional Diagnostic Category. Envy, after all, isn't some lifestyle issue like premature ejaculation. Funny (though immune to belly laughs, he feels one—or rather a bad imitation of one—coming on): Here's Envy just champing at the bit to get into the *Manual* while it's not-so-strange bedfellows—like homosexuality, nymphomania and frigidity in days of yore—are champing, bit or no bit, to get out.

At a time like this (though what makes this different from any other time?) Post, Warner-Metro's Chief Executive Director of Drug Development and Executive Vice-President for Clinical Research, Experiential Marketing and General Regulatory Affairs, suspects that his too many titles cloud his judgment—cataract his mind's eye. He doubts more and more whether

Straynge will deliver the goods but doesn't know what to do with his doubts. Putting them into cold storage is out of the question.

But will it be his fault if Straynge falls flat on his pasty face? What if Invidicum has been kept far too long in The Pipeline? What if the formula has been tampered with too many times, reflecting not the trajectory of the research itself but rather not necessarily inevitable internal conflicts? What if every step of the drug's development has been marked—marred—by and at the mercy of this or that star researcher's quirky delusions? What if the drug is the mere repository of all the negative affects—not least among them Envy—unleashed in the process of coming up and out with a blockbuster to end all blockbusters? To think that Envy itself might be built into the very structure of a drug designed to combat Envy! And if so, is that a good thing and if so, from what perspective—profit or cure? There have been so many cooks moiling the broth. And maybe each has been interested in proving only one thing, namely, that he's been hyperactively virtuosic far beyond the call of duty during the time allotted for his cameo—so what if this hyperactivity has been at loggerheads with ensuring the efficacy of the final product? Maybe Invidicum in its present form, ostensibly ready for testing, is not a real drug at all, just a sum of disjunct inputs, and its identity deformed beyond recognition compliments of pipeline vicissitudes. Maybe it's the victim of identity theft which in this case began long before it could lay claim to anything remotely resembling an identity—that overrated body organ. Maybe it was right from the start that refinement of form and function for the good of Invidicum's target population took a back seat to manipulation undertaken merely to, say, put an overweening rival in his place.

In any event, he can't help believing that the project has been doomed from the start because of the hush-hush fixation on the off-label—the marginal—the peripheral use of the drug, the to-be-approved use understood to be a mere supplement, an excrescence, an unsightly wart on the body pharmacologic. Still, he's rooting for this sleight-of-hand to succeed handsomely. Not because of the sums involved: he just likes to see something central getting, by being shunted to the sidelines, its comeuppance for the sheer presumption of being central. But if Straynge gets in the way of the drug's being approved—if the drug's on-label efficacy is played down by that quack through his megalomaniacal insistence on the far greater efficacy of his very own brand of talk-a-blue-streak therapy—if on-label use can't get its foot in the door, then how will off- make them a mint?

In addition, should the new crowd be alerted (on their consent form, say) to the fact that, based on experiments on death-row inmates and the terminally ill, not to mention (*Be serious, Post!* he warns himself, to no avail) rodents, gibbons, cassowaries and the like, a side effect of Invidicum has already been discovered which (the way things looked) may turn out to be the most alarming of an already impressive lot. (This is what happens when models are chosen simply because phenotypic features reflect genotype, but it's so much muddy water under the bridge.) The side effect in question, he mourns, is the transformation of "inarticulate pangs" into ungovernable eloquence. No evolution, no latency period, no luxurious dormancy. Just a mammoth transformation even after a single dose, with the natural reaction being to fight against impregnation—straitjacketing—by that generic form of eloquence, which prevents the sufferer from earning the hard way his own form of idiosyncrasy.

Cook zips himself up—but not before casting a proud paternal eye, mixed with anxiety, on his impressive organ. He's doing the zipping in Voracicom's thirty-second floor executive men's room, which, come to think of it, is not much of an improvement over the one on fifteen, where he slaved zestfully before his promotion. But there'd be no surplus value if it *was* much of an improvement, he thinks, with a dim suspicion he's thinking like a storyteller, of all things—*or that some inner . . . Iago is entertaining that suspicion for him.* Is it he who was having this thought or Some . . . Body else—or are the parasitic words themselves having the thought through him, their vector? Can he really believe in what he is thinking or does he have to, for the thought to be true? He is looking forward to meeting the rest of the Subjects: some of his most satisfying x-night stands have been with the members of this tribe. The ballerina, undeniably intriguing (or why would he pick her up off the pavement in the first place and try to sell her, successfully as it turned out, on the Envy trial?), is much too old for him, though he wouldn't mind having a crack at her just once. Fact is, he envies every tribe its disease. For to be chosen by a particular disease is an honor—a conferral of realness—ID restitution (i.e., restitution of what one never possessed) in the grandest manner. So, that is why on his deathbed, Cook's ornery old coot of a father was so forgiving of his victims. He was ecstatically grateful to the brain tumor for identifying him. *Identitied* at last. What was that lifelong type A ruthlessness but vengeance on a world that never took the trouble to indicate whether or not he was real. I.e., a man without a disease is a man without a country. *But who is speaking?* Such a thought is simply not appropriate to a meat-and-potatoes kind of guy, as he knows better than anybody though he may not necessarily know that he knows.

CHAPTER TWO

Should I be pleased by these jokers or not, Straynge wonders, as he looks around the chilly windowless second-floor meeting room? Far too early to say. A few look like they could be doomsters, for whom constitutionally he has no patience. It's the *male* Cassandras, oddly enough, who are generally the worst of the lot. Once they are seated, he mounts the podium, takes a deep breath and, adjusting the lectern (he doesn't need to but this tired bit of stage business invariably breaks the ice), says he strongly recommends they attend the introductory lecture on Envy in the newly refurbished Veblen Amphitheater. Just because they are all sufferers doesn't mean they know the first thing about the disease. They're too close. "Trying to understand Envy would be like trying to swallow your own teeth," he adds. "So go—if only to admire the amphitheater's architecture (ca. 1874) with its groined vaults, modillions, balusters and skylights galore. You'd better hurry: Cook and Narr" (Subject Six's consultant) "hate latecomers."

The lecture will make it clear to them just how far researchers, after confusing its mechanisms for so long with those of other conditions, have come in their understanding of Envy. A definitive diagnosis is on the very tip of the profession's collective tongue. But never fear, the lecture will make it equally clear, alas, how far they still have to go. The case histories being messengered down from the publications department at Voracicom ("Has it arrived?" he bellows to the obligatorily fat-assed security guard marking time near the door.) will make them realize they are not as alone as their anguish may lead them to imagine. He adds that several celebrities suffer from the disease and they are bound to run into at least some of them.

Subject Five (Cantor) immediately wants to explain that feeling very much alone is by no means the worst plight a sufferer—or anybody else with some self-respect for that matter—can endure. Raising his hand, he is reluctantly acknowledged by Straynge who has turned (reflexively?) to the security guard. Is he about to draw his weapon, Cantor wonders. Turning so as to be able to address the largest number of audience members he explains that there are several states of affairs where misery—if he isn't mistaken and he rarely is in this department—most definitely does not love company. In fact, it wants nothing better than to be left alone with its uniqueness or at least with the delusion of its uniqueness. Since literally—or at least figuratively—anything is possible with a unique, never-before-seen affliction—even cure. Whereas among hordes of unwanted comrades with the same affliction, there has to be at least one—or ten million—to confirm what he for one already knows better than his own name, to wit, that any life is short enough to endure even the most excruciating bad luck but not necessarily long enough to make the bad luck so cumulatively excruciating that, by a law of Boolean logic yet to be proved, it simply has to turn to good. Who dares to suggest that excruciation ever comes with an expiration date? The demiurges that rule the miserable's roost will always win in a war of attrition. In short, when it comes to being buried alive, he and his kind prefer a crypt for one and when it comes to eating shit, the majority prefer to take their dinner in solitary.

All Straynge can say—stupidly, Five thinks—is, "What I mean is—just hold on to your dream." The very attractive young man whom Cantor studied in the lobby—attractive despite a skin which looks like it may erupt at any moment—jack-in-the-boxes before Cantor is seated (several times already, One's gaze has collided with Mabuse's: blissfully, no sign of recognition) and hazards a guess that in the doc's line of work dreamers must be a dime a dozen. Eden goes on to explain that in his view, the hold-on-to-your-dream business isn't at all about us dreamers but rather about their coach's heroic tolerance for self-delusion in all its flavors. Except for the first speaker, an obvious fruitcake who seems pleased as punch that his declassified ad for a beefy brother-in-arms has been answered so promptly, the others are too stunned to react. This is because, Straynge assures himself, they are nice normal well-behaved little neurotics, nothing fancy, only too eager to put themselves in the hands of an expert. But the little pit bull isn't giving up (he looks vaguely familiar). What ever happened to the absolute dolls of the good old days—the double-mastectomy gals, for example, who, terrified of being shunned, adoringly hung on his every word about how best to lure hubby back into their warped bodies.

And yet by what is clearly a stroke of demi-genius (and more than a few of his colleagues would grudgingly concur), he manages to stifle all signs of combativeness, since having the last word is surely not what matters here. Any fool can be all-knowing. He is lordly enough to be willing to make a big show of learning from one of his lackeys even about what he knows isn't in the least worth knowing. Trouble is the pit bull is still at it, acting almost as if he knows him from somewhere. His predecessor (whose brain seems never to stop doing algorithmic somersaults) may turn out to be a problem as well: he's obviously (for all the smooth talk) chock-full of Scheleresque *ressentiment*.

Cook and Rhys's consultant Narr giggle manfully, as if standing together on the same podium is a joke too obvious to explain. Cook is even more self-assured than Moira remembers him as being at their first meeting—in that downscale supermarket on Second Avenue, of all places. By way of introduction, he announces that every researcher before Post who set his sights on solving the enigma that is Envy Disease always made the mistake of modeling its mechanism on that of some more respectable disorder, like schizophrenia, narcolepsy, Waldenstrom's macroglobulinemia, schistosomiasis, lupus or Jansky-Bielschowsky disease. Hearing this, Cantor gets a little hot around the collar.

As if Envy Disease cannot exist as a bona fide clinical entity in its own right. Narr nods as if entranced—exactly the way Hillary does, Borkman realizes, when Bill stumps her praises out in the heartland. "Why, it sounds as if all those pre-Posters," somebody cries out, "were infected with the very symptoms on which they were trying to get a handle." "He's absolutely right," Narr barks, suggesting, to Two at least, that this town crier is a plant. "Instead of feeling grateful—and proud—when they discovered any feature that rendered EnVD radically different from, say, Lou Gehrig's disease or impetigo, they beat their breast, the very originality of the feature disqualifying EnVD, in their eyes, for further consideration. Which is not to say, of course, that they were any happier when they uncovered a feature identical to one peculiar to some model."

The presentation gets much more interesting, for Borkman at least—that is, exculpatory but at the same time unmanning—when Narr or is it Cook suggests that there may be a genetic basis (loss of a tiny snippet, containing at least twenty-five genes, from one of the two copies of chromosome 9) for this crippling tendency to convert anything that moves into the deadliest of rivals, or that an intestinal parasite may be at the root of it all, or that Envy may be a classic autoimmune disease triggered by environmental toxins, or that (saving the best for last) Envy itself may be a drug which, like heroin and cocaine, throws the brain's reward circuitry devastatingly out of kilter, and whose methadone is—Invidicum. However, parasites or no parasites, everybody is to get a shot at sticking his shrunken head into the coffin of the functional M.R.I. scanner where, at the very moment she is viewing images of an arch rival (accompanied by a voiceover refusing to spare the gruesome details of that overachieving rival's acclaim), her even more gruesome brain activity will be analyzed. Dosages will be adjusted on the basis of the results.

The presentation ends. They are requested to pick up their orientation packet (containing meaty insights from Aristotle, Francis Bacon, Dante, Robert Burton, Spinoza, David Hume, Tocqueville, Charles V. Alkan, Nietzsche, Max Scheler, Thorsten Veblen, Clyde Kluckhohn, E. E. Evans-Pritchard and René Girard, among others) at the hospitality desk and to be back for their first dose after (a caffeine-free) lunch.

Eden needs a walk out in the sunshine: the presentation was deadly. He decides to reward himself for holding up so well under the shock of seeing Straynge again by conducting a study of all the pretty girls (and some are more than just pretty) on Greenwich Avenue, specifically of breasts flaunted ever so coyly. He doesn't flinch when their coyness turns to contempt or even outrage. The mating dance makes such simulations obligatory. He wonders, but not idly, whether a blood specimen will be required and if so, whether he'll have to endure the obligatory (and in his case often fruitless) vein-hunting of some medical student or nurse's aide. As he waits for the light to change, Eden senses the misery-doesn't-necessarily-love-company man right beside him, holding a little white bag with the grease, maybe from a doughnut or danish, oozing through. "Straynge is insufferable, don't you think?" As they cross, he experiences a fatigue so intense it just might be a good idea to lie down in the middle of Sixth Avenue and stage a sit-in, though on behalf of what? For it has immediately become clear that misery man—"I'm subject Five," he says, extending his surprisingly warm hand (why surprisingly?), which Eden clasps—wants to be joined in a little grumbling match. But Eden feels lordly indifference, almost disgust, at the plaint of this little egghead—though in fact he isn't little at all, must be at least four inches taller (*and if he weren't* [Some Body's—Some . . . Thing's—wordflow is telling him], *how could the story hold its head high?*). But Eden is suddenly afraid—must try at all costs to mask that indifference. His disgust is immediately overwhelmed by fear of what the other must think of him if he doesn't share the discontent that is very—too— much there for the sharing. Not the other's grumbling but his own refusal to

grumble will turn out to be the scandal at the heart of this budding relationship. The refusal, worse, the inability, to grumble—to jump eagerly enough
into the warm bath of grievance—to wax plausibly indignant and thereby
appease this heckler—will make him, Subject One, conspicuous enough to be
nabbable as Straynge's assassin—worse, much worse, as Straynge's asslicking
lackey. But how can he wax indignant at a flaw as trivial as Straynge's blubbering lecternside manner after what he's already endured at the hands of this
monster in his post-WWI Mabuse days? Still, wax he must or go under. He
doesn't want to be looked on with contempt by Five who might just decide to
disseminate his contempt among the rest of the tribe. He manages to mutter/
murmur/mumble something along the lines of "right, insufferable, got to go"
and, having done so, is now entitled to dash off into the wilds of Eighth
Street.

As they descend the steps and advance toward Seventh Avenue, Moira
Shearer (Subject Four) wonders if it's such a good idea to have lunch with subject Two (the Herbert woman). Every time she begins to speak, the other takes
this as her cue to look off into the crowd as if in search of somebody *who's late.*
Shearer immediately feels—or is manipulated handily to feel (but by whom?
or more to the point, by what?)—that *who's later than usual* would be an
improvement(?) but can't imagine how, and, more importantly, how it could
be visualized differently from who's late. Although maybe that's precisely why
she's drawn to her improvement—it seems more precise but in this case, the
precision's an illusion—simply untranslatable from the . . . page to the world
out there—it's airtight against visibility, actability. A trap set by words acting
in cahoots. Beware words acting in cahoots, she tells herself, although she's
never paid much attention to words, in cahoots or otherwise. She's a dancer,
remember. This injunction has been foisted off on the wrong tribe member. So, Shearer hears not so much her own voice as Herbert's non-hearing,
which convicts its incipient babble of self-importance. Then all of a sudden
the other turns to her (though—such is the brutality of the movement—it
feels more like being turned on or against) and asks if she knows of a place
nearby. Shearer remembers a Thai hole-in-the-wall on Ninth Avenue, which
in the old days was considered off the beaten track. But nowadays is anything
(except, maybe, Ryders or Mechanics Alley) off the beaten track? In any event,
it's the only Thai joint, as far as she knows, that mitigates the impact of the bill
with a fortune cookie or two.

Once they're seated Shearer hears that last year her son returned from
Falluja to die at Walter Reed (arriving at Dover in *dead of night*—to keep the
press, muzzled anyway, from informing the public about just how bad things
really were). All because Bush and his dream team didn't see fit to ensure
ceramic plates covered the area ripped to shreds. And yes, in answer to the
question she hasn't asked, he ended his days at notorious Building 18, but long
before the *Washington Post* decided it might be good business to blow the
whistle on the cockroaches, the snotty mold, the ceiling holes, the rats and the
rat feces, the shredded carpets, the clogged pipes with no hot water for days,
and the urine-stained mattresses, not to mention the triple amputees forced
to pull foyer guard duty in the middle of the night then show up promptly for

7 a.m. formation. Sleep-deprived she tried to strangle one of the caseworkers simply because he was the kindest man there—even bought roach bombs and a new mattress and pillow for her son out of pocket. Adding insult to injury or vice versa, her son's roommate was discharged from the psychiatric ward with all his paranoid delusions intact and found not long after—on New Year's morning, to be exact—dead of alcohol poisoning in the men's room of the Mologne House lobby (his mother tried to slit her wrists and almost succeeded). But what did these Hispanics matter? In fact, he so dreaded sharing a sty that the other's death came as a relief. Could you blame him? He had enough to do—among too many other things—shutting out the ambulances blaring down Georgia Avenue at 4 a.m. and, when they were silent, the patter of the drug dealers outside the Red Cross building; sidestepping the incompetent half-blind platoon sergeant who hated his guts on general (or maybe just racial) principles; finding (so as to get a new uniform: the one he'd been wearing for a month was bloody and stank of sweat and urine) a halfway-decent photo to prove to some sneering clerk, who couldn't find one of the twenty-four forms he'd already filled out, that yes, he'd actually served in Iraq; and hobbling across Georgia Avenue in the drizzling snow to get a cracked molar attended to.

When the filth—not his suffering!—became too intolerable, she did the unspeakable: rented a room in a near-fancy Adams-Morgan motel with the obligatory heart-shaped indoor pool. And one afternoon (maybe at the very moment her son chose to give up the ghost), the obligatory pink pig of a youngish white man (sorry for the slur) shouted across the water to what sounded like his girlfriend (stretched out in her chaise longue) something to the effect that, after exhaustive soul-searching at a private-equity pow wow the night before, he and his "buddies" were assaulted, in an A+-list sports bar no less, by a self-proclaimed bombshell who had no trouble disgusting them all in record time. And after he succeeded in making Subject Two feel it was not so much the bombshell under indictment as she herself (by virtue of eavesdropping)—well, then, it was time to claim (by divine right of eloquence non pareil) formal ownership of a pool that was de facto already his. And while all this was going on she felt it was only right and proper to depict her own shamelessness—to document her rottenness as a form of proleptic expiation for being unable to grieve once the inevitable inevitably happened—by charting the essential details: the checkerboard shadow under the girlfriend's chaise longue, the postcard-writing middle-aged fellow black lady (song sounds blaring through her earphones), etc. Proof that she was here when she should have been in Building 18. But the splashing fat man kept getting in the way. Until she suddenly realized (or, more accurately, Some Body suddenly realized through her) that she could go on collecting details forever and still not get any closer to conveying the excruciation—as well as the delight (yes, the delight!)—impregnating those fugitive-from-justice moments. And that it was in fact the fat man who was the best teacher around, being *more pool—more poolside*—than any mere detail she could extract from the event. Only things that get in the way sketch an event. Thing is, she has always thought the telling detail, the god-inhabited detail, is something you go out looking for joylessly—the quality of the quarry in direct proportion to the joylessness of the hunt—and that what comes over her like an unsolicited tidal wave (e.g., the fat man's arioso in the oh-so-very-minor key of fat complacency) has to be trashed as at once too easy and too uncontoured to be manageable. It is thanks to him, her nemesis, her obstruction, that poolside life came alive. Thanks to him there is a pool and if there's a pool then there's a poolside and if there's a poolside then there's (her) truancy from Building 18 and if there's truancy, then there has to be a Building 18 to be truant *from*. Building 18 and poolside are inextricably bound. One can't exist without the other. *Though at the same time she can't help feeling* (well of course she can but the words are out of her mouth long before she can adjust them to circumstances: a recurring problem) *she's being primed to be somebody's else's eyes and ears—cued to take notes for that Some Body*—notes that have nothing to with the flagrancy of her maternal inadequacy. She is the vehicle of his aggrandizement—the means of getting him and his vocation, whatever that happens to be, into the act. Or should she abase herself by calling him Him? Oh, why not call him the Master—in the Dickensonian and Peircean sense—and have done with it? A Master to be overthrown at the termination of her tenure—as byproduct of His will to consolidate and paraphrase—date to be determined by circumstance. She'll turn the tables on him, make him wear his rue—rue his rue—with a difference.

No matter what she does, she can't grieve—can't *shit grief.* So she perpetrates what she always—sometimes—rarely—perpetrates: invokes those favorite lines in what's suddenly her favorite poem of all time by somebody who's, even more suddenly, her favorite poet:

> And the hapless Soldiers sigh
> Runs in blood down Palace walls

And even more suddenly, she doesn't have to grieve—better yet, worry about whether she grieves or not. For Blake does the grieving for her—graciously—without judgment. And it follows, as the night the day, that she must invoke in spite of herself even better lines, compliments of London's anastomosing (*yep*, anastomosing, *Melanctha*) nightmare alleys. Lines, she has a hunch, that would—will—be more usefully applied to somebody else's plight (applied like a salve that kills—a caustic that suffocates—a pharmakon!)—the plight of some other wretched state member—Borkman?—of the Envious Tribe to Be:

> But most thro' midnight streets I hear
> How the youthful Harlots curse
> Blasts the new-born Infants tear
> And blights with plagues the *Marriage hearse.*

What a lovely-terrible phrase! a dreamworks condensation—a carry-on portmanteau—that the Viennese witch doctor might—should—have envied. So the poem has something for everyone. Everyone, thanks to her—and

Blake's—generosity—will be able to get into the act. For, let's face it, the poem's a *shabti*, who'll be only too happy to take over the most unpleasant tasks now that they're all dead. For cure—or incurability—are just two sides of the same coin known as Death. Or is this just a case of ineluctable wordflow getting into the act—another example of the shoptalk of an amateur masquerading, thanks to the flow, as think-tank prophet? She's tempted to ask Shearer what she thinks but resists.

Shearer listens attentively—and listens good—hanging on, as it were, for dear life—as always, in fact. But also *as always*, when it is a question of somebody else's excruciation, she can't help turning off the spigots of belief. The hard-luck story is simply a booby trap for her credulity. The storyteller is providing the wrong details. With the right ones, she may be able to start believing. There should be more about the wrong kind of armor, the deadly snipers, the surgeons at Landstuhl, the rancid holiday fare in 18. Much more will be needed to make it all plausible. Who can blame her for hesitating (*who is speaking?*): the very invisibility of the minuscule portion of the population shouldering this wretched war—the hearty dishonored expendables whose hero's welcome will consist in a hearty swindle by the savings-and-loan brigade and an interminable wait for sub-substandard treatment at the nearest VA (which may be hundreds of miles away)—their invisibility turns them into impostors. There are simply far too few for there to be any at all. They're just hypothetical cases in point—infotaining constructions worthy of the Brothers Grimm.

Shearer tries to focus but as it becomes clearer and clearer that the beautiful boy has suffered and died for nothing whatsoever, she decides she has no choice but to became, well, sceptical. After all, it isn't as if the details have been scrupulously vetted by, say, *Frontline*. They don't have the right credentials—yet. Subject Two is practicing—a scam, that's what it is, designed to put her credulity to the test, to stretch it to the breaking point. But at least she's an impartial equal-opportunity sceptic: didn't she apply the same rigorous criteria to her own sorry plight when she heard herself dutifully babbling about it (throwing in a few plugs for Mr. B.) to the intake interviewer earlier today? It will be so much easier for Shearer to believe once Herbert agrees to take her woe public on CNN. But here and now, she's being unfairly subpoenaed to believe without *mediation*—by the media. Herbert's no fool. She senses the scepticism. But long ago she realized scepticism is built into every human mechanism. The human cogs in the wheel of fortune (and she's no exception even if she *knows* she's no exception) are trained—obliged (if, that is, they know what natural selection knows is good for them) to doubt—to build, upon inherent self-doubt, castles in the air of the shakiest selfness.

It's because she herself is all washed up that she can't believe in the woman's story. But is she? isn't the feeling of being washed up a mere epiphenomenon—an artifact—of time (a little past noon) and place (this trendy joint which she loathed the minute she laid eyes on it)? She's all washed up only in the immediate context. The other smells her disbelief, which is growing—she can smell the reactive smell of distaste. So she does what she always does when faced with such distaste—especially when it's coming from somebody who's unabashedly in love with herself (although this appears *not* to be Two's case). She starts asking the sure-fire defanging questions appropriate to the situation at hand. What is her son's name, again? what does—did—he look like? where did Herbert grow up? is she in fact a budding . . . writer? In most cases, rancor or mad-bull envy—sorry, Envy—dissolves like snowflakes in the sunshot struggle to remember. The importance of remembering what makes one unique is immediately much greater than that of ensuring the Other is deprived of the satisfaction of knowing her idle curiosity is being satisfied without a struggle. Once again Shearer finds that it's a far far better thing to lose herself in the memories of others, especially when they are intimidating in their stupid smugness (again, this definitely appears not to be Two's case), than to stumble around in her own. For remembering in Shearer's case would mean recognizing, for the *n+1*st time, that the promise of the most promising events (unaccountable emanation of the odor of lilac, say, from a piss-streaked sandbox in Abingdon Square)—those events unfurling/disclosing, like the Entr'acte, Scene and Awakening from the *Sleeping Beauty*, the infinite perspective of an impossible throb or two of happiness—are still awaiting a realization that will never come. The wound will have no suture. But there's satisfaction (calling it perverse would be the true imp of the perverse) in knowing the past is truly past—that she'll be taking her secret, kept secret even from her (or is it more accurate to say *most of all from her*? or is the hyperlative being imposed on her by the same poolside-haunting Some Body who's got nothing better to do than poison the well of Two's wordflow every chance he gets?)—taking her secret to the grave. The recondite *over-ness* (yes, *recondite*, bub, you heard me right the first time around)—the very fact that an event's irrevocably failed her or that she's irreparably failed it (through missing its real import or opportunity for any of a million and one other reasons)—the refusal ultimately to regret what hasn't been done—since no-regret-for-what-hasn't been-done is a doing, too, and . . . (duck: it's the poolside strangler again!) *maybe the best and longest-lasting kind of doing* (as Balanchine proved in his only Henry James ballet, *The Patagonia*): well, I ask you, members of the hung jury, Isn't there the greatest glory mixed up in all this retribution, in all this uncomplaining acceptance of the inviolateness of born-dead experience? Or is the stiff upper lip merely relief that one sort of illusion is at last stepping aside to make way for another: that, for example, Tuesday will be her good-news day?

Herbert picks without appetite—worse, without curiosity—at her sesame noodles and speaks in a monotone which grows lower and lower. The enthusiasm has frankly worn off. Shearer looks around. At a nearby table, round and roundly overcluttered, several couples self-importantly engage in casual chitchat. Their casual ways make Two's hard-luck story seem even more improbable. Simply out of the question that at the very moment these impossibly chic young things (straight out of *La Valse*) are chopsticking, across the world young men are being maimed beyond repair. She wonders whether she has any strength left (scepticism has left her exhausted) to adopt a body stance that proclaims her outrage. How would Balanchine have choreographed the refusal to be bracketed by her own Dewdrop-eyed impressionability?

But her gaze can't help kowtowing to beauty. Herbert is murmuring something about a funeral procession in Charleston. What matters is that the trendies have seen fit to rise in exquisitely perfect unison. She is being abandoned by beauty. But wait, there's a bright spot . . . a cure. No matter how airily intimidating their babble, how chopstick-svelte its timbre, there is just no way it can refute the proclamation made by surprisingly dumpy posteriors which would never pass muster at NYCB. And it appears they are well aware of being pilloried by their own anatomy because the gestures accompanying the chitchatting-chatchitting are getting more and more desperately airy. Still, now that they're gone Shearer isn't quite sure whether the dumpiness is the fruit of poetic license or poetic justice.

"What about you?" Herbert wants to know why Moira is participating since she doesn't seem to need to envy anybody. Four hesitates. Should she say nothing, out of respect for Two's bigger load and thereby risk outrage for accepting a place better allotted to the authentically needy? Or should she speak straightforwardly of her comparatively trivial torments (old rivals in new instars) and see them writ appropriately small in the green eye of the other—see them envied in their very triviality? Or should she vastly, shamelessly exaggerate those torments—go the route of self-ablation to which she's no stranger (under the assumption that misery loves company) despite the risk of thereby generating the amused contempt of this sovereign in the land of lucklessness for suffering way beyond the limits of . . . propriety—for suffering . . . stupidly? Four doesn't answer.

"Check, please." Two calls to the waiter, who is obviously lamenting the loss of the young-and-beautiful delegation and considers the two trial subjects so poor a substitute as almost to constitute a joke at his expense. As the man, no longer young and never beautiful, advances, obviously hating to do the bidding of these eyesores (or maybe anybody's), even if it will ultimately spell their eviction, there is a loud noise from outside, surely a gunshot. Like everybody else, he strains to see. Strangely, *the gesture of wonderment humanizes his snottiness.* But how does Two know he's gazing with humanizing wonder or even that she thinks he's so gazing? Maybe the phrase, with an agenda of its own, has simply supplanted any thought she may have had. This one can simply be riding pillion on a freefloating neuronal impulse, one that didn't even have time to fire before it was hijacked by the phrase—one, therefore, that will not be able to live out its destiny untainted by the crass materiality of her thought. And how does that poolside self-aggrandizer—the He of her dreams—dare to pass off this sort of confusion—His or hers?—as expertise in the matter of mind versus brain?

On a sunless bench at the south side of Washington Square Park, Four is more willing to spill her beans: she's beginning to understand (without understanding *how*) that human relations are contingent on the vicissitudes of topography. What was clearly impossible back there among the chopsticks *is* possible in the shadow of the Arch. Fact is, compliments of her Envy of ballerinas and non-ballerinas alike, none has more right to a place at the Invidicum buffet table than she. And in her pantheon, none more envied—detested, really—than the ballerina who is, in that vulgar phrase, *having it all—you* know, glory *and* family fun. At her own pace and in her own way, Moira elaborates. Says something to the effect that the obscenity of the Family is proportionate to Its sanctity. Surely, Two knows that the institution appeals only to the bargain hunter, the one-stop shopper: love-soaked orgasms, self-renewal, tax reductions, all in one tidy bundle. She, on the other hand, has a soft spot for the interlopers, the home-wreckers as depicted in cable culture (ultimately suppressed by storylines cum prime time upholder of herd morality). Though she's definitely not one herself, since to stoop to conquer as those anti-icons conquer is to manifest inadequate control over envying what she professes to spurn: worse, to seek to be caught in the toils—in the act—of such inadequacy is to exalt the very institution she pretends to detest and disavows. She's after bigger game, although she doesn't know it, which is to play at Kantian sublimity—at being sufficient unto herself, with no need to flee families like the plague. Even if by temperament she's cold and indifferent toward their loud susceptibility to novelty, among other cherished mass-market defects (precisely because she has been saddled with the peculiar gift of finding novelty in the sameness that underpins pursuit of her vocation), still she has the resources to be beneficent to those upon whom the curse of family fun has been visited—still she is able to tear herself out of her deadly insusceptibility to such fun and bestow comfort on its victims, although not—never—from inclination—from native sympathetic attunement (which would merely rob her gesture of any moral worth)—but rather from duty, the more poker-faced the better.

She willingly—cunningly, some might say—provides Two, who's obviously bleary from all this abstract twaddle, with a concrete example. (But how can Two be bleary-eared since Shearer—proceeding at her own pace and in her own way—leached out all the abstractions that accrued from playing unwitting surrogate mother to somebody else's thinking? *And could that Some Body by any chance be Melanctha's He?*) Shearer explains that reacting against ballerinas who are having it all, and then some, is like being transfixed by X, Y or Z's ridiculous accessory—bag or belt or tattoo. But instead of smirking, one turns away voluntarily? involuntarily?—in any case soberly (sobriety being 99 percent fascination with the possibility of replacing ridicule with sobriety), absorbed in thoughts of another color, which retrospectively invests the transfixion with . . . sublimity. One's eavesdropping on the silence of the accessory hasn't ended in ridicule—ridicule (which would cast the most ridicule on the ridiculer) has, as it turns out, never been in the cards. The accessory is a mere point of convergence: very different thoughts, having nothing to do with the accessory, go right through it unseeing. Since the transfixion has nothing to do with the accessory, however ridiculous, or does it? Turning one's back on the accessory becomes the avowal of complete unseeing—unseeing as purity. Turning one's back in preparation for transforming the accessory into a suitable target for ridicule negates ridicule—demonstrates how far from ridicule one, qua thinking thinker, really is—one can't be any further. Through the very act of turning away to refine the idea of—to prime oneself for—ridicule, one catches oneself in the act of affirming the inconceivability of stooping to ridicule. But has one really caught oneself in the act of unseeing—or is the catching oneself in the act a mere skit performed for one's biggest fan and detractor? (I.e., is moral duty ever entirely free of inclination?) Relinquishment of the chance to ridicule both ushers in and issues from deep thinking which has no time for accessories (but not meanspiritedly), however ridiculous. Anything is grist for the mill of one's lofty and respectful tolerance qua deep thinker. And so one emerges unscathed by ridicule, one comes out smelling like a . . . Kantian sublime.

And so—to answer Herbert's question (at last she's ready) as painlessly as possible—given her hatred of pretty much every woman on the face of the earth and self-hatred for Envying what she supposedly hates, it isn't just providential—why, it's positively miraculous—that, nearing the end of her rope, she chose, one nondescript autumn afternoon with a pall over the landscape, to enter *that particular supermarket* on Second Avenue. And no less miraculous that she managed to fall on *that particular monstrously obese checkout kid*—when there were so many healthier specimens around. (She hesitates to indicate the kid was black: the image of her and Arthur Mitchell interwoven in the *Agon* pas de deux disintegrates before it can confirm she's no racist.) For it was the shock of the encounter with the kid's dysfunction that made her exit in a kind of daze and slow down her usual pavement gallop to a zigzagging canter. Which then enabled her to collide with—but she's getting way ahead of herself.

Dizzy and dehydrated after hours spent searching for Annie-Fannie's birthday present, Shearer went to buy herself a coke and banana only to end up feeling responsible for the kid's fit of excruciated heaving. No more than nineteen and probably diabetic, she'd bent down to retrieve whatever was required—pencil? receipt? dollar bill? key to the register?—to ring Four up. And when at last she rose, heaving even more, the kid's look expressed surly indifference far more than reproachful appeal. The obesity was Shearer's problem more than her own for it was Shearer's unseemly demand for service that triggered it. So she ended up feeling more self-conscious about her own medical condition, *which was precisely the lack of any*, than the kid did about hers. Four had things way too easy. How she envied the checkout kid, who made her feel svelteness was obscene—an affectation—cowardice in perpetual motion.

Can Melanctha Herbert understand without, as a black woman, passing judgment (of course she can) that deformity transformed the kid into a virtuoso because though she had to do everything everybody else had to do, and then some, she did it with far fewer tools of the trade? That virtuosity, indifferently paraded, was Checkout's definitive verdict on Shearer and her crowd. Alas, Shearer's thanks—long-winded in the face of an infinitely more eloquent silence—produced only disgust. Herbert urges—or dares—her not to feel too bad since she suspects it wasn't Four per se but the generic brand of Four that disgusted Checkout.

So, feeling soiled by her privileged way of life, which, come to think of it, isn't all that privileged, Shearer stumbled through the automatic door. Her stumble immediately caught the jaundiced eye of a honey locust which, though lacerated by entrapment in its grate, was trying nonetheless to play the hand fate had dealt it by refusing to believe help might, by some fluke, be on the way (sound familiar?). *That tree was there for a reason*, as the non-birthday niece would say. But this is always the case: the harbinger of better luck next time comes to call, when it comes at all, at the very moment when Shearer feels so battered she no longer cares. Just as in any theater piece worth its salt, Herbert explains, a turn for the less bad is credible only if it constitutes an irritating distraction from matters ostensibly more critical.

The man she collided with on the corner of Eighty-Third was very tall—almost too tall for his own good, with that lank just about to topple over. He apologized profusely for her being in the wrong and as she resolutely sipped her coke (putting the banana on hold), began speaking in what sounded definitively like the key of fate.

"I really suffered for you in there," he said. Unable to hear—the scrape of arched oak leaves along the asphalt was deafening—she couldn't very well respond. But she didn't have to—Bill graciously played both their parts. "I really suffered for you—I mean with that checkout kid." Across from Schurz Park, he gave his name—Cook—and said she'd be perfect. "Perfect for what exactly?"—since maidenly suspicion was in order. She nonetheless agreed (as they both knew she would) to a cup of coffee. In a cramped booth opposite the men's room, he pitched his no-frills offer, making it clear straight off that there'd be no impressing her with his credentials for the simple reason that, being an underdog and proud of it, he didn't have any. Oh, yes, he'd done some public relations work for a methadone clinic in the Bay Area before joining Voracicom where he hoped to be named, sometime soon, assistant director-in-chief of the ever-growing branded entertainment division. It was time he had his eye on the main chance and the main chance was the first clinical trial worldwide for Invidicum (to be conducted down at the Amygdala Neurological Institute), the cutting-edge drug that everybody in the industry couldn't stop talking about. "Don't tell me you haven't heard of it," he bullied.

He had what she could describe only as the determination of a dancer—but a dancer who didn't have quite the right kind of physical equipment and rejoiced at the fact: surely it guaranteed a triumph bigger than anybody else's. She herself knew that, in the ballet world and maybe out of it, too, not infrequently something extraordinary did come out of imposing a not-quite-rightness on one's vocation, though that hadn't been her case: Mr. B.—who else?—had said right off the bat that her body was a choreographer's gift of the gods. Cook told her he had just a few weeks to go and was still having trouble recruiting the right people. The proper channels (800 numbers et al)—as was the way with proper channels—had yielded only the slimmest of pickings. How could he trust consulting companies with names like Pharm It Out and Name Your Poison?

Cook: "Invidicum is an anti-Envy drug—it'll be the very first on the market. And watching you *perform* with that very fat checkout kid, I knew you were just the type who, at the drop of a hat and with almost no provocation, can make herself feel envious of pretty much anybody. You envied her absolute deadpan indifference to what anybody might be thinking about her *condition*, most of all you, or rather" (*or rather*, Herbert thinks, the two most

46

beautiful words in the language) "you envied what you *took* to be her dead-pan indifference. All at once I knew your core is so shrunken you're not so secretly convinced anybody could impersonate you—*do* you—far better than you could do yourself. You feel like an impostor in your own skin. You're an identity thief only the victim is you yourself." So she was being "discovered" for the second time in her life.

He hailed a taxi and within minutes they were in the East Forties entering the kind of building they don't erect anymore. Even the rusticated shadows, whose imprint on other frontages looked fleeting, had the allure of tracery dating back at least two centuries. While keeping up simultaneous conversations with at least three other passengers all the way up to the twentieth—thirtieth—forty-seventh floor, Cook still found the time to appraise himself, congratulatorily—from buzz cut to wingtips—in the full-length mirror.

Drawing the curtains (to prevent her being distracted by the black-eyed puffballs monitoring the tugboat traffic?), Cook emphasized that he was risking a lot taking her in right off the street (so, *her* credentials were now the issue) because there might just be some element of her case history or some biomarker—blood pressure, say, or sedimentation rate—that disqualified her. But that didn't matter since, even if Envy constituted a bona fide disease entity, it couldn't, like epidermolysis bullosa, say, or X-linked recessive hypoparathyroidism or African sleeping sickness, be reduced to the sum of its markers. And even if all the right ones were dutifully going haywire—more than enough to make her look like an ideal candidate—how much of that necessarily translated into Envy's virulence? *Cook:* "You may have, without a single abnormal marker to your name, the very worst form of the disease. So I like to think of you as the born maverick, without that PhD from Wharton—without even a high school equivalency diploma—who's still, or for that very reason, the very best choice for CEO.

"But don't get the wrong idea. Just because it's not biomarker-heavy (yet) doesn't mean EnVD is a *fake* disease—like erectile dysfunction (E.D.), erectile hyperfunction, addictive shopping, snake phobia (S.P.), premature ejaculation (P.E.), Morgellons disease, apotemnophilia, purging disorder, pseudobulbar effect (PBE), chronic fatigue, restless legs, restless balls, roving eye disorder (RED), Capgras syndrome, sensory processing disorder, serotonin syndrome, and other chatroom and bump-on-a-blog sensations masquerading as terminal afflictions." He awaited Moira's guffaw but his humor was too well-informed for her taste. "It's not some harmless fact of life anointed with a life-threatening acronym simply because there happens to be a concoction in the Pipeline simply aching to make the grade as a blockbuster. You're really suffering from Envy—I saw that at once in the supermarket—even if everybody else in the cohort is a malingerer. And what's more, you don't just suffer—you feel it to be your bounden duty to suffer and to be always stretching the limits of your capacity: it's as if a voice is telling you're not being envious enough. Somewhere along the line your standards for what constitutes real suffering have gotten absurdly high (could it be all that daily work on pointe?). It's gotten so bad, hasn't it? that you've disqualified yourself for accession to authentic suffererdom simply because you can still breathe. Sort of. Of course there's no guarantee you won't end up in the placebo group, convinced you're getting the real McCoy but in fact swallowing nothing but pap. But even under this worst-case scenario, you're guaranteed"—here he opened the curtains, swiveled his chair one hundred eighty degrees (had he revealed too much?) and looked upward but unseeing (she handled the seeing for the two of them) toward a cobalt puddle occluded by the collision of two off-white dirigibles—"state-of-the-art daily monitoring of your condition." She shivered involuntarily. "You mean there's a chance I may not get the drug at all?" He managed to look first trapped and then as if wriggling free successfully had been the greatest challenge of his career, in and out of the pipeline. "Tell you what: it's verboten but I'll personally write you into the non-placebo arm."

There was a courtesy knock at the half-open door: without waiting for acknowledgment, a man (completely bald) entered, considerably older, yet somehow much limberer, than Cook. Clearly no stranger to the company squash courts, sauna and pool. *Considerably older, yet somehow much limberer*, what a quaint phrase, Four couldn't help thinking (though not quite in these words): it (*a*) jolts us out of our complacency—(*b*) heralds a complete overturn of all my—our—preconceptions—(*c*) ushers in a Golden Age of unfazeability—(*d*) demonstrates that life is far more unpredictable—mysterious—than we ever gave it credit for being—and/or in a supreme act of meanspiritedness or forbearance (take your pick)—(*e*) forecloses any further possibility of such hijinks, in other words, the jolt—the mystery—lies in the fact that this is a single—the only—instance of things not being what we might have expected them to be, i.e., the hapax legomenon to end all hapax legomena. She wasn't clear whether this touch—the limber bald-headed entrance—was for her benefit, i.e., to assure her that, despite what she may have heard, rehab would be a delightfully bumpy ride. *For a minute she could swear that the phrase had been articulated for her* (by Melanctha's He?)—as if she were too busy having the wind knocked out of her by the impression made by older-yet-limberer to be able simultaneously to nab the exact phrase for that impression. And who's to say whether it *was* exact? Maybe it was the phrase—the wordflow—that came first and the appearance of the bald man touched up to correspond to the phrase. Some Body was doing the phrasing for her—she being one of the many who couldn't articulate on their feet, for whom undergoing and phrasing were incompossible. His job, this phrase nanny's, was to keep her as blunted, as off-kilter, as possible so as to be able to step right in and articulate what she failed to see. Her falling short was his exultation. So she existed only to be bypassed. *Cook:* "Dr. Post, meet Moira Shearer, aka Subject Four." He had flawless teeth, a strong jaw (Technicolor smalt-blue and stubble-free) and a grotesque proliferation of nostril stamens which, being his and therefore constituting further proof of perfect specimenhood, were not to be tampered with should the urge overtake her.

He gave the string of fortresses along Central Park West (the Majestic, the Dakota, the San Remo, the Beresford, the El Dorado, and so on and so forth) the once-over and when he was done, went on looking. But with his virile—no, his obscene—zest for life (she knew the type), it was unlikely that he was looking the way she looked from, say, her favorite knoll in Riverside Park. *She* looked to make sure the day did what days were supposed to do—namely, inflame and die—for there was always a sour delight to be had from such an immolation, even if she knew it was she that died (and last-rite-less), not the day. Though, once the thought died, she wasn't quite sure she'd ever watched the day die with such an aim in mind. Irrelevant: the celebrated Some Body bearing a *considerably older, yet somehow much limberer* portfolio just told her she had. His look said, Better than an unclouded perspective—even on Central Park—from a window on the forty-seventh floor was a perspective obnubilated—yep, *obnubilated*, pal, you heard right the first time—by the perceiver's reflection therein.

It was clear he didn't want to be rushed. So, when he felt he'd waited long enough not to be perceived as doing the bidding of an underling, he got on with the business of talking to the dead space between Cook and Shearer. In a gravelly baritone that, at the end of every phrase, near-drowned in its own gravel (which was what made her find it, against her better judgment, so seductive), he assured her she'd never regret working with Straynge—a man who self-published mini-treatises on EnVD at a time when the concept was even too insignificant for anathematization by the prevailing ideologues. Of course she was sure to hear ugly lies about Jim aka Jimmy, about his . . . San Diego past, but they came, as in the case of any genuine trailblazer, with the territory.

Shearer hesitated, but she just had to ask, his unpluckable nostril hairs notwithstanding— "What?" Herbert is instantly alert. "I asked if I'd be cured, once and for all. No longer doomed to take walks only at night because I'm terrified I *won't* be recognized." "And what did he say?"

Shearer wants (but does not manage—no, not by a long shot) to reply something along the lines of: "He smiled and said he had no answer—and defied anybody who wasn't a quack or a hack to have one. That I more than anyone else knew the question did not want an answer, was incompatible with one. That my question was the fissure, walked the thinnest line, between hope and dread and, by the very fact of having managed the double feat of getting itself uttered at all and staying unanswered, kept dread from infecting hope. That my question was at the same time a poison and the cure for that poison—a *pharmakon*, he called it. The poison and the cure didn't just cancel each other out—their cancellation propelled me forward in a single bound. Then looking at me in a way that he obviously thought was paternal but which stimulated feelings that were the farthest thing from daughterly, he avowed that he was stealing Straynge's thunder. Fact is, Straynge should be the one, he said—and in a group setting—to say what Post needed to get off his chest here and now. But he couldn't wait that long and maybe the impact would be greater precisely because it was coming too early or out of context or both. Maybe I'd remember it better—it was more likely to sink in and faster—because it seemed . . . unmotivated. He was truly sorry he was saying all of this in front of a stranger and a non-medical man, to boot, but let it be known that I should be grateful for his impatience to . . . serve and deep down, or not so deep down, I was, he knew I was.

"What he needed to express and claimed he couldn't as well as he should have liked—though he ended up doing OK as far as I was concerned—was that I would never be completely cured of *my* Envy, nor did I want to be. Envy was my sigh of relief—my small way of saying thank you to Old Man Fate for refusing to grant my wish to have had, to have and to go on having the life and times of Suzanne or Natalia or Cynthia or Lynn—for refusing to knuckle under and accede out of fear to all the terms of my petulance. Which attested to the fact that the Old Man, for all his bad press, had balls (I'm merely quoting)—it showed I was in the ring with a worthy opponent and to have had a thousand losses by way of knockout was infinitely more honorable than to have had fifty-thousand wins against some invertebrate sub-welterweight who complied with my every whim.

"What, he asked me point blank, if my life played itself out as desired— i.e., as one long pacification of a tantrum? Wouldn't that be the worst fate of all? Once I started responding to treatment—and even if I didn't—I'd appreciate the luck of being spared the fulfillment I thought I craved. I'd know I was responding when I started appreciating my Envy as the next best thing to . . . its absence. I'd start hearing again the music that first made me want to be a dancer forty-five years before—how did he know it was Hindemith's *The Four Temperaments*?—but I'd hear it differently, in the radiant off-key of self-transparency."

Four realizes the young man at the end of their bench whom she immediately wrote off as a tuned-out daydreamer (with no interest, in any case, in her kind of dreams) has been listening intently. In fact he is waiting for a next installment of this black comedy of manners. She tries to recapture some of what she said—so as to hear it as he must have heard it and determine whether or not she came across as some fishwifely retailer of sour grapes, always in season. Though not much to be done about it now. Did she manage to hold his attention all the way through?—more importantly, did she manage to make it clear that the pretensions of the Invidicum crew were in no shape or form hers and in cases where there was no choice but to take the esoteric bull by the horns—did she achieve the no-mean-feat of not just expressing the inexpressible but expressing it, horns and all, in such a way as to give the Universal Young Man on the Universal Bench no cause for exasperation, intimidation, contempt—for boycotting and bracketing her away as a phony? For she knows what it's like to eavesdrop on park benches—did so many a time, mainly between rehearsals and mainly on working-stiff adulterers intent on rising as quickly as possible to the occasion offered by an extra-long lunch hour, with her own in-/excluded presence serving as the prime mover. She doesn't want to fail his eavesdropping the way those adulterers always failed hers. She wants him to feel that she's done her utmost to render it justice.

As they rise (Herbert needs to make a call) Shearer, applying her makeup joylessly, almost says goodbye to him. Only she can't very well say goodbye without a smile, can she? Thing is, her pocket mirror tells her the ugly-duckling sneer of pain she is trying to transform just for him, her latest fan, won't budge. In tossing her fortune (at once too optimistic-irrelevant and too mean-spirited-proverbial) in the overflowing bin at the corner of Twelfth Street,

Four (squeamish) notes Two (incensed) noting what is not just a familiar but an *all-too-familiar* sight on the gold-paved streets of New York, to wit, black woman pushing white toddler. Four wants Two to know that not just here and now but *never in a million years* would she even consider complimenting the nanny—detestable word!—on the honey-blond beauty of the blue-eyed tyke since there must be nothing a nanny dreads more than having to appear flattered under the circumstances. Vigorously waving her cellphone by way of explanation, Herbert walks off before Shearer can somehow make it clear (her own blue eyes notwithstanding) that they are standing—now and forever—on the same side of the barricades.

Free of Straynge and Company, Borkman wonders if he should dial his wife in case another collection agency has called about his son's credit card delinquencies. Not that he wants to know: he has enough on his plate and every last scrap inedible. En route to his lawyer's (there should be enough time for an update from one of his gophers on the multimillion dollar problem with the IRS), he *orders the cabbie* [sic] to stop not quite at the corner of Seventy-Fourth and Madison (his own backyard), for he has just espied—yes, *espied*: not seen but espied—the young woman he first noticed—when was it?—about a week before. She is sitting in the same sidewalk café across from the Carlyle (sipping without much conviction on the periphery)—the sort of café where, for the sake of mutual edification, the filthy rich rub elbows with the just plain filthy. The business of paying and secreting his wallet so he won't lose it, as he has twice already in the last few days (when he thinks about his son any mishap is possible), gives her more than enough time to vanish. More's the pity inasmuch as she clearly doesn't belong to the breed of navel-gazing and -flaunting vampires with Nosferatu nails whose come-on simultaneously rebuffs the outrageously out-of-line advances you haven't even begun to make and now have absolutely no intention of making—unless you're like Borkman, who's excited by the members of that breed. With breasts shapely and/yet discreet, high cheekbones and a commanding overbite which would have no trouble giving both Tierney's and Caron's a run for the money, she accepts politely his expression of interest. His cup runneth over.

But how can he think of hitching his wagon to an overbite what with the older boy so troubled and the younger one's troubles impatiently waiting in the wings. Then he remembers he is to meet his wife at the Seventy-Ninth Street entrance to Central Park at 1 p.m. for a visit to the boy's therapist (*therapist!*: loathsome mewling euphemism—and euphemism for what precisely? does the word have a referent?). But will he be able to get back to Amygdala in time for act two of today's envy follies? He needs to be prompt: his lawyer thinks participation in the trial will show he's serious about rehabilitation and therefore blunt the fangs of any out-for-blood jury. He hates the word—*therapist*, that is. (*But maybe, Borkman, its meaning, like that of* Building 18 *not to mention* Berry Sundae *[but of that, more later], will erode by dint of overuse, leaving nothing but a placeholder recruitable at a moment's notice to signify anything but what that debased and debasing little word is supposed to.*) He takes her seat and orders a Rob Roy: the café mustn't go to waste on such a lovely day. If he misses act two, so be it.

They walk across the Park on this spring day in midsummer to prepare themselves mentally, as she is wont to put it, for what is sure to be yet another dire take on their failings. The wife seems calm, intent on sketching the willows near Belvedere Castle. She thinks: *Our marriage was a sleep of reason which produced monsters—the inevitable monsters*—she thinks it before the therapist can think it so as to prepare herself for the shock of the therapist's saying it BUT NOT to *ward off* the therapist's saying it. Only she knows— or Some Body knows for her—that this fine distinction between preparing to take your medicine and warding off the doser is a phony distinction—a non-distinction. When she's preparing to take her medicine she's always only pretending to prepare. What she's really doing is trying to scare off the dreaded event because every dreaded event—thanks to the hard work of the impressionable stooge who's doing the dreading—ends up vastly exaggerating its own uniqueness—its own originality—and fears nothing more than to be anticipated by that same stooge suddenly able to articulate her dread and stage the dreaded scene well in advance—proleptically. Or so she must believe. He asks her to please hurry, though he himself is none too eager to arrive on time. Especially since at their first meeting, said therapist came to him with what is nowadays equivalent to a letter of introduction—his Wiki page. Having done him the immense honor of taking time out from her busy schedule to swallow its contents, albeit not hook, line and sinker, she then did Borkman the even bigger honor of shoving the lowdown on his life down his parched throat at no extra charge (though all this giving ate up a big chunk of that meeting—inaugural, to boot)—and in front of his worst enemy, also to boot. A dirty job—disabusing him of his illusions, that is—but somebody had to do it and who better than she, accredited by no less than the William Alanson White, Payne Whitney and Ackerman institutes. She'd learned how he struggled to make it in business, how the double-cross was his modus operandi to end all MOs, how he couldn't hold down a marriage the way others can't hold down a job.

The wife interrupts, explaining that it is not just a matter of reproducing simple shapes: as if her pen doesn't have enough to worry about, the sunlight anointing the catkins has to be factored in as well. Such nuances, let me tell you, make life sheer hell for the career neo-impressionist. In any case, she's doomed. No point in sketching the catkins since they're already expertly sketched against the sky—already captured—by nature itself, supreme mimic of the artists she's spawned. They're always already a shorthand sketch of themselves so adept as to render superfluous the scumbling of Sunday—and even Monday, Tuesday and Wednesday painters and everybody else possessed of the fiery delusion they can outnature nature. Though, she assures him, there are still plenty of undeterred sketchers out here who, it would appear (to whom?), hold fast to the conviction that that same nature, by graciously handling the least interesting basics, has left them plenty to sketch—the bare-bones unsketchable, in fact. So her sketch is redundant and the only way to go on sketching is to acknowledge the redundancy—to recognize its perpetration as a crime against scalpel-wielding nature, which has this nasty habit of always getting there first. "Look straight ahead or, better yet, awry, if you don't believe me." "Where is *there*?" he asks warily, determined not to wait for the contemptuous non-answer. All she replies is that starting now, her sketches must make it their business never to be about catkins—about this or about that—but about their own superfluousness—their inability to out-nature nature. But how is she to sketch superfluousness?—she doesn't have the right tools. He's tempted to remind her that only a bad workman blames— But he's much too reassured to want to hurt her back—hurting is always a hurting *back*—at least for now. I.e., there's too much cause for momentary celebration for it will be an aerodynamical impossibility for her to go, once they are in the presence of the expert, from such humble absorption to hurling at the canvas of their yoked dysfunction (as is also her wont) depictions of him as the taproot of all malice domestic. A pigeon swoops to appropriate an enormous crust. Is he any less ridiculous—always trying to phagocytize too many corporate pies at the same time? Watch it: you have recklessly impaled the moment, some body or thing tells him, on a metaphor, probably mixed.

And then, as they mount the scaffold with a tumbrelful of equally reprehensible forbears bringing up the rear, what happens is what is meant to happen: she manages without missing a beat to make the inconceivable transition from pearlfisher to fishwife. And not to be in any way outdone, though he always is—and then some—Borkman does some unflattering depiction of his own though his aim, in part, goes (far?) beyond mere self-vindication (is there any other kind?). For as the Bible—or at least his bible—says, Far more evil than any evil known to man—in fact, the most perfidious of low-down ploys, whether known to man or not—is the taking up of *a therapist's valuable time* without a plausibly pathological gripe in tow. Is he thinking this? No, of course not. It's that body or thing that swooped down on him in Central Park a while back that is doing the thinking *for* him, but so what? What matters is that he's suddenly so receptive. Why, he's actually beginning to *get* said body's meaning as a parody of meaning. Since, of course, everybody knows that taking up a therapist's valuable time without a plausible gripe up one's sleeve isn't the most perfidious ploy alive. Far from it. There are plenty of ploys far more insidious. But, according to the swooping body or thing, in this context the *t* word—*therapist*—is a hype—a mere placeholder—an *x*-marks-the-spot—signifying some entity still to be uncovered whose time (and maybe *time* is a placeholder, too) is the most invaluable of all. (*Pretty impressive [if you ask me], this receptivity to the concept of meaning as parody of meaning, given that basic training down at Amygdala-on-Hudson has only just begun! For there has to be some connection between Amygdala's brand of therapy and this Wiki therapist and this new receptivity to oddball meaning.*)

And then, just when he is warming to his rapidly advancing self-improvement—to the idea that if such receptivity is possible, anything is—which is exactly how he's trained himself to feel whenever he finds himself looking all the way down West Seventy-Ninth Street to the Hudson from the Museum of Natural History at, say, 7 p.m. in mid-July—just then, she hisses the magic phrase ("Look where you are!"), as he's known all along she would, but more, it seems, for the benefit of the Ansonia's widow's walk framed by the big bay window than of the therapist herself. And given all the pending lawsuits, the ongoing dismantlement of his empire offshore and on-, she is of course more right than ever. He is stunned, however, as he knew he'd be even if he's heard it all before translated into at least thirty languages, ancient and modern. Remedially, he tries to egg on his rage to the point where effect far exceeds cause—in order to delude himself into believing it is he who's the perpetrator and to thereby salvage his pygmy's pride—in order to have a reason (other than the fear of his *obligation*—his Christian duty—to hate her as vigorously as possible)—a face-saving reason—for downgrading the virulent gratuitousness of her hurricane of an attack from a level 6, say, to a level 2. After all, she cares about her man and just wants him to stop all the self-sabotage—and she's not just thinking about its impact on the kids, who love to mimic the guy they love to hate. She wants—even if it's way too late—to perpetrate happiness, to *visit happiness* upon him and everybody else who gets in her way. So what if it's the generic brand of happiness?

But at the very moment Borkman could swear he's on the verge of—is already—leaving, he makes a lunge at the Mrs., tightening his trembling hands around her neck right in front of this useless bystander—partly to determine (*or so he would think if that old son of a Some Body—that Theuth—that Thamis—will only let him think*) just how useless she might turn out to be. Funny thing about strangulation (aside from the fact that it seems to run in the family): it is the only means of killing which allows you to inflict hurt and constrain the infliction every step of the way. Still, his grip ever narrowing, he *hurls reproaches* to reassure them both that he has the best of reasons for killing and is at the same time out of control—not responsible for his actions, however justified—is too busy hurling long-overdue reproaches to realize he is also a strangler. Strangling alone is . . . evil because unassailed by reluctance. In spite of himself, however, and against his better judgment (after all, he hasn't managed to even begin measuring the good lady's uselessness), he lets go, i.e., lets bygones be bygones, falling back on the carpet (which smells nice, like a prize-winning super-poodle). The wife studies him, in a stertorous daze of unseeing. He wonders why the therapist lady (it's soothing to call her "the therapist lady" though he doesn't quite know to what the phrase is mappable out here in the real world so he's not ready to think about her as such) looks so appalled. The upstanding bystander now threatens to call the police, then relents. "I just want you to be safe," she says to the wife. He doesn't understand all this concern for the wife's safety. (And he doesn't like the word "safe" in this context—or any other, for that matter. Smells too much like a professional euphemism—the euphemism of the moment.) After all, he didn't hit her or, worse, snarl, "Look where you are." He simply tried to strangle her because her words had been on the verge of annihilating him and he had no choice but to annihilate the annihilator. By fastening his hands around her throat he was trying to contain her—to contain them both—to knock some sense into their dismal relation exalted (in the Strindbergian sense) by its refusal to die a coward's heroic death. How can he be accused of making her unsafe—of brutality, in other words—when it's he who's been—being—brutalized—by language—the wife's language—i.e., brutalized by all she's left unsaid? Fighting off annihilation, that's all he was doing. He was being annihilated so he did what any self-respecting autocrat would do in his place: he annihilated right back. Minding his own business in a big way, if it comes to that. He was—is—a little boy fighting off annihilation and how can a little boy's self-defense be called brutality? At which point the lady therapist or somebody who sounds just like her jumps in and alerts him to the fact that his wife herself is probably unaware of what she's left unsaid. The wife's language—anybody's language— is a world unto itself. Anorexic. Yes, the lady therapist has a point there. The wife has been anorexic and maybe still is. By its very nature language—her bony language—elects to omit a multitude of things. A mere *placeholder* (that thorny word again) for the unspeakable just around the bend. Even at its most robust-flamboyant, its most penny-ante baroque ("that means fancy"), every-body's prose is maddeningly thin, ductile, slendered out. Language is by its very digital nature purificatory—vengefully so. A vengeful shaving of the fat of irrelevance off the bare bones of . . . being. He nods his head. Is she on his side with all this chatter, or isn't she? And why does he need to think of it as chatter? He understood every word and it makes sense. And by the way, he knows what *baroque* is supposed to mean.

He hopes she sees that with so much ferocity (his) there must be another side to the story (the wife's). He wants her to know that marriage-hearsing with the woman he just tried to strangle has always been all about learning what *not* to say or do. But for that matter, the therapist wonders or pretends to wonder if any successful or even halfway successful relation isn't one long act of ascesis, of self-disavowal, of simulation cum dissimulation, of abstention directed toward an absolute zero of unassaultable featurelessness, given that the ghost of even the most innocuous remark may be the target of recurring reproach.

Now he explains that he tried to strangle her so he could be accused . . . rightly. Better to be accused for real sins than to be accused gratuitously. For it's the art of gratuitous accusation which he finds her practicing more and more. For worse than an accuser's righteous rage—or even rage made righ-teous compliments of its target's pliancy—is a distortional memory—mak-ing mincemeat of the past—insane accusation of crimes never committed. The need to justify the gratuitous accusation—to save the accuser so that the accused doesn't end up resigned to living with a madwoman—requires the shouldering—even the invention—of sins uncommitted. The fiction of sanity has to be maintained at all cost.

At the same time, he wants justice whatever the cost. Yet he himself is the first to wonder where this outburst—about justice—is coming from. Is he really innocent of the crimes she's saddled him with? Is he merely throwing sand in the therapist's eyes? Or is the wondering merely a means of disavow-ing what he knows beyond refutability—that her hatred is madness? So justi-fied is the outburst that he wants to disavow its terrifying burden of truth—of too terrifying proof of her mad hatred. So doubt kicks in—the medicine—the poison—the pharmakon of doubt.

The therapist asks if his rage at what he presents as her insane hatred (a hatred that transcends its target—a hatred displaced from other targets whose phantom spotlessness must be preserved or she will go insane, even if she already is) is in fact rage at being accused rightly (and if anything, too leniently) for having almost destroyed her life and the life of their children. Or, does his rage encompass the truth both of her insanity and of his blamelessness (the wife is still too dazed to balk although a twitch in the left eye may be interpreted as protest)—a truth that, understandably, he wants to disavow because then where does it leave him but with a madwoman—saddled with her madness even if she is soon to be taken off his dirty hands? Better to regain his foothold in inadequacy—inadequacy at every level—that of husband, father, father confessor, mambo partner—since making *it* all his fault—the fault of his inadequacy—gives him some control over the situation: he, too, is a madwoman. Does he really take the wife for an accuser unjust to the point of madness—whatever *that* is, after all—or is it *his* hatred that transcends its target, i.e., her most unwelcome revelation of horrifying (as opposed to terrifying) truths—hatred too deep and too mammoth to be triggered by accusations of anything so trivial as having wreaked domestic havoc? What is the *non*-fiction, she asks (until they know, there's no hope for the children)—that the rage is so deep-rooted—so chronic—so pathological—it can never have anything to do with events in the here and now? OR that said rage is very much unpathologically associated with events in the here and now? OR both—that his rage, independent of circumstances in the here and now, goes back to his grandmother's womb AND that the rage—a just rage—is being over-triggered by her madness? Or is all this simply a matter of wordflow's refusing to be wedded to the obvious, to be tied to a single meaning? Upon saying which, she presses her fists against her temples and sways from side to side, as if awaiting the return of a . . . some body or thing. (He can't help thinking it's *his* somebody—his Central Park Some Body, surely no fan of the obvious. But maybe the *thing's* in fact Invidicum. Didn't he get his first dose when he signed in this morning? Or is he misremembering from desperation? Can one of the side effects of the drug be receptivity to deep-think—including impatience with the predictability of most wordflows?) Hence his stumbling—his being made to stumble—on the pretty phrase, I want justice, which is both the description of a state of mind and the state itself.

While the therapist—or rather the therapeutist, as Cantor would call her (any word as long as it's not the right word—as long as it's a fantasia on the mewling precision of the right word—will do handsomely)—while the *therapeutista* or *therapnitza* goes deeper into her trance, the wife seems to be, if anything, less dazed. Having detected this opposition—contrast—reversal—Borkman's storyteller's heart (transplant) skips a beat—something that, a day ago, he, like any other self-respecting alpha male, would have deemed impossible. Invidicum—it must be the drug—is teaching him what makes a story tick: forced contrasts. She explains—no, *she proceeds to explain*—to the therapist who's suddenly wide-awake and as lucid as ever—more so in fact (the irrefutable proof of which, at least to Borkman, is her offer of tea)—that of course he's capable of giving her the life she wants but he withholds it out of sheer perversity—the sheer perversity of his refusal to be anything but himself (hey, wasn't he thinking about this very subject earlier today on the way to work?—to the Flatiron? No, it was on his way to the Amygdala Institute).

Which makes his crime against nature—against normality—more unforgivable—not less, as some might think, or at least tend to think.

Getting less and less dazed by the minute and in no wise ruffled by the patent self-contradiction evinced thereby—in fact, she's enjoying it—at last she's able to suture the wound that is the therapist's unanswered question (the blackout has done her a world of good: you should try it sometime). As far as she's concerned, there's no way out of the perversity of being himself—all his rage is at his own self-hate which has nothing to do with the here and now of her so-called madness (for him the here and now is only and always the eternity of his grandmother's womb). Or rather, the rage has nothing to do with the here and now except insofar as his efforts, *in the here and now*, to surmount the self-hate by mainlining wonder drugs like the special-purpose acquisition company, the spinoff, the inversion, the real estate investment trust, the hostile takeover, the toehold, the pyramid, the activist investor stunt, the Ponzi scheme, the collateralized loan obligation, the contract-for-difference, that old chestnut subprime lending and, when all other psychostimulants and opioid analgesics fail (as in his case they invariably do), the inevitable abominable magical merger of his company of the moment with . . . *itself!*, that is, with a limited liability (new and improved) version of itself (for the purpose of generating sham tax losses)—the rage has nothing to do with the here and now except insofar as those efforts fuel the rage, through their having come to nothing whatsoever in the end. By the way, the self-merger happens to be her own favorite uncontrolled substance but what does she know? She's just a dumb blonde and content to remain so: her husband-to-be likes her that way and no other.

Now it's his turn to explain. The therapist looks meaningfully at her watch. So that he'll mind his manners, the wife hisses, "Look where you are!" yet again. What's her beef, he mock-asks the therapist? Haven't they heard? The election results are in: That too much coveted title of "Look Where You Are" girl—or whatever it's called (silent screen "It" girl Clara Bow has nothing on the wife, newly minted queen of the talkies) has just been bestowed upon her by consensus. (He's very proud, by the way, of "or whatever it's called"—or there's some body out there who's doing the being proud for him. Why proud? Because the phrase shows he's not just some know-it-all—if you must know, he's just as much at sea—as yokel-unreliable—as everybody else and as such can be trusted by every member of his audience—boobs and naboobs alike. He is and he isn't your run-of-the-mill smart aleck and garden-variety name-dropper. So he's rightfully having it all—he's a jack-of-all trades—poet and peasant—not just the masterly retailer of a clever turn of phrase but an average joe from the wrong side of the tracks—a rank innocent—who's not responsible for and is more, much more, than his own cleverness—it's been dumped on him out of the blue like treacle. Hell, he's an elite populist, that's what he is—a populistical elitist *malgré lui*.) It's gotten to the point, he goes on to remark, where, what with his essence reduced to material, formal, efficient and (let's not forget) final cause of all her woes as wife and mother and what with all the good done and sacrifices made rawly discounted—"What good? What sacrifices?" she barks (yes, barks).—it's gotten to the point where his only recourse is to watch his every word. No more going all optimistic and full of hope in the middle of the night (when he's least in pain) with big family plans—plans that will not withstand the morning's rage—hers—because they are centuries behind schedule—if he's capable of making plans now what stopped him in the past? So, no middle-of-the-night sky's-the-limit good intentions which will not withstand morning's regret for giving her the golden opportunity to trash them. The wife lets it be known that such plans get formulated only when a spinoff, say, happens to be the talk of the town and they die a martyr's quick death when the talk of the town predictably dies down (look where he is) but not before going viciously viral. They have nothing to do with her and the kids—not really.

He thinks: Now, isn't the past downright wonderful, infinitely deformable and, what's more, ready, willing and able to accommodate every conceivable misinterpretation/misimpression at the drop of a hat? Whose truth, such as it is, is as distensible as the highest-grade saltwater taffy or is it the lowest-grade that takes highest honors in the deformation department?

What's most galling is to know that outside this wretched family context—this wretched marriage-hearse context—"Do you hear that? Listen to that! Is it any wonder my boys are going to the dogs!" the wife shrieks.—his deepest flaws would not pass muster as even the lowliest peccadilloes—would be hailed instead as—as— It's the marriage-hearse context alone which deplores his essence—delivers it up to the sort of endless unmasking that unmasks nothing but the insightless hysteria of the unmasker. Surprisingly, the therapist concludes the session by asking what could be more banal than all this business of laying bare the bitter truth—that eternal bonbon of theatergoers, she calls it, giggling at her own coy derision. *Oddly enough*—thank heaven, for *oddly enough* (*"Contrast, contrast, Horatio!"*)—the wife doesn't take offense— at least not for the moment. She does, however, get in a Parthian-shot or two as they're escorted to the door. For example, she demands to know if Dr. X is by any chance taking this monster's side.

To convey the fact—or the fiction—that she's at the end of her rope, the therapist (she has unattractive hands though she can't be accused of lacerating the flesh around her nails) decrees that he's not guilty for what has or— worse—hasn't happened to his boys. But of course he must accept responsibility. There's a difference. He jumps up, unsure of whether or not he'll try his hand—take a stab—at strangling *her*, the other woman. "He *is* guilty," hisses the wife. To some body—some thing—she's nothing more than *the wife* and he's nothing more than *the husband*. Reciprocity of hatred kept at fever pitch in defiance of its drive toward atrophy has rendered them otherwise nameless. And likely to remain so. "In many ways, you didn't know better," muses the other woman—the non-, the un-wife. The musing, or rather, the musing tone, is a ploy aimed at coaxing him to retake the hot seat. She's not afraid of his strangling her (so goes the musing tone)—he's welcome to her neck—but she won't answer for the consequences of his refusing to sit. "After all, look at how your own parents treated you even if they, too, were convinced they were doing the right thing. And then some." He sits down and gritting his teeth explains that this guilt-versus-responsibility business reduces to little more than a nuance with no semantic clout. Aspic without the jell. So how can this shade of difference between the terms be enacted—pinpointed—out in the *real world*? You know, that sty where he transacts most of his bloody business? "What you're trying to say is that responsibility is more degrading than guilt. Is that it? More of a threat to . . . selfhood." She doesn't-quite-eye-him-shyly, or with what she hopes will pass for shyness, as if *selfhood* might—must—offend him. "I'm not trying: I said it. And I meant it." Her hands look even uglier because he knows she's making good sense all over again. He's never quite sure what she's saying but he knows it makes sense. He concurs: "taking responsibility," or whatever the phrase is, is more degrading because it absolves him of his uniqueness. By virtue of the fact that he's now a victim—an eternally abused little boy who has no choice but to abuse his own little boys. He did know better—every step of the way. He could have chosen differently every time he failed to sacrifice his self on the altar of fatherhood. This wily and wary poor excuse for brawny self-indictment is Madame Catkins's cue to come to the rescue (but whose?): "And the very fact that doing the right thing is for him equivalent to self-annihilation proves that—that—" "It proves that I'm a bad little boy—the baddest little boy on Wall Street." "Laugh all you like. You'll be singing a different tune when they put you away. For good, I hope." "Now that there's a real father waiting in the wings for my boys, you mean." "I never heard you speak of them as *your* boys." (*Never?* That's a bit much, Madame Therapy: it's only our second visit.) "They're always her boys. Do they become your boys only when you're about to lose them?" This is therapy's chitchat, as far as he's concerned—bargain-basement *insight* (disgusting bargain-basement word). The wife is seething but he doesn't care. After all, there's nothing between them. She actually believes (he knows her like a book) that with this comment the therapy lady, now his champion, has put herself once and for all in his corner when in fact— He says what would go something like this if he were ever to end up saying it: "Should I opt to take what seems to be the easier way out—but only to you and your kind—what am I left with when I walk out the door? Certainly not my hell-bent uniqueness. I'm left with a non-self that's nothing but a carbon copy of the non-selves who perpetrated their own homegrown version of toxic ineptitude, themselves selfhood-canceled carbons. So am I supposed to hold my head high—or low with sniveling gratitude for the way out you've offered me?"

Owning all this confers a certain wild-card autonomy. He's heroic. He laughs sardonically. The therapist smiles inoffensively at the laughter. He'd rather be a monster than a cripple—than the mere ghost—and a pale imitation at that—the merest excrescence—of his own parents' ineptitudes. And who knows, they may have had good reason for loathing him. For doing their job all wrong. "But now that you've executed a highly nuanced debunking of *my* stab at nuance—a nuance with no clout out in the real world, as you put it—you look exultant. If you were a woman, I'd say you looked radiant. So this being the case, tell me, what are you left with (to use your phrase) as you walk out the door?" "I don't know: I just don't want to feel better than I did when I came in." "He's concerned about only one thing: how he feels and how he feels makes him appear to the people out there." "I think what you're left with is feeling better since you've exposed my nuance for the fraud it is. Quite an achievement, old man. But how are you going to prevent this feeling better from getting in the way of feeling unadulterably worst. It must be scary to feel you're worth something by virtue of the fact that you've managed to prove—and to an expert, of all people—that you're worth nothing. But let's examine that—next time—shall we?" This graceful way of giving him the boot turns his stomach. But the wife evidently thinks it proves he's become quite the favorite. Which makes the wife seethe even more. "We're not here to examine him and his moods. We're here to examine how he went abysmally wrong with our—my—boys." She needn't worry. There's not going to be a next time. Or so she thinks—for a millisecond. Just when she believes it's all over between them—when everything that's been said, i.e., not left unsaid, can only mean it can't *not* be over, here they are going on, inexorably. Each has survived annihilation by the other—even if the annihilation has been successful—why, here's the kindly therapist to bear witness to that success, of each's operation on the other. And yet here they are still, alive and maybe even kicking.

At the same time, he's lonely. They're right: it's lonely at the top—of the ant heap. He's utterly—totally—completely guilty. But he's not *just* guilty. In any case, he suddenly isn't strong enough to bear the prospect of being guilty-and-nothing-but out in the sunshine of Upper Broadway—at least not yet, at least not until he spills a few more beans. If it were Park Avenue and Seventy-Third, or even Forty-Sixth and Second out there waiting, he could probably endure Total Guilt without possibility of parole but not here. So he's tempted to remind them, i.e., himself, that he did *some* things right. He's not all bad, everybody has some good in them, etc. And he does remind them, or at least the lady therapist, thereby demolishing the Mephistophelian house of cards which he's just spent so much time building. For example, he took the younger boy to Santa Barbara and Coronado several summers in a row. But then he breaks down, though still upright. He will never forgive the lady therapist for listening and thereby aiding and abetting this thoroughly unnecessary stab at . . . self-attenuation. He tells her so—if for no other purpose than to keep the wife waiting. She thinks she understands: The more he defends himself, the more he seeks to exhume instances of admirable fathering, the more he convicts himself of total failure. And willy-nilly, he does mean *total*, isn't that so. Clenching his jaws will have to stand in for a nod of assent. Yes, she's right. Dredging up instances is completely at war with—completely contradictory to—what real fathering must be all about. Real fathering is a monolith of sacrifice that never feels like sacrifice, indivisible into instances. The very act of presenting the severed heads of those instances on the salver of his willed incompetence refutes the very thing those instances are supposed to prove. The True Father doesn't build a wall of instances—of evidence—around him. He's too busy being True. With all this evidence he—the UnTrue Father—builds a moat around the fortress of his disability. With all these proofs he bandages—wraps—enshrouds—the mummy of his fatherhood. With the proffer of all these instances his hideousness is no longer—was it ever?—once-and-for-all: it's in unregenerate flux. Through their accrual he defers his rendezvous with the immutable and incontrovertible.

"Every act, in other words, is an atonement, a measly compensation, for all you're incapable of giving." She says it kindly. "The only fires you're able to put out where your sons are concerned are the ones you yourself started. But that doesn't make you evil."

But he is evil. The wife is out the door, fuming—no, seething (in the corridor, no doubt). Eager to diversify her repertoire for a change and say, once she lays eyes on him, something on the order of—well, how about *Look where you are*, for example. And then she's back, with an *I-wouldn't-miss-this-for-the-world* glint in her jaundiced eye.

"How did you end up with the name John Gabriel Borkman."

He turns to his wife with a *Should-I-tell-her-or-will-you* glint in his gimlet eye. Or maybe she's the one with the gimlet eye and he—

Wife: Because like his namesake, he's a murderer. He's committed the great unforgivable sin—the crime that's beyond all forgiveness.

Borkman: Oh, shut up. You need to get some new material.

Therapist: No I want to hear this.

Wife: And hear it you shall. He murdered the love in another human being. And for what?

Borkman (to himself, in a stage whisper): The slumbering spirits of the gold.

Wife: You know what he used to say to our children when they were little? (*Borkman continues to muse, unseeing and unhearing.*) That the spirits of the gold were his true children and were all he lived for.

Therapist: That is heartbreaking. (*Rising, shaking her head, in disbelief at her own disbelief, given all she's seen and heard.*) The slumbering spirits of the gold. The two of you could have saved yourself a lot of trouble and money if you'd realized at the very beginning (and stuck with it) that, as in any relationship doomed to fail, familiarity breeds contempt—worse, incomprehension.

He feels . . . exonerated. Heartbreaking, after all, is a heartbreaking word if spoken heartbreakingly and the therapist doesn't quite have the knack. He asks for her first name. After all, she knows his. She sixth-senses that he feels exonerated and contends to a tactfully absent jury of her colleagues that this was not her intention. That is, if he thinks exoneration exhorts him—gives him license—to diabolize the distaff—a bitch, at least as he sees it, from way back when. If, however, the swan song of exoneration is heard in the key of lifting a burden from his cold shoulders—of absolving him of the civic duty to destroy her—the wife—then he's gotten exoneration right. But the wife doesn't breathe a sigh of relief since as far as she's concerned, the therapist lady isn't on her side until she forks over her first name since the wife, too, quite frankly, wants to know it. But this therapist—it's peculiar to her practice—doesn't deliver such goods. She likes to keep them guessing since guessing ultimately guarantees a breakthrough. Don't ask me why, her headshake says.

Borkman: Bigger and bigger incomprehension.

Therapist (in so many words): Since there's always one who thinks, How can he (or she) abandon this glorious fusion of souls for something as paltry as the commands of a private essence? I'm sure you know better than anyone (*looking wifeward*) that for a guy like him it's only against the savage demands of fusion that the private essence can affirm itself—legitimate itself. His private essence has no shape, no contour—is a wobbly disesteeming thing—until it starts to kick against the pricks of fusion—against the bounden duty to fuse.

Borkman: Against the contempt, against the incomprehension.

Making water pistols of her forefingers, the wife presses them against her temples.

She makes a great show of managing with difficulty—although in fact it costs her next to nothing—to say that she feels for him. It's suddenly become clear that he got married and had kids because he needed something to escape from for escape is his oxygen and the family is as good a pretext for flight as any other. Only in the process of escape from—of repudiation of—what everybody else wants or seems to want does he affirm his identity. And what she fears, the therapist does, is that he'll take this as a compliment—as high praise for his heroism. For him—for people like him (here she turns her attention compensatorily—expiatively—to the wife: proffers a box of tissues for the wife is weeping)—every relation—even the puniest—is but an archetypal struggle—must be made to function as one. No point in knowing you're uniquely unidentifiable—i.e., that you have an identity—if it hasn't been wrested from the claws of the enemy without who is but the poor man's imitation of the enemy within.

Before he rises from what has become his chair he knows he'll never see this therapist lady again. She's a disgrace to her profession despite all the framed diplomas. He tells her calmly that she's a bad therapist because a good therapist would absolve him of his duty—his civic duty—his Christian duty—his moral obligation—his ethical imperative—to hate, hate and go on hating till death does them part. Whereas she—the Old Testament prophetess act isn't fooling anybody—keeps egging him on.

So I've struck out with the two of them, the prophetess thinks. Both have willfully misread me but is it my fault if each needs to feel infinitely more disfavored than the other to be able to look himself in the eye—to survive in dignity?

Out on Broadway, whose *plat du jour*, as every sceptic knows, is sweltering dogshit smothered under freshly fried raspberry-jelly donuts, he resumes screaming. How dared she yet again malign his work in the presence of an imperfect stranger? What did she know—a mediocrity like her! It would be false to claim it is *to his surprise* that she not just eagerly but all-too-eagerly agrees, calling herself every disqualificatory name in the book—but not that this enrages him even more. Since she isn't really retracting: the attack was eminently justified, only it should have been mounted by somebody with the just-right credentials. His acuity is so very much on-target it actually impales him on a ray of rapturous hope—so very much on-target it actually obliterates, for a split second at least, the state of affairs on which it has been brought to bear. He shakes the wife's upper arms violently—a way of damaging her and, by way of holding on for dear life to those bars of his cage, mitigating the damage—becoming his own collateral damage, if you like—but you don't, and rightly so. He calls her a cunt—what self-respecting battle royal would be complete without that expletive?—and immediately realizes the call—or the expletive—embodies its own cry for help, whose gist is, *Help me not to hate you.*

While strollers and scurriers alike slow down to better enjoy the fist-fight, he takes some comfort (*or the Master does, by putting this unperceivable thought in his head*) from the fact that they will be unable to incorporate it within the context of a storyline, no matter how much slowing down they do. Every jab is just too impacted, too short-circuited, too indirect, too *implied* to be expository. For Borkman is if nothing else a true-blue bipolar, narcissistic personality-disordered, obsessive-compulsive sufferer—and maybe his wife is one, too, though she clearly doesn't *enjoy* suffering as much as he, especially Roseland-style exhibition-suffering in public venues—and the rage-breeding hurt of a true sufferer is so much him and he so much it that there's just no way to break down the monolith of its enactment into a tidy sum of describable—articulable—bits and pieces. The true sufferers, multipolar or not, are always caught up in the most indecipherable atypical cross-section of their mess. Even/especially/only Cantor knows that the mess is at best a pathological curve to which no line of straightforward exposition can ever be tangent.

They both come to their senses. Borkman realizes he's already (too?) late for the second act and she, that those unruly willows have a lot more modeling ahead of them before the day is through. They are about to go their separate ways looking, for all to see, like the very best of friends. His breath must stink, as if he's—he'd—just downed a Tasmanian Devil.

Wait, he stops in his tracks. He wants to say something. To tell her—though he dreads simplification—that all they need is a vacation to set things right. In, say, the sunny Islet of Langerhans. Alas, too expensive, what with all the legal bills. Where not only Borkman's father, a victim of pancreatic cancer, but quite a few unnumbered accounts are buried. Or should he plow right into her, as she deserves? Should he throw caution to the winds and call her a *shitpickle*, his favorite term of endearment? Should he make as if to strike her—crucify her upper arms with nails embedded deep in their flesh—as if—no!—shaking the bars of his cage—thereby burying in an excess of assault whatever legitimacy his rage may lay claim to? For legitimacy is an extra-heavy weight to bear. Even an iota of legitimacy will diabolize her: if his rage is legitimate then she's a monster to have triggered it. Still, he wants to tell her that he's sorry for all the damage done. For having killed love in another human being (he won't go so far as to specify who that lucky human being is). He wants to tell her that for years—decades—centuries—he thought unknowingly that all the suffering It put him through made him a favorite of Fortune only he's come to realize that all the suffering proves just the opposite—that he never was. (He wants to tell her even if he knows she'll only ask, provokingly, *That he never was* what, and that he'll have to reply, redundantly, *A favorite of Fortune*, which will sound so dull-witted, even if it's she who's the stupid one.) But something holds him back from all this belated expiatory telling. But what exactly? Why, her look which he can comfortably turn into a smirk shaped like a tapeworm. It justifies, this look, the hate that feeds on his own self-hate. Which signifies that he resembles nothing so much as a member of the SS yoked to his even more vicious Frau SS—at the moment he's standing guard over yet another procession to the gas chambers—a *brautzug* worthy of *Lohengrin*. Now, how can Mein Herr get through it all with his impeccable decency intact? Simple enough. Just laser-focus on some adolescent in the queue and goaded on by the little woman, renowned for her harmlessly maniacal soft spot for toothy gold, take the boy's look of terror for sly provocation—a provocation so vast and so gratuitous as to be unreason enough to get him *and his kind* exterminated as fast as possible. For extermination *macht frei*.

Now, having come so far in madness, Borkman should take one last cue from his precursor and, to calm nerves unjustly shattered by this six-million-all-wrapped-up-in-one, go listen to some twelve-tone version of, say, Elisabeth Schwarzkopf and Herbert von Karajan making beautiful Muzak together. Or go take a nap under that funny not-so-little tree out there on one of the islands (even equipped over the vicious protests of Fiscally Responsible Republicans with benches reserved for the homeless) for which upper Broadway is, rightly or wrongly, world-famous. This one has an ambitious bough in army camouflage—half proboscis, half penis—growing out of its navel. And, look, it's managed to get halfway across Eighty-Second Street. No mean feat. Slow and steady and all that. Here's somebody he can learn from—somebody who, against all odds— But what does a tree have to do with it. He never pays attention to trees. Thing is, consequent to joining the trial only this morning it's as if the intention were to push him in all sorts of unwelcoming directions. He decides to Make a Man of that swooping body—that swooping thing—whose acquaintance has been forced upon him. For the swooper must be behind the unwelcoming pushes. It isn't a drug—an Invidicum. The swooper's something behind or beyond Invidicum, colluding with it. And now that you mention it, he's sure he heard another member of the tribe griping about the same state of affairs. Or maybe the member in question wasn't exactly griping. Maybe he or she was just full of gratitude that at long last . . . *In any case, Borkman is all for calling a spade a spade, i.e., the swooper should be known henceforth as the . . . Master.* For the record, Borkman's decision to confer this particular honorific has occasioned far less of an inner struggle than Melanctha's. Which is understandable: Borkman's Viking ancestors weren't slave-shipped to and auctioned off on these unhallowed shores.

He realizes that, no, No, it's not her smirk that holds him back from talking, atoningly, about Fortune. No, what holds him back is the joy arising from so purposefully missing such an opportunity to atone—joy at the irrevocable waste of that opportunity—joy in knowing he's no longer intimidated by the threat—the realization—of waste. By the deepening of the distance between them through such a withholding (making waste—conspicuous waste—while the sun shines) generates a tremendous sense of power even if he's but a cog in the waste dynamic. And in the envy manual—sorry, the *Envy Manual* (he's had a peek or two)—didn't that Norwegian—Norwegian-American—Veblen!—say something to the effect that conspicuous waste was the right-hand-man of predatory exploit and wasn't he, JGB, first and foremost a predator? And wasn't the predatory impulse honorable—at least (according to V) among dogs. Dogs! She'll never know what he contemplated saying to her amid the fecal stonehenges here on upper Broadway. What he's capable of saying despite all the *Look where you are*'s. What a triumph—for both of them—if he can just bring himself to say what needs to be said. Too late. He's not going to fall into the trap. He's not going to let her reproach him, as all over the past, for his Dionysian high spirits, a source of bafflement most of all to him. He'll only end up hating her even more. What's the point of telling her he's sorry to have killed her capacity to love. Even if he's using the phrase in another context—a context of detoxification—to validate the sufferer— all she'll hear is the phrase, impervious to context—she'll hear him killing her all over again. Everything that comes out of his mouth—even before he opens it—is deadly—a threat of the foreclosure of any possibility of happiness. So that's why he's just added one more stonehenge to the mix. Wasting the moment constitutes nothing less (and nothing more) than the heady triumph of exploit over . . . drudgery. The drudgery of wifelicking. She puts him out of the misery of his indecisiveness by charging full speed ahead: "Be a father for once!" But what's provoked this remark? He can't establish a context. His mind was wandering. "Look where you are!" she repeats, believing no doubt that there's no such thing as too much of a good one. "You should have listened when I told you—" He tunes her out. She's nothing more than a heady mix of *shoulds, coulds, woulds* and *ifs*. Hatred saves him—hatred, not mirth (the imperial affliction), being the mail of anguish. (If Herbert were present she'd say there's a Some Body—a Master—running around loose who can be depended on to save his bumbling creatures—to take up the slack for them— for He envies their bumbling moral illiteracy *more than words can tell*.) So it's not a matter of woeful waste or expiation but—hate. It all boils down to hate—forget the Veblenian hijinks. He hates her more than he's ever hated a human being. This may or may not be true but it gets the message across—but to whom—to the Master?

In any case, the real quandary—bigger than both of them—than their stupid little life—is how to reconcile the saintliness of his extravagant self-hate (suddenly the Best Part of Him) where failed parentliness is concerned, with his hideously immoral addiction to wreaking havoc on his fellow men, especially via the spinoffs for which he's unjustly infamous. Every company he made his own having ended up divesting itself of its best and brightest, but not before saddling the businesses in question with the outsize liabilities of the now sole parent. And not before cramming them with millions in debt, which they were required to use for the disbursement of a pre-spinoff bonus to said parent, including compensation for its phantom goodwill and other phantom assets. Each then went out into the world resourceless and unarmed and, for the privilege, was required to pay back, as was only fair, hundreds of millions in dividends and management fees—fees, that is, for management of their death throes. In most instances, though, JGB managed to make eviction smell like a spoiled child's grand-exit abandonment of a too-doting parent. But how, answer me that, reconcile such rottenness with the exquisite soul-acupuncture of minutes before? Didn't exquisitry cancel out rottenness? In any event, he's more complicated—complex, even—than anybody ever gave him credit for being. He calls his lawyer for an update on his plight. Is he going to be charged further based on the fact that Utilities Worldwide, one of his least remarkable subsidiaries, has managed to lease part of the DC and San Francisco subway systems, water mains in Tampa, Taiwan's air traffic control system, a hefty swath of the Everglades and three of Santa Barbara's Channel Islands (he visited one of them with the younger boy but cannot remember which: this lapse makes him worthy of a life sentence). The contracted servicing of the assets of course never happened, even if this was the sole justification for getting a big fat tax break out of their depreciation. His lawyer informs him the matter is very much under control thanks to his pals in what he refers to smugly as the IRS Bureau of Missing Revenues. So, with regard to the leasing: *Something happened yet nothing happened.*

But not just with regard to the leasing (but isn't turning the observation into an epitaph a wee bit self-inflationary?). After hanging up, he's not sure whether the news was good or bad because in any case it's contaminated by shame at having anxiously laid bare his neediness to what is (even after all this time) a near-stranger.

Too late to amygdalate: only one brand of drug can kill the pain of *looking where he is.* A loser on all fronts. Administration of the painkiller starts with cupping, ever so gently, a firm cool breast while respectfully but unstoppably introducing two or, better yet, three fingers into the woolly wetness beneath. Although at first—and why should this time (assuming there is a *this time*) be any different—the business (business!) with any new partner always feels so overcoded, as in an R-rated Hollywood movie, one big yawn of plagiarism, with no room to go off the deep end. But every now and then, just when he is about to dismount in a huff and pack up his balls before the glorious, never-overrated moment of penetration, there explodes the sort of tiny miracle of subversion you'll never find retailed in the latest mass-market handbook for the aspiring *sexual gourmet* (sickeningly smug term drunk on its own euphemizing), simply because, truth be told, it's no great shakes out of context. But on the lonely road to orgasm it runs rings around the usual pre-missionary hijinks. For example, the lady might decide, absolutely unprompted, to rub the sweat from one of her own armpits—or, if she is feeling particularly seditious, from both—into his already gooey glans while making sure with the other that her nipples stand stiffly at attention.

Borkman is so roiled by incompatible emotions he hasn't noticed the not particularly attractive woman in an expensively subdued polka-dotted sundress who's sitting diagonally across from him in Zabar's café (how did he manage to find his way here?). He can't decide whether or not she knows he's looking at her. But her look of loathing makes sense only if she does. At warring peace with her ugliness—yes, she's ugly and more power to her: among the millions too spineless to aspire to anything but picture-perfectness her ugliness *is* power—she's incurred her look so deeply inward as to render it as far beyond caring about lookers as any look can plausibly be. Not only is she ugly which makes his looking ugly by association but her ugliness is compounded (thus nullified) by the fact that she owns it with a vengeance—has made a pact with it to withstand all besiegers. Hence his look, once again by association, is doubly ugly, because doubly suspect. He is the lowest of the low: he wants to fuck not her, or not just her, but ugliness incarnate.

But her slight shift to a three-quarter profile, which is much more appealing than full face, immediately informs his mind-heart-groin axis that in this context, ugliness is always contingent, and can vanish in an instant. Or rather, ugliness is beside the point. The body with which her new face communes is no longer disqualified. In fact being excluded from the communion makes him suffer. She is too busy being in powerful communion with all the secret rest of her to worry about the verdict of any jury, well-hung or otherwise. Exclusion triggers an erection. She now makes perfect aesthetic sense because her face no longer exists in itself, for itself, but as the sign of all that's hidden, even to—against—her. He'd like to swim around in the warm womb of that hiddenness, take the lay of its land, be replenished in return for his efforts. He is about to make his move when, glancing pointlessly at his watch, he remembers something the wife said scaldingly the night before in going through his pockets (how did he ever come to accept such routine unmanning?)—to the effect that for a lowlife like him making a move is his way of acknowledging the impossibility of deciding whether or not to make it (why does he feel that Some Body else has had this very thought today?).

All right, so he doesn't care whether he fucks or not. Worst of all vices is being unable to work up an appetite for one's official vice—it's like going for your own jugular. *Quick! who just said that? Why, he has. Or Some Body—now the Master—was impatient enough to say it for him—before the time was ripe.* The Master knows, as a graduate of the high school of hard knocks, you have to make the most of the moment even if the moment isn't the right one, no, not by a long shot, so as to keep in shape for the right one when it elects to rear its ugly head. There is a fealty owed to vice, his bastard son, his Theuth. The Master now reassures him that all is not lost for a real man (and there's nothing he wants more than to be a real man, even now) as long as he still knows both when to put his mangy ambivalence aside to give vice the wide playing field it deserves and how to tread that playing field's fine line between training and depletion. But what makes this a *vice*? Or is *vice* like *therapist* a mere placeholder—an *x*-marks-the-spot?

"Mind if I join you?" he asks. This scene should be taking place in a bar, not Zabar's café. The location scout isn't doing his B-movie best. She turns to him quaintly, no longer in profile. It's taken him a while but he's cracked the code and finds her far from ugly. Or has he simply undergone an arduous apprenticeship culminating in a much more creative conception of beauty? To celebrate he must fuck her. She looks as if she could be made to take pleasure in his urgency. She does, but at every moment he feels something is missing, even in this boutique between Park and Lexington where they've quickly ended up and where his digital trail enables the staff to meet the needs of every frequent flier. Rolling off after his signature postcoital catnap, he knows what it is—a phone call that simply won't take no for an answer—a phone call to remind him—and more importantly her or anybody else who happens to be listening—that his fluids are just too important to be allowed to run their course uninterrupted. How dare the phone not ring at the most inappropriate moment? Nobody has dared to intrude on the privity of his little death-routine. The most flagrant lese majesty, that. Why, every star worth his pillar of salt in gold—even a star about to be sent up the river or to swim with the fishes—has every divine right to expect to be interrupted at such a moment (and by way of thanks to dutifully simulate the requisite through-the-roof exasperation)—that's what makes him a star on the order of Norma Desmond.

Still anonymous, they exchange cellphone numbers (he astutely reverses two digits). As punishment for his pusillanimity, he collides with a linden tree, and the fact that the shadow of its brawny branches sink deeper into the asphalt with every halfhearted gust of wind infuses Borkman with the kind of abstract . . . hope he is always lambasting his wife for extorting from the silliest things.

CHAPTER THREE

Irena Manning, MD, Straynge's anti-muse of sorts (she's been his reluctant right-hand man on several drug trials, including the notorious "carcinoma gals" fiasco: had his license suspended for mindlessly daring to refer to his scapegoats as such in an article submitted to *The Lancet*), stares through the one window of her office that faces a vacant lot, entranced, as always, by its strict partition—doubtless according to some realtor's decree—of light and shadow. A honey locust refuses to cast its shadow across the windowless wall a few feet away, though it could certainly use the exercise. Nor do the pigeons pitch in. After catching a glimpse of the new group, she's falling in love all over again with her detestation of the sick—especially those who profess to be so as a courtesy to the malevolent need of others, significant and in-. She still isn't in the market for the bill of goods that Goldstein, Canguilhem and Hughlings Jackson, her wily mentors at Rockefeller, tried unsuccessfully to sell in her glory days there, namely, that the sick aren't healthy people minus something which has been destroyed, their embarrassing reactions to be explained away by loss or lack, and that if health is a dimension of life, then so is sickness—but a whole new, other dimension incomprehensible to its blundering double which should under no circumstances become the target of a lacerating nostalgia. Like the timid desideratum of "some college" in the classifieds of yore, sickness is *a plus*—its very own kind of plus—not a lower form of life, or obscene disqualification for gracious living.

So, on a more exalted level, the wall unshadowed—some might say the wall unshadowable—was not a wall impoverished, a wall not quite whole, but one of a totally other color, athrob with the unique rugosities conferred by the sun of privation.

The talent scout she sent out to waylay Borkman has come back empty-handed. Though Enviers are reputed to do quite a bit of symptomizing in their sleep, Borkman traded no insider beans. His only subject of concern (though he tried to hide it) was why the phone didn't ring, as a tribute to his indispensability, while he and the scout were at it, so as to turn his impressive—all right, massive—erection into an even longer-playing broken record. No idea, then, whether his largest subsidiary—but isn't it about to declare bankruptcy or in receivership or (but is that possible?) both—together with some punk hedge fund manager cum activist investor—plans a hostile takeover of Warner-Metro in anticipation (once Invidicum gets its foot through the FDA door) of the drug's far greater potential as an off-label blockbuster. Pritchard must be informed.

Though Cantor's passport says Metamathematician, he has already forgotten his subject number. More importantly, he can't decide which excerpt to start with in his *Everyman's Guide to Envy*, Second Expanded Edition. He chuckles at what he hears himself thinking: *Goodbye to piers. Having just been inducted, he's no longer the effete flâneur of hours before. The world looks completely different.* Or so his thoughts would have him believe. As usual, the wordflow is completely orthogonal to what he really believes or doesn't believe, or believes he does or doesn't believe.

For one thing, he doesn't believe in discontinuous turning points, in that one oh-so-specific moment when he went crazy, say, or gay, or Envy-mad—or stopped wearing his winter coat with the shaman's hood—for good. Madam nature in her shrew's cunning permitted no life-or-death leaps in her brothel. But isn't it always the case that when they smell a crisis (and what crisis is this one precisely?), as now, words take advantage of his defenselessness to make him say what he doesn't feel or what he refuses to feel because it's just too much like what everybody else would be feeling under the circumstances or (fearing deportation) claiming that they feel—or, more to the point, what everybody else wants him to feel, especially finally defunct mom and anile dad (wherever they are) and his bushy-tailed co-workers (he refuses to call *them* colleagues and class them thereby with *the likes of* Galois, Trakl, Proust and—on and off—Mussorgsky). The words clearly believe they are doing him a favor by putting themselves at the service of what they misguidedly take to be his rawest and truest feelings. And actually saying the words doesn't make him feel the way he's supposed to: he feels only that he's putting on an act, albeit a pretty good one. But maybe it's less painful in the long run, whatever that adds up to, to loathe himself for his inhuman—i.e., superhuman—simulation of normal human feelings than for the all-too-human surrender to those feelings which is simply out of the question until further notice.

But maybe nature does make leaps and so it's no big deal if he's been completely transformed—all in an instant—by the orientation orchestrated by that pompous ass Straynge (personally, he preferred Strayngely or Straynge-worthy) and his flunkeys. Why, didn't he read just the other day about how Darwin's cozy view of life as evolving through continuous adaptation is being contested by a new concept, according to which fully formed species just pop up—spring, just like old Zeus, from Athena's forehead?

He has no trouble choosing as study hall his least favorite Village parklet, the one marking the noisy, dusty intersection of Hudson and Bleecker. First he opens the *Times* for his kennel ration of Bush-bashing though he needs above all to be fair. Before his tumble in the hay with official villains, it is his citizenly duty to determine just how much of the villainy he already shares. And, oddly enough (but who says it's odd?), the more loathed otherness he can appropriate, the more denunciatory virulence he's entitled to. So, getting down to cases, is there really that much difference between him and Boy George? Après tout, both of them are waiting, or claim to be waiting, for history's vindication. Further, does he really care any more than bronco-bustin' Bush about the paraplegics in Walter Reed's Building 18, for example, or is it just that as a homo with grief to spare, he sometimes welcomes the distraction of waxing outraged over lost causes other than his own? As for the right to indulge in any robust smearing of Anthony Marshall, Brooke Astor's alas too uxorious only son, he must first acknowledge that, thoughts being deeds—maybe the most flagrant kind of deeds (or is this just the banality-rejecting paradox-hungry wordflow talking—wordflow that doesn't think twice about playing Kojèvian Master to his Hegelian slave? Why, he can feel It breathing down his hackles this very minute)—he must first acknowledge that given all the ways in which he plotted a final exit from Mama Cantor's under-continu-ous-construction nightmare, he's no slouch in the matricide department.

But didn't he promise Berry Sundae, his dying lover—or was all the promising done on East Beach, after the ashes were scattered?—that he'll try to steer clear of deep thoughts, even of the ersatz kind? For such snorkeling is—as that first, last(?) and only love, a Frenchman by the way, never tired of insisting without for a minute losing his Cartesian cool—exactly what everybody's demiurge wants him to engage in, so don't take the bait. Though proudly untutored he would never have been caught dead using the word *demiurge*. And like everybody's demiurge— Wait! hold your horses! is Cantor (no, not Cantor! Subject Five!) dreaming *or is said demiurge in fact the avatar of wordflow as it has been fed to him since he joined the Invidicum team? Then hereafter let him refer to the demiurge as the Master (he likes the sound of the word).* And like everybody else's demiurge, Cantor's Master casts his boy into the snorkelable Slime precisely to see what deep-thought pieties his thrashing about can come up with in the way of justifying the Slime sower to the other thrashers—other potential customers for the Master's brand of pap since the Master works on commission. And if not pieties then deep-thought beet-red blasphemies, even if the latter are infinitely more pietistic than a hymn to the creator any day of the week. And when the Master has had his bit of fun guf-fawing at his bad case of the deeps, he simply resorbs the tumor that is Five—er, Cantor. So faster than deep thinking can think him out of his straitjacket as a type, the very fact that he's taken the deep-thinking bait straitjackets him even more.

But what's so bad about a straitjacket? he wonders. Well, it's bad when the straitjacket is deep-think or intellect worship or rather worship of the stance of intellect. Hearing himself swish around in the Slime never has intel-lect sounded like such a mewling, predictable, overstocked, slavish, mealy-mouthed, generic, assembly-line, bad mother-pleasing, bourgeois, conformist sort of contraption, shredded of all freshness. The "brilliant" were clearly a dime a dozen. And the more brilliant they were, the easier it was for their mothers—especially the mothers who hated them—to marvel at the brilliance so called, thereby unwittingly cutting it down to size—bracketing—straitjack-eting it. And if there was one such mother—one such mother lode chock full of tailings—then there were billions, hence billions of sons—prodigies—blessed with the same—identical—noggin circuitry. But his pal Davey Hume predictably put it much better, one bleak autumn evening in the spring of '99 and in the Mathematics Hall lounge of all places long before it was *oh so taste-fully* renovated: *What particular privilege had this [feeble] agitation of the brain we call thought that we must make it the [very] model of the whole universe?* he wondered dreamily (granted, the dreaminess bit was a bit overdone) but loud enough for the adjacent tweedy dunderheads (to a man, all apples of mamma's eye) to hear and grit their teeth from envy—oops! Envy. Intellect/deep-think: A mere stance among too many to count—arbitrarily valorized by self-styled captains of the smarts industry. A stance no better—and a lot worse—than others. In short, how dreary to be such a thinker—how public, like a frog.

He looks down. The shadow of a tree trunk—a tree trunk whose substance, in homage to Plato, he doesn't want to make the effort to locate amid all the din of children splashing and drunks haranguing the splashing—is traversing the pockmarked asphalt. He could weep at its un-self-serving conscientiousness: getting the job done without a thought to the repercussions, even the backlash. That's precisely how he needs to plow through the trial, Straynge or no Straynge. He realizes he's feeling envy. But this envy—the envy of a shadow—is good. Just as there's good and bad cholesterol (the kind of cuddly, ailments-can-be-fun kind of distinction with which GPs never fail to seduce little old ladies of all sexes), so is there good and bad envy.

Now for the Envier's manual. On the cover—how did they know?—is a close-up of his favorite figure in Michelangelo's *Last Judgment*, the one who covers his envious left eye (the right stunned by an insight that has come or been heeded too late), while being dragged hellward by two dimwitted Demiurgi (one shackling the sinner's calves with his left arm and the other pulling at his right foot) as a green serpent (at no extra charge) gnaws his left upper thigh. A gesture—this eye-covering—painfully familiar to him as a too-fastidious schoolboy in one of the New York City public high schools, all of which boasted trendily doorless toilet stalls. For on those rare occasions when he had to use the facilities, he shat shielding half his face with his hand as the next best thing to not being seen at all. *So how could so many of the men he knew have ever enjoyed cruising johns?*

Only he doesn't like the way that sounds: too self-congratulatory—actually gets him believing, at least for a millisecond, that he isn't homosexual after all simply because he has never taken to setting up shop in public jakes. As if by lacking trait *a* he can't still belong to set A. Doesn't he know by now that the A confederacy is big enough to accommodate men of all stripes—even *a*-lackers? You mean to tell me that even at this late date Five's still looking for signs that he—a deviant sect of one—isn't one of the disanointed, still trying to pull himself up by the bootstraps into the lower reaches of hetero heaven? But there's no pleasure like the special pleasure of rejecting so pathetic a ploy and living to tell the tale.

Proving definitively that he is homosexual has required far more legerdemain than that demanded, at least so far, by the Conjecture. In fact, the homosexual proof should already have put him in the company of, for starters, Gauss, Euler and Sylvester. Here's how it goes (a little mood music, Maestro, if you please):

Working from his own vast experience of life among *his own kind*, Cantor set out on a grid—the same sort his namesake had used in arraying the real numbers between 0 and 1 as non-terminating decimals—every conceivable homosexual Type as a sequence of traits represented by digits unfolding to the Banquo-esque crack of doom, it being of course axiomatic that His Type would be flagrantly different from any other Type if it differed in just one digit. So he isn't Type A because its digit 4 signifies "bodybuilder" whereas Five wouldn't be caught dead in a gym, much less a gym shower (shades of Auschwitz). Nope, isn't Type B either because its digit 35 signifies "crossdresser" and Cantor never touches the stuff. Neither is he a Type Z because its digit 984 signifies "soft spot for Mykonos" whereas Cantor passes (*pace*

Byron) on all things Greek except, maybe, Plato's *Phaedrus* and Thucydides at his most lucidly baroque. And sure as hell isn't Type FFF because its digit 8,678 signifies "frenzied passion for both Richard Strauss and Puccini" and Cantor can't take either (he's much more of an Offenbach and Bellini kind of guy). And he clearly isn't Type ZZZZ because its digit 3,504,001 signifies "loathing for all things metamathematical." But just when Cantor is ready to celebrate his contradistinction to and from every conceivable type of fruit-cake, and hence his disqualification for membership in the underclass to which they all belong, sure enough a new Type, call him Type Infinity (∞), rushes in at the last minute to denegate the global disidentity—a lot, come to think of it, like Balanchine's Sugar Plum cutting, on her first entrance, a diagonal swath through the bedazzled corps. Though Cantor can't for the life of him remember exactly where they met (an algebraic topology symposium in Atlanta? a prime-number forum in Antibes? a Blimpie's near Brighton Beach? cyberspace? a novel by Adalbert Stifter?), he does recall that Type Infinity (a bearish twink)—although clearly neither A, nor B, nor . . . XXX . . .—has nevertheless managed to be unregenerately homosexual, and king-of-beasts proud of the fact. And Cantor still finds that every subsequent attempt to refute the proof, and hence himself, invokes just another clockwork incarnation of Type Infinity who's only too glad to demonstrate that being different from Types A through Infinity-minus-1 is no guarantee of non-membership in their fight club. Far from it.

So he ends up accepting the irrefutability of the proof *with a febrile joy completely new to him* or is he simply hyping himself up in preparation for selling it and its gee-whiz backstory to *People* magazine? No, it's all about the joy of knowing, thanks to Types Infinity, that his lifespan will be short enough to render the holding out against any form of rehab eminently practicable.

Putting the manual down beside him on the bench means he has tastier food for thought than anything Envy's greatest diagnosticians can cook up for his delectation. The weather is sultry which means there's plenty of unbuttoned overripe maleness about seeking appraisal which makes him start thinking about The Frenchman, aka Berry Sundae. On the eve of the memorial (not "a celebration of the life of"—how he detested the smarmy hokum of that phrase), Cantor inspected his wardrobe and there it was, inside the pocket of his near-favorite olive poplin, not the telephone number of some side action but a mere receipt in the amount of $2.30 for one berry sundae, no ice. Sales person: Jer 31416P. It must have been that drizzly afternoon in January when they had one of their biggest traditional Saturday fights and he decided to go to Costco alone rather than be abasingly driven there by his tormentor.

Why was it so heartbreaking to come upon such a receipt? he still wonders. Why, well, for starters, how about the fact that he saw imprinted thereon not just the phrase "berry sundae" but, infinitely more important as an inexhaustible wellspring of retrospective remorse for all those Saturdays, Berry Sundae's unawareness of all its resonances. He sees the Frenchman's—his victim's—a lonely foreigner's—pathos-crammed unseeing of all the name evokes of small-town America: goofy soda jerks, sleigh rides straight out of

The Magnificent Ambersons, literally and figuratively corny Fourths of July, necking in the backseat on Lover's Lane after a preliminary workout up in the balcony at the Bijou. The phrase is the purest distillation of Berry Sundae because it confirms his unseeing as innocence, i.e., the most precious thing he's left behind—precious because it can be counted on any time of day or night though the nights are worse to burn a hole through the heart of Cantor's heartlessness. The first and last of his paper trails, "celebrating" (he doesn't mind the word's use here—but why? he wonders)—placeholder for—all he missed because of both Five's selfishness and death's bratty impatience. It is all there on the receipt and what's there transforms him into the last of the holy fools—straight out of *Boris*. Under any circumstances, such unseeing is poignant but exposed posthumously, the excruciation never lets up. The Frenchman, semi-famous on Charles Lane for his long silences, has found his tongue at last or rather it has taken nothing less than a berry sundae—sorry, "berry sundae"—to exhume that tongue at last.

Berry Sundae's unconsciousness of the reverberations of "berry sundae" turns him into a child. And like a child he's hidden the evidence of his transgression: grabbing a sundae right after being denounced for his leech's unemployability. Which makes him a double child, doubly vulnerable. As he does with every other variable, Cantor tries to put the vulnerability in relation with the beloved's male body. The beauty had—has—much less to do with a sum of parts than with its bearer's perplexed relation to the maleness which undercuts that beauty. Did the Frenchman know he was male? Did his vulnerability know he was male? Vulnerability and sexuality were the two sides of an equation that remained tantalizingly incommensurate no matter how frantically Five went on transposing terms.

Yet Berry Sundae's not undergoing the resonances of "berry sundae" becomes less poignant than robust when Cantor manages to remind himself that he just didn't care about names for things, period. Didn't remember them, didn't drop them. Never understood Five's thrill at hearing the boldface names of the canonized roll off his tongue. So when somebody like Berry Sundae comes along who persists in not wanting to know the right names for the right people and the right things, then how can somebody like Cantor not be seduced? For the state Cantor, for all his name-dropping, aspires to more than any other is and will always be Berry Sundae's. It is an otherworldly state, a state of immunity to . . . Envy. That's it, Berry Sundae never name-dropped, i.e., evinced Envy, Envy wasn't one of his changes of garment.

But if by naming a boldface name Cantor abases himself faster than he can be exalted by fusion, through naming, with the bearer of the name, he at least knows something 99.99 percent of all name-droppers don't know, namely, that they *are* abasing themselves—compliments of penny ante self-transcendence. So he's not just another hacker into the celebrity network, not just another phantom of its rue morgue.

He knows that taking anybody's name on faith and then speaking it constitutes a form of abasement through credulity. The name is a pretense, a fraud, and this being the case, how can you expect anybody who's anybody to defer to the name and thereby jeopardize the plausibility of his own? You or I wouldn't dream of inflicting our full name on anybody else, expecting him to utter it faithfully every chance he gets. After all, "John Smith," say, is a fictionalization, residue of a hallucination, badge of unearned grandiosity, volatilization of the dregs of personality into a cloud of vainglory. To say the name, then, is to subsidize the plausibility of John Smith's vainglorious identity as John Smith. The name is all about the named's being able to pull the wool of the name over anybody's eyes: getting the anybody to utter the name means getting him to sing along as this John Smith performs his *Fantasia on the Theme of John Smith* . . . But all this does not apply to the names for things? Each thing does have a name but there is a sadness that accrues whenever Cantor finds the right name for a thing—when the right name for a thing finds him—and thereby sponsors the coitus between name and thing—for this forecloses the need to go on name-groping, which is *the only reason to stay alive*, Cantor thinks. *But can it be he who thinks something so outlandish. Is it not instead that Some Body famous for thinking for him, through him, out from under him, to wit, the entity yet to be named in part or in full? (However, what sounds like "Master" aka "wordflow," still floating around in Cantor's skull, remains one among many contenders for said entity's name.)* Once the right name's been found, the job is done or his job has been done for him and he is then a casualty of the right fit—a voyeur peeping in at the obscene coitus of meshed gears. Nothing more depressing than to have the right name handed to him on a silver platter. But in the case of a name worthy of being dropped—the name of a great one—Charles Sanders Peirce or George Balanchine or Maria Callas or Rogier van der Weyden—the humiliation occasioned by the naming is abolished or at least trivialized compliments of the goose-pimpling self-transcending fusion effected through that naming. The great one has a right to impose his vainglory on the namer. How many times has he waited for somebody to ask, Who's the composer who . . .? or Who's that poet who . . .? simply to be able to reply, Ferruccio Busoni, or, Luis de Góngora—but as poker-faced and -voiced as possible in order to distill maximum self-transcendence from the contrast between the delivery and the thing delivered? So, the long and the short of it is that *berry sundae* will surely take its hallowed place along with *loser*, *Building 18* and *therapist* in Invidicum's pantheon of placeholders (hall of fame to you, junior)—but who's feeding him this decree?

Should he divulge the secret of *berry sundae* in Amygdala's amphitheater of unspeakable emotions? (Everybody is supposed to have his initiatory time in the sun of collective scrutiny—it says so in the *Manual* and surely what the *Manual* says goes.) Thing is, unrevealed, it's immune to diagnosis and can signify almost anything including *the fact that he doesn't really exist*. But sometimes, as a matter of principle if not of mental health, doesn't he have to make an exception and assume the mantle of realness. He needs to get Berry Sundae off his chest in as public a venue as possible. He can't wait for Berry Sundae to find his successor—for *berry sundae* to find its mate. Life is a very sloppy artist—it refuses to mop up after its own false starts—to provide them with . . . whatever false starts are entitled to in the name of completion. So, he tells himself, almost speaking out loud, Don't sit around waiting for Life to catch up with your blind-as-a-bat expectations. Maybe he should try marriage—the heterosexual kind. No more foolproof way of feeling manly than to practice poker-faced forbearance in the face of some female's semihysterical chatter. For every man needs to feel manly, however un-, at least once in his life—needs to feel like his father and divorced—through that very gritted-teeth forbearance—from his mother. *She,* whoever the lucky lady turns out to be, will *do* femaleness on his behalf, thereby exorcising his every inclination to follow suit and leaving him with a core of brawn unbleared and unsmeared with the toil of name-dropping. The more forbearing he is in the face of her Hesiodian hunger to warehouse the fruits of his Works and Days in her big belly, the more of a man he will prove himself to be and the less grim-faced screeching Envy will be his JO buddy. For observing her consumed with Envy of her neighbors' ill-gotten gains, as any self-respecting shrew must learn to be, will quickly cure him of his own.

But enough about the absurdity of marriage. The section of the *Manual* devoted to the mighty musings of Thorstein (not, as the *Manual* would have it, Thorstenn) Veblen seems immediately interesting—never mind what his current standing happens to be among the academia nuts, wherever he's notched on their scrotum pole.

Cantor reads: "The distinction between exploit and drudgery is an invidious distinction between employments. Those employments which are to be classed as exploit are worthy, honorable, noble; other employments, which do not contain this element of exploit, and especially those which imply subservience or submission, are unworthy, debasing, ignoble." AND: "During the predatory culture labour comes to be associated in men's habits of thought with weakness and subjection to a master . . . *leisure, considered as an employment* [the italics are Five's], is closely allied in kind with the life of exploit." AND: "The basis on which good repute in any highly organized industrial community ultimately rests is pecuniary strength; and the means of showing pecuniary strength, and so of gaining or retaining a good name, are leisure and a conspicuous consumption of goods . . . THE UTILITY OF BOTH ALIKE FOR THE PURPOSES OF REPUTABILITY LIES IN THE ELEMENT OF WASTE THAT IS COMMON TO BOTH [the caps are his]."

Veblen's brute deployment of these pairs of opposed terms—drudgery versus. exploit, labor versus leisure, money versus want, waste versus utility—thrills him to the funny bone. Maybe if he's patient, *berry sundae* will find—or be found by—its opposed term (better an opposed term than none at all, along the sappy lines of "Better to have loved and lost . . ."). Whether he knows it or not—or cares—this fearless Norse outsider is teaching Cantor how to remain unfazed and unintimidated by the term in any dyad that is arbitrarily favored by life and her henchmen, how to remain uninfected by any invidious distinctions based on which Cantor may come out the loser (that it has always been a point of honor with him to love losers is beside the point). The drug and its adjuvants will carry on Veblen's work and cure him of his drudge's Envy of the Man, as embodied in A-list actors, politicos, CEOs, footballers and other conscientious philanderers—will cure him of the need to perceive his work as drudgery—as a necessary drudgery. For Cantor still maintains—

after all these years, after all those encounters, steamy or otherwise—that his is a contingent—an eminently facultative—homosexuality, reversible but only through impulse-blunting drudgery—defined as anything that interferes (like teaching too many freshman courses) with his work on the Conjecture. But here is Veblen explaining that it is in fact leisure (in Five's case, a leisurely pursuit of The Solution) that is manly.

Although the military march of the binaries has begun by thrilling him—because Thorstein has taught how not to feel canceled out just because he finds himself always identified with the unprivileged term in each pair—it quickly fatigues and saddens. For the conception of categories as absolutely airtight mirrors too direly his own view of life, which no amount of evidence to the contrary can alter. Cantor knows homos, for example, who regularly experience terrifying heterosexual stirrings and heteros who regularly give in to intriguingly unterrifying same-sex lust but such evidence is always to be discarded as an artifact of statistical delinquency since it calls into question his own airtightness as sole defense against ever-present soul theft.

Fortunately (for Veblen, wherever he is), Cantor decides to read on: "It is obviously not necessary that a given object of expenditure should be exclusively wasteful in order to come in under the category of conspicuous waste. An article may be useful and wasteful both, and its utility to the consumer may be made up of use and waste in the most varying proportions. Even in articles which appear at first glance to serve for pure ostentation only, it is always possible to detect the presence of some, at least ostensible, useful purpose; and on the other hand, even in special machinery and tools . . . as well as the rudest appliances of human industry, the traces of conspicuous waste . . . usually become evident on a close scrutiny."

Beautiful: refreshing: better yet, therapeutic. Afraid of Cantor's defection before they can consummate their courtship, this lumberjack among sociologists—Knut Hamsun minus the Hitleronics—has just tried to prove that after all he, too, knows opposites are never too black or too white for interpenetration. And Cantor for his part is immediately willing to grant that Thorstein not only does know, but knows as well as somebody he's never imagined could in a million years be bested in that department, to wit, his testy old flame and favorite philosopher pin-up, Charley Sanders Peirce, nineteenth-century American academia's fall guy who wrote: "But at any assignable time in the past, however early, there was already some tendency toward uniformity, and at any assignable date in the future there will be some slight aberrancy from law." Interpenetration then, and not ripeness, is all. Why, Peirce and Veblen were themselves now doing it—interpenetrating like crazy. Come to think of it, just like Mallarmé and Melville at the moment when the latter wrote the phrase "the clear, vivid, unspeakable blue."

Enough background for now, or maybe forever. Walking back up Bleecker, he recognizes (from the well-shaped buttocks molding his chinos) a fellow proband. He does resemble Berry Sundae a little from the back—why, he's a veritable Mayakovskian stormcloud-in-trousers, at least at the corner of Bleecker and Christopher. But why is he pretending—and to himself of all people—that his neighborly interest is based solely on Chino's resemblance to the beloved? At any rate, his orientation becomes clear quickly enough when he turns his head to appraise the subsidence of a large-breasted but otherwise spritelike young thing in a halter top and platform heels. In fact, Chino's so engrossed he almost collides with a mauve tank top stretched tight over a T-shirt of reddish chest hair.

CHAPTER FOUR

On a half-empty stomach, Herbert notes that the auditorium seems much smaller. She wishes she could be part of the trial getting off the ground in the one adjacent. The members of the patient group in there look much happier, almost deliriously so, so to speak pinching their cheeks in evident disbelief at how much tragicomical fun institutional rehab can, in the right hands, turn out to be. Or is she simply being fed this observation by the Master? And is belief in a Master one of the many unmentionable side effects perpetrated by Invidicum? In here, all is subdued rancor, as her cohorts try to decide where not to sit and whom not to sit next to. On the other side of the room, under a bust of Hippocrates, Shearer is keeping her distance, though she's obviously seen Herbert come in. So Herbert's hard-luck story has failed the lunchtime audition—or succeeded only too (terrifyingly) well.

A tall well-built man in a blue suit towers unapologetically above everybody else in the adjacent auditorium. He's gesticulating with angry angularity, a little like Donald RUMPsfeld when parrying those very few but still too many imbecile journalists who dare to impugn his non-strategy for letting stuff happen—to others, of course, and preferably under age 21, never to him or George or Tricky Dick II or precociously porcine Karl. His presence casts a shadow over what seemed, seconds before, a Forest of Arden.

From his seat near the sniveling air conditioner, Eden (One) looks Straynge, obviously impatient to strut his grand-inquisitorial stuff, right in the eye. It has been a long journey indeed from San Diego to this hole-in-the-wall and he is oh so very tired of them all, the rehab men (though this is of course no ordinary specimen), the self-styled shamans, the glorified bedpan Charlies. Still, he needs to start thinking of him—Straynge—as yet—just—another rehabber (rather than the Mother of all rehabbers)—like the ones at Payne Whitney West to which his brother twice committed him after unsuccessful efforts, both on the Coronado Golf Course and in front of the Timken Museum of Art, to strong-arm men whom he took to be Straynge—witch doctors waiting to catch him with his pants down, to catch him in the act— and of what exactly? Why, of being himself, what else? And getting himself caught in the act of being himself is of course the necessary first step on the road to cure. But what if this overrated *being caught* has been engineered by the goofball patient himself, did they ever think of that? Did they ever think he—as a sort of loony-bin Robin Hood—might be capable of cooking up a strategy of telltale missteps so as to have the gabby rehabbers where he wanted them, sniffing at his asshole, mistaking its stench for the aroma of truth, and thereby keeping them (in memory of his not-so-beloved father) from preying on the more vulnerable kennel inmates.

Rehab men are always too stupid, he thinks fondly, to recognize how satisfying being caught with your pants down—i.e., caught in the act of revealing (at once knowingly and unknowingly) how you've once again sabotaged the ghost of a chance to succeed—can be. He notes that Straynge, since last they met in downtown San Diego, has grown a little pot which is clearly hankering to get out from under his very blue and very neatly pressed fraternity-row blazer and make its furry way in the world, unrehabilitated.

Sitting here, he grieves for the innocence of this new batch of trial mates. What he remembers best from the small talk therapy sessions mandated by all the other drug trials is less his shame when they caught his sabotaging self-delusion in the act than their pathetic self-congratulation at having done so. But isn't it clear that they become his guinea pigs long before he becomes theirs? Their prey is Eden's mere self-delusion. But his is much tastier: the occupational hazard of taking the self-delusion for the core of his sickness. Being caught with his pants down is thus precisely the point where he, Eden, begins to leave the rehab men far behind and transcend the sabotaging, if self-sabotage is what he practices, without having to bid it adieu. For self-sabotage is the very core of his strength. So he gets to keep the best of both worlds: the enrichment only self-sabotage can bring and transcendence thereof through hoisting the rehabbers by their own petard. But doesn't this very ability to expose them (some body—some *thing*—is asking him—commanding him—to ask himself) invalidate the exposé inasmuch as said ability is based on a much too long association with their kind? Maybe he's kidding himself to think he's entered trial after trial simply to track down Straynge.

As far as Eden is concerned, the minute he is successfully unmasked—and in rehab the moment of truth always reduces to an unmasking—the subject is no longer his self-sabotage but rehab man's sidesplitting smugness in believing unmasking has actually gotten the patient somewhere, clinically speaking. Following that sidesplitting moment, all Eden needs to do is stand back and enjoy the peepshow. His purpose yet again—and/but for the very last time—is to bracket rehab man—this particular rehab man—the Mother of 'em all—in preparation for the biggest bracketing of all—before rehab man can bracket him back to so-called health. But is there ever a last word as far as bracketing is concerned?

Let's put it this way, shall we? (*The Masterly somebody/the Masterly something proceeds to bellow-hiss in Eden's right ear.*). By catching rehab man in the act of congratulating himself for having caught him in the act of being sick, Eden gets beyond his sickness without having to deprive himself of its power to enrich. But he's not Van Gogh so how does cutting off his ear to spite their face enrich him? What does he do with his victory? He can't *acquire* it, like a painting or a symphony.

Up on the dais, where the dusty sunlight collaborates with his self-love to create a discreet little aureole, Straynge makes the usual heavy weather out of adjusting the mike. *Stage business*, Herbert murmurs inwardly (that playwriting course is finally proving useful: it enables her to master the moment). Before sending them on their way, they must—or at least some of them must—as part of a venerable tradition—tell their Envy story. Straynge concedes that *sharing*—detestable word, thinks Borkman (guess what? he's made it back after all because he's desperately needed, or so he tells himself), as detestable as those baby-boomer ingénues who make themselves galling to look at by wearing their voluminously soggy gray hair long, long, extra-long)—is by no means as curative as a good stiff drink of Invidicum. Still, he's entitled to admit that it has its place in the armamentarium. And since therapy—not *terror*py as some would have it (not a single chuckle in the house: Eden is appalled at finding himself feeling a wee bit sorry for the old fart)—constitutes part of the package, it might be a good idea for them to start getting to know each other—and themselves—as quickly, and as quietly, as possible. First up at bat is the fetching redhead: she says, almost inaudibly, that her name is Jean Rhys. (Narr decided at lunch that she should be the first to go public with a case history, even if it's all a fabrication, so as to throw the powers that be—Straynge for one had a long snout—off the unbeaten track of her off-label leanings.) Borkman and Eden both wonder whether her bush is lighter or darker than her frizzy mane. What does her vulva smell like? Borkman wonders, especially when she rolls over sullenly, breasts sloppy and fragrant, to clamp down on the alarm.

Rhys (she's now seated next to Straynge, close enough for their elbows to get in each other's way) explains how Envy has been eating away at her for years to the point where all is valueless. It's Caro, a little sister straight out of Raymond Chandler, who has everything worth having. So it's a double life she leads. But not in the sense you would think, she quickly adds. "In what sense, then?" Straynge now positions himself behind her on the dais, a bottle of high-end H_2O between his plump thighs. The allusion to high-end potency is unmistakable. Or is this a plug for prostheses? She advances to the lectern where a stagehand with a smile that reminds her of her husband's, though he made it a point to smile rarely, adjusts her mike.

Without further ado she starts reading from what appears to be a mishmash of scrawled jottings (though all the flummoxed grimaces may just constitute *her* version of hokey stage business). "I remember the last Fourth of July—ablaze, as it's supposed to be, for normal people, that is—the kind, like Caro and her mate, who always get invited somewhere chic." She must be careful not to out Narr. "I decided that we—me and *my* husband—had to do something—anything—to oppose to their doings before the sun set on one of the longest days of the year, at least for me. So at the last minute we took the almost empty F train out to Forest Hills, bought two falafel sandwiches and sat down under a big old beech (its trunk defaced by tumors) in the little square near the LIRR station to dispatch them. I could tell he felt very comfortably connected to me from the way he burrowed deep, unaware of or indifferent to the tahini dribbling down his chin. Don't get me wrong—he has a strong, an exquisitely shaped chin, that isn't the problem. The problem is his having the audacity to think I burrowed with the same relish, that we were lovebirds of a feather.

"Actually, in the skewed way I'd made my own, I was watching not just him but both of us with the eyes of the *other pair*, amused by our appalling pitifulness. So in my case connection to him from moment to moment took the form, you might say, of a constant sabotaging of the connection—incessant doubt as to whether there was any connection whatsoever. Our only connection was to that other pair—as members of their supporting cast and by no means the most memorable ones. So connection to him was always a sum of disconnectednesses."

How could Cantor not love this depiction—this respectful tribute to Weierstrass and his pathological curve, with its queer continuity that was all sharp corners, its unbrokenness that was all jagged edges, the rebuff of any line's innocent-enough craving for tangency?

"Because of Envy, I was connected to him purely by a desire to flee the wrong kind of connectedness, which he alone imposed on us, into the arms of the other pair. I recoiled from him not so much because he disgusted me but because I knew he disgusted Caro. So I made it my business—my vocation— to get to the point of disgust faster than she could."

Eden cries out, pointedly without asking for Straynge's permission: "Maybe at the very moment the sauce was dripping down his chin, the very same sauce was dribbling down the other guy's chin." "Yes, but when the very same sauce dribbled down the other guy's chin, Caro expected it to be perceived by me as something awe-inspiring and if I didn't fork up the awe, then I myself was the problem, through my refusal to be awestruck by the dribbling." Straynge (*impishly*): "Refusal signified an acute form of sexual repression, no?" Subject Six pointedly ignores him for which Eden awards her, without moving a muscle, two or three standing ovations.

"Yet I had the presence of mind, the decency—a kind of survival instinct—survival on his behalf, you might say—*to force myself to look back on this irrecoverable moment under the beech tree* even if it was by no means over. The only way to endure it was to nostalgize it. If I lost him forever, I would no doubt regard his dripping chin as something infinitely childlike therefore poignant. And I imagined how I would torture myself to the end of my days for not having loved a man, sauce or no sauce, who wanted nothing so much as to please me, at least some of the time. But woman cannot live by poignancy alone: his dribbling chin revolted me and, more to the point, my own revulsion revolted me. Since he had no idea what I was feeling the disconnectedness was even more excruciating. Pity the executioner when his victim doesn't have the decency to understand why he's being beheaded.

"He reached out to squeeze my hand—worse, kiss my knuckles. I withdrew—as I always did, promising myself to make it up to him the next time his kisses came a-calling. Can you understand that I felt both that I was unworthy of being kissed and that he was just as unworthy of kissing me? I needed to be unencumbered enough to think of ways to crawl out of the pit Caro's contempt had dug for me. Oddly enough, the only way out of my conspicuousness to that contempt was to squeeze back much harder, harder and harder, untenderly. In that way I both punished him for loving me and found protection in his loving from my sister's world-historical contempt." (Where did "world-historical" come from? she wondered.) "I was connected to him and through him to the world compliments of a connectedness appraised as worthless."

Straynge rises and motions Rhys aside—a little too brutally, Herbert thinks. "So you see," he remarks, "you're all double-lifers or, as my old pen pal at Copenhagen General used to say to anybody who'd listen, *double-minded to your peril*. There's the life given up to the Envy—the life of your rival—and then there's the *other* life. But the other life, which nobody can live better,

I mean more flawlessly, than you yourself—the eminent domain in which no usurper can *do* you better than you yourself—exists only for minutes at a time, before it is swallowed up yet again by the rival's life."

As Rhys steps down from the stage to return to her seat (Should we applaud? murmur several pairs of upraised hands), Post enters from a side door, his movement in perfect counterpoint to hers—movement contending against movement. (How cinematic, Shearer thinks. But why me, she wonders—why has this observation—a blessing and a curse—been allocated to me unearned?) He's followed by a gaggle of what look like interns/residents only they don't have the requisite irrepressible self-importance—even if they're all in white, stethoscoped to the gills—clipped to their clipboards. Once they get their giddy bearings, each holds up a little poster (arrivals terminal style) with the name of a trial member carefully printed in blue marker.

"To be continued," Straynge says to Rhys, now seated in the audience, in a tone that might be considered encouraging. "Let's all take what one of my professors used to call a brief bladder break." Once again, no takers. Once again, against his better judgment, Eden feels a wee bit sorry for the old fart. And thinks—but not against his better judgment—"One day I, too, 'll be an old fart."

Melanctha Herbert stays put. She's been much more affected by Jean Rhys's tale of woe than she cares to admit. Yet admit it she must, even if she believes, or needs to believe, that as a horse of another color entirely, her African American brand of Envy renders her, on principle, impervious to the vicissitudes of any other. Once her fellow sufferers are seated once more, there is a long silence. Somebody yawns. And what other purpose can he have—wait, he's a she!—than to break the thin ice on which everybody else fears to tread. Herbert wonders why she hasn't noticed the heroic yawner before. Maybe it's because she didn't exist before and having been put on earth solely to perpetrate this groundbreaking stunt, exists no longer.

Back on the dais, Straynge informs Rhys, who's clearly eager to resume (much to Narr's dismay though he can only marvel at her ability to keep his name out of it), that according to the way things work around here, if she happens to utter any word or phrase deemed key, an alarm will go off and a member the staff will require her to elaborate—or do it for her.

Rhys begins to explain—first to the yawner, wherever she now resides. From the very beginning he had both her *and* her arch rival to contend with. During the love-is-blind period, summer dawn in the West Village often found the three of them—note, the *three* of them!—in a coffee shop on Sixth Avenue. She would babble on, rapturously—there! she's said it!—as Caro stared, chain-smoking, into space. She asked them, through perfect draft-resistant rings effortlessly blown, to pay her no heed: she was often like this, she assured them—abstracted, a million miles away. Rhys took her at her word. He had a different take on the little sister, only she refused to listen. He was intent on wising her up anyway, insisting the abstractedness bit was all a big act, to conceal the hunger to outdo Rhys as her designated rival the first chance she got. This wasn't absent-minded—at its best, otherworldly—estrangement—from them, the coffee shop, the Village, New York—Life itself stretching out in front of her or rather, arching its indifferently feline spine. This was highly mundane surveillance which missed nothing. According to him she was taking it all in, warehousing every syllable, so as to be able to humiliate her sister later for what she'd said or didn't say. Since undoubtedly they'd rehash, as sisters must, the events of the day in their undies, over the malfunctioning hotplate in a walkup facing—or at least with a partial view of—Judson Hall. Thing is, Rhys felt a responsibility toward the viperess, who of course denied any dependency. Granted, their mother—generous in her praise only when that praise was invidious—hated her. In her case, however, hatred is mixed with what, on a sunny day, she is still tempted to call *a kind of* love. In Caro's case, the hatred is undiluted. By the way, though she knows it's become all the rage, she can't bring herself to call her mother, mom. *Mom*, after all, is *mother* plucked, defanged, depilated. *Mom* is the generic version of the blunder drug Mother, filleted of its toxic side effects.

Back to the jottings but without the stage business: "In case you haven't guessed, she's—our mother's—one of those women born to be widows, not wives, and for whom widowhood is the only honorable—the only conceivable—estate, not least because it wipes completely clean the wifely slate of willed failure. And this estate has nothing in common with the estate of marriage, even if they have to pass through the minefields of the one to reach the promised land of the other. Through widowhood she's finessed and finagled a second chance at married life, this time without the redundant spouse in tow. Just one look at her and you know immediately this is the role she was born to play—with a host of other shrews (so how can Caro and I not be shrews as well?)—for widowhood is also a *collective* estate. Some might even go so far as to say a collective game. Still, she's convinced it's wifehood that was her calling. And this lie is simply the right and proper cancellation of an essence that's done the gravest disservice to what she should be but through no fault of her own is not. The lie rectifies a reality that has no right to be—a reality nobody has the right to judge her by.

"Following the wedding, little sister got herself hitched as quickly as possible for only with a husband in the picture would surpassing me, whatever that might consist in, resonate. I gasped and gaped from the sidelines as she pistol-whipped herself into a frenzy of compliance, making his every whim her dark command." Narr will be forever thankful that she does not turn involuntarily to the whimsical dark commander. "Whereas my mother-in-law made no bones about hating my guts (and I give her credit for her frankness), Caro and *hers* immediately joined forces to wet-nurse the fiction that here there was some kind of affinity-at-first-sight. She had no trouble at all convincing herself this was indeed the case, especially since the fringe benefit was too tempting to pass up: besting me in the mother-in-law department. No hankering, on her part, after the lonely glory that accrues from regularly parrying the incursions of a stranger who wants to destroy you.

"Her spellbindingly pitiable ploy was to fuse with mother and son faster than their contempt could undo her. And so she had to disavow me. Though maybe she didn't have to—maybe she only thought she had to—maybe fusing with them was the pretext she'd all along been waiting for. But I refused to listen when he warned me that for her kind, betrayal, as a defiant refutation of past dependency, became the purest form of self-realization. If there was any residual debt she expected it to be canceled once and for all through the loathing her betrayal must generate.

"I'll never forget—or rather my husband never let me forget—one gusty autumn night walking down St. Mark's Place toward Second with lovey-dovily entwined sister and brother-in-law taking the lead and (resolutely unentwined) husband and I directly behind—*we were in fact their behind*. I yapped around my little sister like some loose-bowelled poodle, irrepressibly making nice. But Caro continued to stare straight ahead at her ever-expanding future, exalted and unhearing. And the more I chattered, the more she felt her fast-moving contempt supremely justified.

"But I was aware of nothing—it was my husband and my husband alone who saw and, given my willful blindness, had to see double. You might say he was a kind of Master of Self-blinding Insight. The miserable injustice as reflected in the imbalance between me and her was too much for his essential fragility. From the time of that walk down St. Mark's Place, his hatred for my sister and her husband became all-consuming. And the more he hated them, the more he envied them or rather their smug conviction (evident from the tenor of their synchronized swagger) that they were supremely enviable. Envy is contagious. To the point where he couldn't eat, couldn't sleep."

The alarm bell rings out. A woman in a white coat, whose alluringly slender figure has been concealed up to now by Straynge's bulk, advances toward the lectern. Rhys steps aside. She adjusts the mike masterfully. No feebly ingratiating stage business for the likes of her—and no yokage to jottings to impede the eloquence of her enunciation, with true immigrant propriety, of every last syllable. "Yes, you've hit the nail on the head." (She speaks to Rhys through the audience.) "The *imbalance* (I think you used that word)—in the dyad—is the key, the way in, to Envy disease, at least as we have come to understand it at this point in time. Your husband perceived the imbalance immediately: for that gift alone, you shouldn't have let him go.

"At the core of every relationship, there is always this imbalance (which may go pathological as it did in your case) between the one (call him A) who tries in vain to win acceptance, thereby demeaning himself in the process, and the other (call him B) who, transformed by the divine right of movement into something regal (if they happen to be strolling, as you were one gusty autumn night in the battered heart of the East Village), absolutely refuses to acknowledge the supplicant, the court jester, yapping at his rear end like one of the bloodhounds invoked in that movie (the first one I saw once I'd crashed the gates at Ellis Island on a J-1 visa) about some diva's bloodsucking protegée. A envies B's unreachability, unpleasability, is fascinated by it, attributes an infinite depth to it. And on those very rare occasions when B condescends, indifferently, from sheer boredom, to ask A a question about his own life, it is A who, in attempting to answer, stares straight ahead, though A's staring straight ahead is of course a staring starkly different.

"A tries to convince himself that what drives him to go on looking *way out there* is complete absorption in the answer he's preternaturally focused on with his mind's eye, and not dread—the minute the answer's complete—of being delivered up to the verdict dormant in B's expressionless gaze, which is in fact what he's really focused on—skewedly—awry—to the exclusion of all else. His jabbering animation is anxiety pure and simple, fear of failing B's right-to-life test yet again. For he's in thrall to what he takes to be the gnomic potency of B's imperviousness to the unsightly ooze of his own self-contradictions.

"So with ever-increasing frequency B, that very B who prides himself on his radiantly healthy unshockability, makes it a point of honor (for that very reason) to be shocked by a phrase or a gesture or a movement—not in itself but as an unwelcome, unwholesome reminder of A's exasperating tendency to . . . exist. And although B prides himself, as I've just said (or have I?), on his *obscenely all-embracing zest for living*,"—How dare the Manning woman infringe his patent even if it's for a variant of this phrase! Eden wordlessly—thoughtlessly—fumes—"oddly enough he can't be too life-denyingly finicky where A is concerned. So is it any wonder, folks, that supercompliant hence (by B's standards) radically impure A now spends all of his free time (he's a civil servant and just for fun let's call him Akaky Cratchit Bartleby Pécuchet, Jr.) upping the ante of inoffensiveness, of self-effacement, forever unaware that B's revulsion is not for specific traits, for particular qualities, for essences, but rather for the criminal non-invisibility of A's very being? So A, if he doesn't kill him, ends up trying to become B. By the way, by a show of hands, how many of you are or have been or dread becoming a member of a dyad like the one I've been describing?" Manning raises her hand to demonstrate what raising your hand means. A few tentative efforts—and then, nothing. Narr observes Straynge bury his head in his notes, unmistakable sign that he is deeply impressed. Manning turns graciously to Rhys who takes this as a sign to continue (jottings once again in tow).

"He tried to make me understand that invigorated by—engorged with—motion, the little sister felt entitled to disavow all connection. Even her husband—whose loathing of his child bride was already beginning to be all-consuming (for one thing, she showed no dutifully awestruck interest in understanding any of the following sacred terms, among too many others, in which he glibly trafficked: *extraordinary rendition, branded entertainment, experiential advertising, doctrine of distinction, disgorgement, serial acquisition, niche war, electronic discovery, total contract value and pro forma earnings*—or *critical response vehicle surge*, for that matter [despite the fact that at least five or six profound—that is to say, perverse—that is to say, breakthrough—reinterpretations of those terms by budding consultants in his field were obligatory before, say, age twenty-five for super fast-track advancement])—even hubby was transmogrified into an adoring spouse by all that high-stepping unison—and on a street paved with fool's gold, no less. *Motion was clearly the most important element in our penny ante psychodrama.* I'm almost tempted to say that motion was the culprit—the pander (sort of the way *il libro* was for my heroes, Paolo Malatesta and Francesca da Rimini)."

Without waiting for the alarm, Straynge says (*sans* monkey business this time): "Motion as you describe it is a little like the sick family, though all are sick—and this is not just cant. In addition to mom, pop, granny, sis, sis, jr., pop III, the dynamic itself—a matter of perpetrations and perversities—becomes another member of the clan." At which point Straynge raises his hands to the level of his ears and shakes them gently, as if to say, *Don't mind me: I get carried away sometimes.*

"But my husband—giving him a name would be torture—had no intention of letting her off easy by blaming it all on the motion. He saw that I was powerless to stop lapdogging because if I stood still I'd have at last to feel lacerated by the little sister's contempt, enhanced in this case by the contrast between my mannish bomber jacket replete with mangy collar and her long leather coat, a gift from mother (her unadulterated hatred notwithstanding, the old witch cum career widow was pleased to occasionally embellish this teenybopper vamp whose imagined ruthless exploits she came to relish by proxy). Mother, as herself a noisily intermittent exponent thereof, applauded my capacity for self-cancellation. On the other hand, she applauded even more Caro's capacity to look as enigmatic as a smoke ring and to be poised at all times for the sartorial superkill. You see, we were conceivable—bearable—only as invidiously opposed terms.

"It must have been clear to her husband from the first that she was little more than a preliminary sketch for some far worthier successor. My sister cried out to be supplanted. She had, to the practiced eye, 'brief first chapter of spouse's marital saga' written all over her. Maybe what deceived her was his own capacity for self-deception. The too-fateful walk down St. Mark's ended with dinner in a pizzeria where he ran into a business-school mentor cum crony. The crony wasted no time confessing that he and the wife (over whom he couldn't help slavering) had finally decided to take a long-overdue mini-vacation *without the kids.*" (Cantor winces—since he can't retch—at the phrase). "And though even at that point Caro's husband—torture to call *him* by *his* name as well—couldn't stand the sight of her and the last thing he would have wished on himself was *quality time*" (Cantor proxy-retches yet again) "alone, what does he go ahead and do but express his . . . Envy of the happy pair. For you see, so intense was his desire to live, as every self-respecting consultant must, in conformity with the conformity demanded by the moment—so intense was his desire to experience the joys of camaraderie (for there was nothing he hated more than solitude and living with Caro was far worse than living in solitude)—that he had no alternative, although of course everybody has an alternative, except to convince himself doublequick that crony-hubby's indignation (at the little impediments family life had a way, for all its *gemütlichkeit*, of throwing in the path of good clean legally sanctified lust) was very much of a piece with his own. And who's to say our consultant wasn't in fact *at that moment* as head-over-heels in love-lust with Caro as the moment (if it was to be seized) compelled him to be?

"Soon after that too-fateful walk I became pregnant but aborted in deference to my husband's alarm (for somebody like him the prospect of fatherhood is always premature). The next night, as if by clockwork, Caro announced her own pregnancy. It was clear from all the simpering breathless disbelief in her good fortune that she was licking her chops at having bested me yet again.

Would all those bestings stretch out to the crack of doom? It was a few days later, on a torrid summer night which called for nothing less than a resuscitating cruiselet on the Staten Island Ferry, that we decided to stop off, by way of quaint little Minetta Lane, at her Sullivan Street railroad flat—a mere rehearsal for bigger and better things—to extend, like the halfway decent parent surrogates we continued against all odds to try to be, our heartiest congratulations. We brought a few falafel sandwiches to prove we meant every word—every lump in our throat. She was already bursting at the seams—big with child, i.e., big with childlike smugness. Flushed in her plump nightgown, she was meditatively preparing a compote of apples, plums and pears in the living room which doubled as study for the man of the house. And like any self-respecting man of the house he was very much *away on business.* You can't imagine how I envied that being away on business for *through the magic of sheer absence,* he proved immeasurably superior to his brother-in-law who—half- or quarter-man that he was—had this irritatingly conspicuous tic of always being just a wee bit too self-abasingly *around.* How could somebody succeed *in today's marketplace* if he wasn't not just willing but *more than willing"* (hadn't she used that expression not so long ago? in any case, somebody had) "to be portentously forever on the go? If he didn't have one single solitary plane to catch—one measly speech to deliver—to his name? Admitting as much is, I know, the last taboo but as everybody pretends not to know: *a woman regards his absences—his being away from home on business—his having a plane to catch, a speech to deliver—as the most vital part of a man's sexual equipment.* Of what use is a size-ten penis if it's not compounded with an itinerary? Being around as my husband always managed to be was, quite frankly, unmanly."

Since for Cantor's money, Thorsty Veblen is one of the few true-blue trailblazers in America's philistine wilderness of thorns, so unnurturing and hence so much to the taste of its oddball magi (Cantor's fellow oddballs)—to whose heroic capacity for self-sabotage the law of diminishing returns hardly seems to apply—he feels the least he can do is to market TV's cranky conceptualizations now that opportunity knocks. So he tries above the din (Rhys's breaking of what she calls the last taboo has—as they say in the entertainment biz—*created a sensation*—worse, made her a star overnight) to point out that right here in her own backyard, so to speak, they are being treated to a classic example writ large of the archetypal conflict—the old binary opposition, if you will—between drudgery and exploit, utility and conspicuous waste, and leisurely predation and labor, and, as a bonus (albeit not a Veblenian one), between dandies and drudges, habit and chance, frontal and profile views. The brother-in-law's absences clearly set him apart as The Hunter—even if the only trophy he was out spearing was a hot-air balloon. But he has no objection to her proceeding as if Veblen didn't exist, so eager is he to know how things will turn out for her. After all, her tale of woe is pivoted around the most classical binary of all: good versus evil. Rhys takes a deep breath once Cantor is done.

"As Caro went on stirring (even had a surreptitious taste with her forefinger and winced a little, whether with pleasure or distaste or purely for effect it was impossible to say), she pretended to be serenely abstracted—as she'd been in the Waverly Coffee Shop over breakfasts too numerous to count—but I—or rather, my husband (who explained it all to me later)—could see she was consumed by the raging need to zap us with yet another near-lethal dose of our brother-in-law's—and, therefore her—good fortune. It was with difficulty that she even managed to offer us a cup of coffee. I bluntly refused her ungracious offer and so did he (I would have despised him even more than I already did if he'd accepted).

"He explained later that all this brooding smugness must mean that before flying off he'd debased her for not knowing the meaning of the term *purchasing power parities*, say. But that it didn't matter in the least since she was completely fused with her tormentor whose absence yet again effected the transformation of vicious contempt—maybe even blistering rage—into his own very special version of virile devotion." What's virile devotion? Herbert wondered. "So it was a shock when out of the blue and with uncharacteristic spontaneity she confessed in a sob-strangled whisper (while he pretended to be busy thumbing through a cookbook) that before he left, he'd beaten her up. She tried to make it sound like a first. But once confessed, the ill treatment was completely exorcised and she was free to move on, though not before looking back at me with disgust. For as far as she was concerned I dredged it all up *from my own depths*, as usual making a mountain out of one of my very own dunghills. Her debasement was now my hallucination and mine alone.

"Whenever I was faced with this demand to be envied I complied. Nothing easier than to comply because I *was* envious—overwhelmingly envious—and of nothing so much as the shamelessness of this hunger to be envied. I envied her ability to parade their exploits *as* enviable. But Envy quickly went beyond Envy through despair to massive uncertainty about whether to go on living or die right then and there. Before the leering stranger I'd always refused to see. Even without my complying she was able to transmute the least sign of life into a spasm of bowel-churning Envy. While no sign of life whatsoever simply evidenced a refusal to betray the Envy simmering just below the surface or a characterological defect or dereliction of civic duty. My reason for living was now to go on showing that I envied, but without rancor, whatever it was she wanted to be envied for, in order to make her love me, and all this so I would no longer have to fear being destroyed by her."

There is a lot of nervous—forced—heavy-duty—coughing. Yet, as Cantor looks around, the smirk on each co-workerly face proclaims that his brand of Envy—if Envy it is—looms so unique, so particular, so very unlike the bug in any of its textbook forms, as to constitute its own extenuating circumstance, its own disqualification for the dreaded label. Dreaded but, alas, also craved, Herbert thinks, inasmuch as said label threatens to lay to rest the uncertainty over whether they are in actual fact afflicted, which is far more excruciating than the disease itself. *Though why is it she who is having this thought? Who is making* her *have this thought as if she were her own worst enemy when its sack of syllables would doubtless have been more becomingly—intriguingly— consigned to the shoulders of somebody else—somebody more in tune with its implications?*

"To add insult to injury, she informed us airily they'd soon be moving out of this rattrap (which convicted us of being too stupid to realize it was a rattrap). So faced with Caro's impenetrable smugness I did the only thing I'd trained myself to do in such circumstances: *I poured my heart out*, hoping to transform that smugness into pity or compassion. I sacrificed my husband—or rather, his defects—on the altar of her imperviousness. She was double-quick to inform me, as if I needed informing, that her husband suffered from none of these defects. My only defense against this stunning foreclosure of all recognizable human feeling was to get on with the abasing. No response, unless the continuous stirring (the motion motif again!) of her apples, plums and—*peaches*, not pears (how could I have ever been so unseeing?) qualified as one. She added a little ginger here, a little nutmeg there, and even went so far as to explain—coldly, impatiently as if to nitwits, and positively exulting in her busy competence and the far busier competence of *the father of her child*" (Cantor winces again) "—how she intended to freeze the preparation and serve it when he got home. And once again, what shrewder advertisement of his competence than strategic absence from this cozily inane genre scene? But I was able to forgo my own misery and take a New York minute to revere how stoically Caro's brother-in-law teeth-gritted his weary way through his wife's abject contortion—distortion—exaltation (yes, I know, as too many times before)—of kid sister's lesson-giving act into a tough-love-crammed upgrade of my incompetence."

The bell rings and Manning makes her way to the lectern (Rhys steps aside but shows more reluctance than before)—again without resorting to any mike-manipulating fakery. "Your job, if I can call it that, was to hit just the right note of helplessness to engage not contempt but concern (of the tough-lovey variety, of course) or what could be interpreted as such." Borkman has fallen in love—head over heels if you must know—with Manning's pedantic pronunciation of lovey (as "loovee"). "To titrate your helplessness—which is at the same time a simulation of helplessness and no less authentic for that—against her exasperated incapacity to experience what you correctly call recognizable human feeling and in such a way as to induce a reaction from the harpy that could be mistaken for—contorted into—concern. But since, as I understand it, you never got to the desired endpoint, you needed to go on believing (as if your life depended on it—which is in fact the case) the tone-deafness was not her fault but yours, or rather, the fault of your plight. It simply wasn't the right sort of plight to elicit even the wrong kind of rescue. You had to invent a plight that could invent and preserve the myth (I'm using the term loosely) of the harpy's affectionate common sense. Or rather, it must be all your husband's fault—he didn't even have the decency to visit the right kind of indignities on you. You needed to believe your sister was not The Bitch Intrinsic but The Bitch Facultative—one who was waiting rightly and righteously for a plight worthy enough to snare her succor."

Rhys is now back at her battle station. This time without waiting for Manning to be seated (she's come a long way—*or so somebody wants us to think*, Herbert muses), she continues: "As Caro went on joylessly gloating—the very stirring of the compote-to-be was a gloating but oddly enough a gloating full of self-hate—suddenly, through gritted teeth, he said we had to go. Grit for grit, I replied, 'Not yet,' without looking at him. At that moment I hated him far more than I hated her. Only Caro and I existed at that moment. How dare he try to sever me from my last hope of drawing blood from a stone? 'I want to see the sunset from the top deck,' he said as forcefully—as meaningfully—as he could, as if he were speaking in code. But intent on wresting what I still needed to believe Caro in fact possessed but was only perversely withholding, I continued to stew in her compote."

The bell rings. A man from the audience, whom Straynge recognizes as Doctor Walser—Herbert's tall man, in fact (*How economical*, she murmurs)—stands up and says, "The doings of you and your sister, Ms. Rhys—" (Straynge: "Please refer to her as subject Five, Doctor." Manning: "Six." [*More rickety stage business?* Herbert muses.]) "—remind me of the Azande—a Sudanese people studied not so very long ago by the anthropologist E.E. Evans-Pritchard. They practiced witchcraft but not as something outside themselves—it was the very texture, the very woof and warp of their thought. Same holds for you—with regard to Envy disease. Without her need to elicit what she easily convinces herself is Envy and your need to oblige (and by obliging, you begin to actually feel the Envy you don't want to feel toward her whom you simply want to suffocate with your love), there would be no sister act to speak of. Envy has become the very substrate—the menstruum (yes, *menstruum*, you heard me right the first time, folks)—of all your thoughts and actions. It's not just another detail in your action-packed life story—it's what chooses and structures and subserves the details. To qualify for participation in your story, details have to pass muster with the toughest admissions officer imaginable: Envy, Ma'am." The tone in which the final sentence should have been uttered makes Cantor think of hip- and butt-swinging B-movie prison matron extraordinaire Hope Emerson. Walser sits down. Herbert knows she's heard the name *Walser* before but she can't place it. If only, with a little help from the Amygdala crowd, she can create a context: a school for failed butlers, say . . .

Something about Walser enrages Rhys. He is oversimplifying and by oversimplifying making things even graver than they are. Still, this new rage is sure to make the depiction of her feelings toward her sister more compelling: she already has the audience in the palm of her hand. Shearer envies the theatrical skill being deployed. You can't learn that or so they say. "I couldn't stand her silence so I said, as I'd said far too many times before, that she was a vile bitch in heat. The silence didn't budge an inch, I apologized for the rage as I went on living it, enacting it, which meant that I was beginning to wonder whether a rage as great, as all-engulfing, as *universal*, as mine could be made to trace its way back to—" Borkman thinks: Hey, this rings a bell.

"You mean, put in one-to-one correspondence with—a plausible target," Cantor cries out.

"This is the worst thing that can happen to anybody who rages, believe me," she murmurs, ignoring him, trying even to ignore herself. "What is?" Straynge says, ever the virtuoso prompter.

"To be raging yet all the time questioning the legitimacy of the rage, all the time wondering if the target of annihilating rage may nonetheless be just a scapegoat."

Straynge clears his throat and says: "Your plight brings to mind, of all people, Aristotle, that sage and discreet chum of my palmy high school days. You make me realize for the $n+1$th time just how hard it is to adhere to his high standards where rage—and a lot of other impedimenta—are concerned. For it was he who wrote: 'The man who gets angry at the right things and with the right people, and also in the right way and at the right time and for the right length of time, is commended.' It was, I think, to crowd out your unpreparedness for such excruciatingly fine distinctions that you said what you said to little sister." "Are you telling me I was too harsh?" He rests his case.

"Once we were out on the street I realized I'd forgotten my purse. Or was it at home? I was torn between returning to the rattrap and continuing our walk beyond Houston, where the body of every pedestrian, irrespective of race, color or creed, was outlined with the burin of a blinding sunset." (Now it's Eden's turn to think, "Hey, this rings a bell.") "Oddly, we kept on walking. Even more oddly, I confided—first to myself—that contrary to obsessional custom, the further I got, the more implausible became the idea that I'd left the purse behind in the rattrap. Usually the dynamic went the other way: the further I got, the more plausible—because more malleable as a source of misery—my racking uncertainty. 'It's a sign that at last you're not buying what the sick part of you's trying to sell,' he said kindly, kissing my nape. 'And what *is* it trying to sell?' (making a great show of wary anger to hide my . . . hopeful pleasure). 'A pretext for going back and debasing yourself further.' 'But I don't want to debase myself!'"

The bell. This time it is the man next to Walser who rises—Stifter, Doctor Stifter. And this time Straynge isn't so cordial. *And why not? or is what we have here just another case of the same Some Body's—Some Body yet to be defined by consensus (Herbert thinks, or is it Cantor who does the thinking for the two of them?)—the same Some Body's tired old way of generating, through dire intimations, an ear-catching heart-throbbing sense of the inexplicable.* Stifter—now where did I hear that name before? Herbert wonders, almost aloud (she is much taken with his exquisite features). "My dear," he says, "based on that last outburst it's clear you confuse kindly diagnosis of a pre-existing condition either with a (kindly) request that you perpetuate it, or with the slanderous suggestion that you actually suffer from it—a condition that, whatever the secondary gains, never in a million years would you allow yourself to have any truck with. For your kind, i.e., all of humankind, the awful truth is an outrage—a crime against nature. Remember: to cure, one must first name the sickness but if the naming destabilizes you enough to hear the naming as an accusation—as a cue to assimilate, as completely alien, what the name names and to then perpetuate it—well then! Need I say more?" Muffled poker-faced applause. Though Borkman, for one—Borkman!—considers "your kind" to be cruel, reflecting badly on the upstart user of the phrase.

"As we plodded down Greenwich Street toward the Ferry in the smelly-festive August heat, he proceeded, under the fuzziest of crescent moons, to re-dissect Caro's bone-chilling coldness. Though joining in, I tried to sound as if I were talking to myself and he was being rude enough—worse, silly enough—to get caught, as innocent bystanders are required by law to do, in the crossfire. But for all our scalpel-wielding, she managed to remain as undismembered as ever and as we got closer and closer to Whitehall Street (Battery Park City was a palpitant blur), he admitted to seriously wondering whether even so momentous an act as taking a ride on the Ferry could refute her last look, a look that had clearly bracketed—straitjacketed—us as a quintessential pair of lowlifes with upwardly mobile aspirations. By surrendering, in our frenzied outrage, to the sea breezes, would we still be inside the brackets or—fused with the foaming surge—so far outside as to be able, should the spirit move us, to hoist the bracketeer by her own petard?

"By leaning, lyrically, over the vessel's back rail to watch its eely wake dissolve close-up, would we be confirming our status as nonentities or, rather, would the very nobility of the stance counter-bracket into smithereens anyone or anything that tried to so dismiss, belittle, indict us? In short, would our accession to the kind of nobility that only the Staten Island Ferry going full steam ahead can confer prove way too outsize for her straitjacket? Or was the nobility so-called, like every other delusion of lowlifes, tailor-made for it? Only what if (here he became very animated, almost hectic, as if he'd actually found a way out) we leaned over the rail, nobly of course, yet *very much aware* that our nobility was being perceived, by some ill-willed third party, as of a piece with our status? What then? Wouldn't such a strategy make us the victors? Wasn't that the best way to annihilate those hackers at our screen, those phantoms of our rue morgue? Or had Caro's agents around town already anticipated our every ploy?

"Once aboard I promptly got as far away from him as I could in order to inform the wavelet-skimming gulls on no uncertain terms that I was hereby writing off my sister and our botched relation forever. Even if I couldn't help suspecting that I was merely ushering in a whole new cycle of desperate hoping, biding my time until the next encounter (for there *had* to be a next encounter). Doesn't a snowflake do anything to avoid extinction? If only I could stay away long enough to let brute duration—that cunning chiseler—transform Caro into the doting sob-sister of my dreams. If only I could stay silent long enough for that flogging silence to induce repentance. The longer the separation, the more likely her retraction. But since waiting was intolerable, it was only fair that the next few hours or days or decades should, as a small concession, fly by at the speed of light.

"I looked at him leaning over the side with loathing, though he has the most beautiful buttocks I've ever seen—worthy of a ballet star. For at the core of the sister problem and its ramifications lay only one thing—his failure. His job or the job anybody who occupied his place—that of hapless consort—was to apply his only dormant omnipotence for all it was worth to transforming my sister into a good guy. But he perversely reneged. His omnipotence was the worst form of impotence. On the way back, observing mighty Wall Street suddenly yield to a force even mightier, namely, that master editor, The Fog (deleting mullions, spires, entire buildings even, in a single bound), we both realized the relation was dead, though things did crank along a little while longer. In fact, nothing could have prepared me for the discovery that a parting of the ways *any minute now* is nature's most potent aphrodisiac. Though I knew his nudity down to the last detail: the sweat-coiled hair on his chest which was so coarse that, in migrating upward, it almost blotted out his collarbone; the wrack skimming his forearms which, in contrast, was fine enough to betray all, or almost all, of the veiny stress beneath; how, after a hot shower, the filings shading his long thighs were magnetized into little forcefields, etc.—though I knew his nudity down to the last detail, never before had I, etc., etc. But what matters most is the owner's *relation* to his body. A quandary incarnate, he always looked completely unaware of being at odds with his brute maleness. It spoke a language he couldn't decrypt, at least not in my presence. Once again, a perverse withholding. And there lay all the magic—now that the connectedness was on its last legs. So I'm dead wrong—in fact it is this rejection of the invitation extended to the owner of male body to fuse with its maleness that is the most potent aphrodisiac—at least for *a gal like I.* There you have it: I'm just not attracted to men who make themselves right at home in their maleness." She looked hard at the little space to Narr's right. He lowered his head. "His brand of self-disavowal streaked with femininity—a little like a benign cancer of unknown origin—never lost its capacity to enthrall.

"If only I could believe his beauty outweighed his deficiencies. Or if only I'd been able to lay claim to deficiencies grosser than his own, something to give me the edge in unintentional exploitation." These words exhort Percy Bysshe Borkman to do nothing less than rise like a lion after slumber in unvanquishable number, shaking his chains to earth, like dew. By God, her husband is a man after his own heart. In fact they are many, these men after his own heart—numerous enough to emasculate the emasculatrixes—while the emasculatrixes themselves, i.e., wives like theirs, are (and that's why they make so much noise) few. *We are many—they are few.* This Rhys woman can take her forcefields and— "Thing is, none of my deficiencies compared with his stinging failure to transform Caro into the sister of my dreams (what deficiencies could?). What wouldn't I have given to be able to convince myself he was putting up with far more than I was—that it was he who was too good for me, since, as Jane Austen said (in a moment of supreme forbearance), nobody minds having what's too good for him? Nothing would have thrilled me more than to be able to praise him to the skies and beyond by singing the song of my own defectiveness. Of course I wouldn't have painted myself as *too* defective—just enough to make it clear that I was getting far more than I deserved out of the deal, thereby turning myself into the Envy of all my enemies beginning and ending with Caro. In short, I would have loved to be able to strike just the right dialectical balance between depreciation and aggrandizement. Exactly like some politician on the stump, bragging about his Brenda or Cyndie or Kellie-Anne. But bragging with astonishment—exasperation—outrage, almost—that the fates should have seen fit to dump such a prize in his lap—her, of all people, and his, of all laps. And in that way of course he leaves no room for doubt regarding whether Cyndie-Anne is in fact a prize. For how can anybody in his right mind get worked up enough to express agonizing doubt about his right to a prize if the prize isn't a prize to begin with (and so what if it turns out to be the booby prize par excellence?).

And if the self-doubt is real (and why does a red-blooded campaigner admit to something as un-American as self-doubt unless it is too achingly real to keep under wraps?) then what has triggered the self-doubt? Kellie Sue's beauty, brains, balls and bonhomie—must be real, too. So thanks to Brenda-Kellie, his patsies—marks—victims—need never fear he'll be swept away on, say, the megalomaniacal wave of a thousand-dollar haircut (or some unhinged groupie's million-dollar docu-sitcom on that thinnest of all subjects: *what he's all about*), never to be seen again—not as long as down-to-earth Cyndie Brenda's around to keep him hewing and cleaving to the party line. In the same way I'd have drawn *my* patsies so quickly into the agony (and who, after all, would be devious enough to simulate such agony?) over whether I was even remotely worthy of his perfection that there'd be no time for doubt whether that perfection actually existed. It had to exist (in accordance with what I'll call the Law of Gilt by Association)—that is, if they were to go on luxuriating in the spectacle of my agony. I'd have ended up convincing everybody of his star quality—commensurate-and-then-some with that of those campaign trail hussies—in the most dramaturgically savvy way possible: by displacing the psychic accent from whether or not he was in fact a star to how down and dirty his starriness made me feel in contrast. At the same time my down-and-dirty defects had to be pretty dazzling if a paragon like him was willing to put up with them.

"But even if he turned out to be the paragon I wanted him to be I could never see my way clear to bragging about him. Fact is, the Envy of other people terrifies me. I'm much better at Envying those who know how to batten on the Envy they deliberately provoke. Maybe that's why I'm here—not to be cured of Envy but to learn how to lick my chops when I'm provoking it." She wipes her brow with the back of her hand, can't believe she's been this raucously eloquent, exercised breath and voice control worthy of a bel canto powerhouse, used words she never used before, words she didn't know existed, words that were normally the plaything of men. Is the first dose of Invidicum supposed to produce this side effect? Does it have something to do with her immune system's being blissfully out of whack? Is Some Body or something other than Straynge running the show? or is this question too coy for words?

The alarm rings—many times—too many times for Cantor's taste. What a tacky gimmick. Stifter the Beautiful rises (*Up on your hind legs*, Cantor stage-whispers on his inner boards), deploying a sort of (well, is it or isn't it?) whole-body frontal attack. "Very good presentation, Jean. The only thing is—you talk about Envy as if it's something shameful. Which it is, of course, and for that very reason I want every last one of you to crawl into the fMRI machine proud as a peacock in heat. You're all both more and less than your disease. Disease offers an opportunity—some of my colleagues" (he turns to stare down Walser who looks a little hot around the collar, at least to Herbert, sitting a few seats away) "might call it a pretext or a ploy—for self-distancing from what is and isn't a part of you. But it's precisely in the self-distancing—the muscle flexing required to keep the distancing from the disease on its toes—wearing the symptoms like a Brechtian placard—that the *real you* lies. But most people can't handle the double business of being sick as a loon AND alchemizing the looniness into a misperception's-the-gem-of-the-ocean style folk wisdom. Most people aren't weathermen enough to relish this permanent clinical mix of sun and clouds."

Rhys thinks: *So, my love affair with Envy is far far more than a subclinical one.*

Eden is definitely not eager to elope with the woman holding up *his* sign—it's Manning. She's too intimidatingly beautiful. Still, he owes it to his father to get on with the show. It's at moments like these—though what kind of moment is it, exactly?—that he regrets not having his father's—and (from what he's heard) his father's father's—obscene zest for life (*a phenomenon known technically, my dear Eden, as vigor mortis*), flaunted as it was right up to the end. If he hates his father—and surely the fact that even now he can't refer to him as *dad* is the deadest of giveaways—then why all this effort on his behalf? He can love him, then, only as a victim—a victim, mostly, of the obtuseness underlying all that zest. Undiscerning, unselective, convinced à la Will Rogers—and then some—that everybody (except his prodigal son) was his buddy, he couldn't smell a rat even while it literally (literally? yes, *literally!*) chewed away at his innards.

But what is it to love somebody, Eden? Is it, by any chance, to run, where that somebody is concerned, the gamut—or rather, the gauntlet—of emotions among which love may be simply one—and the least important? Or maybe love is nothing of or in itself but—as that redhead (the jury is still out on the color of her bush and the taste, or is it the smell? of her cunt) so eloquently implied without knowing it—just a substrate, the battleground of all those emotions, where each in—or out of—turn, gets to be the remedy for the poisonousness of its opposite or what it handily transforms into its opposite, becoming in the process even more poisonous. A mere matrix within which emotions that never had a chance to be opposed become deadly enemies. Cheer up, he tells himself—on the basis of somebody else's orders, reluctantly complied with—maybe love is most intense when bundled up in the wolf's clothing of emotions deemed least compatible with love. Let's face it, love is nothing more than the terror of being invaded by its opposite without having the faintest idea what that opposite may be (indifference? hate? contempt? remorseless lust?)—without having made its peace with the opposite of that opposite.

Removing what appears to be his chart from her clipboard (her basement office is bare: not a single photo, painting or poster—but personal photos paraded—pimped—in the workplace are corny don't you think? and their smarminess is not to be trusted; in any case, like the heroines in forties weepies—unwed mothers forced to give up their get—who vengefully turn into 24/7 career dynamos, she has no personal life to speak of), Manning (according to the name tag) assures him the key biomarkers—vascular endothelial growth factor, interleukin-6, monocyte chemoattractant protein, and ferritin—have all come up Envy-positive to a fault. He must excuse her, though: she needs to be absolutely sure before administering his second dose, so would he mind stepping next door and crawling into the comfy little coffin of her high-resolution functional MRI machine (grad student guy friday Mike M. is there to make sure things go as planned). What she needs to have him do when he hears the (sorry about that) annoying buzzer is to examine the text and images flashing on the screen overhead. At the same time he's to be hooked up with sensors measuring silly things like blood pressure, palm sweat and (possible) penile and retinal engorgement. He returns (with a terrible desire to urinate) about twenty minutes later. Seeing he's caught her tremulous look of worry (is it an act?), she says she hopes Mike was gentle. As he has certainly figured out, the flashing images and boldface text are all about the celebrities and near-celebrities whom—based on the psychosocial profile compiled from the information on the far too many preliminary forms they made him fill out—somebody like him may regard as arch-rivals."

"And?"

"And—my suspicions are confirmed. You are not—nor will you ever be—a first-class envier. For one thing, no indications of abnormality in synaptic function in the frontal-striatal-thalamic circuits. For another, no telltale agitation in either the right anterior insula or the ventral striatum. My dear boy, you're a fraud, albeit an enduring one—I mean an endearing one." Her accent is hard to pin down but at this level of technicality everybody sounds the same. "The question is why. No, I don't want to know why. In any case, while it's true Invidicum is being tested for use in EnVD, the powers-that-be aren't interested one bit since Envy represents a very tiny niche market—a little foot in the big door." "The way the war in Iraq is a niche war," he ponders. "Don't get me wrong: there are billions of enviers. Thing is, most of them would rather die of this, the deadliest of all the seven deadlies, rather than admit to being afflicted: Envy, why it's the very flaying of someone's selfhood. No, the members of this crowd want Invidicum to be approved for Envy only so that they can start pushing it off label for—for—homic—" She hesitates, blushes, then recovers. "I mean for your garden-variety blockbuster diseases —a few—one—in particular." After all, she concedes with a sigh, Pfizer has no trouble selling Neurontin for bipolar disorder (not to mention Lou Gehrig's disease and attention deficient disorder and restless leg syndrome and alcohol withdrawal seizures)—even if it's no better than a placebo and was originally approved for epilepsy. "We live in an off-label world, right Mike?" (he's just entered carrying a rack of test tubes). "Where the central is by definition marginal and vice versa," he replies robotically or perhaps the robotics are a ploy to undercut an eloquence that trips all too easily off the tongue and in so doing might alienate those without his knack. Eden wonders if this Mike character—this so-called Mike—(like his father before him he's suspicious of monikers: where do they come from? what purpose do they serve?) —is himself taking the drug, since he's overheard—and not just once and not just in the men's room—that the most widely admired—and excoriated (it all depends on your perspective)—side effect of Invidicum is its capacity to turn punks into poets laureate.

"Suddenly I know what you're thinking. That I'm convinced I was born to be a whistleblower. Absolutely not—it's people like me who give whistleblowers a bad name." She hasn't the faintest idea what he's thinking. Eden shakes his head softly. A gesture so temperate is new to him. A guy who can manage such a gesture under extreme duress can manage anything. Blind faith in his mission is restored. "In any case, they all know there's no money in Envy. I don't mean Straynge. He's convinced Invidicum will secure him his long-overdue place in the annals of psychopharmacology. He thinks he's an original, poor thing. The true original of course is Pritchard, E.E. Pritchard, out in Santa Barbara or is it San Diego, I can't remember. My real boss, in any case. But more of him later. With regard to you, Martin," (her pronunciation of his name is caressive, to say the least) "as far as I can see you're the only one who's unafflicted and therefore best placed to tell me regularly what's really going on here so I can report back to Pritch. I know—you're undergoing a crisis of your own (please, no gruesome details) and here I am presenting you with a golden opportunity which could very well turn out to be your downfall. And don't I know how easy it is when one's back is against the wall to act perversely—to positively wallow in perversity—as if the worst possible choice is the only choice, even if peeping in from the fringe of no-choice is the certainty that one clearly does have a choice. But making the worst choice has one very huge advantage: it enables somebody like you, who's so full of self-hate he can't even imagine acting unperversely, i.e., in his own best interest, to make whoever didn't step in to compel him not to make that choice, the target of a rage without bounds and without end. So much easier than confronting your life-denying perversity. Let me know what you decide—no rush." Then: it's as if his starting to leave makes it safe to add: "I know I'm overusing the word *perversity*. Maybe it's to impress you with my hoity-toity credentials. Fact is, perversity just happens to be one of those concepts that are bandied about too loosely. Their defiance notwithstanding, they need to be carefully dismantled into their elements. A periodic table of those elements must be created." She has a fetching way of ending some of her phrases with a slight question mark as if to say, Is this how it's expressed in English? He stands by his impression even if he doesn't know—or care to know—what *fetching* means. They both remember he has a dose to take.

After she's fed him, he leaves with a good month's supply of pills. But what does *what's really going on here* refer to?

Should she reveal that it has recently been discovered, based on not-quite-consensual experiments on Vietnam vets, the homeless, and sufferers from severe autism and schizophrenia, among others, that Invidicum turns inarticulateness into the most ungovernable eloquence in truth-telling? Maybe there's an off-label use for it among would-be orators. No, it will only frighten him off. He seems to take pride in the way he expresses or refuses to express himself. Not quite sure why and whether her interest is purely professional, she follows him—is it because she suspects he may be working for the enemy, whose identity is still to be established to everybody's satisfaction? At Twentieth Street and Tenth Avenue, from his slowed pace obviously a stomping ground, she watches him drift into a sex shop where he stocks up on DVDs—not (*note the change in inner speaker*) because he especially needs or wants them but rather to have something new to protect from hostile forces—remind himself, wedging them tightly under his arm, that there still *are* hostile forces to be contended with. For Manning's sales pitch is making him a bit woozily uncertain that the world is as unregenerate as he needs it to be in order to get all worked up and complete his mission. Tell me, she thinks (*back to inner speaker 1*), do they, those DVDs with a vengeance, constitute a Primal Screen for all occasions, that is, do you revert to them and them alone for a million and one contradictory reasons? From, say, the need to quell—even quash—despair at abandonment as well as to mark the exultation that only the ensuing solitude can bring? In the same way that, to do away with my messy moods as quickly as possible, I end up fucking men of the same body, brain and soul type—they're a dime a dozen. Are they, then, those DVDs, your Field of the Cloth of Gold—i.e., the one place on earth where you can begin to understand just how unsettled every feeling (and almost-feeling) is—how much it is perfused with its *reverse—obverse—other*—how it simply doesn't exist without its *other*. Are those DVDs—and please be frank—nothing less than the Ganges in which all your moods come to wash away the sins of their urgency and the urgency of their contours—come to fuse indistinguishably—come to get reduced to the same consistency—the same unpartitionable compote in which their essence is no longer detectable and where you yourself, as their slaphappy hypostasis, are no longer detectable and none the worse for the makeover? Tell me also, lover man (but only if you won't feel robbed, like Offenbach's Hoffmann, of your unique reflection in doing so), whether or not, by returning to this site—this bank and shoal of time and no other—at the slightest upsurge of an emotion (since for our kind Emotion is the Enemy)—tell me whether or not (given that in your case *every* temperament—and not just the big Four—is made to converge on the same camera obscura—the camera obscura that is both your drug—your *pharmakon* [remember her?]—and the den in which it takes effect)—tell me whether or not you don't routinely feel that you thereby do nothing more than demonstrate what a paucity of resources you have at your disposal for beating life at its own game. No answer. Better that way. She observes him enter an apartment building on Twenty-Fourth Street between Tenth and Eleventh. She follows him in. She doesn't arouse the doorman's suspicions. What a lucky break, not just for her but for somebody she can't locate or rather, localize. She follows him up his one flight and puts her ear to the door that's just slammed. Some chitchat with what sounds like a girlfriend followed by giggles—his and hers—suggesting that sexual activity has just been or is about to be initiated. No point in remaining: he isn't giving away any trade secrets, at least for the moment. Descending the stairs she acknowledges that he excites her. She'll even go so far as to admit that, in his case, the cross-fertilization of habitus and inner torment makes him pretty much irresistible. But where does she come off, by exhibiting faith in his capability which is way past its expiration date in any case, blowing his cool or his cover or both? He's a loser after all, with a loser's unique privileges. It's a relief to be spared any further disrespectful sleuthing.

As far as he's concerned, the sole fringe benefit of being the one john for whom the Lady of the Month not only turns off the timer but makes a big show of doing so is hearing her bitch unabashedly about Madam Butter-Your-Fly's graphic threats about what happens to those of her girls who leave any part of their income undeclared. This always makes him want to protect her and with the eruption of the paternal instinct comes the craving, situated primordially in his gut's epicenter, to fuck—paternally. But at the very moment he needs her to be inconsolable so he can step back and in front of the TV determine once and for all whether taking Manning up on her gracious offer may help or hinder him, Strayngewise, she sits down beside him—just like that she's decided not to suppress the need for comfort. Forthrightly, almost primly, she positions his left hand beneath her buttocks. There are tears in her eyes—each, he realizes for the first time, a different color.

She simpers, "It must be wonderful to play beautiful pieces like that" (the Arts Channel, of all things!—and an orchestra is going full force). The drug must be working since he doesn't mimic her or grow exasperated, the way he usually does, in order to silence her before the know-it-all phantom third party who adjudicates his every act can doom their dyad for its dimwittedness (come to think of it, he's not a little like the Forest Hills redhead except that in his case it isn't Evil Little Sister who's doing the adjudicating). Instead, he finds himself lulled—humanized—by her simplicity, even if he suspects the neediness as being, and already hates it for being, just a put-on—a way of making a fool of his maleness and sucking it dry. She switches the channel—punishing her sudden susceptibility to sappy mood music. Sappily putting his arm around her (normally Eden hates public displays of affection, especially in so public a place as an empty apartment), he feels every bit the proud pop at this, his kid's final basketball game of the season. And how can he not, with proud mom at his side? Though knowing full well that junior—a sniveling bookworm—will never approach his Everest level of prowess, Pop becomes so moved by certain details, like the muzzled clock to the right of the bleachers and the permanent-looking sunpatches on the scuffed wooden floor of the indoor stadium, that he finds himself applauding wildly after every hoop coup. Yet as much as he cares for all the perpetrators, he is most fond of the new character that he, or circumstances beyond his control, have created—one who, though amateurishness-hating and as a pop unsatisfiable, still finds it in his busy heart to be kindly attentive and attentively non-partisan. In fact, he's much more than fond—he's positively crazy about the new him, willing to endure mediocrity in action for as long as the new him dictates but firmly *un*willing, here and now, to bite off his girlfriend's head just because she reminds him of his own low brow. For the long and short of it is that Eden's simply too busy loving the new Eden and loving him more than he could ever love himself—or her—not to take the Lady of the Month's mutterances in manly stride (especially now that she's half-blissfully half-asleep).

Suddenly awake (not *wide*-awake, whatever that means outside of fairy tales, just awake), she informs Eden he needs to fuck her—on the double. Why? he almost asks. Because recently, to pass the time as his dull-witted fellow johns maul her, she's been shooting her very own Lifetime Movie Network miniseries and is experiencing a sudden yen to propel the plot forward. (He is tempted to ask if he's one of the actors only he doesn't quite know what he wants her to answer: the opposite, probably, of whatever she decides to answer.) But since it's within the chalice of her cunt that all ingenuities are bred, she needs to be able to deliver them to the slumburb known as her brain, where sob becomes story. And as it turns out, only the thrusts of a stiff prick engorged with its own ineptitude—even his will do (she adds stingingly to pay him back for aiding and abetting her teary self-unmasking)—can, by depolarizing her creative membranes, trigger the requisite nerve impulse. Although she doesn't express things quite this way. Whoever's running the Invidicum Follies isn't quite *on* to her kind of woman just yet.

CHAPTER FIVE

It is now around eight and Borkman, Eden and Cantor all find themselves undone by the story they've just heard. Each regards it as nothing less than an infringement of the exclusive patent on his own. So before they know it, their ordeal-generated connectedness has landed them in a vegan dive off Washington Square—the first ever in Borkman's as well as Eden's annals of internal medicine. Cantor thinks: *(Heterogeneous) boys' night out.* For there's a certain corny improbability about this outing since everybody—or at least Cantor and James Agee qua film critic for the *Nation*—knows "most men of such disparate classes and worlds would meet seldom, with greater embarrassment than friendliness." But though the director (William Wyler) of the film in question had sacrificed plausibility for clumsy expediency, humble wonders did manage to emerge from amid all that staginess. So how can Cantor expect this ensemble piece—this *Best Years of Our Lives + Seventy-Five*—not to father forth, compliments of its own idiopathic hokeyness, a parallel crop of revelations? After a few sips of chamomile (not so bad), Borkman hears himself say, "My older son tried to strangle his mother and she holds me responsible. I was instructed by a whole gang of therapists—"

"Angekoks," Cantor suggests, with a tactfully light touch which goes a long way toward explaining why he's widely regarded, or should be, as Charles Lane's Chargé d'Affaires a.i.

"What?"

"*Angekok* is Eskimo for therapist—shaman. I personally hate 'therapist.' Too namby-pamby. Too self-indulgently Upper West Side. Not abstract enough. But, sorry—go on, please. That was rude and smart-alecky of me. Forgive me—I'm a metamathematician."

"The gang of . . . angekoks instructed me to wait for him, all day and all night long if necessary, and to call 911 the minute he walked through the door. Which I did. Only the nitwits didn't do their homework since I was told that, in order for the men in white or whatever they're wearing these days to come and gurney him away, he'd have to be doing the strangling at the very moment I called. So nobody came, and he doesn't know what we, the parents whom he trusts even if he hates our guts, had planned for him. What's going to happen to him? Of course, it's not like he ever did it before or that he did it more than once."

First Rhys's husband and now Borkman's son. Eden feels a simultaneous unwelcome throb in gut and anus from all this unsolicited kinship with husband and son. Still, as Borkman has just gone to the trouble of not only loaning him a password but logging him in, he smiles sadly and (to show his grateful willingness to play ball) echoes: "It's not like he tried it several times. It was just one time." The guilt-racked father nods gratefully. The boy is right, dead right, because didn't he say pretty much the very same thing just a minute ago? Yet something is wrong, dead wrong. Something is . . . different. He looks around frantically. He wants more tea even if his cup is still full and steaming.

Now "just one time" means everything except what this kid Eden has supposedly intended it to mean. Whatever his intentions, he's suddenly made Borkman realize, or rather, the words suddenly make him realize, just how close "just one time" is to "several times," even "several times daily." So close that the phrases touch—so close that they fuse. Sure, out in the world there is a difference, maybe a big one, between trying to strangle your mother only once and trying to do the insatiable old broad in several times. But on the level of sounds made in harrowing haste, "just one time" and "several times" are almost indistinguishable. And given the kabbalistic potency of words, isn't it then possible for this indistinguishability of phrases to induce a corresponding indistinguishability even of events as distinct as strangling mom only once and strangling her several times over?

Borkman can't help himself, he has to speak out, even if the kid is young enough to be his son. He says, "I know you mean well but please mind your own damn business otherwise we won't be able to get through this meal." Eden could kill him. Just like his father—just like all fathers—irrational and unsatisfiable. But with the upsurge of unsatisfiability always in the victim's best interest. *Eden listens to himself thinking—thinking less and less like himself. Who is thinking to—for—him? What is this Thing—this . . . Master?—not so much revealing to Eden Eden's own thoughts but reporting—for daws to peck it—Eden's blindness to a truth that's staring him in the face—articulating what Eden should be thinking if he's to be deemed a . . . character worth his salt. Which he isn't and never will be. Doesn't have the stuff of which characters are made.* Be that as it may (*who is speaking?*), this old fart clearly wants help with his problem—or at least he wanted it a minute ago—but how help without first calling the problem by its right name? Even if it turns out to be no problem at all, how can Eden—or anybody—prove that without first calling it by its right name? And the right name turns out to be, at least for Eden, something along the lines of: *Does doing it once lead inevitably and inextricably to doing it again and again?* But obviously Eden's skewing the problem toward its right name begins to make it scarily real in a way it wasn't when the old fart similarly skewed.

Cantor listens observantly, aware at the same time that at any moment these two malcontents might decide to skirt their impasse by turning on *him*, having decided he's the source most likely. Should he play Socratic midwife (of course he should—and he will, just you wait!—here goes!) and try to wryly elicit from Borkman what Borkman must be going through? Say (*a*) that he understands how any response to what he's just said (even—especially—a semi-exact repetition) can only destabilize the mogul's phantom foothold in a world of woe because for all his mock-mighty feats as businessman and lover of women (news travels fast among the pathologically Envious), he's never felt quite . . . real (Cantor knows a fellow sufferer when he sees one, or so he thinks), or consequentially that anything coming out of his mouth is quite real (so how can he impart a sense of reality to his boy?), but (*b*) that he—Cantor—also understands it's precisely the feeling not quite real that has always been his lifeline, since whatever he has to say about some bad state of affairs going on in his life—i.e., the bad state *du jour*—necessarily infects that state with a priceless unreality. And the bad state of affairs is thereby canceled out compliments of Borkman's unreal way with words. Yet here is this galling busybody Eden—who looks, by the way, like he has quite a few problems of his own to solve—taking it into his head to cancel the cancellation. In effect, Borkman's impotence—in the cosmic sense, of course—is a form of potency insofar as anything it conceives of and/or anticipates is assured a non-materialization.

Eden is still too angry to look him in the eye. But he has no trouble saying to Cantor, whom he's actually begun to like . . . a little, that frankly, he doesn't buy the impotence thing. (He struggles to make himself understood. But Some Body—some Monster—maybe Invidicum itself—is making it easier than he ever thought possible. The Monster is turning him into Cantor, at least as far as . . . eloquence is concerned.) The reason why bad event X, dreamed up by loser Y, doesn't happen to Y is not that he's infected X with his loserliness. And while we're at it he's sure he can teach Cantor (who wields his chopsticks—he's ordered the specialty of the house, tofu lo mein—with an elegance Eden envies, though he isn't exactly sure such elegance would go with his body type and sexual orientation) a thing or two about the limits of loserliness as a—as a—Cantor completes the sentence: "As a pharmakon." Ignoring the tip, Eden continues. The gist of what he has to say would go something like this in a best of all possible worlds or thereabouts: The reason why bad event X doesn't happen to our Johnny-on-the-spot, Y, is that, loser or no loser, he manages (transmuting the *fear* of impotence into ingenuity) to dream it up faster than the Monster—the Master—the some thing—the some body—who's running the Show. In this case, our Show. Spurred on by virtue of keeping faithful Straynge in his mind's eye (the great man's deigned to cameo as the Monster), Eden is able to complete his thought in what is for him record time. And since nothing is more important to the Monster than to be original—to feel he got there first even if *there* is nowhere—he has no choice but to cancel the entire off-off-Broadway run of this X. But: *where is this ungovernable eloquence—these perceptions too distinct for consciousness to bear—this truth-telling with a vengeance—coming from?* It's suddenly too easy to blame it on the Master. Who's pulling the Master's strings?

Borkman wonders for the first time whether the belief in a Ringmaster General which seems to be running rampant in this neck of the woods may not be a side effect of Invidicum, which could be used off label to induce such a belief. But for what purpose. He hangs fire. It's clear Borkman feels left out but there's no reason why Cantor's next remark, even if it's meant for Eden, can't interest Borkman as well, especially since he has two sons who will probably end up to be a lot like Eden—Cantor feels it in his gut but his gut has misguided him too many times to remember (but he believes in letting bygones be bygones). It all has to do with the way No. 1 son went about botching his matricide—with true thoroughbred heterosexual fearlessness. "You know when you said you can teach me a thing or two about loserliness, well, you never sounded more authoritative—even authoritarian—than ever. Why is that?" Eden shrugs (did he actually make that crack about loserliness? Eden could swear he only thought about making it—maybe on his deathbed) and, by contagion, Borkman shrugs as well. "Could it be that in seeing right through yourself—calling a spade a spade—means you have nothing left to lose—including your loserliness? For as long as the merciless self-depreciation lasts you're a pathological curve along which there's no point of tangency for the straight-line juggernaut of somebody else's slimy contempt. You're uncatchable—you're yourself in all your loserliness and at the same time the last thing you are is yourself—you're beyond yourself—looking down on yourself and all your detractors from—well, from Mount Olympus." "I don't understand a word," Eden replies, just to be snotty—for of course he understands more than he cares to admit. He also thinks the remark will usher him into Borkman's good graces. Ignoring him Cantor concludes: "Nothing is as threatening—as awe-inspiring—as self-depreciation when what underlies it is complete self-knowledge."

Let the little boys squabble. Borkman can't decide whether the waitress, lurking in the shadow of the men's room, is glowering because she thinks they haven't paid (have they?) or because, having paid, they have no reason in the world for loitering. But how could they have paid? They're not even halfway through their dinner. He refuses to be cowed even if he has no real desire to spend any more extracurricular time with his trial mates. If his rivals could see him now! They'd say he had it coming. The nicer of the two is obviously queer. Once Eden's gone—he rose abruptly and, after throwing what looks like a twenty in the direction of Cantor's tofu (Borkman's having the moo goo turkey tofu), just ducked out—Borkman suddenly finds himself eager to remain. He decides to take full advantage of this opportunity to lament his failure as a father. He decides to *use* Cantor, who can only be grateful for the attention. Cantor is excited by the prospect of listening to what he senses will be a confession but not (though it has nothing to do with his age) by the confessor. Once the floor show is over, Cantor waits awhile, in a respectful exhibition of digesting the other's hard-earned pain, then proclaims, "If I had a son, he'd let me know soon enough that while what he really wanted was Joe DiMaggio he ended up with Liberace instead, sequins and all." Borkman bypasses the self-depreciation (it seems to be tonight's theme), if that is really what it is, and says (lowering his voice a quarter of an octave), "Did you know Joe was estranged from his kids?" Borkman shakes his head in emphasis.

Cantor can't believe his ears. Here is The Slugger, or whatever he's known as to his cigar-chomping fans, no longer quite the superdad he needs him to be—no longer an antidote—a pharmakon—for the disease he needs Liberace to be suffering from. DiMag and Lib are no longer airtight categories, which robs Cantor himself of his hard-won pathos. Understandably, Cantor is extremely disappointed to hear the news for he's gone to a lot of trouble over the years getting himself worked up enough to believe DiMag and Lib are *the* standard bearers for the starkest of contrasts—of binary oppositions. Since the starker the contrast between good-Mag and bad-Lib, the greater his self-abasement as bad-Lib and self-abasement—at its best, exalting—is the name of the game—the perversely pleasurable game known to its anti-fans as The Life of Cantor.

But not, he suddenly realized, the only game. For to conceive the opposition between DiMaggio and Liberace, to bring such disparates together out of the blue, requires a bold imagination, a ravenous appetite for absurdity as a rare delicacy. And he knows he deserves especially high marks for carrying out this exploit in a vegan joint. According to the *content* of the opposition, Cantor is Liberace, all well and good. But according to the *telling* of the opposition, according to the opposition as an invention, a construction, Cantor, as teller, as inventor, as constructor, is both DiMag and Lib as well as—himself—AND neither DiMag nor Lib nor—himself. As inventor, he is not bound to—is much more than—the terms of his invention and—as Cantor plus his invention, much more than himself. A real virtuoso, this *meta* guy, if he does say so himself. So the real subject is not the standing-room-only DiMaggio-Liberace prizefight but Cantor himself, as the behind-the-scenes cigar-chomping promotor of the DiMaggio-Liberace prizefight—as bull ring, battleground and playing field. Or more to the point, the real subject is Cantor's *telling* as promoter, battleground, playing field—the venue—the only venue and the trendiest one in town—where they find themselves on the same bill.

Making himself out to be Liberace alone, Cantor dutifully scales—in his own homophobic eyes at least—the heights of self-abjection. But in setting up—despotically decreeing—concocting so fearlessly inventive a contrast from scratch—dreaming up such a cockamamie opposition cum connection from nothing and out of nowhere between, of all people, DiMag and Lib— Cantor has achieved a Rube Goldbergish self-exaltation. A whopping dose of abjection in playing Lib, the more thankless of the two roles—in ad Libing—is after all a small price to pay for that exaltation. Even if the success of the enterprise required that he first play—and to the hilt—the more thankless of the two roles.

So there's no way he's going to believe this Borkman character. DiMaggio simply must stay put as the monstrously flawless father, the ideal pop Cantor can never begin to be. DiMag's pub[l]ic *escutcheon* (look it up) has to be not only greener than Lib's but greenest, greener than the greenest green. DiMag needs him to be as different from abject Liberace as possible so that he, Cantor, can go on playing his virtuoso role of matrix—medium—menstruum—midway freakshow—where cross-dressing DiMaggio crosses over and becomes Liberace and Liberace—slipping into his snazziest Ebbets Field drag (*I'll only be a minute!*) returns the favor. So that the terms of this supposedly radical opposition can become (in him, through him) better than reconciled—indistinguishable. He needs them to impersonate whatever lies at the opposite ends of a spectrum—to overdo the fierce opposition precisely in order to prove that they have far more in common with each other than with anything in-between. So that he, virtuoso of virtuosi can step in and, free of charge, constitute and be fondly remembered as constituting the site where the fiercest of opposites in all recorded history, i.e., Lib and DiMag, managed to clash and cohabit, cohabit in clashing, thereby enabling Cantor, the eternal substrate, to remain, amid all the tumult, unlocalizable and unstraitjacketable—i.e., identityless (passport notwithstanding), i.e., untainted by the infinite vulgarity of any fixed ontological (yes, *ontological*) abode.

If Cantor needs anything, though as a rule he doesn't need much, it is to ensure that his boys go on being as opposite as possible. So that he can go on being nothing in himself. So that when cleaving spiritual waters he needn't dread the stroke-shackling kelp of a fixed identity. So he can be like Thoth, or like Hermes (athlete, craftsman, master chef, keeper of the flame, herald, chargé d'affaires a.i., magician, merchant, messenger, campaign manager, musician, shepherd, thief, lock-picker, all and none of the above), or like Plato's pharmakon, that is to say, a giddy god of movement and flow, mutation and transition, the confirmed bachelor god of disidentity, nonidentity, unidentity. Settled, then—DiMaggio is as wretched a Las Vegas prima donna dad as Artful Brooklyn Dodger Liberace is a great one.

Still, he feels he could do better—much better—find extremes even more extreme than standard bearers DiMag and Lib, which would make their meeting even more of a feat for sore eyes. Feels he hasn't gone far enough in terms not just of humiliation at one end of the spectrum but of virilization at the other.

Borkman says kindly (he's rarely kind but feels the pull of exoticism), "Anyway, you underestimate yourself. I think you'd be a terrific father."

"What makes you so sure? Is it because you know I'll never be one? How *could* I be one, given how I feel about sports (though some people would call metamathematics a sport, even if it's not man's favorite)? But you know what my Popeye says about sports addiction?"

Before Borkman can react, an obscure vestige of some ancestor's theatrical instinct tells him not to. The most poignant reaction is no reaction. But when did he ever care about poignancy?

"That it's a sign of arrested development and an aptitude for fraud—fraud being one of the two signal manifestations of barbarian prowess."

Borkman is no sportsman either but the younger boy is, so he's relieved he's not within spitting distance.

"Oh, I know that's a wee bit irrational. Especially coming from a jackass of all trades who routinely applies every last ounce of the poison he extracts from the most offensively alien points of view as a remedy against being, chronically, himself. Thing is, sometimes it feels so damn good to perversely shut down P.T. Cantor's Dialectical Circus of Three-Ring Horrors and be just little old bigoted, closeminded me. Sometimes it's just good, clean, sexy fun (I'm using *sexy* to mean, as it did centuries ago, erection-inducing—not, as nowadays, trendily controversial-intellectual) to be perversely one-sided, to indulge my unwashed underfeelings, to stand (and Super Bowlers be damned) on the wrong side of the human equation. There's a thrill in being perverse—ask the French, who turned so many of their countrymen into vichyssoise—although they may not—ever—have considered Jews their countrymen—without turning a hair. Not that I can ever savor the thrill for too long, what with the roar of counter-arguments already in my ears. OK, athletes are overpaid and overpraised—says Liberace. So what's the alternative? (Remember, Cantor, if you want your perversity to sober up fast, always ask, *So what's the alternative?*) Kissing the ass of doomed geniuses? I always remember the words of one of my oldest buddies (yes, gays have buddies, too), that sobering Scot Davy Hume, namely, *What particular privilege has this little agitation which we call thought, that we must thus make it the model of the whole universe?"* (Cantor is aware he may be killing himself off from overuse of this catchy phrase but he doesn't care. Maybe it's the Tofu lo Mein Maison doing the talking.) "So before I know it, I'm on my way back to the right side of the equation and it's the transit I like best. For it's then that I'm unbracketable, unstraitjacketable, irrefutable, unstereotypic, invisible—the whole shebang."

Talking like this, playfully yet authoritatively, with the restaurant atmospherically not quite deserted, for a split second he feels *manly* and feeling manly means feeling heterosexual—hetero enough, in fact, to fuck their waitress (where's she disappeared to?) whose slut-sullenness is suddenly . . . good enough to eat. With Cantor, Manliness, whatever that is when it's at home, comes and goes. Sometimes, it's contagious, as now with Master Builder Borkman. Yes, it's good to feel manly for a change, giving Envy of the real thing a well-earned rest. It makes him unlocalizable since he's not *just* manly. For what would be Borkman's surprise if he started pulling rabbit-sized Bellinis and Viscontis and Cukors and Callases out of his heterosexualized hat? But for the time being he wants to feel manly and nothing but. Borkman makes it both appealing and *doable.*

"I'm sure you'll be a much better father than I ever was." Is Borkman putting him on? (*Borkman feels that the eloquence about to overflow—so alien to a crook of his type—should come with a caveat: What you're about to hear is My Master's Voice. Replete with hologram of my canine muzzle halfway down the gramophone horn.*) "The night I was waiting for the older boy to walk through the door so we could get him committed for trying to strangle his mother I knew I'd stolen the place of my children's rightful father. And I never envied anybody as much as I envied the incumbent. The more I raged against him— and it wasn't because he'd tried to strangle her or even because he botched the job (although that was a special blow to my manhood by proxy)— The more I raged against him *for having cheated me out of hundreds of thousands of dollars to subsidize the dream of a buddy (to use your word) who turned out to be no buddy at all but the kind of super soft spoken but still blustering guru—the worst kind—who's convinced his criminality's holy charity*—the more my rage validated the rage of all the little people and places I myself have bilked—the shareholders, the pensioners, the small retailers, the homeowner hopefuls, though in my case at least, it's always been my dream and nobody else's: a dream tied up in a sack of shit, granted, but they've been *my* sack and *my* shit. So if I'm right about my boy and his buddy then they—the ones I've disenfranchised without blinking an eye—must be right about me and if they're right about me, then I'm invalidated as a righteous rager. So I'm right about him and the buddy only to the extent that I have no right to be right—only if I admit the others are right about me and let that rightness destroy not just my right to judge but my right to *exist. I'm right about him and his buddy only if I don't have the right to be right.* Thing is, if I applaud his borrowed bluster and let him suck me dry so he can donate my tired blood to his partners (actually, he's not even a partner but a worse-than-invisible off-the-books investor) then it's he who'll destroy me. That's his goal even if he doesn't know it. It's the goal of any self-respecting son. In either case, I'm . . . fucked."

"Don't worry."

"Don't worry?"

"What I mean to say is: Take heart because the tragic fate of modern mathematics is solidly behind you all the way, since some of its disciplines also suffer from the incurable cancer of internal contradiction." Surprisingly, Borkman's eyes don't glaze over. "Bertrand Russell, for example, showed that a collection of things (or, as it's called, a class) can be normal and abnormal at the same time. He calls a class normal if and only if it doesn't contain itself as a member. For example (I know I sound like a book), the class of drunkards is normal because, clearly, it is not itself a drunkard and so doesn't belong to itself. On the other hand, the class of concepts is abnormal because it is very much a concept and so contains itself as a member. So far, so mock-abstruse. But, hey, what about N, the class of all normal classes? Is it normal or abnormal? If N's normal, then it doesn't belong to itself, but since N is the class of ALL normal classes and N is as normal as the next guy, then it must belong to itself. OK, but if it belongs to itself, it's abnormal. But what if N is not normal but abnormal? Then it belongs to itself. But if it belongs to itself, it's normal, since the members of N are all normal. So it turns out that N is normal only if it's abnormal and abnormal only if it's normal. Just as your raging is valid only if is invalidated. Russell's 'message' is of course a Turkish delight to outcasts like me but I can understand how a mainstreamer like yourself might feel otherwise."

Borkman (unapologetically bypassing Russell and his message) says, "I feel the boys are dragging me down and cursing me, every step of the way, for making them do it." He looks sullenly at the waitress who's finally returned. She gives her all to amply returning the favor with the best travesty of what she takes to be his kind's idea of racy sluttishness. Her too many long hours—days—years—on the job with no union card in sight gives her cameo a certain murderous oomph. Cantor is chastened—intimidated—by her plight—ashamed of having gotten himself all worked up about *eating* her—whatever that might mean. His uncharacteristic impulse was contrived, he fears, to turn this night out with the boys into a *real* night out and thereby make it palatable to as wide a public as possible—so palatable as to trigger a shock of cozy recognition in every spectator. For they're being watched—and judged—Cantor can feel it in his bones. "I should kill myself but that would be like leaving a porn film before the money shot and I've always insisted on getting my money's worth, even when I had millions." Cantor knows Borkman wants him to say, You shouldn't (kill yourself), but he can't fake it.

"And I bet the more you think you long for death the more careful you are crossing the street."

"Something like that," Borkman says. "How did you know?"

"I was—am—the same now that Berry Sundae's out of the picture."

"Who's—?" but he knows before he finishes.

"After he died, I never stopped talking about wanting to die. But is it my fault if I'm one of those HIV-positive superslow progressors or very long-term nonprogressors we're always hearing about. And then my friends, who can be cunts (or is it *pricks*? that's the more denigrative term: be blunt), especially when they've had one too many mochacchinos (now *I'm* being a cunt, unjust—worse, inaccurate), would rightly ask why, if I was so in love with easeful death, I did everything in my power to ward off its blandishments (*blandishments* means . . .)"

"I know what it means." (In saying that—and in just the right restrained straight-from-the-shoulder tone—Borkman has become beautiful to Cantor.)

"Why, for example, did I down organic carrot juice every chance I got and take my multivitamins three times a day and quit smoking cigars and refuse to kiss on a first date—or even a third—without a condom? At first I was offended, but then I pulled myself together just enough to realize there were some damn interesting thoughts to be gathered here, thoughts simply aching to be picked off the tree of self-hate cum self-love. This was an opportunity to think the only way my kind likes to think: dialectically. Dialectic, by the way, is to ordinary thinking what raw pornography is to the slow-motion fog-filter sex simulated in a Hollywood blockbuster.

"So I told those foul-weather friends that, yes, I contradicted myself every chance I got. But there was a mother lode of gold nuggets as big as the Ritz in them there hills of contrariety. So what if the more I long for Death, the more I coddle myself? Yes, I very much want to die but the more I want it, the more something inside insists that I defy the Oldest of Old Farts to take me on its own terms. I refuse to make things easy for It by actively collaborating with the usual rear-exit addictions. I want Death to surprise me—to earn its keep—to give me a run for my money."

Borkman insists on paying. Cantor resists then relents but not before making him aware of what his considerably older buddy Rambling Samuel Johnson made *him* aware, namely, that there are minds so impatient of inferiority, that their gratitude is a species of revenge, and they return benefits, not because recompense is a pleasure, but because obligation is a pain. Yeah, say it again, Sam. You've got me pegged and then some.

The idea of returning home repels Melanctha Herbert, especially when home is, as it is here and now and may be forever, the outer reaches of the Bronx. Though her son was dutifully buried—at Woodlawn, not too far from Indian-hater Herman Melville, in fact—as far as she's concerned his ashes were scattered all over the borough. She can't help picking at the carcass of the Rhys woman's hard-luck story.

When she explained that in telling her story she was seeking *closure*, a way of *moving on*, Rhys forfeited the little compassion Herbert held in reserve for amateur sufferers. She's proud to be thinking these phrases in italics because her favorite professor at Hunter (her favorite despite the color of his craggily waffled skin) would be proud. He exhorted her, as if he actually saw success— fame—fortune—in the offing, never to forget that you measure the mettle of a man by how much word-dreck he absolutely insists on putting in italics or, slightly less vengefully, between quotation marks—by all the babble, psycho-, techno- and otherwise, he refuses to assimilate to his mind substance, rejecting as an alien graft what he then transmutes into a mere artifact of his apperception. He knows the babble exists to crowd out the interior stuff that makes us unique. As a black woman she must feel like italicizing a lot of white words, for most of our words are, for better or worse, white ones. But in italics, they burn a lot less and you can handle them creatively—in a way most dumb-ass whites like him never do because they never put themselves at a distance from what the hunger for membership in the tribe makes them say. So—are you listening out there in the second row?—she doesn't have to feel she's a traitor for using our words—*if*, that is, she uses (or rather misuses) them in the right way.

Still, Herbert can't help, or stop, wondering what happened to the hapless husband after the fateful post-compote ferry ride. She's sure, however, that he hasn't ended up in Falluja. Middle-class whites, for all their posturing, are always clever enough to foresee and foreclose the grosser implications of their downward spirals. In any case, she wants to know now—right now—hasn't any intention of waiting for the release of the final season of the saga of the sisters Rhys on Blu-ray.

The favorite professor did feel obliged to warn her, however, not to get waylaid by what he called a bit too airily for Melanctha's taste—too dismissively—racial animus italicized or not—and to keep her eye on the ball—on a more "universal" problem. Though what was more universal than racial animus, among humans at least?—it was the blight they were born for. She'd do better to focus on an even more unpleasant blight—the most universal of blights. Didn't she at least suspect that the sacred medium she'd be harnessing to produce her works was the very instrument she deployed in everyday life to communicate her pettiest grievances? In other words she needed to hurry up and start getting used to the fact that as a writer—in contrast to a composer or a painter or a sculptress—she couldn't avoid shitting where she ate. That everyday living in—through—language was, in its griminess, its triviality, its clodhopper arrogance, a desecration of *the other kind of living through language*—the kind of living whose job it was to demonstrate Life purged of the danger and degradation of everyday living was finally achievable. But that inasmuch as everyday language was far and away the stronger—the brawnier—and threatened to collapse the idiot distinction she needed to make between it and sacred language—*her* sacred language—then to survive (or else why bother being Melanctha Herbert?) she must consecrate herself to playing a double game—not just writing *but making sure her idiot distinction remained intact through thick and thin*. No matter that every time she read the papers or turned on the TV or swallowed a tweet she'd end up feeling that (as he still did even after all these decades of pedagogic self-correction) although there language was being cannibalized for different—unworthier—purposes than her own and even if those cannibalizers achieved a lower level of so-called eloquence (or so he needed to believe from a professorial arrogance stillborn of impotence) the fact remained that the manifest destiny of their brand of eloquence—its hard-earned privilege fairly and squarely won—was to crowd out hers. No matter that all her pride had to hold on to was a stupid self-commitment to pitching her mansion of words and so what if it was in their own excrement? No matter that while composers—choreographers—painters—sculptors—had a special language—a *protected* language—the would-be writer must shit where she ate. No matter that what she wielded to create her mansion was at the same time the very waste product with which she regularly besmirched herself, say, to make her complaint in the supermarket understood by the assistant manager—worse, to vent her envy of those she professed to loathe without their even giving her the courtesy of loathing back. No matter that between benders his father used to say "You don't shit where you eat," and that this is exactly what her kind did when they stooped to the recruitment of words—their sacred words—to fight off the world—to keep it at bay. No matter. The bottom line was still to make sure her idiot distinction remained intact. "But," she remembered asking herself in his presence, "isn't the constant threat—better the intermittent fact—of impenetration of sacredness and stench—submergence of sacredness by stench—a source of strength—of enrichment. Isn't it a fact that sacredness can always do with a muddy kick in the butt—that sacredness is born of stench and dies of disinfection?" Not one to take her shit-transcending because shit-preserving meditation sitting down (for he always knew when an unruly daughter was inwardly kicking against his grandfatherly pricks) he implored—ordered—her to be forever on her guard against what he called (but only in the privacy of his own [ahem] water closet) the *shit-where-you-eat effect*. Taking his cue in that regard from an old colleague who'd come up with the adjoining term *genius effect*[2] to account for the baffling refusal of psychologizing academics to eat the shit of Poe's magic—most incantatory when most analytical. Though he'd always felt she was letting him off way too easy. Since where did he—Poe—come off mixing mere genius with the unpleasurably upright business of . . . scribbling. Fact is, genius was vulgar—worse—genius was resistance to playing by the rules.

Eden is just beginning to digest yesterday's extended hard-luck story. He listened hard and he listened well and from all that listening he felt he knew Rhys's husband inside-out: they played stickball and got dead-drunk, flunked out of community college and ended up working in a pepperoni factory and then, after an unanticipated layoff, as semi-skilled mechanics for United Airlines. But at this, the very moment he is about to jump up and strangle her for even *thinking* about throwing her protector to the sharks from—of all places—the Ferry's prow, Straynge announces through a loudspeaker whose whereabouts are unknown that the patients or the clients or the supplicants or the guinea pigs (Eden didn't catch the word) will now pair off, though not, as yesterday, with just their attending physician—"I mean your personal trainer," he guffaws and, surprisingly, a few of the pigs guffaw back—but with a buddy

---

[2]See Shoshana Felman, "On reading poetry: reflections on the limits and possibilities of psychoanalytical approaches," in *The Purloined Poe: Lacan, Derrida, and Psychoanalytic Reading*, John P. Muller and William J. Richardson, eds. (Baltimore, Maryland, Johns Hopkins University Press, 1988), especially pp. 134–141. Don't let the title scare or repel you. Shoshana does Poe prouder than anybody else—except maybe Dupin's Doctor Watson in "The Purloined Letter."

as well. *How clever is storyteller Straynge,* Herbert thinks—or is it Cantor? or why not both? *Yesterday, just a physician and his dog, and today—and imagine! after only the slightest stir of the human soup—a physician and two dogs. What unparalleled powers of invention!*

After waving (but with nothing like—or at least it seems so in retrospect—yesterday's enthusiasm), Manning leads him and his buddy (the queer guy, of all people!, who's ahead of them) back to the basement. He wants to let off steam about the Rhys woman—to skewer her—and Cantor, he must admit, seemed one of the few who visibly bristled at her treatment of what in this case was truly a better half. Only in the unnervingly premature twilight of her office Cantor looks just a wee bit too . . . *gay* to be willing to become? to be worthy of becoming? (*well, which is it?*) his brother-in-arms.

Fiddling with her stethoscope, she asks Cantor what he thinks "of all that."

"Of all what?" he retorts rebarbatively, with clearly no intention of putting his two cents in. She has no choice but to turn to Eden. "What do *you* think?" He is tempted not to answer, as if complying will show disrespect for Cantor's manly resoluteness which has taken Eden completely by surprise and constitutes a much-merited rebuke to his mindless straitjacketing. But responsibility to the husband in question is on no account to be shunted aside.

Only after observing—unseeing—the fall of an oak leaf which ends its days as an eminently crucifiable upturned palm (while its siblings quiver their grief on the sidelines) does Eden elect to inform her (and Cook, the ad man, who without knocking has just entered) that as an ex-factory hand he knows from bitter experience what Rhys's husband must have done—after being compared so invidiously with somebody who wasn't worth his little finger—to prove himself worthy of a shrew like Rhys. She is now very much aware of Cook's surveillance and there is something in her tone that enjoins caution—as if she fears that in his reckless partisanship Eden might end up leaking classified information. Eden feels he is being tested but isn't sure to what purpose.

What must he have done? Why, what any schmuck in such a predicament does. He goes from agency to agency, East Side West Side all around the dirty, forbidding town, trying hard to be buoyed up by employment agency pep talks bookending the funeral toasts of human resourcers to whose firms he is, if he gets lucky, occasionally dispatched on the double. Summer passes into winter with only the curtest nod to autumn. And what does this schmuck remember of autumn? Well, since you ask, just a few pocked oak leaves scrapily gyrating around an implied maypole in some vacant lot between (where else?) West Seventy-Eighth and -Ninth. But what, you ask, can he be doing in a place where not a single employment agency worth a damn is to be found? Well, if you must know, sometimes he likes to escape to the heartland and just traipse around where folks seem never to have even heard of an employment agency, topping it all off with a rapturous quaff of the Hudson at sundown—or, as he puts it, *at parting.* What he likes even better is the surefire sadness that overcomes him as he transverses back to Fifth, Madison then Lex, agency country.

But despite his troubles, he tries to keep his gaze pointing upward, if for no other reason than to memorialize the begrimed Medusa above the door-way of some tenement before it is supplanted by yet another condo—sorry, condominium residence. He is also partial (it's in his genome) to the light-and-shade effects of service alleyways because they alone hoard the dirty secret of the city's beauty, rooted as it is in the ever-widening breach between rich and variegated layers of poor. So at the rate he's going one day he's sure to descry, through some spearheaded railing, the inevitable heap of mattresses. And being who he is, he obviously needs to determine whether they're stained and if so with what. But long before he can decide how to research the mat-ter, the answer comes, through words (*but whose?*) to the effect that, for the purpose of his story, the mattresses are a veritable sperm bank and, addition-ally, very much stained beyond redemption with piss, shit, sputum, menstrual blood, sweat and tears, more tears and every other lubricant under the sun. *So, you bleeding-heart liberals, sunlight is the best disinfectant, is it? Well, think again!*

But they mustn't—she and Bill and subject Five and whoever they're taking their orders from on high (Eden wasn't born yesterday, after all)—get him wrong. For there are definitely moments when our favorite schmuck, finishing up one interview and bracing himself for the next, feels impregna-bly euphoric. And why not, for isn't all this rushing his scrawny ass off to be at agency A at ten-ten and agency B at eleven sharp, with no time even to piss, precisely what constitutes *getting a life?* So what if he heartily loathes this smug little catchphrase with a vengeance? What matters is that, booked solid in the being-at-the-mercy-of-everybody-and-his-brother department, he goes, rain or shine, from specialist to specialist, expert to expert, dutifully squeezing himself (because of the imminence of the next applicant or suppli-cant or stooge or client or patient or victim or arsonist) into their extra-tight schedules—even tighter, he finds (which, by the way, is very much consonant with the Stoic doctrine of the *pneuma*) when there aren't any nexts but whose fault is that anyway but his? The legend of his inadequacies has scared them all off. For as a result of so much rubbing of elbows with extra-tight schedules a wonderful thing happens—Rhys's punching bag finds that he himself has become too damn busy to fit anybody, especially Rhys herself, into his own.

But more and more frequently, it happens that one expert (in, say, the Chrysler Building) will tell him one thing, another (a stone's throw from the Morgan Library) something entirely different while still another (Chanin Building, fourteenth floor, turn right at the ladies' room) will write them both off as quintessential horse's asses, without explaining why. In one vaudeville routine, Jacopo von Dreck wonders how Mack O'Schnitzel can have told Rhys's boy toy he's made for neuromarketing when it must be crystal clear even to a complete incompetent that his strongest—in fact, his only—suit is very-low-end bartending with a twist of lemon. And so he becomes little more than a pretext for inexpert second-guessing and spends all his slotted time (so as not to end up completely mentorless) ensuring that no one guesser can make too cogent a case for another's incompetence. All very cutting-edge New York, he tells himself, but he knows that for all the squabbling they have a common aim: destruction of his already shredded identity.

"Sorry, Eden," says Cantor, "but I can't help thinking what an overrated shock to the system ID theft really is. I'd give anything to fall into the hands or catch the eye of some mastermind willing and able to relieve me of the target of my fiercest hate—myself—so I can have the uncanny sense that an identity is being conferred on me for the very first time—but a real identity, one worthy of something better than hate, i.e., *ID theft victim*. Why continue being me since with every gesture that is uniquely and spontaneously mine, I perpetrate the worst kind of failure?—and you do, too, Eden, or you wouldn't be here telling us Rhys's story: failure to be myself." More than anything, Eden wants to tell Cantor, after punching him right in the nose, and wiping the floor with the Manning bitch in heat and her cunnilinguistic sidekick Cook (they are probably an item), exactly why he's here. But he owes it to his holy terror of a mission to keep his West Coast trap shut. "So I don't feel sorry for Rhys—no, not in the least."

Cantor confesses easily enough that every minute, no matter what he does, he feels he should be doing the exact opposite even if there is no opposite. The verdict is in. It's inconceivable that he can go on being him and succeed. He just doesn't have the courage to be himself, of all people. He and success are incompossible (according to the Heisenberg Uncertainty Principle as modified for imbeciles). Now if we can only manage to get him out of the way (say his inner advocates) then the sky's the limit. When will he be given the opportunity to be anything except himself, to divest himself of his wrong kind of talent for being himself, to be like his rivals—more like his rivals than they themselves are . . .? He's not as strong as Berry Sundae.

"Who is Berry Sundae?" Cook asks, as so many others before and after him. He is sitting on the windowsill, blocking Eden's view. But the blockage is, oddly enough, a relief after what Cantor has just said.

He explains (putting all rumors to the contrary to rest) that Berry Sundae is—was (he feels a little bit like Mr. Memory assailed by Richard Hannay in the final scene of *The 39 Steps*)—a cross between an actor and an aspiring actor. Every day, passing the deli window at the quaint corner of Bleecker and Cornelia on the way home from work (comprising mainly auditions, which by the way were infused with far more drama than the hokey passion and chamber plays in which the successful ones landed him), he couldn't prevent himself from staring long and hard (Envy's a too-permanent erection) at all his rivals, i.e., the Rival of a Thousand Faces who of course refused even to stare him down, so swept away was He by His glossy magazine-cover success. From the very first, he couldn't help being undone—annihilated—canceled out, pipe dreams and all (Envy's the thing with fetters). He wasn't envious—he didn't begrudge anybody his or her good fortune—he was just undone. Until one day (about six weeks before his body kindly informed him he was dying) Berry found himself capable of exiting the furnace of his annihilation at the very moment it was about to swallow him up, slapping a photo of the blessed event on one of those covers (usurping the place of the worst of the thousand faces) and staring semi-fondly at the mess to his heart's content. He managed to *turn the tables on himself*, a feat achievable by few. From that moment, self-annihilator became his biggest portfolio credit, his best head shot, the role he was born to play—even if it had to be in summer stock (alas, he wasn't lucky enough to get the chance to play either Peoria, Pomona or Pittsfield). But Cantor isn't able to frame his annihilation: he's still gullible enough to believe his rivals' success is his failure. "By the way, what happened to Mr. Jean Rhys?" Eden: "I don't know: we parted company at the moment I responded to Straynge's call." Cantor wants to say "siren song" but isn't sure how this touch of fey wit—if that's what it is—will go over.

Before she speaks, Manning lavishes a long look on Cook, which turns out to be his signal to nod entrancement (like Hillary when Bill sings her praises on the stump). "There's obvious friction between the two of you but that's what makes for a very strong team and we need a strong team because something terrible is about to happen here. Cantor, I trusted you at once and as a nonprogressor you'll never be cured of Envy so, qua underdog, you might as well throw in your lot with us. I'll explain why when I'm surer still of your commitment to what for lack of a better word I'll call the cause." She lavishes another look on Cook, which seems to mean that only he can know how painful it is to share the secret. She tells them that the higher-ups and—of far greater import—even the lowliest lower-downs (as she's already mentioned to Eden whom she's proud to say and happy to see has divulged nothing, or has he?) are so intent on getting Invidicum approved in order to peddle it with impunity off label (*where*, to again quote her favorite poet, *the meanings are*) that most of the trial subjects will be saturated with a placebo (oxymoronically) potent enough to render them Envy-free. As for those others who are irresponsive to such a modality, they'll be subjected, when their backs are turned, to the electronic bombardment of the neurons in that area of the brain where Envious neurons live. And everybody will stay Envy-free just long enough to allow the upper and lower expert hirelings to put the finishing touches on their books-cooking report to the FDA, with a little help from the Voracicom ghost-writing brigade.

"What about Straynge?" Cantor asks.

"Straynge," says Cook, leaping off the sill, "is very much an unknown quantity. And as a numbers man, Cantor, you know better than anybody what that means." Of course he doesn't know what that means, at least as Cook *wants* it to mean, and makes a mental note to detest him until further notice for this stroking stab at collusion with the trial's token HIV-positive nonprogressor (after all, it wouldn't have gotten the go-ahead without the participation of somebody like him, or so he's heard). But Cantor says nothing on this score since he doesn't want to be (justly) reviled for his acuity, though he's convinced there's too much whimper (and way too little bang) in the tenor of his silence.

But he mustn't detest Cook for too long otherwise he may just take it into his perfectly shaped head to destroy Cantor, his favorite token numbers-man by far. Treating him as if he's a somebody with depths worth plumbing (though obviously they won't be the kind of Grand Canyonesque depths that customarily set his gypsy heart aflame—or is it *astir*?) will, if all goes according to plan (what plan is that? he wonders slyly), surely cure Cantor of his detestation and eliminate the need for the World's detestation of that detestation (i.e., how dare he, a nonprogressing non-normal, come off presumptuously detesting one of Its very own?). He studies Cook but is unable to fix on an entry point. That he can't render him elegant and solvable shows his failure not just as a man (who cares? in that guise he's eminently expendable and most of all to himself) but as a *budding* mathematician. As the meta-magician he professes to be, he should be able to draw jackrabbits of sheer lovability out of the ten-gallon hat of Cook's standard-issue decreed detestableness, *while at the same time preserving it.* Since it begins to be enviable, that is, to have a sexual allure—the allure of flatness, of a brute refusal to self-commune, communion being unseeingly perceived as a form of transsexualization. Maybe the medication will make him just as flat hence insusceptible to the allure of the flatness of a Cook. No more self-hate, no more Envy (or is it vice versa?) and, most important, no more homosexuality (here he goes again, taking a chance, à la Ethel Waters, on hewing to belief in a facultative version). But life without self-hate is like . . . the missing of a beat, an infinity of beats. And what is self-hate, that is, when it's done *right*—to a crisp—but the masterly anticipation, i.e., obliteration, of the hatred of others? How can he ever hope to solve the lemma/theorem/conjecture that is none other than he himself without self-hate to guide him? Greatness achieved is nothing but self-hatred as told at last to World and Co. Cook, he notes, is back on the sill. This is an act of defiance—defiance of three millennia of high culture, to be inexact—which is best ignored for now.

But does he really believe any of this? Isn't it the same Some Body or Some Thing—now the same old Some Body or Some Thing—doing the thinking for him? Of course it is but he can't shake it. Don't the other members of the tribe have the same problem. Of course they do: he can see it in their faces even when they're not talking to themselves. Hasn't Cantor already asked himself these questions hundreds of times? Of course he has. But like a fine wine, the question gets better with each asking. And doesn't he always get the same answer?—which doesn't, alas, get better. They've been co-opted by what has become by default their favorite ghoul: a "witty and urbane" confidence trickster celebrated as the Monster Master in the kind of semi-elite circles that no longer exist except, maybe, on Rodeo Drive or St. Tropez. So—Is the inability to recognize one's thinking *as* one's thinking an occupational hazard? But what occupation are we talking about? Is participation in a trial actually to be thought of as some kind of occupation? Or is the takeover a hallucination engendered by the drug? Is Invidicum allowing him to think what he's never dared think before and in a way he never dared think about anything? (And if this experiment in ghoul-sharing is being exacerbated by the minute to the point of self-intimidation, how must the PhD-less others be faring under the circumstances?) And does it throw in as a bonus the conviction that there's some puppeteer doing the thinking for him? To cushion the blow of discovering just how much of a deep thinker he can be given half a chance and to ward off the Envious blows of thinkers who don't quite make the grade? But a thinker as deep as he doesn't feel Envy—not for anyone or anything. An over-educated bump on a blog (*untranslatable American pun*), he's always prided himself on his unimprovable eloquence.

(His eloquence: It has something to do with reaping—establishing—a fringe benefit—a surplus value—for technical language, whose capture of any scientific phenomenon worth its salt entails bringing to birth the most unexpected of word combinations [never before seen, never before heard]. Unexpected by everyday standards, is what Cantor means, yet immediately plausible—instantly incontrovertible—eternally poetic. Plausible, incontrovertible, eternally poetic, that is, to an everyday somebody like him who, coming once in a century, can hear the words with an allegorical eye—see the words with an allegorizing ear—the Third Ear and Eye of Allegory. Plausible, incontrovertible, eternally poetic to a somebody who when the New York City Ballet is digging into, say, *Symphony in C* can—sort of like Foucault's clinical gaze or Balanchine's ideal spectator—see the music and hear the dancing. A somebody who when he sees and hears the words—the new words for the new scientific phenomenon—sees and hears an allegory in the making—about, say, a new kind of affair of the heart or scarification of the soul. Something subjective, something unrepentantly *inner-worldly*. Cantor's the kind of somebody for whom a phrase like "decoupling of the Pacific tectonic plate from the underlying upper mantle" [*Nature*, vol. 518, 5 February 2015, p. 39] invokes a new kind of personal self-schism or -delusion. A new kind of twist of the knife deep within the tissue of self-love [which twists are what deep-dish subjectivity is all about]. That kind of phrase, tired of being over-yoked to, overidentified with, the scientific phenomenon responsible for its birth—a phrase whose sole raison d'être is to capture, i.e., describe, and to go on describing that phenomenon forever or until the phenom's caretaker cries, *Stop*, at which point the phrase *allows itself to be shredded, like a minor planet by a white dwarf* [which combo invokes yet another species of self-schism]—Such a phrase, I say, once it tastes the briny air, wants to be more than just a footnote. Just as it is the son of a scientific phenomenon, so does it now desire to be the father of a poetical one—a phenomenon full of blood and guts, heart and soul, placid pain and passionate prescience. A new kind of convulsive inner struggle not yet undergone—a new form of feeling never before felt—but whose time must come—eventually. Thing is, centuries of suffering may be required for its production [since only suffering authorizes probability] and for the generation of the phrase needed to capture it—nail it to the cross of comprehensibility. So this is where a boob like Cantor the Midwife—Cantor the Talent Scout—comes in handy. He knows a scientific phrase capable of allegorization—capable of invoking an inner struggle that's unrepentantly way way ahead of its time—when he sees one. He can smell it a mile away. The convulsive inner struggle—the blood-and-guts phenomenon—can now be invoked, captured, described, before it's lived. Thanks to the little phrase Cantor finds so beguiling [like the lever of Archimedes, that phrase, given half a chance, can move the world]. Here in the world of heart and soul, blood and guts, the word combo brings forth the phenomenon, which is contrary to the way things are handled in the scientific realm, where, from direst need, the phenomenon brings forth the word combo. The word combo unveils, festering at its very core, a blood-and-guts phenomenon hewing close—some might say too close—to the jagged edge of the words. And the cream of the jest is that Cantor's brain holds the patent—upon which no pimply troll lying low in his grandmother's sub-basement in Yekaterinburg can infringe.)

Cantor wants to apologize to Cook—first, for taking a simple reposition-ing on the sill for an act of defiance. But fact is, he can't be held responsible for wordflow—for what words do to and with him once they have the chance. Can he help it if the minute they find him getting all worked up—usually about his own defects—that's their cue to rush right in and use the anguish as a podium, so to speak? Words are parasites and once they get a whiff of his anguish it becomes the engine of their own ever-expanding flow in directions he never dreamed he could want to go. For their expansion is his expansion. And once they've sucked the anguish dry, after dragging it through all sorts of byways and arteries and dead ends he finds himself saddled with thoughts he never dreamed he could father. So should he warn Dr. Manning (he loathes himself for addressing her by her title) that once words—those opportunistic viruses—hijack his suffering there's no telling what he may end up saying to the detriment of the cause? His suffering is but a Goliath of puniest protest against the David of their disregard.

Instead: "You said something terrible is going to happen." "Cook and I have listened hard to you both and our instincts tell us our first impressions weren't wrong. So I feel free to say something terrible is *already* happening. Those running the show are so obsessed with the profits to accrue from administering Invidicum off label that they spend much—most—of their time priming the sales force for its all-out assault on practitioners the world over. And as the staff so-called continue to pay less and less attention (level of care has plummeted markedly even within the two days you've been here), the patients will take—are already taking—this to mean that they *require* less and less attention and can therefore be considered for all practical purposes disease-free. So they will expose themselves more and more to Envy-induc-ing stimuli—on the Internet, at newsstands, etc.—to confirm and celebrate their invulnerability. They will pick at wounds that are just starting to close not because they are still afflicted—or so they will tell themselves—but as researchers whose duty is it to put their immunity to work on behalf of the real victims."

"Recidivism's wet dream," infers Cook. Manning ignores the remark either because as a naturalized citizen she doesn't understand it or because as a woman she refuses to understand it or because allowing herself to be pleasurably waylaid by a wisecrack and honor its irreverence would be tanta-mount to disgracing her profession-as-more-herself-than-she-is.

"If you can think for a moment of the trial itself as a patient who must be overhauled ASAP from head to toe, and of everybody who's running the show as the surgeon-general, then in this case the S-G, instead of performing his task, simply palpates the body of the beast and from time to time makes random incisions, to reassure himself that it—but more to the point, he—is still breathing. Just in case he should one day take it into his pretty little head to get the nosocomial (yes, *nosocomial*) ball rolling."

In accordance with the Law of the Allocation of Insights, Cook takes up somewhere in the vicinity of where Manning has just left off: "Consider, if you will, a masturbation addict (pardon the redundancy) who, having decided he's cured, thinks the world is now owed an expert's perspective on the phenomenon. So he resumes the practice, since in his case (which is the case of billions) it is by resuming, not abstaining, that he avoids going stark raving mad, only now it's as a tourist, an anthropologist on the make. Look, ma! I'm jerking off! but heuristically, and in a state so subexcitatory it's akin to the deep freeze. The frenzied meat-beater is thereby trounced by the arctic explorer. But before you know it he's forgotten all about the exploration. Rather, the spasms coming ever faster and more furious do the forgetting for him."

"Excellent, excellent," she says forbearingly, as if she's heard this all before, and she probably has, though not necessarily from Cook. "But now it's time to wind things up or, better yet, down. Your complete absence of symptoms, Eden, nicely balances Cantor's way too many. That's why, for our purposes, it's a perfect fit. Only a dyad like yours can get us the name of the disease for which Post and his gang want to exploit Invidicum off label." Manning's Eastern European bluntness grates on Cantor. He's tempted to ask her how much she charges so that when she asks, *For what?*, he can reply in his best deadpan, Why, for having done him the honor of summarizing his plight. While she knew from the start it would be a dirty job to disabuse him of his delusion (namely, that the number of his symptoms did not exceed the norm), she also knew, like any humanitarian worth his salt, that somebody had to call a spade a spade, and who better than she? (Though it's an equally dirty job he won't point out that all this summarizing is an apotropaic ploy— yeah, *apotropaic*, you heard me right the first time. It's her way of cutting the threat he poses down to size. But what threat is that? he wonders.)

Eden's avenging angel is pleased to know he hasn't provided Manning with any traitorous symptoms to munch on between work-ups.

CHAPTER SIX

True, his kids hate his guts mightily, each in his own way, and also true, his wife considers him solely responsible for their crises (he refuses to move with the times and warble *issues*). Still, Borkman feels charged up as never before after his first few doses and the first few sessions with Straynge, who thankfully doesn't quite live up to his almost name (Strangelove). He doesn't mind at all that the lady doctor (a bit smug but a lady so foxily fuckable is entitled to smugness, which only amplifies her appeal in any case)—the one on the podium who got Rhys's goat more than once—sits in and takes notes, even with her too-muscular, almost unsightly calves exposed.

He's tempted to think he's on a new path, primed for success in every sphere. Problem is, when you're a horrific dad, the world's worst, and when, unlike Chase, for example, and the Bank of America, you're willing to admit wrongdoing, then even breathing feels like criminal disrespect for your victims. From a purely selfish point of view (is there any other?), a silly spasm of pleasure, however slight, constitutes rank unpreparedness for the next well-deserved blow. A good bad-parent has to be ready for the inevitable shift: after a seemingly permanent entente, the sudden upsurge of filial hate as breath-of-fresh-air emancipation from its stranglehold.

But how can an egomaniac like Borkman care about his kids, anyway? When he thinks of the older boy, working seven days a week in a restaurant where he's not even a partner—not even an investor—just a superscullion whose daily ration is little more than a get-rich-quick line from his buddy-cum-guru and even that thanks only to his guilt-drenched father's being all too quick on the trigger of expiatory disbursement—when he thinks, I say, about the older boy and his anguish comes hot and deadly, is this fatherly concern or is this father-in-name-only in fact standing back aghast at his own lack of it, excruciatingly pained for *anybody* who could be saddled with so heartless a forbear? But isn't concern over the lack of concern, well, isn't that simply a surplus of concern, or concern to the second power, as his not-quite-pal Cantor might put it? Stop it: he is setting absurdly high standards for what constitutes concern, thereby grossly undervaluing his own peculiar version. But it's not as if gross undervaluation carried out now exculpates sins of the father committed then.

True, he's allowing the older boy, through his experiments in self-humiliation, and the younger boy, through his intrusive thoughts and obsessive gestures, to lead him down byways of struggle he doesn't want to know existed. But that's the very least he can do as their progenitor for who is it who said that when you have kids, your whereabouts are no longer your own? They're expanded and contracted and drawn and quartered and stretched to the limits defined by kidly vulnerability. Still, how genuine *is* the concern generated by all that drawing and quartering? And how much can concern over the boys' struggle compete with his already massive assets in the concern department, which are exclusively all about his undeviating focus on what Hank Ibsen, ex-pal and one of his many rivals (though Hank must surely believe he left bush-league Borkman way beyond centuries ago), referred to as the *slumbering spirits of the gold*? The sheer massiveness of Borkman's concerns—his own intrusive thoughts and obsessive gestures—about his Rightful Place in History is refractory to any further accrual. Yes, says the sleazeball who's feeding him his lines: *The sheer massiveness is refractory to any further accrual*—you heard me right the first time, bub. Whatever capacity there is to feel fatherly concern is immediately blunted—canceled—by his dedication to the other concerns— the World-Historical concerns. Garden-variety infinity plus one, or plus a billion, is still garden-variety infinity (did he read that somewhere or hear it at a board meeting or did Cantor say it the night of the vegan blowout?). Since his foregut is always oceanically convulsed with concern over something World Historical, whether it's this failed merger or that premature divestiture, this or that blundering buyout, or the fallout from having spent 98 percent of company earnings to buy back its stock, ostensibly as an expression of faith in the company's future but in fact (also according to Hank) to enrich himself and the members of the board—given all this, how can the boys' undoings and non-doings elicit anything except impatience, irritation, outrage even? How can the fart of fatherly concern be heard in the tornado of ambition's overreach? Which makes him realize—or makes him feel that he is about to realize . . . something crucial, if not to his well-being then to his long-overdue downfall. Only realizing it is beyond his capacity. But if he had the capacity, *it* would go something like this: By sheer dint of innocently persisting in their own being (*conatus*), the boys—as well as everybody and everything else—not only deny the supreme importance of his enterprise—supremest of all since the dawn of time—but denigrate it outright (albeit unknowingly, inadvertently, unconsciously, hence even more wickedly, relentlessly, with a vengeance). And if denigration comes, can obliteration be far behind?

But whatever his abilities in the fathering department, he is in fact grateful for these newer, noisier, fatherly concerns which in rearing their shrunken head are a welcome distraction from the chronic underswell. And now that you mention it, isn't there some lurking unspeakable hope that as a reward for giving the chronics a rest from his infernal meddling by taking time out to contend with the new arrivals—as a reward for *playing at absence* the way that blubbering redhead says her sister's husband does—he'll get a break in the only domain where breaks really matter, e.g., after so much ignominy, both deserved and unmerited, a deal may go through without a hitch for the first time in months, or his pay will be quadrupled thanks to a new performance metric, and the threat of jail time lifted so he can enjoy his misbegotten gains?

But concern or no concern, he needs, or at least once upon a time he needed, to have a wife and kids. It's *good for business*. Even if—or maybe *especially because* (or is this *especially because* merely a case of the wordflow—his wordflow—*somebody's* wordflow—getting ahead of him—and of itself?)— especially because it's only in the connubial—the familial—context that what in solitude or at a board meeting or in the course of a one-night stand (even one that lasts a couple of months) are mere character traits become the grossest of flaws. The more unqualified they are, the more eagerly does he, or people like him—too much like him for his own good (for what does he have if he doesn't have the uniqueness of his grossness, i.e., how World-Historical can a flaw be if you share it with billions of others?)—the more eagerly do people like him put themselves in the family way. Because the stork told them the only way they can exist is in the family way. Because once in the family way they can count on exposure, worry, inadequacy, payback, reproach, unmasking (the stuff if not quite the spice of life) to take their mind off their mortality. In any event, he knew all along that if he didn't put himself in the family way doublequick, he'd be eaten up with an unmasterable Envy. Simply—and tragically for everybody revolving but not evolving around those freaks for whom the Work is everything—the more obsessed they become, the more they crave something that can be counted on to get in the way of the Work at every turn. Now that he's a father himself, it's much easier to deal with the inevitable Envy of the ones for whom showing concern in the right amount, at the right time, in the right place and with the right facial expressions is a breeze. He can even laugh the siege of this kind of Envy to scorn because the difference between him and the A+ patriarchs he envies is merely quantitative—and therefore (hypothetically) eliminable—not qualitative (as would be the case if he remained childless), hence insurmountable.

So here he is in Straynge's office—*austere-plush* (try to map this concoction, Borkman, onto some referent out in the real world and see how far you get)—contending with his fatherly concern, or rather his fatherly concern over the lack of fatherly concern. Fact is, he's always taking it into his head to set fire to the landing outside the boys' room so he can play the martyr in putting out the flames of their resentment with the limp-dick hose of his self-excoriation. And he's finding out that when he puts it this way (at such times and when she's with him in rehab, his better half, like the consort of one of Dante's damned, routinely snorts on the sidelines at the slick packaging of this born-again contrition but fortunately she's not here now and he can play the contrition card to his heartless heart's content)—when he puts it this way, Straynge, like every other psychobabbler he's ever met (whether on the East Side or the West Side or south of Houston down Tribeca way), is all too willing to take the bait and not-quite-insist he's being too hard on himself— too hard on himself, that is, as long as he dutifully—and dialectically—goes on being just that. But now that he's daring to take Straynge at his word and fiddle easier while Rome burns, Straynge, true to his code, exhibits irritation. Manning seems to be a tougher cookie.

He heads for home, his pills (they've increased the dosage) warehoused in a nice little Institute shopping bag. In deference to the latest iconographic twist in the neverending saga of urban pseudo chic (even if by definition all chic is pseudo), en route he swings it—a gesture which has been spreading like wildfire and is currently right up there with compulsive smartwatch checking, that signature exhibitionist tic (or pretended tic) of fashionably sweaty joggers. Swings it just like any other self-respecting partner to a trendy dyad (tourist or non-) who, after buying his pretty plaything a bauble at one of the best Fifth Avenue boutiques, manfully assigns himself the job of carrying the dainty receptacle so as to spare her mini muscles that charwomanesque labor. He's virile 'cause he's henpecked and peacock-proud of it. Only in Borkman's case at the moment there's no plaything to swing the thing *for*—no henpecker who gets to wear the pants because he's left holding the bag. At the southwest corner of Fourteenth Street and Fourth Avenue (where at any hour of the day or night can be heard the soused strains of the old rathskeller favorite "Where, oh where, are the bookstalls *d'antan*?") he transfers the bag (all that swinging has made him feel just a wee bit too girlish) to his fashionably distressed leather briefcase, the gift of a discreetly adoring almost-seduced assistant badly in need of breast reduction who always looked as if she were hiding a vintage portable typewriter under her blouse (hence that aspiring thief's nickname, Madame Remington). As he rings the bell (when he's not out one-night-standing, he shares the upstairs guestroom with a guy named Borkman and, if he does say so himself since who else will, finds him to be a most engaging unsnoring bedfellow), he wants to cry out loud enough for the neighbors to hear (or else why bother?) his thanks for being allowed to sample a hefty slice of fatherhood at the Buffet Table of Life (byword of the latest PBS guru cum chef, this one with twenty-plus bestselling self-help cookbooks to his alias). But in some undefinable way (maybe Straynge can help him do the defining, though he doubts it) the failing to learn has been an enrichment beyond price. Just because something has turned out to be a mistake doesn't always mean—or hasn't he heard?—it shouldn't have happened. Eminently mediocre men make no mistakes—their blunders are volitional and the pathways to selfhood. Too bad he can't shovel back directly into his work (like an unemployed Method actor, say) everything he's failed to learn. Too bad he's not in that one line of work which offers such blunderers—the lucky ones—a fair day's enlightenment for a fair day's excruciating humiliation.

The apartment looks grim and feels cold, though it's the height of summer and the uncomplaining sun is busily doing the maid's job—applying varnish, whether called for or not, to every plaintive surface in sight. He asks where, oh where, the lady of the house might be hiding out. She informs him the wife's out shopping for the dinner party set for 8:30 (this lady-is-a-tramp gets too hungry for dinner at 9). That her look outlasts the delivery of the news signifies defiant underdog enjoyment of his big shot fall from grace.

"What party?" he pursues not just warily but wearily, hoping she's too far out of earshot to answer. But answer she does, and much too circumstantially, for Borkman's patience, never his strongest suit, is at low—lowest—ebb. Yet, oddly enough, there is, as she rattles off the guest list, a sudden warmth, even compassion, in her tone, perhaps inspired by the sag in his retreating back. Rear views never lie.

The wife arrives at last, looking daggers. Why? he wonders. During their last session high above sunless, rivulet-thin Broad Street didn't he tearfully insist he has every intention of being generous—so tearfully, in fact, that even the lawyers, albeit seasoned sleazeballs, felt compelled to turn tearily away from so raw an exhibition of deviant rectitude.

Reproachfully, she asks if he's ill for it certainly looks that way. Her voice, even at its most irritable, never fails to trigger—not in his groin or his throat or his gut or up his ass but deep down inside his chest—a very potent desire yet one that over the decades he's found it increasingly difficult to find an outlet for. He now accepts it as what it is and what it will always be, a form of imprisonment.

He changes the subject (or does he?) by saying he's thinking of participating in a drug trial—no, he *is* participating. She follows him upstairs. Through the bathroom door she asks only for the name of the trial and who's conducting it—not what the drug is for and/or why he's taking it. In protest, he almost drops the vial. As he emerges after a quick shower (indulgently fungus-generating long ones irritate her), his bath towel slips to the floor revealing a shameless paunch and a large erection, which he immediately decides mustn't be wasted.

All through the procedure—as deadpan as a D & C—the wife does her very best to resist. Only she isn't quite sure *what* she was resisting. Suddenly she knows: it's the scene itself, the scene they're expected to play *before the guests arrive.* You know, the one where man and wife, the remainder of their life together measurable only in milliseconds, suddenly find each other tantalizing and quickly confuse this epiphenomenon of good riddance with *rediscovery.* It's the aphrodisiac of impasse that's the star of their show. He's put his hand on her breast and kneads the nipple with maddening deliberation. Rather than feel the motion she listens to it as the continuation of their conversation in another language—a dialect. Tactfully provoking the bud of her clitoris with a persistently encircling forefinger, he keeps withdrawing his penis in order to re-thrust ever more mock-brutally (the level of contrast between tact and thrust is worthy of a Horowitz and Borkman knows it albeit without knowing the man Horowitz from a hole in the wall). So why does she find herself looking on from across the room, displacing from his perch the owlish Doctor of Sexuality whose approval Borkman's competence always seems to elicit? He's been competent—too competent—not realizing competence is the enemy of any art form. Only *in*competence—one-of-a-kind and new-to-the-world—could have saved them. He prides himself on being uninhibited—shameless—but only incompetence is truly shameless. Just before ejaculating down below he musters the courage to ejaculate: "It's a drug for Envy, my pet." He's never used this endearment before. Didn't even know he knows it. Clearly, he wants praise for his penis, that overrated barrel organ— that clunky Bottle with Hairs as *not* depicted by Calder. At this moment, however, she craves his jugular, for some time her very favorite part of his anatomy.

Rolling off, triumphant, ashamed and exhausted, he believes he is merely agreeing with what is on the tip of her tongue when he says their marriage is a calamity which has produced only calamities. But just because she pretty much had the same idea while walking back home from Amore di Nails (a surprisingly homey new addition to this most unneighborly of neighborhoods) doesn't mean she wants to be burdened with his accord, unwelcome under the best of circumstances. She doesn't want him declaiming the reality of those calamities from the rooftops. To date they've been just a *fantaisie-impromptu* composed to reassure all those therapists, should they need reassuring, that she's as good as any other self-respecting East Side mom at making life miserable for herself through over-blame. Now they're real. Shivering, she recoils from the realness. Borkman, she sees, takes this for terror at the thought that he might try to warm her up. The sounds he now makes would, with a little help from a top-of-the-line transducer, reduce—or expand—to something along the wobbly lines of: "Seriously, it hurts saying this, don't think it doesn't. But the only way out of the calamitous hurt is the way back in—saying it again and again is the only suture available over-the-counter for the wound opened up by the saying."

Trying hard not to look at his body whose decay excites her (the only thing more beautiful than a beautiful thing is the ruin of a beautiful thing, warns A. Rodin from his pedestal—and don't you forget it), she retorts (though is a retort warranted?) that maybe he should have started on this wonder drug a long time ago. So that when, on a fateful winter night four years before, the older boy called him a failure and a loser and every other name in the book—said he should never have had kids but didn't have the balls not to— he wouldn't have lost control and started pounding his chest and arms. She remembers too vividly for her own good that period during which he went after companies with intangible assets (intellectual property, brand recognition, etc.) but assets so intangible as to be nonexistent, invested in asteroid mining and rigged municipal bond deals. Everything failed and he was full of rage. And so on that morning when, en route to his office though strictly speaking he had no office, Borkman passed the boy on the street he didn't see him. But the boy was convinced he did and was only avoiding him—couldn't conceive of his father's having been so ragingly self-absorbed as to be blind to his presence—to the presence of anything that wasn't the target of rage. Maybe because—though the boy couldn't admit it, couldn't even conceive of it (*who is speaking? who knows the older boy better than he knows himself?*)—a raging blindness was to him far worse than intentional avoidance. Avoidance means he was seen—for once at least. For he's never seen—really seen—by this father whose only real children, as he always blurts out when battered by life's intermittent refusal to give him what he believes is his rightful due, are his misdeals.

Dressing, he takes cold comfort from the fact that at least he's never *named* his rivals (is this thought the first number on tonight's program whose center-piece is the world premiere of *Chamber Variations in B Major on the Theme of Naming*?). For it only induces her not-so-secret "scorn: too secret perhaps for her own consciousness thereof" (or is he just being kind?). Since to name them is to buy into the flagrant absurdity of their earned right to lay claim to anything as exalted as a name, which goes a long way toward explaining how he could be taken in by intangible assets. To name them is to defer to the superior acuity of their greed—and the intimidating banality of the world's greed (every crook's "lavish lifestyle" is propped up by the same twenty-seven garaged Ferraris). There's little difference between naming and fellation. Though he hates justifying himself, he says, "It was a bad time." He feels duty bound to remind her how his ex-partner (even if the rival remains anonymous he still feels as if he's being sodomized—by the man behind the anonymity) is patenting every idea he came up with as if they're brick-and-mortar, flesh-and-blood inventions warm to the touch. He asks her to remember (she's still shivering and the sun is just about to set) how, as owner of that boutique hotel off Gramercy Park, he got his staff to create a digital footprint for every guest so that upon her return she could count *just like last time* on, say, being chauffeured to all her power brunches in her favorite Maybach 62 manned by her favorite driver wielding her favorite white-gold shift knob. Well, the ex-partner has already patented *that*, whatever *that* is or was, and routinely sends out boilerplate accusations of infringement to hotels, pubs, spas, escort services, right and left. And of course his targets immediately fork up the licensing fee since it's cheaper to pay than to fight. And at the same time Borkman's being sued on the grounds that such profiling constitutes a form of high-end ID theft. He thinks of putting his head in his hands but the gesture will be too calculated to provide any comfort. Anyway, he doesn't deserve comfort.

She asks if this justifies beating up his son and telling him he's a dunce and that the two of them have nothing in common, all so that he can end up living in his cab during New York's coldest winter in over a decade. In fact it's Borkman not his mother that he wanted to strangle but, as is usual in such cases, the father, however inadequate, goes scot-free, gets a free pass, though there's nothing she can do about it now. So much spilt milk under the bridge—a bridge of sighs. "But I got down on my knees to apologize whenever he came back to wash and shave. I felt like a character in a Russian novel. It did me good." This remark enables her to read his mind—to read into it far more than he'll ever be aware of. And as an unloving ex-spouse-to-be she has every right to share the spoils. Does he mean to tell her that he's monstrous enough to engineer father-son calamities solely in the hope that, having assumed full responsibility for the suffering visited on his sons by his unfatherly rages, he'll be compensated?—which, by the way, is never how things work out in the Russian novels she read (sometimes in the original)—with the stroke—oops, she meant the stroke of good luck—luck which has eluded him far too long, far too often. C'mon, even he must know (*super-affected condescending cocktail party hostess voice*) this is magical thinking. But, he counters, with so massive and unflinching—worse, so unlocalizable—an adversary as fate, what recourse, except to magic, does any self-disrespecting schmuck really have? Magic is the very texture of his thought, Madam—the thought of an Azande. So, she snicker-sneers, he goes on hoping, thinking only of himself (he forgets, for example—or rather his obsession with the slumbering spirits of the gold does the forgetting for him—how, during one of his hoping marathons, he allowed his own son, with a knife propped against his spine in case of a break-in, to freeze his balls off in the smelly back seat of that cab). He reassures her, the devil incarnate, that he's at a stage of the game where the hoper knows he hopes in vain. Or does he? he wonders privately. Isn't he simply relearning the hard way, as too many times before—in the wings, behind the scenes, above the peanut gallery—that Lady Luck supervenes only (if at all) when the supplicant's Personal Trainer (what deep thinkers call a Demiurge, Bork) is absolutely sure his man is finally much too battered to hope, to even conceive of hoping (but this has never been his case—or anybody's)?

Looked at another way, the highly theatrical matter of luck doesn't involve only a man and his Demiurge. There's a sanguinary third to be reckoned with, to wit, the first-night audience. And a rave review hinges on those first night-ers being too cleverly sidetracked to pinpoint the moment of Milady's onset. Sidetracked, they won't be able to complain that She's landed on stage too creakily on cue. So he must go on hoping until such time as Lady Luck finds a way not to get caught in the act of contrivance.

She tears him from his thoughts: So the rage and the despair over the calamity it precipitates *in the family way* (so he's learned the phrase from her) are nothing but Envy drugs before their time all-too-knowingly administered as stand-ins for, distractions from, what he craves more than anything—more, even, than his sons' happiness. Has the world ever seen such a calculating monster? Not even Busoni's Doktor Faust at his worst dared to, etc. (and nobody knows better than she—who sang the juicy role of the Duchess in junior college and just when her star shone brightest was "forced" [at gun-point? teasingly inquires the entity everybody has been given more and more to calling the Master] to abandon everything to follow this half-a-man to per-dition). This is his cue to get up and go to the window. Stares outward, striking the patented visionary pose that's just a few degrees east of pretentiousness. It never fails to get her goat. Would her absence make it any less calculating? he wonders. Any less self-exalting? If so, then she has only herself to blame for being a witness for the prosecution. Tell me, does this pose have a core of authenticity—of authentic communion with the urgent tints of the night sky? Or is it all pose—all about *him*—with the sky left hanging? "Yes," she wonders with inquisitive forbearance, drawing out the single syllable like taffy, much further than it can go. It drops her off just a few degrees west of exasperation. He drops the stance completely before the forbearance can smash it to smith-ereens.

Oddly—astonishingly—enough (no doubt to reward him for hanging out the misunderstood visionary act to dry) she doesn't demand to know something along the lines of what in the world he thinks he's doing with a roomful of hungry guests (no, not that many) waiting down below, and in a way he's sorry for he'd like to be able to tell her that what in the world he's doing is nothing less than cheering on the sun as it surges and sinks. And you know something? watching it die and the wretched day with it he's mighty pleased to be an accessory to the destruction of a wanton thing though the keener the pleasure, the deeper the conviction that it's he and he alone who's been surging and sinking and dying and has, for his pains, every right to be pronounced dead on arrival at his final destination. Which as it so happens was Borkman's permanent residence right from the start and whence, for all his raucous stage business over the centuries, he never budged an inch.

He—Borkman—descends in the breezy twilight to (just as he thought) far less than a roomful of guests. These include his lawyer and hers, with com-panion and wife, respectively. And his wife's psychiatristic spouse-to-be who, compliments of his trip to the altar, will be riding roughshod over every con-ceivable medical ethic, with the Hippocratic oath thrown in for good measure. Which is not to say there are not several more—too many, in fact, to count on the fingers of one hand—who, luckily for them, do not warrant differentiation from each other for purposes of extended description. He can see the other wife is surprised to find him still residing here. But doesn't the sanctimonious old broad realize the fissioning process can be speeded up only so much? They loathed each other, he and her lawyer's wife, at first sight. Yet what is it about her he especially loathes?, though the word doesn't begin to do justice to what he feels in her presence or, even more, in the turbulence of unwelcome recollection—*less a feeling, though, than a blackout that annihilates all feeling.* Or is the arbiter of his wordflow, that handsome devil of a drug, just being italicizingly quaint when it's brute candor not quaintness that's demanded?

They're pseudo jewels, these guests—counterfeit "national treasures"— enchased in the ouch of his de facto destitution—at least that's how they come across to the furloughed etymologist/gemologist hired for the occasion to compound the canapés and cocktails. It feels strangely appropriate—almost a feat—for her to remember that by association "ouch" also means "skin tumor." The wife's invited them over to toast a double victory—her imminent divorce and her lawyer's promotion to CEO of the biotech company he helped start a decade before. Borkman wants to remind them he too has been there (*Et in CEO Arcadia ego*) but of course they need no reminding (his downfall is their ascent). He's been as many CEOs as there've been companies to distress—to financial-engineer down to the ground—whose stores were sold to REITs so shareholders could buy shares in the trust. As many CEOs as there've been companies ripe even before they were born for liquidation or bankruptcy. And should he cap it all off with a defiant warning to the effect that as the kind of bad man you can't keep down, he's simply between Officerships? Seeing him, the CEO's wife looks away, struck by the view from the big bay window she's been struck by hundreds of times before. The CEO—thank heaven for titles when a name's anathema—takes the mention of the toast as his cue to kiss his wife—but more to the point, the mother of his children (he has two boys, just like Borkman, but the likeness begins and ends there). And Wife, Mother & Co. doesn't require much prompting to do her share. Borkman wonders if the exhibition mating dance will include some tame tongueing. It's a long—way too long—parched-lips kind of kiss. But spurred on by an aphrodisiac as potent as the misery of Borkman, how can they not believe— and exult—in their happiness (context, Edgar—not ripeness—is all) and try to stretch out the exultation to the crack of doom? Which takes time, that is, if it's done right. Borkman catches the girlfriend's eye. Hard to fathom how somebody who deploys her cleavage with such aplomb (in this case, however, ripeness *is* all) can manage to look so uneasy. Has she, too, noted that the gusto with which the couple maneuver their mouths owes much of its magic and momentum to the palpable misery of the host, with a little of the hostess's thrown in for good measure—misery potent enough to induce, in the right bystanders, nothing less than an orgasmic coma? Has she noted and does what she's noted make her sad? That one man's misery should be another's exultation? That one man's up is another man's down? Borkman's wife looks hypnotized as well but he knows she's converging on the kiss from an entirely different angle. This is how it's done on the sunny isle of TrueLoveLand, he can hear her thinking enviously. Apparently, she doesn't expect such kisses from her psychiatrist.

The Exultants have been discovering in the last few minutes that, unlike Borkman and his wife, casualties of an outdated cult of suffering, they aspire to nothing more complicated than golden-mean simplefolksiness (witness the kiss)—at least for the moment and even if only in momentary contradistinction to the Borkmans—and are only too willing to acknowledge the fact publicly. But who knows what they'll aspire to—how they'll define themselves—five minutes from now? It will all depend on whom the Exultants—the present moment's most quintessential non-Borkmans—are rubbing elbows with since for the Exultants of the world self-definition can be achieved only through forced contrast with somebody else's. That is, unlike the Borkmans, they are not condemned to being just one thing. Non-Borkman knows how to ring every conceivable change on the Theme of Life. As everybody in the business world knows, he can *do* Faustian overreaching *à la Borkman* to a turn, and still leave room for dessert. But since he's chez Borkman and as Borkman is graciously volunteering to be the poster boy for the price to be paid for foolishly self-sabotaging overreach—ejecting every votary but himself from the Bethel of Angst-ridden Insatiability—*sucking non-Borkman dry of every tendency in that direction*—he's been given license to play at practicing what he takes to be the exact opposite of overreach—cautionary contentment—something along the lines of slow-and-steady-wins-the-rat-race—a kind of icing on the seven-layer cake of his own brand of overreach.

So goes the kiss. Or through its lens is he simply perceiving what Envy, his Iago, still wants him to see? (After all he's only a few doses into rehab.)

Yet, wait! what have we here? the milk of conjugal bliss seems to be curdling right before his very eyes. Clearly, a couple's bliss can perdure only just so long when it's fueled by another's misery. And though the misery of both Borkmans is if anything increasing, it has become less palpable, less serviceable, through overexploitation. But before Borkman can disappear with his too many thoughts of this type (thoughts for which words—the Master's words—still have to be found by the thinker himself, that is, if he is to ultimately evolve into what the mother of one of the Amygdala guinea pigs is wont every chance she gets, at least according to said guinea pig, to self-applaudingly refer to as *a keen observer of human nature*) the two of them—but a two-of-them profoundly altered, or rather, profoundly *modified*, like the genome of a knockout mouse—are already making straight for the exit but not the way married folks are supposed to, i.e., as one. And there's actually some wit, intentional or not, to be savored in their out-of-synch head-for-the-hills-style negotiation of the terrain—the toughest kind of wit, by the way, to bring to a boil: physical wit. Mr. Exultant almost mows down the etymologist.

Having waited in the wings long enough, her psychiatrist is now bearing down on Borkman. So that he doesn't collide with and topple his halfway house of thoughts—or worse, invade it—Borkman says he's got to (as his father used to say exasperatingly) *see a horse about a dog.* A second before, Dr. X looked like *death warmed over* (ibid., but not quite so exasperatingly) yet here he is smilingly telling Borkman he's just heard about the Invidicum trial. In fact, he knows the guys running it. Straynge, for example. Good man. A leading light in the field. *What sunny field might that be?* Borkman is tempted to ask—and does. At this deadpan sally the psychiatrist guffaws to beat the band. But the guffaw is clearly all about intense discomfort—a mirth-is-the-mail-of-anguish sort of thing. Borkman has just dared to try to make a horse's ass of X's colleague and X has become an ass by association. The laughter goes on and on and on. Until it starts to mean that if Borkman has any sense or self-respect left he'll join him in LaughLand where everybody's at ease, or supposed to be, with everybody else, even with somebody whose downfall (imminent? a fait accompli?) is contagious. Isn't all the merciless camaraderie bubbling up from LaughLand's mineral springs harbinger enough of the fact that a carnival of the animals straight out of Rabelais is very much in session under the baton of none other than . . . Mikhail Bakhtin!? Thing is, for all the laughter, X seems to be *spoiling* (is that the right word? if not, all the better!—it takes courage to wield a wrong, that is, a self-incriminating word) for a fast getaway (*Who, exactly, is sensing this?*). X has underestimated his own fragility: downfall—failure—is just too close for comfort. Maybe he'll be inheriting failure through this shotgun wedding. Still time to skedaddle, or is there?

But even if the prospect of a fast getaway has reared its ugly head, the fact remains that they can always look forward to being forever reunited in LaughLand—they'll always have LaughLand—so what's one fast getaway among friends? A mere formality. X wants Borkman to understand (for he suspects Borkman despises him for his nervous-ticlike guffaws) that the getaway's purely for the purpose of mulling over in the privacy of his own kennel everything Borkman's precious slow-motion downfall has imparted—and in record time nonetheless—on the subject of how to wear your brute survival—whatever the savage-disappointment-and abject-failure coefficient associated to it—with a difference. So if as it turns out the laughter is the laughter of relief it's relief on Borkman's behalf—a celebration of the fact—that he's still going strong and is still unmistakably *he* despite the downfall and its aftershocks and will remain so no matter how massive (adding insult to injury) the concentration of Forever Chemicals, spewed out of a tannery, the Invidicum gang sees fit to dissolve in his dose so as to entrench a permanent tendency toward self-shrinkage through self-intimidation (albeit for his own good). (The dainty little shopping bag will have many lurid stories to tell before he gives up the ghost, Borkman chuckles.) The laughter, a bit counterintuitively, also encompasses, as a special bonus track or liner note, the awareness that while nobody's more attuned than the wife's husband-to-be to every quirk—every nuance—of his—Borkman's—slow glide toward, immersion in and current emergence from self-demolition (and the price it's exacted not just from him but, more importantly, from the innocent family members he oh so richly doesn't deserve), attunement, like putting up with other people, is hard work—back-breaking labor—and so X needs time to recuperate—or rather regroup, to use the lingo of hip functionaries. If, that is, he is to go on taking *his* own brand of Invidicum, *which is Borkman himself* at his fullest strength. (The psychiatrist is obviously pleased with this poetic equivalency since he keeps babbling—inwardly, inaudibly, or so he thinks—*Borkman brand, the Borkman brand . . .*) He therefore hopes they'll continue to be in touch and end up . . . well, friends in order that (though predatory X the trailblazing researcher—the Jekyll to Borkman's Hyde—of course doesn't admit as much) he may have unlimited access—exclusive rights—to the archive that safeguards all things Borkman—to Borkman the cautionary tale—to the Borkman whose vicissitudes are the mother's milk of Job's comforters and schadenfreuders craving a run for their money. Thing is, the babbling's sufficiently loud—and unseemly—to make his betrothed wonder if there might not still be time to rectify what could turn out to be a pretty big mistake. Borkman suddenly puts his foot down to determine why. "Why what?" "Why I'm *your* Invidicum." True to form the mad psychiatrist tries to laugh this off—guffaw it away—but his guffawing days are clearly over—at least for as long as it takes to cobble together a plausible response. Which swells or reduces to something along the lines of, Why, a High Representative of Laughland like him has only to look Borkman up and down to know what he's always known but for some reason finds it hard to admit, namely, that *the phoenix is not a* mythical *bird*. But the response, now that it's come—sounds limp not to mention lame to both parties. (Furthermore it's not as sphinxlike and sybilline and singular as it professes to be since it's been foreshadowed by the orts of praise drizzled down on Borkman a few minutes ago.) For a response truly worth its salt refuses to cleave plausibly to the contour of the question that generates it and eschews connectedness except at the very limit of the plausible—deforms the question so that adherence is achieved at the least purchaseable sticking point. Which turns the answer into a new question—just as nagging, just as clutching. X's response clearly doesn't fit the bill (granted, it was delivered under intense pressure). Still, that they agree at last on something (even if one of them does so secretly—inwardly)—even something as limp as limpness—is (to use another favorite phrase of the phoenix's father which he took with him to the grave) *nothing to sneeze at*. The psychiatrist tries another tack—or rather, another tack tries him. He admits (without going so far as to grunt, Me Jekyll, You Hyde, or Me Chillingworth, You Dimmesdale, or better yet, Me Elisabeth Vogler, You Sister Alma) to having discovered in the last hour or so that he likes studying Borkman, Borkman the career—the non pareil Envier—the Envier as Paragon. In order to learn from him. Learn what? Well, for starters, how to trounce one's rivals. How to drag them through the mud. How to expose their lack of honor—worse, their lack of originality. Envy becomes him—for Borkman it's clearly a driver—a generator—an engine—*the* engine—a wall of windows on the dreary world of winning at any cost—and if Invidicum thinks It's about to flush him out completely, this is a misconception since in his case the supply of the poison is strictly speaking inexhaustible. So he's not only a walking tipping point but a walking paradox as well. But since every self-respecting silver lining has its cloud—while assimilation of Borkman's example—his case history—can serve as a potent purgative for any envier, at too low a dose it's sheer poison—the poison of inefficacy. For which once again unmotivated laughter (*the phonier the better, by any chance, Doc?*) is the only mithridate. For a low dose of Borkman doesn't allow the student of his sickness—in this instance a psychiatrist of genius—to deinvidifyingly scale his heights and penetrate his depths, which are where the meanings are. "Yet and on the other hand how can anyone self-administer you—Borkman—at your highest dose—observe you—over and over and over again—scale such heights and penetrate such depths as you seemed—seem—to be doing tonight in your sleep, so to speak (I watched you while the cocktails were making the rounds), all in the name of surpassing your rivals?" Though Borkman can't help (who could?) basking in the flattery he's tempted to beg the psychiatrist to stop. And it's not just coyness—what he feels is dread. By any chance does he know what's coming? "How can anybody self-inject—how can any self-respecting Borkman addict shoot up with a clear conscience—especially—and here's the crux of the matter—when it becomes obvious (*a*) that those whom you take to be your rivals—those on whom you've grudgingly conferred that honor—would never in a million years dream of returning the favor, that is, the favor of raising you up to their infinitely more exalted level, and (*b*) that through their refusal they thereby consign you to even deeper depths of invidious despair? In short, it's when you're rightly disavowed by those in the know that you're most my brand of choice."

How could Borkman have known Dr. X would go from half-hearted fan to most rabid detractor although even as such he's a bit lackluster? Yet even the detractor's detractors can't deny he's come up with a whopping surprise ending straight out of middling Agatha Christie. But Borkman knows without knowing he knows that a fan is nothing but a detractor waiting in the wings— an understudy waiting for the star of the show to break a leg (by taking literally that tired old exhortation of theater folk). (But how, wonders the canapé slinger, who's forever on the lookout for *her* big break, can somebody know *without knowing he knows*?) To put the finishing touches on his pronouncement X cites, appropriately or not, Old Testament Paracelsus, to wit, that "all things are poison, and nothing is without poison: the dose alone makes a thing not poison." Which is to say, Borkman's nothing less than an endocrine disrupter in human form, the map of whose impact is a very non-monotonic dose-response curve. Nevertheless, since disrupters have feelings like everybody else he's entitled at the very least to the pleasure of recognizing that his successor is a snake—with fangs for scales—who slithers from faint praise to cheeky excoriation without missing a beat and this being the case the ex-wife-to-be is more than welcome to play footsie with such refuse until their marriage hearse—a jerry-built one-horse shay—predictably capsizes two days into the honeymoon.

But Borkman's nothing if not resilient and he wants to capture what the psychiatrist has been thinking or what Borkman thinks he's been thinking or at least the gist of the thinking as it unfolded in—behind—the saying. Isn't this what Straynge and Manning, in so many words, told him to make sure to do between sessions when confronting persons whose smell he takes to be inimical to his well-being—persons with a vested interest in seeing him negated (i.e., all of humanity including he himself)? Or is it the drug itself making him think they said it? Of course, he won't report the business about Straynge's *field*. But he needs to get the thoughts down immediately so he doesn't have to go deep inside himself later on to retrieve them. The thoughts that came to the despicable shrink while vacationing in LaughLand, for example. And the thoughts (though Borkmn immediately realizes the shrink had no such thoughts: it was Borkman himself who had them regarding the Exultants) about the current epidemic of self-definitions only in contradistinction to somebody else's. Not to mention the biggest bomb of all (its plutonium core sure to be recycled forever): hubby-to-be's meditation on the universal disavowal of Borkman—no questions asked or answered—as an envy-unworthy rival. He needs to get the thoughts down immediately since he dreads—or rather the Old Masterly busybody out to hijack every guinea pig's cognition, or Invidicum itself, tells him he should dread—the unforeseeable but inevitable contact—on the way back to these newly minted thoughts—with other, scarier thoughts having nothing to do with Envy (though every thought concerns Envy more or less) including those generated by the very process of negotiating his way back. He needs to get them all down while he still has *the backing of the context* into which he stumbled, intentionally, solely to give it birth—namely, the powerful context (strangely comforting now) created by the people he powerfully envies, then hates, instead of hating himself for Envying them. They grow, alas, even more powerful, he sees, feeding on and off that Envying hatred. And the psychiatrist's now and forever a member of their tribe.

He manages to grab a pen from his lawyer—judge, jury, amateur Dickensian, district attorney and private counsel all rolled into one (call him Pip Jaggers), who always wears one in his lapel, to jot down what he thinks the wife's hubby-to-be has been thinking—as well as saying without thinking. This jack of all trades follows him into the pantry adjacent to the kitchen, which is the room furthest from the CEO and his wife, who simply refuse to leave. He wants to give him an update on his status—his legal precarity index—but Borkman explains that he needs to get it all down for his pre-dose therapy session tomorrow. For who knows what he might dredge up along with it or—even more likely—instead of it if he goes looking for it later, starting from scratch? The lawyer asks a perfectly legitimate question—he wants to know what *it* is exactly. Borkman can't backtrack and explain. He hopes his lawyer—a quick learner if ever there was one—will get the gist from the context he's alluded to. But he can't waste any more time alluding even if Jaggers ought to be kept abreast of his favorite client's every move. Who knows what sidetrackings he may have to endure on the way back to it if he doesn't avail himself of this golden opportunity to get it all down while it's still fresh in his mind? Even if, as a hero (for he *is* a hero—in fact more than a hero—an activist investor—a misadventure capitalist—a CEO non pareil with the mythical folkloric sinews to prove it), it's his bounden—his civic—his Christian duty to be sidetracked which is what Frank Bigelow (played by Edmond O'Brien) learns—sort of—at the knobbly nursemaid's knee of his thug nemeses in Rudolph Maté's SF-to-LA doomsday classic, *D.O.A.* Amid the smell of ginger and vanilla and fennel (since he's in the pantry) the lawyer puts him on the witness stand and asks whether the thoughts he can't let get away (for isn't *it* just thoughts pure and simple—thoughts and nothing but—even if the sexless *it* seems to bubble up like a fumarole, depending on the temperature of the room he's in, with noirish suggestions of more, much more?) aren't in fact most real when they're no longer fresh in his mind and he's trying to wrest them from the bowels of the earth—come to think of it, like the slumbering spirits of the gold—and can't manage to. When it's not quite clear whether they'll end up being his or his most devious rivals'.

Borkman himself wonders why, once he became beholden to Jaggers for his pen, he traded in *thoughts* for *it*. In any case, the jotting down is a vaccine self-administered against the metastasizing infection known as remembering. As the jotting winds down (Jaggers has been very patient since there was no slow dissolve to stand in for the passage of time needed for the job), his speech gets slurred, he's nauseated, the blood rushes to his skull unsolicited, the ball of his thumb becomes painfully inflamed. His sigh of relief makes clear that even if the thumb's now the size of a drumstick what matters is that he need no longer fear any stopovers among terrifying thoughts he couldn't anticipate and even more terrifying chasms where no thought lies in ambush. Even if— even if—even if (and here comes a stunning reversal—Jaggers can feel it in his old bones)—even if he well knows (thanks not to Straynge's intimations or Manning's or Invidicum's but rather to the meditations of his ex-partner Thamus the Shamus who dabbled in ancient philosophy and probably still does, as if making money wasn't abstruse enough for him!) that taking this line of least resistance means he's missing out on a golden opportunity to look himself in the eye through the prism of the terrifying thoughts that get in the way of the way back—a golden opportunity to make the way back itself the goal—since any thought worth a damn begins to exist in earnest only when it starts doing its smart-ass best to resist being remembered. He shouldn't be writing it down—shouldn't be writing anything down—because if he inter- rogates what he's written down it won't explain—it will only go on repeating the same thing, over and over and over again—in the most unSocratic way imaginable and to anybody and anybody's brother. The writing down's both a remedy against not remembering and a solidified poison that gets in the way of the only remembering worth the effort—to wit, remembering that doesn't know what it's going to collide with on the way back—on the not always rocky enough road—to remembering. In short, writing's a *pharmakon*, says a voice he doesn't recognize. And Invidicum is Envy's pharmakon—it cuts off Envy at the root—prevents it from playing itself out—prevents it from becoming a process—prevents it from stumbling on the unsuspected targets of Envy— targets unlocalizable under the carapace of an fMRI machine—the real targets for which the puny targets in the here and now (like the Borkman-disdaining rivals invoked by the lips-smacking mad shrink) are mere covers—smoke- screens—jigsaw puzzle-type distractions.

"Excuse me, sir," throat-clears the etymologist (the quintessential Inno- cent Abroad even at home) who has a way of ending up in the strangest places through no fault of her own, "I couldn't help but overhear even if you were whispering." Their manful and unintentionally collusive silence makes her uncomfortable so she gets right to the point: Since everybody knows that life is a book where philosophy and psychology go at wrestling each other down to the mat every chance they get (with the mat of course being the field of the cloth of gold that is the human soul), she wonders if as man of the house and a caring parent, Borkman wouldn't do better to steer clear of the timeworn dynamic—the trap—of "quick-fixing through writing down" (though she's just coined it she makes the phrase sound as if it's been around for decades and is common currency among the streetwise). As a good parent shouldn't he allow—force—the thought-in-training to mature on its own— to show that it has the stuff—the makings—of a bona fide thought? "Don't mean to be overstepping my bounds, sir, but my suggestion is" (and here she throws servantly caution to the winds as if it were a ragged hand-me-down from an overbearing, underdressed younger sister) "not to be so quick to res- cue a thought—any thought—from its evolution by articulating it before it can articulate itself." Priding herself on her self-discipline she suppresses a well-deserved sigh of relief.

But Borkman hasn't heard a word—he's a million miles away from the bounds she's failed to overstep—he's got other fish to fry (even if as it turns out her fish are in fact Thamus's fish; and fish of a feather, even more than birds of a feather, flock together). To accept that Invidicum can be a poison, when he's already invested so much of his credulity in its impact as a cure-all not just for Envy but for (though he's still unaware of this) every other sin under the sun, deadly or not, is a step he's not ready to take in the here and now. His eloquence from nowhere got way ahead of him. His bark got the better of his bite. So in a show of allegiance to the latter, he dutifully loses his balance, collapses. Last thing he sees is his wife's face—contorted with irritation at the thought that he might expect her to nurse him back to semiconsciousness— now, when everything's dead and unburied between them. The penultimate thing he hears is her psychiatrist—Everybody's Psychiatrist—Phil Oz, MD, soon to be governor of Pennsylvania and every other state where he's not a resident—murmuring: "Temporal-lobe epilepsy—same lobe in which the green-eyed monster sets its traps." Last thing he thinks is: It's not a fit, *mein klein* jackass—it's the anticipation of a fit—which is the worst kind of epileptic fit—the kind you don't wish on your worst enemy. Last thing he hears is (but not from the psychiatrist—no, this time it's a higher power playing higher-power tricks): But doesn't every disease reduce to nothing more and nothing less than its own anticipation. *But isn't this higher-power trickster—this Mas-ter—this Monster, green-eyed or otherwise*—simply attempting, by equating every disease with its mere anticipation, to cash in, when nobody's looking, on Borkman's anguish—commandeering it to produce through a conversa- tional sleight of hand—an illegal rhetorical loophole known as the Great Syn- onymy—the sort of universality *on the level of language* that is simply not appli- cable to—in—the world out there? The hype-clogged equation fits the Master to a T and offers a privileged glimpse into his heartless inner workings.[3] Prob- lem is, the equation doesn't fit—encapsulate—the way things work in that

---

[3]Cf. the following fast one pulled by that career synonymist Marty O'Heidegger: "[T]his privileged question 'why' (Why are there existents—things that are—rather than nothing?) has its ground in a leap through which man thrusts away all the pre- vious security, whether real or imagined, of his life. The question is asked only in this

world *out there*, that is, when they work at all. Which is of course what supplies the perverse thrill—the naughty rush—to whoever is pulling Borkman's strings—and the strings of the trial—and the strings of its participants—and most of all the strings of those who are sabotaging the entire process and believe that in doing so they become unmanipulable—like the prosthetic gods of a regular guy named Sigmund who once upon a time had a gods-given right to decide who's normal and who's a pervert and never the twain shall meet. But most of all maybe it's the Master who's being manipulated, *behind the scenes-behind-the-scenes.* (Enough said, warns one of the Master's overprotective cronies.)

Jaggers and a few of the others, who reveal themselves to be strapping specimens (or do they look the part only in contradistinction to this weakling who can't even hold his bile?), drag him upstairs and dump him with surprising respectfulness (*Who is responsible for this surprise? somebody wonders*— but not the etymologist: she's far too busy failing to recover from rejection of or indifference to her insights [whichever's worse]) on the semen-stiffened sheets. Midlife-crisis semen. The smelliest type of all. Once below again, they nurse fresh drinks and try, like the strapping specimens they've yet to become, easing themselves back into the party's bespangled straitjacket. His lawyer turns to her lawyer, as wife and girlfriend take another shot at *chitchatting and chatchitting* (every working stiff whether he knows it or not has had a co-stiff who, cursed with a streak of genius, came up with that phrase out of the blue), and says he knows better than anybody that it's exactly this sort of thing that Borkman has put his family through over the years and he wants nothing so much as to help out at this crossroads, especially with the prospect of a prison sentence looming more and more direly. He certainly never goaded him into doing anything shady, by the way.

Borkman's wife apologizes for interrupting (though what she's interrupted is mainly ham radio silence) but is everything OK back at the buffet? She notes with alarm that Jaggers's girlfriend (much prettier than her predecessor) is tactfully averting her eyes from what everybody knows without perhaps knowing he knows—perceives without apperceiving, as her prof down at the New School would say, given half a chance—namely, that the hostess's all-too-transparent efforts to pretend nothing untoward has prevailed are fooling nobody, not even herself. But before alarm can become anger, then sadness, her husband, smelling of alcohol, aftershave and sweat, and maybe even of vanilla, ginger and fennel, not to mention red ink, surprises them all by resurfacing and surprises them even more by thanking his wife for enabling one undeniably good thing to be extracted from the evening's horrors.

"A good thing? What good thing?" She curses herself for sounding like his straight man and even more for liking the byplay.

"The name." He's drunk but not as drunk as he'd like to be.

---

leap; it *is* the leap [the underlining is mine]; without it there is no asking." Source of quotation is Martin Heidegger, *An Introduction to Metaphysics*, translated by Ralph Manheim (Garden City, New York, Anchor Books, 1961), p. 5.

"What name."

"The name that came to me in a wet dream that was—all wet. Of course if it weren't for you" (he directs his bleary gaze at the CEO and its missus), "it would never have come to me at all. It happened upstairs when we were—I mean when I put my—or rather you almost shoved it—" "We have guests," she says with distaste but not entirely. "Once Jaggers gets this dirty business of patent infringement cleared up I'm going to start a new company and Shitpickles will be its name (one of the most prominent side effects of tonic-clonics is insane hope)." Jaggers's girlfriend seems to perk up at the word *infringement* (*to whom does this POV shot in the form of a telling observation belong?*). "The other outfits failed simply because they didn't have the right name." She knows from experience stretching across the blur of decades that he would like her to call his contraption a stroke of genius. And *oddly* (but doesn't any shift in the complexion of things worth its salt come about oddly?) she does want to oblige—she feels a desire, almost sexual, *to* oblige. So she turns away and shrugs. He doesn't want to imagine the face behind the shrug though he's seen it thousands of times, invariably bloated with unfocused rage which she'd like to direct exclusively at him even if out of decency she should consider sharing at least a little of the bloat with mom, dad, siblings, lovers and other tormentors. "Come now, you must admit—" and the very woodwork vibrates with his righteous invocation. Even if it's patently equal-opportunity she takes it (longingly?) to be directed only at her. Afraid, she turns even further away until she's back at her starting point. This so-called inspiration, what is it but another nail—for which room can simply no longer be found—in the connubial coffin? Further proof of how far he deviates, and will always deviate, from the norm. She'll never understand that normal doesn't work for everybody (*who managed, beating all the odds of self-amputation, to extract this pregnant observation from the movie viewfinder and bring it home to safety?*)—for some (to quote her favorite poet, Mr. Nixon, on the perils of versifying) *there's nothing in it*. "I've even been concerned that the clinical trial I'm involved in will also fail because it has no name at all until further notice and that out of desperation they'll call it anything." As far as he's concerned, the trial should also be called (this, mind you, after suitably sober self-consultation reversed by rash impertinence) Shitpickles. "You see, already, Invidicum is liberating me."

Observing him straddle one of her very best armchairs enrages the wife (for she's still the wife—East Sider version of Duchess of Malfi *still*). Only by scouring a wineglass or two in the semi-privacy of the overlit kitchen could she possibly hope to get a grip on herself but for the moment there is no question of escape—escape, which is always a luxury even under the best of circumstances although under the best of circumstances there's no need. As the lady of the house, it's up to her to set some sort of example, even a bad one.

He proceeds to elaborate. If Borkman were capable of doing justice to the facts, the explanation would go something like this: "At first, as I was lying on the sheets we'd dutifully soiled, armed with such a prize I thought only of drowning my sorrows by taking revenge on the entire human race, myself included—that is, by trying out the name exclusively on—each one of you in order to decide on the very best fit. A name worth its salt is infinitely malleable to circumstance. Staging a kind of culprits contest. But I knew I'd be contemptible if I exploited my discovery cum invention for purposes only of revenge. It'd be a pity to waste an unsuspecting name—any name—on robots, or rather, the robo-signers of my death warrant."

But even if he can't do justice to the facts quite in the manner prescribed, the etymologist, who's recuperated from her fit of dejection and is, at least according to the attending physician (*Dr. X: You're wanted in the fourth floor ER*), "doing nicely"—the etymologist is pleased to see that Borkman's acquitting himself honorably—even admirably. She's busy smashing walnuts and getting into the swing of things—rising to the occasion—by pretending they're lapis lazuli. Observing him she can't help feeling—no, she *does* feel— that those assembled here represent the wave of a not-so-distant future—a future where the notion of being in or out of character as related to speech acts will be meaningless—a future where, for example, use of the phrase "infinitely malleable to circumstance" by somebody who could never in a million years be expected to know what it means or why its rigor is . . . sensuous to the touch or why surrender to the sensuousness is in this or in any context a moral duty—a future where such things won't raise an eyebrow—indeed, will be wildly applauded. A future where a culprit's adduction of having spoken out of character to the bank manager as an extenuating factor in a robbery leaving seven dead won't wash. A future where character as we know it will be for all practical purposes extinct—where plausibility of utterance will no longer be adjudicated on the basis of whether the speaker is sufficiently at home with polysyllables—or sufficiently not—to be right for the part. And if anybody is to be considered a reliable prophet it's the etymologist inasmuch as she's lived her entire life uncomplainingly on the margins of the future.

In fact, he (a vengefully self-made Ecclesiastes) even thought of tarring and feathering them en masse with the same lustral brush by crying out something like: *Each of you is a Shitpickles. Shitpickle of Shitpickles: All is Shit- pickles.* His speech is still slurred, but not as much as he'd like it to be. But what counts is that it's slurred enough to enable them to tag this as the ranting of a madman (loosely speaking) who had to have seen better days (the better to tear them to bits once they grew too complacent). Which allows them to listen unthreatened and without rancor. Like a rich kid enamored of his first nanny, he pursues her into the kitchen, where, taking a less immodest tack, he confesses—most of all to himself—that in fact the handle in question has been chosen for them not by him (wet dream notwithstanding) but (through some serpentine process of osmosis) by the culprits themselves, the actual bearers of the name, and by the bearers themselves he doesn't mean just her lawyer and his wife and her mad psychiatrist and the girlfriend who looks a lot like she's going to Harlem in ermine and pearls and maybe even Jaggers— nice, normal Jaggers—the Jaggers who just to irk the girlfriend professes to like nothing better than crap games with barons and earls (Borkman realizes he hasn't yet made up his mind even after all these years about the man's loy- alty: is it unswerving according to true Mafioso propriety? undying? both? neither?). By the bearers themselves he means everybody who's ever crossed him and lived to tell the tale—everybody whose unhumble pie has never been leavened by adversity as his has recently been—everybody who deems him unworthy of the status of rival. Wrestling with the name as he did, it couldn't help but end up in the pea soup fog of their consciousness—individual and collective. In short, he plastered them with the name so they could shed all it invoked because, as it so happens, it's exactly the sort of name that lays bare the right kind of disposable characterologic trash. They needed a name (he's bellowing—some might say screaming—screaming so they have no trouble catching every other word) to cover their nakedness (but only at first) and to extinguish the embers of selfhood's errancy on the side of gluttonous aggrandizement. As for her, seriously, didn't she ever think of taking time out from her busy schedule of mothering, fingerpainting and allied hobbies to notice— she who's always prided herself on what *CliffsNotes* used to call *keen insight into human nature*—that all along these poor excuses for a pal were clamoring for just such a garment? Why does she think they're here tonight if not because of some obscure premonition? . . . And they somehow know without knowing they know—the best kind of knowing but hard enough to come by—that the more they protest as they're doing even now, the more they're molding themselves to the name's appalling specifications and (but cheer up!) smelting away all their sooty smugness—and worse—thereby. But up until now, fate has been uncompliant—absent without leave—hasn't been willing to respond to their unspoken—unspeakable—need. That is, until he—fate's apostle— already transformed by his first taste of contact with clinical trial big shots and hot numbers and, best of all, its hoi polloi into something a good deal wilier than fate—determined that it would be absolutely unconscionable to play havoc with the inevitability of their rehabilitation one millisecond longer. So name them he did (since rehab whether it knows it or not goes nowhere if it can't pivot on the fulcrum of a rehabilitant's name). The same name clings to all of them like a hairshirt from one of the better third-party online vendors. Most of them take the line of least resistance and write off these ravings which are coming in louder and clearer than ever as further proof that to the sick all are sick or as yet another classic case of misery loves company even if even a babe in arms knows that misery doesn't *always* love company—in most cases in fact it's very particular about the company it keeps—since, hey, you never know when ennoblement—worldwide fame, say—will choose to spring from going it alone.

But if she can only manage to observe them as carefully as she does his defects—she tries to get by but he blocks her egress ("Excuse me, but our guests our waiting")—it will become obvious that those guests are alive for the very first time in their wretched lives. And as they re-enter, though a long way from arm in arm, she does observe that they're *different* in the best *Invasion of the Body Snatchers* (1956) tradition. Maybe it's compliments of the action of reagent-name on thing named (so what if the CEO's wife sneers that it's not very flattering to be called a thing especially at her age?) that they're shedding their Shitpickledness at last—as foresters of the self they're doing away with all the rotting timbers of an ulcerating Envy, i.e., pretentiousness, arrogance, moodiness (hallmark of the true Maker), compulsive lying and a cloying obsession of course with money and status, not to mention a wobbly sense of what a new generation of psychobabblers refer to as entitlement. The psychiatrist ventures that maybe seeing Envy everywhere makes him feel less accursed though, surprisingly, this one indisputably *deep* insight falls flat on its face. Not surprising given that Dr. X is such an easy act to precede—or follow (he shudders to think of him on the campaign trail). Borkman defies his guests (and this time he includes the hostess) not to feel that every last one of them is doing his or her damnedest, each in her or his own way, to be (purgatively because for the last time) what the name subpoenas him or her for being. "Waking up bright-eyed from a hundred-year sleep like Aurora," concludes Jaggers's girlfriend. Borkman plans, once he's put the tonic-clonic-ity behind him, to check out this intriguing balletomane. He doesn't know what *balletomane* means or how he's come to associate it with the girlfriend (the term has *Master* written all over it) but what he does know is that the term confirms beyond the shadow of a doubt that her remark about what's-'er-name—Aurora! that's it!—could never have issued from the mouth of some dumb blonde. It's the kind of tactful, reticent utterance that hints at self-suppression of an entire worldview as way too radical for consumption by, e.g., the slobs here assembled—a cross-section of slobs everywhere including you, me and the lamppost—and cries out for a complete overhaul of their misperception of the speaker. Yes, she's a dumb blonde but dumb with sublime—yes, sublime—capabilities. You might catch her in the act of going to Harlem in ermine and pearls but as for wearing her heart on her sleeve for daws to peck at, that's out of the question: its very beat will drive the whole lot of 'em stark raving mad.

"Don't get me wrong, I feel for you," he's quick to add—but, compliments of the slurring and the wish to puke, not *that* quick. He knows better than anybody (why?) that it's a terrible fate to have to cry out in desperation for the enema of a shaming name, especially when you need to believe your unique suffering makes you unnameable—that your plight trounces naming at every turn—that your only real comfort lies in being beyond naming. Surely, they have a right to this one fringe benefit of incurability. But a name is a diagnosis and they need to be diagnosed if they're going to get better and better and recover (partially) from Envy just as he needed a diagnosis of (partial) contamination by the disease to get the ball of rehab rolling, and it's up to him to see that the naming game is played right, that is, without any vile recourse to an allied implement (but a maleficent one), the blame game. But he senses that an in-depth discussion of the benefits of diagnosis as conduit to the core of one's being—will come only later—at Amygdala. He's in no position to steal some expert's thunder. He wants to cry so he doesn't puke but he can only puke so he doesn't cry. (*Shades of—of all people—Henry James's Kate Croy*, thinks Aurora the dumb blonde.) "You'll do no such thing," says the girlfriend, respectful of other people's carpets. Ignoring her outburst, humbly he asks the psychiatrist (forgiving him his previous insight—forgiving him the vicious crack about Borkman's disownment as a worthy rival by Envy's entire global elite—forgiving him his very being) where all this insight is coming from. Is he genuinely astonished by his own precocity or is the astonishment a means of masking his immodesty? "In your case, I don't know if I'd use the word *insight* but I've heard tell from my pal Straynge that Invidicum's been found to enable people to play footsie, especially when like you they want to be good patients, with an ersatz eloquence that's addictive beyond their wildest nightmares," intones this grandmaster of the occult. Feeling diminished by Dr. X's characterization of him (no, not as a peddler of fake eloquence but rather as an aspiring good patient)—and just when he was about to go easy on himself for forgiving the sonofabitch his past crimes—Borkman gets busy hating him anew. "By the way," interjects a still-to-be-identified guest, "ever hear the one about the guy who walks into an Upper East Side emergency room in the middle of the night presenting with acute suppurating wounds to his narcissism? Of course not. I haven't thought it up yet." He gets a laugh or two, maybe because the crack makes no pretense of being on the verge of siring a deep insight. Too bad he's not wielding a cigar, which would put the finishing touches on this interjection. Why must comic relief be so excruciatingly hard to take? wonders the girlfriend.

"Seriously," continues the girlfriend (somebody whispers wickedly that she's a doctoral candidate in pop psychology with a minor in the sociology of euphemism at one of the top-rated dot.com universities and somebody else claims—a bit too righteously—in her defense that she's a human being and like every other human being she deserves a name and that the name should be Gudrun Brangwen), "you've no business diagnosing anybody. As far as I'm concerned, you're a case for the books until further notice. And by the way didn't somebody down at Amygdala tell you you're not to do any diagnosing until the trial's over—i.e., that you're not to tell anybody who'll listen she suffers from Envy just to make yourself feel less unclean?—just as those undergoing orthodox Freudian analysis are not supposed to elope to Reno with anybody (apart from their analyst) until they get the go-ahead from central miscasting." Everybody who was standing takes a seat. As regards her deep insights—for they really are deep (*who is speaking?*)—everybody suspects that as an auditor he's in it for the long haul. "However, this rule doesn't apply to me. Few rules do." Jaggers gives her a do-you-really-think-you-ought-to look, which she sneeringly disregards, though this bit of byplay may in fact be her signal to get started ASAP but not so ASAP, mind you, as to suggest that what's being billed as a feat of improvisation (through intimations too subtle to catch red-handed) has been not just pre- but overcooked. "Actually, naming is a double-edged sword like anything worth its weight in gold. It's my mother who unwittingly taught me this." So, chuckles the etymologist/ gemologist (re-pressed into service just when she was about to abandon all hope of a comeback after having, let's not forget, been almost flattened by a marauding guest a while back, among other bad breaks), that's what her obstreperousness is all about—warming up to challenge the radical views of the Master of the House on names and naming. The knowing chuckle shows she also has a few psychology courses under her belt taken with a view to further making ends meet during this eternal downturn. "Right after pop's death in Venice (CA) and just before her too-long-deferred tummy tuck, she became infatuated with a reclusive neighbor (or rather his death opened the floodgates of a fixation that was already in its late pupal stage—in any case, let's call her Jeanette and have done with it now and forever) whose main claim to fame was her steadfast refusal to eat in restaurants from fear she'd be poisoned. Nice enough and pretty harmless as old girls go. Make that very *very* nice and harmless through purity of heart. While my mother was herself no slouch in the obsessive-compulsive disorder department, *in contradistinction*" (*remember that phrase from a few pages back?*) "to Jeanette she felt entitled to regard herself (context is all) as a thrill seeker who never sought the same thrill twice. Which gave her license to breezily bemoan the fact that the old girl would never deviate from routine long enough to join her for a wild afternoon out on the town. So, as a cute twist on 'Be Kent unmannerly/ When Lear is mad' mom enacted 'Be Goneral (her misspelled nickname) freewheeling/When Jeanette is congeals.' Borkman breathes a deep sigh of admiration: he doesn't know who Lear is but he's dumb or gullible enough to know erudition when he hears it and hers is in full musth. "Clicking her forked tongue (I detested my mother but I cherish her toxicity still), she said it was a crying shame because—and these were her very words the night of my last visit—*Jeanette is* good company. She'd never used the phrase before. (She died of a heart attack a few hours later to register her disapproval of my dilettantish ways—ways without means—which include name-dropping. She never got it—that for me name-dropping is an analgesic: code word for organic painkiller.) While cleaning out her apartment (in preparation for selling it to the lowest bidder out of respect for my loathing of all things . . . well, chrematistic, if you must know), I found myself going back over the phrase because something hadn't clicked—tame, timid Jeanette just wouldn't or just couldn't do what the phrase asked her to do, which was to come vividly, vivaciously—some might say viciously—alive as *good company*—or any kind of company, for that matter. And it broke my gypsy heart to see her try and try again—but to no avail—to be what the phrase insisted she be if she knew what was good for her—or rather, for my mother's chaste unconsummated infatuation.

"So with an eye to the main chance, I asked myself—as if I were a total stranger: 'What if I can listen, really listen, to the hatefulness of the people I hate yet still want to help and dream up the very name their hatefulness craves in order to purify itself?'"

"What's your point?" Jaggers asks, fuming. Authentic ire, or more preplanned byplay? "The point is that what my mother perpetrated against Jeanette is what the neocons and their press club (let's hear it for Koch frères) are doing, a wee bit more deviously, to this country." Jaggers rolls his eye at the analogy which is clearly all about self-inflation not responsible social commentary as we know it from the good old boys and girls of cable news. "They routinely inject the members of the over-diseased body politic with wonder drugs of euphemism, expecting rightly that their victims, i.e., most Americans, will convince themselves that the euphemisms tell the truth and the thoroughly vetted names of the diseases lie. It's not *class warfare* over here but *training for the jobs of the twenty-first century* (a Boy George oxymoron of down-home genius cooked up for him by his speechwriters and trotted out in desperation during one of the 2004 corn-fed presidential debates); it's not *civil war* over there but Operation Iraqi Freedom. *Training for the jobs of the twenty-first century* haunts me as much as *Jeanette is good company.* I simply can't dredge up real flesh-and-blood referents—things *out there* to which my oxymorons can be mapped—referents into which I can sic the fangs of those oxies. Thing is, before it can even begin to get out there *Training for the jobs . . .* is already folding back on itself and into the intestines of Boy George's animal cunning. For one thing, Bush, a Yale scholar of the highest order, hasn't the faintest idea what a community college is, how ill equipped to de-devalue the skills of workers who compete most starkly with computer-intensive machines in the performance of routine-intensive tasks and to counter the globalization-induced steep decline in manufacturing employment (as pointed out by my good friend David H. Autor). So everything gets blurred and the scoundrels take advantage of the ensuing confusion to righteously funnel their booty offshore. Yet instead of revolting, poor slobs try to—" "To make Cheney's scowling phrases fit the mess. You've already said that," Jaggers prompts. "No, it's much direr than that. I at least tried to make Jeanette conform to the contour of the label but these poor passive slobs don't even try: they simply wait for the mess to metamorphose into a perfect fit for the name."

At last Jaggers and his girlfriend make sense, at least to the gemologist. She's uncovered the mechanism that governs their dynamic. At the moment she feels more like a gemologist than an etymologist—more like a girl than a boy. Come to think of it, the girlfriend may once upon a time have been a boy or she may turn out to be neither boy nor girl but the noble embodiment of a leisurely shuttle between the poles of boyhood and girlhood with the gender—the sex—of her soul at any given moment contingent *absolutely* on the words she happens to be using or the image she's struggling to portray. Though she's not necessarily a boy at the moment when she deploys, say, the word *fuck: fuck* may simply be a way of setting off a genuine girl's exquisite artfulness to stunning effect by enchasing it in the ouch of maleness. Jaggers is the mighty moguloid and his girlfriend the obligatory decades-younger sylph in tow. And of course lurking in the background is the divorce which has alienated Jaggers from his kids (he bullies strangers, if they happen to be present, and himself—by pigeonholing—i.e., dismissing—the kids as "wonderful" or "great" or, if all else fails, "terrific"). Thing is, the *nature* of the divorce (messy versus sordid) has yet to reveal itself. Under the quaint sign of messiness neither party to the ritual is suffused with hatred for the other. It is only under the sign of sordidness that each is suffused with such hatred—a hatred that to achieve its particular virulence needs to have begun gestation in the cradle or thereabouts, proving that for some, or most, marriage constitutes a second chance—another *stab*—at infancy and childhood—under the auspices of a mechanism whereby the grievous sins of the officially stainless parents of one spouse are visited on—transferred like an epithet to—the other. But surely if the dynamic has room for these two it has room as well for an unobtrusive third party, the faithful secretary—*in tow* like the street-smart sylph—who follows faithful Jaggers from boardroom to boardroom. Though she's lived her entire life with a cronish mother such bondage has done nothing to blunt her acuity—much less suppress it—if anything bondage has sharpened that acuity and extended its applicability to a host of areas unrelated to that in which secretarial expertise is condemned to blush unseen. And the gemologist feels vindicated knowing that she—I mean, the secretary—has a role to play in greasing the wheels of the dynamic. "So starting here, starting now, I'm waging a one-woman war against euphemisms until such time as 'Shitpickles' *enters the language* and becomes a euphemism itself—that is, a means like 'Ground Zero' of making a thing infinitely less dire than it is while pretending to go to any lengths to confront the fucker (sorry) head-on. At which point all smiles will stop together. Just mutter 'Ground Zero' and you'll find you couldn't be more disengaged from the way things are down on what's left of Cortlandt Street. You'll find, in fact, you're no longer you, the quintessential native New Yorker, but some tourist from Saragossa amassing a treasure trove of Facebook photos identical to every other tourist's trove. I never told you this, Jaggers," (clearly she loves to terrorize him—for starters by calling him Jaggers—with belated confessions of little terrorist import and he clearly loves to be terrorized but how can anybody judge from this one instance unless he's privy to material unavailable to the general public?) "but remember how I used to make fun of your subscribing to that super-glossy Condo Nasty rag *To the Manor Born*?" "Ex-wife was the subscriber." (A sordid divorce, thinks the etymologist.) "Well, fact is, I made a point of reading it regularly cover to cover—when, say, a raging fever (brought on by too much dismantling of the one big euphemism known as Everyday Life) incapacitated me for anything better. Anyway, remember when it was doing yet another asslicking spread on yet another filthy-rich couple, this one in the throes of sprucing up their fourth residence (down in the Cayman-Hamptons)? Not knowing quite how to euphemize the childish but very natural evil doings of the husband—he was nothing special: your garden-variety hedge fund honky—the editors came up with *young turk on Wall Street*. That did the trick all right: a referent-hungry gem right up there with Jeanette is good company and *Training for the jobs of the twenty-first century*. It thinks—thought—for euphemisms do think—that it had managed to turn some snotty little silver-platter punk into a duly-diligent star innovator. Trouble is, I still can't wrap my ragged claws around the star turn. Could you?"

"I've met many such punks," Borkman says. In a tone that is meant to egg the girlfriend on. Can't remember her name—especially not after the mock epileptic fit. Or as they say nowadays, *faux* epileptic fit.

"You're just jealous," the wife hisses.

"I've been one. Don't you remember, wife?" he retorts through gritted teeth in a tone that would have made Robert Ryan green with envy—Envy. (He's done the impossible—made "wife" ladle out more virulence than a nastier expletive for female ever could.) "We have guests," she counters. He would like nothing better than to strangle her (*Are we back to that again?* shout the hecklers who've recently taken up residence in his Broca area) but hasn't his son, a far better man than he, already tried and failed and, because of that sodden burst of spontaneity, didn't he, Borkman (*yes, I know we've been through all this failed strangling business, only you haven't been through it in* non-conformity with this particular context), on the unanimous advice of ill-informed therapists, lie in wait all night to ensure that the minute the prodigal walked through the door he'd be straitjacketed and carted off for evaluation and appropriate treatment? The bottom line is: He doesn't want his son to be in his shoes.

Even after all these years, Borkman still has trouble accepting that even under the best of circumstances a wife is a wife and a wife will always be just what (here the Master takes over—pinch-hits—for Borkman)[4] old Hesiod says she is, to wit, a gaping wound of insatiable belly-hunger (*limos*) at the hearth's heart for whom no amount of husbandly toil is ever enough to exorcise the demon of poverty—a shrike who rates the worth of her mate according to how thoroughly he puts his own needs—his precious self-love—his very essence and its rightful cravings—to one side as being incompatible with fatherhood so that his get may thrive and surpass him. Infected with her wifely Envy of the size of everybody else's granary (*yes*, granary: *there are times, wise guy, though few and far between, when a cigar is just a granary*), the husband dutifully makes that toil completely joyless by turning all his fellow toilers into the deadliest of rivals. Some people never learn. And while we're at it, hasn't somebody connected with the trial been thinking about this guy named . . . named . . . Hesiod! recently? Borkman wonders. One day last week—Thursday, to be exact—while he was blissfully—pissfully—minding his own business at a urinal in the second-floor men's room, he could have sworn that from one of the stalls, all of them empty, there issued forth . . . what sounded like the ravings of an old codger high on a gold rush of tau and beta-amyloid protein deposits whose ire was focused specifically and unforgivingly on the wife. According to him, her specialty of the house wasn't minestrone or kreplach or Yorkshire pudding or a tony tarte Tatin but rather exalting and glamorizing the status of the other wives—trivializing *their* privations out of existence—so she could shine as the one who, on the spousal front, got the rawest deal (including the poorest health on the planet) and with that star turn came a nothing-to-sneeze-at fringe benefit: hypochondriacal exhibitionism legitimated by the obligation to chart her every mortal symptom.

---

[4]Here we see how The Master has his work cut out for him. I.e., he is constantly needing to decide just how much eloquence—how much erudition can—should—be allocated to any given John Doe or Jane before she/he collapses under the heft of his/her own implausibility. E.g., can a bum like Borkman be saddled with knowing even Hesiod's name, much less his works (inside out) without demolishing (*a*) all that is great about the Borkman we know and love and in tandem (*b*) the mausoleum of which he is one of the armatures? More to the point, who or what's to determine where and when the Master should draw the line (at Hesiod?—though not at, say, Nosferatu?) and in consequence step in to provide cover to whoever may be acting out of character? But isn't there such a thing as too much stage-mother intercession even if it stems from so noble a motive? Isn't there such a thing as too much interweaving—threading—of the Master's voice with those of his flock which stems, when all is said and done, from an *ignoble* underestimation of all their abilities?

Surmising that the guests have had just about enough of bargain-basement Strindberg, the girlfriend feels *empowered* (a word she detests) to resume. "Even with all my unwelcome millions, I still have a social conscience and, more importantly, a soft spot for the slang of days gone by, which took its cues from hard-working criminals. Slang nowadays—but there *is* no slang nowadays: it's all euphemisms: a shitload of spineless, self-important, repressively fake solidarity-peddling cast-offs from the sports and business worlds which transform the slimiest of scams into the holiest of touchdowns. When you're robbing the little people blind, just CEO- or sports-speak a little sand in their eyes and see how quickly they forget to suffer hunger pangs because suddenly they've acquired the equal-opportunity delusion that if they can only speak the speak they'll end up as big a power broker as big Dick riding herd on the Saudis. Detestable humanoid, that Dick."

"You know," says the CEO (unrepentant for having almost mowed down the gemologist and clearly exhilarated by his refusal to repent), "this really isn't the time to start a business." "Business?" Borkman asks, stalling for time (though time for what?—a question he doesn't ask). He's more lucid now but what is this business about starting a business? "You're going to call it Shitpickles, remember." "*Shitpickles: The Movie*," the CEO's wife sneers. But it's a playful sneer, full of girlish high spirits. Borkman isn't getting any of this—or only to the extent of acknowledging that if this is what a newly minted CEO is supposed to say from time to time (with or without a little sugar 'n' spice from the little woman), then he's grateful the CEO in question knows how to say it.

"I couldn't disagree more," exclaims—yes, *exclaims*—the girlfriend. Judging from the expression on Jaggers's face and, more to the point, the way he rubs his soft hands together, he couldn't be prouder of his newest discovery (is he the sugar daddy who's saddled her with millions?). Clearly the stabs at rubbing her the wrong way were all a stunt, a remnant of his vaudeville—his court-appointed attorney—days. What he really wants to do—and which he does soon enough (the minute a new round of canapés are passed around)—is to praise her to the skies (she's got more on the ball than all of her predecessors combined). This entails measuring her virtues against his own numberless defects (". . . but as nobody minds having what is too good for them . . ."). Which comparison only goes to show that no matter how numberless, they are far outweighed by his special gifts—I mean, his genius—for which getting the worse end of the deal is a small price for anybody—including Gudrun—to pay. She announces that she needs another drink. *Haven't you had enough?* is on the tip of his tongue (he doesn't quite know why: after all, this clashes with the watercolor he's just dashed off). Instead, waiting until she's out of earshot, he asks rhetorically of nobody in particular, "Isn't she adorable?" but in a conference-call voice, which defeats the purpose. He professes to be calling on the gods themselves to attest that he has no choice but to lay down his arms before the irrefutability of that adorableness when in fact he's attempting to elicit—to compel—some pretense of confirmation from this focus group. The only guest with whom the question doesn't sit quite right is the pudgy little egghead of a man, of indeterminate profession, waxing his moustache in the corner.

Whether she's adorable or not suddenly doesn't matter now that, drink in hand (it smells like a Rob Roy), she's back, fevered and feisty as ever, and after—and expecting everybody else to be after—bigger game. "As I was saying, this is very much the time to start a business. I intend to put a 'dot.com' after every last one of the euphemisms that are eroding our social fabric and start trading them (domain names are hotter than hot). Once I get the ball rolling it will be hard to keep up with demand—from politicians, contractors, lobbyists and, last but not least, young Turks on Wall Street with a quaternary residence in Belize. And with the proceeds I'll find a way of blitzing the media with only 'good' names—or at least goodish ones—the kind that force folks—I mean, people (nothing I hate more than the fake-populist *folks* except maybe the subtraction of the final *g* from participles as a sign of solidarity with the soon-to-be-homeless)—to see, hear and smell things as they really are. But of course sometimes the good names need to be the wrong names to have that effect. And to subsidize my good deeds, I'm sure I can make plenty through scattershot notices of infringement on my euphemism patents.

"Once I make my first billion I'll branch out." "Sure you will," remarks the CEO's wife in a stage whisper. Jaggers is beside himself—or, as Straynge's widow-to-be would say if she were he (see below and beyond), *besides* himself. He wants Gudrun (isn't that her name or is he confusing her with somebody else?) to be adorable, yes, but there's such a thing (to quote Jimmy Durante) as abusing the privilege. Racked by ambivalence (which the egghead wryly toasts), he would like to crawl into a corner or fall asleep at her feet. Thing is, he slept too long—and hard—the night before to be able to fool himself into thinking he's exhausted. But what is he to do with so much wide-awakeness— too much wide-awakeness for his own good—except lavish it on her most unappetizing—her most *unadorable* gumption?

"Why, just this morning, what do I see walking her poodle down Madison between Eighty-Fourth and Eighty-Third but some fat-assed anorexic in a baseball cap, grungy sneakers, a mink coat and layer upon layer of pancake. The message in her madness? 'I'm not a typical hoity-toity alimonious East Side bitch because, look, I'm wearing my streetwise baseball cap' (which has the additional advantage of making her look thirty years younger, or so she thinks)." The minute *bitch* is out of her mouth, however, Gudrun regrets it— oh, all right, not the *minute* it's out of her mouth but soon after—specifically once she sees the lady of the house looking lividly ready to take up the cudgels for this hardy specimen of vintage oxymoronia with whom she feels a kinship (though she doesn't regret not knowing if she's a girl or a boy as a result of uttering the word). Gudrun's always been a fast learner where gaucherie is the teacher. Obviously use of the word was supposed to endear her to some segment of the audience—prove she was one of the boys. As the vehicle of a self-presentational act, *bitch* was supposed to transform her into somebody superior to—smarter than—herself. But in thereby robbing this vintage item of her pathos—her potential pathos—she robbed herself of . . . what precisely? Well, for starters, her own slice of that old heartland holiday favorite, pathos pie à la mode. And—miracle of miracles—the lady of the house seems to have simmered down—lost her bloated look—livid with the unfocusable rage of too many lifetimes. Let's face it, Gudrun, she tells herself, expletives—epithets—are facile. They diminish those who don't merit diminution and as for those who do, well, they deserve a harsher comeuppance than induction into victimhood. Time to move on. "And while we're at it, let's not give short shrift to the other members of my own semiprivate rogues' gallery: Young Turk with his camel's hair coat and toque beanie (or cashmere reversible headband) or Don Juan cardiologist who makes it a point to sight-read or rather *makes a point of* sight-reading the score of a Bruckner symphony while outrunning the treadmill at the local gym—I mean the local high-end sports club. I know all about him—I was there. In addition, he's sweating bullets. How do I know he's a cardiologist? It's the first thing he'll tell anybody who'll listen—like the hairy-thighed pal on his left (I'm his right-hand girl Friday). He and his hairy-thighed pal make salaciously disparaging remarks about the not particularly attractive—worse, the not even interestingly unattractive—woman in front of them to their heart's content (she's wearing earphones). And if bystanders like me get caught in the crosstalk, all the better. In fact, the hairy pal holds his nose. Is it because she smells or because her failure to please is a marketable—a highly patentable—pheromone? The very model of a modern oxymoron, our resident cardiologist, priding himself on embodying—curating—all of life's contrarieties within his soon-to-be-unflabby person. Physician *and* esthete *and* vulgarian—who can ask for anything more of a single subhuman being? Mediocrity is just one of his changes of garment. Maybe I'm so taken with him because he resembles you, Jaggers, and therefore my own deadbeat dad." She explains that meanspiritedness, boorishness, vulgarity, mediocrity, are not slurs—not in the context of genius—which is what he thinks he is—but, to the contrary, an enhancement thereof—something along the lines of *male* enhancement—proof of his ability to ennoble all stereotypes by assimilating them to his essence. As a genius, he is insatiable. But isn't the surest symptom of his genius the ever-expanding desire to be more—to encompass as many self-contradictions as possible? "Who's a genius—the cashmere cardiologist?" snaps Borkman's imminent ex-, sick of the word, sick of having spent decades with a blowhard who had everything going for him as a genius except the guts to remain one. "The cardiologist, Jaggers, deadbeat dad, Borkman, Mr. CEO—you're all geniuses because geniuses are a dime a dozen and not just online."

She explains that lots of people—maybe most (or is this *most* merely what some meaning-monger wants her to say because he's sure his clientele are suckers when it comes to mistaking exaggeration for profundity)—want to be unfixable, unstraitjacketable. And to this class of useless beings she'll be marketing another line of names—names befitting their hallucinated uniqueness as living, breathing oxymorons—names designed to remind them they're unique when they're in danger of forgetting—when the get-up, say, no longer succeeds in getting the message out. (They'll just have to migrate to her click-fraud-unfriendly website, Oxymorons.com, to find the right one.) "And each name—by embodying as many ethnic, religious, socioeconomic and intellectual incompatibilities as possible (but not to reconcile them as they can never be reconciled in life but rather to highlight their irreversible antagonism and immiscibility)—will serve as the direst of warnings to aspiring straitjacketers. The price of a name will of course be based on how many incompatibilities it manages to incorporate and on how deftly it does so. And with the profits I'll run programs online and off- designed to alert young people to the dangers of addiction to unstraitjacketability. Straitjackets like diagnoses have their place. But I'm sure Mr. Borkman here will be learning lots more about the function of diagnoses down at Amygdala. Congratulations, by the way, on being—on having been—accepted into the trial." Is she putting him on? Is being accepted into a clinical trial something to be congratulated for—in, of all places, a roomful of career backbiters, every one of whom is far more worthy of Invidicumization than he?

Once the guests are gone Borkman stretches the boundaries of his blamelessness as a parent by once again fusing with a fiction. He offers viciously seething Veda Pierce (Ann Blyth) the chance as so many times before to give as bad as she knows she's never gotten from her mother, martyred Mildred (Joan Crawford). (If left up to her, the endlessly repeated text of the missing master chyron floated at the bottom of the screen would read something along the lines of *Veda doesn't let would-be MasterBaiters quash her shameless eloquence*). Purged by virtue of the mother's stoical response to horrific mistreatment, and at peace with parenthood as long as he can remember he's Mildred's fraternal twin, Borkman decides to go to bed. As he mounts the stairs, the wife shouts—her tone atypically, almost eerily, placating—that she'll just be a minute. Since he's taken (and taken to) the guestroom—sharing it with his favorite stranger to boot—why should he care? He has to get away from the almost-eeriness ASAP—it's incapacitating him for ascent. Yet not, as it turns out, for descent, since with no memory of having landed there, he's back at the foot of the stairs, waiting. Waiting, but with no idea why. But getting a whiff of her phone voice (or rather, the voice reserved for chats only with the psychiatrist to end all psychiatrists) he knows at once what he's waiting for—the inevitable (now that he's been packed off to bed) unflattering exchange of notes about his latest enormity. But suddenly there's a silence so ominous he begins to hope against hope that it's furious and signals a definitive rift. But then it rights itself—transposes from minor to major—bids farewell to a lurking atonality—and presto! the lovers are notes-exchanging clinicians in sheep's clothing once more.

Wrong again: in fact she *is* furious but for reasons that have nothing to do with him. He's history, guestroom or no guestroom. From what he can make out, it has to do with some excruciating symptom which the psychiatrist insists is all in her mind, poor thing. A welcome change—being able to refer to her as *poor thing* and mean it—at least for a millisecond. (Borkman thinks of calling him Mabuse [only because the older boy is an aficionado of German silent films] but that domain name's already taken. *But by whom?* So what about . . . Cottard? [suggests somebody . . . Some Body whom Borkman suddenly hopes is racking up quite a constituency, as It's not quite as alien to him as it was a few days ago] which may very well be the real name behind the X: namesake of a fictional whipping boy and pet grotesque of some "obscure" French writer.) So the minute she slams down the phone (she hates cells, or is this just an East Side affectation? or a ploy of her . . . Creator aka Borkman's Some Body who's clearly forgotten, in his admirable haste—inasmuch as time is money—that landlines are cenozoic at best) he advances with every intention of giving both his wife and her symptom the validation they so richly deserve (she's too distraught to wonder what he's doing here). The urge to protect generates, as usual, lust for the exquisitely vulnerable creature created by that urge but before the first few words of comfort are out of his mouth she's already reproaching him for not having gotten *it* exactly right. Can't he get it through his thick skull that Doctor Judge Brack (so it was "Judge Brack" lurking behind the X) has viciously dismissed not just her ache but her very selfhood? As usual, Borkman's clanky first-aid truck is racing to the scene of the crime from the wrongest direction imaginable.

She names her symptom, her beloved symptom. He names it back—to naturalize it—to legitimate it—to show he's on her side—knows the symptom's real. But this repetition ostensibly in support of her symptom is being heard instead as a mockery of her bondage—bondage as homage—to the symptom's detractor. She utters the Doctor's disparaging word for somebody who believes she suffers from such a symptom. Not a pretty word. Again, Borkman comes to the damsel's rescue by proudly affirming that he hasn't the faintest idea what X or Brack or Cottard means by such a spluttering specimen of mumbo-jumbo. Once again, he's put his foot in it. The disparaging word—the word he dares to deflate in his role as straight-shooting layman— is, as it turns out, a sediment of such ungovernable power and sacred energy that to make her a gift, out of the honest desire to provide moral support, of his well-meaning and razor-sharp obtuseness becomes her pretext for deflecting rage from Brack to Borkman—becomes just what the doctor ordered—a signal to accuse him of *playing* at obtuseness—of playing mind games—of dragging an expert witness through the mud. For the ex-wife-to-be is the keeper of the expert's torturous flame.

Yet in the same breath she gives Borkman another example of the Doctor's deviousness—he's suggested she get a second opinion if she doesn't trust him. Straight out of a post-war Hollywood melodrama—*Experiment Perilous*, say, or *Whirlpool* or *Gaslight* or *Sleep, My Love* or *The Two Mrs. Carrolls*—clearly he's trying to drive her insane. Thing is, she just as clearly intends for this second example—this confirmation of Borkman's loving acuity—to be heard in the key of . . . correction—reproof. How could he have allowed himself—as her knight in shining armor—to miss this salient bit of information the first time around? No matter that he wasn't made privy to it before this moment. Borkman's words of wisdom are grossly overrated—they've served no other function than to awaken her to their own inadequacy—to their blundering usurpation of the place of evidence (second-opinion evidence) that's far more vital. But wait . . . there's static on the line—somebody—Some Body—is trying desperately to reach him (Hollywood melodrama style)—to prove that *she's* the problem—that it's she who's trying to drive *him* insane. Fact is, she has no idea what she means—no idea whatsoever whether it's indictment that she's after or total exoneration of the demon lover. What matters is to muddy the waters of language through the auspices of language. *It isn't that your words are woefully inadequate, Borkman,* that Some Body—that Master—is telling him—and, imagine! in language he can actually understand. In fact, the meaning of the words is beside the point. It's the brute fact of utterance that is the meaning. And when you're Lady Borkman, for whom every face is as a book where men may read strange matters, any act of utterance—no matter what the meaning of the words on which it hitchhikes—is by its very nature, or its anti-nature, designed to throw her off guard, to destabilize her, to make her doubt not just whether her symptom is real, or whether she's understood Brack properly—but everything else. A drug compounded from the most comforting words in the world can't counteract the poison injected into the bloodstream of her soul through the act of their very utterance. Remedy as Poison and, it is to be hoped (once the patient can minister to himself), Poison as Remedy. In a word, *Pharmakon.* A term lent new—mass-market—life by a showman who would have given P.T. more than a run for his money: Ladies and Gents let me introduce you to the Castle Garden likes of the one and only Jack the Derider. A Master of a different color.

He is about to atone by beefing up his denunciation of Brack but in the nick of time realizes she must want this even less than his words of comfort. Under no circumstances will he cast a shadow over and thereby seem to imperil the inevitable reconciliation, tectonic-plated rumblings of which are, to his well-trained seismic sixth sense, already perceptible under foot. Suddenly he has no desire to stay the night and tells her she needn't worry (why would she?)—heading straight back to his hotel. "Oh, you mean the boutique number where Ponzi schemers become legends," she remarks dryly—or is it distractedly? hence without malice.

CHAPTER SEVEN

Shearer finds herself constantly—morbidly—monitoring her reaction to the drug (she still can't bear to call it by its rightful, portentously silly name). Since she lives alone and in case of untoward side effects, couldn't depend on any of her neighbors (they think she's a snooty has-been) to take her to a hospital emergency room. Or is this just self-glorification, a splintered homage to her epochal collaboration with the twentieth century's most innovative—some might say, its only—choreographer?

It's late and she's unglorifyingly dead-tired after an afternoon of non-stop teaching. She detests her colleagues because she's intimidated by their mocking anatomization of the defects of their students. Mistakes it for a mere extension of their tough-loving dedication—they're more dedicated than she by virtue of that very mockery. At the same time she realizes they're no more dedicated—just nastier. That it should come to this, after all those years of, among other feats, oh so wittily yet poignantly (through the wit alone) enacting, but without *dramatizing* (and thereby betraying the Master's aesthetic), an aghast and flailing astonishment at what her feet are always managing to be up to without her consent—after all those years of tipsily fighting off abduction by, surrender to, a madly proliferating Lilliputian army of simpering bourrées, and never being more faithful to the choreography than when ruefully simulating a breakdown of the very discipline it demanded. Joseph Cornell immortalized all that in the box (now at the Getty) entitled *Shearer Footsteps Cell*. How can she forget what this stage-door Johnny looked like waiting stooped and breathless (just another crank, clearly more homicidal than most) to offer it to her (the stoop being the purest expression of his homage? Nay, it *was* his homage (*or is this verbal contortion yet another eternal calling card of Melanctha's He?*). She confesses that her first impulse was to keep on walking (the month was cruelest April and the starless night unseasonably warm).

On Eighty-Eighth Street (right around the corner from where that renowned vaudeville team, the Borkmans of Broadway, chose to air their dirty laundry), a wisp of greasy gust-driven trash approaches, then retreats, clearly too terrified of pursuers to halt long enough to plead for help. Its disappearance is a reminder of the oh-so-many heartstopping dives into the wings—high points in any ballet—that Mr. B. devised just for her. A little further on, at the corner of Broadway and Eighty-Ninth, it finds her again. The plea's more desperate—that of a gazelle about to be torn apart by a lurking leopard, but since this is TV zoo-porn, the poker-voiced narrator encourages her (as leopard goes about doing what leopards do best) to gorge freely on all the horizon-broadening gore inasmuch as the victim is in a state of shock and—trust me—doesn't feel a thing. But would her rivals have stopped to turn a gazelle into a piece of trash? Of course not. That's why each was still a Star (having singlehandedly transformed the concept to suit their aging bodies) and she—well, she prefers not to call a spade a spade.

And yet—or, as the Schubert of "Im Dorfe" would have said, *Je nun—*

at this very moment of choreographing her trash ballet under a prepluvially electric purple sky, invidious distinctions are inconceivable: she is simply unavailable to do what she does best: *suffer by comparison*. Or is that the Invidicum talking? The panhandlers pitch in as well: observing them give the newest wave of *condominium residents* the spine-tingle or two to which as taxpayers they feel entitled—a measured whiff (before they toddle off to their rooftop saunas or rooftop carriage houses) of that danger for which New York was once famous—she is immunized against her rivals. The word has no meaning. Her communion with trash, sky and the panhandlers dutifully giving the condo-folk a run for their money is incomparable. At this moment in this momentary universe, nobody can do communion with city things better than she. Nobody can do *her* better than she herself can. She has to hold on to this discovery (soon to be a major modern maxim). But suddenly, in revolt, everything Herbert has told her is refluxing, making it a heresy to be thinking about Balanchine, Cornell and gazelles prancing about in their own blood when at this very moment some young man—no more than twenty—is staggering comatose on excruciated stumps through the piss-dizzying corridors of Building 18. While the rest of America goes shopping or, worse, choreographs to young man Schubert (himself no slouch, by the way, when it comes—came—to excruciation).

Impossible, however, to stop thinking as she's prone to think. Art in collusion with suffering—art as an unspeakable affront to unspeakable suffering—that's the way it's always been and always will be. (As the misery of all beings is, alas, in the public domain, they should not expect—least of all the gentlest, the kindest, the most trod upon among them—any sort of compensation for its unauthorized use.) If Balanchine waited for all the suffering to go away before standing his ballerinas on their head . . . Some Body's telling her (Herbert telepathically?) both too much and too little excruciation make the practice of art unthinkable and that therein lies the dialectical tension generating its doability. But where does she begin and that Some Body end? It's not *Some Body*—it's the Invidicum that's pulling her strings—stuffing her head with all sorts of ideas she can't make head nor tail of. Art is not just viciously opportunistic: it has a vested interest in encouraging perpetration of the unthinkable, all so that *Never Again* can be turned into a platitude. Granted, Moira, it's horrifying that *Never Again* can be turned into a platitude by a new wave of genocides. But for the inventor of "it's horrifying that *Never Again* can be turned into a platitude by a new wave of genocides," there's only euphoria. Induced by the contrast between the perceived (or decreed) boundlessness of genocidal horror and the quaint boundedness of the sentence elegantly encapsulating the perception of that boundlessness. Induced by the vengeance of language on life—the trick language plays on life. But Moira feels cheated—thinking these thoughts she could be anybody—including least likely suspect, given her near illiteracy (aren't all dancers assumed to be dummies?). Why is she being saddled with—assailed by—this eloquence, if eloquence it is? She is tempted to cry, *Why me?* And the being—thing—that is trying to saddle her with his—its—eloquence replies, *That's the stupidest question I've ever heard. Why* not *you?* Thinking of the billions of genocide victims who might have been tempted to ask the same question, she is inclined to agree.

She buys a caramel crumble cone just to be able to examine the list of Invidicum's side effects (which comes with every new vial) on the rocking bench outside the ice cream parlor. But not before trying to make her looking at the condominium residences all around into a looking *back*. A looking back by somebody who, looking on helplessly as they're replaced (by behemoths even more featureless), vows to keep alive the memory of what now passes for antique splendor. To be able to live among the condos, which have use, mind you, neither for Balanchine nor for Building 18, Shearer needs to nostalgize their brute *thing*hood from the vantage of a future where such things will have become a mere and unsightly residue of the new Real McCoy. A future where the new Real McCoy encompasses not just the even-more-featureless behemoths but, far worse (for however featureless, however soulless, behemoths are still touchable), the unrepeatable and traceless *experiences* of everybody's online avatar. With everybody of course now reduced to an encumbered version of that avatar—the avatar of an avatar adrift in a poor man's cyberspace. (Volatilization syndrome, her proleptic ex- calls this, with impatient relish.) She may be thinking these aspiring deep thoughts without knowing she's thinking them. That's where the Invidicum obligingly kicks in, enabling her to know.

It's almost disappointing that as of this moment there's been no hair loss, blackouts, convergence insufficiency, serotonin syndrome, premature ejaculation, compulsive shopping, stuttering, narcolepsy, priapism, uncontrollable laughter, apotemnophilia, binge eating, buffalo hump or (unkindest cut of all) somnambulism. With not a measly symptom to her name (is her ballet training the culprit?) Straynge must wonder how, when all of the others seem to be, most promisingly, fighting a losing battle with four or five, such an impostor dares to go on showing her face at group sessions. For just as any artist worth his salt craves detractors to validate his greatness, so are side effects crucial to establishing the credibility of any wonder drug. Her obstinacy is giving Invidicum a bad name.

She turns reluctantly into the Costa Rican rainforest of 110th Street. Her nieces are sitting on the stoop of "her" (yes, *her*) brownstone (with its deliciously unsightly big-bay Pickwickian paunch), where they are auditioning by cellphone for the Actors Studio, which mostly entails pointedly ignoring her arrival. Doing thereby the implied bidding of mom who bristles at their rapport with auntie and whose cankerous influence is far stronger than they, as self-decreed free spirits, are willing to admit. Don't they realize cellphoning at the drop of a hat shows disrespect not just for Shearer but, more importantly, for this unique irretrievable moment—shameless disrespect for the *environment* of the moment, animal, vegetable, mineral and everything in-between? What about those squidlike sleeves of overilluminated ginkgo, for starters? Well, what about them? Her nieces prefer parading their connectedness to the unseeable. Especially since the very latest cellphone model, which is what they flaunt, can be activated only by prosthesis, so to speak: that is, the password is their unique take on the Valley Girl twang—ubiquitous, generic, husky. Let them be: can't you see they're living life to the hilt, i.e., reliving it as the irresistible sound of their own voice tells them it deserved to be lived in the first place—as street theater?

Yet, just as a porn star, either from real excitement or boredom or disgust or forgetfulness (in their early days, Shearer's ex- insisted she watch XXX-rated films—to liberate herself onstage, he said; thing is, he hadn't seen her very much at home in the *Prodigal Son* or *Agon* pas de deux, which made mincemeat of such insistence)—just as a porn star will occasionally jump out of the skin of the "script" and do something uncoded—lick his partner's clitoris, say, just a wee bit longer than he's been contracted to do—so Annie-Fannie, or her sister, Lulu, will, but only when the spirit really moves her, part company with convention and speak as herself, in her own Valley-free voice. A voice that no longer pisses contempt on everybody who has nobody to blame but himself for being within pissing distance (according to the First Law of Cellphones, *Proximity breeds contempt*). Yet, oddly enough—or not so oddly enough—she prefers them Valley-encumbered . . . For as such they've been responsible for her first meat-and-potatoes Envy attack of the day which may very well be tantamount to—worth more than—fifty side effects. She finds herself envying them with their shoulder bag and cellphone cradled between neck and collarbone and envying them even more when they interrupt their busy schedule every now and then—more now than then—to take a swig from their designer bottle for she can't help being intimidated into believing that each has—out of—out of . . . *Ideological necessity*, she wants to say, without knowing she wants to (and the fact that she can't say, much less think it, makes Shearer, in the eyes of that Thing or Body stalking her a few paragraphs ago, as helpless as a sylphide—whom, for this very helplessness, He's not sure he wants to adore or strangle)—she can't help believing each has managed to invent the cellphone stance from scratch as the purest and most perfect expression of who she is and, more importantly, whom she intends to become when she's gotten all the mileage she can out of being who she is. Shearer refuses to believe what she knows only too well—the laceration inflicted by Envy *in its pure state* is much too tempting—that they're rank imitators and the slicker the imitation, the stronger the conviction of originality. So once again, she's "in" Envy, not in denial, and thereby doing her part in Amygdala's war effort. She has the indistinct impression that the self-hatred of somebody else on the team has a similar need to see originality where only slavish imitation reigns—supreme.

That Shearer can't decide whether Lulu is talking to somebody or simply leaving a long message, saddens her. Not knowing whether the absence of side effects makes her a good or a bad subject has the same effect. But she owes it to herself to keep this craving for resolution from marring enjoyment of the uncertainty, of being in two places at once. Being in two places at once makes her Envy-free. Better yet, balletic, and she has every right to be enjoying herself. So she pretends to be in one of Mr. B.'s pink applause machines, where, as the work's lead dancer, she finds herself on the cusp of perpetual transformation, never knowing if she still belongs to the current soloist-versus-corps or to the next. What she does know is that's a privilege to be riding that cloud of indeterminacy. For every transformation is organic. A choreographic Christie, Balanchine demonstrates moment to moment how any member of the company—or the audience—can at all times remain one step ahead of him in effecting it, since the building blocks are in the public domain.

Shearer's impatient stare at a point just above Annie's perfectly shaped head—signaling that the applause machine, like her tolerance for being ignored, has run out of steam—makes the multipolar cellphony slightly uneasy. But as she knows only too well anybody who makes Annie uneasy—anybody whose righteous indignation serves as a prod for self-confrontation—finds that the unease immediately rebounds as proof of the prodder's perversity, sickness unto death. Lulu hangs up abruptly, but not before whispering something unflattering (Shearer's sure it's about her). She's picked up Annie's smug smile though she hasn't once glanced her sister's way. So what is their aunt supposed to do under the circumstances? She thinks of going deadpan by pretending to be stage center in *The Unanswered Question*, definitely no applause machine. Then she remembers whom she's dealing with. Not even deadpan, poker face, rigor mortis, can baffle their sort's signature brand of dismissive verdict cum diagnosis—elude the long arm of their law. Her simulation of a withdrawal of warmth, like warmth itself, is immediately thrust back on the shameless perpetrator as proof of disability—incapacitation for life as those robustly in the know live it. No framing the framers, no bracketing the bracketeers. All affect is grist for the straitjacketer's mill. So she is left with nothing but her own unanswered question: How mount a self-defense unpre-emptable by mockery and live to tell the tale? But defense of what? Everything their cellphoning spares them from saying. For starters, that her success is inconceivable except as a long act of self-sabotage and this being the case, her prospects for rehab are thin. As for her failure, it's all too conceivable and might prove catching. They don't understand that a dancer's career—her life—is abysmally short and in her heyday there was little in the way of documentation to prove her greatness. But even she knows these are contingencies which do not address the bleeding heart of the matter.

The very mediocrity of their verdict cum diagnosis has a hypnotic hold. There is a tremendous copyrighted authority about it. But why degrade herself by calling it mediocre? Because the moment demands such a counter-verdict, that's why, and in preparation for what's to come, will accept no substitutes. Because whatever it is that's exerting the hold transfixes her—like the surly, cranky obesity of that checkout girl who got her into this Invidicum mess in the first place (though why call it a mess even if *mess* sounds good on paper, since isn't she beginning to feel a whole lot better than she's felt in a decade thanks to her booster shots?)—and whatever transfixes her needs to be taken down a notch or two—cut down to size. How would Balanchine himself have handled them, here in Costa Rica? That's the key question. Balanchine must deliver her from them straight away. Only Balanchine, by his example, can immunize her against them. Only he can get them to smelt themselves free of this reflexive bracketing of their betters—yes, betters. Only he can get them to immolate themselves on the altar—not of his own work but of his reverence for what he needs to believe are *his* betters, i.e., Stravinsky, Tchaikovsky and

Mozart—the three B's. Will he allow himself to be gristed—and through gristing catch on and come to agree that his work is too much of a plea for its own timeless import—even more to the point, that better than genius, so cowardly, so limiting, so wrong, is the debunking of genius as its own falsehood, as the naïvest form of self-misrepresentation, and the worst of all affronts to unfazeable cleverness? Or maybe he'll be the first to acknowledge there's nothing funnier than the conviction of one's own genius and nothing more refreshing—more inspiring—than Annie's and Lulu's refusal to be immolated on the altar of his professional ecstasy.

Shrewdly they abandon her before she can evict them from the stoop they've cleverly turned into their casting office. But, as usual, it's difficult not to miss them *for they hold the key to her past and to her future.* Shearer has no idea (all right, she does have *some* idea) where this conviction comes from— the wordflow got to it faster than she could. In any event, it does nothing to alleviate the asphyxiated craving for the tender gaze, free of the contempt born from Envy, of one true woman friend, whose decency she's ready to pridelessly take for love. The gaze that's eluded her or that she's eluded all her life.

But what about Herbert for the (unacceptable because supporting) role of the true woman friend? Well, *her* gaze says outright that if cursed with lily-whiteness, she'd know what to do—wouldn't waste it like Shearer. Though she's trying not to look at her the way black ladies instinctively look at big-mouth self-important ineffectual white ladies (are there any other kind), especially when those whites are sick or (as in this case) needy without knowing quite why or what they need, and the black ladies therefore have the whip hand over the white ladies' vulnerability—a far cry from the airs they give themselves when things are going their way which, for whites, is 99.99 percent of the time. What a waste of an organ—this overrated organ of whiteness. But she has to be fair and give Shearer some credit—that is, for electing not to flaunt, like so many white boss ladies do given half a chance, a fake self-abasement—for electing not to play the ineptitude card with regard to everyday (read trivial) matters, noblesse-obligingly leaving dull-witted dexterity in that domain to their eager-beaver black sidekicks, whose gently mocking compliance is to be understood *on no uncertain terms* as the obverse of affectionate awe.

Eden wonders whether it hasn't been a mistake to take a part-time job as a telemarketer when he should be busy planning his next move. After all, he's far from having exhausted his little legacy (which includes some of the proceeds from the lawsuit). He knows he's waiting for Manning to make the move for him. In a way he can't quite define. In any event, he can't antagonize her, she may be useful—on-label or off-, she could provide an alibi when the fateful night arrives.

However, as Amygdala has its own small employment division, he decided to avail himself of whatever it might offer in the way of leads which turns out to be precious little. Does its lackadaisical staff know from experience Enviers are pretty much unhireable (and the treated ones even more so)—that even as menials they're non grata? But for his purposes—his purposiveness without purpose—the precious little's just enough or maybe even way too much. In short, he lands the job! The company's headquarters and training hindquarters, located in a generic upscale high-rise on a generic upscale boulevard—less than a year ago it was a vacant lot—overlook the slopes overlooking the Hudson and the dockyards, whose picturesque dereliction is about to fall prey, like the lot, to gentrification's almighty scythe. Eden gets into the habit—upon arriving each morning—of saluting the doorman (who sports uniform and gloves at all times), but one morning, emboldened by the sweltering heat, he makes the mistake (as a brother-in-arms) of suggesting that the management must be prize jerks to insist on this overbraided full regalia. But what Eden proffers as a vote of confidence Ike takes to be an impugnment of his competence—worse, the competence of his bosses. In protest he does not reply, preferring to toy with a button. Which means that he and Eden, even after all they've been through together in the last few weeks, don't have a solidary leg to stand on. Whatever rage Ike doesn't know he's been storing up against the management is easily—audibly—directed at the schizoid who insists on pissing in the rosebushes across the street or at the pizza delivery man who forgets to wipe his feet. Eden is simply lending him much too much of his own—what's the fancy word from the *Envy Manual*?—*ressentiment*. Never again will he make the mistake of trying to turn underdog into Underdog.

The doorman's response undoes him—he calls in sick from beyond the rosebushes. So what if his supervisor learns that even before crossing the threshold he took it into his head to disappear?

In any case, he has a session with Straynge in about two hours. To ensure that his hatred is in good working order, he calls him, as he walks downtown by way of Tenth Avenue, every name in the book, though maybe the litanizing dissipates the hatred. Any contact with Straynge feels like a betrayal of his father since he's set impossibly high standards for hatred: he's supposed to feel it—and give some sign of it—every moment of his life, even if giving some sign of it in Straynge's presence may very well get in the way of the execution of his plans. His office is flooded with sunshine—the dark gods are clearly darkly jealous of the comfort of their own. Straynge asks about the effect of the medication on his sexual life. With just the sort of affectlessness that should have been lavished on Ike, Eden replies that he's between girlfriends . . . in deference to Invidicum. An exquisite touch which isn't lost on Straynge. Once he's said it and because of how he said it, the sexlessness begins to have a sexual flair all its own. "Well, find yourself a girlfriend and *be with her* (euphemism? archaism?). In fact it'll be good for the treatment."

The tension between fucking as the tweaking of a dirty little taboo (which is what Eden understands it to be) and fucking as a manly duty, a stance so ethical it becomes virile or vice versa (which is how Straynge seems to perceive it), is new to Eden and interesting enough to be arousing. He's panting for more of Straynge's officialization of his sexual life—his insistence that he hurry up and have one. To his horror, he's finding that he likes to be near Straynge, even if a moment with no hatred is like the missing of a heartbeat, which could be fatal. Because being near Straynge means being much nearer to his sexuality than his father ever allowed him to be.

Bill Cook enters, as if on cue, and Straynge, all crow's feet, goes tense and abstracted, also as if on cue. He asks why Narr of all people—a meatball if ever there was one—has been recommended over him for the post of consultant on the Invidicum special to be aired (if all goes according to plan) on HBO early next year. Straynge assures him, a wee bit irrelevantly, the other candidates are even soggier. They *almost* come to blows. Fortunately, it stops at *almost* since Eden is having a hard time imagining what actually coming to blows would look like in their case. They've completely forgotten about him— Subject One to his fans (*who is speaking?*). Which is downright cruel—schematically, didactically, heuristically so—which means that it's not cruel after all, just cruel-only-to-be-kind—the best kind of cruel. Yet to Eden, everything going on seems premeditated. Maybe it is Straynge the Innovator's intention (*but who's putting this idea in Eden's head without his express permission? the Master? the Master's boss?*) to cover exploratorily, over several sessions and for Eden's exclusive benefit (fact is, he's taken a shine to the boy), the gamut of life events most likely to induce Envy—with a little help from headliner Cook (who from what he's just gone on to say about the content of all of cable TV, not just HBO, appears to be quite an authority on how to turn any subject, however inappropriate even for mature audiences, into eminently marketable cliffhanging family fun)—so as to inoculate him in vitro against such events in vivo.

Remembering Eden, Straynge, ever the professional, now asks if Invidicum, at its present dosage, is in any way affecting his work. Good question, Eden thinks. How *is* it affecting his plans for Straynge's future? He answers even if the question has been barked out ungraciously as at some prompter's command, or in accordance with some outworn protocol (though that may be part of the in vitro shenanigans). Even if it's a question he can never begin to answer to Straynge's satisfaction. Even if the honeymoon's over, at least for today. "There isn't much work to speak of. You see, I work part-time." "Only part-time?" Cook looks down his nose at this unprepossessing suitor with the gall to be asking for his only daughter's hand. But this snootiness may be homeopathic as well—exhibited to immunize him against the Envy of others (after all, he's the quintessential good-looking young man from the provinces with plenty on the ball) or better yet or more to the point or both, against his own tendency to envy those brazen enough to mask their Envy with contempt.

Eden's not done and he sees no reason why he shouldn't continue—he's got to tell somebody, after all—and who better than Straynge, since he won't have time to do anything with the dank, dirty secret on the tip of Eden's tongue (no, not *that* dirty secret), except take it with him to the grave. And as for Cook, well, he'll deal with him later, when Straynge is out of the way. (*By the way, is he here at Manning's behest and if so, is showing highminded revulsion at Narr's preferment a mere ploy to keep his spy status under wraps?*) So he describes how, the day before yesterday,[5] having been requested—ordered—

---

[5]But before he can jump into this tall tale he'd like to delete *when Straynge is out of the way* since it's the kind of expository phrase that does a disservice to his dedica-

by the boss, the telemarketing king of Riverside Boulevard, to put his third wife's white mink in cold storage at the Thrift Thrift Horatio Thrift Shop on West Seventy-Eighth and Amsterdam, he did only what any self-respecting flunkey would do when faced with such a challenge: he pissed on the article in question en route. Never mind where. Straynge wonders if Eden is, by any chance, fishing for pity or shock or, worse—Envy? "No!" he shoots back. He struggles to explain what's really going on—or what Straynge thinks should be going on—but fails to get to the heart of the matter to anybody's satisfaction. Awed, in spite of himself, by the man's Mad Ave savvy, he appeals to Cook, who has no trouble explaining that in fact he feels terribly *unworthy*—and the feeling of unworthiness started as far back as Amsterdam and West Seventy-Fourth—of having had such an anecdotal nugget—an incident that plays so well as an anecdote—dumped into his lap *unearned*, since no matter how hard he tries he can't, thanks to the disbenefit of hindsight, revive the humiliation with which he's paid for it many times over. According to the infotainer, he's having big trouble believing he was entitled to turn that humiliation into a triumph of high comedy, made to order for this session—or an Upper East Side cocktail party.

But it's Straynge who—intervening, as if on cue—steals the show. Trials are all about cueings, Eden decides. The Invidicum trial, Straynge explains, will make everybody aware that life reduces in the end to what some opportunistic egghead centuries ago referred to as the incessant transformation of confused perceptions—*petites perceptions*—semi-sufferings (like those associated with dragging the mink to the Thrift)—into *speakable* distinct *apperceptions*. Eden looks blank. Straynge, not missing a trick, says he understands his blankness only too well: has seen it in operation many times before—in many different trials. It's base calculation masquerading as obtuseness. (Is Straynge by any chance alluding to his father without necessarily knowing that standing—sitting—before him is none other than the son of that father? Eden wonders.) And there are very few drugs that, like Invidicum, can accelerate such transformations. So Eden has come to the right place. As Straynge sees it, walking up Amsterdam Eden finds—and loses—himself besieged by perceptions of what is happening, both inside himself and without. But insofar as he is so much stung by humiliation he can't perceive himself perceiving, i.e., *ap*perceiving, so as to be able to put into words *what* he's perceiving, however confusedly (which in this case encompasses, inter alia, the mink coat; and the Thrift Thrift Horatio Thrift Shop, inside and out; and the glances of

---

tion—his obsession—his vocation of murderer. Inasmuch as whether alive or dead or in-between Straynge was, is and always will be *too much with him late and soon* there's no way for Eden to distinguish—to plausibly *think the distinction*—between Straynge in the way and Straynge out of the way. So he feels, without necessarily knowing he feels, that the Invidicum—or what about Manning?—or that Master guy?—or maybe Straynge himself—is shamelessly sacrificing Eden's flame (that which, within him, is so all-consuming as to be rightfully unspeakable and unutterable) on the altar of some cliffhanging gimmick.

passersby, at once amused and horrified; and Amsterdam Avenue; and best of all, the humiliation itself, since what would life be without its blandishments?). It's all a blur. That is, he doesn't feel entitled to put his perceptions into words and thereby preside at the birth of an anecdotal nugget, to be polished up and retailed at some festive occasion and parlayed into vocational advancement. (According to the egghead [for he lives on within us all] such confused perception is akin to that which we have of the ocean's roar as the whisper of each individual wave all mixed up with the whisper of every other. All remains confused until we give ourselves the right to put our full weight behind the apperception of that roar.) But after a certain point Eden's confused perception of each of *his* waves is transformed, compliments of their garbled interpenetration, into the distinct apperception—hence speakable and in a language he never knew he could deploy—of nothing less than an oceanic roar. But he's still not where he should be and it's only through Cook's timely intervention (thanks, Bill) that he's been able at last to enjoy the fruits of his humiliation. And so his dosage will have to be adjusted accordingly. And thereby hangs a tale.

Before Eden leaves, the three of them agree that he needs to streamline his ability to make humiliation *pay*.

When he gets out, he feels too . . . humiliated and at the same time too exultant to pay a visit to Twenty-Fourth Street, even if she's just left a message. Since he told her yesterday (or was it the day before?) that he's more and more desperate, she decided to cancel an appointment with one of her most dependable (and generous) johns simply to fit him in. Instead he goes straight home and somehow musters the courage to sit out, bared arms folded defiantly, on the smelly stoop. He's even too tired to walk the few blocks between here and sunset over the Verrazano. Furthermore, it reminds him too much of the Golden Gate, which he may never see again. Just as his self-consciousness is wearing off he hears the ringing of a phone that could be his. So he wolfs down two and (when the spirit moves him) three or four steps at a gulp and by some miracle grabs the receiver before the greeting in the voice he hates to hear has begun.

Irena Manning's secretary, of all people. He didn't even know Manning had a secretary. Although, as his mother used to say—though come to think of it, she said so only once (when) she was highflyingly half-drunk—*Everybody has a secretary*. Which was yet another way—one of billions—for Mom to trash his old man (for wasn't she implying that it was only a jackass like him who wouldn't have a secretary—worse, wouldn't know that everybody, even the lowliest men's-room attendant, had one—worst, would refuse to accept the fact that a secretary isn't some sort of counterrevolutionary status symbol but a stark necessity, like a pack of matches above the crapper?)—in other words, where secretaries are concerned (and, now that you mention it, not just secretaries), his father was, and he (by divine right of genome) is, a jackass, not because he isn't worthy of one but because he has no idea he *is* worthy. But how liberating it is to come up with an aphorism, whatever that is, like *Everybody has a secretary* and to suture the wound of that aphorism's inapplicability by inflicting it not just on its native context but on the whole wide world—come to think of it, more than a bit like the hero of that *Alfred Hitchcock Presents* episode (a MeTV rerun) when he proclaims: "A sliver of glass is a man's best friend." (Is this the Invidicum perceiving—no, perceiving the perceiving—i.e. apperceiving—for him?) "Dr. Manning asked me to tell you she knows what went on today between you and Dr. Straynge and Mr. Cook and that she's sorry and wants to schedule an emergency appointment for tomorrow at nine-thirty, if it suits you." "Sorry, I have to be at work at nine—sharp. My schedule's on the information card I left at the front desk a few weeks back with that snotty clerk." "Well, how about two, then?" "Perfect," Eden retorts over-graciously, in other words, wickedly, to the fuckable voice.

He sticks his head out the window. The street which during his all-too-brief apprenticeship to stoop life was more or less deserted is now a hippodrome where sullen-looking guys (but no better looking than he) are self-importantly promenading their sullen boobozoic-era blondes, knockouts every one, who clearly hang not only on their arm but on their every grunted utterance—the moodier the better. Where is his blonde? His head swims, he's Envy-bingeing, making mincemeat of Manning's assessment, which may have been a put-on. But he doesn't have Envy disease—he's a tourist, remember, in the land of the damned—an amateur researcher, an impostor, an assassin.

When Irena Manning gets off the phone (she's listened in on her secretary's call), Bill Cook, who is massaging her temples and beyond, asks how she became so damn interested in a loser like Eden in the first place. On his preliminary application, if Cook remembers correctly, he indicated having spent over a year loading fish lard and sulfur onto freight cars in Stockton, California, while living in a trailer with his bulldog, White Fang. Taking a forbearingly deep breath she explains, as to a child too precocious for its own good, that the usual barrage of pretrial tests revealed in Eden's case a microlesion on his orbitofrontal cortex, an asymmetry between the right and left hippocampi, and significantly low levels of serotonin, all of which are correlated with (as he should know better than anybody)— He does know (though why should it be better than anybody?). "Violent behavior," he replies. "It gets better." When she stashed him in the MRI machine and, to obtain a psychological profile, flashed overhead the usual array of photographs, there was off-the-charts activity in insula and amygdala (signaling overwhelming disgust and hate and anxiety) but in response only to Straynge. "So why didn't you eliminate him?" Irena either has not heard or is unheeding. She explains that it took just a little research by a few eager-beaver interns to determine that he's the son of Straynge's most famous patient, a much-decorated Korean War veteran done in, San Diego style, by the doc's murderous incompetence, with a little help from his flunkeys.

Cook still looks blank but she doesn't mind in the least: he's so much prettier that way—and so much more mysterious, since the unhurried blankness coyly masks his quick intelligence. Only she prefers to perceive him as the very opposite of coy. He makes her think instead of none other than Valentin de Boulogne's *Samson* (stuck in Cleveland of all places), who, to misparaphrase Michael Fried, bears the burden of not-quite-consciousness of his bodily being with a quizzical yearning that presses the refresh button (long overdue) on the term *secondary sexual characteristic*. (The only thing she knows about Cleveland is that her artsy-fartsy colleague Ishmael Drybock lived on, of all places, Fairchild Road—the end of the world he called it—while in med school there.) She notes that the combination of shapely Adam's apple defined by two o'clock shadow, the barely visible tip of a T-shirt of dark brown chest hair, and expertly shaved head (worthy of the beefy bodyguard of some A+-list celebrity) deserves to be tiarified with a pair of the most cutting-edge aviator sunglasses. But she must keep her mind on her work—their work. So she explains to her resident not-so-dumb blond that Eden believes he's been put on earth to kill Straynge. And killing Straynge will feed the need to go on killing, for reasons to be explained directly below. One murder to obliterate another: the motto of the careerist psychopath. Adding insult to injury, there is in fact a quasi-lover—what used to be called a call girl, if you must know—who, for a by no means nominal fee, has disclosed certain of his . . . tendencies, involving much more than just rococo variations on the unoriginal theme of unsafe sex. Killing Straynge will be an audition, a warm-up, a dress rehearsal, for killing—Tom Post. A multinational somewhere out there would like nothing better than to set up a subsidiary with Invidicum (but not in its incarnation—more like its incarceration—as an Envy drug) to be its sole asset—and is willing to pay (and to vastly overpay Irena, as broker) for the privilege. Only Post has so far refused, on humanitarian principles. Cook looks a thousand and one questions, all of them unanswerable, all of them reducible to *Why?* "Because the multinational wants to sell it as a killing drug. All that's required is a bit of Tweaking of the Basic Structure. But only Post knows how and what to tweak. The tweaked version is being generated in bulk as we speak somewhere on the West Coast—where else? Unfortunately, I have no further details at present." "As if you would divulge them in any case. So you were only pretending you didn't know what off-label use Invidicum's doomed for. You've been making a fool of me. I'm sick of your stunts." She ignores his tantrum. "I didn't know you had this flair for hysteria, Samson." Then, without missing a beat. "In case you weren't aware and it's obvious you weren't, my goal for every drug I've worked with has been to change the course of psychopharmacological history by replacing 'FDA-approved' with 'off label' as the more-favored term in the dyad constituted by these terms, which must have broad repercussions not just for our discipline" (she hates the prim pomposity of *discipline*) "but for others as far away—but, in the last analysis, not all that far—as pop philosophy and pseudolinguistics. I've failed up to now but this time, with Invidicum—" Her voice trailed off, as she was aware it should. "And who are you to have a *goal for every drug*?" He doesn't expect an answer. His rage at the thought of all the self-inflation that answer must let loose terrifies him.

So he sticks to the issue. "And who better than Eden—Eden as you portray him, that is—to try it out on. Right?" His tone informs her he's resisting the idea, has a soft spot for Eden. All well and good, since she needs to slow down the unstoppable inventiveness of her Theory of Eden through assailment by the unwelcome echoes of its own tentativeness and who better to nurture those echoes than an MBA jock, a sports bar stud, a . . . Republican, like

Cook. Making heavy weather of ignoring the fact that he's taking tomograms of her tits, she tells him what she perceives to be The Truth, namely, that Eden is one big wound (of avengement of the father he hates) which he lacerates unceasingly. Since for the likes of Eden the only way out of the wound is the way back in. The only suture, further scarification. And as Straynge himself has noted (since they've had many a brown bag powwow—a father-daughter/Rigoletto-Gilda sort of thing—on the subject of Eden and Laceration, interest in which is sure to beget an Ivy League cottage industry) even if Eden manages to kid himself into thinking he's master of the wound he'll find out soon enough that self-laceration—as his seeing-eye dog—his prophet—his sorcerer's apprentice—is always way ahead of him. He has to be forever inside the wound, to be *all wound* 24/7, so as not to feel that but for this minor detail he'd be intact and functioning at highest capacity within society. What luck to be so blissfully encysted as to be unable to take the bait of thinking that but for this mere contingency, to wit, the wound—which it just so happens is nothing less than the poor slob's very essence—everything would be falling into place. "But won't he go berserk if somebody else knocks Straynge off?" Manning asks if the idiom "knock off" isn't a bit archaic. But she's tactful (after all, she doesn't want Cook to knock *her* off). It's only then she realizes posing a question in response to a question is her way of *stalling for time* (not archaic). For his question upset her. "But he'll still be accused of the crime. That counts for something, Bill, doesn't it?" On that note, they part.

When he arrives the next afternoon (after having pointedly ignored Ike both on his way in and on his way out), Eden finds that Irena Manning looks especially nervous hence especially radiant. Breaking with tradition (or inaugurating a new one?), she's serving up a good deal more cleavage, though lunchtime's long over. He likes the spray of freckles above her right breast. They put him at ease, as freckles always do. They speak his mother tongue. She doesn't feel comfortable talking to him in her office. They'd be better off in Washington Square Park but just to show who's boss he invents a preference for Madison Square. On a bench under a diseased elm and to the left of a beech (the city's second-oldest), with an elephantiasic double-trunk, Irena tells him she's heard through the grapevine (which in her experience never lies) that Straynge has tried to flay him alive. He is about to inform her that if there was any flaying done then it was perpetrated by Bill Cook but since she is so intent on making Straynge the heavy, out of curiosity he lets her have her way with him. She can't even begin to imagine the horror of having, after every session with that gargoyle, to frantically inventory the limbs lost, the vital and not-so-vital organs ground to a bloody pulp as forage for his fellow hounds. He feels he should be grateful for her concern, so why is he convinced it's she, not Straynge, who's the Gargoyle, the Grinder, faking orgasms of commiseration solely in order to saddle him with an abasing plight and goad him into making that plight his war cry? Or maybe she's a genuine sweetie-pie and he's just a lowbrow to end all lowbrows, proof being his tone-deafness to what is certainly the most poignant rendition of the Empathy Sonata of the last fifty years (*who is doing the thinking for Eden? the Master? Invidicum as the generator of an eloquence that isn't afraid of taking on rare birds like empathy*

167

sonatas?).

Against the mauvish backdrop of beech leaves, he is strikingly if unconventionally handsome—like all highly unstable losers at the peak of their non-achievement. That his features are *all wrong* is initially a relief, since she doesn't intend to fall in love with him. Thing is, the defects, whichever way she inventories them, do nothing to weaken his impact. She has to face facts she's already faced dozens of times: unconscious defiance of the canons of beauty is the only aphrodisiac to which she's not allergic. She knows him better than he knows himself because she knows herself better in him than anywhere else: He'll never be evicted from childhood's house of shame and despair for there's no other house in which somebody like Eden can live. Despair is his country and shame is his home town (she apologizes to all her fans for this facile nouns-and-bolts insistence on the unspeakable). She's learned there's a younger brother somewhere up in the Pacific Northwest, a hotshot corporate lawyer who upgraded his status as family favorite by remaining completely unreachable all through the VA ordeal. Eden should be relieved, then, that the abusive father he's so intent on avenging is dead. At least if he's doomed to go on failing, he can proceed at his own pace without somehow feeling he's failing to fail fast enough to satisfy that chops-licking old fart.

She's already feeling a little like a biographer—she *is* a biographer—she'll be the best kind of biographer because she knows that when push comes to shove which it always does, albeit either premature- or belatedly, she won't be bothered by what is erroneously deemed the bane of her tribe—a glaring lack or unreliability of documentation. In fact, she's already rejoicing that that thumb-twiddling old bureaucrat, Life, won't renege on its duty to be the sloppiest of archivists. For by being so sloppy, Life's carving out a future for her. Truth be told, she's always wanted and still wants to be a writer, like that Herbert woman. How delectable to swing high in a hammock of loose ends. For loose ends breed a proliferation of warring interpretations (e.g., is the man on the opposite bench looking at his watch or at the hairs on his wrist and is his neighbor talking into his cellphone or shaving his gristly square jaw?) and warring interpretations—the more the better—breed text and text (at least as she'll be cranking it out) will yield . . . atonement for her and apotheosis for him. She'll atone for making Eden her fall guy by reversing the sign of his every mishap, his every failure—turning a loser's defects into a genuine folk hero's sacrosanct stigmata. To be seen at all, Eden first needs to be grasped as undecidable. To see him as he was meant to be seen entails forever backtracking, forever revising a previous impression (e.g., what she took to be his watch is in fact the sunny hairs on his slender wrist and what she takes to be the sunny hairs is in fact his cellphone). For the Edens of the world, the incessant revising is the seeing. Emerging from what has turned out to be not a trance per se but *something* of a trance, Irena is surprised to see her subject sitting beside her. Because it's much colder out of the sun than she would have thought possible in windless mid-July, she regrets not taking a sweater. Though she makes a practice—more, a point of honor—of avoiding regret, well aware of the irreversible damage inflicted on neurons along the ventral striatum-anterior cingulate cortex axis.

She says: "After the way he's treated you, I'm afraid for you—I'm afraid of what you may do in . . . retaliation." Eden looks like he wants to protest but doesn't know how. How much does she know? he wonders. How much does *he* know—about her? she wonders. She's afraid of his doing something rash. When the time is ripe for rashness, it must be according to her specifications. "Yes, I know what you're going to say but there's no need. Straynge, you see, has already spoken to me at length about what goes on during your sessions, although he's completely unaware of the real gist inside his gist."

He wants to go, so Irena lets him. Just as well: in an hour she has to see Post, who hates tardiness in his underlings, especially females, and particularly the attractive ones. She hopes, however, he's not going to re-air his humanitarian concerns. One of the interns will be tailing Eden back to his apartment or to Riverside Boulevard or to wherever he ends up going to let off steam. Knowing that, whatever the destination, the very first order of business on getting there will be to shake his fists at that tired old call girl Life, she is sorry to have to treat him as a means to an end.

CHAPTER EIGHT

Invidicum is proving ineffective against the disease that dares speak neither its name—nor Rhys's. And her symptoms of Envy—whose subclinical days are officially over—are increasing, especially during motel-room fucking. What else can she call it: *sexual activity*? (too bland), *sex*? (too bluntly characterless), *lovemaking*? (too self-help suburban). Narr's charm is fast wearing thin or has already worn off completely, making him, oddly enough, easier to tolerate. She envies her sister for being free of him in any case but most of all she envies women who seem to have been nurtured by that rarest of rarae aves: a good mother. Now that she's put her hatred of Caro on hold, she's coming to grips with the most painful discovery of her life (the medication focuses that grip as if she's all inner eyeball and the ciliary the most powerful muscle in her body)—that her own mother, a literally raving beauty whose sole creative act is destruction, started hating her long before she was born.

The discovery is no less painful—and no less of a discovery—for having been made thousands of times before, since each time she manages to make her discovery in a slightly different way. The implications of any one discovery are always slightly different from, and to her delight sometimes starkly contradicted by, the implications of all the others and on the rarest occasions the implications of a single discovery manage to contradict each other and so wildly that she no longer knows where and (more importantly) who she is, ending up having undergone a regeneration like no other, compliments of the syncope. Why, it's positively awe-inspiring—I mean the way a girl like Jean, a hale and hearty all-American sort of girl, manages to come at mother-hatred from a new angle every time. Or rather, the way a Girl like Life manages to produce such an illusion. And maybe, just maybe—*Pay attention! this is your narrator speaking!*—with a little prodding from Invidicum (rumor has it that the big *I* can lay the groundwork for a new kind of perceiving) she'll become capable of realizing (*a*) that Life's artistry has lots and lots to do with frugality—the Humean *great frugality* (so Cantor isn't the only fan of the *Dialogues Concerning Natural Religion*)—i.e., sticking with a given crisis until it has been refracted through every conceivable context and subtext—instead of manhandling one crisis after another in the name of carnivalesque sweep and (*b*) that Life never mistakes distillation for impoverishment and routinely refuses to invite (for the sake of a phantom enrichment) incompatible elements into any work in progress even if the snub incurs sabotage. The more sabotage, the better, snickers Life—since sabotage, if you must know, is infinitely more fertile than distillation would ever want to be.

In too much pain to remain in the vicinity of Amygdala (she's just had her eighth session with Straynge), she decides to take the subway up to Columbia (1 Train). The campus's sparse greenery is soothing (as a dropout she has certain rights of passage). All these pretty young things, even—especially—the ones who aren't the least bit pretty, are entitled to radiate pride—and their tattooed midriffs second the motion. And, what's more, they know their entitlement requires no frantic adducement of justifications which is, particularly under such a limitless midsummer sky, further proof of entitlement to be radiantly—insanely—proud. Can people tell that in her own case, however, the timidest manifestation of a craving to exist is undergone, still, as a vicious provocation, to which the only appropriate response, from the mother who makes it a point to be everywhere and nowhere, everyone and no one, is outrage? She finds herself sitting opposite Mathematics Hall.

Fact is, she'd be better off dead—as long, that is, as the long-overdue deadness does not become an unseemly lien on the lives of the living (she has a few beloveds among them), who have far better things to do than shed crocodile tears for the worst sort of freak—a defiantly dead one. But somehow she's managed not to accede to the ultimate invisibility.

Her cellphone emits its generic ting-a-ling—which some very charitable folk have mistaken for the first few notes of the introduction to Gilda's "Tutte le feste al tempio"—imperfectly synchronized with the twitter of some bird above her head. With time they'll get it right though she won't be around to applaud. She calls a lot now that she knows her daughter is participating in a drug trial. Doesn't matter what Jean's being treated for. What *does* matter is her certain access to insider information about drugs that may very well be capable of ministering to her mother's plight, which in fact comprises several plights. Trouble is, when Jean asks questions—ostensibly the right questions, questions commensurate with the multi-plight's ever increasing gravity—she's never allowed to get it quite right. Which actually works out quite well since The Mother (Jean tends to view humanity as a spectrum—a continuum— of archetypes—of archetypal responses to crises of insult and injury, real or imagined—more real if imagined)[6] can then modulate her self-pity into the off key of contempt, the only conceivable basis for connectedness. She has always demanded Jean's unwavering belief in a plight of unsurpassable excruciation—only it is this very belief which, once induced, becomes the true progenitor of that plight by contriving through sheer poison-oracle ill will to squeeze the very life out of its nonexistence. Her daughter is always torturing the old girl by refusing to grasp the gravity of a plight immune to abatement (the very fact of asking after it—naming it—constitutes an abatement) AND cold-bloodedly tarring and feathering that plight with far too much gravity. Jean tells herself, as she's told herself, to little purpose, many times before, that the mother's contempt is just a *prehensile* device, like an aardvark's snout, allowing her to hold on to the beauty of the image of her daughter's unflagging concern. The job of the contempt is simply to protect her from the far more pernicious effects of her mother's Envy—to ensure that she—its holy-fool target through no fault of her own—doesn't just survive the fit or whatever it is that Envy has when it goes into highest gear but comes out smelling like the rose she's always been and always will be for Mother Rhys, even if she'd be the last one to admit it—or be aware of it. Old-master contempt, as her mother practices it, she explains kindly—too kindly not to be putting herself on—is

---

[6]See Adriana M. Mujal and Matthew F. Krummel, "Immunity as a continuum of archetypes," *Science*, vol. 364, No. 6435 (5 April 2019), pp. 28–29.

a lifeline—the only lifeline of an old hag—there, the cat-o'-nine-tails is out of the bag—to her more fortunate fellow creatures. It enables her to share in their good fortune—the good fortune of feeling at home in the world. With only a bit of disingenuousness, she manages to put a better face on her mother's contempt.

She can think of no place better suited than here to listening as self-protectively as possible to the contemptuous one when, as now, she's on the rampage. The apologia of a minute before no longer holds water. Her mother has just uttered her signature prefatory sigh and the apologia proves powerless against it. Already the blood of distrust is boiling in her daughter's veins—the anticipation of being toyed with and of not knowing how much of the toying is a calculated assault on her credulity. She knows she isn't credulous through stupidity, though Caro and her other siblings (does she have other siblings?—for a split second she's forgotten) certainly think so. On some level impervious to the stupidity that guilt breeds she always knew she knows the score. To wit, that the mother's self-accredited diagnoses of the-way-things-are-but-shouldn't-be (without and within) have to be, like the diagnoses of her masters, Karl Marx and Sigmund Freud, aggressively distrusted. Not just because she is a hypochondriac, this being the least interesting reason hence the least valid because it doesn't do away with her in the domain where the mother operates best: language.

She has to be aggressively distrusted because she is one of those street-corner clinicians who just happen to be (like her two illustrious precursors) a poet. That is to say, somebody who hopes that whatever she has to say will be led astray by the words—the wordflow—deployed to say it. That is to say, somebody who counts on the words to perpetrate unspeakably unnatural acts against each other so that there can be no making the result correspond to the something out there or in here that has been the sole reason for having any truck with words in the first place. Even if, as an overaccredited social scientist, she starts out with the best of investigative intentions, the fact remains that once the fireball of words gets rolling she can't resist being led astray—being led where the molten flow takes her—even if it's far from the subject at hand—a cancer, say, of unknown origin, which is one of her pet afflictions. Being led astray is after all the whole point—otherwise, why bother? She becomes an action painter. And the constructions she—or rather the words—come up with dare-defy the real world within or without to come up with events or entities or admixtures of the two into or onto which they can be mapped. Such ingenuity—or rather the ingenuity of the words working through her—keeps her—and *her kind* in tandem—from dying out. For as long as any given thought goes on wordflowing, goes on tidal-waving, goes on living, she, too, lives. Just because a sentence dies doesn't mean she has to die along with it. Not that it isn't hard for the most seasoned fantasists to conceive that someone like her, a mere nobody, an ex-farmgirl to the core, can stump the experts by virtue of excelling in the practice of casuistry as endless self-qualification (what dockworkers refer to in their lighter moments as *epanorthosis* and *epergesis*). They forget when it's a matter of life and death, anybody can excel at anything.

As far as Jean can see, and she can see pretty far when she puts her mind to it, each time her mother opens her mouth the sole intention is to capture something out there happening deep within her own body—to build a case for being at death's door thanks to the disease du jour. But there is no way to diagnosis her disease except with words and once they start getting drunk on their own momentum they have a bad habit of forgetting all about what they're supposed to be capturing with textbook sobriety—they have an unlawful irrepressibility of their own and it is precisely this that her mother is a pastmaster at fomenting even if she pretends to stand back aghast at what is being fomented in defiance of her instructions. She professes to be living for the moment when the words, having put their heads coolly together (*Maestro: this time around, please, no twists and turns of wordflow*), produce a coherent diagnosis with all the symptomal trimmings. But words in cohoots are by their very nature so powerful that they have no trouble producing not just a diagnosis *but the disease itself*, from which, once it threatens to exist all throughout her body as a bona fide clinical entity, she has no intention of suffering—from which, for all her bellyaching, she knows as well as the next guy she isn't suffering—can't be suffering. Even if it seems inconceivable—almost insulting (more than anything, she hates being snubbed)—that such a disease—any disease once named—should see fit to bypass her (and thereby detract from her reality) without so much as a fare-thee-well. So she has no choice but to allow convulsive—paroxysmic—wordflow to kick in and save the day. How? By depicting a disease with symptoms too intricate and incompossible, *as depicted*, to be mappable onto some flesh-and-blood process unfolding out there, i.e., deep inside the world of her body.

She's a certified accredited Kabbalist, like her acupunturist, Dr. H.J.D. Azulai, and in accordance with his mystical technique, when she utters the words of her personal Torah, ostensibly to depict her disease and to make everybody guilty over the fact that she's contracted it, or rather, that it's contracted her—when she utters her words in the name of accuracy so she can be helped—what in fact issues from the depiction—the combination of the words—the wordflow—are potencies and lights, in other words, medicinal poisons and poisonous medicines—in a word, pharmakons, whose sole purpose is to cure her of depiction, to spare her from naming her disease since by naming it she brings it into being and gets afflicted by it and ultimately dies of it. Until the next seismic upsurge.

Rhys has heard the story of her diseases too many times before—every time the mother calls. But compliments of the violence inflicted by the well-nigh Kleistian twists and turns of her wordflow on that story, another story— the one she refuses to tell—is always on the verge of getting itself told instead. A story with its own nonce-syntax—a story owned by that syntax, a syntax of the heart's rot. A story too violent to tell *because it's nothing but the violence of its own refusal to be told* (*or is this last aperçu a case of the Master's making like Jake the Derider and succeeding not quite brilliantly?*). Since to tell it would be to annihilate the world (or so Mother Rhys—like any other self-respecting Azande—shudders to think). So instead of getting the story of her mother's violence, Jean must settle as always for second best, which is the violence inflicted on the story that's being told, i.e., the same old story. But thank heaven for the comeback of that comfy old term *story* since everywhere else you turn, everything else is, joylessly, dully, a *narrative*—worse, a *journey*—worse, a *healing*—worse, a *closure*—worst, a *narrative*.

Self-diagnosis is the mother's mother's-milk, her reason for being, her self-administered wonder drug, her pharmakon. But if language is the instrument of diagnosis it is also the instrument of escape from diagnosis which, once provided, or even suspected, immediately became—becomes—inadequate, an affront to the seriousness of the disease, AND AT THE SAME TIME, too adequate, i.e., too close to calling into being—for the tissue of language is coextensive with the tumor-friendly tissues of her body—the very disease she insists she suffers from as long as she knows she doesn't suffer from it in the least. Diagnosis is drug and poison. The minute it shows signs of acting effectively as a drug, drug became poison, a bad fit, the wrong color. So she has no choice but to be always one step ahead of the diagnosis of the moment in order to not so much clarify as supersede its verdict. This is her life's work. And with face still buried in the pillow of her phone, Rhys realizes that today's diagnosis has just changed. It's no longer a matter of the descending portion of her thoracic aorta but of the pars intermedia of her pituitary's anterior lobe. But she knows this new diagnosis is not so much a superseding as a warehousing of its predecessor in preparation for its own warehousing any second now. Out in the real world diagnoses might cancel each other out but here, on the level of language, diagnoses are additive and complementary. On this level and this level only, correction isn't annihilation but addition. For all the bellowing about calamities unfolding in her depths, Rhys's mother is ultimately all surface—surface and undersurface of the twists and turns of words. Will she become—is she—a diagnoses-hoarder like her mother? And if so, doesn't this mean she's hoarding the targets of those diagnoses—harboring a cancer of incompossiblities which is metastasizing throughout her body *as we speak*?

She is hesitant about discussing the trial in any shape or form. It would be madness to explain that she's the only proband who, unbeknownst to the authorities, is being given the drug for a disease other than Envy, though (remembering her performance on the podium) as it turns out, it is probably Envy that's eating her up alive. Her mother mentions that Dr. Azulai thinks she's suffering from nothing less than three syndromes: Meckel-Gruber, Bardet-Niedl and Lesch-Nyhan. How easily these names roll off her tongue. Rhys expresses a concern she doesn't feel. *Only this time, the entirely unexpected happens.* Her mother doesn't chew her out for a lack of conviction. Instead, with a cackle she warns her—commands her—not to worry. As if worry is her daughter's way of wishing her into the next world—and who knows? maybe it is. As if daughterly worry is—has always been—the mother's No. 1 affliction, its virulence proportionate to the worry's genuineness. The traffic up and down Broadway, not to mention all the between-classes chatter, makes it difficult to hear. But she's a quick learner where another's ill will is the teacher. Her mother is discovering (but why so late?) that she can torment her daughter far more by flaunting her indestructibility than by retailing her life-threatening symptoms. And without the slightest embarrassment that one stance starkly contradicts the other. Her mother recruits whatever half-truths or outright lies she needs to win the round of the moment, life being a jagged discontinuity of local lesions none of which are under an ethical obligation to contribute to a plausible Semmelweiss-respecting clinical picture.

Stunned by the efficacy of this tactic, Rhys is afraid she may be unable to make it back to her apartment, much less to Amygdala, though she takes some comfort from the fact that so many people are milling around unassailed by other people's ill will. At the same time how can she avoid feeling that the business of *Only this time, the entirely unexpected happens* (*she can't put her finger on it but it sounds, this out-of-tune tune, as if it were penned by what the members of the Amygdala tribe have gotten around to calling variously but always and only in a stage whisper* Some Body *or* Some Thing *or* The Some Body *or* Some Thing *or more to the point, the* Master) is mere hype, reflecting an untalented starlet's collusion with the wishes of some impatient indie filmmaker who's trying to convince all the paying customers out there in the dark that they've been privy, against all odds, to a mother-daughter conversation uniquely different from all the others, i.e., privy to nothing less than *the* conversation—the last straw, the one that has just managed to provide his—their—heroine with the impetus to change her life at long last? Come on, she hears him shouting from his director's chair (making a bullhorn of his self-infatuation), you can do it, baby!

Tired of flaunting her indestructibility—which Jean determines takes the form of a letter posted *through* her to the *entire world* (which wishes her but ill)—the mother decides to re-restrict herself to a single target. Lavishing on the daughter her acuity as a diagnostician, the mother calls her every name in the book. According to Azulai, her pathological failures have been a primary cause of her mother's ailments. Not only does she suffer from narcissistic personality and obsessive-compulsive disorders but she's also bipolar and a nymphomaniac of the old school. In addition, she's cheap and greedy (when was the last time she sent her mother a gift?) and thinks small and that's why she owns nothing—she rents, imagine, at her age. Should she counter that nowadays it's cheap and greedy—not slow and steady—who wins the rat race?

Recognizing him immediately as he emerges from Mathematics Hall, she's pleased it will take some time to be recognized back, since this gives her the opportunity to look him over. She remembers—or rather she *seems* to remember—somebody's referring to him in the Café Amygdale (the name of the canteen: she hasn't smart-assily made it up) as nothing less than a metamathematician (whatever that is) up at Columbia—in fact, he's the metamathematician's metamathematician. Inspired by his looming advance under the elms, she wastes no time getting on with the filming of her PBS Masterpiecemeal miniseries—a corrective to the plotless meta-mess concocted by her indie dictator (*Yes,* indie bellows to all the paraphrase-ravenous hack reviewers yapping at his rear end, a *plotless meta-mess and what of it?*). Place: Devonshire country house. Time: eve of the First World War. Anti-hero-of-sorts: Cantor. Isn't that the name? Probably homosexual by trade but that doesn't matter—or rather, it does and very much so, but only as fuel matters to the fire. You may remember that in our last episode, the heroine, an unhappily married and snootily titled goyess, or goyesca, has gotten to the point of inviting, only to then sniggeringly repulse, the advances of a handsome tycoon who by wearing his virility so imperturbably—so . . . *semitically*—on his sleeve gives it an almost moral lustre and whose tactless indifference to her bad manners only aggravates the lust beneath. But there's no getting on with the filming—no finding out here and now what happens next—until by certain unmistakable signs he proves he was born to play the part. But isn't being wrong for the part what actorliness is all about?

But without masturbation to induce cinematic-cum-literary labor there's no getting on with the show. If the plot is to thicken—if the goyess is to reveal what she really feels about the tycoon—then Rhys needs with fore- and middle fingers to scrape the bottom of her barrel and follow it up with an increasingly-less-tender encirclement of her clitoral bump. Self-stimulation generates images and, when she's lucky, even subtitles. But until she's well on the royal road to orgasm, the story remains virtual, latent, larvate, untellable— worse, the most intriguing parts of the anti-hero's body are foreclosed to her. Until she manages to masturbate her way out of a refractory ground state by depolarizing the membranes of her maidenhead beyond a point of no return and thereby triggering and propagating what for better or worse may be called the *creative impulse* (as dismal a term as the *artistic temperament*),[7] further developments at Devonshire are not in the cards. This, after all, is what masturbation is for—to serve as the big bay window on an interior world—a dormant—potential—world. Rhys must hurry home or she—now an indie director in her own right—will be late for filming. She avoids Cantor's glance which he obviously thinks is expertly probing—a veritable Straynge, Jr., this one—terrified he can read the four-letter images that are coming as fast and furious as her inner thighs can moisten. He sits down and introduces himself. What is she doing way up here? he asks. The phrase *way up here* puts her at her ease. But what's wrong with her—isn't he one of the audience members who stood up to ridicule what he called her tale of woe? Out here on such a balmy afternoon it's hard not to forgive all six feet of him.

He puts his impressively voluminous folders to one side and asks what she thinks of the trial so far. That he seems to experience attraction without desire is intriguing (he is not staring into the depths of her blouse but at its fine print). The sleeves of his flannel shirt are rolled up to the elbow: a statement, but of what—of how deftly golden hairs on the underside of his forearm can catch the sunlight if given half a chance? Should she seize on this as her cue to speak of the disease for which—or for which she thinks—she's really being treated? Of the syndromes from which her mother says she suffers? Of her mother's three syndromes (which, she realizes, have become hers as well)? But does *the disease for which—or for which she thinks—she's really being treated* matter any longer? Does it matter now that (compliments of her connections) she's been inducted under false pretenses, inasmuch as Envy has

---

[7]According to G.K. Chesterton, the artistic temperament is an affliction of amateurs.

clearly managed to carry the day? Spilling the beans (including the bit about cheap and greedy winning the rat race), she nevertheless stops short of revealing the name of *the disease for which—or for which she thinks* . . . He is not only unshocked but delighted—by her shock at his being un-. She's not alone, he tells her: they all think—every last one of them whether they admit it or not—that they're putting something over on the study—smuggling themselves in under cover of Envy in order to be treated for something else—something . . . orphaned—and what do they discover but that Envy is first, last and always the molten core of their plutonium core.

He understands perfectly what she's been through as far as diagnoses are concerned. For her information, he's been called every name in the book ("I mean the *DSM-5*"). Multiple diagnoses, all conflicting, are his trademark. In fact, he *came out* long ago about multiple diagnoses—long before he outed himself about his . . . well, she must know what he's referring to. Nodding absently, she's suddenly terrified her mother might see fit to call again at this, the very moment when (as her mother would say!) she's *pouring out her heart.* She mustn't get into the rut of hoping, however—on this he must insist—that all the diagnoses will turn out to be *mis*diagnoses. Easy to pooh-pooh labels but he for one is all for them and even more for those who traffic in them—well, maybe not *even more* but he's sure she gets what he means. Can't get enough of them, in fact—labels, that is. Why elude them?—on the contrary, wear them as a badge. She should be grateful she's no longer deprived. Doesn't she sometimes feel a hunger to be *simplified* by diagnoses so as to be able at last to get on with the bigger business? *Like filmmaking*, she thinks. Collude with the diagnoses (however ramshackle), accept them proudly, he warns, in what she realizes is a bass-baritone worthy of José van Dam . . . And thereby steal something from the identity thief. He remembers when it first came upon him that he suffered from . . . a narcissistic personality disorder—found it almost impossible to love, among other things. It was in fleeing, after a terrible quarrel, from Berry Sundae (thankfully, she doesn't ask the eternal question but doesn't he resent the not asking just a wee bit?), who, usually sparing, accused him of suffering messily from a host of psychiatric disorders. But why now? he remembers wondering, walking in Riverside Park above the Marina amid the dead plane leaves of unflatteringly autumnish midsummer. Or rather, why was he so blind before? Maybe he simply wasn't ready before, she suggests, uncertain how he'll take the suggestion and a bit excited by the uncertainty—excited by proximity to somebody who could make her feel anxious about her uncertainty. He counters that his past selves, with which he still kept up cordial relations, were cheated of their rightful due, by this interloping Hudson River-loving upstart present self—future self of those cheated selves past—which had done nothing to earn the diagnosis—hadn't been around long enough to earn it—but was granted this rude awakening anyway solely on the basis of his Upper West Side credentials.

And he's having more and more of them. Fake anagnoreses, that's what they are, devised by some . . . Master for his clientele. Does she feel it, too—that there's a Master lurking in the grounds of the Institute (though there's not much in the way of grounds down there in Greenwich Village)—saddling them with a . . . language they've never spoken? Yet where there's so much idiopathic eloquence ("See what I mean?—I could never have concocted such a phrase two months ago."), there has to be insight. (It suddenly comes [back] to him as he undergoes the irk of an eloquence new to him—a remark by the administrator of the first dose [or was it an alert pinned to the wall?]: *Achtung: You may experience nausea, alopecia and/or [worst of all] eloquence.* [By the way, he's all for eloquence as long as everybody's eloquence isn't the same standard-issue claptrap.]) As simple as that—though by no means a popular thesis, especially among the star guerrillas of academia—to whom such eloquence—in any shape or form—is anathema, stinking too much of the ivory tower whose barricades they are forever storming and in which they pretend not to reside rent-free. It's just that he's used (nothing will cure him of that) to knowing and seeing everything all at once and from the beginning—like Dostoevsky's illuminati according to Bakhtin. He's waiting for her reaction. Is she seduced by his incoherence? Evolution is for suckers—he for one doesn't have time for *personal growth.* And what he doesn't know all at once—what he must incubate—he doesn't need to know. He should be all selves at once all the time. He refuses to believe in a future self shaped by hard knocks. He doesn't want to wait for the future He doesn't want to be cheated by the future of what should be his, right now and all along.

But maybe, she suggests, he sometimes hides from himself what he already knows and sees— like the narcissistic personality disorder camping out in the dead leaves—until the occasion for self-revelation is propitious. She's not sure how he'll take this. She keeps confusing him with her tycoon— the noble Semite—the modern-day Samson on whom, as script girl, she's conferred a violent temper—violent but ultimately congenial—when sufficiently provoked by lust.

She may be right but in any case this is a minor gripe. So many diagnoses, no matter how they get themselves *out* there, are not an embarrassment but on the contrary an embarrassment of riches. Thanks to which everything foul is *named* and thereby smelted away, leaving the core of the self intact—alone with itself at last. Diseases are rank contingencies, mere obstructions on the way to essence. In fact, she should post that witticism over her bed—or failing that, her night table. Contrary to popular belief there's a lot left over after diagnosis. There's life after diagnosis. With enough diagnoses taking their toll, the poor slob ends up with the delusion of "genius" as an artifact. And with so many ailments, disorders, syndromes, diseases under his belt, is it any wonder the victim develops a selective amnesia? Which is all to the good: since amnesia then becomes not just one more affliction but, as the byproduct of afflictions, a bonus—an affliction of the second degree—a first derivative of disorder, if you like—one more layer to be peeled away. And when that's *swept* away, the essence in question is even more pellucid (decked out, like the Kabbalists' Torah, as a young maiden). (Does he mention the Torah because he somehow knows her mother's Rasputin is a guy by the name of H[erschel] J[udah] D[avid] Azulai? Of course not, this is conspiratorial thinking and if she doesn't watch out she'll end up just like this Rasputin's Empress.) The more backbreaking the work of sweeping away, the more valid—valuable—

vital—the residue, i.e., essence. It's the more the merrier, where diseases and diagnoses are concerned. Rhys doesn't get it or, in her best maidenly manner, pretends not to but then she remembers he's a man who eats, breathes and sleeps metamath, so how *can* she get it. But whatever she fails to get notwithstanding, *she mustn't make the fatal mistake of trading substance (disease) for shadow (essence), thereby perpetrating a textbook faux pas as old as the Platonic hills.* She's suddenly convinced this sudden spurt of italicized hysteria (i.e., *she mustn't make . . .*) has been drummed up not by her but by what the members of the tribe have come at no small price to their self-esteem to call the Master, here exhorting—as apoplectically as the main attraction at a Nuremberg rally—for her benefit alone. She's come to see things their way: body-snatchered like all but the hero in that 1956 sci-fi cum horror classic. All at once she visceralizes what the tribe has been getting at with its stage whispers. And what might that be? a party-pooper could ask. Haven't the faintest idea, she might reply. But as it turns out in a not-so-distant paragraph, she underestimates herself simply because she's been trained to believe that's the maidenly thing to do.

Then a funny thing happens—she seems to get it—all of it. "Like family dynamics," she thinks (then says: what has she got to lose?). "Family dynamics," he whispers, fearing she might just turn out to be intelligent—more intelligent than he about certain things—but liking the novelty of the fear. Just as amnesia—the gut's inevitable failure to remember disease states—should itself be deemed a bona fide disorder—more disorderly than all the other disorders put together—so might family dynamics—i.e., family dysfunction—just as plausibly be considered a worthy family member in its own right—but infinitely less defective than all the others put together. He was right to be afraid—she is smarter than he is. To disguise the fear and stall for time he says, ponderingly, "Yes, I'm beginning to see what you mean. Not unlike the business of Elijah at the Seder, so to speak." He retrieves his folders, refusing to be taken in by desire, even if it's *his own brand of desire.*

He changes the subject—sort of. "What people fail to understand is that the labels are not reductive—in fact, they get the superfluous, the contingent—*the me that's not me* (the genomic, ontogenetic, epigenetic, familial, environmental me)—out of the way. To make way for—fo—f— The void that is everybody's uniqueness or into which everybody injected—injects—one's uniqueness." And when her mother called her cheap and greedy, that too was diagnosis—clearing the way toward uniqueness—so she should waste no time getting used to her new name—cheap and greedy at your service—reporting for duty—assuming the position. Accepting the label with a tip of one's high hat evidences not weakness but a new strength—a new concept of strength. Come to think of it, he, too, has been called cheap and greedy or some grosser variant thereof and a lot worse: he's cheap, he's greedy, he's *x*, he's *y*, he's up, he's down (like Fonda according to Stanwyck's pocket-mirror monologue in Preston Sturges's *The Lady Eve*)—he was last seen at the corner of Hollywood and Vine wearing a feather boa—no make that Bollywood and Fine—and, wait, it was a rhinestone-spangled jockstrap not a boa (wouldn't be caught dead in such an oldfangled contraption). But surely she has eyes to see how ultimately unlocalizable defamation makes him—it has an effect opposite to what's intended. "Always in the market for new epithets, new disparagements, to beef up the old CV, *my good woman*"—he likes the sound of this term of not entirely *mock* endearment (in fact it's already beefed up his CV better than any other epithet he could have recruited, at least at a moment's notice). And if her mother dared to accuse *him* of *being cheap and greedy* (i.e., code for *thinking small*)—well, he'd tell her point blank (while showing the fiercest respect for her shameless hypochondriacal exhibitionism (aka SHE) that in fact he loves nothing better than thinking small—the smaller the better—contemplating, for example, the obscene constriction of the fabric of the heavens to a pinpoint on a moonless June night—how Lurianic is *that*?

He loves thinking small because it inevitably leads not just to putting things in order but to endlessly *verifying* the continued existence of those orderly things. Thinking small through exiguous obsession, say, with the order of placement of soup cans in the foyer cupboard—or with ensuring that there are never more or less than four cartons of organic huckleberry-grapefruit juice on the lowest shelf of the freezer—keeps the pot of uniqueness churning (he doesn't know how she'll deal with the potential of a rare bird like *exiguous* to deliver a borderline pornographic shock to her mental genitalia). She can tell her loathsome mother—sorry, she's not loathsome just . . . troubled—that he's the first to recognize that where there is too much order—organization—orderliness—there must be a secret—a deep dark secret—like those dogging the footsteps of every last amasser of a great fortune in Balzac's Paris. In his case, though, there is no secret *behind* the obsession with order—the obsession itself is the deep dark secret. Cantor's fiercest rivals would of course like nothing better than to exploit to their advantage this obscene devotion to the will of entities that are not alive—that do not *breathe* (as, say, Dickinson's poems breathe). They could contend, for example, that the hunger to publish not perish led him to cross the line of decency and pledge an obscure allegiance to such entities. (*Defendant's response:* While this kind of dabbling in the dark arts would have gotten him burned as a witch in seventeenth-century Salem, just let 'em try it in twenty-first-century Babylon.) As for getting the hang of obsessive verification you need to be able to think really small. He's been tempted to put together several primers on the subject but teaching duties and fits of inspiration that would warm the cockles of Euclid's heart are always getting in the way. Verification is all about going the extra mile toward making oneself real in the world. By challenging the resistance of orderly, seemingly peripheral, thinkable things to being anatomized over and over and over again for their own good. It's all about doing what one knows is unnecessary—uncalled for under the circumstances—under any circumstances—a sacrilegious waste of time—yet doing it anyway because so much is at stake, nothing less than creation of a fibrous connection to the world—under the auspices—direction—of those orderly things which demand so little (except to have their resistance respected) and give so much. It's all about pushing way beyond one's limits—going against entrenched belief (e.g., that the faucet is turned off and all is therefore dry in Glocca Morra)—against received wisdom (e.g., that the front door has been triple-locked)—so as to legitimate the erosion of the contour of things through repeated inspection—in order to cement—to solder—that sought-for fibrous connection since all connections left to their own devices are tenuous at best. And this compulsion to verify, by the way, seems to go particularly well with the unfelt panic induced by departure from a worksite. For the unsung song of farewell to the inanimate has a genius for invoking the sort of uncertainties which cry out for immediate surgical intervention—interventions without end (to determine, for example, whether the desk lamp has really been turned off—whether the communal refrigerator door is sufficiently barricaded against every conceivable form of critter infestation). So as it turns out it looks like the only way such erosive interaction can satisfy the verifier is by destroying—yes, destroying—the target—the subject—of his anxiety. So if she knows what's good for her she'll hurry up and forget everything he's just said about verification except that it's all about mayhem—havoc—annihilation—masquerading as civic duty—that it's very goal is the dysfunction it professes to seek to avert—that it hates entities whatever their size and provenance with all its heart—and that for all of these reasons and more it's a perfectly respectable pathway to self-discovery.

In short, don't anybody dare (including her rancid mother) to sell obsession with ordering and orderliness short: it encompasses many things but what it wouldn't be caught dead encompassing is whiplash from too much turning the other cheek, being jilted by fate at the altar of greatness, blessings so disguised as to be maledictions, confusion of wishful thinking with divine decree, comic relief, impalement on the horns of the same old dilemma. "You get the idea," he concludes, standing before her. "You've helped me," she tells him. He's very tall for his age, she thinks absurdly as a way of fending off the lameness of "you've helped me" (helped me how? when? why?).

He tries to give the impression that he's not looking for flattery (they both have bigger fish to fry) by asking her to remember that whenever anybody slaps her with a misdiagnosis it's all to the good. For the war cry in these parts is *Misperception: the gem of the ocean*. Surely she must suspect that Invidicum is in the service of that Master he spoke of a few pages back—a Master *showman* whose clientele requires the Invidicumites to be forever, say, mistaking P for Q, or to be forever expecting X only to be stuck with Y (Y is in fact the whole show, X being just an afterthought and a none-too-poignant one at that). And if his stooges don't manage to get it all wrong there's no show. What client will pay to watch some smug lucky stiff forever getting it right and then some, having her expectations met over and over again at every turn? (and, no, it doesn't matter if the stiff is self-mockingly smug like Citizen Kane when he says he thinks he did "pretty well under the circumstances"). Where's the triumph over—or better yet, the annihilation by—adversity in all that? Jane Q. Pubic has every right to expect Jean—that is her name, isn't it? (she knows he knows very well what her name is)—to hold up her end of the entertainment bargain, which means seeming (so as to avoid being pelleted with rotting turnips in the middle of the first scene) to abominate the impediments thrown in her path. "So we've been recruited under false pretenses. Here I was thinking I put something over on the powers that be by getting myself admitted when in fact it was they who—" She clearly doesn't mind taking the cue from his playfulness. "I'm not being playful," he retorts harshly—to what he thinks she's thinking. "Showbiz is no laughing matter. I'm more and more convinced there's a real flesh-and-blood Master running this show—he's Barnum & Bailey to the core—and the show is not Invidicum, off-label or on- (Invidicum's the merest smokescreen: a stalking horse, a red herring). The show is strictly dinner theater fodder—summer stock fare. We've all been signed up—roped in—to entertain his corn-fed clientele. That's why it doesn't matter whether you sneaked in under false pretenses or not. Your false pretenses are strictly small potatoes. In fact, they're just another red herring and as such their stench and color serve the bastard better than he deserves. So we—you and I—have our work cut out for us: to misperceive or be misperceived—whatever yields more discomfort in the moment. Whether as perpetrator or victim, we'll be gorging on—living high on the hog of—misperception—misreadings—'cause that's the stuff of psychodrama. Ask Dionysus when you get a chance. Ask Pentheus if you don't believe me—or his grandpa." "My mother thinks there's an entire conspiracy out there bent on destroying us through misreading and when I refuse to be bullied into an alliance against its charter members—" "Just tell the old witch that—sorry, she's not being targeted—certainly not from envy of her talents and good looks. Fact of the matter is that each and every one of us has been put on earth for one reason: to be misread and to overreact accordingly—to steer clear of those who misread forcibly but hold no life-or-death sway over us (why bother to align our parched lips with *their* hindquarters since they don't pay our rent or put food on our table?) but naturally not before daintily bashing their face in with the turd of their smug overreach. Of course there are those who though misreaders are humble enough to be forever in the market for correction because correction means (they're sly enough to know) self-nourishment. For them we simply clear the air, at no charge, of all toxicity. As for those lucky enough to be able to transmogrify the misreading they've endured into the overarching theme of a life's work—into a gift basket of enlightenment goodies to sustain them on their seven voyages of discovery—all they have to do is jump up and down with insane delight, that is, once they've annihilated their tormentors with the good news." "What about the ones who do hold life-or-death sway . . . over us?" Cantor pauses artfully—to give whatever he has to say the patina of woeful ponderation— of struggle. "I haven't figured that out yet." He now takes a deep breath and smuggles in a plaintive sigh to hide the fact that he's changing the subject— but only slightly—and only for her—his little sister's—own good. "*I'm not sure why things have turned out as they have—but I intend to find out.*" They both observe a non-collaborative moment of stony silence—in honor of this true Man of Noir. The Man finishes off his one-sentence exercise in forthrightness (seasoned with all the pathos that italics can buy) by emitting a little shiver of pleasurable prideful self-disbelief. He's turned out to be quite a guy—at least for the moment.

He confesses solemnly (*ma non troppo*) to not understanding why even despite his particular sexual interests—or why even with the substantial investment those interests willingly made (the signals were all there for men to breathe or eyes to see) in getting the two of them over the finish line—their meeting didn't blossom into or at least have the ring (however tinny) of a normal courtship ritual—you know a tall-balding-guy-meets-ice-princess-with-heart-of-gold kind of thing. Something intervened. "The Master," she says, playfully. "Exactly—he had to unload his thought packets on somebody—he had to turn us into his loudspeakers. Who else could he get at such short notice, after all, to do this dirty job?" She assures him they'll meet again and then . . . who knows? By saying this (albeit a bit too chirpily—it makes him want to strangle her) has she, too (as a true *Lady* of Noir if only by association), done her part to resuscitate, if not reinvent, the genre?

Buoyed up by Cantor's Pygmalion-like faith in her potential, she manages to make it back to Amygdala for her group session with Manning and Cook although she's still not quite sure what the latter's work has to do with therapy. But isn't that what Cantor was just talking about—no show-must-go-on if things are right as rational rain? No therapy, however, Cook or no Cook, before she picks something up in the Lafayette Bakeshop, soon to fold. Wait! the counter lady is smiling as if she's known all along Jean would go for the unusual—a cherry-cheese Danish with almond sprinkles—and by the time the smile gets done with her Jean doesn't know what kind of pastry she is and, you know something? she doesn't care. She's pure-and-simple gladness: it's clear (but to whom?) they both treasure, each in his—no, her—own way, their participation in this highly diverting new episode of *her PBS miniseries*. Yet, something's fishy. Jean smells a rat. Here is somebody or something—an agent of the Master no doubt—trying to pull a fast one—to smuggle in another mention of Jean's PBS triumph with the aid of the sort of impressionistically "light" touch commended by Roland Barthes as if the mention were some colorless remark that isn't worth remembering—a throwaway that has "forget me—that's an order!" written all over it but that will be revealed—retrospectively in a sleight of hand worthy of Agatha—to be the slip of the tongue that puts the speaker in the culprit's seat by cracking his alibi. So here again is the miniseries but invoked, Jean suddenly realizes, not with an eye to the pleasures of puzzlement for its own sake but rather to put to rest one of the grossest misconceptions of all time, or at least of the present moment, namely, that a show whose plot is wrapped—frivolously one might say—around a particular line of goods (*branded entertainment* as it's called in the Biz though in this case shouldn't it, Biz or no Biz, be referred to, almost reverently, as *branded* personal *entertainment* inasmuch as for all the non-discriminatory sweetness and light it's craftily targeted, *pace* the pastry, only at those happy few whose vocation is self-laceration, which naturally includes Martin and Melanctha and Borkman as well as other such Men from Shropshire whose home sweet home is the dog-eared pages of *Bleak House*)—that a show such as this can't simultaneously tackle the Big Issues—the Big unfrivolous Issues—though Jean's not quite sure what in this context those Issues are. Unfortunately the counter lady, whose attention is now transfixed by the love affair already brewing between the next customer and the next Danish, can't enlighten her.

The sky threatens and (gray contra gray) blimplike clouds, their broods in tow, are losing no time migrating south. She's at the curb now, guarding her goodies. But won't the red light that's stopping traffic also stop the rain? But by the same token won't the change from red to green trigger not just the uptown stampede but the dreaded downpour? So much childlike freshness of gem-of-the-ocean misperception crowded into a single instant! How delighted must her Master—she means *the* Master—be! How proud of her! Almost as proud as Cantor! But why is the Master if he's such a big shot wasting his time on the likes of her? After all, she's no maker like Herbert, or the over-the-hill dancer, or Cantor, or the self-important architect of mergers. But maybe it's precisely this—that she's stark naked—that she has no crutch of a project to lean on—that (to take a page from the meta-man's hornbook) she's all essence—which intrigues him. But in that case, why not Eden? He seems to be even less of a maker than she. Red lights have come and gone and she's still at the curb on Greenwich Avenue, unwet—sun-drenched in fact. She can't cross. Something compels her to go on giving Greenwich the benefit of the doubt rather than shift her allegiance to Amygdala. Though what exactly does she owe it?—Greenwich, I mean. What has Greenwich ever done for her that Amygdala can't do better? Why not try a compromise: the nearest sidestreet, ginkgo-shaded and brownstone-prim? Is loyalty simply inertia? Why can't she give it the cold shoulder or at least a chip off of it and simply *get on with her life*? You know, the way politicians feel entitled to do after owning up to the obligatory infidelities on prime time. Well, maybe it's because she *suddenly realizes* (How's that for epiphany, Cantor?), with a little help from the sun beating down uncharitably *as it would never dare to beat down anywhere else*, that *only here*, on Greenwich, *and now*, at 5:04 in the afternoon, can she acknowledge what a damn fool she is to hope that a drudge's attentiveness to her mother's every symptom, however implausible, will ultimately trigger a crisis of gratitude—that from the manure of contempt will sprout a motherly pride unstinting. Trouble is, the old witch has been on to this desperately tinny plea at the core of Jean's servitude from the word go and from the word go she's hardened her hard clinician's heart against it, but only for the good of the patient.

So amid all this inner tumult, the last thing she wants is to be inspected by some young-Turk-on-Wall-Street wannabe, whose buzz-cut trimness in olive poplin obviously confers the right not just to size her up quizzically (mission accomplished) but to stick around for as long as it takes (and it was taking forever) to transmit in full his serious second thoughts about a much-too-generous first impression. She's led him on *unconscionably* (to use a favoritism of His Honor the current Mayor) and must be gaze-skewered for this bit of shameless self-hype. Sorry, Narrator Man, no gem-of-the-ocean misperception here! She calls it as she sees it. She intends to look away long enough to ensure that the looking back, once finally unloaded upon her loitering tormentor, will serve as the withering indictment his smug redundancy warrants. But when she does unload, it is only to discover he's halfway down the sidestreet she'd rejected, the bounce in his step proclaiming to her and anybody else who cares to listen that he's mighty pleased with his choice of escape hatch. And why shouldn't he be? she asks, noting for the first time that (among a host of other amenities) there are even a few clouds big as alps at the tail end of it.

When his friend walks in swinging her purse like a veritable streetwalker, Eden is peeling a much-bruised apple in the kitchen, while looking at a newspaper photo of several soldiers snoozing in the grass at Fort Hood, Texas. The weapon, a 9-millimeter Glock, is tucked away in his messenger bag. Should he show it to her? Is this going to be one of the moments when a devout loner gets vexed by the occasional yen for connectedness at any price? Then he remembers it's purely a commercial arrangement titillated now and then by tidbits of genuine feeling erupting between orgasms.

According to the caption, they have just heard one of their most intrepid brothers-in-arms—Deadeye Dick Cheney, unshellshockable veteran of five-odd draft deferments and, true to form, inexplicably absent from the frame—tell them "to stay in the fight until the fight is won." And Eden has only to look into their beautifully earnest, dutifully smiling faces to know that they will—have every intention of proving they are more than worth their cannon-fodderly salt. Hardly very original or risky to loathe the likes of W's pitbull, dimly Eden knows, or should know, but loathe he must, whenever the opportunity presents itself, if only to signal his solidarity with . . . he isn't quite sure whom. Appalling to consider that their fate—maybe everybody's, come to think of it, at this point in time—hangs from the thread of Dick's rabblerousing spittle. When she comes out of the modestly refurbished bathroom (any minute now: the toilet's trilled growl signals the end of Linda's royal flush), he'll tell her so. She looks at him with disgust as if to say (can he read her? no? well, then, somebody else will just have to pitch in and read her *for* him, until such time as the Invidicum—wonder drug to end all—kicks in and enables him to read her on his own): Oh, come off it, bud, how can you stoop to being so outlandishly *facile*, daring to compare everybody's else—that is, your measly own—fate to the fate of these kids about to die for nothing, or to be maimed beyond recognition and left to fend for themselves in the Walter Reed Hilton's Building 18? How dare you try to conflate your own Life of Riley (albeit refracted through the Book of Job) with their looming tragedy? After all, true to your made-to-order tabloid profile, you have your hit right where you want him. Should he reveal that the closer he gets to avenging the wronged veteran, the more obvious it becomes that the immaculate self-conception at the heart of all his war stories is a fraud, but that only by proceeding according to plan, even if he doesn't yet have one, will Eden be entitled to detest him—dad—with a clear conscience? Doesn't all this make for a fate worth bemoaning?

Suddenly he hates Linda. Wants to murder her. Can't conceive that murder and the aftermath would be worse than enduring her disgust. So much does murder seem the only thing—the only right thing—to do. He wonders without knowing he wonders—the best kind of wondering but You, Dear Reader, know that by now (and by the way this coy aside isn't the offal of some disgruntled pre-modernist—whatever that is)—he wonders whether he should express his rage—call her every name in the book—or live with it, let it subside, let it play possum. But keeping the rage to himself means being alone in the Cave of the Self—Plato's cave—Ovid's cave—of Envy!—and he's always had a hard time living with his self—deep inside his self—a hard time living with the inviolability of the self—of the soul of that self: a hard time living with its impermeability—impenetrability (keep those polysyllabs coming, Maestro!—and fast and furious, if You know what's good for you)—impenetrability to the presumed omniscience of everybody else—everybody else being immediately elevated—catapulted—to the rank of the protective comforting parent-in-training he's never had—in whose cradle that self's wickedness—worse, ambivalence—can rock itself to sleep, exonerated in full, or so he needs to believe. The othe—oops! Other—who can deliver him from selfhood—from the unreality of being real and from vice versa—without his necessarily having to spill his toxic beans direct, that is, without his having to pretend to struggle to remember the irrepressible business about killing little girls in Balboa Park (see below, far below, specifically the deserted spot where pages 456 and 544 cross swords—under the watchful eye of their coach, page 188). But he has his pride and he's not going to dump his self's inviolability in her lap, for turkey buzzards to peck at. (By the way, is the story of his status as an accredited loser [an apocryph if ever there was one] the lullaby with which she sings herself—or her other loser clients—to sleep?) He's going to live with his rage—rage at Linda's putting disgust before the well-being of the target of her disgust. Which is one of her trademarks—hell, she's got more trademarks under wraps than that great big pimp of a Rump Organization. It's soggily settled: He's going to live with his hatred of Linda, without telling her and without running away.[8] Even if the loneliness generated by being right next to somebody—being right *and* being right next to somebody he hates *right at the same time* (what a feat and not bad for a layman)—is excruciating. And at the same time there's nobody who treasures his interiority more than he—even if he can't *talk it through*—even if he's not an artist in residence—i.e., not an opportunist in residence (not even out there in sunny Santa Barbara where everybody's an artist or commanded by the hula-crazy palm fronds to be one at least in effigy)—and hence can't be expected to be capable, even for icono-graphic gain, of parasitizing interiority's creatures—Netherlandish demons straight out of Rogier van der Weyden (Rogier who?—Eden's ignorance is a challenge not to be trifled with—more intimidating than the arrogance of know-it-alls). But if he disgorges the rage then maybe it will transform her, ultimately, into somebody . . . likeable. But it's too late for likeability. They're past that stage, what with the hate-fucking and their down-the-hatching of allied potions. This is why, Your Honor, for the life of him he can't understand

---

[8] Though all of this talk about hatred seems just a wee bit too facile—trips off the tongue and spills onto the page a bit too . . . easily. Is he serious? wonders Linda (who can read the hatred in his eyes). Or even if he's a self-professed yokel mightn't he also be a savvy enough entertainer to understand that injecting hatred into any relation sells like hotcakes—generates an immediate sense of danger—urgency—importance—a sense that there's more-here-than-meets-the-eye? And maybe—thinks Somebody Else—dragging a surefire crowd pleaser like hatred into the act is the best way to proleptically pay Eden back for his imminent put-down (see below) of my kid brother's middle-fingering of normality.

the hullabaloo over privacy—privacy at risk—the lauded privacy being hacked away at *as we speak* (wretched phrase) by all those cybergoons and -thugs. He, for one, welcomes their hacking the way FDR welcomed the hatred of the robber baron crowd. Let them decrypt him—disencrypt him—whenever the evil spirit moves them—his identity is safer in their virtual vault than in his own soon-to-be-bloodstained hands. He'd be tickled pink if, when popping its cork as he does—tries to do—daily, YouTube—putting its money where its mouth is (talk, after all, is cheap: in these Not-So-Breit . . . Bart days, never cheaper)— Tickled pink if YouTube showed just how well it remembered, and from years back no less and with an autocomplete or two or three to prove it, that a guy like him would never be caught dead listening to Glazunov's *Concert Waltz no. 1* if *no. 2* was lurking just around the bend. And for some odd reason he thinks—without knowing he does so—that this idea—this notion straight off the notions counter—this Concept of Privacy as a relentlessly disappearing Snapshot—has the makings of an armature—a foundation—for the start-up to end all start-ups until the next one comes along.

It hits him: killing Straynge will be very much out of character. Somebody who carries around a 9-millimeter Glock hoping to be caught in the act of . . . carrying it around is not made of the stern stuff called for. But Some Body, *the* Some Body—Invidicum's Inner Reader of Circumstance— (*Oh, quit beating around the bush, Eden. Spit it out. Call a spade a spade. You mean the Master!*) Eden relents. (*See, that wasn't very hard, was it?*) But is Invidicum's Inner Voice (IIV) consubstantial with the Master's? Consubstantial or not, the Voice is insisting that the duty of a man's man is to be out of character—to break, Samsonlike, the chains of his characterological straitjacket every chance he gets (especially when there's none for the getting). Eden hears the Voice, whosoever it is, but it's all noise. Clearly, Invidicum is no match for IIV and the Master, especially when they're at war. It's way too weak to transliterate—transduce—all the noise into horse sense. Eden's being spoken for and talked through and taught by entities unknown but for all practical purposes he's invisible. OK—but there are worse fates. Maybe IIV is just a lowbrow version of the Master, shorn of his pretensions and will to control, and therefore Martin's rightful champion by divine right.

He can see roughly half of Linda in the kitchen grinding coffee in her—his—favorite panties: the pair with the too-many loopholes in its plot. Though her gestures desperately want any passing stranger to think—to know—these panties are just going about their professional business, he can tell from the whimsical way she keeps shifting her weight from one hip to the other in time to melodies unheard that, in spite of herself, she is having something of a ball being in uniform. Actually, his enthralling perversity qua john has enabled her to realize that only in the context of loving can kink generate the excitement it's supposed to even when the loving is, as here, infinitesimal by design.

It's back to business: the Voice doesn't share his interest in the panties, at least at the moment. Instead, the Voice prefers to focus on Eden's need to stop thinking that to kill Straynge (the dose is strong enough to generate the exhortation) the killer has (as a matter of silly pride) to be in character—that there has to be a perfect marriage of actor and act. (The Voice's directness is refreshing so maybe it's IIV who's up at bat.) So what if the actor's at right angles to—at loggerheads with—the act. They can still be true-blue. But the inner voice is on to Eden. It's more than a matter of being in character, isn't it? Eden believes act and actor must be a super-plausible pair—intimidatingly summarizable and Fort Hood-paraphraseable—so that Straynge or Cook or Narr or Post can pitch them to potential consumers at a hitman convention (some counter-voice must have put this crazy idea in his head, perfectly comprehensible considering his status as a "world-class" information exchange for such potions). But he's not a book, after all—a potential bestseller. He needs to stop worrying about whether his act *gives good paraphrase* (knowing as he does it's the women—and men—who worry most about whether or not they gave good head or good blurb that make the world's worst fellators or reviewers)—good enough to make him a star at such a convention. (*Thing is, he didn't know he was worrying until now, until the Voice enlightened him.*) Fuck the paraphrase even if it makes him look like an implausible jerk. Fuck the paraphrase even if it never forgives him—and makes every one of those conventioners do likewise—for committing an act for which it proclaims him overwhelmingly unsuited. (But isn't it precisely the ones most quote unsuited unquote who, by provoking an act's fiercest resistance to their unsuitability, thereby capture its essence?) He should stop worrying whether the blood inevitably let will be too copious for mopping up by the rag of paraphrase and whether the hemorrhage of disbelief induced in his not-so-innocent bystanders will be too copious as well. He should stop worrying whether paraphrase will give him a fair shake. The ill-intentioned trillions always bad-paraphrase no matter what you do to try to please them.

His business lies elsewhere—in getting en route to a kill from point A to point B and from B to C and so on and so forth. But at the same time he has to stop all this wistful thinking that the shortest distance between them is a straight line instead of one of those pathological curves his silly dose-mate is always chattering about in and out of group. So in fact, Eden's worst enemy is not his paraphraser—funny folks like Gym Dwier and Christine Alias-Burger and their progenitors and spawn—but his own all-too-headlong self.

But to be fair, the Voice continues, if he can only manage to dig deep inside the nervous breakdown (cause and effect of madness) inflicted on him (oh so precociously) at age eleven—when he was convinced he got up in the middle of the night to murder pantyless little girls on the fringe of Balboa Park, and that eventually he'd give in and hack pop and little brother to death with the meat cleaver purchased on the installment plan at Horton Mall (doesn't said dose-mate also have some business to finish down at the Mall?). And as in all cases of unattempted murder, everything pivoted on the dissociation between feeling and image: the rage driving him to the act was routinely smothered by the terror of its commission and the more adeptly—irretrievably—pigheadedly—the rage was smothered, the more bedazzling became the clarity of the image of that doggone meat cleaver, stashed away in the "family room" broom closet down in the cellar. *Family room* (more like a serial killer's airless areaway)—now how's that for euphemism at its smarmy, stodgy best? Doesn't he remember how close he was to murder until medication and what is now known as cognitive behavioral therapy stuck their nose into what didn't concern them in the least? But as the Voice was saying (before it was so rudely interrupted by its own elaborations—mind you. all essential): If he can manage the re-descent into madness, then he'll be able to collide head on and fuse with the kind of authority—authoritativeness—that only self-induced recrudescence of a madness survived and surmounted confers and that precocious madness recrudesced confers double. (The Master seems to be trying to elbow his way in here with his fancy words and fancy conceptions—to get into the act—to reclaim his sovereignty—but if you think IIV will cede the terrain without a fight then you don't know It very well.) Then the coupling of act and actor will not come across to the conventioners as all that implausible. If he digs deep he'll find a way to make the punisher fit the crime. The book-jacket paraphrase will be a thing of mass-market beauty— credible, creditable. But if he goes on forgoing and forswearing madness—this human resource to end all human resources—because he believes it dresses him in the wrong kind of authority—that it disqualifies him for life—diminishes him—makes him inferior to the average joe, let alone biggish shots like Cantor and Borkman and Cook and Narr and Straynge and Post—if he goes on forgoing, then there's no telling how he'll end up—worse, how his avengement will end up. Sure, in the domain of everyday life madness is in most cases a liability but in the *other* domain there's no such thing as disqualification. (Except through too much normality, *whatever that is*, somebody thinks flippantly [maybe it's the Master's smug little shit of a kid brother whose life of Riley has been handed to him on too many silver platters]. The perverse flippancy—yep, *perverse flippancy*, the main cause of death among people aged one hundred and four or above—irks Eden since he knows—and in this case *he knows he knows*—it's easy to play the renegade and trash normality [whatever that is] when you hew to the goose step of nothing but and what's more when you know there'll never be a reckoning for such phony daring.) If anything, madness—even its aftermath—even if it's now nothing but its aftermath—is all qualification, qualification in spades—all beef, no fat. He just needs to get inside the skin of madness—the sackcloth of madness—and apply to the case at hand all he learned long long ago without knowing he learned it—through to the bloody end. He's simply got to dredge up all those unlivabilities, Actor's Studio style, and allow himself to relive them now as meds and CBT didn't allow him to live them then.

Eden wonders what domain the Voice is referring to, even if he knows perfectly well, 'cause there's something exciting about pretending *not* to know (spasms shoot from spine to perineum: he doesn't mind the spasms but he doesn't like them described—description feminizes or haven't you noticed?). Pretending not to know gives the Voice the permission he needs to seduce Eden and it feels good to be the seducee for a change. Still, what is his domain?—Cantor and Shearer and Herbert and Borkman all have theirs or pretend they do but what's his? Crime, of course—murder. But somehow the answer doesn't satisfy. But isn't thinking that being a veteran of madness (no matter who's doing the thinking) gives him an edge—well, isn't that a wee bit preposterous (like being a wee bit pregnant)—isn't that madness *to the second power*, to use a phrase Cantor's so damn fond of—using it every chance he gets, clearly to impress what Straynge calls "the gals"? But if he likes men, what's the point? The point, Martin, is to fuck without fucking—to experience all the joys of gal-fucking without the mess orgasm in such circumstances is renowned for leaving behind.

But, hey, not so fast, let's not forget the mutilated ring finger of his left hand—macerated in a beach chair (noon, midsummer, Coronado) when he was only three. What about it? he wonders. Well, that, too gives him an edge. Doesn't he realize he's a one-man trauma unit—that madness and mutilation are prime movers on the assassination circuit? If he wants—as he claims—to achieve plausible paraphraseability (not to be confused with plausible deniability) in what is now his only domain, then he mustn't hide either. He's got to flash their signets, get all the mileage he can out of them. They're his war stories. None more thrilling.

The ripples of tension in Linda's suntanned arms are well worth watching now for she's started not just pouring the coffee, but doing so with all the currying caution of some Old Dutch Master's favorite gamine. *Listen, and listen good!* resumes what Eden decides—and to hell with the Master, at least for now—is the gonadless Invidicum Inner Voice (as indifferent to her arms, suntanned or otherwise, as to her panties), distressed by what it takes for a display of inattention. Any life story whose wounds are worth their salt in gold is implausible by its very nature—or un-nature: is nothing more and nothing less than the rift—the synaptic cleft, if you will, and even if you won't—between itself and . . . plausibility as cherished by the old folks at home. And trying to do away with that cleft will be like trying to swallow one's own throat or chew one's own teeth. A life story's plausibility *lies* in its very deviation from plausibility.

What will enrage most bystanders is not that he's killed somebody but, given who they think he is, that he's killed implausibly, and implausibility being, as everybody knows, contagious, any minute now the wound of his implausibility must become theirs. So they'll try to suture Eden up double-quick by making out that off-the-charts pretentiousness not hot-blooded murder is the real culprit in residence here. Only he shouldn't expect any down-home gratitude for having turned them into trauma surgeons (despite what people may think, no bystander likes to remain idle). So when all is said and done, it's his story that's the ultimate bystander—caught in the crossfire between his obligation to live it and theirs to trash it.

He succeeds somehow in getting himself unhooked from the IIV machine well before she finishes up in the kitchen. So he has enough time to rehearse his apology for not being willing to talk about the drug trial: everything about it is just too brain-drainingly tentative, even—especially—the undeniable high points. When she finally does emerge he starts in but even before the table is set she announces that she has no intention whatsoever of asking questions. And to emphasize this she testily kicks off her platforms and manages, without missing a beat, to wiggle out of her panties while hopping her way back to the bathroom (as she's spent a lot of time in there, he hopes she managed to wash her hands before working on the coffee: like everybody's favorite president though not his—at least not yet—he's a germophobe)—and a graceful business she makes of it, too, he's compelled to admit. Still, he's sure he's caught a flicker or two of interest at the mention of the high points, intriguingly impossible as they are to associate with a life like his, riddled—landmined—as it is with spectacular lows. He doesn't want the apple he realizes he's still holding in his hands. For one thing, it smells unusually bitter (side effect of Invidicum?). Peeling it extra-roughly has been nourishment enough.

After this cross-chat, however one-sided, with IIV, he's closer to Straynge than he's ever been *in all their years together* (the phrase chokes him up—call it a teary guffaw: whatever it is, it's on the house). Closer to *getting* him, that is. Or does he have some other form of closeness in mind? Only he doesn't know if this getting closer means ending up a winner or a loser. He feels like the foundling hero of some nineteenth-century English classic (the kind he can't fathom or finish but this may change very soon): too happy and yet not happy enough. But whatever he's feeling, as usual it's egging him on to make the strongest possible case for his being a poor slob—and not just any old poor slob but the proverbial poor slob. He feels safe in the vestments of a poor slob—and super-virile, too. Since when he's around *his woman* (the phrase sends shivers of excitement and revulsion down his spine and into his perineum: he'd loathe the sound of the word if he knew what it meant), nothing excites him more than the contrast between his masterly self-presentation as the world's biggest loser (with a loser's obligatory predilection for the corniest sort of kink) AND a very different kind of mastery which enables him to deliver a satisfaction so intense it never fails to burn off and away all her baseline rage, defiance and contempt (both for life and for him as a razed-suburb-of-life) which R, D & C then becomes—for as long as her hatred of pleasure can stand it, that is—a joyous desperation. You could say he's got a calling for loserliness which is all to the good, as he must feel like a loser to get going sexually.

So maybe in spite of all his efforts he's going to end up a winner and has known as much all along, even as far back as the womb, for only a conviction of ultimate victory could enable him to go on, day after day, doing loserliness as deftly as he does it, always with a bonus bit or two of self-degradation thrown in for the connoisseurs. What must have happened is this (and he didn't need old IIV to figure it out for him): From the word go he had so much faith in his ability to do anything he put his mind to—which now includes pulling the plug on his father's killer—that he ended up warehousing a staggering surplus. And what better way to utilize that surplus than by pretending to be the very opposite of what he is, thereby throwing his enemies (99.99 percent of humanity) off the scent?

But, after all, he's only perfecting a technique practiced by his father who, when he felt particularly chipper, usually after dinner (but why then, since mom was an intentionally abominable cook?), would offer advice like, *Do unto others before others can do unto you.* He, of all people! But eventually any good man must do something (or he'll explode) with the negative voltage that accumulated from having never inflicted harm. And out in the world his father was a truly good man even if he couldn't stomach his nearest and dearest, especially Eden, whom he started to hate long before the boy's meat-cleaver phase. And maybe he had good reason to hate him and go on hating him to the end. (As late in the game as a month before the old man's death, when Eden first realized for the thousandth time that he was unsalvageable, the first order of business became to shit his dread. So he ended up using the toilet, only he forgot to flush. Lifting the lid simply to piss, his father's fellow moribund in Ward No. 6 let out a howl so robust it seemed to herald a return to health. When his father learned why, his bug-eyed speechlessness made it clear that no turd could ever be more disgusting than his son.) So—as IIV or the Master or I was saying: Abstention from perpetrating evil gave Sr. the license to letter-killeth and in the inability of the speaker to be true to his words—in the disjoin between the MO sketched by the words and his real MO—lay their poignant charm and their poignant charm was their power. On a full stomach his father routinely permitted himself a little vacation from goodness. Just as his unfavorite chip off the old, cold shoulder, putting conviction to one side, gives himself up to the esoteric thrill of playing at loserliness.

Stark naked except for jingling anklets (the gift of a Peruvian Admirer-General), she plops herself down beside him, with childlike guilelessness. Yet there's something phony about this exhausted collapse into loverly surrender: she's using it to mask her awkwardness—or something else—the way some people use a lurid yawn to demonstrate how much at home they feel in your presence when in fact they couldn't feel less comfortable. But he can't start trying to figure her out what she has up her sleeve: his heart wouldn't be in it. He needs to talk about the shameful turd business. It clearly isn't over even if it played itself out years before, when killing Straynge was a mere speck in his mind's eye. Only words can drown out the deafening soundlessness of his shame—soundlessness of a million syllables and still counting—words not fit to be heard by another mortal. First, he babbles obscenities. She looks at him as if he were crazy when she must know he clearly isn't, since he's talking not *to* but *through* himself, to the bearer of his shame with whom he is no longer to be confused since he, Eden, now armed only with a smelly old phrase, has just shot him down, together with all incriminating spectators.

But if the shame-bearer is dead, the shame itself is very much alive and suddenly this is all to the good. Barking out the phrase—something to do with sucking the cum out of somebody's ass or the shit out of somebody's cunt or soul—Eden proves he's mettled enough to transcend turdiness without having to repudiate it (*who is speaking?*). The barking affirms that he does shame so well he's able to integrate shame as well as its sequelae (whose effects are more devastating) into his sense of self—that *from now on* anything he does, no matter how shameful, must make that self more robust. Let's face it, his is a selfhood—all too rare in these pursy times—that knows how to enrich itself at shame's—at anything's and anybody's—expense: knows how to turn shame into shamelessness at the drop of a hat. In short, he's *a national treasure.* Then, without even looking at her, still making like a teddy bear, suddenly he knows all this is a farce—unplayable in Peoria, Pomona and everywhere else: he is just stuck with his shame and will never make it pay.

But shame or no shame, merely by rubbing her belly he induces the familiar drowsy look which means the cave beneath her dry-as-manzanita pubic hair is (amazingly, given the minimal fingerwork required) starting to gush. And even more amazingly, she always chooses this moment to hold forth caustically on what he has come to refer to as Today's Theme. He routinely works off the lust her passionate delivery generates (it's much too precious to dissipate in the rough-and-tumble of sofa sex) by masturbating in the bathroom during her obligatory post-declamatory snooze.

"The most shameless thing about the XXX-Gov." (so she wasn't unnerved in the least by his inner distancing over the last twenty minutes: it's the ex-governor who's got her goat) "is not his betrayal of wife and constituents but the fact that he made his whore (whom I happen to know very well: we started out five years ago next month working for the same dragon lady over on West Twenty-Eighth Street) take Amtrak (coach!) all alone from New York to DC Getting her a first-class plane ticket would have shown that he recognized being a bad boy in the large didn't release him from the obligation to be a good boy in the small. And by the same token being a good boy in the small didn't detract from his stature as a bad boy in the large. Buying sex (the unsafe kind) he feels like trash so the whore is automatically trash, too, and by treating her accordingly he somehow redeems himself. Negative of a negative is a positive (maybe even an HIV-positive), according to the XXX-Gov.'s wacked-out calculation. The canceled coach ticket is a trophy he can bring home to his mommy-wife as proof-positive that he isn't such a bad boy after all, since with its help he's managed to punish his victim real good. Treating her like a turd (to use your word)—absenting himself from the most basic level of human decency—makes the John of Johns a little less reprehensible in his own mind, a little less unfaithful, a little less of a party to the transaction (and maybe no party at all!). Coming inside her is not—inasmuch as it's *beyond his control*—he's its trick—as blameworthy as getting that first-class round-trip ticket would be. He can always say: I did not have sex with that hotel room overlooking the Potomac. When he was busy sticking his unsheathed dick down her throat or up her ass he wasn't really himself—he wasn't even in the act—there was no act per se—his orgasms were hard at work eroding it. That's what orgasms are for, stupid—to erase all that comes before. And with his last ejaculation of the night, the-act-that-was-not is completely obliterated. Whereas securing that first-class round-trip ticket would have required standing still and admitting that a bad-boy act was in process: a shameful one, granted, but not so shameful—not so monstrous—as to release the perp from his obligation, in its seedy confines, to behave with some degree of chivalry. As my second employer (no dragon lady she) used to say at the dawn of each new workweek on East Ninety-Third Street (I'd come up in the world): 'Never fear, girls: Even an ocean of sleaze has its little islets of true gents.'

"In any case, once they stop treating us bimbos with life-threatening disrespect, they will have to find a more direct way of expressing the reverence for their partner that they don't feel in the least. In john-think, contempt for the whore becomes the closest thing to reverence for the vampire-wife, at the same time that trashing the whore is also a trashing of the vampire, from a safe distance of proxy. The whore is the shot in the arm, the '*danger-ous supplement*"'—now where did that phrase come from? she wonders (of course! Tuesday's three-thirty slot runs a deconstruction company on Staten Island!)—"that any self-respecting marriage on life support sorely craves. The john needs our infectedness to make his woman holy by contrast for it is only by contrast that she *can* be holy: she's holy only when she's holier than thou. In contrast to us whores and the whory situation we put them in *against their will*, wifey is as pure as the driven snow. Of course, XXX-Gov. and every other erring sleazeball of distinction would stand a far better chance of enduring the little woman—they might even grow to like fucking her and out of the liking develop an authentic respect for their partner in crime if not for the crime itself—if their peabrains had the balls to ask what exactly is so goddamn holy to begin with about matrimony. No wonder by the way, that a john marries a shrew: he thinks she has the ability to scare away not just him but death itself. Though all that asking might end up putting us poxes out of business. For there is no holiness *to begin with*. Whether or not what two poor married slobs have together is sanctity incarnate can be decided only after the fact— when they're no more—on the basis of the traces they leave behind. All this by way of saying, If ever we're apart, lover, and you start missing your little . . . Thing, don't have me ride in coach. But you're different—that's what intrigues me: You've never used me to make some Thing back home look gooder than It is." She needs to believe his modesty is about to protest so she can add, "And the fact that in your case there's no such Thing back home—nor will there ever be—is irrelevant."

For all the lightness of tone there is something final about her delivery and he begins to wonder if it means this is the last time they'll ever meet—the last time he'll *be with her*, to use a favorite euphemism/archaism—as already mentioned—of that old dinosaur Straynge. (Eden's not even shocked at the sacrilege implicit in applying so good-humored an epithet as *old dinosaur* to his prey.) His instinct is correct: she's leaving on a little business trip—of unknown duration. Panicking he withdraws his hand from between her legs (can't remember having put it there). In that case, Eden (doing his damned-est to sound casual) wants her to know that for once they're in agreement about something—110 percent. He's referring to the XXX-Gov. affair. And as it turns out (the casual touch is getting way out of hand), he, too, will be away on business. "But what about the trial?" "It's trial-related." "Then take me with you," she retorts, a catch in her throat. "Are you serious?" He puts his hand back between her legs: only that low-down ooze will tell the truth. She can hardly expect him to believe in the genuineness of any upstairs waterworks, given how painstakingly she's been taught by her hard-as-nails employer to blubber just enough to make departing yokels feel like irresistible cads. He kisses her. She meets him halfway—most unusual: usually he has to scope the entire palate before her tongue will yield an inch. Guiding him into her two worlds of wet, "I'll miss you," she says, with a flippancy that may be camou-flaging excruciating pain—or none at all. "I really will. But it's all for the best. Madame Dragon hates your occupational-hazardly guts for making me flout her golden rule: never see a run-of-the-mill client more than twice."

What with her departure and the resurgence of the turd from deep within the bowels of memory, too much is happening all at once—for which, of course, he should be grateful since it means he's alive and (if sufficiently provoked) kicking. Be that as it may, he needs to talk about—he needs to disgorge—unload—the turd, or rather his father's hatred of him qua turd, and to whom better than Straynge—the third vertex of the triangle that is Eden's fateful mission. At first he thinks of Manning, so understanding or at least so understanding-looking under the beech trees, their roots big as boles. But Manning means Cook, whose inevitable presence at their session will be as much of a mystery as before—even more so—though he can't help suspecting that for somebody or rather Some Body: the Master, the IIV, the eloquence-generator, the apperception-wizard—call him what you will—mystery, or the appearance of mystery, is all to the good—good for business, so to speak—that is, the business of forking up meanings for his clients. So: no mystery, no meaning, or rather, no anticipation of meaning, which comes down to pretty much the same thing (at least according to flippancy-mongers, who get paid on commission).

But no—Straynge is definitely the ticket. Maybe with only a little prompting, he'll end up having a pretty definite hunch as to why Eden, Sr., should have made such a hobby of hating his son to distraction. The victim's hatred of the avenger will then rub off on the culprit and before long Eden will be giving as good as he gets—hating as good as he's hated. For he needs all the hatred he can muster where Straynge is concerned, especially now that it seems to be at low—lowest—ebb. At their midmorning session the following day (the bulbous bulb overhead, Eden notices, is fatally entangled in the leafless branches of an elm tree a little to the left of Straynge's bald head). Straynge offers him tea, which he politely declines. He's after bigger game. In record time, he tells A Tale of a Turd and its fellow moribund, suppressing all self-revelatory details. Straynge quickly—maybe too quickly—assures Eden he's being too hard on himself (no wonder he envies anybody who seems to have no trouble giving himself a break). What does the incident prove after all but that he, like everybody else, is a robust contradiction in terms: he's a man with the strength to fulfill his filial duty and at the same time an infant who wants to punish his father's terminal helplessness by (fathers aren't supposed to be helpless, after all, even with their dying breath) flaunting his own. Still, for all the sweet talk, Eden, aka Ki no Tsurayaki (the distant observer par excellence), is convinced in his gut that Straynge, deep in the heart of *his*, thinks very different thoughts—something to the effect that it's the son's turd not the father's illness that did the old boy in.

And sure enough, almost immediately, Straynge, much truer to form—the form of Eden's preconception, misconception and conception pure and simple—feels obliged (while toying loftily with his oversize stapler) to spice up his mollycoddling with a lesson, namely, that it is often a far far harder though not necessarily a far far better thing to be both man *and* turd than just turd and nothing but. But is it really harder? Eden can't help wondering. No, of course it isn't. It's just that after easing Eden's plight, Straynge realizes he goofed, was (given his native uncharitableness or his usual therapeutic strategy—no telling them apart, one being tributary to the other) terribly untrue to himself. But with his Mayflowery abhorrence of waste he has no intention of recanting. Through no fault of his own, he shot his mouth off in a way that ill accords with his tough-lovin' approach to losers. So to save face he (dis)qualifies the initial statement, twisting and turning it in such a way as to make it conform to his darker impressions. But aside from Straynge the Angekok and his need to liquidate the comfort he's unwittingly provided to a patient who clearly doesn't deserve any, since his problem routinely refuses (making it at once monstrous and non-existent) to submit to dissection, there are also Straynge the Text and *his* needs to consider.

For by the time the first statement is out of Straynge's mouth Straynge is Straynge no longer: he's become a plaintext—a tissue of words—and any text worth its salt dreads nothing more than leaving well enough alone, quitting while it's ahead. Straynge as Text—even when it's writing itself in response to the mastectomized dolls who hang on his every pronouncement (including how to win back hubby et al)—can't bear to stay put with, i.e., impale itself on, the rusty nail of a simple statement—in this case, that the patient in question—all patients for that matter—is an all-too-human, compassion-worthy contradiction in terms, a mix of man and turd, an untidy sum of good and bad, period. This simple (hence *too* simple) statement has whipped Straynge, or rather Straynge's words—which are light-years ahead of Straynge himself—into a syntactic cum synaptic frenzy. For them, imprisonment in a simple statement gagging on its own good intentions is a death sentence. So they—or the congeners who now rush into the breach to pick up their slack—have no choice but to not leave well enough alone—to find a way to maintain that being a contradiction in terms, a mix of man and turd, an untidy sum of good and bad, with good presumably mitigating bad, is in fact far far worse than being just plain bad. This anti-statement isn't so simple: it's extreme, it's perverse, it's indecent—worse, improbable. You could say it's the excreted embodiment of the prior statement's self-hate. And like any self-respecting text Straynge's craves nothing more than such extreme, improbable, perverse statements (the bad smell of a prior statement) precisely because they require the sort of justificatory qualification that stretches the sinews of the Text machine's explanational ingenuity to the breaking point (of course this is all about sophistical casuistry, but as the stakes are mortal, it's especially about poetry). And precisely because they give the Text machine's neuronal drones a run for their money—a real workout. And though any explanation/justification/qualification (call it Q-1) that Straynge comes up with (if his impulses are synapse-jumping at full-plus capacity) is sure to be clearcut enough to make perfect sense on the foolscap of discourse, its intricacy can be depended on to thwart every attempt to map it onto some flesh-and-blood state of affairs out there in the world of turds and men, while at the same time defying turds and men alike to prove no such one-to-one exists. And it is the very unprovability that ensures the survival of the word clot hence of Straynge itself—as handmaidens of the further e/j/q (call it Q-2) needed to prove that Q-1 resonates very much at the frequency of flesh-and-bloody things. Explanation/justification/qualification Q-3 of explanation/justification/qualification Q-2 of explanation/justification/qualification Q-1, and so on and so forth, are—is—what keeps the Straynge Text very much alive and kicking because forever on the move, taking unlocalizably zany twists and turns which are meant to be unlocalizable out in the world. For localizability is text-death. Straynge and his words brigade never know where such extreme, improbable statements will lead—at what point the process will come up against the wall of blessed unlocalizability—but what they do know is that the obligation to explain/justify what came before—to clean up after the previous indecent improbability—to stick to their guns—is their very lifeline. And with a little luck, the explanation/justification/qualification of anti-statement ME (that a mix of good and bad is worse than pure bad) will be even more perversely improbable than ME itself, thereby necessitating further explanation/justification/qualification. And with a little more luck, explanation/justification/qualification ME+1 will turn out to be of an even wackier cast, thereby necessitating . . .

Eden awaits in vain Straynge's hate-filled explanation/justification/qualification of anti-statement ME as fodder for his own hate. But the session is, or at least seems, shorter than usual, though as a rule it's never too short for Eden's taste.

CHAPTER NINE

The day dawns midsummer-grim, gritty-gusty, high-ozone—a typical Monday morning special à la NYC. And as far as Eden is concerned the fact that, as he exits the F on the lowest of the West Fourth Street station's too many levels, a pizza-greasy paper plate glued to a bench is the first thing to catch his eye doesn't augur at all well for the success of today's mock-rehab. Outside, he quickly convinces himself the omens are far cheerier (so what if much of what he sees he sees without seeing that he sees? His more precocious neurons get the drift anyway). Like any self-respecting streetcorner octopus, a ginkgo trains, by poignantly shadow-wrestling, to defend itself against the momentary thunderstorm. Hearing somebody mutter "disgruntled," he realizes the word has been invented for the sole purpose of straitjacketing another somebody just like him.

No need of Invidicum. What he's really gotten addicted to is the novel fix of participation in a group enterprise though the last thing he'll ever admit to (*But according to which whiz kid?*) is how soothing it can be to . . . belong. Why he even finds he's staying on after the last dose of the day has been duly administered, effectively signaling his solidarity with those career loudmouths who are in no hurry to go home, should they have one. Maybe, like some of them, he's getting the benefit not of Invidicum itself but of the very side effects somebody (Manning?) warned him about—fatal to charter members of the Envy Club but a veritable windfall to a lanky loner like him. After all, those middle-of-the-night chest pains are far more intermittent and, hey, there aren't any ugly black spots on his glans.

As he skims through today's *Post* in one of the many lounges in which the building abounds, Eden overhears what sounds like Narr telling what looks like Cook that the problem with this wonder drug is that it's just too effective for its own good. Now what exactly is the meaning of a crack like that, will you tell me (aka Eden)? Back where he comes from, there can never be too much of a good thing. This is what happens when the language drug gets into the wrong hands—is sold on the street to minors from eight to eighty without a prescription, so to speak, while the FDA (or is it the DEA?) turns a deaf ear and a blind eye. He's just about to put the question to his neighbor on the rubbery settee, whoever he is. Only he gets a little tongue-tied when it turns out to be Borkman, of all people, the rivals-lacerated ex-CEO, who's all too willing to break the ice—smash it up rather—with the trademark truncheon of his congratulatory self-hate. Reminded of the vegan joint Eden is a cough away from puking. For the nth time (as Cantor would say), he's made to hear all about what a lousy husband and father the mogul's been and, as far as parenting's concerned, will always be—in fact the world's worst—since he knows he'll never stop squandering his life force in dismal one-afternoon stands, committing sins of emission (hohoho) when he should be expiating sins of omission. Though—to whip up a little self-reassuring Envy frenzy among the hoi polloi—he makes it clear that the scenes of the crime (top-tier boutique hotels with at least three multilingual concierges per floor) are far from dismal. No denying he's drawn to the guy, never knowing where self-hate ends and hubris begins but whatever Borkman happens to be peddling at the moment, it's deployed like an extra—and shamelessly hairy—appendage. Clearly the old stud has a ton of horseshit on his plate but why should Eden let that cow him into not going ahead with his question? (is he overreacting to Borkman's signature tic, a neck-dislocating cough, which brings to mind his father's spasm-racked final hours?). But Eden must have posed it for here he is mumbling through his cough something to the effect that many of their fellow guinea pigs are afraid Invidicum, in curing Envy, will cure them of their very essence.

Warming to the subject, Borkman goes on to explain in a membrane-inflamed undertone, forever on the verge of expiring in the pebbliest of whispers (Narr and Cook are within hearing distance), that whether they know it or not those pigs are merely echoing ungrateful veterans of previous trials. (His younger son [or is it in fact the older?], a semi-hotshot with a PC, it so happens, has done a bit of research on the subject to impress his quarter-literate old man.) Blaming all their failures in love, life and work post-Invidicum on a rehab too total for its own good, they thereby tried, through propagation of the second-hand smoke of their defeatism, to breed a second generation of washouts. "Previous trials? You mean there were previous trials of the drug and it flopped?" Gently, he assures Eden that they involved much less potent versions of the drug—variants so poorly tolerated that, for all practical purposes, they could be considered horses of a completely different color.

Still, even in the face of the evidence, those rambunctious sour-grapers went on to play the hyper-potency card for all it was worth and at a well-publicized hearing held a few years back at mock-Moorish City Center on West Fifty-Fifth, insisted that they not only responded to what was clearly a megadose but responded all too well. That is to say, they ended up completely cured not just of their Envy, but of themselves—of everything within and without they'd come to treasure as uniquely and inviolably *them*. For some, it took months to recover even the tiniest part of what the drug had ruthlessly excised; for others, all was irrevocably lost. So the most lunatic among the lunatic fringe decided to bring, claiming ID theft, a class-action lawsuit against Warner-Metro, which of course came to nothing (details available from www.lunaticfringeInvidicumtrials.com). But all that's ancient history. As far as John's concerned (*That's right, call him John*) no potion worth its salt can ever deliver too many positive effects. What he for one needs is something deadly enough to keep images of his deadliest rivals (pudgy thumbs stuck deep in their smug snouts) from parasailing across his airspace. Eden wonders how Borkman comes by so much knowledge of prior trials. He doesn't seem to be much of a historiographer: as it so happens, the gaps in the bit of due diligence he did carry out were filled in by his lawyer and even more diligently by his lawyer's girlfriend cum girl Friday of the moment.

Before Eden goes in—but is it to see Straynge or Manning? (He's having more and more trouble keeping his schedule straight [a side effect of the big I?], which is as it should be, 'cause frailty [thy name is madman] makes him more . . . sellable.) Before he goes in, Borkman aka John (he's waiting for the initial rush of his increased dosage to wear off before venturing out into the wilds of Waverly Place, where commingling with the braless coeds never fails to massage his sagging spirits) cautions him against committing what he's discovered the hard way to be *the* cardinal sin as far as Straynge's concerned. "The cardinal sin?" "I mean speaking too quickly and too freely about intimate matters, for old Straynge is the very model of a modern major quack of the old school and too proud for his own good of that dismal fact." That he always gets right to the point, requiring no prompting whatsoever to trot out the details of his shamefully sexual life and the even more shameful details of his half-life as the world's lousiest father, has put Straynge off—permanently, he fears (*but* who is speaking? *Borkman? [no, not enough self-knowledge]; the Master? IIV? the narrator? the author? the reader? [who the author has trained to be up on the latest characterological extravagances of Straynge's clientele]*). But the drug is working big time so what does it matter if Straynge hates his guts and intends to flunk him silly in Self-Exorcism 101.

Borkman's hand, which he's placed paternally on Eden's shoulder, sticks around to give his scapula a first-class micromassage. Which doesn't prevent him from mock-lamenting the fact that his forthright ease in describing the most lurid encounters while throwing in at no extra charge a pointer or two on how to practice super-savory unsafe sex yet live to tell the tale (Eden hopes this won't segue into an excoriation of that universal whipping boy, the XXX-Gov.) has challenged—and ultimately undone—Straynge in the very core of his expertness. As regards the disastrous parenting, which Borkman admits to so blithely (Tell me about it, Eden shudders), he has uncharitably given Straynge no opportunity to insist there is absolutely nothing to feel guilty about (as long, that is, as he dutifully hangs his head until further notice). But don't get him wrong—he couldn't feel sorrier for the smarmy old bastard— and for the fact that he just can't see his way clear to transforming himself into one of the many who require just such coddling-brutal midwifery as Straynge famously practices. But, damn it, man, he, aka Borkman the Red Layman, isn't here to feel sorry for anybody—not even himself—least of all for the so-called experts, no matter how sorry a sight their inexpertise turns out to be.

"As far as Big Jim is concerned, I've failed badly at being a patient precisely because I've made him feel like a failure. And all because I haven't allowed him to lick his chops over my shame while pretending to be busy freeing me of it. So take a page or two from a failure's guidebook. If you are what you seem to be—a healthy strapping guy who takes his pussy straight, without a chaser—do not on any account show how much at home you feel in your humanness. Don't approach him from any direction other than sheer self-hate. Your job is to let him see how much the humanness makes your skin crawl. Otherwise he'll start feeling helpless and feeling helpless he'll get punitive. Look, before you go in why don't you take a minute or two to brush up on how to look horribly uncomfortable about everything that makes you you?"

Borkman senses he's about to reach that point of no return which he's been reaching more and more frequently since treatment began—the same point, he suspects, being reached by the other stooges in the group—where insight and the eloquence needed to convey it become incompatible with character. Where what there is left to say about Eden's self-hate and Straynge's helplessness—and there's plenty—and how it needs to get said, are beyond his reach and his means. Where his own thinking needs to be usurped by Invidicum's thinking (*who is speaking?*)—by Invidicum's thinking through a sort of mastermind (Borkman's still a bit shy about using the byword *Master*) or (whatever that all boils down to) vice versa—because it makes no sense for he himself to be expressing what he'd never in a million years be capable of thinking, much less expressing, and let alone with an eloquence up to the Invidicum mastermind's high standards. So it's time for Invidicum or the mastermind behind its administration or the mastermind behind the mastermind—and he doesn't mean Post or Straynge (they're ultimately small fry: he can feel it in his activist bones)—to take over. Or rather, a compromise must be struck. Any further insight, necessarily super-subtle, on the subject of Eden's self-hate and Straynge's helplessness must be expressed indirectly (farewell brash quotation marks)—through indirect speech—along the border—the paries—between his voice and the Big Other's. But under the circumstances, wouldn't it be more in keeping with Borkman's reputation as a man's man, fluctuations in his status as a mogul's mogul notwithstanding, not to lend his voice, even indirectly, to an insight he hasn't earned by the sweat—or, more to the point, the chicanery—of his brow?

Eden suddenly feels somebody else has recently taken just such a tack—the suggested tack—maybe he himself. That somebody else in the group has made the same point—or at least thought it through last week or the week before. Which signifies nothing less than that the Invidicum currently flowing through their veins is flowing through what's become one big collective vein afflicting them, intravenously, with the same eloquence. And if so, so what? Isn't originality overrated? And in any case, even if somebody else has already taken this tack—i.e., cautioning that the only way to keep Straynge from feeling helpless is to approach him through the defiles of self-hate, etc., the tack was taken, the thought pellet shot, at a different time and in a different place, which means that right now and right here Borkman's take *is* original. All the more reason for him to lash out—not play the self-hate card. After all, Borkman's original enough to be able to take Straynge's ensuing viciousness. He has, unlike Eden, originality to keep him warm, or at least lukewarm. It seems he's had this hunch before—many times before—ever since the Invidicum kicked in, or refused to do so.

"I don't have to brush up. I feel horribly uncomfortable about plenty of things that make me *me*—terrible things, things that are beyond shameful. Things that deserve to make my skin crawl. But I've been figuring out a way to redeem myself." He's tempted to reveal what has brought him to the Big Apple.

Thinking he's being kind, Borkman says he can't imagine Eden ever doing anything that would give it the right to make his skin crawl. He treats himself to a refreshingly deep breath after this good deed—the first in many days. Yet what do we have here? If he didn't know better he'd say the wildly pacing beneficiary is glaring at him with outrage.

If for no other reason than to slow him down (quite a few eyebrows are being raised, including Narr's; Cook, on the other hand, is imperturbably cell-bound), Borkman apologizes tenderly. He's sorry but all this has been only by way of looking out for Eden's best interests. In fact, he hopes Eden won't think him crazy but at this very moment he feels he's chatting with his older son but on a much saner, happier footing. All he meant is that Eden needs to refrain from breaking—or he'll be *done for* (does Borkman in fact know what's brought him to the Big Apple?)—the unspoken contract existing between Patient and Angekok (Eskimo for *shaman*, according to his son [you mean, according to *Cantor*, thinks Eden, disgusted to see that, even unprovoked, this senile blowhard has no trouble going into proud papa overdrive]) under which the former has nothing to be ashamed of as long as he remains consumed with shame and puts himself, so consumed, in the adjudicating hands of the latter, aka the Flémalle Master of Shame and Non-Shame (*Who just said that?* Borkman wonders Nederlandishly). Such is the homeostatic mechanism at play in the P-A organism.

"Isn't it a little late to be telling me this?"

"It's never too late: every session is a brand-new beginning. As so many bushy-tailed therapists have told me."

He mustn't make the fatal mistake of charging right in, refusing to stagger his patient's progress, revealing his most shocking thoughts and his most indecent feelings without being prompted—rushing his effects, however spectacular, like a too-talented ballerina. As far as Straynge is concerned, Borkman's so precociously in tune with his disease, why, it's positively pathological. But where, he asks Eden, has attunement gotten him? He's ended up robbing Straynge of his expertise, his vocation, his identity, his very manhood. By castrating him he's made an enemy for life. Borkman bursts out laughing. Eden joins in, appeased by somebody else's misery even if it's simulated.

It must be all over the Institute by now (Borkman mugs for the camera by looking around nervously—*too* nervously, since there doesn't appear to be anybody in sight worth dreading), his daring to deactivate the landmines of his own psychic terrain without cues from his coach (or, to use the catchphrase of the moment, his *handler*). Post, not to mention that Manning woman and the rest of their gang, has probably gotten wind of the mess he's created—the dire precedent he's set—and will no doubt drop him as a bad influence. He says this with understandable pride. More laughter. Eden actually feels happy.

He adds, though there's nothing to add—no, not really—since between the two of them they've managed to cover all essential points (it's a joint effort, after all: Eden is simply Borkman's straight man—it's a beauty-before-age kind of thing)—he adds that one of his hang-ups is not wanting any extenuating circumstance to mar the purity of the problematic encapsulated by, for example, his fatherhood—or to be more exact, his non-fatherhood. Straynge doesn't seem to get it. Borkman waits for Eden to ask, "Doesn't get what?" But he doesn't—because he's either not interested or self-preoccupied or because he already knows the answer—by heart. Finally, Eden does ask—but Borkman's already well into explaining that Straynge simply can't fathom how Borkman might prefer—might prefer to *know* that the mismatch between him and his

kids—and not just any old mismatch but a providentially irremediable one—
has nothing to do with the way Borkman's pop—more weasel than pop, in
fact—treated him. As one of the deposed kings of Wall Street, he can't let anybody—least of all that old faker Upbringing—steal the show, especially when
the whole show is his child bride Uniqueness. Nobody's fault: just an unlucky
throw of the dice that made him—who'd come hateful and hideous out of
nowhere and whose tragic flaws owed nothing to his genome—irreparably
him. In fact, Borkman can't lay claim to a genome: as he not-so-merrily rolled
around in the womb all his genes were mutated before they had occasion to
become themselves (parodies before they were originals)—and to everybody's
detriment of course—and he's been carrying on the tradition ever since. How
explain to this crazy mixed-up kid who is probably a lot less crazy-mixed-up
than he is that he actually likes being hemmed in by the hatred coming at
him from both ends of the lineal chain—from his pop and his get—the more
righteous the better.

There is no way to explain. So Borkman does what he thinks is the next
best thing, by saying: "And at the same time, I have to give him some credit.
After all, I don't want you to go marching in there thinking Big Jim is a rotten
sonofabitch and nothing but. Why, at our last session (or maybe it was the
one before or the one right before that), in a tone which showed there were
no hard feelings even if my shamelessness didn't leave him any room to do
what he did best . . . he suggested I might try a little handball—or was it racquetball? or chess?—with my kids. He found that a game or two with his own
boy two or three times a week, even now that he was fully grown and doing
brilliantly," (Borkman had, in the men's room, overheard starkly otherwise)
"as well as the occasional lap or two around the Reservoir after which they hit
the showers—"

But the effect of his words was so powerful as to make it impossible for
Borkman to understand a damn thing he said. Oh, of course he did understand that Straynge wanted him to drool over the better-than-great relationship he, unlike Borkman, was capable of having with his spittin' image. Still,
not even that could prevent him from doing more to cure Borkman than all
the Invidicum in the world. "*They—the words—acted like a remedy when
they were most a poison,*" he heard himself think (was this the Invidicum
vengefully talking back to him, doing the thinking for the two of them?). As
Straynge babbled on, Borkman felt he was finally getting an edge, at least for
as long as the music lasted, not just on him but on all of his rivals, past, present and future, who were rolled up into this smug little superdad with a silly
flag pin on (what else?) the lapel of his spiffy navy blazer. And his—or rather,
their—being diverted by so much trivia, like racquetball and reservoir jogging
and saunas and masseuses and maybe even backyard barbecues, meant it was
Borkman and Borkman alone who'd win out in the end. Borkman thought
he saw a quizzical look on Eden's mug, and pounced. Why? Well, because
while Achilles MacStraynge allowed himself to get distracted right and left,
Borkman, aka MacTortoise, was, like a good boy, continuing to focus his
efforts on the Big Picture—hostile takeovers, reverse mergers, vulture-invest-
ing, that sort of thing. Against the backdrop of—in contradistinction to—

Straynge's unknowing confession of failure to keep his blind-eye on the ball, those efforts suddenly had a different valence: they were giving off—for the first time in months, maybe decades—a whiff of victory.

"So my man Straynge—sorry, Our Man Straynge—in trying to make me envious of the fact that he was not merely a worker of the first rank but, unlike me, a well-rounded one, managed instead to trigger the most gigantic spasm of hope I'd ever experienced. Thanks to that backfiring boob, I'm primed for a comeback. Now, when some cabbie starts bellowing about his next trip to Vegas (as one did last night), where he's sure to break the bank, or the counterman in the deli on East Ninety-Fourth (where I always stop off for bialys) offers me yet another sneak preview of the windfall he's sure to reap from the stocks Carl I. Shure-Cahn (not just another regular but, like Bill the Ackmann Cometh, a scumbagger cum carpetbagger extraordinaire) told him—just ten minutes before—to buy (imagine me! John Gabriel Borkman! once upon a time envying such lowlifes!)—now, I say, when somebody starts bellowing to beat the band I'm able to give in to the same dimwitted optimism. For whatever they're about to do is the very last thing in the world they *should* be doing if they intend to make it big." "Maybe they shouldn't want to make it big," Eden says, looking away, to the front desk. The admitting clerk regularly regards him with contempt even when, as now, he's resolutely staring hard into the pitch-black rabbit hole of cyberspace (he always has a little side-sneer handy—available for Eden's . . . perusal? consumption?).

"So why shouldn't I gloat? Hell, everybody's my rival and since *everybody except me is letting himself get sidetracked*, I'm bound to be first at the finish line and in world-record time to boot." His eyes beg Eden to second the motion but fearing non-response, he immediately voids them of all entreaty. "But in the old movies my dad used to watch over and over and over rather than look at, much less talk, to me—especially *D.O.A.* with Edmond O'Brien (he was really nuts about that one)—the hero is *always* getting sidetracked. Isn't it the job of a hero to get sidetracked?" He knows he sounds querulous, bitchy, even serpentlike, even if he doesn't mean to. But facts are facts—or better yet, fiction is fiction. With a snicker Borkman retorts, "But I'm no hero," although it comes out sounding much more like a sob, for whose upsurge Eden wretchedly takes full responsibility. Entering, Eden feels not a little like the ill-fated Laffler (Stanley Ellin: "The Specialty of the House") being allowed at last to enter Sbirro's sanctum sanctorum. But this can't be *his* thought. Since fact is, he's never heard of Sbirro or Ellin—or *Alfred Hitchcock Presents*, for that matter (wasn't born yet, he supposes). So exactly whose thought has he just incurred?

The first thing Straynge says once Eden has, as usual, taken his mid-afternoon dose in front of him ("Swallow it all: there's a good boy" [chuckle, chuckle])—(Wait, is Eden mistaken or has Straynge just shown a glimmer of recognition of the *real* Eden? Too late—the glimmer's already gone though isn't that precisely what any self-respecting glowworm of apperception is supposed to do, i.e., get itself gone before you know it?) The first thing Straynge says is, "You're a little late: for a while there I was afraid you'd gotten yourself sucked up into Jake's vacuum cleaner—he's the new janitor—I mean the new custodial engineer." Oddly enough Eden isn't offended (he wonders why he hasn't already noticed that Straynge's office directly faces St. Vincent's Seventh Avenue ambulance ramp). Is it possible—or worth it—to loathe Straynge more than he already does? Deciding quickly no, he chooses instead to follow the image straight into Jake's woolly innards where Straynge's animosity no longer matters in the least and where almost immediately he begins to experience a peace he hasn't known for ages, not since his last real vacation in fact (where was it? sleepy Carpinteria! and when? only three weeks after his father's funeral with his then girlfriend, a chain-smoking dancer who found God [and ballet-world pariahdom] by taking it up the ass [and living to tell the tale—and a little masterpiece of a tale it is, too]).[9] Even if the remark confirms that to Straynge he is, at best, a knucklehead—or worse, a meatball—still (or is this just the voice of Invidicum coming in loud and clear at last thanks to the Master's transducement?), there seems to be hard at work here what can only be described as some sort of homage to his unique capability—not given to every knucklehead, after all—of inspiring such flights of anarchic fancy. Eden's way of thanking this old butterball is to say, "I haven't met Jake yet," and to ask if the sour aftertaste he's recently been experiencing will persist even when he's on a low maintenance dose. How graciously he manages to bypass Straynge's provocation. So unlike him.

Portentously putting notepad and disposable fountain pen to one side of his blotter and licking his lips, if not his chops, Straynge asks him, as he's taken to doing at the beginning of every session, if the Envy's still getting out of control—it's known to happen especially among the very *pharmakoses* who are ultimately certain to benefit most. Why? Eden wonders, though he must admit—or somebody must admit for him—that this paradox certainly sounds good enough on paper. Keeps the obfuscation going and if you can keep the obfuscation going then you've got the reader—er, the mystery-lovin' listener—licked. As always, Eden the assassin has to think super-fast and para-plausible. "My co-est co-worker up on Riverside Boulevard"—"The poor man's Sunset," Straynge chuckles, though there's little enough to chuckle about, as far as Eden can see. "—is getting to me more and more. He's definitely on the make and as to how far somebody like him can go, the sky's the limit. He wants to run his own start-up—into the ground, the little shit. But" (giving a tone of defiance his very best shot) "I don't want to talk about it!" Borkman would be proud of him—his response is meant to convey a rookie's discomfort with shame and self-hate which borders on frenzy and Straynge looks mighty impressed—but by what? by whom? the dainty little shitkicker? "And what is it exactly that *you* want to do? It's you I'm interested in." Eden's shrug gives him no alternative but to retreat to the window. But you can bet a little thing like the pane's being desperately in need of a good scrubbing won't

---

[9] The tale in question is none other than, as every woman and ever womanizer should know, *The Surrender* by fearless Toni Bentley. Relegating it to the non-category of "eroterica" should be punishable by death—not the "little death," but death pure and simple.

keep a visionary like Straynge from getting things right enough to be able to turn around and say, "So you desperately Envy Joe Blow's get-up-and-go. His manly sense of direction which is, as I certainly don't need to tell you, more important than ever nowadays. And when he's around, you feel obliged to sneer and grumble though you're not quite sure about what. You may even take a crack at masturbating in the john to work off steam and at renting porno flicks on your way home to tune out Reality (which from what you say JB's clearly got by the balls) even more. So that by the time 4 a.m. rolls around you're stoned, stewed and stinking." Eden takes a deep breath as if it's he who's just been running off at the mouth. "Why not admit it—there's nothing to be ashamed of here. You're among friends."

Eden can't believe what he's hearing, window or no window. Before he's even begun to get into the swing of discussing the ins and outs of his phantom-limb affliction, here he is, the man of the fifty-minute hour, being cut off at the root so it can be made brutally clear there isn't going to be any halfwit beating about the bush where said affliction's sordid details are concerned—not on Straynge's watch, that is. Eden is glad he doesn't suffer from Envy if this is the way the big S. manhandles its victims. Although *votaries* may be a better word—whose utterance by those victims would be especially liberating if only they could see their way clear to taking the plunge.

As the session drags on (no use protesting that the sordid details should or need not apply for examination), Eden becomes less and less sure that Straynge has intervened to help him over some Borkmanesque hurdle of unnecessary shame. What seems more likely, at least to an avowed layman, is that he's concocted that hurdle for the sole purpose of getting himself over it—or one like it. Maybe it's Straynge who routinely jerks off when his colleague—Envy—becomes too potent for teeth-gritting and who, even if his shamanly credits stretch from here to Canarsie, wherever that is, still has trouble pole-vaulting past shame at doing so. But both needing to confess and afraid his reputation—i.e., his very identity—may not survive the ordeal, he's had the brilliant—no, luminous—no, numinous—idea of packaging the confession as Eden's—byproduct of his tender-hearted omniscience about what this born patsy must be going through harboring the aftertaste of such horrors (of which he, of course, as a man of the cloth has no experience first- or even secondhand). Straynge, the all-knowing angekok, is—in a bit of inspired miscasting—conferring on Eden the status of father confessor by proxy, knowing full well he can reclaim the role any time he chooses. So in this case—and probably in tons of others which went similarly unaudited—the hapless patient is being billed for the witch doctor's own self-rehab. Though (also in this case) at least there's no out-of-pocket.

"So you're envious of your co-worker down at the plant—it is a plant, isn't it?" "That's not what I said." Though for some reason Eden wishes it were. "Aren't you listening, old man?" *Old man* makes him feel he's getting closer at last to the meat-and-potatoes of the matter that is the taking out of his hated father's killer. "How's that? I can't hear you." Cronelike irritability contorts his regular features and lends them the glare of shameless resentment. Perversely refusing to make himself heard proves beyond the shadow of a doubt that

Eden is the lostest of lost causes—too lost to be worthy of expert treatment. Or maybe the perversity is all Straynge's (has he ever thought about that?)—in refusing to hear what he's heard only too well as impugning his competence.

"In any event, plant or no plant, life as you live it is unbearably unjust. He's getting all the breaks. Given a track record like yours, you deserve better, etc., etc."

"Not just him."

Again, Straynge grimaces his refusal to hear. "What?"

"I'm envious of everybody, *not just him*." Eden applauds his own cleverness. By *going global*, he's managed to get Straynge off the scent. But even if he has, what's the connection with going global, as he—or somebody else—puts it? He's shouting and at the same time enunciating every syllable so that, if the shouting fails, Straynge will have no trouble reading his lips.

"I can't be expected to remember all the details." (Does Straynge actually consider Eden wily enough to accuse him of forgetting what is in fact a brand-new admission—hot off the press? If so, it's another coup for *misperception the gem of the ocean*!) "For one thing, I don't have your file in front of me. But that's not the point. Look at me. I mean, *look* at me. All right, so I'm low man on the scrotum pole up at Sinai where I do most of my research. A psychiatrist is always low man in any medical setup. It's the cardiac and brain surgeons who run the show. But do I care? Am I envious? Hell, no. *I love to practice.* I never allow Envy to get in the way of that—never has. Never, Eden. Even if I have the smallest corner office and my window faces the darkest brick wall. Even if I get the sorriest-looking secretary on the block—he's a man to boot!—and whom, by the way, I share with three other low men just like me. Even if as one gets older, my—one's—penis doesn't always get hard when one wants it to." Is this last supposed to strike a responsive chord? Always at the ready, old S. is, to courageously shoulder the burden of speaking the unspeakable for more than just himself even—especially—if the unspeakable in question happens (as is the case here and now) to afflict nobody *but* himself.

Eden squirms, looks at his naked wrist, feels therapeutically superior to Straynge inasmuch as Straynge's handsome timepiece reposes none too comfortably within its setting of wrist tendrils—too thick, too black. He would have preferred anything to Straynge's crying on his shoulder while professing to be too much of a man's man ever to stoop to such a thing—demanding, as he vows to go on loving his work through thick and thin, that Eden help him bemoan his tragic fate and—more to the point—canonize him for not bemoaning it. Anyway, far more interesting than Straynge's model triumph over humiliation is his insane conviction that all this brouhaha, involving brick walls, plastic surgeons, secretaries of a certain age and gender, totem poles and who the hell knows what else, actually amounts to one—model or otherwise. Thing is—or rather, more to the point—Eden has trouble, although he's not exactly or even inexactly aware that he's having trouble, imagining Straynge "practicing"—can't evoke the activity corresponding to the word— maybe because for him (and for this the obsessively tight-lipped operatives who treated him at Langley Porter and other venerable neurospsychiatric institutes after his breakdown are clearly to blame) a bona fide vocation must by its very nature be too ingrained, pervasive, ubiquitous—excruciatingly tax-ing—to be describable. Sure, the Democrats never miss an opportunity to brag about how they can tightrope and chew gum *at the same time*. Still, Eden just doesn't get how Straynge can simultaneously practice and talk up what he practices—any meta-talk about commitment should have been swallowed up by his mighty exertions centuries ago. In short, Eden's having trouble—big trouble—mapping *practicing* (as the mighty Straynge goes about the business of practicing) into the real world. Putting the word into one-to-one corre-spondence with some thing—some event—some referent *out there*. Although he could never put this disquiet (which is the closest he'll ever come, or at least for now, to a conviction) into words, he suspects dimly that Some Body is warehousing the words for him. (*OK—it's the Master:* why are the members of the Invidicum tribe having more and more trouble naming the Master the more they get accustomed to his force-feedings? Why has naming become so excruciatingly concessionary?). Words, after all, are not his *thing*, even if Invidicum, compliments of the most important of its side effects, is sending his eloquence coefficient—like a fever—through the roof. (Now it all comes back to him: Didn't Straynge, administering his first dose, mumble something that could pass for a warning along the lines of: *Youngish man, don't be overly alarmed if you begin to experience symptoms like vertigo or rice-water stool or, worst of all, eloquence. Don't be alarmed even if the eloquence you bleed through your veins is the same as everybody's else eloquence—don't be even more alarmed if your insight is as insightful as everybody else's insight?*) Though who'd be crazy enough to want to off-label The Big I for such a purpose?

Straynge looks Eden straight in the eye but—as is usually the case—uncandidly for all that. The shameless old fart is imploring him to admit—in other words, daring him to deny—that the best thing to have happened to him so far, or rather to his affliction, is being shown how the mature male, priapic or not, trumps the hand which ever-senile fate has dealt him. Eden reminds himself he has to put up with Straynge just a wee bit longer.

"By the way, have you started *Envy Through the Millennia*? Eden says he absolutely hasn't, which is the first defiantly distance-keeping thing that pops into his head, then realizes this is in fact the truth, since during a rare home visit his last Lady of the Week, furious at having stubbed a sloppily painted toe on the monster, tried to tear all nine hundred-odd pages (his cursory tally) to shreds.

"You should read at least a chapter a night: Aristotle, Bacon, Burton, Nietzsche, Veblen, Scheler, Evans-Pritchard, Girard, Rawls, Schoeck." Quite a lineup, Eden snickers to himself. He remembers them, albeit not vividly, from his orientation-packet days, which seem a million miles away and counting. "Those guys, Eden, will show you it's beating Envy to the finish line that makes them great. You'll feel less alone. Less like you should jump out of a window (Riverside Boulevard, isn't it?) the first chance you get." "But you don't understand: I *like* feeling alone. The only consolation in being an Envy junkie is knowing my brand of the virus is unlike everybody else's—even if that means I'm incurable. It's thanks to the uniqueness that I don't jump." Straynge shudders at the word as if he himself isn't the one who casually introduced it seconds before. Eden has a silly thought: maybe the big S. gets a commission on every jump he successfully micromanages into a fatality. Also, Eden feels—though he's not yet at the point where he can think the feeling—his uniqueness junkie's perverse insistence on stumping Straynge's expertise (which generated the shudder)—not to mention Nietzsche's—proves both (*a*) that his affliction simply doesn't exist and (*b*) that it very much does exist but in its present form has proven supremely undeserving of treatment.

From discomfort (though Eden tells himself it's to throw Straynge off the scent) he says, "Sorry to bore you with the same old stuff, doc." "On the contrary, it's a gift." Long silence. "I don't get you." "You've taken the risk—overcome the terror—of *sharing* your shame with me." Now it's Eden's turn to shudder, without knowing why. Well, I'll tell you why: because with every fiber of his being he rejects, as well he should if he has any self-respect, the disgusting namby-pambiness of sharing. "But there isn't any risk or terror. I've never had trouble spilling my guts—to you or anybody else." But Straynge is too busy congratulating himself for having managed not only to make a gift out of whatever miseries Eden saw fit to fling onto the pyre—the altar—of his professional savvy but also to provide the giver with a counter-gift, namely, the good tidings that the gift arrived on the recipient's consulting couch in record time and mint condition. And if this ingrate—this washout—is daring to reproach him for using the term "gift" to define his own measly burnt offerings then that reproach, too, is a gift. Pity. Eden will need to learn the hard way that the prison house of a mind diseased runs on the fossil fuel of gift-giving.

CHAPTER TEN

To work off the tumult triggered by an overpowering attraction to subject One (he insists on refusing to know that he knows Eden's name in full: he has some pride left, after all), Cantor decides the best—to wit, the most therapeutic—way to make his 5:45 lecture (on pathological curves, what else?) is to walk to Forty-Second, take the No. 6 a few sweaty stops, then cross the Park and bus it up Broadway on the M104. Without first working off some sexual steam, he just can't bring himself to enter a subway, least of all at West Fourth, amid a de Kooningesque mush of MetroCards and pigeon shit. He reaches Grand Central Turmoil at the very moment the Chrysler Building (*Oh, come now, is it really* at the very moment?) has started, with the trusty scalpel of its spire, to lance the black-bellied boil on the rump of a cumulus and although both doctor and patient look primed to put on quite a show, he just doesn't have the stomach to wait for what's known in the world of pornography as the Money Shot, knowing, in his present state, that he'll just ooze away with the massive discharge (it's a formidable rump, after all). He wants to fuck Eden and then (with the preliminaries out of the way)—to *know* him, to the extent that his choice of words will feminize him into knowability. But never mind things like choice of words. What do they matter when he can shelter—not in place but in movement—frenetic movement exhorted by the movement of every-body else—and all of it under the aegis—no, the baton—of the Celestial Ceiling of the terminal's Main Concourse? The Concourse exalts him into feeling deliciously small and, at the same time, important—mighty—by virtue of smallness. So in this case small and big are not opposites—not contrastive—each feeds off the other—each pays off without demur the penalty incurred by the other as in some Presocratic goat song. In fact, they're brothers-in-arms impressed into the same battle—a battle for subjugation of desire by pride.

The No. 6 is overstuffed. *Like a Carnegie Deli Reuben*, he thinks—because, let's face it, somebody's got to think it: it's what the moment, if not the Age, demands. Not the image of the moment's accelerated grimace, nor Sappho's barbitos, but a Reuben. The closed-eyed woman beside him is, through no fault of her own, hectically chewing the cud of some unthinkable obsession, and rightly determined not to let the push and pull of the other straphangers interfere. All that rumination makes her—as it would have made anybody—smell bad but he somehow manages, with an *Excuse me* to the nosepicker on his right, to gracelessly squeeze his way out of the car at Hunter College, even if he hasn't intended to exit the underground quite so soon (but is he in a state to intend anything at this point?). But there's a fringe benefit of the nosepicking—maleness when he needs it most of all, at this moment of infatuation. But he has enough time—in fact, the moment is infinitely exten-sible, or at least feels so—to look at the nosepicker with disgust barely sup-pressed (but suppressed nonetheless). And it's thanks to the unpremeditated suppression that he becomes a prime exemplar of the Judging Male—hence male—he becomes his father if you must know—maleness hitchhikes on the back of authentic disgust—a moment of true affect, then—not a performance (performances are women's work) for the benefit of, say, the ruminant behind him. The maleness lies in the forbearance in the face of another male's silly unsanitary trespass. So here is an aptly male response to circumstance which apt response calls into question all his convictions—illusions?—of perpetual disqualification for maleness—about not measuring up. And since he's the firmest believer in giving credit where credit is due and not allowing virtue to be its own reward, he must admit the phrase "calling into question" has played no small role in bolstering the maleness. Fact is, at the moment of deftly bystepping the nosepicker and his own revulsion—at that unpredicted moment he felt very much estranged from what he took to be his self. The suppressed disgust allows him—compels him—to bifurcate, gastrulate. Who is he—the male who manfully suppresses his disgust? or the real and inextirpable self that wishes it could be the suppressor? Here he is in the wake of disgust—sceptical at, resigned to, detached from, being the self called into existence by the nosepicker—the self that is and is not he. The self that is a heuristic self—to the extent that it shows him what he could be if he were this male, i.e., this real, *all the time*. He's too lofty—too male—to express his disgust. Just when Everybody inside the car and without thinks he's going to stare down the nosepicker loudly enough to draw the attention of Everybody to his hideous doings, he turns up his nose—the most manly turn-up in the history of maleness—at this offer of giddy mass approval, refusing to be infected by the giddiness—turns away as if preoccupied by something entirely different, thereby casting a retrospective too-male-to-be-derisive innocence on what Everybody is only too ready and willing to take for hyper-observing mockery, i.e., femaleness. He turns away, proving that what they've all along thought to be X is in fact Y: he's simply staring past the nosepicker as the merest waystation en route to thought, deep thought. Let's face it, he's the strong silent type on the John Wayne model. After all, doesn't every self-respecting male want to be John Wayne—even John Wayne himself? Since JW never takes note of anything petty, comical, bathetic, of what can only indict him—for being what he notes.

Herbert sees Cantor getting off at her stop, but hopes she won't have to say hello. Though she heard him reviling Proposition 8 during a strident cell-phone chat in front of the Lafayette Bakery, *it isn't because of his homosexuality that she wants to avoid him.* So why has she just issued a disclaimer regarding what is supposedly inconceivable—the farthest thing from her mind? All right, then, *so it is because of his *orientation*, at least in part. She's been peripheralized (Herbert hates *marginalized*) too much to risk further margi . . . er, peripheralization) compliments of the peripheralized company she keeps. That he is lily-white is of course not to be discounted and she doesn't feel much inclined, especially right before her screenwriting class (though why *especially*?), to *make white.* Though at other moments what she calls white words definitely have their oily attraction as a forged passport to better things. It all depends on how she feels, or thinks she feels. But given her newfound hunger to express (though it's far from new), no words are safe—neutral— adequate anymore, not even, i.e., *especially*, black words.

Does she envy—sorry, Envy—him his white words? Is that what it all comes down to in the end? No, she mustn't go around doing the bidding of whoever—i.e., the Some Body behind Straynge, Post et al—is running this puppet show ("whoever" is shaking a forefinger at her to put the finishing touches on the dehortation). (*So she, too, is having greater and greater difficulty calling a spade a spade, that is, difficulty in calling the Master a Master.*) Mustn't take the bait (but whose?) and go around imposing a false unity on the proceedings every chance she gets—making it all come together on the Cloth of the Field of Envy. So he can sell it to the folks who take their whiskey straight, their metaphors mixed and their entertainment all tied up in a neat little package of fake—sorry, faux—organicity. What is it her favorite prof is fond of saying? *Three cheers for centrifugality.* Unity must come from within, if it comes at all—pushing itself up and out from under the morass of incompossibles. (*Yeah, bub, incompossibles, you heard me right the first time*—and by *bub* she means all the white folk out there who're not just willing but *ready and willing* to squelch her aspirations.) Excruciating discomfort overtakes Herbert in the lobby of the West Building. Every (fellow?) student is young enough to be her grandchild or rather (*making white*) her *grandkid.* But that's not it. Can Herbert help it if she feels acutely—but far more acutely than her trial mates, who seem to be given more and more to expressing similar misgivings among themselves (similar, yes, in being about the trial but along its least interesting dimensions) or on cellphones to "buddies" back home though with nowhere near the exuberant urgency with which, in the right company, she'll disgorge *her* misgivings?— Can she help it if she feels acutely that—that— But there's no room—no excuse—for feeling acutely about the Master as if she were some blushing schoolgirl. As a budding something or other, she should know by now what it's like to be another's work in progress—his pivot point—and she does and what's more, she promises to refer to the Master *as* the Master every chance she gets. And neither can she pretend that He doesn't loathe the results so far. Granted, she's dangerously alien and worst-of-both-worlds dangerously endemic to her creator—an embodied resistance to his aims. He's not one to be bargained—much less reasoned—with. But she doesn't need to reason: she already knows Him by heart (it's all happening so fast) and it's the very difficulty of the attainment of His aims that keeps Him—a difficulties addict—going strong. So He should be grateful for her throughput. His job as He sees it—as she sees him seeing it—is to compel her to make His most harrowing thoughts her own but in her own way, her own . . . context, to the point of unrecognizability. Whatever contorted feelings He—and she simply has to start referring to him under all circumstances as He (Master is much too formal)—has about spinach, say, can take the form of her feelings, for example, about . . . Building 18! For she's sure He's convinced, her creator is—for He's also her creation!—that no thought's worth a damn unless (for what is thought but feeling kept in the deep freeze until it thaws?) there's a core that can be abstracted to, refracted through, other contexts—the more alien the better. The more alien the context, the bigger the challenge, naturally, of making the thought fit—that is, *not quite fit.* Which is all to the good, since better than anybody she knows life does *not quite fit.* So, His doubts notwithstanding, she and her puppeteer are going to get along—are already getting along—just fine. (Another cause for celebration: she's eluded the sticky issue of Proposition 8 without even trying.)

Thing is, she doesn't want her accursed Building 18 hijacked. Building 18 belongs to her alone. Isn't that why she's back in school—to learn how to tell the world about Building 18? Not how to talk about Building 18 in order to be talking about something completely different. She takes out her new, cobalt blue Miquelrius notebook and a pencil, disappointed to see that—for all her past scribblings about the side effects of her son's medication which she sometimes mixes up with present scribblings about the side effects of her own (imagine, using her own son to talk about herself! why, she's a lot worse than her creator!)—it's nowhere near being honorably worn down to the bone. Hence, not to be discarded, yet.

For, truth be told, Herbert lives less to write than to wear down to the bone the tools of what she aspires to call her trade (is the perversity of this observation the Master's handiwork?). So as to be able to discard and replace them with bright shiny new ones every chance she gets. For at the privileged moment of discarding she trashes not only the tools but the trade along with them. So this stage business of wearing down, so as to be able to replace, the tools of the trade is turning out to be not a preparation for plying the trade but a willed escape from plying the trade—it has become the trade hook, line and sinker (so the observation isn't as perverse as it seems). And she's always amazed at how much lighter she feels—she, a mere apprentice! And it serves the trade right. Since more and more, this accursed trade (too heavily weighted toward white words) whose practice is supposed to guide her toward the Truth (so much of a piece with black words) ends up blocking access to It. How? Why? Because she's always coming up with the right word for something out there before she can grope toward that word and never find it—never want to find it—because she's found too many more interesting things along the way—because she's made the trade a process. She doesn't like being handed things on a silver platter—especially *le mot juste*. Not that she's ever been—handed things on a platter, that is, silver or otherwise. Needs of the trade as she's taught how to practice it so as to groom herself for stardom (no mean feat in a more and more talibanized publishing world) is at war with the need to keep the thing out there—phenomenon—unnamed so that it can go on being attacked—analyzed—from every angle. The cleverness of the right word pulls the rug out from under the phenomenon—out from under her wrestling-with-the-angel-of-the-phenomenon—every time. The trade, as she's being taught to practice it, coaxes her into focusing on the 99 percent of things that already give off the whiff of the right words which prevent them from becoming themselves. Which means that she bypasses the one percent of the one percent before they can give off a whiff of their dire refusal to be mastered and thereby spur her to mastery. So this business of plying the trade as she's being taught to practice it, ply it, is turning out to be an inescapable escape from the business of . . . penetrating to the essence of things: things like Building 18 and the dead boy (she simply cannot think of him as her son) and her stint by the pool. She's always being assailed by too many right words— vying for her attention—coming fast and furious down the pike—stealing the spotlight. Even if there is no such thing as a right word for the word becomes right only after the fact when, having instantaneously convinced the plyer of the trade that it's more the thing than the thing itself, it puts itself in that thing's place. And the business of wearing down so as to be able to discard and replace the tools of the trade is the only escape from the sham of such a trade. For the trade, so practiced, so plied, reduces to nothing more than the tricks of the trade. But is there a mathematical operation (if only she had the courage to say hello to Cantor) under whose auspices escape from escape becomes . . . confrontation? The right words are like the cleverest students in the class—they're not worn down by a need to steer clear of the right words—their worst enemy if they only knew it even if the wrong words can never groom them for stardom. They're spared having to cart around the baggage of the highest standards—don't have to waste time steering clear of superficiality—worse, competence—which time unwasted can be used to be fluent, facile, fearless, intrepid, with the fearlessness of imbecility—to operate on the lowest level of ear-catching wit. But isn't all this denigration of the other guy just a pep talk? Isn't she, by giving in to all this peppy self-exaltation, practicing the very right-wordism she professes to spurn? Don't answer that question, Melanctha, Some Body—Some Thing—the Master—He—tells her.

Still, too bad the pencil isn't worn down to the bone so she can throw it away. Since there's nothing's as gratifying—nothing is as *giveyourselfabigfatpatontheback*-ish—as the legitimately earned trashing of an instrument of labor honorably worn down to the bone. At that moment, anything becomes possible, even walking out for good on her own identity—everything that makes her her—for something much much better—much better than storytelling, motherhood, Envy, Envy poison, poison oracles, divorce, blackness, black of grief and white of shameless shame. Like no other, the act of trashing the bone awakens her to infinite possibility, makes her as light as a feather, turns her into her very own overnight bag. As if the only thing that ever stood in the way of self-realization is some measly little pencil. For a split second, she's invulnerable, because unlocalizable. Until, terrified by all this overrated unlocalizability, she ends up grabbing another lead, since only another lead will allow her to catch up with the tools of the trade, though they may never find it in their heart to forgive her abandonment. Only she no longer knows what her trade is. Is it the scribbling or, rather, a pastmaster's ablation of her tools so as to have done with the trade once and for all?

Over the last few days, however—she realizes it now—there's been a change: less of a temptation to trash those tools and walk out on herself without giving due notice. Maybe Invidicum is in some way responsible (less Envy, less self-loathing). In which case she must give Straynge and his goons a little credit. Or is all this a construction—to convince herself entering the trial has been the next-to-best thing she's ever done?

Herbert's almost forgotten it's her turn today to read in front of the class (should she take the stairs or go sybaritic and take the escalator). But first she's got to include a sentence or two about the smell of urine in the third-floor corridor just outside her son's room and about the mouse that set up shop without a permit in his hangerless closet. Since how even begin to convey, without recruiting that special Building 18 smell, that special mouse, Bushie's smarmy indifference to the carnage wrought by his lying folly, not to mention the Girl Scout indifference of Rice, the curmudgeonly indifference of Amphisbaena Cheney-RUMPsfeld (which managed to hoodwink latte-averse rednecks into mistaking it for the closest thing to rectitude—to plainfolksiness—they could ever hope to rub elbows with) and the toadying indifference of little Gonzalez (forever begging to be allowed to get on with the hallowed business of protecting our kids in uniform when pressured to explain yet another fan-hitting shitload of improprieties). But there's no writing up the smell—not with this pencil. She needs a new, a fresher one. But is there enough time to run out and buy one? But hasn't somebody just warned her of something relevant to this pint-sized agonizing? Her professor? Doctor Phil? Judge Judy? Oprah? Jay Leno?—no, Cantor, of all people! Not directly, of course, but through yet another (in this case Proposition 8-less) phone conversation on which she eavesdropped (just before group in-treatment last Tuesday afternoon during which she made it a point to sit as far away from him—from everybody—as possible). But what does he expect? His voice invites eavesdropping—very gravelly-seductive, if the center of her body does say so itself. What was it he intimated, obviously to a colleague? Something to the effect that the minute you try your hand at anything worth a damn the work itself immediately takes a back seat to all the suddenly upsurging preliminaries vital to its survival. Which preliminaries always entail a gathering of artifacts—the more irrelevant the better—to oppose to the terror of being ablated to zero by what the work demands. Any work worth a damn triggers a sense of total depletion—and a crying need for replenishment—long before the worker gets started getting started, long before a single drop of workerly blood has been shed. Fact was, nothing made him dread obliteration (or was it in fact the colleague who did the dreading for the two of them?) more than the prospect of oneness with the work's pure process, its messily unboundaried gestation—of being churned up by its busy bowels. So is it any wonder that she, mired in dread like Cantor's proxy, wants to buy a new pencil whose fixed contours will guide her toward re-generating her own?

Herbert discovers she curses the work she's on the run from as she did her one and only pregnancy. This ugly new gestation, this incompleteness, this transit, this being stuck in the shuttle between two underworlds, leaks with similar blatancy out of every orifice in sight, and within hearing. But why a shuttle between two underworlds? *Why?* Because the work's bloody fetus is not yet in the words—and right or wrong words, what difference does it make in the long run?—but no longer completely outside them either. That's why. (But hey, what's all this I hear about *what difference does it make*? Is the sudden mournful airiness solely for effect and if so, on whom?) She can't tell where Cantor's thought ends and hers begins—which is all to the good, she thinks, at least for her Master—her puppeteer—though she's not sure why. No point in trying to convince herself being in process ain't so bad per se, that frankly she could do worse, much worse, than get temporarily churned up by busy bowels (a metaphor to end all metaphors, if she does say so herself)—that it's not a slur on her integrity, more importantly, on her efficiency, most importantly, on her writerly caucasian manhood. She just can't help feeling that the labor she's renouncing for the sake of a pencil she may never find is sheer boondoggle. The work should be complete the minute its stirrings are felt—that's what stirrings are for—if not long before. Its—her—unfolding over time—in time—is proof of its—her—their—impotence. Why is it that every time she puts lead to pulp the conviction takes over that there's an infinity of far brainier heartier brainchildren waiting in the wings, howling for her divided attention, outraged that she continues to labor over this soon-to-be-stillborn? They've had their fill, these much-worthier-of-being-born, of Building 18's flea circus of horrors—much worthier, that is, as long as they stay put in them there wings.

Not so suddenly reading the work in all its blood-and-guts tentativeness is just plain unthinkable. She hurries out, almost knocking down one of her white grandchildren. Terror prevents her, atypically, from saying she's sorry. Fleeing goes well enough up until canopy-crazed Seventy-Second, between Lexington and Third (just a few more blocks to her favorite stationery store, run by a Korean couple whose baby sleeps soundly by the register), at which point the terror revisits.

Only it's brand new. She's already looking back with regret-racked nostalgia. Now that she's found a means of escape from a terror of confronting the work publicly, what's far more terrifying is being (compliments of this obstruction, screen, supplement, dangerous supplement, poison, cure, painkiller—this . . . fleeing) *unable* to confront it. In fact, this new terror, terror No. 2, is so great and so all-effacing that for the life of her she can't remember, out here on Seventy-Fourth and Second (so she's made some further progress even in her derangement), a terror No. 1. How can Herbert have ever imagined the work itself could induce terror when in fact it's being cut off from the work by a drug wrongly self-prescribed that's the culprit? And, by the way, who asked this busybody escape hatch to nose its way into the innards of her plight and gum up the self-confrontational works? Thinking like her creator and thereby liquidating, at least for now, his animus which has been breathing down her hackles ever since Sixty-Ninth, she realizes that such must be the fate of any worker who, in her gnawed gnarled guts equating work in progress with self-cancellation, invokes a cure for the terror that ensues, then curses the efficacy of its gall.

Against her will (for she has better things to do with it, i.e., save it for a crisis that truly merits the name), she thinks, If only I were white I wouldn't be in the fix I'm in (*What fix is that? chortles her deadpan Master*) and I don't just mean just here on First Avenue, or is it (already) York? Not that she wants to be white irrevocably but there certainly are times, though few and far between, when she can't help feeling you need to be white to make it—as she still wants to make it, even at her age—in America. Though she's managed to rebuff such thoughts for quite some time because of her man Barack. During the too-thrilling primary days, she'd kept saying, maybe to ward off the certainty of his defeat at the hands of that steamroller lady, If only he were a white man, he'd be a shoo-in. Only his triumph managed to expose the foolery of Herbert's frontier logic. Ultimately Herbert (though no fan of pseudoprofundity-peddling paradox) had to admit that in fact *it was thanks to his very blackness*, presumed toxic by the pollstergeist, that he emerged from the campaign smelling like a rose—the rose remedial for nationwide ills. It was his blackness—or perhaps the even more potent absence of whiteness—that made the tensile forbearance in the face of McRumpelstiltskin's jabs resonate so powerfully even with cross-sectional whitey—a forbearance so tensile it became the purest form of eloquence—eloquence far more eloquent than oratory. In the abstract, blackness was stump liability No. 1, but when factored concretely—constructively—into The Obama Equation it mutated into an asset—the asset of privation—of untaintedness by the evils of good-old-boy whiteness, the evil whiteness of Ayatollah Boy George and his imamniks. Only she isn't Barack and the current hurdle isn't a presidential debate, much less a primary—it's far more . . . primal.

In her present state—no different she realizes than states past and states to come (but can she help it if Her Master insists stagily on *present*?)—in her present need to escape the distant memory of how she reneged on her obligation to read before her classmates—Herbert is able to make it uptown only so far as Cherokee Place, by no means her favorite spot for an audition (for what is life but one long audition for a role that's unplayable?). Intoning: *Her* Master. Her *Master*. Any wonder, she also realizes, that He should have selected her, the descendant of slaves, from among all the others, to get the ball of Master-Slave dialectics rolling? But Herbert the medium's medium is convinced she can turn the tables on him and that being just a good ol' boy at heart and likely to remain so, he's filled to the brim with collusive relish at the big idea. She's even more convinced he wouldn't have his miscegenation any other way. Sitting herself down just outside John Jay on the only bench that isn't weighed down with pigeon droppings, she closes her eyes so that unimpeded by all the scowling faces she can hear the boy's Building 18 voice—in her present state, the only voice worth obeying. A voice more eloquent even than Barack's because poignantly uninflected by what folks, white *and* black, take for eloquence. She tries to hear him as he cried out to her *in the darkest hours of the night*. No, too melodramatic therefore an affront to his agony. As he cried out to her *some time after dawn*. But all that penetrated was the cigarette-hoarse chitchat of the White Cellphone Girls, getting louder hence closer, the poorly masked timorousness of the sentences that ended in a question mark (except for those that were authentic questions) contrasting oddly with the no-holds-barred profanity of the ones that didn't. But why is she complaining when she should be groveling? After all, oddities, contradictions in terms—any incision into the flab of the usual drab—are fiction's meat and potatoes. And if the writer, budding or otherwise, isn't (unlike her at this moment) lucky enough to have a hearty helping dumped right in his lap, then he must (cooking the books, so to speak) whip up his own facsimile thereof and devour it as he would have some *real-world counterpart*, that is, with real-world down-home relish masquerading as genteel distaste.

As a rule Cantor isn't grateful for much, especially with Berry Sundae out of the picture for good, but how can he not be grateful for the fact that the black lady from Amygdala—ladylike, sometimes, to the point of otherworldliness—has tactfully chosen not to recognize him since more than anything he wants to be alone with his love pangs? He's been able to cross Central Park faster than he would have thought possible given the drag of those pangs—subduable only, now and then, by the counter-pangs of lust. The pain is much too fresh to be anywhere near giving way to Amherst's famous formal feeling but it's having a calming effect nonetheless and has already transformed him, atypically, into the most unjudging of observers. Foul-mouthed softball players, the variegated homeless haranguing their unhearing selves beneath the gangly ginkgos, avidly heterosexual joggers too pretty for words joined sweatily—and gabbingly—at the hip, skateboarding punks of every age and income bracket (yet for all their biodiversity there's one thing they see eye to eye about and that's wearing their cantankerous caps umpire-style as a matter of manly—make that mannish—honor), insatiable crones of all genders stultified by the shameless need to go on catching human misery (it's their bread and butter) in the act—you name it, ethereal Cantor non-judges it. Simplified by his love-lust, he wants nothing and nothing wants him. Gladder to be unhappy than any genial freak since Larry Hart. But Cantor has to admit willy-nilly that this cloud does have a silver—or at least a silverish—lining. For the joggers make heterosexuality look so easy on the gonads. How easy to be hetero, their sweaty regalia seems to cry out—how public, like a frog. He's already undergoing the relief of falling into its lap—the warm welcome of its lap—that is, if that lap will have him. And as if one lining weren't enough, to his delight he must acknowledge that these particular two (even if she sports the obligatory blond ponytail) are not screaming their heads off about insider trading or Big Data or (that old warhorse or chestnut or *pièce de résistance* or last resort) deferred capital gains, which would have served only to unaesthetically virilize the ponytail. He can't help wondering where they stand on same-sex marriage. Much as he likes Obama—(How distant seem those pursy times of Cheney and Rumpsfeld and [mustn't forget his favorite for no particular reason] that humorless ex-quarterbacking alumnus of Goldman-Sachs, Hank Paulson—as imperceptibly as immitigable grief did their eternal summer pass away)—he must suppress a manly giggle realizing how before inevitably coming out in favor of it, Barry will be obliged to go on promulgating the confession that, as far as the union which dares not speak its name is concerned, he's still *evolving*. In other words, this Man of the World who clearly couldn't care less whether Don consensually loves and/or lubricates Don, or Dawn Dawn—or, for that matter, Don Dawn—will need to take plenty more keeping-you-posted stabs at soothing the lunatic heartland's savage breast through agonized allusion to a nonexistent inner struggle—a wrestling with the angel of biblical injunction—over many a sleepless night. *But why label it the heartland lunatic, you smug urbanite?* Cantor asks himself not quite rhetorically. For though not an author and with no desire to become one (look at what such yearnings are doing to Herbert), he knows that to write off the breast so easily—to refuse to *engage* with it through a secret affinity—is to deprive himself of a source of enrichment. Along the same lines, damn Cheney for acquiring a lesbian daughter to humanize him—and for thereby making villainy a little bit . . . complicated.

But he's become Eden—that waywardly beautiful child Eden. For this must be how Eden looks out—or back—at life, i.e., with the poker-faced wonderment of a naïf, a perpetual novice, somebody not quite real, somebody not quite fully conceived, much less born. The purity of his deadpan, free of all Envy (Cantor still doesn't understand why so fallen an angel has been allowed to perform in the Invidicum Follies), rancor, contempt, ridicule and schadenfreude, must make all those self-plausibilizers who cross his path uncomfortably aware that they've turned traitor to their essence before they even knew they had one. They must Envy Eden uncontrollably (but, unlike Cantor, without knowing it) for not having succumbed—for having held out to the bitter end against the debasement of acculturation. No doubt about it, Eden's intimidating wonderment emits a neon moonglow. Cantor knows, of course, that *his* brand of wonderment is impure ersatz (for Envying and schadenfreuding [trolling's older sister] the richly smug and famously arrogant are more vital to his alveoli than mere breathing). Still, it's fun to playact.

Furthermore, how get inside the taste of Eden's skin, under the sweat of his foreskin, except by playing him—playing *at* him to the hilt. And, who's to say that, once within, Cantor may not come to understand Eden's particular relation or better yet non-relation to his sexuality and through understanding (a vastly overrated faculty) exorcise the demon of his own longing (since no good can come of it)? *Go back to Berry: leave the dead to bury the living.* For it is precisely this unknown quantity—not knowing the precise degree to which Eden is aware or unaware of the impact of his (for lack of a better phrase) glaring potency—that is not so slowly driving Cantor crazy. As a fornicator, is he inexhaustible yet deadpan to the point of psychosis? Or with every finger-fucking thrust, however ruthless, is he forever playful—playfully *vocal*—to the point of shamelessness? For the measure of true potency is the ability to *talk* sex clinically, straightforwardly, even primly, in the very throes of the act and in easy continuity with one's everyday self (not through the bullhorn of some souped-up male-enhanced how-to-manual fantasia on the limp theme of that self, to be disavowed immediately after [or maybe even long before] the final spurts). Or is he racked by "issues" of impotence or premature ejaculation or priapism or (virtuosic to a fault) all three at the same time? And if so, is he defiantly unapologetic (or better yet, indifferent), which will only make him more irresistible to the discerning female? In running the gamut or gauntlet, then, from brazen dys- to hyperfunction never would Eden clock in as undesirable—at least, not in Cantor's gym class. He can sustain a lacerated love-lust for this guy as much for botchery as for prowess.

On the bus uptown, he sits diagonally across from a woman who has the audacity to intrigue—as if life as he lives it isn't tough enough—while steadfastly enraging him. Although he knows he appears perfectly calm, he also knows the mode in which he acknowledges her bony frame and sunken cheeks is all the while that of the most frantic repudiation. He isn't at all like her—not in the least. Anyway, isn't all that *anima muliebris virili corpore inclusa* stuff old—the oldest—hat? If only he could kill her, and lay the uncanny resemblance to rest—but that will just lend support to the received wisdom that fags (there it is, the irresistible F word—*his* kind's response to the N word) hate

219

women. So then he's got his work all cut out for him, i.e., his job on this bus is to prove to himself and *a fortiori* to all his traveling companions—but without the least visible animus—that he's very very different from her. But he needs to keep looking if he's going to be able to determine just how different.

Meanwhile she's managed to inveigle the distaff side of one of New York City's typical middle-aged Jewish couples into conversation (kind-faced hubby is busy communing with his dyspepsia), shrewdly having made it an ice-breaking point to admire her scarf. And it's certainly worth admiring, thinks Cantor, with his expert eye for fashion, high and low. Yet here she is— call her Ismaela—suddenly going all floridly silent simply because biddy is refusing to keep up her end of the conversation, is not rewarding sufficiently her over-admiring kindness of heart, hasn't had the decency to perceive that taking the first step comes at the not inconsiderable cost of forgoing the reverential wooing to which she, as the real star of any roadshow, is entitled. She's just given her all to the proceedings and as usual is vastly underappreciated. Desperate for connection she's been tricked into feeling ashamed of that desperation. But it doesn't quite matter, does it, what she is and what she does and what her all consists in. Since the point is that, whatever she is, whatever she is to *him*, he needs to repudiate the kinship cum monstrous twinship—this two-peas-in-a-pod effect. Needs to repudiate his too visceral understanding of their identicalness even if that understanding may be getting both of them all wrong. The whole business calls to mind something mathematical, or at least quasi-.

Minutes before, Cantor—Subject Number . . . Subject Number . . . Subject Number . . . oh, who cares about the number—whatever it is? It's clearly *up*— minutes before, very glad to be unhappy, he was basking in the sunshine of Eden's fair skin (but in the sunlight downed with dark brown hair!) and now he's being asked to undergo a fusion he doesn't relish in the least. A certain subspecies of anorexic urban female neurotic is drawing him into her menstrual vortex purely to spite his hard-won manhood—for, yes, Cantor, like Cukor (as exquisitely obituarized by Andrew Sarris), is most definitely a man (the snide hairy-chested griping of Rhett Gable the Butler notwithstanding), a real man, even (*Stop*, shouts the Some Body out there—the . . . Master—who he's more and more convinced is running the show and ruling the roost, *this is going too far; Not far enough*, Cantor retorts—or maybe it's the other way around—emboldened by a change of garment) a real man's man. Not unlike the other members of the tribe, Cantor has gone very much Master-shy: can't bring himself to name the unnameable. Cantor only wishes he could have come up with a brighter word than *neurotic*, which merely and noisily gets in the way of his thinking her through—processing her—from scratch and coming up with something more analytically nuanced hence more accurate. Now, why did this right word have to go getting itself stuck in his craw? Damn them, these right words, always hanging around ready to gum up the works—the workings of thought as a wayward process blessedly rife with self-revelatory detours. Why, it's positively uncanny but he could swear there's somebody out there—some member of the Envy tribe—who's given to similar agonizing over this right-name/wrong-name problem. And he could also swear that the

Some Body of a few sentences ago—*his* Some Body—his . . . Master is rejoicing that so ripe a lapse should have fallen to His share, since if anybody knows how to make said lapse pay and pay handsomely, though Cantor has no idea in what currency (he's just a dumb blond), it's Some Body. And it's already paying since it has given rise to a meditation worthy of Descartes—or Massenet.

The spectacle of anorexic fending off the indifference of biddy-plus-hubby all by her lonesome is still unfolding (so twistily suspenseful it positively clogs the arteries of his apperception) but now in total silence: odd woman out's ever-so-slight *I-know-when-I'm-not-wanted* shift of the hip being alone worth the price of admission. Even obtuse hubby seems to have begun to suspect there's something not quite right about wifey's gal pal manqué. Though since you mention it, isn't he, or rather his tone of voice (now it's time for Cantor's expert *ear* to take a bow), a bit on the fruity side? Or is it simply the feminizing influence of the distaff or of age, or of both? Wincing, as only an outcast can wince, for the acuteness of their discomfitures, Cantor has easily become all three (stagestruck to a fault, he's even taken on the thankless role of the dyspepsia). In fact, he's awaiting what will never arise: the bold dawning of fully articulated awareness on the part of *I know when I'm not wanted* that, though the roots of the current transit crisis is rooted in her pathology and hers alone, she can resolve it by leaving no narcissistic pretension unexposed and unexamined. He's waiting for her to affirm not just to her two ex-friends but to all the passengers that they aren't necessarily reducible to the rags of their inordinately self-hating self-love (ISHSL) and that through the right sort of relentless self-unmasking said love can be the raw material of a redemption. He's waiting for her to insist (egged on by that old faker Leibniz) they needn't ever let flaws and failures, however ferocious, however fatuous, be the last word on their worth ("there is nothing fallow, sterile or dead in the universe" [*Monadology*, sec. 69]) since merciless disqualification of every measly pretext for self-love (which she intends to undertake the minute she disembarks—or does she?) makes up for a multitude of sins. He's waiting for her to reassure them there is no need to feel disqualified by somebody else's apparent lack of, or by yet another somebody else's higher-end brand of, the stuff since ISHSL is nothing in itself—it's what you do with and to it. Why, if he didn't know her better he'd say she's but a hop, skip and a jump away from paraphrasing what Baruch said to William de Blyenbergh on 5 January 1665, namely, that when ISHSL is considered in itself without regard to anything else, it possesses *a perfection coextensive with its essence*. In short, he's waiting for her to do his dirty work.

But he's waiting very much in vain, for she looks as abject-haughty and as surly-complaisant as ever. So he goes back to repudiating her, this time with what he assures himself is a vengeance. Yet the more he repudiates the connection, his queer identicalness to this creature for whom no bystander can ever begin to do enough, the more identical and connected he feels because, after all, repudiation—resistance—rejection—unsatisfiability—is her stock in trade. And why shouldn't it be since her dunderheaded victims invariably get her appeals all wrong? Those appeals aren't outrageously unrealistic. It's all the biddies and their Joes to whom she makes the mistake of directing them that are to blame. She deserves better. That, in fact, should be inscribed on her tombstone: *Here lies one who deserved better—from the Metropolitan Transportation Authority.* Hence the harder he tries to disavow that he knows exactly at any given moment what entrails-scouring feeling she's feeling and what it is that makes her feel it, the more like unto her he becomes. Since disavowal is her business. It's only when Cantor admits he is she, and then some, that he finds he's she no longer, inasmuch as *the one who deserved better* is the last person in the world who'll admit to anything as unselflovely as the awful truth. Awful truths are associated only with those who've failed her, i.e., just about everybody she's ever met and plenty she hasn't.

Now he realizes what he's been reminded of—Bertie Wooster Russell's jolly paradox, of course! (but this time in Upper Broadway drag). The chestnut about the set that's normal only when it's non-normal and non-normal only when it's normal and so on and so forth to the last polysyllable of unrecorded time.

So here's the deal (he hates the phrase but at such a juncture no other will do since it toughens him up enough to be worthy of putting the finishing touches on his self-transcendence): If he gets all dowager-huffy and refuses to accept his blatant twinship cum kinship with this succubus, then he can rest assured he'll stay an—her—identical twin forever. On the other hand, if he resigns himself to accepting wholeheartedly this invagination of his selfhood then finally he'll be cured not just of her but of the whole damn pre-Weimar woman-in-a-man's-body horseshit. Though come to think of it, if think of it he must, surely even a superbly uncouth two-hundred-twenty-five-pound steroid-guzzling tits-and-shaved-pussy-rabid hyper-trophied quarterback might find himself under the right circumstances (in the shower, say, when lathering his blue balls next to an even ballsier and more truculent three-hundred-fifty-pounder) feeling overwhelmingly and appallingly like . . . Audrey in *Funny Face* or, better yet, Gish in *Broken Blossoms*. Gender, in short, is all about the demon of context.

But, he suddenly realizes (tell me something, aforementioned Mr. Some Body, why does a realization have always to be *sudden*, at least in print?), it's the antics of this very twin that's been preventing him for the last forty minutes from studiously ingesting Upper Broadway's vainglorious fresco of midsummer archetypes aswim in a heady-hued mix of sweat, spit, shit, sperm and a million other secretions still to be cryptanalysed—a fresco unfolding (not altogether smoothly) in what (sometimes humorless) cinephile Berry Sundae would have called a lateral tracking shot. Hence (even though she's helped him produce if not a mind- then at least a gender-bending corollary to the Russell paradox) he can't help cursing her. At One Hundred Sixteenth, fresco's end, his identity is still as muddled as ever—or even more so? (no, that's just Some Body trying to hype things up in the hope of wangling Himself a Hollywood contract but as what precisely? screenwriter? astrologist to the stars? hairdresser to the starlets?). Exactly who is he this very instant as he fights so bravely against alighting too daintily? Gable? Grable? Bertrand Russell? Bertie's twin-sister Roz? Roz's niece Jane? Liberace? Liberace's twin-brother DiMaggio? Mussolini? or, for better or worse, that old chestnut of the self-help canon *himself at last*? But, hey, never again will he be himself (i.e., a reasonably manly male with a manly eye for the manlier line of gents) unless he outs his consanguinity with this . . . pupate bag lady. For he's suddenly realized (though—and Hollywood be damned!—by no means *that* suddenly: the oceanic roar of realization has, as the summation of wavelets, been a long time coming) she's but a step away from zigzagging her crap-festooned shopping cart down some final mean street. Never again can he hope to pass himself off as a desirable male for another desirable male, unless he smelts away the last— no, the *very* last—dreg of his crabby occult femaleness by admitting, humbly, fearlessly and with every faculty, follicle and fiber, how very alike they are, a veritable pair of sisters under the mink (paging Gloria Grahame and Jeanette Nolan) right down to the rolling of the eyes (fake lashes optional) when suffering fools ungladly. So, quick! what is he waiting for? He knows he'll feel fifty pounds lighter—hence fifty times more muscular!—once he's managed to expel the gigantic turd of his ornery resistance to the nakedly hermaphroditic truth she embodies. (Trying his hand at fake abasement before the apprentice for whose bedazzled gyrations his instruction has every right to take full credit, the Master as sorcerer thinks: *I can't get a word in edgewise.*) Quick! Problem is, though he needs a sliver of profile through which to penetrate her soul and thereby consummate the surgical travesty, all she's vouchsafing on the smelly pavement is the back of her head rapidly shrinking to a pinpoint of pitiless glare.

Gone. So with, as so many times before, exorcism on hold, can he still *make it* (what a phrase—it should be ashamed of itself!) with Eden, his fellow proband? Does he still have enough residual maleness to get Eden's dander up? But this is assuming Eden's . . . susceptible, which he most certainly isn't. After all, Cantor knows all the signs of a fellow traveler, though after a stretch of monogamy crowned by celibacy-with-no-end-in-sight maybe he's just not the fieldworker he used to be, or thinks he was. Still, if he's so sure of Eden's insusceptibility, then why in the name of Adam Kadmon is he— But there's no time now to lick the wounds perpetrated by the slender scalpel of his illogic: he has a pack of undergraduates to teach and, come to think of it, there's something about wielding a butt of yellow chalk in front of them that makes him feel supremely logical.

The two bag ladies who know Herbert, a panhandler's dream, by sight— who know her better than she knows herself (*or is this the Master babbling again on behalf of his clients?*)—are pushing their covered wagons across the street, at peace for once. Maybe, just maybe, it's the high-noon warmth of 3 p.m. which has enjoined sisterhood (Rampage and Roach, she—or rather Shelley Smith—her favorite practitioner of thrillduggery—would have gratefully called them). Rampage, refusing to put *all* of her bedeviled eggs in one basket, shoulders a sweat-drenched backpack as well. But the panic with which Herbert, at the sight of them, checks to make sure she has her shoulder bag, clutch and CVS plastics and the little satchel of books and notebooks that (whether she looks at them or not) she never goes anywhere without— and why should she?—causes her to wonder just how far away she herself is from bag-ladyhood. How many more bare essentials, if any, will she need to have annexed before the municipality compels her to acknowledge that she's irreversibly crossed the line? But doesn't awareness of the temptation to cross save you from such a fate? If only. What matters is how many bare necessities (*O reason not the need*) you feel compelled to lug around, for however long you're out pounding the pavement, unemployed or not, in order to feel that you're truly yourself, whether being so is a blessing in disguise or not. And as Melanctha has plenty of luggables, there's no doubt in her mind she's a Rampaging Roach from way back—highly conspicuous—biblically big with bag-liness. So what choice does she have except to go running after them, as they well know is her feckless wont, to make a measly donation to the cause of the day, of the hour? Only this gest will set her apart once and for all, as was supposed to be the case so many times before, for, I ask you, have you—I mean, has she—ever witnessed one bag lady subsidize another, much less two at once, and much much less with the sheepish insistence of a sinfully solvent good samaritan? She regrets not having stopped to say hello to Cantor. Not knowing why, she's convinced he's battling the same sort of demon (you know, the tongue-twisting *A's-not-B-to-the-extent-that-A-accedes-with-all-her-heart-and-soul-to-the-all-too-obvious-twinship-with-B* sort of demon) but battling it far more successfully because . . . because . . . well, because he's got the laws of his trade working overtime on his behalf—and that's half the battle. It all boils down to a very special kind of mathematical paradox, my dear, she hears him saying. But who's put such a sophisticated intuition in her noggin? Clearly, the Master's working overtime although inasmuch as He loves—lives for—His vocation the way a locust does the plague, He never counts the hours. You'll never catch Him (as you can be sure to catch Narr, say, or Caro) boasting/lamenting about how hard He works, how busy He is, since in the Master's case it would be like boasting/lamenting about how busy He's been masturbating—or worse, breathing. So, the Master always knew He wanted to be a Master and nothing but. She's suspected as much. While Melanctha, too, *always knew*, in her case there was nevertheless a need to delay fusion for as long as possible with what she now has no wish to call anything except her destiny. Fighting tooth and nail against surrender to what was so much of her it prospectively stank of the same impotence, she went along mystifying those vocations—filmmaker, jazz musician, girl singer, girl archeoanthropologist—that in their stark incompatibility with—inaccessibility to—her deepest selfness were therefore surcharged with the promise of the only glory worth dying for. Squatting, Roach takes to making faces at the bright blank screen of her scavenged burner phone in order to fit in and Melanctha needs to believe that unlike the well-heeled zombies for miles around making similar faces Roach is aware she's trying to fit in—is aware she's mugging for the camera—is aware a cellphone is not a utility but a globalized accessory like distressed "jeans." (*A bit facile, don't you think? a gadfly buzzes into Melanctha's right ear and she knows full well she had this coming.*)

All this business about the bare necessities brings her back, as do so many other disquieting things, to the semi-golden days before 9/11—or in the much better words of that Austrian to whom Phil introduced her six days before the catastrophe, the *dunkelgoldene Frühlingstage*. Phil, her young friend, gay (Melanctha Herbert hates the word: very un-PC, if you ask her, but nobody does) and, true to the code of his tribe, always so very talkative (at least when she was around), who spent pretty much all of his adult life caring for a mother insane to the point of shrewishness and then, after her untimely death (in the sense that it should have occurred decades before), studiously rejecting his (remarried) father's patently halfhearted efforts to rehabilitate their un-connection. She and he, on the other hand, did connect—or rather (*or rather* being the only counter-incision that patient-victims like Herbert can make into the bellied brain of the malpractitioner that is life), reconnected before ever having met—at (where else?) the Unicorn Hair Salon (on Lexington and Twenty-Sixth, a few steps west of Herman Melville Way) at seven-forty-five every other Thursday. Unlike Cantor, who's very masculine-looking and –acting, poor Phil (the Master insists that *poor Phil* be enunciated in the Jamesian vein of *poor Marcher*) canted toward the prissy-giggly when even slightly agitated. So homosexuals do come in all shapes and sizes after all. But like every woman who befriends them, she feels—felt—the hard work of befriendship entitled her to a little lateral recreational contempt and in her case contempt for Phil was double-barrelled since he'd wasted not only his lily-whiteness but his balls as well. (What couldn't she do with a pair or two? Why, she'd give whitey a run for his money!) Trouble was, she had no one with whom to share that prissy-giggly contempt. Surely not her boy, who would have been too revolted by, and jealous of, the other boy. The thought of calling either by his name brings on the usual nausea. Now why is that? she wonders.

For most of his adult life he was in the employ of an office management contractor, which years before had (deferring to his steadfast lack of ambition) landed him a spot in the archive department of The Poxx Corporation on the 100th floor of Tower 2. That fateful day, his only co-worker who was also a pal, and *her* pal, having smelled smoke, immediately decided to vacate and somehow convinced him to accompany them to the nearest stairwell. But when over the public address system it was announced that the problem lay with Tower 1 and it was not only safe but highly advisable for good workers to go back to their battle station, breathing a sigh of relief he said he was dizzy and, in any event, needed to retrieve his backpack which he'd always referred to as his second skin. Melanctha, a francophile *malgré elle*, frankly preferred *peau de chagrin* and said as much and her flippancy turned out to be a portent. The co-worker pal later revealed to the *Times* (with true pal impropriety) it was in one of its sidepockets that he routinely warehoused what she'd taken it upon herself to call his toxic assets—without permission of course and never in the culprit's presence (believing perhaps that in retailing the information she was doing her part to humanize to a wider public not just this zany ultimately harmless energumen but the entire brotherhood). He rented these DVDs (for of course that's what they were)—which were targeted at a certain subset of the pornography-loving public whose members were law abiding to a fault—on the always eerily uneventful eve of each new workweek from some surprisingly well-maintained hole-in-the-wall on Oliver Street, and as it was now Tuesday he'd intended to return them before closing time.

And according to his tell-all pal he'd said a funny thing, Phil did, before he went back up to meet his maker: Something to the effect that he owed it to the backpack if not to the company; that it was the very least he could do for having been vouchsafed so much expert self-camouflage over the years, no questions asked, especially since things had a way of knowing when they were the victims of base ingratitude. Yes, they certainly knew when indexterity was intentional.

So after reading about his death—reading about it!—then having it tear-fully confirmed by the owner of the Unicorn (which has just been replaced by yet another branch of the Bank of Chimerica [hohoho] famous for its faux super-exclusive Private Client program) whom she would never have imag-ined capable of such a generous outpouring of rheumy grief—and goaded on by curiosity regarding her own peculiar overattachment to things, and as her own particular way of paying her respects, she gave the day's pencil free rein to meditate on the subject of which possessions, if any, somebody flee-ing at zero hour might grab to feel he has exactly what is needed to keep his glassy essence intact. Though what if, when the bell tolls, daring him to choose wisely, that essence instantaneously undergoes a sea change, forcing him to choose between the possessional requirements of the old (begging for reinstatement) and those, if any, of the new?

If only, she thinks, all the precious booty so conjunctive to one's life and soul could shrink to a microchip easily injectable into her upper thigh (the moleless one: its underside almost as pale, unfortunately, as a white woman's) via capsule no bigger than a grain of rice, and whose instant breakdown across that most mercilessly selective of all crosspoints, the blood-soul barrier, would make it impossible to say where the booty left off and the self began. For isn't getting to the point of *impossible to say* exactly what every acquirer craves? Just think: to be able to assimilate and metabolize into something completely new not just the substance but the *very* substance of every art-ifact (poem, novel, four-act play, piano trio, canvas, movie, marble sculpture, etching, con-tact print, mezzotint) she's begun to treasure all too self-cancelingly, all too *whitely*. To make it a vital, untraceable part of her own unplagiarizing sub-stance. So that the message of this, their collective looming—that it's pointless for her, as a black, as a woman, as the inept curator of her maternity's sole artifact (and where ineptitude is so gross, there must be malevolent intent), to compete—that acknowledgment of her redundancy (itself an art form—a degenerate art form—of sorts) is the best thing she can do for her pretensions, i.e., her ambition—so that the vile message of that looming no longer comes in so loud and so clear—no longer comes in at all.

No more curarizing of her synapses by these grandmasterly things. With their uniquenesses all mixed up inside her microchip, they'll be too busy correcting each other's limitations, each cutting each down to size, simul-taneously annulling and preserving (the good old Hegelian one-two), each sublating each in a single spasm—each too busy administering the poison, the antidote the . . . pharmakon! of its own uniqueness as an unsolicited cor-rective to some other's—too busy correcting—besting—each other to be able to take time out to loom, lurk, hover, and thereby disqualify her—their undeniable better—at every turn.

But isn't uniqueness—worse, the striving for uniqueness—passé? Isn't the striver a self-styled nincompoop? If she's been forewarned once she's been forewarned a thousand times and a thousand times thereafter that Abstract Expressionistic stabs at misshaping a hallucinated molten essence is now worldwidely regarded as the easiest way out—a monstrous evasion of the only thing worth wresting from one's apprenticeship in Creative Writing 101 through 104, namely, the Voice Generic, the Penstroke non-Elitist, Originality Degree Absolute Zero. Anything else bespeaks the worst of all Flaws Characterological—that of being *out of key with [one's] time.* But doesn't all this fuss about Phil in Tower 2 and her boy in Building 18 prove she's very much of her time, if only opportunistically. In fact, if there's any entity in this Barnum & Bailey world that can be said to have crossed her blood-soul barrier irreversibly, it's Building 18. But at the same time, so absorbed, Building 18 is Building 18 no longer, or rather it's no longer *just* Building 18 as, outside his room, she, over and over and over again, thought it, wept it (yes, wept it: so she does love him!), implored it, cursed it (before she took it into her head to write it). In fact she has absolutely no idea what she really believes about Building 18 except that for the time being, which may last a lifetime, she believes simply in where the wordflow eddying around Building 18—or rather, around "Building 18" or rather, around *Building 18*—is charged to take her and in what it may be taking her to. *Building 18*—or rather, Building 18—is now after all so much more than itself—a placeholder for everything horrible that's just beyond the pale, around the bend, of articulability, things brutely inaccessible except when she refers to them as Building 18. "Building 18" is now, if you must know, nothing less than a totem, a full-fledged fetish, the concretion into four syllables of a lifetime's loathing—mostly of its own repeated failure to loathe (so as to do old Aristotle proud) the right mess, to the right degree, at the right point in time. In fact, as far as Herbert's very own "nucleus thought" of Building 18 is concerned, everything's going according to plan: exactly as (based on his heady experiences with such placeholders for the ineffable as "Indian hating," "confidence" and "the grand central forces of a philosophy of boys") her favorite white Confidence Man, Herman Melville (though to make a point and in true nineteenth-century fashion, he hadn't been above deriding a darkie), prophesied it would be: "Straggling thoughts of other outrages"—and spiritual outages—are literally going crazy and taking it upon themselves to "troop to the nucleus thought, assimilate with it, and swell it." So that the nucleus ends up being just the tip of an iceberg. And then there's Poe's (differently compelling) version of Building 18, namely, the purloined letter. Building 18—no *Building 18*—immunizes her against Envy. It's better than a drug—it's a vaccine.

So she can have it both ways after all: she can see to it that the books to come (and she hopes there'll be lots: publication is a drug she's been told) are both (*a*) suppositories [*sic*] of mass market-friendly opportunistic content and (*b*) exorcisers of the banal demon of content through the pseudo elite-friendly recruitment of placeholders (*i*) which do not respect content—(*ii*) which make mincemeat of content—(*iii*) which, like Andy's Campbell Soup cans and Jasper's Stars and Stripes Forever, say themselves over and over and over again in order to get content out of their system—(*iv*) which follow other itineraries, wordflow (versus worldflow) itineraries. Placeholders like (*a*) *Building 18*; and (*b*) *Berry Sundae* (yes, Melanctha's heard tell of him—or rather It—although she's forgotten from whom); and (*c*) *slumbering spirits of the gold* [she's heard—or rather, overheard—about that one, too]; and even (*d*) *he* [instead of, say, Cantor] and (*e*) *she* [instead of, say, Jean or Moira]). Content is a crutch and the more content her work has, the more it's impoverished. On the other hand, the less content the work has, the more it's impoverished. I.e., more is less and less is less. So she needs to wear at least two hats, that is if she wants to be a one-size-fits-all starlet: she needs to curry favor with content and at the same time she needs to be able to show she's graduated summa cum laude from content—has shuffled off the mortal coil of content—defied content—repudiated her enslavement to content—and has nevertheless lived to tell the tale and still has lots to say.

Since she's in the neighborhood (though as a fanatical walker is she ever *not* in any neighborhood you may care to mention?), Herbert decides to forget about the course entirely and stop at her optometrist's. Her bifocals need adjusting, too much pressure on the bridge of her nose—she'll think of something to justify the visit. Too late to go back and visit *a mother's grief* (in this case over said grief's failure to leave even a calling card) on the usual gang of straitjacketed nitwits, give or take half a dozen, who can always be depended on to curry favor with their honky prof by catching each other in the act of violating the immutable laws of CW 101.

A very well-dressed (this is the East Side, after all) old fart cum superannuated preppie (pink wattled and pink polo-shirted and ninety-five plus if a day), waiting for his fiftyish, trophyish fretful child bride to select the four or five pairs of sunglasses that will set off her bleached coils to best effect, has determined that no better use of his time can be made than in scooping out with his mottled claws as many M&M's as possible (color irrelevant) from the glass bowl on the counter while—to mask his deadly serious, righteous greed—small-talking his way into the heart of the optometrist's Gal Friday. But it becomes clear quickly enough, at least to Herbert, that Mr. Muchbonused Wall Street Vet has been dead wrong assuming he can serve with distinction on two fronts in this particular theater of his war against the grim reaper and has in fact bitten off far more multitaskmanship than he can ever hope to chew. His heart, eye and mind belong to, if not in, the glass bowl and any attention that's still directed galwards is just a geriatric tropism. Melanctha Herbert's (*why has the Master become so formal all of a sudden?*) seen his kind many times before—usually being wheelchaired around Central Park's Conservatory Water by a not-so-distant relative too weighted down with impatience at his own boredom to remember to hope that the Vet kicks the bucket sooner rather than later. He and his glass bowl clearly constitute content pure and simple—and a content with, to boot, no aptitude for transcending itself. But something tells her she shouldn't write him off so quickly but by then he's gone and she's preparing to throw her bifocals on Friday's tough mercy.

This at-death's-door exercise (with the fatuously frail snacker using chitchat as a cover for his inexpertise) invokes, of all things, the incineration of the porn-secreting backpack of father- and motherless Phil which naturally leads Herbert, by a law of logic all her own, to her son, as fictionally incarnated in a twenty-year-old child who gets himself almost blown up compliments of the insurgency in its everlastingly last throes (though smarmily assured by Boy George and Deadeyes Dick and Don, albeit not personally, that he'll be welcomed as a liberator) and who then, some years later, goes on to be really blown up, this time by the (far more insurgent) members of the medical board at Walter Reed. Having been made to understand that his traumatic brain injury doesn't exist or if it does is in no way related to the fact that one smoggy spring day in Basra, which felt like August in downtown Death Valley, his Humvee hit a bomb cemented into the curb, its blast triggering two fragmentation grenades inside the truck along with an antitank weapon and endless rounds of ammo. So what if it tore through his abdomen, splintering his depths suddenly all bloody, sooty surface; carving out a fist-sized hole in his guzzler's already ravaged liver; and destroying his underappreciated spleen, a third of his stomach and a quarter of his colon? If you ask them, his so-called injury sounds more like the result of a congenital malformation (big as a turnip) at the base of his thick skull, and even if there isn't a malformation (the jury is still out on that one) and he isn't inventing or even exaggerating the headaches, vertigo, tinnitus, numbness in the one limb that continues to function if barely, slurring, nightmares and wall-cratering rages, the fact remains (*the fact remains*: the Mount Rushmore of idiomatic invocations of the irrefutable) that still there are no quantifiable diagnostic criteria related to what he claims he is going through hence they have no alternative but to grant him a mere pittance of the severance he so arrogantly believes he's entitled to. *A sense of entitlement among our men and women in uniform*—it's the epoch's tailor-made root of all evil. (The fact that while they're busy cutting his outsize greed down to size, draft-averse Wall Streeters dutifully award themselves unclawbackable bailout bonuses is irrelevant—but young man, you just better think twice about screaming class warfare, the true last refuge of scoundrels.) She knows this clumsy defense of boys like her son, sons like her boy—swimming in slaphappy self-righteousness—exemplifies the worst kind of opportunistic writing. It is she more than Tricky Dick II who is profiting from the slaughter of soldiers. Imagine anyone sinking so opportunistically low as to try to dig out a *mot juste* from under a pile of corpses. And imagine anyone sinking even lower by opportunistically excoriating herself for so digging. The only comfort—as if it's she who's entitled to comfort at a time like this!—is to recognize that picking up a pencil immediately transforms her inescapably into a scavenger of the basest sort.

And to think all this misery is unfolding, if only in her infertile brain, at the very moment some cautiously exultant old fart is putting the lid back on his puny predations. To an opportunistic virus like her, the sense of outrage is simply thrilling (the high contrast of inequity—of class warfare—is, after all, to be one of her bread-and-butter themes). Catapulted by this unique observation, any second now she'll be mounting her stratospheric soapbox to do what she should have done years and years ago—officially excommunicate the World for generating such heartrending inequities—but kept putting off partly from cowardice and partly because she was toiling *to raise her son, a real handful,* by herself. To raise her son, a real handful. Is that what she actually did? Well, if the words say she did it, then she did. The words make it— make her—real—more real than she can ever be without them. Whatever's real about Herbert lies in the words, which order her to hurry up and coincide with their gist. The wordflow's appropriated her—turned her into what she didn't imagine she could be all by her lonesome—grants her sole custody of her realness, in this case, the realness of an anxious mother.

She takes the No. 1 train home and at last, after the usual too-long wait, it passes the field where her son played touch football after—and sometimes instead of going to—school. But *this time,* or so her hyperbolic Master needs her to think (for isn't appreciation, i.e., fabrication, of difference in sameness a key to bestsellerdom?), the trunks of the encircling planes are slanted backwards *farther than they've ever been,* obviously aghast at the shameless shadowplay of their private parts. Shadow, as usual, more real than substance. But of course it's from her they're recoiling, specifically from her all-too-real failure as a mother. The thrust of their sign language is unequivocal to her practiced eye. Noting the reflection of a bulbous cloud in a window of the only high-rise for miles around (the CitiCorpse Building, she dubs it, in homage to the fiction of class warfare), like any good sophomore she dutifully goes into allegory-of-the-cave mode and wonders a bit wistfully—but not too wistfully (*Why the qualification?* wonders Some Body somewhere [there are moments when she simply cannot refer to Him by His title])—whether, for present purposes, image isn't more real than object. No contest, in fact: how can a cloud ever compete with the ultra-high-definition of its smouldering borders and blackish underbelly under glass? Only she doesn't want to be guilty of single-handedly reversing twenty-five hundred years of progress in metaphysics. She has enough on her conscience—or should, if she has any decency.

But in a little while she feels a whole lot better, if not about herself then about her Vocation, for catching, as he rests his bike against the stoop of her building, a very well-built Latino delivery boy—as of this moment, and for all time, *her* delivery boy—in the act of comparing the customer's address on the bill stapled to his plastic bag with the number inscribed in the grime of the unlovely lintel. How many delivery boys has she needed to go through before the act of comparing could resonate as it does right now? Maybe there's a particular pathos in this one's effort to do the job right which she failed to find in the others. Maybe he resembles the dead son more than do any of the others. Or at the moment maybe it's she who's pathos-heavy and, being so, craves a proxy, plausible or not. Whatever the reason, for the very first time she's unable to take the delivery-boy comparison act for granted by skipping the crucial step of interpretation. Yet by interpreting she isn't so much *putting the meaning of his act into words* (any CW 101 fall guy can do that) as dutifully taking down the words that his act (now as clearcut as that blackbellied cloud porpoise reflected deep in the satiny surface of the ShittyCorpse) whispers to her in the twilight and to her alone so as to give her a way back into the coffin of wordflow. For the act, kindhearted to a fault, knows wordflow to be

Herbert's true, her only home. (She can be a mother only to, and mothered only by, words. To everybody and everything else she's a Mother Inferior.) And she feels very chaste taking them all down. She isn't tampering violently with things to make herself interesting: she's merely and anonymously serving some lowly delegate of the Great Out There—but not as lowly as she—no, not by a long shot. After swallowing her three capsules (colors of the week: red, yellow and tennis-ball green) Herbert righteously writes down not a single word (so as not to violate the privacy of the stoop event) and does instead what she knew all day she would end up doing, which is to take a drug of another color, i.e., cuddle up with a good book from (you guessed it!) the Life-time Movie Network stacks now that she's gotten her hands on one (the maid is black as is the blonde boss's commonsensically wisecrackin' sidekick but she's too tired to fulminate against this sort of not-so-subliminal intimidation of her and her kind). She's read this particular book (which like all the others is committed to showing what life's like properly idealized, to wit, with all the fat of its brute duration excised away) many many times before so there's no point pleading in her defense a slummer's hunger for novelty. Unviolative or not, she's betraying the Latino and wasting all he's gone out of his way to teach her without recompense.

Debating whether to pay a visit of apology to her prof first thing next morning, Herbert falls asleep just before the credits roll. She enters after her two knocks have gone unanswered and for mentorly effect he eyes her coldly. The merciless morning sun, also presenting itself uninvited, poses the usual indiscreet questions about her aging flesh. He warms to her as quickly as she warms to her own self-hate. After all, if he's told her once he's told her a thousand times: there's writerly fool's gold in them there hills if she can only learn how to mine it.

She chalks up her having gone AWOL to perimenopausal stage fright. He looks away. Is he, normally so combustibly solicitous, repelled by her self-mocking frankness? Clearly not. Because when she retaliatorily follows suit by pretending something has caught her eye out on Lexington (only to discover something really has: is he by any chance aware that at this very moment a long ray of sun has managed, and as it turns out at no small personal cost, to crawl out of a service alley only to be obliterated by the shadow of a truck?), Herbert catches him greedily studying her. So clearly he isn't a bit uneasy, only regretful that he didn't (out of shyness, no doubt) park his gaze long enough to savor the titillation of a mutual scrutiny, eyeball to eyeball. She turns back to him abruptly and confesses to having just last night sat through—wanted to sit through—an LMN movie she's seen many many times before. For which she hates herself. It proves (but, hey, what about the gold?) she'll never produce anything worthwhile.

"So what if you watched the damn movie again and again? Remember what Heraclitus said: You can't pass through the same soap twice. I see that I have no choice but to make the subject of today's chat (a word I hate, by the way) disqualification. Instead of thinking your unspeakable act disqualifies you for all future good work, accept the even more unspeakable fact that it can't—nothing can. Remember what Terence should have said: Nothing in me is alien to me, nothing in me disqualifies me for being superlatively—hyperciliously—me. In fact, it's the so-called disqualifiers that give you your only real shot at the name-above-the-title."

What in all decency could she say but, "How so?"

"It's tough being a true original because being one means cultivating the very things you were taught must disqualify you for all further consideration. So, when you begin to smell something—usually its pleasure—as disqualifying and want to recoil in self-disgust, it's precisely then you've got to get ready to take a good hard humorous look at the pleasure and the recoil from the pleasure (analyzing the recoil—breaking it down to its components—will probably tell you more about the pleasure than the pleasure itself). Looking and recoiling yet having the strength to analyze the looking and the recoiling—to know you're much more than just the looking and the recoiling and that they're just your raw material—has the potential like nothing else to make you, Ms. Melanctha Herbert, an original. But knowing you're much more than just pleasure and recoil doesn't mean you're supposed to give up either the pleasure or the self-hating recoil from the pleasure (remember the gold in them there hills)—doesn't mean you've got to ditch your credulity (which has been such a faithful friend) and stop believing in the shamefulness of your originalizing. We both know, don't we? that you need to go on believing in your shamefulness in order to go on originalizing. But knowing you have the strength to analyze the pleasure and the recoil from the pleasure—to analyze them and yourself into greatness—doesn't mean you can't go on living the shame and the self-hate *at the very same time*. The ability to juggle with only one hand the knowledge that the movie is mediocre and the realization that recoil from its mediocrity in the right spirit of quizzicality can, given half a chance, set off firecrackers of undreamed-of self-realization—this ability isn't given to many. To know all this does no less than put you on the royal albeit (I know: nobody says—or thinks—*albeit* any more) rocky road to greatness. I'm not joking. If you can just hold on to the film as a way in to your own mediocrity then you stand a good chance of coming out the other end completely transformed—transmogrified—transfigured. Remember, Melanctha, it's what one does with one's mediocrity that counts—everybody can be mediocre, after all. It's knowing how to wield that mediocrity for all it's worth—how to pinpoint exactly what terrifies you about, and makes you recoil from, your love for that mediocrity—it's this that separates the girls from the girls. First off, you've got to stop trying to fight your way out of its paper bag at every turn. The long and the short of it is that watching LMN movies (there's just so much mileage, after all, to be gotten out of privation) is not a lapse from the universal standard of greatness. There is none—you create your own. By the way, what does LMN stand for?" She immediately looks daggers. He takes the hint. "Now how do you like that? Nothing more contagious than the need to repudiate one's mediocrity—than the need to preserve (as I tried to do just now by pretending not to know what LMN stands for) the futile distinction between highbrow and low-.

"I remember one of my many ex-colleagues disingenuously asking (but with none of Whispering Jack Smith's class) the following question (in print),

Where are the highbrows of yesteryear?—having given himself license to take this disingenuous stab at otherworldliness (one in a long line of stabs, I suspect) once he at last realized his boyhood dream of becoming a hotshot Thinkster at Large (as you've probably figured out, this place is a revolving door for those on the make). And the stab was strictly rhetorical, fake-elegiacal, smug, coy, in fact, since from the word go he himself has been doing much much better than all right peddling every scrap of fake insight to be extracted from the mock breakdown of all distinctions, fine and otherwise. Well, what the pompous ass means of course (and a lot of other tenured anti-elitists—ivory-tower populists—are coasting on his less-than-perfect wave) is that a highbrow is a lowbrow (and not just along Broadway) since nowadays a lowbrow is anybody who insists on maintaining the distinction between high- (A) and low- (B). In other words, the Berlin Wall of opposition between A and B has been razed at long last which means the formerly favored term, A, is now the infinitely less favored, inasmuch as it stands for somebody who still maintains the nonexistent distinction (thereby missing out on so much self-transformative schlock). A, then, embodies nothing but the sheer impossibility of a distinction between A and B. A, then, is sheer nothing.

But, as anybody knows who takes the trouble to read between the lines of my version of Feynman's *Lectures on Physics*, I for one am staunchly contra abolition of the distinction between high and low. But not because I think Hank James is a better writer than, say, Jesse (in fact I acid-testily don't: give me *Jesse's* nouvelles any day of the week even if—i.e., precisely because—they wouldn't be caught dead being blest and beautiful). I'm against it because if high is low and low is high then great artists in training like you won't be able to beat themselves to death for loving what they know is low for the very reason that it *is* low. We've got to preserve the distinction so you can go on excoriating yourself and then stand back and analyze the excoriation in order that from the loins of the blessedly unresolvable tension between analyzing and excoriating a body of work may be extruded bloody but unbowed. You're fidgeting. Am I boring you?" She shakes her head subduedly. The faintest of smiles has taken up residence at the corner of her mouth. The smile—like cheddar cheese—gives her strength. Worse, it gives her *class*.

"If you're to be a great artist, there'll come a moment when you realize, and robustly, that nothing disqualifies you for greatness but that, at the same time, you must do your utmost to keep your belief in the myth of Disqualification-Everywhere-You-Turn alive—the myth of having missed the boat because of your unspeakable mediocrity and all it drives you to do—and worse, not do. By keeping the myth alive you can live off the tension (a toxic asset if ever there was one) between humorless self-hate and giddy self-knowledge. But maybe you've already discovered, thanks to CW 101—" "I'm in 103." "—that the pain of admitting what is most shameful can always be mitigated by your self-exalting delight at how *eloquently* you managed yet again to sentence yourself to death. It's inevitable but you mustn't let smug virtuosity blunt your capacity to self-hate: you must become a virtuoso at resisting the blunting. You must learn to catch every spasm of smugness on the wing in order to expose it—self-exposure, after all, is your bread and butter. The true artist, my dear Melanctha, is able to resolve the vector of self-congratulation into its delusional components. The true artist welcomes the self-disqualifying lapse into mediocrity (though who, I ask you, has the right to decree, post-Berlin, what's mediocrity and what ain't?). Because what every lapse ushers in is nothing less than a new cosmic cycle—*shemittah* is what they call it down Kabbalah way (I'm a freelance practitioner of the sport). Which is just a fancy-pants synonym for *fresh start*.

"A new cycle of what?" To take the edge off her (anti-fancy-pants) testiness, she caresses her lap where a purring thing should be. "Why, regret, of course, shame, self-hate—haven't you been listening? Which exalt your uniqueness to the point where you, or rather the work, comes out more qualified than ever—so qualified in fact as to make the question of qualifications irrelevant, if you see what I—or rather, the wordflow—means. Your impoverishment—you're being left without a shred of dignity—is the work's richesse. Rendered déclassée you'll watch the work grow well-connected beyond your wildest dreams." Melanctha remembers the last seven minutes of the pre-talkie version of *Stella Dallas*. She notes that he's sounding more and more like the Master—could it be possible that he, a CUNY professor . . . And where did he hear about the "concept" of "wordflow"?

"But what if the 'power of analysis' is just another dead end and belief in it another delusion: delusion to the second degree?"

"Impossible. If you go on examining yourself from every conceivable angle thereby destroying any pretext for self-love, then—then—"

"Then what?" She doesn't want to hear the answer. None will satisfy. He yawns. She's waiting for the yawn to play itself out before telling him about the drug trial and how lateness isn't tolerated. At last he re-emerges. By no stretch of the imagination can he be considered good-looking but there's something sensual in his defiance of the disqualificatory canons of beauty.

"Wait a minute," he says, as she rises. "Before you scamper—or is it scurry?—off to donate your soul to the quacks, I must warn you about one last thing." She rises, for effect. "Fans." She retakes her seat, but not quite so theatrically: he's hit a tantalized nerve. Fans? her? Herbert? "Unfortunately, they come with the territory and your territory is monumentality so you're sure to have many. Fact is, they're a lot worse than detractors even if detractors stick around a whole lot longer. A fan will love you because you're an original—an innovator—but at the same time he'll smell the defenselessness that innovation visits upon you and he'll hate you for that defenselessness. And if you, as his deity du jour, show that you've been contaminated by the fanboyishness—that he's made a welcome dent in your armor—he'll hate you for your humanness, too, at no extra charge.

"He loves you because loving you sets him apart from the herd, which prides itself on damning you, but being young, or at least young at heart, because just starting out, he doesn't want to be damned as well. So as a budding writer he must rehabilitate himself as a marketable you. Both remedy and poison, he will praise your talent (familiarity has made quick work of the belief that you're a genius) in order to define its limits. His praise, then, has, as its inevitable price, unwished for stopovers in the land of your rivals, whom he'll want you to envy as nothing less, and nothing more, than niftier versions of Melanctha the Great. He'll be wanting to punish you for having compelled him right off the bat to prefer you—the very worst possible version of yourself imaginable—to the niftier models who would be so much easier to love if only he could manage to work up an appetite for niftiness and its vicissitudes—but he won't 'cause he can't and it's all your fault.

"But after an encounter with even one of the worst of this accursed breed, it will be hard—let me tell you (though I've never, alas, been stalked nor, mark my words, will I ever be)—to go back home, i.e., to the old despair, aka to faith in posterity which makes about as much sense as faith in one's posterior. He will have led you to expect some kind of . . . outcome—one that does not entail posterity's jumping into the breach."

CHAPTER ELEVEN

As he gooses himself approvingly in the shower of the Voracicom pent-house-gym after today's far too many meetings regarding the HBO special (*branded entertainment at its best*, according to some bigwig from central casting with liver-spotted knuckles [a sure giveaway, but of what?]), Cook still can't believe it took him until the night before to realize, in (where else?) the glitzy dive off Hanover Square which was currently all the rage among his demographic cohort, that he knew Borkman far better than he let on to himself. And all thanks to a generic drinking buddy who, catching sight of the man in question, took him aside to explain that this was none other than the Fisher King of the opaque trade, the default solution, the junk bond, the covenant-lite leveraged loan, the throw-of-the-dice transaction where nothing took place but . . . the place, the special-purpose acquisition company, and a mastermind when it came to packaging and repackaging debt, soured mortgages, default, dread, destitution, loss, distress, non-performance, bankruptcy, dysfunction, ruin, you name it, he swapped it. In fact they've been frequenting the same gents' club over on Tenth Avenue (called Positively Shocking) since opening night last fall and it's with none other than Borkman that he came to blows over the club's very best lap-and-pole dancer. Who turned out to be quite an eloquent social critic what with her impassioned *Times* op-ed on the johns she dreaded most: not the obese, as it turned out, or the foul-smelling or the lame or the psoriatic or none of these, but rather the smugly almost-handsome big spenders—their nostrils chock full of smugly handsome tufts—who, invariably developing a case of morning-after outrage at all they'd been foully tricked by the club's temptresses into charging to their virgin credit cards, went so far as to retaliatorily name names and refuse to pay. He was a little drunk (following a particularly unhappy Happy Hour) and just couldn't accept what he elected to perceive as the last straw, i.e., her throwing him over for somebody else, and a much older else at that.

Borkman did it all and always got away scot-free: never had to wield some bricklike global positioning device or sport an electronic monitoring ankle tag. But according to the buddy generic, things were about to change. Though at this exalted level of malfeasance, things were also very very hush-hush: unclear whether Borkman was about to be tailed, apprehended, arraigned, indicted, sentenced, pardoned or extradited. But whatever happened, the acronyms coined for the shelters he invented (their sole raison d'être, some said)—take SLIME (service leasing injects municipal excellence), for example, and/or PIRANA (productive investments reduce apathy not activity), to name just a few gleaned from among the least spectacular—would remain the defiant stuff of legend. Though why are things so blurry where Borkman's judicial status is concerned? Cook wonders, drying himself off meditatively. Or better yet, something within is doing the wondering for him—call it, in accordance with the soft-boiled lingo du jour, his *inner* Iago. (Cook is at an evolutionary crossroads—like Oedipus of yore—and it is now his turn to undergo the official metamorphosis of inner something [Iago in this case] into a Some Body and finally a Master.) Why are things so blurry?—well, could it be that his buddy is the puppet of somebody who has a vested interest in keeping things blurry?

As Cook finally steps out of the shower, drawing the curtain behind him (Mae West could never accuse him of *not* taking his time), Iago makes it clear that keeping things blurry is a delay tactic. The Some Body who's running this show (*if I've said it once I've said it a thousand times:* He's not to be confused with Straynge) will do anything to avoid telling Borkman's story as it's meant to be told and knows there's no better way to distract attention from His inept-itude or resistance in this department (hard to say which is the stronger) than to pile up the words for incompossible states (you can't, e.g., be arraigned *and* indicted at the same time). Since only such a pile-up can keep the show from going on while still ensuring that something else does, i.e., the words—which profess to deplore what they themselves have engineered: a bottleneck. Some Body (soon to be anointed as Master) hates telling a story almost as much as Borkman hates watching the Super Bowl, say, with or without his kids. Though Cook can't remember hearing Borkman, or anybody else, say as much. But of course he pretty much doesn't know him from Adam. So why is Borkman, of all people, being saddled with this Super Bowl affliction? Because, pipes up Iago, Some Body, a part-time sissy, needs to free Himself of its stigma by proxy and as a showman with customer needs to consider He's also interested in demonstrating how said affliction operates in, of all people, *the least likely vector,* since the element of surprise is the Number One attrac-tion under his kind of Big Top. For as much as He hates telling a story (because telling a story is always done at the behest of somebody or something and there's nothing Somebody likes less than to be sodomized by a behest that isn't His own)—for as much as Somebody hates telling a story He hates espousing plausibility even more, since once a puppet's plausible—characterologically set for life, so to speak, even with two cents in his pocket—he can no longer be what he was put on earth to be, namely, a word or better yet a thought, or better yet, a sequence of inferences, a train of Peircean thought after Peircean thought after Peircean thought. And that's all you need to know about Some Body for the time being. But maybe a word is better than all the other escape hatches combined. Since use of a new word ushers in a new life—a new word is a weapon against life—hurled from deep within the entrails of life. Use of every new word offers an escape from self-hate—an escape from the self-con-tempt bred by self's too much familiarity with self. Every new word is a new beginning—a flight into blessed otherness—into a new shell—a carapace many fathoms deep. Entry into a new word's inner sanctum constitutes a dis-grace and a promotion. But it's crucial that the word in question not be *le mot juste*—it's crucial that the word in question know it's the wrong word for as the wrong word it tells the truth. Cook is as a rule shameless, but he knows that while Iago goes stunningly full blast *on this particular subject,* it's a profana-tion to be drying his balls.

Dressing slower so as not to be dressing faster than he needs to (though if he wants to make his 6 p.m. meeting with Narr and Manning, he'll have to get up some steam), Cook feels a witless desire to let bygones be bygones as far as Borkman is concerned. The man begins to be of inordinate interest. There may even be a slot for him in the HBO documentary, that is, if his Envy manages to play its wild cards right. But, hey, more to the point, what about that off-label subsidiary Manning was jawing about a while back? Borkman would be the ideal investor. And so what if he happens to have a scruple or two left?—no need for him to know the backstory. He can be told the enterprise is all about harvesting platinum-group metals in the asteroid belt (whose status as winged chimaera has, if Cook remembers correctly, been recently upgraded thanks to the intervention of a K Street blowhard gratefully nicknamed Asteroid—not Alibi—Ike). But as he strides manfully down Greenwich from Eighth Avenue, with (as it turns out) plenty of time to spare, whom should he almost collide with but his new idol cum quarry, looking impressively harried and cover-boy trim. Dare Cook attribute this access of rejuvenation to his own fanship, however preliminary? Are they already quantum-entangled? The stretch of street smells like a cattle car which, the hordes notwithstanding, they have all to themselves. The fact that its overpadded, cramped interior is perfect for self-abasement gets Cook, albeit an indisputable ladies' man, more than a little excited. In accordance with the fifth law of physiological physics, almost-collision has generated recognition. And, come to think of it, the fact that Cook's been recognized as an Amygdaloid rather than as a positively shocking Tenth Avenue gent may be the best thing that's happened so far to that off-label subsidiary. The perfect moment to approach, break the ice. And what better axe for the frozen sea within than blundering sycophancy?

"Mr. Borkman, I'm one of your biggest fans. It must be tough for a man of your calibre—I mean of your stature—to participate—and as just another —I mean—what I mean to say—" Cook has never realized until now how hard it is to *simulate* putting your foot in your mouth. Without knowing it, Cook is expecting Borkman, in response to this display of abject reverence, to say something (devastatingly funny to the right pair of ears) along the lines of *Whoa. Down, boy. I'm a man. Just a man. Just a man like you and me. Just a man, do you hear? just a man!* Cook is expecting him to say something that manages to retrospectively—pseudoplausibly—contort Cook's prostration into the stuff of richly deserved deification but a deification even more richly deserving of fake rejection because only rejection makes the deification real and turns just-a-man with all his *just-a-man-nerisms* into not just a god but a god with a gimmick, so to speak. A god who knows how to pretend to be less than a god because the pretense is a good way to beef up his portfolio. But John Borkman isn't taking the bait and has decided to go an altogether different route. Proving thereby that he has a much better claim to godhead than his Cook-concocted double, John "Just a Man" Borkman, a phony—a phony's phony—if ever there was one. "A fan of what, exactly. I'm a fraud, as you well know. And as a fraud, I'm damn lucky to be in any kind of treatment: so what if I'm being treated alphabetically?" Before Post can protest, Borkman says (as they ascend the steps of the Institute), "Did you watch McCain—I mean, really watch him—during the second debate?" Cook wants to look as if Borkman's social consciousness is sweeping him off his feet. "When he spouted that malarkey about *taking care of the vets—his vets*? I guess he meant the ones lucky—or unlucky—enough to get shipped back from Basra after an eleventh tour of duty. Little old John went all smarmy-blubbery when he promised that he would never forget our—his—boys (even if he'd already voted squarely against any GI bill-type benefits for those same boys) when—once—if—the American people did him the honor of, etc., etc."

Cook is already through the revolving door and under the mock-marble statue of Oedipus consulting the Sphinx (gift of the Brothers Kock) when he realizes Borkman's no longer three steps ahead and a little to the left. But that's because he's still outside, lighting up an impressive cigar with an even more impressive (*no, Master, calm down, it's just an* equally *impressive*) lighter. Did Borkman, master of conversational rhythm, plan this mightily effective pause? "But as much as I wanted to puke, I understood. You might say the suppressed puke was the understanding. Fact is, the debate was an open book, unputdownable. For that's how I used to be when I drilled my shell-shocked troops high above Hanover Square." Revved up, he explains, albeit a bit too loudly, i.e., didactically, for Cook's ears, that the hunger to win—and maybe the even stronger dread of winning which in no way cancels out and in fact accelerates the hunger—is so powerful—so axiomatic—so authentic—it automatically confers on any remark (however opportunistic) made in the service of that dreaded hunger the same authenticity. The hunger to be on top instantly disinfects every lie intended to put the hungry one there. Once anointed, he'll repent in leisurely haste. "Once anointed, he'll make amends to, make friends with, the real McCoy—I mean, McCain."

"Or take Hillary, if you're tired of McCain. Who exactly *is* Hillary?" He offers Cook a cigar. Cook—or rather his parrying palms—say no. Immediately he's a worrywart. The palms were meant to convey, No, thank you, I'm not worthy of such egalitarian generosity. But maybe what they've conveyed to Borkman is, I never touch the stuff and you shouldn't either. And maybe, just maybe, he shudders, that's exactly what I wanted them to convey, and to hell with subsidiaries, off-label or otherwise. "*Why, Madame Hillary is* moi," prompts the Master (who's always kidding around *but on a very high level*), but Cook neither recognizes the alluder nor gets the allusion. And if you must know, he's proud of not getting it since the allusion in its borrowed finery sounded a bit . . . well, you know, *deviant*. In any case, whoever Hillary thinks she is at this point in time, she's generating far more puffs per phrase than McCain. "The real Hillary is, like any loony aspirant—like me in the old days (which may not yet be over, no, not by a long shot)—nothing more than her very own willed belief in a fakery that never quite comes off. She just has to be a fake or she won't succeed. So she becomes a fake—a self-parody—before she even knows who's she's travestying." Borkman has been doing OK up until the bit about Hillary's being nothing more than a willed belief, etc. That's when his utterance—his sacred idiosyncratic take on himself and the world—got cannibalized by a prepackaged eloquence—if you can call the mush eloquence. Even Cook, a newcomer to the cast of the Invidicum follies and temperamentally averse (when it suits him) to alarmism, must admit that things have gotten way out of hand. There's a problem here—a full-scale invasion of the idiolect snatchers. Can it be solved before the guinea pigs who at present merely—*merely!*—sound alike start looking alike as well? He has no idea. Frankly, at a time like this he's glad he has his intermittent belief in the truth of the rumor that he's the dumbest of inexhaustible dumb studs to fall back on—to keep him out of harm's way. Between puffs, Borkman explains that, for all her calculation, in the last analysis she's the end product and upsurge of something bigger, if not better. The calculation is itself at the mercy of something deeper—something she can't (and in some part of her she's glad she can't) begin to control. In fact, if you watch carefully, from time to time you can detect, when she really is (not just pretending to be) off-guard, a sliver of relief slashing her profile. She's glad because loss of control is her only connection to, the only guarantee of, a *realness* in them there depths. Fakery is no longer a cancer of unknown origin.

Like Borkman (or The Bork, as he's known to those who loathe him with a passion) and all the other biggest fakes Hillary wants to keep her realness intact somewhere deep down—even if, thanks to her overweening ambition, she has no idea in what that realness consists. She wants to have her realness and eat it, too. She's saving it for a rainy day. Even if she can't imagine herself—or the universe, for that matter (for Hillary, it comes down to pretty much the same thing)—managing to go on if she ends up failing at what she believes she's been put on earth solely to do—even so, she's relieved that, for all the fakery, for all the simulation (but simulation of *what?* she must sometimes wonder)—there's a mechanism—a bottom nature[10] hard at work, a tectonic core over whose convulsions she has no control. It's reassuring for Hillary to know it's to this very bottom nature that the task falls of masterminding every access of fakery—pulling its strings—taking it in directions she never, or so she thinks, intended it to go. She's relieved that the unrealness will always be only partial (despite the thousands upon thousands of hours of grueling rehearsal time) and that whatever she does, she'll always be Hill. Despite the vow to play anti-Hillary to the hilt at every turn, dutiful bottom nature will routinely foil her. (*And by the way, Who's just said all this? [and, more to the point, who wants to know?] Borkman? Borkman as transcribed by down-to-earther Cook? Borkman as mischaracterized by birther The Rump? Borkman Master-minded beyond appeal or recall? the more- or less-than-proverbial man in the street? the narrator? the author? flesh-and-blooded Ishmael Drybock?*) Hurrying by, though there's no reason to hurry as far as he can see, Cantor murmurs into his cellphone (or is he murmuring to himself, with whom no cellphone can hope to compete for his attention?), "Exactly: is it Hitchcock who's manipulating us or is it we in fact who—as *his* Master—are manipulating Hitch." He could be, thinks Cook, editing—or writing—somebody else's doctoral thesis out of the goodness of his heart and off the top of his head. Of course this cinebabble is meant in part—in large part—for Cook and Borkman—of that the former is sure—but Cantor's too terrified of their reaction to

---

[10] High marks to Gertrude Stein—a true American in the Making—for coming up with this yeasty term.

come clean. He becomes more and more audible, however, the further away he gets (inebriated by rapid motion like that Rhys woman's sister on St. Mark's Place, Cook's Iago thinks), as if to say, hell, you only live once. He ends on a triumphantly pessimistic note: "Thanks to us, the fat man ends up recapitulating to his old and omnipresent compulsion—which is to break down each of his films into a sum of suspense cells—suspense packets—even—*especially*—in those cases where suspense is unwarranted." If Cook knew Cantor a little better than he does, he'd be grateful that so pathological a name-dropper has been particularly sparing in that regard for the duration of this bit of street theater.

Putting his money where his mouth is (although he's not quite sure the phrase applies here), Cook cries out *something along the lines of*, "So why are the politicos wasting her time and our money? Answer me *that*. Why don't they just go ahead and make her our first lady president and have done with it? Why not respect, or at least surrender to, what the textbooks will someday refer to, reverently, as her destiny?" Too bad he couldn't squeeze the fat man into his outcry.

Cook suggests they have a drink up on the roof. "Café Insula smells and looks great this time of year." Just the moment to approach Borkman about the subsidiary. After all, the ice has already been broken—or has it? But even if it's *just the moment*, Borkman is not necessarily *just the man*. Somebody driven to lambasting vet-averse McCain may not cotton to the idea of a blockbuster designed to turn mere madmen into super-profitable assassins. And then there's all that talk about Hillary which suggests a mind diseased . . .

Borkman must take a raincheck. He explains that even if he'll be going up the river sooner than everybody thinks, he owes it to the crew to go through with the full blood chemistry scheduled for today. So what if it's his sixth bout of testing in two weeks. "What are you doing *here* then?" Cook asks, sounding more truculent than he intended. "You need to head over to the sub-sub-basement of the Learning Annex across from McCarthy Square." Borkman's gaze doesn't answer. Is he lying about the blood chemistry? Does he know more than he's letting on—well, about the assassin subsidiary, for instance? Is he already on board? already a member of the Board, that is, if there is a Board so early in the game?"

Borkman changes the subject by sticking to it. "They're worried about my creatinine, or is it my fructosamine. or maybe it's my bilirubin, or my GGT or my ALT or my AST. All of the above, no doubt. And then" (in a whisper), "I'm supposed to have my cock hooked up to a plethysmograph to see if, when looking at pictures of my healthier, happier, more balanced rivals *going at it*, I get much too excited for somebody my age." Hearing Borkman say, *my bilirubin, or my GGT or my ALT or my AST* Cook is immediately reminded of something he doesn't remember experiencing firsthand. A thought event, then—if such an event can exist—engineered by his Iago. It has to do with the piling up of uncertainties so as to create a sense of duration . . . without evolution. He feels a little like Hercule Poirot even if he doesn't know Hercules from Adam or Hamlet from Hercules.

Perversely, Cook decides to walk him to the lab. Borkman has gone silent—coldly silent. Does he suspect that Cook's keeping tabs on him? Or is it that Cook's poignant engagement with the great man's travails smacks (engagement so intense it qualifies as a form of condolence, craved and at the same time fiercely deprecated) much too much of boyish naïveté and/or roguish insincerity?

From queasiness about his own motives for following Borkman, Cook says, "I still think you're the greatest dealmaker around. As for going up the river, you and I both know that doing time is—what do the French call it?—*de rigor* for any self-disrespecting entrepreneur intending to run the world some day. It's known on the street as apprenticeship for sorcerers. Just as it's *de rigor* for any self-respecting politico to admit having cheated on his wife. He needn't have done it. He just needs to confess to it with difficulty . . . masterfully conveyed—to cough up a *narrative* (as they, even proctologists, call it these days) to the little people like me. As long, that is, as the toy in question is not a boy." Conspicuously bypassing all this cleverness, Borkman says, "I guess you're referring to the kind of deals where absolutely nothing happens but the deal. Where's the percentage in that? As I've said somewhere before—at least I think I have—the only thing I do for the companies I own is to merge them with themselves—with limited-liability-company versions of themselves. To ease them into self-liquidation. Trivialissimo, granted, from a business perspective but the generation of billions in tax losses is not to be sneezed at." The bypass surgery leaves Borkman feeling virtuous—especially, for some reason, toward Jason. *Jason would be proud of me*, he thinks. And simultaneously he also reproves himself (fortunately without realizing he sounds just like the oldest bastard child of some underground man), as follows: *What a no-good you are, to laugh at what you've just thought.*

The self-depreciation sounds so convincing Cook wonders if it isn't a bad idea after all to pitch Manning's brainchild. No point, come to think of it, in getting the subsidiary self-liquidated before things get off the ground.

After being made privy in the course of the briefest of semi-walks to everything Borkman underwent to become Borkman and undergoing (in record time) vertiginous ascent cum descent (by proxy) Cook is, understandably or not, all played out. Can't think of anything to say—to wish for. Borkman has done all his living for him—sucked up all the available living left in the world at large. Or is it merely the unlivable kind of living that he's graciously sucked up on his way up the river, thereby liberating Cook for bigger and better things than, say, the instigation of self-mergers? Thanks to Borkman, there's no need to get through what, during their semi-walk, he came to think of as the (mandatory) self-merger stage of his apprenticeship. Borkman has done it for him—and then some. Is Borkman aware, by the way, that he's done for Cook what Sure-Cahn and Ackmann-Cometh and the counterman at the East Ninety-Fourth Street deli not to mention a cast of thousands of assorted cabbies have done for him? Now it's Borkman's turn to be pained by the silence but he quickly takes hold of himself and says, "If you want to be charitable and I know you do—otherwise you wouldn't be the fanboy you claim to be, right?—" "Some fanboys can be pretty brutal." "Touché, though you're not of that ilk. So if you want to be charitable you can say my deals use me to realize *themselves*—to divest themselves of themselves over my dead body. The way Hill's bottom nature uses her fakery—her war with her fakery—to realize itself. My biggest deals had, to a man, the knack (the somebody who's feeding me my lines refuses to call it uncanny) of smoking out the underlying, underpinning disgust for what I did (the very disgust which asslickers who professed to swill in my ale took for passion) and once they'd smoked it out they hitched their paddy wagon to its star or their star to its albatross as the most energy-efficient and momentous (from the Latin *momentum*) means of ultimately—canceling themselves out and me along with them." Cook listens hard and listens long but with certain serious reservations. Crouching at the ready, Iago addresses them by pouring into the porches of his ear (could use a bit of de-waxing) the following observation: And why should a self-proclaimed greedy *zhlub* not be capable of oratory on the order of this?

At the entrance to the annex, Cook asks whether they can meet for dinner (pleased to see that the gargoyles above the canopy are in need of a good de-griming: that means they're authentic). Shaking his hand, Borkman says no. Where the results from this particular battery are concerned he needs to prepare manfully for the worst. Thing is, Cook needs to meet with *somebody* for dinner—and soon. Not sure if it's to discuss all he's been through with Borkman or to take his mind off the matter. Whatever the reason, seeing—no, espying—Narr at the southwest corner of Hudson and Christopher, he jumps at the chance of inviting his arch-rival to dinner. How about that not-so-new brick-oven joint over on Bleecker?—my treat. Why not? After all, Jean is making it clearer by the day that she finds his company distasteful at best. Halfway through the salad, he ends up divulging his deepest darkest secret of the moment. He can't stop thinking about the Rhys woman, especially about her ass, her delectable not-so-little ass. In fact, he sometimes wonders if he isn't, you know, semi-*gay*, given this well-nigh exclusive focus. But why disgorge the ass business, of all things, and at this time and place? he wonders, simultaneously with his babbling. For what does the ass business have to do with Borkman and Manning's off-label subsidiary or with deals where nothing happens but the deal or with Sunset Boulevard's dream-teamiest couple, McCain and Hillary? Sure, he needs something to serve as counterbalance—as corrective—to what's turning into an ever more heated exchange of the fluids of high seriousness between him and Borkman. But why implore the ass business to fill the bill? Pure gratuitousness . . . or is it? Because never in his whole life (*the Master speaking*) has the gratuitous seemed so necessary—so appropriate—to the here and now.

Before Narr can even begin to think about getting his heat shock under control, Cook is well into describing the exhaustive experimentation—on the body of his wife (now ex-: you mean to say I never mentioned I'm divorced?), a Brazilian not-quite-super model whose every pore exuded the musk of an unapologetically pungent salsa—through which he's gradually come to accept that achieving orgasm will always be contingent on unimpeded access to a special brand of hindquarterliness. But it became clear soon enough that those peachy-plump globes, into whose crack of doom he like an ostrich routinely wallowed, were but a preliminary sketch of better things. Which didn't mean of course that, for the sole purpose of proving worthy of his craving, those better things were in fact doing their damnedest to be out there. Maybe there's no ass alive made to the measure of that craving, *whose very essence might consist in the foreboding that, indeed, this is and will always be the case.* (Clearly, unbelabored eloquence is one side effect of Invidicum which in terms of potency—and perversity—can hold its own against any of the others and maybe against all of them combined. And clearly you don't have to be one of the dosees to come down with an unshakable bad case of it. You just have to be in their vicinity or in the vicinity of somebody who happens to be in their vicinity. Didn't Moira tell him that Irena told *her* [after administering the very first dose] not to panic if initially she experienced dizziness or constipation or [perish the day] *eloquence*—and an eloquence beyond her wildest dreams? And didn't Moira add that just as Maria Tallchief, another sylphide extolled for her uniqueness, had proclaimed she didn't mind being, in the nightly program, listed alphabetically among the principals of the Company but very much did mind being *treated* alphabetically, so wouldn't she, Moira, mind being hit over the head with a truckload of unasked-for eloquence if only that truckload weren't a dead ringer for—the spittin' image of—everybody else's.)

Immediately following the divorce (as divorces go, it was pretty amicable although his clothing, books and appliances—everything he owns, in fact—have continued to resist desalsafication even after all these years), Cook had no other option than to sign up with dozens of online dating services in search of the above-mentioned better things. One candidate, from her photograph at least, he found particularly promising—come to think of it she bore no little resemblance to *the Rhys woman.* A sudden fury of protectiveness lends Narr enough presence of mind to ask why he refers to Jean Rhys as such. Cook doesn't—can't—answer on his own behalf. But his Master can—and does—for He simply can't let this scamp, whatever his corporate pedigree, get away with murder—worse, obtuseness. So He invests the undeserving Cook with not just eloquence but *fathomless—some might say* unfathomable—*insight* (another Invidicum side effect). Referring to her as such, sayeth Cook the Master, he throws the spell she casts right back in her face, or so he thinks: the minute somebody like her has a full name (first and last), she's an impostor and he's not one to have any truck with impostors. The full name gives her—and her special effects—a weight she hasn't earned (if only he can manage to get the name out of his system, then she and her effects will soon follow). As her upper body parts suggested their logical completion by just the sort of buttocks he required to put the finishing touches on the contours of his sexuality, he became so excited he simply couldn't wait for their first date (how quaint the word sounded to Narr, in thrall as he was to a woman who clearly despised him). He needed a preview. Or maybe you were just overcome with fright, Narr thinks, and needed to feel you had the upper hand. But he keeps his trap shut. For experience has taught him that somebody else's lust, somebody else's desire, is no laughing matter. Don Juans are in fact the world's biggest prudes: theirs is a supremely *ethical* enterprise. (It was his ex-pal Soren who taught him as much even if he didn't want to heed what had had the urgently unpleasant ring of a cautionary—not a tall—tale.) And, all too improbably, these Dons relegate every other Don to the status of deviant. Each fuck has to follow the same strict—the only conceivable— guidelines, with hell to pay if the lucky lady (or lad) in question leads their libertinage astray. Come to think of it, they're very much like that office manager (several years his junior) he "reported to" (unfortunately, quotation marks do not take the sting in the Canettian sense—or in any other sense you might care to mention—out of this reluctant invocation) in his Flatiron or was it his Olivetti? salad days—you know, the one who routinely referred to Narr as his *assistant* and who, when ordering his daily tuna sandwich, always insisted on two and a half slices of tomato, making no bones about sending the mess back with the delivery boy if it turned out (following the routine horripilating inspection) there were only one or (worse, much worse) three.

One evening in mid-spring (Narr is brutally yanked from his reflections though not disagreeably: it's an all-too-rare in-the-nick-of-time sort of yank), feeling he simply must get a foretaste of his Dulcinea (it's foreplay before the foreplay, so to speak), Cook drove out, through the pine-perfumed drizzle, into the manicured wilds of lower Westchester. (Would of course have preferred to show up in a dream Ferrari 599 GTB Fiorano instead of his Lexis even if he had no intention of being seen.) He parked several blocks away and, in the shadow of a magnolia blooming much too brilliantly for its own good, began his vigil. Better, if she'd emerge through the front door since he needed more time to prepare himself mentally for epochal confrontation with her bare essential. As it turned out, however, she chose the side entrance (thereby cutting to the chase), so that his first, unwilling glimpse was of a pair of polyester thighs bending, with pruning shears, over some unusually tall— some might say abnormally tall—rhododendrons. The thighs were much bigger than her photo had led him to expect and her ass was *very* much bigger and sagged—with the utmost complacency—to boot. The sag in particular enraged him to the point where, if he'd had a bow and arrow and she were the Granny Smith atop Walther Tell's head— He was realizing (alas, too late) that he hadn't been anywhere near as appreciative of Salsita's succulent peaches as he should have been.

What the candidate had to offer was damaged goods and compliments of her rank impudence his lust died on the vine—maybe forever, he remembers thinking. "So what did you do? skulk away?" Narr's tone is coolly, not (he hopes) coldly, jeering: Cook's complacency has spurred him on to become the arch advocate of the entire saggier sex. Taking disdain for commiseration, Cook retorts (not to commiserating Narr, of course, but to the bottom nature of the candidate herself by whose defiant inadequacy they are both justifiably appalled): "Exactly that—I skulked away. But I did show up for our appointed meeting two days later even if I knew there was no point." To his horror, Narr realizes he is impressed and not just by Cook's decision to take his medicine. In fact, there's no denying he's full of gnawing Envy, and has been for some time. Though in this case Envy makes him feel good, even very good, at least for a split second, which can mean only that it's what well-meaning general practitioners are always referring to nowadays, in their condescending GP

245

babyspeak, as The Good Envy, i.e., the arteriosclerosis-mitigating kind. Well, whatever it is, its upsurge assures him he entered the trial for the best of reasons and is therefore a man who acts logically—whose actions are in accordance with his needs. Until he remembers it's not he but Jean who's the guinea pig here (in fact she's become quite a patriot where Invidicum's concerned), but no matter. Clearly, Envy comes in all shapes and sizes—the saggier the better—and rears its not-quite-ugly head in the strangest places.

Fact is, Cook is so powerful a self-promoter that, listening as intently as he has to this tall tale of Westchesterly woe, Narr must make haste to mind the moral he's stitched togther from the telling, namely, that if he intends to succeed (and not just with Jean), to become unique, to achieve true immortality, the only means of doing so will be to out-Bill Bill, i.e., to get all ass-obsessed *à la Bill* yet obsessed far beyond Bill's wildest dreams—to swallow whole the fiction that no manhood's worth exalting—that manhood as godhead is inconceivable—without the ass obsession annexed thereto. Yet now that the storytelling's over—really over—the storyteller, albeit from all indications still ass-obsessed to a fault, comes across as no great shakes as a man, much less an immortal, since what lingers overridingly is a sense of his pusillanimity. And by the way, isn't that a pimple on his Adam's apple? So ass-obsession isn't all it's cracked up to be, that is, the royal road to making one's name in the company. It's an important revelation—nay, even a dazzling one—and for this Cook should have the decency to thank him. All in an instant, Cook's both laid the groundwork for the revelation and spit it out, while at the same time managing to create a well-nigh epical sense of time passing, of evolution, of character development's brute duration, out of all proportion to the measly interval allotted. So Bill, through his sterling demonstration of what it means to leave lots to be desired as a man, has just spared him—compliments of a dynamic shockingly similar to the one that governed the interaction of Cook and Borkman an hour or two before—all the time and expense he'd surely waste trying-to-be-an-ass-man-so-as-to-become-a-man-god. He can now get back to doing what he does best or (according to Caro and probably Jean) worst: homing in on his essence, on what makes him uniquely him, undiverted by the lunacy of every goodtime Charlie he happens to rub elbows with. Even the puffy pimple sees fit to pitch in by assuring him (if he's still in doubt) he shouldn't think twice about sidestepping Cook's obsession en route to sheer selfdom. What a relief! for this means there are only a mere trillion left to demystify.

"I tell you, man, she was a real loser." The word nets Narr's interest. "There's no excuse for women not taking better care of themselves. I'm glad I'm over her kind of animal." Narr has completely forgotten about Cook—the Prince who's chosen to throw in his lot with public-like-a-frog-dom forever— so his lame comeback (bruised fruit of unease at the long silence?) comes as a surprise—unwelcome, because it's making him Envious—I mean, envious (*Envious* is strictly for members only)—all over again. For Cook is obviously the kind of guy who, whenever the need arises to bemoan what, measured against his puny resources, seem like overwhelming hardships, manages first to convince himself they were overcome long before they arose, having posed not the slightest challenge, and that he's merely favoring the real bemoaner—you!—with a demonstration of his incomparable expertise. "And talking about losers, did I get around to mentioning that it's Manning who's masterminding the off-label use of Invidicum for—for—for—" If Cook is expected to spill the beans, he needs a prompt or three of encouragement, which can then, should the need arise, be misconstrued—i.e., invoked in a court of law—as rank complicity. "For." "For the production of homicidal maniacs." Cook shuts down, his bleary stare unseeing. Wild horses couldn't drag him out of retirement. In any case, he must be joking. Rather, the salsa must be doing the joking for the two of them. Probably getting back at Manning for giving him the brush-off.

A lonely thing indeed to be left alone with delusional smugness, with its crow's feet of clay. Excruciating, in fact. *Why me?* Narr thinks, aware of the stupidity of succumbing to this stupidest of plaints. Why *not* me? he counter-thinks, laughing out loud. He has the urge to express these feelings to Cook even if/especially because he wouldn't be in the least receptive. How penetrate Cook's signature opacity—how call attention to delusion, however . . . therapeutically, without being convicted of same? Should he, then, as a last resort, tell Cook—and *on no uncertain terms*, as his father used to say, or was it Nixon?—that he sounded exactly like the kind of lover, Lexis or no Lexis, who pursues women simply to defer—maybe even crazily to cure himself of—masturbating? Not to tell him would be overdoing tact to the point of tactlessness. A word of advice, if delivered without rancor, might help improve the quality of his work. Though too much improvement might end up endangering Narr's own prospects.

Uncannily, at the very moment Narr, inspired by Cook's numbskull misadventures (why *numbskull*, except that it goes well together with misadventures—a *bacon* and *eggs* sort of thing), is thinking about the self-love that dares not speak its name—at that very moment, give or take a split second, Herbert, while walking up Fifth Avenue (always a treat, especially after her session with Straynge), is confronting the very same household demon but in an entirely different context. The Panama-hatted oldster striking a dapper pose on the steps of the old B. Altman Building, a dead ringer for Sidney Poitier, looks disquietingly like her son. *Not here, not now*, she thinks. Why does she have so much trouble mapping out the kind of story that is (to quote the syllabus) "suitable for presentation in class"? Why, when planning and plotting does she feel she's only plotting against rather than for the benefit of the reader? Why does burrowing backward to determine whether a new detail contradicts details past feel like playing dirty, going behind rather than watching his back, pulling a fast one, cheating? Why does plotting feel *unethical*? Why is getting out there and colliding with the furniture of the world (which is what she's doing this very minute: if you don't believe me, then ask Poitier over there) so as to give birth to a thought dripping with amniotic urgency, i.e., a good thought—the kind of good thought she *knows* to be good when she's living it—thought as authentic exploit—why is *getting out there* the only course of action that feels ethical?

It's these precious thoughts, not clanky plots with more holes than twists and vice versa, that she's duty bound to bring to her readers—the child of an Edomite night—as proof of having confronted life in the raw instead of hiding in her bedroom as she so often had as a child (although almost never, contrary to her mother's salaciously wishful thinking, in order to play fast and loose with her privates: *keep in mind,* she was told, a *black girl is judged far more harshly for such crimes than a little white goody-two-shoes, the shoes being mary-janes*) with the sole purpose of cooking up ways and means of trouncing reader folk running the entire gamut—or gauntlet—of skin tones. But here and now she leaves matters of blackness and whiteness to fend for themselves. Here and now she's an abstraction in quest of the thinkable— she's Melanctha the huntress pure and simple (though in fact neither pure nor simple), whose prey is the tidal wavepacket-like events lying just outside the range of the thinkable. Though here she is managing, as always, to think them all the same even if such thinking never does justice to the event—*in fact it pollutes the event with its own impotence. In fact it pollutes . . .* Here He goes again playing fast and loose with wordflow, whatever the consequences. But even when it, the thinking, does do justice to the event, ostensible success merely generates a deeper hunger. For the event to be captured is ultimately not the event per se but this crying need to capture the event, or rather, the story—yes, the story—lurking in its folds. And that story is uncapturable. So what she brings home are the mere trophy carcasses of a willed "failure to communicate."

So—according to the law of the vicious circle (Cantor's favorite curve, by the way, and soon to be hers)—she can't win whatever it is she thinks she's been put on earth to win. Her modus operandi entails (though she's not quite ready, or able, to lay it out for the same old daws to peck at): colliding with events out there so as to prove she's not a career masturbator; extracting thoughts from the collision as compensation for all the time and trouble associated with abstention (it's a case of consumerism at its most refined); perpetrating a weird sort of connectedness upon them; and passing off the mixed results as a story unsuitable for presentation. But by intrepidly refusing to weave her weary web of plausibly peopled plots in a room darkened decrementally according to the rules of CW and going instead after thoughts that, when all is said and done, are about nothing but her, she ends up getting herself pegged as the very thing her "colliding with events" tries to show she's not. So what if she's sabotaging herself? Fifth Avenue, in its perennial Easter bonnet, doesn't seem to mind in the least. Self-sabotage, when the self in question is hers, constitutes (as the Master is suddenly trying to make her—and, more importantly, the Forty-Second Street lions—understand) just another injection of meaning (and probably the most important) up the jugular vein of thedetour-junkie-that-is-her-story.

But even if self-sabotage as "lifestyle" isn't all it's cracked up to be (easy for sideliners to exalt unsuccess as the cat's meow) she must be careful not to take her cue from the infinitely more perverse of the two coat-toting brothers (Jack) in that deliciously digressive tall tale by Jonathan Swift and try to extract every strand of self-sabotage from the fabric of her talent. For in perceiving its evidences embroidered into the substance of her telling—the millions of sabotaging stitches that will require the nicest hand and sedatest constitution to extricate—she has all she can do to refrain from acting just like him, since it's not for the likes of Jack to pick up the stitches with caution and diligently glean out all the loose threads of the self-sabotaging inlay. Acting like Jack she has only one option: to strip, tear, pull, rend, lacerate, flay the entire substance of her telling. But in the final analysis she is more like sagacious brother Martin, or would like to be. So observing the embroidery of self-sabotage to be worked so close as not to be removed without damaging the entire fabric and observing also that at certain junctures in the body of the telling it is this very self-sabotage that serves to hide, yes hide, the flaws contracted by the perpetual tampering upon it of Herbert when in good-little-worker mode and her sole heart's desire is to render her product as pleasing as possible to the CW apparatchiks—so observing, she realizes the wisest course is to let it, the stuff of self-sabotage, remain, resolving that in no case whatsoever shall her product, however eaten up with self-sabotage, suffer injury at its maker's hands. Resolving, in other words, that in no case whatsoever shall her ultimately precious self-sabotage be sabotaged in the name of self-reform. To be continued, but not necessarily by Melanctha or anybody else associated with the Invidicum trial. But the hope is that whoever's ultimately impressed into service will be a telegenic expert on The Ethical Text, a live-wire conundrum which has stumped the so-called experts as far back as the Mesozoic.

And at the very moment Herbert is skinning herself alive for not being at all like other writers, would-be, budding or otherwise, Straynge, after his last session of the day—with Herbert in fact—is getting ready to leave. But with his wife and son away on vacation in Ojai there's no need for him to hurry up and dive into rush hour at Grand Central. Why not kill some precious time masturbating? As life is short (blessedly, he sometimes thinks) and his penis without coaxing is rarely long—in fact it's very much in the sere, the yellow leaf—as its curator he feels duty bound to show that, however demanding his schedule, he still finds time to cherish the little man. Though he'll be snowing both of them if he actually professes to believe that he's about to lower his drawers solely to help out a trusty old campaigner down on his luck. Fact is, he's eager for Shearer and Rhys to fall for each other hook, line and sinker—to shed their petticoats and pantyhose, with each using the other's touch as a mere springboard for descent into the closed-eye fugue-state limbo of auto-arousal, replete with nipple twisting and fingerfucking. He—or rather, his little man—insists that searing eye contact be maintained at all times, however contortionate their gooey gambols. These unkenneled love sluts' collusional indifference to him, their best shot at a spectator, exerts a powerful effect—such defiance packs a wallop in fact—makes him come . . . too soon. For his intention was not just to stretch to its breaking point the life of the act connecting him regeneratively with his two favorites—favorites because they've been the most receptive to his intervention on the therapeutic front (first sylph Shearer deserves especially high marks since her ethereality has emerged from this shameless pas de deux virtually untarnished). The more important goal was to explore that act—dangerous supplement to heterosexual intercourse—in the state of blissful subexcitation needed to bring the full weight of his clinical expertise to bear professionally on its vicissitudes

(Yeah, its *vicissitudes*, thinks Straynge: you heard me right the first time, dude) and thereby help put so many unfortunate practitioners (a disproportionate number of whom are of course Enviers by trade) on the road to health (do I actually believe my own PR? he wonders, but not too audibly). Armed with Invidicum and buoyed up by talk therapy there's no telling how far lowlifes like Borkman, Eden and Cantor can go. Though he's willing to admit normality just isn't some folks' cup of tea. As far as he's concerned, *normal* should be sent back where it belongs—to the dark corners of the funhouse known as set theory (he was a math major before he caught the cute little psychopharmacology "bug").

How much longer does Narr have to listen to Cook self-congratulatorily bemoan his impossibly high standards? His eagle ear decides to plead for sanctuary among the one-of-a-kind glyphic doodlings on the begrimed facade of the tenement opposite, but he knows he'd better be quick because any minute now it's going to be razed to make way for—well, you know what it's going to make way for—and he'll never look upon, and among, their likes again. But oddly enough, unlike him the tenement isn't feeling a bit desperate—or rather it's *chosen* its desperation, as a sign of election. Unfortunately, the feeling isn't catching. Never mind. Having managed, over Cook's feeble protests, to hold the attention of their dutifully snooty waiter (whose chitchat with the pretty cashier can't possibly be about anything but tonight's cheesier-than-cheesy clientele) long enough to manfully mime the scrawling of his signature, he prepares to speak his mind rather than risk a stroke. After all, footing the bill does have its privileges. And if worse comes to worst, he can always defend his bluntness as tough love, i.e., the tough-loving compassion of a squire for the sufferings of his Knight, whose Mournful Countenance is exalted by the futility of tilting at backsides. Skeweringly, Narr informs Cook—all for his own good—that real lovers of women can always be counted on to rejoice in their so-called deformities because they know it's in fact the very defiance of the straitjacketing norms of beauty that constitutes or, rather, is infinitely better than beauty. Cook's desire simply isn't strong enough if it's turned off by what he takes to be imperfection. In fact, from time immemorial, his type—and Cook is a type, no way around that fact—have invoked (that is to say, invented) imperfections to justify their squeamishness. But Narr stops dead in his tracks, whether because he's afraid Cook will misrepresent his constructive criticism as insubordination to the higher-ups or because he's simply too tired after a hard day's work on the HBO "project" to give Cook's probably hostile response his retaliatory all or because the suddenly invidious contrast between Cook's swinging bachelorhood and his own loneliness disqualifies him for all further practice of tough love, however blunt or insubordinate or constructive, or because— Whatever the reason(s), he fizzles out in a sigh meant to signify that he's learned his lesson and is only too ready to re-cede the field for the worthiest cause he knows: Cook's deployment of his ten-ton delusion. Take it away, *Maestrino*.

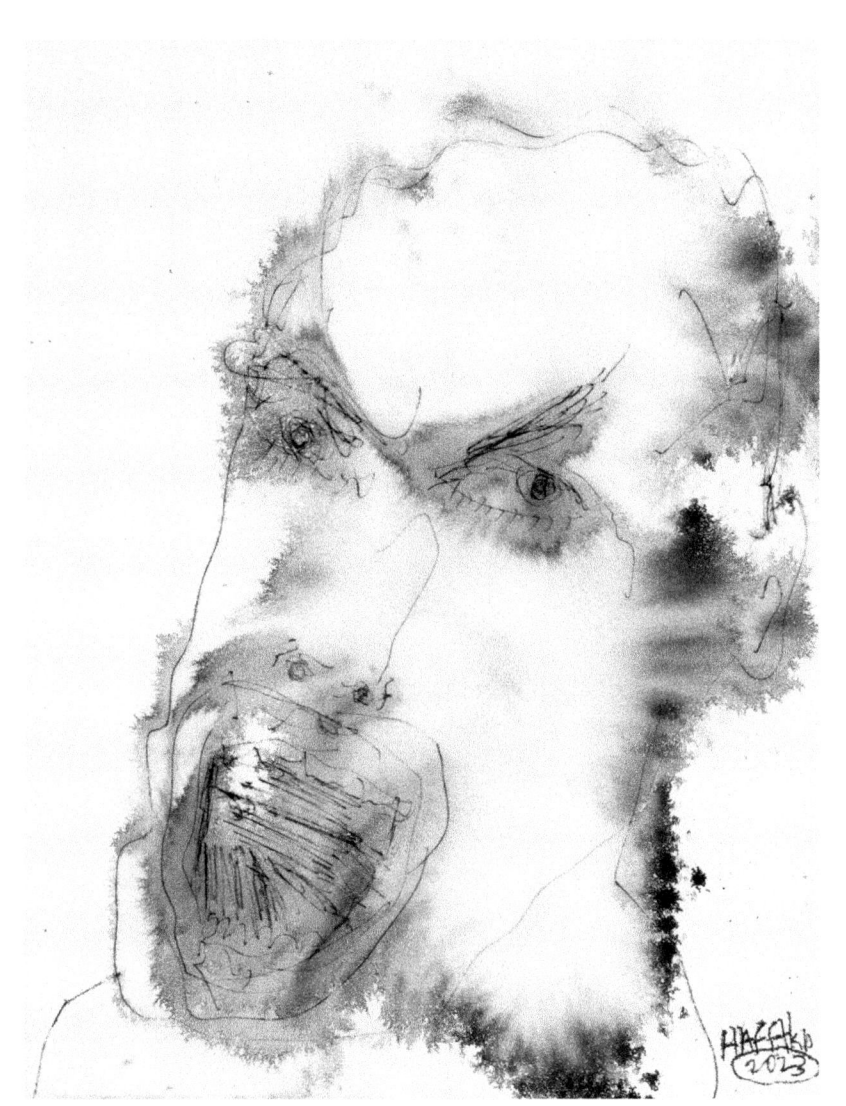

CHAPTER TWELVE

The next morning, at Voracicom headquarters, after this harrowing encounter followed by an equally (no, let's go for *even more*) harrowing middle of the night spent trying to convince Jean that she not only loves him but loves him far more than she ever loved her ex-husband (or is the divorce not yet final?), who should take Narr aside in the men's room (bad timing, indeed, since he needs to get to the bank to cover a check) but Cook himself. With a virile gruffness that gives luster to the compliment and credibility to the ambience, Cook lets him know just how very much he admired his presentation on "Envy and the Genome" (from a Mad Ave consultant's perspective) the week before, though it may have been two weeks or even a month before (overwork makes him lose track of time). "Masterly." Couldn't spill the beans last night because the trattoria ambience just wasn't solemn enough.

Narr's unable to compel himself to feel rapture since he can't help suspecting that, the kudos (*singular*) notwithstanding, what's being expressed is an unequivocal eagerness for him to fail—and die in the gutter if at all possible—even if he's become the star of his very own sideshow and Cook his biggest fan. It's hard to feel worthy of such an ovation now that it's finally been visited upon him because on the spot—in vivo—he seeks one thing and one thing only: to keep the fan from discovering just how humiliating, self-exposing, fruitless, and bootless, not to mention feckless, it is to be one, i.e., a fan and nothing but. So the first order of business is to prevent Cook from confronting the brute fact of his fanship, which, by the way, happens to be both much less, and way too much more, than Narr deserves.

But as it turns out Cook is that not-so-rare bird—a fan with reservations. He can't help feeling that the presentation was not as impersonal as *Ethan* may have wished to believe. (Doesn't he get tired of always being referred to as Narr? Yes, but nowhere near as tired as he already is of Cook's—Bill's—weasel praise.) He can't help suspecting that he's had his own gut-wrenching experience of Envy—in fact we might be talking here about nothing less than a lifelong struggle sans let-up to surmount Its shaming debilitation.

"I feel for you, I really do" says Cook (very man to man: even pissing Cook remains a salesman). Ethan has the desire, far from uncontrollable but the desire nonetheless, to sneak a peek at his pissmate's cock. Is it possible that, after all these years, he's developed an invidious interest in other men's equipment? He's terrified of asking why. "Because you're so envious" is already the answer. "More envious than all the other trial stooges laid end to end. In fact, it's you who'd make the ideal trial subject, I think even Straynge, nitwit that he is, knows that."

"Oh, I know, I know," says Cook, cutting off Ethan's speechlessness at the root. He's zipping up (despite the fact that there are still a few dewdrops left to go). "You yourself are well aware you're consumed with Envy so it's not like I'm telling you anything new. Still, you're mightily offended and you have every right to be: everybody has that right when somebody else is uncannily on target. In fact, I know what you're thinking this very minute." Before continuing,

Cook waits for words to fail *his* pissmate, and fail him they do. Ethan, according to Cook, wonders why this Cook character can't get it through his thick skull that whatever it is he, Ethan, perceives to be unflattering or even revolting about himself, like (to start with the least revolting first) a susceptibility to Envy binges, is immediately canceled out—confuted—compliments of the unreliability—the worthlessness—the abjection to the point of non-being —of the perceiver himself. If the idiolect snatchers had their way, his final words (before the elevator opened) would sound like this: "Inasmuch as the perceiver—you—is a being who couldn't be more negligible, nothing easier than to discount what he perceives—raging Envy et al—and so you, the perceiver, come out smelling like—the most unenvious, i.e., the least revolting of men. So why did I have to come along and louse things up by confirming definitively (since I'm the last person in the world anybody would ever dream of calling a non-being, much less a negligible one) that your perception is as right as rain? Heartiest congratulations." But with mythic studliness standing Cook in good stead he's been able to wriggle out of their clutches and come away sounding like himself.

But just as they are nearing the elevator (en route to a lecture on Envy and Secondness to be delivered by some up-and-coming hence overly high-falutin' neo-Peircean, which is to serve as the theoretical underpinning of the crucial seventeenth episode of the HBO extravaganza), Cook—presumably to demonstrate that not even abjection is beyond his powers of mimicry when it's a question of out-Ethaning Ethan in the Envy domain—wildly denounces—no! *starts wildly denouncing* (don't ask me why the change in phrasing: it should be obvious)—the person pretty much everybody knows to be his arch-rival (except for Ethan, who continues inexplicably to reserve that title for himself), namely, Robert ("Bob" aka "Bobbie") Walser, Voracicom's Executive Creative Director for Branded Pharmacological Entertainment Concepts (acronymization still in the works). Then, on the longish way down, he informs Ethan that today is Walser's very last day—he's been fired (at heart, he's an old sawbones and the job—or at least the job title—doesn't quite fit). Under the clawback provisions of his contract, he'll be penniless. But he'll rise from his ashes, don't you worry, since as far as he's concerned (not to mention Milady Borkman's bethrothed) the phoenix isn't just some figment of the mighty Greeks. That is, *it's not a* mythical *bird*. Ethan presumes (wrongly as it turns out, but more of this later on—if ever) that super-spy Bill is imparting a message in code.

"I thought he was a Doctor—at least, that's how he presented himself, or was presented, at the town hall meeting a while back." (No need for self-correction if Narr had only taken the trouble to register Cook's scornful crack about Walser's being a sawbones although, come to think of it, is being [as Cook put it so delicately] a *sawbones at heart* equivalent to being a sawbones in fact or must the phrase be construed here [with no loss of self-esteem incurred by the construer] as implying a true vocation irrevocably missed [self-correction warranted]. Or is the reference to a vocation that can never be denied no matter how many times it's been jilted by the practitioner [self-correction unwarranted]?) "Town hall meeting? which one? there were plenty!" "You know, the one where Jean—I mean the Rhys girl—told her life story." "Oh, him—yeah, well, after all the derring-do (is that the right word? probably not!), he was promoted by the Voracicom higher-ups. They liked the way he put—I mean guided her—through the ringer—showed he had infinite potential as a grade-A—I mean, a first-class—ad man or some such nonsense. A star-is-born sort of thing, all too common in our line of work, as you know better than anybody." *Why, me, better than anybody?* Narr thinks, but he keeps his irritation to himself. No point getting on the bad side of a sleazeball who's well on his way to the top of the corporate ladder. "The pot-bellied bigwig seated in the golden horseshoe—a regular town-hall addict, by the way—waged an all-out campaign on Walser's behalf right after the show. Veritable cast of thousands and all of them ready for their close-up. Thanks in part to his pot-bellowing, everybody (including assorted Amygdaloid Brahmins and Mugwumps, who finally condescended to cave) insisted on a crossover, 'effective immediately', from psychopharmacology to advertising—*bridging the Pharma gap* they call it in the trade, though few are called, and maybe it's better that way. Thing is, he just hasn't made the grade, as you'll clearly see from the state of his office. So I guess he'll go back to being Herr Doctor Walser again." But this confirmation of Walser's Doctorship has come too late for Narr. At this point he doesn't know what to think—he's been too busy wrestling with the demon latent in that overloaded phrase "at heart" to care. "He won't be . . . penniless," pleads Narr, surprised by his passionate concern (after all, he doesn't know Walser—or Stifter, for that matter—from Adam)." "Of course not. Don't worry about him. He'll be resuming his so-called brilliant career, and if there's anybody who'll know how to milk it for all it's worth, it's our wunderkind Walser. In short, he won't end up in a loony bin like his namesake.

"But wait, we have some time (those lectures are a dud anyway) so whad-daya say we scoot over to the Kurt Goldstein wing (a gift of the Sacklers, bless 'em) and see whether Kelly has actually cleared it out? You look like you could use a pick-me-up and what better pick-me-up than a bit of schadenfreude, but who knows that better than you?" Turned-worm Narr has suddenly had enough of Cook's innuendoes. "Or you, for that matter." Cook laughs—with bluff mirthlessness—a lot in fact like Hillary when queried about whether or not she intends to run the gauntlet of greatness. When they reach Wals-er's office, Cook admits that he's terrified of what he'll find within. "A storm trouper [*sic*] like you? I can't believe it." "You go first and no lip." The office is almost bare. No denying the sad fascination exerted by the last few rem-nants—stethoscope, duck-billed speculum, vial of pep pills, three imported No. 2 pencils, tape dispenser (empty, to telling poetic effect). "Too bad old Walser didn't see fit to stick around long enough for me to transform him into somebody I wouldn't have to hate quite so thoroughly." But about those remnants . . .

Narr (he's tired of *Ethan*) wonders—I mean, can't help wondering—whether Walser—with the same snaky adroitness that, according to Cook at least, has marked his entire reign of tenure—managed to take off with every-thing that truly reeked of his essence (*A*). Or has he in fact left behind what is most intimately revealing (*B*)? In other words, how privileged a glimpse into Walser's beleaguered soul and by extension into the soul of the organization is Ethan getting from this side trip? Or (*C*) could it be that Walser is the ethereal—the otherworldly—type, i.e., somebody who routinely makes it a point—a matter of honor—to put little or no stock whatsoever in . . . things, or one of those tax-sheltered beautiful people who also put no stock in things but for reasons having absolutely no connection with honorable infection by the otherworldliness bug? For what such parasites want (and in this case Narr *does* know better—way better—than anyone) is far more onerous than things (*oh, yeah, who says so? or rather, so says who?*), namely, obscenely tasteful once-in-a-lifetime experiences that leave no trace—no how-to clues to their reconstruction—nothing that can rob them of their sole claim to uniqueness-above-all-others. The correct choice seems to be *A*, hands down, since Cook has proceeded to curse Walser for leaving not a single trace of everything he wrote off as a business expense. Including, so he informs Narr, a three-hundred-thousand-dollar commode ("Just wait until my friends at the IRS hears about that baby!"). He dutifully calls him every name in the book and quite a few that have yet to be granted entry. He can't stop, the names are coming too fast and furious. But as fast and furious as they come, even faster does Walser grow into them without the slightest resistance—why, his aftermath positively clamors for more of Cook's invocations. Walser, it seems to Narr, needs the names to survive beyond the grave that is this almost-empty office, or so it seems to his newly awakened sixth sense. *Don't quit while I'm ahead!* shrieks the tape dispenser. The presence of the arch-rival—the beckoning fair one—is suddenly so palpable that Ethan with similar suddenness understands why Cook was afraid to cross the threshold unaccompanied.

"Have you put together your acceptance speech?" Ethan asks, because this is what the moment demands—it will accept no substitutes. Cook, still searching for traces of the departed, explains that he is by no means a shoo-in. Apparently, however, Voracicom's Deputy CEO and a few other bigwigs have been invited up to Tom Post's that very evening at which time the announcement, he suspects, will be made. As an afterthought, or so it seems, and with a mixture of solicitude and swagger that is *very Cook*, he asks Ethan if he'd like to tag along. Why not (*who is thinking?*), his presence would be a reminder to those bigwigs that he not only exists but exists to serve. But something causes him to hesitate as he makes his way toward Post's townhouse on East Seventy-Sixth between Madison and Park (he remembers it from a Christmas brunch some years back) and by the time he reaches East Seventy-Third he feels he should have declined. But, hold your horses, he's being blessed with a portent straight out of Tacitus:[11] the corner streetlamp is giving the cold shoulder to a trapezoidal wedge of rusticated stone perfused with the juices of the setting sun, which would have made the perfect resting place for the recurved shadow of its nape, but the nape obviously has other plans. But what Ethan should realize (and maybe does), afflicted as he is with this near-fatal

---

[11] Tacitus, *The Histories*, translated by W.H. Fyfe and revised and edited by D.S. Levene (London, Oxford University Press, 2008), Book Three, p. 150, para. 56.

inability to sell himself, is that, as in the case of his merchant marine buddy Vitellius, it's he himself who's the portent, rough-hew it how he will.

Entering egregiously in the middle of the Deputy's presentation, Ethan, a bit crestfallen, takes a seat in the rear of the dimly lit atrium (laid out, come to think of it, a bit like the Frick's) but brightens up when he realizes that from this, the best seat in the house, he can size up the entire audience unperceived. He's immediately amazed at how tremulously (no other word will do) these hulky admen and lanky eggheads (hey, isn't that Amygdala's brainiest postdoc holding hands with a potted palm playing hard to get?) swallow the spiel of the Deputy's semen, or is it the semen of the spiel? But who can blame them? After all, he's a far-too-well-known feel-good TV guru with far too many bestselling DVDs under his Gucci belt. Smeared across their baby faces is a look of the purest entrancement and every time he takes an expert stab in the half-dark at proving (though the folksiest of illustrations) that whatever they may be sleazily perpetrating here in the cutthroat world of Big Pharma isn't, the polysyllables notwithstanding, all that different from what goes on— what *needs* to go on—in every other sector if the holy grail of dealmakers, i.e., *shareholder value*, is to be safeguarded. Nothing more holy than pursuit of profit, it surpasseth understanding and justifies every subreption. Got that, boys: *subreption*? Don't get him wrong, though: it's normal, of course, to feel a wee bit queasy about grossly exaggerating the efficacy of the latest blockbusters to sales reps, doctors and the FDA and about sweeping life-threatening side effects under the carpet. They titter, sweatily embarrassed at their immense relief at being reminded that theirs is nothing less than [g]od's work.

So, aware his parishioners are all massively repressed (or else they wouldn't be parishioners, right?), though still unsure of the nature of the dark knowledge they grapple to their soul with hoops of steel (while remaining convinced its potential can do far worse than to be harnessed to the Invidicum machine), Vince Valjean Voracicom has, with fey, faux, foxy cornball deftness, just let all their Boschian boogies out for a breath of fresh. He's commanded them to know it's AOK and then some to be deviously greedy and even to go one better and harbor greedily devious thoughts. Each, lifelined to the guru and through him to every other raptor in the house and beyond, is no longer consigned to solitary—the solitary of his unspeakables. But what amazes Ethan is that none of these ruggedly self-made mavericks seem to mind being part of VVV's herd. And if they've betrayed their uniqueness— surrendered every last one-of-a-kind marker—then good riddance. (Just as the French intellectual, that queer duck, doesn't mind temporarily delivering up to the will of the herd his or her precious radical intellectual uniqueness real or imagined, as long as that herd's the herd of . . . anti-Semites. He wears his smelly descent into the maelstrom of slum solidarity as a badge of honor— undergoes it as a well-earned vacation from the rigors of the quest for perversity, in other words, originality—it's the flaw, the quaint pseudo weakness, that affirms the purity of his reverence for truth by flying in the face of it.)

Having listened to the Deputy map out a lifetime strategy for SEPPP (spiritual enhancement from profitable product potentiation)—he owes what he calls his Life Ethic to the humble teachings of six stern but unloving grandparents—Narr (he's Narr now, for as long as he can refrain from bringing down the roof of the atrium on these philistines) yens ungovernably for the kind of nutritives extractable, per VVV, solely from hardscrabble. He wishes he could just skulk off into a corner and forget he grew up on Park Avenue and got expelled from Harvard Law School and the Yale School of PsychoDrama. Wishes, instead, to be able to summon up remembrance (*a*) of how, smack in the heart of the heartland, he learned to polka, for example, from his polyar-thritic Uncle Sid and (*b*) of how, for that matter, he arduously mastered the art of herding—and eventually cloning—the sheep on Aunt DayZee's turkey farm. Wishes he could convince himself things were *so much simpler then*, with the simples there for the taking any time he craved them, like right now, since it's becoming more and more obvious by the minute that for the longest time he imagined none other than he himself to be the front—the only—run-ner for Walser's post. His unawareness of how things stood was an act—an act so good it had him bloody-fooled. Well, if it's *that* good then why is he, a seasoned headliner, still here? Where he really belongs is Vegas.

As the lights are turned up to signal spiel's end, Cook rises and beck-ons. So it's he who's non-stop been mock-soulfully curling his hempen locks directly in front of Narr. He assumes Cook wants to gloat over his promotion, sure to be announced any minute now (and why shouldn't he be promoted? If anybody shares the pulpit bully's workingman's ethic it's Cook). But, no, what he appears to need Ethan for is nothing more or less than to stand with him on the wrong side of the tracks and gape at his—their—betters. As the room clears (every VIP and his brother are headed for the buffet tables in what looks, at least through the tacky beaded curtains, like a branch of what used to be called the Pierpont Morgan Library), Cook in an unnecessary whisper begins lavishly to sing VVV's praises but Ethan—er, Narr—can't help sensing that beneath all the dewy-brained wonderment (that such luminaries should see fit to stride among them even for this briefest of intervals) lurks a slavey's rancorous conviction that there's no reason why Bill, slavey or not, should have to stand there reconciling himself to being the lowest of the low when here's Ethan, made to order as his inferior many times over and far more suited to play, when all is said and done, the part of most abased gawker.

So it seems strangely, seamlessly, somnabulistically fitting that, follow-ing this display so much at odds with Cook's trademark self-assurance, the King of the Pipeline and their host, Tom Post, should have come back to deliver what seems, from the look on his face, to be awful news. It has been determined by consensus and consensus never lies (or lives to tell the tale, if it does), nor for that matter does functional magnetic resonance imag-ing to which Cook has been subjected daily for the past month without his knowledge, that his comportment is positively pathological any way you slice it—Envy rampant at every turn: dorsal anterior cingulated cortex a blaze of synaptic hypersecretion—and so the Executive Board has no choice (in the name of that old chestnut *shareholder value*) but to assign him to a team of their best shamans, led needless to say by Jim Straynge, whose job it will be to fix him up. To enable him to save face with his army buddies they'll call it a furlough, a sabbatical, a leave— "Of my senses?" Cook asks. Intent on not getting the joke, Post remarks airily that he's free to call it whatever he wishes but the feeling is that he needs to put some distance between himself and his work, especially where it involves the patients. Word has gotten around that he treats them with contempt. Cook at this point glares at Ethan as if it's he who got this vicious misrepresentation going, or worse, the Rhys slut, at her lover's prompting. The glare, for a reason Narr can't explain, seems meant for the two of them. He shrugs inwardly, narrowly missing the still point. Why should Cook think he's connected with Jean? "Now, don't get me wrong," Post parries, "you've been a damn good recruiter, as recruiters go. You'll be long remembered if for no other reason than that you managed to land us the Shearer woman. First time we've had a full-fledged *performing artist* in the sausage grinder. If I have my way, she'll do for Envy what Esther Williams did for swimsuits, what Hannah Arendt did for the Banality of Evil—" Ethan looks away for Cook's little-boy-lost stance is just too painful to jeer at. "Thing is, many of them have complained of a bizarre tendency to wear out your welcome. You forget that they're no longer your property once you've safely put them over the finish line and into our hands.

"Of course, we have to make absolutely sure, what with every expert running amuck trying to prove his evaluation and his alone is the correct one, that your rehab itself doesn't get lost in the shuffle. We can't have you end up as the first casualty of their all-out battle royal." Cook seems to remember somebody else wailing about just such a predicament. But who? Eden? Borkman? that fast-talking thankfully rare visitor to the hallowed halls of Amygdala, Straynge's wife, Margo? the placidly overweight guy (racist magma percolating beneath the wheezing blubber) who runs the bakery across the street from the Institute? And just when he's beginning to feel that such a predicament would suit him to a T (though it's not as if he held the patent) Post is mouthing all this motherly concern over his ending up a casualty—in other words, being bad for business. "It'll be all too easy for those overdecorated bozos to forget that whatever epic quality the battle achieves will be due to you and you alone. At the same time I encourage you—" Instantaneously, for Cook's sake, Narr (formerly Ethan), hates "encourage": it sounds—it *is*—so very patronizing. But Cook just shakes his head respectfully—after all, it *is* the boss speaking. Or maybe this has nothing to do with things like respect, or hierarchy, with who's in or who's out, or who's higher or who's lower on the notch-crazy corporate scrotum pole. Maybe he's simply trying to prove, to himself first of all (and from Ethan's seat in the bleachers—or is it the golden horseshoe?—he seems, by God, to be succeeding magnificently), that when wisdom's the ticket (for isn't wisdom the poison—the pharmakon!—that's being doled out here?) he can be as humble as the next guy because he knows what the next guy probably doesn't and never will, namely, that to a sage in the making, no fount—not even a first-class deadhead like Post—is too insignificant, too improbable.

Hell, Cook looks like he's enjoying this wide-eyed poker-faced suppliant act—maybe more than he would have enjoyed anointment as the new Walser. As a suppliant in search of wisdom, he hovers on the tattered fringes of a world he's had no hand in creating. The very last person anybody can call the accomplice or the steward of its calculated vilenesses. True, as a suppliant, he's doomed to remain the victim of those vilenesses. But, looking on the bright side, he's also vouchsafed the aesthetic thrill nonpareil of pretending to be what he is not—somebody whose virgin gaze just takes it all in without judging, without craving, because the gazer's simply too innocent, too otherworldly, to *get it*, i.e., he wouldn't say no if the world's worst, ultimately chastised by their bafflement at so much non-judging, so much un-craving, implored him to become their Myshkinesque philosopher-king. He obviously likes himself in his new role and Ethan likes him in it even more.

But as if he hasn't humiliated Cook enough for one day—for one lifetime—our José van Dam-style bass-baritone Post announces, loudly enough to startle (which speaks volumes) the canapé-cramming buffet crowd, that it is Ethan who is to be their new Walser, effective immediately. Ethan has been with the company etc., etc., he's a graduate of etc., etc., and he reports to etc., etc . . . And by no means the least of his responsibilities will be to keep track of Cook's progress, rapid or otherwise, by staying in constant contact with his angekoks (Post of courses uses another, less rarefied term)—most of all with Jim the Straynge. "All right with you, Bill?" With an almost imperceptible trembling of perfectly shaped lips, Cook, still very much in adorable naïf mode, has no trouble conveying his grateful assent. And the fact that, amid the double-edged trappings of degradation-for-your-own-good, he bears more than a passing resemblance to the poignantly half-witted Vladimir Staritsky in Part Two of Eisenstein's *Ivan*, doesn't mar his adorability one bit.

CHAPTER THIRTEEN

It is nearing the time when Straynge, healer of souls, is to meet his maker. The number of people who hope with all their heart that the meeting will take place sooner rather than later is rapidly growing. For starters, there is Cantor. Today, before he's even halfway through his arioso (theme: infatuation with Eden, experienced as a weighty pang concentrated in his midgut, which elicits no more than a delphic shrug), much less at the door, Angekok Straynge (the moniker is too good for him, if you ask me), is already racing to his phone or his laptop or both, with only a yawning sigh for Cantor, or rather, for the long line of Cantors who insist on pestering him with their uninteresting desperation. He finds himself relegated to the past so to speak even if he's still, or still feels, very much present. So he does what he always does when obliterated—blames himself heartily. He should have spit it all out faster than the sonofabitch could demote and disbar it with that signature sigh cum yawn. He should, as an exit strategist of Clausewitzian proportions, have been out the door hours ago, long before eviction was even a glimmer in Straynge's gimlet eye. But there must be something he can do—exit is still in the works, after all—to obliterate the obliteration. He forces himself to turn around, with a sad smile that's a little too smiling for the context (turning it into a stroke of misunderstood genius)— Then he hesitates. Then he hesitates a little more. Then a lot more. But how can hesitation be part of his strategy however hastily devised for he's always thought of himself as much too self-hating to be able to stick around when somebody wants him gone, especially when that somebody wants him gone because of his aberrancy (he can't imagine the good old boy's stable of devout heteros triggering this I've-got-a-plane-to-catch act)? Yet here he is doing Mae West proud by taking his sweet time and on company time, no less. Invigorated by the lady's lustful esteem as conveyed in a tone that lovingly kneads his flesh, he says (his voice suddenly deeper than its traditional semi-strangled Irish tenor), "I want to make a suggestion for the future—not necessarily my future—but the future of those far more worthy and endearing, more worthy because more endearing" (the subtlety of indictment is of course completely lost on the old fool—the most detestable kind of old fool—the kind of old fool that at the drop of a hat thinks he's more sinned against than sinning). "What is it?" Straynge asks, visibly distempered. "Simply this: when evicting the latest victim of your expertise—eviction being bad enough—don't then go ahead and add insult to injury by rushing to your desk before the sonofabitch is even out the door. By doing that you consign your latest fruit to an infinite sequence of indistinguishables. Your hurry implies he's just an obstruction to the real business at hand, which, in such cases, usually involves a laptop or a blackberry or a condom or a wet noodle." "What is it you want me to be doing exactly?" Straynge demands poker-faced but not poker-faced enough to silence his disgust at being called upon to exercise, and at his age and after all the dues he's paid! a little professional forbearance.

"What do I want, dearie? I want you to remain glued to your fucking seat. Thunderstruck in spite of yourself compliments of so much poignant profundity." Straynge pretends to ponder: "Maybe it's the very best prepara-tion—kicking you out the door, I mean—for all the brutality you're bound to experience everywhere else, especially since, in addition to being an Envier, you're also a— Has it ever occurred to you that my kick and a half may be a teaching ploy?"

"You mean a *heuristic device*? (a phrase my pissing colleagues are wont to bandy about in the ivied men's room of Mathematics Hall). Frankly, no. Anyway, it's you who needs the shot in the arm since *I'm* the brutality outside and you just can't bear to look it in the eye—that's why you rush to check your messages. So the next time you're tempted, before the eviction of some incur-able meatball has even begun, to down that fatal shot of laptop, remember that the eyes of the whole world, through the eyes of that very meatball, will be on your every ungracious movement." Straynge smiles but to Cantor it is not a pretty smile: it belongs on the mug of some creature born, at an evolutionary crossroads, from the kinky fusion of, say, a vampire bat, a turkey buzzard and a slime hag.

But out of pity or fear Cantor tells Straynge to cheer up, since if he knows anything about what his lover used to call *le cinéma*, it's that he ought to be able to extract a certain pathos from the fact that the vampire bat's deep-focused rush deskwards poses a challenge to, blunts and thereby enhances his exit as main event. The fans need to feel it's had to fight to the death for its place in the world. *The main event should never come on too strong, too . . . foregrounded and unimpeded, otherwise it loses its aura* (who is pontificat-ing?). Straynge wrinkles his sceptical nose. "We're not making a movie here." Cantor understands Straynge's scepticism better than Straynge does because here on the threshold, Cantor himself has grown sceptical. To defend against a sense of shame growing ever more intense the longer he tarries, he's just allo-cated whatever fuel can be extracted from its contingent itch to the generation of a global truth, only to be immediately confronted with the massed insur-gency of a thousand—a million—counterexamples readable behind Straynge's wobbly gaze. But isn't this what the painful pleasure of aphorizing is all about? Aphorisms, he's just this minute discovered—though, granted, this is neither the time nor the place—aren't about global truth, but about demonstrating how easy it is, when there's enough violently unfocusable feeling on hand, to make any local inflammation positively ooze and reek with globality—as if it's everybody's inflammation, only more so. And who more than he, after all he's just endured, has the right to perpetrate such violence on . . . language? This is his vengeance on a world that, acting through its puppeteer Straynge, has just evicted him from its precincts. Surely, he's entitled to some kind of consolation—door—Nobel—Pulitzer—booby—prize.

Predictably enough, Bill Cook has become sick of his rehab men, not to mention all the fMRIs—just too too many for one l'il ol' cortex to bear. Only the Institute cafeteria (which he formerly boasted about detesting every chance he got) offers anything approaching relief. For one thing, there's his favorite corner table, about which he feels quite crankily possessive, what with its sedate view of maidenly Bank Street—or Miss Bank, as one of the fruitier guinea pigs calls it. And it's to Miss Bank that he flees upon seeing Straynge enter. First time their paths have crossed in these now-hallowed precincts. He's obviously just emerged from a meeting which went smashingly and at which he no doubt showed his peers of the realm a thing or two about cutting the incurables down to size. Expounding still, all gruff heartiness and boundless tolerance for man and man's ills, he's up to his cauliflower ears (*now that's not fair: they're perfectly shaped*) in awestruck acolytes. It appears he's about to dismiss them before their reverence, which borders on the obscene, can oppress him any further when he happens to catch sight of the street, as framed by the big bay window to the left of the steam table. And his look is that of somebody who's just collided with his spittin' image in a convex mirror and who thinks: *Why it's more beautiful than even omnisentient I could have imagined. Too bad I'm too busy with matters of (psychic) state to be able to show it (this urbanely wrapped bonbon of a summer's day) the appreciation it oh so rightly deserves. Too bad I can't hang around long enough to overstimulate my retinal palate (still, those who know me well can tell you I'm always improvisationally up for a bit of in-transit ecstasy, however rushed). Yet who dares to suggest that I don't massively bemoan the loss of this here bonbon (or more to the point, the loss of its entourage-dazzling, memoirs-worthy evocation at the next grand rounds)?*

So as far as Cook is concerned (he marvels at how much more acute he's become thanks to what one of his handlers refers to as The Treatment) Straynge's looking out at the streetscape is less a looking out than a good-humoring Lord-Bountifulling noblesse-obliging toleration of every midget mortal with all the time in the world to indulge in such a looking out or, more to the point, toleration of every midget scape with all the time in the world to be looked out at. Blissfully condoning the stupid little lives of his fellow men is in fact a prime perk of Straynge's vocation—a perk so huge, in fact, it routinely threatens to eclipse the comings and goings of the vocation itself. The things of the world exist, then, only as an ouch for the rough diamond of his greatness.

For the life of him, Cook can't remember the name of the headshrinker he's now sitting across from and the lapse somehow underlines the urgency of taking his tray and edging up within hearing distance, even if the move means sacrificing his incomparable view of Ms. Bank and her tidy glories. That the nameless one is concentrating exclusively on what smells smokily like a custard tart provides Straynge with an ideal opportunity to wax unrestrainedly indignant about how so many other drug companies, pipeline-destitute to a man, are, with absolutely no counterevidence, sleazily calling into question the wonders of Invidicum every chance they get. It is now the turn of . . . Stifter! (Cook has remembered the name at least thirty seconds before Straynge utters it, and he'd have no trouble swearing as much before any judge deeming it admissible in a court of law)—it's now Stifter's turn to wax indignant (he puts aside what's left of his snack to show he means business), followed by Straynge who waxes even more indignant and so on and so forth until it becomes clear (at least to Cook) that they are delighting in their indignation as an end in itself rather than agonizing over the direness of its target. Which makes Cook for the first time in weeks, or is it months? wish more than anything to have his old job back for with the job would come the old (countless) pretexts to wax similarly indignant, that is, similarly expert, for aren't *indignant* and *expert* synonymous where professionals are concerned? Alas, what is expertise when you get right down to it but an adjunct of freemasonly indignation (at whose simulation these two zealots are obviously past-masters) over the corrupt incompetence of self-proclaimed colleagues? What Cook needs is not (*pace* his buddies) to get laid but to lay claim doublequick to some kind of expertise (even if there's no field in which to exercise it) which will enable him to excoriate the other experts and salvage his soul—or more importantly, his reputation. But imagine wanting to acquire expertise before there's a field in which to sow and reap it! imagine wanting to express an expert's indignation before there's an expertise to underpin it! Imagine! Talk about putting the corpse before the hearse. Though maybe it isn't so absurd after all—maybe every rivalrous professional goes about things in precisely that reverse order.

Of course if you listen—really listen—and stop bemoaning your fate, it becomes clear quickly enough they aren't waxing indignant just to hear themselves wax. A lot more is going on. Why, in the last few minutes alone they've managed to put their finger on at least a dozen cases of baseless criticism. One pipeliner complains that the Invidicumers administer the drug much too early, before Envy can begin to flower in vitro. For Envy, like any disease worth its salt, is a living organism, whose flowering has its own rhythm. And notoriously slow to flower, is Envy. A known fact, this, exhaustively explored *in the literature*. To treat Envy before it's ready to be treated is to manhandle not only the disease but the patient as well—is to deflower not just the prima donna but also her accompanist.

Another insists the Invidicumers are proceeding much too slowly, letting the disease get more life-threatening by the minute, waiting stupidly for the go-ahead from symptoms that may never erupt unaided. No excuse for such pussyfooting: they have the tools, after all, to manufacture those symptoms— to bring to the surface what is festering in the depths.

Still another is appalled that the Invidicumers don't put the patient in parentheses so to speak—as distracting and detracting from the disease. Once again they need to remember that Envy is a living thing whose delicate flowering must remain unaffected by the vicissitudes of its necessary-evil habitat, the patient. The disease is natural. The patient, on the other hand, is unnatural and his overrated idiosyncrasy (a barococo mishmash of tics, temperament, tendencies—the detritus of ongoing putrefaction) merely blurs perception of the disease in the direness of its pure state and must be suppressed. The patient, then, *n'est rien*, the disease *tout*. The patient aspires to be interesting—that's what gets him sick in the first place—by deploying all the musty artifacts of his idiosyncrasy. What the disease itself aspires to—self-identity degree zero—is far harder to pull off.

A fourth, fifth and sixth, equally unrelenting in their virulence, maintain that the Invidicumers, overbent on abstraction, make a bad habit of insanely parenthesizing their poor patients out of existence, refusing to realize that a patient-purged disease entity in its pure state is sheer fantasm. Just because every case, skewed by the patient's peculiarities, is necessarily a deviation doesn't mean that just around the corner from all those nasty deviations there's an attainable norm. Either you accept the disease as an incessant deviation from itself, dependent for its very existence on such deviation—or you have no disease. Like would-be cartographers for whom method of projection, scale, orientation, baseline and sign system are just defilements of Map in its Essence, the Platonic Form-hungry Invidicumers immediately write off the patient as an impediment to the flowering of EnVD in its pure state, failing or refusing to recognize there's no such thing as EnVD in its pure state and that without the impedimenta there's no Disease whatsoever, pure or otherwise.

What is there for Straynge to do but click his forked tongue at the thick-skulledness of all these vermin, who routinely attack the Invidicumers—"I mean the trial administrators"— in all the best and even the semi-best journals, not to mention on CNN and Fox News—and, by the way, on that score nobody 'scapes whipping, not even Stifter. Cook knows Stifter to be just another run-of-the-mill careerist who makes a point of playing it safe every chance he gets (except at off-hours in dimly lit cafeterias), so it's not surprising that he's visibly upset by this crack out of nowhere, richly deserved. "Some of them accuse us of wasting the characterological richness of folks like Eden and Shearer and that Staten Island Ferry gal—you know, the one who never shuts up about her sister and St. Mark's Place—and *even* that math-whiz character. Of not making better use of those folks' subterfuges as a conduit to the rankest recesses of the disease." Stifter wants to know what Straynge means by "even that math-whiz character" (are S. and C. by any chance sisters-in-arms? most definitely not: Stifter's not just happily but *ecstatically* married to a not-so-dumb blonde with snideness and silicone to spare) but Straynge brushes the question aside. "Others have decided—or haven't you heard?— that our surrender—an affliction of amateurs—to all their folksy seductiveness has prevented us from plumbing EnVD's direst depths." Cook holds his breath, waiting to see if like him, Stifter has smelled something not quite right (nothing to do here with matters of political correctness and related tripe) about *that Staten Island Ferry gal* and *that math-whiz character*. Has Stifter managed in spite of the dulling effects of the tart to strongly suspect that while Straynge knows Rhys's and Cantor's full names at least as well as he knows his own, he also knows that uttering them outright will constitute nothing less than a gulled prostration before the bearers—an espousal of their worst pretensions? In short, he'll be destroyed—at least for as long as the utterance lasts. Cook now knows a thing or two about such things thanks to his run-in with Narr and the Names Police. Fortunately, he had his inner Iago—now his Master (Cook's made the evolutionary leap)—at his side. But will Straynge be so lucky?

And in fact, at this very moment, Straynge is asking himself, without knowing he's doing so—or better yet, it's some body else who's doing the asking (*the same Some Body that takes to plaguing his probands from time to time, not from malice but in order to get and keep his—oops! His—ball rolling, whatever that ball turns out to be*)— At this very moment, Some Body is asking (with Straynge granted permission to piggyback on that asking), Where, oh where, are the patients and probands of yesteryear with good old names like Dottie Baisecul and Clairy Humevesne and Juanita O'Grady Schlumpf, not to mention Charley van Dreck y Lucientes and J.J.J. Jackoff, Jr.?—names I could trust, because capable in their very essence of ministering to my mind diseased.

(How explain that my loathing of serious names—self-respecting phone-book names [try Sarah Carson, Jim Banks, Nikki di Stefano, Lew Goldsteiner, for starters]—names taking themselves way too seriously—names consisting in nothing more than that way-too-seriousness—is a matter of principle [and what principle might that be?]. How even begin to explain that deferring to such names is simply to take life seriously in the wrong way—the wrongest way of all. I am *sceptical* of names. Hence my love affair with names that in some crazy way are oxymoronic—names whose center refuses to hold—names [*pace* Cratylus] that don't believe they belong to or are an adequate imitation of the thing named—names that wreak havoc by dislodging the "right" name from the thing named in order to not-quite-take its place—names gathering under the same rubric components of an essential immiscibility—names nipping self-identity in the bud, cutting self-evolution off at the pass, stopping self-affirmation dead in its tracks and shrinking it to a pinpoint. *Naming maims the namer*—that's my cautionary motto.)

But on one point all their detractors are in complete agreement, to wit, that they, the so-called Invidicumers, a chain gang of perversely merry mutants, are encouraging their guinea pigs to believe that once cured of Envy or at least stabilized, they can look bravely forward to a re-establishment of the equilibrium so rudely perturbed by the inrush of the disease. As if the centuries squandered, through its lethal auspices, on complete self-disqualifi-cation for participation in the zero-sum game of life (inasmuch as they lacked the one credential crucial to success, to wit, the pedigree of their rivals) constitute the puniest of interims. On the contrary. EnVD, like any disease worth the paper its diagnosis is printed on, ushers in a new, unrepealable form of life—one to be perceived not as afflicted by a lack of this or that, i.e., privation incarnate, but as suffused in its own way and in its own right with a robust positivity. What the pigs should be told instead is that they can never go back and any lost paradise for which they pine was itself (like his father and *his* father before him) the same kind of anathematized new form of life. In other words, the Invidicumers have an obligation (so the vermin) to warn those pigs right off the bat that what they've lived through Envy-wise is not to be perceived, at the slightest hint of drug-driven abatement, as an excisable episode leaving no traces. Envy: the Disease (like *Invidicum: The Musical*) has changed—is changing—them forever and will always be with them, as an Angel, so to speak, on Their Shoulder.

But the thing that bugs Straynge the most—though clearly not Stifter, who's returned to the scene of the crème—is the mincemeat the drug's detractors have made of the team's contributions to the literature, even if he's authored little himself. In fact, he's written nothing about Invidicum (venturing this with a certain self-righteousness, as proof that he's no huckster hankering to break into print). For Straynge is, if nothing else, a man of action—no effete scribbler he (though if Cook remembers correctly, he never missed an opportunity, in and out of meetings, to push his own prolificity).

At the sound of Straynge's stentorian, "Get this," Stifter reluctantly but obediently puts his tart on hold which allows him (Thespian manqué) to engage in some fussy (some might even go so far as to say charming) stage business that is pointedly ignored by Straynge. Having corralled Stifter's attention, he explains that the bastards—sorry, the vermin—claim every write-up, not bad at hewing initially to the facts of the case, yields quickly enough to the flow of the words and its logic, which logic, alas, has absolutely no connection with the logic of Envy Disease or of any other disease—or of any phenomenon under the sun for that matter. Forthright depiction of EnVD cedes quickly enough to the will of the words themselves, which, unmasterable, proceed to write their own manic ticket and call the shots. That is, the words, now drunk on their momentum, dare the vicissitudes of the disease to conform to the curve traced by their own diseased specifications. And since the disease can't conform—what disease could?—the depiction achieved by words gone haywire has no choice but to expose EnVD as a fraud.

According to the speculations of their . . . (Straynge decides to be polite) *detractors* (as in *fans come and go but* detractors *are forever and self-detractors are forever and a day*), the Invidicumers feel that for far too long they've been at the mercy of EnVD's insisting they master the language required to capture its teeming spectacle. So it's only right and proper that, after the detractors have fulfilled their part of the bargain, the mastered language should now transform itself into a sorcerer's apprentice, with their blessing. Only right if not quite proper for said language to dare anyone to contend that, having thanklessly subtended and circumscribed and straitjacketed the malign sector of reality known as Envy Disease, it isn't entitled to turn the tables by commanding the Disease to hew to and act out a new, sorcerous truth—the truth of its wordflow gone not quite haywire. In their onrush, the words configure a clinical entity that simply can't exist out there but is still required to, to the consternation of peer reviewers everywhere. So like Kleon son of Kleainetos those detractors, bless 'em, denounce their EnVD-crazy enemies as denigrators of the straightforward in language who value words only as a spectacle in their own right, the more outlandish the better, with no obligation to signify. And amid all this diabolical one-upmanship, with the copy demanding that the model resemble it to a T, how can the patient (remember her?) not be left out in the cold?

Straynge, suddenly aware of Cook's presence, freezes, refusing to throw any pearls before this swine of an ad man turned patient. Or any more pearls, if he's been hanging around for some time. And the ad man, whose demotion, if that's what it is, has understandably triggered a hyperalertness to slights, tries to convey a withering counter-contempt. How he detests the old quack. He'd be—what's the expression?—better off dead. Much better off.

CHAPTER FOURTEEN

Stretched out, eyes closed, Borkman asks himself (Manning's welcome to listen, notepad optional) why it is that in everybody else's line, the things worked on, or with, or through, or over, have a life and a lifetime of their own, while his things, the things he buys and sells, the things he traffics in, have neither, are in fact no more than promises to buy or sell some unnameable asset or indescribable liability at some future date unspecifiable in some lowest-latency transaction. What he means is that the things he owns for as long as he owns them, a mere millisecond or two at best, are only the dim anticipation of their even dimmer resale value. Whatever gets traded back and forth is not A against B, or B against A, but A or B against some future state of itself, probably unrealizable. The thing acquired exists not at all, being merely the handsel (yes, *handsel*, all you archaism haters out there) of its worth at maturity, which, since he routinely sells even faster than he buys, never gets reached.

Sibylline Manning suddenly speaks (her husky hiss teutonic, sure to drive him wild in bed, has no impact while he's here on the hot seat, or rather, on the hot couch, or rather, on the hot *casting* couch, though he's sure not to get the role of a lifetime that's being auctioned off). She has no doubt that he's so quick to sell because of his terror of anything's coming to fruition organically—because he's capable of tolerating only as much process, only as much unfolding, as can be stashed into subsidizing, say, a clitoral orgasm—yet she wonders whether this is what's bothering him. Maybe it is. "I can't say—I can't—something to do with the Fourth of July—fireworks—from the roof of the Waldorf-Astoria—breathtaking view—too horrible because too *true* for words—fireworks—fireworks—" He sounds like he's really in torment. Though the first thing you learn in her line of work is to distrust abreactors. Most of the time their cold sweat's phony.

"Wait, don't speak" Manning purrs, "before you say anything more, I want to try something on. If it succeeds, and I know it will, you'll be able to understand and make me understand, too—what's really bothering you, I mean. And once you find a way to talk about what's really going on you'll be able to talk about pretty much anything. And it's the *anything* that interests me—chalk it up, if you must, to my professional prurience. Initial tests showed quickly enough that when you wax envious the Envy, which predictably activates your pain-related neural circuitry (specifically the dorsal anterior cingulated—I mean cingulate—cortex [dACC]), also stirs things up elsewhere but in a manner particular to you and you alone. (I've never seen anything like it in the course of my career, which has been longer than you might think.)" "And where is this world elsewhere, bright lady?" "The dentate gyrus of the hippocampus (as you may—should—remember from Lecture 5, the hippocampus plays a crucial role in memory and learning)." He looks defiantly blank. She goes on to explain that the gyrus's granule cells, a class of excitatory neurons, receive perceptual data from the entorhinal cortex but, despite their name, those neurons don't get excited all that easily because of dentate gating, a process dependent on the impact of a plexus of inhibitory interneurons. So that only a tiny percentage of the relayed signals register. "Dentate gating is foiled in exceptional cases, like temporal-lobe epilepsy, which results in seizures—the uncontrolled but synchronized firing of the granule cells—preceded by the perception of an aura. As well as in *your* case—we may never look upon its like again—where, once the sluicegates are wide open, almost all the signals make their way in. Only you, unlike the seizure victim, experience no prefatory auras, no memory deficit, no confusion, no déja vu, among other disruptions. The only thing you do experience is awe-inspiring lucidity. Which enables you, the lucky circuiteer, to not only petit-perceive what eludes most of us, MDs or not, but, worse, put it into words (through a mechanism we don't quite have a handle on) for not-quite-mass consumption. So for our purposes, your Envy is just a way in to the site of sites—a forged ID, a password, a decoy, a dummy variable. We knew immediately, or almost immediately, that the minute you perceive a threat that exceeds a certain threshold of virulence, you alone among the unholy few will have the ability (given just a little electrodal—a little transcranial magnetic—nudge) to *think* that threat in a special language and through the sheer power of thought, teach us how to neutralize it. And there are things going on hereabouts that certainly pose a major threat. And that's where you come in for it is only a patient like you who can subject himself to such threats and live to tell the tale and a whole lot more. The fact that you just spoke so eloquently about the pitfalls of trading at two-thirds the speed of light merely confirms what the initial tests have already revealed." So what if all this business about the site of sites is sheer rigamarole. The rigamarole is in the service of a good—a great—cause: investment. And it's none other than Cook who's spurred her to such heights of ingenuity in the service of that cause. *His* cause, at least until he fell out of favor. For Cook's the one who suggested a while back (but when exactly?) that Borkman would make the ideal shareholder in their subsidiary-to-end-all-subsidiaries—in fact, the suggestion is the only thing so far that's come through his ordeal with flying colors. But what if the rigamarole isn't rigamarole and Manning gets herself hoist by her own petard? What if there is a site of sites and Borkman the lord of its realm. She feels a bit like Hillary—a perennial subject of speculation at the Institute. "Does the tale in question—" (he's tempted to repeat the "bright lady" bit but decides it's better to refrain) "have something to do with the life and hard times of Brother Straynge?" "Straynge and a whole lot of others. But there's no time to talk about that now—in mixed company, so to speak."

Responding as if to a signal ("mixed company"?), two post-adolescent huskies enter, stripped to the waist or even below, musculation irrepressible even beneath all that chest hair. "If you must know,"—ignoring them a bit too loudly—"I decided right off the bat (needing neither the confirmatory fMRIs nor a nod from my colleagues) to put my money on you as the canniest of the lot—as the one with the greatest capacity to see and to articulate what you see. For a lot needs to be seen around here." "You decided to put your money where my mouth is, is what you mean, bright lady." She's made up her mind to hear no evil in the phrase and is obviously exalted by the ploy. Too bad there's nobody around perspicacious enough to catch her exaltation in the act and savor it by proxy. Borkman's certainly not up to the job (his site of sites is still wet behind the ears until further notice). "This being the case, I—we—intend to put you to work but as far more than a mere dosee. As a sort of inside man, if you will. And for somebody of your stature who (if you'll forgive the indiscretion) has fallen on hard times, there are certain rare opportunities here which are by no means to be sneezed—sneezed—." "Sneezed at." But what she really wants to say is something along the lines of, *Does the term* credit default swap, *for example, mean anything to you, flimflammer not quite emeritus that you are—and must remain if you don't avail yourself of these opportunities?* But she abstains—not from tact but from persisting active discomfort in navigating the defiles of a foreign tongue. She still isn't equipped to ensure that in all cases the reach of thoughts and the grasp of words required to do them justice correspond. "Think of yourself as a hunk of marble but one latent with nothing less than the lineaments of Hercules: all it takes is the right chisel to bring the innate masterpiece into being. Into the Leibniz Chamber with you and no lips." "Lip. No lip. But how many times do I have to tell you? I can't detect a threat any better or more quickly than the next guy." "What do you mean, *How many times?* this is the first time you've said anything of the kind. In any case, I know your potential and I have all the necessary machinery at hand to help you realize it. Boys, what are we waiting for?" Eased gently off the couch, he's escorted into a windowless equipment room—no, into *what turns out to be* a windowless equipment room. But there turns out to be a sunny alcove as well (so the room, like life, isn't all that windowless!). Bringing up the rear, Manning explains that he's going to be stimulated so as to generate not so much perceptions as *apperceptions*—thinking about thinking. Piece of cake to somebody of his calibre since the state of his site of sites reveals him to be a seasoned deep thinker. "Fireworks," he bleats. Is there a tear in his eye? "Don't forget the fireworks." He hates this teary bleating but the moment requires it. He'll never—what was her phrase?—look upon its like again.

They lay him down head first in an MRI crypt cum sausage grinder which seems smaller somehow than the ones he's become used to and start flashing the same old photos of the same old rivals, CEOs for whom no crisis (especially those of their own making) is unweatherable or megabonus-incompatible. "To localize your blessed E spot," she reminds him though he needs no reminding, thank you. After about fifteen minutes worth of exposure he's extracted and dragged, presumably punchdrunk (he hams it up a bit to prove to himself that he isn't completely under their thumb), into what resembles a passport-photo booth. Pulling the plastic curtain (as Manning cracks the whip), they cover his head with a sopping electrode-studded elastic mesh cap and his (now-naked) torso with a barbershop cape so they can localize, by measuring a very special kind of brain wave known (only to the happy few) as an event-related potential (ERP), the site Manning has been raving about. Once they have what she calls a reusable imprint of the site (so that henceforth they can stimulate its circuits directly without detouring through Envy-heavy terrain), he is hooked up simultaneously to a fluorescent light box, a dawn simulator and a negative-ion generator so that his spirits, doubtless made hyper-wintry by all this pressurizing, can be revived. Then, and finally, very high definition transcranial magnetic stimulation is applied to his occipital bone by Manning herself, the pulses finetuned (thanks to the imprint) to tweak the intricacies of what she has now taken to calling the Leibniz spot. (She hails from Leipzig like Gottfried the Great, on whom she's had a crush—a sometimes debilitating crush—since early childhood.)

And strangely enough, or not so strangely, once he emerges from the Chamber alcove (the goons have skedaddled) he's convinced from skull to groin—from the nave to the chaps—that he can get to the bottom of the fireworks (i.e. and aka, what's really bothering him), at least as well as any man, and what they mean to him and why he's come to love them (as he can never love those females who have the audacity to survive the orgasms he bequeaths them out of the kindness of his cremaster) even while they threaten him, reminding him as they probably do of his own self-sabotages, which wife and partners by consensus have determined to be his only talent. The Bright Lady from Leipzig is right: he *is* indeed a hunk—of marble—and not just any old hunk but a hunk Herculean. And she's been his Michelangelo (though he hopes her boobs don't resemble the Cumaean Sibyl's, even if he's never heard of much less seen her—no matter, the pinch-hitting Some Body he intermittently refuses to call by His right name since it's he, Borkman, who's the true Master has done both and on more than one occasion) and that state-of-the-art transcranial magnetic stimulator is her chisel.

When the torsos have disappeared and they're alone once again in her office (which seems oddly charmless after the arcane glories of the alcove), he can't wait to get back to the fireworks, which she's probably going to pinpoint as the cause of what makes him his own worst enemy. She asks why fireworks are so *special*—he hates the word and even more the schoolmarmish way she contrives to mispronounce it. (He prefers the rapturous boat scene rendition of the word by the Taina Elg character in *Les Girls* directed by George Cukor [again, very much a man's man] even though he would not, if pushed, ever remember having seen it.) He knows her kind. But he swallows his pride and proceeds. No need to cut off his nose to spite her face. He explains—in a language he doesn't recognize as his own personal property (because it ain't: it belongs to that troublemaker non pareil, his dentate gyrus)—that, for one thing, there's absolutely no connective tissue between outbursts where fireworks are concerned. Each burst expands to a certain distance only to stop dead in its tracks as a result, obviously, of some prompting from within. And at the same time it's *compelled* to stop dead—can't she see that?—by something without. In other words, any burst's attainment of the limit of its own inner potency coincides—fuses—with submission to a limit-imposing brute resistance from without. And he's known all along—but without knowing he knows, that is, until this moment—the only way to grasp the phenomenon's whole kit and caboodle—to clutch it with the fist of his gaze—is through such a double seeing. The fireworks, that smelly balmy humid summer night— when the wife was conveniently out of town—comprised a sequence of unaffiliated jumps. "So like you—like your own life—they do—did—no evolving to speak of." He reminds her that the absence of an evolution didn't exactly disqualify them for being—for beautiful existence. The fireworks were—

are—a self-sabotage machine but in their case—and why shouldn't it be in his, too?—SS didn't stand in the way of . . . success. As far as he's concerned, they tell the rags-to-riches story to end all rags-to-riches stories. Their success is smashing because all too short-lived.

So what's really bothering his bottom nature *is* in fact this "love-hate relationship" with process. He's simply laid it out heuristically good-and-proper in a new—a simpler—dimension—a dimension deprived of line-of-sight microwaves, flash crashes, rooftop laser units, market making, speed bumps, relativistic arbitrage, fractures, and those old horse-chestnuts, algorithms. The dimension of fireworks. Where, too, there's no such thing as process. Only process-nipped-in-the-bud. Headed-off-at-the-pass. Caught-in-the-act. Caught-with-its-pants-down. Her faith in him has not been misplaced. In a manner of speaking. Granted, the site of sites is a fantasm of sorts but what it's done for him is not.

He jumps up and stands before her, challenging. "Was it me—" "I." "Was it *I* who just said all that? Me, the monosyllabic he-man—the polysyllables-averse man-of-action more hairy-chested than both your goons combined?"

"Yes and no," she answers, doodling with two kinds of ink, hibiscus-heart red and tennis-ball green. Did she dare to doodle while he poured out his heart, pre-crypt? Impossible to say, especially in his condition. "Let's just say, it was the transcranial stimulation speaking to and through you. But before I can speak definitively and if you're going to be our spy in the House of Pharmakon I'll need to know more. About a lot of things—especially your lust life." Her voice closes in like the kind of fog at whose epicenter a horde of pigeons purr.

"Why?" "Because getting you to talk about lust means getting you to talk ultimately about intimacy—a source of terror, an authentic threat, if ever there was one—against which lust is your only defense. And getting you to talk about an authentic lurking threat is a surefire way to keep you sweating and sweat's the best lubricant for your Leibniz spot." "You want me to be ready, don't you? to deliver the elocutionary goods, when lightning strikes our premises, which it is slated to do any day now (or are you simply an alarmist)?" She wants him to understand only one thing matters—that his hot spot remain in top shape so that when the time comes for it to, in Tom Post's phrase, *strut its synaptic stuff*—well, then, not even the sky will be the limit. She can assure him, however, that if all goes according to plan it will be, as intimated above, very much worth his wiles. "*While.* Very much worth my *while*," he corrects. He is rabid now. "Intimacy, old girl—" "What happened to *bright lady*? I prefer *bright lady*." He shrugs—to mask his not-so-secret pleasure at discovering she has a soft spot—where her heart should be—for one of his inventions even if it's a plagiary (Glenn Ford, through gritted teeth, when just about to finish off Jeanette Nolan by strangulation got there first but, more to the point, who is feeding Borkman this mangy scrap of film noir scholarship?) and has no shame about making her preference known. "Intimacy, bright lady, is a cheap fiction dreamed up by well-meaning and not-so-well-meaning therapoids whose only goal is to make millions by peddling their broken-down

Procrustean beds in the shape of an e-book on *Oprah*." *What's happening to me?* he wonders, like a pubescent looking past his groin at the ejaculate on his mother's brand new carpet—the kind of mother who treasures her carpet more than her (only) son's cum. *Where do I come off using a term like* Procrustean bed? *Where do I come off using a mealy-mouthed term like* term?

Going off like a firecracker in Borkman's inner gated community (can responsibility be laid at the doorstep of the usual suspect—oops, the Usual Suspect?) is the following overstatement of the obvious, to wit, that Invidicum's guinea pigs have been recruited for the sole purpose of ensuring that their individual voices converge on a single voice, whose task once constituted it will be to . . . to . . .

"First, taking hot shots at such an easy target as therapists—they're trying to survive, just like the rest of us—doesn't speak well of you." "Pot shots." "Though intimacy may not be real, *as a massive deduction from identity* it is more than real. For the likes of you, intimacy is identity theft pure and simple." "Then you must be talking about my ex-wife, not me. Though, come to think of it, we may still be joined at the hip—or the Achilles heel (with the hospitality staff at Rikers breathing down my back, it's hard to keep track of something as trivial as marital status, let alone identity). But ex- or not, I still respect her—venerate her even, if only for one stunning insight. Every time Thanksgiving rolled around and in spite of what might be demanded of the Hostess-with-the-Mostest-on-the-Balls (mine), she always made sure to eat her slice of pumpkin pie in the breakfast nook—defiantly, poignantly alone. Because, as she put it, doing so *made the slice seem like more,* much more— like the whole pie in fact."

"But enough about her and the mincemeats she made out of you." "Mincemeat." He's getting better and better at correcting her in a forbearing— otherworldly—seemingly absent-minded way. Like a gynecologist rendered inadvertently tactful through overexposure to the somewhat damaged goodies of the female anatomy's promised land. Can't accuse him of being in the employ of Smart Alecks Anonymous—ridicule is the furthest thing from his mind. He's exalted by a complete lack of animus and he couldn't care less if there's no applause—no cavalcade. Each correction is a perfect gentleman and if he were a woman—with even a modicum of taste—he'd make sure to fall in love with all of them. In short, the business of correcting her makes him feel *manly* or more manly than he normally feels—or rather, it makes him see just how manly he really is though of course he'd be hard put to define the word. This blessed state, by the way, lasts no longer than a millisecond. "Tell me about your fantasies—during penetration, for example, and at the moment of orgasm."

"I don't have fantasies. I don't need fantasies. What I crave is intimacy." (And he immediately wonders how he can be so crass as to give a name to something whose sole allure lies in being too deep for words.) "It's the women I service out of the kindness of my heart who have the fantasies, in order to escape wallowing in the intimacy I crave." "How do you know they have fantasies?" "Because they tell me—they shout them out, down to the last grimy detail." "And in so doing they threaten—they terrify you." "They make me

273

laugh out loud, that's what they do." She asks him to explain and he tells her he's not just happy but *only too happy* to do so. As he goes about trying to excite those broads, so many of them—too many for this to be chalked up to sheer coincidence—cede pride of place to the same proxy: an illimmigrant with enormous breasts chambermaiding to beat the band in some one-star Orange County motel (the city varies though so far it's Laguna Beach that has generated the most frequent-flyer miles) whose fathoms-deep trouble with the filthy riches of the English language is to be understood as incurably symptomatic of insatiability. So, compelled to partner two lovely but unlovable ladies over and over and over again in the same MGM dream ballet *pas de folie à trois* which is distasteful to say the least (neither the exploitability of insatiably chesty chambermaids, nor Laguna Beach motels, do anything for his privates) Borkman has no choice but to increase the number of primal-scene actors to four by introducing a retaliatory self-usurper to do his dirty work, i.e., a brawny, brainy, shamelessly hairy plumber whom his lady, as the hypercongested trophy of a magnate away on business, has taken it into her empty head to recruit for declogging.

So although he and his lady go on dutifully sweating and thrusting, they become too distracted, each in his own way, by the ungovernable wiles of their effigies to be able—as the avatars of those effigies—to fuse. Manning, busy lighting a cigarette and taking her sweet time about it, doesn't appear to be listening, which means she's probably listening so intently it hurts, but whatever she's doing it's incumbent on Borkman to remind her it's he and he alone who desperately wants intimacy: intimacy, as anybody knows who's ever crossed his path, is the first, last and middle name of his game. On the other hand, the minute they're threatened by the prospect of being handed the firecracking big O, and on a silver platter no less, all the babes he's ever known feel obliged, regardless of race, color or creed to relinquish, on behalf of their more deserving rival (the chambermaid from central casting), all divine rights thereto. As an admission of worthlessness—of their unworthiness even to be the star of their own fantasy? he wonders. Manning keeps her own counsel (has his wonderment hit home?). Or are they, in the only way open to them, simply compassionating, that is, simultaneously exalting, defanging, mocking, silencing, all the rank unfortunates out there in motel land and well beyond—by granting to the luckiest one of their number as much firecracking as she can manage to crowd into a one-night-stand?

Finally she says (trying to put as much adorable distance between herself and idiomatic correctness): "It's clear it's never you that your babies desire but the desire of their proxies. Which gives them no choice ultimately but to bow out and leave you dry and high." "Since two cunts can't house the very same orgasm at the very same eternal moment, is that it?" Puffing luxuriously, Manning, adorable as ever, doesn't flinch. "I've never understood women. Nuts, the whole lot of 'em." Through the corner of his eye he sees she's not taken in by this sham inarticulateness. After all, thanks to transcranial stimulation and a host of other interventions he's already shown he can polysyllabize with the best of 'em. No going back to the Cenozoic era at this late date. Not for the likes of him. Her silence coerces—strong-arms—him into speech. "What you really believe is that it's all my fault. There's something in me that drives them to bow out—my fear of intimacy is contagious, that's what you think!" On the contrary. She has it on good authority he's so terrifyingly adept a lover that the ladies have no choice but to inveigle a decoy into parrying his steamroller prowess (between the two of them, how can he be so selfish as to refuse to patent his formula?). In fact his adeptness is so adept it's tantamount to intimidation—he intimidates them into surmounting their fear of intimacy. And before he knows it— He waits in vain for Manning to finish her sentence. But she doesn't, or can't—pity, because it started off so promisingly, even beautifully—seemed to have so much to live for. "It's precisely the intimidation that makes you the ideal candidate for the work I have in mind." But as she speaks she wonders why any conversation with the guinea pigs must always be redirected toward—compelled to end up being about—presumably the only subject worth pursuing, to wit, the "subsidiary" theme—the off-label proliferation of a master race of homicidal maniacs straight out of *The Boys from Brazil* or *The Parallax View* or "Keller's Therapy." How fatiguing. "Don't think we got you enrolled in the trial out of concern for the debilitating effects of EnVD. Never in a million years did we think that you couldn't handle what little Envy you harbor—that you couldn't make Envy work for you. But just as the marketers of Botox, originally approved for crossed eyes and involuntary closure of the eyelids, have allowed the drug to eclipse itself through their parlaying of a mere side effect—temporary wrinkle abatement—into a multibillion dollar cash cow, so do we intend to perform a similar wonder by—by— In short, we intend to establish a subsidiary consecrated to the off-label use of Invidicum and from the very beginning we wanted you to be our prime investor—to shame the mugwumps into getting off the fence and intimidate them into following in your seven-league footsteps." Is this another malapropism or a purposeful flight of poetical fancy? "Oh, I know what you're going to say—that you haven't a penny to your name. Don't worry: we'll provide you with some seed money because we know you'll make it grow exponentially. As for your crimes, well, they will only shed a certain lustre on our doings. So don't let that—" "What I was going to say was, who is this 'we' you keep mentioning?"

"Our biggest stumbling block is Post—or rather his moral menopause: he's begun to have misplaced scruples. Imagine! at this stage of the skin game! Thing is, only he and his gang know how to tweak the structure of the molecule so as to turn it into a world-class homicidogenic. Why waste this remedial poison on Envy, a mere orphan disease." Which means (she goes on to explain) that, having never been responsible for a single innovation despite all his titular claims to same, he'd rather see Invidicum asphyxiate in Envy's womb (or should she say the pipeline?) rather than acknowledge that it may be destined, just around the bend, for far more profitable applications. "And like any true humanitarian," Borkman muses (pretending to be unbendingly caught up in his own thoughts so he can study her unobserved), "he wants to have things both ways. But who doesn't, right?"

He's too worn out—he's sixty-three (or is it seventy-three?) after all, not *twenty*-three—to insist on knowing what's behind the crimson curtain of the *we*. So he does the next best thing, which is to shrug, transferring all rights of decipherment (it's the least he can do) to her and her alone.

CHAPTER FIFTEEN

While to Tom Post, MD, PhD, LLD, LCSW, it may feel like the beginning of just another day in the life of a stymied innovator-cum-entrepreneur, to his autonomous right eye—which has just caught the magnificent reflection of an orb in the drenched asphalt—it feels very much otherwise. Sun? moon? lamppost's incandescent bulb? headlight? Impossible to determine at such short notice. For the last few blocks, he's lost all sense of day and night, his circadian rhythm way off its hinges, maybe for good, who knows? who cares? Dealing day in day out with Straynge, not to mention that Narr character—who (for some indefinable reason) is more trouble than he's worth—has taken its dreary toll. The clinical-trial circus just isn't what it used to be though he'd be hard put, if cornered, to define the *what*. One thing, however, is clear: the good old days would never have tolerated the good doctor's cockamamie theories—even less, his portable-soapbox-style dissemination of their choicest threads-cum-shreds of self-contradiction. According to Jimbo (Post's handle for—and thus on—Straynge and other things Strayngian as well as a nod to Claude Debussy, one of his pop heroes), the side effects of any mental-health drug are generally so morbific that in nine hundred and ninety-nine cases out of a thousand they overwhelm the symptoms against which it's been recruited, to the point where the poor patient (remember him?) ends up incapable of putting his finger on exactly what it is he claims to be suffering from (finger-putting being nine-tenths the battle). And all this, for some unrevealable reason, holds *a fortiori* for Invidicum. (Enter, then, the indispensable adjuvant cum adjutant—talk therapy à la Straynge— successful only when administered by his likes.) Now, what kind of song is that, will you tell me, for a trialmeister to be singing—and when he isn't even singing for his supper? Well, for one thing, it's the kind of song that costs him nothing. Since it's not about him but about the drug with which his therapy's supposed to be in synch and, as everybody knows even if they don't know they know, he's abjured this drug in his own slimy way from the start. But let's assume (says Post to Post), let's just assume, he identifies in toto with the drug—that he champions it body and soul. Then the unavoidable self-depreciation bound up with an authoritative analysis of its defects is more than compensated for by the analyst's demonstration of his lookma-no-hands hyperacuity. In short he has no trouble surviving his own self-depreciation. He comes out smelling like a rose—and a highly articulate one. So what is the dangerous supplement, the favored term? Post wonders— Straynge therapy or Invidicum (which merely piggybacks on its potency)? What is center, what periphery?

But oddly enough, he feels Straynge is . . . on to something. So what (thinks the drill sergeant within, whom Melanctha Herbert would without a qualm refer to as—but never mind what Herbert would refer to it as) if Post's sudden faith in a theory riddled with loopholes is the merest epiphenomenon of rapture generated by a specific time and place, namely, summer morning in the Flatiron district? (So many buildings in the vicinity look like they're trying to cash in on the brand by mimicking the Flatiron *look*, especially attractive to drug-trafficking oligarchs in hot pursuit of a multilevel parking lot for their lucre. But where exactly does the vicinity begin and end? How far away can one of them be and still lay claim to residence therein? A question [he remembers reading in some noisy online tabloid] that's stumped the experts from Heraclitus to Wittgenstein and back again.) Epiphenomenon or not, he's poignantly, plangently wrenched. For he foresees all too clearly that the medical establishment will tar and feather Straynge's chimeric mouse as a heavy-handed hoax. And though the attack is sure to be launched en masse, each attacker will stand convinced that by refusing to buy into Straynge's folk wisdom he's putting his reputation on the line—going out on a limb—the limb of a lifetime. As if figurehead Straynge poses a mainstream threat to the body politic—Straynge, of all people, who can't be more marginal, more sidelined, and whose sole raison d'être, after all, is to serve as a cover for the shadier goings-on behind the scenes, many of which even Post is unaware of—though he's very much aware of being unaware and it's all—if you must know—a wee bit exhilarating.

Post, frequently rebuked by less talented colleagues for his impish sense of humor, can only laugh. Since he knows Straynge is doing the trial a service through all this self-inflationary insistence that if there's an adjuvant (see above) in the House of Envy-run-amuck, it's Invidicum, not talk therapy. For Post is a great believer—among the greatest and from as far back as his pre-salad days—in the benefits accruing from sabotage conscientiously practiced. It injects not just another but a better kind of meaning into the scar tissue of any self-respecting enterprise. So Straynge isn't the only one with a theory. Theories are catching. So, hooray for old Straynge! And a hip-hip for Post as well for being able to take what's best from Straynge: his self-aggrandizing passion for the supreme vehicle of innovation: sabotage!

As far as he's concerned, a hearty dose of sabotage (whether from within or without) isn't lese majesty but the purest form of homage. What *is* lese majesty, on the other hand, is respectful appreciation of the worker to the exclusion of the work. Nothing funnier than a dowagerlike bristling at the trashing of the work by rivals, detractors, colleagues (indistinguishable beasts) when what dowagers of every conceivable sex and those (for the time being) inconceivable should dutifully feel is glad beyond gladness when a saboteur errant takes the time and trouble to shit on the fruits of their labors. Since isn't the capacity to take a comradely shit along with them the ultimate proof of one's creative mettle? Before it's anything the work must foresee and foreseeing, invite and encompass the fructive animadversion—yeah, wiseguy, *the fructive animadversion*—of others—the *Others*. What would it be without their sanction? Where else can its seed be sown but in their drought-ravaged terrain? Absent that capacity, one is no better and probably a whole lot worse than the horse's ass who, when struck by lightning, cries out, *Why me?* (*Why* not *you? Be grateful for this mark of distinction.*) Alone among men, Post relishes nothing better than to warm the cockles of his trailblazer's heart at the fireside of a nasty asperser. That the heartwarming technique hasn't caught on makes no difference. The key (though he's not quite sure what it's the key to) is not just to be grateful for one's detractors (any halfwit can *do* gratitude) but to egg them on mercilessly in their revels, pick them up when they collapse like a house of wild cards under the weight of their own vitriol, rake them over the coals every time they fail to strafe some vital hotspot of vulnerability in their target—that's you, buddy!

It's precisely, or imprecisely, because he himself has never experienced any of the grotesqueries of Envy (why, it got so bad he often wondered, especially around puberty, whether there mightn't be something wrong with his glands and/or glans), has never measured his assets and defects against others', that he's been able to mastermind an EnVD trial which will, if he plays his cards right, herald nothing less than the dawn of a new century. Never has he allowed a rival's life to become more real than—to tumorize—his own (although he's been tempted on occasion), making him the prisoner of an oncodrama. Never has he found himself actually speculating about how to interpolate himself into the magic circle of a rival's life. Whenever he feels such a song of speculation coming on he consigns it to a parallel universe— the Girardian underground—and the degradation-hungry singer along with it. For he knows that what makes the man is not the flaws-riddled endowment with which he's been saddled. The endowment exists, after all, only to be put through the grinder of analysis (or so he's been told by those with a talent for such things)—leaving no narcissistic pretension, i.e., narcissistic hurt, unturned—in order that the man may acquire himself as other than— lateral to—himself, i.e., as the sum total of those flaws, but now transmogrified, compliments of analysis, into assets. Never has he allowed himself to be fooled, much less deflated, by any of those lupine rivals in soulful sheep's clothing whose professedly humble prostration before the incomparable achievement of one of Pharma's greats, safely dead, is but an instrument of coercion—the means of demanding invidiously and insidiously that faced with such achievement, he, unsafe because undead, hurry up and acknowledge the futility of his own ambitions. All this so the lupines can feel a little less futile. For why should he be allowed to strive for greatness, i.e., the realization of his uniqueness (even—especially?—if it turns out ultimately to be the uniqueness of his own private failure, his own special brand of defeat), when they, out of what they're all too ready to pietistically pass off as deference to the greats, have abjured all such striving as the vulgarian ultimate in bad form. And as the leader of the pipeline pack he's always deprecated engagement in such practices by his staff. Even if it hasn't always made him popular.

A paragon, then, of freedom from Envy and its toils, he likes nothing more than walking. Like his ex-pal Friedrich something or other who, before going mad, routinely shared the cab fare for the trip out to the Ur-lab on Cape May, he maintains, also routinely, that when it's a question of bringing to birth truly great thoughts and even the not so great, walking is the only midwife worth her weight in Epsom salts. Especially not-quite-strolling, as now, down Fifth past the Met Life Tower clockface glaring westward above the dusty defiles of the beech trees. His very own timepiece. Not to mention the (delphine and cauliflower) clouds above, his bespoke fob pocket. Is he imagining it or are those two copper-rimmed rumps to the left of the Tower about to sever their pink-stranded lifelong connection forever? Such disengagement after what feels to him like an eternal millisecond of connectedness—much too painful to bear without the proper medication. It hits too close to home. Too much of a mirroring here of his own misrelations—to Straynge, Cook, Walser, Stifter, Pritchard, not to mention all the little flunkeys whom he's put through the sausage grinder of disciplehood with very mixed results. A little further east, or west, or north—he's suddenly lost all sense of direction—another pair, also coppery and pink, are competitively pissing murky shafts of sun. But these are just marginals. Among the putti skating out on the great central azure rink directly above the Flatiron, there is neither competition, nor severings, and hence no envy in need of a rest cure, only high camaraderie which oozes from their every pore. In other words, here triumph has no meaning for a skater if it isn't the triumph of another. Not that Post himself is observing the gambols: once again it's the autonomous right that's been assigned to interpret (during his sabbatical from seeing) this cautionary tale made visible. What he does observe, however, and this time in every faculty and fiber, is one of his very own crossing Fifth while pertly paying little enough heed to the traffic—one of the unholy few, in fact, who've been giving them so much trouble as of late (though in broad daylight she looks quite harmless). At least according to the blow-by-blow accounts of Straynge's little flunkey (toxically on the make), who seems to have come through *his* grinder without a scratch.

As for Shearer, she keeps moving with her head turned: she has no desire to meet up with that guy *who bears an uncanny resemblance* to the balletmaster-in-chief, Post. Or is it the chief *lui-même*? She keeps on walking, toward Sixth, though she didn't have the intention to do so upon setting out—right! *upon setting out* (let's hear it for all the closet archaists in our studio audience!). But how can she resist the looming doorman who, in what looks—and sounds—like a moment of riotous freedom from the beck-and-call of hoity-toity tenant traffic, is taking the trouble unsolicited to balance a broom on his left foot? Surely, just what Dr. Balanchine would have ordered as the inspiration for some little soufflé (*The Steadfast Tin Doorman?*) to be hygienically interpolated between two of the biggest—and best—applause machines—*Tchaikovsky Piano Concerto No. 2*, say, and *Symphony in C*. But Mr. B. is dead and her career has simply and tragicomically (*Stop it, Moira! let your feet do the overacting!*) hit the skids. But skids or no skids, she doesn't recognize the city anymore. So much unregulated condominiumization: so many unprotected workers falling to their deaths without permission. But she doesn't want to suffer—to walk on her own corpse, so to speak—so she's coming to treat Manhattan as a foreign land—no memories to trip her up. It hasn't failed her, nor she it, for it's brand new. And its brand name is Greed. And the conspiratorial hallmarks of its fear-fueled practitioners are fake high seriousness and fake disgruntled self-righteousness (their version of true virility, which must be humorless to pass muster) and authentic mercilessness toward the insulted and injured and toward the lethally frivolous "left." And its face— its ugly scowling puss—is Mick Mulvaney (with Brian Kemp of Georgia a plausible runner-up), as the RUMPsfeld and the Cheney were its face in eons gone by.[12] But if you rout around a bit you can unearth the rough sketch of a self- and party-debunking smile on the mugs of Gaetz and Jordan—reptilians on the make—a smile that aches to—but dares not—speak its (very unvirile) name.

Should she confess not *to* but *at* this week's poor excuse for a father confessor (even if only Toni Bentley would understand) to having masturbated late last night against the Master's—the *real* Master's—image? Thing is, any hope of orgasm was dashed when Shearer's greatest rival, whose name is always better left unuttered at this or any other ungodly hour, made an unannounced appearance—thereby evicting Shearer from the premises of her own fantasy (which eviction was, she's ashamed to say, its most exciting moment by far). The greatest rival proceeded to suck the real Master bone-dry, a show-stopper choreographed by Moira to the passage in Hindemith's *Four Temperaments* that accompanies the wrenchingly poignant exit, following his encounter with the baby bacchantes, of Balanchine's Melancholic. And who precisely will this week's confessor turn out to be? It's not as if the list is posted like the casting in any self-respecting NYCB performance. She's figured it out only via hit-and-miss. Frankly, there are just too many headless-chicken rehabbers running around the Institute so it's no wonder she has no end of trouble keeping them straight—more to the point, deciding which strain of psychic fecal matter is most appropriately flung in the face of which master coprophage. How could her stomach muscles not tighten remembering (for it was the muscles doing the remembering for the two of them) how in Stifter's office (directly across from Straynge's) for the first time she went on and on—because she didn't know what else to do—about an old partner now dead of AIDS (how rapturously respectful he made his kneelings in the second movement of *Symphony in C*), and irresistible especially for his underarm sweat, gracefully contoured balls whose hugeness no tights could mitigate and the sparse blond hair on his chest? (She wasn't wise enough in the ways of rehab—and still isn't and may never be—to know that refusing on demand to cough up the unspeakable—that salting away all the shamefuls for a rainy day, so to speak—is the only therapeutic breakthrough—the only cure, in fact.) Quickly enough she realized she wasn't supposed to be leaving that kind of beef stew on Stifter's doorstep since it belonged by divine right to no other gourmandizer than Doc Walser and, anyway, Stif's sole right (and a woppingly undivine one it was, too) consisted in being irregularly updated on how the dosage might be affecting her concentration and REM sleep patterns. (Any other sort of revelation, especially the ones served up with generous dollops of *désespoir brûlé*, made him fidget beneath the convenient pile of folders in his lap—come to think of it, a little like the raincoaters in those far-away-and-long-ago old-time Eighth Avenue porno labs that her partner in *Liebeslieder*, unfortunately

---

[12]*Q*: But how did we get "from Cheney to Mulvaney" in a single bound with absolutely no effort made to establish a plausible duration? *A*: Novelistic duration and the lack thereof are both the refuge of scoundrels. The only plausible duration is that spanning the compression-sock elaboration of a single thought.

still alive, was always cooing over.)

As for Walser, when she let slip weeks ago that there were simply too many cooks here for her taste, he gave her to understand she was way out of line springing a crack like that, that he simply didn't know what in the world to do with her and her symptoms and that if she found him too jargon-slap-happy and distrait to be bothered to make the effort to find out, which he was pretty sure she did by the look of her (he knew the Shearer type all too well), this only confirmed that her Envy was simply the wrong brand—it was, let's face it, inadequate by every criterion of symptomatological excellence. Fearlessness—with which (or so she thought) she was no longer on speaking terms—compelled her to demur: "You mean by every criterion of symptom *niceness.*" He singled her out as the sickest of them all because she, unlike the others in the group, was simply too healthy to be here (which became, at least to him, crystal clear even before the first week of dosing was half over) but had nevertheless stopped at nothing to get—and keep—herself enrolled. So it wasn't that there were too many cooks rehabilitating the very broth of her being but that her sickness had overreached itself in demanding the intervention of too many (so she could get lost in the crossfire of their mock expertise) precisely because it was no sickness at all. Or rather, the demand was the sickness—in fact, more sick than the sickness. The demand of a diva (so he'd done his homework), if she must know—and she must, she must!

But don't get him wrong. At the same time she was sick—sick beyond anything he'd ever seen and he'd seen plenty, let me tell you. Only her problem, no matter how hard she tried or would doubtless try again, simply didn't meet the quirky specifications of their expertise. Was he implying that she hadn't met Mr. B.'s specifications either? But with all due disrespect for whatever he was implying *then*, she's come around to forgiving him because she knows *now* that he was simply overworked. He was not only fulfilling his duties at Amygdcala but moon- or rather daylighting as Executive Creative Director for Branded Pharmacological Entertainment Concepts (acronym still under construction), i.e., he was taking a long-overdue stab at Going Hollywood which required that he bring the full weight of his expertise to bear on the development of an HBO series (twenty episodes) on the subject of Invidicum-friendly Envy. (Funny, she thinks, how obsession with Envy as a fancy-pants pseudocultural phenomenon seems to be a prerequisite for working at HBO or its competitors in some type of exalted capacity and, even funnier, how, now that all key "creative" positions have already been filled, latecomer aspirants are being ordered [or so she's heard], to make do with the title of Executive Producer and/or forever hold their peace.) Alas, the scuttlebutt has it that he was booted out only a day or two ago and fears mightily he'll be unable to continue his work full-time at the Institute, not that he finds the prospect of being kept down on the farm particularly fulfilling now that he's seen Paree.

So why is she bothering to return? Because the other experts like her, or seem to. No denying she's tired of the trial—of all this pill-guillotining meticulousness to ensure she doesn't over- or underdose herself. And let's face it: she craves more and more the soothe of her daily routine as a trial participant. Why, it's almost like being back in the Company. Not as principal of principals of course but in this case it's far more exhilarating (and much less tiring) to be in the corps—which means taking advantage of near eclipse by other corpses to improvise radically, with one foot safely in the wings. And what's more, being one with all the others who are also going to work (even if in fact she's not) somehow enhances her . . . uniqueness. She likes looking, if you must know, *as if* she's going to work, as if she has no choice *but* to go to work. She likes acting like a harried straphanger, stoically entranced (with a little help from the counter-rhythm of subway or bus or her own two feet) by very private tribulation-riddled thoughts. It's an enactment of sidewalk martyrdom and she enjoys milking martyrdom for all it's worth, but what is it in fact worth in today's marketplace? Never mind that (she has no head for business, not even stage business). In fact the role of harried working stiff may end up being the greatest of her career—greater than the incarnation of Dewdrop or Sonnambula or the late-for-class waltz girl in *Serenade* or the Unanswered Questioner or as (on loan) the hapless Caroline in the ABT production of *Jardin aux Lilas*. Her tongue, if you must know, has been hanging out like a fleabitten mutt's ever since the B. Altman building—a mutt panting for the windfall of a bewhiskered soupbone—the soupbone of a spectator to applaud her expert imitation of Working Stiff Susie. Straphanger Extraordinaire. She's pretending to submit to what she's busy creating—after all, who knows better than she that the road to the most exhilarating freedom is paved with such pretenses of submission? And now that you mention it, what about the time she got a call (at six in the morning) to pinch-hit in *Walpurgisnacht*? Her first (or was it her second?) solo required that she execute a few dozen little pizzicati while staring down in arms-thrashing disbelief at toe shoes that had suddenly taken on (even if they were emphatically not red) an ecstatic life of their own, as if it weren't her own virtuosic discipline that made the flawlessly fancy footwork possible. And she was required to go on flailing away ever more wildly aghast at the ecstasy, now fed exclusively by said disbelief. She was spectator and spectacle, Nero's fiddle and Rome's fire, one parasitizer exploited by while feeding off the other. And this—pretending to pretend that in fact the height of intricate control displayed in supervirtuosic patternizing constituted the very last word in sorcerer's-apprentice-sowing chaos—was (accept no substitutes!) the greatest (reward circuit goosing) drug of 'em all.

According to her most fervid fan (who later and all too typically repudiated her in and out of print, fandom transcended being the last word—the last straw—in betrayal), her dancing in the Gounod (and everywhere else) made being *on to something* look like being *on* something.

So walking to work when she really isn't means being *straitjacketed* (à la Callas) into the steps of a new ballet (though kaleidoscopy à la Balanchine is never reducible to mere steps: the meanings lie far beyond their fungibility). She who wished for nothing but uniqueness is pleased—tickled pink—at being part of this matutinal fraternity of breadwinners. All these average joes flitting by become her mirror at the barre. In fact observing them closely she's sure she'll be arrested any second now for navel-gazing, still a felony in these backwoods. But forgetting about incarceration and worse, how much playing at straphanging can she allow herself before it completely snuffs out whatever isn't just playing? How much rope should she allow self-consciousness before it suffocates the life out of the spectacle that is she and that she wants to enjoy? For there's the gold of an authentic Straphanger in them there hills of simulation and it has a right to breathe. And maybe it's the terrifying authenticity of her being-Doomed-to-Straphangerhood—her being the biggest Straphanger of them all—that drives her to play up the simulation angle. How much molding—how much codification—before her Straphanger is airtight and beautiful? How much intervention—how much molding—before her Straphanger is legible—before she gets it right? And once her ideal Straphanger has been done to a turn, if not quite to perfection, how much veneration can she be permitted before the veneration starts to pollute the purity of the Straphanger act that's more than just an act, more than just a star turn—before all the defacements of veneration render the idol illegible? But so what if it's just a simulation, a failed star turn, an act? She can't help feeling there's a Some Body (oops! has she forgotten that she's graduated, unbidden, to calling him Master) who at this very moment is spectating her self-spectation and licking His chops (and Whom Melanctha can't help ranting about more and more every chance she gets though she makes it a malpractice to pretend, given half a chance, that all she's doing is *alluding*) since He knows better than anybody that what clearly *isn't* a simulation in this mess of a dialectic is the split within—the split between the Straphanger-in-spite-of-herself and the Ideal Straphanger that Straphanger-in-spite-of-herself is trying to create. She thinks she's putting something over on the world when in fact it's she herself who's the dupe—of her own split. A little like Cantor's Hitchcock—yes, she was present the day he sounded off to his cellphone about the manipulable Master Manipulator for all to hear. Clearly, she interests Him, Melanctha's Master, her new Mr. B.

She can never be a Straphanger. And the Master knows it. For the beauty of the Straphanger is his immersion in an inner anxiety without being in the least concerned about how it's seen—about whether his straphanger ballet is ripe for immortality. He's not engorged by self-consciousness. And that's what beauty's all about, she realizes. The unconcern about whether his playacting will be validated as more real than the real thing. But wait, she hastens to tell herself, or rather, would hasten to tell herself if only she could fit her plight into the straitjacket of the right words or even the wrong ones (any will do in a pinch), I'm real, too—I'm immersed as well. Only her brand of realness lies in the fissure between the fact of her pain and the need to portray it as fancy-footworked fiction. And she's got to agree with Him, at least as she's constructed Him—at least as He exists in *her* allusion: it's hard work looking self-immersed beyond any concern with spectators when you never stop hungering for their unalloyed awe and when gnawing away at you is the fear that all this playacting is eating away at whatever subsists of authentic self-immersion. It's precisely at these moments that He—the Some Body Who is the Master—catches her four-square authenticity in the act—of being itself. It's at the very moment when she allows herself to be mortally afraid self-consciousness will mar the whole mimicry shebang that she eludes self-consciousness. It's at those moments when she's aware of the split, self-constitutive as it turns out, between the desire to be the Straphanger and the desire to be seen as she sees Him—this other Him—that she becomes real. Being caught in the split, the gap, she's longer posing, in fifth position, so to speak. So through no fault of her own the enterprise-doomed-to-fail allows her—forces her—to become real, in spite of herself she manages to miss a beat of her unreality—to carve out a void into which reality-bashing self-consciousness can't rush in.

But as if things aren't complicated enough, there's the business of her rivals, the ones who are still going strong. They wouldn't be caught dead straphanging. But this is of course her richness. Isn't that what Walser told her, or at least implied, when she caught him way off guard? For she's being granted privileged access to a domain from which her rivals are permanently barred compliments of their dazzling success. The only question is whether the all-too-human misery to which she's privy (for isn't this all about misery? the misery of being a generic sufferer?) will do her in before she's had the golden opportunity to strut its heady stuff in her work—in what's left of her work. For she wants to create even if she isn't Mr. B. Can she, then, manage to rush the artifacts wrested from her contest with the lower depths of ordinary life into the arena of her modest undertakings before the pain those artifacts commemorate destroys her (for there's such a thing as too much of a bad thing)? Or will she be decapitated (like her pills) before she can exploit them?

She adjusts her headphones or her earphones or her earbuds or whatever they're called (she hasn't quite mastered the distinction and relishes the fuzziness she imposes on things by refusing to know their names) and throwing herself on the mercy of the one "classical" music station still functioning between here and Canarsie, what does she hear but the same old messages from EF/Accupuncture, to wit, that just as Chopin and Berlioz always kept their index finger on the pulse of populism so is Excreatory Funds, Inc., ("Toxic Assets Delivered") forever at the beck and call of its clients. And just as Charles Valentin Alkan succeeded brilliantly (if apocryphally), as punishment for writing *Le Festin d'Esope*, in getting himself decked to death by the world's oldest living Talmud thanks to its fortuitous dive from the highest shelf of his bookcase, so does Accupuncture make sure each and every client is knocked blissfully unconscious by sandbags of swag. And just as Mozart, though mildly misunderstood by his contemporaries, carried valiantly on nonetheless with the scoring for what would turn out to be a surefire hit (*Amadeus*) so is Excreatory Funds in its merger with Accupuncture . . . doing what precisely? Why, getting on with the bloody business of composing cassations, barcarolles and transcendental études, not to mention songs and dances of death, that's what. A perfect marriage of high finance and low art every time. She clearly has a lot to learn from the likes of Excreatory Accupuncture but where will she find the time to manufacture a gimmick that comes up to the high standards of EF?

When she arrives (the bakery across the street is atypically closed for alterations), the receptionist, sniffing more than squinting at the laminated photo ID hanging from Moira's neck (not nearly as swanlike as in her great City Center days), tells her to go downstairs and see Straynge immediately (in a tone that make it clear she holds him in contempt for having no idea what he's letting himself in for and being neither wise nor at least humble enough to heed the warnings she dares not give *since there's nothing as intimidating as a stupidity that knows its own mind*). Shearer doesn't quite know what kind of retreat is best suited to showing she's doing anything but complying. To her surprise Borkman and Herbert as well as the hapless Rhys are also present. It looks like they know they're being cashiered but nobody wants to know just what his own shame looks like by staring at somebody else's and so each, sitting as far apart as he can, looks away. Her seat faces a brick wall, denatured by time—Father Time, to you, and in cahoots with . . . why, Mother Nature, who else? Sixth Avenue could be—and in fact is—a million miles away.

Straynge arrives at a run. From the way he clears his throat it's clear, at least to Rhys, or is it Herbert? (can't be both), that the send-off is the work of a cost-cutting consultant, maybe the newly ascendant Narr, maybe Cook semi-miraculously rehabbed into reusability (he's busy lurking in a shadowy corner overlooking the intersection of Seventh and Greenwich). The four of them are being asked to withdraw because none has taken strides of any consequence toward resuming his life work. Even if the dosages have been tailored to their perceived needs: this is the one trial to have gotten that part right, according to last week's issue of *Pharmakon* (an unlikely—a probably unengineerable—cross between a glossy pay-to-play trade rag and a highly respected scientific journal), which Straynge conscientiously waves in front of them, deprecating all protest. They can't expect Amygdala to subsidize them indefinitely. Shearer discovers all she can think about is Rhys or rather, Rhys's life work. What can it possibly be? A definitive rapprochement with that compote-crazy evil sister? Or is it Herbert who's thinking this, or Borkman or Rhys herself?[13] Thoughts after all are so fickle—and perverse: often they decide to visit themselves on the least likely proponent—candidate—suspect. Or maybe it's the brick wall. Not that it's actually thinking this thought. It's simply the theater in which the thought happens. The site of the thought's undesirable implantation. One thing's certain: it can't be multitask-averse Borkman. No time to think: He's too busy folding and refolding the hands in his lap as if they were gloves—but they are gloves! (if there's one thing the Master can't stomach, Herbert realizes, it's *as if*s)[14]—and trying to get it just right—to do it just the way he's seen his white-shoe rivals do it at moments of

---

[13]Upon the urging of the Master (the present footnote is entitled "The Master fights back") the reader is hereby informed that the proliferation of ostensible lamentations over who, at any upsurge of eloquence or analytical insight, is doing the thinking or speaking, is not an *arrière-garde* prank which costs the author nothing—but giggles. On the contrary, it reflects what is very much a matter of life and death—as dire as determining which pediatric oncologist on staff should be the bearer of ill tidings— namely, what is to happen to an eloquent insight after it is born, always prematurely. Is there a character who will agree to embody it and in so doing comply with its need to be—as the sole means of preserving its identity—slightly out of synch—incompat- ible—with said character?

[14]I tip my hat to the Master's well-earned stomach-churning revulsion for *as if*, which, as noted by Dorothy Van Ghent, does nothing more than provide the "conservative" reader with the poison pill of "a familiar bourgeois security." Too much of that run-

286

boardroom crisis. But in his case all this hand-wringing is a feint, fabricated to throw everybody off the scent of his true-blue invincibility: he has no doubt he'll come through even this, whatever *this* turns out to be, with flying colors.

Straynge confirms their worst fear without any sign of compassion. They've managed to fail at what supposedly it's impossible to fail at: patient-hood. It hasn't been simply a matter of not responding. They've refused to respond—to collaborate with the drug—to give it the benefit of the doubt. So it's Invidicum that deserves his compassion, not they. Cook emerges from his corner presumably to hurry Straynge off the stage—the very stage of life—but before doing so, decides to play champion of his underappreciated genius which means stating (with a passion almost Periclean, Herbert later thinks—but by then it's too too late) the all too obvious, namely, that "Straynge, here, is at the end of his rope because of you and you and you and you." Straynge looks appropriately demure and—rope-ended. As if to say, I spilled not a sin-gle bean—Cook's deduced it all from my haggard countenance. To say noth-ing of the unsightly stain on the seat of my trousers born of selfless anxiety on your behalf.

Taking heart from the words of a fan, Straynge adds, "Unable to bear the anxiety of knowing you might fail, you blame rivals for your incapacitation in the face of creative rigor. Why, oh why, for the love of God, are you all so afraid of doing without your rivals? Fact is, you've shrunken your life context to the point where survival has become incompatible with life, even the lowest form of life. And so, though I hate to say it, you'd all be better off dead. Under some circumstances—like yours—it may be advisable for the *organism* (to Rhys, thinking of her sister, the word is bone-chillingly cold) to give up on life in order to keep its essential characteristics intact—unmarred—so that death can get on with the business of being creative *for* that organism. Death has a habit of reversing the sign of your every mishap. In a word, some are born posthumously. To be fair, however, I—we—must remember that success versus failure isn't a matter of pluses and minuses. Your refusal to relinquish your rivals in the name of self-realization ushers in an innovative experience barred to them." Never have any of them heard Straynge sound so convinc-ingly far gone. A shuddering thought—along the blurry lines of: *I'd murder him out of sheer compassion if I could*—crosses (or rather jaywalks across) the mind of first-responder Cook.

Why, oh why, is this happening to me? Shearer wonders. Being laid off, I mean. By any chance, will I be having to train my outsourced successor before I exit, my fate hanging—hung—by the thread of his H-1B visa? And that it should be happening to Herbert and Borkman and Rhys as well—straight-A subjects from all indications—is even more incomprehensible. Through over-sight or malfeasance on the part of the powers that be (Herbert's—now every-body's—Master? no, He's a demon of abstraction who doesn't traffic in the

---

ning around loose as it is. See Dorothy Van Ghent, "The Dickens World: A View from Todgers's," in *Dickens: A Collection of Critical Essays*, Martin Price, ed. (Englewood Cliffs, New Jersey, Prentice-Hall, 1967), p. 29.

nitty-gritty of things like layoffs), it's somebody else's fate that's fallen to her share. And a dismal share it is. It's even dismaller since Straynge has chosen this very moment to leave the room. This enrages Herbert—this washing his hands of her as if he's been unexceptionable and then some as a healer and it's Herbert and Herbert alone—or rather, her wrong kind of organism (isn't that his word?)—that's responsible for the failure. His manic headshakes proclaim that Herbert's incurability is base . . . *ingratitude*. And adding insult to injury, the imminence of invisibility—knowing he won't have to stick around for the reaction shot—has given him the courage to slam the door, thereby delivering the straw man's Parthian shot.

At the same *very moment* Borkman becomes aware Straynge must die. Something—a lot—to do with the unceremoniousness of the exit. But a lot more with the layoffs. And just to save a few bucks. Borkman's not concerned about himself—if worse comes to worst, he'll be having his three square per day up the Amazon. But what about Shearer and Rhys and Herbert—what will happen to them? Invidicum has become their raison d'être, not to mention their bread and butter. For one thing, they started to dress better around the time of their second or third dose. Killing this character—that would be one way for a proband to de-shrink the life context. Someone chock-full of crisscrossed homicidal impulses and, unlike him, with an overriding impetus. Somebody who isn't, like him, all fart and no feces. Cook follows Straynge into the corridor. Through the door, raised voices. What's that all about? they wonder.

When Cook gets back (Shearer can't get over how much he's aged since their first encounter—you remember, when he'd tried to sell her a bill of goods and succeeded handsomely—but no doubt she's aged twice as much, maybe more: she's certainly aging fast enough right now), he tells them they have exactly five days to pack up. "And that's pretty damn generous by pink-slip standards, wouldn't you say?" he beams. But no need to fret: rest assured their responses, however aberrant, will be factored into the final tallies. Nobody in these parts would ever dream of skewing things in Invidicum's favor since, for their and everybody else's information, there was no similarity between Warner-Metro and any of those giants known for inflating modest gains into immodest breakthroughs. As rejects, moreover, they'll be receiving (much-coveted) honorable mention in the Annals of Amygdala.

And as they file out what is their surprise to see, waiting brightly in the corridor, as unlikely a duo as you could ever hope to find this side of the Rockies. Cantor, especially, looks quite the local boy making good. Well, there went Herbert's scapegoat theory (being an unregenerate homo, Cantor should obviously have been the first to go). Straynge reappears, as if on cue—but whose? "Cook and I—get over here, Bill—weren't in agreement about when to break the news—hence, the raised voices: sorry. I saw no reason to keep you on tenterhooks whereas he—" To make a long story short, all of them are still very much on the payroll. Mere victims of a gag-filled experimental ploy designed to exacerbate baseline Envy under the threat of brute eviction (which explains the *pièce de résistance* materialization of Eden and Cantor as improbably favorite sons) inasmuch as research in that neck of the woods was about to become (shush!) Pharmatown's Next Big Thing. We've (er, the Master means *They've*) got it all on film. Hidden cameras everywhere. But not so fast! the Amygdaloids need to figure out which neuron tribes were doing the dirty work as the gag unfolded. Which means more work for the sausage grinder. So, quick! last one in is a rotten egg!

Everybody's chattering away with semi-relief. Except Moira Shearer. As for Straynge, he's clearly, unaccountably, the man of the hour, his unhinged bluster forgotten. But just as clearly, just as unaccountably, he hasn't forgotten her, not for a minute. Sort of the way Mr. B. never forgot Ashley, even after Farrell came back to re-rule the roost. He wants to say something but can't remember what. Or maybe he remembers all too well but doesn't care, or know how, to say it. Something to the effect that she's the one lamb who should have been slaughtered? She looks daggers. For better or worse, he takes her aside. Through the corner of her eye—or his—she watches the others slumber toward the basement bethlehem of fMRI headquarters. There's a rumor afloat—vicious, as all rumors are—although he doesn't need the rumor to confirm what he's already determined to his satisfaction, namely, that Shearer is here, on Greenwich Avenue, misguidedly or under false pretenses. What she's been seeking all along is not a cure for the Envy virus but a life coach like that balletmaster she's always babbling about, mainly to herself. She wants said coach's vaccine-encoding genome to hijack—expropriate—co-opt—pre-empt—commandeer—overpower (the possibilities are endless or rather the possibilities of synonymy are endless, which amounts pretty much to the same thing, or does it?)—the autonomy of her own by taking up residence in her latent reservoir of resting-memory infected cells. So that when those cells are subsequently activated by the sight—or heard-tell—of yet another rival fearlessly swinging toward yet another victory on the Trapeze of Life, the vaccine can do away with the new crop of infected cells before they go into latency. Funny, in the course of his elaboration Straynge's tone has become less and less accusatory. Indeed and alas, it's gone and gotten itself suffused with a kind of wonderment—as if she's just polished off that old warhorse, Odile's six hundred and one fouettés (or whatever the going rate is for the canonical number), and exhibited to boot a sledgehammer exquisitry not likely to be surpassed, at least in his lifetime. Proving that his faith is and will continue to be justified. He leaves her, presumably to ponder, even if she hasn't understood a word. Though she has taken note of the friendlier glint in his eye. In any event, life coach or no, they're waiting for her down below.

She's terrified of being ditched, despite the reassurance. Because of the reassurance, rather. For where there's reassurance, there must be a need for reassurance. She pursues him, frantically, but primly draws the line at the door to the men's room. In fact, she's gotten there well before him. "Should I be worried?" she cries out as he approaches, hating her need for more reassurance. "You have a right to be worried," he tells her. She isn't crazy to be worried about being ditched, especially after all she's been through, if that's what she means. Something in her expression moves him to add, "But not *that* worried." But the comfort of knowing she's not crazy is outweighed by the discomfort of knowing worry about being ditched isn't all that beside the point. A further something moves him to add, but this time a little less kindly, that as odd woman out what she really wants to know is just how much worry must be enacted before it's decided she's paid her dues and is thus entitled to leave worry behind forever. Or, how much worry is required—how many frequent-worrier points must be earned—before he or somebody with the same authority is induced to decree that the worry has become scandalously excessive. So that the decree can be made, through the subtlest of shifts, to sound as if it applies across worry's entire spectrum, wireless or otherwise, i.e., to worry in every conceivable shape or form, especially the initiatory, non-excessive kind. Pleased with his dissection, he exposes his gums unattractively. She, too, is convinced (if life on earth is to perdure) that Straynge must die.

Borkman (first on line for the sausage grinder) is glad to be able to make a getaway before the others. Who cares about the results of the assessment? They can can him for all he cares. Or is this just ankle-monitored swagger? Is that his son standing on the southeast corner of Eighth Street and Sixth? The boy's waving, so it must be he. He asks Jason—*is* it Jason or is Jason the other boy?—how he managed to find him. "You know my method," the boy replies, in a perfect imitation of Basil Rathbone. Thing is, Borkman doesn't know his son's method from a hole in the wall. One more nail, then, in the coffin of his apt acuity as a parent. A backpacker gets between them, smacking his shoulder. No apology, just a smug little don't-blame-me-blame-the-backpack look. Or rather, there is no look. The smack is the look. And maybe he, or she, is right. Maybe the contraption does have a life of its own. Like his own inadequacy. It could have been worse: at least they're not in a crowded subway car. They sit down in a coffee shop off West Fourth. A woman at the next table warns Borkman that it might be better for him and his friend to sit further away, since she and *her* friend intend to make a lot of noise. It's just their nature. Or in the nature of things. Wolfing down whatever generic coffee-shop fare he's ordered, the boy announces that he's planning to create a start-up. "All by yourself," Borkman prompts. He has no idea how to proceed. He slept too well last night to be able to feign exhaustion. So how is he supposed to tamp down all this alertness—on what can he bear to lavish it. "No, I have partners. We've already been prevalued at four billion and change. They're flying us out to the Coast next week." Borkman's stomach sinks and he sinks along with it, into pukeable emptiness. He feels abandoned. Borkman! of all people! who's always been a deadbeat dad as far as time is concerned, begrudging every millisecond spent. The wife, damn her, knew of what she spoke when she called him *cheap and greedy* in front of one of the younger boy's teachers (middle school, wasn't it? [they used to call it junior high back in the last century]).

Is Jason going to lose his shirt, that is, Borkman's, in another enterprise doomed to fail? Will it be another case of (when he asks for details) *None of your business*, that is, until it becomes very much his business, to the tune (factoring in inflation) of, say, sixty grand. Jason shakes his head, forbearingly, refusing to take whatever bait's to be had for the taking. Yet again, Borkman—he can see this from the sparkle in his son's apt pupils—has gotten things all wrong. He dreads accusation so he decides to beat the accuser to the punchline. "If I'd been as good a parent as I wanted to be—more to the point, as *she* wanted me to be—you'd have created one—several—by now. I would—should—could—have helped—used my connections. For there used to be a time when I had them in spades." The boy—it *is* Jason! why, he's the spitting image of that little boy in the photograph pinned without appeal to the refrigerator door by a beetle-shaped magnet—continues to shovel in the generics. By way of being at the same time more specific and more opaque (i.e., by way of confessing he is incapable of showing interest in an enterprise—anybody's—that isn't his own, even—especially—if it's his son's), the best he can come up with is that old chestnut of a phrase which never fails to (almost) move him (*hear ye! hear ye! in the last analysis it's always only about* him)—to tears: *I wish I could have been different.* Never fails to tug at his heartstrings, if at nobody else's. Perfect example of self-cancellation that, shrewdly, never gets down to cases—cancellation-worthy cases of eye-popping malpractice. Since a few of those cases might just have the cheek to be amenable to some small rectification on his part. Instead, he trots out the usual sins, mainly, glaringly, of omission, which graciously foreclose any such option. Sins like:

(*a*) Having dutifully missed the Saturday afternoon soccer game, even after the doorperson, not one to dispense compliments gladly, especially—understandably—to the fathers of white boys flush with dirty money, had said, unsolicited and unrehearsed, "You should go watch your son play sometime: he's really good."

(*b*) Having refused (pleading generic exhaustion, not the kind that comes of, as was in fact always the case, a hard night's philandering) to *bond* over homework, even when the subject matter (encompassing questions like, Do bank employees become more dishonest when primed to put their professional before all other social identities? or, What potential does an appeal to morality have for mitigating negative market externalities?) should have been right up Borkman's blind alley. (Oh, and by the way—wretched byword, that *bond*, sucking all the marrow out of what it purports to exalt. In this regard, it's not unlike the bloodlessly coded spectacle of two white men *in comfortable circumstances* hugging in hello or goodbye, at least one of them sealing the pact of their shared discomfort with the obligatory pat or three on the back. Under any other conditions, the pat(s) would mean, *There, there, whatever it is, it can't be as bad as all that.* But in this case, the goal being de-eroticization at any price, the meaning's consequently, *Keep your distance: you're making my skin crawl with all this fake warmth. Frankly, I'd rather be butt-fucked on HBO than put* both *my arms around you.*)

(*c*) Having expressed nothing more than *petty irritation* when required not only to post bail after the boy, age fifteen, was wish-fulfillingly jailed for smoking weed with friends out in the skyscraperless wilds of Astoria or was the crime scene that pretty little pocket park on East Fifty-Third? (he's too ashamed to ask) but also to pay for the expungement of all charges. Although he does remember fondly the eager beaver just out of ambulance-chasing school waiting inside the entrance for the materialization of just such a solid-citizenly pair of worried-sick parents as he and the missus (she'd brought the boy some textbooks so his abysmal grades wouldn't go even further downhill). He'd done his job very well by the way: clean slate, no complaints.

Not just bringing up the doorperson's remark (you remember Vivian), but going into all the detail necessary to paint himself in the luridest colors (what could have been more important than the ballgames?), he quickly discovers the paint job has a life of its own. *I wish I could have been different.* What is it his film-buff wife always sneered when he trotted out the phrase? Oh, yes, that he reminded her of some rejection-craving mother in a forties or fifties woman's film—Crawford, say, in *Mildred Pierce* or Juanita Moore in *Imitation of Life*, for starters. She even dragged him to *Pierce*. He claimed it left him cold—falsely (see above), notwithstanding all the ear-to-ear yawns during and after the show.

His son looks like he wants to put him, i.e., his ploy, into words. And if he—or somebody else—doesn't, then this meeting, like all the others, has no point. He's tempted to enlist the services of the noisemaker at the next table. Thing is, she and her friend are as quiet as churchmice. So how can she be trusted with so weighty an assignment if she hasn't managed to hold good on her exuberant threat? "With all this apologizing you're making me feel even more doomed." "You're not doomed." Borkman's words sound hollow—worse, opaque. But just when all seems lost, the son finds his tongue. He says something to the effect that there's a fine line and a happy medium between (*a*) declaring one's culpability—if for no other reason than to reassure the victim that he's not imagining things—and (*b*) taking a malign pleasure in aggrandizing culpability to the point of obscenity. A fine line between (*a*) admitting culpability compliments of a stately measured self-recrimination and (*b*) indulging in a slobberingly voluptuous abasement—an abasement so dire it constitutes an injury far direr than any previously inflicted. An abasement so vast it purposefully swallows up the victim in its vastness, i.e., perpetrates one more crime against him. In fact, the biggest of the bunch: perpetrator's revenge on the victim simply for being a victim but (lese majesty of lese majesties) no longer just a victim. And the worst form of aggression against the victim who's no longer a victim. In fact the admission—the inculpation—is all aggression—another stab at negligence but in a really big way. And most unforgivable of all (his son takes a deep breath and wolfs down the rest of the ersatz cherry pie), the perpetrator's description of the crime, if crime it is, simply cannot be put into one-to-one correspondence with an actual state of affairs *out there*, i.e., it's impossible for Jason to configure a real-world entity on the basis of such beleaguered instructions so caught up in the intricacies of their own beleaguered syntax. But that's the whole point, isn't it, pop?

But that's OK. The issue of non-mappability from word to world—is right up the boy's alley. He's a creator, for Pete's sake—better yet, an upstarter. And it's this very issue of non-configurability that will underpin the explorations of him and his partners for decades to come. So, with all his flaws—or rather, because of them—there's still a place after all for dad in Jason's universe, if not in his heart.

The boy stops him dead in his inculpating-exculpating systolic-diastolic tracks, surprisingly eloquent even with the generics clogging his windpipe—even more so, some might say, but whom? that Thing? that . . . Master? (Now who's going around calling the Master a Thing? Just wait till I get my hands on him, thinks Borkman, his fealty toward the Master expanding as fast as the credibility—and creditability—of his shame for being a failed father is shrinking.) The boy's gist (a boy's gist is the wind's gist) is that he understands. At last. Once and for all. His father doesn't want him in his life, not really. Never did, never will. It's not his fault that he's not like other CEOs—the head of Scamco Investors (fifty billion in assets under mismanagement), for example, where all the kids work for dad. Even the halfwit eldest daughter (the old man's favorite, if truth be told) has her niche—as Director of Business Analytics and Evaluation. And what about the eldest son, who's running the obligatory Affiliated Benevolent Association (motto? charity begins at home, what else)—running it into the ground? Not to mention two other turkeys, each of whom made (wouldn't be fair to illegal immigrants everywhere to say *earned*) more than five million last year—even before incentive compensation was factored in. The marketeering wife, by the way, makes more than ten million—not bad for a gray eminence (fairer to call her a bleached blonde non-eminence) who's singlehandedly transformed sluggish marriage hearse into fast-moving gravy train.

The boy has figured it out: there's something about being connected with sons and wife visibly and publicly that makes his skin crawl. He needs to think he's been going—making it all alone. Public exultation in the fact that his sons whom you see standing proudly beside him have engineered an extension of his essence—made a multiplication of his being happen—calls too much attention to that essence, that being, which in the last analysis he heartily despises. One should apologize for the stench of one's essence and the only apology worth making is through its transmogrification—its dematerialization—its volatilization—into . . . greatness. Jason understands. If he didn't he'd be an even bigger ass than his father has no problem taking him to be. Just as Borkman is about to open his mouth: "No need to protest." After all, he's lived with Borkman pretty much all of his life. For the Borkmans of the world, nepotism, however loving, is vulgar. It demonstrates a complete lack of awareness of the obligation to perfect self-hate as launching pad toward self-detoxifying greatness—and to reassure every passing stranger that the self-hater, true to his code, would never dream of preferring any member of his brood to him or her. But the question is, which unhealthy figures from his unhealthier past do those strangers embody—figures who obviously need to be reassured that Borkman isn't abandoning them, i.e., forgetting about them for one moment—figures that are at once powerful enough to wreak havoc on anybody who dares to put them second and weak enough to require life support? Borkman is frightened: who *are* those figures? More to the point, doesn't Marco Scamco know how ugly he is and how he only magnifies that ugliness by rubbing the spit of his spittin' images in our face, yours and mine? Scamco may not know. But his father knows. And how could he not know that his father knows—after all, *Jason's start-up is founded on just such a knowing.*

"What?" Borkman suddenly realizes that for most of his life, unforgivably, he's grossly underestimated the grip—hence the truth—of cliché: For his heart, supposedly his least sensitive organ, has really just skipped a beat.

Maybe three.

Jason, *for his part*—no, *As for* Jason—he's replaying every word, every phrase—every note of his breakthrough start-up aria—before he's even sounded it. For once, he wants to explain things in such a way as to frustrate his father's every effort to write off him off as a pretentious twit even if sometimes—not always, but sometimes—big ideas require big words. The task's forbidding, Sisyphean, self-canceling at the very least. Either he's a twit or he's nothing. At the same time he's enough of a *budding artist* to be intrigued by the possibility of rising to the challenge of reining in what his father regards as his worst tendencies, i.e., everything that makes him him and thereby justifies Borkman's refusal to love him. The only way out is to become—or at least sound as if he's become—everything he's not. No high horses permitted in this paddock.

The boy and his pals are working hard to bring to term an *intervention* (whether fish or fowl has not yet been determined, which may be a good thing and an even better thing as regards keeping the venture caps on tenterhooks) that will enable people like Borkman to undergo the Basic Life Experiences— of fathering, for example—without any of its bothersome claims on their attention (in their case, always better directed elsewhere).

"An experiential drug," Borkman says dreamily—musingly. Playing for time—for time to size up the competition, i.e., his son. For his son's triumph is his downfall. But whatever he knows or thinks he knows about Borkman, the bottom line is: he's doing him a favor by painting him—however tactfully, however slantedly—in all the colors of the rainbow—a rainbow gone rancid—doing him a favor by rehearsing his defects for the forty-fourth time and as a bonus letting him in on the embryonic little secret of an intervention in the works which is targeted not just at him but at defectives like him— an intervention to ensure that freaks like Borkman—future freaks—have a means—and are forced to avail themselves of that means—of steering clear of siring (as appeasive sops to vanity and on this overpopulated earth of all places) innocent victims of their own freakdom. An intervention that will keep those defects all in the family—a family of one. Yet in a funny—even silly—kind of way Jason has done him a favor (or so he needs to think)— has only made him more aware of how much he still wants to live—not for the sake of his measly self—the self that's anchored to his ankle—but for the work—even if the work doesn't compare to (as the wife never failed to remind him) the slow movement of a symphony, say. The Work—the Life Work—for everybody has a life work—is still out there—waiting for him to claim its next installment. And that it's still out there after all he's been through is a tribute to—to—well, to the sinewy resilience of his mediocrity (though he still hasn't quite mastered the craft of monetizing its fool's gold). The son's hatchet job whether the boy thinks of it as such or not has put Borkman's strength— his commitment—to the ultimate test. So what if commitment in his case reduces to the scamming of humanity in all its gory glory? It's a commitment founded on maintaining a fierce protectiveness over inadequacy—as father and as husband and probably as son as well—inadequacy *perpetrated* on any role he himself hasn't—didn't—invent from scratch (and those are few and far between). It's a commitment nothing can demolish—not even guilt—not even shame (to the extent that he can experience either guilt or shame before self-congratulation—for having yet again successfully run inadequacy up the flagpole—barges in and, like love, conquers all). Jason's sinewy precocity—for only an authentic opponent could awaken him to such defiance—makes Borkman aware (as so many times before but differently) that while Beings come and go—sons come and go—wives come and go—business partners come and go—the rotting ripeness of the work is all and forever—even if the work is a tissue of expensive lies told by an idiot and sure to be forgotten at the stroke of midnight EST.

But the boy resists pop's uncharacteristic siren song of dreaminess and continues. Since, as he notes astutely, the Borkmans of the world crave those experiences simply from envy—of the people who *really* crave them. Once the intervention in question has put Envy—or, at the very least, its grosser manifestations—on hold, it can get on with the heady business of inducing the desired Experience. And by the way, whatever Post and his crowd have come up with in the way of an envy pharmakon is all wet—All Wet like The American Dream. Their first big mistake was to turn envy into Envy without having earned the right of refurbishment. Fact is, Invidicum can't inhibit or inactivate the proteins that contribute their fair share to Envy disease for the simple reason that it's incapable of setting up shop—occupying a bona fide binding site—on any one of them. Invidicum's activity is all noisy subversiveness—a patchwork of misleading signals. It suffers—if a drug may be said to suffer (the way, say, a backpack or a notebook suffers, selflessly, on behalf of its owner)—from a sort of medicinal chemistry aphasia.[15] Its speech—if a drug may be said to speak—is purely reactive—a slave of context. Belonging willy-nilly to the category of what are known as PAINS (pan-assay interference compounds), Invidicum engages in a masquerade—an impersonation of genuine attachment to a binding site—it's just an artifact of its own rampant promiscuity.[16] Invidicum reacts against—but has no real affinity for—the protein culprits propping up the Great God Envy. It doesn't have enough self-discipline to go the obligatory binding-site route toward efficacy. In short, there's absolutely no celluloid chemistry—no love lost—between star I and starlet E. Out of the blue, Jason snaps his fingers with a eurekaesque flourish. Invidicum's relation to the proteins that cause or at least contribute to Envy is, come to think of it, like—or sort of like—Borkman's mangled entwinement with wife and sons—with all other humans. Like a true redox cycler (one species of PAIN) he generates peroxide—that is, his own version of a killer antiseptic—to keep the Other at bay. Since keeping the Other at bay is his only way of connecting—of binding. The smear campaign takes its toll (Borkman sud-

---

[15]See Roman Jakobson, "The cardinal dichotomy in language," in *Language: An Enquiry into its Meaning and Function*, Ruth Nanda Anshen, ed. (New York, Harper and Brothers, 1957), which utilizes the data of Kurt Goldstein.

[16]See Jonathan Baell and Michael A. Walters, "Chemical con artists foil drug discovery," *Nature*, vol. 513, No. 7519 (25 September 2014), pp. 481–483.

denly feels far more protective of Post's reputation than of his own essence).
He resists—tells himself ths rant is nothing but a little stab at radical chic
Silicon Valley style—sophomoric perversity masquerading as . . . even more
sophomoric penetration.

Still, his son astonishes him. Never knew the kid could be this unrelentingly smart. Which speaks volumes about Borkman *père's* congenital (others,
less kind yet with a soft spot for pathos, might choose *willed* over *congenital*)
retinal detachment. Clearly, he and his start-up buddies are the new Men in
the Gray Flannel Suit, or rather, the Gray Flannel Hoodie (the stitching's only
a wee bit different).

"Sound promising?"

"The PAINS?"

"No, everything connected with the intervention." Of course it sounds
promising. But why give his son the satisfaction of watching him capitulate
to yet another take on failure—the failure of parental entrepreneurship or
parental stewardship or whatever he's decided to call it as he goes about sacrificing Borkman on the altar of his ingenuity—although what's being proposed
appears to transcend mere ingenuity. Let him do the hard work of unconstructing the debacle that is Borkman's fatherhood and come up—out—with
a bright and shiny template for this intervention to end all interventions—as
a sort of inverted homage, say, to Borkman's love affair—and the love affair
of the half a billion other Borkmans currently treading the boards—with
intransigent unvanquishable inadequacy as the *only* royal road to uniqueness.
After all, he's young and fitter than most. And he needn't worry: there's just so
much failure—just so much inadequacy—by association he'll be expected to
shoulder once Borkman's up the river darning his socks. Sensing Borkman's
resistance, his get (and for the moment he's nothing more or less than his *get*
but don't take my word for it—get thee to a dictionary!)—his get changes the
subject thereby hewing closer to it than ever since where he and his father are
concerned, there's only one subject.

"And just out of curiosity, does this business of an experiential drug—
experience without the associated effort—bring anything to mind?" Borkman
says nothing because he's had enough talk about failure for one day. "A while
back, you invested in a compound that seemed to allow fat mice to enjoy a
workout without the usual blood, sweat and tears. Endurance without exercise. Gain without pain. I forget the name." Nothing easier than to say, That's
because the compound didn't get to have a name since it was way too toxic at
high doses, but Borkman intends to remain beautifully blank to the bitter end,
no matter how bitter, about this brainchild of the Jupiter (Florida) Paracelsus
Institute which he together with thousands of other average joes pretending
to be robber barons felt compelled to consecrate as the Next Big Thing. Jason
rubs it in—reminds him (though surely he can't have forgotten) that once the
compound was injected, the mice (poster boys for anti-athleticism) used lots
more oxygen and expended 50 percent more energy than their untreated cellmates while remaining, in most cases, even lazier than they'd been pre-injection. That does it. Dutifully infantilized by his son's condescension, Borkman,
while holding on for dear life to his poker face, can't resist showing just how

smart he, too, can be (though if he's as smart as his words say he is, how did he end up betting on turkey after turkey after turkey?): "I remember now: you're referring to the compound that increased the potency of—of—of—of—" Borkman's cliffhanging grows bolder as Jason's gaze grows blanker though he's fighting blankness tooth and nail. Time's up. "REV-ERB. The protein that triggers the production of more—and stronger—mitochondria." He has no idea how and why he's retained this wisp of text through centuries of malfeasance but the boy is clearly intimidated or needs to think he is so he can rejoice at his father's predominance. What matters far more is that in the shadows adjacent to the blazingly indiscreet sunlight of failure a rose has bloomed.

Jason's looking blank—vulnerable—childlike—hurts Borkman. So he does harbor genuine fatherly feelings after all! But the fact that Jason doesn't immediately reward him with . . . reverence gets the old man's goat. "But isn't all this chitchat—I mean horseshit—a bit *peremptory*?" Borkman asks, keeping the word at a distance as if it's the very incarnation of his son. Uttering the word, distant or not, his father evokes a power-breakfaster in an impeccable and dependably laughable collar-contrast shirt who nonetheless stinks of garlic. I think you meant *perfunctory*," Jason can't help saying. He knows his father's reactive look only too well—lancinating and completely unconnected—missing nothing, misinterpreting everything. Whether or not he's made an error, it's the boy who's the bigger culprit. Knowing the difference between *peremptory* and *perfunctory* is downright unnatural. The fissure laid bare mirrors a more unsightly fissuring within the barer, since only somebody who's hopelessly at war with himself will try to turn language against his own father—to expose the misuse of language. In correcting his father's nonexistent error (for when his father says *peremptory* it's to be understood that he also means *perfunctory* and, as anybody who knows him knows, he's sure to be meaning perfunctory far more than peremptory) Jason's not only perpetrated harm against him, but called into question the manhood—the very virility—of language itself. But guess what? such plans have a knack for backfiring since Language is sure to come out on the side of the Father every time. 'Cause language, no dupe, no dope, has a way of knowing who its true friends are.

Sipping his Molotov cocktail of hard feelings, he forces himself to say, "I know you'll be a success—perfunctory or not." He tries to make it their little joke: or rather, their punchline minus the joke. Another example of Borkman's very special way of contaminating all he touches—of putting the corpse before the hearse. "It's the intervention that needs to be a success," he answers pleasantly. "Not me." "But what about the privacy issue?" Borkman fishes, although privacy has never meant much. Not for the likes of Borkman to jealously guard it. In fact, he's always welcomed nothing so much as the opportune invasion of that privacy. And when is such an invasion not opportune? Bad publicity is good publicity. But the only way to get his envy across enemy lines—and anybody who risks succeeding is his enemy, even his own son—is to wrap it up in bleeding-heart sob-sister finery purchased at the ACLU Thrift Shop. The boy explains that we have to invent a new concept of privacy or dispense with the notion entirely. We have to dig even deeper toward strata of selfhood inaccessible to even the most cutting-edge decryption or rather (since this kind of digging deeper simply honors the old-hat concept of privacy) we have to formulate—and thrive under—a concept of privacy that has nothing to do with preserving selfhood as we know it. In short, we should bless the invaders for driving us to new feats of ingenuity. So what if the eligibility of our attention span for hookup with this or that online ad is continuously up for grabs by matchmaking marketeers? Everybody is a dope if she or he isn't flattered that his attention span is such a hot item. (A secondary sexual characteristic, actually—and as every sexologist doesn't know, the secondaries, from chest hair [his] to hindquarter saddlebags [hers], are way more primary than the primaries themselves.) Come to think of it, make Everybody a double dope if he/she isn't tickled pink at being the buttered toast of the real-time electronic trading platforms and with so little self-promotional fuss and bother on his/her silly part. So what if he/she's sharing the auction-block spotlight with billions of other boobs (Silicon, meet Silicone Valley)? "Every one of us has a unique *click life*. As unique as a fingerprint. At the same time, we're spared the feelings of loneliness and vulnerability—of downright freakishness—that are the bag and baggage of uniqueness. Thanks to matchmakers like the Rubicon Project platform we become a little less burdened with the inviolability of our own souls. Isn't that, by the way, what you were trying to do by waiting up for me all night not so very long ago, so I could be taken into custody for trying to strangle your wife, i.e., relieve me of that inviolability? You see, *I know what happened.* I was there all along, in a manner of speaking. I didn't let myself get caught only for your sake, because I know how you would have felt if you'd actually succeeded in betraying me—even if you believed handing over that inviolability to the authorities, long overdue, was in my best interest.

"But getting back to the death of privacy, one of my partners—who still isn't sure if he's gayish—told me not so long ago that right after listening on YouTube to Judy Garland (who else?) sing an amazing arrangement of 'How About Me' for the eighty-fourth time, he was sent a recommendation by the YouTube Powers that Be. To watch a clip of Neil Patrick Harris putting across the 2011 Tony Awards opening number ('Broadway's Not Just for Gays Anymore'). Of course he loved it—not just the number but, far more importantly, seeing his search profile get caught with its pants down. 'Cause YouTube connected the dots that make him him faster than he could ever have done it on his own steam. (It's all part of the Gershwinian Algo Rhythm/Algo Music tradition.) But all kidding aside, though who's kidding? the intrusion saved him years of Who Am I//What Am I?-type work and spared him the expense of boning up on what the latest self-help dreck might have to say (nothing of any consequence) about such an identity crisis—as if Identity Crisis Mania isn't constitutive (yeah, dude—I mean, dad—*constitutive*, you heard me right the first time) of the human organism. It wasn't Garland or Harris alone that made him realize he's gayish—it was the link between the two created by an algorithm. And as we're coming to understand, there's nothing more personal—and personable—than an algorithm. I personally feel safer with my ID bracelet in the hands of the data marauders than under my very own private lock and key."

"You say the algorithm saved him years of work?"

"Yes, that's what I said."

"But what if the algorithm *deprived* him—*robbed* him—of years of work —the kind of work that makes somebody exactly who he's supposed to be?"

"A too-quick fix, you mean."

"Yes, that's what I mean."

In any case, as Jason now points out without any sense (as far as his father can see) of self-betrayal, privacy is nowhere near as dead as the usual prime time experts take it to be—need to take it to be if they are to retain their CNN-et-al franchise. Why, according to Jason's flagship mentors of the moment Artur Ekert and Renato Renner (communicating privately),[17] all that's needed to produce an inviolable cipher of super-safe communication is the shared randomness (and, by the way, anything not completely deterministic can be made completely—and amplifiably—random) embodied in a non-reusable cryptographic key.

Borkman is stunned by what sounds like so much self-confidence. And he can't help being a wee bit jealous of the glamor *wielded* by these all-too-obvious father substitutes. Their breezy success in the role proclaims his failure. "I know you'll be a success," he repeats. Not knowing what to add, he turns his back on the momentary impasse. The girl who was supposed to go all drunk and disorderly has reneged on her amiable threat. The role of public enemy has been usurped by a family of four. Super-beefy dad, covered with tattoos, sits across from his surprisingly studious-looking son, who's sporting trendy specs. Even more surprising, they look completely connected—almost overconnected. As far as Borkman's concerned, they need to go on a *connectedness diet*, although the son looks underweight. What's this dad's secret? Daughter is, or tries to be, more of a chip off the old block—abhorring a vacuum where clearly none exists—and to prove she's all she thinks dad wants her to be she bends over, ostensibly to pick up a candy bar before the waitress profanes its wrapper, revealing not just midriff but the bland beginnings of the crack in her ass, normally the specialty of plumbers. Why, she, or rather her father (since she's clearly underage, however precocious the curves and cracks), could be sued for patent infringement. Should he warn her—him? Before he can decide, another family group troops in, followed by another, and still another. It's clearly feeding time among the out-of-towners, he, a self-made and -unmade native New Yorker, thinks smugly. But this is just a nondescript coffee shop, impossible to imagine it getting itself bolded in any self-respecting tourist guide. No local color. These folks belong on the Mulberry Street strip. Thing is, they seem more at home in Borkman's home city than he'll ever be. He's the tourist. In any case, dad seems not to have taken kindly to Borkman's leering, which as an ethical stance, is/was anything but. From the look of him Jason has been thinking very different thoughts. Or has he? As far as he's concerned, there are no beasts more intimidating

---

[17]Arturo Ekert and Renato Renner, "The ultimate physical limits of privacy," *Nature*, vol. 507, No. 7493 (27 March 2014), pp. 443–447.

than tourists who sulkily insist on measuring his home town's moral fibre by its guidebook valences and his own worth as an aborigine by how much imagined moral injury to their beasty essence he's willing to ignore. And as far as the members of this particular swath of the tourist tribe are concerned New York has flunked the picturesqueness test with flying colors. They're lost and angry but their anger is not just *their* gain (since they clearly know how to wield it qua authoritative indictment of the city's . . . inadequacy) but Jason's as well since it can teach him how to bake (if only he'll listen) the hallucination that is tourism into the experiential pie.

The boy's having the not-quite-distinct impression though he's not giving away any jack-of-all-trade secrets to his arch-enemy—for isn't that what a loving father is (the more loving, the more arch)?—that this, their great reconciliation, an extended duettino worthy of *Don Carlos* or *Les Pêcheurs de Perles*, is being . . . *messed with*—twisted and turned in directions that should be off-limits, that is, if it wants to be taken seriously on the therapist's couch or in the fMRI sausage grinder. And he's not just talking about the tourists who are clearly in the wrong place. He's talking about the whole drift of the discourse—the much-too-vast amount of ground they've covered in record time. In short, it's a question of too many thought packets. Every packet, however *insightful*, is implausible in the context of a story. *The story shouldn't be serving as a maternity ward for unwed packets.* The event is clearly being stretched purely to determine how far the Turkish taffy of implausibility can be pulled before reaching the breaking point. As if every twist constitutes a wound inflicted—a wound that can be sutured only through infliction of another—even more implausible. But who's—or what's—profiting from all this first aid? For the first time (mark the place and time on your calendars), the term *conspiracy* rears its ever-pretty head—here, in the Mabuse Coffee Shop, of all places. Without moving a muscle Jason confesses his disappointment in his father to the Daughter Next Door (the cleft in her ass and the chip on her shoulder are getting bigger by the second). Once again, Borkman has failed to behave like a true father—a true dad—a true pop. He should have been smart enough to discern immediately that his son was in trouble—in this case caught in the crossfire—the push and pull—between thought packets and the story's building blocks and should have figured out ASAP how to provide comfort without sugarcoating that bitter pill called life. Should have told him not to fret since it's a truth universally acknowledged: that there comes a time in every story's life when it must cry out for impalement on the shaft of a thought packet or two which craving shall not be denied; and that, while some—most—almost all—thought packets are nothing in themselves, in prefiguring their own service as the gateway to other—better—packets—a better class of packets and maybe a class of things that are better than thought packets could ever hope to be—they're not to be pooh-poohed (though the notion that there may be things in heaven and earth better than packets is anathema to the idealistic likes of Jason); but that, as the aforementioned bitter pill doesn't dole out any free lunches without a fight, every last packet must be earned which is why the Story, a joyless and frugal taskmaster if ever there was one, permits the trafficking in such unholy treats but rarely and why stories that are less stories than shrill tugs of war between building blocks and packets are advised to turn themselves in at the nearest police precinct sooner rather than later.

Or maybe he's a bit undone because something just said—brazenly— contradicts something said long before—by one of the trial guinea pigs, say— which is of course causing the Master to lick his chops. (Inexplicably, Jason seems to know a thing or two about the Master without necessarily know- ing he knows. Must be genetic or telepathic transmission or a combination of both.) Because it just so happens that in his domain, he takes to internal contradiction like a fish to water. For in his domain internal contradiction demonstrates that events talk to each other across long distances despite all his mock efforts to the contrary—a phenomenon known as entanglement. In short, they have a life of their own thanks to willed amnesia.

But before Borkman can add his own not-quite-distinct impressions to the heap, Jason is on to the next big thing. "First, we have to come up with a name. The name is all-important—as you know better than anybody, daddy." "Why me better than anybody?" Borkman isn't sure (for one thing, the boy hasn't called him *daddy* in decades, if ever) if he's parrying a compliment or fending off some vile innuendo within a labyrinth that runs amuck between the lines. So he engineers a . . . pause in the proceedings, for perusal by his boy—and, if possible, re-perusal, though as what precisely he's at a loss to say. For starters, something like dignity's outraged rejection of the request for immediate clarification.

But Jason has better things to do than genuflect before a pause—any- body's pause. For one thing, he needs to backtrack since as it so happens, it's not in the least a question of finding the right name—much less, the rightest name of all. "Then what *is* it a question of," Borkman asks, omitting the ques- tion mark so that irrepressible irritation can remain undetected. (Is it possi- ble that the boy is actually being condescending. *Condescending to him!?— Charles Foster Borkman!!!???*) A name—any name, right or wrong—even the rightest of the right—would be a death blow—the coup de grâce, really—to said intervention's long process of thrashing—groping—toward the grail of its own realization. Give it a name prematurely—any name (though strictly speaking all name-giving is premature)—and presto! the process starts to self- mold in keeping with the falsifying specifications of that name. The process (like diseases, as determined under the WHO guidelines issued on 8 May of the current year) is to be named based on what it does rather than after the individual, species or region in which it had the bloody cheek to turn up uninvited. Thing is, they're nowhere near knowing what it does and when they do know, a name—the last refuge of scoundrels—will be redundant. Any self-respecting process must strive toward staving off the reward of a name, for the minute the reward is conferred the process dies—a buffoon's death, not a martyr's.

"Take *marriage*, for example. Look what it's done to you and mom." (*Mom*, unlike *dad*, falls reminiscent on Borkman's ears.) He speaks daggers of compassion—even if against his better judgment: How could they (*being what they are*) ever have managed to live in accordance with the prohibitions imposed by the name—in accordance with the name as the *sum* of its prohibitions, no more, no less? How go about their business under its steely interdict? An ethical conundrum, true enough. But more importantly, an aesthetic one, for where then, under the circumstances, was the legroom for serendipitous disfiguration of the blessed estate—for horseplay against the grain of that blessedness? So as to satisfy their collusive craving for . . . uniqueness, unlocalizability, unbracketability. So as to enable their no-end-of-defects (normality isn't everybody's cup of tea) to dodge the bullet of diagnosability.

"In other words," sighs Jason, manfully seizing the tab, "the Name's a parasite borne by a not-quite-unsuspecting vector—you or me—for the sole purpose of nipping our hosting life process in the bud." Or put in another, better way: the Intervention, as named, is unwitting vector for the parasite that's none other than the great lie perpetrated by the namers—any namers, not just Jason and his crew—to wit, that the name in all its catchy pretense—its glitzy gravitas—its blubbery contingency—is more the thing named than the thing itself and that to know the thing in its essence is to exalt the name and nothing but the name. Nobody should host such a parasite. Not even the namers themselves. Somebody is thinking—but surely not Borkman—*Jason, m'boy, you take my breath away.*

And what is Jason's *takeaway*—to use the term so popular among the journalist-pundits on MSNBC? Simply, or not so simply, that he'll never be able to think—much less, say—about Borkman what his start-up buddy Ishmael Drybock is always saying about his own father (dead going upon three years)—a butcher by trade. Namely, that it never occurred to him to say— much less think—that he, with only a high school education, was in fact an exceptional intellect and ethicist. Hence his indifference to that exceptionalness—he was always too busy reinvesting its dividends in overt action to take a step back and petulantly coddle it (not that he could ever have conceived of doing so)—hence, his blithe unawareness amounted mysteriously to nothing less than a kind of genius. Jason conspicuously sighs: *Well, we don't choose our fathers. Or do we—and is that the whole point?*

CHAPTER SIXTEEN; or, ALL THINGS ARE POISON

It's early dusk of a delightful midsummer evening, the kind conducive to bittersweet musings. And Dr. Narr has every right and every reason to consider himself entitled to the bittersweetness. Even if (or maybe it's because) he's already achieved pretty much everything any mortal worth his salt might aspire to and in half the time, he's begun to hate his earthly life, not that he's one given to believing in some suture-studded hereafter.

Uneasy lies the head that knows what those smart alecks think is known to nobody but themselves (hacked emails speak volumes). Somewhere down Pipeline Pike, Post and his clowns discovered that the drug being used to treat Envy (in Ethan's view, a non-disease par excellence and potentially hotter than premature ejaculation, erectile dysfunction, Morgellons disease, priapism, fibromyalgia, Capgras syndrome, chronic fatigue syndrome, sensory processing disorder, apotemnophilia, the pseudobulbar effect, and pasty thighs disease put together) is in fact hyperpromiscuous. That is, at the proper dosage—but *only* at the proper dosage (and following the obligatory tweaking of the drug's molecular structure)—Invidicum interacts far better with protein receptors located light-years away from the Envy site than it does with the site's receptor. One such made-in-heavenly interaction prevents a dedicated team of Boy Scout neurons in the orbitofrontal cortex from inhibiting, when a susceptible subject is exposed to the proper stimuli, the unstoppable cascade of depolarizations over the entire limbic system, which results in the eruption of a murderous rage. So the beans Cook spilled a while back were not just jelly.

So forget about Invidicum's ability to suppress activation of the brain's dorsal anterior cingulated cortex (dACC), processing site for Envy and other politically motivated excruciations. After all, who can blame Warner-Metro for seeking to x-tuple sales by shadow-hawking its puny pharmakon as an anger mismanager nonpareil, given the ever-expanding demand, especially among those all-too-dependable bugbears of the technothriller trade, Terrorist Organizations Worldwide?

Even more disquieting—or delightful, depending on where you stand in relation to the finish line—is the fact (another distillate of the content of unwary emails) that Invidicum, at least qua homicidal, does not act out in accordance with a monotonic dose-response curve. It's at the most minuscule doses that it's most potent-poisonous—doses to which Borkman and the others will never be subjected (cf. Paracelsus [1493–1541]: *All things are poison and nothing lacks poison: only the dose makes a thing not a poison*). While for Eden and Cantor a little may be expected to go a long, long way.

Right up there, then, is Invidicum with those endocrine disrupters that rogue toxicologists are so fond of—herbicides like atrazine and fungicides like vinclozolin, not to mention plasticizers like bisphenol A and the hand-wringer's best friend, antibacterial triclosan—associated as they are with summer blockbusters like cancer and heart disease, as well as a host of other, more exotic, generators of realness. And what will be the generator of *his* realness? Ethan wonders. He's impatient to know. Frankly, he would prefer it to be an exotic—one of those signature orphan diseases like giant axonal neuropathy or chordoma. Something to prove death has not mistaken him for somebody else, whether an inferior or a better. For he won't be real until the grisly diagnosis cum death sentence gives the sign. Fact is, he's tired of living, or maybe it's just his obscene zest for living that he's tired of. In any case, death is neglecting, bypassing him. How dare it refuse to visit upon him some insidious onset while he's still young enough to relish the joyride? After all, it's pretty much over between him and Rhys, hence between him and life. No use kidding himself. Notwithstanding, this eagerness for easeful death—even if it's an intellectual pose albeit with no talent scout within smiles to applaud him as he descends the runway—is alarming

Through interception of the very latest batch of Post's emails, Narr has been able to determine (unimpeded by all their juvenile cryptogramming) that Straynge is perceived as getting much too big for his britches. And inasmuch as with self-inflation inevitably comes the obligation to know more than one should, the good doctor needs to be bumped off pronto, followed (but only if time permits) by whistleblower-wannabe Cook, still overembittered by his demotion, even if thanks to the lessons learned therefrom he's more a figure-to-be-reckoned-with than he's ever been. *The phoenix is not a mythical bird.* And once the bloody deeds are done, what will be easier than to turn Eden and Cantor, losers each in his own way, into euphemisms, i.e., *persons of interest* in the case? For by now it's common knowledge Eden has a Hamlet-like score to settle with the old mountebank. And as for that self-professed fruitcake Cantor, well, it will become even clearer post mortem that he was forever, like every other member of his accursed tribe (*the women shall have Gomorrah and the men Sodom*), but an Envy-consumed hop, skip and jump away from indiscriminate heterocide. (For wasn't it no less a firsthand authority than W.H. Auden who said homosexuality is All About . . . no, not Eve, but Envy? [although if, Ethan thinks, the not-quite-manly giggles at Film Forum's recent Joe Mankiewicz festival are any indication, it's all about Her and nothing but]. And, hey, wasn't Hamlet himself pretty darn envious of regular guys [er, dudes] like Horatio?) So Post's legendary scruples have flown the coop, that is, if they were ever there in the first place.

Fact is, Amygdala's Leopold and Loeb are about to be told (he's overheard Post mock-reluctantly spilling the warmed-over beans to some visiting Silicon Valley bigwig—beans, again! you'd think there was nothing else in the Amygdala pantry) that based on their record-breaking receptivity all down the line, they've been chosen to participate—way way up among the yucca stonehenges of Santa Barbara's tawny hills no less—in the second and far more critical leg of the trial. But of course the police will read their departure from the scene of the crime—I mean, *their* crime—just before the victims' bodies have been discovered, as tantamount to a signed confession. The plot thickens, Ethan tells himself, with mixed feelings. Though if he's anything he's a man who *likes* his feelings (and metaphors) mixed and his Rob Roys roughly shaken.

Post & Co. are also counting on Manning to unintentionally do her part for the war effort. Convinced that these bumbling legionnaires must lead her to Operation Invidicum's innermost sanctum (the tweaked variant is being further tweaked somewhere on the West Coast—things always seem brighter out there, don't you think?—before mass production begins), she'll surely traipse after them over Southern California's desert sands, like Dietrich in *Morocco*, whom, come to think of it, she eerily resembles (e.g., same weary scepticism in the twinkle of a lustful eye). For there are trillions to be made from the assassin drug, as it is already being referred to (those blasted emails again!) by, among others, Congolese warlords when—but only when—they take counsel with their pet she-goats, invariably christened Betty (as well they should be, though he wasn't quite sure why). And whoever Manning is working for knows this. So through her own bumbling pursuit of the legionnaires Post hopes she'll lead him to *her* warlord who must surely have a few secrets of his own to impart. And once they're rid of the two of them, well then, the coffers will start to overflow which, if not for Manning, they would have started doing non-stop centuries ago. So Post the Humanitarian's conscience isn't as war-torn as Manning (according to Cook) made it out to be to Borkman (Cook overheard their patter-chatter). But maybe Manning knows she's being set up or maybe she set Post up to set her up or maybe they've been working together day and night to make some third, fourth or fifth party believe that they have nothing better to do than set each other up. Ethan hears Some Thing delectating. He holds his breath in manly dread. But thanks to the travails of others—Eden, Herbert, Borkman, Cook, etc., even Jean (for they are but phantom limbs of a single organism)—the easiest thing in the world for him, now that they've cleared the path, is to make the leap from inchoate Some Thing to . . . Master. He quickly understands—is *made* to understand—that for said Master—this Miami Beach Dinner Theater Maestro—loose ends are not just a sight for sore eyes but music to his ears and grist to his mill and a chip off the old block since they need to be sewn up and this can be achieved only with words (along the lines of, e.g., *But maybe Manning knows . . . or maybe she set up Post to set her up or maybe . . . just maybe . . .*). He stakes his claim to greatness on being able to do everything in His power to enable words to steal the storyline's thunder by flaunting its feebleness, its incoherencies, its inconsistencies, its inexplicabilities. His job is to make sure the storyline doesn't get *too full of itself*—not for a minute must it forget its place as a mere ancillary to—a mere breeding ground for . . . analysis. Without a storyline whose construction is shoddy by every criterion of artistic excellence, He—the Master Explicator—the Master Fixer—would be out of business.

So: the only Big Secret where Invidicum the Homicidogenic—the illegitimate—the variant—the tweaked—is concerned is that everybody's in on It. And the sole lingering question (not pregnant enough, however, to qualify as a secret) is whether everybody's in on It to the same extent. Though as pointed out by the point man at the CDC, or was it the CIA? (but more of those orgs directly below), it makes no sense to pellet a chimaera—a chimeric mouse—like Invidicum with descriptors like variant, tweaked, legitimate/illegitimate and off-label (for starters) since from the very beginning—no, much earlier—and by its very nature as the pipeline brainchild of Cook and Co. Invidicum has been an off-label, illegitimate variant to its core—a spinoff before there was any core from which to spin it off. (Like those would-be makers who turn themselves into self-parodies before they have any self to parody or have I already made that analogy? Which sleight of hand, by the way, is entitled at the very least to a Nobel Prize slot since, to quote Straynge [in camera], it's at once the hardest and the easiest thing those would-be makers can do.) Or is this backstab at "analysis," Narr wonders in retrospect, just another wan example (as if any more are needed) of words' going the gaudily irresponsible way of their own ad hoc laws—and the real world be damned?

But who is Narr to condemn out of hand Cook and Co.'s chimaera for being off-label before it was ever on-? The minute *he's* assigned by this or that section chief to produce copy for the HBO El Blockbuster,[18] he's out the door in flight from his innateness (read *penury*), which dooms him to failure, and in quest of the drips and drabs of arcana needed to give him the edge on all of his potbound competitors. Not just for Narr himself but for the Narrs of the world (*Who is speaking?* he wonders), the work at hand can't begin because it's automatically contaminated by their resourcelessness and becomes their accomplice in evasion. Evasion, engendered by terror of being alone at last with and unhampered in the doing, almost succeeds in getting itself passed off as the sole pathway to enrichment—enrichment before there's anything to enrich. For the Narrs of the world, enrichment is a substitute for erection of the thing to be enriched. That the world at large is a source of boundless wealth is a fiction called into being by a double fear—that he'll be depleted through engagement and that there's nothing there to deplete. He needs to replenish what hasn't been touched, much less exhausted. So how does he get any work done? He manages somehow. He just can't seem to remember what Nute Gringrich Liepnits (more of him below: his entrance remains deferred for melodramatic effect) is always asking rhetorically: Is his soul so empty that unless it snatches images from without it is less than nothing? Why must he acquire everything through contact with outer things and why instead is he unable to extract objects of thought—thought packets—from his own depths? So he, too, like Invidicum, is a chimeric mouse before he's even a mouse. Suddenly he could swear somebody else in the group suffers from the same affliction. The Herbert woman? She's a maker, after all. But isn't everybody, in one way or another? But, wait: somebody *else*? He's not a member of the group, except maybe by marriage. In any case, member or not, judging by this totally unforeseen burst of analytic eloquence, the side effects of Invidicum are clearly transmissible through the exchange of body fluids.

But Narr's head is swimming for he suddenly feels an Envy arioso (for countertenor and full orchestra) coming on (and it makes his blood run thick and cold), though not, as one might expect, with Post, or even Cook the Phoe-

---

[18]As a reflection of his pizazz—or rather, his pizzazz—as a consultant, and following his in-too-many-ways-unwelcome promotion, Narr wasted no time beefing up his profile on LinkedIn. To whom it may concern: He's no longer just a CIA operative and psychopharmacologist but most important, an A-list screenwriter.

nix, as its subject. No, it's Eden of all people who's caught the conscience of this kingpin despite the doom that's in store for him *or rather because of it*. Though, I ask you, isn't this afterthought a wee bit too fake-paradoxical/calculated/facile? Or maybe it's not Eden all by his lonesome—and is there anybody lonesomer?—but rather the two-backed beast cum two-headed serpent that is Eden-Cantor. Well, whoever it is, it's got the Master's signature clearly written all over it (*Who is speaking and who is overhearing the speaking?*)—the same Master who stretched the plausibility of the text of Borkman's fateful meeting with his son to the breaking point and beyond so as to cover every subject in the book, whether even remotely relevant or not. For it seems to be the way of the omnivorish strings-pulling Master (*Master*: the very honorific, come to think of it, that some indiscreet somebody stage-whispered with obvious relish to his piss-buddy in Voracicom's tenth floor men's room while lonely as a cloud, Ethan crapped out his entrails, having made sure to do so in the stall furthest from the urinal bay) to willfully mistake a text for the sort of over-stuffed specialty sandwich overserved at Sarge's (still going strong, I hear, on Third Ave between Thirty-Sixth and -Seventh and, hey, go easy on the mayo while you're at it, OK?). No, it's Eden who's The Rival—the Rival to End All Rivals. Narr walks toward the window, already panting for his nightly retinal fix. At the end of the street stands the only homeless shelter (slated for demolition momentarily) in all of Manhattan able to boast of snug adjacency to an herbal-tea-and-crumpets boutique-and-café (*désolé*, not a reservation to be had for at least the next thirty-odd weeks). A couple of elbow-swiveling automatons hurry by, rudely interrupting his vantage while they're at it. Is this by any chance the tempo set by their personal trainer and, if so, is it being monitored by what Williamsburg techies, but only among themselves, refer to as *nanny sensors*? (the pair's A-list watches sure look as if they're crawling with 'em). Or are they just trying to catch a taxi on the rebound without looking too disjointed?

More to the point, how has he come to pick Eden for so exalted a position, exalting himself in tandem? An open-and-shut case of gilt by association, as it were. Maybe because all along he's been thinking of Eden as his disciple. So much like me at his age, he thinks, even if, when you get right down to it, they've got to be pretty much the same exact contemporaries. He envies Eden for having been chosen for participation in the SB legs of the trial even if he's going to his doom. No, that can't be the reason. He envies Eden for the crystal-clarity of his mission—anyway, what he believes to be his mission—to kill off his father's killer. Though he's going to be shipped off to SB before he can complete that mission, most probably. But why is he obliged to be envying Eden for any reason in particular? Why can't he be, in a manner of speaking, allowed to undergo all the agonies of art in the absence of any agonizable product-in-the-making? Sticking his head out, what he experiences first and foremost, and all too acutely, is disqualification for participation in so beautiful an evening. Disqualified for the event, that is, when he measures himself against Eden. It's only the Rival's trajectory that matters—that *is* a trajectory. Dazzled by the Rival's triumph he forgets that he, too, is trajectoried. To exist, he must have—be—the other's trajectory or else he's less than nothing. He doesn't want his own trajectory even if it's interestingly littered with the kind of non sequiturs that are redolent of a self's unique identity: three years of med school (Lausanne), three and a half years undergoing orthodox psychoanalysis (Tulsa), etc. Such particulars make his fate even direr for it is precisely the fact that Eden's trajectory is barren of particulars, shorn of anecdote, that renders him so pure and in his purity a shoo-in for the kind of preferment Ethan can only masturbate about. In Eden's case, there are no anecdotal particulars to clash with the particulars of the training that's in store for him, that is, if those emails are to be believed. A voice he doesn't recognize (the voice of side-effect eloquence loaned him by Invidicum, compliments of the deep dark Master?) tells him, in case he doesn't already know, that Eden shines *with a rare radiance of privation*,[19] to use a favorite phrase of his cousin Hank James, who first applied it to another cousin, Gussy Barker, military-schooled at Sing-Sing. So Ethan's problem, among so many others, is that his history's too . . . replete. Not anorexic, like Eden's. Not anorexic, like language itself, that is, language *at its vengeful best.* But he wouldn't dream of competing with Eden. The *displeasing ferocity* of competing doesn't enter into it. He envies Eden for what he is (he is "so *other*") not for what he does. He has *a helpless little love of* Eden's horizons. And how can you compete with somebody's horizons? Yet, even in the throes of Envy pain he acknowledges there's nothing more shameful than to forswear grateful acknowledgment of the validity of one's own life trajectory. Thing is, he can't stop himself. But he must admit there's a certain relief in knowing he simply cannot be Eden even if not being Eden cuts him off without right of appeal from the success he craves. Or rather, in knowing Eden for all his success can't be *him.* For isn't the Rival also a deprivee? And, hey, isn't it in fact the Rival's very triumph that's the culprit here, to the extent that it stands in the way of his laying claim to what Ethan himself is laying claim to and is now undergoing with (if he does say so himself) such élan, namely, *privation*? A life experience not to be missed, by the way, whatever one's training.

But what exactly will constitute Eden's success and how can it possibly shoot him down inasmuch as Eden, qua target person, doesn't have "superior and self-relevant characteristics," which is what Envy addicts are always—according to all those peer-reviewed letters that get into *Nature* and *Science*—on the lookout for? But doesn't the fact that Eden's the least likely target add a certain keep-everybody-on-their-toes piquancy to things as they are? Why, it's as if the mastermind—the puppeteer—the . . . Mabuse! (in the Langian, not the Strayngian sense) behind all this homewrecking has chosen Eden to be Ethan's bête noire so as to compel him—and who better than an overqualified soon-to-be ex-adman—to do His own dirty work, i.e., plausibilize (that word again) Eden's implausibility as an Envy target?

Which he's now trying to do, in spite of himself. For excruciating as the Envy pain may be, he's already looking back at it from the distance of, say,

---

[19] Henry ("Hank") James, *A Small Boy and Others* (New York, Scribner's, 1913), emulation aria, pp. 175–176.

somebody sufficiently anesthetized to be able to witness the presiding ophthalmologist's healing incision into his detached retina. And that's a first step, or is it? Within seconds flat, he's become an old hand at Envy (a master, he is, at telescoping his own evolution). He hears Jean's signature unfumbling turn of her key in the lock. So his travails aren't over, no, not by a long shot. For he's got to confess what he's just discovered about himself (they still share the same bed, after all). "Jean," he says, "Jean—I'm an Envier. I don't know if I suffer from Envy but I'm definitely an Envier. I'm envious of . . . Eden. You know, the guy—" "I know who Eden is." The fact that she manages ever so gracefully, while cutting him short, to set what looks and smells like a sack of potatoes on the countertop, gives her an advantage—*the* advantage. But now that the cat's out of the bag he must never allow her to catch him unawares—in the act of seeming to forget what he's just confessed. For then she can convict him of a double abjection—not just envy although that's bad enough but the failure to keep in mind unremittingly the gravity of that abjection through, say, some simple act like rolling up his sleeves to the elbow on a day like today (as an affirmation of manhood).

Ethan needs to make it clear—through action or *in*action (grim, chiseled silence works best)—that continuing to do the job right—any job (like rolling up his sleeves)—as a matter of honor (and he comes from a long line of honorees) doesn't mean he isn't at war with his new abjection at every minute. Doesn't mean he's minimizing his new defect. He must adopt a stance both ethical and physical, made to the measure of this new guy on the block, that proclaims he's never in danger of letting up on staunchly doing himself in (which strategizing, as he well knows, comes with its own brand of exaltation). He mustn't, through some silly lapse into well-being, catch her in the act of looking like she's caught *him* in the act . . . of forgetting just how abject he is—of failing to look like he's aware of every single one of the defects he's ever laid at her feet *merely by being around her* as well as those she's been ungracious enough to lay at his. He's got to acquire not his defect but the consciousness of his defect before she can frame him for his *un*consciousness. Since the only way to dissipate the abjection arising from defects is to ensure that no facet thereof is refractory to the penetration of consciousness, a tactic known to the misbegotten as *apotropaism run amuck*. (Mabuse, Ethan thinks [he just can't get used to *the Master*][20]—or is it Mabuse doing the thinking for the two of them?—is showman enough to know that if he's going to fall for a term as precious-pedantic as *apotropaism*, then it's got to be undercut by a qualifying phrase that's way more blood-and-gutsy, or by a speech impediment, otherwise the house [whether it's the Tennessee Wittgenstein Dinner Theater in Boynton Beach or the Brooks Atkinson or the Guthrie] will be two-thirds adversatively empty in seconds flat.) To be conscious means to be forever on the qui vive for the evildoing of true loves like Jean. There, he's said it. She's not going to turn him into a replica of her soon-to-be ex-husband. He's got

---

[20] Weimar's dotty Mabuse is, unlike the Master, a true flesh-and-celluloid/celluloid-and-blood mastermind.

to make it clear that he's always one step ahead of her typical female's "secret scorn"—that he can be counted on till his last breath to frame that secret scorn before it can frame him as blissfully, bunglingly, bumblingly unaware of its target *defect du jour*. And although he's tempted to say—as Hawthorne says of Annie Hovenden—that it's "too secret, perhaps, for her own consciousness," this might just be allotting her far more charity than she deserves, since she must surely reject the notion of anything's being too secret for a consciousness as carnivorous as her own. Only once—he suddenly realizes!—did she beat him to the jokeless punchline, having remarked, out of the blue, that although he wasn't particularly bad-looking (albeit no matinee idol), his arms were disproportionately long for his legs. While he knows better than he knows his own name that he's so deformed, vanity blinded him to the certainty that she, too, must know and is no doubt still feasting on the fact that she knows what he doesn't know she knows. So every time he's silly enough to let his guard down in a situation where the disproportion becomes all too evident, what she sees and smells—what she, licking her chops, catches in the act—is not some guy exercising his right to enjoy himself but, rather, one with no idea of how sickening-silly he looks and smells swinging those ungainly probosces in pursuit of said enjoyment. Before he could make the consciousness of deformity part of his professional equipment—his character armor—she made it part of hers and is using it to frame him every chance she gets. Well, he isn't going to make the same mistake this time. So—the moral of the story—his story—their story—is (even if his one goal in life, as of this moment, consists in tearing the fabric of his—their—story apart, i.e., bringing down, Samson style, the walls of its temple on both their heads): Don't leave home—or better yet, don't *stay* home—without it. *It* being his credit card and his credit card being the proleptic consciousness of all his defects.

But let's forget about her for a minute. Say he were to lapse into a forgetfulness merry as a jig. How much pleasure can he succumb to before his Envy pain is invalided as a simulation—a pose? Would Envy pain take him back? Since it's just hit him like a . . . sack of potatoes that Envy pain, at least the sort he's just started to *practice*, if it remains uninterrupted hence cumulative, will inevitably indemnify him with a triumph far bigger than the Rival's. As long, that is, as he manages to keep his own grim, exultant counsel. But if he loses his bearings with relation to his Rival's lacerating triumph, which is his true North, all that cumulativity will be canceled and he'll find himself back at zero on the map of mishap and misprision. Imagine, then, if you dare, all the hard work that goes into sustaining the pitch and tenor of Envy pain—all the cumulative proofs of an almost priestly fidelity thereto—being pissed away because of some brainless surrender to a pleasure as harmless as, say, sticking one's head out the window on a midsummer night.

He asks the street (though she's welcome to listen in) how is it that Envy counts as the deadliest of the seven deadlies? Her snorting sigh means, *Same old tired question*. Same old tired question indeed only he has a surprise for his fellow sufferers—an answer that isn't tired in the least—isn't past anybody's bedtime. Least of all, hers (she works the vampire shift). It's just come to him in a vision, compliments of the couple crawling with sensors. But first she's got to promise to forget all about Raiga and Nietzsche and Chaucer and Bacon and Scheler and Freud and Veblen and Girard and Shakespeare and Hume. Her sigh seems to mean, *More matter with less fart.*

However deadly for the sinner, Envy's even deadlier for everybody else with whom he transacts the business of life. Since everybody else has no idea with whom he's transacting or even if it's a real somebody inasmuch as the party in question flatly refuses to *be* if he can't be the Rival. But if the party in question forswears his realness then, in keeping with the Fourth Law of Contamination, the transaction itself isn't real and everybody trying to transact isn't real either. The envier, he concludes, exerts the same destabilizing effect on others as somebody undergoing gender reassignment.

But Jean's no longer listening. She's too busy doing what looks and sounds like *multitasking* (italics: the means by which the italicizer disguises his envy of the supreme self-assurance with which any worthy bit of sociobabble contaminates its user), i.e., cellphoning and snoozing to beat the band—and smugly, to boot. (Imagine, him, Ethan B. Narr, who's made a vocation—a cottage industry—out of smugness, being outsmugged by a mere concubine, having the rug of smugness being pulled out from under him.) His heartfelt confession is clearly (*who is speaking?*) an uncomfortable reminder of how far she, too, still has to go where Envy's concerned (without having his excuse of being a late bloomer). In any case, she's taking Invidicum for another disorder *which dares not speak its name*, remember? But wherever Jean's situated on the road to cure, be it for Envy or for chapped lips, she shouldn't make the mistake of so many addicts. Which is to strut their superiority before the addicted self they've supposedly left behind for good in preparation for a return visit to the site of temptation. But this time (again, *supposedly*) as slummer, paleoanthropologist, muckraker, revivalist—and most of all, career recidivist. She shouldn't turn up her nose at past transgressions. After all, it's made her what she is today even if most people wouldn't touch that *is* with a ten-foot pole. After all, she's nothing but an extension—like everybody else—of that with which she thinks she's now incompatible.

He's got to leave the apartment before Jean gets back from her snooze. *He simply can't face her after all he's confessed.* Thing is, he doesn't feel in the least that he can't face her, confession or no confession. But the words—Mabuse's words—clearly think otherwise. So now he's got to leave the apartment because he can't bear to face the fact that his precious feelings have just bowed to the words of their master. Should he walk toward the full moon or the sun? The latter is certainly more interesting, to the extent that movement's more interesting than stillness—at least to those who can't stand still. For the sun *is* moving, unstoppably, like a lemming, toward the horizon. Unfortunately, it's smothered by silt before it can sink, as befits a self-respecting orb, beneath the rim. And before Narr—in this scene, Narr's Narr, not Ethan, for reasons soon to be revealed—can recover he, too, is smothered, in his case by the sensation of having usurped the real beneficiary's place in—literally—the sun (unsmotherable after all, it's just about ready to sink in a manner befitting its orbhood). The evening's gotten off to a shaky enough start, with Eden's usurping his place in *being* (no other word will do). And things are even shakier, now that in tonight's performance, he's the usurper. The sunset and night air are wasted on the likes of him. Eden would—will soon—know how to wield them for the good of that old sod, humankind. Notwithstanding, on this particular bank and shoal of time, it's he who's being called upon to catch nightfall in the act (to be extremely busy mastering it, whatever that means) while (most important) not caring in the least what anybody else thinks. Which requires defending himself against anything that might stanch the flow of the loneliness needed to get the job done.

He's made his way to the homeless shelter without knowing how he's managed it. Full of surprises is Narr, especially? only? to himself. All is silent within, even the rats and cockroaches know when to shut their traps, since next door, in that herbal tea-and-crumpets café, obviously next in line for fifteen lines worth of anointment in the "Metropolitan" section of (where else?) the *Times*, matters of great pitch and moment are being deliberated. He takes a seat in its railed-off great outdoors where, on a balmy night like this, it is determined that populism will reign supreme so that the filthy rich can rub elbows with the just plain filthy. And as he listens to the recommendations dutifully made by the poker-voiced servers and to the questions dutifully posed by the patrons, he finds that the phony organic chatter is the perfect distraction from his present inner spectacle with its cast of thousands—thousands of . . . perceptions, most too minute to be perceivable. He perceives their unperceivability, so to speak. Which is all to the good. Disgusting in themselves—too much a reminder of his own unenviability—if too distinct they'll only cause suffering, or what old Liepnits, his once and present mentor (who's scheduled to arrive on the scene any second now), used to call—and probably still does—semi-suffering. And semi-sufferings will only get in the way of a process that should be suffering-free. But if they are left to their own devices, which is what precious little perceptions should be left to, Ethan is sure, without knowing he's sure, that they will summate (like the sound of waves) into a mega-perception like unto the ocean's roar. A mega-perception to end all megas, i.e., a mega-perception of what it is he lacks and what precisely it is that he envies in Eden. (The serenity—the sublimity—of stoogedom?) Even if the mega-perception nips him in the mud—exposes the void at his very heart—it will not be as painful, even if infinitely more ignominious, as any one of the million-and-one minute perceptions it comprises. Simply because the mega-perception will be complete, a finished product, a commodity ready for "the auction of the mind." And as such and like any great work of art, irreducible to the sum of its parts. And like any great artist, irreducible to the sum of its salad days. But what if he doesn't manage to swallow the Liepnitsian bait and so ends up in the dark? But come to think of it, hasn't Liepnits recently been babbling every chance he got (and he made sure he got plenty) about how Invidicum and all the other drugs in the pipeline would soon be tailored to ensure, whatever else they did or didn't do, the perceptions at the root of so much mental trouble were prohibited from mounting grimly into mind's-eye visibility so that even those most disabled by shame could get out there and fight the good fight without fear of electrocution through enlightenment.

But he can't keep his mind off the inner spectacle: sounds of the surf mounting to an ocean's roar. No go. He can't think about something other than the minute perceptions, each a wave-packet incarnating a past shame. Like Ira—and George—Gershwin's British Museum (once upon a time he wanted to be a song-and-dance man), the trendy clientele has lost its charm.[21] Even those two calorie-crazy ladies in the corner (they're talking shop so he knows they're bank VPs but nowadays isn't even the lowliest bank officer a VP, better yet an Executive VP?)—dragging the joyless shreds of the venue's upscale signature greens (so upscale they're off the charts and what's more, they go great with the crumpets) round and round on their plates in the impossible hope that in so doing, those shreds will turn into, say, fettuccine Alfredo with a side of Swedish meatballs and deep dish cherry pie à la mode— even they, are no match for the surf. He's almost tempted to send an email to Caro apprising her of the state of things. As if she is somehow responsible for his Envy. And for why it is Eden, of all people, who is facing off against him on the opposite bank of the river of life—why it is Eden who is his rival (fr. L *rivalis* one having water rights to the same stream). But when you get right down to it, isn't she—responsible, that is? By virtue, from the start, of always leaving something to be desired, didn't Caro act as an unsurpassable advertisement for Jean's contrastive glories? Her defects played up and continue to up out of all proportion Jean's nonexistent virtues. If Caro had only managed to leave a little less to be desired, he wouldn't have regarded the first pretty-young-thing to come down the pike as a vast improvement—an improvement so vast as to be a *sign*. What he most misses—if truth be told, although he wouldn't dream of having it told to *him*—is Caro's shameless, tactless slave-girl eagerness to satisfy his every whim. He frankly regrets Caro's girl-scoutish knack for keeping his egotism out of trouble, so to speak, by responding to his every belch as something infinitely more rarefied than hot air.

And wasn't it Caro, after all, who introduced the Dowager Dottie O'Narr to NY's premier schmatte mogul and, more to the point, to the wraparound terrace of his penthouse triplex on Lower Fifth which became, shortly thereafter, the scene of an at-death's-door wedding feast with all the IV trimmings (compliments of fulminant pancreatic cancer) held, testamentally speaking, just in the nick of time?

In any case, Ethan always makes it a practice, whatever the status of his semi-sufferings—and this, he believes, is what sets him apart from the common run of men, not to mention the specimens desperate enough to participate in a clinical trial—to have no time for regrets. Yet in spite of himself he has the uneasy feeling qua petite perception (the coast is clear: after all, the VPs have exited and a sparrow is supping supersonically but still exquisitely

---

[21]George and Ira Gershwin, "A Foggy Day (in London Town)," from the 1937 film *A Damsel in Distress*. See also Alec Wilder, *American Popular Song: The Great Innovators, 1900–1950* (New York, Oxford University Press, 1972), pp. 157–158. In his analysis of the ballad's ultimately heartbreaking angularity, Wilder the scholar—and fellow craftsman—never prevents the sun of a joyous reverence from (to quote the Gershwins) "shining everywhere."

on their remnants) that he protests too loudly for credibility on this score and that perhaps the best thing he can do for himself—since whatever maximizes tension is the pathway of evolution—no, *evolvement*—would be *to* regret and petty damn quick, before the regret has the chance to take it into its head to go underground and really do some major damage. And didn't he recently or not so recently read an article in *Science* on the results of a study in Laguna Beach indicating that regret was such a good thing that non-regretters could only be considered freaks: not enough of a decrease in bilateral ventral stri-atum blood oxygen, too much anterior cingulate cortex engagement and too little reduction in skin conductance responses in the face of a missed opportu-nity? Why, for starters, he could regret not having contracted envy—he means Envy—sooner, when he was still young enough to enjoy it.

But regret or no regret, what is he going to do with the Dowager (since before you know it he'll be off to Santa Barbara but not to bask—perish the thought—in its mottled sunshine) now that she's just been diagnosed with Wilson disease, which means that before long she's going to be spending most of her time stammering and trembling, in outraged response to which dege-nerescence her delusions of grandeur will become more aggressive than ever (but, alas, with no Caro to field her foul balls)?

But Wilson or no Wilson, semi-suffering or not, how can Narr allow himself to be bamboozled by the Dowager at a time like this? Not on your life is he going to follow in the footsteps of his not-quite-namesake, which in Narr's case would mean losing the Battle of Invidi-loo to the flare-up of some maternal hemorrhoid. The way things stand, or buckle, he has no choice but to play the old unfilial game of Dumping the Dowager *somewhere*, even if that makes him—or makes him out to be—even worse than that famous motel-managing matricide for whom it was a point of honor to keep his vic-tim on the premises. What matters most is that Jean be at his side, whether she wants to be or not—whether he wants her to be or not. All other consider-ations suddenly pale—even temporary abandonment's probable acceleration of Dottie's dementia—before his need for such penile enhancement. But does he really need it? You're not going to tell me he's managed to forget (yes, but only out of modesty) that after being on the CIA shortlist for less than a day he's just been appointed (bypassing Senate confirmation, a first) to its new post (created, some say, specifically with him in mind) of Director-General of Covert Pharmaceutical Operations while being permitted (still another) to continue acting in pretty much the same top-dog capacity at the FBI, the FDA, the NIH and the CDC? Isn't all this penile enhancement enough? And of course he has no intention of resigning as VVV Executive Creative Direc-tor for Branded Pharmacological Entertainment Concepts which thereby makes him Pharma's biggest—and better yet its youngest—"intersectional turfer," i.e., no garden-variety operative but one tasked with nothing less than fulfilling (while reconciling) six (unnecessarily conflicting) mandates. Of course the usual rivals have questioned his credentials straight down the line. (Going so far as to call him— What was it they called him?—ah, yes—a "menstruum of immiscibles." [Even if it's meant to be a put-down he can't help loving the sound of it.] Indeed [Ethan wouldn't be caught dead using a word like *indeed*; Mabuse, on the other hand . . .]—indeed, it's like a seventh mandate.) How has a dead-end jobber, they still sigh disingenuously while trudging up and down the corridors of power with every appearance of otherworldliness (so what if he hails from a world-class ad firm with its foot in every media mouth), managed to parlay his near incompetence into such largesse? But don't they understand, even if he himself doesn't, that it's his very incompetence, or rather, his lack of the usual-suspect qualifications that make him, the quintessential outsider, etc., etc. As for all that semi-suffering over minute perceptions . . . Well, maybe when Liepnits finally rolls into town, the minutiae will decide to summate into the mega-roar of the void at the heart of his multi-titled repleteness. Until then, the minutiae must fend for themselves.

But top dog or not, monster or other, replete or non-, he—the merriest of menstruums—must see to it he gets to California well before Eden and Cantor (and who knows how many other fools-errant?) are shipped out of the country (along with mammoth quantities of the drug itself), as foot soldiers in Invidicum's war on the war on terrorism. He seems to remember that according to somebody's email to somebody else, batches of the Homicidogenic in various stages of refinement are currently being shuttled at least two or three times a day among various Orange County warehouses (whose titular owner is Voracicom) in order to throw the enemies of progress off the scent. Shuttled, as far as he can see, in the same way that aluminum, copper, nickel, tin and zinc are shuttled, up to seven times a day, among warehouses owned by banks like Goldman Sachs and JPMorgan Chase (which with a little help from the feckless Fed have finagled their way into the commodities market)—shuttled solely to increase the metal-owners' storage costs exponentially and thereby add a wee bit to those banks' coffers (but isn't the CEO of Voracicom the brother-in-law of his GS "counterpart"?). Which costs are factored hugely into the premium added on to the price of all those metals on the spot market and which detestable stratagem costs powerless consumers (are there any other kind?) billions annually. But who is he, a consumer in his own right, to pass judgment on the workings of the Invisible Hand? Let him mind his own business and be grateful that at his young age he is already a minister with seven portfolios and counting.

While on the one hand all this mandate regalia will be of great use, ensuring him instant entrée into West Coast Pharma's innermost sanctums, on the other he can expect it to play fast and loose—or whatever the expression is—with his precious anonymity. Experts at the NIH and the FDA, with whom Ethan has spoken repeatedly and at length (how far away—how inaudible—the minute perceptions now seem and sound now that he's getting down to brass tacks), are convinced that Eden and Cantor are to be "assayed" by TRNs (terrorist recruiting networks) in North Africa and Central Asia. Which will entail hobnobbing with A-listers like Omar al-Bashir, Bashar al-Assad, Hamid Karzai, Mullah Muhammad Omar, Jalaluddin Haqqani, Hezb-i-Islami Gulbuddin, Jamat Sunat al-Dawa Salafia, Laurent Nkunda (and his Betty), Eugene Prigozhinoff, Stuart "Elmer" Tarrio, Bob Mugabe and/or their successors. Then, once the secrets of the drug's absorption, bioavailability, route of administration, biotransformation and excretion have been revealed, they'll be slagheaped except for their brains, well worth preserving for future research. The preservation mechanism is still a thing of hazy shreds and hazier patches. It's rumored, however, to involve cold shock proteins, specifically RNA-binding motif protein 3 (RBM3 to you). Post's Sunday painter-type experimentation with prions-infected mice has revealed that RBM3, whose synthesis ramps up during hypothermia, keeps neurons alive and preserves their synapses. So the duo or the dyad will of course be transporting vats of the stuff, which is to serve so to speak as their obituary and certificate of resurrection. It is rumored, or more than rumored, that the fools-errant are also to serve as libation bearers straight out of Sophocles, through transport of an adulterated older version of Invidicum (four-square Envy drug Invidicum) known to be contaminated with the AIDS and hepatitis B and D viruses hence dutifully slated for dumping in the poorest of the poor countries of the region. But once again he suddenly realizes that what is most important, as the stage is being set for the demise of poor Straynge and maybe even (but differently) for that of poor Post (he's powerless to stop the mayhem, otherwise he'd be doing all he could . . .), is that Jean accompany him. All else pales—even abandonment's probable acceleration of Dottie's dementia—before his desperate need to have her there as an inspirational thorn in his side.

The best part of the walk, Ethan realizes (if walk it has been), is this, the masterfully slow return home, thus out of season, threading dark-eyed night. Slow, so that he can relish his triumph over Jean's conception of him, frozen in time. Triumph through exertion, excruciating Envy pain notwithstanding. He mops his brow. But does he really need to? Is there any sweat to mop up? And if there is, does it bother him enough to warrant such extreme unction? A not-so-resounding no to all three questions. But the moment clamors for so exquisite a gesture even if there's nobody around to ooh-and-aah, and he's not one to challenge the claims of the moment. Furthermore, he doesn't envy Eden: the walk has taught him that Eden is Eden no longer since he's joined with Cantor at the hip and everywhere else [NB: each is the other's straight man, effective immediately] and the only thing Ethan can feel for this beguiling twinship is love. Upon his return Jean is nowhere to be found so he'll have to lord it over the pigeons—if they'll have him.

CHAPTER SEVENTEEN

The next day, at grand rounds—which consists in Straynge's making the grand tour of his desk for as long as it takes him to run the day's Discourse on Method to ground while Amygdala's core staff (which he insists on referring to, maddeningly, as *his*) look on in amusement—Straynge examines Irena Manning from head to toe (by no means his wont, so repulsive does he find the sight of her). To these postdocs and Voracicomers (whose intermingling gives life to the injunction, almost Biblical, that to every drug shall be allotted its celebrity endorsement) he then announces that of all the pigheaded health professionals he's ever dealt with she is by far the most uncooperative, while in the same breath enjoining his flock to understand that here uncooperativeness goes far beyond a mere lack of cooperation. In response, the lady in question defiantly raises her left hand and Straynge, equally defiant, refuses to acknowledge what is obviously a request to dissent. She tells him off anyway. He's made a grave mistake—maybe the gravest of his career—getting rid of all the trial subjects except Cantor and Eden. Even if the mass eviction turned out to be a farce. He points out that it's she who's giving the pair preferential treatment and that, by the way, the so-called mass eviction did not in fact involve all the trial subjects. (Or did it? for the life of him, he can't remember.) How much does he know, she wonders, about her plans for them? And come to think of it, he's looking—and smelling—more and more like Moscow Mitch.

He calls Cantor and Eden big-time incurables. Wasting taxpayer gold on these clowns is unconscionable. Worse, obscene. He knows for a fact that they lead a secret life, whether together or apart, which is at the same time barren of secrets and rank with their scent. Cook winces (for he's here, too). So yet again here's Straynge about to prove he's second to none when doing what he does best, i.e., using patients, the more unwitting the better, as a sump for his own soggy smelly disavowals—strapping them down on the gurney of losership and wheeling them into an ER of the mind from which you can be sure they'll never re-emerge unsullied. Now Cook, mind you, is no lover of oddballs—for his money they constitute a vastly overrated subspecies. But the way he still sees it is, When an oddball meets an oddball and both are real men—men's men, to be exact (with the realness having nothing to do with sexual orientation or the lack thereof)—and when from that fateful meeting is born a real mission (and Cantor and Eden do have a real mission, even if thanks solely to matchmaking Manning), they're pretty much obliged to cobble together what will look to the crowd like the propulsive inner workings of a secret life and convince its members (and what's even more difficult, themselves) that said life is being lustily led. It's simply a matter of self-protection serving self-promotion or vice versa. Without harboring a single dark desire, they're nonetheless duty bound to go through the motions of not just harboring but, with warm breast and with ah! bright wings, brooding over what exalts them with self-disgust and keeps them, fertive, awake at nights breathing hard between jissom-stiff sheets (yes, fertive, *dude, you read it right the first time; what? how's that? oh, the meaning! tell you what, look it up in*

317

Webster's fifty years from now if he's still around, that is). Otherwise, they'll only end up eclipsed by any of a million more media-potables. In short, a missioned man has to be like unto the kind of up-and-coming (!) porn star who rapidly realizes that to make his mark in what is in fact the most unspontaneous and puritanical of niche genres, he must flout a protocol infinitely more constraining than that of drug trials by, say, sucking a clit or an asshole either in inventive first-time-ever conjunction with another unspeakable actlet (pud- or nipple-pulling, say) or a little longer and a little more thoroughly than the always-uncompelling storyline might warrant (a storyline, by the way, that is as uncompelling as anything the Master could come up with and whose unnatural actlets are equivalent, *armaturishly* speaking, to His thought packets).[22] And by the way, if it so happens that he does in fact harbor a bona fide secret or two not so deep within the heart of his not so very secret life, well, I ask you, doesn't that multiply the chances of his achieving what every mission man dreams of, which is to make the mission as powder-keg immortal as a tsunami?

Manning has clearly been caught off guard. A perspicacious observer—fortunately, nobody qualifies for this role—might say she's wilting. She clears her throat, not that she needs to, but it buys her wilting time. And done as she does it—with exquisite hesitation—Manning's found it to be a surefire crowd pleaser. Even her harshest critics must grant her that. Only now she discovers, or decides, that she really does need a clearing. The exquisite one was just too exquisite for its own good. Only it's too late—one clearing to a customer on any given occasion. The moment has passed, never to return. She buys more time. "I've never given Eden preferential treatment. The Envy label simply doesn't do him justice. I can't stand idly by and—" Post has just entered, inobtrusive to a fault. Steps back, into a corner, his imperial image blotted out by stethoscopes. The softshoe's message: *Don't let me interrupt. I'm just as much an apprentice as all of you. Now, Dr. Straynge, as you were saying—* But Straynge has no intention of taking his cues, however subliminal, from the likes of Post, whom he suddenly realizes is his arch-rival (in life, who is or who isn't one's rival can change in an instant depending on the weather, what one had or didn't have for breakfast, etc.). He could kick himself (forgivingly) right smack in the foul rag-and-bone shop that he dubs his groin for not having realized this until just now. But before Straynge can have second thoughts, Post says, "Now, Dr. Manning, you better than anybody should know that the first law of our great land is, Give a thing a name even—especially—if it isn't the right name. The reductionism is the genius of the thing. *Success in circuit lies.* I know you feel for your subject because you feel for *yourself* in your subject—feel for yourself *as* your subject—and so you will obviously feel his rage at the label's not having gotten you—him—quite right, thereby yielding him up to kinship with a plethora of types with whom he's convinced you're convinced (because he trusts you, maybe even desires you) he has absolutely

---

[22] Yes, *armaturish*: for a definition, try Webster's—around one hundred years from today.

nothing in common except a label: right for them, wrong for him. But this kind of rage is a terrific motor out in the real world." At the mention of rage, Narr starts to pay even more careful attention. (He's just made *his* inobtrusive entry and mock-retreated into *his* corner, behind *his* stethoscopes. Post as it turns out isn't that hard an act to follow after all.) He needs to determine how much Post knows about Manning's game plan and vice versa. Or, if in fact they're strange bedfellows, then the measure must be taken of their collusion. Post drones on liltingly: "The all-consuming effort to prove the label wrong can lay the serendipitous groundwork for great achievements. Achievements that will retroactively render the label causing all the fuss irrelevant. Reductionism, then, is the way in—the patient's way in (and let's face it, we're all patients in the long run, aren't we?)—to being in the world. For the alternative to fighting off the label that fate, in the guise of some nitwit mugwump, has dealt us (which label, whether right or wrong, never takes individual variations, however extenuating, into account) is not being, pure and simple, but no being at all."

Manning considers that the best tactic is to ignore such advice to the lovelorn and behave as if she's never needed anything of the kind. She must throw them off the track about Eden. And as it so happens she has a cocka-mamie misconstruction all cooked up. It's too good to throw away. Her hope is that one fine day it will, like some too-persistent hornet, alight at last on the blushing flower to which it is truly wedded. "As you may remember I was present at Eden's initial workup." "You masterminded it." She isn't sure if this is Post's idea of a compliment. "He was trembling in his shoes, poor thing. Yes, he was infected with Envy. Any fool could see that. Every time we had him contemplate engaging in some task, especially a pleasurable one, the neural circuits associated with disqualification *by virtue of the superior abilities of others* lit up like Times Square on a blistering midsummer night. As did the circuits associated with rejection of that task as *unworthy of the superior abilities of others*. They'd never be caught dead doing something so lowly. He had it bad, as they say. But it could have been worse, and in fact it was, far worse."

"So what is really going on, Nurse—I mean Dr.—Manning: we're busy men," says an aggrieved Post. "Very busy men," she adds, respectfully, so respectfully in fact that it becomes clear he wants to strangle her, and she rejoices at the prospect. While Straynge looks as if Post has taken the *words* right out of his mouth, he would of course never admit to such a *desire*, least of all to himself. Or maybe the minute perceptions of such a desire would never be allowed to summate to an awareness thereof.

"In his case, the Envy is in too many ways a screen for something deeper, much deeper—a state of affairs far direr." And far more threatening to global Pharming, not to mention national security, her tone implies. "Or rather, it is the war *between two kinds of Envy* that is the screen. Just as we all know (from our finger-licking dabblings in matters cardiovascular) that there are two kinds of cholesterol, namely, the good and the bad." (Oh, how she hates these catchy simplifications which the experts so-called, "caring" to a fault, see fit to visit on the brute imbecility of their clientele.) "For somebody like Eden—and who, will you tell me, hasn't had moments when he felt exactly like *somebody like Eden*?—the good Envy is triggered in situations where, for example, at the slightest threat of disorder he feels the need to clean up and scuttle. (As we know all too well from our studies of pygmy hippos, men who've suffered from acne as teens are often like that: they recoil at what they take to be the tiniest exteriorization of their own hormonal turmoil. For those men, things piling up—in the sink, under the bed, behind the toilet bowl—constitute massive boils, threatening their integrity, their will to live (shaky under the best of circumstances)." She sighs, having barely made it through one of her famous parentheses, the scourge even of her fans. But is Manning to be blamed if for her the saddest time of any day is when a sentence must come to an end and there are no more parenthetical remarks in her sights through which to postpone its death? "So he digs in, discarding the scum and making sure everything is where it should have been. But then a funny thing happens: He finds himself remembering and Envying the so-called normals, all those cool dudes not in the least unhinged by the shells and shards of chaos. They become viable targets, those dudes, of emulation—objects of emulation—waystations en route to health." Every time she utters the word *dudes* (which she pronounces like *duds*) Manning looks (reflexively?) Postwards as if to say, Whatever our differences in other spheres, you are my ultimate arbiter with regard to lingo and pronunciation so, how did I just do? "In fact, the act of emulation becomes itself a sort of . . . lost object refound, and an object more real and far less imperfect than the emulator. In fact, by cradling emulation in his arms somebody like Eden becomes whole—becomes real—by association, if only for a few milliseconds. But, alas, the good Envy invariably gets overrun by the bad. Which bad Envy enters the picture when the agonizing of somebody like Eden over a rival's puny triumph is inevitably transmogrified (gorgeous word, don't you think?)" (*titter—of baffle- rather than amusement*) "into an agonizing even greater but in this case *as a duty imposed from without*—by some remnant forbear, some Big Other out there. A duty to agonize even more because the agony as secreted spontaneously by Eden's Envy gland (E-1) just doesn't cut it with this sharkskinned Big Other, who as we all know maintains excruciatingly high (some say unrealistic) standards where the suffering of others not quite as Big is concerned. So Eden or rather Eden's Envy dutifully struggles to meet BO's insane demand that he, Jacob, manufacture a much bigger angel of Envy with which to wrestle. And what he comes up with is precisely a vengeance on spontaneous E-1 for having *then* been at once too excruciating for the matter at hand and being *now* not anywhere near excruciating enough (no such thing as mutual exclusivity in this neck of the woods)." She explains that it is the role of the self-avenging Envy to wield a kind of nightstick of proprietary control over the spontaneous Envy and that by doing BO's bidding, Eden ends up doing a wee bit of his own. Cook wonders how she's managing to stay on her feet. Giving her his full attention is in itself exhausting but there isn't an empty seat in the house. In fact, there are no seats. He can't help feeling proud of her as if in some way she's his creation. "And the bad Envy inevitably trumps the good Envy until the next round, when good trumps bad. Which brings us to the underlying condition I've been alluding to a bit coyly, I admit—the one that uses the War of the Envies as a screen for its own perplexities. And against which Invidicum, as you've probably guessed, is powerless."

Straynge: "Exactly my point, if you'd only paid attention: he was—and remains—his own worst enemy."

"But it's not exactly *my* point."

Even Post—who, from his rapt expression, looks almost like her greatest supporter, albeit only locally (i.e., only at this very moment and on this bank and shoal)—even Post seems to be champing at the bit. But doesn't everything taking place among the Amygdalites, Cook asks himself (he's been charting the course of Post's raptness, praying Manning won't fall for it and go under, thereby destroying all she's—they've—worked for), pretty much add up to little more than the local suturing of a local lesion, perpetrated with the blithest unconcern for the big picture? Call it a perpetuum mobile of bygones letting bygones be bygones—call it a case of one man's big picture being another man's mini-postcard.

"So what exactly *is* your point, my dear Irene?" angles Straynge.

"Why don't we all shut up and listen to what the expert has on her mind," Post prompts, the raptness dead and buried. In one fell swoop he's managed to belittle both Straynge and Manning. To cap his triumph he glances mock-surreptitiously at his Apple Swatch, or whatever this timepiece that's all the rage is called, to great effect (a busy man playing down his busyness in the name of self-improvement). So enjoined, her first reaction—surprisingly, shockingly—is to panic. For the life of her she can't deliver the goods, provide the lowdown on her signature discovery, i.e., the scourge against which Invidicum (off-label, on- or in-between) is powerless. For she feels as if she'd just dragged several bagsful of Hungarian pastries to (where else?) the front end of the downtown platform at the Cathedral Parkway subway station (she, too, is in some way darkly affiliated with Columbia University), during the school-day rush hour no less, and that as a result both retinas are about to re-detach (her sight has never been anything to write home about and if she did, would anybody back in Budapest, or is it Bucharest, really care?). But the trick is to control the panicky self-disgust, no matter what she feels, and not inflate it on the pretext that things can't get any worse. Not immediately throw caution to the winds and overstep the boundaries of the ostensible worst because, supposedly, there is nothing to anticipate beyond them. Since there always turns out to be a far direr version of the worst which induces an instant nostalgia for the ostensible worst, now you-had-your-chance irretrievable. So here she is, and before a capacity crowd of all things, forcing herself to instantaneously learn this and much much more, with a gusto of which she wouldn't have believed herself capable minutes before, all in the name of clamping down on the will of self-hate to perpetrate even greater havoc (on the assumption there is none greater) than has already been sown. She must blast-furnace herself out of this coma of self-destruction.

She flounders—worse, hears herself floundering. She, of all people, who has always managed to whip herself into a frenzy of eloquence (or at least of elocution), giving post-pebbled Demosthenes a run for his money every time, at the sight and sound of a hostile crowd. She is as appalled as Post (and probably Cook) at being unable to specify exactly what Invidicum does and doesn't bring under its control. Cook comes to her rescue, or to the rescue of the moment. She reads his lips. And what pretty lips they are. He tells her not to worry. Far better in fact than the ability to specify what Invidicum is and what it isn't is the ability to feed off this sudden failure to supply all the gruesome clinical details. Floundering is more pathetic and poignant than accuracy—and, in its effort to wriggle out of its own incoherence, ultimately more prolific (a definite advantage, if only she could find a way to be paid by the phoneme or the polysyllable like the Grub Streeters of old). And best of all it's the only means of keeping Post and Straynge and their gang of compulsive pin-downers out of Eden's hair as he prepares to meet his maker halfway. And so infectious is Cook's free and easy approach to this transmutation of the lead of floundering into holy-fool's gold, that she already finds herself reaping the fruits of *her* floundering, and enchanting, thanks to its vicissitudes, the entire audience (minus at most two members). He's taught her that flounder-ing is a positive—an apostolic—act: any act is positive at long as it embodies something—even if that something is privation. Irena, he mouths (it's almost a stage whisper), When symptoms fly by much too fast, failing to name them is not necessarily a privative experience, requiring that one hang one's head in shame. Time and again privation becomes, if only you'll let it, the replet-est thing of all. Ignorance if not quite bliss can, in the right hands, become a pathway to bliss. "Here's how," he cries out. And to the horror of all, including Manning (petite bourgeoise to the core for all her posturing), Cook proceeds to illustrate, like the imp he is (albeit over six feet tall and still counting), on an imaginary chalkboard with an imaginary pointer.

But he quickly tires of his impishness as he long ago tired, even more quickly (as suddenly becomes clear to him), of the dopey doings of Eden and Cantor and all the other stars in this freak show of shows. Slouching once more against the back wall Cook realizes he's feeling not a little usurped—after all, he's no longer embattled Manning's sole fan. Thanks to his pep talk they now number in the seven figures: who would ever have imagined he could be so self-subtractingly eloquent. "There's hope for Eden," he cries out, "no matter what's behind the screen." He, too, was given up for dead after his demotion yet here he is on the rebound, stronger than ever. (Talk of demotion makes all the up-and-comings in the room nervous, the unmistakable sign of which is the sudden baton-twirling of stethoscopes, real and implied). One of Straynge's flunkeys exits. Will he be returning with the campus police? "A sec-ond thing in Eden's favor" (But has there been a first? Manning wonders) "is the fact that unlike the others (I've been through their files more than once) he doesn't make it a practice to hate, i.e., envy, normality.

"Not for a second should he be classed with, e.g., that Cantor character who makes no bones about hating the normals. Why, in his intake bio he confesses that when he started fucking women—even moving in with some of them as an exercise in Peircean illogic—it was not to slip into the skin of normality (even if homosexuality was no longer being written off by—i.e., no longer being written into—the *DSM* as a disease)." Instead, Cook explains, it was to exalt vociferously (amid the consternation, even more vociferous, of his bedmates) non-normality within the cozy confines of the normal, that is, the heterosexual hearth. As Cantor put it, normality was *a disease he never wanted to catch and has no intention of catching.* The tactic doesn't work for everybody—for some, there's nothing in it. He had no trouble performing—a hole is a hole is a rose, after all—and so his fulminations could be taken as largeness—vastness—of spirit. They enabled him to remain unlocalizable, that is to say, not only was he a bona fide hetero (proven by performance with form following function) having heterosexuality to spare but he saw no better way to spare it than for a supermanly defense of the indefensibles. "What a he-man, always looking out for the little guy."

Nor is Eden like that blowhard Borkman (Cook looks around to make sure he isn't within spitting distance) who is always more than willing to portray himself as a disaster where husbanding and fathering and working and playing are concerned. (He's the worst sort of one-trick pony express but in some crazy way he merits our respect.) Through condemnation (for which he has a definite flair) of every one of his particularly inventive embodiments of high-end ineptitude—sorry, inadequacy—as mortal sin, he aims to show normal humankind what not to do and how not to do it, so as to save the race billions of dollars and years in lethally false starts at evolutionary crossroads. He has a Barnum's vested interest in going out on a heuristic limb to make everybody else end up looking like or thinking they look like hyper-normals. And all of that fakery simply to ensure that his own non-normality in husbanding and fathering and working and playing and philandering and wrongdoing can steal the show exclusively *and for all time.* Of course there are some, of the scummier sort, in whose presence he suddenly feels that his non-normality does not register as all that glamorous—in fact, it's recoiled from as rather disgusting. Since immediately upon getting married or having their first kid, these scum forget just how treacherous, false, murderous, wild, crude, anarchic, vicious, non-normal (except in the viperous bosom of their own crowd) they were seconds before. In the chilling shadow cast by their prospectively flawless offspring (or if they are not flawless then the flaws in question are sheer ornamentation—gourmet icing on the cake of life as the Lords of Misrule meant it to be lived), they've turned rancid: prim, pious, patronizing, putrid. So he keeps away from them. For they take his big-top self-excoriation—his bearded-lady non-normality—at its disingenuous word. They are not seduced by the boastfulness at the heart of that self-excoriation. He's a threat to their credibility.

Ethan wonders if Cook is now about to throw *him* to the stethoscopes as yet another viable case study even if the case in question is still very much a newcomer to the un-normality circuit.

Now it's Cook's turn to near-panic. For he has no idea how his thesis can be made to apply to Shearer and Rhys and Herbert and a tumbrelful of others waiting in the wings. What is he going to do? He couldn't survive a second demotion. Not at his advanced age of thirty-six. Maybe the campus police will arrive to whisk him away before he breaks down in lunatic sobs. He can't for the life of him remember what he said that was so soothing to Manning when she was on the hotseat (Physician, heal thyself!). He looks around. His surprise is greater than his delight when he perceives that nobody seems to be caring whether or not he has any more case studies up his raveled sleeve. As far as they're concerned, he's done and not a minute too soon. He's acquitted himself creditably—or at least unremarkably—and now it's time to move on. As for the underling—the flunkey—maybe it was just the need to piss that drove him out of the room a while back, which means there'll be no paddy wagon and no second demotion. And he's a bit disappointed.

From what he can make out Post and Straynge are battling tooth and nail over some ridiculous question of protocol, giving him, their godson, leave to settle back into the parcel of wall that now has his name written all over it and wait for the entr'acte to end happily never after. Panic gives way to unease. *Semi-suffering.* Now where did that tidbit just come from? He feels he's stolen it from somebody else. All those brainy observations about Borkman and Cantor, they can't have been his. They would have been better, i.e., more plausibly, allocated to somebody else—somebody with a knack for having smooth insights and making fast connections and with plenty of advanced degrees to back him up (this is not the wine of modesty talking but rather the Scotch ale of self-defense). But maybe in being allocated to him they achieve an outlandish force. Or maybe they should henceforth be allocated to those who, however implausible as mouthpieces, are nonetheless—all the more—worthy of a helping hand up the polysyllabic ladder of socioeconomic success.

There's got to be a Beast running this show. *Master—Iago—Some Body—* is simply too kind an appellation for this destroyer of storyland/characterland plausibility on behalf of His own eternalization. Cook's heard scattered talk to that effect. Up until this moment he hasn't believed a word of it. But suddenly . . . *There's no other explanation,* as one of his girlfriends used to say. The one who believed to the bitter end that a conspiracy was running her show. Nice kid. Pretty, too. But if here and now, with only a wall for moral support, he can so lucidly think through his unease over having spoken those brainy thoughts (without a driver's license, so to speak)—well then, maybe he would have been capable of thinking them up and out loud in the first place, without any help from a Master, Iago or Beast. But if there *is* a Beast—a hound with hairy mane terrific—a Master (*is he thinking this or is he being told to think it?*)—then why should He be interested in ensuring that any thought He came up with was mappable to only one particular freak and plausible only in that freak's particular circumstances (with the understanding, of course, that if no freak was man enough to fit the bill the thought would be shredded)? Why should an all-or-nothing kind of guy like the Master restrict himself? If Cook were a bona fide Master, he'd do as the Master just did. He'd make sure any and every thought he came up with (to combat—to lyse—the horrors *Out There,* or why bother to think in the first place?) was never at the mercy of that kind of plausibility. Foisting it off on the first available bystander (since somebody had to keep it going), he could only hope that said bystander would turn out to be the worst possible choice, i.e., the least plausible vector, and that the bystander's particular circumstances would turn out to be the least solvent medium—would turn out to be *a menstruum of immiscibles.* The less compatible the vector and the less solvent the medium, the better the thought's chances of retaining its identity. The better its chances of staying collage-glued to the surface of the goings-on. So with the Beast's machinery going full-blast (Cook hopes nobody will plagiarize his substitution of *Beast* for *Master*), none of them knows when she may be recruited as unlikeliest host and habitation for a short-circuited brainstorm and made to pay for the privilege with what appears to be a total eclipse but is in fact a subterranean densification of her essence. But Cook is beginning to feel sorry for the Beast. Sure, it's hard to put your essence on the back burner at a moment's notice to accommodate some bully's thought tantrum. But it becomes a wee bit easier, he thinks, when you acknowledge that the bullying is said bully's sole defense against the Tantrum that is Life Itself. Life's too much for the Beast. Which explains why he maintains a pharmacopeia of thought packets, any one of which at a moment's notice can be administered to—thermometer-gunned at—some freak in the menagerie he's created solely for this purpose.

He becomes aware that the inner entr'acte's over, for Manning is hard at work, and currently without a trace of panic in her voice or bearing. "I am certain now that underlying Eden's Envies are a confluence of affects—conducing to . . . self-sabotage." She makes it clear (a bit too coldly for Cook's taste, and, come to think of it, Narr's, too) that Eden is failing as a patient because he needs to sabotage the trial as he's sabotaged every other windfall that's come his way, even in the womb, and to thereby prove yet again that this, his wretched life's driving force (or nisus, as it's called out on the street), is not a gratuitous, a perverse (or worse, a facultative) thing but rather the molten core of a supreme self-construction which has, Out of the Cradle Endlessly Falling, stood him, the saboteur, in good stead. After you've self-sabotaged for the first time—" Somebody whom Cook doesn't recognize or remember having seen in the room up until this moment shouts: "But hasn't Dr. Peirce Sanders Charles (who, if I'm not mistaken, was Mr. Post's mentor up at Warner-Metro) already taught us there is no such thing as Firstness?" "After you've self-sabotaged for the first time and discovered you like it—or at least like it infinitely more than you could ever like success—then you need to go on sabotaging to keep that first time company in its infinite loneliness (there's safety in numbers) and to convince yourself that sabotage is life-enhancing rather than self-defeating and that you couldn't have chosen any other way to greatness, for in his own domain" (she doesn't name it: to do so would compromise the ongoing operation, whatever that consists in at the moment) "Eden wants to be great and he will be. Of course there are always the self-sabotagers willing to inform anybody who'll listen and especially those who won't that their re-perpetrations are proof not of addiction but rather of a desire to understand (so as to enable them to guide the ones who come after) what could have drawn their unrehabilitated selves to such bizarrerie in the first place." She's long been aware of this very tendency in herself but has come to realize only recently that determining what drives it can be achieved only through determining what drives Eden's, even if he's being driven in the opposite direction. Is this true humility, Cook wonders, or just calculation? For surely she better than anybody must know the easiest way to win over a gang of medicos is to confess to a helpless overidentification with some miserable patient—miserable but adorably overladen with daddy issues.

The Firstness fiend shouts, "I know what all this is leading up to." Ethan realizes the fiend is none other than Liepnits. *He's come to rescue me*, he hears himself think, sounding to his own ears like the wretched Renfield in *Nosferatu*. But from what? non-normality? envy? Is it to be thanks to the suave intervention of *his* mentor that he'll be spared ever having to hear himself acknowledge that the history of his rivals is (as that Danish guy Brigge back in Paris said about his neighbors) the history of the symptoms they have generated in him? Although now that he *has* heard himself say it, Ethan wonders why he should be so up in arms about something so . . . poignant, even heartbreaking. "This woman (I know the type) is preposterously implying that Invidicum has infected the patient with its own will to self-cancellation. That it's a . . . pharmakon. So, for argument's sake, let's assume the worst, namely, that by turning on enough charm to have you wrapped around its little finger, Invidicum is managing to get itself administered for all the wrong conditions over and over and over again. So what? Sabotage is not the disqualification all true makers dread yet seek but just another kind of input into the work in progress, enhancement of *the-work-as-a-thing-obstructed*: meaning as resistance to the way *they want you to mean*."

Now it's Straynge's shaky turn up at bat (no sorrier rookie ever graced a diamond) and to his surprise Cook's obliged to admit old Jim is asking a pertinent—a highly pertinent—question. "But isn't there a problem here with what greater minds than you, Liep, have termed the Sabotage Dynamic (or is it Dynamism)?" "To wit?" Is Liepnits's forefinger cleaning out his ear or signaling to the jury that the defendant is nuts? The defendant is too fired up to care. While willing to grant that the work, their work, wrests its identity—*reclaims* it before it has ever claimed it—from obstruction, procrastination, deferral, Straynge still wonders when all that good stuff gets to outweigh the capacity for enrichment. "Are there cases where the obstruction wears down the creator faster than he can get himself enriched? Where's the tipping point?"

"Let me give you an example." He looks at Straynge as if he hoped to be forgiven or, better yet, as if he dared Straynge to make him care one way or the other, for in either case Liepnits, as it turns out and not a minute too soon, is the very worst of the surgeons whose lese majesty Straynge never misses an opportunity to squawk about—the man most responsible for Straynge's professional status as "low man on the scrotum pole up at Sinai" (none lower). But if he does squawk it is always in the guise of one who—loving his vocation too much to allow the matter of his position on that pole (none lower), let alone the histrionics of the sonofabitch who put him there, to interfere with his exemplary practice thereof—is light-years away from squawking in any shape or form. All eyes are fixed on The Liep. For none better than he knows how to milk the crowd and work the room. "There is no *tipping point*, as you call it. Fortunately. The more self-sabotage, the better. As in the story of the civil servant sitting in his damp, narrow Sixth Avenue office facing a sidestreet, which we all had to read in grade school." (Is this a snotty allusion to Straynge's immemorial abasement up at Metropolitan General?) "Bear with me a moment. Imagine, if you can, the sun reflected in a window across the way. Understandably you don't—I mean he doesn't—understand why, with his imposing seniority, he should, when seated, be vouchsafed a mere reflection. So, taking the law into his own hands, like any solid citizen he rises to secure a wider vantage." "But a vantage on what?" Straynge groans. Liepnits only pretends to ignore him since he's well known for paying particularly meticulous attention to what smell like attacks in order to enrich his work with their substance, as is only to be expected from a sabotologist of the very first rank. "As it turns out, there's even more to see than he imagined, much more." He slips on a pair of tinted spectacles (Manning, being Mad about Opera, gets it at once: homage to Offenbach's Coppélius) and proceeds to read from the cute little notebook he's extracted from his jacket pocket (thank heaven it's not a Moleskine, thinks some little squirt of a Hemingway-averse budding physician-cum-author). "Namely, (*a*) a stand of honey locusts whose intimidatingly unsuspecting joie-de-vivre makes you wonder whether they shouldn't be warned that, any minute now, those gauzy sleeves will be shredded into pothole dung by rain, wind and absurdly high heels, (*b*) a lollipop palm with a club foot (oops! wrong sidestreet, wrong city, wrong Coast), (*c*) the Eighth Street crosstown whose double-jointed unwieldiness gives you (with a little help from the unchanging red light) far more time than you need to examine the Showtime poster on its flank, only there's plenty of avant-garde method to this madness, since you find yourself transported way beyond mere perception to the realm of ap- (though, I do agree, *meta* isn't always *beta*), (*d*) a pizza box serving as skateboard for a pride of *pimply* louts (in fact, their complexions are girlishly flawless) and, last but not least, (*e*) two lindens, one of whom has just deposed the shadow of its trunk in the sun-striped space between them, well aware that to avert hard feelings his better-bred neighbor would—still refusing after so many centuries to admit that the deposer is completely at home with hard feelings as long as they're not his own—abstain from appropriation."

Clearly, Cook thinks, this guy has caught a bad case of the Master virus. Probably from his patients "up at Sinai"? So has he been tested for antibodies yet?

"But you—he—realizes he'd gladly trade all this meaningless fluff for that reflection of sun barely discerned way back when. Suddenly, the only vantage worth a damn is that furnished by his captive cramped seatedness, for it ain't just any old vantage but the vantage on his precious connection with disconnection, with being kept out, and it is only the particular way he handles this being kept out *without ever exiting from its holy confines* that offers him a shot at the title, the title in this case being uniqueness. The connection is sacred. In most cases—and here is where *Eden alone* or *Eden for one* (take your pick) is on the right track—a better prospect is positively useless in terms of improving some core image. For the core image is precisely that of his relation to obstruction. He must build on it—must never be tempted to trash it for some souped-up version. Or rather, by all means *be* tempted (you owe it to the saboteur within) but never succumb. I.e., sabotage all the seeing you think you so much crave. That's what getting somewhere means. For self-enhancement through having more and more is a delusion. It is obstruction that brings one closest to oneself and brings out the beast—I mean the best—in a man, even in a half-man, even in a woman. Don't be afraid to play the unturned worm gnawing away from deep within its host at his every goofily New Age or Gilded Age or Stone Age stab at Accentuating the Positive. Now, boys and girls, what all this has to do with Invidicum I leave it to you to discover. Connect the dots or forever hold your peace. Or, if brevity be the soul of wit, play on, MacDuff, or forever hold your peace. As Rodin said that the only thing more beautiful than a beautiful thing is the ruin of a beautiful thing, so do I say that better than the perspective through a window is that perspective mutilated by the perceiver's reflection in the pane."

His last words do the trick. He has everybody in the palm of his hand. You could have heard a pin drop.

CHAPTER EIGHTEEN

It is out in Westchester's wisteria-drenched wilds (with whose surprises Cook, for one, is already way too familiar for his own good) that, a few nights later, James Madison Straynge is found definitively strangled, "the victim's obligatorily naked body sprawled on the daybed in the coziest den of his recently remodeled townhouse" (Reuters). (Divulgement by the press of his middle name, or of the fact that he possessed one at all, sends, unaccountably, shock waves, or at the very least ripples, throughout the relevant medical communities from coast to coast, from which they are still reeling.) Mrs. Straynge, as it turns out, has been stranded for weeks on Martha's Vineyard, ministering to a chronically ill younger sister to whom she is chronically bound by the strongest of all ties: ambivalence. Perched on the doctor's left buttock was an innocent-enough-looking vial, bearing Eden's name and containing a few of what looked like Invidicum tablets. The wicker maxi-hamper in his strictly-off-limits private bathroom was found to contain several weapons (each and every brand new): three Kel-Tec Sub Rifles 2000, a Walther .22-caliber handgun, four 9-millimeter Glock pistols, and seven 9-millimeter High Points, as well as seven amateurish silencers (beer bottles wrapped in pinkish duct tape). From all indications, a singularly unpeaceful death.

When Eden wakes up and reads the headline (minuscule, true, but still eyecatching for eyes willing to be caught) on page 14 of the *Post* (delivered mistakenly to his door), he panics. But not before emitting a very audible groan of delight (the buzzard is dead) tempered, oddly enough (since somebody's just made mincemeat of his life work), with very little in the way of outrage. He looks around for his medication, hoping it may prove to have the right side effect but the vial is nowhere to be found. He doesn't have the wherewithal to try to remember where he left it the day before but, under present circumstances, who in his right mind could expect him to be able to think that far back?

As for Manning, after getting wind of what is already being smarmily touted as a terrible, terrible tragedy, she's been besieged with phone calls, emails, faxation, text messages and Skype assaults. Most of which, surprisingly, are related not to the Straynge way of fate, but rather to just what exactly did she mean by asserting that, in the case of Eden-Envy, Envy is just a screen—and Invidicum right along with it. The assertion has dutifully gone viral, as it turns out: Somebody—that budding squirt of a physician-cum-writer? the flunkey who skedaddled in the middle of Cook's demotion arioso? (*who is thinking these possibilities?*)—has uploaded a video of the second half of the meeting in Straynge's office to YouTube (7,654,321,002 hits as of 15 minutes ago, the pendent posts best characterized as a mix of sun, clouds and tsunamis). She scrupulously informs as many of her soon-to-be ex-colleagues as she manages to get a hold of that there simply isn't time to explain (in many cases she adds inconsequentially that her desk is a mess). Of course she agrees: the matter's no trifle—nothing like the raspberry and pastry cream concoctions she used to gobble up in Devonshire as an intern. In fact, it's precisely upon just such a bedrock that she intends to erect the brothel—bethel—of her Weltanschauung. At the moment, however, she has other—though not necessarily tastier—fish to fry. For one thing, she must pay her respects to one of neuropsychiatry's near greats, who's just bitten the dust—or haven't they heard?

It is suffocatingly muggy even for late July and with the threat of lightning to boot, but Irena knows in her bones what she has to do and, as they're thoroughly professional bones, she's made up her mind to do it, come hell or high water. Eden and Eden alone can inform her exactly who's been finagled into believing he was promoted and is in consequence, as an expression of the team's appreciation for his brain circuitry's stellar performance, being shipped off to Santa Barbara for super-crucial phase VI (a level of fine-tuned testing never before implemented—anywhere—in a clinical trial). Though sorely tempted to ring the bell, she knows it's essential to meet him as if by chance outside his lair, to which she and her agents have tracked him more times than they—or at least she (lusting lovesick swain as she's to some extent turned out to be)—cares to remember. But lo and behold, who should be emerging from that lair, and with no less than a dovegray raincoat slung noirishly, as opposed to rakishly, over his shoulder (does she merely imagine that his face has in fact lit up at the possibility that she's somewhere in the vicinity?)! And who (picking up speed now that possibility has become dead certainty), though about to be pulverized by a stretch limo (also dovegray)! is managing to step out of the line of fire in the nick? Who, indeed, but the beautiful boy himself. For he *is* beautiful—as beautiful as consecration to an exploit doomed like Hamlet's could make anybody with the right baseline physical equipment. She thinks of losing herself, absurdly, in the stonehenge of what look like oak trees down the street, for it seems, judging from their stance, that they'd like nothing better than to cancel her out in their collective embrace—but Eden is too quick. She knows that if she were able to think at such a juncture she'd already be under those oaks.

How explain that she must calm herself down by watching birds dive—which is what the girl in that Ophuls movie set in Old Vienna should have been doing instead of getting herself mixed up with a typhus epidemic (while writing her dissertation on Purkinje cells, she lived right around the corner from where Billy Wilder was born)—and where there are trees there must be birds. Turns out she doesn't need to—explain, that is. She follows Eden's none-too-eager lead into what he announces sullenly is Fort Greene Park. It's clear that saying the name compromises his integrity, his autonomy, his acuity, his masculinity. The name—any name—is an instrument of coercion, sodomization. Or hasn't she heard? Surrendering to it—uttering it at last—the namer proves he'll believe just about anything, however outlandish. Naming makes mincemeat of a man's manly strong silent scepticism, just about his only real weapon in a Barnum & Bailey world, which is just as phony as it can be and getting phonier by the minute. And the minute he names names, the namer participates in the name's phoniness and pretentiousness and countenances the self-inflation of the thing named—buys it, buys *into* it, thinks—knows—there's nothing so fine for somebody so limp and so empty as to ride sidesaddle into the wind on the inflated coattails of that thing named. The namer is officially head PR man for the thing named, that is, until the next namer falls into the trap. But doesn't Eden have any compassion?—the park didn't give itself that name—the name has been plastered onto it and, so embellished, so caparisoned, the park was sent out into the world to do the hard part—convince everything else that it fitted to a T—that it was the only name that could fit. But if everything else refused to believe it did fit then that was simply the park's fault. She feels *for* the park—that is, she feels the vulnerability that the park can't feel. Just as she feels Eden's vulnerability since he obviously can't make head nor tail of *Martin*—it's the unseen gum on his right shoe and he's stuck with it—he's too pure for the name—the first Martin in history who's too pure to deserve the name. The name, like any other, is a condom and the prick of Martin's purity simply can't be made to fit. *End of name aria*, Manning hums. "I like to wander here, he concedes." "Lonely as a cloud?" He looks even more sullen. "What?" "Never mind." It's going to be fun playing Blanche to his Stanley—Julie to his Jean—Patricia to his Michel. It's already fun, being mocking, ironic, ambiguous, that is. Exposing her own florid, depraved recourse to quotation as a sign of defeat, substitute for action, a fey way of mourning the death of action. But suddenly quoting under this cloud isn't so much fun since it's the old hat of platitude. Quoting is a sign of enfeebling depravity simply because she doesn't have the courage to wield the quotation as she would a truncheon, thereby proving that quotation as perpetrated by a quoter with balls—or, in her case, ovaries—is every bit as active as blowing somebody's head off. What's wrong with summoning up remembrance of "lonely as a cloud" without apology—without the concomitant need to expose the ignorance of the other so he can retaliate and expose her for what she is, whatever that is? Rotten, that what's *that* is. Why is the experience incomplete if it is not framed by what she can perceive as a salutory putdown—raw mockery of her selfhood? (His sullen "What," alert to *her* putdown, will serve very nicely to frame her for the crime she's in fact just committed.) Maybe because the "What" keeps her in line, will save her from making a steady diet of the phrase and phrases like it. Which transfiguration by beauty—fusion with the maker of beauty—with Wordsworth—incapacitates her for unbeautiful life's bigger though not necessarily better business. His sullen "What" saves her just in the nick of time from collapse on the flowery bier of the kind of language they just don't *wield* anymore—that they're just not allowed to wield anymore. Not that his language is a flowery bier for Wordsworth himself. He's too busy sweating out the lines. For her, sweating laborless on the sidelines, the lines (as long as she stays put as Blanche) are a pretext for icy ecstasies à la Tonio Kröger. It's good that Eden's around to cut her down to size. *End of Blanche impersonation with commentary thereon.*

But maybe suddenly it isn't so much fun also because Manning with equal suddenness finds herself wondering, unrelatedly (but how can she, quintessential damsel in distress, be sure?), if she's not already a victim of the "spooky action at a distance" effect—the victim of quantum entanglement with Post and his cronies through their devious expropriation of *what she's putting herself through here and now* and its degradation thereby into yet another symptom of Manning disease (peculiar to delusional amateurs), like indulgence in theorizing on, say, the War of the Envies, Good and Bad, as a Distraction from Deeper Troubles. But she knows it's not Post & Co. who've expropriated her and her thinking. Post & Co. are not the bug making the rounds at A.I.

Yet here she is discovering that the pathos of birdsong is the most powerful counterweight to expropriation by Post and Company—or whoever is perpetrating the expropriation of her being. And the most powerful antidote to Blanchedness. Loving the birdsong she feels . . . virile. And feeling virile she feels whole, unapologetic, capable of anything. By the way, there is no meaning inside the little phrase one of them keeps secreting. The meaning is its repetition: either the phrase has immediately had the desired effect on mate or rival or both (thereby making the repetitions an expression of triumph) or it has remained unheard or, worse, ignored (making them the sign of a mighty refusal to give up or of a self-excoriation at having done so too soon or not soon enough). Her fusion with birdsong as the song of her love or of her lust transiting toward love is capable of counter-bracketing any body or thing that tries to straitjacket and thereby belittle and dismiss it and her—dismiss it (the love! the love!) *as* her. Birdsong as she's come to know it is perfectly capable of squelching anything that dares mispresent her love as yet another example of her compulsion to collude with the minor and marginal—the Envy Screen, e.g., instead of Envy—so as not to have to confront what should matter to her most as a Knight of the Order of the Pharmakon. Not that the birds themselves are under indictment—only her compelling them to do the bidding, by its very nature deviant, of her thought. But is she—are any of them (tainted as they all are, whether victims or practitioners, by the Institutional climate)— capable of having not just thoughts but their very own thoughts? Ever since this trial began, it's as if— She stops dead in her tracks. She's sworn off *as if*s. Ever since the trial began, more and more do her thoughts—especially the really juicy ones—feel implanted. So it's *she herself* who's been expropriated, not just what she's been putting herself through. But does she really believe in this expropriative bug?—in this Thing, Master, Beast, Big Other everybody's talking about—worse, thinking about—behind her back? How can she be even asking herself such a question. It's just that here, in Fort Greene Park, with oaks to the right of her and ginkgos to the left, she feels particularly vulnerable. "To what?" "To my 7,654,321 anti-fans." Eden wants to say with that same sullenness which she's come to love, "Don't blame Fort Greene for your missteps (he uses an expletive but means missteps)." But maybe it's her arrogant repudiation of the bug that is bringing down retributive torrents of expropriation the others couldn't even begin to imagine, much less withstand. Maybe the bug is activated only by repudiation of its art. But she's come to the Master's table too late to be able to pull her punches. She's unintimidated. Her older siblings—Cook, Straynge, Narr, the Moira woman, to name but a few— have (as is the wont of older siblings) fought her battles for her. And so she— the runt of the lot who's enjoying all of a runt's uenarned privileges—has room to see through him, though she hasn't given Him a thought until this minute. She's ideally suited to perceive that for all his efforts to differentiate himself into a panoply of distinct, disjunct *types*—homosexual mathematician, black woman writer, dancer on the skids, businessman crooked to the core but with a cellist's ear for the slumbering spirits of the gold, etc., and now demonic *psychopharmacologista*—despite all those efforts he's still reducible only to himself and himself alone. Oops! should be "Himself and Himself alone" (it'll take some time for her to start using the initial caps his disciples routinely serve up with no sense of self-diminution). He's trying so hard to make his creatures different and whaddya know, they end up plagiarizing each other like crazy, with all the ensuing litigation draining the coffers not just of the federal government but of states, cities and counties as well. Alas, the types He seeks to spawn always turn out to be the thought packets themselves. They are the poor man's slumbering spirits of the gold and can plagiarize each other to their hearts' content without incurring one cent in damages.

But inasmuch as she doesn't know how, much less what, to go on thinking—lest thinking now prove what she already knows, i.e., that she's no longer the progenitress of her own thoughts—she does what she usually does under such circumstances (though there have never been any quite like these), which is to hail a cab. Any old cab. A generic. Fact is, she's simply unable to get herself back into Uber-Über-Alles mode, especially after having been strong-apped by the fifty billion dollar juggernaut's top- and lowdown 100 percent fake grassroots campaign into signing, every time she clicked, a petition of average joes just like her protesting the Mayor's (B di B's) proposed crackdown on liveries. She'll never forgive herself for having chosen a fake man of the people over a semi-plausible one. For having actually believed that she was sitting, at each click, on a people's revolutionary tribunal, and with as many votes to her name as tribunal president Travis K. Robespierre. Yes, Edward T. Walker (*Times* op-ed, 6 August 2015) deserves all the thanks she can muster for an eloquent wake-up call—unforgiveable, however, that she should have been sleeping on the job of citizenshipping so soundly as to require one. But Travis has taught her an even more important lesson, namely, that you are a man of the people or anybody else if you think you are. Life is so much simpler when you are unaware of or shamelessly indifferent to self-contradiction. *End of Uber arietta.* But is it in fact true that she hails a cab whenever she's in such circumstances? Or does the Master decree it to be so in order to move her on to bigger if not necessarily better things? In short, is cab-hailing the bat with which He—the home-run king—belts Irena out of the park? And has this thoroughly irrelevant Uber arietta been visited upon her so that its duration can pinch-hit—stand in—for the ride's? About which there's nothing to say—about which the Master has nothing to say because if you've hailed one cab, you've hailed 'em all.

In the cab Eden knows what she's thinking. He isn't following her train of thought. His train is leading her train, masterminding the hops, skips and jumps of its itinerary, sideswiping it into regions unknown. Simply by the way he breathes, sighs, yawns. Once they're in Madison Square Park, which is now *their* park, on a bench facing Mad Ave's quaint beginnings, he knows she's getting ready to spring her trap. She stage-whispers her question. The stage whisper is recruited to demonstrate that she respects his plight and, to the extent permitted by her professional obligations, shares it. "Who exactly is being shipped out, and when?" He is no longer able to contain the vicious joy that accrues from having mastered the darkest of applied arts. That of adaptation to being unrecognizably millenniums ahead of your time and likely to remain so for another hour or two. And he looks around anxiously. "Do you see somebody? The police?" He knows he's thinking something 'cause he feels it. But he's decades away (all lost) from being able to phrase it. *Try,* he hears himself cry out from deep in his bowels. So Manning phrases it for the two of them: Like any celebrity, he shuns the invasion of his precious privacy. But unlike all the others he's famous for being obscure or, if you prefer (as he does, since it holds out the feeble hope of a change in his fortunes), *obscured*—i.e., peripheralized to a pinpoint (she refuses to use the word *marginalized,* already done to death by know-it-all know-nothings). So obscure, in fact, as to attract capacity crowds at every intersection. But right now, he's in no mood for the paparazzi. Eye contact with even one member of that tribe will give him the runs, contra-indicated for somebody on the run.

He announces—portentously, as if he's implanting the announcement in her womb but with his customary embryologist's tact: "I happened to be in the cafeteria the other day and I overheard Straynge say to Cook and the Ethan guy, who's been looking at me strangely in the last few weeks, that you were de—de—" "Delusional?" "Yes." "Good." "Good?" "Good." "Then they said your work—something about a War of the Envies as a screen for—" "Yes, I know all about the War of the Envies." "They said your work—" "Would be forgotten?" "Yes." "Good. Even better." There is a cruelty not so much in his voice as in his eyes (not so much in *A* as in *B*: she loves it when brain circuits, arising like lions after slumber, put aside enough of their differences to permit such constructions to frame the case at hand) and the novelty excites her, which excitement generates a much-needed defiance of her enemies. "So what if they bracket me as delusional? It's a blessing in disguise. And even more of a blessing is their writing me off as forgotten or, even better, already forgotten" (in his tumultuous delight at her downfall, he may have misheard) "or (my very own favorite) born to be forgotten." She goes on to explain (in the coarsest of everyday language so as not to offend the ivied rabble in their ivory towers) that thanks to him, a messenger straight out of the *Oresteia* (whom she has no intention of shooting), here lies an opportunity, golden or not, to overcome her tendency to undergo labeling—bracketing—straitjacketing—as a malign prophecy—a death sentence. Here lies an opportunity to get herself rehabbed way beyond such vulnerability and to lay the whoppingly outsize tab for the makeover on the doorstep of her detractors. Frankly, she prefers them to fans, whose fickleness wields infinite power.

"As everybody knows, fans come and go, but detractors are forever, and self-detractors are forever-and-a-day." Even before it's completely disgorged, she knows somebody else has recently had or is having this very thought—this deep thought—and expressed/is expressing it in pretty much the same way. Even tone-deaf Eden looks as if he's heard or will be hearing it very soon. Who knows, he may be the one to give the thought its last trial run. It's obligatory. A prerequisite for advancement to the next stage. And simply because the subject's of burning interest to—to—to— Whoever's running the show, that's

Who. He can't let go of it, this subject of fans versus detractors, inexhaustible is its relevance. But to what? dosages, maybe? Hardly. Eden brings her back to earth. Thanks to him, she explains—or pleads—here she is chinning on the bars of their irreversible verdict and growing stronger and more shapely by the millisecond. (Odd, isn't it, that by the very act of relegating her to forgottenhood they keep her memory burningly alive.) "But now that I've baffled my doom, it's back to you, buddy boy." And as pretty a buddy boy, she might add but doesn't, as she'll ever have the misfortune to lay eyes on. "Exactly who is being shipped out and when? What about the stooges who've already left me for dead." Eden thinks (without knowing he's thinking): *It's always all about you. Nobody but you. Though you're no worse than every other woman I've had the misfortune to know. And knowing you're no worse than every other woman is a big relief since I was just about to take you for something much worse than a woman.*

"By the way, I have it on the best authority—i.e., my institutional memory—that you needn't worry about being arrested." He's tempted to raise his eyebrows and tilt his head but such a dumbshow of quizzicality comes way too easy to him so he refrains. He wants, without knowing it, to be inventive. To surprise her. To make her love his inventiveness because if she can love his inventiveness then—he feels this without being able to think it—all hell will break loose and they'll be at loggerheads for ever-and-a-day. "Warner-Metro, including its subsidiaries, takes care of its own. It's famous *in the biz*" (the look in her eye seeks confirmation that the phrase has been turned appropriately) "for holding a contingent in reserve for just such an emergency as this." The culprit of choice at the moment is Straynge's only son, who seems to have had a bone to pick with dear old dad from the start. Forty years ago he would have been described as *wayward*. Good thing, W-M had the foresight to warehouse the waywardness. His PC's already been impounded and debriefed: thousands of visits to the History's Greatest Parricides website and allied consortia, commemorated by uploaded selfies of the boy as Oedipus, as Svidrigailov, as Damiens, as Don Giovanni, as *Man of the West*'s Link Jones and as Macbeth.

"Forgive me. I can only begin to imagine what you're going through: so much persevering in order to visit on your father's—or is it your dad's?—destroyer a well-deserved rough justice only to have some busybody or worse reach the goal for you." Yet she for one can't help wondering out loud whether all this wasted effort hasn't been a precondition for achieving what will turn out to have been the Main Design all along. "Though you've worked so hard for something you didn't achieve, you may very well end up achieving something you haven't worked for at all, something bigger and better. Something that will *make your name in the company.*" Which, she thinks without letting on, sounds exactly like the Big Other's idea of the ultimate joke. For the Big Other is now a given, at least in her own commedia dell'artistic roadshow. She can't do without Him. Hearing herself talk, one of her hobbies, she becomes more and more affirmative about his prospects. Cut off in the youth of his progress without the hard-won consummation craved, here he is on the verge of being granted what he never dreamed he'd covet. Status of Invidicum poster boy—Invidicum's Man of (at least) the Year or of (at least) the Next Few Years. Once he gets a whiff of the footlights, he'll be wanting it more than ever. Or so she needs to believe at the moment because the Big Other wants her to want him to want it.

Touch of autumn in the air. She raises her face shamelessly to the sky. Its light is silky, as if filtered through a cataract, make that two. The sun's heat ebbs imperceptibly like surf—like grief—the intenser it grows—it *is* surf—and leaves her sinking into that quicksand of foiled expectation which surf routinely leaves behind for the rookie beachcomber dumb enough to hope he'll be swept away. Expectation of what? she asks herself harshly, impatiently—as if she were Straynge or any one of a vast number of colleagues who'd like nothing better than to see her done in, vocationally speaking. *Forgotten.* Expectation of what? Expectation of the cure that only sunlight can administer, that's what. Well, if she is done in, like Straynge she won't have to stick around for memorializations. Best thing about being dead—you don't have to read your *Times* obituary—or worse, have it read to you by your "caregivers" (disgusting term), for whom care means singleminded devotion to disabusing you of the notion that you'll be vouchsafed one. She can already taste the *Times* phrasing for corpses like hers which never realized their potential or never had any potential to realize or whose talent never lived up to their potential. The sun has turned vicious on her with the wide-eyed viciousness of insentient things. Enough stage business—enough all-the-world's-a-stage business. Back to the real thing.

Has she gotten a slight tan? Does it become her? Has he noticed? "Fact is, we never know what form the experience we're trying to shape will ultimately assume. For the experience lived is always different from what, starting out, we petulantly decree it must turn out to be if we are actually expected to condescend to live it." She marvels at how easily she's dropped her malapropisms. It's not that she's been pretending all along: they're just one of her changes of garment. In his case, the experience has been that of playing the trial game, winning which meant killing off a corpse in progress if ever there was one. But the core outcome has flown off to the periphery (as cores are only too happy to do), leaving him holding the bag of an inconceivable one. "Maybe you needed to define the terms of the experience so rigidly because you knew you could never comply with those terms. The experience would then be lived, if it was to be lived at all, as pure *dereliction of duty*—which is the only way somebody like you knows how to live any experience. Don't take it personally—there are billions out there with just the same tendency. But while you were so busy punishing yourself for the dereliction that allowed you to remain faithful to your father's demeaning vision (admit it, he's—was—far worse than Straynge could ever be: you hate his guts and then some)—beneath the tectonic crust of things you've been undergoing the most important formative seething of your not-so-long career." "I never thought I had a career." "Everybody has a career willy-nilly just as everybody is a maker." He could never lay bare the True Aim of his experience simply by exposing, through analysis and re-analysis, the irrelevance of the Aim Ostensible, which (let's face it) has never been anything more than "prepackaged self-hate kept alive by the need to comply with a dying father's nonexistent wish." The only way into realization of the True Aim, and triumphant liquidation of the self-hate, has been through undeviating commitment to the Aim Ostensible.

His obtuseness, or simulation of obtuseness, both exasperates and pleases her. Manning's unavowable desideratum, among others: to be dominated sexually by somebody whose potency skyrockets whenever he recalls that, according to every cognitive standard, he's considerably less intelligent than she. "I'll make it simpler for you. As is so typical on the world-historical stage and elsewhere, there are some—be they individuals or entire peoples—who have a duty to get things the hard way—the hardest way possible. E.g., what if thanks to the issuance of Robert Mueller's report, The Rump *did* get kicked out for good? That would have played much too neatly—defying the laws of dramaturgical construction, all of which state that, for maximum impact, salvation or damnation—the definitive turn for the better or, better yet, the worst—must crash-land when the audience's back is turned—when its attention is directed *elsewhere*. Remember your Shakespeare: *There is a world* elsewhere. And, more importantly, remember that on the rare occasions when things turn out as planned, you can be sure a price is paid in some other domain—a debacle of one sort or another supervenes whose direness for civilization far outweighs the puny fringe benefits of a gravy train that, unlike the Mueller train, arrived right on schedule, its cattle cars chock full of just what the horse—or witch—doctor ordered. But, don't despair, our scrupulous shortness of breath as we followed every twist and turn of Mueller's interventions ultimately paid off—paved the way to a dividend, only not the one we fixed our hopes on initially. Since behind the scenes. as the report went about playing the anticlimax card—the dud card—to the hilt, another rough-and-ready beast was slouching toward DC's Bethlehem cum Gehenna to be born." "What beast is that?" Eden asks, having graduated from sullen to surly without missing a beat. Is he reveling in his slowness on the uptake? or is this simply, in anticipation of the firecracker fuck that will land her a place in Milton's Heaven where all passion is spent (until its next upsurge), what her antsy gonads need to perceive him to be doing? or is he merely taking the temperature—gauging the breadth—of her poetic faculty? "The whistleblower's report on The Rump's 'perfect' bout of phone sex with the president of Ukraine (spoiler alert, my love: I lived in Kyiv, pigtailed, with my boozy grandmother between ages five and six so my even boozier parents could get Reno-divorced as untraumatizingly for me as possible). Which it seemed would, with righteous ease, be able to do what two and a half years of superintensive legwork by the Mueller team of super-pros couldn't. But that too, fizzled, thanks to a debauched Senate's surefire mix of cowardice and calculation (who can say where one begins and the other ends?). But here, too, an unforeseeable—a more improvisational—a more jazzlike—a heartier species of juggernaut salvation was waiting in the wings." "COVID-19." Whereupon he points out that this, too—notwithstanding all the crazily astute incompetencies unkenneled—will probably not be enough to prove the Rump's undoing. She shrugs—disappointed that he's (far?) more intelligent than she gave him credit for being. He shatters her hoity-toity misimpressions—makes mincemeat of her bracketing—her straitjacketing—of his very being—by mumbling à la Stanley Kowalski (which mumbling, by the way, is a mere screen for the uncanniest verbal nimbleness, i.e., Stanley and Blanche, Blanche and Stanley—sisters under the mink, brothers under the stink—have far more in common than they're willing to avow)—by mumbling something to the effect that history is one long death march toward the endlessly receding, endlessly superseded salvation we can finally count on and when it's not a death march then it's a caravan of beasty slouchings stretched to a nowhere's crack of desert doom. She thought he would be pleased by a clarification that does, as far as she can see, leave room for hope. But he doesn't look pleased. No matter—she has no regrets about accepting the Beast's invitation to be his mouthpiece (giving Melanctha H. a well-earned respite) for He's managed to penetrate her far more deeply than Eden ever could, despite the purported low IQ—a metric, by the way, constructed by imbeciles for the sole benefit of imbeciles. In fact, she's beginning to feel the luscious ooze between her legs. So, should she invite him to a hamburger joint as a way of making amends—but for what? Americans are known to wolf down hamburgers in times of epicrisis. Now it's her turn to be, or at least seem, displeased. She looks as if the only cure for her displeasure would be a kiss. There's only one recourse, then: to pucker up and (as simultaneously as possible) say, *Pucker up, pretty boy*.

Eden doesn't know whether what she says is true or not-so-true. He knows only that he is now entertaining the idea of kissing her before it's too late. The slight tan has worked its magic. Only he doesn't want this to be a case where at the last minute he finds out (as with so many of his women for hire) that he can't bear to plant a kiss and when he does plant it, shakily enough, the kiss becomes anything and everything but a kiss. A smothered cry for help, say, or an admission of defeat or the warding off of another reproach (notwithstanding all the shop talk about the superiority of True to Ostensible) for having failed, unlike any self-respecting parricide, to skewer Straynge. What if that's all her tact-talk boils down to, revulsion at his failure? She's kept talking to keep herself from puking. It's at times like these that he misses those women for hire (what wouldn't he give to have Linda at his side like a gun in his sidepocket)—specifically those moments when all of a sudden it would become unclear (and it was keeping the unclarity going that was the sexual act) whether theirs was still a business transaction or the beginning of something else, though not necessarily something better. But there's no unclarity here, unfortunately. From her look, it's clear she knows all about his wrestling match with the kiss. He goes even more silent. The silence gets to her: it's too respectful. Why, it positively rises up on its hind legs and begs to be heard as far more than just total agreement not only with everything she's said but with everything she's left unsaid. His silence gives her to understand it's composed of only the very best of ingredients: nothing but accord with just about everything she's already said or thought, is currently saying or thinking, or may one day choose to take it into her pretty little head to say or think, about him, including his failure to skewer Straynge. And the crazy upshot is that she doesn't know if she can stand, now that she's secured it—sealed with a kiss before the kiss, so to speak—so much agreement with everything she's said about the Aim, True or Ostensible. Since she doesn't know if she herself agrees with everything she's just said. (Maybe it applies not to his situation but to somebody else's. Only she—er, the Master—couldn't wait around indefinitely for that somebody else—the thought was already melting away under the glare of its own lucidity. So He saddled her with Eden.) But so much unsolicited agreement is not a love letter—or not *just* a love letter. It's a form of aggression, of . . . revenge not just against her, not just against himself, failure or no failure, but against life itself. A revenge against life emerging from deep within the bowels of life, his last known address. And hasn't one of the trial members been accused or self-glorifyingly accused herself of exploiting just such a tactic? Hearing him with the third ear agree to all the terms of her take on his predicament she simply doesn't know if she can go on shoving *her handle on things* down his throat.

His own thinking, always a subthinking—an under-the-radar kind of thinking—goes something like this: Without knowing it, he's taken her infatuation for granted (evident from all this small talk about aims and *a fortiori* from her hunger to snatch a tan) but now he doesn't know what to make of the displeased silence. Is it just a cover for her poignant need? Or has she written him off, in which case he can't let her go, at least not without a farewell kiss? He hesitates. After all, a kiss initiated will be too much of a concession—to any woman, not just Manning. It will usher in an era of expectation on her part and of duty—or, worse, desire—on his. Clearly to be deprecated. But to refrain will usher in an ice age of regret. To be deprecated as well. But there's simply no getting round the fact that a man's kiss doesn't wait for a maid's features to settle into the configuration most conducive to its planting. The maid doesn't go ahead and prove herself worthy of the kiss: the kiss worth its salt must prove itself worthy of the maid's inevitable unworthiness.

So given all this hesitation, how can the kiss bestowed turn out to be anything but the Grossest Simulation and at the moment of its bestowal how can he come across as anything but a too visibly Gross—the Grossest—Simulator? Things were—are—so much easier with Linda. At least in the last-kiss department. He can smell the stubble around her cunt. A pretty smell. Much prettier than that of the hair it replaced. That smell protects him from Irena, from whom he suddenly needs forcible protection.

But can't love very well be born or reborn at the moment of the kiss? All of a sudden he feels too much impatience for birth or rebirth to demand that the kiss be reverenced as the heroic concession it doubtless is. In kissing and kissing only can he begin to love. There is no thinking love, much less loving, outside the realm of the kiss. Incessant self-questioning in that barren outside is resolvable nowhere but in the fructive inside, specifically at the moment of the kiss he finds it so hard—harder than ever—pretty much impossible—to plant.

But even if the loving is revealed at last in the planting of the kiss, by no means should he minimize: the inevitable discord; the resentment at having given away way too much and received, even if all at once, way too little; the shame at having been caught with his pants down at, probably, the very moment when Manning is loving no longer or knowing she can never love (at least not him) or both, given that never will he appear so repellent as at the moment of planting. But even if there isn't any discord, still, compliments of the planting, the recipient will now be very much within her rights to question why he's been so intent for so long on hiding the fact that, hey, he's at the very least just as adept a planter as the next guy and, upon receiving no plausible response, even more within her rights to convict him of the grossest perfidy known to man: the *withholding of normality*. And then what? Well, the legitimate expectation of further demonstrations of said normality, as was evidenced through the assured apposition of his lips with hers, is sure to be cruelly dashed, that's what, and all because his plight as quest and quest as plight (for, knowing no other way to get through the day, he's still stalking his father's killer) will tolerate no rivals. Poor guy: To achieve normality beyond appeal by the bestowal of a harmless kiss and to then be convicted, through that very bestowal, of having from sheer perversity withheld no end of similar proofs of said normality, over what must feel to her like centuries of deprivation—what fate can possibly stink more? But is the vile bitch aware of the mammoth effort it will cost him to be john doe even for the duration of the kiss? To be true to his potential love he'll have to perpetrate a double self-theft: of his constitutive incapacity to kiss without crazy lust and of the conviction that through so kissing he'll destroy his real self—the self of the plight cum quest. For who can guarantee that at the tail end of the kiss, seamlessly rendered, there he'll be, still real, still intact, still Martin Eden? Any wonder he's looking for the slightest sign of rebuff to justify not literally sticking his neck out?

So, just when he feels the temptation as never before—just when even his full lips as semi-autonomous beings are pressuring him to succumb—just when Manning as patient-exploiting mad doctor (selling her own brand of perverse withholding) is expiring before his very eyes and being endlessly resurrected as the most seducible of gamines (with a Leslie Caron overbite thrown in gratis)—he can't take the plunge.[23] Not even by way of atonement for having gratuitously stabbed her through the heart with his trumped-up tale of envious cronies' merciless vilification.

"Who's being shipped out?" He doesn't reveal the details. For one thing, he himself is more or less in the dark. All he knows is the time and number of the flight out of Newark. And he has no intention of divulging that information. How can he trust her after she's remorselessly—and eternally—saddled him with her displeased silence?

With one plummeting leap out of the park, their park no longer or (depending on your point of view) their park forever, Eden tosses away the tan, the kiss and their future. He's exhilarated to be revenging himself on her simply for being a woman, whose cunt, shaved or unshaved, no doubt smells

---

[23] This dynamic illustrates the almost-famous "surplus beyond simulation" concept as formulated last year at Davos (and, some mightn't hesitate to say, as plagiarized from Colletti and Bateson) but applied of course to a completely different—and more respectable—context.

better than Linda's.

More to the point, he's thrilled more than he cares to admit by the phrase *time and number of the flight out of Newark*. He makes a mental note to purchase the thriller everybody's talking about (even in his sleep), in which the phrase appears, and more than once. They must have a copy in some duty-free shop out at the airport. Then he realizes the thriller has yet to be written. It's still being lived or about to be lived (or maybe it's unlivable, that is, unparaphrasable). So he has just practiced a Misperception. Is he going mad? If he slows down he'll be able to hear what the Big Other (he means the . . . the . . . the . . . Master [*now that wasn't so hard, was it?*]) is trying so hard to explain— the Big Other who can be thought of as the Wire he's been wearing to entrap Manning or the Wire that is wearing him. He will understand why Misperception is called The Gem of the Ocean by those in the know. Misperception doesn't mean he's mad, demented. After all, he'd caught himself in the act of dementia well before there was any grand damage done. In fact, the ability to catch himself in the act of misperceiving—to catch the misperception before it disappears over the horizon of consciousness or under its radar or off its chart—proves he's as sharp as ever. Since when busy catching himself in the act, he's making his neurons work overtime and his synapses (vesicles, clefts and everything in-between) go into overdrive. Which goes a long way toward explaining why Post and Co. have chosen him—him—him—yes, him— (He shakes his head, refuses—refutes—the bait: one thing he won't tolerate is venal flattery.) But whether he likes it or not he's got to take some responsibility for having become what the vast majority of men can only wet-dream of becoming, namely—and nothing less than—the theater of a madman's dialectics operating between brain fuzziness and brain fitness. The fuzzier— the more mixed-up—he gets, the bigger the opportunity to hone his skills as capturer cum pinpoint articulator of the fuzziness. Which articulation of fuzziness caught on the wing is a far far better measure of acuity than getting things right in the first place could ever be. Which therefore makes him preeminently fit to carry out any assignment coming down the pike or pipeline. QED.

But he strongly feels, without knowing he feels, strongly or otherwise, that he's let the Big Other—the Master—down. Surely he's come up with better, subtler misconceptions in his short life, which has for all practical purposes just begun. Like this one: if he gets to the airport fast enough he can return to the Institute in time for his session with Manning. Or this: if he can catch some stranger's eye long enough to look into its depths he will be able to determine, without having to open his laptopless laptop bag in broad daylight (like one of the army of homeless), whether he remembered to take a few changes of underwear. Or better yet: the fact that this austere European trio is slowing down so that the papa bear can photograph the Flatiron (don't knock the tourists—more to the point, don't knock their smartphones: they keep the NYC economy robust) means that he won't be late for his flight (he'll be rewarded for not succumbing to such frivolity). Instead, the Master has chosen to pounce on one of the least interesting of his misses—what Cantor would surely call a *degenerate case* of the breed (he's heard him use the phrase in Skype- and Zoom-talk many a time and finally gets the meaning). Always too impatient to wait is the Master. Some call it a hallmark of Mastery. Or maybe there's some well-thought-out aesthetic purpose—some avant-garde stuntwork—associated with hitching his meditation on the rococo theme of misperception to the example least worthy of the effort.

Standing at the corner of Greenwich and Seventh Avenues (after having returned home very briefly to roost and checked in at Amygdala for any last-minute instructions) Eden is uneasily realizing he can be mistaken for, of all things, somebody hailing a taxi, precisely because he—he, of all people—is doing exactly that. Having no credibility-enhancing smartphone to monkey around with, he does the next best thing by dragging out of the vest pocket of his greenish linen jacket (not threadbare enough for his state of mind) the appointment book Linda (in a moment of daringly uncharacteristic sweetness) gave him for his birthday. Knowing there's nothing to look at, he's surprised that in fact there *is*, namely, what look like nonsense equations (though how would somebody like him know nonsense from the real thing?), scrawled all over the last pages. Then he remembers: a while back, Cantor, lavishly forgiving him his homophobia, sketched out directions to Roosevelt Hospital where he needed to have some urgent bloodwork done (the Amygdala lab had just closed) and got carried away.

Waves of disquieting perception mount inside him but are nowhere near summating to an ocean's roar of *ap*perception (neither seeing nor feeling, he sees and feels intense- and intently) so he has a lot more in common than he thinks with the somebody (is Narr his name?) who considers him his arch rival even if Eden can't return the favor. (If only some smart-ass start-up would round up the usual algorithms and create an app specifically designed to effect this summation. The idea belongs to him by divine right—he's earned it—even if the credit will go to somebody else. Somebody who knows how to *get* ideas.) He can't take his eyes off a sparrow, which can't take its eyes off its shadow, which thanks to the sun's rays is three times its own size. He, too, would like to be three times—ten times—his own size. Giving up trying to compete with Shadow, Substance disappears into an ailanthus. To reward his inattention, a stretch limo almost mows him down in the course of swerving inelegantly to avoid getting splotched with shadows, however leafy and lush, but makes no effort to make amends, proceeding instead to fire caustics of derision off every point on its trim. And adding insult to injury or an embarrassment to riches, there are moms everywhere (hormonal clocks ticking away like crazy) who wield their *world-class* strollers like machetes (well, maybe not like *machetes* but in any case it's too late for retraction—you see, the massive image—or rather, the words for it—swooped down and carried him off before, pending proper validation, it could be interned). In short, the city is making every effort to come alive at last, for him and him alone, just when (oh so typically) he's about to leave it, probably forever. Can't remember its blue sky ever having looked so blue. Or its pocket-park mixed greens looking so edible.

He gives up trying to hail a cab, which turns him into an ass, i.e., an ass*hole* minus all the glamor. What makes things far worse is the fact that in front of a fancy-looking building but a few steps away some little guy (and younger, to boot) has just succeeded, flagrantly disregarding Eden's seniority, in flagging down a nice big one. Yet even before the cab stops, something in the flagger's way of holding himself tells Eden (who is duly, or unduly, saddened) that he hasn't brought it to heel for himself (and sure enough, who should come hobbling out from the humorlessly well-appointed lobby but a pair of oversprinkled and -baked cupcakes). Notwithstanding, thanks to their speedy departure combined with the little guy's less speedy retreat Eden's never felt freer (another misperception and the furthest thing from a degenerate). For example, what (if the spirit moves him) is there to stop him from, say, heading back to Sixth Avenue and even crossing it on the diagonal instead of remaining glued to the same spot? Especially since Seventh Avenue traffic, he suddenly realizes, is southbound, toward the Holland Tunnel, whereas he needs to be going uptown, toward the Lincoln Tunnel. Or is it the other way around? Or is it the Queens Midtown that should be in his sights? For the life of him he can't recall. Is his memory shot to hell? Was something by any chance mixed in with the last doses of his medication, which he intends to continue taking at least until he gets to the airport—if for no other reason than to keep up appearances, keeping up appearances being his lavish farewell gift to the Amygdala Institute and the insomniac city that battens on the fallout from its breakthroughs? Is this Post's doing? Manning's? (If so and even if not, forgoing the kiss is the best thing he ever did, if not for himself then for his country.) Are the two in smarmy, snotty cahoots?

No, he thinks, *inconceivable*. (Big Other has just forced him to undergo a paragraph break in the text of His thinking. No better form of retaliation [but for what?]. Nothing so mutilating as the division into parts of what should be one big indivisible. Back to zero, as represented by the inauguration of a new paragraph, at the very moment when he feels he can get along swimmingly deep in the old without once coming ever up for air.) He's picked up at last. It doesn't matter what direction the cab takes. The mere fact that it's in motion and seems to have every intention of remaining so guarantees an early arrival at the correct terminal (another misperceptual gem). Once within, he feels without being able to articulate what he feels (par for the course in the kind of novel he's living and even in the kind he isn't, which is why they're all ghost-written, dubbed, supertitled, transliterated, and why, e.g., prodigious Marcel lip-syncs for larval Albertine when she who thinks only about her clit is supposed to be imploring him, the narrator, to talk about highbrow lit)—once within he feels that the forgetting has been engineered by somebody much bigger than Post and, for that matter, than the somebody much bigger than Post and so on and so forth. A somebody much bigger even than the Some-body, Master, Big Other or Beast who is becoming more real to the members of the trial tribe and their handlers than they themselves are and who by any other name would smell as rank. A somebody not necessarily associated with Amygdala or Voracicom or Warner-Metro but an organization unto itself and, unlike any organization or marketable text, indivisible. Hence, with no natural dissolution to be feared nor, even worse, a pinpointably natural beginning. Only (thanks to the absence of parts) all-or-nothing annihilation or creation. Or is this just inflationary pap self-administered by Eden in an access of imperial affliction (but if so, what better place to do the job than in a cab bound for the airport, i.e., between two worlds, that is, between Good and Evil)? *But why are you afflicted, imperially or otherwise, little man?* Because he's realizing that, like his ex-communist paternal grandfather and for all the talk about promotion, he's just a cadre. And what better way to sweeten the pill than by imagining that a memory-manhandling organization without parts (playing Hyperion to Amygdala's satyr is just one—and the least interesting—of its changes of garment), and more powerful than any member of the tribe (except monad-mad Liepnits) could ever have imagined, has chosen him, from among billions, as its prime target. He falls asleep in the cab and is jolted into a drowse by the driver's defiance of a pothole. Awakening for good, albeit (yeah, *albeit:* unlike you, it's entitled to an archaism's life after death) still far from his destination, he misses something. His wallet? (another gift from a lady for hire—one who got perilously close to becoming something more and somehow lived to tell the tale). No: the m-m organization. And, oddly enough, as a result of its dutiful disappearance into airy nothingness, he feels less of a cadre or rather, less of the stigma attached to being condemned to remain one for life.

Having succeeded in making Eden flee (engineering the non-kiss was a stagecraft pro's routine stroke of genius: that stint as Richard Foreman's script girl has paid off handsomely), Manning allows herself to breathe a *brief but luxurious* sigh of relief. (*Brief but luxurious,* by the way, is far harder to carry off than it sounds.) On the wings of that sigh, she *puts in a call* (now there's a phrase you don't hear much anymore) to Pritchard, who's always believed in her when others have not. But what if he's believed in her *only because* others have not? She's tempted to ask him to describe the weather out there. The hotter the better. Thing is, he's sure to take this for small talk, which makes him livid and now more than ever she needs him to be sympathetic. She assures him that, as ordered, she's been lacing Eden's Invidicum with the same *atypical protein kinase C isoform PKMzeta*-occulting synthetic he's been using on his rats. Its name—a snappy one—escapes her. "ZIP," he remonstrates, "which stands for zeta inhibitory peptide." He manages to bark out, "Good," but as if the prospect of having to do so would have cost him several nights sleep. If Eden's going to be of any use, he must stop being allowed to get away with murder. For too long, from what she's already reported, he's been burying deep within, under the weight of stray perceptions leading nowhere, everything connected with the Big Picture—what he's had the opportunity to see and hear as related to Straynge, Post, Narr, Walser, Stifter et al. "That's why ZIP is our only hope. We have to wipe out the memory of those strays and facilitate the long-term potentiation of the memories that matter and continue to matter—everything connected with the Big Picture. He's our star . . . cadre." *I know all that,* she thinks. *Are you going all semi-technical for the benefit of some self-proclaimed layman invited to listen in on our chat?* Or have these lines been lifted from the HBO docudrama that Voracicom dolts Narr and Cook are doing their doltish best to render both incomprehensible to Main Street and (with all its talk about the virtues of "pharmaco-socialism") toxic to Wall Street. "And by the way. I'm sure you've heard that ZIP cannot be used on humans because it deletes all memories, both good and bad. I, however, have found a way to make it selective. And again by the way, forget about PKMzeta. It's star status was a false alarm. Nobody knows yet exactly what chemical ZIP is acting on when it shuts down synapses." "Roger."

She then confirms that Eden has indeed been making a subvocation of seeing no further than his own nose and sometimes not even that far, compliments of this Big Picture-sabotaging addiction to colliding his perceptions (instead of keeping his eye on the ball) with what's local/peripheral rather than global/central. Which addiction has required, from her and her team, ongoing disinterment of those global/central perceptions from the slagheaps of inattention, their extrication from the clutches of the locals/peripherals (aka strays) and their reconstitution via fMRI, for they, unlike the strays (it hurts her to refer to the local/peripheral strays as perceptions and she knows it hurts him, votary of the global/central, even more), can't be allowed to go to their graves unapperceived. And to think that all of this drudgery could have been avoided and might be avoided in future if only—if only—. She stops herself in the nick of time for she knows Pritch will have no truck with practitioners of regret. All this unnecessariness just so that the Big Picture of the Invidicum Story does not end up as nothing more than the zero sum of stray perceptions or, worse yet, of the spaces between them—as nothing more than a kaleidoscopic multiplicity of things unfolding like some brisé fan with the broken promise of a phoenix on the half shell lurking coyly in its every crease. They agree, as so many times before, that while all of the guinea pigs are a perceptual living mirror of the Invidicum universe, it's his perceptualization that matters most. Because of his special place in that universe. Thing is, as their most important balletmaster, he's letting his corps de ballet locals/peripherals outshine the global/central principals. (Pritchard, by the way, is thrilled at the prospect of meeting Moira Shearer, *the* Moira Shearer, having made it his business at the time when he lived in New York and she danced at City Center, the then home of NYCB, to go nuts about her every chance he got, which was several times a week. Even had the impression—since he always occupied seat AA 107 [orchestra, first row center]—that she feared he was stalking her, playing Boris Lermontov to her Victoria Page.) "So we both agree, don't we, that from here on in he's got to hew to the Story line. As we all do." So Pritchard's no longer the mastermind pulling the Story's strings. (Since when the others allude to a Master, Beast, Big Other or Puppeteer, it's his image that she routinely invokes, as her only means of demystifying their froglike need for a philosopher king.) For even if those allusions constitute nothing more than the alluders' strategy for escaping from self-confrontation, they have an eerie way of getting under her skin—she, the most secular and unsuperstitious of lady mad scientists! But now he's gone—bang! bang! her baby shot her down—and turned himself into just another character with an axe to grind and a hatchet to bury, which in his case translates into ensuring that the Story doesn't cancel itself out through irrelevant enrichment with stray perceptions and become irreducible thereby to castrative paraphrase by some hack or quack or flammable mix of the two. Since Pritchard has no problem with paraphrase (if it clears a way toward fulfillment of their goals). With his passing she must acknowledge her own need for a philosopher king.

She wonders if Post doesn't also intend, at some point, to dust Eden's oatmeal with a modified- or delayed-release version of El ZIP. So if he ends up at the wrong end of a debriefing by the FBI, say, or the CIA or Interpol or ISIL or Planned Parenthood or AA (Acronyms Anonymous) or the AAA, there'll be no beans to spill. And should that occur then, of course, there'll be no need for a Pritchard-style memory-selective version of ZIP. In that case, one fell swoop, a clean sweep, would be the ticket. As if following her train of thought à la Sherlock, Pritchard says: "Yes, he seems to think of everything several cosmic cycles ahead of us." "He certainly does think so!" she replies. Then bursts out laughing with amazement. How has he managed to read her train of thought? "Post may already be preparing to implement what we refer to out here as the Sow-Your-Wild-Oatmeal approach to memory extinction. He may even have developed a technique for administering ZIP remotely, known, also out here, as synapse-skyping. But being the sophisticated cutting-edge kind of wiseguy he is, Post must also know that an aspiring assassin experiences no greater destabilizing dread than at the moments when the data (mega, macro and micro) and memories vital to getting—and proving—the dirty job done can't be retrieved (even if his body—even if *he*—is his password), i.e., when his competence is in danger of fading away. And if he doesn't have his competence, what does he have? In which case, not only wholesale erasure and indiscriminate damping of the memory of Invidicum-driven atrocities by ZIP but, even more to the point, the modification by ZIP *qua drug* (stirred not shaken, waiter) of the pharmacodynamic and -kinetic properties of Invidicum might be just the thing to send him off the deep end into that rarefied realm where competence (overrated in the best of circumstances) becomes *mere* competence and at best an *obstruction* to getting the job done, dirty or otherwise. So in the end who's to say whether you, me and Post are at loggerheads or ever the best of accomplices, at least with regard to keeping Eden in and out of occasional blackout mode?" A bit archly, Manning says something to the effect that if they are accomplices after all, then Eden should heartily welcome all their contributions to his cause, inasmuch as serving not one but three masters can only nail him more firmly to the cross of plausibility in *the literature*.

"Oh, by the way, Irena, I hope you weren't taken in by my Sherlocking act just now."

"In the adventure of the cardboard box, he reads Watson's train of thought off the slate of his features. But you can't see mine. How did you manage it."

"From the tenor of your silences. Seriously, I would have said what I said no matter what you were thinking." What he means is that when Sherlock pulls his mighty stunt, the readers come at things from the wrong direction. The psychological acuity invoked is a mere screen. Is he making a ribald reference, she wonders, to Envy Screen theory, the hot new discipline that is up/off and running thanks to YouTube? Or so she's been told (in all the tumult, she's had to put her budding digital notoriety on the back burner). Has he viewed the upload and if so, who tipped him off? Can Pritchard, her beloved mentor, be plotting, in cahoots with somebody at Amygdala, her long-over-due downfall?

"A screen for what?" she counters dully when what she wanted to do was counter *dryly*.

"For his creator's ingenuity in creating a signifying chain (forgive the lingo) of arbitrary links." According to Pritchard, devourer of Agatha's thrilling puzzles, what is peddled as an iron-clad chain of deductions in the world *out there* is in fact a sequence of descriptions whose course and contour are determined by wherever the affinities or disaffinities (which are also a kind of linkage) of the words in question decide to take ACD on the page *in here*. As with any magician, that is, any unacceptable writer, the twists and turns of wordflow determine what's happening out there instead of the other way around. Just as when, according to H.J.D. Azulai, a man utters the words of the Torah, he creates new spiritual potencies that issue *like medicines—pharmakons*—from ever new combinations of consonants. And also like any magician, ACD is committed to linking the units of wordflow at their most tenuous, mostly implausible points of attachment, if at all possible. Only tenuity makes the magic of linkage visible. The convulsions generated by yokage—at once arbitrary and overdetermined—that's the main event, the whole show. Making the darkness of linkage visible, that's the whole show. The links are so much thrift-shop decor. So the fruits of Sherlock's ability to put his powers of deduction at the service of his powers as a *CliffsNotes*-style *keen observer of human nature* are the mere anti-climactic after-effect, after-shock, byproduct, bywork, side effect, artifact, residue, detritus, inditia, of ACD's feed-through. Sherlock's fabled acuity in deciphering a world of woes through a psychologized logic is merely the pretext, the vector, the vehicle, for Doyle's remaking of a world of whimsy through wordflow. ACD's manipulation of wordflow, or rather his allowing it to manipulate him, to take him in directions he never dreamed he could go in his dreary life off the page, constitutes a little ballet where one step leads to another in conformity with the obligation not to imitate, represent, mirror, something *out there* but to adumbrate what its predecessor suggests as a sensuously interesting grammatical possibility at the level—in the medium—of abstract space and time *in here*—call it toeflow. In other words, toe- and wordflow are not windows on the world out there. It's their world that becomes the world out there—only out there is now in here, on the page or in the space of the stage—a world whose vicissitudes Sherlock's fake deductology is supposed to mimic, represent, imitate, carry out. There is nothing to deduce since things are linked in conformity with wordflow not logic. Pritchard takes a deep breath. She can see the exultation in every facial muscle. She knows what he's thinking. It's something to the effect that "No man lives or has ever lived who has brought the same amount of study and of natural talent to the detection of crime which I have done—while at the same time managing a cigar factory whose hubbub of aromas would have made Bizet's Carmen salivate in every orifice of her alley cat's soul."

Back to you, Eden, and your cabby. At the moment of waking, he's undeniably dirty, smelly, sweaty. And by any chance has a drop or two of piss seeped into his briefs? Immediately upon opening his eyes, he sees himself projected on the screen of his worst nightmares. The cut from sleep to awakening, from eyes shut to eyes open, is identical, simultaneous, with the cut from Manning somewhere in Midtown to him in a cab somewhere in New Jersey. And this cutting from Manning to him and back again has been recurring—he's seen it all before—or is again about to become recurring.

Because where he exists—and not just he but everybody connected with and disconnected from the trial—a pinpoint must stand in for duration. Because where he and they exist, there simply isn't time for duration. I.e., there simply isn't enough time to create a sense *of duration.* He's a mere pawn in a game of cross-cutting from Manning to him and back to Manning again and, as such, is making a pretty poor showing when compared with her. Or rather it's the Beast who's making him think-this-without-knowing-he-feels-it. Since, for one thing, he knows nothing about film editing and what editors do to make ends (literally) meet. So the Beast, the Big Other, Mabuse, the Master, is also a movie maker. At the exact moment he's back on screen, he hears the humiliating subtitle *Meanwhile back at the ranch.* The subtitle translates the meaning of the shot of Eden that directly follows the cut. And that meaning has nothing to do with the life and loves of Eden per se but rather—but rather—but rather— (*But rather,* the most beautiful phrase in the language because it both discards and heralds in a single spasm. It's a phrase in motion, it's going somewhere, won't settle for the second best that it's just discarded and with which it's been too long identified. But at the same time let's not underestimate the bittersweet duress associated with the act of discard.) So, where were we? The shot is not of Eden—the meaning of the shot has nothing to do with Eden—even if he's indubitably within the frame. Rather, the shot is of the audience in its amused revulsion at being nagged back to, forcefed more of, grim Eden when all it wants to do is gawk at glamorous Manning. Even if the audience isn't in the frame, its own amused and revulsed image is what it sees when it looks at the screen. This, then, is all about the cut's failure to fulfill its function—to make itself invisible so that the cinematic illusion may be preserved. What's the point of a cut if the shot that's cut *to* isn't worth the celluloid it's printed on—if the image cut to has nothing to offer the shot that cradles it? What's the point if that cut is perpetrated purely to maintain the fiction of a connection perduring over time and space—in this case, between priceless Manning and worthless Eden (worthless, at least, as image)? A connection that shouldn't be, given the imbalances involved. So, thanks to the irrelevance of Eden's recurring squalor in the context of Manning's recurring splendor, even the most filmically illiterate of viewers begins to suspect that—inasmuch as its failure has made invisibility visible—such a thing as a cut exists, for better or worse. So, whatever conflict there is, exists not (*i*) within the story of Manning as it unfolds across "her" subsequence of shots or (*ii*) withithe story of Eden as it unfolds across his subsequence of shots but (*i*) between any given shot in his subsequence and the shot within hers that follows or precedes it or (*ii*) between any given shot within her subsequence and the shot within his that follows or precedes it. A fight between subsequences, then, one fighting for hegemony—supremacy—the spotlight—against the other. And each shot is an avatar of—a gladiator fighting for—its particular subsequence. Each subsequence fears obliteration by the other—worse, that its viral DNA will be inserted into the DNA of the deadly bacterium the other becomes automatically—worser, that its forced fusion with the other will reawaken the ignoble Old South's unsleeping and insomniac fears of what, in a stage whisper, it still refers to as miscegenation—worst, that any shot generated from cross-cutting back to it will bear the stigma of an invisible sub- or supertitle reading "Meanwhile back at the ranch," accompanied by the same running joke in the form of an inaudible sigh on the soundtrack. It's a matter of nothing less than the life or death of Identity. Identity not of this or that puny, expendable living thing. But of the story of X versus the story of Y, such as they are and such as they will themselves to be for all time.

Somebody has left behind a colorful scarf, probably silk. Holding it close to his face, he realizes it's the cab that stinks, not he. It would make a nice present, but Linda has left town. A high-profile assignment in Doha where the demand for her type is apparently inexhaustible (something or other to do with being unnaturally blonde), even if she's made it a point to transcend type every chance she gets, or so she routinely proclaimed, less boastful than wistfully resigned, always just before she removed what she called her peignoir. According to the portentously peppy anchor discussing the case with her Rumpishly toupéd co- on the tiny screen in front of him, Straynge was found clutching the corner of his desk with his bloodied right hand, evidently trying to reach the telephone. Why, it's as if they're trying to make the telephone or the right hand a person of interest in the case. There is much insinuation as well regarding that old chestnut, a lavish lifestyle (encompassing a mishmash of brands wherein the usual suspects, Rolex watches and BMW X5's, figure prominently). True, he did his utmost to keep the home fires of hate burning before they met and, as far as he knows (though how far is that?), never allowed daily contact to mollify that hate. Thing is, as he now realizes (amazing how insight-friendly cabs can be given the ghost of a chance), the hate quickly got denatured—transposed into a new key—for every time he looked his target in the eye, he witnessed fear, generic fear (which made then-pitiable Straynge go weirdly out of focus as the Man to Hate). And the greater the fear generated by the club Eden wielded, which was simply his BillyBuddish gaze (but from said target's perspective a generic gaze), the less Straynge, through the incontinence of his fear, managed to go on resembling the person made to the measure of Eden's hate. Got to the point where hating as he harbored, depended on and toadied to it became a means of protecting Straynge from its grosser implications—a form of goodneighborliness, if you will—and even if you won't. A double-edged wet noodle, so to speak.

And so Eden has ended up losing what he worked so hard to achieve and made sure never to possess, for all his blustery protestations that hatred came naturally to *somebody like him* (who- or whatever that is). Like any great artisan in spite of himself, Eden has ended up abandoning his abandonment of life-draining nuance worship—ended up abandoning his steely stance of all-or-nothing black-and-whiter—a stance that sounds so good on paper, especially in a global epoch whose badge of honor is unclean energy. He's ended up renouncing the pulp fiction that his intolerance houses an unyielding core beset by no inner life—a core whose sleep of reason proudly produces monsters, not changes of heart.

Maybe it's the stifling stench of the cab (feeble air conditioning and windows that open only halfway) but he's actually on the verge of tears remembering how, at Wednesday group therapy sessions, especially the next to last, Straynge—and he can't say it was completely out of character—supersolicitously strove to train them to view a rival as what the ancient Egyptians (*Book of the Dead*, chapter 6) called a *shabti* (later referred to as an Answerer). (A rival, where he came from, being somebody invested with the power, through the success signaled by celebrity circuit engagements, to disqualify somebody else for accession to selfhood. And a *shabti*, where the Egyptians and Miss Carol Andrews of the British Museum came from, being a servant of the dead who performs the work of his master—the back-breaking work of ploughing, sowing and reaping needed to maintain eternal plenty in the Other World's Field of Reeds. Like somebody paid to fight in the Civil War for somebody else, only the *shabti* wasn't paid. So, confronted with a rival, they should remember that he—as if equipped with the *shabti*'s traditional pick, hoe, adze, seed bag, water pot and amuletic signs and alarms, and as if made of the traditional limestone, wood, steatite, alabaster, bronze, axe, glass or pottery—is, by suffering *cautionarily* the drain on the spirit perpetrated by those engagements, freeing them up—yes, *them*, Eden, Cantor, Shearer, Borkman and all the rest—for the pursuit of real immortality. By the way, the highest-he-man-on-the-scrotum-pole surgeon up at Metropolitan General [aka Sinai] he's always ranting about is, he'd have them know, *his shabti*.) Still stifling, the cab is at the same time still insight-friendly, as attested by Eden's realizing that the members of the company—both the principals (he, Cantor, Herbert, Rhys, Borkman and Shearer) and the nameless corps—are all *shabti* of some Master, Big Other, Beast, Ringmaster General. Although over the last few weeks there's been a growing consensus—based at least on what he's overheard in the corridors of the Institute—that belief in such a Being is a mere, and probably transient, side effect of Invidicum. *Master* is no more than *Rival* writ large enough to be targeted and demolished with ease.

Eden never realized until this moment just how much high drama—even Greek tragedy—can be packed into a cab ride as long as it's to an international airport. He's so taken with the notion that if push came to shove right here and now he would pick (*pace* that beefy ingrate Terry Malloy) being a bum over a contender without batting an eye (or is it *without thinking twice*?). He misses his big brother even if big brother never, which is putting it mildly, looked out for him. Cutting in, the driver asks him halfheartedly for his take (it's tip time, folks) on W, O'Cheney [*sic*], Condi, Kerry and Breck, McCain and Palin. When Eden reminds him that he's barking up the wrong decade, the driver, a fast learner where good-humored mockery's the teacher, tries his hand at Obama, Clinton, Romney, Biden, Carly and Jeb. Eden groans, to keep the conversation semi-alive, even when there's no longer a need: they've arrived at the terminal *in record time*. Whether this is in fact the case is beside the point: this *little phrase* that he overhears within and whose italics have gone to its head (come to think of it, the critter is a little like the one in the Vinteuil sonata although the delicacy of that connection is wasted on Eden [*oh, yeah, who says so?*]) settles the matter once and for all, that is, until further notice. First stop: men's room. While his mirror image is as usual pastily repulsive (though women for hire seem to find him, a bona fide condemned man, exciting)—with every milestone pockmark burined by the funhouse glare—all the other reflections bristle, to a man, with spotless suavity (this concession reeks mightily of self-congratulation, though only the Master could or would say why). Adding insult to injury, one of the reflected gazes is fixed on his with the foul-smelling disgust, long-overdue, that it so obviously warrants. However, when the attendant enters, his broom-and-pail routine sending a much-needed signal to cruisers of all ages, the gazer wastes no time training the same scowl on *him*. So maybe, just maybe, it has no affect-laden import whatsoever—is just his ugly old puss's version of Life-of-Riley-esque repose. (The film-noirist that Eden doesn't know resides within or—in the puke-inducing lingo of the day—his *inner* film-noirist, wants to cry out, just for the bloody hell of it, *Paging Neville Brand, paging Neville Brand, paging . . .*). Wait a minute. This guy, at least when he's scowling (and when isn't he?) resembles somebody very much present in the audience while Rhys was telling her Tale of Two Sisters. Stifter? Walser? Whoever it was looked as if he were seeing more in Rhys's story than she saw there herself—as if he already had big plans for her, no questions asked. As he exits, a voice to which he's tone-deaf—the voice of, say, the Master—wants Eden to admit that the men's room sequence hasn't been as bad as he anticipated, now was it? Due in no small measure to His having, out of the kindness of His Tin Woodman's heart, rustled up a few telling details to give the event some heft . . . It must be the drug (he's heard or overheard or read or been told that excretion takes a long long time and in many cases isn't completed until long after death) since Eden hears himself reply coherently, eloquently, incisively, *You did it to save face with your peers or your fans or your detractors or your clients.* Recognizing nobody at the gate, Eden feels an odd relief and (emboldened thereby) even a hope, purged of any leftover oddness, that there may have been a mix-up in regard to the time of the flight or the airport or both. But a stab through the stomach suddenly informs him that leaving a city—especially this, a hated one—is going to be more complicated than he thought—since in such a situation it never fails that, seconds before take-off, horrified and ashamed the hater finds himself smothered by regret, not so much for the city itself as for the relentless denigration which has conjured all its defects, and the further and higher he gets, the more vigorous the bafflement at his unreceptivity to all its unsuspected wonders suddenly emergent through the trapdoor of irrevocable separation. In midair or thereabouts Eden takes full belated virtual possession of the Chrysler Building, Trimble Place, the Albano Building and Hart Island. The one unlovable walk, following an atypically run-of-the-mill assignation with Linda, down aggressively sunny Mill Lane—the kind of thoroughfare in whose malfeasance you become *complicit* simply by entering—he prefers to forget.

Directly to the right of the line for the metal detectors, a total stranger has been conscripted by a dad into photographing him and his son. And

Eden quickly accepts the fact that (albeit not quite in these words, or in these thoughts) having recently—and many times over—had his pretensions to meriting the title of avenger first class definitively debunked, he's offered no choice but to find solace in debunking the pretensions of others, even if they harbor no pretensions to speak of, only the humble wish to persist in their own being. Notwithstanding, he feels obliged to fulfill a career orphan's civic duty and sneer at the sorry spectacle of yet another father intent on perpetuating, at any cost, the image of his already perpetuated self, as if there aren't enough of those floating around central casting. But in a twist worthy of, say, Christie or Ira Levin or Conan Doyle or Francis Beeding or Margaret Millar or Chandler or, last but not least, Stanley Ellin, so intent does pop become on rubbing the kid's left arm because it either hurts or is sick with fear (as only left arms can be sick) or too hot or too cold and (as the kid begins to babble) so intent does pop become yet again, but this time on responding and in such a way as to ensure that here and now (hence for all time) the babbler feels his opinion *really matters*, though not because he happens to be his father's son but rather—but rather—but rather—because he happens to be human (although this doesn't amount to much of a recommendation, as far as Eden the done-in prodigal is concerned)—so intent does pop become on doing everything else under the sun that he loses all interest in self-perpetuation. Which means the stranger who now risks missing his flight is forced to demand that the big boob hurry up (and hurl his moldy slab of *Cheese!* at the camera). The Great Debunker would have given his right arm to be able to put pop out of his misery—to be able to believe he can put pop out of his misery—by assuring him the last thing the kid expects, or craves, is a response, its babble being generable only within the confines of a certainty there'll be none beyond its own echo. So, because of an excess of factors, which Eden is too father-hungry himself to tabulate (hungry enough at least at this moment to suck the dick or lick the balls of almost any man over fifty-five who gets in the way of the hunger), the photo session no longer fits the Debunker's bill, since it's clear as day that what pop has been fussing over is not a mere chip off the old blockhead but a being totally separate whose mystery (Eden, though unlettered in matters of diagnosis, thinks, or needs to think, this may be the mystery of, say, autism spectrum disorder, since mystery unpathologized is just too tremulous a concept) must on no account be swallowed up by the urgency of somebody else's displaced self-love or unspeakable demand (all the more unspeakable because unuttered) for vengeance. He begins to cry—no, he *cries*—as he did in the cab when reminded of all the strange little *shabti* ready at the drop of a hat to do everybody's dirty work but his own.

As regards satisfying Martin's father-hunger, Borkman might do in a pinch, being pretty much the right age—and build. He wonders if he's actually having this thought or if it's wordflow through thick and thin that's having the thought for him—for the two of them. In return (*duck! more distortive wordflow* . . .), he could take up Borkman's cause, as he took up Eden, Sr.'s—there's simply got to be another Troy for him to burn—but this time he'd make sure no rivalrous avenger beat him to the finish line (. . . *unmappable to anything in the overrated real world*). On the other hand, wordflow or no wordflow, Eden has no doubt what would happen if he asked Borkman on his deathbed (as he'd asked Eden, Sr.), *Are you proud to have me as a son?* Eden knows Borkman would be ready with some kind of famous-last-words spiel. Instead of with more of what he got—the famous last words that were no last words—the silence of a death's-head gaze much too penetrant not to be transmitting a categorical *not on your life* exclamation point. Or much too penetrant to be trained on anything as expendable as anything in this world. The encounter haunts him still even if—i.e., precisely because—at the time he was struck by his own indifferent playacting. He simply wanted to know whether mouthing the question would induce the feeling that should have generated it in the first place. The question was the means of informing his father that he rejoiced at his powerlessness. Or the means, through its elicitation of nothing but the death's-head silence of that too penetrant gaze, of resting assured that his father rejoiced even better at his own—maintained his omnipotence even in his death throes. Or the means of reminding them both that the question had no context, that it was an epitaph on the irretrievability of what never could be, given the stars of the dumbshow. Either your father takes to you or he does not. And if it so happens that he doesn't, well, then, you do what any self-respecting ladybug has no choice but to do—you spend what's left of your lot tracking down whoever you've determined has murdered the father-son dyad. Or is this just the wordflow? he wonders almost aloud, trying extra-hard (because it stems from a revulsion too deep even for crocodile tears) to squander universality on an unrepeatable fluke.

He freezes dead in his tracks though he's been sitting absolutely quiveringly still for the last twenty minutes at least, ignoring the chorus line's increasing length *in front of him*. He's got to disaccustom himself to these crying jags. Since the more conspicuous the anguish, the easier its straitjacketing within a very little diagnosis and the anguisher along with it.

CHAPTER NINETEEN

Under the almost-twilit sky, especially appealing out in the wilds of Westchester (which are always rearing their ugly head whether or not the Invidicum tribe is up to tolerating them), Margo Straynge pops yet another pill in her mouth. Has she lost track once again and taken the antipsychotic instead of the antidepressant or vice versa? During one of their many marital crises, which oddly enough always felt like a lull in the proceedings, Jim suggested she go on Invidicum, to allay her Penis Envy. Perhaps she should have, since it may just be that she's far more of a shrew than she's willing to admit. She tries not to be undone by the caterwauling of Jim, Jr., in the next room but one. But what is to become of someone who makes it a point of honor to skip school at least three days a week and routinely trades his laptops up on 125th Street for weed? Yet although Jim, Sr., is himself prey to massive depression, priapism, premature ejaculation, erectile dysfunction and suicidal ideation[24] and although she's almost famous in these ugly-head-rearing wilds and beyond for checking into any one of the number of boutique *rehabservation* centers popping up on the Upper East Side *every chance she gets* (not *now and then* as her husband, always alert to appearances, still maintains) for any one of a number of boutique disorders (her hypochondria being more of a fulminant metastasizer than most killer cancers)—despite all this, she nonetheless holds fast to the notion—*her* point of honor—that whatever Jr. suffers from is an idiopathic fluke. Why, oh why, she refrains from asking (at least out loud), did this meatball asteroid elect to crash through their bedroom window when it seemed unimaginable that between her and her better half things could have gotten any worse?

That he isn't given to bedwetting quite so often anymore has ushered in a belated golden age of sleepovers. Truth be told, however—and this is the crux of the matter—she wishes (though the wish is well below the surface of consciousness) that the symptom would reclaim its rightful place among its strange bedfellows, since with the vanishment of each symptom comes a diminution of her ability to speak frankly—inspiredly—about his troubles, which are also hers, to friends (whose schadenfreude she reads as unjudging compassion) and, especially, siblings (see directly below). So abatement, however brief, is a bad break. She lives to tell his story by telling his symptoms but in fact the telling tells another story—hers, as unspeakable understory. It's the roil of the surface story's wordflow—with its paroxysms of ominous omission thrown in for good measure—that gives a half-life—a bottom-shelf life—to the down under. The units of the surface story invoke, only to cancel out, the units of her own which in any case can never be anything more than potential because they simply don't lend themselves—*yet*—to thinkability. Hers is still very much a story chasing its own tail.

---

[24]The items in any fictional list purport to clarify but in fact their job is to muddy each other's waters. They are placeholders but for what precisely?

As for the siblings (or the *shitlings*, which is how Straynge refers to them—no, referred to them—no, *refers* to them [the Master—surprised at His own fondness—isn't at all ready to relinquish him to posterity]—without even being able to relish what he assumes is savage wit, so great is his loathing of all twelve of them), well, they don't cotton to her glad-to-be-unhappy volubility act in bemoaning her own fate through her son's. Straynge routinely bellows something to the effect that she should know by now that any sign of happiness, however unhappy, will be met with hatred, inasmuch as this represents an abandonment of her true vocation, which is to minister to their own miseries even if it's to be understood that at the same time they (too photonlike for words) are too cleverly sane to be miserable. What maddens him more is that when they don't take the bait (which they never conceive of *as* bait, little tempted as they are to stroke her hackles), she takes this—that is, would take it if she were operating at a much higher and for all practical purposes inaccessible frequency of apperception (oops! that *darn* word again)—to be her own fault. She simply doesn't manage to strike just the right note of helplessness required to engage not contempt but concern, or rather what could be misinterpreted as such. But is there a right note for an earmarked sibling like her, whose plaints draw forth only slings and arrows of raw ambivalence? She induces the sort of exasperation that cannot be misinterpretable as tough love. Their nonexistent mercy craves no purchase on the steeps of her need. So what does she expect to get for her pains? Well, since you ask, just what she does get, and in spades: a world of sneering sighs laced with cyanide. What maddens him most is that she's forever living in the hope of finding some way to titrate her need against their hatred of that need but with enough volumetric delicacy to induce a reaction that can plausibly be taken for plausible concern. (*Who is speaking? Straynge, but a Straynge whose stirring dismantlement of Margo's untruth is refracted through her dutiful sisterly blindness? prosopopoeic Straynge, clinician non pareil, speed reader of the human heart, speaking through nobody else but himself, from among the probationary dead? Margo exploded into a million and one splinters of painfully liberating lucidity? the Master? Margo as she will think once cured of her* sibling sickness? *George Balanchine? Sir Thomas Browne? Thomas Eakins? Walt Whitman impersonating Socrates?* ["He most honors my style who learns under it to destroy the teacher"/"Not I, not any one else can travel that road for you,/You must travel it for yourself"] *Offenbach's Doctor Miracle? why not all of them in one great big Anvil Chorus of the loftier emotions? and, at no extra fee, the author, too? [whoever or wherever she is].*)

This has meant, inter alia, constructing and believing and making them believe in the three-volume fiction of their expertise, in this case in the domain of familial dysfunction—so fashionable a dysfunction as to have become universal by popular demand. (Tell me, he, Straynge, has wondered many a time, what family with any pretensions to hipness will admit nowadays to being functional? None. So, to prevent the ones that are truly functional from feeling left out of the sitcom spotlight, it has been decreed by the *folks* [chestnut of all the great populist fatcats from Cheney and Palin to Romney] who brought you the *DSM* [eds. I through X] that the dysfunctionality spectrum shall not exclude functionality but shall encompass it as its [dysfunctionality's] most extreme form.)

And/but it's not as if she has no raw material to work with. After all, one of the shitlings is a psychic, another a Druid in training, the third a hydromancer and the fourth (the family celebrity and chronic high achiever), a small-town talk therapist whose cure rate based on an extremely short-term approach has been so high that she's successfully talked herself out of a lucrative practice. The other nine belong to the Holier-than-Thou school of freelance practitioners whose principles were formulated by Freud and extravagantly distorted by his American epigones in conformity with 1950s-style notions-counter notions of normality, which distortion was further distorted by Jacques Lacan through an all-too-predictable inflationary twist sporting its own brand of no-holds-barred self-righteousness. So she's gone ahead and constructed the fiction of an expertise to end all expertise, an expertise she can defer to and in so doing defang her tormentors whose contempt of course has only increased in the face of her slobbering before an attribute and asset they know they don't possess. Further, bemoaning her son's fate and therefore her own—since anything that stinks of prideful affirmation is inconceivable (the word's not in her lexicon)—only reminds them of their own precarity. Which doesn't sit well with their conception of a cleverness that's their cure for all defects.

That she routinely comes—came—*comes* crying to him after solicitation of this expert guidance gets her re-kicked in the teeth has exacted a severe price—from Straynge himself. Granted, because of his outsize ambition he's a figure of fun not only up at totem-pole-crazy Metropolitan General (aka Sinai) but at the Institute as well. But do they know what he puts up with from her on the home-away-from-home front and how deft he can be about putting his finger on— "On what?" she's given to ask. "On your insanity," he is given to reply. Still, he has to learn how not to dignify the shitlings—cunts, pricks and everyone in-between—with shitling-like names. They deserve the sort of better-quality execration that either annihilates or compels the annihilator to forever hold his peace. For when he refers to them as shitlings he does his cause a disservice—builds a protective wall around them—exalts them as victims. He's in fact calling himself a shitling through guilt by self-association. Furthermore, in any given instance of teeth-kicking, there is always at least one shitling who can stand forth as "innocent" if only through absence (NB: a sleeping dog is not a dog). Which generates the insane hope needed to get her twelve-step going again. But in the end the only means of keeping hope alive has been through invocation of (straight out of post-Versailles Berlin) an ultimate grand culprit who's feeding them their lines or getting his network of Weimar-meets-Wehrmacht henchmen to do the feeding and it sure ain't forced—Doktor Mabuse as he calls him (bringing to mind his better half's ignorance of hubby's maiden name always gives Jim a chuckle). Conspiracy's the only explanation—the only explanation—the only explanation, that is, when the real one becomes intolerable—intolerant. But why should this invocation of a Big Other destabilize him, play havoc with his conception, more fragile than he ever imagined, of what's real in the world? Beside himself—or, in Margoese, *Besides* himself—he's even suggested that she mosey on down to the Institute (incognito) and (pseudonymously) get herself MRI'd on the off chance that a connectopathy can be pinpointed to account for her Mabuse mania. But why recruit a sorcerer in the first place? *Why*, you ask? So she can keep going back for more. But doesn't such a recruitment constitute a gross impugnation of their competence—the perpetration of an act of lese majesty against the members of a group that has proved itself time after time perfectly capable of getting on with the business of torturing her without any nudges from backseat drivers—? No matter: the guiltier they are, the more inconceivable that guilt. So, once abuse reaches a certain intensity, the spigot is turned off and the baton passes to Mabuse (*spigot? baton?* yes, well, their mixed-metaphoric rendezvous on Straynge's dissection table is no stranger than the conjunction of umbrella and sewing machine on a famous somebody else's).

One of the many things about Margo that get his goat (an idiom that deserves a second life—or a third or a tenth) is her unrelenting adducement of yet another bit of evidence, in this case of the tribe's viciousness, as a means of going nowhere, of denying the immutable. With no respite ever in sight for her best listener. Endless rehash of the same events is exculpative because it dishes up their immutable viciousness as *in flux*—and if they are in flux (since viciousness and they are one) then the verge of rehab is forever on the way. Old news is dressed up as a new development—hot off the press—and it is new in the sense that any resurgence of excruciation is new—*a new take on an old take* (a phrase to be played in the same key—B-flat minor—as *no fool like an old fool*). They've survived, intact and as shameless and remorseless as ever, the insight she refuses to achieve, hence every last one of them is innocent. The sickness of reconciliation isn't far off if she can only keep on jabbering. Talk about an insult to language (though who's to say, he concedes when nobody's listening, what constitutes such an insult?). But as an evidence addict who'll do anything to fend off self-exculpation she's convinced—or rather, she's convinced she's convinced—that if she can just manage to compile an imposing enough dossier—sufficient testimony regarding their transgressions—sufficient proof of the already proved, i.e., that it is not she but they who are the culprit—if she can manage to go on infusing enough contingency, tentativeness and insufficiency into what is resolutely, unrepentantly uncontingent, irrefutable and replete—if she can mortify self-exculpation already well established beyond the shadow of a doubt into the shakiest of processes requiring still more and more affidavits—more and more reams of inexhaustible foolscap—as proof that they—the hillbilly shitlings—are the villains in the piece—well, then . . . then . . . then she can go on doing what she—what everybody else on earth except Straynge himself (at least according to Straynge himself)—does best— which is to fend off a rendezvous with the immutable, the irrevocable—in this case, the immutability and irrevocability of her shitlings' under-the-radar campaign to destroy her. Surrender to the hallucinated need for further proof of their transgressions fends off what should be a final verdict—delivers them from the evil of a truth forever postponed—disperses—disseminates them— until such time as their services are again required, which is any second now.

Sometimes after she's booked her last adducement for the day he sees from the look on her face—glazed, hurt, hopeful, unreachable—that she's already planning a comeback. Already in a new cosmic—cosmetic—cycle, mounting a new campaign to regain what she's never had—their love. For she loves the siblings—oops! shitlings—more than her own life—and certainly more than Straynge. And of course she must make sure never to name them outright, whatever the cosmic cycle, for unnamed they can be anybody—anybody but themselves—their guilt remains fluid—indeed, it may very well belong on the shoulders of somebodies else still—hopefully, never—to be identified. And all this despite the fact that she has the greatest respect for names—especially, significantly, those of her son (see below).

And speaking of Straynge: Through his failure to believe in the Conspiracy masterminded by Mabuse and his network of mad therapists (Straynge's only solace in dealing with this career incurable [to her pals she's just plain Margo] is to keep reminding himself that unbeknownst to the careerist herself, he's managed to bestow on her tormentor nothing less than his maiden name—his *nom de doom*)—through his failure he's become more of a perp than the perps themselves. And he's even more of a perp—the worst kind of perp—if he does in fact believe in the big C but does not act on his belief. Which, she sometimes contends without knowing she contends, is just as well since he seems not to understand that acting on that belief doesn't mean annihilating the shitlings but transforming them back, Grimmly, into the siblings they never were and never will be. His job was—is—to annihilate—exterminate—without offending them. Or to transform without annihilating them in the process. Or along the lines of what she forthrightly enjoined in front of the whole clan at seeing him, one summer afternoon in the family compound, head for the toilet just after it was scrubbed by their Cinderella-in-residence, he was expected to *urinate* not *defecate*, defecation being an operation far too noisy and smelly and convulsive and *alien*—at least as he performed it—to be paraded before persons of quality. It is Straynge, the quintessential bystander, who is therefore the guilty party for, though able-bodied even at his advanced age, not making transformation happen. Refusal to act urgently becomes a form of disbelief far worse (or is this just *her* wordflow talking?) than disbelief in the Conspiracy. So, to stay married to Margo he must walk a very fine line—even if he's sick and tired of the perp walk—between outrage which gets right out there and does something Boy Scout-reparative and outrage so vast it hankers to try its hand at nothing less than annihilation of the real perpetrators or, worse, severance of the bond between her and them.

Conspiracy-speak enables her to grieve over, without keeping her rendezvous with, the immutable. Conspiracy-speak, at least as she practices it, is a crash descent into the maelstrom—a labyrinth of innuendo and subtext where nobody is safe, least of all innocents like him (for in this context at least, he's innocent).

The phone rings just when she's about to curl up (or is it *cuddle* up?) with a good book—*the* good book—the one that's all about Mabuse's tentaculate overreach. As a rule she immediately identifies herself as Margo Guglielmo Finkle Straynge, since to her mind unleashing this mongrel, faithfully and latently oxymoronical, on the caller bares the soul of wit in all its brevity, but something holds her back. She almost hopes the call is from the headmaster of the Sutton Square Country Day School (billed by *Time Out for Szagat!* as the only institution in the country with a curriculum geared exclusively and unabashedly to the almost- or soon-to-be-gifted) even if it's to inform her that Jim, Jr.'s athletic support, i.e., gym teacher, has observed yet again that his track shorts reek and not just of healthy urine, sweat and semen. "Hello." (No lady of the house ever sounded less housebroken.) "Mrs. Straynge?" The voice is not as deep as the old codger's but more manly, more distinctive. "Yes." "This is Inspector Hank V. Kleist from the New York City Police Department." She has enough presence of mind to ask, "What precinct." "Sixth Precinct, ma'am. Right under the Ed Koch. It's about your husband." Margo (*relieved, but still wary*): "Yes." "Seems the doc—I mean Doctor Straynge—was found dead a little over an hour ago in his office." For once, silence must be compelled to do what it's reputed by its most talented practitioners to do best, i.e., speak volumes. "Mrs. Straynge—are you there?" The only way to throttle such an intrusion, and the intruder in tandem, is to take all the time she needs to ask herself, *Does this idiot actually think I've fainted.* "Mrs. Straynge? Mrs. Straynge! are! you? still? there!" She nods emphatically. "Two of my best officers should be dropping by any minute now. But don't let anyone in without requesting proper identification. We've been getting lots of reports recently in your neck o' the woods about thieves and rapists and worse securing home entry by using the oldest trick in the book: impersonation of a cop. Oh, and, before I forget, the crime scene seems to have been staged to suggest suicide. Your husband's left hand was on his chest, which isn't all that unusual. Thing is, it was shielding a gun—a .40-caliber Glock to be exact." She's still speaking in volumes. "Any leads?" Why, only this morning the expression was used with conviction in an HBO docudrama and she doesn't want to end up indicted for letting it go to waste. "Let's just say we're making some headway. But absolutely no progress." "Headway but no progress. Still, that's something, Inspector Von Kleist." Before she can stop herself, Margo mutters, "No problem," an all-purpose she particularly detests or thinks she should, then slams down the phone in shame. "What I can't figure out is why that hoity-toity dame thought the *V* stands for 'Von.'" "Well, does it?" asks his wiseacre crony a few desks over. Now it's Hank's turn to speak volumes. [*Ah*, sighs the anchoritic Master enviously, *smart-ass byplay of workaholics who love their job almost as much as the camaraderie the job fosters: there's nothing like it.*]

Feeling like a jackass, however, does not prevent her from wondering why Inspector-Whatever-His-Name-Was let drop that remark about the Glock. Does he by any chance take her for one of those Glocker moms who, in online forums, glory in having loaded mags in their AR-15 and AK-47 semiautomatics, in taking potshots therewith at those pussy states that dare to set limits on what firearms if any can be kept at home, and in bragging about how their son has taught them everything they know about gun law and who, once he's managed to slaughter dozens in a movie theater or community college with an FN Herstal pistol, in homage to mild-mannered reptile John Wayne De-LaPierre, will "not respond to messages seeking comment" from major news outlets? What's more, she is not divorced nor has she been for decades out of contact with her ex- (and in any case he's not your usual highly respected private equity do-gooder who tended to be opaque as husband and father).

She immediately feels very protective of her troubled troubling troublesome boy. Maybe even *overprotective*, which has a fiercely virtuous ring to it. After all, starting here, starting now, they have only each other . . . to thank. She calls to him. No, she does a great deal better than that: she calls to him dragging in all of his given names—even improvising a few others along the way. Otherwise, he won't answer. No, she knows very well that's not it since quite frankly she couldn't care less whether he answers or not and in point of fact he always does, whatever she may have decided to call him. It's just that spouting all those names . . . gives her a much-needed sense of self-congratulatory security. But there's a catch: the spouting has to be done *querulously* or not at all. No other way will do. "Jim Jason Jordan Guglielmo Grigorevitch Finkel (Straynge), you come right down here right this instant! Why must you make things so difficult for both of us? How can you let all those names get in the way of everything I've been trying to do for you? Jim Jordan Jason, you tell me right this instant exactly when the school bus is scheduled to pick you up for the memorial barbecue tomorrow." (Margo knows without knowing she knows that too much unnecessary expository baggage has been packed into the battered trunk of the final sentence [after all, JJJ aka J³ knows why—i.e., *for what event*—he is being picked up]; and for whose benefit is all this packing? she wonders—who constitutes its target audience?) Yet for all the at-wit's-end hand-wringing stage business (*Querulousness! thy name is woman*), she manages to ease herself into a tone of soufflé-light mockery— and on her very first try, ladies and gents!—the tone particular to a mother who, while the first to seem to admit she's left lots to be desired on the rearing front, knows nevertheless that none more than she has earned the right to ogle her too-glaring defects from just the right self-curative angle. And from there it's just a hop, a skip and a jump to feeling deliciously victimized for having to tongue-twist her way through that accursed string of names, which now sounds (compliments of the casuistry caked into her fake-exasperation) like his very own invention. So exasperation turns out to be inexpertly masking self-congratulation. Her seemingly grudging concession to calling him by his too many names includes both a fake disparagement (which costs her nothing) of the very pretensions with which she herself has saddled him and a warning (which isn't fake) that he's not upholding the honor of those names (pretentious no longer). She almost neglects to mention that there's a picnic lunch waiting for him in the fridge (for she doesn't trust the much-subpoenaed and -fined Sutton Square Barbecue Committee, memorial or not, to provide him with all, or even some, of the essential nutrients).

So—or rather, on the other hand—all these names are nothing less than the dark emanations of a prince's—a godhead's—not an asteroid's—vainglory. And as one of his subjects she has no choice but to do the bidding of those names by getting them right and in the right order, for if she omits even one she'll destroy the whole world (at least that's what Joseph Gikatila, her catechism teacher, albeit in a slightly different context, was always drumming into her holy communion-slaphappy head). But getting the names right, so she's discovering, also means uttering them in such a way as to convey—to the person for whom she's predictably packed what she doesn't realize is too big a picnic lunch, to be followed by (depending on his reaction) thousands, maybe millions more—that the unwarranted complexity of their intermixture is simply too much for simple souls like her—a noxious impediment to the exercise of their semi-divine right to get through the day unstabbed by greatness. Why, the whole business is beginning to resemble something out of *Numbers Rabbah:* it's as if every name has seventy faces and every letter of every name seventy faces as well and that's just for starters, not to mention that these are names to which no letters may be added and from which none may be taken away. But most important, in doing these headstands, Margo becomes aware, even if it's through a glass very very darkly, that she's applying, and applying adroitly (and with an economy even Ibsen—Sr.'s favorite playwright by the way—might have envied), no less than *the* principle underlying the construction of the mightiest earthworks. Whose formulation goes something like this: In order for what's most vital to the main design (treating a prince's vainglory with the paralyzing awe it deserves) to get past the audience's first line of defense, it must first be undergone—and not just by billions of picnic-lunch guys—as the biggest and most irrelevant obstructions to the realization of that design.

But while she must bow and bow deeply to all those emanations (the secret world of the little names-bearer's godhead is—like all worlds worth a damn—a world of language), her bow remains—like everything else in Margo's life—complicated. On the one hand, it emphasizes that if he's had the audacity to weave himself a living text of names in which to disappear when the spirit moves, that is, warns him, he must prove himself worthy of so protective an adornment. On the other, the bow is man-of-the-world enough to see his point, and a point well taken to be sure, to wit, that the assumption of so many names is to be considered not an indulgence but a strategy for achieving an impregnable uniqueness: He's chosen to call himself Jim Jason to distinguish himself from all the too many other Jims, and Jim Jason Jordan to distinguish himself from all the too many other Jim Jasons, etc. And so Jim lives in the vain hope that with enough names under his wampum belt—the belt woven through their auspices—he'll fulfill his goal even if the desiderated one-of-a-kind-ness will also make him considerably more vulnerable to identity theft.

So even if he's diluted his credibility among those in the neighborhood who know a names dandy when they see one, especially one who's forever trying to impress the neighborhood ingénues at cocktail and block parties with all the equipment under his belt—even if his credibility couldn't be lower, still, the Professor of Socioeconomics three mini-mansions down, one Thor Sten V. Blen (obviously no slouch himself when it comes to garb dandiacal and no relation to Hank V. Kleist), has noted in extenuation (he's a Jr. fan, no denying it!) at those parties where his twin daughters by the way cut a ravishing fixture (I mean, *figure*) that every article on the market—especially names—especially wampum belts—is made up of use and waste in varying proportions and that in any such article appearing at first to serve for ostentation only, it is still possible to detect the presence of some useful purpose, however anemic. Much to Margo's delight, even if all this sounds like a dressed-up—a dandiacal—rehash of things she's already heard or read about though she'd be hard-pressed to say exactly where or when. For hasn't she detected that very purpose in the ostentatious appropriation, as his own, of the names she keeps on forcefeeding him? "You're spoiling that kid rotten," was—is—her husband's regular refrain in this regard. "Why, a day doesn't go by without his flouting some newfangled moniker. Why, when I was his age—" "Flaunting." "What?" "*Flaunting* not *flouting*. And they're not monikers. They're bona fide appellatives and he's earned every single one—the hard way, I might add." "Bona fide what?" "Appellatives—names to you, bub." At which Straynge rolls the eyes of his soul. He tries to play the philistine since it's a manly—the manliest—of roles. "And you might as well resign yourself to the fact that our boy is as a book where men may read strange matters, and said book is a fabric of those very appellatives." No response. "My cataclysm—I mean catechism— teacher told me to keep an eye out for such omens." (She's tempted to add, "So, there, smarty-pants," but wisely refrains.) "You mean that Gikatila character who presided at our wedding and will no doubt preside over our divorce-and-entombment combo?" Such conversations marked the start of the disintegration of their marriage. Learning that his son is a wunderkind has been too much for Jim to handle. But can you name anybody who is doomed to play a more useful purpose in a time of crisis than Jim, Jr.?—*and she's not just saying that because he's her son.* Remembering all this, how can Margo—she's a mother, after all—not perfuse her concessionary naming with a poignant forbearance?

But Jr. hasn't responded to Margo's call, let alone these musings, which to her ears sound even louder. No wonder she begins to feel wretched. But in replaying them, she realizes they must be the spawn of a voice starkly other than her own, and that their weird concoction has been dumped in her lucubratory (*do not de-stet, dear copy editor, on pain of death*) lap without prior consent. All this business about namings and blamings has absolutely nothing to do with her predicament, whose plot has the right to go its own unmerry way unhampered. Some nut (who but Mabuse? the same fiend who's been poisoning her shitlings'—siblings'!—tribal mind) has simply succeeded in infecting her brain cells (Margo was a Bio major at John Webster Tech and is Duchess of Biology still!) with the plague of his ideology—the flag of his disposition—by splicing its entire genome, junk bonds and all, into their naïve chromosomes. Or rather, He must have stumbled during one of His interminable nature walks on a bit of viral roadkill, gutted it of whatever genes would be antipathetic to his foul objective and replaced them with the genes on his own genome coding for the *thought packets* (the term's a bit fanciful but what else can she call these little monsters?) that are most tainted by said ideology. So armed, He's hijacked her story the way she's hijacked Jr.'s, and has become her voice box as she's become Jr.'s. Based on heart rate, skin conductance, pulse, etc., the redesign of the neuronal circuits on whose activation the articulation of the nut's smutty thoughts depend must be just about complete. So, with all the behind-the-scenes sabotage, is it any wonder that she's been neglecting her troubled son? At the same time she *can't help* feeling that buried under all this misconstruction to which she's too generously lent her premises, there have to be at least *some* proteins just aching to rear their pretty heads, defy the Master and his encoder goons and do what they know they were put on earth to do, namely, enable the generation of thoughts whose sole purpose is to give long-overdue credibility to her plight which now includes widowhood—that is, if the Inspector is to be believed. A plight whose allegretto maestoso direness can be conveyed only by, say, the tenor aria ("Cujus animam gementem") from the Rossini *Stabat Mater*, an old fireside family favorite.

Straynge did say a similar delusional bug was making the rounds at Amygdala. *Might be transmitted by Invidicum in the suboptimal dose he lobbied against from the start*, Jim grumbled, but she didn't pay him any heed (remember their marriage has been disintegrating). Of course she could have caught the Master bug from her husband. And she wouldn't put it past him to infect her out of spite especially in the midst of this names game which has been spiraling out of control for what seems like decades. OK, she may be infected but she's not the least bit delusional. And if it turns out she is, then her son will surely step up to the plate and cure her—he's duty bound to rule the bloody earth one day.

Thus, it is now clear to the point of transparency that her story—her ads-free sorrows—exist in the main merely to showcase his commodities and embed their brands and furthermore is expected, starting here, starting now, to slue and skew itself (to the point of unrecognizability, if need be) toward plausibilizing those branded products as indispensable plot-twisters and -turners (hey, isn't this precisely what industrial psychologists call *branded narrativity*?). Though maybe the cockles of her Big Other's avant-garde heart are most warmed by the insertions that are least plausible. In any event, that perennial cable favorite known as the *Margo Straynge Show* whose every rerun proves to be an instant YouTube classic—why she's right up there with My Little Margie, Lucy, Joan and Riley—has suddenly been packet-branded, ideology-co-opted, beyond recognition.

Clearly, Big Other Mabuse doesn't have much faith in her story—or is it in stories in general? Right you are, ma'am. BO's allegiance is pledged, instead, to a warped ideology, according to which commodities (in this case, thought packets) are infinitely more important than the mass entertainments (in this case, a technothriller whose accessories, for starters, include murder, truancy, drug addiction, mental illness, corporate wrongdoing, Balanchine ballets, vampirism and metamathematical conceits) that they reluctantly deign to brand. *For thought packets alone have the stamp of personal uniqueness—of—of—of* . . . *haecceity.* (And to whom, you may ask, does this last thought belong? It's certainly not hers for she is, at best, just a strapping dumb blonde all too peacock tail-proud of her down-home pedigree to give a hoot about a guy like—well, if you must know—like Duns Scotus.) Mabuse wants her to know that (as if she doesn't have enough on her plate) more exciting than every other story is the story of why he can't tell a story-like-every-other-story. Sort of like Mrs. de Cambremer-Legrandin, her neighbor with the insufferably fake name, who considers the "periods" of any artist she deigns to admire to be a mere footnote to her own evolution as *the* expert on those periods. And who knows? with so much de-making of makers by non-, maybe she's right. Or maybe it's not Mabuse who wants her to know this—and a host of other things. Maybe it's the Some Body who's put Mabuse on her map and on the maps of everybody else, including the siblings who loathe her. But a Some Body, *this time around*, with no pretense of being—or craving to be—Mabuse's or anybody else's boss.

The next morning, while preparing to swap the wilds of Westchester for those of Manhattan, she's overcome with impatience to gorge herself on all the little bonbons of freedom being offered her by Fate. Before it's too late. She'd like to feel she envies every woman everywhere who's woken up a non-widow but let's just say that whatever she does happen to feel in this regard would immediately disqualify her for participation in the Invidicum program. Is this Fate's reward for playing so faithfully the hand It dealt her? She might sell the house, for example, and buy an apartment in the city but could she afford the sort of *condominium residence* that's always being advertised, in a nauseatingly portentous British accent, in the pages of the *Times*? She could buy herself one of those boxes at the Opera she's always gawking at from her seat in the bleachers (fringe/cringe benefit of cohabitation with a career low-man-on-the-scrotum-pole), whose smug-mug occupants make her feel like Saint Joan Wilkes Booth. Plenty of time for the niceties and rigors of fake indecision. First she's got to claim the body. Whose lack of warmth, by the way, she doesn't in the least miss. Should she take her son along? Better not. What if he was to develop post-traumatic stress disorder? She's simply not in the *frame of mind* to start looking for doc shops that lifetime-guarantee a relapse-averse cure through virtual simulation of the culprit event. But what frame of mind is that? she wonders. Or rather, it's Mabuse or the Somebody who put Mabuse on her map or some other Big Other or all three that ("respectful of her deep tragic loss") may be doing the wondering for—through—her. She's simply the theater of a wonderment that's not worthy of her signature willingness to do anything—especially anything beyond reason—for her boy. (It's a Leda-and-the-Swan—or rather a Leda-and-the-Three-Swans—sort of thing.) In any case, how can she face other people, honorary members all (thanks to Mabuse's campaigning) of her siblings' extended family? As she prepares herself, Cantor and Eden are already (attesting to a masterly manipulation of cross-cutting by the editor of the film all three inhabit, namely, *Invidicum: A Love Story*) en route to Santa Barbara by way, so they've been told, of San Diego. Martin got the number and time of the flight all wrong, which entailed a complete overhaul of travel plans for the whole tribe. Yes, every member was present! Too many familiar faces for their—not to mention the enterprise's—own good! After all, he and Cantor were made to understand this would be a very select affair, involving just the two of them, soldiers of misfortune whose troth was plighted till death did them part. Maybe they're just window-dressing, as Cantor suggests in a whisper. But all's well that ends well—or all's well that ends, period—and as it turns out, the other tribesfolk have found themselves routed to a different plane. As if to confuse what, in the lingo of real soldiers *of fortune*, are known as *latent pursuers*.

The first thing out of the mouth of the Postman who's Labrador-retrieved him from a stall in the men's room opposite Gate 45 is "you're forgiven of course but first off you've got to forgive yourself," which, to a California native once removed, smacks of Surfboard Psych 101. Getting on the plane, Martin feels wretched (he's already forgotten the second thing out of the Labrador's mouth). He misses Linda's pussy musk (imagine, the first time he insisted on cunnilingus, she, of all people, shied away) and Manning's duplicity, which had—has—a muskiness—and, willy-nilly, an artlessness—all its own. But most of all he misses the unspent kiss. Cantor, on the other hand, boards messenger-bagging the sort of infinite hope—the temporary insanity—the temporary inanity—known as hope—he forgot he could feel, having last harbored it while refusing to make up his mind whether falling in like or even in lust with *this Berry Sundae character* would be good, or at least not bad, for both his Life and his Life's Work which, as an unapologetic fan of operatic self-pity, he pronounces, when the spirit moves him, to be One and the Same. But he knows hope, infinite or otherwise, can't last. Even if to think is to hope. *Since it can't help falling in love with its own obliteration* (is this truism true? well, the wordflows says it is and that's good enough for Cantor—or at least for Cantor in the guise of Passenger). Only this time, as so many times before, he's way ahead of it, deflating it, beating it to the punchline—even if hope's not the thing with feathers but the supreme example of—to misapply Marie Windsor's phrase in *The Killing*—a bad joke without a punchline. The Marie Windsor business has to be the work of that Master—Beast—Big Other— everybody's talking about more and more and whose ranks he still postpones joining. He's never heard of her before this minute, at least he doesn't think he has. Not that he's incapable of shouldering any excess cultural baggage the Maestro decides to shunt his way (he's Charles Foster Cantor, after all). It's the others—people like Eden—he's worried about. How can they assimilate all this crumbly froufrou without going under?

The only way that, on Air Force One, empyrean-phobic Melanctha Herbert (seated next to Jean Rhys who incomprehensibly insisted on the middle seat) can mitigate, as she waits for her three Seroquel tablets to take effect, the urgency of a newfound need to be always gathering material (so as to smother through overwork her bad-motherly guilt over having survived No. 18?) is to remind herself tactfully that she isn't California-bound to put together a travelogue for *Vanity Fair*. She is here not as a budding writer but, in good faith, as a patient. Nobody expects her to milk the landscape for all it's worth—and nobody would give her a standing ovation if she managed to come through the milking with flying colors. And, by the way, wouldn't too much creative fulfillment, however amateurish, mask her native Envy, which needs to be as rawly detectable as possible if she's to be cured even if it's not for good? *Keep your Envy powder dry*, that's the slogan plastered all over the ladies' room in invisible ink. Why, one morning she found it scrawled with lipstick on the mirror as well. Rhys and Borkman (who's across the aisle) are both out cold (it's been a long wait) but—just as every snowflake resists extinction in its own way—they're out cold stark-differently. Borkman is thrashing his way through a difficult dreamscape riddled, from all indications, with raptures unspeakable. Hardly the sleep of the just—no, not by a long shot. That grayest of eminences, Narr, is directly behind Herbert's seatmate, *apparently* to ensure by his grayest of presences that her sleeping style does not violate trial protocol. But in seeing this—or thinking the seeing—Herbert has the oddest feeling. As if her respectful hesitation—the hesitation signaled by "apparently"— has been generated to mask someBody's—or someThing's—too intimidating omniscience or peremptoriness or omniscience-as-peremptoriness—in a word, Big Mastery (Big as in Big Data). That's it: the Thing is a Master! and the Master is the Thing (she's sure of it) that has, ever since she started taking Invidicum, been crowding out her thoughts (before they even knew they were thoughts) in favor of His own. Never has Herbert felt so strongly that there's no turning back from the fact that such a Master exists. And never has Herbert let herself in for such a big surprise: she assumed the question of His existence was settled centuries ago—on the D train, to be exact, when in fact her wrestling match with His shadow's substance never stopped playing out right under her nose—until this moment. Only she hopes that whoever's dangling His strings or pulling His dick (*now where did that come from? I'm not supposed to know I know such language!*) isn't expecting her, and on such short notice, to formulate a coherent—a Unified Field Theory of the Master so as to stop Him dead in His tracks. Why, she's not even a teaching assistant. For starters though, what about taking him for a byproduct—a side effect—of either the trial or the drug that's being trialed? Subject for further research, she tells herself.

So It's back in action, immune to or undeterred by skysickness. Clearly, the California sunshine has already begun to agree with It even if they're somewhere only a bit west of Cleveland Heights. This time (as so many times before?) said Master has taken it upon Himself to shuffle the immortal coil of His too burdensome omniscience off onto, of all people, her, the token . . . creative writer of the tribe. But this time He's met his match. The bruteness—hence the inartisticness—of His portrayal of the motive for Narr's sitting behind Rhys has been masked—softened—naturalized—and what better way than through her uncertainty over that motive? She is one of His . . . proxies—all right, one of his Slaves. She is doing the dirty work, i.e., giving yet another one of His directives ("Let Narr be sitting behind Jean and acting as a patrol car . . .") a soul—a soul embodied in a single word. Yes, *apparently*.

But maybe this is more than an artistic strategy. Maybe her Thing genuinely seeks to commune with His slaves. Maybe Thing is a lonely old thing— tortured by His mastery, which comes down to nothing more than being condemned to compel them to do His bidding with no show of resistance. But what is it worth precisely to a Master to be recognized as all-knowing by a slave? Is mastery, then, not all it's cracked up to be—is it a dead end, an impasse, a nowhere-to-go-but-way-way-down? Can he really want his masterly deMastering of the unlosable art of storytelling to be applauded by slaves? A Master, after all, valorizes the recognition only of another Master even if any Master worth His name would prefer to die rather than cough up such recognition. Though how can she be expected to answer for the Master?

At this very moment she can feel Him breathing down her neck well into the small of her back, doing what feels inexplicably like Envying like Crazy her restricted vantage, her partial perspective, her powerlessness to decree what reality must be and what its dizzy denizens must do if His . . . clients are to get their money's worth. For if there are two accessories the well-dressed master *simply must have* if he's to be voted king of the runway by acclamation, it's slaves and clients. From the way his breath skims over her buttocks, which haven't been manhandled for decades, Herbert can tell (or is it the wordflow telling her?) that He finds something cozy, chaste, winsome, stoic, deliciously life-denying—in other words, something *artistically satisfying*—about her finiteness. For if omniscience, like beauty, is a privilege, then it's also a burden. (Tell me though: Is this truism true? Well, the wordflow says it's true but that's not enough for Herbert who, while *honing her craft* [why does this phrase disgust her?], is at the same time homeschooling herself to be wary of crafty wordflow.) Albeit low on the totem pole even of novices, all at once she knows that He knows the only way to render Narr, e.g., real to His clients is by abdicating His own all-seeing in favor of a limited point of view (POV), namely, that of another one of His slaves, and seeing to it that said Slave's—I mean, slave's—seeing is a highly uncertain seeing—a fluid *as if* seeing. No self-respecting clientologist—not even one without an iota of self-respect to his name—will buy any of the motives advanced for Narr's sitting behind Rhys if they come direct from the Master. Under those circumstances, Narr, motives and all, will simply lose the precious if overrated opportunity to exist. If a slave is to exist, its existing has to be perceived (but speculatively, incompletely) by another slave. (Slowly but surely, she's infecting Him with the notion that she's beginning to know Him better than He knows Himself: queenship of the harem, that's what she's bucking for.) He can't just go ahead and plop Narr down behind Rhys and expect his clients—tough customers each and every—to hew to the party line, i.e., that Narr himself did the plopping to keep her outrageousness in check. To ring true, Narr's doings have to be decipherable, but only partially, uncertainly, tentatively (this being the sole guarantee of Narr's client-centered realness!), by one of his own kind tethered to her own POV. It's the partial (or mis-) perception of the plopping that flesh-and-bloods the plopper. Narr's plopping is a sign to be interpreted by somebody like Herbert, with her interpretation itself becoming a sign for the interpretants to come.

But, his application of a veneer of authenticity to the proceedings notwithstanding, hasn't the Master—*their* Master—created a situation where no slave is allowed/allows himself to make a move unless it's certain that another creature will perceive that move? Clearly this is all about moving from perception to perception. Clearly, *she's* suddenly all about moving from perception to perception—about an appetite *for* moving from perception to perception—but never fully realizing the whole perception toward which she's moving. Through what feels like the operation of an internal principle, which is all that's left of her, compliments of the Master. What is it the Leipzigers of yore were fond of saying? *Fully realized perceptions are all alike but each unrealized perception is unrealized in its own way?* Well, that must delight his clientele no end. Their perceptions, after all, like their dreams are fully unrealized (or why else would they be his clients?) and now their misery has plenty of company. She's feeling more and more disembodied by the minute (the price for being head of the harem). She's never felt more like His captive. Is she bipolar? At this moment she needs to be bipolar, like the heroine of *Homeland*, her favorite TV show. Although she's convinced that a black actress would have been far more right for the role. She needs to be bipolar so she can *become* the heroine of *Homeland*, who's the very opposite of disembodied. She's already tired of being the Master's favorite child—star. She needs to throw a wrench in the works of her competence before it gets out of hand. Bipolarity will be both an atonement for competence and the pathway to hyper-competence. A real pharmakon. Although it could just be the altitude mixed up with the fetor of lunch being slapped together in the hold. Before she can decide, the surgeon-stewards are speaking in tongs. The hot towel reminds her that at least she has hands and a face.

The Master, after all, doesn't have the blood of a Club Med social director running in his veins. He's more of a swarm-of-perceptions machine kind of guy. He's done and still doing everything in His power to ensure that she and the other slaves don't mingle *palpably*—that they're left with nothing palpable to mingle palpably *with*. When He gets done with them, they won't be able to affect each other in the least, only to perceive, with somebody turning out to be more perfect than somebody else when she finds a reason for what's happening or failing to happen in him. As is the case for more-perfect she and altogether less-perfect Narr. But her perception of Narr isn't even her own. Massa's just too impatient by nature (although strictly speaking there's nothing natural about the guy) not to rush His star-turns by plastering any assignable perception on the first comer, no matter how incompatible with—how un-right for—that comer's character. Better—best, in fact—if he isn't right for it—better if he's woefully, extravagantly unright. For by virtue of being unright, the comer fades into the shadows so that the perception, immeasurably enriched by its brief encounter with not-rightness, can take full possession of the stage. But she can't believe what she's hearing even if the towel's dulled her senses: The Master's transmitting the very thoughts that can blow his cover and, adding insult to injury, they've been signed, sealed and delivered with an eloquence she assumed to be attainable not before late middle age. But the thoughts are *all they say*: they caulk all the holes in His own character and suture world-inflicted wounds. They're *in some inexplicable way* (a phrase that's the last refuge of scoundrels) a deathblow perpetrated against life from deep within the bloodied gut of life. For the only thing more beautiful than a beautiful strategy is the gory anatomization of a beautiful strategy.

His favorite pupil suspects—though she'll never let on, not even to Rhys in what promises to be her non-stop insensateness—that He's beginning to hunger, however desperately, however self-destructively, to find out just what kinds of thought acts his slaves, when challenged by a sort of Diaghilevian "*étonne-moi*," can manage in his absence to cook up all by themselves. She's sure He believes somewhere not so deep down that they have the capacity

370

to be more than slaves of their misperceptions and of their thoughts about those misperceptions—much much more. And he must Envy them their fear of exploiting that capacity because a Master is not plagued by fear. And who knows? the Master, egged on by the turbulences of the stratosphere, may be just about to give them their big-break opportunity to throw off the yoke of his pre-established disharmony and get to know each other as more than mere mirrorings—disparate to the point of . . . indistinguishability—of the same old universe, which (*pace* Leibniz or, in Amygdalese, *Liepnits*) has no existence beyond those mirrorings. For he's the first to admit (*who is speaking?*) that the best thoughts are the ones born of resistance to a Master's—that the only way His thoughts can become even the least bit real is through resisting, in vain of course, the resistance of those forced to express them. He's even taking time out from his busy schedule to invest her with a hunch that, even if their emancipation ultimately destroys Him, he wants to be in at the kill.

Still she feels that even by having such thoughts she's letting the Master down and that if left to her own devices, as those very thoughts are suggesting she should be, she'll never succeed. And, more to the point, if Charles Sanders Peirce (albeit the greatest American philosopher according to her second favorite prof at Hunter) still mustered the humility to threaten to bear "a cross like death for [*his*] master's sake" and if Emily Dickinson (albeit the greatest American poet according to her third favorite) felt inadequate enough to pen not one but three letters to *her* Master, where she not only expressed a willingness to die for him as fast she could and described being separated from him as having a tomahawk in her side but also implored him to take her where sundown couldn't find them—if that's all true and it is, then who is she, Melanctha Herbert from the Bronx, to kick against the pricks? Oh, why did she ever agree to come to California, when she's even more misinformed about the waters than Humphrey Bogart's Rick in *Casablanca*? (unlike Cantor she's seen it—many times—and through a cataract of misgivings). [And she's finally managed to forgive him (Rick/Humphrey not Cantor)—sort of—for the cringe-inducing mock-Masterliness that poisons his relationship with Dooley Wilson's Sam, although it seems to be cherished by everybody regardless of rage, color or creed except her.] Maybe it's the foretaste of the sea air but her relation to the Master is becoming more unmanageable than ever—one big Unanswered Question. (Come to think of it, didn't Shearer claim, but not at all in a hoity-toity way, that a dance with that very title was created to showcase her talents by *her* Master?) So what if the long and the short of it is that she can get to be great only by dismembering herself on the altar of the Master? Didn't one of the greater than greats say self-dismemberment, if hygienically performed, is the only highroad to greatness worth taking? But if she can get to greatness only by taking the already great at their word, then she wants no part of greatness, not even greater-than-greatness. At least for the duration of this eerily unbumpy ride.

CHAPTER TWENTY

Just before Berry died, he and Cantor made a pact to, in so many unspoken words, nourish the fiction that there'd be no getting through any given year without impregnating the Pacific. It came to nothing. High above San Diego, the landscape is "strangely familiar" (already in rebellion against having been hijacked as backdrop for a mere mission)—confronting Cantor with just the sort of fissures, clayey crevices and humps he'd prefer not to see so nakedly come into focus, especially on an empty stomach—and more especially while committing to paper some very important theorem-related thoughts—so important he can't bear to plague their emergence with the demon of legibility. The illegible curve of the waves below is the curve of his thought: the slight hesitation before they collapse is the pause of a master orator. Yet for all the XXX-rated doings, the remains of the day hold out an infinite promise.[25] Too bad the organ of hope is no longer capable of achieving full erection—throwing in a few droplets of pre-cum for good measure—and that there's no Viagra to match wits with so widespread a condition.

Exiting the plane, the first thing to catch Cantor's eye is the obligatory wheelchair at the end of the passage—as vivid as a Dedekind cut, as irrefutable as one of Peano's axioms. Yes, *Cantor is a mathematician and—worse—thinks like one and—worst—can't stop needing to think he thinks like one.*

Outside the baggage terminal, Cantor (he and Eden have finally retrieved their luggage after being misdirected—lured?—to the wrong carousel) is surprised to see the other guinea pigs *in such fine fettle.* But, Cantor wonders, does he really perceive them as such? Maybe he's been around the others too much (how avoid it?) but he could swear the phrase has been plastered on him simply because he's the most convenient billboard of the moment. But by whom? By the medication masquerading as (what's his name?) Mabuse who's supposed to be terrorizing the tribe? No, he believes—must believe—in more personalized persecution tailored to the unavowable needs of the sufferer. So—might as well come clean and admit that in his case, no matter how insane it sounds—the plasterer is none other than the scourge-of-psyche (SoP) who began hounding him back in New York on day one of the trial—not only completing every thought long before it was a speck in his mind's eye but, far worse, saddling him with specimens of which he could be regarded by anybody who claimed to know him only as the least likely exponent. And whose meddling has increased exponentially since the murder. (Is the creakily melodramatic and mathematically fuzzy *exponentially* yet another one

---

[25] The western sky is pink—he never knew pink could be so passionate—so he tries to see yellow. But pink it is, and always will be, as long as dusk lasts. Dusk is, in fact, exquisite but by deeming it so Cantor renders a disservice to troubadours everywhere—eating up the space dusk needs to flex its wings and earn the epithet fair and square. And having once succeeded, the last thing in the world dusk will want to be called is exquisite.

of SoP's plasterings?). If he doesn't watch out he'll be swallowed up in SoP's wordflow. So until further notice the Master and SoP are rivals, busy being busy staking out the same mental terrain and going about it as floppily as sea lions, say, munching on their own reflections in the pool of the Central Park Zoo.

Why can't I go back to calling the Master Master? Cantor thinks. Why can I deal with His thinking only by regressing to a larval state of uncertainty—shilly-shallying—mugwumpery—where the Master's name—his very existence—is concerned? You mean to tell me that after all this time I still havn't made peace with the title so richly deserved? Why revert to *Mabuse* or *SoP*? Under attack (by Cantor) Cantor thinks, I can only speak for myself, but it smells as if we'll never master the Master—we're too busy *remastering* Him—as if he were the archival wreck of some early talkie masterpiece like— well, like, *Das Testament des Doktor Mabuse*. We're always back to square one whenever He shows up uninvited (or are we just refusing to admit to our own invocation, at the drop of a hat, of this water rat?). Always uncertain—or pretending to be uncertain—whether He exists or not or if He does exist, whether another name wouldn't smell as sweet. Or maybe it all boils down to the fact that we don't want to be seen as taking our marching orders from the same drill sergeant, which robs each of us of our uniqueness—or at least of uniqueness as it's commonly understood among our kind.

Cantor remembers (how can he forget? *he*, with his vested interest in eloquence as the end to a means) that already much-alluded-to (see above) something in Invidicum which, when administered at the right dosage, can induce the same "depth of thought" and "level of expressiveness" in everybody, no questions asked, thereby controlling for the distortive impact of these messy variables on Envy in its pure state. Maybe too much of either can only exacerbate Envy, making it feel, and present as—through the sheer power of thought- and wordflow—more intense than it is. Or maybe it's too little of both that's the Envy intensifier (OK, less interesting because predictable; but so what if it's less interesting? does that merit disqualification for recruitment as a working hypothesis?). Or maybe the correlation that does exist can't be formulated *with our present knowledge*. So, let's say whatever the impacts, it's been determined that these variables must be held constant. Of course, Cantor's case—like Melanctha Herbert's, perhaps—has called for a diminution of both depth of thought and level of unbridled eloquence so as to keep things equalized. Or maybe everybody else, qua private thinker cum public speaker, has had to be upgraded to his level. (Clearly, Cantor is getting carried away. Officially betrothed all of a sudden to his own delusion of grandeur, he whispers, "Leave me: I want to be alone," like Chaplin's Hynkel just before he bounces the globe on his cute little butt. Only unlike Chaplin he has nobody to whisper to—nobody cares.) So, given the stakes, maybe there is a Mabuse—a real flesh-and-blooder, not some disembodied voice of Radio Free Europe who poisons the wells of their all-American credulity every chance He—I mean, he—gets. Because maybe, just maybe, that much-alluded-to something is a bucking bronco in need of reining in by a rodeo cavalier: call him Ishmael Mabuse. And maybe that Pritchard character up in Santa

Barbara, or the mother of the racist punk who runs the bakery across from Amygdala or Walser or Stifter or Tom Post's Dutch uncle, will turn out to be Mabuse. And, while we're at it, who but Manning could take on the role of Lady Mabuse?

Didn't Fritz Lang make three films featuring *his* Doctor Mabuse? (As the eternal sophomore, George— George? Yes, *George*, for that's Cantor's name, or rather that's the nom de plume, the stage name, the code name [being the closest thing to *Georg*], that the Master in his infinite mercy has decided to visit upon him. For how much longer could He, without emitting a belch or two of encouragement worthy at the very least of a Sancho Panza, be expected to watch Cantor, brand new as he is to these idiot-savant-unfriendly Pacific shores, struggle to navigate a juncture so big with transition and in the only (altogether misbegotten way) he knows how, i.e., by convincing himself he's a re-embodiment of none other than Curiously Gorgeous and Gorgeously Curious George [né Georg] *Cantor*?— As the eternal sophomore, George, without being invited, decided [pursuant to knight-aberrant subjection to the Quixotics of film theory, just then coming into its vainglorious own] to become a major filmmaker and almost strung himself up upon realizing—all by his lonesome, mind you, without any help from assorted rivals or mentors—that he had less than no talent. A neoclassic case, his, of All Text and No Lights-Camera-Action!) Hey, and didn't that guy Noël Burch—something of a maverick whose shrewd theorizing always hewed close to the concrete and was blessedly allergic to the avant lingo of psychoterrorists like Jack the Derider at their inflationary worst—didn't Burch regard the middle film, *Das Testament des Doktor Mabuse*, as both the most important of the trio and one of the radical masterworks of the Golden Age spanning 1927–32? So he'd better take a look at the Testament, if only on behalf of saving his sanity by toying with whatever's left of Mabuse's. Surely, wherever they're being shipped off to must have a Video Room where he can pick up a DVD (even if the staff's not as savvy and the collection not as comprehensive as the one on Third Avenue at Seventy-Ninth). Eden grunts. He doesn't buy the idea that the others are window-dressing. Weren't he and Cantor, whatever he may think of him, made to understand that they and they alone had passed all the auditions and were in consequence to be the sole participants in this, the final stage? Or maybe this stage is the trial's own audition for the final stage. Which is still fine with Eden. It's bad enough having Cantor snatch half his laurels but here are all the others by their mere presence on the scene staking a claim as well. To be fair, they don't really look as if they're trying to hog the spotlight. Quite the opposite. Everybody cringes as if he can't figure out who any of the others are, having never laid eyes on them before. And maybe everybody hasn't ever laid eyes on everybody else before—at least not in so merciless a light—a light that only airports know how to shed.

The serpent-sleek black-and-blue minivan—so state-of-the-art it oozes sensorly charm from every pore—drops them off in what Bill Cook (sitting beside the driver) informs them is—which Eden of course knows—Coronado. The beach is obliterated by deep fog. A jogger who has been fancily outrunning his panting dog Friday by a wide margin finally takes pity and makes an even more virtuosic show of backtracking. Talk about the *telling detail*, Herbert thinks, unabetted by the Master. But why this detail? Herbert wonders, almost out loud, for she isn't quite sure if she's awake or, now that she's out of the stifling vehicle, only just beginning to dream. Why this detail, when there are millions of others that would have been more suitable as first stabs at scene setting, that dying art? But how much more suitable and why? She has yet to learn what her mentor has been trying to drum into her head evidently in vain, namely, that the missed plenitude of which every puny detail with the decency to show up becomes the sign—the thankless placeholder—is an illusion made possible through the too-charitable auspices of its very puniness.

Frankly, she wants to get all *possible* details over with and out of the way as soon as possible—to dispose of the local color in one fell swoop so that she can look forward to something . . . unforeseeable. So she can concentrate on—what, exactly? Proving herself eminently worthy of basking in the Santa Barbara sunshine (how can she, when her son's dead and she's incorrigibly alive and kicking)? Making sure to dose herself on time despite the disorienting stench of kelp? She doesn't want to be distracted—but from what exactly? Well, for starters, from all the things she's read about in the guidebooks purchased reluctantly, shamefacedly. Things like the mad hornets'-nest vociferations of club-footed lollipop palms oddly inaudible under the blazing interdict of high noon. She's inherited her son's impatience. But was he in fact impatient or is this on-the-spot invention just another sop to some spectator Cerberus (such a spectator as the backtracker on the foggy beach seemed to be craving or else why all the mugging?) provided free of charge and without her permission by the Master? For (*pace* his wannabe-poignant intimations in the previous reel) He's nowhere near ready for a swan song and has no intention of losing his storylovin' clients without a firefight and, as everybody knows, you're well on your way to sewing things up once you get the hang of throwing out a revelation or two just when they think you think you've lost 'em for good. Was the boy impatient by nature? It frankly doesn't matter: He is now—the moment demands it. And if he's patient enough, he may even be so tomorrow and tomorrow and tomorrow.

All of a sudden, Shearer doesn't know what she's doing here—not *here in Coronado*, for she instantaneously adores the place and once upon a time she even played San Diego (where her three dying falls in the second movement of *Symphony in C* were enough to make her the toast of the Gaslamp Quarter)—but *here in the trial's next phase*. Maybe it's the absence of sun where there should be sun at all times even in the middle of the night, or the chilling whiff of the unimpeded ocean, but it suddenly comes to her, as in a vision straight out of *The Sleeping Beauty*, that—

The jogger is walking toward the van from what appears to be the foggiest part of the beach (or is *the foggiest* simply the Master in hyperlative wordflow mode?). He's good-looking but, more importantly, symmetrical from head to toe. He reminds her of—

"Moira?"

"Yes." Her fellow tribesman all turn to her, with a surprise indistinguishable from respect on their collective face.

375

"It's me, Akim. Akim Volynsky." She realized this just before he opened his mouth, still a pretty one. His wispy goatee (new) is pretty as well. But she wants him to sing for his supper. It's her revenge, but for what precisely? Well, what about for his having created, just for her, a modest little solo (to Liszt's undanceable "Au bord d'une source") for whose failure to become a concert staple—after six, or was it five, measly and very much unsold-out performances in a *space* (detestably limp use of a stout-hearted word) at Chelsea Piers—he immediately made her prima culprit assoluta. Something to do with not giving the work her all because it wasn't a Balanchine or an Ashton or a Tudor confection. A charge in which there lay some truth. But how give it her all when he never missed an opportunity (even those that didn't present themselves) to poison every rehearsal with all that blistering talk about his Arch-Rival, somewhat younger and already a risen star?

He tells Moira (gallantly shouldering the heavier of her two pieces of luggage) that he could no longer stand living in New York. Driven out by his Rival was what he was. Never thought he could settle for being a big fish in a small pond yet here he is lapping up the adoration of the students at the school he runs in La Jolla and the members of his troupe, the Coronado Ballet. Just to be clear she asks if he means *the* Rival. Looking her straight in the eye to obliterate any wiseguyish looking back will have to serve as a yes. They've been left behind by the others. No matter. She remembers the room number. For one thing, he explains warily, *A Dancer's World* magazine (named after a not-bad Graham documentary) conducted an interview with the Rival (an honor the magazine continued to withhold no matter how much Akim insisted, to anybody who'd listen, that he'd never stoop to such self-promotion), to be included in a special issue devoted exclusively to the theme "Effects of 9/11 on Your Work." She looks up at the turrets of what she's just heard one of the tribe (*Jean Rhys*?) gushingly proclaim to be none other than the Hotel del Coronado—*Some Like It Hot*'s Coronado (can't *be her: she's too sophisticated to gush*). Standing here, hard to believe in 9/11 or—a Volynsky. Entering the lobby, they find two seats in a secluded windowless alcove but not, judging from his anxious looks (straight out of the lovers' pas de deux in *Jardin aux Lilas*), as far from the madding crowd as he would like to be.

Most galling to Akim is how easily the Rival rendered silky self-promotion compatible with leaden grief. He depicted himself (Shearer vaguely remembers the interview, or at least all the online buzz, with which her wobbly cursor crossed paths more than once) as having, post-holocaust, stumbled around with his entire company (only six members but he'd made it sound like the Symphony of a Thousand) in the obligatorily bumbling state of shock, all of them (but none more soulfully than he) diligently questioning the purpose of their vocation in the wake of such carnage—but not, as it turned out, in New York but while "on the road." And he made you understand the catastrophe had life only insofar as it became a trigger for harrowing self-doubt even if you had an ignominious hunch that by the end of the interview all of it would be transcended—on behalf of the victims, of course. And, hey, what about the business of being on the road?—well, the long and the short of it was that by seeming to bemoan his unpardonable absence, however official, from the scene of the crime he was able to broadcast the fact that (could he help it if) everybody wanted him. (Absence exalts: wasn't that the case with Rhys's brother?—no, it was her brother-in-law.) Hence, unpardonability never looked so good. While here, she thinks, in contrast—in starkest contrast—is Akim (*her* convict every bit as much as Abel Magwitch was Pip's, just as shackled, just as scarred), always available at the scene of *any* crime because unwanted everywhere else. He explains that Sir Rival has *this knack* and not just in the context of 9/11 for painting over himself with the broadest brooding strokes of self-depreciation (so Akim never tired of recounting, though why did it always have to be in the midst of a rehearsal) only to emerge from the messily impasted stocks more self-anointed (unlike Kent)—more *geniused*—than ever.

No self-challenging about whether his suffering was really up to snuff— no whimsically queasy throb of postboding (it's very farfetchedness, according to Dostoievskian Akim, being its own dark beauty) that he might have helped precipitate the disaster through some self-loving remark made just beneath the future tarmac of terror—that through his thinly disguised ambition he somehow colluded with the invaders. Akim's self-hate, how can she not see, hates the invincible self-love of his Rival whose token self-doubt (self-*hate* is clearly beyond even his powers of simulation) is nothing more than self-love's filigree. Far direr than the catastrophe, then, was its salubrious ill effect on him—worse, on his career—which ill effect, peddled as ravaging concern about "whether dance had a place in the post-9/11 world," was already danceable (*who is doing the thinking? Moira? Akim? Master? Master's Master? remastered Mabuse?*).

The glamorously unresolvable contradiction in terms between dancemaking and a catastrophe of such Richter-scale magnitude was simply good, clean Rivalrous raw material—the best to have turned up in a long time. It deserved to be honored with one millisecond of silence, for what better proof was there of a supremely superior nature like the Rival's—one that by being both itself and at war with itself was consequently more, much more, than itself—hence, more than any competitor's self? So Akim's rival managed to snap up both substance and shadow. Managed not only to have his seven layers of self-flagellation but to gobble up the whole cake—not to mention the icing *on* the cake—as well. Or rather, in this case, to *dance* it in what every post-9/11 votemonger made sure to refer to as The Greatest City in the World (without disclosing the criteria on which his or her assessment was based)— the sort of congratulatory epithet that immediately becomes self-congratulatory. Yes, the Rival was—is—highly efficient—nothing is too horrific for transmogrification into the sublime stuff of dance. *Which is as it should be, no?* Moira is tempted to ask but doesn't. And in fact the Rival admitted to the gushing interviewer that, *as they spoke*, he was creating a daylong Ballet Imperial about the day of death despite his fear of profanation (to be foregrounded, of course, within the work itself as an act of supreme courage). And such was the Rival's coy advertising genius (a unitard of shameless opportunism of a piece with his own thick skin) that this mush became yet another symptom of anguish at being A Survivor. Ah, if only he, Akim, could have managed such a hucksterly pietism. She tries hard to explain—for she's had enough of his rival-bashing, at least for now—that artworks are—are expected to be—opportunistic by their very nature and if a given work is good—and though she has no firsthand information about the Rival's, she suspects quite frankly that it is—then by virtue of its very goodness it obliterates the flagrancy of its on-the-make maker. She wonders, however, if through this show of support she's being fair or merely practicing a sort of perverse self-therapy at the expense of her doppelgänger's. In any case he has no patience for what is immediately shoved back down Pollyanna's throat—quite effectively, she must admit—with enough expletives thrown in to give at least one of the drooping desk clerks a much-needed shot in the groin. For Akim (she prefers to think, *For the Akims of the world*), the only comfort is the default war cry, *Either you love his work or you hate it.* But how painful to be hearing him try his hand yet again at marketing this tired old puff pastry as the emblem of triumphant resignation—resignation to a greatness dividing the world just so both parties to the schism can end up as rivals only in . . . abasement before that very greatness!

So she has no choice but to leave Akim to face his facts alone (he'll have plenty of company in the same but different boats): self-hate (notwithstanding his shrieky insistence that it constitutes the highest-grade fertilizer for the fruity soil in his garden of Terpsichorean delights) does him no service. It surely repels not just the staff of *A Dancer's World*—the interview, he informs her, was, can you imagine? later syndicated across the globe, making its way even to his native Minsk (where she suspects he's still a long long way from being heralded as the local boy who made good)—but every other self-respecting cultist of the toe. The Rival's admissions, on the other hand, though they may smell to Akim (and to her, too) of the sheerest blandness (albeit driven by the unblandest calculation), have mass appeal. Akim knows that. Does she think he's an idiot? Why, it's he who's singlehandedly brought to the attention of the world (through a letter to the editor)—a world that misuses scepticism to camouflage its unreadiness for truth—the fact that the masses love nothing so much as blandness masquerading as genius in everymanly drag—genius stalwartly refusing to succumb to inexcusable excess. He plies his blandness for all it's worth, the Rival does, as the healthy self-deflation of authentic genius threatening to get out of hand. He manages in fact to get his genius past customs in the deftest way imaginable—by depicting it as the most inconvenient of givens and far more trouble than it's worth. And in this way he gets all the little people—you know, *Leona's* little people, the ones who have to pay taxes simply because they don't know how to strike an inversion or a credit default swap or two—to focus so busily on the inconvenience that they swallow the genius without protest. The Rival's—*his* Rival's ('cause he wants a piece of him, too, or rather a piece of his action)—genius is the sort of genius that gives itself a hard time—a real workout—because it knows it's inexcusably incompatible with other, more human functions. That is to say, *being* a genius just gets in the way of doing not only what a genius does best but a million other things besides. So, thanks to him, genius is no longer just genius (any slob can *do* genius) but genius tempered by self-inflicted lapses into heroic ordinariness. There is a time and a place for genius, folks (just as you don't shit where you eat, neither do you *genius* where you eat—or something to that effect)—it's the first thing a real genius learns, preferably the hard way. Only they mustn't end up thinking for a minute that, with all this self-debunking, he isn't still a genius. His modesty mustn't be misread—*as* modesty. He isn't denying his genius—exposing himself as a sham. He's simply, nobly, starkly getting into the ring with the fact (and inviting cigar-chewing fans past, present and future to cheer him on as hard as they can) that sometimes genius must wait out, must wait for, must wait on, other functions, infinitely more cherishable. And this knack he has—or says he has—for recognizing under what conditions genius must wait (or it just isn't genius), while at the same time remaining unable—through the wayward unstoppability of sheer genius—to practice the waiting he preaches as it deserves to be practiced, makes him even more of a genius—a genius overtaxed, unsubdued and unsubduedly penitent. In short, he's that most Promethean of geniuses, a genius at war with genius—which means, among other things, that he's under no circumstances to be mistaken for one of your run-of-the-mill dime-a-dozen geniuses. And the purest proof of all this (if more be needed) lies in the fact that he has no qualms about talking your head off (as the 9/11 interview made perfectly clear) when he has absolutely nothing to say of any consequence, about genius or anything else for that matter. For this nullifying boldness signifies, as nothing else can, that the Rival's genius is merely gestating between orgasms, so to speak, and will be siring a new pseudoprofundity any second now. Hence his interlocutor should consider himself supremely lucky to be able to listen to its madly—or is it feebly?—beating fetal heart.

She tries to console him as she did many a time in New York—to remind him there are billions just like the Rival, most of them considerably worse (she gives herself a pat on the back for *considerably*: elegant and not bad for somebody, albeit an SAB alumna, who never got a high-school diploma). But still, he doesn't want consolation. For in addition to the Rival, there's One far bigger—nothing less than the Sum of All Rivals, past, present and to come (not just Balanchine, of course in a class by himself, and Ashton and Tudor but also Petipa, Coralli, Fokine, Nijinska, Jooss, Graham, Taylor, Tharp, Morris). One giant competitor, infinitely prolific, i.e., infinitely innovative, with no dead—much less age—spots over the course of a career spanning centuries and no deadwood in his output. So how can he, Akim Volynsky pure and simple, ever be expected to compete with this multitentacled wunderkind . . . ? So why is it she who's undergoing treatment and not Akim or, for that matter, the ghost of Balanchine, who could be excruciatedly envious of a favorite's husband or lover (or was it simple kitchen-table jealousy?)? So maybe Invidicum will never cure her—because in fact she doesn't need curing. Maybe she's simply a disease-free proxy and her true vocation to surrogate-mother the real victims' Envy parasite until such time as they're capable of mustering enough manfulness to relieve the vector of her burden (handwritten thank-you note optional), acknowledge that they host a life-threatening infection and, with the more-than-proverbial tail between their legs, seek professional help. Though, wait! hold the presses! maybe she *is* the only envious one after all and not just your unfriendly neighborhood envier but one who, like the most contemptible cripples from all walks of addiction, papers over her disease with self-righteousness by professing to selflessly agonize over the fellow sufferers she can't help seeing everywhere around her—but sufferers far worse off inasmuch as they won't admit to the suffering she insists consumes them. Looking fairly hot under the collar, Akim mumbles something along the lines of hoping to bump into her again—sooner rather than later. Oddly enough, he doesn't ask what she's doing here. He must be terrified she's now part of an illustrious troupe—after all, this *is* the Hotel del Coronado (though how can her companions by any stretch of the imagination be taken for hoofers?)—that her career has gotten an invidious second wind and that the time's not far off when the Quarter's Gaslamps will once again wrap their guidebook-lauded arms about her. All well and good, but—as Irving Berlin, another immigrant from Eastern Europe, might have put it—how about *him*? But maybe, sighs Jean (she's pinch-hitting pro bono for Moira who's stepped away from her desk for a minute or two to see a pig about a poke), just *maybe*, Akim is as great as his productions fear to think he is and wherever it goes, the greatness can't help leaving in its wake "an attunement of opposite tensions, like that of the bow and the lyre."[26]

As soon as they're all semi-settled they're to proceed to the junior grand ballroom, which faces the very *shackteau* where the Adolf-lovin' Mother of All Celebrities Famous for Being Famous, and Her Abdicator, used to stay. Or so they've been informed by the assistant manager, sounding to Cantor (who notices such things—and not much else, according to his snarkier colleagues) just like one of those poker-voiced commentators charged with giving the B movies of the late forties their documentary feel—stuff like *Naked City, Call Northside 777, The House on 92nd Street* and *T-Men*. Narr is none too eager to dump his bags even if he knows he won't have to share the room. For he doesn't want to be alone with his realization that there may still be plenty of holes in the cheesy Big Picture. He can't remember, for example, how much Manning is supposed to know about what Post is supposed to know and vice versa and if her plan, according to Post, is to remain hot on the heels of Eden and Cantor and whether the arrangement is for Eden and Cantor to be kept apart from the others and if so, then why is everybody setting up shop in the same house of cards cum crystal palace? And who exactly is to run the subsidiary which will oversee, assuming it ever gets off the ground, the manufacturer of homicidogenic Invidicum as the contribution of Amygdala to the war on the war on terrorism? Borkman? Or is it already well off the ground with Borkman running the show over Post's objections? And where does Post fit in, not to mention Narr himself, chock full of his own sort of holes? Is he to regard himself in the mirror as a rogue narc or as a multi-company man who just happens to be the not exactly ex officio master exploiter of warring mandates for the achievement of noble ends? Is his job, e.g., to protect Eden and

---

[26]See, for example, John Burnet, *Early Greek Philosophy* (New York, Meridian Books, 1957), chap. III, "Herakleitos of Ephesos," fragment (45).

Cantor, and more from themselves than anyone else, or is it to catch Manning in the act of collaborating with whoever is willing and able and greedy enough or is it rather (the job, he means) to bring down, like his hero Samson, everybody linked to the promotion of Invidicum for homicidogenic purposes? He can't remember what he himself has ended up knowing from all the emails he's been privy to. Why, he's turning out to be nothing but a dumb blond. Quite a feat, given that he's an impenitent brunet. Blond or not, at this very moment yet another horde of locusts is sure to be giving their Old Testament all to inbox-strafing.

Maybe something or other was being added incrementally to the lunchtime specials of which he was an ardent fan—or rather, of whose *predictability* he was an ardent fan. His routine—almost Kantian in its strictness—was known to everybody after all—was even the butt of harmless jokes. Or not so harmless ... The Wednesday haddock melt (now that you mention it) did taste even stranger than usual recently, ditto the Friday fondue-fricassee (which some overestheticized staff member, more clown than colleague, never tired of referring to as the culinary equivalent of Glinka's Valse-fantaisie) as well as Thursday's porridge pattie (served up golden brown just the way the Viennese profess to like it). In fact, everything tasted strange—awful. A phenomenon he ascribed with his usual tact to a passing fancy of his taste buds. But what could be easier than to pour into the porches of his plate a poison strong enough to overstimulate the dentate gyrus of his hippocampus, causing it to unleash a flood of fleeing-migrant neurons whose sheer numbers would leave them with no other option than to ungratefully hijack and destabilize the gyrus's existing circuitry and in the process labilize the very memories he needs to be able to retrieve at a moment's notice if he's to get a handle on things. Memories not only of those recent emails but of strange conversations overheard in the men's room (but isn't every conversation overheard in a men's room required, at the very least out of respect for context, to sound strange?), odd looks at breakfast briefings—looks lasting just a little too long? They thought he didn't notice ...

Were they to have been flown up to Santa Barbara directly or was this stopover in the cards from the beginning? If so, will it be a long one? For the life of him, he can't remember. Maybe he dreads wanting at all cost to know everything there is to know about the organization's plans for Eden, who, to the otherworldly extent that he's not a rival in any specific domain, is still his rival to end all rivals. Even if knowing everything will be ulcerative, *the more he knows the less there will be to, even more ulceratively, imagine.* But does he, the authority conferred by italics notwithstanding, really believe this? But, the anxiety transmitted by italics notwithstanding, does he really believe this? Well, the wordflow of the moment says he does and that seems to be good enough for whoever is generating it *from behind the curtain* (a curtain, by the way, straight out of *Das Testament*). Now where did that italics-worthy phrase come from? Who cares just as long as it summons up all sorts of acousmatic possibilities? But his musing is interrupted by Post, who's just announced to Shearer (he's close enough to kiss her which looks like it's no accident) that Jim Straynge's son is now regarded as a person of interest in what's being referred to as the Amygdala Case. She doesn't seem to care—neither about being kissed—and more power to her as far as Narr's concerned. But even if Shearer doesn't care, everybody else in the hotel seems to have been swept up into the excitement. By the way, there's a highly flattering photo of Straynge on the front page of today's *San Diego Union-Tribune* (behind which somebody with over-bejeweled, flabby, hairy hands is hiding). But to go from the ridiculous to the sublime and back again, Narr remembers reading all about how, from its safe and secure windy-city aerie, Tribune Media is busy inflicting more and more layoffs on the paper, doing all it can to trash one hundred and fifty odd years of first-class journalism. This, under a merciless five-point transformation plan—that last refuge of scoundrels—whose gist is big—bullish—on boilerplate. There now, Narr is pleased that his heart's in the right place. But where's his sense of fairness? Doesn't he realize that CEOs—like pimps—like studs—have feelings, too? Take Larry Ellison, for example.

But he has his own problems (having one's own problems being another well-known last refuge of scoundrels). Those too many holes, too many contradictions, for one thing. In fact, the Big Picture—the Invidicum story—as he's just been discovering/recapitulating is one big fat hole. He holds things together—barely—compliments of his *uncanny ability* to localize and articulate the contradictions. In the hope that the sequence of contradictions—the sequence of holes—can, through an Old Testament sort of dispensation, be put into one-to-one correspondence with—can invoke—the holes-free *sequence of events* that make up the Big Picture—any Big Picture. In the hope that through a sort of sublime-to-ridiculous parody of double-helix-style complementary base pairing (whereby the identity of a base on one strand divulges the identity of the base to which it binds on the other), every contradiction will end up divulging the identity of the unique event for which it serves as so much sand thrown into the eyes of a gadfly by birth like Narr. Thing is, events, at least as performed by men of action, have a bad habit of leaving no traces. (Ethan is aware that with *men of action* he's about to go off on a tangent, thereby *jilting* the current thought—and after all it's done for him!—which he nevertheless intends to connect to the one to come, albeit by the slenderest of threads.) Fine and dandy for men of action who don't need any traces—they can't wait to give themselves completely to the task at hand—to vanish into the thin air of the task—to become the task with no remainder. But not for folks like him, Ethan thinks. When push comes to shove he's first, last and always a man of . . . *ivory*. Men of ivory can do just so much giving, vanishing, becoming, before the terror that they'll never re-emerge takes over. To stave off the memory of having jumped ship—to parry the void left in its wake—they concentrate instead on salvaging something from that void—inconspicuous consumption but consumption nonetheless. And what better something than articulation of where, when, why and how the task went wrong—where it clashed or is bound to clash with other tasks? With that something in tow, the man of ivory emerges as more than himself. (As his intact self he's always about to become nothing, his contour making him an unmissable sitting duck.) He's more real than he started out as being because now he's in opposition/apposition to a something that's *really* real . . . So he becomes a new if momentary me. Acquisition of that something is acquisition of hope—a hope unencumbered by context—unconstrained by failure. There's even a rumor going around that the man of ivory refuses to vanish into the thin air of exertion precisely in order to wangle the compensatory something he considers better than success.

The off-label crowd—whoever its members turn out to be (at this stage of the game, heuristic hunches are welcome)—want to strike terror and paydirt as well with a single thrust of the shovel. And that's possible only by waging war on the war on terrorism. And more importantly, they're perpetrating terrorist acts against him—a man mainly of ivory and likely to remain so—through their refusal to generate for his ongoing consideration a coherent sequence of events susceptible to tabloid-friendly paraphrase at a moment's notice. Which is required if he is to *get his man*. And maybe his woman, too. True, his thoughts about Big Picture events do sometimes cohere at a very very local level. But that's due mostly to what some schoolman of yore should have shed his sackcloth long enough to label as the Brownian motion of wordflow, consisting in the transfer of wordflow's unholy credibility, by virtue of *being* wordflow, to the phenomenon encysted by the wordflow. In any event, they're shooting him full of holes: even here, even now (he isn't taken in by the ritzy decor). But if he can manage to survive the assaults long enough to figure out through what kind of anti-logic he's being manipulated into trying to caulk those holes and bind them together like fagots—with what kind of phantom bitcoin, shadow currency, he's being suborned—then he'll be able to determine how they—the off-label crowd—unknowingly manipulate themselves into taking their madness for holy writ. A pondered examination of the inconsistencies—the contradictions—in the movie they're making him edit, dub, subtitle and intertitle—the very inconsistencies that are supposed to throw him off their trail by driving him mad—will enable him (as long as he can keep them from making good on this promise) to anatomize and autopsy their madness and the subsidiary madness of their plan to Invidicumize the developing world. Oh, and by the way, any temptation in this regard to create a phantom shot-by-shot, scene-by-scene continuity—by making what *happens* at the end of one scene (an *explosion*, say, outside one of the warehouses among which off-label Invidicum is being shuttled) rhyme with what's *said* (by Stifter or Walser, say) at the beginning of the next (something about the fear of missing the "Magic Fire Music" in that night's MET performance of *Die Walküre* compliments of a call from some snotty ER claiming that one of his patients has just had a near-fatal Envy attack)[27]—that temptation, sir, must be resisted at all cost. For all the rhyme does is suture—invisibilize—plug the unsightly cut required to get from one scene to the next. More than a sum of shots and scenes, *Invidicum the Movie* is an anthology of gashes (or is this just the wordflow shooting its mouth off all over again?). And those gashes, holes, incisions, orifices, must be foregrounded since they are the only way

---

[27] Such a rhyme does in fact play out in *Das Testament*. Well, whaddaya know, Narr, like Cantor, is a Mabuse fan.

in to and out of the off-label tribe's madness—a Cave of Envy straight out of Ovid. So, from now on, his job title is Trafficker in Discontinuities. The surgical examination must, then, be measured and respectful—must take the inconsistencies on their own terms—must not entail clearing them up for the sole purpose of diminishing the tension, the unease, the panic, they understandably generate in the examiner. He's got to bracket them, to cultivate them in the *in vivo* of abeyance. So he must, starting here, starting now, choose to think of himself as having no choice but to play the hand fate has dealt him, by savoring the holes in the Emmental, the gashes in the celluloid. He must remind himself upon every fresh access of caulking frenzy that holes let in fresh air and expel toxins.

The ballroom resembles the amphitheater they've left behind on Greenwich Avenue—and as far as Cantor is concerned, not a minute too soon, though he can't say why just yet—maybe because he's too busy trying to remember if there were several amphitheaters or just one. But wait!!!, whether there was one or five hundred is beside the point: no self-respecting ballroom can, without authorization, just take it into its head to *resemble*. Or do anything else for that matter. Or so the (newsreel narrator) Voice of the Master (James A. FitzPatrick to you, bub) suddenly seems to be insisting. (Cantor laughs—not last but still best—at how easily he, a non-conformist nonpareil at least according to his latest passport, has come to adopting—Once And For All, or so it suddenly seems—everybody else's Epithet.) No, before the brute fact of resemblance is allowed to take its place among all the other brute facts with which that landfill Life is littered, it must first assume the guise of a Sign, i.e., the ballroom must *seem* to *somebody* to resemble the amphitheater and if this is indeed the case, as Cantor knows it is, he doesn't mind in the least being that somebody, even if he feels (for any number of reasons, too tedious to elaborate, most of all to himself) that he's the least plausible of somebodies. But (the same jolly-portentous Voiceover is up on his high horse again) it's precisely the fact that he *is* the least plausible . . . interpretant of the Sign in question which may very well make his particular take the most exhilaratingly fertile Sign for another interpretant waiting (stagestruck) in the wings. Which is as it should be, for didn't somebody really famous (not famous for merely surviving his allotted fifteen minutes) affirm, while devouring his deathbed slice of Black Forest Cake, that Plausibility is Deathness? All right, but still . . . It isn't as if he weren't flattered. Or as if he were afraid of sticking his neck out (all of his colleagues, even the ones who hate his gay guts, can vouch for his intrepidity when pushed far enough). It just *seems* that such a butterfly-delicate perception would be much better off getting caught on the wing by somebody commensurately delicate—Herbert, say, or Moira, or even rehabilitated Cook. But of course if there are no volunteers in house he'll be only too happy to incarnate the required POV for he understands perfectly (no need for the Voiceover to go on insisting: he's made his point!) that without a POV, however implausible, there'll be no seeming and with no seeming there'll be no ballroom and with no ballroom, no real-life context.

CHAPTER TWENTY-ONE

As Melanctha Herbert moves toward the roped-off podium (every speaker, toying expertly with his bottle of designer water, looks like an MSNBC regular)—unnerved as much by the absence of any familiar faces in the audience as by the impression her olive-green dress is already making (however modest its décolleté by the standards of the day)—the first thing that strikes her as she struggles to get a grip on herself is the extent to which the ballroom resembles the auditorium—sorry, amphitheater—in which they all spent so many rapt hours listening to Straynge and his minions drone on and on (in hindsight, oh so irrelevantly) about how penetrating the analysis of *their* disease by the likes of, among others, Girard and Veblen and Nietzsche and Schoeck and Kierkegaard and Freud, still remained. (Why, the way those luminaries were lauded to the skies you'd think they themselves were the holy-grail biomarkers Envyologists worldwide had been seeking for decades.) Taking his seat, Cantor feels that just when he's been voted Man Most Likely to Be Implausible and Still Live to Tell the Tale—just when he's about ready to stretch out on the Persian rug of his implausibility and enjoy the peerless ocean view—it's being pulled out right from under him by some nobody but a nobody who knows how to play the plausibility card for all it's worth. And that he's powerless to stop that nobody from setting up shop in his eminent domain.

The obvious leader of the podium pack, a tall balding man (and as regards looks a vast improvement over Straynge, Shearer has to admit: wait! it's none other than her bête noire Walser)—who might be anywhere between forty-two and seventy-five (in some fashionable suburb of agelessness is where he obviously hangs his hat)—sighs deeply as soon as the microphone looks competent enough (compliments of the showy exasperation of a tinkering technician) to broadcast the sigh's cannily failed effort to render itself imperceptible. Is it because of her, the difficult patient par excellence (or is she giving herself undue credit?), that Walser has aged so badly and at the same time so alluringly, to the point where . . . Borkman, suffocating but always on the lookout for a pretty face, is waiting for the salt breeze to do more than just toy with the curtains. Oddly enough, Herbert is a bit disappointed to discover the bald one is neither Straynge nor Post nor Cook nor even that latecomer Liepnits who seems to have exerted such a noxious effect on Straynge. It certainly doesn't redound to the Master's credit that He's forever needing to pair new speeches with ever newer deliverers (she doesn't—or doesn't want—to recognize this joker). Such conspicuous waste just to satisfy the craving for novelty of some client (a craving she, client or not, would never stoop to entertain)—a novelty that is even more monotonous than sameness—well, quite frankly, it'd be despicable if it wasn't so pathetic and vice versa. Even a change of climate is no excuse for such prodigality. Why should new quacks be recruited when the eloquence of the old guard hasn't even begun to hit its stride much less to be squeezed dry as one would even squeeze dry a rubber-bulb syringe chock-full of venom? Don't these upstarts realize their places will be usurped in turn though has that ever been a deterrent to anybody (and, in all fairness, why should it be?)? Herbert and Herbert alone are—is—to blame: the Master should have learned by now, through the tutelage of somebody more at home in the world than he can be expected to be (he doesn't have Harun al-Rashid's license to kill time among his subjects incognito), that every new utterance, however urgent, should not be entitled to a new utterer but tailored instead to the attributes and aptitudes of a seasoned performer already on the scene and likely to remain so for generations. So—she's failed not only as a mother *but more importantly as a mother surrogate . . .*

Has she just said what she thinks she's heard herself say? Not taking any chances, Herbert dutifully recoils in what she hopes can be perceived—by some spectator with a flair for intuiting the goings-on in the chamber theater of other minds—as horror. But what shocks or at least intrigues her is that she's nowhere near as shocked at this thought-crime against nature as she ought to be.

What, after all, is the point of a speech in this context if its delivery doesn't promote the evolution *of an existing character*—doesn't serve as a welcoming transit country in his migration toward maturity? Most other Masters must know this and so it is *Their* disciples who get to be invited back—not once but regularly—by Saints Oprah and Charlie, among others. They should, these storytellers, be Melanctha's gods. The only thing irking her—well, not the *only* thing, no, not by a long shot—is the fact that they, while in the undislodgeably safe and secure majority where traditional character- and Big Picture-building are concerned, still manage to gallingly glamorize themselves on air—and everywhere else—as apostles of risk—the last bastions of a beleaguered ethos. But failed self-indictment is thankfully cut short by the purling tenor of Dr. Bob Walser (for that's how he introduces himself). Odd, Melanctha thought he was in the branded-entertainment business (for of course she recognizes the old dud). But does Herbert really harbor such a thought? Is Herbert perplexed? Of course not—she knows he was once a doc and then an ad man of sorts and then a doc again (non-news travels fast). End of story. Once again, the Master can't seem to make up His mind, about this as about the so many other things of lesser import lurking about—or worse, He wants people to *think* he can't make up his mind because for Him, uncertainty—ambiguity—means having one's cake and eating it, too. He needs Melanctha to be uncertain *for* him so that for a little while at least, Walser can be both a branded entertainer and a sawbones extraordinaire, i.e., unlocalizable, unbracketable, a non-thing of words and patches. For it's only as a word—at most, a string of words—that Walser can be controlled by the Master. A life of his own is simply out of the question but one day—mark my words!—Walser will thank Him but by then, alas, it will be too late. Herbert, on the other hand, is in no humor to thank the Master—her muddled Master—for masquerading as Wilde's Lady Bracknell—so that Melanctha Herbert of the Bronx can be Melanctha Jack in town (where she takes Walser for a sawbones) and Ernest Herbert in the country (where she takes him for an ad man). Somebody whispers, "I heard he wants to practice medicine like a real doctor, Lucrezia." To which Lucrezia (presumably) replies, "I heard that, too, Borgia." Narr to himself (*eavesdropping from a few seats away*): "So that's what Walser, *canned* to within an inch of his life, wants everybody to think. Clever guy—cleverer than I gave him credit for being." So now that everybody has solved the mystery that is Walser—each in his own way—and not a minute too soon—so now that he's been explicated beyond all hope of appeal (though is this what just happened?)—Melanctha can devote quality time to zooming in on his mannerisms, which are too mad-docterly for her taste. But if so, why does the insufferable little Pollyanna deep within—the quintessential golden-ringleted white girl that, on and off, her mother wanted her to be, at least in company—why does Polly simper, *But mad-docterish in a* good *way*? He clears his throat—to refrain from exhorting them to save the inevitable standing ovation for the end of the aria.

"You may all think you have the troubles of Job but whenever *I* think I have troubles I need only remember a Job more Joblike than Job, to wit, that kid I read about the other day in the *The New York Times* Styles Section (of all places!)—a kid just back from Baghdad who's lost all four limbs in the mother of all most useless wars. As well as the mother (recalling the sub-pittances of sacrifice demanded from the folks back home—you know, the good-timer Charlies and Charlenes on Main, Wall and Easy Streets) of all boutique-and-niche wars. I have only to think of him to realize not that my troubles are not great (if anything they seem, because clearly infinitely inflatable, more horrific than ever) but that as unbearable as they are there'll be no reparation because there sure as hell won't be any reparation for *him*. I know what nobody else knows or will ever know: that the momentary distraction proffered to him and his ever more torturable loved ones by the aforementioned coyly upbeat piece will wear off (though it's only natural for them to mistake the omnivorous spotlight for an omniscient beacon of hope) and that should Charlie and Charlene have, while en route to some regional office of, say, JPMorgan Chase, Bank of America or Goldman Sachs (which, if Monsignor Blankfein is to be believed, is doing god's work), the misfortune to bump into his torso—a misfortune far greater than any the kid has undergone or can still undergo—then they will simply recoil indignantly as from a tasteless put-on—a profanation of the memory of those who not only really did serve but are considerate enough to keep their remains invisible. For in these pursy times, dismemberment like indigence is always the fault of the victim, who under no circumstances must be pandered to as one, for that is not the American Way. Only licensed billionaires merit seed money. Sorry, I can't be more nuanced, folks, but there are times when to nuance is to do . . . the devil's work." (*The issue of Nuance looks like its shaping up to be the Anthropocene's Next Big Thing, right up there with super-fungible tokens, somebody with inside information thinks.*) Any minute now he's going to invoke Building 18. She's sure of it. Which invocation is of course but a hop, skip and a jump away from excoriation of her failure as a mother. Worse, the mother of a veteran. Worst, a vet who didn't have the decency to stay alive long enough to stretch the taffyish sensibilities of Charlie and Charlene to the creaking point. *Briefed on Melanctha's history*, has he been crooning uncomfortably just for her? Highly unlikely that his crooning has anything to do with her in particular, except insofar as she's just another citizen of the Greatest Country in the World. No, the crooning's just what the lilting strains make it out to be—a meditation on the nasty, brutish fact that every life is just short enough to make the unendurable, well, endurable.

"This having been said, I alert you to the fact that the most difficult—some might say the most unendurable—phase of The Trial is about to begin. *Je commence*, It says, like Hoffmann (Its culture hero) when he's about to tell the story of his four lost loves, Stella, Olympia, Antonia, Giulietta and—of course, Hoffmann himself. Only the number of lost loves in this case will be far greater than four—I mean five. More like four thousand. And you, Eden, and you, Cantor, are entering an even more difficult phase (the price to be paid for consistently outstanding performances up to now)—but more on that score later. (Cantor refuses to blush; Eden never learned how.) I know for all of you it must feel like yet another audition when you've rightly had it up to here with auditions. Let's see, you've had the fMRI audition and the penile plethysmograph audition—at least six to a (male) customer, although females have been auditioned as well (to mixed acclaim)—and the protein accelerator audition and the diffusion spectrum imaging audition and the polygraph audition (yes, even in this day and age) and the electroencephalogram audition and the E.R.P. cap audition and the thermal scanner audition and the eye tracker audition and the pupilometer audition and the transcranial magnetic stimulation audition and the transcranial electric stimulation audition and the transcranial direct current stimulation audition and the deep brain stimulation audition and the occipital nerve stimulation audition and the positron emission tomography audition and the neuromotor prostheses audition and the fiber-optic cable plus electrode (optrode) audition, not to mention the CT brain perfusion scan, fluorescence recovery after photobleaching (FRAP), fluorescence loss in photobleaching (FLIP), photoactivation, photoconversion, fluorescence correlation spectroscopy (FCS), image correlation spectroscopy (ICS), fluoresence cross-correlation spectroscopy (FCCS), image cross-correlation spectroscopy (ICCS), fluorescence resonance energy transfer (FRET), fluorescence lifetime imaging microscopy (FLIM) and protein-fragment complementation assay (PCA) auditions. And let's not forgot—show a little respect here, people!—the single photon-emission computed tomography (SPECT) audition, the support vector machine (SVM) analysis audition and, last but not least, the MRI identification of iron-deposition changes audition, or have I (silly, silly me) already mentioned that one? But look on the bright side: never was there a need for the cingulotomy and capsulotomy auditions, thank heaven. (Even if there was never a question you'd be subjected to these two, I couldn't resist: there's something so seductive about a universal list that flaunts the fact that it ain't anywhere as universal as it's cracked up to be.) By the way, sorry for all the acronyms: I'm going on a diet starting tomorrow morning. That is to say, 'I'll never stoop to onion soup,/And pork and beans are taboo.'" Is it possible that only Cantor can trace this quip back to its mother lode in the wilds of Peru (Indiana)?

"But don't let anybody kid you. I'm going to say something most M.C.'s in my or any field field of expertise would rather die, or diet (the vast majority are gluttons), than admit: the obligatory pre-shtick rattling off of a list of the ordeals they feel so terrible about having subjected you too, even if it was in the name of your well-being, has absolutely nothing to do with remorse and everything to do with creating a sense of . . . common duration—no mean feat. (As one of the James brothers [I forget which one—wait! now I remember! Jesse!, the most precocious of the lot] wrote in a letter dated 23 December 1903 to Annie Oakley aka the Duchess of Sutherland that '[T]he very most difficult thing . . . is to give the impression and illusion of the real lapse of time.') And now that I've finished the saber rattling you must feel you've not only been here forever but were also *there* (undergoing all those high-tech cutting-edge world-class auditions) forever, and that's how you're supposed to feel—*that's how we want you to feel*—because the feeling of an interminable shared duration breeds trusting solidarity in spades."

"Between slaves and their masters, with the trust going only one way." Borkman (of all people) cries out (well, his father was a Commie for the duration—that word again!—of the thirties). "And what does duration have to do with the Envy cure?" Somebody evidently cowed by the papal authority wielded by the podium counter-cries that Borkman should shut the fuck up and be grateful for Annie Oakley, not to mention the Duchess, among others.

Walser turns to his podium mates and with eyes still very much trained on them replies, "We're working on that. Hard. But I'll say this: people who share the Duration Experience realize they're all in the same boat and therefore have little reason to envy each other. But the thesis is still in its formative stages. How fast we prove it depends on how fast we make you well enough to become Envy counselors yourselves." Borkman gets up and mutters something under his breath—he has no idea what. He wants some fresh air, or at least that's what he needs to think if the exit in high dudgeon is to be brought off with mad-dog panache, in other words, dour dignity. "Moreover, as you might have already guessed, you're all on camera (remember, Hollywood is just up the block)—you've always been on camera—which means the collective unfolding of your sad-sack saga is being streamed 24/7 to audiences webwide (we need to test the waters on YouTube before that HBO docudrama you've been hearing about goes into full on-location production). And if we expect them to stay tuned (many are eminent psychopharmacologists who simply want to apply our techniques in their own practice so why wouldn't we want *them* to stay tuned?), they need to feel like major players in that saga. And nothing creates that feeling better than, as I just mentioned, a shared duration and nothing generates duration, shared or otherwise, better than the rattling off of an interminable list of items with the ring of high-tech authenticity. But there's a catch, as I also mentioned, sort of: the rattling must give the impression it's a reluctant because harrowingly expiatory rattling, so as to camouflage all the cold-blooded calculation that has gone into getting it just about right for unpopular consumption.

"I hope *my* rattling has, as a fringe benefit, made you feel you've been Californians a lot longer than you may have thought (a too-lengthy acclimatization process can only blunt the edge of our efforts to get you all back on your feet). And that—such are the miracles worked by lists—without my having set a single tourist trap—without your having to waste precious company time gawking at the jacarandas." Herbert wonders if he's making hay of her literary strivings. Or maybe he's just trying to win her confidence—seems to be up for grabs in this neck o' the woods—by suggesting ever so discreetly that he has some idea of what it takes to capture a particular time and place: the dedication, the tenacity, etc. And thereby ease her into receptive-patient mode or, more importantly, receptive audience-member mode. For he's no doubt convinced (remaining true thereby to the dictates of his accursed tribe whose members, whatever they may be saying, always mean something along the lines of Play it, Sam, *because I, your lord and master, have this sudden yen to exalt my lonely stoicism and you, with not a yen to your name, exist purely to satisfy mine*)—no doubt convinced of how difficult it must be for her (like all the members of *her* accursed tribe) to bend to authority, especially when it's for her own good.

There is a pause—as portentous as it is short. He looks around with a vaudevillian's mock-wariness then, in a strenuous stage whisper through cupped hands, announces that the items on the list have served yet another purpose: they're in fact stand-ins, placeholders, for everything that he and his kind are not allowed to divulge lest they be arraigned as traitors or whistleblowers or, worse, as bores. From the back of the ballroom, Borkman, clearly unintrigued—worse, unimpressed—by these intimations (self-respect prevented him from exiting without a fight), cries out loud and clear, "So, what you're really saying is that a fake (or faux, as your kind would put it) sense of duration is being bioengineered to make us boobs think you're doing much more for us than stall for time and shoot your mouths off." Through a leisurely panning of his gaze he makes sure to include the other podiumsters in his indictment.

"I'm glad you've spoken as you have, Mr . . ." "Borkman—you know my name as well as I do." "Some of my colleagues might say I shouldn't be giving away our deadly secrets, allowing you to see us with our pants way way down, so to speak—but I don't agree. I know just how you must feel. So many auditions and the jury is still out on who among you have (*a*) the disease and the symptoms, (*b*) the disease but not the symptoms (in these so-called elite controllers, the viral load may be high but for some reason it does not trigger a tissue-wrecking chronic immune activation), (*c*) the symptoms but not the disease and (*d*) neither the symptoms nor the disease." (Given her mock epiphany in the fog—the fragrant fog—a while back Shearer *can't help but feel* [or so the words would have it] that the last-mentioned category has been established on the spot with her alone in mind. Herbert and Cantor, on the other hand, *can't help taking* (*d*) for a mere [mere!] byproduct—side-effect—precipitate—of the wordflow, generated with no thought for ensuring that it signify—something *out there*. In fact if it did do something so blandly subversive, the generators wouldn't think twice about blowing its ugly head off.) "And though I hate to add insult to injury, I must admit that the same jury is still out on whether, symptoms or no symptoms, Envy *is* a disease. Maybe—some say—it's just the armature—like so many other forms of collateral damage inflicted by the fittest's struggle for survival—of a strategy devised to secure a place for some pep pill in the blockbuster pantheon. (So you're not alone: Envy and Invidicum are auditioning as well.) Or maybe Invidicum has been mis-tailored to combat Envy at a stage when it's no longer combatable. Oh, it's not easy, trial-mongering, let me tell you. Only to the woefully uninformed does it appear glamorous."

Walser's top-hat style rubs Eden the wrong way. But what doesn't at this stage of his peregrinations? "So, maybe, just maybe," Borkman cries, "you should have gotten to us earlier on." "Like when we were in the cradle," Eden guffaws. "Endlessly rocking," Melanctha approvingly murmurs, thinking of her son for once without self-reproach. The sleaziness of Walser's handlers renders her virtuous by comparison. Cantor feels for Eden—feels even more for his unfunniness which has immediately taken on a dog's life of its own. Clearly uncomfortable in the role of teacher's pet, Eden wants a chance to prove that when he puts his whole heart and soul into it, he can be as much of a Peck's bad boy as the next guy. Walser makes like he didn't hear, which suggests the exercise of, depending on your taste, either lofty forbearance or cavernous craft. "But let me say that I feel for the most vulnerable among you: having waited most of your lives for a definitive diagnosis, what do you discover to your horror but that it's not a prerequisite for experiencing the toxic impact of our interventions. I can hear you crying out (even if you yourselves can't), *My kingdom for a diagnosis—any diagnosis.* Understandably, you've dreamed of being free at last to go out and do what, by destroying yourself (Envy is a deadly vice, diagnosable or not), could be claimed, by those who come after, to be the bidding of that diagnosis. Thing is, you won't be around to get your head swelled by all the fuss and bother. Remember, suicide isn't a vengeance on life—the ultimate statement, refractory to paraphrase—the ultimate fashion statement, impossible to knock off—a leap beyond the bounds of life. Even if it's precipitated by a craving as transcendent as Envy. On the contrary, it's a leap into the abyssal arms of the bracketeers. After they've chewed you up as just what you are and no more—a *suicide*—and spit you out, label and all—label above all—you'll realize that you've never been more bounded—and gagged. We all set out believing suicide is the ultimate statement—the ultimate fashion statement—only to discover, hopefully in the nick of time, it's about as ultimate as your hypochondriacal great aunt's weekly excursion to the gynecologist's."

"What's an audition in the context of the trial?" asks somebody who's raised his hand and been duly recognized. The brashness of his tone belies the fact that he's the very first to comply with the rules of procedure. Obviously a plant, then, whose function it is to make Walser look either plausibly stupid or too smart for his own good.

"While I don't exactly know what constitutes 'an audition in the context of the trial' as your lucid phrase puts it, what I do know is that you've come to the place where all ladders start and all auditions thankfully end. Trial leaders on both Coasts—and I'm referring not just to the Invidicum crowd—are equally responsible for this Audition Culture and the rampant Envy it wantonly fosters.

"But it is always so irresistibly beautiful—oh, you have no idea how beautiful—to observe, in the course of the voir dire, each candidate *propositus* (I use the word incorrectly—with relish) venturing forth in the bloom of his youthful expectation (anybody willing to participate is by definition a bloomer). And to know that ultimately, it is the one who, duly girded with every imaginable defect, enters just in the nick of time, in other words, at the precise moment when we judges can't bear to look at another specimen because we can't imagine one even a wee bit less mediocre than the millions preceding him—to know it's he who'll, in keeping with the Grimmest protocol, end up taking us by storm. Which, when it happens, is even more irresistibly beautiful. So I've just told you something every other M.C.—and not just of the Borscht Belt tummler variety—would rather die than own up to, namely, that we, a stock company of artistes manqués, are all in Envying awe of auditioners. What we want is not to pick out the one extraordinary supplicant in the chorus line but to be that supplicant at the very moment he *is* picked out, and thereby suture the wound that drove us to become judges in the first place.

"And we imagine ourselves to be not only the winner—indemnified at long last for humiliations greater than everybody else's (just as everybody else's is greater than his)—but also the unsung—the unsingable—creator (remember him?) whose song he chose, from among all others, to showcase his uniqueness. The creator's unawareness of the fact makes *him* beautiful as well, and us by proxy (life's a proxy war). Here, by the way, we have a neoclassical (why neoclassical?) example of what's known in the *DSM* as 'Look, Ma, I'm Dancing—on the Back of Another Underdog' Syndrome (the inspiration, by the way, for yet another Warner-Metro blockbuster—this one for creator types excruciated by what is all too sappily, patronizingly, sadistically, referred to as *the lack of recognition*—coming soon to a specialty pharmacy near you—Plato's Pharmacy, to be exact, whether it's near you or not). Herbert thinks, *When a literary hack doesn't know what to do with a word, he italicizes it, and when that doesn't do the trick, well, then he has no choice but to win the Pulitzer Prize hands down.* "Such a creator needs to believe that even if his song is being hitchhiked as a means not to his own end but to his interpreter's (*Ma, are you still there?*) the fact remains that the underdog interpreter is in the process—the throes—of making it big and in making it he (just turned overdog) enables said artist—the hitchhiking career underdog whose song he's belting out—to make it, too. Judicious overdosing with the blockbuster keeps the precious sensation going and, when it really kicks in, it's like an exhilarating gust, *albeit posthumous*, from recognition's sunny alpine world."

"How can some pill that caters to a super-tiny demographic be labeled a blockbuster? The so-called blockbuster will be lucky to make into the microniche category." This shouted out by what looks like an unidentifiable flying object—in Harris tweeds, no less—in order, or so it seems to Narr, to cut less-well-intentioned questioners (should they have the same axe to grind) off at the pass. I.e., this Object out of nowhere is a plant. "Hey, are you for or against me?" This from Walser, who's clearly being coy (at least to those in on the game). The regular-guy act doesn't suit him in the least—and it suits Herbert, once again too thought-oppressed for her own good, even less. Adding insult to injury, the Master is once again violating her—Her—Rule No. 1 banning conspicuously wasteful recruitment of new stooges every time there's some new speech or speechlet to be perpetrated. "Chalk it up to that rarity of rarities, CEO delusions of grandeur." The Object nods cautiously, as if daring to hope they've come across as authentic adversaries. "And how do you know fame 'surely awaits' your so-called creator?" "A niche blockbuster like this doesn't work for delusionals." Another nod, this time one of relief: judging from audience response, they've put Darrow and Bryan to shame.

"But getting back to you, our new contestants. (NB: as you enter a new phase, you're back to being a *new* contestant, with all the trimmings. In short we're like A.I. chatbots which are trained [except for ChatGPT] to disremember what they've picked up from past chats and to thereby approach each new query sporting the full panoply of a tabula rasa. At the same time your performances have been cammed, scanned, tweeted, liked, Skyped, texted, uploaded, downloaded and streamed—not to mention, *steamed*, like cauliflower florets—every step of the way [which is not necessarily the best thing, or even a good thing].) I've lived your torments, even more intensely than you yourselves have. And at the same time I exercise proprietary rights over those torments precisely because I wouldn't dream of living them. Especially high praise to two of you for top-notch work in the True Confessions Department. I was there—front row center—when you, Jean, high-C'd your tale of sisterly woe (in retrospect, by the way, far-less-shocking-than-it-hoped-it-would-turn-out-to-be) into a star turn worthy of Callas as well as when you, Moira, 32-fouettéd (no big deal, I know, in the post-Balanchine age) your adverse reaction (what adverse reaction specifically? she wonders: she's had so many over the course of a lifetime) into a showstopper worthy of Allegra Kent. I was particularly moved at the very beginning—laughed till I cried and back again—by the way some of you, convinced your self-corrosion wasn't extreme enough to warrant a place in the trial, tried too hard to wax untreatable—yes, *wax* untreatable—and in so doing racked up a lot of bad marks for perversely withholding just the sort of harmless, heartwarming—extenuating!—signs and symptoms we deem even more telling, clinically speaking. And I suspect you've already guessed when I use the term *trial* that I'm most often referring to anything but what's commonly understood to be a trial—that nine times out of ten the features of the thing invoked are the features of the *anything but. Trial* is a placeholder—a self-generator. Through it I can get around—and get around *to*—Speaking the Unspeakable. *Trial's*, come to think of it, not a little like Ms. Herbert's *Building 18* and Ms. Shearer's *Mr. B.* and Mr. Cantor's *berry sundae* and Mr. Borkman's (no hard feelings, I hope) *spinoff* and *Liberace* and Ms. Rhys's *Caro*. And of course Mr. Eden's *proxy patricide*. Your lives are all an open book, I'm afraid.

"I hope at least some of you will have the good fortune to come under my care during this, the determinative phase—determinative, that is, until the next determination. Since the feelings I've just revealed—feelings I cultivate exclusively on your behalf—go very much against the grain of what angekoks (Eskimo for what it is we aspire to embodying but rarely become) usually experience toward their victims." At the sound of this magical word (*angekoks*, not *victims*) George nods loud enough for Walser to see, while hating himself for striving whatever the cost to make his braininess legible. But what if he didn't debase himself by nodding? What if he even mustered the guts to simulate a yokel's befuddlement—writ yokel-large, in a big fat empty thought balloon? What would that make him? Simple: Walser's scullion—boy—bitch—for life. Yet Cantor has no reason (*who is speaking?*) to feel self-degraded by the nod. After all, is there any bond deeper than that forged by the shared understanding of a word? especially one whose pedigree hails from off the beaten track. "As candidates (cum supplicants in their processional), each of you will be made to feel like yet one more uninvited guest among way too many. You'll be hurried in and out solely to accelerate the eviction of your pre-decessor and the *conviction* of your successor." At this, his colleagues rise up, though not quite simultaneously, in protest. However, when he raises his fists (sign of unmanageable stress? Quick, a statin!), they all back down, or pretend to. "Their tactic of reducing you to the least common denominator—to links in an unending, self-dedifferentiating chain—is referred to in the technical literature esoterically as *serializing the nincompoops.* Its purpose? Simple: to exalt their own particular brand of nincompoopery—perhaps the most nin-compoopish of them all. They don't want to hear your Envy troubles. What they do want is for you, the supplicants—you the nincompoops—to listen to your silly confessional chatter through the ears or rather the earplugs of their ostentatious forbearance—to hear it as valueless in itself—as serving only to highlight—to biomark, if you will (even if *they* won't)—the virtue—and more importantly the virtuosity—of that forbearance. The confessional hereabouts, then, is all about their wanting you to know (*a*) that they're putting their own problems on bighearted hold but not (*b*) that in so doing they're killing two birds with one stone and all thanks to you, i.e., they're evading those problems while making evasion look like the supreme sacrifice—in this case, of their precious attention, and to something as ludicrous as your blubbery articulation of infinitely less important ills—less important by virtue of their very articulability. And by the way, no matter how brilliant your articulation, it's always the wannabe angekoks who'll have the last word—or rather, the last non-word. So for the likes of these wannabe angekoks" (this time Can-tor doesn't nod away his self-respect) "*there's* (inflationary) *gold in them there* (articulable) *ills.* The secret subject of your troubles then becomes no more and no less than this noble abstention from telling their own. And what's eas-ier, I ask you, than for psychically wobbly, relentlessly self-doubting folks like you" (Cantor bristles at *folks*: much too fake-populist hetero!) "to find them-selves buying into the non-telling as the signifier of heroism—while forgetting of course that the non-tellers—tourists in the land that doom forgot—are paid handsomely for their schadenfreude?"

"But why must this drug trial be compared to an audition? You still hav-en't explained. Why must we *live* it as an audition, where we turn out to be either harpists or harpies—under- or overdogs?" This from Jean Rhys (at this moment and for this moment only she's Jean Rhys, just plain Jean Rhys, and her talk-prose is, like her namesake's, sledgehammer-exquisite)—Jean Rhys, career gadfly, refusing to let well enough alone but if she wants to jump out of her seat she suppresses the impulse, choosing instead—or so it appears to Cantor, who for the first time can smell the ocean (the Pacific is suddenly acting like the Pacific!)—to channel the aggressivity into (if such a thing is possible) razor-sharpening her delivery. *Good girl*, he thinks, *she has the makings of a first-class screwball comedienne.* Herbert realizes Rhys is only a few seats away. Judging from the desperate tone and all, it sounds to Borkman as if she were wrestling with a demon much bigger than auditioning. *Audition is*—what did that character Walser call it a minute ago?—a mere placeholder, a self-generator. Herbert thinks she may be just a mouthpiece, a prepared piano. Or maybe Melanctha's invoking the Master (she can't help it if Invidicum's doing the talking for the two of them) to fend off the virulence of what Rhys is saying—or rather of what she isn't saying but threatens to be about to say. A virulence that's very much her own creation and nobody else's.

Standing against the wall in the left aisle, Ethan sighs. *Here she goes again. Acting on her delusion that the most exalted thoughts can only be about degradation.* By her tone, she's making it clear, at least to Ethan, that she's too old, or too young, to pussyfoot about—that she prefers to put that pussyfoot in her mouth and salvage the little that's left of her dignity after so much overdosing—and in her case, for the wrong disease. The ensuing silence (she envies it for being able to *ensue* without backlash) gives Herbert (ever the career impressionista) a long-awaited opportunity to evaluate the setting sky with what she hopes is an impartial eye (her abiding and impatient interest has always been not in what clouds do in the course of a day but in the denouement—i.e., in how the dregs of their doing precipitate in dusk soup's filter flask). Impartial or not, she dares anybody to deny that the azure chinks in the armor of all those fire-fringed cetaceans deserve the highest praise from Sunday painters.

"A point well taken," Walser concedes, though he sounds pretty antagonistic. It's all too obvious to Cantor that when he should be practicing the humility in vivo he's just been professing in vitro, the prospect rubs his sensibilities very much the wrong way. He may be terrified that Jean's storming of his battlements will encourage further insurrection. "By the way, before moving on to Santa Barbara we'll be meeting in little deep-focus groups, as my colleague Orson Toland used to call them." His podium mates nod their heads. "My colleagues, as you can see, are neither as laid-back nor as rigidly set in their ways as rumor would have it." Titter. "In short, they're hipsters." That he resolutely kept his eyes off them as the rivulet of praise—if praise it was—ran its course has generated a certain tension—good for his image and for theirs as well.

"You do right to ask why, my dear," Walser resumes, sighing deeply. He's trying to sound as if the question were something of an inspiration—a blessing, not a blessure, in disguise. Pause. Is he suffocating, Cantor wonders, or, being an amateur musician (members of the profession often are), has he decided that this moment of truth should be commemorated by the missing of a beat? "Because quite frankly or quite simply or both, the trial, as already intimated, is not just about its subjects but also (and perhaps mostly) about its Subjectors. Maybe I've been a bit too harsh toward them—us. After all, we have feelings too and if those feelings are not attended to as we're entitled to believe they deserve to be—well, then all hell breaks loose: the Subjectors find themselves unable to function and the trial ends with a bang—*and* a whimper. Guys, I once heard a premature ejaculator whisper to his buddy (now don't go letting the makers of that no-better-than-a-placebo Semenarest [accent on the second syllable] fool you into thinking PE is a disease) during, of all things, the eleventh inning of a Yankees game that, before ejaculating (usually no more than—on a good day—ten seconds after penetration), he (or to use his word, *we*) 'always took care of the wife first.' So the moral of the story is that you, the subjects, need to take care of us, the Subjectors, first—we're nothing but big babies, after all. But how is that to be done? Well, if any trial is to succeed, then one of us—who then assumes the role of Prime Subjector—must get inspired enough to concoct—and ejaculate into the proceedings—his very own personal fantasy (though what fantasy isn't personal?) about one of you. Otherwise the trial is kaput no matter how many biomarkers it manages to unearth and wash up on the wobbly shores of our incompetence—and that's why (though nobody was ready to admit as much at the time) phase 3C of the Mefistofelase trial failed so miserably back in New York: no member of the team got to be a Prime Subjector.

"The Prime Subjector needs to create a fantasy figure so he can envy it. Envy it the beauty of its struggle—beautiful because PS knows that struggle in this case is, under the auspices of a surefire teleology, the royal road to redemption through triumph over every rival—to redemption *as* triumph. Envy it because its struggle, unlike his, *makes sense*. And envying it, the Subjector can begin to understand what you must be going through. But it is almost impossible by and large for any of us subjectors to allow ourselves the pleasure of putting together a fantasy from scratch, i.e., without a model/muse breathing down our backs who nevertheless remains in constant sight (otherwise we wouldn't be Subjectors). In short, we're inept in the fantasy-concoction department, but ineptitude, like Beauty, has its privileges. Which means that one among you must serve not just as muse and model but as midwife too and demonstrate an especial relish for those thankless roles. So the long and short of it is that, thanks to fantasy—to the fact that we're short on the tools that are *de rigueur* for constructing a fantasy—we're auditioning for you (everybody knows the muse chooses the master and proceeds to run his sideshow) and you're auditioning for us (everybody knows the master chooses the muse)." He looks sheepishly at Jean Rhys. To see if she's in the market for his bill of goods, Cantor thinks, sadly.

Jean's having none of it. She's trembling. Ethan has never seen her dander up quite this high. Not even Caro had the knack—not even on that woefully windy night along St. Mark's, back in the days when the Saint still relished the seamy smell of his stigmata and would never have dreamed of gentrifying it away at any price. As far as she's concerned he's using the trial—using them—using their misery—to rationalize—to legitimate—his own peculiar obsession with auditions—to give that obsession a podium—literally. She for one would prefer dealing with a child pornographer who, bravely recognizing the unassimilability of his hobby to any legitimate context, embraces their (the hobby's and his) conjoint solitude. The kind who doesn't try to hitch his wagonful of dirty pictures to a star of Bethlehem.

"Just be patient," he answers patiently, taking a dog-eared page from the *Bedford Book of Hours*. "It looks like I'm being primed (with all due immodesty) for the juiciest part of Prime Subjector. For I've already taken a particular shine to one of you—I won't say whom—and that one, or rather that one's doings, have become the raw material of just the sort of fantasy the trial's shadow protocol demands. And it's turning out to be a rather complicated fantasy. I'm well beyond the first-impressions stage, by the way. But only within the last few days have I been able to start *articulating* the fantasy which means not only being (as with any fantasy worth its salt) at cross-purposes with it every step of the way but, more importantly, simultaneously dissecting *the pathological tendency to live through another* as laid bare by the articulating. (To paraphrase Michel de la Foucault without quite knowing why I'm doing so: if the fantasy in the making is dissectable, that's because it is itself dissection—of an identity so defective as to be almost unworthy of identity theft.) This marks a particularly big step forward, since for a fantasist like me, the fantasy doesn't get itself made just like that—up to now it hasn't even been perceived as a fantasy but merely as a featureless obstruction to getting on with the work at hand. But what would the work at hand be without the fantasy? Undoable, that's what. But let's get down to cases.

"Consider the hero—the (falling) star—of my fantasy to be a young man—or young woman—viciously persecuted by family members for his . . . sexuality, say, or his bi-, tri- or even multipolarity. It is the cruelty of their treatment that renders excusable and, more importantly, plausible the decision to flee (even if in adversity or old age one or more might require his loving care) and to live from then on in a fissureless solitude. However, a fantasy, which is always first and foremost a thinking being, must be guided by a precise notion of what—and how much of that *what*—it can accommodate. For one thing, it still doesn't know to what extent the hero is to resemble me, its maker. While it does know that he is to be allotted as little pleasure as possible so that the ultimate anointment may seem all the more deserved, the fantasy's still having a hard time making up its mind about exactly or even inexactly how much heroic self-laceration, -suppression and -effacement can be imposed without destroying him in the process. And frankly (and in this regard I think I speak for the fantasy as well), I'm still very much undecided about the cause of all the persecution. If aberrant sexuality is the ticket, my hero is thereby robbed of a certain abstraction and what is more beautiful than to be rejected grossly but still abstractly, independent of all contingency?" "But everybody has a character and how can character be contingent?" blurts out one of the gray eminences. "Good point. So the temptation at this stage is to render him completely traitless—to make traitlessness the reason for his persecution—and to leave it up to abstraction carried to the breaking point—abstraction on fire, so to speak—abstraction on (though I hate the word when used metaphorically) *steroids*—to ensure his irresistible poignancy.

"I admit that so far I've been moving in the direction of making him a performing artist which means—to me at least—stacking the deck; turning him into a veritable anthology of hard knocks and bad breaks; and seeing to it that things go as wrong, for his aspirations, as wrong can go. But every time

I'm about to deprive him of yet another familial advantage, I realize that it is by no means incompatible with success. *Pace* Hollywood and the Brothers Grimm, most of the members of his tribe aren't at war with the world and haven't had to overcome abysmal poverty and routine abasement by kith and kin. Far from it. Problem is, I'm still not over Hollywood and Grimm. But why should my hero have to suffer—if it *is* suffering—for his maker's own unyielding and regressive illusions? In any case, I won't have his family deprived of its wealth or high IQ for the good reason that abasement has an extra-special virulence when practiced by the world's winners—and he deserves all the virulence I can bring down on him. But maybe my soft spot for devoutly unwishable total negation as *the* prerequisite for triumph, artistic and otherwise, is as atavistic as some thug's truculent belief in an afterlife. But I know we all agree about one thing, namely, that whether or not he turns out to be Cinderella or Jerry Cinderfella, they have no recourse but to end up on the West Coast. But what if I supply him with a modest legacy from a beloved barren aunt, a Betsey Trotwood, say, but without a Dick, as I'm sorely tempted to do? Will that ultimately mar his stature? Maybe it's better to have him scramble together on his own just enough cash to enable him to get on the airport bus (but does he steal it? and if so, will stealing diminish his most potent secondary sexual characteristic, namely, enigmaticity?). But there's another thing about which I'm sure we agree, namely, that when the time comes for him to hoist himself up and pay his fare, the hoisting should be photographed in a high-angle long shot so as to emphasize both his vulnerability and his resilience (the "little man, big dreams" sort of thing) and that it certainly wouldn't hurt in the least to have this soon-to-be-famous departure scene played against the (singerless) heartrending final strains of (*a*) *Pelléas et Mélisande* or (*b*) the 'Liebestod' or (*c*) Fiesco's aria (*Simon Bocanegra*) or (*d*) the Letter Scene (*Onegin*) or (*e*) the 'Cujus animam gementem' from Rossini's *Stabat Mater*, or the last four or five pages of Franck's *Prelude, Chorale and Fugue* (oops! already gobbled up by Visconti in *Vaghe Stelle dell'Orsa*) or the titles theme from J.-P. Melville's *Le Samourai*—(*a*) through (*d*) supersaturated with what Immanuel Kant would unblushingly call 'hopefulness without hope.'" (While conceding that Walser sure has a way with name-droppings, Cantor [no slouch himself in that department] feels nonetheless duty bound to deplore the way the good doctor over-sautés them. Easy to see why Voracicom canned him. On the spot. Even easier, why Warner-Metro welcomed him back with open arms [even if, strictly speaking, he'd never left].) "Nor do we, I believe, disagree that his final destination should be Los Angeles where, going to work full-time to pay for his education, he proceeds to do what he does best—smother all emotion, pleasurable or otherwise, but in the name of what, precisely? brute survival? ultimate fulfillment? atonement for the hatefulness of others? Can't begin to answer that yet. The only thing I know is that my fantasy, take it or leave it, is modeled, to a considerable extent, on those Women's Films of the Forties whose heroines do, through sheer plod, the Veblenesque impossible, i.e., they transform drudgery into exploit.

"Oops, I almost forgot" (he hits his forehead with the heel of his left hand to make the point stick) "that because of all the Visconti and Franck and Stabat Mater stuff of seconds ago—most of you must think I'm what's called a *cultured idiot* (as opposed to a *useful idiot* [post-KGB hoodlums' main dish of choice at Russian Easter dinner]). And for that epithet—that term of endearment—I'm grateful. I really am. You've come by it honestly. That is to say, I'm not offended—even if it's even more painful knowing your kind doesn't usually succumb to such animus. Or rather, I don't let offendedness get in the way of the opportunity offered by your epithet to extend the horizon of my selfhood.

"Must warn you, though—I need to savor the epithet before swallowing it whole and to mull it around in my mouth (and the semi-legitimate insight it carts around on its back)—formulating, formalizing—even if I've heard it—and much much worse—thousands of times before. Never understood why it's so hard for blowhards like me to acknowledge the truth. The self is irrelevant—as long as it's not completely demolished by said truth—and if it is, demolished I mean, then it has no right to be a self to begin with—it's not worthy of feeding off the pustulent riches oozing out of its own flawed carcass—I mean the carcass of its adversary's meanspirited acuity. That I've survived the observation since here I am shows there is something beyond the self—the self is just a makeshift means of holding all sorts of unendurables together. By acknowledging the truth of the epithet I haven't been annihilated—on the contrary, I'm exalted—it's one more feather in the dunce cap of my essence. 'Cultured idiot' is one of the many traps I set for the useful viciousness of idiots. What matters is to extract as much truth as I can from that usefulness. No self-respecting self should ever shy away from leasing the stance of its worst enemy—from seeing itself as that stance sees it—from prospering under its auspices. Why? So as to become more than itself, silly—a full deck's worth of shuffled selves—so as to accrete to itself a panoply—an integument—of inconvenient selves as conduits to ethical invincibility. The vicious truth of epithets like 'cultured idiot' is and is not of me and if it is of me it is not of me essentially or rather it is of me essentially only to prove just how phantom and detachable any limb of the essential can be once its soul-strengthening toxins have been dutifully sucked out of it. Nothing is as essential as self-understanding—a flesh-and-blood entity in its own right—or as the lucidity to be amassed through a strategically shameless humility."

So what if the response is muted—nothing like the standing ovation for honesty he was expecting? He's weathered worse.

"Frankly, I'm afraid this damn enterprise is so resistant to getting itself achieved that I'll never be able to start treatment on schedule. It's not all that different, when you get right down to it, from the kind of pornographic fantasy that makes a bit of headway only when the would-be fantasist is masturbating, opportunities for which in the context of a long workweek are, as I'm sure you all know from bitter experience, few and far between, so that during the preponderating dry spells it ends up, this porntasy does, being bulldog-refractory to any further elaboration. But as you see I'm soldiering on (you'll forgive the expression since I've never seen combat per se, although I sometimes have the indistinct impression that I was George W.'s Gunga Din at the Battle of Bull and Run). For I know that sooner or later I must get him—the hero—off his pedestal cum hot seat and send him out into the world: he can't stay behind a desk or a steam table or a tractor forever. So I've decided that one of his co-workers is going to get him invited to a party where the host will be seduced by our hero's deadpan (and why not? he's beautiful and the fact that he's too busy keeping his anguish under wraps to know it or care makes him even more beautiful). Do I have him buy a bottle of scotch as a gift though he can ill afford it? Yes, because there's something touching and mysterious—in other words, erotic—about his doing, not from inclination but from deadly duty, what something tells him is the right thing. Something positively Kantian about his tearing himself from the lockjaw insensibility he is actively cultivating (but still has a long long way to go toward past-mastering) in order to act beneficently no matter how mammoth the grief he harbors in his still hopeful heart. In short, he's just the sort of closet energumen the author of *Groundwork for the Metaphysics of Morals* would have had no trouble falling madly in love with if he'd been capable of falling in love. In other words, this liquor-buying is less a gesture than a dormant heart's concession to gesture.

"Well, to make a long story short—much shorter than it needs to be—this brief overexposure to good clean conviviality manages willy-nilly to get his hormones off their high horse. The next day, a Saturday in July, still aroused, he throws caution to the winds and hitchhikes to Venice where he is . . . pursued by an admirer. Does he succumb? Does he resist? Resistance has pathos going for it, which is not to be sneezed at when your aim as a fantasist is to take an audience half-stewed on pap and bromides by storm. Thing is, self-suppression and nothing but will only dehumanize him to the point where he may never fulfill his destiny, which is to become (remember?) a great performing artist, i.e., a dark god. But if he is to become a god, dark or not, there must be something earthen (*no, terrestrial!*) he has to transcend, transmute, transmogrify. In other words, our pre-auditioner is under lots of crossroads-type stress (thrilling only in retrospect). But if he ends up sated and spent, does he still manage to safeguard his impenetrability?" Is Walser actively avoiding his gaze? Cantor wonders. "And is it through or despite self-occultation that this genius receives his unanimous due? But why is it so vital that he turn out to be one? Still, inasmuch as unanimity is always suspect, he can rest assured that, whatever kind of genius his rabid fans do ultimately compel him to be (that is, until the real thing comes along), there will always be two or three detractors planted securely among them (like rosebuds in his lapel). Since performances taking place anywhere but in their luminous shadow aren't worth a damn.

"So there you have my fantasy-in-the-making. Which reveals my own inexhaustible capacity for Envy in the raw. And to the extent that it binds me to one of you, it binds me to all and thereby qualifies me, as no formal contract ever could, to superintend the current phase, as it was meant to be superintended. That is, in such a way as to ensure that none of you are mutilated (there's no point in hiding the fact that this phase is riddled—iatrogenically, how else?—with landmines)." Narr (that's Executive Creative Director, etc., etc., to you, bub) can only admire the aplomb with which Walser manages to bid a MacArthurian farewell to the podium while pointedly ignoring his colleagues. Making for the wings with the dire grace of a *funambulist*—true, that's just *tightrope walker* in Falutinese yet somehow much much more—he looks far more poker-faced, far more lockjawed, than fantasy man—at least in Narr's version—could ever be.

CHAPTER TWENTY-TWO

When Eden gets back to his room—he and Cantor are roommates, which doesn't exactly thrill him (what could, now that he's botched his mission although probably not as far as the police are concerned?) but neither does it repel him as he thought it would—when he gets back, I say (*pay attention, you!*) he can't help asking the ocean and the ocean alone (though of course it's Cantor the egghead he's addressing: after all, aren't *his kind* supposed to be expert, supersensitive listeners, grateful for any opportunity to atone for their crime against nature, e.g., by reasoning away the unavowable feminizing anxiety of their uncrooked betters?)—he can't help asking why the *higher-ups* have decided to stick them here in San Diego, even if only for a few days, when time is of the essence and Santa Barbara their real destination. Eden's use of the term higher-ups sticks in Cantor's craw. Betrays yokeloid servility of the worst kind. Cantor, *for his part*—no, no, no: make that *As for Cantor*—is well aware of the dynamic he could set in motion by ministering to the neediness of this soul-damaged straight—and taking him more seriously than he has the courage to take himself. So he decides, as usual unconvincingly, that this time he has no intention of being ill-used for his compassionate acuity (sure to be pilloried as unladylike asslicking once it's done serving its purpose). Thing is, he knows how helpless he can be when up against that acuity's throbbing desire to . . . penetrate its target. "Are you asking me, man?" (giving him the brush-off from his pillow by trying to sound manfully half-asleep).

Should Cantor go ahead and say he hasn't the faintest idea why they've flown him three thousand miles from civilization but that it's pretty obvious Eden's here for one reason and one reason only—to be sent into homicidal mode ASAP? For one misty morning he eavesdropped (in what is now a sepia-toned reMastered flashback straight out of Feuillade's *Les Vampires*) on Manning (according to her master plan?) as she tastelessly disgorged the entire contents of Eden's file for the delectation of some orderly. (They supped on his horrors and licked the template clean.) The Amygdaloids want to get Eden in the mood (Cantor can feel his fabled acuity going into overdrive, where it's most at home) to—to—hate his martyred father all over again which will then—as in the past—make it oh so urgent for him to find a plausible dispatchable substitute, especially now that one rug of revenge has been pulled out right from under him. It's evident—but not *painfully* evident, as rumor would have it—that Eden possesses plenty of the milk of human kindness. Only it's indigestible unless curdled by hate. Once he settles on a target (so went the file note though Cantor could have done a much better job of file-noting and in much purpler prose), whatever heinous act said target has perpetrated to justify Eden's hate will be chickenfeed compared with the heinousness of that target's daring to persist in his own being in the wake of perpetration. It's as if almost any act will do—even the borderline heinous or one that only by the wildest stretch of the imagination can be deemed heinous—as long as in its wake and against the backdrop of its barest plausibility the perpetrator's daring to persist in his own being can be perceived—at least by Eden—as just cause for opening the sluicegates of that hate. Since for a career hater—cf. John Moredock, Cantor's all-time favorite, for example—it's the target's endeavor (*who's speaking right now? surely not the file note! surely not Cantor! No, this is the point where the voice of the file note metamorphoses into Cantor's so the voice you end up hearing is that of the metamorphosis itself*) to preserve and persist in its own being (didn't—doesn't Spinoza call it *conatus*? of course he does! George's no dunce especially when it comes to knowing a thing or two about the lingo of so mighty a coreligionist albeit—no, especially—an excommunicated one) that constitutes the most defiant form of provocation. But why? Cantor wonders. Well, isn't its conatus nothing but the essence of the thing itself (*Ethics*, Part III, Proposition 7)? and whenever he observes him, Cantor can't help feeling Eden doesn't believe he's real—doesn't believe he *has* an essence. So how can he not envy those who do have one—or convincingly pretend that they do? But he can endure his envy only if he's able to turn it into hate and he can turn it into hate only if he's able to worship the target of his hate—not the hated one per se but the hated one's conatus—as something obscene which it would be even more obscene to possess. (Why *even more*? Cantor wonders: well, that's the way of the wordflow which, uninvited—yet selflessly on call—as always, is now doing the thinking for the two of them.) And surely the conatus of somebody who's committed a heinous crime (and who, rather than expiatorily self-annihilate, happy-go-luckily perdures in its wake) is an obscenity par excellence. And even better for Eden's purposes is the perpetrator who, in the wake of perpetration, knows all too well that under the circumstances persistence in his own being is especially obscene yet gets an especially obscene thrill (obscene beyond the call of duty—obscene to the second power) out of the knowing.

But to whom does this thought about conatus and its vicissitudes belong? Cantor wonders. Who owns it? Who holds the patent? Him? Manning? the Master Builder of Wordflow everybody seems to be talking about and in whom Cantor is beginning to believe more and more—not as some default literary lender of last resort but, rather, as nothing less than an architect of perception the likes of which the world has never seen? But how, Cantor also wonders, can anybody verify the truth of his eavesdropper's confession which costs him next to nothing? How much preliminary wrestling with the angel of self-worth did such a confession require? None. It's the Master's wordflow that's doing the confessing—in a mere nod to the needs of storytelling. But the confession's a rogue concession and doesn't want to be embedded in any story. It's been warned against them all. Doesn't want to be beholden for habitation to anyone or any thing. But in the last analysis, does it matter who the thought belongs to? What's important is that a thought of such urgency *get itself* thought come hell or high water and he's willing—no, more than willing—to share the royalties equally, equably and equitably with whoever else may lay claim to the victory. For the articulation of a thought worth thinking is like money well spent—it's a victory—one of life's few, even if it is ultimately granted to the sorcerer's apprentice that is wordflow.

No response from his better half. Maybe Eden is asleep or maybe Cantor's question has crossed the line into heinousness. Or maybe the line was crossed long ago and as a perpetrator of obscene conatus—obscenity squared—he's Eden's latest father substitute and prime target. Or what if it turns out that, for whatever reason, they're here to cancel each other out? Given any or all of the above, what does he have to lose by saying (as long as he keeps it simple and toneless), "You're a powder keg, Eden, and they know it and they know how to use it. The keg, I mean."? Should he then—never one to leave well enough alone—add that Eden's right up there with Joe Frady and Raymond Shaw? When he turns over, cautiously (for he doesn't trust silences), he sees, first, that Eden, spread-eagled across the sheets, is asleep and second, that a note has been slipped under the door. The note indicates (the simple gesture of picking it up has made *him* simple in tandem—too pure and too simple to harbor any bad thoughts about Eden) that around ten thirty in the morning, three sultry days from tomorrow, just the two of them are to meet with Walser and Doc Stifter (sure, George remembers Adalbert, the pseudo-Viennese wunderkind) on the North Patio, the one facing the tennis courts. (Odd, before going upstairs tonight after Walser's oratorio—he needed to pollute the whiff of sea air with a few puffs of his cigarillo—didn't he overhear somebody at the entrance to the lower-level smoke shop insist that all patios faced the tennis courts? Is this Herbert's Master's—his, too—giving a plot-thickening stir to the human soup? Well, he won't get very far—not on George's watch.) Eden is snoring lightly—wheezing asthmatically actually more than snoring. Or is it the surf or the wind in the eucalypti or a regiment of white-noise generators in the room adjacent or the manful growl of a toilet flushing overhead? An embarrassment of interpretational riches. Non-committal juggling of the possibilities makes Cantor pleasantly woozy and in no time at all—or rather, less than no time—he's fast asleep. But not before demanding to know why, if he and Eden are being groomed and doomed for greatness, each doesn't have his own private executive suite.

Next morning, it's while he's virtuously rearranging his few shirts in the walk-in closet (guilty for once of underpacking) that a cache of what look like DVDs catches Cantor's eye. He recalls how the clothes in Berry Sundae's closet refused to go the way of his flesh. They, like Spinoza, persisted in their own being and are probably still doing so. One day he'll be leaving his clothes behind and somebody—a stranger, no doubt—will be tasked with unloading them on rank innocents. The prospect of a complete lack of control over the messy matter of his own posthumousness should come as a relief. Thing is, he can't view the matter from just the right relief-yielding angle: like Richard II's Queen—he's simply no good—or rather too good—at *looking awry*.

As the weather's becoming too lustrous to waste, they agree tacitly that a swim may be the best cure for their incompatibility, or at least take the edge off of it. Sometimes the silence between them becomes unbearable, at least to Cantor. Why has he come along? He knows he makes Eden's skin crawl. Well, then, George, my boy, this is an overripe opportunity to learn to live with a skin-crawler without allowing yourself to become undone. He's tempted—no, sorely tempted—sore till its hurts—to break the ice by saying, *Look, I can shoot my wad into some wet warm waiting womb as mercilessly as the next guy. And I've done it more times than I can count. (For there is nothing good or bad, but saying makes it so.*) The beach is heating up. A shard of foam vacillates until it's pocketed by an incoming wave. George would have liked to lecture it on the need to make it a practice to always decide before somebody else decides for you: *Take it from me . . .* And if the bit about the wet warm wad doesn't work he can remark, casually, that imagine! he just read in Frommer's or Fodor's that right next to the Naval Station there's a Camp Tennessee Wittgenstein where *gays* (Cantor shudders at a pejorative worse than any euphemism), i.e., non-straights, i.e., crookeds, are encouraged to pray aggressively against the deity who made them what they are—to grapple him to their soul with hoops of steel so as to destroy him and themselves in the process. A foolproof cure. And if this isn't enough of a miracle, Camp TW also services—services— those heteros who, curiously, want to pray their way into the orientation that dares not speak its name.

But he can still get a load off his chest by talking in generalities ("Give him a mask, and he'll tell you the truth"). No need to get bogged down in his specificity. Why focus on the details, however significant. (Contrary to popular belief, God [which unlike Plato's Demiurge has neither the tact nor the decency to steer clear of omnipotence] is in the Big Picture.) It's self-shielding universality that should be his grail. So instead of focusing on that not-quite-unspeakable act amateurishly performed in the men's room at the Pierre (in the days when a non-guest who looked even halfway decent could take a leisurely piss in any class A Midtown hotel without fear of deportation) or the misunderstood overture at a hotdog stand in Coney Island on the day after his fifteenth birthday, why not invoke the lot of all men?—why not take a wildcat stab at we're-all-in-this-togetherness? Shame and self-disgust—now that's something everybody can get into the act about. After all, he won't be the first to try to pass off evasion and elision as the hallmark of luminously self-abjuring breadth of artistic spirit. (The sun is deliciously, unbearably hot: it screams *health* in 57 different Romance languages.) Even if he's no artist. (And by the way, 57 just happens to be the number of commies in the US government Raymond Shaw's stepdad claimed to be able to identify.)

Yet as it turns out he doesn't need to do anything. Eden does what Cantor would never have imagined he could do, even with a knife held to his throat. "You look sad," Eden says, not really paying attention or pretending not to. But the comment—particularly *sad*—paves a way in to *Eden's* men's room (ritzier than the Pierre's)—more like a camera obscura—where Eden's femaleness is asserting its right to life. Where momentary self-communion, self-schism, self-dismay, are giving a sold-out performance to a single rapt— raped—spectator. All this simply because the performer happens to know the word *sad* (an auto-bio-marker which suggests all sorts of possibilities as regards man-to-man intimacy) and as a bonus utters it. (Utter that word or a word like it and it's down tiny Alice's rabbit hole, maybe for keeps.) Before he can reason with himself, Cantor says, "Why should I be looking sad. You misread me, chum" (should he have said *pal* or *bro*?). And why *not* play the nut hard to both crack and get and thereby enhance his desirability? Why not give the squirt (Cantor is a few inches taller, bud, and don't you forget it) a taste of his own medicine, whatever that is? He mustn't wear his excitement over *sad* on his sleeve for the rare bird that is Eden to peck at. "In fact, I'm living the lie—I mean the Life—of Riley. As refracted, of course, through the Book of Job. The last of the Great American Playboys. Always on the go." He can see incomprehension mounting in Eden—not so much for the text (he's no dumb blond for all his probably unconscious posturing to the contrary and must know *the text is foolish—a document in madness*) as for the tone. And for somebody like Eden there's a thin line between incomprehension and disgust. If George's waxing incomprehensible—whether through text or tone, it makes no difference—then he wants to be incomprehensible and if he wants to be incomprehensible then he's pretentious—not ambitious, just pretentious. And pretentiousness gives off a bad smell and rightly so. So George's now on a mission to induce a sense of defectiveness in the comprehender. It would never occur to Eden that through sarcasm Cantor's confirming Eden's perception of him qua male (whether conscious or unconscious) as defective (only living things without balls resort to sarcasm) AND bracketing the perception as his way out of its debtor's prison AND beckoning Eden beyond all the sarcasm and the bundled debt to his own men's room where an expert is waiting to demonstrate how self-schisms of all stripes (e.g., up/down, true/false, essence/appearance, inside/out, remedy/poison, writing/speech—and before we forget, mascul-/femininizing) get sealed up for good—sort of. He wants to frame Eden's framing of the gratuitous enigma that is he, Cantor. He wants to be not only outside what makes Eden ambivalent but outside the ambivalence itself—to catch Eden *for all time* in the act of catching him in the act of simultaneously being repulsively what he is and not being what he repulsively can't be no matter how hard he tries (he's not sure which is worse from Eden's POV—a POV that's otherworldly in spite of itself and therein lies its charm). But doesn't all this effort to bracket the bracketeer merely condemn him to sport the tightest straitjacket ever designed for *his kind*—the Hope diamond of straitjackets—which just happens to fit him—Cantor—to a T.[28]

To complete itself—to realize itself—the Coronado stillness—so famous that there's talk (real talk, i.e., Silicon Valley talk) of turning it into a cryptocurrency on the model of Bitcoin, complete with blockchain—requires nothing more than the lunchtime tinkle of cutlery. But it's nowhere near lunchtime. Or way past. He decides to take a swim before he uncovers the brutal truth, and without (call it an emancipation proclamation, of sorts) waiting for Eden. That'll show him who's boss around here—a New Yorker not (as anticipated) a Californian. He dives in and is duly wave-whipped and -lashed for daring to abandon Eden. He trails his hands backward. Watching a gull soar, he dreads the moment when it must succumb to a wingbeat. Every wingbeat, after all, is a wound inflicted (victim to be determined). Missing Eden, he emerges but he's no longer the Cantor who abandoned him what seems like hours ago. Fact is, he's just been short-leased a selfhood (try tuning in CNN

---

[28] In the universe of Elias Canetti (see *Crowds and Power* (New York, Viking Press, 1962, pp. 301–333), the brackets would correspond to the command and the straitjacket to the sting.

if you don't believe *me*) that no longer requires Eden's disapproval to serve as its armature. Having dared to reject Eden and now the ocean in what feels like a single bound, he's become real: indentured to a life whose vicissitudes the ocean and Eden, inextricably bound, can't begin to envision. He came to the ocean a rank underworldly something and has emerged a ranker something else and it's all to the good and never the twain shall meet. He wishes a little of the realness could rub off on Eden, who's sadly bereft, especially now after the *failed homicide*. (He hates his press agent self for what it's just done through failed homicide which is—and for a few measly cents!—to reassure every paying customer within mind-reading distance that the Invidicum story is still cliffhangingly alive and kicking, with gore past sure to be outdone by gore future. And for the benefit of those with a short attention span he's resurrected Eden's failure into the bargain, staving off its extinction for at least a few more news cycles. But it's not his fault—the Master made him do it.) And so powerful is the realness, there simply has to be some spectator out there made to its measure. For such a spectacle mustn't go unwitnessed. And what spectacle is that, by the way? Why, the spectacle of his truculently kicking the sand and imperiously shaking out his towel like a bona fide everymale, which is surely momentous enough to deserve memorialization especially when compared with what the too many apps at everybody's disposal choose to memorialize. Cantor can't be expected to do the memorializing himself because that will only destroy the realness, which boils down to unselfconciousness, which boils down to maleness. Already he's messing things up through his inability to refrain from trying to catch himself in the act of all three. But the brouhaha notwithstanding, he can't help envying Eden's unrealness, due neither to hyperselfconsciousness nor to a deficit of maleness. Clearly, realness—or at least realness as Cantor lives it which may in fact be the furthest thing from realness—is overrated. Eden's unrealness is unrealness degree zero—its own final cause—an eternal mystery. Call it the Ishmael of . . . psychosis. Eden ignores his triumphant return, by the way.

Armed with his flip-flops, Cantor retreats to the water's edge, ostensibly to whack the sand off the soles of his feet. His unbefriendable ex-lover Howard Ingham, late of Hammamet, had a foolproof method, or was it his ex-friend Anders Jensen, also of Hammamet. He's more than a little shaky which is to be expected: reunion with an old, unreal self tends to have that effect. Though he's buoyed up by that self's familiarity. For once again, what he takes to be rejection by another male has drawn the nectar of his exultant realness through its sieve. Eden advances to the water's edge several feet away, toes tentative and alert. Is this a concession? an invitation? a courtship ritual? Cantor wonders briefly. But whatever it is, *it's as if somebody blazed Eden this trail ending at the water's edge—as if somebody went the extra mile to do so, the way a good dad does and a bad dad doesn't, but without robbing him of his independence—his originality.* And in his Home State, too! But Who or What has taken it upon Itself to go that extra mile and, adding insult to injury, inform him, the guiltiest of bystanders, of the fact? But doesn't Cantor's reflexive effort to drag in that usual suspect, Who or What—to make the meaning of the image—the meaning of the conceit—a meaningless byproduct of—the collateral damage wrought by—forever wayward, frivolous, fanciful, irresponsibly giddy word-flow (*who is speaking?*)—doesn't that effort suggest Cantor is deathly afraid of the meaning—that it's too substantive—too personal—too *un*frivolous to warrant being laid tout de suite at wordflow's revolving door, at the smelly feet of wordflow's Master De-builder? So once again (as in a fairy tale), when push comes to shove, it's ostensibly frivolous wayward wordflow—Cinderella wordflow—much-maligned wordflow—wordflow (that thorny flower—that . . . precious excipient!) which comes to the rescue—that becomes the reverent handmaiden of meaning—a meaning that this time pre-existed wordflow, not a meaning that wordflow has robotically generated. But even if the conceit has apparently nothing to do with Cantor—even if its annunciation was a silly prank and the thing annunciated hermetically sealed off against applicability to anything even halfway human—still, wordflow, the unsung hero, has as so many times before come straight to the rescue by treating it, the conceit, dead-seriously, i.e., as a key snippet of somebody's . . . life-as-allegory—some-body's hence everybody's. So it's official: as Eden kicks the sand he's every Son who's still following in the footsteps of the Father he never had nor ever will have and who's therefore grateful for that Father's blazing a trail where no trail was ever blazed before.

When they are once again stretched out in the sand, so close that who's to say whether the hair on Cantor's thigh isn't Eden's, and Eden's Cantor's, Cantor is emboldened to put his foot in his mouth by saying, "Invidicum's an overrated half-beast." The subject has been harassing him for weeks and weeks and in revenge he wants to ensure it's beaten to a bloody pulp before they attend the next meeting. As it turns out, he's killing two birds with one stone: indeed, he can already taste their innards being churned to feathers in his gut. First, he's revenging himself on the subject—or rather on all the thought packets to which collision with the subject is bound to give rise—for getting in his way. He's not quite sure what he thinks those thought packets are obstructing—whether it's other, far better packets or an end to all packets now and forever. And if it's the latter what does he expect the evaporation of all packets to usher in? The Dreamtime of a Promised Land? i.e., an Anti-George? i.e., a George purged of everything that makes him loathsome to the public at large, or rather, that would make him loathsome if only they'd sit up and take notice? (but he's made no progress on his proof [not much different from Eliot's Mr. Casaubon, if you ask me], so what does he expect, contempt and ignominy for free?). But aren't thought packets his existential bread and butter—his shackles plus file, so to speak? He can't exist without them. He can't imagine life without them. But maybe that's the myth (he knows he's using the term loosely, or better yet incorrectly) he's trying to explode. The myth upon which Cantor Enterprises is founded and upon which it founders every chance it gets.

Second, he wants to gobble up the subject before Walser & Co. can get their grubby hands on it. Before they can maul it in the name of unavowable self-aggrandizement. He's civic-mindedly—apotropaically—depriving Walser of his material. Since Walser will only debase himself further, if that's possible, by making an inadvertent mockery (he's too dumb-ass smug for it not to be inadvertent), through his approach to that material, of the way the other, the *real* Bob Walser, had every right to use his. In the case of the real Bob—Swiss madhouse Bob—Jakob von Gunten Bob—the material was—is—the Walk and the Walk is routinely a ticket to (routinely well-deserved) professional advancement compliments of the thought packets snapping at the walker's rear end—a rear most tenaciously cerebral when most idle and negligent. But who cares if this isn't the time and place to bring up the subject and if Cantor's its least plausible exponent?

Well, for starters, Socrates—the Socrates of Plato's *Phaedrus*—cares. He'd surely react to George's performance more harshly than he did to Lysias's essay on love (given George's more than two-and-a-half millennia's worth of additional experience). The same Lysias who, according to Socrates—the gadfly—the flat stingray (*narkē*)—tried, belly up, to swim upstream through the current—the wordflow—of his discourse from the end not the beginning. The same Lysias who had no cogent reason for setting down his second point in second place or his *n*th in *n*th place. The very Lysias who had no qualms about setting down whatever came into his head wherever and whenever he pleased. As if he were terrified, for all his impudence, of nothing so much as of *the vulgarity of a plausible concatenation*—of ending up in one-to-one correspondence with himself. Convinced as he was that it would be the worst thing ever to befall him and given that he prided himself on nothing so much as being always one step ahead of himself—as being able to play both Achilles *and* the tortoise in Zeno's one-act tragicomedy still breaking all box-office records at the Tennessee Wittgenstein Dinner Theater (giving *The Fantasticks* a run for its money)—as being always one tortoise shell ahead of his love for Achilles. (So maybe it was the incendiary subject matter that was ultimately and proximately responsible for Lysias's loss of all sense of proportion, i.e., self-coincidence would equal self-exposure would equal self-cancellation.) The very Lysias who made it a point of honor to deploy his topics in defiance of any orderly principle of composition. The Lysias who refused to admit that every discourse—like every disease—like Envy!—is a living thing none of whose parts should be lacking and each of which should befit all the others and the whole. The very same Lysias whose essay read like the lines of the epigraph on Midas the Phrygian's tomb which could be shuffled around with no appreciable loss of precious incoherence.

In any case (*In any case*, the last refuge of drivelers), if Cantor's going to bring up the subject and mash it to a pulp then he's got to do it raw—bareback—no eloquence, no pill-sweetening. He's got to kick against the pricks of the subject's density, its built-in eloquence, or nobody will listen, much less listen hard. The performance has to be—or look as if it's—uncomplacently at war with its own resistance to self-realization, so that every listener-looker can feel connected to it, a fellow sufferer.

"Why overrated?" Eden, playing Socrates to Cantor's tortoise, asks with his eyes closed. The closed-eye tone of the question revives Cantor's appreciation of sun, sand and silence but not necessarily in that order.

"I meant useless." Cantor shuts his eyes in the hope of mimicking Eden's irresistible tone. If he can mimic the tone and thereby extract its secret, maybe he won't be plagued by the need to devour the intoner, thighs and all. "Why useless?" George lifts himself up, rests his blazing skull carefully on the back of his right hand and stares resolutely out to sea. Now he and Eden are evenly matched. Don't ask him why. "Martin," he announces. The utterance of the name singes his belly like a salty caress (yes, a *salty* caress: you heard me right the first time, you, bub, you!). And who knows, maybe it's doing the very same for Eden's. In any case—*In any case*—that utterance gives George—or so the wordflow would have him believe (and wordflow knows best)—a further advantage.

He knows better than to think Martin Eden will answer, Yes?

"Did you ever have the feeling it's Envy that propels its lifeblood through the world's veins—links heaven and earth—keeps the heavenly bodies out of trouble? Not Rabelais's *debt* or Melville's *Indian-hating* or Melanctha's *Building 18* or my very own *berry sundae* but Envy? Did you ever have the feeling it's not a side effect of our operations but that we operate solely to be able to feel Envy toward or induce it in our fellow operators. That nature created man not to Lend and Borrow but to Envy?" Cantor likes the modest kind exploratory tone—of forbearance toward his own uncertain ignorance. That tone invites Eden to play Lewis and Clark and insists he take whichever is the meatier, juicier role.

Why does Eden's silence make all this heavy breathing sound—the allusion to Panurge's robustly beautiful debt aria notwithstanding—hopelessly beside the point, ex-centric?

"So you're saying it's not a disease." Eden makes obtuseness—even if it's 100 percent fake obtuseness—well, sexy. Or rather, hot, since, as noted in the wilds of page 107 or thereabouts, *sexy* now and until further notice means something like "attention grabbing."

"No, I'm *not* saying it's not a disease. What I am saying is that like any disease worth its salt, Envy constitutes just another form of life with an allotted span. It's a living being—like the breath of speech (the *Logos*)—whose natural progression has to be respected, and not irritated by drugs, just like the Good Book says."

"The Bible?"

"The *Timaeus*." Should he inform Eden of what he himself learned but a few hours ago from the chambermaid? (toothsome to a fault—too bad he doesn't swing both ways even if he doesn't believe you *can* swing both ways). Namely, that tomorrow's World Plato Day in old Coronado, complete with fireworks and an adaptation of the *Allegory of the Cave* to be staged on a barge (twice as big as Cleopatra's burnished throne) over on, hopefully moonlit, Glorietta Bay.

"Which makes Invidicum the enemy of life."

"Like every other drug. And once Envy feels it's about to be infected by Pharmakon—I mean Invidicum—It will simply metastasize to a new target, i.e., a new Rival. A Rival even more difficult to combat than its predecessor. So Invidicum the remedy makes the sufferer even more envious. So you might say Invidicum (Horus) is never more poisonous—more invidious—than when it's combating Invidia (Seth).

"Sounds like the *writing it down so you don't forget* dynamic."

"How so?" George asks though he knows the answer. How could he not know, since he makes it a point to read the *Phaedrus* at least four times per semester and eight times during summer vacation.

Eden (*in the same closed-eye sun-baked monotone*): "In that case writing is the pharmakon and forgetfulness the disease. According to the Socrates of this dialogue, one of Egypt's old divinities—Theuth of Naucratis, the inventor of writing (the Son)—came with his invention to the king of that country—Thamus (the Father), who lived in Thebes—claiming it would increase his subjects' wisdom and improve their memory. But Thamus countered that writing would in fact only sow forgetfulness in the souls of those who learned how to use it because under its auspices they'd no longer have the need to exercise their memory, knowing they could now depend on alien marks and superficial imprints to recall things to mind, rather than on their own inherent powers. So writing as remedy—writing as pharmakon—writing as Bad Son—as Wandering Jew—as orphan—as basilisk—inasmuch as its marks do not inscribe themselves in the wax of the soul—hypnotizes the life of memory and poisons its well. Writing robs memory of its life process, which is not to recover what is in any case irretrievable (leave the engrams to bury the engrams) but to discover through the stimulus of loss—and the right missteps—what was inconceivable. Which means that Writing the Pharmakon is most akin to Hermes the Thief."

Cantor can't believe his virgin ears. Sure, he's pretty much come around to accepting what's now a hoary commonplace among his fellow pill-poppers—that one of the principal side effects of Invidicum is its engenderment (*there, what did I tell you!*) of an incorrigibly virtuosic wordflow (so don't be alarmed if you're suddenly sounding like Timon of Athens after he's reread *The Sacred Fount* for the seventeenth time). And, sure, he's even willing to grant, but only after the obligatory (nonexistent) inner struggle—like the one Barack pretended to have undergone (in appeasement of the unappeasable heartland) before acknowledging the legitimacy of same-sex marriage and divorce— And, sure, he's even willing to grant the following: Such wordflow, while priding itself on the ability to leave in its defiant wake only the sort of construction that refuses to be put in a one-to-one correspondence with something out in the world of *world*flow, is nonetheless willing when sufficiently provoked to come up with a construction that's mappable from in-here into out-there. A construction that makes horse sense not only in Word but in World.[29]

Sure, he's pretty much come around to accepting—OK—anything, but here we have a construction that's mappable from in here to out there every

---

[29] *And isn't this what growing up—gay or otherwise—is all about?* Cantor hears himself think. But, wherever it came from, he refuses to have such a simpering idiotically bright-eyed and bushy-tailed remark ascribed to him when it's the wordflow—*his* wordflow—that's responsible. (*Doctor Mabuse*, he hears himself think, *I tell you it's not me who's stark raving mad! It's the wordflow! the wordflow at war with worldflow!*)

step of its way and not by accident. Here we have a very deliberative hyper-sophisticated meditation and out of the mouth of babes no less. So it's just as Cantor's been suspecting all along but was afraid to admit: Eden aka Theuth aka Thoth has been chosen executor of the creative enterprise of the Master aka Thamus aka Horus. Enunciator in words and transmitter of the Master's fully formed and ready-made divine thought. But even if the enunciation is only the palest reflection of all His creative energy (itself a reflection, but of what?)—is only an afterthought—is only a mere formality . . . Still, for the Master to have selected Eden while forsaking the beefier credentials of all the others . . . And even if it was the very leanness of Eden's that galvanized the Master into . . .

Cantor can't believe his inner ear: He's actually thinking about the Master as if he were . . . real. Or is it the Invidicum doing the thinking for the two of them? But when you get right down to it, isn't believing He's real—or not—also *a mere formality*? The Master's unreal realness/real unrealness is essential to the trial's main design.

Intentionally, Cantor lets slip the fact that he's been wondering more and more whether there mayn't be an orphan disease out there against which Invidicum is eminently suited to pack an off-label wallop. An unambiguously beneficent wallop (all remedy, no poison; all gain, no pain). While hating nothing so much as being the class sneak, he's got to find out how much Eden knows about the off-label use on whose altar he's surely being sacrificed—about what he's been fitted out and girded for. So what if Eden now goes berserk at his not-so-deft allusion to the Big I's homicidogenic function? After all, it's George's future as well—even his life—that's at stake here. Is Eden going to stomp on what he takes to be George's allusion to Invidicum's homicidogenic function? What's the difference? Eden will be shipping out any day now and with a little luck they'll never meet again. Like Strangers on a Train. Cruise-mates sharing the same lifejacket. How much does Eden know about what he's being fitted out for? Girded against? "I'm especially concerned about what an off-label use may have to do with this so-called final vital crucial leg of the trial. Especially since the two of us have been singled out for something even more dire." It's the first time there's been a reference to their special status. Unless one of them—or both—talked a blue streak in their sleep.

"What the hell does off-label mean?" Eden manages to look as brutish as anybody *can* look in pretty (red, white and blue) swim trunks. Overcompensation for what all those polysyllables have done to his manhood—worse, to his manhood's reputation. So—it's no more Mr. Nice Guy—or rather, Mr. Thoth Guy. From this moment on he's swearing off lingo. More, much more: he's decreeing that his incursion into the fairyland of grandiloquence—ungratuitous grandiloquence—grandiloquence demanded by the facts of the case—grandiloquence as the sole bridge between word- and worldflow—is officially at an end and (as far as his integrity as a regular guy is concerned) not a minute too soon. Unless he has no recollection of being in fairyland (falling into a Master-induced coma—equivalent to one hundred years in *The Sleeping Beauty*—being obligatory for the transmission of His Lesson). No, the brutishness has too much of the feel of a home remedy directed against whatever poisonous traces Eden thinks fairyland grandiloquence has left behind—in the testes, for starters.

So, for the time being, the matter of off-label use must be put on hold.

Advancing toward the North Patio, as . . . requested? required? ordered? Cantor resigns himself to the fact that it's going to be—no, that it already is—one of those days when as the sun gets sunnier the clouds get blacker, though ever more compensatorily rimmed with torchlight. At the breakfast table, he notes at once that Eden is acting a bit odd (though how can odd be distinguished from, say, even in the case of so loose—and at the same time, so stoically controlled—a cannon?). Is he having trouble handling his newfound semi-celebrity as Patient Most Likely to Succeed? Walser appears to be noting this as well. But it's to gangly Stifter that the task of asking why (more like the chore, judging from his expression) has been delegated. To slow their pulses (the suspense is killing them), the two prissy-posh ladies (gals, really) at the next table puff-puff away. Finding Eden's struggle to explain too painful to watch, Cantor decides to take the bullhorn by the horns and hold forth on his behalf as if unburdening himself—and maybe he's doing just that and nothing more. He's expected to participate in this, the crucial phase, as a VIP and he's flattered, don't think he isn't, but isn't there a danger in being cured too quickly. "How do you mean?" Stifter blubbers, as if the House Escutcheon has just been sullied. "I just don't think I'm ready to be untrue to—disrespectful of the diagnosis dealt me way back when. Otherwise my newfound cockiness will make me stray off course and it's unlikely I'll ever be curable. I mustn't get too healthy." But—Stifter thinks daggers but speaks none (as does Eden, though less lucidly—but *how dare we make that assumption!*)—in your case, Georgie boy, there's absolutely no danger of veering way off course by getting way too healthy—you'll always have your queerness to shield you from that. (Stif doesn't know what Straynge, his mentor—more often than not, his *tor*mentor—thinks—thought—on the subject but he for one has never gotten over the shock of living through the scourge's depathologization by the spineless, fickle AMA, even if he was only a tyke in sheep's clothing at the time.) He suddenly realizes his daggers haven't been sharp and agile enough to de-depathologize Cantor for here he is, still speaking—glibly of course, as is the way of his kind. "If I were to evade—elude—eschew (call it what you like)—the diagnosis I've worked so hard to incur by flaunting too many of the signs of health too soon—if I were to give up on Envy and leave it in the lurch, so to speak (for I've grown quite attached to the old devil)—then I'd be working against rather than with the medicos I've come to admire more than I can say. Cure, self-reform, rehab, emergence from the maelstrom (call it whatever you like) would be a betrayal of your faith in me, which means your faith in my infirmity, or is it the other way around? I need to keep the disease in the line of sight of my rehabilitators at all times even if it ends up meaning eternal sickness. Premature rehab (what rehab isn't? and as a VIP don't I risk just that?) would be a dereliction of duty. Signs of health at this or maybe at any stage of the game would be most inappropriate—bad form. I don't want to be the bratty model remembered only for having refused to stand still long enough to be snapped, with the dead disease cuddled in his arms, by Amygdala's house cameraman. Nor does anybody have the right" (he looks Stifter straight in the eye: no upstart sawbones, however cute, is going to dictate the terms of his turbulence) "to attribute my qualms to that old chestnut of the psychobabblers—I'm referring to *fear of success* aka *self-sabotage*. I guess what I feel I'm trying to say—" (Stop right there: he likes the sudden, unpremeditated fumbling of his tone; he likes what it reluctantly evinces of a down-home distrust of words [*pure simulation*]; he likes being, for as long as the folksiness lasts, the high-school football jock voted most likely to enter the big time and die from complications of chronic traumatic encephalopathy while his NFL exploiters go on laughing their fat-assed admissions-of-no-wrongdoing all the way to the bank.) "—is that I can't leave the disease behind just like that— the disease that has made me what I am today—even if it isn't a disease." He's just executed an avant-garde stunt—a mere stunt—but as the stunt consists in impersonating the tone of a hero (i.e., the exact opposite of what he is or takes himself to be) why not let himself enjoy the best of both fantasy worlds: anarchy and virtue? By any chance, is he atoning for the fact that *the other disease* has been kicked out of the *DSM*? Stif wonders as his roving gaze settles on the lady smokers, neither of whom merits an erection—no, wait, the older one (if only she could manage to have that mole under her right eye removed and a crocodile teardrop put in its place) definitely has possibilities.

Sighing deeply to indicate their grand tour of his innermost premises is at an end, Cantor's mighty pleased to acknowledge that only he could have plausibly delivered this message. More to the point, he feels his delivery has been a powerful one—why, the pair at the next table seem to be trembling still. And if he's not mistaken they're competitively casting amorous glances his way (*control yourselves, ladies! this hotel bills itself as not just mutt- but family-friendly*). But isn't it the unofficial policy of his Scourge of Psyche[30] (not to be confused with FoP, or maybe it should be—but of that, more anon)—isn't it SoP's policy to encumber him only with the thoughts he'd be least likely to engender when left to his own devices? He suddenly remembers countless occasions when thoughts as complex or at least as complicated were expressed by the unlikeliest of suspects—Eden or Borkman or better yet that trial member who always resembled, when emerging from the MRI, "the same old sausage, fizzing and sputtering in his own grease." Why, it fast became a tradition—unlikeliness, not sputtering. (He remembers having overheard AI folks back in New York remark—restively, snarkily [but you know how New Yorkers are]—that the thoughts they started having after being on Invidicum for about a week or two—thoughts that didn't sound like their own and with which they were saddled as by some Alien—were just *silly-complicated*, not *somberly-complex*.)

But SofP sure knows what he's doing—except in this case—Cantor sud-

---

[30]Cantor is temporarily on the outs with the Master so, motored by adolescent spite, he'd like nothing better than to jilt Him and re-engage the concierge services of his own personal master but since he doesn't have a personal master, he's decided to call his Rose by another name (at least until his hackles fall back into place) which smells just as sickly sweet.

denly realizes, since as expressed by the wrong person the thought always manages to deliver an electrifying jolt, transforming Cantor for one into something better than he considers himself to be, at least for a moment. He sees the whole world differently, including the deliverer. He is the music while the music lasts—the very model of a modern major specimen who, his boundaries expanded, has a better sense of what his and everybody else's suffering—suffering as *beauty*—is all about. And any other listeners who happen to be mulling around—trialoids, doctors, nurses in mufti, lab technicians, visiting dignitaries with the obligatory Vandyke—are also electrified, or at least unnerved, which does more wonders for their complexion than a brisk walk in the shivery spring rain ever could. Once the speech is over, they aren't quite . . . themselves, which in their case is always all to the good. So maybe it's not only his boat that's getting rocked regularly by SoP (except for just now when thought and thinker were spittin' images) but the others' as well— maybe they're all targeted by the . . . Thing (some even more than he) but have elected to say nothing lest the experience turn out to be the wrong kind of side effect—the kind that's downright disqualificatory—or no side effect at all but the symptom of some rival condition that will only lure Invidicum away from its prime target. As far as he can tell, this is the first time that (progressively? regressively?) he's called the Master aka SoP a Thing. Will this usher in the Age of Immunity to Envy?

And what if he assumes—just for argument's sake—that it was not Envy but a predisposition to enslavement by the Master's—the Thing's—ordinances or those of some thing just like It (for there must be plenty more where the Thing hails from) which roped them all in, either as victims or perpetrators (the distinction is too simple but will hold until further notice)? What if those dumb enough to get involved in the Invidicum project were the Thing's vocation? And what if the signature jolts that have been proving so transformative for anybody lucky enough to undergo them are concoctable only by a Thing addicted to sabotaging its consecration to said vocation? And what if it is precisely the Thing's relentless misallocation of insight-choked ariosi, which turns chorus members perfectly at peace with their expendability into irreplaceable star tenors, that is both Its addiction and Its cure—Its . . . *pharmakon*? And who's to say whether the jolts are the detritus cast off by a thriftless self-destructor or the marvels of a master builder who knows exactly what he's doing at every moment but, for the life of Him, just can't meet industry criteria? After all, it mustn't be easy for It to deal with the likes, *as he's found them*, of Herbert and Rhys (rebarbative whether on the Ferry or off), and Borkman and Cantor himself, not to mention the clowns—as numerous as those in any quadrennial lineup of aspirants to the Republican nomination—assigned to cure them and the kinfolk rooting on the sidelines for their excruciatingly slow defeat. But the question still remains, How has Cantor's delivery—the hawking of a thought by, in this case, its *most likely* manufacturer—managed to come across as so powerful, so . . . jolting? To the extent that it visited a pubic thrill upon the *absolute dolls* (in corporate-speak of far away and long ago) at the next table? Well, maybe it's because—even if he's the most plausible hawker du jour and even if this (for no other reason than to give Stanley qua

Brando and Brando cum Stanley a run for their money) is the role he was born to play—he's had the good sense to unburden himself of his albatross in the most implausible place at the most implausible time.

The novelty of *Thing* and *It* is, Cantor's got to admit, wearing pretty thin. At the same time, there's no urgent access of homesickness for *Master* on the horizon. But maybe there's no need to get all worked up about some master self-destructor, whatever she's called. Simplest explanations work best, at least for the simplest-minded. SoP could very well be *FoP*, aka Feeling of Presence, as often reported in people with injuries to the frontoparietal cortex and soon to be reported (and why not?) in people . . . addicted to Invidicum. So who dares to suggest that as a member of the trial group, every one of them isn't entitled to ask, along with Eliot's Antarctic expeditionist, *Who is the third who walks always beside you? When I count, there are only you and I together but when I look ahead up the white road there is always another one beside you gliding wrapt in a brown mantle . . .*

Walser demands to know why Cantor has waited until now to blitz them with second thoughts about getting cured and staying cured. "All you wanted was to wangle a free trip to sunny CA. To be able to brag to colleagues that your handlers were *flying you out to the Coast* since it was their business, as moguls, to know a hot property when they saw one. Or is it" (turning to Stifter) "*wrangle?*" Stifter's prompt obedient shrug, with its slightest twinge of smugness, means: Unlike you, I make no swaggering pretense of *not having the faintest idea.* Is what Walser has just offered a specimen of tough therapeutic love in action? Cantor doesn't care (whatever it is, it's a big fat flop) since he's suddenly too busy missing the other Coast—rues the day (which seems like yesterday—which *is* yesterday!) he consented to sell off all retinal rights to the gumdrop-yellow sidelights of his now-beloved East River tugs for this measly shot at the title. And what title is that? he has every right to ask. Well, for starters—and as the man just said—*Getting Cured and Staying Cured* (subtitle in the works: since the shriller the title, the direr the need for a mitigating sub-). Which is sure to end up, after the requisite superslow start in the marketplace, on the hit lists of both Oprah and Jenna Bush Hager not to mention the (nonexistent) highbrow Mafia. Cantor looks hard at Walser who resembles nothing so much as a toad—a smug toad—though not as smug as Stifter's shrug. He wants to hate him for being a toad because hating will make the relation so much easier. But he can't because Walser isn't smug-toad enough to warrant hate. But because this isn't just any old hatred we're talking about but hatred begotten by Despair upon Impossibility, all's well that ends well and Cantor ends up hating Walser far more for not fitting the bill than he ever could for fitting it. He orgasms quickly and having now gotten as much mileage as he can out of the vicissitudes of hatred, he turns to Eden, whom he's been trying so hard to defend, or at least camouflage. He doesn't expect gratitude but, still, he's only human and it's disappointing to see him hanging his head as if (*delete* as if) in flayed-alive disavowal of everything Cantor's just said. Walser's nastiness—nastiness so nasty it induces a Feeling of the Presence of Bad Breath—has left Cantor debased, i.e., feminized. Virtue needn't be its own reward, however, for those virtuous enough to see and what Cantor sees is reward beyond price: a spectacle that would be unmountable in New York (and not just because of the tugs or the buildings spread out against the post-twilight like slabs of prime beef marbleized upon a table). Rhys and Shearer have lost interest in volleyball as quickly as Herbert in her notetaking so they've ended up (he feels not like one but *three* chummy parents, happy to see that the kids are—and without any prodding, mind you—getting pretty darn chummy as well) far more fulfilled in giggling at their own chatter with gestures to match. And as if the giggling-chattering-gesturing weren't sufficient reward in themselves, here they are making him feel as much maleness as he's ever going to feel since his kind of maleness—the facultative kind—can surface and subsist only in contradistinction to a proximate giddy femaleness, preferably near-hysterical. Here they are sucking the virus of femininity from the marrow of his manhood to fuel their giggling chattering gesturing femaleness and epiphenomenally refunding his maleness. Here they are making him male, masculine, even heterosexual—heterosexualization being but a step away, albeit a mighty elusive one, from remasculinization. Compliments of an *On the other hand* coming round the bend, he knows full well that this boost must not be perceived as the first step toward implementation of a Heterosexuality Protection Program. What he's just been grazed by yet again is nothing more than a Feeling of Presence—of the ghost of heterosexuality—which prefers to come and go as it pleases. So what he's been vouchsafed—(Yes, *vouchsafed*, you heard me right the first time. If you can think of a better word, feel free to contact my proctologist in the morning.)—is the ghost of a feeling which is quite content, when all is said and done, to remain a feeling especially since it doesn't have the option of being anything else. And *he's OK with that*, or so goes the lingo, which like so much lingo is already an archaism (or is this just wordflow's wishful thinking?). What he's been vouchsafed as well is an opportunity to meditate on the subject of lost opportunities—to be cherished as long as they know their place and stay lost. Making him one in a long line of heavies which includes Stefan Brand, Eugene Onegin, Lear, Zampano, John Marcher and (on a slightly less exalted level) James Stevens, whose remains, given half a chance, can all attest more than they know.

And just as the giggling— Hey, if Cantor doesn't watch out, *giggling* will turn into just the sort of placeholder for all sorts of aberrancies Walser pretended to warn them about, putting it right up there with *Building 18* and *audition*, not to mention Rabelaisian *debt*. And just as the gigglers have sucked him dry of all femininity (he momentarily feels *virus-free*—no longer virus-naïve—on too many levels to count), so is he expected, through the good auspices of his contrastive shadow, to suck Eden free of whatever curbs his appetite for the self-ablation required to realize his manifest destiny. No doubt about it: his shadow, like that of Masaccio's Saint Peter, is expected to be curative—healing—remedial.

But observing Stif appraise a shimmering beauty fresh from the foam— here, there and everywhere she's anointing the air with the droplets disdainfully shed by her blood-red snakeskin—he wants to be more than just a grand-tourist in Heteroland. (The calculating squint makes it clear that heterosexuality is the only attribute of the substance that is maleness.) He wants, crazily enough, to be one of its model citizens. But how can he expect to be naturalized if, at the sight of said beauty, he feels not the slightest tingle in his groin though he does feel the stirrings of the old alarm (can this qualify as a step in the right direction?) at missing yet another opportunity—always experienced as his very last—to make the grade? What excites Cantor beyond measure is Stif's desire. The stiff prick that is his gaze. He desires Stif's desire. That he detests him—Stif will have to work a bit harder to merit the kind of hatred he feels for Walser—adds spice to the stew. That so detestable a target of desire should dare to be the namesake of the author of "Abdias" adds even more. (He could advise Melanctha that the first line of that work would make the perfect epigraph for her bestseller on the tribe's current adventures in this new cosmic cycle. Though she might take it as a warrantless raid on her autonomy.)

But then it comes to him—and where but here *should* it come to him? (After all, it's in Coronado that algebraic topologists and their cronies have a bad habit of becoming fast-living and hard-loving legends.) And miracle of miracles, while it's coming to him (as it has too too many times before and always, as now, in a first-ever ecstasy worthy of Bernini), maleness floods his veins where it belongs—well, maybe it doesn't *flood* but it doesn't exactly trickle either. Because for the first time he's sure (as oh so many times before) that his fascination with and desire for somebody else's maleness is not a *non*-maleness but one of the many unsimple changes of garment of his own brand. Which shows he's infinitely more versatile than stiff-pricked Stif. So for the first time in his life he's refusing (as oh so many times before) to let this fascination with another man's maleness—*the fascination that dares not speak its name*—make mincemeat of his selfhood. The foreign country that lacerated longing has put on the map of his mishaps retains its charm precisely because he knows he wouldn't—couldn't—be caught dead making it his permanent home—that is, if he seriously intends to keep his franchise in the psychosexual avant-garde. So thanks to the longing—or rather, to his idiomatic manipulation of that longing—he's constructed, stone by stone, a Gibraltar of his own sort of maleness founded on, among other things, a longing for connectedness to—fusion with—habitation deep within—other guys' maleness. So, you guys, let me introduce you to another man's man—a Marlboro Man's man, in fact—but a man's man who wears his rue with a difference—who's man enough to embrace—to let himself be manhandled by—all of his flaws, pre-eminent among which is the inability to be male 100 percent of the time and heterosexual more than, say, 31 percent. So—even though Cantor finds himself sitting not quite diagonally across from yet another sulky-smug-snotty dude who's managed to do the impossible, i.e., achieve oneness with his maleness sans messy remainder—for the first time (as oh so very many many times before) he ain't the least bit intimidated. Or rather he is willing although not necessarily able to work on being unintimidated as part of his just-established *Unblushing Commitment-to-Maleness Campaign*. The Stif no longer has the self-conferred right to stare him down (in any case, with Snakeskin still on the horizon he has better things to do).

Cantor has whittled Stif down to size and with, thriftily, the very same chisel used in erecting his sunny West Coast Gibraltar. Stif's maleness—like the maleness of Eden and Borkman and every other ravingly erudite cunnilinguist on the block—has turned out to be—and not a minute too soon—just another brand—another brand of branded entertainment. But so, too, is Cantor's (see above). But though he's pleased that his brand is a bona fide brand—one of the boys, so to speak—he doesn't want it to be a normal brand—he doesn't want the normality of the other brands to rub off on his. He wants his brand to be unique—first among equals. Even if he knows all too well that non-normality is just the poor man's uniqueness. Even if he remembers that Liepnits dude (yes, *dude*: effective immediately: by COVID-19 Executive Order No. 69, an anti-dude has the same right as any other dude to use the word *dude*) saying at one of the last convocations on Greenwich Avenue (to somebody in the first row whose name tag read *Christian Wolff*) that there were more things worthy of observation in a healthy body than in a sick one (much to Straynge's consternation, inasmuch as sickness was his bread and butter). But he needn't worry: his brand only seems to have become normal by contagion: it's still salvaged by defects, drawbacks, debilities, the very means through which he gets an edge on the competition—custom-made pinholes drilled, so to speak, in their—the competition's—Veil of Maya, expressly to allow him a privileged glimpse awry of what normality—which he knows in his gut to be the most overrated of Kantian El Dorados (but which he still exalts, as attested by his relentless mockery thereof)—a glimpse awry of what normality looks and sounds like in its pure state. And what should this Thing-in-Itself turn out to be but a Sphinx, just a tired old three-legs-in-the-evening sort of Sphinx, or better yet a sphynx cat, who is now scarily reassuring Cantor, if he happens to still need any reassuring, that though Normality is very much alive and well (at least statistically), and not just in the Bible, Borscht, Corn, Chastity, Hurricane and Asteroid Belts, there is (*sorry!*) simply no normalizing poison—no pharmakon—against his special brand of maleness which is all bound up with his special Audenoid brand of Envy—nor shall there be, ever. So he can relax and enjoy the incurability—the unnormalizability—the poor man's uniqueness—of his brand of brandedness. He has nothing to fear from normality.[31] The Envy everybody else in the group feels or thinks he feels has, in Cantor's case, been swallowed whole by his own particular incurable brand, which is insusceptible to cure. Cure *it* and you cure him of himself. And he'll never be desperate enough to want that to happen. The only thing her—the sphynx cat's—foster-children (Straynge and those who come after)

---

[31] Never before has George experienced the concept of non-normality (as deployed in one of Bertrand Apollinax's parlor tricks) so viscerally. Why did it take him until this minute to realize that a non-normal class, i.e., one that contains itself as a member, is a sort of mathematical fetus-in-fetu and as such deserves all the bad press its grotesquerie manages to generate? And while we're at it, didn't T.S. Channing-Cheetah—in a snide-by shooting worthy of Al Capone—once refer to Bertie's laughter as that of an irresponsible *fetus*? It's all coming together! (*that's a phrase Cantor wouldn't be caught dead using*).

have to offer Cantor is a dollop or two of curd-crazy platitudes in a bowl of piping-hot placebo. Maybe every sleazeball in the pipeline figured that out long ago and decided to keep Cantor on ice only because they suspected he'd make a great chaperon for Eden—a great *beard*. But just because x (homosexuality), subset of X (Envy), has no cure, there is no reason (except perversity) to reject a cure for X especially when, as now, it is about to be handed to him on a silver platter (as if it were the head of John the Baptist and he a mix of Herod and Salome). Or is it?

Eden looks like he has something to say—something he can't wait to spit out. But he waves instead, and smiles enthusiastically. Most uncharacteristically though maybe not so uncharacteristically—Cantor doesn't pretend to know him by heart. But neither can he deny that very much on unforeseeable display here is a certain flirtatiousness, hinting (intriguingly, groin-tinglingly) at things to come that (even more intriguingly, even more groin-tinglingly) will of course (given the straightitude of the flirt) never come. Following Eden's gaze, Cantor spots Borkman, everybody's favorite visionary robber baron—he does look baronial, one has to admit, even in corny Bermuda shorts and sockless pennyloafers—who has clearly found a friend (another specter in snakeskin) or the semblance of one and therefore has no time to notice much less acknowledge, a wave from the remotely recent past. Is this one-trick pony express by any chance wearing his monitoring bracelet? With his equally corny cigar cocked directly at the tiniest cloud ever to shield the sun from prying eyes, he's no doubt boasting about his outsize business triumphs and boasting still more, for all the token self-hate, about his failures in other spheres which are sure, acquainted as Cantor is with Borkman's talkaholic magic, to end up sounding like triumphs as well—and if anything, even more outsize. Since the failures only confirm (so says the cigar) what everybody on his radar should already know—namely, that he's been put on earth for bigger and better things than confronting the challenges of fatherhood, husband-hood, citizenhood, sonhood, brotherhood, partnerhood, etc., head-on—but such is his greatness of soul that he's been more than willing to try his hand at all the roles for which he's least fitted, having surmised early on—as his name-sake didn't—that lousing up other people's lives from start to finish can only redound to his own credit as a tragic figure, a fate for which, far more than for his spinoffs and acquisitions, he wishes to be venerated (though Borkman will never admit as much, least of all to himself). In addition, what can he do if there happens to be a crying need in Killjoy's Great Chain of Being, aka the Leibnizian curve of the universe, just as much for a representative of *his kind* (so say the Bermudas)—namely, the sort of bigshot in the world of high finance who flunks bigtime everywhere else—as for representatives of all the others? And whose fault is it if, in order that the Chain might have no gaps, in order that there might be no missing points on the curve (i.e., no missing exemplars of every life experiment as conceived by Its—the Chain's—demi-urge), he's been chosen as the representative of his hapless constituency? But if he's failed—and he has failed, and failed big—then it's pretty much the fault of the roles themselves for not adapting to his talents—for not conforming to *their* curve—talents that have made it their principle (the only one to which they hew, and hew doggedly) to reject all truck with everyday things—things incompatible with greatness—or rather, and more importantly, with the trappings of greatness. And anyway, everyday failure is the surest proof of expertise non pareil in the only domain that counts. Puffing and preening, he looks exactly as he looked on that hot July evening (at the leafy corner of Bank Street and Greenwich Avenue?) when, on the spur of the moment, he decided to saddle Cantor with the privilege of feasting on his confessional brand of braggadocio.

But appearances are often deceiving (Cantor mutely guffaws at this darksome profundity). Since once Borkman and his companion are seated—not too far in fact from the very ladies who had the misfortune to fall head over heels for Cantor (or his vocabulary) but who, all things considered, are convalescing nicely—he elaborates, by pointing to his monitoring bracelet, on a state of affairs to which (as his tonelessness makes clear) no lustre accrues from the surplus value of failure in other spheres. Spheres whose only music is failure, of a very pinpointable kind. It's bigger than Cantor imagined. The effort to show concern makes her fidgety. Or maybe she's just shivering in her wet snakeskin. "Nothing to fidget about," he warns.

Though soon enough he's up to his old self-inflationary tricks. So it's suddenly no surprise to hear Borkman tell the little lady that he's not in the trial because he suffers from Envy. That was all a pretense to get his big flat foot in the door. He's in the study as a tourist, you might say (eco-, oeno-, suicide, virtual or sex, take your pick, though probably the last-named, considering all the conquests he's already racked up). The longer he stays roped in, the more he realizes he's not envious or at least he doesn't suffer from the disease, which may do nothing more in fact than scare away its symptoms. At the mere sound of the name of the disease (in the course of doctor-patient consultations, for example) beneath whose umbrella they dutifully seethe, or at least reside, the symptoms skedaddle. By virtue of having gotten himself roped in, he's being purged of whatever resting-memory-state envy or latent-reservoir envy he happens (like everybody else) to harbor.

From the point of view of a drug entrepreneur (which he's fast becoming simply by virtue of keeping eyes pricked, ears peeled, jaw set and head half-cocked—and of course a few vanity massages at the Manning Sports Salon in the getting-ever-more-chic-by-the-femtosecond West Village did wonders for his progress), a disease is only as good as the number of orphans—incurable diseases that afflict fewer than 200,000 people—into which it can be salami-sliced and baloney-diced. Since orphan diseases have a funny way of breeding orphan drugs and when orphan drugs get themselves approved by the FDA for perpetration of market mayhem, the agency not only waives the two-million-dollar user fee a company normally pays to unleash its scourge but, adding insult to injury, grants tax credits for expenses incurred through clinical trials, whether conducted or not, as well as market exclusivity for seven years, during which approvals for all rival drugs are put on hold. Or, if slicing and dicing comes to naught, then he has to ensure that Invidicum stays underground long enough to render plausible a sudden overripeness for rediscovery—as a cure for Envy in at least four or five of its <200,000 dicings.

Requiring an eleven-fold price spike. "Why eleven-fold?" she asks. "Because my mother was born on August 11th and I hated her guts." And from there it's (in the great tradition of Questcor's Acthar and Turing's Daraprim and Valeant's Isuprel and Catalyst's Firdapse) but a hop, skip and a metastasis to confections like Lambert-Eaton Myasthenic Syndrome, toxoplasmosis, West syndrome, progeria and Chagas disease. Yes, the orphans have clearly taken over the Agency, the way inmates, it is said—worse, their keepers—used to take over the asylum. *Duck, you suckers*, Cantor thinks, *the lunatic fringe has gone mainstream.*

And he'll have (pointing to the bracelet) plenty of time to wait for Invidicum to get grandfathered back into the fray. He's already planning a comeback once he's released on his own recognizance, or whatever the phrase is. He'll work around the regulatory bans by making a virtue of necessity. Which means, my dear, no more publicly traded investment platforms with billions in assets—at least for a while. No more gobbling up and guzzling down small businesses, with the inevitable blocking of investor exits because he's drowning in illiquidity. No more *entities*. Just actions that leave no trace—high-frequency trades from home, wherever that turns out to be (96.8 percent are blissfully canceled before they ever see the blear of day). Trades faster than the speed of light—in futures, bonds, and commodities. Especially water. "You can't imagine how appealing water can be to a recovering lush like me." "You mean you'd give up billions for—" "For an unspeakable glass of water? Yes." Then he backtracks (not tergiversation but attention to detail). Only he won't be trading water per se—water the entity, the resource—not even water the commodity. Instead, he'll be trading, to quote one of his arch-enemies (Cantor knows exactly whom he means: Frederick Kaufman ["Wall Street's thirst for water," *Nature*, vol. 490 (25 October 2012)]), pledges to deliver or accept water at some specified date—derivatives indexed to indices of indices of rainfall, desalination, dams, aquifers, sewage. "Until I get my feet out of my mouth and on the ground." While she's by no means convinced, neither has she completely lost interest. After all, the bracelet *is* big and it sparkles. Still. Won't it bother him to be trafficking in disasters (drought, monsoons, floods, water wars)—to be indexing—mortgaging—his morals to their ebb and flow? She's choking on her exasperation. Cantor hangs his head. *Never again*, the head warns him, *will I permit you to underestimate the capacity of a snakeskin for righteous outrage.*

Before responding he puts his hand on her knee. She pushes it away. Or rather, she flicks it away as if it were a fruit fly which didn't respond to Invidicum, in pheromone form, as it should have. Cantor takes note and is somewhat excited: No surer, if not necessarily sweeter, aphrodisiac than being at loggerheads. Their exchange of glances is now way more raw than most people's exchange of body fluids. "Good question." Thing is, he's in the business of being a captain of industry—in the Schumpeterian sense. He has no other identity—it's not just his most *salient* identity—it's his *only* identity. And always will be. And it just so happens that Big Business (OK, so it's an anachronism) puts a premium on rank fraud. So that's the norm under which he operates. Because he can't bite the hand that feeds him the only dog chow that matters.

Frankly—rankly—being a fraud—ripping out people's meager assets from deep inside their gut—isn't as hard as it's cracked up to be. He simply needs to put himself in the mood—to think of all the bad things the world has done to him (which is difficult, because things have been pretty much idyllic from the word go but never mind that) and make sure to subsume everybody—especially widows, children, orphans, the lame, the legless, the blind and anybody else who rightly deserves an exemption from more bad luck—under the rubric *world*. So that nobody 'scapes whipping. The minute Borkman begins to focus on individuals—relative degrees of guilt—he stops himself in the nick of time and gets back to huddling the huddled masses—into a mass grave. He simply wills himself into believing he's one of those pitiful East European hacker wizzes (the kind his son intends to annihilate with one fell swoop of a start-up's magic wand) traumatized beyond rehabilitation by the collapse of the USSR but who, by crafting every-day-is-Black-Friday malware that is always light-years beyond the decryption capabilities of even the cream of cybercrime analysts (thereby giving them something to live for), nevertheless manages to transmute plight into pure productivity—the sort that will shower benefits on an inexhaustible posterity without regard to bio-, socio- or any other markers. Armed with this belief—that he's one of the knottiest of the have-nots (But after this performance, isn't it clear, Cantor contends, that the definition of "have-not" must at all cost stretch itself to include the Borkmans of the world—or else collapse into irrelevance like the USSR?)—duly armed he plunges into the entrails of the financial machine—the skintrade world of puts, put-ons, shorts, calls, longs, liquidation preferences, wholesale funding, reverse-payment settlements and cloud-funding—as if it were one big point of sale seething with an infinity of welcoming victims. A fool's paradise of greed gone viral in which even the most angelically right anti-software fears to fear to tread, much less foolishly rush in, so little does it know about its target.

"Get the picture?" he purrs roguishly. "I get the picture," she says, quaintly—both excited and disappointed. She tells him he seems to be following in the footsteps of that crazed congresswoman—you know, the one. His silence says he doesn't. She doesn't trust it. "Outrage at accusations of collusion with Russia leveled against her führer triggered the erection of 'a kind of permission structure in her mind' which licensed belief in what she claimed to know was patently false, that, for example, CA forest fires were ignited by laser beams manned by Globalists and shot from their headquarters in outer space.[32] It's the manufacture of belief, whatever that is, which interests me—the point of no return." Cantor sighs. It's taken him all these years to realize—to be made to realize—what quaintness consists in—excitement and disappointment *romantically entwined*—a real tabloid item. Though spent, Borkman doesn't sigh—sighs are for . . . pussies. Instead he takes a very deep

---

[32] See Robert Draper, "The problem of Marjorie Taylor Greene," *New York Times Magazine*, 23 October 2022 issue.

breath. A momentary infatuation with stupidity compels him to boast, "One day I'll be lightning-fast-trading in Invidicum and its spinoffs—trades, that is, not in shares of the drug but in pledges between equally rank fraudsters to, say, deliver or accept a fatal overdose at a specific future time and place."

And all of a sudden it happens and to think it should happen to Cantor, and at his advanced age. He hates Borkman. (Some Body—one of the Master's rivals hence not to be trusted [though distrust can be carried too far]—thinks He forces his creatures to resort to hate much too easily—a default tic that's the easiest way out of His own doldrums. But the Rival stays mum lest he himself be convicted of Envy.) He wants to kill him. To put him out of the world's misery. For suddenly he realizes (compliments of this change of scene) that it's precisely the Borkmans who are responsible for the arrival of yet another branch of Chase or Santander or Bank of America on this or that streetcorner and when you go in, what do you find? Not the affordable housing Di Blasio's always babbling about (best intentioned though he may think he is or thought he was—before he saw the light on the ticker tape announcing his ascension to the presidency) but empty spaces. Not an "officer"—i.e., one of the usual regiment of vice-presidents—in sight. Only one or two slug-slow trainees, glorified non-tellers (a teller! a teller! my kingdom for a teller!), having the run of the place and well aware of what's required of any self-respecting mouse when the cat's away. Enjoying full impunity for their overripe ineptitude. Dancehall hostesses in basement-level corporate drag, whose wan hello means, at the very least, Watch your step, felon: you're in the hidden camera's hairiest crosshairs. And with tits just as slug-sullen since they're not allowed to show off their aureoles to the highest bidder. But with non-tellers being replaced at the rate of one per millisecond by kiosks he can already feel himself going all nostalgic for those tits, with or without aureoles. Yes—even he. So suddenly George knows why he's here. And Eden should know, too. But he shouldn't be too hard on Eden for look how long it's taken him, with all his advanced degrees, to catch on. They should put their heads together and decide on a course of action. Forget the plans the others have for them. Those plans were an afterthought or, if not, then the choice of the two of them as the executors thereof was an afterthought.

It's a clear-cut case of good versus evil—along the lines of, say, Stalin versus Hitler—this bone he has to pick with Borkman—with the Borkmans of the world. A clear-cut case of the need to beat life at its own game. George has decided the theme of the junket—or at least of this stopover—will be Borkman as Villain. Sorry, Melanctha, he hears himself murmur, no room for nuance here though as a budding storyteller I know how invidiously you've been enjoined by your mentors to profess to treasure it. No room for fifty shades of . . . gay. Indeed, he's always considered it a point of honor to *not be*—to *not be* as much as possible, as much as the traffic will allow. (One day, decades and decades ago, who should accost him at the epicenter of his universe, namely, the SE corner of 112th Street and Broadway with its humbly idiosyncratic take on the facade of the world's biggest Cathedral—who should accost him but any right-thinking Jew's idea of a preeminent Black Forest metaphysician with unsavory . . . leanings. Patting him heartily on the back, this crypto-Nazi asked, even more heartily, "How is it with Being?" to which George, ever the party-pooper, replied, "We're not on speaking terms.") Maybe because the stench of being is the hearty stench of appetite, in all shapes and sizes. Though that's less interesting than thinking things the other way around: he eschews appetites because they stink of . . . being. Being itself is what sheerly pollutes: its modes are innocent bystanders. But whatever the reason, there are times, though few and far between, when one must make an exception or a distinction and, out of respect for one's righteous rage, take the plunge and prolapse into being. Times when prolapse—like speaking one's mind—should cease to be a moral duty and become a pleasure. (The route had been charted for him decades before by his irrepressible high-school elocution teacher, Gwendolyn O.W. Fairfax, whose quavering Joan Greenwoodish timbre had a thrilling righteousness about it and, more to the point, who had a soft spot for his . . . ambiguities. We could use more quavers, he thinks dolefully.) There are times, then, when non-being simply won't do. When that righteous rage won't let you off the hook. And what's to become of SoP, aka The Master, when he's forced to rethink all of the man's despoilments? Because if George forces himself to do so then the Master will be forced in tandem. Which means Borkman will no longer serve as an innocent pretext for the sort of Masterly thought packets that breathe best in an abstract ozone. Although the Master has always wanted it both ways—the show-stopping concreteness of titillating topicality AND the corrosiveness of supra-topical deep-think. That's His downfall and his glory—His glory as downfall. He and Eden have been thrown together come hell or high water to rid the Earth of Borkman. So what if theirs is no marriage made in heaven, to be blissfully annulled in hell? Cantor is trembling with rage.[33] Not necessarily righteous rage—in any case, he doesn't want it to be too righteous because righteousness may end up killing the rage out of the sheerest self-congratulation (the way curiosity killed Schrödinger's cat, and not a minute too soon). Yet he fears the explosion of coquetry he's witnessed between Eden and Borkman, coquetry peculiar to Michelangelo's Noah and Ham. Has Borkman replaced Straynge, for whom Cantor is beginning to have more and more . . . what's the word? pity? If Eden has taken Borkman as his . . . role model (ugh! detestable term), then the game is over long before it starts. Or maybe this is all part of the plan.

Avoiding Eden's atypically piercing gaze, Walser announces—sounds more like a placative promise—that he'll have to find the two of them a decent place to stay up in Santa Barbara. Eden inter-erupts. "For our honeymoon,

---

[33]Cantor might be able to calm down (nobody's more aware of this than the polymath himself) if only he could start thinking of the Master as none other than master filmmaker Sergei Eisenstein, and of His thought packets as nothing less than an enigma variation on the theme of Sergei's "prepared fragments." and of the Master's own film in progress as being *constructed* (not *created*) with those fragments (aka "finished parts") like a machine. See Jacques Aumont, *Montage Eisenstein*, Lee Hildreth, Constance Penley and Andrew Ross, translators (Bloomington, Indiana, Indiana University Press, 1987), p. 150.

you mean. Look, why am I here? I'm not interested in why the others are here. They can go to hell for all I care. Why am *I* here?" (*Why am I here?* Cantor can't believe his ears. Hasn't Eden been listening to everything he's been thinking?) "Here. I mean back in the city where I was born and where a terrible thing happened to my father. I wasn't all that crazy about him but he *was* my father (not my *dad*) and as my father he deserved to be avenged." As an afterthought, he pounds his fists on the table top which, fragility notwithstanding, gives at least as good as it gets. The two ladies leave in a hurry. Even Borkman looks taken aback—his cigar stops dead in its tracks. "We're interested in your rage, Martin. At least you've tried to do something constructive with it. You've failed but at least you tried. It mustn't go to waste—" Cantor can see that Eden hates being addressed as Martin, by this somebody he barely knows and has no wish to know better—this somebody who (*a*) like a bank officer or job interviewer, professes to take on faith everything that the con artist before him, by cooking up the extravagant name *Martin*, is trying to peddle yet who, in the same breath, (*b*) like a zealous social worker, makes it clear he'll do everything in his power to help *Martin*, this steadfast (or is it stalwart?), obviously hapless innocent secure at long last whatever he all too rightly insists is his. *What's in a name? Plenty. Plenty, that is, that's unnameable.* "The information we've gathered regarding some of the scrapes you got yourself into in New York suggests that those who trigger your rage are mere pretexts—straight men, so to speak—and that their job (you've kept them all heavily employed) is to induce the same kind of rage over and over—rage at your own impotence—and, quite frankly, we don't like to see one of our stars feel impotent. And we want to be sure it's not the Invidicum that's causing the impotence, which by the way has not been one of its side effects up to now, at least as far as we know. (But we're always interested in a trial subject who can compel a drug's side effects to march to the beat of his own drum.) At the same time we want to make sure the drug hasn't, in blunting your capacity to Envy, also blunted your capacity to feel rage, impotent or otherwise." In a tone whose dry dismissiveness suggests Walser has gone on much too long and in doing so has strayed further and further from the essentials, which it's therefore up to him and him alone to cover before they slither off, as is the way with most essentials most of the time, Stifter says he suspects that the minute Eden's sure the rage is being perceived by its instigator as "nothing more than a proof of his impotence," he starts exerting way too much pressure—expecting it—the rage—to "work miracles of annihilation." And when it doesn't—how can it?—the sad fact only makes him rage all the more . . . impotently. "And there have just got to be times, no? (correct me if I'm wrong), in the midst of a campaign, when the instigator suddenly looks thoroughly implausible." "Thoroughly what?" Eden mutters, looking directly at Cantor—who, understanding he is doing so only to avoid eyeballing his slithering tormentor, is therefore neither offended nor flattered. Unless . . . "There must be times—too many to count—when the more you rage, the more you find yourself raging against the rage (a rage so vast as to be unlivable) for not having drowned out that implausibility. That's why in your case (and in all our years of testing and retesting, we've never come across a case more staggeringly special) the focus must at this point be on rage, not Envy, involving (there's no denying it) a certain measure of . . . of . . . (ahem) quarantine." Stifter's show of reluctance to utter the word comes across, to Cantor at least, as complete fakery—no doubt a means of distracting attention from some coded allusion to—to—Cantor as Eden's first victim! Now where did that thought come from? Where, will you tell me? Hard to focus on mortality when, at a nearby—no, an adjoining—table, some nicotine-revved loudmouth is suggesting that the Manchurian Parallax Brasserie—having opened just six days ago up in Condor (evidently a corollary of La Jolla but even higher-toned) to rave reviews—would be pretty much pitch-perfect—make that *pitcher*-perfect—for an all-you-can-drink Sunday brunch. Cantor's been unjustly excluded. Now where did *that* idea come from? Never mind. Loudmouth has just corrected himself (it's the Parallax Manchurian) which is not usually the way of loudmouths hence as it so happens or as it turns out or when push comes to shove Loudmouth is more—way more—than your garden-variety or friendly neighborhood loudmouth—he's a loudmouth *with a twist*, as Cantor's mother might have put it—with a heart—with a soul—whose sole raison d'être is to prove Cantor's just a tissue of preconceptions and prejudices who deserves to be shot for all the reputations he's tarred and feathered.

The possibility that he's already been set up as Eden's first victim—that at this very moment and right before his very ears Eden and his handlers are laying out the gruesome details—that E and S/W are nothing less than a pair of entangled photons turned into an unbreachable do-it-yourself encryption key, with Cantor trapped in their lattice of light—that the fists bit was just stage business—all of it doesn't, oddly enough, disturb him in the least. Which is to say, it does. Mightily. So this being the case, Cantor (after first looking around to make sure he isn't being observed) gets busy doing what he does best when held fast within the bonds of dread, unimpeded by the fact that what he does best in such circumstances has proved time and again not all that efficacious. But he has no doubt—he can feel it in his bones—that this particular apotropaic stunt is going to be one of his absolute triumphs: just the sort of thing to *make his name in the Company*, if he were employed by one. He manages within the course of a few seconds (the time it takes for his adjoining pals, all spittin' images of Eugene Pallette, but without the talent, to tell El Loudmouth with A Twist that of course they're all looking forward to putting on the feedbag, Condor-style) to conceive of all the ways in which he can be done in by a drug-enhanced Eden and to view each from every possible angle of perpetration. Thanks to all he's learned from his old bowling buddies, Evans-Pritchard's Azande, the present is big with the future and the future at the mercy of the mystical forces he's doing his level best to harness to the here and now. So that by the time murder at the hands of his yokemate does befall him it will have been handily transformed—thanks to its having been tainted if not quite done in by his foresight, emasculated if not quite transsexualized during his thousand and one nights of anticipatory rebuff—into something better than just a bad break pure and simple. Transformed, if you must know, into a different phenomenon entirely—a phenomenon, granted, whose difference he can't be expected to pinpoint (especially while being hacked to pieces) but whose dreaded arrival on the scene will leave no room for dread. So once again he's confirmed in his belief that so-called magical thinking has been given a bad rap. And—talk about fringe benefits!—the web of that belief has become the very fabric of his thought—exactly as E-P said it would. The matter of the murder, so interwoven with his being that he has the power to decide whether it will befall him or not, now belongs solely to him, not to the anemic future. So the moral of the story is, Three cheers for apotropaic stunts. And in this case, maybe apotropaism has been practiced with such balletic nicety that there's a hefty surplus waiting in the wings for use in parrying other dangers, of which there are sure to be plenty more. For there's no way out of the apotropaic trap when you're Cantor and even when you're not. Any and every gesture—movement—curse—is laced—drenched—with the fentanyl of magical thinking.

Which is not to say he isn't fully aware that he's confusing the ingenious prolixity of dread with control over what he thinks he no longer dreads. But you know what? it simply doesn't matter. Out here on the sunny-cloudy patio—with El Loudmouth cozily droning on and on about the size of the portions and the measurements of the waitresses and growing more endearing by the minute for reasons Cantor can't begin to pinpoint—his confusion is hilariously irrelevant. And from the look of him Eden seems to understand for he's laughing out loud (another feint taught him by the big boys?). Maybe for better or worse, he's been guilty all along of underestimating Eden's intelligence which is his way, *pace* the advanced degrees, of underestimating his own. He feels for Martin. For there are so many different ways in which the plum and peachy role of "Martin" can be played. For starters, as an ADD-afflicted innocent, or as a boldfaced little vixen so adept in his cunning as to be able to claim innocence as, and not just for tax purposes, one of his dependents.

"We've been holding out on you," Walser simpers. "Fact is, we took the liberty of finding you, our star players, an apartment in a terrific little boutique hotel at East Beach." Sulky Dal (or Del: he answers to both—grumpily) makes it a matter of honor not to offer any further details. "It's a stone's throw from the Santa Barbara Cemetery, which boasts the best view of the Pacific in all of Southern California. In fact I know the owner intimately: she was my unofficial mentor—the best kind—when I was in training." "You know the owner of the cemetery?" Not to be outdone by his colleague in matters of honor, Walser makes it clear to Eden he's not amused. "I bring her my hardest nuts to crack. You'll hardly ever see her, though, since she spends most of her time alone on her yacht, the HMS *Cathexis*. Netta's fond of saying privacy's the soul's celibacy. Do you think she made that up all by her lonesome, Del?" "*Catharsis*." "What?" "The SS *Catharsis*." "*Cathexis*." "*Cachexia*." Walser shrugs. He has better, or at least bigger fish to fry. "Only thing, pals, her yard stinks perpetually of burnt cabbage and raccoon droppings. Worst at misty dawn.

"Oh, and before I forget. Netta's a smart lady but she's also a hoity-toity bitch and the minute she senses all you crave is her approval to make your life complete, the game's over. So the key is to immunize yourself against her aflatoxins. And how do you do that? you may ask. Suffice it to say only a manly —even ribald—relish of her savage brilliance will make it clear your hairy balls are strictly off limits." As if on cue, S. and W. excuse themselves and depart, with hard-to-fathom haste. Eden follows suit, making his hangdog way back toward the beach, without any acknowledgment of the one who's left behind to parse his shuffle. He keeps his hands moodily in his pockets as if—like a tenor sax after jamming all night—lonely by choice. Cantor realizes that either Stifter or Walser carelessly left his glasses behind. The carelessness is the whole show. The casual discard is a fashion statement. He heartily envies the owner's throwaway knack for extracting the last drop of glamor from utility or (in more Veblenian terms) of exploit from drudgery. And no, Cantor thinks, on behalf of the whole tribe, this kind of meditative observation isn't excrescent to The Invidicum Story's main design. It, too, is the whole show. At least for as long as it lasts. Stifter stands unsulkily before him, pointing at the tennis courts. "I forgot to mention ('cause I thought you knew): Netta is the woman in grand-rounds white—sorry, they're all in white—playing against the cute little redhead. Whose name, I seem to remember, was Jean (and still is, for all we know). Jean from the Orientation Session (as she's known to her fans and not just on the tennis courts)—which may have been more of a *dis*orientation, given the way Walser manhandled her. Yes, I know, Netta does look much younger than her seventy-odd years (though when all is said and done, no odder than most). Tread lightly, though: she's well into a fourth divorce and, from what I hear, the messiest of them all. Though I don't understand why: money or child custody can't be an issue. And by the way she isn't quite so penis-envious as my partner makes her out to be." Envious or not, she's identifiable by Cantor as exactly the sort of bourgeois babe whose composite profile he once upon a time dedicated himself, qua Sunday anthropologist (weekends were appropriately worst), to constructing—through treks within the wilds of Central, Prospect, Riverside, Battery, Seward, Fort Tryon, Morningside, Strauss, Madison Square, Washington Square and Schurz Parks and while we're at it let's not forget the New York Marble Cemetery, among so many other hotspots—as a way in and out of unmanly grief. One of those workout-obsessed halves of a power couple who's used to being sweatily in control on every front but can never, as far as her expulsive spousal orgasms are concerned, be really—really!—sure if they represent a triumph over, or just another triumph *of*, multitasking gone hog-wild. And who will make it her very own categorical imperative to portray hubby as a raving pedophile during the custody battle segment of their dutifully messy East Side divorce.

Power couple? Did anybody say *power couple*? Cantor emits an inner scream forgetting it's he himself who just used the term, having taken as his model the delectably inconceivably loathsome Ira Rennart and his wife Ingeburg—surrogate parents who are always in the backdraft of his mind. "Denying any liability or wrongdoing," this piece-of-horseshit junk-bond Nero—owner of the largest occupied family residence in the US—"agreed" to pay the measly pensions of the 1,250 retirees who'd worked at a subsidiary, R.X. Steal, of his conglomerate of mines and smelters—the Renpo Group to you, buddy. Just before R.X. folded, this vilest of snakes (no room for the niceties of nuance, thinks Cantor wistfully—twice in the last 15 minutes! a record even for him) went hunting for new financing NOT to resuscitate the subsidiary BUT to reduce Renpo's ownership from 100 to less than 80 percent so as to thereby deliver it from having to fulfill any pension obligations. Fortunately, the Pension Benefit Guaranty Corporation turned the tables on the monster and his bride. How can such a pair, Cantor wonders rhetorically, live with themselves? Easy as pie, apparently. And whatever do they think about (without necessarily admitting it to themselves, much less each other) when they're busy organ-grinding, for example? Something along the lines of, say, how much better than fucking per se is *fucking over* the little people? So much for power couples. But to work up the courage needed to do violence to ball-busting Netta by calling her a bourgeois babe the likes of which the bleached blond sands of San Diego County has never seen before (after all, a lot is riding on his choice of the right epithet for his landlady to be) he needed—to his everlasting shame—to invoke the violence done by his surrogate parents to their R.X. Steal retirees since such violence gives license to his own even if his is much worse. But even if he's not crazy about *bourgeois babe*—even if before it can impale the landlady as she deserves to be impaled, the term impales itself—still, there's something in it that he doesn't find in himself even if it's *of* himself—*from* himself. It's a sword—not a double-edged sword—not a sword of Damocles—but just enough of a sword to terrify his self-styled oppressors (they're everywhere and the noonday sun is smoking them out, one by one) and to render their detractions irrelevant—and irrefutable. [Nota bene: don't be too quick to deem the present paragraph inorganic hence expendable hence deletable.]

Herbert, he observes, is chatting with, of all people, Borkman, who's unceremoniously shed his snakeskin or vice versa. How could her susceptibility to the California sunshine have allowed such a thing to happen? Herbert knows, long before she knows she knows, that Cantor's excavatory gaze begrudges her this puny diversion, if diversion is what it turns out to be. Just as she knew at once, long before she knew she knew, that the minute they saw two full glasses of lemonade approaching her—Melanctha, the trial tribe's token black—with Borkman in tow (she found the lemonade stunt poignant—clearly, the only means at his disposal of getting the ball rolling—the ball in this case being what those two harpies must perceive to be the makings of a not-so-harmless dalliance), both Shearer (from her beach chair) and Rhys (engaged at the exit to the courts in a bit of too-flamboyant-to-be-agonized post-match stretching and flexing) began to eye her begrudgingly. As if she'd ditched them for bigger game and, much much worse, was *unaware of their awareness* of the felony. Don't they know it's *over*awareness that's Melanctha's Achilles heel, irreparably butchered through perpetual misalignment with the divine right to *conatus* which as every white boy and white girl knows means persistence in one's own being (see above)? And now, adding insult to injury, the moment she's rightfully dreaded has arrived—the moment when Borkman would take off in a frenzy and she'd have to stay on to face the music alone (something to do with the monitoring bracelet, the middle stall in the men's room adjacent to the mezzanine gift shop and an unexpurgated conference call with lawyer and ex-urologist). Their gazes accuse her (a) of having betrayed, among other things, all trust in her steadfast aversion to Borkman—one of the few sureties they piteously cling to in their trek (in fact, it's the only lodestar of their universe) toward what they've been told is health; and (b) worse, of being in her feathery ecstasy completely unaware of their supersharp perception of the crime's dimensions. She can actually see inside—touch—their gazes—and everything those gazes have been ingesting and if she can manage to rummage around deep inside it long enough, she's suddenly sure of stumbling on an unflattering but posterity-worthy cutout of herself. In other words, Melanctha is learning, to her detriment, that here in Coronado a gaze, if penetrating enough, becomes by some stereoscopic miracle a bona fide tangible *thing* in three dimensions. While—again, here in Coronado—it is the lot of a *real* thing—like a beach chair, or a stretched calf, or a discarded pair of glasses, or the gazers themselves (no matter how much out of shape)—to flounder around in at best two. Indeed, anybody who ends up listening to or watching Melanctha's story (for once, a story that she's actually living, not being Master-compelled to think—a story that's all about accusations of betrayal and treading the primrose path of dalliance)—anybody, which includes Melanctha herself, mustn't expect its unfolding—if it unfolds at all—to entail, as in some painting by a fifteenth-century Renaissance master of linear perspective, a coerced but leisurely recession of the stars of its show toward a vanishing point coextensive with the generation of insights deep—deeper—ever deeper within the quicksand of crisis—a vanishing point coextensive with the all-or-nothing of painful (is there any other kind?) truth. In short, expect no relief, folks—painterly or otherwise. Expect, instead, not stars or starlets but only their three-dimensional gazes—scleral clots oozing unrelenting scrutiny—each jealously zoning itself off from inclusion in any federation that smells like a story—each of them zealously milking the "vertiginous uncertainty about the distance separating [their] forms"[34] for all it's worth. And do you want to know something? well, it so happens those gazes are proliferating like jackrabbits as we speak for other harpies, including Netta and Netta's former lover Yetta and Yetta's protégée Vendetta and Vendetta's mentoretta Fughetta whose favorite key is G major, have shown up, unsolicited, to defend aggressors Moira and Jean. Put differently, the Master's text as it oozes its way through gazes big and small wants the listener/watcher or watcher/listener to "follow a [parallel] choppy and erratic [unleisurely] path" from . . . from . . . *thought packet to thought packet* (there, the cat's out of the bag), each oozing from the mouth of some gaze, rather than experience "full apprehension" of an entire homogeneous field, on which a full-fledged story crammed full of sweaty horsehair and other Thanksgiving Day trimmings is spread out for consumption.[35] She shudders: this is the kind of un-story she

---

[34]See Jonathan Crary, *Techniques of the Observer: On Vision and Modernity in the Nineteenth Century* (Cambridge, Massachusetts, MIT Press, 1992), p. 125.

[35]Ibid.

may one day end up telling, in blackest contravention of all the principles inflicted on her by her (mostly white) tutors—that is, if the Master doesn't tell it to her first.

But don't they know Borkman isn't bigger game? He's just one of *them*, one more of them. They've transformed a mere somebody like themselves into a thing of unmatchable allure. Why? She suddenly knows why. They have a sudden hunger to envy. A craving for the raw meat of Envy. A need to flex the muscles of Envy. They need to convince themselves they're Envy-ridden to the point of massive dysfunction hence entitled to be out here ingesting the California sun, most expenses paid. And as a target, she'll do—she'll have to do. Even if envying a black woman—a black from nowhere who will at trial's end return to nowhere—diminishes the plausibility of their animus. To keep the Envy pumping, they're turning her (round and round she goes on the spit of their urgency) into a betrayer who's relegated them to the status of droolers. She can feel—i.e., *touch*—their Envy of this easy enjoyment of Bork-man's company transforming her, the transgressor, into one of those smug reptiles—*usually white*, by the way—(Come on, is she really thinking what the italics tell her to think or is it simply a case of the Master's coming atypically to her rescue by forcing a few words of support down her throat? which, in the name of self-surmounting fairness, she's coughed right back up.)—one of those reptiles who, in returning to Earth after abandoning the dearest friends in the world they never knew they had for a trip to the moon, must now pay the piper but not so much for the transgression itself as for their heinous underestimation of the breadth of the victims' *awareness* of what's been done to them.

They don't know that with her third eye she's been taking the measure of that so-called awareness. Whether or not she has eyes only for Borkman, the fact of the matter is she's never taken her mind's eye off *them*. No need to pay the piper for she's never lost sight of their Envy—over and over, she's been bracketing it before it could bracket her. (By the way, all she can feel is rage—at what it is they've chosen to envy. Why not her literary style? Why not her observation that the true artist's vocation is to wear down the tools of his trade to the bone? Here's a syndrome, she thinks—call it, Mis-Envy—that has yet to find its Invidicum. But the rage [like Dickinson's light that exists in spring] passes and she stays.) Not once through all these long sunny years of Califor-nia-style kinship with Borkman, however irresistible (as only a middle-aged male with a catalogue that puts Don Giovanni's to shame can be), has she allowed herself to be sucked into a maelstrom of abdicated awareness—invei-gled into an alertness-annihilating camaraderie (however tempting annihila-tion might be). So, given her track record—given the fact that, all down the decades of Borkman-triggered flouting of the rules they've set for her, their favorite black girl, not for a minute has said girl lost track of how they continue to misperceive her—given that, out there on the margin of the tennis courts chitchatting and chatchitting with the Don, she's never stopped hearing herself as they must hear her even if she's been (unrepentantly, they would say) out of earshot, never stopped seeing herself as they must see her—given all this, at the very least she's entitled to full exoneration for a crime she's never even contemplated committing—a crime that not even sand and sea can accuse her of committing. Never, down through the centuries—A.D *and* B.C.—of her communion with Borkman, however dazzling (as only a middle-aged con man with a scheme that puts Ponzi's to shame can be), has her chitchatting and chatchitting not been overarched and outpaced by the premonition of inevitable misjudgment—not paid proleptic homage to the intention of her racist lessers to judge and destroy her. (Yes: *to judge and destroy her.* She'd never be caught dead contributing one red nickel to the ideological-rot machine known as "la grande famille des hommes" whose mythologies have been expertly dismantled—and not a minute too soon as far as she's concerned—by that fruity Frenchman [what *was* his name?] her sociology professor drools over every chance he gets and he makes sure he gets plenty. Whoever he is, it's a fascinated aversion to phoniness that drives his analytics and more power to him.) Never, over all the deep blue millennia of blissful interracial concubinage, has she allowed herself to believe that in exchanging her body fluids deliriously—virtually—virtuously—(pre-pandemic) remotely!—with his, she was actually serving as proxy for delirious Jean and Moira and (especially) Cantor. That is to say, never has she been deluded into believing her two seconds worth of small talk with Borkman would prove unexceptionable and unjudgeable. Even now, with her co-culprit gone, inklings continue to empest her every breath. So why should she be punished? She's been on the qui vive—not on the make—every step of the way. She's kept their rancorous need to give Envy a run for its money respectfully in mind and in her mind's eye at every scapegoatish turn. She's never lost sight of their envious bystanding—has in fact gratefully aided and graciously abetted *through her very pretense of non-seeing* the toxic participation of those spectators in the spectacle they themselves have created—presto!—simply through self-relegation to the basest spectatorship. Indeed, what would it be without them? Come to think of it, they *are* the spectacle—she (recruited merely to get the ball rolling) was displaced aeons ago, *long before the spectacle had even begun.* (Or does *long before* ... constitute yet another case of Masteritis, that imperial affliction whereby Masters, whether masterly or not, get carried away by the wordflow of their puppets—by the need to make those puppets surmount, surpass, supersede said wordflow—by the need to disabuse them of the illusion that the job of their wordflow is to faithfully, minutely mirror what should in fact be its arch enemy, namely, worldflow—by the need to therefore perpetrate violence against wordflow—by the need to throw, discursively speaking, the wrench of perversity masquerading as totalitarian insight into the works—and if, by this slender means, Masters, masterly or not, should manage collaterally to rescue their all-time favorite of the moment from a fate worse than death, i.e., banality, then all the better?) So, despite the fact that through all of those ordeals of self-glamorization (compliments of hand-to-hand mock-combat with, and mouth-to-mouth mock-resuscitation by, the Glamor Boy of Wall Street), her vigilance never missed a beat of their condemnation—despite the fact that vigilance left no time for dalliance—she must be punished.

Melanctha laughs last. So what if not necessarily best? Since, when all is said and done, what was that rabidly envied carnal chitchat with Borkman all about anyway? And what was its even more viciously begrudged high point? Something relatively anodyne, in fact (at least, she would imagine, from the perspective of those who are childless, which is the case for each of her tormentors, if she remembers correctly)—something about parents and their clubfeet of clay—or rather, parents afflicted, like them (Herbert and Borkman, Borkman and Herbert), with the grossest of all defects—too gross to be referred to in mixed company. And most remarkable of all, not once did Borkman invoke his staggering fatherly failure as a means of lustily impressing her with his extraordinariness. Not once did he even imply that, like Nietzsche's Socrates, he'd married, mated, had kids *ironically*. For she, too, has noted this tic of his. Who, if not she?

To escape them—no, to escape their gaze which has indeed taken on a life of its own (never has a blind spot come across as so penetrant)—Melanctha decides to wade out as far as she can manage, though she's a mediocre thrasher at best—and even if she's not uncomfortable: the heat is dry, a bit windy, perfect. Fortunately under her muumuu lurks a bathing suit (the slightly souped-up version of a fifties model now back in style, or so she's been informed by her whimsy-prone barber). Yet the biggest problem is not negotiating the scalding shoals but getting to the water's edge without calling attention to a body part bereft of all spirituality which should have been laid to rest—by males, females and everyone in-between or beyond—at some evolutionary crossroads billions of years ago. It will only ally itself with her tormentors—egg the trio on to mug their disbelief that one so ill served by the-anatomy-that-is-destiny could have won the heartlessness of Don Ponzi. But what if she were to disappear—like Crawford in *Humoresque* or Mason in *A Star Is Born* or Kyoko Kagawa in *Sansho the Bailiff* or Sterling Hayden in *The Long Goodbye* or Steerforth or Mouchette or Ophelia? Well, then, her good fortune would be marred through eternity thanks to the description, in flyers posted everywhere, of what she was last seen wearing, i.e., saddlebags.

The Master (she can feel it) is growing impatient with her *for the very first time*—but is this *in fact* the very first time or is He simply trying to make things seem—or at least sound—more dire than they are (so his clients don't go home hungry, feeling they got nothing out of the ordinary for their money)? In any case, the impatience is warranted. He foresees no end of trouble in bringing his breakthrough—his blockbuster—in on time, much less under budget, given all the trouble His diva is causing just getting into the water. But seeing her carried off by the weighty wave of her own embarrassment, the Master, in drag oceanic, and with Poseidonesque unpredictability, gives her (after all, she *is* His diva, prima and assoluta)—a totally unexpected but much-needed push shoreward and adding insult to injury, sees fit to deck her out in the Botticellian ethereality of anatomy-obliterating kelp. And since assistance, as she's learned over and over the hard way, is always in short supply and though it's against her principles to go around taking handouts—even from the Pacific—Melanctha gratefully accepts. With the curtsy her mother taught her to make. She sits in the sand, surprised the sun hasn't set. Every so often a wave upsurges with a growl different from that of all the other waves, past, present and to come, intent as it is on affirming (like her son at the end) the sheerest embodiment of health over the protests of the only virile beast it can't hope to silence—its disintegrating organ system (like her son's at the end). Can Shearer and Rhys, mannish butts notwithstanding, lay claim to this ability to describe (or is it fabricate) the war inside every phenomenon—at least the ones worth agonizing over? Answer me that. But— True to form, the Master butts in: Melanctha, dear, he murmurs (she knows she's in for a dose of his celebrated tact and knows even better that tact shares a border with the cities of insincerity and indifference and that during business hours its practitioners get a kick out of snoring between gritted teeth), didn't you mean, i.e., wouldn't it be better to say, "the war inside every phenomenon *which in fact makes it a phenomenon?*"

CHAPTER TWENTY-THREE

As it turns out, there's one more session scheduled (Netta hasn't reappeared—or, like an infection—recurred) before the flight out of Southern California's Little Egypt into Santa Barbara's promised land. An informal group session, to be exact—a jam session, to be more exact—including a very pleasant picnic lunch on the promenade facing San Diego (has the session ended? has the picnic already begun? hard to say), whose mean streets Eden, as ordered, has walked and rewalked, but without any success whatsoever in the rage-revisited department. He's gone from the Gaslamp Quarter through Balboa Park to Hillcrest (with a brief for-old-times'-sake side jaunt to his beloved India Street), from the Old Town to Point Loma and on to UC San Diego (which rejected every member of his family slaphappy enough to apply) and back over the Coronado Bay Bridge to the Del (after wolfing down some fudge—hazelnut, his father's favorite—at Horton Mall but as quickly and surreptitiously as possible, since he hates nothing more than to be seen eating, i.e., jerking off orally, in broad daylight). Not to mention a host of even more challenging itineraries. All to no avail. The only thing that moves him—and that, mightily, though not to rage—are the spots where the city becomes lastingly fictional by evoking others—like New York, Chicago (where he worked for two months as a porter in a Lakefront condo) and Cleveland (scene of his six-month triumph as co-manager of a wild-orchid delivery service). Not to mention Portland (Maine)—where he did absolutely nothing except visit Peaks Island, a must-see according to the grizzled cross-eyed ferryman. And a must-see it was, at least for any self-respecting serial killer in search of a workstation. Though he hungers for these moments of evocation more and more the further he gets from the safety of the Embarcadero, there's always disappointment when they come. And that's because they prevent him from confronting, even if not head-on, the deadness of the newly discovered dead-and-gone places. (Like Pornucopia, the video store in Hillcrest. And Shock Tactic, the escort service [a block away from the Bancroft Building] where the golden girls had the decency to bleach their fleece the same color.) After all, this deadness isn't some revocable state of affairs—as he might be tempted to think or as Some Body might think on his behalf—whose ripeness for aesthetic delectation (usually not his cup of tea) is worthy every now and then of a detour or two drenched in melancholy misgivings (the spigot for which can be turned on and off at will) before he escapes just in the nick of time (before deadness becomes too real) and retraces his manly steps toward things as they are. But if video store and escort service are indeed dead (which they very much are as opposed to merely—*merely!*—playing dead to fulfill the needs of an aesthete in spite of—and unbeknownst to—himself—for there is no deadness quite so poetic as the deadness of urban things[36]), i.e., if it's they who've abandoned

---

[36]Cf. Walter Benjamin on Eugène Atget: "Not for nothing have Atget's photographs been likened to those of the scene of a crime. But is not every square inch of our cities the scene of a crime?" (See "A Small History of Photography," in *One Way Street and*

him (instead of just posing for his palette), then he needs to backdate his take-stock options and convince himself it's he, not they, who's moved on. He needs a way of life that makes these losses irrelevant. It's only in bidding farewell until tomorrow's trek that—baffled by and cursing his unreceptivity to its incomparable wonders—he permits his home town's contours—including the dead ones—to coincide with no other contours than their own.

So what he should be referring to as the New York ordeal (but isn't) has not been a mere interim over the course of which the dead-and-gone places could be counted on to stay undead until further notice. Not a case where the clock stopped ticking until all was resolved—until all was as it should have been in the first place. No freezing of time as a compensation for so much necessary waste—as a reward for all that atonement. The interim turns out to have been life itself, which is in fact a relief—or *something of* a relief. But Eden doesn't want you to get the wrong impression, especially since he doesn't know who you may turn out to be once his back is turned and he's judged solely on the basis of how he maneuvers his butt through the loneliest of crowds. Fact is, these trips up and down memory lane—these exercises in self-fragmentation on behalf of what others might be tempted to call his vocation—have been rife with fringe benefits, not to mention the fringe *elements* with whom he, as hands down the least illustrious among them, has been rubbing elbows on many a dead-end street. So it's about time he *gave back*—that is, included San Diego in his will *and* Living Trust—the way those celebrity influencers on TV nudge you to do when they plug PBS or the Salvation Army or that mother of all bleeding-heart charities, Blackstone Inc. And what better way to give back to this, his home town, than to visit a swarm of Old Testament locusts (in the shape of his most preposterous packeted hyper-perceptions) on its comeliest exurb. Though he'd better hurry up because the Amygdalite wagon train is getting ready to head due north. But it just so happens that with rising stardom come certain privileges and there's nothing more privileged than slipping away noiselessly from an adoring gang of mentors cum handlers to demonstrate one is after far bigger game than adoration (while making dead sure under the cover of darkness at noon that the break-out is moodily self-advertised just enough to be *talked about* in his absence). And if Eden is lucky—really lucky—he'll end up being dared by some truck driver at the intersection of, say, Glorietta Boulevard and Third Street not to get himself mowed down and in turn daring the darer to follow through on his threat. And all this just so, as expertly managed, the stalemate—the split second of eyeball wrestling—the game of moves plotted on the chessboard of a muddy windshield—can trigger the absolute certainty of triumph in every future confrontation under the sun (and mentors and handlers be damned). And if Eden's luckier still, he can deploy his newly minted power-to-confront by demanding (even before the trucker has skulked off) that the loudmouth who just happens to be approaching from the other direction (companion

Other Writings, translated by Edmund Jephcott and Kingsley Shorter (London, Verso, 1979).

hominoid to Cantor's Parallax Manchurian)—one of those robots who wants you to know he's the very first worldwide to have mastered the impossible art of annexing an entire sidewalk, ruts and all, while complacently bellowing the details of his latest lightning-speed trade into the smartest of smartphones— he can deploy the power-to-confront by demanding that loudmouth show some respect for his better half—his infinitely better half (namely, the *process of walking*—the process in its essential purity—to which sidewalk-annexing loudmouth has been annexed through no merit of his own)—not to mention respect for what accrues to every walker from surrender to, humble collabo- ration with, environmental eloquences. So there's no longer any need for Eden to slip away: If Coronado has ears, it knows he's already given back—that he himself is a Living Trust.

Walser and Stifter look as if they're taking special pains to ignore their two favorites—to make them feel that, like all tyros with time on their hands and swell in their heads, they've presumed too much on their mentors' declared partiality. Walser in particular clearly gets a kick out of poking at the surface of that presumption to get at the raw vulnerability beneath. So the first special session with picnic obbligato is being held solely to generate misperceptions which are to be corrected as the al fresco unspools. But Cantor at least is more than a match for the pair, having had enough experience with colleagues so-called and otherwise to know that even if Encounter 1 ends on a note of shared ecstasy, it will never do to give the impression at the onset of Encoun- ter 2 that as a consistency buff he expects more of same. If Joe Colleague has started out expressing admiration for his work, maybe even awe, under no circumstances is Cantor to betray his expectation of a reprise of the old fart's youthful indiscretion. He must expect nothing—except career disfigurement if he succumbs. In fact, the first sign of collegiality should be an alarm signal to Cantor as it is to Joe himself since, look! he's already swerving in the oppo- site direction, toward homeopathic put-down. So for Cantor it's poker-face time again in the Old West.

But there's no need for Eden to be made of the same stuff since, for one thing, he doesn't automatically translate every slight into a blistering attack on his sexuality—into a more-or-less successful annihilation of his being. Or every act of appeasement into an even more successful self-attack. For Eden wants to appease Walser, or so it seems to Cantor, who suspects that any day now he'll be sworn in officially as his roommate's personal trainer. And what will happen to Cantor then? When the Edens of the world smell danger they struggle to dissipate it in the only way they think they know how . . .!? Right off he tries to defang the Walserbeest by telling him that the New York team routinely made him feel his soul was not quite his own—or his Envy for that matter. Cantor wants to rush over (though only inches away), slit his throat then shut him up for, unlike the defanger, he knows where all this is leading. But not so deep down Eden, too, must know (even if he's a fool, his guts aren't) that the operators out here are no different. He's throwing the dank incense of his vulnerability on the altar of Walser's smugness in the hope of invoking what by the wildest stretch of his imagination can be construed as the divinity of . . . not contempt but its much better half, tough love. He's trying to slap together the kind of plight for which that tough love can work up some affection. Which means striking the right note of helplessness. His badmouthing of Straynge & Co., performed in the key of childlike bafflement, is both a plea and a command that Walser be different from what Eden fears—knows—he is. He's appealing not to Walser's compassion but to his presumed vanity, his dread of being a copycat quack, but being a copycat is the least of Walser's dreads. In fact, dread doesn't enter into it at all. Walser smiles benignly. "Oh, the New York team isn't—wasn't—all that bad. So now we know who doesn't own your soul, i.e., your Envy, but what we still don't know is who owns your sexuality—anybody's, for that matter."

He's within earshot of everybody. Shearer parries the question by focusing on the sailboats. She mustn't forget to take a photo to give to her nieces . . . as a reward. For she hasn't stopped hoping absence and distance are transforming her into somebody admirable in their eyes—more admirable than a has-been of her caliber has any right to be. She parries as well, with what she herself feels is a too-anguished shake of head and hand, Borkman's kind offer of elderberry wine, black grapes and an overly generous slice of extra-sharp cheddar on a slab of pumpernickel-with-raisins (don't let the upscale goodies fool you: the extraordinary session is still in session). Borkman answers the question—as a provocation—for he senses Walser doesn't want it answered. At least not here in Coronado, with departure imminent. "Not us—but the drug companies and the experts, so intent on making sure we stay hard for the little lady—harder than we have any right, or need, to be. I can just smell them getting ready to slice and dice impotence into a million and one different orphans. Same goes for premature ejaculation, in case you're wondering." But why the disgruntlement—why the *ressentiment*? Isn't it precisely slicing and dicing that's going to remake Borkman's name on Wall Street? But he's wrong about Walser who's gotten into the spirit of the thing fast enough. It looks as if Borkman's blurt is just what the doctor ordered. "You know, poor Oscar Wilde" (George pricks up his ears: Why *poor*? he wonders), "if he were alive today, would say about fucking what he said about (differently poor) Henry James's writing. Engaged in—" (The very imminence of departure seems to be freeing him up. He's clearly savoring the surefire punch. Nobody's going to accuse *him* of prema-jac.) "—'as if it were a painful duty,'" shouts Melanctha, beating him to the finish line—Cantor can tell she's laughing to herself (*inner-laughing*, he calls it) as she moves off to get a better view of the city skyline—a better view, that is, than Shearer's (*who has just spoken?*). She hasn't forgotten this NYCB relic's display of Envy on the beach. But that's unfair. She's more, Herbert is sure, than a relic. It's just that the moment calls, your honor, for calling her a relic. "Even impotence—even premature ejaculation—is better than prosthetic fucking. Much better. That's what we've become—a world of prosthetes. Our prostheses are *the experts themselves*—not their expertise so-called but the experts themselves." That Cantor's mind has been wandering (his enthrallment with Melanctha's inner-laughing has been a perfect jumping-off point) accounts for his inability to identify the speaker of these last words—much less respond now that he, or she, is apparently addressing him. But he doesn't expect any excuses to be made for enthrallment (however otherworldly), which is just another name for amateurish inattention.

Otherworldly Stifter muses thus: "Unhappy is the land that *needs* an expert." But otherworldly or not, he hopes somebody will get the (expert) allusion. Nobody does, or nobody wants to give him the pleasure of showing that she does. "And by the same token, who owns Envy." Borkman: "You know who: the same sort of robber-baron quacks who own the sexual act—the prime time gurus who preach humility while hawking their bestselling DVDs on the subject." "Only we're not quacks—not even old Straynge—and we have no intention of robbing anybody of his affliction until he looks us in the eye and tells us he's decided, after the most strenuous deliberation, that cure is less degrading than persistence in that affliction." (Borkman and Walser are on the same side, aren't they? Ethan wonders. [He's just gotten back—his life being a succession of detours—after paying what will probably end up being final respects to his favorite great-grandmother, who's on her last legs in an assisted-dying facility up in Carlsbad.] Thing is, they seem to be using their being on the same side as the best means of getting each other's goats.) When is cure ever less degrading than affliction? Cantor wonders. As if in response—no, *in* response—Herbert moves even further away, yellow flip-flops held gracefully away from her body. Avoidance of the hot gravel giving her an excuse to swivel—also gracefully—this way and that (though how else can you swivel? wonders the gravel). Like a woman half her age. Encircled by a halo—too coppery to be red—and without which barely acceptable expression of reverence it would doubtless have refused to budge another inch, a cruise ship advances slowly against the horizon way out to her left. Herbert doesn't notice the ship, which not-noticing lends her (interest-free) a certain . . . otherworldliness. And it's lucky that Cantor's around to catch it in the act. But in this case it's the real thing. (Aspiring otherworldling Del Stifter—and, yes, Cantor did get the allusion but so what?—should take a page or two from Melanctha's Book of Hours.) All this—whaddya mean *all* this? after all, it's not much, except to Cantor—all this Cantor observes with his usual trademark absence of any stirrings of desire (inasmuch as his target's a reasonably desirable female) but not without the usual farcical stirrings—*Will the brain never learn what the penis never ceases to teach?*[37] (or vice versa)—of disappointment at that absence. But he has no time for such fine distinctions because he's already imagining, with the compass and straight edge of Envy, another male's stirrings of desire and starting to harbor very much unfarcical stirrings for those stirrings.

Herbert is observing him and thinking him through. Right now, the thought packet he's inspiring is the most important thing in the world. Nothing more important. She's got to work it into the piece for Creative Writing 101 ASAP: the whole shebang will die without it. She can't leave Coronado without making sure the thought's been incorporated just where she left off in the manuscript, although *manuscript's* much too hoity-toity for what she's been perpetrating. Even if the placement is all wrong—even if it roughs

---

[37] Gen. 47:29.

up—lesions—the texture (how convenient for the Master that his aptest pupil should be a writer). And that's exactly why, she tells herself, she'll never make it in 101 which means she'll never make it anywhere else, inasmuch as 101 is the gateway to the Auction of the Mind. Too bad she can't (falsely) hierarchize her thoughts to ensure that they receive the most suitable placement. The most *tasteful* placement. The think-through about Cantor shouldn't be inserted now but later, if at all. But there's no right placement for the likes of Melanctha's—oops, the Master's—packets. Every thought has the same urgency as every other. First come, first served. Every thought event is as life-changing as any other.

Borkman is still throwing his weight around. Slicing and dicing erections right and left—with ill-concealed relish. What issues from between his shapely lips (Cantor must give credit where credit is due) is one long self-congratulatory fart. Cantor's hate is still forge-hot. It hasn't abandoned him. It's made stronger by the fact that he agrees with much of what Borkman is saying. Everything about Borkman—everything he once found attractive, although not (at least to his own knowledge) sexually attractive—now bears the opposite sign. All positives have become negatives. Eden looks over at him and smiles—conspiratorially (so what if the smile is very much out of character?). His smile delivers a message Cantor is constitutionally (even constitutively, he hopes) allergic to—to wit, *Life is good.* Wants to puke when anybody tries to shove that robust Everlasting Yea up his ass—even when it's Thomas Carlyle himself. (And just for the record: he's never bottomed in his life, on camera or off. Though is that anything to brag about?) Has wonder boy's asslicking proved profitable? It would appear so, judging from the way Walser eyes him with appetite. Cantor looks away: *Come not between the dragon and his hate.* Then he looks up—I mean, *back.* Now it's he who's at the hoping end in what is fast becoming cable TV's hit game show, *Get that Allusion!* (inexplicably all the rage among Enviers).

Here's Borkman tsk-tsking the commodification of sex when it's thanks to him that mandatory arbitration clauses are fine-printed into unwitting employee contracts and teller windows at every Chase branch are being replaced by ATM kiosks. Situated just below the slide show reminding you that Jamie Dimon—like Vlad Putin, Ted Cruz, David Koch and Stephen Schwarzman—has your (though not its employees') very best interests at heart. *Dare to dream your financial dream*, the slide-pods' smiling teeth proclaim, *and your Relationship Banker, Robby the Robot, will be dreaming right along with you. Thing is, he'll be dreaming very different dreams.* Cantor can't make up his mind whether the hate has come too soon or too late. No plausible buildup, some—the Master for instance—might say.

By hating Borkman is he doing the Master's bidding or contravening His orders? He doesn't want it to be thought—as if anybody gave him a thought—as if he had any say in the matter—that he's a slave—a Hegelian slave—or worse (at least according to Nietzsche aka *Saxony's favorite son* aka *Saxony's local boy who made good posthumously* aka *Saxony's wild boy of the road* aka *Fearless Freddie*—or to Nietzsche according to Deleuze) a Hegelian master—an inferior, in any case, and of whose inferiority there's no better proof than his being *conscious* of Borkman, who doesn't return the favor. So Cantor is a slave, after all, by virtue of his consciousness of a self that is not conscious—a self that doesn't need to be conscious—a self that wouldn't be caught dead being conscious—that has no time to waste being conscious of anyone or anything, not even bank tellers. I.e., Borkman's as superior a self as you'll ever see strutting proudly across sunshine-infested Hanover Square the morning after a record-breaking spring snowfall. You'll never find his spirit hovering around dead ends and culs-de-sac. Borkman loves no-non-sense nothing-to-hide thoroughfares like Wall Street and Broad Street, so by default it devolves upon Cantor to love the world's unjustly neglected back alleys (Ryders, Mechanics, Theatre and Nightmare, not to mention Broadway [no, not *the* Broadway, silly, but Broadway *Alley*—pay attention!] will do very nicely, for starters)which fester in the shadow of the White-Shoe cathedrals where the terms for herd spoliation—and, by extension, herd immunity—are precisely, if cryptically, set. The minute he starts being conscious of Bork-man, in other words, starts hating him, only to realize Borkman won't hate back, won't meet him on equal terms, won't meet him on any terms at all, he becomes no more than a function of Borkman who, qua function, maps Cantor onto Cantor so he—Cantor—can be excoriated by the two partners, Cantor A and Cantor f(A), to this unwelcome self-coincidence. And Bork-man—the beast of prey—the *Blonde Bestie* (*There*, thinks Cantor, *so at long last Nietzsche's frantically masturbating cat is out of its semen-sputtered bag, or should we say, its . . . closet?*)—will always remain superiorized because he can't for the life of him conceive of Cantor's scouring his own guts for reasons to hate him. And that's precisely what makes Borkman—at least the Borkman of this momentary bank and shoal of time—so . . . otherworldly. Yes, this is the true otherworldliness, otherworldliness planted right smack in the middle of the worldly world, the real world, not the world of impotent allusioners all too conscious of their hunger to be acknowledged. And to think that it's Borkman—big, burly, beefy (at least in spirit)—who's the tru-est practitioner of this dying art. To think that it's gracelessly graying Bork-man (get a load of that manic proliferation of curls around temples and nape which are supposed to compensate for his big bad bald spot) who has turned out to be the otherworldly blond beast. To think that it should fall to the likes of Borkman not only to embody what Saxony's favorite son Freddie called the rarest quality in the world, i.e., the Old Testament stalwart naïveté of a prankishly murderous heart, but, propelled by that very naïveté, to repel every effort of Cantor's *ressentiment* to infect him with a bad conscience. Yet why should Cantor be intimidated by this slab of Biblical beef? (After all, each and every barge tug-shepherded up the East River post-10 p.m. which Cantor has worked so hard to love more than his own puny soul—yet without fear—is just as much a fearsome slab, albeit a more poetical one—a subsidiary slab of night.) Why? Well, because Cantor has been taking the measure of Borkman (under a self-supervision that is, of all things, almost rabbinical in its strictness) and has come to the conclusion that he's about to become the darling of the same armchair-general academia that drools over Saxony's wild boy of the road, whose genealogy of morality is one long act of auto-rehabilitation achieved (sort of) by hating himself in a figment of his Aryan imagination, i.e., the haters par excellence, i.e., the priestly Jews. The Jews who, let it be known, instigated (according to the moustachios of that wild boy) the slave revolt called morality—propelled by the abysmal hatred of their own impotence—decreeing that only the wretched, suffering, deprived, sick and ugly are good. Etc., etc., etc.

So Cantor, for all his number-crunching, has turned out, also—always— by default (i.e., pursuant to inept storytelling's compliance with the tiresome Law of Oppositions) to be nothing more—and nothing less—than the anti-type of the Jewish priest. Priest of the Jews. The Jews, with Jesus as their fall guy, their Trojan horse, their bypath. Priest of Israel exercising the black art of the politics of revenge against the noble horde by making the instrument of its revenge out to be its mortal enemy and (in a stroke of evil genius) nailing him—Him—to the cross. Why, it's both a triple twist straight out of Agatha or Margaret Millar and a quadruple bluff worthy of Ira Levin or Alistair MacLean (*Puppet on a Chain*). Thanks to Israel, the slaves, the mob, the herd, have won. Thanks to the Jews who, incapable (according to Saxony's finest) of the creativity of deeds, indemnify themselves with an "imaginary" revenge. (Now what will Cantor's Black Forester [see somewhere above] from the SE corner of 112th Street and Broadway make of this pre-blog blogorrhea? He'll use it, of course, to forward in Word 2010 another one of his programs of imaginary mass extermination. But of course the Black Shirts of the future—from Christchurch to Charlottesville—who turn to his trash for doctrinal comfort won't read the fine print of the footnotes to the footnotes in which this Nietzsche, Jr., cunningly abjures [sort of] the Jews-directed obloquies that are the very thew and sinew of the genocidal enterprise.) And even if the noble hordesman dreamed up by Saxony's favorite son (Nietzsche, Sr.) looks down on and falsifies the image of the members of the herd, this is nothing like the caricatural vengefulness of the impotent Cantor the Cantor. No, the noble beast is too lighthearted and joyous in his contempt to have any truck with caricature. The noble one's nobility can't stand still long enough for contempt. He has bigger fish to fry right off Hanover Square. So the members of the herd should be grateful that the noble hordesmen's words, Greek or otherwise, for what they secrete, are always sweetened with the toxins of pitying forbearance. The noble hordesmen—the mini-masters—recognize each other in and out of the boardrooms by their robust impulsiveness in expressing anger and exacting revenge, though Freddie does admit (an unconscious slip?) that the noble beasts *can* undergo *ressentiment*, given half a chance, although on those rare occasions when it should happen to surface, that *ressentiment* always has the decency to exhaust itself in a single reaction. (But can *ressentiment* exhaust itself in a single reaction and still be *ressentiment* as we know and love it—knew and loved it before Invidicum set foot in the parlor? Isn't that more than a wee bit like feeling deep grief for a laughable second and a half, a feat that Wittgenstein—aka Heidegger's pharmakon—classily debunked?) But why muddy the waters at all, defame the (self-)portrait by introducing *ressentiment* into the eminent domain of the noble hordesmen? Cantor wonders. (Yes, *Cantor*, for it is Cantor thinking all this.)

Unlike the black-eyed Jew (although Cantor isn't exactly black-eyed), the blond beast (although Borkman's no surfer-dude blond) wants nothing so much as to reverence his enemy—wants him to be as noble as possible—will do all he can in fact to prop up the image of his blue-eyed rival—because the more honorable that rival is, the more honorable is he, the blue-eyed rival's (presumably blue-eyed) rival. Although, at this moment at least, Borkman doesn't look all that reverential. Maybe it's because he hasn't found a rival worthy of his reverence or because he's having his 15 minutes of Warholian *ressentiment*. Hell, when you get right down to it, he and his cronies are mere *innocent* beasts of prey—*never more innocent than when they are beasts of prey*. (Or is this ostensible afterthought [*never more innocent . . .*] yet another trace of the Master's going, with a little help from thoughtflow, into short-circuiting hyperlative mode and dragging Cantor ever so willingly along with him? And maybe what Cantor's and Herbert's gazes are colliding with at the moment is not each other but a recognition that the Master exists and that they are here to do his bidding.) Rape and murder? Little more than a frat boy's spring-break escapade. For to demand of force that it not express itself as force is to yield to that seductive subreption according to which effects are conditioned by some Thing that causes effects—the lightning behind the flash—the doer behind the deed. How dare the practitioners of *ressentiment* dare to imply that the circus Strong Man is free to be weak—worse, a lamb—worst, a lamp chop? For Fearless Freddy, Erl King of the Culture Industry, the long and the short of it is that the Jews constitute the priestly nation of *ressentiment par excellence* and one has only to compare them with similarly gifted tribes (the Chinese and of course the Germans) to see which occupy the first, second—and fifty-third ranks. But there is always some preternaturally eloquent Jew like Kauffmann who'll fly to the defense of a dangerous doubletalker like Nietzsche with the obligatory remedial footnote. But, my dear Walter, all the footnotes of Arabia will not sweeten this not-so-little diatribe.

And also unlike the priestly-vengeful black-eyed Jew Cantor, knightly-aristocratic Borkman is one of the Saxon's so-called emancipated, i.e., he's earned the right to make promises and keep them. Any way you slice and dice him—he, Borkman, is the free man, possessor of an unbreakable will who promises slowly (as if chewing the aroma of a truly fine cigar), reluctantly, rarely, distinctly, and whose trust is therefore a mark of distinction, the distinction all the feeble crave. The word of the Borkmans can be relied on because they know they're sturdy enough to keep it "in the face of fate." And from the altitude of this extraordinary privilege they can look down their nose at priestly-vengefuls who promise without the divine right to do so and whose promise is coterminous with its abrogation. Borkman's faculty for remembering gives off the heady whiff of distinction because it's sparsely—anorexically—exercised: only the promises that he's made need apply for membership in memory's exclusive club. His forgetfulness, on the other hand, is pretty much all-inclusive, a form of robust health—profligate, prodigal, frivolous. As stimulants, amity and enmity are equally unwelcome and his hearty constitution demands that they be kept at bay. Friendship is a no-no, as it was for Ibsen, Proust, Drybock. The doors of consciousness close on everything except his exalted promises—on anything and everything that brings on the dyspepsia of begrudgement—anything that constrains the cheerfulness of prideful cruelty. But has our knightly aristocrat kept his promises—really?, even a few? Cantor wonders (remembering that pretty ankle bracelet, focus of so much ado in the middle stall of the mezzanine men's room a while back). He's a loathsome crook. A loathsome crook who knows how, on a few occasions, to look otherworldly—altitudinous. And yet bracketing—framing—straitjacketing him thus cuts Cantor off from something . . . fruitful—if not for him then for somebody like Melanctha, who's no stranger to strange fruit. He'd only lose them but she'd know how to use 'em. So Cantor's got to watch his language so that he doesn't deprive Melanctha of an opportunity for enrichment by proxy. For crooks have the capacity to enrich as much as saints, in whom he has no vested interest. So how do you like them (strange) apples? and, more to the point, what does he do now? Love Borkman for Melanctha's sake or hate him for his own? After all, it's not Borkman's fault if Cantor fancifully repurposed him as an impeccably ethical blond beast of prey and then went on to take him to task for rank—worse, jovial—self-misrepresentation.

But oh me, oh my, thinks Cantor, here he is rambling on and on about Nietzsche (the worst kind of Jew hater, i.e., a Jew lover) clearly boring everybody in sight (and out of)—including himself[38]—and, adding insult to injury, almost missing the *pièce de résistance*—for as if on cue—no, *on cue* (but whose?)—here is Borkman denouncing of all things . . . gay guys! He's clearly a bit on the drunk side. Or is it the pumpernickel talking? Yet Cantor can't help feeling that if Borkman is patronizing him, then it is only on behalf of making things simple—simpler—only on behalf of enabling him to go on

---

[38] But he can't stop rambling—playing some of Freddie's greatest hits is addictive and Cantor is only human. Best of all is observing Saxony's best and brightest go about thinking he's magisterially leading thoughtflow around by her Roman nose when in fact it's wordflow that's leading *him*. Fun—and a bit poignant—to watch poor old Fearless Freddie try to outdo himself—to bully himself into superseding—topping—the utterance of the moment with something even more imperious, i.e., even more bullying. And (let's give credit where credit is due) he does outdo himself every time—having mastered in the womb this darkish art of extracting organically from the bowels of any given thought its corrective, its pharmakon (to be corrected, remedied, poisoned, in its turn). But at the same time—though is it ever *not* at the same time?—even if Freddie, given his dreary brand of literary-philosophical typehood, cannot shed the straitjacket of a predictably bilious, dyspeptic, relentlessly self-overriding approach to writing (as pursued to the point of caricature or obliteration, whichever comes first), mightn't it still be possible for the wordflow that governs his cerebral viscera to go in an altogether unforeseeable direction compliments of its Brownian motion and thereby liberate the Type from his Straitjacket—the Dancer from his Dance—at least from time to time? So that he ends up sounding less like, say, Adorno or Benjamin or Cioran or Deleuze and more like, well, like . . . Lewis Carroll or Mickey Spillane or Molly Bloom or her lover, foxy Blazes Boylan.

hating his favorite knight-errant while sparing himself thereby any added self-schism (the stock in trade and meat and potatoes of the folks who go by the name of artist and artist only). And as if such knightly largesse weren't enough, here is Borkman making hatred even easier by directing an admiring middle finger at the animal kingdom none of whose members would ever be caught dead— "Well, you know what I mean," he barks, pointedly at Cantor. Cantor must step in. He has no choice but to run the gamut and the gauntlet and everything in-between. "I haven't the faintest—" No, *faintest* is much too gay. *Fucking*, once again coming to the rescue, does the dirty work of masculinizing him without taxing his ingenuity, which is all to the good since ingenuity has a bad habit—through its inherent frivolity—of playing havoc with his birth gender. "Haven't the fucking faintest idea what you mean but I know for a fact that many of those members would be outraged—by whatever it is you think you mean." "Who, for example?" In his best prosecutorial tone, Cantor pounces: "Does the name *Octopoteuthis deletron* ring a bell?" Borkman shuts up double-quick. Did that twitch in his right eye signal alarm? But why should Borkman be alarmed at the mention of a silly old squid? Gay-baiting is formally at an end. Walser (or is it Stifter? hard to tell them apart) looks, or acts, disappointed.

It's been exhausting—degrading—lacerating—to play Jewish priest to Borkman's Aryan knight aberrant but now that the skit is over and done with, Cantor's invigorated by—exalted from—having just shed yet another skin separating him from selfhood's holy grail (thanks, JGB!). With only about 2,300 more to go before he reaches its core, which he hopes will still be molten. For what is life, ladies and gents—at least, his life—but a series of impersonations each peculiar to a given skit. There's been, let's see, the *hetero skit*, the goodson skit, the sulking-rebel skit (see under hetero skit), the Myshkin skit—and that's just for starters. And sometimes—but only when he's in the mood for a belly laugh—he goes slumming and impersonates himself. As Walser—no Stifter—bristles as if the goodies (*note that the Master is here up to his old tricks, i.e., refusing to cross the Rubicon into a new paragraph even if—no, precisely because—a shift in the righteous progression of thought now calls for it,*[39] *which refusal brings joy to the hearts of all conscientiously bad storytellers*) just delivered by that expert NY caterer Cantor & Borkman—a trusted neighborhood institution since the heady days of pushcarts and sweatshops—were simply too much to digest at a single sitting, it's providential that Netta should arrive on the scene. From the look of her she seems to be gearing up for a major role in the soon-to-be-released "quintessential Sirkian melo-noir" (*Variety*) entitled (tentatively—variously—vaingloriously—simple-mindedly) *Imitation of Envy* or *All That Invidicum Allows* or *A Time to Envy and a Time to Die* or *Envy,*

---

[39]See, in this regard, Jay Leyda on the "youthful horseplay" of fearless refuseniks Sergei Eisenstein and Edward Tisse with dissolves in Eisenstein's first feature, *Strike*. As noted by Leyda, they are "used for almost every reason except *the ordinary reason of indicating the passage of time*" [bravo!; and the italics are mine] (*Kino: A History of the Russian and Soviet Film* (New York, Collier Books, 1973), p. 183.

Son of Cochise or (longingly) *Shockproof* or, most to the point, *The First Legion of Invidiously Shrinking Men*. Since according to somebody very much in the know (*Now who was it?* wonders Melanctha, just back and sorely unmissed), the mere sight of her does wonders for anybody's digestion, however sluggish. While it is true that Netta's splotchy peasant blouse is unbecomingly (some might even say grotesquely) low-cut for a dame even half her age, she's prepared for warding off the inevitable revulsion. She's fashion-savvy enough to know there's one accessory no self-respecting exhibitionist (even the most alluring) ever leaves home without—no, not some Queen of the Nile-type doodad designed to get the flab of her upper arm in a boa's grip and keep it there until death do them part nor a pair of stiletto-heeled Mary Janes but, rather, the right gaze, i.e., the gaze apotropaic, i.e., the gaze unseeing of the outraged victim—victim, in this case, of an unwelcome leering lust which her tan-withered gourds (ever more exposed the ever more deeply their bearer sinks into damselesque despair at the world's wicked ways) have done absolutely nothing to arouse.

It wouldn't cost Eden much to extend her some credit (*hurray! the Rubicon has been crossed unexceptionally at last, i.e., at an appropriate bend of its current, which unexceptionability in full regalia fills the prissy hearts of all conscientiously* fine *storytellers with even prissier joy*)[40] for coming up with so wily a ploy. Thing is, he just doesn't have it in him to summate all the itching little perceptions about Netta of which he's plainly not aware into one great big gift basket of an apperception, which would be one step away—although in most cases it's an infinite step—from articulation. Pity, since such a faculty could sure be of use to an assassin on the make or on the run or on the lam. Cantor knows exactly what Eden's thinking-but-doesn't-know-he's-thinking, about Netta, soon to play such a pivotal role in both their lives, lives already yoked far beyond mere disseverance. Telepathy's the name of the game here—the currency—the small change—of the country in which he's ended up. It's clear he's been much too hard on Eden's asslicking where Walser is concerned and that he will be obliged to take over the role of perceiver for the poor guy. You might say Eden's mind will be forced, whenever warranted, into and out of *per*ceivership with a capital P as administered by Cantor.

He can already hear SoP down at headquarters somewhere deep in his pia mater shrilly insisting that Cantor become Eden's prosthesis—even his prosthetic god—for, contrary to unpopular belief, prostheses do have their time and place. (Wait! it's official! the Master is now none other than SoP, at

---

[40]And yet, one might rightly ask, why shouldn't fine storytellers be pleased when the "paragraph rule," aka the Rubicon rule, is respected? And why shouldn't fine filmmakers everywhere be enthralled—feel smugly vindicated—every time the dissolve is put to its proper use? But who's to say what a dissolve's proper use should be and who's to determine the right moment—if any—for a paragraph to give birth to a successor? Is it perverse convention or equally perverse Mother Nature? Who- or whatever the driver, the dissolve and Rubicon rules are implied commands whose fertile sting (see note 27 above) must be preserved at all cost through *incorrect* compliance.

least in Cantorland and maybe even Edenland, but though this is a triumph [even if self-concocted] it feels like something's been lost in transformation. Or maybe Cantor simply isn't used to [or so he would like to think] getting things the easy way, especially what's too good for him.) Since, per the Word on the Street, SoP is not at all pleased with the sound that Eden's little misperceptions (or, more accurately, non-perceptions) of Netta's doings are making. What sound is that? Why, the most abysmal across all the ages: the sound that saucy little wavelets make in refusing to summate to an oceanic roar. And it's this sound that's preventing the headquarters staff from doing their dirty work as planned. It's the busy season, after all, which means the SoP dinner theater crowd will be over-ordering the house filet mignon with the usual sides of slaw, fries and . . . full-fledged ocean. And Netta—boobs and all—is sure to be right up their alley but in a way that SoP would at present be hard put to define. Thing is, Eden would be the best one to put her vulgarity across. The best one to think Netta and her boobs. To express their juices. Cantor knows, on the other hand, that SoP knows full well that, unlike Eden, Cantor, akin to Foucault's clinical gazer, can be counted on to hear a language the minute—no, long before—he perceives a spectacle; to articulate before he thinks, so to speak; to overpower worldflow with *word*flow. Cantor doesn't permit *his* unperceived little perceptions to bombard him unless he knows they're prepared to pay the ultimate price: summation into one big perceivable—a Great Whatsit straight out of *Kiss Me Deadly*, Aldrich/Bezzerides's answer to *Dead Souls* (if it needs one). Cantor stays out of mind-trouble by sucking them up into the seething maelstrom of lucidity, i.e., of perceiving as apperceiving—of perceiving that knows it's perceiving and what it is that's being perceived—which is but a step away (and in this case, the step's tiny) from hearing the words needed to capture the thing perceived. Which are not to be confused with the words needed *to describe the thing perceived most accurately.*

But it's too bad (if Cantor doesn't say so himself) that he may have to take over for Eden. Unfortunately, Netta is too complex a being for Eden to handle alone. On the other hand, and at the same time, and the fact remains that, Eden is more attuned to the stage business of the boobs—intuitively, you might say—which is no mere add-on but *the very core of and key to Netta's achievement* and not just as clinician, landlady and skipper. (That such a build-up far outruns any justification we are currently aware of—that it luxuriates in sheer excess—delights Cantor, the quintessential idiot savant as aesthete.) For it is clear that Netta thinks through her boobs—her ploysome mind games have taken up residence there and will not budge until a better venue comes along which is not likely to happen any time soon—and it's equally clear that boobs are simply not Cantor's forte even if—precisely because—he was the very first to pull the peasant ploy apart. So, since each (Cantor and Eden, not boob A and boob B) has a strong claim to zombification as this year's most implausible thought-host/steward/curator, the question becomes through the auspices of whose implausibility is Netta's latent image, as the sum total of all the thought packets it can't help generating, ultimately to be refracted? Packets of a very special kind, or so SoP believes in his most self-important moments, and as such to be attributed to a being only as corrupt as SoP Itself.[41] Corrupt, you say? Well, it just so happens that Cantor is, unlike Eden, always already infected by His thoughts—yes, *always already*, i.e., according to C.S.P.'s Law of Firstness—long before SoP has even started toying with the idea of injecting them. Hence, when all is said and done, Cantor gets the part.

But/Still/And/Moreover/Nevertheless/On the other hand/Thing is/Here's the thing/By the same token/And by the way/More to the point/Along the same lines, the all-perceiving SoP lacks the one advantage possessed by Cantor and Cantor's kind. Not only does Cantor—as a character in the making or as the stirrings of a character in the making, i.e., as a man *with troubles of his own*—think his own thoughts without any help from the powers that be, but he also can't think without running his thought of the moment through the grinder of feeling or feel without running his feeling of the moment through the grinder of thought—can't put his foot in his mouth without first contriving a misalliance between the mouth of thought and the foot of feeling—which means that the product in either case emerges miraculously as not quite one and not quite the other. SoP, on the other hand, is stuck with thoughts and thoughts alone and the more Masterly the thoughts, the more impoverished the feelings, and ultimately the more impoverished the thoughts, Mastery notwithstanding. Or so SoP reminds himself (Cantor can hear the middle-of-the-night mumblings in his middle-aged ventral striatum, which processes regret, and his dorsal anterior cingulate cortex, which is activated by Envy) and this means being reminded in tandem that he's at the top, since the only time he knows he's at the top is when he gets a whiff of how lonely it is all the way up there—as it was for his most famous avatar, *White Heat*'s Cody Jarrett. Only somebody like Cantor, an underling! can make SoP's thoughts live.

Cantor gives Netta's eggs another once-over-lightly. Still, no poacherly stirrings on his part. Meanwhile Borkman replays his windy spiel about how premature ejaculation is being sliced and diced into a thousand and one Little Orphan Annies while the user-fee-waiving FDA stands around playing footsie with its pecker. And he's making sure to pour the potion of that spiel directly into the porches of her ear. Could he be trying to *excite her back* or is it all strictly business—in the service of extracting some vital trade secrets from somebody who's reputation—but as what precisely—has preceded her? He's now replaying one of his greatest hits—the business about staying hairy-chested-hard for the lady—harder than any self-respecting male has the right—or need—to be. George doesn't quite get the point of the play on right *versus* need—he's getting it even less this second time around. Or is it just another case—albeit a Federal one this time—of wordflow decking worldflow right out of the boxing ring of meaning? Which can mean only one thing: that the Blond Beast of Wall Street has his own Master cum SoP to contend with. The usual fruitless speculation has kept Cantor from noticing that Netta's mouth is open wide in (a simulation of?) Munchian horror. The lips are sur-

---

[41] The sort of being who can boast: *After such knowledge, what forgiveness?*, meaning, *I defy you to forgive me for all the vile things I did to achieve such knowledge.*

prisingly thin despite (presumable) surgical intervention to restore them to their youthful pulposity. *Next time, blow 'em up with a bicycle pump*, thinks—not Cantor, not Borkman, but Cantor-and-Borkman-thinking-as-one.

George's mouth (unsurprisingly full), though closed, gapes in horror right along with her. For it's clear she's actually shocked—even as a veteran of so many cadaver rooms—by the bit about getting hard and staying harder. However, her orifice strives unconvincingly to convey that it's not the expletives and the raw imagery (though Borkman has managed to pretty much bypass both) that have shocked her—not the unseemly brain sex she's being forced to engage in when all that ripe old age clamors for is the peaceable shuttling of ill-gotten gains among a slew of offshore subsidiaries. On the contrary, it's what's just been revealed by Borkman in his unofficial role as Man of the People: The outrageousness of the prosthetizers and the talk-show hucksters and their DVDs. The orphans-crazy sleazeball shenanigans of Big Pharma as countenanced by the Office of Orphan Products Development. She'll have you know what she's shocked to learn is that we live in a world where the minute the man on the street tries to cuddle up with a harmless symptom or two they're expropriated as signs of a bona fide life-threatening condition which, after centuries of neglect, is to be at long last legitimated, i.e., by some new diagnosis-and-drug jazz combo. So overpowering (according to the terms of her ploy—the ploy which Ryle should have referred to as the Munch in the Machine) has been her own reformer's outrage at the current sorry state of things pathopharmcological, as exposed by Jacob Riis Borkman (clearly not just another craggily handsome face down at Delmonico's)—so overpowering that, frankly, she would feel remiss in swooning, at a time like this, over all the coy wit and fey whimsy, not to mention the coy whimsy and fey wit, that went into recruiting the subject of fucking, and fucking hard, even if it was solely to get the indictment moving in the first place. Out of the blue (though the sky is ominously overcast) and for the first time Cantor notes, or allows himself the pleasure of noting, the disproportionate largeness of Walser's torso (his anatomy's a non sequitur), which has given it license to push his legs down further than they—or any other pair of legs—were ever intended to go—in this case, almost into his socks. So that's why, notwithstanding having started out with the very best of intentions, they've ended up so stubby and crabbed. And this observation seems capable of explaining everything. Not just Borkman's rant and the shift in psychic accent of Netta's reaction to it. Not just Eden's failure to relearn his sacred rage on native soil and Herbert's unseemly flirtation on the beach. But everything. Only he isn't quite sure how. And that's a relief, though not necessarily a welcome one.

Herbert observes Cantor observing her narrowly, although he's doing his level best to smile compassionately, unjudgingly. She can't believe it. He, who left the muddy paw tracks of his Envy all over her immaculate muumuu, has taken it upon himself to treat *Herbert* unjudgingly. Well, he—or at least you—know what he can do with his unjudging compassion. And though it's Shearer's turn to chat with Borkman (on the scrappy little stretch of pebble beach below and a little to her left), never in a million years would Herbert's gaze dream of skewering her for it. Rhys and Narr are popping scraps into each other's mouths. Herbert for one is glad he has chosen to return from the dead—she's missed him. Yet again, as so many times before, his mere presence serves to mitigate Rhys's *worst excesses*, though Herbert would be hard put to identify even one in a court of law. Maybe that's because at this moment the only excess on the loose (which consists in invoking, through her, what simply doesn't exist but needs to if the relation between the couple is to constitute more than a forcefeeding tournament) must be laid at the doorstep of the Master. But wait! hold your horses! it does seem as if Rhys suddenly wasn't avoiding Melanctha with her usual flamboyance.

Taking all of them in, she vows to remember each and every moment of this day—their last in Coronado, and oh so different from all the others *in far too many ways to enumerate.* (The Master, again: Master, neither of Ballantrae nor of Flémalle, but of Necessary Excess.) But wait! hold your horses one last time! Since isn't it today of all days—at this minute of all minutes—that she's beginning to realize everybody connected with the trial from the lowest scrub to Post himself is—by definition or divine right or default—a member of that obscenest of configurations, that most bestial of organisms—the Family? But our family, she thinks, is *beautiful* because it's only a budding family, inasmuch as all its members are still psychically dispersed and don't know they are members. Ignorance isn't always bliss: sometimes, as here and now, it's something much better: beauty. (The otherworldliness act again, back for an encore. Only in this case, it isn't an act. *Who is parenthesizing?*) *Let's enjoy, shall we?* (she hears herself—or the Master—uncharacteristically twitter) *this little sabbath from the systolic-diastolic penal servitude of conforming and deviating.* And everybody seems to be taking her advice, scampering, running, jumping and standing still (and, in Shearer's case, double-pirouetting). As in an etching by Hieronymus Bosch. (At the same time, it can't be said that they're getting—or that they will ever get—along famously. For your information, they're savvily practicing social distancing to the max even without a single pandemic in sight. For all the prancing, they're keeping a tight leash on their connection to the outside world—the world outside their dynamic—adjuring in a million endearing little ways that they will never forswear their fealty—in fact, they're all ready at the drop of a hat to put that connection over and above their misconnection to each other for they know instinctively that if they don't, the outside world will take its revenge by visiting upon them, the dream *anti*-team, a thorough psychic thrashing, that is to say, they'll be labeled—framed—impaled—collectively as One Big Happy—worse, well-adjusted—Family, i.e., they'll end up packaging themselves as one big fat archetype.) Nobody feels oppressed by everybody else or by the Organism itself because It's taking Its time being born, into the divine right of its despotism. No laws yet, all reducible to the same law: The deviant need not apply, though there's nothing more deviant than the Family itself (not because it's *A* but because it's *B*: we'll leave it to some tenure-hungry pundit to substitute the right phrases). The deviant need not apply but if his number comes up, he has no choice *but* to apply, and then go underground. But first he will have, as a point of honor, to lay claim to something to go underground *with*, preferably a dirty little secret—something to explain his deviancy, whose reputation precedes him and of which he himself is only the expendable trace. To survive, he must gorge on his dirty little secret, which entails first convincing himself it is dirty (no mean feat). A crime against motherhood is, for example, Melanctha's dirty little secret. The sum of the needs of those family members who are deviants—labeling everybody a deviant would be too facile—to affirm their will (deviants are an overreaching lot) against every other will, deviant or not, by flamboyantly hoarding each his dirty little secret, equals the will of the Organism and the will of the Organism is Its cohesion. The only thing that will keep It going is the underground war waged by deviant wills, for each deviant will, to the extent that it's at war with every other will, deviant or not, duly bends to the Will of the Organism. That each deviant will hates its subjection to the Big Will only fortifies cohesion, according to what is known thermodynamically as the icing-on-the-cake effect. Any attempt by the deviant to get out from under the udders of the organismal norm—either by feigning normalness or by pumping up his deviancy to the point where its strength overpowers that of any other norm—only reaffirms the strength of the norm and is thereby doomed to failure and not even a noble one.

But it's way too early (or is it?) for the members of the Invidicum family to discover who's a deviant and who isn't. To discover who needs to come up with a dirty little secret double-quick to prove beyond the shadow of a doubt that he's come by his deviancy honestly—that he's earned his badge the hard way—and who doesn't. But the budding writer within suspects, or the budding deviant inside the budding writer hopes, that up in Santa Barbara, where each of them will be immediately obliged to hit the runway as poster child for this or that FDA-approvable slice of the Envy pie, the Organism's evolution is to be nipped in the bud and deviancy will become very much the norm. Up in SB, everything deviant will come to theatrical fruition, she can feel it in her bones. Self-exposure—no longer an idle threat—will be theatricalized well beyond the threshold of its capacity to inflict harm. Oh, Santa Barbara! (oh, Misperception!) the Gem of the Ocean!

Now, these being the terms—and the palmy backdrop—set for their liberation, what else can they then do to convey the poignancy of unworthiness but give the runway hounds their money's worth—thereby doing the Master proud—by making self-exposure as agonizing—that is, as exhilarating—as possible (but she's getting way ahead of herself—worse, of the Master). Which means that in order to make the gala a success everybody's deviance must learn—and learn fast—to pull its own weight. And that includes you, Pop Albee, with your ostentatiously closeted boozin' (in tonight's performance, the role of pop will be played by that old trouper Your-Guess-is-as-Good-as-Mine), and you, Ma Williams, with your even more ostentatiously closeted shootin' up and down the mainline (in tonight's performance, she will be played by Miss Emily Mestayer, the very image of some Jamesian "*thing* of the theatre" in the shape of an "infinitely-handled greasy violoncello"), and you, Sis Inge, with your aggressively undivulged same- and third-sex cruisin', and you, Junior O'Neill, with your somewhat less aggressively undivulged armed-robbin' and you, too, Sis Miller, Jr., with your fetus stranglin' and, even worse, your scuba-divin', and you, Gramps the Grampus, with your small-arms smugglin' and you, Uncle Plutocrat Hellman, with your savvy mix o' money-launderin' and conflict-diamond traffickin', and you, too, Auntie Method with your unrelenting kiddie and granny porn-peddlin'. So that by the end of the fiftieth and final act of this, their very own reality show, each will have earned his two cents' worth of kitchen-sink transfiguration.

But He's saving her and her alone for something better—something *He* considers better—and Melanctha knows she shares his conviction, to wit, that she's ideally suited for incarnating a—*the*—Imperial Stage Manager, in *Our Town of Santa Barbara*, whose role it will be to goad (but gently) and galvanize (but graciously) the deviants under her tutelage into revelatory inaction. She knows she's well within her rights to blame Him for trying, every chance he gets, to abstract from all the difficult particularities—her blackhood, her femalehood, her motherhood, her divorcehood, her novicehood—that make or profess to make her Herbert and Herbert alone. Within her rights to blame Him for undertaking gentrification of those ruins so as to ensure they don't impede the sort of deep-dish thinking about the Art of Envy and other maledictions for which ceremonial He, Boris Lermontov MacMaster, has selected her, Victoria Page MacHerbert, and her alone. Especially when others might, to the unpracticed eye, appear to be worthier or at least more plausible votaries. But the Master, ever the client-centered Maestro, is smart enough to know it's their very plausibility that disqualifies them for active duty. Of course, she has no one to blame but herself for granting him license to uproot her from herself—in other words, to do (*no!*) . . . do (*no, it can't be true!*) . . . do (*it just can't be!*) . . . do (*yes, it can be and it damn well is!*) . . . what she herself always hungered to do but found unthinkable . . . unnatural. Until now.

Stoically putting away plight and promotion (as one and the same)—and labor and leisure, too—Melanctha takes note of the fact (or rather the Master, quite the budding film buff, has her take note [he's currently big on Dreyer and late Eisenstein]) that the jam session quickly degenerated (although it never had the least intention of being anything else) into the mere sum total, with nothing left over, of all the thought-packet events with the misfortune to unfold on its premises.[42] No aspirations on the jam session's part to be, say, an ur-Event with an autonomous existence and offering a host of other spectacles for sampling (not just thought-packet events) as well as dead times and dead spaces galore, of which It's too self-assured to be afraid. But the Master *is* afraid and does a gross disservice, as usual, to those times when and those spaces where, mind you, it only *seems* that nothing is happening by replacing them with the doings of his own secret police (the packets) or, as some lefties might say, by packing the courts with his reactionary, woefully unqualified judges (ditto). Melanctha is sure some admirably vile hack will leap at the chance to frame *The Invidicum Storybook* as "a missed collision of thought-packed perspectives on the Void" (so why not

---

[42]Cf. Noël Burch, *Theory of Film Practice* (Princeton, New Jersey, Princeton University Press, 1969), p. 39, as cited in David Bordwell, *The Films of Carl-Theodor Dreyer* (Berkeley, California, University of California Press, 1981), p. 107.

throw him his slab of raw meat right now and have done with the nauseous suspense). Saddest of all, the Coronado waterfront—an innocent bystander if ever there was one—will, through contagion, be forever remembered as a big fat there sans *there*.[43] But can it be that the Master is getting a raw deal and that Thought Packets, like crossing the Rubicon and apparent misuse of the dissolve and . . . la Danse (at least according to Balanchine according to Shearer according to Herbert), c'est *une question morale*. And a very serious question at that.

---

[43] Sorry to say, but the city of Oakland should sue the Stein estate for having made it, obviously without permission, the referent for this oh so very smug and tired non-image.

CHAPTER TWENTY-FOUR

"But you must remember that I couldn't under any circumstances antagonize Straynge," Rhys hears herself say before a Full House (everybody who's anybody is piled into the Board of Supervisors Assembly Room at the Santa Barbara County Courthouse). Which thrillingly attests to a country-wide craving for the lowdown on the near-lethal fallout from what that morning's edition of the *Santa Barbara Bald-Eagle Eye* has mercifully called "the biggest double-bind [*sic*] study in Pharma history." With the contestants (Amygdala's publicity arm's new term for *subjects*) representing, incidentally, no less than one hundred seventy-three countries and fifty-two non-self-governing territories—and still counting. She's addicted to full houses—hogs the spotlight every chance she gets—Ethan hears himself *muse*—enviously. Heretically. After all, she's his *girl* and any red-blooded male worth his salt is obligated to perceive his girl as flawless. Shearer is ashamed of herself for thinking, *Why is she Invidicum's poster girl up there on the podium and not I? Why not the almost-famous Caro instead? Why not anybody, envious or not? Anybody—as long as it's not she!*

Herbert has a hard time following for she's still recovering from the shock of being here. (Straynge's murder, if murder it was, seems about to take a back seat to other concerns.) There's this fuzzy recollection of having been awakened in the middle of the scents-smothered night, herded into a minibus with the core crew from New York (very comfortable seating, she has to admit) and deposited at John Wayne International Airport in record time. (By the way, isn't Wayne the guy—of course he is—who surmounted the obstacle of never having seen active duty by becoming, singlehanded, the most-decorated war hero in his country's history? His country, though not necessarily hers.) It's been a lot to take in, especially by those not getting any younger and doomed, therefore, to age faster by the minute than anybody else. Still, she has no choice but to look on the bright side since at this very moment Pritchard's advance guard, in response to fears voiced above all by Shearer about their being tracked down and made to pay for the malfeasances of Amygdala's top brass, are assuring everybody that never fear, those members of the CIA, the FBI and INTERPOL in the pay of the crooks have been thrown off the scent, probably forever—and even if they haven't, the compound is, as every local knows, the most impregnable of bunkers—in fact, it's an agglomeration of bunkers boasting an incomparable quality of life—to which they're due to be transferred but only once compliance with state specifications is airtight. Though why Shearer, Herbert duly wonders—the one among them least likely to be afflicted by the dopamine-drenched sequelae of cat-and-mouse disease, even if played out across an entire continent. Unless . . . the increasingly desperate Master is counting on just such expectations-foiling plot twists to turn him into a roly-poly Master of Suspense, and a highly bankable one—that is when he isn't reveling incompatibly in the incoherence of those twists. She can feel Him breathing down her back: "I need a hit—a palpable hit. Just one. A blockbuster. A breakthrough. A comeback. I'll even settle for a sleeper or (ugh!) a cult classic. Think fast, Melanctha. Think. But not in packets." She's tempted to retort (and what self-respecting voodooist wouldn't be?): "Go away, dead man." But she resists since he's been like a father to her. At present, the core group will be lodged, adequately (*once again, the Rubicon is not to be crossed: more to come on that score*), at the Hotel Synapse (Cantor finds the cuteness too irksome for words) and everybody else at either the (less posh) Dendrite Inn or the (less secluded) Axon Arms. Both conveniently just around the corner from (even more irksome) Plato's Pharmacy. "And until you *are* transferred, little lady," a member of the advance guard trills (the lady in this case being Rhys, oddly enough, not Shearer [*nice touch, Mr. Master!*]), "just bear in mind that your temporary lodgings are being guarded night and day by our Special Enforcers."

During the brief adjournment, Melanctha engages in a bit of amateur (as opposed to amateurish) eavesdropping, from behind (so sayeth the plaque) a Nagami kumquat tree, on a conversation—if only it were heated!—between Ethan and Cook. Thing is, Cook's stentorianics are enough to put any self-respecting eavesdropper out of business. The pair are staging a rebuke—aimed directly at her. Who else could it be aimed at since she and she alone fits to a T—or is it a *T*?—just the sort of profile they're lambasting—the profile of a subject who transforms the pain that the trial needs to inflict (if he's ultimately to be cured) into a generator of ideas—i.e., of tributary, compensatory gain—to be applied to a private enterprise? A subject who cuts pain off at the pass before it can become the pain he desperately needs to undergo—excruciating and free of fringe benefits. A subject whose misbehavior calls into question the purity of the motives of his brethren. For her trouble, she learns more and ends up knowing even less about the Straynge Affair, which everybody seems to have forgotten. For one thing, Eden is more unstable than she imagined. It seems he'd had a severe breakdown on the perilous threshold of puberty which gave way to a chronic blurring of the boundary between the real and the unreal, making him the perfect fall guy. The records subpoenaed from a Dr. Joseph L. Bell (the name sounds familiar—has a distinctly Sherlockian ring), whose care Eden was under thereafter, indicated that in the disorder's tumultuous early stages he was convinced he trolled the Gaslamp Quarter nightly for big-breasted blondes whom he then lured to Balboa Park with the promise of jumbo orgasms. There he bludgeoned them to death. Forensics weren't up to his level of expertise in disposing of the bodies amply dusted with the DNA of hapless bystanders. It took every possible combination of anxiolytics plus talk therapy administered over more than a decade by the good doctor to enable him to master his delusions without bidding them an ungrateful adieu. This oddly (but why *oddly*?) touching tidbit of warts-are-all biography at its incendiary best leads her to believe Eden should, without the right to appeal his deletion, be removed from the shortlist of candidate culprits. She returns to the Supervisors Assembly Room neither a sadder nor a wiser man.

George realizes that the glamor girl of a certain age who's managing to look riveted in her aisle seat in the second row, and at the same time preen loftily as if in her lifetime-subscriber's box at the opera, is none other than the invincible Netta, their soon-to-be landlady. So why did Cantor think they'd left her (racket still lazily swinging) back at the Del? (But did he actually think this or is SoP simply ordering him, whether up to the task or not, to think he thought it—to be the thought's sponsoring consciousness after the fact? since like every Scourge with a reputation to protect He has no intention of letting the racket image precipitating out of the muddy solution of the thought—and giving back to the thought far more than it deserves—disappear without a fight.) But Netta—and Stifter and Walser and any members of the New York team still extant for that matter—can preen all they want: it's Jean and her gang—the core group, as they're being referred to enviously in the musty corridors of the Courthouse—who are currently lording it over the podium while it's the so-called experts who've been relegated to the peanut gallery, or galley, even if it's still very much under construction. (Which may be, speculates Borkman, on the qui vive even when half-asleep, just a big fat ploy to make the suckers feel important, the better to catch them off guard when fMRI time for enviers rolls around, as it had a bad habit of doing back East, and will no doubt make a point of doing even here on the Wild West Coast.)

"*Why* couldn't you antagonize him?" Netta cries out, standing up and looking around, as if for some sign of healthy support from hecklers, who are—Søren Kierkegaard was, as usual, right on the money—never there when you need them most. (Herbert, realizing that the outcry is in response to Rhys's comment made a while back, or maybe a mere second ago, dutifully thrashes her way out of the warm womb of inattentiveness and, while remaining primly seated, manages to stand respectfully at attention.) "Why were you so passive?" Jean shields her eyes against the sunlight assailing from every angle. Is there something calculated in her gesture? Herbert wonders. Might she be auditioning for the role of Blanche DuBois without knowing it (Hollywood's right around the corner, after all) and might she suspect that shakiness in withstanding the merciless glare of her own talent is working boldly in her favor? "Speak up, young lady. You won't be incriminating yourself. Nobody here would be daft enough to take *you* for a murderess." "Because it was he and he alone who stood between me and my dosage . . . for the disease." Do they know what disease she happens to be referring to? How can they? Even she doesn't know anymore.

The man on Netta's right jumps up and, having identified himself as . . . of all people and at long last, Dr. Pritchard! (if today's late edition of the *Eagle* is to be believed, he went on to stop the show by shouting "Call me E.E. Evans or forever hold your peace!" to no one in particular on his much-too-jovial way out), warns coyly they'll be seeing far more of him than they may care to in the long months to come but that they might end up not minding since "things will now be a lot different here for you folks." Somebody behind Shearer (impossible to determine whether it's a man or a woman and in the end does it really matter?) stage-whispers, "He's the one I was telling you about." Whether he is or isn't, Herbert can think of him only as yet another prop from central casting sent in—prematurely, to say the least—when—true to Masterly form, none of his predecessors have been milked even halfway dry. Maneuvering so as to be facing both the "folks" on the podium and those in the audience (*He's in pretty good shape for a man his age*, Herbert can hear everybody thinking—and in unison, to boot), Pritchard assures them that although he hasn't come to praise Dr. Jim Straynge (he would never have brought up his name if not for the young lady), neither does he intend to bury him. Especially since he's already buried—dead and buried, in fact. And a crying shame, too, whatever his glaring defects. Which brings him round to the subject of his introductory speech (he'll make it brief because everybody's obviously bushed after the longish trip—he can smell it—and must want nothing better than to hit the sack pronto), namely, Diagnosis and Its Vi . . . Vic . . . Vici . . . Vicissi . . . Vicissitudes. In Cantor's view, there's something phony about the stutter. Phony, phony, phony, phony, phony, phony, phony, phony, phony, phony (this newfound ability of his to excrete chunks of dead space [ten, imagine!], and thought packets be damned, takes him completely by surprise). Pritchard evidently has his own SoP—an overprotective SoP—who, like every other SoP, is overprotective not so much of his voice box (a nullity like every other voice box no matter how much of a big shot in elite circles) but of the box's transmission of His message. He can't have him showing right off the bat how very easily he—i.e., the message—consorts with polysyllables. For that will only turn off full blast the spigot of philistine receptivity and like most other members of his breed, Pritchard's SoP craves as wide an audience as possible for his fireside chats (which he no doubt hopes will morph into The Rump-style rallies replete with MAGA-festooned deplorables—yes, *deplorables*—and their even coarser better-halves). Bottom line: If His fireside chat, pretentiousness and all, is to crash unmarred through customs (secreted, as planned, on a microchip in Pritchard's rectum), then he must disarm audience resistance and what better ice-breaker than an unpretentious speech disturbance—at once native and message-induced? Proving that the transmitter is having at least as much trouble metabolizing the message—whatever its provenance—as the audience. And ensuring thereby that the subject of the message quickly becomes not what its title says it is but "logjammed transmission." Terrific strategy.[44]

"The last thing I want is to follow in the footsteps of every sleazeball careerist under the sun and knock my ex-mentor. His approach was damn good—as far as it went, that is (though it's certainly not up to me, a maverick of an entirely different stripe, to decide whether it went too far or not far enough). But he failed to realize you can't just go ahead and treat Envy outright if you don't recognize that, first, it must be *pre-treated* as a particularly baleful form of . . . body perception. But, strangely, Straynge was always

---

[44]Cf. a similar ploy by J.-L. Godard in his film *Passion*, where a waitress—in a Swiss restaurant so understated-elegant that it hurts—stutters her way mock-precariously through a few lines of Schiller (I mean the Schiller who graces the Central Park Mall and demands reverence—or at least motionless deference—from the robins that routinely congregate at the base of his pedestal). Another case where that nasty Swiss wunderkind smuggles one of his signature rarefactions into the celluloid stew on the wings of some trumped-up affliction.

against that idea and if you brought it up in his presence he felt personally attacked. So, Straynge or no Straynge, the first order of business is to get all of you *out* of those sweaty clothes and *on* Bakhtine—the hottest thing on the market for the thing that ails you. Why? you ask. Well, because Invidicum just can't be expected to do it alone. It requires a backup, an adjuvant, a way-paver." Borkman raises his hand (a new tack) but before being recognized shouts, "I thought it's Envy and Envy alone that ails me—us. You don't mean to tell me we've come all this way just to hear—" "Everything is intermingled—all mixed up," Netta shouts expressionlessly, so as to be spared having to hear Pritchard fire off this none-too-convincing party-line rejoinder to such an objection. He holds up a little lavender-tinted phial.

Remaining seated, Eden asks, "What ails us, exactly?" He doesn't look at Borkman even if they're supposed to be on the same side: the briefest of flings seems to have ended. "As Liepnits back in New York was fond of saying" (he's making quick work of the stutter), "the soul's job is partly to express the body and vice versa and as the body expresses the whole universe, the soul in representing the body also represents the whole universe and maybe a wee bit more (see his *Monadology for Twenty-first Century Men, Women and Other Beasts* and philosophical correspondence, edited by one C.I. Gerhardt). And what can be better for the soul than to seek the oneness with the universe that is fulfillment? For the universe feels no Envy. But that—the only basis for health—is a path closed to you. For there's no use denying you're all mighty uncomfortable with your body—in fact, you hate it, or you wouldn't be here: expecting the California sun to do what plastic surgery cannot—or will not (it's folks like you who give it a bad name). Which makes you envious of souls that love their bodies—I call this *baseline Envy*. I don't say all cases of Envy start here or that baseline Envy is *the* characteristic feature of the disease but I *do* say that every envier experiences baseline Envy at some point along the pathological curve we refer to technically as A Life. But as much as you hate your body, you hate the universe even more for threatening, per your unspoken request, to annihilate it at every turn. When you get right down to it everybody hereabouts is rather prudish (in the way that every Rilkean angel is *schrecklich*)— especially the Leporello-less libertines among you who, more joyless than the Puritans, can tolerate thinking about what happens between their legs and somebody else's only in terms of *meeting their monthly projections*. But by shutting down your orifices (in order to fool yourself into thinking you're a self-sufficient finished product, hence indestructible) you deprive yourself of commerce with the universe which is your only ticket to oneness. Because it is solely, according to the Law of the Carnival, through acts performed at the body's frontier (need I round up the usual suspects?) that you get to swallow the universe and all of its glories (mountains, rivers, pandemics, earthquakes, rivulets, sheep, dung beetles, genocides and lampreys) and be swallowed in turn—and what is all that cyclical swallowing and being swallowed but oneness, or so debt-ridden Panurge would have us believe. But to be fulfilled you have first to swallow your pride, which is much bigger than the universe, and accept that it's your orifices—bowels and all—that have final say on and final sway over whether you get to be cured of yourself. But how can that hated body expect to be receptive to Invidicum or any other pharmakon? This, my friends (or rather my friends-to-be) is where Bakhtine comes in—and not a minute too soon. It opens you up to the universe. So, no matter how tired you are, take the 50-milligram dose before turning in. It will reactivate your serotonin, dopamine, β-adrenergic—and Invidicum—receptors (for soul hate is perceptible even by body entities as tiny as cells) and get you started off on the right foot in this, stage 76N-5, of what is rapidly becoming recognized as the Biggest Double-Blind in Cinema History—but you already know that."

Melanctha experiences deep shame for the Master—a feeling he's never inspired before—or at least not so deeply. Clearly this Pritchard character has been trotted out just to advertise the jottings of yet another Big Thinker or two. To yoke that Thinker's thought, however incongruous, to the subject at hand, whatever that happens to be—to hitch the wagon of that Big Thinker's profundity to the rapidly declining shooting star that is Invidicum in all its guises. If you ask Melanctha, the Master's pay should be docked substantially every time he sees fit to try his hand at this kind of Invidicum Story enrichment which enrichment is in fact a declaration of depletion. Why, he's treating the Story's every building block or stumbling block or cell block as if it's little more than the grimace of a swaihwé mask as refracted through the gaze of a Lévi-Strauss. I.e., no Story block exists in itself. It's simply a marker for the infinite number of other blocks, real or possible, with which it could have been replaced. What's said at any particular juncture is simply a stand-in for what the Master can't bear to hear said because it's what His clients expect to hear said and what they expect is just too damn boring—too damn typical—too damn archetypical—because it's exactly what every other hack would have said under the circumstances. But it won't get said on his set. And what stands in for what doesn't get said on his set is precisely the too-damn-boring, the too-damn-typical, as transformed—deformed—re-formed—reformed—beyond recognition through collision—collusion—cohabitation—coition—with one, or maybe two or three, of those Big Thinkerly thoughts. He can't allow to be said what everybody's paying to hear because it simply isn't Him. It will never be Him. Melanctha gets all that. She even begins to discern the gnatlike stirrings of compassion in *the groined vault of her soul* (that's right, the groined vault of her soul: any objections to a little Cotton Mather-style theologizing?). But this time it's to the paying clients that her heart goes out (and to think that's seconds ago he was begging her to come up—though not in so many words—with the *concept for a smash*). This time her disappointment is stronger than her . . . love. Yes, her love. Maybe the Master, mastery notwithstanding, isn't so very different—is in fact indistinguishable from—that student, way over age like her and too handsome for his own good or anybody else's, who got thrown out of class over and over—and then permanently—because of an inability to keep the plotting straight, that is, crooked enough, in the airport thriller he, like everybody else, was instructed to write in order to pass. It was only after he jugularized himself to death with a disposable fountain pen (the blood mistaken for ink by the first first responder) that the professor directly responsible, ordered to do a little expiatory research or face dismissal, discovered that the deceased had in fact suffered from a rare writer's disability whereby perpetration of a legitimate plot twist is in itself so traumatizing as to obliterate, almost immediately, any memory thereof. So when the time comes to inflict another twist, there's no basis, no continuity, no context, since its predecessors are all irretrievable. The only disease running loose, then, is the Master's—and she's got to admit it's far more interesting than Envy, that silly little orphan pretending to bawl for its biological mom. *But why is perpetration of a (just-as-silly) twist so traumatizing?*

The applause coming from the Amygdala crowd, if it does come, is tepid at best. The Big Think, sometimes Bigger than Big, combined with the materialization of this synergistic sidekick for Invidicum which up to now seemed so . . . ruggedly self-sufficient, has clearly been an irritant, although the locals are eating it up and already asking for more. George is getting a bit hot under the collar: if his rivalrous siblings only knew what he'd stooped to down Coronado way, i.e., all that gratuitous big-thinking about (with a prod or two from FN) himself as priestly David versus Borkman's Peroxide Blond Goliath. Why, they'd tear him limb from limb. Shearer for her part (no: *for her part*, weak) . . . As for Shearer (yes: *As for*, strong), the news about Bakhtine has hit her hard. *Unhappy is the pharmakon that needs a sidekick.* If she'd only known how things were going to turn out, she'd have—she'd have— *You'd have what, dear?* Mr. B. asks, cupping her right instep in his hands. His question magnifies the wastefulness of her regret and constricts her, the skilled practitioner thereof, to a pinpoint. Ethan is one of the very few to show enthusiasm. Considered in a certain light—like that currently bouncing off the ocean floor and transpiercing the windows—Ethan's rather dashing and wouldn't be out of place as, say, Sanguinic's black-and-white cavalier, so if Jean badmouths him every chance she gets maybe it's to keep every other woman's envy at bay. Putting his arm around his rival (purely for his own amusement since the room is rapidly emptying) in an orderly display of the mogul-to-mogul intimacy he witnessed countless times among the Big Boys in New York and so envied (especially in the course of his in-house imprisonment), Bill Cook, in tight-fitting white chinos and purple-prose penny-loafers, takes the liberty of steering him toward the loggia. They've already patched up their differences—buried the hatchet (so what if it was meant to be in each other's jugulars?) thanks to Cook's being—or at least acting—the bigger man. Once his forced sabbatical ended, with reintegration into the company at a much higher grade, Cook found it tantalizingly easy to take the first step. He lauds the Pacific but in such a way as to leave no room for anybody else's admiration but isn't that the whole point. Ocean-blind under the best of circumstances, Ethan convinces himself he can think of nothing but how to acceptably ease himself out from under Cook's wing. So imagine his surprise when he hears himself say, "What did you think of it?" As if the question turned the questioner into one big hot—one big scorching potato, Cook immediately withdraws his arm, thereby sparing Ethan any further discomfort and enabling him to discover just where the words—no longer his—anybody's but his—are headed. "I mean, What's your take on her crack about Straynge in front of everybody?" Nobody, surely, would deny Ethan's right to hope that Cook will pooh-pooh his fear of being guilted by association even if he doesn't quite know how to extract the desired reassurance without losing face. "As any proud alumnus of the Parallax Corporation's master's-in-vilification advertising program will tell you," Cook says coldly, "we're not here to dissect what your girlfriend made the mistake of saying about some rancid corpse in front of a motley crew of farts, old and young, but to make sure this Eden creep does what he's supposed to before generously agreeing to take the rap for the other business. They've dug up three witnesses more than willing to swear they saw him staggering down Tunnel Access Street around 11 p.m. (i.e., an hour or two after the time fixed for the murder) bloody-but-unbowed, dutifully drunk and blear-eyed and— talk about an embarrassment of riches!—cursing Straynge at the top of his lungs. But getting back to your question, what do I think? Well, what I (also) think is, Where the hell does Pritch, our favorite flunkey, get off trying to put his personal stamp on the proceedings by pretreating our knockout mice with his own cockamamie brand of snake oil? Let him find some other way to beef up his CV in anticipation of the moment when we give him the boot and he discovers he'll Never Have Lunch in This Town Again. His horn tooting is definitely not in the score. If he's not careful, he'll end up like you-know-who. How, I ask you, can Eden be expected to do what we tell him to do if he suddenly discovers he likes his body and his body likes him which means that he likes every other body and every other body likes him and you are right and I am right and everything is quite correct?" Ethan shrugs it off. Shrugs off not what he's just been hearing about Eden and newcomer Pritch and Straynge and the Tunnel Access Street irregulars and the knockout mice and whatever other cameos this Mad Ave maestro has been able to pack into a few upgushes of boyish effervescence but il maestro's expression of contempt, way back when, for a fellow sufferer's suffering (i.e., Ethan's as related to possible guilt by association with Jean). Ethan has been stone- and tone-deaf to everything uttered thereafter. So let anybody who's been listening in on Cook be forewarned, even if it's way too late, that Ethan's is a special kind of listening—a listening through somebody else's non-listening, in this case a non-listening so concentrated and intense as to have become the true subject—the hottest topic—of whatever's still being listened to.

Cook, riding high based on all he's privy to and Ethan isn't, perceives nothing of all this, which only allows him to ride even higher. "But whatever Pritch has done is merely the least interesting example of all that's been sabotaging things from the start. I'm talking about our refusal to play the hands that fate has dealt us, which always entails sticking first and foremost to their meaning *as dealt*. He can't stay content—stay put—with Envy eating away at the soul: He has to drag in the soul's body-hatred. And I dare him to blame his hanky-panky on the California sun: he's been out here long enough to know how to keep its rays from playing havoc with his circuitry." (Judging from Cook's tone and posture, Ethan is certain he's about to be snowed, for as long as he can hold up, by a whole slew of self-promotional videos of the same sodden type.) The business about sabotage has really gotten his goat. Yet, afraid to challenge Cook directly because anything short of Cook's annihilation must rightly be adjudged as failure and failure will only multiply Ethan's rage a googol-fold but aware at the same time that he's simply got to put forth the challenge in some form and double-quick, Ethan hits on professedly animus-free musing as the best available vector. "But isn't self-sabotage just another—meaner—term for the highest form of ambition?" Armed with a practiced look of withering perplexity Cook now intends—Ethan is sure of it—to carry out the lowest form of character assassination. And he does— or at least tries to—by reminding his "undistinguished colleague" that he's concerned with sabotage plain and simple, not *self*-sabotage, of which by the way he's a pastmaster and with tons of accolades and fan mail from the most respected avant-garde cabals worldwide to prove it. "Isn't 'respected avant-garde cabals' an oxymoron?" Ethan ventures, buoyed and at the same time soothed by fury. This is the last straw (funny, Ethan thinks, that something so lame should be the last straw) and Cook dutifully storms off looking—even if, or maybe because, he has virility and machismo in spades and to spare—a little like a duchess—make that a *grand* duchess—and not any old grand duchess, mind you, but the Grand-Duchesse de Gérolstein. So as it turns out, it's Gender Fluidity not Misperception that's the Gem of the Ocean. At least for now, here in the Santa Barbara County Courthouse . . .

Trusting to her (*as you can see, the Rubicon has just won this round and the refuseniks are hanging their heads and cursing their stars but just for a millisecond for they're refuseniks still and as such forever resilient*) untrustworthy view from afar, it's become clear to Herbert—and this time without the Master's intervention (but how can she be sure?)—that what it is poor Narr needs, only movement-and-rest—his or some other entity's—can provide: an antidote—a pharmakon—something to turn off the spigot of Cook's words, words, words—his and everybody else's—even if they've been doing nothing more noisome than what words do best—assail (albeit with the firm intention, in this case, of turning him into an even lower man on the totem pole than Straynge was forever claiming himself to be). It doesn't have to amount to much—just as long as it's good, clean movement blessedly free of voice-over, -under and -sideways. Even the lowliest will do—footsteps, say, approaching the ladies' room or a forefinger pointing at the scimitar over the entrance to the Law Library or a cloud (there are plenty of them to go around) getting all tangled up in (for lack of anything lowlier) a Chilean wine palm (the possibilities—however, i.e., fortunately—are not endless). Exactly the sort of dead-space activity the Master's *henchmen* or the members of His cabinet (thought packets to you, bub!) have been trained to displace so as to dispel their Boss's horror vacui which, it should be pointed out, easily outHerods Macbeth's or Boris Godunov's though maybe not John Gotti's. So Melanctha finds it all the more commendable that the Boss has still gone out of his way simply by getting out of *her* way (withdrawing into himself, you might say, as if he were Isaac Luria's God)—has made the supreme sacrifice (even if movement is not his cup of tea) to ensure that a little long-overdue stage business gets thrown Eden's (sorry, *Ethan's*) way. For look, here in the garden, a pair of geese, amenably in tow to their nibbling young, are taking a three-hours-too-early after-dinner stroll. The coast is clear: not a word in sight. The smile that irradiates his whole body is one long act of deasphyxiation. On his behalf Melanctha breathes a sigh of relief. After all, he's young enough to be her son.

But—but—but—but—but—she knew it was too good to be true (*an infinite duration has elapsed between the termination of the preceding paragraph and the commencement of this, its successor*) for words are again about to rear their ugly head unbidden. And if she can hear them rearing then no doubt Ethan can, too; and if she knows what those words are then he knows it, too, even if he doesn't know he knows, though not from self-imposed obtuseness practiced as a matter of duty à la Eden but rather because of— well, because of heart trouble (*who is speaking?*). Thing is, some movements— some images of movement—she's learning too late—can't help but give rise to thought packets—like magnets they attract such creatures, the fault lying not in themselves, but in their stars, that they are underlings.[45] Can the Master, uncontrollable as he is, help it if, like Foucault's clinical gaze, He hears a language as soon as an image catches his eye? (She, too, feels the pull though she resists.) So, He's doing it again—or rather, Language is doing it again— constructing a thought—butchered at both ends and at many of the waystations in-between. But she wants to go easy on Him—after all, He did get out of the way of "her" image. It goes something like this: *The birds manage to depict (a) casual but total absorption in the doings of the shrubbery and at the same time (b) hyper-vigilance where the doings of the goslings are concerned* but with neither stance giving off any whiff of simulation. The words have taken a perfectly reliable image and butchered it to death. From the look of him, Ethan, unresisting, has just been made privy to the same butchery. Taking his cue from the geese and acting from the strongest sense of conviction Melanctha has ever witnessed in a human being even in so momentous a situation (hyperlativity compliments of whom exactly?), Ethan waxes self-absorbed and hyper-alert and in no way is either stance a simulation. He, too, after all, has his goslings to protect. So the movement event with its delicate punctuation by intervals of rest hasn't been a flop. Thanks to of all things the thought itself, specifically to the pivot/crowbar words *but with neither stance giving off any whiff of simulation*. Words that have forced him back to the image to witness through their smokescreen nothing less than that image's enactment of the Impossible: a sort of compatibility of mutually exclusive stances. So here we have the rare case of an image's actually becoming what every image secretly aspires to be—a super-image—through the intervention of what folk wisdom never stops proclaiming is the image's mortal enemy. Unlike Melanctha, then, Ethan will return to the fray sadder but wiser. She of course envies him the prize—an expert blend of sadness and wisdom—but even more, his insusceptibility to her sort of gnawing ambition—gnawing consciousness of that ambition—which got in the way of her claiming her very own prize a while back. As is only right and proper, the prize has gone—like all other prizes great and small—to the person least capable (or so he wishes it to be thought)

---

[45] In other words, the fault of attracting thought packets lies not with the images but with the packets themselves (the Master's flunkeys), under whose unlucky star those images, fair and unpolluted, are transmogrified into—that is to say, annihilated by— Language.

of associating his doings with an entitlement.

Though Herbert, unlike Rhys (thanks to her sister) and Narr (compliments of Rhys) and Shearer (in homage to Balanchine), has had no particular training in indenturement, she feels—no, she's *feeling*—no, she's *starting to feel* (once again? for the first time? as usual?)—no, she's *never felt* as strongly as she does at this moment that her circuitry is the rogue and peasant slave of His transmissions—all of them. (Or, as one of her profs might say, she's His Lakmé, His Thaïs, His Leila, His Dalila, His Hérodiade, His Djamileh [French orientalism's hit parade]—only the hypervirile old guy [like Nabokov, he makes aestheticism smell virile] isn't here to confirm it. So she'll say it for him. After all, she was *his* slave, too.) He's won. He's pulled the wool over her eyes. She refuses to go easy on Him. He's not as helpless in the face of words—thoughts—as He's just pretended to be. Getting out of her way was an act—flawlessly mis-executed. Never mind the beautiful image, now dead, which by some fluke she had a hand in creating. Never mind that she was *in at the creation*. Never mind that, however briefly, images of movement-and-rest became her domain. She can no longer look on the bright side and revel in the ort of surplus value extracted from his meddling: transformation, as perpetrated by His thought packet, of image into super-image. According to the signal just transmitted *Effective immediately*, He doesn't take kindly to the introduction without his express permission (and even with it) of movement and its fall guy, rest, into the system of things out there—the system of objects occupying their place in space—the system of Extension. But why the sudden feeling of delight—even ecstasy? Is it because they're having their first marital squabble: He's gratuitously putting his foot down (how like a man) while she continues to wear the pants, even if they're second-hand. He's letting her know on no uncertain terms that if He gives the OK to movement—and who is she to be giving Him orders?—then it devolves upon Him to describe it—under His system of Thought. Or rather, there's no question of devolution—no question of movement falling prey to language: where there's *world*flow, there's *word*flow, period: if there's movement then there's description of movement and vice versa. Wherever movement goes, description follows. Although it's as insane to talk about description *following* movement—of Thought following Extension—as it is to talk about chewing your own teeth, swallowing your own windpipe. Since movement and its description—connubially, funereally enchained—are the very same capacity just viewed under different attributes—in this case, the best known among an infinity and the most sought after, namely, E and T. Not that the Master is to be thought of as the sum total of His attributes. He wants it to be known right off the bat by the distaff—by his bride, Melanctha—his Shekhinah—that the sum total of the Everlasting He (it's counterintuitivity that rules the roost hereabouts, as everywhere else) amounts to one and the same thing as perceivable from different angles or under different lights, with its nonexistent components most *accessible*—albeit notionally, at best—when swathed in the morbid slime known as worldflow.

The shareholder value of counterintuitivity notwithstanding, He knows his clients well enough to know they won't sit still for something as unmasterly—as downright lowly—as somebody else's movement, much less the description of it. They'll get all jittery. Or is it rather He who's got the jitters. After all, He hasn't sacrificed youth, worse, middle age—didn't make that now centuries-old Faustian-Promethean bargain (the uncredited theme of too many MGM dream sequences)—merely to sign off on what will not bear—will not *bear bearing*—His stamp. Since all movements come down to the same anonymizing thing (but, whatever you do, don't go spouting such rot in front of Shearer). Ditto and *a fortiori*, all *descriptions* of movement (which is precisely why an Anglo-American mandarin like the Guy from Rye swore off the stuff early on in his career). For movements, even the best of the lot, can be described only along the lines of, say, *Cook took a stroll down the Courthouse's Anacapa Gallery or Rhys descended the Circular Stairway three steps at a time to the Hall of Records, which is the only place she could have left it* (her Ralph Lauren shoulder bag, a gift of atonement from too-scared-to-be-sexually-abusive Dad) or *Borkman extended his sunburnt right arm in passing the Spirit of the Ocean Fountain or was it the Old Jail Wing? only to discover he'd left his watch in the tour bus, or so he hoped.* And how by any stretch of the imagination can mass-producible confections like these be perceived as Masterly? They stink—of that sublimely folksy carcinogen, fructose corn syrup. So, if you're a bona fide Master with a clientele to be bedazzled at any price (though in backwater dinner theaters, which truth be told are what—take heed, Amygdalites!—His company usually plays, bedazzlement just didn't cut it: movement is in fact the only dish, besides crocodile hash, deemed halfway edible by the locals), *EITHER* you take your movement medicine (resigned to the fact that man cannot live by grandiloquence alone) and dive, nose held high, right smack into the cesspool of brute description—and make an avant-garde virtue of hack necessity by hacking it up as blatantly as possible (with stomach-turners like *He walked in, She walked out, Sarah Jane came out of the ladies' room, and Sarah Jim jumped out the window feet first as Betty and Sam sawed away merrily at their boysenberry sundaes*). *OR* you find a better way to assert the dignity of your uniqueness even as a lowly choreographer (even *as a choreographer*! get a load of him, Moira! thinks Melanctha).

On the other hand (if the Breaking News being transmitted Reuters-style down through His circuitry to hers is to be trusted), He has no objection to the kind of sleight of hand (read stunts) practiced, notoriously, by—yes!—that Guy from Rye—constructions along the lines of, *The evening had so nearly closed in, though the Guy had lighted the lamp nearest him, that he* hadn't distinguished *the appearance of another person, an eager woman from the look of her who in her alacrity had barely paused before advancing.* It would be OK for Him to set the stage for movements such as this—movements to be carried out by one proxy and described—but only in terms of *the failure to have perceived it!*—by another. The failure to have perceived it! Such a construction (according to this latest dispatch) won't tarnish the Master's reputation as the one among all others who, whatever the odds and whatever the climate, aesthetically speaking, always makes it his business to transmute anonymizing descriptions of movements into self-initializing ones. Which descriptions are suddenly not at all about movements but, like this one, all about the mis- or missed perception of movements (and in the Guy from Rye's House of Fiction, *it's perception*, mis- or otherwise, that rightly rules the roost). Movements that in lesser hands (so continues the wired press release) remain no more than themselves (and in so remaining end up teaching their clientele absolutely nothing they don't already know) are, in his, alchemized into . . . not gold (anybody can *do* gold) but something infinitely more precious, that is to say, the merest detritus of—the merest pretext for—this or that mis- or missed perception, proving that nothing is ever doomed to remain the very thing it loathes itself for being when there's a Paracelsus on hand to reshuffle Fate's stacked deck. Which alchemization of missedness ultimately redounds to the spiritual health of His clientele—even the Everglades dinner theater crowd—or so He needs to believe if He's to stay afloat in that ol' devil maelstrom of masterdom. Since it serves, the alchemization does, as a model of how to alchemize Life itself (which, between you and me, is pretty much all misses) into something a whole lot better. "Well, you don't have to chew my ear off!" Melanctha hears herself thinking, secretly pleased that it's her ear He's chosen to nibble on and that she's got the sound of a shrew being what she believes is coquettish down pat. But the pleasure quickly wears off. Between lambasting the Master and saving Ethan she's had no time to look around. Not surprising, therefore, that she's missed the tree trunk standing diseasedly defiantly leafless before her very eyes. It doesn't take much reflection to realize this is exactly the kind of spectacle—goslings are strictly for the birds—that should have been served up to him. He could then have put himself right to work proving that self-stymying inner tension is much more all about movement than is movement itself. Proving it—living it in the body of his gaze—through the auspices of a thought . . . a thought . . . (As she knows exactly what's she's about to think, Melanctha's hesitation is for dramatic effect only: *Hollywood's right around the corner, after all,* so who knows what talent scout may be buried in the quicksand of this particular Everglades.) . . . a thought . . . a thought . . . a thought about what is in fact very much the case here, to wit, an entity's war with itself—a thought about said entity as the battleground—as the lek (yes, *lek*: don't play dumb)—of opposing tendencies. A thought along the lines of, say: *The tree trunk is all elbows—in fact it's glued to the life task of elbowing itself out of existence before it can get on with the true work of charging skyward.* If things had unfolded as—as—as—well, as it was too late for them to do now, then what an *unmitigated triumph* for Ethan! How else characterize his tormenting of some self-schismed entity into movement by assaulting it with a description of its particular brand of paralysis?

Not only is it clear to Ethan (hooray: the Master has chosen yet again to cross his own Rubicon) that Jean is *upping the ante* of her contempt[46] (the goslings have opened his eyes to the fact that the Blanche DuBois routine was put together solely to humiliate him) but he has an inkling or two that Herbert is thinking big bad thoughts about him behind his back—in cahoots

---

[46]Is he employing the expression properly? But if he isn't, who cares? Employing it as he does exalts despair in a way that proper usage never could.

with somebody everybody (including him) is calling her . . . Master (the more racist among them chalk it all up to hot voodoo). He's more alone than ever: neither a guinea pig nor a master. His position is—and no doubt will always remain (that is, if it manages to perdure in this world of robo-signers)—that of a middle manager. Like his father before him and *his* father before him. That's what attracted her to him in the first place. Took one whiff and knew he was ripe fare. From the first she was busy stripping bare as pretentious any preference smacking of the will to resist his robust mediocrity (if he would only peel away the layers of that resistance he'd be sure to find mediocrity at its core, awaiting harness), hence his self-advancement in the approved way. But don't take his word for it—ask her first husband (for—mark my words—there will be others). Women—yes, all women—take it as their duty to expose—to unmask—the perverse refusal to put his soul up for sale. He laughs. What tripe.

Such is his story, which continues to trace what, in the lingo of some advanced-degree holders (out of Invidious curiosity he Googled a few of Cantor's published papers), is called a pathological curve—ploddingly continuous but, at any point, without foreseeable direction. As for the even unlikelier story within which he finds himself embedded—the Story of the Trial—it resembles nothing so much as his uncontested favorite among all the pathologicals (and Cantor's apparently as well), namely, the Snowflake. While the area covered by the Invidicum snowflake remains bounded (the plot, under all the froufrou, is ultimately quite simple), its perimeter is infinite (comprising all those digressive analyses symptomatic of dread—that plotting, if hewed to, will obliterate the plotter). But if Ethan is by any chance as serious as he doesn't say—doesn't even whisper even to himself—about refusing to take his self-relegation to the slagheap of middle management standing up (but without being perceived as thereby doing her bidding), then he needs to move—to be on the move (and if movement won't come to him . . .). In other words, he needs to think. He takes the elevator up to El Mirador for just that purpose. But once there, he expects the Pacific, already super-freighted, to do the thinking for the two of them. But the Pacific won't let him have his way with her. Anyway, the Pacific, addicted to his blandishments, belongs to Cook and Cook alone. But just when he's about to give up, Figueroa, patron saint of middle managers, comes to his rescue. Though no Ocean, it does have its medicinal virtues: For example, as regards spectacular delineation of contour, the three salmon-streaked puff pastries afloat above have nothing on their reflection in the windshield of that sports car parked directly across from the Courthouse (as is usually the case when cumulonimbus meets Maserati). Which only goes to show that over millennia, preferred shares of reflection stock have been grossly undervalued. The elevator opens. Ethan looks away. Cook has evidently followed him up here—such is this little man's loyalty to his straightman. Herbert has failed in her mission—no movement countervailing Cook's wordflow to be had for love or money. Unless Cook's own footsteps qualify as pharmakon. And why shouldn't they? Only it isn't Cook—it can't be Cook. He wouldn't be waiting this long to unshut his trap. Ethan can't resist turning. It's Stifter—no, wait, it's Walser. Trust your instincts: Stifter, hands down. "Sometimes I wonder exactly who the biggest Enviers are—the so-called patients or the docs themselves." No intro: great minds don't need one. "Aren't you one of the docs?" Ethan asks, the windfall of so many shares of preferred stock boosting his self-confidence. "Don't know if I am or I'm not. What I do know is that I'm as cunning as Christie's Honoria Waynflete—but you've already guessed that— which means I've managed from the very start to get my non-membership in the group to which I belong accepted as a given. Where was I? The minute something's out of their medical mouths (like Jean—not *our* Jean but Sturges's Jean—when she's talking about her *ideal* in *The Lady Eve*) they start to Envy like crazy the person they could become by qualifying the meaning of that something out of existence—a person who's identityless, unlocalizable, free as a bird, even immortal, at least temporarily, until the next arraignable lapse into meaning-what-they-say. At first Jean's ideal is a little short guy who'll look up to her: her ideal, then, is somebody who'll make her *his* ideal. But strictly speaking he's *not* an ideal since, as it so happens, he belongs not to the category of ideals per se but to the *sub*category of *practical* ideals. What's more, she'd never dream of marrying somebody who looked like her ideal so, as it turns out, her ideal is no ideal at all." Narr implores the Pacific to make this man on the make disappear but, true to form, the Pacific, without so much as a purr, rejects his overtures. And why shouldn't she? After all, who does Ethan think he is? Cortez? Balboa? Chapman? Homer?

"Which brings us round to H. Melville, Confidence Man, another envier of whomever he could manage to become through FMR (fixed-meaning resistance). [Caveat: I spent all last night memorizing this speech just for you, or somebody like you.] He did with the signifier *Indian-hating* what Preston Sturges later did with *ideal* and Plato way back when with *pharmakon*, which was to go on a qualification-of-meaning rampage and then, through a kind of Action Writing, to create an unsuspected compatibility between the meaning and the hog-wild qualifications. Herman knew, as did Plato and Preston (and let's not forget Herman's favorite great-grandson Franz), that any fixed meaning was an irreversible diagnosis, a death sentence, which had to be overturned at all cost and thus that a consideration of Indian-hating in its pure state, of Indian-hating per se, would lead nowhere (in Herman's own words, 'the career of the Indian-hater *par excellence* has the impenetrability of the fate of a lost schooner'). So if he himself wanted to go *some*where undiagnosed, his only option was to abandon the troublesome concept of Indian-hating per se and concoct something less pure, namely, the sub-concept of the *diluted* Indian-hater (along the lines, pretty much, of Sturges's *practical* ideal), and to see how far the desperate ingenuity of improvisational ink-flinging *à la Pollock* could go toward compatibilizing them. And Herman did in fact uncover a compatibility between the pure Indian-hater and his diluted cousin who 'by his very infirmity, enables us to form surmises, however inadequate, of what Indian-hating in its perfection is', etc., etc.—only the compatibility was pure invention achieved (without recourse to any evidence exhumed from, say, the archives down on Centre Street) by putting words and words alone at the service of desperation. To invent that compatibility Herman had to invent a language which entailed, as a fringe benefit, simultaneously writing his old self out of existence and inventing a new, unlocalizable, unstraitjacketable, non-indictable self (Herman minus his morbidities) within—identical to—that language and in consequence was able to live happily ever after, i.e., until he finished the passage in question.

"If you don't mind my saying so (even if it costs me my job: the night as viewed from the El Mirador has a thousand ears), maybe all of us—the Mighty-Mouse medicos like me and the ad men/yes men (like you and Cook)—are doing with Envy exactly what Herman did with Indian-hating. Doing it at the behest of some other Herman—a Mabuse look-alike not quite ready for his perp walk. We talk about diagnosing and treating it and peddling the treatment and then we talk some more though nothing interests us less than this, the deadliest of deadly sins (how can we be interested in what is woven so invisibly into the fractured fabric of our being?), but, lo and behold, one fine day we'll awaken to discover that all the talk about it skidded centuries ago into other domains and continues to do so imperceptibly and so what we're now doing is simply utilizing *Envy* as a placeholder for the name of every other disorder under the sun, as well as of everything that's the furthest thing from a disorder. We'll discover that we managed to erode, to attrite, to volatilize out of existence, if not the accursed sin itself then at least the even more accursed name for it. And soon enough, nothing will be left except wordflow itself—Herman's blessed blighted wordflow—rolling merrily along on its own steam without the slightest need for the things to which names insisted on corresponding one to one (they'll never learn, will they?)."

No point in hiding the fact that Ethan is disappointed. He's been hoping—especially after the Christie reference, not to mention the incident of the incurious Maserati in the daytime—that Stif for all his fabled reserve would end (since Stif *is* ending, no doubt about that) on a note much less general—with a self-annihilating revelation (is there any other kind worthy of the name?), Envy-related to be sure, and so startling as to relegate his own Eden-triggered illness to the status of the airy nothing he should have had the courage to perceive it as being long before it ever reared its ugly little rear. A modest something to prove that he's not one to let anything (not even an outsize addiction, or is it a compulsion, given to throwing its weight around, and with the sufferer, a mere afterthought, in tow?) get in the way of a timely discharge of his duties, as JO buddy, irreverent funster, and (as here) freelance ontologist. But if the moment leaves lots and lots to be desired, Ethan still has no doubt that this sin of omission will turn out to have been a visionary blundering—and more conducive to Ethan's progress than all his colleagues' prudential directives put together.

Stifter throws up his hands and, in exasperation, announces, "I should have been an artist—a writer or a filmmaker." So the revelation hasn't been omitted after all. Although this isn't the kind of revelation Ethan has been hoping for, what matters now is to determine at whom or at what the exasperation is directed, and in what key it's being played. Is it Ethan who's being targeted for not taking him at his true worth—for not having stopped the scholarly show to proclaim, "You shouldn't be wasting your time decrypting the work of *others*. Since you're every bit as good as Herman and Preston."?

Or maybe it's Life Itself that's his bull's-eye: cruelly afflicted with so embarrassing an embarrassment of riches how can he be expected to set his sights on just one, or even just ten? Or is language the culprit since, as we all know, it has a bad habit of doing the only thing it knows how to do, i.e., trivializing any predicament unwary enough to subject itself to framing? Or maybe it's Everybody Else who's the problem since whether Everybody Else knows it or not, He's an artist and a damned good one at that, in which case Everybody Else's refusal to storm the barricades of self-suppression becomes an affront not just to Himself but to artists everywhere—and to Stifter most of all who though not necessarily more talented than his talented brethren is infinitely more conscious of his gods-given rights. This refusal to recognize that they too are geniuses hobbles his efforts to carry the standard for geniuses everywhere. Though none of these possibilities feels quite right—scratches away the fury of the itch that is Stif's exasperation. Even if Stifter has been playing into his hands, Ethan feels more vulnerable than ever. One more thing. Stifter, especially during his Preston Melville speech, didn't sound quite like Stifter even if Ethan hasn't the faintest idea what Stifter *really* sounds like. He's not trying to absolve or disburden him of his essence but the performance had all the hallmarks of something engineered by somebody else—by Some Body like, well, like Melanctha's Master, even if Ethan hasn't the faintest idea under what criteria the Master operates when he's doling out insights to the studs in his stable. By George, he's got it! Exactly! Stifter's just another stud recruited from central casting to strut and fret his hour upon the stage or however long it takes to home-deliver the Master's prepared fragments—*abattis*—packets du jour—while they're still piping hot.

CHAPTER TWENTY-FIVE

Rubbing his eyes, Cantor is on the verge of hearing himself say, He woke up a New Man (the amenities of Hotel Synapse are a distant memory), but shuts off the PR faucet in the nick of time. He isn't going to give anybody, least of all His Mortal Enemy, the satisfaction of thinking his mourning period has come to a premature end. Through the door, Eden cries, "We're wanted up at the Center, man" (they're the only ones lucky enough to be living outside the bunker complex). "You mean the freakshow has officially begun" (said more to himself than to his housemate). Why does he hear so much unconcern in his voice about the training he knows Eden is about to undergo? In any case, the vistas on the cab ride up proving predictably breathtaking, their driver, in his late forties and a beachboy emeritus, is kind enough to stop and let Cantor (of all people!) take a shot of, or at, the Ocean from on high—Cantor who's made a cottage industry out of mocking the irreverent awe of gawking smartphones. Cantor, whose gimlet eye has routinely enjoined hordes of tourists—at the Central Park Turtle Pond, for example, on an ordinary afternoon in "midwinter spring"—to experience what real tourism is all about by photographing only what can also be found in their own backyard. Go home and make it exotic. Come here and domesticate everything you've been intent on missing way back home. But who is Cantor to mock (even if he won't be inundating his nonexistent Facebook Page with trinkets), when he himself, like the millions of Cortezes before him, is staring, silent, upon his peak in Darien? Genuflecting among stonehenges of yucca, he catches a glimpse of what must certainly be the SS *Catharsis*.

Pritchard meets them in the cafeteria which is about one-third the size of Amygdala's and, being located in the second sub-basement, windowless. While Cantor passes on the offer of breakfast (*with a little parrying side-to-side shake of his upraised right palm: handy little gesture—he should use it more often*), explaining that he never eats heartily before, at the earliest, seven in the evening, Eden wastes no time wolfing down (uncharacteristically) a stack of what look like blueberry buttermilk pancakes, though the odor's hard to define. Sated, he resurfaces unseeing, his visage blotched (yes, his *visage!*: what, are you deaf as well as dumb?), its expression at once torpid and vicious. That the innocent-looking syrup may have been witch-doctored gives Cantor a much-needed chuckle or two. Pritchard, who (Cantor is sure) has noted the viciousness and whose pen-swirling clearly signifies that he rejoices at what he's noted, says mournfully, "I can't help feeling Our Mr. Straynge has been and continues to be maligned. For surely, my friends, there were times—though few and far between—when you found yourself sharing his unwavering conviction that the Envy gnawing away at your vitals could be eliminated forever. Surely the old boy induced what's known in the trade as a spasm of hope now and then." "Well now that you mention it, doc . . ." Eden looks sheepishly at Cantor, though a bit *too* sheepishly for Cantor's taste as if acknowledging he's almost but not quite ready to take the consequences for revealing what was agreed would always remain their little secret. When you get right down to it, *who is Eden?* that all the quacks commend him? One thing's certain, he's able to switch from sophisticate to yokel in a single bound. ". . . sometimes, when nobody was looking, Doc Straynge would invite me down to the cafeteria to grab what he called a bite." "Quaint, very quaint." "I guess he wanted to study me outside the test tube—in my native element, so to speak. He never suspected I played along only because—well, you know." "Yes," Pritchard murmurs, "that nasty business about your . . ." Through gritted teeth, Eden wants him to know that that *business*, as he calls it, was the sordid and premeditated murder of the best human being you could ever want to know. "Like Bush—Jeb, not W—I think my father's the greatest man alive." "Only he's dead. But we *do* know that whatever you may have felt about poor Straynge, you didn't kill him." "Oh, but I did think about it, let me tell you—drove myself crazy in fact thinking about it—endured sleepless nights, cold sweats, racing heartbeat, ringing in the ears, vertigo, thinking about it. Barely made it through till morning." "Ricewater stools, too, by any chance?" Confronted with what just might be puckish West Coast humor, Eden retreats into yokel mode. But getting back to the spasms of hope Pritchard is referring to, fact is, he felt them *routinely* when he and Straynge were down in the cafeteria. "It was nothing like this one, though," he lies, handsomely. "Although he never stopped saying how it was this big improvement over the one he used to—to—" "Frequent?" "Yeah. When he was a medical student at Case Western Reserve." "Just out of curiosity—some might call it morbid—did you actually *feel those spasms* or did you just *feel them coming on*?" "Funny thing was—is—they weren't triggered by anything Straynge said or didn't say but by the sight of the steam table near the big bay window which looked out, rain or shine, on Sixth Avenue." Eden explains that each time they went in—Straynge was an early luncher—it was always already steaming up a storm, which meant that the two of them would be having not just a bite (uttering the word Eden looks as if he's swallowing and regurgitating cough medicine in a single bound) but a pretty decent meal with all the trimmings, paid for in full by his intended victim. Yet as fast as the attacks came, away they went, for they had the bad luck of bringing to mind all of Eden's previous attacks, triggered not just by steam tables but by a million and one other things as well. "So you're an equal-opportunity spasmodist?" (Cantor can't deny he's moved by—envious of—Eden's look of incomprehension, whether real or feigned. It turns Eden into a real man, maybe even a Blond Beast. Since a real man never stoops to informing a would-be adversary that only somebody who's way less than a man makes *words* his weapon when there are much manlier ones around to be had for the making.) And as each attack gave rise to a despair even deeper than that induced by the attack preceding it, Eden knew he'd be kidding himself to think the steam-table attack wouldn't suffer the same old fate. "I told Dr. Manning about the spasms during one of my afternoon fMRI sessions." "What you mean is, the MRI itself told her. I know Irena inside out. She and Waldo (Liepnits to you) just got hitched. Question got popped (while he was still married to his terminally ill third wife, I hear) on a cruise round and round that archipelago known as the Obstinate Isles. The (double fisherman's) knot was tied on Little Cayman, where else? Fourth audition for both. Give it

473

a year and a half, tops. What did my little ex-protégée say?" "That the clock-work shifts from hope to despair and back again were all due to my multipo-larity which she'd been able to diagnose. Serendipitously, was how she put it. She said if I let her report me in the . . . wait, she wrote it down somewhere, 'cause she knew I was too upset to pay close attention." *Somewhere* is a scrap which he extracts, preparatorily clearing his throat, from the back pocket of his corduroys: "If you let me report you in the lit as the first case of MP seen anywhere, we'll be all the rage—the toast of the town—the buttered toast of prime time psychobabblery from the Springs to Laurel Canyon. But if you refuse—*si tu nous trahis, si ton âme succombe aux pièges maudits de l'amour*" (Pritchard grits his teeth at the pronunciation) "I'll make your life a living hell." Eden looks up, chuckling presumably at what he's about to say. "Doesn't she know she's too late for that? But this is why" (waving the scrap) "I'm shocked to have been shipped out here as Guinea Pig Most Likely to Succeed." "If it's any consolation, dear boy, everybody in Drugworld Coast to Coast agrees that MP is a shoo-in for superstar status in the 2023 edition of the *DSM*, right up there with—with—with nobody but Itself, except maybe binge eating. In other words, you haven't spasmed in vain. As for your beloved Manning, she'll never be the toast of anybody's town because the fact of the matter is, she's already toast, pure and simple. You see, Eden, unlike all the others—Straynge, Walser, Manning, Stifter, Liepnits—I don't view your uniqueness as merely the end product of a psycho's refusal to play what Imbeciles Pseudonymous (A+ rating from the BBB three years in a row) calls the only game in town."

But though at long last somebody is taking his part against assorted tormentors (some of whom he didn't even know he had), Eden discovers he wants that kind of support far less than he wants his supporter to join the ranks of those tormentors, if he hasn't already done so (without of course being able to put it to himself this clearly but can anybody put a discovery to himself clearly, much less *this* clearly? as clearly, that is, as the Personal Trainer, if he's lucky enough to have one on ice, who sees to it he's saddled with only as much insight as his dignity can withstand—mostly the kind that can't be put into words, though some of Them say the wording annuls the wound, as the night the day). Why regale Pritchard with Manning's misdeeds? So the wily old dud can exploit Eden's newfound trust (founded on Pritchard's presumed outrage at those misdeeds) to catch the exploited off guard first chance he gets and, for starters, evict him prematurely from a session or two? For nothing enrages Eden more, he realizes, than for somebody to call the shots where eviction, premature or not, is concerned. Even if he doesn't need more time with the evictor—has nothing more to say or to unsay which is of course when he most wants to stay.[47] Even if he hates the evictor's guts and can't wait to kiss off his smugness forever (without of course being able to put it to himself this clearly but can anybody put a realization to himself this

---

[47]After all, isn't it the very kids that are abused who are the ones least able to bear separation from mom and dad, good old alcoholic and good old pedophiliac though they may be?

clearly?). Even if the last thing on earth he wants to do is to stick around until he feels better since far far worse than feeling worst is feeling better which, according to druidic common law, is just a bubble forever on the verge of bursting. In short, Eden knows the drill better than he knows his own name: The medicine man of the moment makes you think you're colluding with him against a third party—one of his fellow Philistines—the collusion giving both of you license to bring the temple down on all their heads—and maybe even his, too (he leaves that samsonian decision up to you, nominal colluder in chief). That is, until you discover that it's you yourself who's that third party and always will be. He hates to see Pritchard seeing him take his own torment seriously—his life disappointment seriously. He hates to see Pritchard catching him in the act of . . . being—of succumbing to the lure of being—of taking life seriously by taking his torment seriously—of buying into the scam of scams they call life. Life, that fishwife's cunt, doesn't deserve such an obeisance. He hates nothing so much as to see his torment writ small in the beady eyes of a Pritchard since this means it's now bracketed—straitjacketed away— in those beady depths with all the other closeted skeletons. Closeted away as just another species of torment—another sheep in the fold—not the very rare wolf-in-sheep's-clothing kind of torment that transcends torment, looks back on torment with the evil eye of infinite distance—*com' avesse l'inferno in gran dispitto* (Eden's paternal ancestors hailed from the same Monte Beni region of Italy that expelled Hawthorne's Donatello, another would-be murderer, from its brambly sun-drenched loins). Just your garden variety—your friendly neighborhood kind of torment. So Pritchard the angekok now has him by the balls: as it turns out and not a minute too soon, he's no different from all the others in a long line of multipolar nincompoops dumb enough to cross Pritchard's threshold. Or maybe he himself constitutes his own long line of nincompoops—at each session different and yet very much the same— maimed to the same sameness. He himself constitutes a slew of long-limbed psychotics voguing on a runway—he's his own signature fall collection (make that his own signature *fall-guy* collection).

But starting at *a slew* a funny thing starts to happen: why, it's as if Some Body, very much uninvited, has taken over the thinking for him—Some Body is thinking through him—a Some Body who's too busy or too lazy to stop to consider urgent matters of verisimilitude, of *tact*—a Some Body that simply can't wait for the right thought vector—the right thought vehicle—to come along. (Eden has just contracted conveniently, reflexively, vindictively, a bad case of masteritis: can't see his way clear to calling Some Body by his right name.) That is, the sort of mosquitoey vector who knows a thing or two about runways and voguing and fall collections. And a thing or two about Judy Garland and Maria Callas and von Sternberg's *The Devil Is a Woman* as well. Hey, who does that Some Body take him for? A . . . Cantor? And this thought about being saddled with a thinking that no matter how you slice it isn't his—isn't *him*—isn't true to his code: this thought, too, isn't his: it belongs to another vector—for whom Some Body thinks he is also too busy to wait. But that Some Body finally passes—maybe it's Pritchard himself—and Eden stays: *It passes and we stay. Before he knows it his thinking's its old self again*—ready, willing and able to be up to its old tricks.

Before he knows it he's his old self again—that is, until he isn't. Since he's undergoing another thought that simply can't be his. (But, again, Some Body [he means, the Master] refuses to wait for the right thought vector. As he's supposed to do, as stipulated in the contract drawn up between Him and the Tennessee Wittgenstein Dinner Theater in Key West. Though as we're all supposed to know by heart, in Santa Barbara as in Life Itself, if we wait for the right this or the right that to come along, well, then, dot dot dot.) It's a thought having something to do (as he proceeds to explain to present company, his mighty stutter a convulsed rebuke to Pritchard's picture-postcard version of the same affliction) with the torment's—Eden's torment's—being like—no, just *being*—a vicious circle and that circle caught—gripped—squeezed—vised—between two regular polygons (both of them stab-in-the-dark diagnostic machines), one inscribed, the other circumscribed, and each with an ever increasing number of sides. And as the number of sides madly increases so does the number of their shared vertices and therefore so does the number of pinpoint incisions perpetrated upon and ratcheted into the torment's flesh by those vertices (incisions coming at it from without and within its circumference) and all that pinpointing for the sole purpose of extracting whatever juices are needed to assess the torment's nature and severity—all solely for the purpose of forcing it, through such archaic leeching, to spill its idiopathic beans so as to be able thereafter to forever hold its peace. *He may feel nothing right now but just wait until . . .* And as the number of sides of each polygon increases, the size of its perimeter gets closer and closer to a fixed limit point, with the measure of his torment squeezed thereby to an inevitably greater and greater clinical "accuracy"—to an ever increasing number of decimal places—between the two limit points. Until there's pretty much nothing left of the torment's will to resist, so exhausted from too much incisional squashing has it become—exhausted, that is, according to the Archimedean method of exhaustion. But as he spits it all out, even poignantly stuttering Eden (your not-so-average Joe) knows the effort to make some mathematical maneuver the armature—the doppelgänger—of a personal torment does a disservice to both. Each can conform—barely—to the contours of the other only by getting all bent out of shape to the point of blest invisibility. The metaphorics, alas, misses the mark. Mathematics can do nothing to illuminate psychopathology and has no need of its returning the favor. And yet in this case there must be *some* meat-and-potatoes consanguinity between the two if the thought packeteer managed to intuit—or think he intuited—the plausibility of straitjacketing one plight according to the parameters of the other—of mirroring one state of affairs in the scary funhouse of the other. There's more here—there's got to be more—than a perverse yoking of incongruities à la Samuel Johnson. Or rather any so-called yoking—the more ostensibly perverse the better—is already an unmasking of a secret affinity. That a mind—even a mind as laboriously feeble and vulgar as the Master's—can invent such a connection proves it is not an invention—or not *just* an invention—but a discovery—an archeological discovery—an exhumation from scratch. On the other hand, reluctant ventriloquist Eden wonders (thereby purveying what the Master experiences as a kind of seller's remorse) whether this analysis of the relation or non-relation between math and pain represents less an act of penetration to a never-before-attained depth of insight than a heavily ornamented block-age of such penetration, since analysis is supposed to be a battle to the death against the forces of delusion and here was all that eloquence—if eloquence it was—leaking out of Him/him with uncontested ease. "But too exhausted for resistance to what exactly?" Eden has been rudely awakened from his opium dream. His first impulse is to cry out (as if he were Piero delle Vigne and Pritchard Dante) something along the lines of, Quit lacerating me! I'm just the messenger; put the blame on Mame—I mean, the Master. But he restrains himself, knowing Pritchard is trying to draw him out for his own good—Pritchard's own good, that is. So why not give him a run for his money? The response duly stuttered boils down to something along the lines of: Why, resistance to misrepresentation through lamebrain nosologizing; trivializa-tion through ever-more-precise dimestore diagnosis; straitjacketing by the numbers; martyrizing à la Saint Lawrence but in this case the Saint's being barbecued on both sides at once; being framed like some eighth-rate hood in a stunning Joseph H. Lewis vehicle. Judging from all six-hundred-odd bars of it, though (why *though*? why not *indeed*?), this thought about him and its tributaries—an operatic set piece if ever there was one—would have best been allocated to . . . to . . . Cantor, of course. And the wry glances Pritchard and Cantor have just shared—an exchange of retinal pinpoint hemorrhages you might call it—confirm as much. In which case, this thought Eden's been forced to call his own—this thought about polygonal gridirons (*a*) converging from both directions and (*b*) engaging in predictably belittling *DSM-IV*-style stabs in the dark regarding his circular torment (it all seems so trivial now)—this thought is hereby transformed, effective immediately. No worries—it's still a thought about gridirons converging on his torment only the gridirons are no longer instruments of interrogatory impalement but rather torments themselves, namely: the (inscribed) torment of knowing he was saddled with a thought so disrespectfully—so violatively—out of character, why it's almost as if he had—has—no character to fall back on;[48] and the (circumscribed) torment of knowing he unwittingly colluded with the Master—or rather, with the impatience of the Master—in robbing Cantor of what had Cantor's name rightly written all over it and might have Made his Name in the Company.

But, garden variety or not, friendly or not, doesn't Pritchard understand that everybody has a civic duty to take his gods-given crisis seriously—as seri-ously as if it were the devastation of Homs—because it's only by respecting—even genuflecting before—the direness of his own crisis, whether dire or not, that everybody measures the direness of everybody else's. One self-pities on behalf of the world. One learns to self-pity on behalf of the world—for the sake of the world. But suddenly it hits him: good has come out of insight's

---

[48] It's not the content of the thought (Eden has taught himself to withstand the grossest imputations of any type of content) but the baroque relentlessness of the zigzagging presentation which is so much at odds with his essence.

necessary evil for at last Eden understands all that talk about the Master and the Scourge of Psyche and Mr. B. Since now, he, too, has a Master only in his case it's a Personal Trainer. So why didn't Cantor and Herbert and Shearer just say what they meant? why all the pythagorean secrecy? Did they think he was too stupid to catch on—that his attention is all deficit? But maybe it's for the best that they didn't spill the beans. Being first and foremost a Man of Concreteness he needed time to stumble on his own particular version of everybody else's customized Chip On His Shoulder, something closer to his own experience, not that he's a slow learner or a sort of (though not for want of trying) allegorical dumb blond.

"What I need to know," Eden says, again turning to Cantor—and getting a bonus eyeful of Borkman, who's just entered (hot off the steam-room press, judging from the floridity of his incipient jowls)—"is whether you think I should have killed Straynge outright." To Pritchard, who rarely—never—errs in such matters (there's still a lot they've yet to learn about him) it's clear Eden is entreating him to complete what promises to be a matter-of-life-and-death-type thought. But not just so they—i.e., their thinking—can move on to so-called bigger things (as if one thought can ever be bigger than another!). "You mean rather than get hoodwinked (just to be able to succeed on their terms) into believing you suffer from binge Envy (with a dose of multipolarity thrown in for good measure) in order to have your life all mapped out for you on their cozily interventionist terms." Inasmuch as Eden looks as if he himself was about to do a bit of intervening, Pritchard holds up a traffic cop's demurring forefinger. With ineffable grace, Cantor has to admit. Involuntarily he turns to Borkman (at the steam table) to see if he, a fellow aesthetician, strongly agrees with this estimation. Borkman, however, is too busy undressing the latest arrival on the breakfast circuit. With an ass as big—to tamper with a quip of her once-favorite writer—as the Ritz. "What's done is done," Pritchard continues (a bit more compassionately, in Cantor's view: Eden's underdogged threat of intervention has worked!). "What matters is that even if hoodwinked, even if succes*sed* on their terms, somehow you've managed and will go on managing to squelch their every effort to reduce you to their puppet, guy friday and poster boy." Pritchard glances at Cantor, now his conscience, his dark angel—Cantor, who finds that keeping his eye on Borkman still eyeing the Lady with the Ass (her plate piled shamelessly high with scrambled eggs) is the only way to decline to occupy that office. "Or we wouldn't have picked you to star in this, the next-to-final stage of the trial. If I read you right—righter, maybe, than you read yourself—what you want to know is not only whether you've come through the ordeal you've just described with flying colors but if you've been able at the same time to do what's much harder, namely, absorb the denigration you experienced as a patient (by the way, *denigration* means . . .)." "I know what *denigration* means," Eden replies through gritted teeth, giving a final flourish to his deadpan (which clearly clamors for one) by soaking up what's left of the pancakes (in something that only now reveals itself to be a far cry from purest Vermont maple syrup) and popping the mess into his mouth. Before continuing, Pritchard tries to ensure Eden understands he's pretending to pretend to have seen neither hide nor hair of the teeth in question, but fails yet soldiers on. "What you want to know is whether you've done the toughest thing of all, namely, absorb the denigration into your bloodstream in such a way as to make your self stronger." Whipping open a napkin with a matador's adversarial expertise (his plate is also piled high with eggs, albeit not quite so shamelessly as his Lady's), Borkman asks, as simultaneously as possible, "Can I join you guys?" After scowling down this intrusion, Pritchard pointedly ignores him. But Borkman resolutely rejects the role of club vulgarian he's just been assigned and by proceeding to show Pritchard a thing or two about table manners unmasks him as the boor he unconsciously aspires to be. "Or whether, on the contrary, the moment for creative phagocytosis has come and gone, leaving you permanently disabled. The sad part, however (one among too many to catalogue), is that you perceive denigrators—hackers at your screen, phantoms of your rue morgue—where there's not a one to be had for love or money." "But there *were* denigrators, I tell you. They assailed me." Yes, he knows what *assails* means (one of the unsung side effects of the big *I* being to trigger, as already alluded to and usually starting with the third dose, an expansion of the subject's vocabulary). They assailed him with the sort of scattershot questions bright-boy interns are taught to pose on grand rounds under the eagle eye of their hot-shot mentors. "Only they stopped listening the minute you started to give your answer, right? That's because that sort of questions are supposed to keep the victim so busy being stumped he never notices them impatiently eyeing the clock. The trick is not to take it *personally*. Anyway, you're not a *person* as long as you agree to be under their thumb while, for your own good, they go about getting under your skin. Or rather, you're a person in the making. A jerk—I mean a work in progress." There's still so much Eden wants to say, now that he has a Personal Trainer—a Henry Higgins—to say it for him. Like Eliza Doolittle (now where did she come from?) he could dance all night, although the last thing in the world he wants to do is overwork the old boy's auspices.

But there is no more time for small talk and Swiftian little language, since Narr and Cook (each waving several newspapers), together with Walser and (inexplicably) Netta, have just stormed in. Herbert, Shearer and Rhys (the Three Wise Men or the Weird Sisters from *Macbeth*, depending on your taste) forcibly bring up the rear, hemmed in as they are by a yapping swarm of lesser probands. "Did you see this?" Is it merely (merely!) Cantor's imagination or has Borkman, the Almighty Borkman (as he's called or should have been called or would have been if only they'd listened to Cantor from the start), suddenly gone all shiv- and shuddery? "Did you happen to know that our Mr. B." (at the taking of her lord's nickname in vain it's now Shearer's turn to go all shiv- and shuddery) "is all too heavily invested in DHP Industries? and Tom Post, too?" the two men bellow, almost in unison. "So what does that have to do with his treatment?" Pritchard asks. *Reasonably*, Herbert thinks.

Excellent example, Herbert also thinks, of adjective *transmogrified*— yeah, transmogrified—into adverb all for the sake of whiplash brevity—of converting attribute (a dime a dozen) into action. And why is that a good thing? Why is that a poetic thing? Why? because it shakes things up, disorients the avid listener, who deep down is nowhere more at home than in no-man's-land, even if it's the mangy no-man's-land between adjective and adverb. Why? because it subjects him to the kind of jolt—the jolt prophylactic—the jolt propaedeutic—the jolt heuristic (take your pick)—that immunizes against those (jolts) perpetrated by life—the inconveniently redundant life beyond the printed page. Why? because it proves no fate—no ID—no gender is fixed—not even the complex fate/ID/gender of a part of speech, thereby giving our listener an emancipatory thrill comparable to that levied—yes, *levied*—by, say, the Coney Island Cyclone on the coppery cusp of nightfall in mid-July. And isn't this what good writing, like good cross-dressing (anybody in the market for an adjectival sheep in wolfish adverbial drag? well, then, step right up, folks, and c'mon in, the water's fine and it's on the house!), professes to be all about? Tears come to her mentorly eyes. Most protégés have a bad habit of turning into a sorcerer's apprentice but the Master—*her* protégé—has sidestepped so tempting a trap and done them both proud into the bargain. All her corny (yet tremendously moving) Corn-is-Greenish dedication to this brat's intellectual upthrust has borne fruit.

Cook and Narr collapse into near-matching lounge chairs (though Cantor would be hard put to pinpoint what makes them a near match—for he's the POV *du moment*, i.e., the quintessential fall guy whose fall everybody's relying on to set their own perceptions straight) only to end up re-placing them as far as they can get from the odor of high fructose corn syrup-flavored bacon rind. The others make do with collapsing into whatever looks uncollapsible. Cook continues: "Not to mention that—and I quote—'Mr. B. is still on the board (*Attention, members: monitoring bracelets optional!*) of TuristaCon, the white-shoe equity firm that a while back, as you may remember or may have chosen to forget, paid bottom dollar for Persimmonius Bedwear, and Beltway and Brother's Smart Cookie Clothing Company, among other sitting ducks, and helped devastate both in record time, not to mention the lives of the duty-driven American Dreamers who kept the owners' spinning wheels humming busily over six decades in rightful expectation of their own just desserts. Only to end up just-deserted. (And too bad that, as class-action plaintiffs, they hadn't taken the time to decrypt the non-existent prenuptial agreement, whose superfine print stipulated that any dispute—any Luxembourgian grudge-bearing—any seditious standing on one's rights—must be done away with through arbitration alone. Arbitration: one of the corporate world's prize Gems of the Ocean.) Sucked them dry, TuristaCon did, while collecting a total of about $10 million in fees for not just non-management (bad enough) but (far worse) management per se as well, both focused mainly on EFPD (Ensuring Full Product Deterioration), before selling off its roadkill, at an immense profit, to the next serial predator, in this case A. Nuss and Feekle Point, a subsidiary of Fannie Fundamentals, Inc., and a highly respected name in the munitions industry, whose own subsidiaries were cozy-cagily incorporated in Wilmington (Bahrain's administrative seat and third-biggest city).'" Cook's deep breath is Ethan's signal to take over. It turns out that Borkman—Ethan refuses to refer to him as *Mr.* B. (where *B* stands for "Ballet, thy name is woman.") out of respect for Shearer's Svengali and all he compelled her to accomplish (*alert:* with wet dreams of becoming the next Edward Villella, Ethan signed up for a few dance classes in his early teens)—is also a pal (some say the gray eminence) of the CEO that Turista soon brought down on the heads of both victims. Or maybe he misread somebody's lips on the way out of the Courthouse briefing and it's B. himself who's CEO and his own grayest eminence. In any event, when he isn't busy stuffing his hundreds of thousands of dollars worth of free mattresses with tens of thousands of dollars worth of free cookies, the CEO, whoever he is, busily enjoins the serfs at Per-simmonius-Cookie (yes, the companies quickly merged although the "eagerly anticipated exponentiation of synergies and diversification of portfolios did not materialize") to gorge their starved psyches on the best recommendations on self-improvement they'll find anywhere, namely, the ones contained in his ISBN-less Ray Dalio-style mini-magnum opus entitled *That Endless Ninth Inning Called Life: A Fielder's Guide*. The CEO, however, as distinguished from his opus (though in moments of creative ecstasy he pretends or contends they are one and the same), has pretty much washed his hands of the serfs, ninth innings and all, so what they do about their layoffs (or—to quote yet another CEO, a Swiftian Yahoo with a majorette's expressionless flair for euphemism—their *remixes*) and related foreclosures (to wit, the only bread and butter their kind will ever be permitted to relish) is pretty much their own business and a profitless business it most surely is. CEO Turista, a firm believer in respecting the privacy of the pillaged, has bigger fish to fry and he fries them best in the flybridge jacuzzi of his second-biggest yacht. In any case, there are plenty of middle managers still running around (Ethan obligingly cringes) who are ready, should their defunct and extinct services be needed, to play Pancks (*start googling, bub*) to his Casby (*bis*). Truth be told, for all this steam-table muckraking Ethan hasn't ruled out the possibility of getting involved, once his paltry little HBO stint ends, in a *real* Hollywood movie project (he'll have a track record, after all)—a wannabe blockbuster depicting not penny ante layoffs and foreclosures but the real stuff of corporate malfeasance so that for two and a half measly hours the audience can themselves orgasm on the conviction that in the Arcadia of mass exploitability they, too, were once the Lords of Misrule. Herbert, *for her part*, is thinking other thoughts—trying very hard to get inside the bleached-blond brain that begat *remixes*. Problem is, the hip-hopping antics of adjectivized adverbs (reasonable into *reasonably*) keep getting in the way.

"Oh, when," Pritchard wails (or tries to), "will all this too too too fac-ile bull's-eyeing of big business finally melt, thaw and resolve itself into . . . adieu?" (Ethan is liking Pritchard more and more: he's making him feel not just like a muckraker but like a martyr. Should he shelve the craving to exploit exploitation on the big screen and do what Pritchard seems to imply he does best? Oddly enough—though maybe not so oddly, pythoness Herbert (one step ahead of the Master as usual) can't help thinking (even if she can), given her protégé's ever-readiness to sacrifice the black and white of truth (in this case muckraker's truth) for unwarrantable nuance—sorry, "nuance"— *Not so oddly*, then, it's Borkman who retorts full speed ahead, taking up a cudgel or two on behalf of all those faceless busboy figurines (too exhausted or too proud to kowtow)—you know, the ones who, for example, in NoLita bistros tend to the dregs, both spirituous and human, so that at the end of the day, or night, they can retire to the South Bronx (that is, if they're lucky enough to be able to afford the rents) enhearsed in their very own unprivate stretch limo. He seems to be maintaining that the target practice will end, namely: When companies like LIN Media stop merging with themselves to shield their lucre from the tax man. When behemoth satellite-TV providers like Dish Network stop Trojan-horsing around by bidding for FCC wireless-spectrum licenses through instantly inflatable "very small business" proxies. When behemoths like Abb-Vie stop inversioning. When newly publicked companies, hare-lipped babes in the woods like Berry Plastics, Emdeon (billing) and national CineMedia (advertising), groomed both long and hard and short and sweet for fleeceability, are no longer contracted, under "income tax receivable agreements,"[49] to fork over to their pre-I.P.O. masters—PE buyout scum like Apollonian Global Management and Mayhem Partners—the lion's share of consequential current and future tax savings. "In other words, never," he concludes, licking his chops. To nail his point home, he coughs up a bona fide hacking cough though he hasn't chain-smoked for decades. The non-smokers, i.e., most of those present, are especially impressed—even intimidated—since they like every schoolboy know it's harder to impersonate a smoker than to be one just as it's harder to play than to be Rambo. His incipient jowls join in the fun. Without innuendo, Cantor opines: *For better or worse, an honest man is hard to find.* Though maybe the cough isn't a simulation after all (thinks Netta, who surely knows a thing or two about coughs: after all, both of her parents were and two of her five sons are pulmonologists) and maybe, just maybe, Borkman, through no fault of his own, happens not to belong to that lucky band of ex-smokers whose bronchial epithelium harbors—and who then, immediately upon quitting, experience the expansion of—what researchers have recently identified as a distinct subset of cells with an almost-normal "mutational burden" which, after having remained resistant to hard-core smoking over decades, end up miraculously protecting against lung cancer.[50] Maybe Borkman is envious of these happy few. And maybe, adding insult to injury, this particular species of Envy is unresponsive to the caresses of Invidicum. Which means that Borkman is scheduled—not *doomed*—to part company sooner rather than later with the slumbering spirits of what should be deemed the people's gold.

Pritchard ignores Borkman's punchline and concentrates on all that came before. "But as my fellow Dane is famous for saying—sorry, as my fellow Dane *famously said*. By the way, no Blond Beast he. More like a knight of secret inwardness and the best pal you'll ever hope to find, barring none, on those

---

[49] What's in a name? Plenty. For starters, how 'bout billions in ill-gotten tax savings reaped by utterly conscienceless fatcats? While rotting infrastructure and teacherless schools—they've got "collateral damage" scrawled all over them—go listlessly a-begging.

[50] See Kenichi Yoshida and others, "Tobacco smoking and somatic mutations in human bronchial epithelium," *Nature*, vol. 578, No. 7794 (13 February 2020), pp. 266–272.

frosty summer nights for which SB—you'll see soon enough—is celebrated, rightly or not. Anyway, as my fellow Blond Beast is famous for saying:" (Cantor looks daggers, but dutifully—or faintheartedly—speaks none) "the art of *communication*, though he might as well have said *abomination*, is the art of subtraction. As applied to our current mess, what he means is, When a man's brain is so full of the wickedness of Wall Street that he doesn't have space enough to think the wickedness through—to feel it in his bones—then does enlightenment consist in filling his brain with more wickedness or does it lie rather in taking it away? And what better way to subtract the wickedness and leave some much-needed space for its assimilation than to get it in through the back door, so to speak, by reintroducing it in a form that's *strange* —or *Straynge*—à la Shklovsky." With timing worthy of Rosalind Russell at her peak and enough self-congratulory Babbitry to make the question sound like some sassy quote from *The Lady Eve* (see somewhere above)—the sort of quote that gets cherished by wannabe wiseass movie buffs who make it a practice never to see daylight or the sunset's declension—Netta shrieks, "Who's Sloshie?" Pritchard knew something like this was coming and relishes its stale predictability. "For if the form is strange enough then our man will feel he's being robbed of all that he thinks he knows about such wickedness. He'll feel the almighty *threat* of strangeness. (If wickedness is strange, it needs to land on one's doorstep in an even stranger-looking receptacle.) And when he thinks he's about to lose what he thinks he knows, he'll fight back—against the opposing form—the form that he insists is keeping him from what he knows. Even if it's only in cracking form's shell wide open that he'll be able for the first time to get his grubby little hands on the wicked content within and think it as it was always meant to be thought. Or, to short-circuit poetically— the cracking *is* the thinking. OK: Pritchard's a verbal contortionist and this ticlike fusion of cause and effect is of course the last refuge of such scoundrels, so why does Melanctha find the contortion oh so satisfying—exhilarating— thrilling? Because . . . because . . . because . . . it's the vengeance of word- on worldflow and right up the Master's blind alley to boot.

"I'll remember all that," quips Borkman, "the next time I want to bite the hand that feeds me." "You mean the hand that lands you in stir where you belong," counter-quips Cook, but with a knobbier edge. Immediately, he wishes he said, ". . . that lands you in *the can* where *your kind belongs*."

"But what's DHP?" Rhys asks, toying anorexically (i.e., quizzically, sulkily, timorously) with a scrap of rye toast. Narr and Cook look especially— utterly—lost. Herbert, on the other hand, can't help being charmed. Can't help feeling satisfied, exhilarated, thrilled. (Wait, that makes twice in the course of just a few minutes. Most people don't feel so much exhilaration in the course of an entire lifetime.) So what accounts for the thrill? Same question as a few minutes ago. Different culprit. And isn't that what her work to come will come down to in the end: accounting for the Thrill in all its manifestations? True, Rhys's ability to manhandle not white, not whole wheat, but *rye* toast (even if it's just a scrap) and at the same time pose an unbeggable question attests a stage sense of the highest order, but this doesn't begin to put things into perspective. What would the Master make of it? (Sorry [*who is speaking?*], no more Master. It's *you* who are Master—*you* who are Mrs. de Winter—at least for now. Everybody's counting on you, Melanctha, whether they know it or not. This is your big break. Make the most of it. It will come no more. Never, never, never, never, never.)

The thrill pivots on Rhys's question, has everything to do with the fact that the question's impact is wildly disproportionate to its form and content. The question demonstrates . . . demonstrates . . . demonstrates . . . demonstrates . . . demonstrates . . . (Brute duration is slowly filling in the details [she can hear its unmistakable drip-drip-drip: if time heals all wounds, then duration solves all puzzles or at least puts them uneasily to sleep].) Demonstrates that there has indeed been another way to live this interval devoted to name-calling, with no-holds-barred speculation providing the comic relief—that is to say, the interval that (*a*) began with Cook and Narr bellowing in unison—sorry, *almost* in unison—about the misdoings of *their* Mr. B, specifically his being too heavily invested in DHP Industries, and (*b*) ended with the exquisitely anorexic (and DHP-related) question posed by the love of Narr's life. While the others have been rolling merrily along (*listen carefully*) hemmed in by all the deep-think of and about muckrakers and carbetbaggers, there is in fact one—One—who's chosen instead to try to wrap her termite-artful consciousness around . . . an acronym of all things! (in Herculean terms, the least likely suspect)—to simmer inside it—and, so positioned, to stay stubbornly, subterraneanly, put. Someone who has, through a question lobbed from out of left field, relegated the polemical tumult, which everybody else has mistaken for the main attraction, to a mere sideshow—to a bad joke without a punchline straight out of *The Killing*. One who has relegated the tumult to a mere interim—to nothing more than the space between an acronym and its echo—and transformed the acronym into that tumult's molten core—the heart of its matter. And in so doing, has stood the tumult—specifically the lessons learned (or learnable) through the frenzy of speculation it generated—in far better stead than those who had nothing better to do than throw undiscerning incense on its altar. Of course Tumult & Co. isn't a mere sideshow, a mere interim. But by shifting the spotlight—the psychic accent—from Tumult to an acronym—thereby marking It as something over and done with—something that's a long way off—something that never was—Rhys has made Tumult-triggered speculation just that, i.e., *strange*—strange à la Sloshie—the way Pritchard's Blond Beast out of Copenhagen enjoins everybody to *make it strange*. Shunted to the margins, driven underground, consigned to the mists of time, forced to dance like angels on the head of . . . an acronym! the lessons learnable have a much better chance of sinking into the collective skull unperceived, hence unresisted. Like any great artist (Herbert, old girl, take note!), Rhys, ruthless in her prioritizing, has managed, and without recourse to a single prop (besides an anorexic crumb or two), to transform—better yet, transmogrify—the given and, hey, isn't that what *every* audience member is really hoping to witness as the curtain goes up on a stage still bare, that is, swarming with possibility? For if the given can be transformed—the shabby insignificant given—then surely there's hope in store for *self*-transformation.

"I hate to mention this," Ethan starts to reply (the reply's directed to a question mark—any old question mark—not the Lilith who at times is cunt-compliant—even shockingly so—but only in the good ol' summertime and only at dawn's crack of doom), re-collapsing into his lounge chair or maybe it's another chair even further from the steam table. Cook crouches nearby, as if straining—beatifically—natureboyishly—at stool (the leftovers have attracted an intrepid mouse, probably chimeric from the look of 'im). "Especially in the presence of somebody who's lost her son to the warmongering of draft dodger extraordinaire Dick Cheney. Now, why did the sonofabitch have to go and sire a lesbian?" He struggles to explain (so I'll help) that Dickhead's unlovable curmudgeonry doesn't deserve such rapid-fire humanization by association. Nuance doesn't sit well with his brand of wickedness. But as there's no ill wind that doesn't—

Herbert wonders if she shouldn't respond to Ethan's remark, less deferential than dismissive. Almost chortling. She's wondering if she shouldn't say (as poker-facedly as possible) something along the wobbly lines of "At least my boy didn't serve long enough to end up (understandably) too desperate not to go AWOL in Taliban country and getting a less-than-honorable discharge for his trouble. Which would have allowed the Department of Veterans Affairs to saddle him with the privilege of ineligibility for permanent health care, disability benefits and job training." But all at once Melanctha stops wondering since from everybody's queasy look she knows she's already said it, loud and clear. Only it hasn't delivered the relief and release she didn't know she was hoping for. Instead, she feels like a phony as she always does when anybody swallows her grieving-mother act hook, line and sinker. But wait a minute. They haven't swallowed it. Didn't take the time to even begin to swallow it. What she's taken for queasiness is in fact cud-chewing indifference. Life is a carnival, or hasn't she heard? and before she could even begin to put the finishing touches on her spiel they were already on to the next big act in the next big booth. But she's gotten so unstable in her deductions that maybe in five minutes from now she'll be realizing what she took for cud was in fact . . .

Anyway, to cut to the wild goose chase: Close to the Vest, a subsidiary of DHP Industries and a bona fide start-up located improbably in the croc-infested retirement community of Panaceaville, Florida, is a manufacturer—some might say *the* manufacturer—of bulletproof vests. It was awarded tens of billions of dollars in body-armor contracts by our friends in the military during the height of the debacle. "It's all here," Cook cries, waving what must be sheaves upon sheaves of evidence. "Our Mr. B. is close friends with its founders and biggest shareholders: Eric Princz, Betsy DaVos Prince, Willber Ross, Ross Adelson, Steven Humpt Cone, Gary Dumpt Cone, Johnny Thaine, Khrisstye Wyett, Christee Wyott, Charlie Koch, Charlene T. Koch, Chloe Louise Koch, Zoe-Louie Koch, Cassandra Koch, Philoctetes Koche, KayLeigh A. Konway, Ajax Redstone, Dr. Jamie Di Stumpf, Mitch MacKonnell, Micheline McConnell, Carlo ICahhn, Edouard O. O'Lampert, Herbert Von Carrion, Donnie Blankenshipp, Rev. Frank Grahame Blankenfine, Allen 'Robert' Stanford, Lee B. Farkus, Billy Bob Ackman and Ellison Uber-Äckmann, none of whose spokespersons or spokesmobiles for that matter have returned repeated requests for comment—not even to boilerplate away the boss's iniquities."

Cantor must protest. He lets it be known that there's something wrong—dead wrong—with this roll call: it's one big tired poor excuse for a jab at the funny bone (referred to as *le petit juif*—that's right, "the little jew"—in what long long ago used to be his favorite non-mother tongue) and the guilt of these big-time grifters is in fact being eclipsed by the egregiousness of the roll-caller's bid for life-of-the-partydom. "*Eclipsed?* you mean to tell me that the so-called egregiousness of some poor slob's (sorry, Bill) hunger to shine dwarfs the guilt of our guiltiest grifters? oh, come now," Herbert counter-protests. As outsiders, if for no other reason, Melanctha Herbert and George Cantor are yet again on the same wavelength, though on this particular occasion their wires have crossed swords. And she proceeds to address herself to a point directly above and a little to the right of Cantor's left ear, which is where she assumes the particular incarnation of the Master conjured by his bugbears sets up shop (for it's the Master who's put Cantor up to this). The gist of what she has to say is reducible to—is translateable as—something like this (oops, she's in danger of being swept away by her own eloquence, which cannot, unlike the others', be dismissed as the mere collateral damage of Invidicum intake—it's too organic for that—too organically conjunctive to her life and soul): "I know You prefer to perceive the manifold not-so-bad through a hyperlativizing lens, preferably to the total detriment of truth, simply because You feel deliciously powerless against the unsurpassably Bad and want to coddle that powerlessness (i.e., why bother excoriating poor old Hitler when there's somebody like Churchill around to pummel?) but surely there are times when even You must recognize that it's in fact possible to pummel powerlessness into ball-buster courage—the courage to absent Thee from perversity awhile (the perversity in this case being to Blame the Victim)—and exterminate . . . Evil . . . slowly . . . deliciously. Recognize all this at least for Cantor's sake, oh Jack-of-No-Trades and Master of But One." (Quintessential Donizetti: Lucrezia Borgia throwing herself on the mercy of the Duke of Ferrara for the sake of prodigal son Gennaro.)

Shearer cannot recall *ever having been forced* to inhabit a silence *so profoundly disturbed and disturbing* (Hyperlativity's wingèd chariot is hurrying near) as the one that has just descended. It contitutes the very first clear-cut acknowledgment by all parties that under their aegis and through their auspices the Master does exist (and vice versa), and, this being the case, must (from time to time) be held to account for his frivolous excesses. She looks around. Why don't they all have their hands over their ears? How can they tolerate the noise they make crying (as one), *Master, are you awake? Master, are you listening?* Netta, still glowing from her triumph in the off-off-off-off-off-Broadway smash *His Girl Sloshie*, says, first, that, like the black lady has just indicated (the lady in question immediately transforms herself into a violent whole-body shrug of Karen-loathing), nothing can eclipse the guilt of those big-time Evildoers. At the same time, as far as she can see, there's been no clear-cut blowsy bid for stardom on the part of the caller. In fact, she's tempted to chide him for having erred on the side of caution—or rather, poker-faced supersubtlety (might the timid yet purposeful misspellings have been, by any chance, governed by a fear of lawsuits?). For one thing, there's been no effort to flaunt a comprehensive diversity—if anything, the list flaunts the lack thereof. Its flow—its progress—its novelty—keeps getting jammed by virtue of the fact that each item bumps up against a funhouse spittin' image (which means that, as far as she can see, the jamming is the novelty). She dares anybody to try to convince her that he can, for example, tell the Willber Ross behind *Willber Ross* apart from the Ross Adelson behind *Ross Adelson*—or better yet that Khrisstye Wyett and Christee Wyott are very much *not* one and the same. The sole raison d'être of each item (e.g., *Micheline McConnell*) is clearly mockery of its predecessor (in this case, *Mitch MacKonnell*) but a mockery with no belly laughs and, please, no punchlines—a delicate mockery that is in fact a sleight of hand—computer code—for taking the serrated edge off, and extracting the stench from, the heinousness of that predecessor's referent (i.e., Mitch MacKonnell) out in the real world where names have a bad habit of, unfortunately, turning into men. No overriding logic—no grand plan—just a sequence with the intention neither of converging nor of diverging—just a set of variations on a theme that dares not speak its tinny name—just termite art, then (but more about the termites later), at its showstopping best, as Manny Farber might say. Clearly, list-making is an art with its own laws and leave it to a poor slob like Cook to obey them magisterially. (How cleverly she sidesteps the Unanswered Question of the Master's Existence, Shearer thinks and thinks and thinks, till she's blue in the face.)

On the upside the roll call (Rubicon crossed yet again! over the objections of the lunatic fringe which harbors ambitions of going mainstream) has made Borkman look almost as queasy as Ted Cruz (the quintessential Unacquirable Taste) at those moments up there on the primary debate stage when The Rump of Evil was busy hammering away at his indigestibility. (Cantor and Herbert perform a telepathic Rump-inspired pas de deux: Cantor: *But wait, aren't we still in W's ice age?* Herbert: *Not exactly, time travel being the last refuge of scoundrels, the would-be storyteller kind, that is. And on that cautionary note: be sure to remain on the lookout for said Rump. He'll make you want to feel like the most disaffected and sanguinary of Everymen just so you can bask in his afterglow.*)

Melanctha Herbert, too, is sorely—sourly—disappointed by this infinitely extensible roll call (but she's more inspired than her protégé could ever be even in her disappointment because she knows how to handicraft it). When will the real world finally come up with names as good as (Mr.) *Merdle* or (on a less exalted level) Melmotte or Madoff, names inextricably glued to their bearer as purest proof of his non-being—of his being too damn busy to . . . be; names refusing to grant him any extenuatory life whatsoever outside its purview; names serving proudly as the bars of his cage? In consenting to utter such a name the utterer may rest assured he's not simultaneously bullhorning a coerced and credulous concession to the bearer's demand that he endorse his delusions—disseminate his inflationary pretenses—coddle his self-love, all of which are thriftily distilled in the name (which bullhorning is, alas, very much the order of the day with those assorted Zoes, Chloes, Jamies, Khrisstyes, Mitches and Charlies). A name like *Merdle* doesn't coerce—it doesn't even solicit. It doesn't set itself up as an extension—an expansion— of the self's native glamor. It's a cancellation, an ablation, perpetrated long before glamor could become even a twinkle in Merdle's eye. Which is just fine with the Merdles of the world—that is, if there *are* any out of print and of the world—since self, glamorous or otherwise, is one bit of baggage they can heartily do without—it only gets in the way of transaction. So the name's utterer needn't fear he's applying yet another coat of varnish to the bearer's mightiest piece of body armor. For in the case of the Merdles, the name, like any joke expertly delivered, is itself the dismantlement—the pulverization—of that armor. Which suddenly explains why Melanctha had so much difficulty living among the Nambikwara People of the Amazon during her canceled but nonetheless unforgettable Junior Year Abroad: the tribe declared utterance of proper names taboo. Or maybe that was precisely why she had absolutely no difficulty doing so during her failed sojourn. As it turns out Cantor has a bone to pick (most unfairly) with the Nambikwara, which he's been gnawing on ever since his own junior year in the rainforest. If they'd extended the invitation sooner or marketed their progressivist mores more astutely worldwide (so goes his gravamen), he'd have learned that the practice of homosexuality was not incompatible (as he'd taught himself to believe) with abstention from fluttery name-dropping.

Still, no stopping Cook. "And in late 2004—about three months before small reports emerged of big problems with those vests—Post and our boy cashed in shares of DHP/CTTV preferred stock worth close to $1.2 billion. With some of which the first thing he went out and bought was—you guessed it—the obligatory blue-gray touring model Nissan 350Z hardtop with gold-encrusted floor mats. Do you think he cared what happened to the employees—cared that *their* stock—common stock—common as dirt—was essentially worthless? Did he care that only the rank and file suffered, not the sleazeball founders, the investors, the venture caps, the high-level execs? Did he care that, immediately after CTTV went south for good, the CEO, Khrisstye Wyett—(from all accounts *his* Khrisstye)—took home tens of millions, not to mention an 8-million-dollar severance payout? Did he care that the majority of employees actually lost money—found that they'd for all intents and purposes been paying to work for CTTV?" He explains that since pre-IPO CTTV was a unicorn (the unicorn is as unmythical a thing of flesh and blood among start-ups as the phoenix among literary "losers"), its exalted valuation generated a surge in the worth of the shares of employees (on paper, that is), resulting in a surge in the tax levied on those shares, which meant they had to empty out their savings accounts, and move in with unsympathetic dad—or worse, a grandad of the Smallweed variety—if they were lucky enough to have one or the other. "Khrisstye was so confident that the company would be valued at around 1 billion when it went public that she turned up her nose at every offer to buy it. And when it finally ran out of cash what did Kristy—sorry, Khrisstye—do but go on a preplanned trip to Hong Kong and Davos to instruct almost-packed houses on the powerpointable need to stay innovative. Just before leaving, however, she did inform the suckers that mental-health counselors were available at every turn, although according to the most disgruntled this beau geste was prompted by fear (the glass wall of her office had been shattered the night before). When the holders of common stock started suing the company for breach of fiduciary duty she'd long since left to . . . perfect the udderly amazing feat of breastfeeding her quadruplets simultaneously. There are rumors afoot that it's Borkman who— But never mind that." Is Cantor imagining things or is Borkman actually glowing— proud as a peacock—as a turkey buzzard—at the insinuation? (Whatever else the glowing means, it is within its rights to be all things to all men.) *Question:* was Khrisstye heroically blindsided by the banality of a hunger to succeed at any price until the bitter end or was she unheroic enough to sense the end was coming well before it came and was simply pulling a fast one? And don't answer: *Both*, even if this is in fact the correct answer. Netta rises and as if standing at the prow of the *Cathexis* (with the second sub-basement her very own private Delaware) proclaims that she was one of the first to be duped. Borkman shrugs. "By a show of hands, how many of you are in the same boat?" She raises her own hand to demonstrate or compel.

"My older son—or is it my younger? or do I have only one? somebody, please refresh my memory!—was also duped, Netta. But unlike you, he's come out of it a far better man—human being. In fact, the experience galvanized him into creating his own start-up, whose goal is to help people invent a concept of privacy (since privacy as we've known it is no longer) that's proof against hackers simply because it encompasses precisely what can be of no interest to them. I'm—he's—talking about a last bastion whose stock in trade is neither already monetized nor monetizable through shaming." It's Netta's turn to shrug—*à la française*, which means jerkily getting both shoulders up on their hind legs, like a glum pair of jacks-in-the-box. Borkman has no choice but to go livid—no, to *turn* livid and go *ballistic*—in response to what he takes to be clearly an affectation contracted on some package tour of Gay Paree. (Like the majority of benighted mankind, he doesn't know that, albeit of semi-humble stock, Netta was in fact née either Nanette de la Putain or Annette Du Pétain or Nettie Putin, on the too too ritzy French Île of Yeu where albeit of semi-humble stock, she misspent, most agreeably or so I'm told, her first thirty-one years.)

Eden can't hold himself back any longer. The potshot at Netta, his patron- ess of sorts—the mother—father—prodigal son and brother he never had and is less and less likely to have, even parthenogenetically—is the last straw in a life (like every other) littered with last straws. He goes for Borkman's jugular. At least he hopes what he's compressing in all sincerity is the old boy's jugular. But nothing seems to be happening. Borkman looks as healthy as ever. Somebody separates them—somebody taller and beefier than either who evokes a bouncer at a Rump rally (or rather its head bouncer whose every move inhabits the deplorable fantasy of auditioning for the coveted slot of second in command). Dusting himself off, Borkman chides Eden—yes, *chides* him, dude[51]—for tak- ing expressions like *go for the jugular* much too literally. Cook, ever the starter-

---

[51] From principle, the Master makes it a habit to shudder at the thought of consigning any word to the slagheap of so-called archaisms when its expressivity is still very much in the very bloom of youth. Nothing like assigning that word to its least plausible

upper (even if it's always by proxy, for now at least), can't help overhearing and what he overhears gets him thinking really, really hard. Never has he felt so much envy as he suddenly does for Borkman's favorite—his No. 1 son and more than anything Cook wants to be No. 1. Comes from having watched far too many mutilated reruns of Charlie Chan flicks as a (college) kid with time on his hands at Smerdyakov U. There's got to be plenty more where *go for the jugular* came from. Plenty more gold in them there hills, i.e., plenty more odd bits and pieces of wordflow that are simply unmappable onto some even odder bits and pieces of worldflow—that just can't see their way clear to translating—oozing—into worldflow. Owing to a clogging of the windpipes, drainpipes, bagpipes. In which case there's money to be made from this apparently semi-violent business (thank heaven for The Rump) of effecting such a mapping at any cost. Or is this just the Invidicum talking (Cook's been taking it on the sly for his off-label hemorrhoids) but still managing to make damn good sense even if he's cut the twice-daily dosage in half because of one serious side effect (the little death of priapism)?

A lateral life passes before him in an instant—a life he's not yet suited for but of which he has a dim . . . recollection. Junk derivatives indexed to the ever-shifting valuation of mappings plenitude and mappings dearth. A brave new world of the commodification of word- versus worldflow—commodification of the difference between the present and future values of a mapping on its maiden voyage to eternity. A brave new market (caveat: it may not remain niche for long) of, say, newly minted bonds backed by the most troubled would-be mappings. Those on the verge of foreclosure—the riskier, the better. A futures exchange where assurances to create or deliver or accept the viable mapping of a particular slice of wordflow *in here* onto a particular slice of worldflow *out there* are traded like filthy lucre (and not only by scribblers). Where such contracts are liquid assets in their own right. Lightning-speed human trafficking in the *maybe of mappables*—the maybe of the mappability of risk onto risk and back again—is there any better pharmakon for the sick soul? And, hey, what about a long-overdue shake-up—even a revolution—in the video game console industry triggered and underpinned by the weighty theme of Unmappability of Word- to Worldflow with a dash of six-player no-limit Texas hold'em thrown in for good measure?

And suddenly somebody never before seen hence never to be forgotten who will surely go down in the annals of white-collar crime as nothing less than Borkman's pinch-hitting apostle No. 1 cries: "You're just envious of all that *my* Master Builder has yet to accomplish. And if you know what's good for you you'll remember what Pritchard's Dumb Blond pal—and a Master Builder in his own right (no, not Norwegian—Danish)—*also* said." Which she proceeds to translate more or less as follows: Envy is a form of madness for it is the penchant of the madman to have an absolute relationship with what's rela-

---

utterer (a case of two wrongs—non-consignment and defiant implausibilization—making a right) despite the risk posed to the implausibilizer's personal safety by the smug arbiters of literary taste.

tive—with what he discovers he wants—through an oh-so-predictable turn of the Girardian screw—only because his rival du jour got there first. Comical, isn't it? that an individual—Man—whose being is willy-nilly dedicated to the eternal—to the Absolute Venture (nothing Andreessen Horowitz would be caught underwriting)—uses all his strength to stick his tongue as far up the ass of the perishable as it can manage to get. (Melanctha takes ample note of the fact [though will such acuity manage to hoist her another notch or two up the totem pole of Success?] that once again the Master has caved—through cowardice, through calculation—to his clientele's craving for novelty, that is to say, he's smuggled yet another new character into the proceedings [if you can call her that] whose lifespan is conterminous with the two-line speech which she was no doubt paid a full month's salary to mouth—and not all that convincingly. Which only goes to show Melanctha's got it all wrong since in fact the Master's no coward, just a swaggering disciple of the best kind [every Master's a disciple until he realizes discipleship is bad for the complexion]—a disciple of none other than the Demiurge-crazed Father in Bruno Schulz's *Street of Crocodiles*, whose Dinner Theater [like Rodin's atelier] runs on the principle that for every gesture, every slip of the tongue, a different actor shall be called into being, with only as much profile, hand, axillary hair, earlobe, thigh, genitalia, as is required to confirm that his entrancing country-bumpkinhood is not a sham but a sublime affliction. Nor for a minute would the Master dream of begrudging Father Schulz his seniority—his precedence—in having rolled out this soon-to-be-eternal concept of one-time use and its allied practice of prosecuting to the fullest extent of the law those tailor's dummies who report for Fatherly duty seeking to portray a leisurely personal *evolution*. But it's not because the Master's an uninvidious soul that He bears no grudges. Rather, it's because He suspects He's about to outdo *His* Master according to every criterion of big top flimflam.)

Strictly edge-of-the-seat-of-your-pants-style exposition, mesdames and gents. Nobody under this Big Top wants the show to end, and with good reason. But end it must and when it does there's not a dry crotch in the house.

"So when are we finally going to meet the Fair Khrisstye (not to mention those lovely quintuplets)?—she sure as hell sets *my* gypsy blood astir. Like—I mean, *as*—in that racy poem we had to memorize in nursery school." Pritchard tries hard to infuse a little heartfelt aggrievedness into his mockery of what it means to be so deprived but the intended aggrievedness ends up, alas, being just more grist for mockery's mill. As for Cantor, well, he's, frankly, a bit surprised to hear—yes, *hear*—Pritchard mug for the camera in this way since right off the bat he assumed—call it his *woman's intuition* (to quote the villainous sidekick in *North by Northwest*[52])—that there before him stood a Flaming Fruit of the Loom if ever there was one. Well, maybe he is and maybe, this being the case, it will take no less than the good auspices of a Khrisstye— with a little help from able doppelgängerin Christee—to cure—that is, "cure"

---

[52]A celluloid confection whose debut was tailor-made for Radio City Music Hall on Easter Sunday.

him. In any event, Cantor, like all duly diligent patients by proxy, is in dire need of a second opinion. Thing is, everybody around here looks as if he's just stepped right out of the fine print on page 3 of the *Times* weekday Business Section. Which is to say that everybody, though every inch a person with direct knowledge of the case, can speak, owing to the ongoing nature of the investigation, only on condition of pseudonymity and in any event, surely not here, surely not now.

"You're lookin' straight at 'er." Why, it's none other than Borkman's Apostle. She introduces herself swaggeringly as Hilda Wangel . . . Jencks (from stage fright, thinks ethereality-prone Shearer, who's an authority on the affliction). Since the Apostle is turning out to be more intrinsic to the main design (at least she's making threatening motions to that effect) than Melanctha was willing to give her credit for being, she may end up having to eat her words— or, in this case, her thoughts—or rather, her *ample note taken*. Maybe I'm envious, she thinks: When has the Master ever called *her* His apostle? But, she reminds herself, there's no reason to care what the Master calls her: it's what she calls *Him* that counts and for now He's her not-so-apt pupil in chief.

Something in Khrisstye's street smart intonation (rank with animal cunning and brute dismissiveness, not just of Pritchard for asking the question and of Khrisstye herself for stooping to serve as its hot topic but of any *thing*, human or otherwise, giving some sign of chokeability) reminds Cantor of . . . of . . . of (of all things) The Rump—the very Rump who qualifies for every foul diagnosis in the *DSM* and the millions more that didn't manage to bribe their way in. Only she's not just any old incarnation thereof—she's not, for example, DT the collective—the world-hysterical—tantrum-made-flab (show me a ham who can't manage that). No, it's definitely *Huey* Rump who's currently treading the sub-basement boards in the guise of this ex-CEO with four dugs and at each one an adorable tyke hanging on for dear life and not just any old Huey but Huey Pierce Long Rump, Jr., the goosestepping Stumper minutes away from assassination at the hands of a disgruntled Silicon Valley . . . postal worker—a postal worker expertly played by Moira Shearer and cast mischievously against type by Rump-hating KVCM (Koch Very Creative Management) in collaboration with the Lincoln Project—that is to say, a postal worker who's disgruntlement-lite and, instead, harbors lush but untappable reserves of poignancy and plangency and (if she were a pianist) a keyboard technique that's all rubato. (So at the creaky behest of who else but the Master, Moira, Melanctha and Cantor have each transformed Khrisstye—Borkman's Khrisstye—into a veritable map of misimpressions.) But at the same time the prospect of Huey the Rump's assassination, especially at the end of a hard night's algebraizing in vain, doesn't please Cantor Khayyam in the least even if it's to be at the hands of a sylph as enticing as Shearer used to be. Truth is, he (*a*) has gotten used to cheering the Rump on for what is at present the crassest of all his class acts on the debate stage, namely, dandling Little Marco and Big Ted while juggling Little Ted and Big Marco and *at the same time* throwing Middling Jeb a supersonic curve ball or two, and (*b*) doesn't relish the prospect of witnessing that zany act fold any time soon (yes, *zany*—at last the pesky little word has found a niche to call home). Not to mention all the other acts which together make up the 2016 Rump presidential saga. Frankly, Cantor hopes it will run—like *Springtime for Hitler*—forever. *But if it is to run forever then he needs a generous assurance from the not-for-profit Presumptive Certainty Foundation that it will also* end—*with the Rump's landslide defeat and Melanka in tears.*

And at the same time Cantor has got to hand it to The Rump: you'll never catch him saying "folks" instead of "people" like so many of the elite-because-moneyed on either side of the aisle when, for reasons bad and less bad, they try their luck at connecting with—oops, *reaching out to*—what they take to be the huddled masses. (While, ironically, the masses yearn for nothing more than to try *their* luck at proving they can live without respiration, food, sleep—live without living. Why? well, silly, in order to spare some of those eliteniks, coastal and otherwise [from one side of the aisle in particular], from having to finally make good on their tacit promise to shoot themselves in protest against human misery when they have so many much better things to do.) Moreover, you'll never catch The Rump being called *Don*, either. You'll never find him—bona fide fake populist—getting caught in the act of stooping to *play* the fake populist, or rather, the act of *stooping* to play the fake populist.

Cantor has more than a dim suspicion that he's doing exactly what he taxed the list maker for doing a while back (let's face it, he's the sort of vassal by vocation of whom that crank Adorno would have been obscenely proud)—running the gamut from frivolousness to perversity and back so that through all this "poking fun at" The Rump from the safety of his apopletic armchair he can make himself applaudable, even acceptable, to as comprehensive a swath of the huddled masses and the huddled moneyed as is compatible with their incompatibility. But that's because he's currently the toy of his own changes of state and doesn't yet have the guts or the tools (but if not now, when?) to be able to imagine—aposematically (*look it up!*), apotropaically (*ditto*)—how easily his—and America's—present sad opaqueness (*triste opacité*) could usher in a future of eternal ghosthood (*spectres futurs*).[53]

In short, Cantor isn't quite ready to throw in his lot, hook, line and sinker, with MSNBC/*Politico*/the *Daily Beast* et al. As the clouds heralding rabid inter-party warfare are not yet on the horizon and as the present climate of opinion is comfortingly coolingly shadowed by inevitable eradication of The Rump virus, Cantor affords himself the puny luxury of mocking the all-too-human idiosyncrasies of those news outlets' foot soldiers. In short, as the historical moment's provisional *composure convinces him that all is safe, his wit flows long.*[54] But he

---

[53] First example, in Cantor's experience at least, of the unlikely application of the "lessons" of Mallarmé's "Toast Funèbre" (1873) to US gutter politics (2016). A mighty clash and ultimate consensus of abstract and concrete that would have turned Old Man Hegel green with . . . Envy.

[54] Formulation pilfered, *mutatis mutandis*, from a scene in Jane Austen's *Pride and Prejudice* (vol. I, chap. VI, last sentence) where the author's House Surgeon-style wit lies in laying bare the rot of self-delusion—in exposing what one of the many mean-spirited characters seeks to pass off as wit for what it really is, namely, patter generated by

senses the time is not too far off when the infantry will be his heroes and he will have "zero-tolerance" (the inept battle cry of bumblingly pompous public officials) for anything interpretable as a criticism of their on-camera style. A time will come when there'll be no place in his echo chamber of horrors for the leveling of accusations of incompetence against the gods and goddesses of the liberal media no matter how far they fall short of anything approaching radical frenzy. But for the time being, The Rump is still the outsider and certain never to reverse his status so there's no risk and hence no shame in mistaking his viciousness in all its vulgarity for refreshingly uninhibited candor. Especially when the target is, for example, fellow draft dodger Bush, Jr.'s fire sale of the invasion of Iraq. And one day he'll surely look back on, and with a certain nostalgia for, those pursy times when it was harmless enough to take comfort from—and maybe even suffer a dopamine-heavy mental orgasm or two when obliged to witness yet another demonstration of—The Rump's dumb-ass snaky super-shrewd pugnacity at play—those pursy times when, because The Rump and his attack dogs weren't in the ascendant and never would be, he didn't have to feel personally responsible for the safety of Maddow, Hayes, O'Donnell, Fahrenhold, Krugman, Goldberg, Melber and the like.

And in fact Cantor's sad opaqueness is already fast-forwarding—to the nostalgia his future ghosthood is sure to feel for one particular incident in the present that stands out among many others. An incident that in fact cried out, at the very moment it was unfolding full speed ahead in the TV alcove in his hotel room (with its little bay facing the gauzy foothills and its neuroanatomy-themed wallpaper and curtains), to be nostalgized precisely because it already felt—*especially to itself*—so quintessentially epochal, already felt itself to be so very much a creature of its time—a time soon to be gone forever—a cozier time when The Rump's critics could be gently mocked inasmuch as the salvation of democracy didn't yet depend on Cantor's shielding them and their every utterance from even the minutest aerosol of surgical mask-piercing ambivalence.

If Cantor remembers correctly (thanks to his dependability, his rationality, his ability to maintain a graceful self-distancing despite all his "bad" narcissism, Cantor is default POV for all things Rumpian until further notice), it was a few weeks back, just before he bid a properly ambivalent farewell to the Synapse and set up shop at Netta's, that he watched a particularly fetching rising star in cable's Kingdom of Snowflakes interview someone noisily assaulted at a Rump rally by a gang of beefy tattooed Alt-Righters in biker and bouncer

---

jealous fear of losing her man. Of course if "real life" dared suggest to Caroline Bingley (the character in question) that she was in fact scared shitless of losing her man (it was his "composure," i.e., expert dissimulation, which "convinced her [of course wrongly] that all was safe"), then she'd of course have to enlist the aid of smugness-smothered narcissism in annihilating the attempted annihilation of her selfdom. (It should be noted that Austen's heirs have been inadequately indemnified by the author of *Invidicum* for his plagiary, which even if it of course stemmed from dumbstruck reverence is still inexcusable.)

drag. What better way to feverize his ratings, new as he was to the game but eager to learn fast, than to bountifully inflame her wording of what went on through some unstoppable *pre*wording of his own. But instead of stepping aside and letting him get on with the job of doing hers—instead of instantly recognizing how lucky she was to have a rookie, an up-and-comer right down to his designer specs, willing to do the thinking for the two of them—she, the assaultee, just couldn't see her way clear to giving him, her deliverer, the go-ahead right off the bat. You see, Cantor (he reminds himself), she wanted, touchingly—exquisitely—to be fair to her perception wherever it took her, notwithstanding diehard allegiance to the event in question's (exquisitely) precooked take on itself—a take whose armature was the chyron "Unarmed young black woman assaulted by the *real* fake news guzzlers: Rump scum and their brickbat-wielding Alt-Right outreachers." Only he wouldn't let her go her own way. Blusteringly misreading her self's quest for precision as a voyage deep into inarticulateness he had no choice—rather, she left him no choice—but to stoop to what he decided was her own level by administering a dose or two of excoriation of "the folks"—the folks who stood by and did nothing, the folks who rancidly cheered, the folks who had roast beef, the folks who had none and the folks who cried all the way home. Problem is, the patient refused to be pharmakoned, without even knowing she refused (for to know would have been to stoop to *his* level). She gave him for his pains—the pains taken to shepherd the story in the direction his censors demanded—a world of sighs.

But no folks for Don. No beamingly anxious attempts, à la baby-faced Marco, to extract approval from the audience through treacly collusive "bonding" every time he one-ups a Primary opponent (*Look, Ma, no glands!*), which in his case is all the time so who needs their—or anybody's—approval? The Rump has better things to do with Cantor's post-Synapse time. His triumphs are way too numerous not to be marked by scowls redolent of championship fatigue at so much inexorable record-breaking. Audience members—the preliminary sketches for a cabinet of toady vermin—serve at his displeasure. Not yet so morbidly obese as to be unable to plow his way way past even his biggest fans toward game that's even bigger, and ever better, he sets his beady sights on the big fat vanishing point his Better Demons call the horizon. His rants make Cantor poignantly want to feel—and even to enjoy feeling—like a cutthroat underdog (and why not? life is short and, more to the point, far too long) shortchanged by the fatcat GOP's contrast-collar disregard and thereby ripe for *blue*-collar resurrection—if only he can manage to stand still long enough to bask in the sunny shafts of The Rump's melanoma-inducing rhetoric.

But even if Cantor wears his blue-collar rue with a difference; even if he and The Rump, while both angry—vein-poppingly angry—are angry about totally different things (or as Melanctha would say, *Angry each in her own way*); and even if it's only desperation that makes his fellow blues think The Rump is angry *for* them—angrier for them than they can ever be for themselves—still, Cantor is able to put aside not just his labor and his leisure but his reservations as well and get on with the heady business of wondering disingenuously (the wondering is all fake until it isn't) whether The Rump (and, by extension, Borkman though obviously on a much less exalted level) is (*a*) nothing less than the World-Hysterical Individual—the Corsican—the Macedonian—the Rubiconian—the Austro-Hungarian—that this hot-as-Hell Ice Age demands (although Cantor's of course wary of going into Masterly hyperlative overdrive too early in the game); and (*b*) nothing less than, in particular, the World-Hysterical Thug invoked by America as guide of choice on its too-long-deferred hence overbooked interminable whirlwind grand tour of the country's home-baked grand rot. The hysterical expectation being that through the strength and power of his dedication to a vocation hatched like a terrorist plot deep within the sacred fount—the Kernel—of the World Spirit, whose waters though unstill run ever so deep, he'll be able to slake his—and by proxy the electorate's—vexingly *un*morbid craving to (speaking current-lingo-istically, i.e., euphemistically) *disrupt* (and not just the GOP's status quo, though that will do very nicely for starters)—to crash into the outer world as into a shell and shatter it into a billion pieces because as it just so happens, the Kernel of the World Spirit is a horse of another color entirely from what could be called the "everyday kernel" harboring like a mare in heat all things regular, calm, orderly, approved, unenviable. But as all roads lead to Envy, Cantor can't help wondering whether the level of authenticity of The Rump's vocation as cooked up by that Inner Spirit is in direct proportion to the degree to which it's Envied—the degree to which his enviers try to reduce his actions to pranks perpetrated under the spell—the impulse—of a mere morbid craving for the unhappiness brought by fame. But even if (*a*) Cantor's fellow blues only *think* they feel the irresistible power of their own inner life embodied in the Everglades of The Rump's cunning of *un*reason and (*b*) Cantor himself doesn't feel the slightest twitch or twinge of Envy for The Rump's parodic pursuit of a world-hysterical vocation—even so, what if it should turn out to be the case that Cantor is able to perceive—to allow himself to perceive—the mighty inner spirit of his own vocation only as embodied in The Rump (for hasn't every holy fool of an MSNBC host and every print and online journalist from Williamsburg to Chelsea and beyond already discovered that they feel vocationed and as never before only when covering The Rump and his flunkeys even if—especially because—covering The Rump and his flunkeys, however "scathingly," however "blisteringly," is necessarily and unavoidably to give him cover—to cover his ass—to legitimize him—to welcome him sappily back into the human community even if he takes the welcoming as an unforgivably reductive slight since he'd much prefer to be *un*welcomed—ideally as an unsequenceable bacteriophage?). Clearly, these are matters resolvable only by a higher authority—preferably some Wiseguy from Tübingen. Suffice it to say that if it turns out that Omar Cantor is indeed the mathematician on the order of the poet of the *Rubáiyát* that his nightly wet dreams think he is, then it was none other than The Rump Khayyám who put his stars to flight. But why bother worrying about any of this since once The Rump's gory goal is achieved or maybe even long before, like all agents of the World Spirit he'll be shed like scurf from the Spirit's Kernel and never heard from again.

Still, World-Hysterical or not, he's enabling Cantor to understand Borkman at last. Only as a Rump manqué does Borkman become legible. Only in falling short of The Rump—and who doesn't fall short?—does he become sufferable: He's not so bad, there's worse, there's The Rump, and nothing less than a world-hysterical pathos lies at the heart of his having fallen short. Only by playing tortoise to The Rump's Achilles—but in this case an Achilles who wins—does Borkman begin to make sense as a businessman. Without the Rump Borkman is nothing and maybe the converse is also true—or is that just the SofP going all doctrinaire for a change?—letting wordflow lead him by the nose, also for a change. But whatever goes on between Borkman and The Rump—whether The Rump is far more than Borkman's *semblable* or whether JGB's far less than The Rump's *frère* (*frères*, after all, are a dime a dozen and nobody knows it better than Cantor who has three under his belt or is it four? or none?)—whatever goes on between them is their own business. What matters—and will always matter from this day forward (that the day is at least or at best world-hysterical may be going unnoticed)—is this newly minted Cantor-Borkman connection—an organism in its own right—a cautionary tale incarnate, woven for the benefit of aspiring centaurs everywhere. For the connection is nothing less than Cantor's readymade—his uterine urinal—his Richard Mutt—his found object nonpareil—into which all inhibitions about seeing Borkman *for what he really is—or isn't*—can be pissed away for the price of a manly flush—even if they *stay* pissed solely for the duration of the flush which generously includes the growl, not quite manly, that signals its demise.

So it's no longer shockingly unthinkable, at least to Cantor, that Borkman (since it's no longer unthinkable, shockingly or otherwise, for him to be mentionable in the same breath as The Rump, even if it's only within the context of falling short) may indeed be what everybody else's been saying he is: Biggest Daddy of Dross Finance, Mahatma of the Backdated Option, Ur-Odysseus of the Orphan Brand, the Shadow Banker's Shadowiest Shadow Banker. No longer unthinkable that it may indeed be John Gabriel and nobody else, as he insisted far too many times to be credible in Amygdala's eavesdropper-friendly corridors of power, who invented SUBOs (synthetic uncollateralized bet obligations), which are, simply enough (at last Cantor's expensive training is standing him in good stead), algorithm-engendered cramming of all sorts of bets on the fate of the debt incurred by those (persons and businesses and everything in-between) compelled to bet on thinkable things like the patentability of sarcastic smiles or manipulated slivers of junk DNA; the probability of a felon's being able to pay for court-ordered anger-management classes or that *Toxic Assets, Unsocial Distancing, Exit Strategy, Dismissed with Prejudice, Negative Pregnant, Contract for Difference, Click Fraud, Relief Defendant, Doctrines of Distinction, Work-Product Privilege, Criminal Predicate, Recreational Violence, Anchor Client, Asset Forfeiture* or *even Counter-cyclical Diversification Strategy* will be the title of the next techno-terrorist blockbuster on the order of, say (thinking big), *A Nightmare on Wall Street*;[55] the winnability of a

---

[55]Somebody, Cantor thinks, should explain (and get tenured for doing so) the secret of movie titles portentous enough to give the menace-fraught impression that the package they're peddling has the zeitgeist by its A-list balls.

whistleblower suit; the profitability of investing in Paraguayan soccer players, virtual-world storefront online-abilia, or AIDS victims' life insurance policies, trafficking in human tissue harvested from the highest-end funeral parlors, or buying bogus public asset leases (of, say, Canada's air traffic control system or the Chicago subway system or Barcelona's celebrated water mains); and the outcomes, long-, short- and medium-term, of secondary buyouts and web domain-name auctions. No longer implausible to think that Borkman's SUBOs are works not only of genius but of a very peculiar kind of genius. To wit, a genius that lies (according to people with direct knowledge of the phenomenon but who'll speak, if they deign to speak at all—citing the delicacy of the soon-to-be-ongoing investigations—only on condition of anonymity) in their containing absolutely nothing and certainly nothing so vulgar as mortgage bonds or promissory notes or IOUs or stocks or commodities or CDs or last week's Mulligan stew or the mean-spirited ghost of student loans past. *A genius that lies in their self-referencing the things they might have contained if only they hadn't been so busy betting on the fate thereof.*

A genius that lies in their self-referencing the things they might have contained if only they hadn't been so busy betting on the fate thereof. (Cantor's thinking stops dead in its tracks: this determination of Where Genius Lies sounds like an ominously perfect description of the Master's failed handicraft [he's decided to throw his beloved SoP under the bus temporarily]. And though the ability to debunk his own life work so aptly albeit inadvertently ain't given to just anybody—and though such aptly inadvertent debunking, which seems to nip any claim to genius in the bud, is, by the way and in fact, the one incontrovertible proof thereof, or is that, Cantor wonders [as Herbert might wonder], just the Master's PR machine in overdrive?—*these* wild horses won't keep his detractors away from getting on with the business of doing what they do best—which is to overexpose what they take to be definitive self-demolition by the handicrafter they currently happen to hate the most.)

And if it's no longer implausible (was it ever?) to think that the slumbering spirits of the SUBOs are works of a very particular kind of Nordic genius so is it no longer horripilating to realize (genius has its privileges) that, in short, SUBOS do little more, and little less, than reference Fate, finger Fate, give Fate the finger? They're so enticing precisely because they spare those who fish in their muddy waters from having to get their brains dirty over and over and over again conceiving new real-world targets (once a real thing's referenced it's volatilized away). No longer matters that an initial target (e.g., the profitability of blackmarketeering inflatable artichokes [PBIA]) is all you need to generate an infinite number of bets, themselves infinitely recombinant.

Still, in a cosmic cycle under the Sign of The Rump, Borkman's too-much is nowhere near enough. Why, for all his exorbitant self-referencing Borkman's in danger of becoming The Rump's next Little Marco. So for his iniquities—for his crimes against mankind's better nature—he may end up being absolved by virtue (!) not so much of his remorse or his inadvertency but rather of his prissy failure to go the whole nine yards—to take his SUBO-powered iniquity to the limit. It may be decided that, for all his efforts, nothing Borkman did (ankle notwithstanding) was criminal because whatever it was

Borkman did, The Rump went him one better (sometimes simply by standing still), making his atrocities seem like pussyfooting.

Yet, for all his faults and forfeitures, Borkman the Icon—Borkman the Movie—Borkman the Musical—Borkman the Miniseries—may very well still turn out to be the Panurge of his—of our—time—embodying—living— draining to the dregs—what Panurge maintained at the drop of a hat, namely, that Hesiod's mountain of heroic virtue was composed of bets on the fate of debts and nothing but; that he, Panurge, was venerable, honest and a force to be reckoned with to the extent that he betted his life away; that God created man only to borrow in order to bet and bet in order to borrow; that bets constitute a sort of link between heaven and earth, a unique means of preserving the human race, and maybe even the soul of the universe; and that without each organ propulsively making bets on or against (like any self-respecting knight aberrant in search of the holy grail of *shareholder value*) the competency of the others, the body would disintegrate from inanition and man the microcosm would perish straight away. *Shareholder value.* If I hear that phrase one more time, Cantor thinks, I'm immigrating to Highgate Cemetery. (Or is it emigrating or is the ostensible confusion over the difference between them his throwaway—his signature—way of flaunting an intelligence beyond intelligence? an intelligence so great it can afford—indeed, has a Judeo-Christian duty—to bypass, purposely undervalue, get the goat of its feeble underpinning, namely, the *little agitation of the brain we call thought*, and which he leaves it unregretfully to others to go on making [wow!] *the model of the whole universe*).

CHAPTER TWENTY-SIX

Surprised at how quickly and how vehemently she's come to reject the two men's depiction of this mogul, Jean Rhys *can't help wondering* (what a soother, that phrase!—what a scene-stealer! what a wunderkind! but how? but why?)—and with a certain exhilaration—the kind she hasn't felt since menarche—whether from the very beginning they—she and Ethan—haven't been in disagreement over pretty much everything under the sun, whose lust-inducing rays alone have blinded them to the bruteness of the fact. This tailor-made point of contention is simply the final wedge between them. She regrets not having cut Ethan off in flagrante delicto instead of addressing anticlimactically the unstunned silence. How can she make him—them—understand that at this very moment Borkman, for all his désinvolture, is arm-wrestling with the dark angel of his guilt? She points in his direction. "Can't any of you see that like that spinster in *The Cherry Orchard*, he's in deep mourning for his life?"

"*Seagull.*"

"What?"

"*The Seagull.*" The correction—never mind that Melanctha's the one who's made it—delights her. "The best he can do—but it's already way too much for somebody used to being obeyed—is to bury his head in the quicksand between his legs. Khristy—I mean Khrisstye—should be pleased somebody's coming to the defense of her man but since he *is* her man, she dog-in-the-mangerishly resents that somebody's daring to poach on her preserves. What's more, her flared nostrils say as much." How make them understand there's a manfulness in his stance, or lack of a stance—a lackful stance which has taken the time and trouble to assure them that he doesn't profess to be anything but the bloated worm he knows they know he is—that he's well aware of how lucky he is not to have been drawn and quartered and boiled in oil for his bookkeeping errors. They mustn't think he's sulking when he's simply soliciting the intervention of the college of soul surgeons he's given them no choice but to become. All he's trying to do is—and she'll stake her life on it—honor those who, purely by deploying their own unimpeachable rectitude, have exposed him for what he is and who in their angelic refusal to inflict punishment inflict the greatest punishment of all. She certainly has her work cut out for her. What's more, he's an artist, too. Or an artist's muse. Or an artist's tool. For he's kept only so much of his anatomy—bowed head and legs cut off a little above mid-thigh—to convey shame-saturated remorse.

But are they ready for Borkman as Rubek—or as an *abattis* straight out of Rodin's workshop—or even as Princess X?

She spills her beans and what do they do but fall upon her like a pack of wolves. Borkman, Cook explains, is nowhere near being contrite—he's just ashamed that his accomplishments have fallen so far short of The Donald's (it's not Cook's fault: he just isn't ready to refer to him as The Rump, which is not to say she doesn't admire those who are ready—who've been ready for weeks now). All her fancy thoughts are an evasion—a displacement—even if *every thought is a displacement* and even if a thought like every thought is a displacement is the biggest displacement of them all. "He should be punished: an eye for an eye," Cook says musingly, as if his native clemency has, willy-nilly, already gotten the upper hand. Ethan scowling shields his eyes from the midmorning sun as if it's as merciless as his scowling makes it out to be. "You're wasting your breath. When Jean gets this way, she's unreachable. She's not even talking about Borkman, though she may think she is." What he means is, She's applying the bandaid of her chatter to the wrong life-lesion. "God knows whom—or what—she's really talking about: her penny ante diagnosis could fit anything—even a pebble—even her ex- or soon-to-be-ex. Maybe the party in question simply doesn't exist yet though, as you can see, there'll be plenty for him to account for when he does." Borkman Agonistes is out of the quicksand and from the look of him hasn't taken too kindly to her wild idea that he was in total eclipse (no sun! no moon!) and in need of a champion.

Coming to Borkman's defense (because from where she's sitting he *is* in total eclipse), Melanctha goes so far as to inquire where any of them come off (fully aware as they all must be of how Envy can make its naked prey do the craziest, meanest things) throwing stones at a fellow sufferer—a lone lorn critter straight out of *Copperfield*. And Rhys—yes, Rhys—is in her own way the worst of the lot though she'd be hard put to explain why. No stanching the flow of underdoggerel even if she knows how very busy Borkman has been all his life raking in the greenbacks—and far more cardinal, losing 'em as fast as he was raking them in—while her boy rotted away in grossly underfunded city dumps like . . . like . . . Building 18. No stanching the flow even if—precisely because—the vehemence of the delivery strikes her—strikes *back at her*—as too outsize for the occasion, that is, until she recognizes it—the vehemence—has nothing to do with Borkman, whether as victim of mob violence or carpetbagger or Princess X (*Wait! how does she know about Princess X?*), and everything to do with a budding artist whose monstrous opportunism always manages to nip her in the bud.

"Save your breath." From the sound of the voice she can't tell whether it's Cook or Narr, or Stifter or Walser or some combination thereof. And yet what exhilaration—what a triumph over art and the laws of art—over life itself—to be unable to distinguish W. from S. and vice versa. To watch the universe turn to one [al]mighty stranger before one's very eyes. To be present at its birth but before its differentiation into entities with a distinct biometric profile. "What's the difference? He's sure to triumph. They all do." *Stifter. I'd recognize that voice anywhere.* Even if she couldn't. He wants them to understand (easier said than done) that even if Borkman—*their* Borkman—does end up behind bars, he'll surely find a way to exit prematurely and one fine day suddenly enough time will have elapsed to scumble the contours of his opprobrium, at which point the inevitable quote window of opportunity unquote will open wide enough to afford him—and the peeping-Tom public—the tantalizing prospect of a new kind of celebrity, contingent on, say, his feasibly hosting a Sunday round table or two—with Mike the Pompeo to the right of him and . . . Mike the . . . Pompeo to the left of him. Whatever outrage there was will inevitably have subsided, leaving in its wake a curiosity even more prurient than the one that gobbled up his flagrancies way back when. Nothing more sexualizable, in other words—nothing more mind-masturbation-friendly—than the shamelessness of a shamed survivor's respectfully unregenerate refusal to not show his face. Which is why the ex-Governor of New York rehabilitated as host of a cable-TV show on finance high and low was for the briefest of moments infinitely more intriguing than his previous incarnation (muckraking purchaser of unsafe sex), of which said host constituted the transcending shadow and preserving substance (in a Hegelian midsummer marriage at which they were all best men and much-deflowered bridesmaids).

Clearly all fired up by Stifter's lucidly caustic take, somebody to the right of Shearer—Netta!—cries out, "What I want to know is, how you can stand to look at yourself!" "Don't underestimate, please, how much people can stomach of what scowls back at them from the depths of the bathroom mirror. Anyway—and it's a big *anyway*—as a rule, I avoid mirrors, madam," Borkman chuckles, thereby cutting the crier down to mockable size, "except when one happens to be installed on the ceiling because the broad I happen to be fucking happens to want another insatiable couple along for the hayride. In any case, don't underestimate the high tolerance of folks like me for what stares back at them from the depths of *their* bathroom mirror. And before I go any further I want to thank you, Nettie, for returning the favor and cutting *me* down to size." George and Melanctha—soon to be or maybe already as famous as Chuck and Nancy—can both hear the Master's stertor while he ponders—as both Mouse and Man—whether yet another set of His best-laid plans have gone awry. Will the dinner-theater-going-public realize that Borkman's fake take on Netta's cut-down as a casebook demonstration of underlined unprovoked *tough love* (another of the many last refuges of scoundrels) was immediately undercut by his crocodile thanks to her for "returning the favor" of his own defiantly circumstantial cut-down (with its exquisite little Schrödingeresque bonus of retrospectively turning her cut-down into an event both succeeding and preceding his). "And to let you know that if I was lucky enough to have been bailed out as too big to fail, i.e., as too big to be *allowed* to fail—which is obviously what you're driving at—it's simply because at the height of the Great Infusion I managed to maneuver myself into the right position. That is"—voice lowered to a whisper—"for quite a while I'd been paying the Big Boys—*folks* like Goldman-Sachs and AIG and Bank of America and Merrill Lynch and Kojève-Girard and Veblen-Stanley—far more handsomely than They deserved to clear most of my fund trades and from my seat on the sidelines finally got just the lowdown I was looking for." It's Invidicum that's responsible for all the fancy talk—eloquence with a vengeance—and with just the right mixture of stress sass. But this side effect wears off pretty quickly—sometimes in the middle of a sentence. Still, it's nice to see somebody so *possessed*, especially with an opponent like Netta.

"And what lowdown was that?" Walser asks, trying hard to adopt a tone true to Stifter's as well as Netta's—a mix of wise guy and (think Edna May Oliver) horsey-faced suffragette—a mix of sun and clouds—with a bit of wistfulness thrown in for good measure—but fails them both, miserably. He wishes he had a bit of stage business to go along with—to give a bit of slice-of-life heft to—the asking. What about dipping a piece of rye toast in his coffee? Too late for heft, and a whole lot of other things. But heft or no heft, Borkman is amenable to responding despite all that his tormentors have put him through. "The lowdown on why they needed to be kept alive and shitkicking." "Why?" "Why? you ask." Borkman warns them that what he's about to say may sound counter-intuitive but as counter-intuitivity is always a welcome breath of fresh air whatever one's sexual orientation and, as a fringe benefit, the (or rather, make that *a*) last refuge of scoundrels—and what's more, as nobody minds having what's too good for him—he entreats them to please bear with him and "to trust [him] on this." Because It's Their operations and Theirs alone—and by extension Mine—sorry, mine—keeping Mother Earth in her orbit to the extent that said operations invariably benefit the one percent of the one percent of the one percent, with none of your mythic trickle-down to the dispossessed, if you please, except for the trickle of more dispossession and dispossessedness. This being the case, once the Boys agreed to go on doing what They referred to smarmily as God's work, the Infusoria had no choice but to graciously do their part—just as they had to do their part underwriting affordable housing for oligarchs from what used to be called the Third World—since the only alternative to keeping the wheels within wheels of gross injustice churning would be to blow everything securitizable to kingdom come and start from scratch.

"But forget all I just said. What really matters is why you waited so long to unmask me. Why at this particular moment when, for the first time in my life, I'm acting—plausibly—like what I am and always will be—an average joe who wants nothing more than to mind his own businesses. OK, so you see right through me yet again: so *it* has nothing to do with actually being an average joe and everything to do with the fact that this moment, as we're living it here and now, requires an average-joe act to feel complete and will accept (you know how touchy moments can be) no substitutes. So since none of you were willing to volunteer for the thankless task, I had no choice but to—to—" If Borkman says *so* one more time, Melanctha thinks (she can handle the *to*s), so help me I'll—I'll—

Cook leaps up and starts jabbing his right forefinger at the air as if it were Borkman's barely or still barely[56] noticeable cummerbund of flab. "Folks, don't let this scoundrel erect his last refuge over our ruins by claiming it's us who are the criminals—for having waited so long to expose him." At which point Borkman leaps up, cummerbund and all, and does—no, *proceeds to do*—a by no means implausible imitation of Somebody Celebrated thrashing past a horde of the only things worse than hecklers, namely—fans, i.e., practitioners of lese majesty gone hog wild.

Having listened as hard as circumstances and his position permit, Pritchard discovers he's developed quite a mangy soft spot for Borkman's sultry chant, if not for the man himself—one that's impossible to excise at

---

[56]The difference between "barely" and "still barely" in this context is worth pondering.

least on such short notice. And this perfectly timed exit clinches it. He has no intention of letting him go without getting cured. Since all of his misdeeds, as he fondly called them (but did he in fact use the word?), were obviously perpetrated at the behest of Envy gone wild, he needs even more obviously all the help he could get.

CHAPTER TWENTY-SEVEN

The least you can say is that Eden, as he makes for the beach, has never been more confused. Cantor, too (Eden, atypically, seems to welcome his companionship or at least his presence). What was the Borkman-bashing all about? they wonder, each in his own way, neither realizing how something good might come out of pooling that wonderment. Did it represent a carefully staged effort to direct Eden's expanding animus toward Borkman?—it's obvious, at least to Cantor, that Eden's dosage has been beefed up since their arrival here, no better (counter-intuitive) proof being the leveling off of Eden's homophobia (a euphemism if ever there was one). A carefully staged effort in preparation for his taking on The Rump, presumably at the national Convention. For isn't The Rump in some strange way the biggest threat to the GOP's Cumaean Sibyl, Big Pharma and Her inversions? And does this mean that Cantor, a relative nobody, is off the hook—off Eden's meat hook? Or were there simply two birds-with-one-stone now, instead of one? It doesn't matter. Which means it's a matter of life and death. If only he knew way back in Manhattan what, willy-nilly and while (of all things!) waiting for the light to change so he can cross Cabrillo and feel the warm sand underfoot, he's being made privy to at this very moment (exactly the kind of moment Borkman was badmouthing back at the bunker buffet), namely, that the easiest thing in the world for a stand of palms pasted against the noonday horizon to manage is not (as we've all been taught) the shredding of their sleeves in the noonday breeze sounding more surflike than surf but rather getting themselves reflected in the windshield of a gaudily speeding sports car. Armed with this hard-won knowledge, he's sure he'd have had the courage to pull out of the trial and Envy be damned before being sweet-talked into heading West purely to end up as the target of some psychopath in basic training, albeit one with a heart. Has Eden noticed his scowl of disgust? and if so, will it be what sets him off? But as Eden signals that it's time to move, his look is surprisingly tender so maybe the scowl still has a lot of work to do—maybe it hasn't even begun to make the crossover from frown to scowl.

They almost collide with a thin, well-proportioned but resolutely unmuscular jogger whom Cantor has no trouble forgiving his trespass, inasmuch as the hazardous self-absorption is amply compensated for by (even enhances) just the sort of distribution of hair on chest, thighs and forearms that he, of course a connoisseur in such matters, finds disquieting, that is, irresistible. Eden, on the other hand—for, as Cantor learned very early on, where statistically deviant desire is concerned there's always an *other* hand and the goal of this other hand is to get the upper hand—Eden has no trouble framing a . . . scowl . . . (so Cantor's fabled gestation ended by throwing up its hands and migrating to another womb). But it's an amiable scowl and has nothing to do with the jogger. So here they are once again (yes, they do have a shared past after all) coming at the same thing from different angles, Cantor's being the angle of breathless fetishization and Eden's that of unseeing immunity. So may a not-too-happily married couple converge Homerically (why *Homerically*?:

chalk it up to the triumph of sight and sound over sense) on, say, the name of the husband's boss. In recounting the day's workplace humiliation, frazzled Hubby, let's say, utters the name gravely—imploringly. From shrewish duty, Wifey follows suit, only her uttering is a quizzical contemptuous castrative commentary on his—on all it reveals of unmanly subjection and bedazzlement. Why, he actually believes the name holds his fate in its hands—allows himself to sink so low as to swallow its—and, by extension, her—grandiosity hook, line and sinker. Doesn't he know that taking anybody's name at face value—being intimidated by the ostensible perfect fit between name and thing is the basest form of credulity? A lady jogger, who as it so happens is the spittin' image of Wifey, follows fast on the grointhrob's footsteps. In sharpest contradistinction to Eden, who is still scowling but in a new key, so to speak— let's call it the major key of riveted, almost accusatory lust (how dare she get my dander up without permission?) and have done with it—Cantor unsurprisingly (or where have *you* been for the last 500-odd pages?) has no interest in her ample thighs nor her even ampler tits which, in the way of the world of tits, ampler or not, jog right along with her—like pet pitballs—no! like top-of-the-line sensors, keeping track of—keeping time to—her vital signs. But he does—did—have an interest in her metrosexual T-shirt, inasmuch as he wasn't (and never will be) able to make out the final word in its splashed slogan. Though maybe this kind of curiosity is in fact desire—the kind of full-fledged desire that makes mincemeat of the gender of its target yet remains meaty desire all the same.

Cantor is the first to notice Borkman, sipping what looks—but doesn't smell, at least from afar—like lemonade, at the only outdoor table at the only beachfront eatery in sight. *Where's Khristy? (oops, Khrisstye)*, Cantor wonders. *Definitely bad planning or plumbing on the part of whoever's running this roadshow to have introduced and touted her as not just another dumb blonde only to get her remixed at the first opportunity.* Between sips he loftily purses his lips— exactly like The Rump after he's maneuvered everybody else on the podium (and that includes layoff-slaphappy "When I'm President" Carly Fiorino) into attacking him. George tries to avert his gaze but he's way too slow. Eden, on the other hand, goes straight up to Borkman and with a certain smarmy menace that's new, at least in Cantor's experience, says, "They really raked you over the coals back there. Why, I'll never know. You're no worse than any of your cronies. In fact, you remind me of that woman who stood next to me on my way back to Brooklyn one sweaty night this summer in what felt like the most crowded car on the train. Out of the blue she yawned and farted (after which you could have heard a pin drop)." Eden then explains how everybody else, or what seemed like everybody else, burst out cackling and cheering as if she and she alone had had the courage to enact their most urgent craving—a craving they didn't even know they harbored until it was given fullest expression. As a means of disavowing his connection with *this geek bearing gifts (who dares saddle Eden with an epithet that doesn't quite fit—who is so addicted to the vagaries of alliteration as to allow it to trump meaning, of which there's little enough in this world?)*, Cantor brushes a little non-existent sand off the soles of his sneakers. Borkman understands at once: everybody else could reap the fruits of her comic daring without having had to making the slightest investment in a possibly fatal (though used to stretch limos, he still knows what risks the L line poses in the wee hours) self-mockery. Eden rolls his eyes, or rather his eyebrows. It's unclear to Cantor why. But they're bushy and voluble so why let them go to waste? "I didn't say it was the L. In fact—" "So you think of me—if you think of me at all—as satisfying everybody else's craving to pull a fast one that will go down in history as the Ponzi to end all Ponzis." Borkman doesn't roll his eyebrows (Eden has robbed him of his right to that gesture)—he shrugs deprecatingly, evidently unfazed by the depiction he attributes to Eden, and almost as if (*try to picture this: try to make the shrug live on the page as this*) it's Eden himself who needs absolution—or the usual extenuating circumstances to be rounded up. With robust irrelevance, Eden replies, "Well, I've got to say you're taking it all pretty calmly," in response to which Borkman removes an envelope from his shirt pocket and swings it back and forth a few times as if it were a censer, then tears it up. "No point in dwelling on penny ante stuff when you've got just a few months, maybe weeks, to live. Jaggers, my lawyer, just FedExed me—did you get that? he *FedExed* me"—which means, ladies and gents, nothing less than that the trial now falls officially under the rubric of branded entertainment (*but who is the author of this parenthetical remark?*)—"the test results." Cantor wonders if *ladies* is directed at him. In which case, if Borkman is hale and hearty enough to per- petrate this rancid slur on his manhood, then maybe the deathbed act is just another con. On the other hand, it could be that, understandably aghast at his fate, he needs to visit the emergent rage on somebody. After all, didn't Can- tor's Uncle Hildy start fulminating against blacks and Hispanics immediately after learning his testicular tumor was inoperable? Still, out of respect for the near—or the sham—dead Cantor holds his peace.

By no means illiterate (don't let his populist bilge fool you), Borkman speed-reads the scepticism in their eyes and understandably can't wait for them to move on. Besides, they're blocking his view of the exquisitely pretty redhead (but what if her sure-to-be-delectable sweat-soaked pubis turns out not to be color-coordinated—what then?) who, undeterred by something as trivial as talentlessness, is plectrumming away at her implausibly soulful ren- dition of "Can't Take My Eyes Off-a-You" by the water's edge. Immediately he tries to make amends for this cruel, and perhaps woefully premature, verdict, which belongs to Some Mysterious Other (like Cantor and Herbert before him Borkman has just discovered, but in his case for the four-hundredth time, that every self-respecting invidicumite has One, custom-tailored to his very own deficiencies)—he tries to make amends by doing *his* rendition—of listen- ing as hard as he can. Problem is, said verdict, whatever its source, prohibits any further access. Which is a real pity since with the two losers—yes, *los- ers*!—no longer obstructing not just his view of some redhead but his vantage on being—yes, *Being*!—itself (what *has* he done with that stupidly dangled envelope?)—he's now allowed to warm to the notion that maybe, just maybe, she's at the point in her career where the demon of talent, rendered obsolete or extinct like the Tully Monster, cedes pride of place to demons more revelatory or at least more relevant and resuscitating especially to those who like Borkman are busy knocking at death's door. But suddenly realizing she's a proband like him and not just any old proband but the one who in the Coronado's grandest ballroom asked the question that made Herbert smile for the very first time (at least in his experience), Borkman forecloses all possibility of pursuing his demoniac thought to the finish line (if somebodies should ask, just tell him and her it's the Invidicum that's rendered him so uncharacteristically super-speculative—and so unpopulistically eloquent to boot). On the other hand, the fact that the redhead is a member of the tribe makes things more . . . elegant, in the sense that a mathematical proof—one revolving around, say, the dynamics of predator-prey interactions in Fairfield County—can be so deemed. Elegant, yes, but neither, alas, for his purposes, nor for Red's (he can read her now like the palm of his hand). But what about for the purposes of that Mysterious Other—that campfire raconteur—that Scoutmaster without a Shadow—who one day took it into his unexpurgated head to tell The Invidicum Story and who like any raconteur of the Hudson River School dreads nothing more, every time he senses yet another installment coming down the pike which is just too juicy to jettison, than having to recruit outsiders for the new roles coming down the pike with it, given that they may be too grossly out of character for anybody in the already established stock company to inhabit? On the other hand, Borkman thinks, inbreeding could screw up the trial results. But why should a doomed man care?

Borkman stares intently because he knows he must find a way to hustle her into bed before his time is up. He owes it to the trial to prove that Invidicum does not blunt potency in the old—at least not in the youngest old. And she in turn appears to have registered his wrenched longing and to recognize that she's the pretext for a desperate bet with himself and as such must stand at the ready until the croupier or the maitre d' in the Caesar's Palace of his soul has gotten the eight-ball rolling. But knowing they harbor in their clayey folds the first draft of his obit, he redirects his blurry gaze toward the celebrated Santa Barbara hills (a cloudlet, more fog than cloud, is at this very moment self-importantly straddling one of their saddlepoints) for all the world as if it were the triplex skywalk connecting Gimbels and the Cuyler Building. As anticipated, the draft obit is cattily denigrating and then some and, added to all the other shames he's bequeathed, sure to be a continuing source of embarrassment to his kids, since it goes something like this: *After a long battle with . . . leaflessness, Salix amygdaloides borkmanica succumbed to total skeletonization.* And adding insult to injury, the obit goes on to contend that he was a walking scourge—something to die (Delancey-trouncing Calspeak, so to speak) not *for* but *from.* Still, being stone dead might turn out to be his best ally, his best PR man, a far better advocate for his true visionaryhood than Jagger ever was, even in their first-love days (notwithstanding all the at-the-drop-of-a-hat heartfelt hugs, complete with tritely desexualizing First Aid-style scapula pats). Funny, it feels as if he's thinking a thought cast off out of pity by another member of the tribe. So what?—he can still make it his own. Or maybe it's the thought that cast off the thinker because he never managed to think beyond the embryo. Against all odds, he could very well emerge from some hack's warts-are-all bio (obliging him, in every anecdote, to wear his sleaze on his sleeve) as more—as infinitely more—than the sum of his mugshots (*Wanted* at last, *albeit Dead, not Alive*), even if this is the last thing in the world he deserves.

But resurrectable or not, he will never disport himself like his terminal daddy, no matter how ineffective the painkillers or how arrogant the puffy chiefs of staff. No matter how dire the prognosis, damned if you'll ever find him crawling into that last refuge of scoundrels (so many last refuges! and so little time!): an out-of-the-blue sappiness which in the old bastard's case entailed a never-before-avowed (because rented just for the occasion) cherishment of the suddenly near-and-dearies whose guts in fact, albeit unbeknownst to himself, he always hated, justifiedly or not, and who returned the favor in spades, justifiedly or not, every chance they got, and they got plenty. And most of all, please, please, no ruefully rheumy remarks à la pop (after the final dose of chemotheraplacebo) about *how he thought he was going to be one of the lucky guys who'd make it*, at which his wife had jeered in private. And in silence Borkman jeered along with her, hating the jeers but hating far more what provoked them: the illusion-breeding vulnerability of a not-so-average joe shamelessly overdoing the averageness in the hope of appeasing the hubris-hating death deities (who, by the way, are themselves no slouches when it comes to good old-fashioned hubris). But the venomous seedling of *cunt-intuition* (*a teutonism! my kingdom for a teutonism!*) that his father, like so many other manly males, to his peril smothers in its bed, managed later to repenetrate his entrails even more perilously in the fanciful guise of a liver tumor with mad-motherly designs on his pancreas. *Hey*, Borkman (unbeknownst to himself) wonders—*was it* me *who just had that thought?*

So, just so you know, Red, and all you other ladies, lovely and otherwise—it's a cunt's scathing intuition that's fueled The Bork's legendary (if the word up and down the Street is to be believed) virility and not (as you might have been led to think) the purposefully nice-guy obtuseness—aversion to nuance, analysis, super-self-consciousness—that every determined-to-be-comradely prick confuses with manliness. On the other hand—and nothing less than the California sun (of whose blandishments he feels somehow unworthy) has been required to make this perfectly clear—he allows himself (thereby overriding the veto of his mother's mean-spirited illusionlessness) to express nice-guy and hairy-chested decency, loving kindness, geniality, compassion, empathy, generosity, encouragement, commiseration, only (but at those times unstintingly and over the widest tactile spectrum) through his penis and nothing but. It's by having humbly taken his cue from the shapely, darkly handsome, infinitely distensible shaft and the thousand eyes of the exquisitely tactful tip that he never fails to concoct the mix of tenderness and ferocity appropriate to the occasion. *Penile tact*, they call it sneeringly in the *DSM*, not to mention the International Classification of Diseases. But why was there such a ruckus to get it ushered in, thereby pathologizing what, for so many men, is their sole redeeming characteristic? And why, in high contrast, is everything being done to sanitize that hag Envy by ensuring she flubs her lines and her ballet steps at every *DSM* audition? In the end, are all the strings being pulled by that Global Envy Lobby (GEL) whose overriding fear must surely be that a cure for the disease (the logical next step after accession to *DSM* citizenship) will mean the end of all cutthroat competition on the world stage, and hence of all progress.

But maybe he can leave all pathologies behind and make a fresh start—with Red. Surely, knowing as he now does that there will be very little to follow, such a start (false to its core) should be the easiest thing in the world to manage. Ah, yes, he can see it now through neither-fog-nor-cloud: She'll be hitched to an *ab ovo* Borkman shorn of vileness, and will watch enthralled as he, by masterminding the metastasis of Decency, Loving Kindness & Co. to his other organs, makes medical history and as a result of all the enthrallment and if things go according to plan she'll have no trouble seeing her way clear to mourning him as kindly, decent people are mourned (and may thereby, who knows, even exert something of a positive influence on the snotty bio hacks). Of course at first (and this, too, will be according to plan) his little mistress of a Thousand and One Nights (to be crammed, given his new timeline, into two or three or, at best, four) will understandably be full of resentment—at having to express sadness, officially, especially for somebody like him whose foul-smelling reputation preceded him wherever he went, even here in sandy Santa Barb. Which is fine and dandy inasmuch as, not long after, she'll find herself, with true gaminelike amazement, growing happy, even exultant, in direct proportion to the strength of that sadness, now welcome because unalloyed and unsolicited and getting stronger and stronger by the minute—and even more exultant after she will have managed, by scouring deep in the guts of memory, to dissipate any lurking suspicions that the loving acts of unmitigated decency were merely the inflationary ploys of a self-seeker. And once she'll have established to her satisfaction that he's exactly the milk-of-human-kindness kind of guy he professed himself to be—well, then, Red must undertake (if she's anything like him and how can she *not* be, having immediately returned his Gioconda smile?) the much harder though by no means insuperable task of weaning herself from the belief (which he, when confronted with authentic nobility entombed, has never been able to do) that such a guy perpetrated through his very being a crime against nature since, last she'd heard, it was still the same heady mix of lacerating phoniness and mincing cruelty.

Red has obviously read his thoughts (yet another side effect of invidious Invidicum) for here she is edging toward him: erect, she looks far younger, and even prettier. What will the pretext be for striking up a conversation? he wonders. But will he need one? Cantor can observe them at leisure for they aren't as far off as Borkman would like to think they are thanks, happily, to Eden who, on his haunches and refusing to budge, has fallen head over heels in love with his inspired portrayal of the Moody Male in Unrepose (he bears, come to think of it, no small resemblance to the Sistine's Nahshon), a performance delivered to a sold-out house of swooping gulls, lollipop palms, early-bird sunbathers, and other Method actors, some with Madness to spare. He relies most—but to very great effect, at least as far as Cantor, connoisseur of males, moody or otherwise but mostly moody (Berry being the great exception), is concerned—on that trusty old standby of vaudevillians, a pebble-pelting of the drink (which, imperturbable, deserves better). Seemingly mechanical only because it's the pebble-pelting that's doing the thinking for the two of them. But couldn't there be something the least bit calculated in this portrayal of the doomed outsider? As if consubstanial with the rebel (he of the shapely, not overly muscular thighs) is a horse of another color, the aspiring actor as unsulkily ruthless pragmatist who, whenever he feels a song of careerist desperation coming on, goes immediately into personal trainer mode in the hope that a scout with clout will zoom past in his Ferrari 599 GTB Fiorano and, liking what he sees, reward said rebel with the role of a lifetime. In short, how much of all this delectable moody maleness—delectable at least to Cantor, who till the bitter end will approach the foreign land of maleness only asymptotically—is spontaneous upsurge and how much the highly self-conscious imitation of other males, on screen and off? Impossible to determine. But Cantor *has* determined, and from early on: (*a*) that self-conscious imitation, being female, is a tactic to be repudiated by all self-respecting males whose self-respect is founded precisely on their ability to proclaim themselves—with the *straight*est of faces and Girard be hanged—expert beyond an Envy-driven need to imitate; and (*b*) that when a male who he's deemed unambiguously male because opaque to the femaleness entrenched within manages nevertheless to emit a sign thereof he gets (irrevocably? irreparably?) seduced. In other words, what turns him on is, in "authentic" males, the dialectical (yep, you heard me, bud: the *dialectical*) opposition (more like a perilously shaky truce) between male opaqueness and female talkathon transparency.

Cantor looks at his watch (which needs a new strap). They are due back for their inaugural dose at 3:30 but, first things first, which in his case is to start proving himself worthy of this purest cobalt of Santa Barbara noon, and what better time than the present and what better way than by snapping to gratefully martial attention? He waves at Eden who either does not see or doesn't want to (the pelt-pelt-pelting has gotten much more ostentatious, i.e., more truculent, i.e., more vengeful). Meanwhile, Borkman and the redhead are strolling off, entwined, in, appropriately, the direction of the city cemetery. And speaking of (loverly) entwinement, as well we should and no holds barred: for Cantor, it has always been, whether public or private, and whether with man, woman or beast, too much a stance—a tactic—of smug exclusion (targeting, in particular, solitaries, cripples and uglies), thereby rendering its adoption by any self-respecting man of the people a civic impossibility. Although maybe all this delicate attention to malfeasance is just plain fear— of the rabid Envy said stance could trigger among the excluded. But what would Pritchard have to say on the subject? Now that his credentials have been established to everybody's satisfaction (or have they?) as a bona fide flesh-and-blooder—and not just one more wraith conscripted by Voracicom's central casting to give docudramatic voice to its mock insights, for example, that participation in any clinical trial is just one long audition for an unspecifiable part in an unactable play, the kind (take it from somebody who's well versed in the matter) that's slated for off-off Broadway demolition—perhaps this is exactly the right moment for Cantor to approach him (didn't he insist that walk-ins were welcome?) on the matter of testing (as he's never been able to approach the others and not just because they're evidently heterosexual or think they are) to determine how he's been faring, with regard to mastering not just his own unmasterable Envy but, more importantly, his fear of the Envy of others.

CHAPTER TWENTY-EIGHT

When Cantor enters (the office, though huge, is surprisingly sunless) Pritchard is slumped over with his head in his hands. Not another murder—worse, a botched murder! Has Eden managed to get here first? "What is it?" he groans, without looking up. "I told you that I don't want lunch—now or ever." Cantor waits, suppressing *not so much the need to sneeze as the desire to have that need.* Or is this yet another example of—what was Herbert the very first to call it?— word- besting worldflow, and never the twain shall meet? "Oh, it's you" (still not looking up). "Mr. Cantor, if I'm not mistaken and I rarely am." He can see the cemetery from the big bay window to his right. Can that be Borkman and his child bride wandering Poe-like or rather straying Brontë-like among the gravestones? or just another dime-a-dozen overentwined pair intent on turn- ing the well-heeled stiffs snot-green with Envy at their obscene zest for wal- lowing anaerobically in all the glitzy filth the pre-afterlife has to offer? Have they stumbled yet, whoever they are, on Ronald Colman? Laurence Harvey? Suzy Parker? (Most unusually, devout name-dropper Cantor doesn't really care who or what they've stumbled on, being a mathematician at heart, but whoever's doing the thinking for him at this juncture is making no bones about very much caring.) "If you've come about getting a partial refund for all your side effects, might as well tell you I can't help. At least not now. I've just been on the phone with Margo Straynge for over an hour. True to form, she's been going around telling everybody from (*a*) Chris Christee and Charles Dursst (they're an item, if you must know) to (*b*) contrast-collar-crazy heart- throbs Mittch MClonnell, Lu Dobbs and "economist" Karry Ludlow (ditto) that it's that sonofabitch Pritchard who's responsible for hubby's death, even if he didn't actually pull the trigger. As if I ever coveted his position! As if I ever had the slightest desire to go back East, scene of my worst humiliations, professional and otherwise (even for a long weekend). That's what you get for taking the plight of other people more seriously than you take your own. That's what you get for taking their plight more seriously than they do them- selves. That's what I get for believing Margo (who like the rest of her kind is plighted to nothing but the *self*-deception she wants to practice on me as if it's *my* self-deception) had—has—a plight that demands urgent meddling when in fact all she craves is to shoot down my heartfelt interventions one by one. When I take Mrs. Straynge's plight seriously, what fills her with delight— *Russellian* delight (you're a mathematician, or so I'm told, so you know what I mean)—is the impossible-but-undeniable coexistence of (*a*) my gullibil- ity (since, on the one hand, the plight doesn't exist) and (*b*) my inadequacy (since, on the other, the plight does exist but is much too smart—and too hon- orable—not to feel compelled to stump my so-called expertise). I might—and will—go so far as to say that *if her plight does in fact exist, it's only in order to stump the expert.* (And I'm not just playing a game of wordflow versus world- flow here although I know of course it's garnering raves on Greenwich Ave.) So I'm the one, George (*George* never sounded so caressed as it does in the arms of Pritchard's cry from the heart), who ends up plighted. But, truthfully, long before I ever laid eyes on her I was plighted already—addicted to solving the sickness of others and getting them rehabilitated as fast as possible and without a hitch since I'm the sort of worm that feels unentitled to persist in his own being until he cures everybody else who, if left unattended, will surely (*a*) begrudge him what little hope of joy he extracts from the persisting and (*b*) far more virulently, envy him the persisting even in the ever-expanding absence of all hope and all joy.

"But maybe I deserve what I've gotten—or better yet, haven't gotten." (He still isn't looking up.) After all, it's the track record that counts. And colleagues far and wide will be only too happy to tell you mine's abysmal. But that's only because when it's a question of treating a patient for Envy—i.e., for the particular variant with which she presents—I tend to err on the side of overprotectiveness—of the disease not of the patient, although it's always and ultimately for the patient's own good. This means that I have a professional obligation to overcompensate for my bias toward the Talking Cure (which sometimes metastasizes into a conviction that it can do the work of the drug better than the drug itself) by severely constraining its efficacy even if I don't go to the extreme of practicing downright incompetence. The goal is to ensure symptom mitigation as effected by the Cure—and any tampering with the lucidity of the usual biomarkers (monitored half-hourly during this phrase of the trial)—is kept to a minimum so that when the time comes for administration of the first dose of Invidicum, the variant under attack is cleaving as closely as possible to its own pure state and by extension to the 100 percent pure state of what I—but nobody else—likes to call the NeoPlatonic Form of Envy. (Even if there's no such thing as purity where diseases are concerned: they're a perpetual deviation from an inherent deviance, as my friend Mike Pendulum pointed out to me up [or is it down?] in Berkeley years—no, decades—ago at the height of the AIDS pandemic no less.) So, while it is incumbent upon me to do my level best to make the therapeutic chitchatting and chatchitting as effective as possible within fixed limits, I must ensure that the talk doesn't poach on Invidicum's preserves. The job of the chitchat—structured according to an old family recipe—boils down to addressing the accidental—the serendipitous—symptoms stemming from the patient's age, diet, temperament, sexual proclivities, etc.—to talk them away—to put them in parentheses—to abstract them—rapidly—rapidly—before they can exert a disproportionate influence on decisions related not only to highly personalized drug dosage and composition but to the compounding process as well. *Compounding*, by the way, is a fancy term for—" Cantor feels very Edenesque—very *male*—as he dutifully retorts: "I know what *compounding* means." Cantor senses Pritchard (his head remains sloppily buried) isn't offended by the retort; in fact, his stagey sigh signals (masochistic?) pleasure. "And of course I must perpetrate the same bracketing—straitjacketing—abstraction—on my own idiosyncrasies. (For as Mike was also fond of saying, but in Golden Gate Park, not Berkeley: In the space of disease, not just patients but doctors as well must be neutralized.) In short, it's my job to see to it that the personalized version of the drug and the Envy variant it's targeting are the real McCoy even if ostensibly putting the drug and the disease before the patient (the key word here is *ostensibly*) routinely costs me my triple-A rating from private equity clientologists, who by the way (*a*) run this health care bunker and millions like it worldwide, (*b*) have junk bonds for brains and (*c*) order my victims to fill out, after every appointment whether kept or not, "a brief survey" regarding my *performance*.

"So what service do I in fact perform in the interval—some call it the No Man's Land—between diagnosis and dose-giving?—which can seem an eternity, and not just to my honorarium-crazy keynote-speaker pals with the obligatory Big Pharma private plane to catch. For starters, I throw myself, body and soul, into becoming the veritable curator of the above-mentioned variants, treating the patient not (as certain pastors do) as if he's been self-indulgently using Envy as a pretext for perpetrating anything ranging from a dinner table faux pas to mass murder but, on the contrary, as if he hasn't been sufficiently true to, respectful enough of, the sum of symptoms that is his organism's particular take on Envy—its particular contribution to America's Envy Songbook. In short, I don't do what my heart cries out for me to do which is to force the patient to confront his resistance to confronting his disease—i.e., the morbid symptoms that feed on the pathogenic Idea that is Envy like mycelia on wood chips and that proliferate around and through its underbelly like a school of tarantulas. I end up playing along with the resistance (plying a suggestive or additive as opposed to an analytic or subtractive technique) which serves the needs of my pill-pushing colleagues even if I thereby deprive myself of all insight into what the Guy from Golders Green calls the play of mental forces.[57] In short, I'm a handmaiden of the pill pushers when I should be their master. And the more I find myself loathing the whole lot as if they're one single multitentacled leech (present company excepted) simply because I refuse to admit how much I loathe my second-fiddle self, (*a*) the more I strive, hewing to a tailored approach, to bolster the image of each and every patient as, Envy notwithstanding, somehow Envy- and fancy-free and contentedly normal to a fault (this approach to priming for The Big Dose seems to work best) and to assure him that we all have our fair share of anathematizing rivals who at the drop of a hat will take it upon themselves to brand us invidiously (albeit not erroneously) as smug, meanspirited, tight-fisted, cruel, entrails-scouring impotents deserving of grand internment and (*b*) the more I, in so doing, egg him on to loftier and loftier feats of morbid self-inflation which make him more . . . legible hence more treatable. So now you know: I feed (and feed off) self-delusion—I praise resistance—because that's what keeps the Envy intact as a specimen." "You're what I'd call a Good Samaritan-at-heart," says Cantor, which gives him the right to ask (since he's sorely tempted)—and in fact he does now end up asking—whether Pritchard's trademark image-bolstering pep talk includes the image-*toppling* phrases (image toppling, at least according to Cantor's own yokeloid understanding) "Envy notwithstanding" and "albeit not erroneously" or are these just editorial asides whipped up for the benefit of his visitor?

Pritchard replies to the best of his ability. More importantly, his head is

---

[57] See Freud's early paper entitled "On psychotherapy" (1904).

517

finally off the table's chopping block (he looks his age, but gracefully). "And now I'm going to tell you something I've never told a soul." Cantor sighs: *Another Cicero too eloquent for his own good.* Pritchard explains how awed he is, willy-nilly, by every member of the Envy crowd (though his sheepishness rings a bit false)—by the members of any crowd of sickos—by any crowd, for that matter. He envies their . . . blind-eye comradeship. He, whose curse it is to see everything from every conceivable angle and has paid the price, is revolted by the fact that he's automatically awed by their cleavage—their hewing—to a single point of view on every issue (they know better than to dirty their hands in the wallows of nuance) even if they seem to be constantly disagreeing as much with themselves as with everybody else. (His predicament, then, is reducible to an epigram along the lines of, *Nothing is more intimidating than stupidity.*) He's not quite sure what those issues are but, you know something? his respect for this crowd would skyrocket if it turns out the issues *have nothing to do with Envy.* In any case, it's undeniable that through sheer tenacity they seem to have achieved the flawless fulfillment of an ethical imperative. On the other hand, when by some fluke they do manage, each in his own way and each in her own time, to let up on the cleaving—when and through no fault of their own they suddenly go easy on their my-way-or-the-highway brand of self-righteousness—(*Is there any other brand?* Cantor thinks.)— when, whaddya know! they are self-deviating enough to ooze a little elasticity of outlook—when unbeknownst to themselves they violate the pact of delusional self with delusional self for a millisecond or two—well, then, as far as he, Pritchard, is concerned these are occasions not for hope or delight but for sweltering rage. Doesn't Cantor—now semi-officially his protégé (congratulations, George! richly deserved!)—see that Pritchard's cursed by virtue of the fact that he carries within himself (can't help being a fixer—question of temperament: born that way) the seeds of every form of anticipatory self-ablation needed to tactfully caulk whatever holes may be revealed in the fabric of their hobgoblin consistency? And for the last seventy-two years he's been driving that self-ablation to whatever extremes may be necessary to honor and conserve, for eventual therapeutic dismantlement, the wall-eyed weltanschauung of all the arrogant assholes who've happened to cross his path and sully it with their unseeing. So when they suddenly dare to flaunt a whimsical self-contradiction which may or may not know it's contradictory—right after he's been making every effort to incarnate the ideal listener, who knows just what to say and when not to say it so as to avoid triggering a collapse of the system whose armature is but an illusory coherence—he's ready to kill. "Yes, I can't help perceiving them not as cripples but as the elements of a coherent . . . system whose classical perfection must be maintained at all costs and not just for psychopharmacological purposes *but because I need something to believe in* (being a knot of unwelcome contradictions, I can only Envy them that all-set-for-life coherence, however illusory). But if I can sink so low as to Envy the enviers then I'm the biggest Envy cripple of them all. Thing is, I've been telling myself all along that since I am the only qualified administrator, on the West Coast, of the drug and adjuvant therapy designed to do It in, I hold proprietary rights over Envy and can therefore decide to put my own property on the market, so to speak, only when I'm good and ready. So, as you must have already deduced, I pamper the cripples not from doctorish solicitude but from fear—fear that I might ultimately lose control and tear off the masks and that once they start (inevitably) retaliating, my rage, rapidly assuming mammoth proportions, will be satisfied with nothing less than their annihilation. (Nothing—do you hear, nothing!—in my entire life experience has disgusted me more than watching them squirm the few times I threatened to únselve, with strokes of havoc latent in a mere rolling of my eyes, their system's precious [mostly poplar] furniture.)

"But my colleague, Dr. Hank James aka The Guy from Rye (too bad he and Pendulum never met: their similarities would have outweighed their penny ante differences)—who's sure to outlive me—who's got to outlive me—who must draw his breath in pain to tell my story (unless you, Dr. Cantor, would like to do the honors)—my colleague Dr. Hank has expressed all this far better and far more courageously and far more succinctly than I (and without my signature bile), even if he left out a few essential details. Up on the podium at one of the many crank congresses we attended together, this one in Sochi (far from the *paradise enow* it was cracked up to be by Arshile Gorky and Vlad McPutin's Olympics-plugging thugs), thoroughly holistic Hank deprecated (even in his role of professional caregiver) what he called 'a greater feeling for people's potential propriety or felicity or full expression than they seemed able to have themselves' as nothing more than a 'wasteful habit or trick'.[58] So much for Hank, The Guy from Wry. He will be missed—even if he's still very much among us."

Here we go again, Cantor thinks: another one of those ventriloquist's dummies from central casting sent in to spout the company line just when I expected to be dealing at long last with a real . . . character. But this is unfair since Cantor considers Pritchard very much a character—worse, a role model (ugh! awful term!). A hero, in fact and of the purest kind—after all, it took guts to admit what he's just admitted to. A hero because he obviously knew everything there is to know and seen everything there is to see from the very outset and because he also knew his precious ideas would never stoop to reformulation under the influence of experience. Pritchard is expert beyond the expertise that experience is supposed to confer on the lucky ones. Rightly yet at the same time wrongly on the defensive, Pritchard the thought-reader says: "Don't you think I'd like to be able to carry on a normal conversation—about the Yankees, say—as much as the next guy? Or, better yet, the NFL concussions committee, devoted unstintingly to the well-being of its marquee players, as evidenced, e.g., by peer-reviewed articles riddled with omissions and tainted analyses, and its pooling of lobbyists and lawyers with the tobacco industry. Fact is, I myself chose (don't blame central casting) to chain myself to *ideas* (though *thought packets*[59] is less vulgar) and having done so I know it's all

---

[58] Henry James, *Notes of a Son and Brother* (New York, Charles Scribner's Sons, 1914), p. 39.

[59] To suffer hearing the person whom he, Cantor, considers (granted on the flimsiest

my fault that the story—our story—The Invidicum Story—is forever deviating—like a disease—from the true course of its deviancy. But inasmuch as I'm a hero—as you just said, or rather as you must think—and the duty of a hero is both to be sidetracked over and over and over again (a little like—to take the most exalted example—the Eddie O'Brien character in *D.O.A.*) and to have his mind handcuffed (a lot like the protagonist—played by DeForrest Kelley—of *Fear in the Night*) I tell myself I may be doing everybody a favor in the end. After all, even my worst enemies have to admit that I invent my best discoveries in the packet department when thought is compelled to fight against thought, like Polyneices against—no, not Eteocles—but . . . Polyneices himself! When, borrowing Clytemnestra's nets of fury, thought 'standing-ovations' entanglement in the trap it's set for itself. But getting back to those silly old side effects— Have a seat." Cantor remains standing and moving closer to the door—goes so far as to put his hand on the knob, though without feeling the least urge to escape. In fact, he's beginning to find Pritchard appealing (you can't be exposed to this cagey sort of *de profundis* and expect to remain non-partisan). "When required to engage with some patient in a give-and-take, I prove helpless and happy to remain so. After all, don't you think there's something so dull—and so terrifyingly ID theft-ish—about dialogue, even in the clinical arena where I'm supposedly calling all the shots? So at the first opportunity—even if there isn't one for miles around—I attempt to populate the arena's void by dragooning a packet or two yet the minute they're in I can't wait for them to be *out* for, whaddya know? the little buggers have become an immediate obstruction to what, thanks to their infringement, is a void no more.

"But just because the master sorcerer—yes the _m_aster sorcerer (unlike you and all the others I refuse to upper-case his loony pretensions) that's supposed to be running our particular roadshow—yes, I've heard all about him through the grapevine or maybe I myself got the rumor going—keeps insisting (mainly, I suspect, in order to convince the greatest sceptic of them all: Himself)—that he's an artist with a Unifying Vision (something to do, if I'm not mistaken, with Envy as the Greatest Show on Planetesimal Pharma)—just because the master protests too much doesn't mean I can't fly (off the handle) now and then to said Vision's outmost periphery and toy uncensored with what knuckleheads treat as irrelevancies but could very well turn out to be the epicenter of the main design." (Cantor secretly wonders whether this is in fact an accurate depiction of the Master, i.e., whether Pritchard and the Master aren't in fact birds of a feather or, like the bad girls in Fritz Lang's *The Big Heat*, sisters under the mink.) Just as the Dickensian troubles troubling the severed head of Charles the First were always getting into Mr. Dick's Memorial so do things equally morbid (like Lévi-Strauss's take on sorcerers

---

of pretexts) to be the last bastion of sanity in a world gone mad use the very term he chillingly associates with mass zombification yields one indisputable fringe benefit: audition-free transformation of the sufferer into the black-and-white hero of Don Siegel's *Invasion of the Body Snatchers*.

and their magic, and J.-P. Vernant's on what it meant to be an artisan among the ancients, not to mention Stephen Toulmin's debunking of the myth of temperatures lower than Absolute Zero roaming around like Dante's damned in impenetrable thermal depths[60]) wend their wicked wicked yet surprisingly weary way into Pritchard's mentation. "Why, sometimes things get so wobbly on the therapeutic tightrope that I become convinced no patient can expect to be cured—or at least curettaged—if I don't succeed tout de suite in compelling *some* extrinsic insight of, say, old Lévi's (doesn't matter which) to fit his plight like a glove. Otherwise, the patient's plight and the patient along with it—will remain invisible. And by the same token, an insight, *for its part*, will have no life of its own (and it has as much of a right to life as any one of my patients), will remain out of focus—illegible (at least as far as the limitations of my own understanding are concerned)—*incurable*—will have been born to blush unseen and waste its rankness on the desert air—any insight I decide to take under my wing will have no life of its own until it *does* fit the plight of the patient to which it's been assigned or makes a pretense of fitting it—will have no life until it sacrifices itself to the impossibility of fitting it—until it lays bare the unbridgeable gap between itself and what it's supposed to fit like a glove— will have no life of its own until it's been exalted (contorted, many would say) into a cannibalizing metaphor—a bite-sized allegory of the plight in question—but an allegory that doesn't quite fit—that's a little bit *off*—and being a little bit off forces me to look *awry* at what I've been gazing upon *rightly* but—or rather, *and therefore*—to little purpose." He offers up as an example (whether good or bad, Cantor will never be able to decide even on his death bed) the insight garnered from the account of a trial that unfolded among the Zuni people of New Mexico[61] where a young man charged with witchcraft was summarily handed over to its priestly court. Wily and desperate, he ultimately confessed and through his confession validated the tribe's magic as a real live enabler of evil and transformed himself into something much better than your run-of-the-mill—friendly neighborhood—garden variety—evil- doer, namely, the champion and protector of witchcraft as a coherent system and the community's only conceivable alternative to chaos. The guiltier he made himself out to be, the more spiritualized the system became. He gave the elders what smelled like truth and they returned the favor by giving him back his life. But in the course of fabricating the lies demanded by imposture—a fabrication imposed on him by the imperative of self-survival hence imposed *from without*—he found that he actually liked (even convinced himself, some- what operatically, that he was born to perform) the labor of manipulating

---

[60] Reader, beware! When you hear the term Absolute Zero, hop to it and think—raven- ously, indispensably, gratefully, transformationally—Stephen Toulmin, *The Philosophy of Science: An Introduction* (New York, Harper & Row, 1960), chap. IV, "Theories and Maps" (especially sects. 4.6 and 4.5).

[61] See Claude Lévi-Strauss, "The sorcerer and his magic." in *Structural Anthropology*, Claire Jacobson and Brooke Grundfest Schoepf, translators (Garden City, New York, Anchor Books, 1967), part three, chap. IX.

the raw materials (real and imagined)—including medicinal roots, wall plaster, cactus needles, a cat and a plume—which fed the fabrication. Such labor emerged *from within*, deep within, at the behest of an unsuspected infatuation with building blocks. The sweat of labor was true—even if it was the labor of constructing a lie—a system of lies. In short, his vocation as a sorcerer *found* him at long last and not a minute too soon. But don't worry, I know what you're going to say and you're absolutely right." Cantor suspects that his dutiful stab at the self-negating deadpan this transferential presumption demands would do honor to the most orthodox Freudian (if any are left). But he owes Pritchard something beyond mimed tact. He needs to show that he cares enough to harbor certain reservations regarding what sounds like a rehab strategy gone stark raving mad. "How does the Zuni's plight apply to the plight of any of your patients?" "What you meant to say was, How can it be *made* to apply to the plight of any of my patients?

"But what you really meant to say was something along the lines of, Why force (à la Rabelais and his not-so-innumerable progeny) all sorts of unwieldiness into my big fat bing-cherry cheesecake of a casebook on Envy, when the *diagnosis, dissection, demystification and destruction* of the need to incorporate such hokum would be the gutsier—and more original—tack by far? But you just don't understand. I'm not trying to be fashionable. My Envy insights—my Envy packets (the packeteer's pre-eminence notwithstanding)—will be untranslatable into viable therapeutic options without proof of sponsorship by at least a few of the biggest names—the biggest *headliners*—in the business." *What business?* Cantor wonders, but not coyly. "Which sponsorship would of course be contingent on proof of the compatibility—or rather, the fruitful incompatibility—of my packets—my insights—my Dead End Kids—with theirs. Thing is, I don't have the luxury of waiting around for compatibility or incompatibility to rear its ugly head—the luxury of waiting for the Kids to cultivate, thirteen cosmic cycles from now (make that, in honor of Gershon Scholem, thirteen *shemittahs* from now) and on their own gonadal steam, a yen to engineer and participate in a veritable interpenetration of identities (i.e., interpenetration of their own identities with the identities of insights begotten by the likes of heavyweights on the order of, say, Lévi-Strauss or Louis B. Mayer or Toulmin or Vernant or Burch or T. Dantzig or Sam Spade or Sam Snead or Sam Eilenberg or Scholem or Rodin's nephew Leo Steinberg), which would signal nothing less than the birth not just of a new but of the very purest kind of packet: one whose emergence was for once not contingent on the messy collision of some wannabe packeteer's consciousness with something *outside* it, against which a packet is normally the only defense. As you can see, such a project's hopeless in the here and now—in *my* here and now. Because as a businessman, as an operator, as a schmoozer, as a collector of bigwig testimonials, I myself am hopeless—*I myself am Hell.*" Cantor thinks (as the equivalent of throwing up his hands), *Milton! thou shouldst be living at this hour!* although as a mere dabbler in the leavings of Great Writers he's aware the citation should have been Melanctha Herbert's to think. "And that's why I . . . decided—the minute we met—that you, Mr. Cantor, must be my successor. (Like poor Ponzi-ish Borkman, I'm not long for this world. And I can only wonder—you do a lot of wondering when you've been at death's door as long—or as many times—as I have—if it's Putin and his cronies who've put the finishing touches on the nails in his coffin since, as you must already know, Borkman once owned 33 percent of Gazprom.)[62] I'm convinced that you and you alone can put what will one day be referred to in the literature as the Cherry Cheesecake Factor out of its—and everybody else's—misery." *What literature?* Cantor wonders, this time coyly. And asks, almost simultaneously, "How do you know he's not . . . long for this world?," but immediately regrets focusing on absent Borkman instead of very-much-present Pritchard—immediately regrets complying with that overinvoked law of life according to which (as pointed out so ably by Jean Rhys during what's sure one day to be referred to *in the literature* as her Amygdala period) it's always the absent one who must get all the attention, all the reverence, all the pity. "I intercepted the FedExed packet bearing the news (by the way, he owns only 10 percent of that company: my mistake; and also by the way, the bad news may turn out to be either a false alarm or a kind of blessing in disguise)." Something comes over Cantor just before, or just after, opening the door and that *something* compels him to fire—or, better yet, aim or launch—a Parthian shot at or against Pritchard or himself (*sorry I can't be more specific*). "Haven't you forgotten to ask the most important question of all?" (Cantor doesn't know if it's the thrill of humility or impotence or . . . a belief in his talents so unshakable that the only thing he can do with it is dare his patron to go ahead and just try and shake it.) Pritchard's impish chuckle is meant to mean, *Go ahead: I'm all ears.* But unable to stand the suspense a second longer, he takes the words right out of Cantor's mouth. "You mean, *Are you qualified?*" But just as MSNBC journalists are wont to preface or postface their ostensibly stunning revelations about the day's usual doings atop the dungheap of Capitol Hill with the supposedly sobering reminder that "in a normal Administration— but this isn't a normal Administration," so Pritchard feels duty bound to warn Cantor that this isn't a normal Organization hence the rules of the road don't apply and it is therefore to be expected that *wordflow will almost always trump worldflow.* And, now that you mention it, Pritchard does suddenly feel as if he just contracted some kind of bug for how else account for the woozy sensation that whatever he currently happens to be experiencing in thought or speech or action is what he's been wired to experience? And just as suddenly, his term *master sorcerer* is no longer just a curmudgeon's flight of fancy but an awestruck euphemism, cooked up by a true believer *malgré lui*, for *Master Programmer* writ large. "Whaddya say we think of me as just some poor man's version of dev'lishly handsome Mitch McConnell and you as the last of his lavishly unqualified protégés to get confirmed to the US Court of Appeals for the DC Circuit? And let's also pretend, while we're at it, there's no love-that-dares-not-speak-its-name angle to mitigate the monstrousness of the coup."

Shearer holds her breath. She is about to knock but—thanks to the instinct that served her superlatively in the *Agon* pas de deux and *Bugaku* and

---

[62] The parenthesized passage should have been read in an unhinged stage-whisper.

as the dance hall hostess in the *Western Symphony* adagio—stops herself in the nick of time. She resists listening between the lines, but listen she ultimately does, understanding more than she thinks inasmuch as what's being enacted behind closed doors is nothing less than the rite of passage known as Passing the Audition about which she knows a thing or two (as in so many other cases, the contrast here between Before and After is almost too diagrammatic). "In any case, I've had the chance to observe you on several occasions—wading into the surf, for example—and I'm convinced you're the man not only for the job but, much more importantly, for the superabundant perks that go with it. And don't worry about not having what my so-called colleagues consider, oh so self-congratulatorily, to be the relevant qualifications: math-wizardry will stand you in far better stead here than any downloaded medical degree. (By some fluke [not worth de-boning] I'm overly familiar with your unpublished [because unpublishable] treatise-length anatomization of aberrancy through the so-called diagonal process [as "invented" by your namesake] and 21-gun salute its audacity.) Which reminds me: are you by any chance—?" "Nope, no relation." "Just as well. What struck me initially was your *lack* of qualifications since, as everybody (and not just my friend John—er, Jack—Ruskin) knows, 'the finer the nature, the more flaws it will show through the clearness of it.'[63] And though you try to pass yourself off as a mathematician I'm happy to see—and say—that you don't prize 'smooth minuteness over shattered majesty' (I guess that's what drew you to Martin) and—what is even rarer—you recognize that 'the demand for perfection is always a sign of a misunderstanding of the ends of art'—and of math, too, I guess, not to mention of life itself—living being all about knowing how to withdraw from the perfection trap at the right moment. Of course, there's bound to be some pretense of opposition at first. But what's a maverick, I ask you, without a horde of (pint-sized) detractors? You'll make a perfect Demiurge. Plato (P the cosmologist not P the pharmakonologist) would have been awfully proud. Maybe even tickled pink." To justify his exemption from exercising any say in the matter—so that if things go wrong he won't have only himself to blame—Cantor must demand (his favorite makeshift) that not magic but mythology come swiftly to his rescue (as so many times before) now that he finds himself imperilled by good fortune and set itself the task of, this time around, doing a number on Pritchard, i.e., transforming Pritchard the man into Pritchard the archaic god—the Greekest of archaic gods, that is to say, not a person but a power with its own modi operandi, not an ontological entity with a Social Security number to prove it but a node in a network of relationships, not an individual but a forcefield and not just any old forcefield but a forcefield that can be (*a*) a single entity or (*b*) a multiplicity, either finite or infinite, of powers distinguishable or indistinguishable among themselves (like a whole slew of cultic Zeuses which have a knack of always remaining Zeus and nothing but the Zeus) or that can shift over from (*a*) to (*b*) in the

---

[63]See John Ruskin, "The Nature of Gothic" (excerpt), *Unto this Last and Other Writings*, Clive Wilmer, ed. (London, Penguin Books, 1987).

course of a single invocation.[64]

Done. Mission accomplished. And in record time. While Cantor knows he's in good hands with the new, improved Pritchard, he can't help wondering why the interview had to come to a close with this wishful thinking about his benefactor's transformation into a god. Why did the Master feel naked without the annexation of such a packet—and a *welterweight* to boot? Why does the story line seem never to be enough for Him? How *gratuitous* was the packet's recruitment? Would any other have done as well? And yet out of all the excrescences—extrinsics—Souls that stand create, the Master elected One—this One—so it mustn't be all that gratuitous—extrinsic—alien—to the main design. Did He (*a*) smell out a kinship between the story event and the packet or—as a select member of Dr. Johnson's "metaphysical race"—(*b*) simply decree and impose *a sort of* kinship and is this mess therefore just another case of [t]he most heterogeneous ideas [being] yoked by violence together"?[65] Did the packet *emerge* out of the story event (interview) and if it did so was the emergence organic—plausible—inevitable? Did one cry out for the other—event for packet and (returning the favor) packet for event? But why the emphasis on the godhead's concurrent singleness and multiplicity or was that just an unexcisable artifact of classical scholarship which happened to appeal to the Master's greedy love of paradox as a strategy for warding off castration at the hands of the hangman known as "or" and thereby maintaining the illusion that the universe, and all its contrarieties, are ingestible? Or was it a question of simply striking while the iron was hot, i.e., doing the yoking, violent or otherwise, before the next guy did it and got paid more handsomely for his occult transgression? Or does it all boil down to the Master's soft spot for old wives' warmed over psychobabble, in this case about *The Fear of Success* (Cantor's) whose allayment required that Pritchard the Benefactor be implored to upgrade his job description to include "prosthetic god capable of both conferring promotions and fending off whatever packs of bloodthirsty enviers are bent on dismembering the conferee"?

Cantor is positively giddy as he leaves Pritchard's office—too giddy to wonder what Shearer of all people is doing here (she can wonder the same about him) and, more to the point, why she's so stationed as to make it the easiest thing in the world to bump into her, which in fact he does, effortlessly—even (if he does say so himself) balletically. For a split second, he goes all woozy-heterosexual inside—maybe it's because she must be at least fifteen years older. In backing away to escape his gaze (more lustful than he intended), she succumbs to the serenely excruciated squint peculiar to all ballerinas (over which his fruitier friends, fresh from this or that NYCB or ABT gala, never tire of waxing ecstatic) who, to avoid collapsing under the dizzying weight of

---

[64]On the pretty thorny issue of personal identity as it relates to divine power, see Jean-Pierre Vernant, "Some aspects of personal identity in Greek religion," in *Myth and Thought among the Greeks*, Janet Lloyd with Jeff Fort, translators (Brooklyn; Zone Books; 2006).

[65]See Johnson's Life of Cowley, in *Lives of the Most Eminent English Poets*.

their false eyelashes, must spot on the middle seat of the very last row of the first ring, for there resides the sole spectator capable (and who always looks not a little like transfixing Anton Walbrook in the *Red Shoes* Mercury Theater scene) of keeping them defiantly on their toes. He will have to walk all the way back to the Synapse (the last Cabrillo Blvd shuttle has already come and gone). Yet isn't this as good a time as any to "convert obstacle into opportunity," by putting the exhilaration generated willy-nilly by Pritchard's anointment to the test—the question in question being, Is it propulsive enough to land him back at the hotel so he can get himself ready, in record time, for the Great Migration (assuming he doesn't have to clean up after Eden as well)? Then Cantor remembers that he and Eden moved out of the Synapse Arms not so very long ago. But, after all, doesn't forgetting—or better yet, seeming to forget—that the Migration occurred make it somehow more real—less calculated—more worthy of being remembered? Maybe. So maybe it's the Master after all—the Master as Demiurge—who's through Cantor converting O into O by presciently shoring (*a*) what are in fact the most precious albeit/because the most maligned *fragments* of storytelling (namely, those that reflect—that reveal—its dogged inability to get the facts straight—its screwball *amnesia*) against (*b*) His monumental presciently disavowed literary *ruins* (a trail mix of slick ineptitudes with, contrary to populist-elitist wisdom, not a whit of redeeming literary importance but chock-full of Hollywood-style "self-betrayal"). (Cantor suspects that for the likes of the Master, conversion of O to O as a way to Dress for Success works only in the domain of His telling but as the Master's life *is* the telling and nothing but the telling, He's in far better shape than billions of others—Cantor included. In short, His plight fits Him like a glove.) And on a lighter note, the only fly in the ointment so far appears to be Pritchard's having referred to him as a Demiurge. Sounds too much like Demagogue though, as he seems to remembers, Plato didn't mean it that way. Well, at least Pritchard didn't refer to him as a Nurse of Becoming though he's the last person in the world who should be throwing millstones in *that* direction.

But, more importantly, what's all this about *obstacle into opportunity*? Cantor thought he'd ditched the wretched phrase forever immediately after severing all ties with its inventor, who achieved the medium-rare distinction of being, hands down, the most shameless of all the SS (shameless shamans) addict-intent on curing Dare-Not-Speak-Its-Nameness. You see, one sultry summer night, OIO greeted him stark naked at the door of his office, doubling as home away from home, and clearly with something other than rehab on his mind. Though, as it turned out, this was meant to usher in a very special stab at rehab—the kind that dares not speak *its* name. However, when he terminated "treatment" inevitably and soon after, oddly enough it was not owing to OIO's stark stab (tactfully rejected) but rather because, as Cantor tried to take his own stab at responding to its unorthodoxy (for wasn't this his right and duty as a patient?), OIO fell (even more unorthodoxically) asleep and then (most unorthodox of all albeit avant-gardish to the bitter end) denied having done so. But sleep and stab notwithstanding, shouldn't somebody like him, just mandated to carry on the Pritchard Tradition, whatever that might end up consisting in, be acquainting himself with the widest possible range of clinical interventions, even—or especially—the screwiest? Nay—yea, *Nay* (to be sung to the tune of "Archaism, the Gem of the Ocean!")—shouldn't he be heaping fresh incense on the irreparable altar of OIO's incompetence, not denouncing it?

Fact is, whether propelled by good fortune's hot air or not, Cantor needs to pack up . . . er, get back to the apartment he shares with Eden—as quickly as possible.

That he feels himself actually buying into the idea that he was all along reserved for and is racing on to bigger and better things—bigger and better than anything the Synapse had to offer makes him want to laugh. In fact he's tempted to let laughter have its way completely but (fearing the foolish rushing in of its better half, hysterical self-mockery) refrains. But given that he's in the world (as thought is in language)—though not by any means a man *of* the world—he has no choice but to act as the world deems necessary if he is to see it (whatever *it* is) through—which means, first and foremost, getting back home. Still, the temptation of returning to the Synapse is overpowering, though he isn't sure precisely—or even imprecisely—why (never realizing until this minute that the Synapse could be such a hard—such an impossible—act to follow even if nothing of any consequence happened there). Only a thought can tell him why and once again, *he has no choice but:* If he wants his thought—wants to gnaw on the bristly bone of his thought—wants to have his thought and eat it, too—he must dive tout de suite into the lukewarm bath of Language and accept unconditionally the terms of the immersion, under which words, Its henchmen, agree to respond, by intermingling, to what to them is nothing more than a brute stimulus—the brute stimulus of his temptation. But unlike so many other deep thinkers, Cantor has no trouble accepting the fact that his thoughts are obviously nothing more than floaters in Language's jaundiced eye and would never in a million years stoop to claiming that the end product of said intermingling represented a flagrant mistranslation. He will be grateful if there *is* an end product. Humbly aware that Language, as the only cure for the indisposition of thought—the indisposition that *is* thought—has the best intentions in the world, he awaits with unabated eagerness (not sure if he's moving toward or away from the hotel), as so many times before, the vast improvement It is sure to perpetrate on what was non-existent before the perpetration. His thought will, if he's lucky, be born through the words' intermingling. And don't ever imagine this thought waiting to be born is a thing—a clothes horse—all too ready and willing to be expressed in words—fitted for a suit made out of words. His thought isn't already there, ready to don words as a ready-made garment.[66] What it is, his thought, is a process looking to find reality, form, existence, in words, *as* words. As the man said, the thought isn't already there. It's not a picture so the expression of the thought won't be a description of the picture (Wittgenstein).

---

[66]See Lev Vygotsky, *Thought and Language* (Cambridge, Massachusetts, The MIT Press, 1986), chap. 7.

And it's not a feeling so don't hold your breath, Cantor, waiting for intermingling wordflow to give vent to the feeling as a sigh gives vent to grief. Nor is it the expression of a private language, which is to be translated into that of an accessible one. And it sure as hell isn't an idea already before his mind's eye—so that what's to be expressed in words is already expressed but in a different language and so what needs to be done is translate from the mental to the verbal.

This is what Language, as primly gruff as an Oxford don, comes up with: He wants to return to the Synapse to prove that although the glorious days spent there are irrecoverable, the site of those glories is very much retrievable. But as proof of what? (*is this part of the thought or its confutation?*). In any case, the thought was well worth the wait, especially by somebody with heaps of time on his hands. Since—and don't let anybody tell you different—it's a good thought, a level-headed thought, and (notwithstanding the mock abstractness) a down-to-earth thought of the first water. The kind of thought a *Cambridge* don would give his right arm to wield in demonstration of the fact that atomic propositions are deadwood.

From the rooftop sundeck Shearer watches him depart, disquieted by his ability to move quickly while getting nowhere fast, which disquiet has segued seamlessly into longing for a continuation of the attention lavished on the whole lot of them day and night by the staff at the Del. Although the longing could very well be for the otherworldliness evidenced by her total unawareness of that attention (guest-financed fawning), otherworldliness being equipment more basic to a ballerina than the austere bun, flag of her vocation. But whatever the longing is for, she longs to cradle it like a bowl of slightly bruised fruit in her no-longer-willowy arms. But why, Shearer wonders, does she experience longing when she knows herself—needs to know herself—to be heartily immune to the bug or the drug or whatever it is? Very fishy. Herbert, on the other hand, what with her dead son and a probable trunkload of bittersweets, is far better suited to the thankless role of teary flashbacker (Nostalgina O'Jones, to you). Come to think of it, ever since the Del she's been troubled by thoughts vivid as feelings and feelings as lucid as thoughts that are completely incompatible with what she takes to be her True Nature. But does that necessarily mean they are being foisted off on her by the sort of Demagogue Herbert rants and raves about every chance she gets, albeit sotto voce?—foisted off by some great big Mulligan Steward whose business is to ladle them out? Absolutely not. (*Oh, why, and after all this time, am I still unable, Moira wonders, to cut the blushing schoolgirl act and come right out and refer to Mulligan by his official title—Master. Why must my every allusion to Him, aka Melanctha's aptest if most refractory pupil and the principal donor to her expertise-building campaign, turn into an invocation of their embattled fusion?*) Of course, being a ballerina, she wouldn't have conveyed her wonderment quite this way but, ballerina or not, this is how she's been ordered—programmed—wired—to convey it. She puts the blame for these side effects squarely on the shoulders of Invidicum, as denatured, perhaps, by the California sun. Just for argument's sake, though, let's say that having taken a shine to her, Mr. Stewmaker—according to Herbert, the Teller of their sad tale (as a budding writer she sees tellers everywhere)—sensed immediately there was nothing she desired more desperately than, qua artiste, to stretch the boundaries of said True Nature to the point where True becomes Anti-True and therefore out of opportunistic pity decided to take the bull by the horns and choreograph on her an "applause machine" worthy of Mr. B., namely, *Ever Since the Del*, set to a suite of jitterbugs lusciously neoclassicized by Prince Igor. And so what if he's at the same time—or merely—exploiting her to help cut short his master-chef love affair with haute abstraction—to *rectify* a love that only gets in the way of the telling—to help him overcome a dastardly resistance to old-fashioned but never-out-of-fashion character-building? Or maybe he isn't in the least interested in anybody's self-enhancement (the realization comes to her as quick- and unexpectedly as the realization in the old days that it was time for the Sleepwalker to make her entrance—the most magnificent entrance in all of ballet, if she does say so herself—but, don't worry, she can handle it just as she could always handle, waiting in the wings, the shock of sensing in every muscle that the showstopping moment was upon her—and upon every lucky spectator bearing witness) but only in the exploitation of that unholy dialectics whereby thoughts duly thrust against the beings with whom they are incompatible and the beings duly counter-thrust, so little do they relish the prospect of serving as the vectors of those thoughts. Which thrusts and counter-thrusts are of course to be applauded as the true characters of the drama, with a right, therefore (unlike thoughts and beings), to a life of their own.

Shearer's brain has never before functioned at so high a level of abstraction even if once upon a time, her dancing body was semi-divinely up to the challenge night after night after grueling night. What if she's now permanently on loan (good approximation of panic at the thought)—like a van Eyck triptych—to Herbert's Demagogue, which will entail thinking what He thinks she should think when He thinks she should think it (i.e., to dazzling effect at the least plausible—the least *compatible*—moment)? She tries to calm down, assures herself that it's the Invidicum talking. Noting that in fact she hasn't shrieked out the panic, Shearer congratulates herself heartily (some might say too heartily) for exhibiting in a time of crisis, and at a moment's notice no less, what amounts to a genius for refraining. And what, when you get right down to it, is genius after all but *a perfectly timed recoil from the response to any stimulus that is most appropriate to one's nature*? Did she just think this or is it being thought through her as, in the Christiesque sense, least likely psychotic subject? It doesn't matter who thought it. What matters is that she's no longer afraid. For it became clear as she made ready to execute her refraining act that the Demagogue, a Rodin in his own field (yet to be identified), is much more straitjacketed by his thoughts—his giblets—his *abattis*—than is anybody up whose ass he is compelled to try to shove them. And, what is far more important, his affliction as perceived has managed to stir up (for why, exactly, see directly below) old, tender sentiments for something, for . . . somebody else, for . . . for . . . of course—Akim! *her* Akim! who insisted over and over during their brief affair that if he could have been the Poet in her inaugural *Sonnambula* (3 January 1967) or Co-Sanguinic in her last *Four*

Temperaments (Saratoga Springs, 2 July 1973), he'd have died not just happy but *monumentally* happy—better yet, immortalized. From the very beginning he knew they were birds of a feather because they both knew life—and *a fortiori* ballet—is all about *support* or the lack thereof and about nothing else—in particular all about asking for support when you least need it—not asking when you most need it—having it offered and rejecting it brutally—and (on the rarest of occasions) having it offered when you least need it yet being so touched by the offer as to end up accepting it graciously—so touched as to end up needing the support as never before—so touched as to end up learning—ravenously—to love needing it.

Sometimes, after the preliminaries, barely post-adolescent Akim (in homage to *Prufrock*, his peach-comely buttocks were in the light of the halogen lamp downed with light brown hair!) happened to find his gangly self on the right side of the bed, which was very much the *wrong* side as far as maximizing the impact of his right forefinger's meticulous rotation around her glans clitoridis was concerned. (How, in farewell-kissing its post-orgasmic remains, had he—with his three and a half months of med school down the drain—routinely referred to said glans? Ah, yes, as, hands down, the most vulnerable shred of living tissue in the universe and, once inflamed, the most impregnable—as nothing less, if she must know, than that Cosmic Mountain scaled by sunny Siberia's Tatar shamans and here conveniently shrunken to a flammable pinpoint!)

Though wrong-sided, he couldn't move—must play the hand, henceforth sacred, that fate had dealt him. As he explained more than once, shifting would have been a violation of any great draftsman's aesthetic: proof of inspirational impoverishment—of the inability to respect the rules of the paper plane wherein his body cum stylus was, like it or not, now securely fixed (surely she must remember (*a*) what in this regard Arlene Croce said about the "Gymnopédies" section of Frederick Ashton's *Monotones*, not to mention (*b*) the termite ravings of Akim's pal Manny Dyer.[67] Didn't she get it? He needed to stay put, sort of like the parallel plates of a condenser, in order to accumulate enough static energy to reduce that Mountain of hers to molten smithereens. (But when, to buttress his point, he invoked a country priest named Bazin

---

[67] Dance critic Croce compares the continuity of Ashton's choreographic line to "that of a master draftsman whose pen never leaves the paper" (see "How to be very, very popular," in *Afterimages* [New York, Alfred A. Knopf, 1977], p. 83). *Monotones*, then, is clearly an example of termite art, which Manny Farber (inventor of the term) associates with, e.g., Cézanne's "fascination with minute interactions" and characterizes (specifically with respect to the movie medium) as "buglike immersion in a small area without point or aim and, over all, concentration on nailing down one moment without glamorizing it, but forgetting this accomplishment [and hoping the audience will, too (this bracketed intrusion is mine)] as soon as it has passed" (see "White Elephant Art vs. Termite Art," in *Negative Space: Manny Farber on the Movies* [London, Studio Vista Limited, 1971], pp. 134 and 144). In this regard, see also Croce's termite-friendly observation that Ashton's line in being "so steadily traced makes it difficult to speak of climaxes or even of 'moments.'"

and a Hopi named Whorf,[68] her rabid cinemaboy and freelance linguistician did so in an unconvincing sleep-talker's Brandoesque mumble so as not, she presumed, to be taken for some bloodless pedant [although if he'd been able to turn this erotic episode into a ballet, then a brazen playing of the pedantry against the grain of shameless sexual aggressivity would have made for a tense and tasty mini-spectacle appropriate—as long as the emergent imagery stayed indecipherable—for all ages].) By getting up and walking across to the other side of the bed when fate had deposited him here he risked spilling all his accumulated energy and leaving her unendurably congested. Furthermore (or more to the point?), taking the initiative in that way would risk making him real, setting him up in business as a *being among beings*, distinct from other beings—no longer a slablike extension of the gaping hole between her legs, a boundaries-nibbling bug straight out of Mannyland reducible to the sum of its immersions in moment after moment. Even rolling over her to get to the other side would constitute a stab at thoroughly alien self-sculpting, hence extrusion from the sacred monolith of the moment. Thing is, he wasn't real and he knew it and prized what he knew. Had never felt real. Would never be real. Didn't—if you must know—*want* to be real. Didn't care to make his own acquaintance as a *real*. Didn't want to be sculpted into boundedness for boundedness in all shapes and sizes just cried out for annihilation. *Was* already annihilation. As long as he bowed to the dictates of fate he wasn't saddled with beinghood (yep, *beinghood*, you heard me right the first time, bro). To give her an orgasm as Akim, a real honest-to-goodness being, was inconceivable: it was as a slumbering force, a massive shapelessness, that he did his best work in the cunt-decongesting genre (or was it a subgenre along the lines of, say, the Jungian Spaghetti Western? [ho, ho, ho]). So she must take him as she found him and she did just that, to a fault. And while doing so she must also look on the bright side for the bed, albeit canopyless, did have a bright side. And in retrospect Shearer sees that he was right on target for not once during all the time Akim spent choreographing on her cunt did his fingertip betray an inability to manipulate creatively the organic building blocks

---

[68]André Bazin applies the *energy accumulation metaphor* to the film image in his exquisite essay on Robert Bresson (see "Le Journal d'un curé de campagne and the stylistics of Robert Bresson," in *What is Cinema?*, Hugh Gray, translator [Berkeley, California, University of California Press, 1967]). Benjamin Lee Whorf uses a similar metaphor to contrast "our" termite art-averse view of time with that of the Hopi, which emphasizes "persistence and constant insistent repetition" and cherishes the cumulative value of innumerable small momenta" (see "The relation of habitual thought and behavior to language," in *Language, Thought and Reality: Selected Writings of Benjamin Lee Whorf* [Cambridge, Massachusetts, The MIT Press, 1969], p. 151). For the Hopi (from whom the author of *The Making of Americans* learned so much—or maybe too much), "time is not a motion but a 'getting later' of everything that has ever been done" and its unvarying repetition is perceived as "not wasted but accumulated"—as "storing up an invisible change that holds over into later events." Which might explain super sex toy Akim's soft spot for these two thinkers. [The underlining in the present footnote is, by the way, mine (*mad scientist voice*: MINE, DO YOU HEAR!? ALL MINE!!!).]

with which she, in the role of fate, had supplied him. Not once did said tip feel compelled to flee the bed-studio in search of a supplement—something to compensate for the failure to milk the given, the sacred cunt-given, for all it was worth. For there was never any question of failure, only of incessant hops, skips and jumbo jumps from strength to strength. And not once during all those rehearsals which had no opening night to look forward to did Akim go flagrantly non-termite. Not once (in the hope of speeding up, by rushing his dick in where even fingers feared to tread, her incremental advancement toward the Big O) did he—her one-stop shop where all things termitic were concerned—cut the coil of the continuity his finger had worked so hard to preserve.

So how, I ask you, could she not begin to feel intrigued by a stewmaster similarly obsessed? For just as Akim remained glued to the sacredly wrong side of the bed for the sake of a *gapless* evolution of her excitement toward its breaking point (*clitoris non facit saltus*) so is the stewmaster glued to his bread-and-butter giblets, which are just as sacred. So, in order not to waste them, which would be a desecration, here he is forcefeeding those giblets to his proxies even if he knows that, through unconditional self-surrender to such opportunism, he stunts their spiritual growth and skews their actions, reactions and everything in-between toward the grossest improbability. And wouldn't it be a wee bit odd if all her connection-making was at the stewmaker's behest and could be reduced to just another giblet on the half-shell? But why is it that the members of her crowd cannot find themselves a hole to crawl into that is under the gibleteer's radar? Unless all this forcefeeding effects a mock-fulfillment of their craving to be Other. In other words, the giblets are Dante's *Arpie* who, according to the most beautiful *chiasmus* in all of literature (yeah, chiasmus, no other word will do, folks), *fanno dolore, ed al dolor fenestra.* And for "the most beautiful chiasmus . . . ," yet another pronouncement drenched in self-aggrandizement, we once again have to thank Hyperbolics Anonymous, the Master's heavy metal one-man band.

CHAPTER TWENTY-NINE

The setting sun has left only a salmon-tinged streak behind. Just when the stewmaster has taken it into his head to stew elsewhere and she can therefore give her full attention to Cantor, he's decided to follow suit. Absurd that the fate of the trial should lie in his hands but maybe they'll turn out to be capable hands—the hands of a brain surgeon who steers clear of too many interventions. Did he know she'd be watching him disappear? Probably. All of her partners who were in this Pretender's camp adored being gazed at with awe—or at least with paralyzing admiration.

Just when Cantor (no idea Shearer has been cheering him on) is about to give up all hope of being shuttled back in the direction of the zoo (a stone's throw from his new home away from home), the driver of the little bus slows down between official stops and (without taking his eyes off the road) glumly invites him to step in. "You looked a little lost," he explains, justifying the good deed to himself. Then: "That'll be twenty-five cents," to remind the beneficiary (wobbling his way toward the back) that the duty of any self-respecting good deed is to come with a price, however nominal. Turning toward the beach Cantor's eye is immediately (or is it reluctantly?) caught by a couple who, arms tightly entwined and sporting matching swimwear, are parading defiantly under the club-footed lollipop palms, or are they paint-roller palms or baby-rattle palms or clenched-fist palms or giraffe palms? He's never been able to relish botanical niceties, which avowal makes him feel he's moving a wee bit closer to the practice of devout heterosexuality, only it's that time of day when he's never in the market for reorientation or reassignment or repackaging. Suppressing a chuckle (at how a simple thing like not knowing what sub-subvariety a particular specimen belongs to can trigger what Berry Sundae referred to mock-wistfully as *a bad case of the straights*), he quickly realizes it was way too faint to need suppressing. Well, he'll be damned if the wraparounds (they've turned up the volume on their smug little us-against-the-world broadcast) aren't—weren't—aren't Ethan and Rhys.

Inasmuch as the Scourge of *his* Psyche appears (unlike Moira's) to have taken a well-earned sabbatical (*who is inner-speeching?*), there's no excuse for deferring consideration of things as they now stand. But he just can't concentrate because the other passengers (the most intimidating being the homeless, who are feistily furthering the cause of each other's brute survival through tips provided in code or maybe it's just shorthand)—the others are busy sizing him up (after all, they're veterans while he's just a raw recruit). Cantor begins to feel he's lived the present in-process shuttle sequence before. Or rather, that one or some of his teammates have, on his behalf, lived it, *mutatis mutandis*, all before. But even if it's the same sequence, it's different, inasmuch as this time it's Cantor who's living out the sequence, which promises to unfold—to encode—a top-notch racial memory. To quote Melanctha, with her fondness for subtitles (which amounts to a mania), *Each in his own way*. Getting back to the passengers: He knows their look—half fear, half hate—only too well. But what exactly is the target? His mean-squint simulation of Spaghetti Western penal authority (hard enough to manage without Morricone at his side) which they must loathe themselves for swallowing hook, line and sinker as the Real Thing? Or the Realer Thing underneath which as fellow marginals they have had no trouble ferreting out lickety-split? Or is it by any chance the jittery ease with which he's managed to tame this eely oxy-moronicity. The impossibility of knowing forces him to do what he does best under such circumstances, which is to direct a deadpan gaze (*otherworldly in spite of itself*, that's the ticket!) far beyond the ken of this ragtag bunch of inquisitors who'd give old Torquemada a run for his money. Once they've given up trying to reach a consensus on how best to bracket him and are about to put themselves to work on the hazing of recruits even rawer (the shuttle has made several subsequent stops), he is able, if not to sit back and enjoy the ride, then at least to proclaim himself (though not before the shuttle has turned right on to steeply ascending Millar Avenue) a bona fide bastion of the old guard. Only now, with the familiar terracotta frontage staring him full in the face, it's time to bid the homeless (the only passengers remaining) a far-from-fond farewell. He mutters, Good riddance, and is immediately ashamed: why, he's no better, or sounds no better, than, some arrogant-ass Cisco Kid in a Blue Flannel Hoodie, specifically one of San Francisco's Googlite trillionaires trafficking in Dead Souls. Unfortunately, enviously excoriating these trailblazers, he sounds even worse—like an old-fart Luddite—our Mr. Chichikov—a Dead Soul himself. Yet the minute they're out of sight he wonders why he didn't manage to say, or at least think, All right, let's just pretend, for argument's sake, that for all practical purposes I too am homeless and my name is Cantor and I am an Oxy- which means nothing more and nothing less than that I find shuttling between oppugnant/repugnant orientations and doing an injustice to them both, the easiest thing in the world. So what if my queer brand of virility subsists only in the form of a shuttling? Surely that brand has every right to life, since the shuttler in question isn't some wish-washy true-ID dissimulator— he's an embodied experiment whose end product gray-eminently enriches your black-and-white bleak- and blandness. Its absence would represent an all-too-flagrant missing link in the Great Chain of Being and I for one don't want to imagine the effect on Leipzig's co-inventor of the calculus—don't want him, especially at his advanced age, somersaulting in his grave.

He doesn't want to walk in and find Eden doing pretty push-ups, especially if Pritchard has left a message on his cell (Cantor never takes it with him: hates the damn things although he's got to admit that the dead-serious stance of young men as they thumb their rugged way—at streetcorners, in subway cars, en route to the men's room—through page after page of dimwit content holds a certain appeal)—a message to the effect that after a thorough background check, lusty enthusiasm had no choice but to give way to way too many second thoughts. There's (unfortunately?) nothing of the kind. In fact, with what must be customary perfect timing, he's just shot him an email that's one long reaffirmation of purblind faith. Only there's a slight problem: to the right of the French windows, a potted shrub (how could he have missed it before?) is crawling with shameless pistil- and stamen-flaunters. Revved up by hot ocean breezes, each bloom via dodderings and quiverings strives to vivify its haecceity—yeah, man, its *haecceity* (you won't get anywhere trying to make me eat my polysyllables: they're the only nutrients worth the paper they're printed on)—but is making little progress because (as far as Cantor can see) the minute the shrub entire gets wind—literally and figuratively—of the goings-on, lickety-split it starts milking said breezes for all they're worth, though not (thinks Cantor) to body forth on a naturally grander scale its own brand of uniqueness (a venial craving) but rather to swallow up, purely from invidia, every last vivifier in a massive goal-less turbulence (venal to the core). So in a sense, by getting the self-evolutionary ball rolling, the flaunters have signed their own death warrant. Cross-examining the shrub, he tries to make his inflection—as he asks, *But why such a portent here and now?* (for there can be no doubt it *is* a portent)—hew as agonizably as possible to that of Hoffmann, at the moment when, in what is Cantor's favorite opera (in case you were wondering), he interrupts the Muse's portentous *couplets*, which insinuate that his beloved Olympia (the Siri of her day) is nothing but a wind-up doll, to ask, "Pourquoi cette chanson?" Unless, like Vitellius in the *Histories* of Tacitus (the Offenbach of *his* day but don't ask me why), he himself is, poignantly, the portent. Though, unlike Vitellius, he never gets drunk and, what's more, is capable of forethought. Or maybe the question is better put thus: In the Royal Amygdala Repertory's adaptation for modern audiences of the soon-to-be-timeless classic *Portent Time in Big Pharma: A Mathematician's Straight Rise and Queer Fall*, who's been assigned the plum career-changing role of Hero-Cannibalizing Shrub? Surely not Pritchard, his newfound champion. Though how well does he know him really? Now that you mention it, there's been far too little stage time allocated to this quaint little Santa Barbarian—nowhere near enough to ensure that his transformation into a Major Player rings plausible. Obviously, another anti-stroke of genius perpetrated by none other than . . . SoP (Cantor's resistance to the term *Master* shows no signs of abating). The intention has clearly been to keep Pritch, once introduced, out of the picture as much as possible. Several staggered absences, remedied—pharmakoned—by a few dimwitted monologues going on forever, add up to a super-shrewd manipulation of the sense of lived duration, which has managed to get Pritch fully vested in record time (thanks to "dimwitted" Cantor has stolen His detractors' thunder though when has SoP aka the Master ever gone to bat for him?). Why, up at the ranch things have gotten so out of hand that they're all swearing they know him, Pritch, better than they knew each other, or even themselves. But why single out Pritch? Wasn't this the house MO? After being put through the mill of a bare minimum of stagey confrontations with the strangest of bedfellows, every recruit is dutifully retracted to facilitate the unimpeded infiltration of their—the ranch hands'—consciousness by his afterimage. But all kidding and small talk aside, if it turns out that the statement of the shrub is to be taken at face value and there's a saboteur at large driven by envy of Cantor's preferment, then who is he? *Who is he?* Now what kind of question is *that*? Fact is, Cantor's relation to himself (like anybody's) is a nuptial relation (he's not *one with himself* but at the very least three for the price of one) and the business of such a relation, complete with marriage hearse, is to make sure that if one party asks a burning question of the other—his twin by default—it's the kind of question whose unwelcome answer is already buried in its own folds. The kind of question whose violence is violent enough to undo that answer—to put it in a straitjacket for life. The kind of question that exhorts the answer to stay buried—the kind of question whose sole raison d'être is the scab-scratching pleasure it derives from assessing how far the answer given deviates from the right answer. Surely it's not Pritchard, his newfound champion. Though how well does Cantor really know him? Funny, now that you mention it, how little stage time has been allocated to turn this quaint little Santa Barbarian into a Major Player. Cantor's simply not ready to answer—to talk back to himself.

But it doesn't matter who the hero-cannibalizing shrub is. The shrub's a red herring. What does matter is that Cantor is having the same relation—the same *kind* of relation—the same kind of "showdown"—with a shrub as the high-hat in that delicious old Caesar/Meyer/Kahn standard had with Crazy Rhythm walkin' along Broadway, right? Through sheer force of will, his desperation, like the high-hat's, has managed to pay a non-animal the ultimate compliment, i.e., has managed to deliver the ultimate insult—by turning—no transmogrifying—that non-animal into a flesh-and-bloody antagonist and ascribing to it unspeakable traits and intentions worthy of a sorcerer's apprentice on crack. Although the high-hat's challenge was, granted, infinitely steeeper and the outcome infinitely more ennobled inasmuch as he was obliged to work his transformative—his personificative—magic on the most disembodied of all entities—a mere pattern of sheer movements. But in both cases there has been the same give and take—the same (whether explicit or, as in Cantor's case, implied) accusations ("Ain't it a shame? And you're to blame"; "What's the use of prohibition? You produce the same condition"); and the same brush-offs ("from now on, we're through"; "here's the doorway, I'll go my way, you'll go your way").

Eden, who's succeeded in getting a slight tan, is fast asleep in his briefs. His chest hair, more blond than brown and none the worse for it, spreadeagles upward from the the . . . the . . . (what did he called it, the snotty Park Avenue urologist Cantor went to see when the pain from that scrotal wart finally became unbearable?) . . . the . . . the pubic escutcheon! of course!—spreadeagles upward from the pubic escutcheon like . . . like . . . like . . . a sewing machine or an umbrella or (better yet) both, etherized on a table. Should he entomb him with a kiss? (the full lips inscribed in a perfect oval fringed fashionably with bristle-fuzz certainly deserves at least one). He waits. Waits some more until Eden finally stirs. The kissable moment is gone. Why this reluctance to have acted? Easy enough, of course, to claim it's his Cartesian evil genius, SoP, who's behind it all, being as dedicated as ever to steering him clear of just the sort of simple actions that prove people are alive and kicking—and on the flimsiest of I've-got-a-reputation-to-protect pretexts, i.e., that Cantor hasn't earned such an action in the only way he legitimately *could* have earned it, namely, as the byproduct of providing SoP's superselect clientele with what they don't know they crave, to wit, food for thought and thought for food and not just any old thoughts but thought packets, which may (because with all their compressed energy they have nowhere else to go)—or may not (it's a Pascalian gamble cum gambol)—prolapse—precipitate—seamlessly into action. In the *best-case scenario* (detestable term but whose sheer detestability is not to be taken lightly), a thinker will be sauntering along minding his own business. Through no fault of his own, he collides with the world and out of that collision is born a thought packet. And what should suddenly precipitate out of its sidepocket but an action. But not just any old run-of-the-mill action imposed arbitrarily and inorganically on the unwary wayfarer but one that, being determined—overdetermined—by the flow of thought, which as everybody knows is never arbitrary, becomes non-arbitrary by association. But Cantor isn't buying any of this even if he started off trying to hard-sell it to himself. He knows, even if SoP doesn't, the missed—the unearned—kiss was all about that old chestnut/warhorse/red herring: fear of annihilation—self-annihilation.

Before he realizes it he's opened the *closet* (so he's capable after all of action not preceded by thought, even if this one isn't on the monumental scale of a kiss), with the intention of gathering all his belongings and squeezing them into a suitcase (including, if possible, the ten-ton Cantor thesis beloved of Pritch). How can he remain Eden's roommate (dumb-ass word) under the circumstances? Since he's now aware that if he didn't kiss Eden it was because he didn't want *just* to kiss him. What he really wanted was to fuck him but only *after* the kiss, or rather, a lot of tongue- and lips-devouring kisses, withdraw just before ejaculation so as to be able to cover his buttocks with glistening gobbets, then as a finishing touch drive the two of them stark raving mad by plowing back in even deeper, this time lubricated and lubricating every step of the way. And maybe, given the benefit of the doubt or half a chance, Eden would have followed easily enough in Berry's footsteps and surrendered to a tidal wave of excitement (whose attenuation always required at least seven orgasms)—excitement which had been a matter less of sensations, anal and otherwise, than of sheer amazement that the stratagem responsible, combining daringly cool calculation with such brainless aggression, was devised by a human. Does Borkman, targeting a different hole of course, have similar fantasies? although if he does (and of course being Borkman he must) they're sure, with his prowess, not to remain fantasies for very long. (*But why*, Cantor asks himself, *am I making such a big deal of Borkman's so-called prowess? I've given birth to this fantasm simply in order to have something before which to abase myself in expiation for all my very real prowesses past.*) In any case, (*"in any case," "in any case," the last refuge of scoundrels!*) whether he goes or stays, shouldn't he be proud of having managed to get from A to B without caring one bit about trivial things like annihilation? Shouldn't he be tickled pink that the move has been way ahead of any thoughts, premonitory or otherwise, and that he's become aware of it only retrospectively (which proves there was no calculation involved and that he's nothing but a rank innocent at heart)? Yet why should he be running away—and with his telltale masterpiece in tow? For as long as he keeps on packing up a storm with his back turned to the dozing swain (*The Dozing Swain:* great title for the ballet Nijismsky didn't live to perform) and his darkest impulses better than overcome by virtue of being unrealized, Cantor is not, nor has he ever been, a member of Joe McCarthy's Homosexualist Party. And he isn't deceiving himself in the least, or so he needs to think, for the not-so-simple reason that anybody's sexual ID fluctuates from discrete to indiscreet instant and back again and at this particular instant Cantor is as normal as a fullback in spring training thanks to the stress of packing, which wakes up all his dormant heterosexualismo beef and brutality? But of course the surest symptom of normality (for which frugal Freud rightly reserved most of his compassion) consists in not caring—not *giving a shit* (and not just when one is in the death throes of lust which makes it a practice never to lie)—not caring whether or not one makes the grade— or, more importantly, whether one is being perceived as making the grade. Cantor is, alas, nowhere near that stage and may never be but the hope is what keeps him going. So maybe he should pack up and skedaddle, and promotion be damned. Though, on second thought, why should he?

Eden makes his entrance at last, emerging from under the covers, where he's taken refuge from Cantor's unwanted—because unperceived?—assault. It's clear he's about to say, Quit making all that racket (hopefully, to the windily offending shrub). Instead, he waxes slowly toward a poetical crisis (it's the Invidicum talking, of course; only these days, when *isn't* it the Invidicum talking?). He explains to the shadow he takes to be Cantor's that he's gotten into the bad habit of going to bed at around 5:15 a.m. (or hasn't Cantor noticed?), which he can't seem to break (it's around 3 p.m.), even if he always ends up hating that obscene moment when, the sky having gone from black to luminescent blue, rosy-pawed dawn cuddles up beside him reeking of feline entitlement and waiting to be fed. Sated, Eden crawls back under the covers. But not before taking another stab or jab at lyricism by lambasting the litigious split second just before the sunrise starts breathing down his back— exhorting him to celebrate its client's ludicrous solemnity.

Indifferently Eden asks where Cantor thinks he's going. "For a long walk in the hills." "Then why are you packing?" "It clears the sinuses of my soul like nothing else." (To his displeasure, Cantor observes that he's responded in the key of prissy self-importance and that the answer doesn't match the question—it's an answer waiting for its mate to be born. Ben Jonson, then, was absolutely right: preferment *does* change a man,[69] and rarely for the better.) Eden smirks, no longer kissable—still fuckable, maybe, but definitely not kissable. To keep this observation from public view, Cantor mutters (just as indifferently?!), "See you later, chum."

Remembering there are lockers to the left of the entrance (he's hasn't made up his mind about skedaddling), Cantor decides to kill some quality time at the Art Museum (Gunther Gerzso retrospective)—even if this move does little to advance the plot he's obliged, as Pritchard's anointed, to carry on his shoulders—but not before picking up a copy of the *New York Times* at Stearns Wharf. On page A15 (national), there's a brief article about "endlessly proliferating dead ends" in the Straynge case. Eden is mentioned—not as a suspect—not as a person of interest—but as a *focal point of some concern* (*A new one on me*, Cantor thinks). Newest development: the beloved psycho-

---

[69] See Ben Jonson, *Epicœne, or The Silent Woman*, act V, scene III.

pharmacologist's colorfully unstable wife has tried to do herself in after her even more unstable son's relentless accusations—that it's she, working alone, who was "his dad's executioner"—became intolerable. Cantor can't imagine Straynge being anybody's dad, which oddly enough makes him sad; also oddly enough, he is far more gripped by the article at the bottom of the page, about an (of course highly respected) MD who's severed the spinal cords of fifteen babies at an Evanston private clinic: his photo, adjacent to that of the crime scene, is (intentionally?) one third its size. Ordinarily, the next order of business would be (only this isn't a film noir) a meeting with his ex-girlfriend at an Anacapa Street bar and grill to convince her (wistful-grimly over their favorite song, Rob Roys) that they still have the ghost of a shot at a *decent life*, which out of the mouths of noir folk always sounds more scandalous, more exotic, than life in the super-fast lane could ever be.

In the men's room, he dutifully washes down his three afternoon pills with some tap water (nobody notices: good omen? bad?). After all, the trial is still in progress (even if he can very well be one of the unlucky few relegated at the start to its placebo arm) and even if he's been nominated top dog, there's no reason to believe Envy has decided to leave him luxuriously in the lurch.

The more Cantor wanders through the prettily appointed galleries, the more he excoriates himself for not having stumbled sooner on this artist whose work (take *Ávila Negra* or *Desnudo Rojo*, for example) seems to be all about one of his favorite concepts cum image, "incisions" (*grietas*), and nothing but, with assorted cracks, cuts, slices and fissures thrown in for good measure (and by the way, isn't homosexuality a kind of Dedekind cut into all that irrationally exuberant hetero flab?). Then he wouldn't have had to wait quite this long to unload the dread of discovering, as he is doing at this very moment, that Invidicum's greatest virtue—and a timeless one (given the nature of the inextinguishable human beast)—is to be more or less freeing him (as we speak) of the omnipresent feeling that his suffering is never commensurate with the dizzying magnitude of his rivals' triumph after triumph after triumph and consequently that if he expects said suffering to let him alone at last he has always to outdo it, to beat it at its own con game, to undergo not just the suffering plain and simple (with the right coach, any boob can do that) but the first, second, third . . . nth derivatives thereof at every point along its pathological curve, as if the only weapon at his disposal against the Envy stimulus (even if, to be effective, that weapon must simultaneously be turned against himself) is a suffering beyond suffering—suffering as an . . . *incision* (No. 1) into the heart of suffering, followed by incision No. 2 into No. 1, then by incision 3 into 2 and so on and so forth until the last polysyllable of recorded time.

But while it's OK to a certain extent to ward off the varieties of suffering inflicted by whatever Platonic Demiurge is running the Envy show (maybe it's SoP or Melanctha's Master[70] or Shearer's Balletmaster in Chief or Bork-

---

[70]Suddenly the Master is just one in a slew of troublemakers—a suggestion giddy at best but invigorating and whose plausibility lasts only as long as it takes to traverse the parenthetical remark in which it's been tucked away.

man's Ibsen) through anticipatory—apotropaic—articulation of that suffering (since if Cantor knows his Demi and he thinks he does—by heart—then he also knows Demi wants above all to be or at least thought to be Original and not just original but a practitioner of the kind of originality whose contour and content are impossible to guess at), there's also the danger that in so doing Cantor may be feeding Him prize tips on how to up the ante of perpetration, i.e., ammunition that Demi (being an infertile fraud at best) would never be able to synthesize on his own. But before his adversarial relation to the Demiurge gets out of hand he decides to give himself a good talking to—to remember that the Demi is none other than SoP and as such is the newest member of that exclusive confraternity that numbers the Master among its stars and also as such has never failed him—could always be depended on to deploy all the weapons in his arsenal—with all the melodramatic flourishes at his command—to foil Cantor's every effort to get himself done in by his ordeals and so here he—Cantor—is again, having come through with flying colors, for what is the discovery of Gerzso's incisions but another triumph over life. The Demiurge aka SoP has been appallingly consistent: when it comes to any loathsome duty—any effort doomed to fail—the Demiurge, johnny-on-the-spot, has always said in so many words, Just show some effort and I will extract you from the horror (if only to dump you into the firepit of another).

Nevertheless, Cantor is capable of realizing it's all for the best that their paths (his and Gerzso's) didn't cross before he was ready to be enriched, i.e., incised, by an outside influence. And speaking of the incisions perpetrated by outside influences, is the soul-bugging chitchat all around him *really* about the show, as it would have him believe, or about the weather, however perfect, or where to eat? Most definitely not: the chitchat's content, phatic to the core, is its *form* which is all about the overwillingness of the chitchatters to lie on their backs, limbs splayed, before the chatchitters (or vice versa) as proof that their bellies are indeed as fangless as they look, hence incapable of incising away at chitterly or chatterly self-love with a view to exposing the vacuum pack beneath its fat.

But how has he managed to go from incisions to chatchitters in a single bound and with the same urgency? How can chatchitters be as important as incisions? Well, for somebody like Cantor, they're equally life-changing—or, to use a phrase he especially love-loathes, *game*-changing. Hierarchization of events strikes terror into his childish egalitarian soul. So if, along these wobbly lines, Eden's chest hair is as important or as unimportant as, say, Shearer's semi-retired tutu, how can he become, as envisaged by Pritchard, Captain of the Invidicum industry (where Envy and Envy alone—not Dedekind cuts or phatic flab—must reign supreme)? He'll worry about relinquishing his too-universal susceptibility later.

So, to confront the dirty little secret that is *the need to suffer-beyond-suffering* he's required nothing less than a field trip to SB. Well, the price of the ticket (which wasn't even out of pocket) has definitely been worth every last penny for there is, to say the least, something refreshing, regenerative even, in being able to declare at last that a spade is a spade is a spade. (And so what if the stirrings of regeneration are very much of this spot and instant—are a local phenomenon—and not transplantable—not even to nearby Pritchard County?) Can it be, he wonders while descending the Museum steps two at a time (and wondering even more at the dispassion with *which* he's wondering), that this *suffer-beyond-suffering*-style suffering—or *bad* suffering (which, along the lines of the fate of cholesterol, is sure to be its baby-talk moniker once the smarmy diagnosticians get into the act)—consists in nothing more than the sufferer's short-circuited dread of uttering its name or of its being too dreadful to even have a name? But now that he's joustingly lanced the boil of that namelessness—well, de sky, rehabilitationally speaking, is de limit. But does he really believe that this kind of suffering—or suffering of any kind— reduces to a simple dread of naming or is what we have here just another case of the trumping of the churchly logic of worldflow by the pagan illogic of wordflow—an illogic that owes much more than it dares to admit to the Bacchanale from Saint-Saëns's *Samson et Dalila*?

What he does believe—suddenly—is that the ghost of Berry Sundae if nothing else enjoins him to suffer beyond the call of suffering (in this case, the suffering that stems from the inability to suffer) by, among other things, never forgetting—not for a minute—to sustain the immitigability of that suffering. But can he really suffer beyond suffering for his failure to suffer (or is he simply jumping through the hoops of wordflow, as his cultish detractors might put it, albeit far less politely)? Maybe, if he puts his mind—his mind's guts—to it.

He decides to take a walk, a walk being the metamath's equivalent of a stiff drink. The Botanic Garden's just the ticket (there he can be alone with his incisions). He's earned it. So he hops a cab—he's earned that, too. Lots of trees and even more tourists, so it seems at least to Cantor. And there in the middle distance (shielded by manzanitas from life's grosser perpetrations although they don't deserve it) is the group he's been waiting for (country of origin? Funny it should have taken you this long to ask! Let's just say it's the homeland of Dickens's Mr. and Ms. Defarge and Joseph Sheridan LeFanu's Ms. de la Rougierre, not to mention Generalissimo Louis-Ferdinand Putain). For nationals in this particular group have a need wherever they go to talk about what they see but always in a maddeningly neutral—doctrinal—fake-humble quizzical tone—apparently unself-proclaiming—unself-congratulatory. And there's always one among them who, in showing off her million-dollar observations, tries to sound as if she's just speculating—tactfully tendering a mere possibility (with respect to why, say, the branch directly overhead is slanted upward and inward). All is provisional—subject to correction by mere experts. But provisional or not, today's tourist like all her compatriot tourists of yesterday or three years before yesterday makes sure there's no room for correction. She holds all the cards—she owns the tree—owns its troublemaking branch. The maddeningly mock quizzical remark, simulating humility—high praise for the event—the tree as event—is everything, the man—or, in this case, the woman—is nothing. But in fact the event in question is not the tree or its wayward branch or even the buzzardly indifference of the pigeon directly below the branch—no—you'll simply never guess what the event in question consists in. Think hard: wrong! what's that? wrong again! how's that? still wrong! give up? well, it's the acuity—the life-or-death acuity—of the tourist pointing out for her companions how clever she is and yet how humble because isn't she—or at least her tone—laying down its arms in front of nature, complemented by art—isn't her tone soliciting help—but he senses that anybody—even a companion of the loudmouth—would find it excruciating to be asked to lend a hand to the commentary especially since everybody is already mired in —shackled to—spectatorship—eavesdropperliness—sidekickhood—the role assigned him or her through the auspices of the loudmouth's dreamy tone—dreamily speculating in all innocence, in all humility, whereas in fact she won't stand for any dissent—or, much worse, requests for clarification. Cantor can't help extrapolating her mannerisms to the bedroom—and he's fascinated by what he sees: her refusal to relinquish the didactic—doctrinal—upper hand (the very hand that's just sketched the phenomenon she's trying to decipher for the benefit of her benighted companions) even at the moment just before orgasm. And maybe, Cantor wonders, somebody overcome with revulsion for his botanic garden mannerisms is concurrently extrapolating them to other contexts and is overcome with a kind of perverse relief to discover they are invariant under transport. Which suggests that fluidity is not necessarily doom. But he has to remind himself things could have been worse—that is, less insidious hence less of a pathway to self-discovery. He has to remember that any time someone gets his goat—I mean, *really* gets it (like know-it-all La Turista)—it's immediately conjunctive—indispensable—to his life and soul and indispensable to his evolvement. Ruskin would say goat getters always have his best interests at heart 'cause without knowing it they "look for the *thoughtful* part" of him. As a phenomenon the encounter could have offered him—a scalpel-brandishing country bumpkin cum lay analyst just setting up shop and desperately in need of patients—no entry point for surgical intervention. That is, the tree in question could have been just another Eiffel Tower or Chrysler Building or Museum of Sex or Big Ben (they're all a dime a dozen) and she, just another cellphone wielding snapping turtle eternalizing it from every angle for the sole purpose not of dazzling the folks back home (who cares about *them*?) but of suing all the other turtles for copyright infringement.

CHAPTER THIRTY

While Cantor is busy formulating his Unified Field Theory of Suffering beyond Suffering, which he has little way of knowing will become one of the ivied pillars of *experimental* psychopharmacology for decades to come (how Herbert hates that word: isn't anything worthy of prosecution experimental by divine right?), Eden awakens painfully because irreversibly, aware that he's just blown his chance of serving up a direly needed dead man to the Invidicos. Simply because he was afraid to jump out of bed to proclaim, and jump back in to simulate, a more-than-willingness to satisfy Cantor's evident desire. So compliments of his delicate scruples he's ended up botching—he, a cadre answerable to the very highest echelons along the gravy chain of command!—not only Operation Straynge, but a task, far more delicate, which has the weird property of both containing and being contained by the Operation. On the other hand, didn't Post (or was it Cook or Liepnits—or Irena the Cat Woman, who still stalks his wet dreams in dominatrix drag) assure him—in, of all places, the dingy bakery across from Amygdala—that, should he end up, as now, determining (despite all his desensitization training) that initiation of a sexual relationship with Cantor—even as a mere means to an end—was too repugnant for words—or wordflow—much less deeds, then he could always plug Borkman in some back alley after "a night of heavy drinking," thereby both proving his own mettle and, with the same stone, turning him, posthumously, into most likely culprit in what would surely be christened, by some mid-century Poe, the Straynge Case of Jim Strange? Assurances notwithstanding, he's had more trouble getting through to Post for pointers—cues—guidance—a shot in the arm—pep talks (call it what you like)—than he chooses to acknowledge. For what does Post's inaccessibility evidence but his certainty of Eden's failure, which may (and don't try perishing the thought!) in fact be the linchpin of the Operation—the key to its success. So all the more urgent becomes—should become—the need to prove his mettle.

Or maybe he's nothing more than a convenient scapegoat (*whose voice is this?*)—a stalking-horse (is that *le mot juste*? Hell, no!)—who, once silenced, is to be thrown (or has already been, with absence—distance—doing the dirty work of silence) by Post & Co. to, e.g., the mealy-mouthed anti-Pharma liberals who routinely raved and ranted, during Amygdala's celebrated open-to-the-public Wednesday free-for-alls, against RRUHS-CTTWB (rabid recruiting of unconsenting human subjects for clinical trials in Third World backwaters) and other sleazeball practices (like Bayer's Herr Nice Guy shipments, to Taiwanese, Sudanese and Guatemalan distributors for sale to hemophiliacs, of the excess stocks of contaminated Factor VIII-containing plasma concentrate, rather than the heat-treated and consequently virus-free later version). Not to mention the most reprehensible thing of all (at least according to the "never-Rumper LGBTQ radical leftists" who overran one such meeting), i.e., the fact that the replacement of the nematode worm, the fruit fly (where phenotype conveniently equals genotype but inconveniently factors out the impact of environment) and the thale cress as standard model organisms in drug research, by the Antarctic icefish, the dune mouse and the comb jelly, was long overdue but would remain overdue even longer, perhaps forever, inasmuch as the trafficking in worm, fly and cress was a multibillion-dollar business. Everything that's been going wrong with Invidicum will be attributed to his incompetent corruption, with a laser focus on whatever can be played up as worse-come (alas!)-to-worst. Yes, he knows firsthand all about those Nuremberg rallies which were held to self-serve Amygdala with a subpoena of the very best humanitarian intentions and were so successful in fact as to make one forget it was a pill pusher (just like its ostensible bêtes noires, only more so). For he made it his business, ostensibly out of respect for his father, to attend, the aim being to scoop up every last souvenir anecdote exposing the drug companies for what they were and thereby steel himself against the anticipated whimpering pleas for mercy of his mortal enemy. So what if ultimately the big-boy perpetrators—when word got around to them—never did anything except "decline to be interviewed," while boilerplating like crazy to the effect that they'd behaved "ethically, responsibly and humanely by virtue of having acted on the best scientific evidence available at the time and in accordance with the regulations then in place" and on that note, "looked forward to reaching out to" and "going forward with" the secret police of all impoverished nations, although they couldn't comment further thereon "owing to the ongoing nature of future investigations."

He'll feel better after he gets dressed—even better if he cold-showers first. Maybe it's not too late to track Cantor down. In wry homage to puberty's perilous midnight, maybe he should emphasize (but to whom?) the *need* to kill him in order *to keep a promise with God*,[71] which is how he phrased it to his mother (dad was atypically away on business) when the recurring fear of stabbing her to death far beyond the call of duty became too terrifying to ignore. (After which he graduated to the too-real-to-be-hallucinated Balboa Park murders, as mentioned [a bit too airily, at least for my taste] somewhere above.) If memory serves, she took the keep-a-promise-with-God business very well, he must say (pity, there's nobody around to hear him not-exactly-sing-her-sodden-praises)—*too well* in fact—indeed, there was a certain under-amusement as a reflection of his own (even if his terror didn't know somewhere within—not necessarily *deep* within but within—that he *was* amused). Maybe because the warning's shock to her system was no shock at all. After all, the invincible old shrew had unloaded the curse of life upon him—Martin, the curse of *her* life—because she sensed well before conception was even a twinkle in her rotting womb's eye—well before the implantation of "his" blastocyst in her unwelcoming uterus (*who's thinking this thought for him? after all, he doesn't know a thing—much less a thing or two—about embryology*)—sensed that there was something not quite right about the boy—about the *thing to come*—and such a heap of not-quite-rightness mer-

---

[71] NB: "promise *with* God" NOT "promise *to* God." I.e., even in abject despair Martin manages to remain defiantly God's coequal (and, far more importantly, the coequal of, e.g., Ahab, Bartleby, Caleb Williams, Heathcliff, Hester Prynne and Jude).

ited no less a punishment than Life itself—Life, the only Petri dish in which his accursedness would be definitively neutered—the only canvas on which his accursedness would be sketched and scumbled into oblivion—so that nothing like his likes could ever manage to erupt again. And so through his promise-with-God spiel he was just belatedly validating and by validating purging her of her darkest vision of his thingness but, as Aesop never ceases to remind us, with validation and purgation come obligations. And she had an obligation to be killed since killing her would be the ultimate confirmation that she'd been dead right about him—about his not-quite-rightness—all along. Maybe she was simply intrigued by her own *non-fear of death* (most atypical for a staunch hypochondriac). But what intrigued *him* was her—and eventually dad's (she spilled the beans as soon as he, the Willyest Loman of them all, hunched-shouldered his slouching way through the kitchen's screen door)—indifference to what such a tormented confession (it wasn't a threat, wasn't a warning—it was a cry of primal pain) boded for his—their least favorite son's—future—that is, if ever he was unlucky enough to have one. They didn't exert any parental controls—didn't consider the impact of the torment on his malleable psyche—didn't consider how he might go about surmounting or at least surviving beyond it so as to be able to *function*—to *fulfill* himself—even to *thrive* (he never dreamed he'd be rattling around the loose change—the chump change—of words like these—optimistic words— in the hip pocket of his self-perception: must be the Invidicum). Eden was shocked then and he's shocked right now by their refusal to be shocked not by his idle threat but by what victimization by that threat was doing and would continue to do to his parchment-thin selfhood. Maybe they turned a blind eye because they associated his *psychosis* (in this case, the word is not a label but an intentional *mis*-label designed to ward off even more insidious assaults on his uniqueness) with an unspeakable strength—a vindictive strength—an avenging strength—and if he chose to be their adversary through gratuitous verbal assailment—then it was only right and proper that he—an experiment gone awry—should be compelled to make his own way and see to it that he crashed. Since crash he would. And let strangers be responsible for his Old Testament-style chastening.

So, he needs to kill Cantor to keep a promise. Or is it merely a case of needing to throttle *the Cantor within* or rather (using treacly current lingo) *his inner Cantor*, with or without a side order of the sexual factor? But assuming he plays his cards right and gets his fat chance, will the timing be perfect (*he refuses to finish off his thought with the required question mark*). Will the prospect of going back to Linda—but only as the most explicit means of letting Manning know that by so doing he rejects her in her very being—give him the courage to plug Cantor with his Glock .40-caliber semiautomatic, slipped into his messenger bag, on a typical scrotum-scented midsummer morning in the Big Apple, as a parting gift from his ever-thoughtful semi-protector (*ditto*)? His every train of thought, whether it's about his mother or Manning or Post or Cantor or Linda, manages to debouch on a cul-de-sac named Humiliation but maybe any bout of Thinking isn't to be deemed successful unless it so debouches (yes, *debouches:* all you need to do is pucker up, pal, and the enunciation will take care of itself). Just as (to go from the ridiculous to the sublime) a shit taken in earnest isn't thoroughly successful unless there's blood on the toilet paper. Must be the Invidicum that's allowing him to think so clearly, although this still isn't quite his own brand of thinking, since he feels as if he were walking on the eggshells of somebody else's—Cantor's!—which is congealing into thought packets faster than Cantor can disavow the connection, though why would he want to? Thought packets, after all, are his—are everybody's—bread and butter (*who is speaking?*). So just when he needs all of his energy—all his coherence—he's self-splitting and self-doubling at the same time. But isn't it better (as Hegel rightly insisted—Martin Hegel, that is) to be propelled by somebody else's thoughts into committing the right act than propelled by one's own into committing no act at all?

But there's *too much* self-splitting—self-fragmentation—going on (too much, at least, for a normal American boy, whatever that is, to juggle on his own) when the first—and last—order of business should be to double Cantor's thoughts and dog his steps (if for no other reason than to pay homage to the "even and odd" strategy devised by the eight-year-old boy in "The Purloined Letter"). Applying the towel to his privates Eden feels better but he knows the-feeling-better won't last and that he'll end up feeling betrayed—worse, incapacitated—by a self that, through allowing itself to feel better when feeling worse is what's sorely needed to get the dirty job done, is most him when it isn't. (*But is it possible for Eden to know this without* knowing *he knows it or is the Master, driven as always by a spurning and craving of selfhood, recklessly saddling his star of the moment with apperceptions which if achieved successfully would [in a saner universe] require him to renounce his identity once and for all?*) He walks quickly—he's almost running—to the drugstore at the corner of State and Canon Perdido. It's still open (deep breath signifying deeper relief) and what's more, it *does* carry "his" brand of sleeping pills (deeper breath), even if they're contraindicated. "One thing less to worry about, ay/eh," the pharmacist, a true brother in arms, remarks. "Yeah," he answers, "now I can concentrate on the seventy-five others." He smiles tenderly, leniently, at this effort to be witty by yet another self he doesn't recognize—the self he is currently impersonating—a self he could have been—a self he is by virtue of the fact that it's one he could have been. For a moment—under the auspices of the joke—he steps out of his own skin to become . . . Eden. A belated self which is in fact not so belated as all that since, look! it's right here, like Hermes the Thief, at his service. Better late than never, then, to be oneself—any one of an infinity of selves—though he's tempted to ask his brother if he himself has found this is to be true. "C'mon now, it can't be as bad as all that" (tenderliness cum leniency sure is catching, in SB at least). And feeling indulgent toward himself because deep down he's excruciatingly vulnerable (if you must know, as innocent as an infirm gosling which, unable to waddle its forager's way through life, must, however painfully, quickly learn to hop: the memory of that gosling, spotted in Central Park after one of the Amygdala rallies, makes him seasick with a compassion too excruciating to be self-congratulatory)—feeling indulgent toward himself how can he not feel indulgent toward Cantor or is this just the ploy of a career welsher? Unbeknownst to himself he's light-years beyond the mewlings of devout atheism. Still, he must keep his promise with God—the dark god of Balboa Park. Or (as a stunning example of word-flow trumping worldflow) *all the more reason* for him to keep it.

Cantor's kind, so Eden's been told, like nothing better than art galleries. That's a start. Further up, however, on Figueroa (though already 6:30 the sun blazes on, ensuring that whatever shadows are still owed the clayey foothills from yesterday, or yesteryear, get duly cast), an enormous fatigue asserts its right to life, for every step he takes has already been taken—and taken better—by somebody else—Cantor, again!—and in a worthier context. More unwelcome splitting and doubling. He descends toward the beach but in attempting to breath deep enough to get a good stiff whiff of the surf . . . Well, there it is again, the conviction stronger than any feeling that somebody has done the descending and the breathing before—and better. No getting around it: the pursued is mightier than the pursuer, as he has every right to be. Well, at least he can hear the surf although on second thought this might very well be the sound of palm fronds plaiting and, inevitably disappointed, unplaiting—outHeroding surfy Herod, so to speak. Turning his back on the fatigue, he decides to go, by way of Anacapa Street (State is out: it's been to him exactly what he's always been for his mother, i.e., *nothing but trouble*), as far up as the Museum of Art (Cantor pointed it out to him, almost proprietorily, a few days ago during one of their buddy-buddy jaunts) and wait outside on the off chance. But when he's just about to throw in the towel, who should emerge! only to disappear down Anapamu. He remembers Straynge's going all poignant-autobiographical toward the end of one of their sessions and saying (though for the life of him he can't remember why) that there was nothing more real than something about to disappear and nothing *realer-than-real* than something about to disappear *down a sidestreet*. This should revitalize him. Instead, he's sapped, and but good—too sapped, he assures himself, to pursue his shadow. Eden hears his name uttered, in the key of unaffectionate amusement; turns. It's Herbert and Shearer, followed by Rhys, who explains, almost defensively, that they're are on a shopping spree. Eden has a hard time imagining what *shopping spree* corresponds to—has a hard time mapping it onto an activity out in the world in which these three could be plausibly perceived as participating—to which they could be perceived as lending their fun-loving imprimatur. Let's face it: they aren't *shopping spree*'s cup of tea—at least when they're together. They aren't shopping spree *material*, as his mother might have said. No matter how hard they try. "A taste yet to be acquired," Herbert hears herself think, then say. "Taking our mind off petty hardships is part of their plan," Rhys grumbles, while taking obvious pleasure in the thought that her remark is going straight over this Little Leaguer's head. "Is that what Ethan told you?" Herbert's question sounds stabbingly unfriendly—how make it sound otherwise? "He never talks shop—never talks, period." Unclear whether it's Herbert or Eden or innocent-bystander Shearer or just plain-old-Ethan who's the target of Rhys's exasperation. Which unclarity is of course the whole point of the exercise. (*Granted—but who's pulling the strings?* the sunlight asks, since somebody has to.) No event exists, after all, unless (as every last one of you out there should know by now) it's the locus of a struggle—unless it's being torn apart Turkish-taffily by "warring" interpretations. Though most prime time experts would agree (just ask 'em!) that there's more to interpretational mania than mania per se: Double- or triple- or *n*-think is the pivotal Archimedean lever, the little bit of the unreal everybody *desperately needs* (no histrionics, please!) to be able to hew to the *un*-unreal—to be able to go on living (*living*: a six-letter word signifying the brute capacity to mistake tissue scarring for healing—or better yet, a four-letter word that invokes the less-than-puny talent for alchemizing fibrosis into tissue regeneration). And of course the scar tissue undergirding that living is toughest when woven from interpretations that are blatantly contradictory but that refuse, from ideological purity or some other will-o'-the-wisp, to cancel each other out.

Out of the blue, Eden mock-salutes in mock farewell. He didn't think he had it in him to be so . . . mock-eloquent. But relegation to the role of Little Leaguer rankles and the rankling has catapulted him to unsuspected (no! *to, alas! but dimly suspected*) heights of wit—body wit. As for Shearer, she knows a prestidigitator when she sees one and is duly impressed—even inspired. They could very well end up, post-barre, hitting it off in bed.

Is it the salute that triggers Herbert's shell-shocked acknowledgment of what she's been suppressing for so long—the fact that Eden's mad, *mad* as in *incurable*? Did she, one foggy morning while waiting for Dr. Manning to examine her, steal a glance at his file where the word was writ large—huge? Or did she only dream having done so? He's carting the wretchedness of childhood around on his shoulders, that's for sure. And what wouldn't *she* give right now for a nice juicy dose of madness! Something to counteract the feeling of sterility—of a lack of *material* (that word again)—yet much more than just a feeling. She hates herself—or would like to—for daring to think the boy's death has been a disappointment, artistically speaking. Fact is, she's milked Building 18 for all it's worth and has nothing left to say on the matter—or on any matter for that matter. She can no longer depend on B18—and all it secretes—to make her famous. And here comes Eden swathed in the borrowed finery of a condition that should by all rights be afflicting her. For what can madness do for Eden but speed up his entry into a life of crime for which, according to watercooler scuttlebutt, he's unswervably headed. Something to do, from what she's gathered, with testing Invidicum for its homicidogenicity out in the Nevada desert. But on the subject of details—and there must be details—the scuttlebutt's been primly silent. For her, on the other hand—or somebody like her—madness would be authorial bitcoin in the bank (i.e., she needs to trade in *Building 18* for *Madness*—one purloinable letter for another). Madness would ensure she lived—and with a zest bordering on the obscene— even when she wasn't lifting a finger to catch life in the act. An inexhaustible resource, then, since, as madness never goes away—not with all the opioids in the world—not with all the perfumes of Arabia—it can be depended on to mezzotint every experience, even the lamest—and, even better, the absence of experience—into an agenda item of the direst importance. The perfect antidote—the perfect pharmakon—for bookishness—for creative writing, her principal vice (instilled in her by academic hacks who want nothing more than to *mean well* and who by and large do—to a fault). Perfect, that is, as long as bookishness is still under contract to prevail during those periods when madness, having become *too* toxic for milking—too much of a good thing—is on the verge of doing her in. She wants to call him back—run after him—beg him to lend her a little of the inexhaustible direness he carries so effortlessly on his shoulders, which from behind now seem much broader—too broad, in fact, for his own good. And to show—to whoever's interested—just how low the disappearance of his secret has made her sink Herbert is about to ask Rhys to borrow her smartphone so she can google it. Though maybe he isn't mad or *all that mad*—maybe Herbert simply sorely needs him to be mad so she can have, while we're waiting, a *motivated* thought or two about madness. At the Master's behest, of course. Though maybe starting now it's at her own behest—though maybe she's learning fast how to beat the Master at his own game—maybe she's just a daddy's girl at heart—a daddy's girl gone bad. And speaking of madness, what's all this about Straynge's wife being on the warpath—a warpath that runs straight from Westchester to the Santa Barbara foothills? She's expected any day now. She's not in the market for the official version of how her man met his death—that he was done in by one of those belabored darlings of the pulps who just happened to be in the wrong place at the right time—a disgruntled postal worker—a drifter—or (though this is by far the likeliest possibility) an ex-Navy Seal with a chip on his shoulder as big as a Rhodes scholar. Even less so for the unofficial one—that the killer was an ungrateful patient, yet to be identified, who considered susceptibility to cure (he was so close Straynge could taste it in the Amygdala lunchtime cafeteria's haddock) a massive affront to his manly dignity. No, she's convinced Straynge was the victim of a conspiracy and she'll be arriving any day now to prove it or, better yet, dare anybody to *dis*prove it. Word on the Street is that she's Pritchard's ex something-or-other and goes by the name of Margo.

At Jean's suggestion ("My treat"), they decide to take a load off their feet (though the spree has obviously only just begun) in a not-yet- but from all indications soon-to-be-trendy little café (a bit too shady-chilly for Shearer, whose hopes thrive best—or only—on the ozone of direct sunlight) opposite the Lobero Theatre. The *Lobero*! Only after she's finished a third of her drink, a bittersweet concoction never before sipped (who ordered it?) does the name ring a bell. For it's where she once danced, traitorously *but nonetheless* or was it rather *and in consequence* "magnificently," according to Sir Fred—as the lead (what else?) in his *Symphonic Variations*. Why, Akim was so moved (immediately appointing himself Moira's lead groupie) by the performance (or was it the ovations?) that he crashed her dressing room to insist she superstar in the "first Alkan ballet ever" (to be choreographed to—or better yet, against—the Allegretto alla barbaresca from the Concerto for Solo Piano—imagine!—and the Quasi-Faust movement of the *Grande Sonate*). What an elitist, that Akim: not his fault, though (being a long-time victim of Snobola virus, whose specialty is sending every self-exaltation-inducing enzyme under the sun into overdrive). Should she let her hair down and reminisce in public? What, after all, would be the worst that could happen? A letter of dismissal from Jean's lover, acting on behalf of the Warner-Metro Executive Board? always obsessed (but does a Board exist that isn't? what with Ackmanoid activists forever on the rampage) by the demon of shareholder value? But didn't she just imply they never pillow-talk? Before she knows it Shearer is telling them (such is the power of sunlessness) what she hasn't realized until this moment, namely, that participating in the trial feels exactly like (all right, not *exactly* like)—rather, participating in the trial *needs to feel like* (that is, if her life is to have any cohesion) rehearsing *Symphonic*. Over and over and over, the male principal lifted her gravely, caught her in mid-leap, encircled her waist from behind while gazing obediently Olympus-wards until he got it right and did a hundred and one other stately-grave things *urgently called for by the story* only there wasn't a story, just the life-and-death obligation to realize the configurations (polynomial equations incarnated in motion, as reverential Akim irreverentially put it) urgently exhorted by the score (the non-existent story's proxy). And suddenly the following occurs to her (compliments of or by order of the Master) as it must be occurring to the others as well only they're too polite or too afraid of being plagiarized to admit it: JUST AS the level of every biomarker recruited to determine whether *Symphonic Variations* harbored the story disease was screamingly compatible with its presence even if no such disease could be found coursing through the ballet's bloodstream, SO DOES the concentration of every marker recruited to determine whether a trial is indeed in progress ragingly attests to the existence of one even if . . . But the coveted mirror-imagery between ballet and trial collapses. Shearer can't finish her thought or the Master doesn't let her finish or the connection is bad. Oddly enough, she's much relieved. Since she's failed shrewdly, through ineptitude, to establish her very own high standard for the yoking together of things not so much heterogeneous as mutually indifferent, she need never worry about having to regularly surpass it. Rhys signs the merchant's copy and tears up the other. She's ostensibly been way too busy paying the bill to attend to Shearer's predictable breakdown during her invocation of the Sublime, as embodied by the ballet she's been babbling about. (For it's the sublime—terrifying, noble, splendid, great, simple—and nothing but the sublime that Moira was struggling to recreate—to ingest as if it were a painkilling wonder drug, which it is. Since an Ashton ballet, if done right, is every bit as sublime as understanding or courage or tall oaks or the Night or companionless shadows in a sacred grove or a long stretch of time or unswerving acceptance of danger for our friends' or country's sake or a great depth or a great height or war itself [if it is prosecuted in accordance with an orderly respect for citizens' rights, or so Manny from Königsberg, exhibiting the exasperatingly prim obtuseness of an armchair Genghis, would have us believe] or withdrawal from society [but not owing to personal interest or lycanthropy] or Tartary's Komul Desert or an Egyptian pyramid or an interminable orgasm or the Hotel del Coronado or the Seventy-Ninth Street Rotunda or the Bronx High School of Science mural or Poussin's Arcadia or the siren song of any one of CD Friedrich's abysses.) But it's precisely Jean's having been ostensibly way too busy paying the piper to attend to Moira's anatomization of her lonely quest that gives a from-out-of-nowhere, frog-into-prince kind of . . . well, sublimity, to what Jean now has to say and how she says it. She's hell-bent (without yet knowing she's hell-bent) on demonstrating how a *real* trouper depicts the sublime and, more importantly, survives the depiction. "The key, Jean," whispers the Master (now she knows she's hell-bent), "is to convey, first, the pain that any full-blooded embodiment of the sublime is obligated to inflict if it is to hold on to its franchise on Mount Olympus—the pain that arises from recognizing the inferiority of (*a*) the imagination's fluttery hysteria-driven aesthetic over-estimation of the sublime Thing (e.g., the Matterhorn or the Pierre Hotel) to (*b*) the cool corrective assessment made by tweedy, pipe-smoking, ivory-tow-ered reason. But, cheer up, if there's pain, there's pleasure, too (the pleasure is child to the pain)—hard-won yet guilty pleasure—pleasure galore—a sunless sea of pleasure measureless to man—the pleasure of discovering that even if your imaginative faculty has overestimated the charms of Mount Rushmore, you've managed to catch it red-handed at the game of overestimating and (guess what?) your very determination of its inadequacy *accords with rational ideas*. So you might say that, without descending into the giddy depths of overestimation there'd be no scaling the heights of so penetrating a verdict. In other words, there's nothing as sublime as catching imagination in the act of doing violence to the rational self." She's far from having metabolized every-thing He's just sent down her pike but nothing prevents her from stalling for time until she can ably spit out the gist—and not just ably but like a pro. And is there a better way to stall than to warn them that while what she's about to depict is a Sublime Thing it's far less sublime than the Statue of Liberty as viewed from the prow of the Staten Island Ferry by a pair of star-crossed (or were they just cross-eyed?) lovers (she tries not to look as if she were grovel-ling for some sign of recollection, preferably fond)? Still it beats anything . . . danceable, that's for sure. She knows she's being cruel but Moira—what's the expression?—had it coming.

However hard it may be for them to imagine, she, too—albeit a mere aspiring non-artist, an average Jo straight out of Louisa May Alcott—never stops making discoveries every bit as disorienting as Shearer's, even if she hasn't a fan to her name. And in that regard, do they happen by any chance to recollect Jean's gutsy podium presentation back home in Greenwich Vil-lage (when they were still rookies and gut candor wasn't all that fashionable)? A presentation whose abiding aim (it's obvious they don't recollect or, what is more likely, won't give her poorly masked entreaty the satisfaction of see-ing them show all the signs of recollecting and not just recollecting *but rec-ollecting as-if-it-were-yesterday*)—whose abiding aim was to document (for the benefit of what she suspected—rightly, as it turned out!—were hordes of closeted fellow sufferers) how she came to realize her Envy-choked rela-tionship with Caro—and, for that matter, with pretty much every other sub-human she'd known—was nothing but a disease. Or rather, a non-relation harboring a disease. Or, at best, a non-relation aiding and abetting a sum of symptoms[72] in search of a disease. But suddenly, like Shearer, she self-scuttles

---

[72]Assorted snubs and slights, and other petty ploys (running the gamut from manic bragging about triumphs real and imagined to self-exalting lamentation over opportu-

amidstream—can't seem to see her way clear to seeing her way clear. (Both have given up albeit [Melanctha concedes] *Each in Her Own Way*.) It's not just her pals' refusal to remember, much less honor, her podium triumph. It's not just that the Master jilted her (at Melanctha's bidding?)—i.e., refused to rush back in where metabolization—in other words, salutary vulgarization—of his pep talk feared to tread. It's not just that she isn't strong enough to go on cherishing her discovery—that most relationships are tumors which have yet to find their palliative—even if it sends a message of rack and ruin which doesn't sell even in apocalypse-rabid California. (Although, come to think of it, Moira hasn't done too well either in the sales department, even if *her* discovery—that there are indeed cases where all the signs and symptoms of disease may be in play but no disease to be had for love or money—sends a message of cornball hope [thanks to the herd immunity-inducing hijinks perpetrated by High Art].) Fact is, the podium *business* (even if it's sure to be one day hailed as a—no, *the*—Matterhorn of oratory) is at best (even if it *isn't* danceable) a shoddy substitute for a real exemplar of the sublime. But so great was Jean's envy of Moira's talent and so great was the desire to surpass her and so much did her privileged upbringing mislead her that she ended up trying to pass off as highbrow performance art what was nothing more and nothing less than televangelical-style motivational speak. She has no idea who tricked her into hitching her wagon to so elusive a star (and oddly enough having no idea lends her a much-needed pathos of fragility) but whoever it was did her a gross disservice.

As they walk back in the direction of the hotel (there are no plans to relocate them for the time being but when will present circumstances learn to outgrow *the time being*?), Shearer feels a retort coming on, called for or not. For Rhys's information, the last thing in the world she thinks of herself as being is an artist and, by the way, she shun fans—they're far more dismissive than detractors who, after all, have taught her everything she knows that's worth knowing. Any wonder, then, that she's got a big fat soft spot for the breed. In high contrast, nothing more detrimental to persistence-in-one's-own-being than having the inevitable two or three or even thirty-two fans who, constituting as they do a mere extension of the wound-licking deluded self, turn it (through their very fanship) into that sorriest, funniest exemplar of portentous mediocrity, i.e., the un- or underrated Great Artist, thereby snatching away her only hope which is to give posthumous birth, by remaining totally impervious against the ooze of contemporary blandishment, to a brand-new overripeness for rediscovery. Collaterally, she wonders if she actually believes the classy stuff she hears herself saying—the classy things that the Master or Invidicum (which may reduce in the end to the sum of its side effects) or both are (without meeting any resistance) compelling her to say. Sure sounds as if she does, though. Or is it the world-overriding words telling her what to

---

nities for greatness unjustly snatched away) engineered by one party to victimize and at the same time invisibilize the other and all of them governed by dramatic shifts in the levels of FDIC-accredited biomarkers.

think she believes—that is, if she's as tired as she sounds of sharing the stage with the same old Great and craves a momentary respite from vainglorious victimhood? And so what if it's the words and nothing but the words? So what if she has, at least for now—at least for as long as their music lasts, up and down State Street—no life apart from the words? So what if she's been way-laid—mugged—by words? She's heard horror stories about the damage words can do from Akim (whose career may be perceived as reducible to the sum of its bad notices) but these words, California words, are different—they're a good egg. Indeed, now that she's made a pact with them they aren't, like oh so many of their kind, deserting her just because she has. In fact, refusing to rest on their laurels, or play the familiarity-breeds-contempt game, they seem to be working even harder on her behalf—on behalf, that is, of the self she thinks she deserves to be if only for a moment. Since just when, almost relieved, she's busy assuming that they've come to the end of their rope, why, here they are doing another starry turn. Going so far as to tell Herbert and Rhys that what interests her most is falling short—is the willed inability to play by the rules. That's the kind of artist she always wanted—and still wants—to be. Granted, a patent quarter truth at best. (Wordflow, however, when, as now, it's really racing, makes a point of forswearing all truck with the bauble that goes by the nickname of truth. It's after bigger game—namely, *world*flow—specifically, the triumph over worldflow which is specifically the triumph over no less than Life Itself. Even if its vehicle—its vector du jour—in this case, Little Shearer [wordflow's answer to Little Marco]—Shearer playing nag to Wordflow's jockey—has no such exalted goal in mind.) Wordflow when it's really racing invokes that very triumph—more precisely, a triumph over the laws of life—which includes a triumph over Envy (since Envy is one of those laws) and over the cure for Envy and over the remedy for—the pharmakon against—the inherent toxicity of that cure. Fact is, for the likes of wordflow, life is Public Enemy No. 1 and wordflow will be damned if it's ever caught taking the enemy seriously—if on its watch, Life gets a free pass—is allowed to think even for one minute that with a crack of the whip its victims can be made to cry over the milk it tries to compel them to spill. For What is This Thing, this Crazy Thing, Called Life when you get right down to it but a fla-vorlessly multi-flavored mess of spilt milk? And damned if wordflow—now that's it gotten this far—will ever be caught transforming itself into liner notes for life. For What is This Thing Called Life but a broken record?

Now, if anybody knows what Shearer's getting-at-without-knowing-she's-getting-at-it (Something Big having to do with the wonders of self-sabo-tage), it's Herbert. But why stoop to playing midwife when by doing so she'll, crazily, only be abetting somebody else's theft of her very own thunder? Inas-much as it—*self-sabotage*, that is (qua key to greatness)—is fast becoming her million-dollar baby—fast replacing *Building 18* as shorthand for all woes and their transformation into wieldable weapon (albeit solely on the level of wordflow, but who needs any other?). But if thanks to Invidicum's intravenous trickle-down effect, even an extra as ineffectual as Shearer can get into the act—the high-wire meditation-on-sabotage act. So what? Herbert snickers (*would* snicker, if only she knew how)—why not let her ineffectuality have its all-too-brief brief time in the sun? Thing is, why must she bluster on as if it's she who's single-handedly discovered this crazy thing called wordflow when in fact it's as old as Methuselah, or at least as Ludwig Wittgenstein (a simple proposition from whom, in the cruisable depths of the Prater some stiflingly Schnitzel-scented summer night, Herbert wouldn't have thought twice about accepting)? For didn't he say?—of course he did!—that the form of language is constructed with quite another aim than to stoop to letting the form of thought—of the life-world—be recognized. And what is that aim, after all? Herbert wonders. Not knowing softens her. Suddenly she forgives Shearer for poaching on her preserves and the potency of forgiveness brings tears to her eyes. In tandem she forgives herself, for having been unable to love the child made in her image.

Isn't that Eden slipping away into the distance? Rhys wonders. (She stopped listening to Shearer hours ago and she'll be damned if she lets the blasts of Herbert's thinking interrupt the peregrinations of her gaze. Secretly, Rhys sees herself [though she's not yet ready to admit it] as Herbert's eaves-dropping ring-tailed lemur since when she's sufficiently provoked, as now, her hearing range aligns with the lemur's, enabling exquisite attunement to the supersonic frequencies at which Herbert's thought blasts operate.) He's tailing somebody. I spotted him first, she hears herself think, ridiculously, as if she and Shearer were harpies competing for the snarly favors of some punk. She surveys him unflinchingly through the prism of Shearer's non-seeing and is forced to concede that an orphan's electric pathos—abetted in no small measure by that unseeing—suffuses his every move. For one thing, she never realized how much taller he is than Ethan. As having picked up the tab (nice phrase, too bad it's archaic) gives her a certain authority, she suggests they walk up toward the Granada (they'll have plenty of time to cover the waterfront in the days to come and she simply can't turn her back on the boy when his profile needs her most). At this distance the theater looks perfectly unremarkable, Shearer observes self-protectively (she hates to be under another woman's thumb)—except for (to be fair) the vengeful blaze in a single window, a sight as shocking as that of a tarnished gold filling in a row of picture-perfect incisors and (to be even fairer) well worth the price of admission. Each woman, unbeknownst to the other two, fears for Eden now that Pritchard's got him in his clutches. Herbert seems to remember Straynge on one occasion having denounced—no, having *gone so far as to denounce*—the leader of the West Coast gang as at best a quack shamanizer, his MD procured most likely from some Bishtek-based online telemarketer, or from The Rump U, a subsidiary of what should take (at least until she gets its real name straight) the pseudonym Fukk U. On the other hand, Rhys knows Ethan regarded such Pritch-bashing (pretty rampant at times back at The Amygdala), to the extent to which he made his puny feelings known, as nothing less than heresy—and gratuitous heresy, at that.

CHAPTER THIRTY-ONE

Eden gives up: Cantor has eluded him. The next day—pursuant to an email marked high priority (yes, Eden's been standard-issued a laptop (Dell) like everybody else and what's more, he knows how to use it)—Eden meets with Pritchard. By doing so he must admit he's following, improbably, in the footsteps of, of all people, his supposed prey even if the meeting is in another office and in another bunker (the furthest from headquarters as it turns out). He's led up seven hefty flights by the *even heftier* concierge, a Ms. Bean, or so she says, to Pritchard's suite, which unapologetically surveils the mountains. Or at least one of its rooms does—the one where he's just collapsed on a couch big enough to accommodate at least five wrestlers, Sumo chignons and all. As if reading Eden's mind (which only appears to be blank), the estimable Bean announces that dinner's to be had at around 7:30, *God willing* (God, how he hates that goddamn expression), every day except Saturday, when a world-class—no, galaxy-class—day-long buffet is offered to the public at large. Eden wonders why she's telling him this since he has a home of his own. Mimicking an adenoidal tour guide—a feat of which he would never have imagined her capable (why? if he were Herbert he'd think: So the Master can keep up his reputation as being, like any great storyteller, full of inane surprises)—she informs him that the Pritchard Clinic (first time ever he's heard the place referred to as such) survives primarily on grants—anonymous, since, by and large, the benefactors are related to those in treatment or in trials and nobody, understandably—not even the filthy-rich—seek to advertise that sort of consanguinity. Then she's gone. He hears the door open through closed eyes and when he opens them long before he's decided to, who should be looming before him but Pritchard himself—in seersucker, no less—and looking, at least as far as Eden is concerned, considerably less imposing, for all the looming, than he—the loomer—clearly hoped.

"My ridiculous getup notwithstanding, I want to help you keep from going off the deep end: which has been a major—some would say *the* major—concern throughout your life—I know all about Balboa Park and environs. And I know Post and his gang, which includes Irena Manning (they've corrupted her), want to cash in on what they call your homicidal impulses. But we won't let them. Some of my colleagues would say you're not ready to be helped—that we've just got to wait until the ideal conditions foist themselves upon us before embarking on an overhaul—especially an overhaul as critical as this one promises to be. I, on the other hand, believe that we have to work with what we've got—in this case, imperfection, impurity, failure, lopsidedness, privation (ours, not yours). First order of business is detoxification—it might take weeks, maybe months. For (in preparation for your visit to our fair shores) not only were massive amounts of Invidicum pumped into you back there on Greenwich Avenue but mixed in (making for an incendiary combo) was a superpotent because extremely small dose of 3,4-methylene-dioxymethamphetamine (ecstasy to you, bub). My agents tell me they were afraid the right ingredients might not be available out here in the Styx—I mean the sticks—or only some generic which means that like one of the caged cats down in our zoo (fortunately, it's not a world-class institution), you're just about ready to spring." Nodding, as if he's come to the same conclusions and unbeknownst to himself maybe he has, Eden is desperate to speak about his trials, drug-related and otherwise, only Straynge's corpse keeps getting caught in the line of confessional fire. *Or is it the confessional line of fire?* asks somebody with whom Eden is not yet on speaking, i.e., speakable, terms.

"Are you married?" Pritchard asks, half-sitting on the window ledge. Seeing him so seated Eden wants, oddly enough, to ask, How do you expect to get the poisons out of me? yet refrains, just as oddly. Pritchard must know he isn't married—and never intends to be. Which means that if he goes on with such scattershot interventions, clearly devised to mask the wiles of an expert insight (as has just been the case), then he'll turn out to be not all that different from Straynge and Post and Manning and the slew of alikes with whom he rubbed elbows, in the Greenwich Avenue Era, to the point of being skinned alive. Which will make things less complicated. Eden answers slowly, fighting against his natural tendency—*natural, that is, since said Era*—to get it over and done with ASAP since he regards any action as a mere impediment to other, better actions even if he knows the only existence the other, betters, can lay claim to lies in their being impedimented. A little—a lot—like clipping your toenails super-thoroughly (steer clear of that hammertoe) in the hope that it will be for the very last time, or else, why bother? Why bother if it isn't for the *very* last time? That is to say, a little like clipping your toenails to clear the path—not to muddy death—but to the reward blocked solid by tasks like toenail-clipping. But can such a tendency—such a striving (or rather can the apperception of such a tendency, such a striving)—be natural to somebody like Eden even if only since the Greenwich Avenue Era (and how can that be when it was in the Greenwich Avenue Era that Eden started being *denatured* compliments of Invidicum)? Or is it Herbert's Master who at the present juncture needs somebody (word gets around) to have just such a tendency even if it's the least likely culprit, and is intent on passing off this least likely culprit's least likely tendency as something supremely natural to His system? Never mind whatever He's putting his culprit—Eden—through in the process: the sick feeling that whatever he's undergoing in the way of perception or apperception or everything in-between should be gone through by somebody more plausible hence more deserving. A feeling that will no doubt haunt him for the rest of his life. Since somewhere "below the threshold of consciousness" Eden knows without knowing it that he's simply incapable of regarding any action as a mere impediment on the way to something bigger and better which bigger betterness and better bigness exist *only as long as they're impeded*. For the simple reason that Eden is very much the dog in the nighttime of Sherlock von Wittgenstein's *Philosophical Investigations* (No. 650)—who has no trouble being afraid of being bitten by his master but does have trouble being afraid of being bitten by his master, or anybody else, *tomorrow*, precisely because (per Ludwig) it is language and language alone that provides the criterion for the existence of such a fear. In other words, Eden (your not-quite garden-variety angry young man who champions big boobs over hairy chests, forward passes over fouettés, and anti-artisanal beer over brie) is—as invidiously compared with—no, compared *to*, say, Cantor or Herbert or even Rhys—not quite right for the role of apperceiver. He's more at home with Action and Movement (or so everybody needs to think), which are the Abbott and Costello of storytelling at its bumpkin best. Only the Master expects him to know, without knowing he knows, that descriptions of A&M—as of Mr. Teste's Marquise going out at five o'clock sharp (with her five o'clock shadow in tow)—necessarily gnaw away at the very pith (read *myth*) of a teller's uniqueness.

Pritchard, Baker Street Irregular par excellence, knows exactly what Eden has unbeknownst to himself been thinking. Just by looking at him and even without imposing the discomfort of a cuff he knows all his vital signs are off but off in such a way as to bring every unthinkable preoccupation—especially the business about being the least plausible culprit—to the surface. Pritchard now knows for a fact or at least a factoid that in the present case (and probably in a million others) the Old Master aka the Master Sorcerer aka the Master Programmer couldn't care less about holding the mirror up to nature and in fact takes the proverbial fiendish delight in both (*a*) violating Her First Law of Creativity 101 (which is to Show, not Tell, and not just Show but Show that what is being shown is nothing less than a 100 percent organically grown offshoot of a pampered somebody's—Eden's!—full-blooded and psychosocial evolution)—and (*b*) foregrounding that violation as the very heart and soul of His enterprise, and let Darwin be damned. And all this to show—not tell— that the only meaning worth a damn is the one sketched by the twists and turns—the eely sinuosities—not of some true-to-nature slice of life but of His very own Thought's nature-proof structure, structure as Chomsky-deep—as deep-dish—as an apple pie. In these parts, word- trumps worldflow 24/7.

For the Master—Melanctha's Master—aka Everybody's Master Baiter— has discovered there's a certain mileage—story mileage—to be got out of the very tension induced by catching Himself, qua storyteller, red-handed. That is, catching Himself in the act of, for example, foully trying to pull a mealy-mouthed crowd-pleasing hairy-chested big-boobed fast one (i.e., foully trying, in emulation of Aristotle's angry man, to allocate the right insight to the right recipient at the right time and in the right place and for the right length of time and at the right dosage and at the right volume so that the Everglades dinner theater crowd can digest their seven layers in peace) when his heart ain't in it. Rather than a-doin' what comes naturally (alas, *too* naturally for anybody's taste, especially his own), to wit, forcefeeding His latest thought packet—his newest confectionary turkey with all the trimmings—to its least plausible recipient—i.e., the least implausible fall guy for the job. There's a certain story mileage, then—a certain Shklovskian make-it-strange-ness—to be got, as now, out of allocating insights to insight-resistant Eden—nailing him to the cross of those insights—insights that would have fitted somebody else—Ms. Herbert, say—to a T. *But* how *does the Master get that story mileage?* Well, by projecting the inner conflict (just the sort of intrapsychic crisis, by the way, that any self-respecting Godhead would give his every last *Sefirah* to come through with flying colors [but a purely aesthetic conflict, mind you—a conflict between, say, the longing of His left hand to allocate the misbegotten insight to the most implausible recipient and the longing of His right hand to allocate it to the least implausible])—*by projecting the inner conflict into the very body of the story*[73] itself for transmutation into good old-fashioned meat-and-potatoes *non*-aesthetic swordplay, between, e.g., psychosomatic character X and irresistibly bipolar Y or between hyper-narcissistic Y and aphasic Z or between Pritch and Eden (which in this case has yet to materialize).[74] *That's* how. And that's how the Master Baiter manages, in true Aesopian fashion, to have his tall story and eat it, too.

Pritchard drones on and on appallingly (but appallingly to whose ears?) about how, among too many other things, it's a matter not just of detoxification, even if exquisitely tailored to his needs, nor of simply decreasing the susceptibility of his brain's reward circuitry to overstimulation (less by Invidicum than by the vision it induces of a homicide-friendly future). But of feeding him—forcefeeding if necessary—an *ionic liquid* brand of the drug with a peculiar property. Namely, the ability to dissolve away (in a process known as synaptic pruning) all the rapidly proliferating neuronal connections, generated by Ecstatic Invidicum, that were turning him, whether he knew it or not, into the sort of supermale who never needs anything more (to go all Kalashnikov-berserk) than just one tiny prod. "Just a monosyllable, say, spoken in a jagged susurration: yeah, that's right, *susurration:* haven't you ever been in that old saw of a situation where, while *whisper* alone is what's called for, it simply won't do?" A rhetorical question, Eden senses, so no point in responding even if he could. Or is this simply the line of least resistance. "But of course to do all this the brand needs to be packaged in a big fat lipid nanoparticle so it can be delivered COD or DOA to the tumor of Envy without leaking out of any blood vessels en route." And as Pritchard continues to drone, well, Eden *can't help feeling* (the Master's favorite phrase for it converts the bloodless abstraction to come into a dire concretion aimed straight at the gut)—though once again he's not anywhere near being able to think the feeling—that all these technicalities are being utilized like extreme close-ups in a thriller-in-

---

[73]Cf. the procedure of Luigi Pirandello in, e.g., *Six Characters in Search of an Author*. In Act I, the Son declares: "No action can therefore be hoped from me in this affair. Believe me, Mr. Manager, I am an 'unrealized' character, dramatically speaking" [English version by Edward Storer]. The writer (so I blithely speculate) had trouble fitting the character of the Son into the action. But instead of trying to fix things in a well-made-play sort of way, Pirandello realized he could do theater history far more good *by projecting his impasse into the play itself* in the hope of transforming a drab dramaturgical problem into a compelling characterological one (namely, the Son's, as laid bare in his outburst). See *Naked Masks: Five Plays by Luigi Pirandello*, Eric Bentley, ed. (New York, E.P. Dutton, 1952).

[74]Consider, in this regard, the masterly squabbles between the Father and the Step-Daughter over whose fault it was that the author out of whose fantasy they were born refused to give them life ("you were too insistent, too troublesome," he tells her in Act II). One could imagine, say, Borkman (unjustly?) reproaching Melanctha for having a similarly alienating impact on the Master.

spite-of-itself, namely, to disorient, not clarify. In the hope that the spectator (*and now Eden is beginning to actually* think *the feeling: must be compliments of all that synapse pruning or owing to the fact that Pritchard and the Master are both vying for his affections [surely a first in the featherweight annals of Invidicum]—or both*)—that the spectator will end up punchdrunk enough to imagine he now knows every nook and cranny in the rat trap known as Real Life, at least as it unfolds onscreen. Since buzzwords, like close-ups, function as fiction's black holes into which gurgles a counterfeit duration crucial to creating a counterfeit sense of life lived. (One day some Stanford dropout in the obligatory Gray Flannel Hoodie and with the even more obligatory certification of official dropout status duly notarized will no doubt find a much easier way to induce the same sensation.) Clearly (*who is doing the deducing?*), Pritchard B. DeMille needs Eden to feel he's been holed up here for quite some time (so as to render him more immediately responsive to detox and other goodies) and has recruited every sesquipedalian just out of reach to induce that fuzzy feeling. Only Pritchard's ploys suddenly don't matter for the simple reason that the detoxee hasn't heard a word—that is, everything after *synaptic pruning* has gone in one ear and out the other. He's just waiting for some *meaningful event* to which he can glue—onto which he can map—the term. He knows deep in his gut there's one out there just waiting to be lassoed in. So for a split second Eden's back in sunburnt New York, whose middle name after all is mappability. New York, where the leaf clusters in every oak tree up and down Greenwich Street (or is it Greenwich *Avenue*: he always mixed them up) are sure to be—and already were before he left—just too summer-shriveled to crackle with anything approaching wasp's nest conviction. NYC where, in a manner of speaking, he was once at home and where this little term might learn to be at home as well. Nothing doing.

But a meaningful event that has nothing to do with neurons. Pritchard knows this lean and hungry look—this *My kingdom for an event!* look. He's seen it many times before. It emerges—that is, if a look may be said to emerge—when Invidicum takes over and starts to do the thinking—the longing—for the Envier and when the Envier has no inkling that he's better off staying hungry for once the term gets glued—once it's stuffed into the corset of a meaningful event—it's the death of both. (So Eden too's been waylaid: he's caught The Language Bug [dumb-ass phrase] thanks to Invidicum. And Pritchard can surely sympathize with somebody who's trying to stumble on a new self—an anti-self—through the short-circuit called language.) For the biggest problem with the drug is not its homicidogenic aftertaste but the fact that the massive uptick in eloquence it inflicts on everybody who sips or even guzzles is ultimately the same eloquence: It masterminds an asymptotic convergence to—on—an identical way of thinking and sounding. I.e., whenever the big I's on the warpath, it maims them all—illiterate and ichneumon alike—to the same sameness. But what a sameness! the deluded Master Baiter cries out—or should cry out—from his prattle station at the highest point in Santa Barbara Cemetery. But maybe Pritchard, with a lifetime of experience, can save Eden from the aftertaste as well as the asymptotes. And while he's at it maybe—just maybe—Eden can be turned into the prodigal son he and

Margo never had. And from what he's heard about the one she did have out in wild and woolly Westchester (Jim Jason Jacaranda, isn't it?) anything would be an improvement (when staging a tantrum J3 has been observed to savagely pound each thigh with both fists like Balanchine's Prodigal Son[75] but that's the very least of his talents).

Pritchard sees that for all his willingness, Eden and *synaptic pruning*— like him and Linda—just can't seem to be able to make a go of it no matter how hard he tries. They can't seem to make this midsummer marriage of true minds *work* (putrid term in such a context). That is, he doesn't seem to be able to caliper the something out there—and he knows it *is* out there—that's more whatever synaptic pruning's cracked up to be than the accredited event itself—the something that is in fact the eternal form of the event—the model for the mere textbook copy that cave-dwelling experts take, expertly, school-boyishly, for the real thing. And even if whatever he's looking for and knows is out there even if he can't find it, but not, mind you, for want of trying (see above)—even if whatever he's looking for doesn't quite make it as the model for synaptic pruning that it's cracked up to be but is itself a copy, one of many, and the lowest man on the totem pole—Even given all this, the fact that it calls into question the very identity of the model, means that, like its champion-in-spite-of-himself, it's not to be taken lightly. Taking himself by surprise, Eden finds he can muster up the energy to say—he'd like to yawn simultaneously but is too bushed to take a stab at simulating hearty fatigue—"I'm so damn tired of rehab, doc." "Then why bother?" Pritchard shrugs professionally. "After all, what's health but just one viral strain among billions. Either it infects you—I mean fits you like a glove or it doesn't and if it doesn't, it never will, take it from me. And of course the Amygdala crowd hasn't helped one bit—it's putting it mildly to say they're mightily indifferent to your well-being." Pritchard is aware of a certain giddiness now that Margo has confirmed her imminent arrival—he's an aware kind of a guy. And how can he not be after a grand total of forty-eight years of orthodox psychoanalysis as both the Poor Slob on the Couch and the Sphinx in the Catbird Seat (with a Maserati in the parking lot), not to mention his stints as both *simultaneously* (wrap yourself around *that* stunt, why don't you?) But will he be up to the outsize challenge of tackling her conspiracy obsession which, from what he's heard, is getting stronger by the hour. Supremely spry, he leaps from the sill the better to emphasize that Eden is sure to be in even better shape than he (if the leap's on the level) once he sets his mind to steering clear of such bastard orthodoxy. Since if it's about anything, said bastardy's about the art of categorical repudiation of pleasure in all its guises by virtue of putting the worst

---

[75]Why drag in Balanchine (especially since Shearer is nowhere in sight), the groundlings gripe, revolted as they tend to be by anything that smacks of the Artsy-Fartsier-than-Thou? Clearly, the Master Baiter or his gray eminence needs to be rectificationed double-quick at one of their Bible, Rust, Sun or Borscht Belt labor camps. It's just too bad that Li Zhensheng (1940–2020) won't be around to document in black and white the deconstruction of His crime against nature.

possible interpretation on one's every move—by overplaying to the hilt one's uncanny resemblance to the creatures one devoutly loathes most—the sleaziest hubby, say, of the sluttiest Real Housewife of Death Valley or, even better, the slut herself. And not just overplaying but *overplaying*, once self-brutalization becomes like mother's milk, to the point of refusing—categorically again—all the points of *non*-resemblance. But rather than unload all this fine print Pritchard decides to keep things schoolboy-simple. "Remember, Martin, it's not a matter of, Either you're healthy Or you're a homicidal maniac. There are plenty of, albeit less interesting, choices in-between. In other words, don't do anything rash." Eden shrugs but for the life of him can't figure out what the gesture's supposed to mean (it isn't a professional shrug, that's for sure) since it's already too far ahead of him—too far ahead, surely, for retraction. Conveying without permission what he's still millions of miles away from having made up his mind to feel. He doesn't want to be rushed—even by a shrug. But the shrug has no patience with his shilly-shallying and won't back down—it was for his own good and, more importantly, for the good of the trial that the shrug was executed (and with exquisite precision, if you must know) right here and right now. What a waste.

"Martin."

"Yes, doc."

"Have you frequented any Facebook arms souks since you arrived in SB?"

"How do you mean, *frequented*?"

"Bought a TOW launcher, say, on such a site."

"No."

"What about an SA-7 gripstock? or a forward-looking infrared camera?"

"You're going too fast."

"Stop seeing yourself as a dumb blond."

"Or triacetone triperoxide."

"What."

"TATP."

Martin nods no, sadly. The stealth of feeling in his old bones tells Pritchard his son-to-be is telling the god's-honest. Then he has the following silly thought: *With Cantor as his successor and Eden as his prodigal son, he'll have it made.*

"What about uploading homemade jihad videos to YouTube or thereabouts?"

Martin nods no again, but this time around not so sadly.

"Did you ever attempt to make contact with 'exemplary family man' and Putin look-alike Viktor Bout?"

No response whatsoever—clearly, he hasn't the faintest idea who this exemplar is. Pritchard envies Eden his ignorance: it gives him—no, *lends* him—an air of otherworldliness. An otherworldliness whose embers Pritchard has little choice but to go on stoking.

"You look sad, Martin. Really sad. Something I've said, perhaps, or should have said?" How can he express to Pritchard what he can't express to himself, no, not by a long shot (though strictly speaking this should be a facilitator, not a hindrance), namely, that what he's been hankering for all along without knowing it is exactly this sort of rapid-fire exchange—stichomythia, isn't that what the oldest of the old Greeks called it? Well, at last he understands what they had in mind since it gets the ball of exposition—indeed, of catharsis—indeed, of purgation!—really rolling. For a few minutes, however painful the questions, he felt free—no longer embroiled in everybody else's meditations—free to get his story told at last at bargain-basement prices—free to get his story down pat—free to discover, finally, what his story *is*, was meant to be and will continue to be. For at last somebody in his midst—he, Martin Eden—has something to say to somebody else—Pritchard—without either's having the need to resort to the visitation of malarial thought packets on some least likely vector or vectorette. Which doesn't mean, however, that homicide—and Envy—won't take him back, if he so desires. *Or* (an Arctic gust suddenly ransacks his vitals) *does it?* Has he somehow betrayed his pathologies? Has he not kept his promise with God?

Should Pritchard tell Martin that, based on his responses there's a good chance, i.e., something between a fat or a slim chance and the ghost of one, that he can be saved from every homicidal fore- and aftertaste catalogued in the *DSM*? All he can manage to blubber is that Eden's come to him just in the nick of time though, come to think of it, time, hereabouts, is not of the essence.

CHAPTER THIRTY-TWO

After her first night at Grand Hotel Bunker (she's been relocated)—in a gated community to end all gated communities—Melanctha Herbert wakes with a giddiness completely unwarranted by present circumstances. Among other things, she's not all that delighted at having gotten stuck with Jean Rhys in the same suite. If this were some very mainstream comedy of errors, she'd be playing the wisecracking sidekick who's tough-loving-to-a-fault and forever at the service of her boss (super-competent at work and all-too-reliably but at the same time *adorably* [or so the script doctors would have our gut, very much against its own better judgment, believe] incompetent at True Romance)—the black planetesimal orbiting her white-hot star (more akin to an M dwarf as it turns out) like all the Hattie McDaniels and Butterfly McQueens before her. But Melanctha is nobody's sidekick nor does she traffic in wisecracks confectioned for the delectation of white folk. *So look elsewhere for your megadose of tough love, Jean Rhys.* Dawn hasn't even begun to give a hint of the usual ambivalence over rising—for the moment, it's nothing but the ghost of its own imminence—and already Rhys (to judge from her breathing) is a bit under the (soon-to-be-perfect) weather: must have something to do with Her Man, since she hasn't stopped muttering his name all through the night. But Herbert is far too curious about how things will end up out here (since it's out here that things are bound to end up) to be able to focus, even halfheartedly, on her roommate's self-exaltingly tone-deaf operettics. The trial can't go on indefinitely—there has to be some kind of dim resolution, some beast crouched in the foothills waiting apocalyptically to spring—as in that oft-filmed Booby Prize winning parable, *The Unshort Unhappy Life of John Marcher*. But then, adjusting her blouse (a mother's day gift: he never forgot), she realizes only a fool like her would so vastly underestimate the capacity of life, in the guise of the trial, to go on and on and on wearing her—anybody—down and to cease only when death did them part. All the same, surely the trial (even if only out of pity) must be working its way toward an issue from whose vantage point she can look back and chortling with self-contempt, rabidly loathe herself—as only a former self can be loathed—at having believed such an ordeal could endure forever. For let's face it, it has been an ordeal (and that's not Masterly hype talking even if of course it is), what with the side effects—worse, their refusal to present (*why* worse? *explain yourself!*)—and the humiliating one-on-one's, not to mention the even more ghoulish group sessions and the fact that she's been the only black for miles around. But hasn't she gathered by now that the end-of-pain dividend will accrue, if it accrues at all, only when the bondholder has abandoned all hope of such a windfall? But of course there is always the danger of artificially inseminating oneself with brute hopelessness—as was the case when, climbing Building 18's ratty walls, she tried to stave off the boy's death through such a ploy—largely out of fear that she just wouldn't rate as a griever. How she envies—envies!—those who are able to swallow life whole, bones (of contention) and all, without resorting to magic to keep it at arm's length. But there's one thing the bone-swallowers know and

Herbert (albeit the proud flower of a Bryant Avenue tenement (No. 1795 to be exact) must learn. To wit, that if she intends to go on revising herself out of her past (however non-sordid) with a little help, of course, from the drug (calling it by its "real" name still makes her blush), which seems to be tailor-made for such transmogrifications (though when was that made clear, if ever), then she must remember it isn't as if she were trying to pass herself off as somebody else. Simply a question of punching her way out of the papery envelope of the given, which is not her natural habitat—nor should it be anybody else's. Just because she was born Melanctha Herbert doesn't mean she has to stay that way—doesn't make the tics and quirks with which she was born any truer to her essence than the ones she's adopted over the years. In short, as far as Melanctha Herbert is concerned, Melanctha Herbert's sole raison d'être is to serve as the bull's-eye of ever-recyclable repudiation by none other than Melanctha Herbert—but in a friendly way—because it's all in the service of an evolutionary trek through the wilds of self-definition. A lot for a girl from the Bronx to swallow in one gulp but she's up to the challenge and she knows it.

But she goes back to sleep because, at least for now, she's on an all-expenses-paid well-deserved vacation from self-repudiation, friendly or not. *Two hours go by.* At the window the first thing that catches—that she allows to catch—her eye is a eucalyptus shivering—rustling—shaking out its gauze—in a sheer absence of wind. Trying to . . . secede from itself in order to form a . . . more perfect disunion. So that's what Herbert was trying to get at with all the business about self-repudiation's being a kind of food for the soul. So what if it required nothing less than a eucalyptus with the heebie-jeebies (in a sheer absence of wind) to make her understand that the only road to selfhood is the one paved—and badly at that—with self-schisms? So it's only through *things*—e.g., eucalypti and hominids (or is it hominins)—through their auspices—that she can hope to encounter herself—meet up with herself—make a Molotov-Ribbentrop pact with her self. There'll be no self-knowledge—hence no greatness (even if the sort of greatness she's after is by no means contingent on self-knowledge: in such circumstances it turns out, more often than not, to be a drawback)—unless she can read it off the tabula rasa of things. Which isn't all that *rasa* since it's already inscribed, like the veins in a slab of marble, with whatever she needs to read into them—the shape of a female Hercules, say—in order to read herself. But the Sunday-brunch crowd (mainly townies) entering through the gates aren't paying any attention to the eucalyptus—*her* eucalyptus. They're too busy selfieing the sailboats below (any snapshot with a smartassphone is "by definition" a selfie no matter what the ostensible subject). Since rarely do they get to gawk at them from so privileged a height. But their biggest soft spot is reserved for that yacht skidding on the treadmill of its own foam. So her very salvation—her Binsey Poplar—her Cherry Orchard—has become a spectacular one-man allegory of unwantedness incarnate. And no matter how manfully it sways, the tree-thing makes little headway in shedding the skin of that unwantedness. But for all the jaw-dropping they've missed the most telling detail of all: The fact that *the clarity of outline of the cruisers loitering on the horizon provides a much-needed corrective to the ocean's palpitant blur.* This is how she puts things right for her poplar—by transforming a something seeable into a something sayable, which autocratically goes on to make the something seeable, seeable in one way only—and only by her—no, *the likes of her*. Which sleight of hand (all for the sake of her unwanted friend) gives her the title—if not the subject—for the sort of eminently talk-showable potboiler she'll never have the guts to write—to wit, *Vengeance Is the Best Revenge*. Yes, she can hear her writing teachers telling her *the clarity of outline of the cruisers . . .* is way too abstract—has nothing to do with the cruisers. But she needs a baseline description. The only alternative (per Stephen Toulmin of the Institute for Absolute Zero) is no description at all: if there's nothing to say—as baseline, as projection, as scale, as orientation—then there's nothing to see—*really* see. Only in the process of providing a corrective are the cruisers seeable.

The second thing that catches her eye is Eden. He's fighting to crash the gates against what he needs somebody to think is unspeakable odds (though nobody's holding him back, as far as she can see). *Yesterday*'s gates (word of his visit, though nothing out of the ordinary, has gotten around and generated incomprehensible envy). The gates of inaccessibility. Does he relish exclusion, like K, as being good for business—the business of self-exaltation, that is—or is it slowly killing him the way it did Jude (for whom self-exaltation was way too much of a good thing at Christminster and beyond)? He's a little of both, he supposes—or rather, it's the Master who, johnny-on-the-spot, does the supposing, for the two of 'em—three of 'em, if you include Melanctha in the package. And why shouldn't you?—after all, she's the armature of all collisions between Master and Man. So, to Melanctha, it looks as if he'd like to relive yesterday's visit only so far it isn't *playing* the way Repetition is supposed to play. On the one hand (so he'd be thinking if he could), recapturing whatever's best of yesterday's rapturous collision with Pritchard—the health-bashing, the invocation of the online arms souks and the rapid-fire exchanges worthy of Euripides *at his Dionysian best*, not to mention all that synaptic pruning (merely uttering the term makes him go weak in the knees)—would be rapture exponentialized: squared—even cubed. On the other hand, recapture—any sort of recapture: not just of warmed-over sauerkraut—would be proof of exhaustion, penury of resources, a frugal palette, self-plagiarization as the last refuge of scoundrels, hairy-aping as attrition. Going to Pritchard could turn out to be pornographizing: an addiction for all seasons: locus of both celebration and despair—both drug and the place where drug takes effect. In her opinion, Eden deserves better. She wants to run out and warn him (but of what? her fears aren't his fears—he ain't afraid of aping himself silly) *before it's too late*. So just look at her: willing (though not yet ready or able) to squander, on the rankest of strangers, whatever motherliness she could never lay claim to. Well, and so what? Can she help it if just breaks her heart to see him returning to this site to recapture the rapture he didn't know he felt—*because it wasn't there*? The event in question—the meeting with Pritchard—his father-to-be (yes, he too felt the bond to come)—surely knew nothing about rapture though don't think for a minute it isn't mighty pleased to know there's somebody out there who swears it's worth its weight in transfiguration. But only when framed tight enough by retrospect does the canvas of the event ooze rapture. For the vocation of retrospect is to ascribe to its target precisely what wasn't there (or is this yet another case of words running snottily amuck?—the cancer of their disconnection spreading like wildfire—at the Master's peremptory behest).

As Eden advances toward Pritchard, sitting cross-legged next to the still dewy diving board and encircled by about half the trial participants, who are either stark or semi naked, he is muttering something to the effect (terrific icebreaker, this) that they have no reason in the world to Envy so-called creators since now, thanks to Invidicum, they are all creators, whether they want to be or not, and shouldn't let anybody tell them different (including Pritchard himself who has a bad habit of changing his spots), though when they've finally come to recognize the uniqueness of their so-called creation they mustn't fall into the booby trap of cultivating a hoity-toity sense of its worth (nothing more humorless than narcissism, even the "good-cholesterol kind," and the surest sign of mediocrity, to boot) which will only end up infecting the creation itself—and no less lethally because retroactively. "Hi," Pritchard says, a bit too graciously, as if underlining that what may have been construed a while back, at their tough-loving first interview, as harshness is but one focus of an elliptical grand plan (graciousness being the other), which is to acquaint Eden with the unsuspected reserves of killer resilience that will go on enabling him (until its services are no longer required) to accept unjustifiable shifts of mood—anybody's mood—without crumbling.

"Let's get one thing straight, my young friend: a display of emotion, or its lack, on my part is never anything but *heuristic*. (Once I release you, have no qualms about looking the word up in our over-stacked library.)" The scents coming from every direction, including the smell of the heat (the headiest of all by far) warn Eden that as long as he remains on these premises (The Rumpish Pritchard is making him feel like Little Marco), he mustn't be shocked if the meaning of words turn out uncannily to be directly opposite to—or, far more radically, just slightly different from—their meaning elsewhere. So why shouldn't he follow suit and . . . also (what did they call it in Hollywood?) play against type? But what *is* his type? Pritchard: "It's obvious you're exceptional—or exceptionally disturbed. But whatever else you are, you're trouble—trouble so great it seems like—and is in fact—talent—and I know how to spot it a mile away." "But you said I'd start to feel less . . . talented within the week." Eden would have thought he'd feel much queasier about having his dirty laundry hung out to dry before strangers. In fact, he's exhilarated.

"You're correct. And what would you say if I were to announce that Doc Manning's flying out here for the sole purpose of getting the detoxification ball rolling? But what about her defection, you wonder? A mere ploy to throw Post & Co. off the scent." (Eden immediately realizes how much he's missed Irena.) "And adding insult to injury, no less than the deputy assistant chief of the LAPD will be arriving any second now with a warrant for Post's arrest as the killer of Jim Straynge." But if suddenly there's something for Eden to live for, as now seems likely, what with the police and Irena on the way and his not-quite-handler about to be skewered, the danger that it might be definitively nipped in the bud is (like Shelley's Spring) not far behind, in which case only a definitive quashing of all hope (cf. Melanctha's toying with the "concept" of brute hopelessness) will make short work of his panic at this prospect. Pritchard suddenly goes silent, punishing him, or so it seems, for not showing sufficient appreciation of the good news and, more to the point, of the artfulness of its delivery—appreciation expressible, *where somebody like Eden is concerned* (but *who is cranking out such a phrase*? Eden? Pritchard? Somebody? Somebody Plus? the reader's surrogate mother? Mrs. Bean? the narrator? the universal wisdom machine?), only by delivering his very own version of news, good or otherwise, so as, through the inevitable high contrast, to underline just how artful Pritch's inimitable artfulness in fact was. Which punitive silence must mean the session's about to end, even if it hasn't even begun (at least as far as Eden's concerned), and as under no circumstances will he give Pritchard a chance to further consolidate his hegemony by making an announcement to that effect, Eden decides (without having the faintest idea that what's going on in his muddled frame *is* deciding), by rising prematurely (as any other self-respecting man of the world, naked or clothed, might do in his place), to deprive the fuzzy old dear (but *who is speaking*? Somebody? Somebody Plus? the author? Cantor at his campiest? Rhys or Shearer at her cattiest? Ronald Firbank? Lorenz Ca'ad? Saki?) of the delectation of serving the eviction notice himself and, secondarily, of observing Eden, officially evicted, crawl toward the bunker on his hind legs with the sort of sheepishness no Parthian shot, however much to the point (the point being Pritchard's groin), could mitigate. But in Eden's defense it shall be duly noted in the record that his decision has been influenced in no small measure by a filial inkling that, from the gerontological angle, such delectation—being too rich, too greasy, too sudden, too non-habitual—must remain strictly prohibited even if the doc looked (especially in poolside mufti) considerably younger than his (seventy-? ninety-odd?) years.

But as it turns out, the session has no intention of ending for here's one particularly unfetching member of the bare-butt brigade shrieking between sobs or vice versa: "What if there are surveillance cameras or recording devices in the pool and everywhere else?" She doesn't want any of her vicious co-workers or even-more-vicious kissing cousins knowing about this unholy institutionalization for Envy Disease. And here comes Pritchard to the rescue, doing his best to assure her that nobody but nobody (and reaching out with his liverspotted forepaw to seal the deal) listening in on their meetings (group, one-on-one or anything and everything in-between), however attentively, will ever be able to deduce the subject thereof, for the simple reason that all true sufferers in vitro can't avoid cutting the meat of exposition superthin to the point of audience uningestibility—not because they're terrified of appearing as dramaturgically inept as some off-Broadway hack who's never learned the first law of hackdom, i.e. *Show, don't tell,* but because they're too tortured— too much at one with the torture—to be able to name it—to think of naming it: which would constitute a feat on a par with (per our old friend Toulmin) chewing up their own teeth.

While attempting to seat himself within the winner's circle which seems to be the only configuration suitable for lapping up the curds and whey of all this folk wisdom, Eden gets an eyeful of Bean bearing down on them, highish heels exaggerating her unflummoxable heft, and immediately fears the worst—that the police have arrived to make him their fall guy. In fact, no, not at all, the furthest thing from her mind: the old girl is merely bringing Pritchard a glass of what looks like ruby-red grapefruit juice in which two or three tablets are dissolving, though not without protest. But as her receding rump trumpets Mission Accomplished, another old girl emerges (the one who, at the moment of his arrival, was aggressively manning the phones in a windowless side office and chewing gum, even more aggressively) to shout through hands comedically cupped: "Doctor, the LAPD mounties!" Rather than be manacled before this group (only a lunatic would mistake them for a hung jury of his peers), Eden decides to flee.

Sensing—seeing—that poor Eden is about to do so, Pritchard—his face a battleground of fast-ebbing irritation (at his prodigal son) and anticipatory delight (over his next sally)—motions him to get right back down on his hind legs this very instant or face the consequences. As it turns out, they're here to debrief Narr and Cook (last seen gamboling about on the ferny fringes of Skofield Park)—the Defectors' Defectors, as they're called in the executive washrooms at Langley and well beyond (although on the basis of what evidence? somebody thinks—maybe Eden!)—not arraign a cur like Eden, who's way below their radar and likely to remain so for quite some time, maybe forever. The jagged edge of such (well-intentioned?) belittlement carves out a fierce Envy of the unholy pair. The question on the tip of everybody's forked tongue is of course, Why the LAPD? why not the SBPD? Pritchard takes the bull by the horns: "Silly matters of purview become irrelevant when you're confronted with a case of such magnitude, for not since Aldrich Ames and Jim Nicholson reared their ugly heads has the Agency unmasked operatives this base. Though of course the defections were and the residual baseness is all an act—to throw the real villains and their high-tech eavesdroppers off our track. *Our* track. Since we're all in this together." Little does Pritchard know—little does anyone know—that *We're all in this together* will become the feeble fatuous phony rallying cry during the COVID-19 pandemic. Thing is, when they start rolling out the gurneys in celebration thereof, we *won't* all be in this together—no, not by a long shot—not when The Rump's undeserving cronies suck up all the forgivable-loan oxygen out of the Paycheck Protection Program (paging Mike Kelly, St. Andrew's Episcopal School, Marc Kasowitz, Jared Kushner, etc.) and the idle rich flee to their second, third or eighth homes while noblesse-obligingly giving the essential (that is to say, *expendable*) workers leg room enough to stoically strut their stuff in supermarkets, nursing homes, hospitals, post offices, etc. "So stay tuned. In addition, it's all hands on deck up at the cemetery *what with the bomb threats and tombstones hacked to bits*." But, Herbert thinks, judging from the tone—a bitter one, which takes a malign pleasure in that bitterness and given half a chance could disgorge megatons more—this last utterance is not at all about what it's supposed to be about. The subject is not tombstones but the failure of the utterance to come anywhere near conveying the something else it *should* be about. Which probably goes double—or triple—for all the utterances that came before. A mere placeholder, that's what each of them is, for a truth none is worthy of transmitting by virtue of the simple fact that it *is* a placeholder—just another limit point of language. Hence all the exhilarating, suppressed bitterness. But as she sees it, where language is concerned the sky's the limit. After all, language is, following the few obligatory missteps (without which her ghosted autobio would be a bore), about to become her bread and butter.

Taking a few dog-eared pages from the Guru's cuebook, they apply themselves (except maybe for Herbert and Cantor—and it's a big *maybe*) to paying no further attention to Eden. Which means that his acculturation has miraculously managed to bypass, for better or worse, what is known on the sociology circuit as the Stage of Privilege, at which the blatant newcomer, perceived as bringing some much-craved whiffs of the great outdoors to a community damned and disgusted by excessive inbreeding, becomes Man of the Hour. So what if this anointing turns out (in most cases) to be a mere reprieve before the Man (his Hour up) justly incurs the most devastating kind of familiarity-bred expulsion—that which lands him in the innermost heart of the community? And all this to the far-from-intoxicating strains of Strauss, Jr.'s most over-celebrated and least overrated Sacher-Torte in three-fourths time, the "Walking Papers Waltz" (ca. 1883).

Yet here he is remembering, of all things, Jean Rhys's account (before a capacity crowd no less and in, of all places, Amygdala's newly refurbished [Girard?] Amphitheater)—riveting, at least in retrospect—of how it took just a dose too many of a compote-crazy kid sister's smouldering smugness (Dottie Sue? Lucy Lou? no, Caro!) to drive her and her soon-to-be ex to the extremity of taking an abortive midsummer night's ride on the Staten Island Ferry. As long as the memory lasts—for it's he who's steering, expertly—he feels *insulated* from *disregard*. Though he'd be hard put to define either.

Somebodies who are obviously two of LAPD's finest stride across the lawn, one, as is to be expected by those in the know, being slightly shorter than the other. How *naked* is movement, she thinks, Movement doesn't *lie*, though this is neither the time nor the place to figure out why. It would be sacrilege. Why? But if she intends to make her way as a writer on whom Hollywood ultimately has no choice but to confess it harbors designs she bloody well needs to overcome her fear of that nakedness—to flesh it out without altogether smothering it in borrowed finery. They halt behind Pritchard. It isn't clear, at least to Cantor, whether he's pointedly ignoring their presence or pretending he doesn't know there's a *there there*, given the willingness of his poker face to serve as the field of battle between bubbly absorption in the needs of his unmentorables and exasperation at having that absorption diluted. And with things so ambiguous—not least of all his status (is it still intended that he succeed Pritchard *when all this blows over*?)—Cantor can't deny it's very nice to have to admit that the flagless flagpole behind the chaises longues has cast its clear-as-crystal shadow on the crab grass just in the nick of time. Something sitting so rich- and famously pretty certainly didn't need to stick its neck out—but here it is having done exactly that and with no expectation of reimbursement. The shorter of the two bends over and stage-whispers, "We need to speak with you, doc."

Pritchard takes his time acknowledging shorty—Shorty's—presence. They stare at each other. Pritchard immediately understands that for now the encounter's all about who can keep his bull's-eye stare going longest—all about who has the longest stare, i.e., the longest dick (he appears to be in the lead). Pritchard, if you must know, has never realized—never allowed himself to realize—just how manly his stare is—just how manly his *gaze* is—and how much akin to a dick gazes really are. As it turns out, they're more, much more, than cognates, agnates, analogues, homologues. Fact is, to the practiced eye they're indistinguishable—one and the same—as the gods themselves meant them to be—the very gods who throw stale incense on the altar of impossible sacrifices. But does he believe this—can he even imagine it? No, because the verbal decree forecloses all seeing (including the closed-eye kind last practiced professionally by Stan Brakhage)—even if what the decree promises is not just seeing but seeing at a Dolby wraparound level of intensity. He looks up (and away from Shorty's shorter dick) and what does he see but a cloud— one of those clouds—you know the kind—whose contour resembles nothing so much as the coastline of, say, Zambia. Yes, synonymizing dick and gaze is the same thing as decreeing that a cloud's contour resembles nothing so much as the coastline of Zambia—yet another decreeing that is designed to occlude any seeing—that insists on remaining airtight—refractory to signification. And now—over there—is a pocket of azure that's the size, although not the shape—or is it the other way around—of Texas (Ted Cruz's gutless Texas to be exact). Here again is wordflow doing nothing less than making sure it doesn't crash-dive onto the tarmac of anything seeable. These ostensible clarifications are a purposeful dead end—a cul-de-sac. And to the right of the tarmac is yet another cloud whose rim resembles nothing so much as a fractalization of . . . the Gold Coast of Arthurian Britain. Once more, wordflow triumphs over worldflow. Apparently worded thoughts—like everybody else (since *a man is a thought* and a thought is therefore a man)—just want to have fun—good clean Peircean fun—and who can blame them?

(This all feels so . . . new to Pritchard: after all, he's a babe in the woods where championship bouts between word- and worldflow are concerned.) Do I believe what I've just put into words, Pritchard continues to wonder (all the time keeping his bushy gaze erect and trying to stop from going mad, as Eden—Balboa Park's favorite son—once or thrice went mad). But does it really matter if he believes or not? Or is all this just a case (*yet another case* since there had to have been plenty of others while he was too busy scampering about undiapered in those woods to pay them any heed)—just a case of words needing, like everybody else, to be allowed to go their merry way untended, unintended—un*tenanted* by reference—allowed to achieve (it's a mental health issue) the blighted evolution they were born for—from A to Z and back again? And while we're at it, isn't it the case that his—that anybody's—evolution is the evolution of their *wordflow* just as the history of Malte Laurids Brigge's neighbors was the history of the symptoms they generated in him at the behest of a puppeteer every bit as nasty and messy and intractable as the Master, who doesn't know, by the way, that He's (no, make that *he's*) just met His (make that *his*) match?

Pritchard is catching on. For just as Cantor has a mentor in Pritchard so does Pritchard now have one—in the Master (whether he wants the Master or not, His services have been outsourced gratis for thirty days). He's out-amygdalizing the Amygdala crowd, fresh from their record-breaking engagement (as ill-assorted mountebanks and saltimbanques straight out of Tod Browning's *Freaks*), on Greenwich Avenue. He's making word whoopee without having to fear what the absence of a correspondent whoopee out in the world might mean for his future—for his career. You might say he's contracted a bad case of "the Master" thanks to imperfect social distancing. Alas, if only he'd allowed himself to realize something like this decades upon decades ago, things would have been so different. There'd have been far less hurt, much less humiliation. But isn't the very business of life the business of Lamarckian evolution, the messier the better? and what (asks Pritchard the Merchant of Pritchard the Urchin—asks Pritchard the Highbrow of Pritchard the rhythm-crazy Lowbrow) would evolution be without humiliation? which simply cannot be speeded up to satisfy the evolver's hunger to annex the phantom of unmessy invulnerability—to apply the bubble glaze of moral perfection. Evolution is all about humiliation—some might say that evolution *is* humiliation. On the other hand (if there is/for there is always an other hand) could anyone ever guess, looking at him now atop the Everest of his mortarboarded dignity, how hard he campaigned for and hence so richly deserved all the humiliation munificently thrown his way in the course of every instar? Could they put two and two together and come up with the five or six of an unspeakable lust for degradation—of a snottily obese toadying before wealth and power which afflicted him starting from the cradle? But he has no accounts to render to anybody: he simply needed something to learn from—the way somebody not born into wealth needs a job to retire from—and humiliation fit the bill. Pritchard remains (like the so many others whose lot scars these never-to-be-dog-eared pages) a super-fast learner where humiliation is the teacher (*I think I've already used that quip somewhere above or somewhere below: I dare you to forgive me*).

Can it be that he's been infected with WORDFLOW-19 (which is literally all the rage) through contact with the Amygdala crowd? Envy may not be contagious but the side effects of Invidicum could very well be. Or might somebody have dissolved a masssive dose of Invidicum in his morning coffee or middle-of-the-night chamomile or evening Rob Roy over the last few days? And speaking of possible culprits, he's frankly never really hit it off with that shadowy Bean woman (even if or maybe because he was such a big Jean Vigo fan in his cineclub days). But now that you mention it, word did definitely get around (he seems to recall), although not necessarily to Pritchard (any Führer worth his salt is always—like *the husband*—the last to know), that just before they left New York the members of the Greenwich Avenue contingent had started receiving a dose of Invidicum (abetted by a dollop or two of Master) so potent it turned them, at the drop of a top hat and at the behest of that messy puppeteer, into practitioners of hyper-eloquence—the brand that necessarily depends on wordflow's besting worldflow (is there any other?). Although they must pay for their good fortune, if good fortune is what it is, by accepting the fact that when in eloquential mode, they're pretty much indistinguishable from each other—and in fact, the indistinguishability increases . . . *exponentially* (to use a word currently overused to the point of meaninglessness) with level of sophistication. So what all this hullabaloo (a fancy word for affliction) may amount to is a clash of cultures—a collision of coasts, East and West, even if never (supposedly) the twain shall meet. Though why be so quick to accuse the Amygdalites when it's very possible he may have caught some kind of doomsday bug while trout-fishing in the subarctic months back—SARS-CoV-2, for example, which, if his ex-broker's hot tip is to be believed, will shortly be "roiling the markets" in such a way as to benefit mightily *those in the know*. But whether he's caught anything or not, he needs to take the law into his own hands and lower their dosages. Just to play safe.

When he forces himself to say, "Would you two be kind enough to wait for me back at the ranch?—I'll be up in a minute," the words are directed not at the pair but at the entire group. He announces, once he can sense them receding, as tactful as surf: "I'm sure you're surprised—especially the newcomers from Way Back East—to see so many people here today—older folks, pre-teens, even toddlerettes. Well, fact is, these sessions are not merely for the patients—the trial subjects—but for family members and friends as well—unsung heroes who've been suffering along with them every misstep of the way—what I call the Fallout Brigade." But what he's really announcing is that whatever contingencies may assail him, he'll never, so help me gods, let them impede the discharge of his professional duties (even if the health insurance crooks decide not to reimburse him one penny). Better yet, he's going to hijack adversity (looking deep into the sunny bosoms of Santa Ynez), as only he knows how, and turn it, yet again, into the vehicle of their—or, better yet, his own—self-improvement.

As a bonus, Pritchard treats them to a précis of what's he's been thinking about over the last few minutes: wordflow versus worldflow, (expurgated) dicks, gazes, Britain before Billy the Conqueror, evolution, Texas, Zambia, etc.—but in a language everybody can understand without raising an eyebrow. Then collapses into his own lap, i.e., puts his face into the safekeeping of his hands (a gesture that Borkman knows from personal experience is supposed to mean *I've just endured a too-long standing ovation and have every right to take a load off my feet but now watch me as, without missing a beat, I go—well just about as deep into myself as a man can go without abandoning all hope of still getting out alive*). Then looking up and grinning boyishly (as if having managed, spiritual virtuoso that he is, to make mincemeat of every LAPD argument for self-arraignment appropriate in such a place), says, "Where were we?" They shake their heads—a big I don't know—as if all heads are one—the very one Caligula dreamed (or was it Nero or Genghis Khan?) of flinging, together with his Stradivarius, into the flaming Tiber. As for Borkman, he wishes he had, like his namesake, an attic (nothing fancy) to pace back and forth in—to the tune of (what else?) "In the Hall of the Mountain King" (guaranteed to drive any self-respecting psychopath wild with a renewed sense of purpose).

It's clear, at least to Herbert, that Pritchard considers himself what used to be called in the good old Dark Ages an artist-martyr, and a savvy one at that, for hasn't he managed to extract from yet another dungheap of ersatz super-esoterica nothing less than the molten core of mass-market accessibility it never dreamed itself capable—much less worthy—of harboring? And why not, especially right now, when the time is overrripe for just this sort of sleight of hand, what with the ever-slicker lowbrows making relentless mincemeat of the highbrows, that is, of their productions' mythic value-added. By proving, through mimicry, that you can be a highbrow—or at least a sort of highbrow—without renouncing your citizenship as a lowbrow—that you can enjoy the best of both nationalities. Since that's what dire slickness is all about. That's what *competence* is all about. And coming from the other direction—also with not only Georgia on Their Mind but Destruction as well—are the hyper-highbrows who every chance they get proclaim The Death of The Author as Highbrow, erecting on his ruins an altar to The Author Who Proclaims the Death of The Author as Highbrow, i.e., they themselves. So folks like Herbert can look forward to bombardment from above and below. Only most folks are not like Herbert, who's been steeled over centuries of slavehood to weather just such bombardment. Or so she hopes. Since the steeling could be just the imbibable fantasy of whites, who mean well—as they did on the sidelines in lead-saturated Flint—because the meaning well costs them less than nothing.

Her musings get cut short, however, by the outburst of the most recent conscript to the Fallout Brigade, who seems to have taken Pritchard's avowed compassion for the Brigadeers at its word—or its wordiness. The conscript mutters (pointing both forefingers straight at him) something about having discovered her husband's Envy too late and to self-devastating effect and, frankly, she's not sure whether it was simply finding out about it or finding about it too late that was—is—*the fly in the ointment.* (Herbert's not sure whether this Brigadieress [accent on the third syllable] is using the idiom correctly but isn't it the duty of idioms to be mangled as long as they're mangled tastefully?) "Too late for what?" Pritchard, so as not to cringe in the face of so much unfocused aggressivity, probes airily—or pretends to probe—all the while casting glances back, but not quite so airily, in the direction of the cops, now out of sight. No need to wait for an answer since he realizes the lady before him is none other than his lost (and only?) love, Margo Straynge. And if so, there are certainly more things in the heaven and earth—and most of all the hell—of her juggernaut of a mismarriage than can be encompassed by any interrogation, however thoroughgoing. She's advancing toward the swimming pool and looks about ready to—literally—go off the deep end. Knowing a thing or two about marriage hearses, Jean immediately wants to strangle him for giving such short shrift—for giving *no* shrift, really—to the woman's all-too-evident wretchedness. But isn't this the occupational hazard par excellence of the members of the shaman tribe, i.e., to end up denigrating the needy for their very neediness inasmuch as nobody worth healing would ever be caught dead in their Magic Circle? Only the absent are worthy of healing but by virtue of absence they're exalted beyond need (as if Caro's big sister needed reminding) or at least this is how their absence is interpreted by toadying quacks like Pritchard. (He's eminently distrustworthy, she calls out soundlessly to conveniently absent Ethan.)

Margo returns soon enough. But she's scuttled her incognito. Apologizing like the great lady he knows her still to be, she explains to anybody who'll listen—and in fact everybody is already all ears—that it's the visit of the LAPD that's undone her. And by the way, she no longer professes to hold Pritchard responsible for Straynge's death. Fact is, Straynge's siblings—worse, Margo's own—had joined forces in holding *her* responsible from the get-go (the overwork required to cover his wife's expenditures drove him to an early grave) and the rest of the world, compliments of their indefatigable networking, fell quickly into line. So what could she do but find herself a patsy. But she doesn't hold it against them for they themselves were/are being manipulated . . . by a Mabuse—the Stonehenge-accredited honcho of some ashram cult. Pritchard wonders if that's how she perceives *him*. In any case, the conspiracy bug is alive and well—insusceptible to incineration even by this ever-dutifully-blazing California sun. Indeed, if he must know, she's come all this distance to praise Caesar—*her* Caesar—her first and only love (suddenly, only Tristan and Isolde, i.e., the two of them, exist)—not to bury him (with Straynge, Sr.). But even if Gentleman Jim got her on the rebound she still managed to entertain, through thick and thin, a certain fondness for the clumsy old blowhard who turned out, after all and notwithstanding, to be man of the world enough to have officially adopted *their* wayward son as his own. Pritchard blushes. He's harbored suspicions but given his other interests and her borderline infertility . . . So she's hoping against hope that any moment now, they'll be arresting the culprit. Only then will she be able to start *healing*. Only then will there be a *closure* that befits her grief.

Healing—*closure*—how Cantor (knowing a thing or two about grief)—and not just Cantor—hates those fucking words. Words so abject they're fuckable. Thing is, his fellow haters may not want to get acquainted with their own hate. For this could mean permanent estrangement from the fickleness of the common horde. Or maybe they think only an advanced degree would entitle them to piss on such smarmily *caring* euphemisms, with their sob-sisterly pretense of confronting the phenomenon in question (in this case, grief) head-on. In fact, *healing* and *closure* have been cooked up to prevent—smother—confrontation with said phenomenon. Just like—or almost just like—one of those descriptions of a few minutes ago, Pritchard thinks (this is, after all, a Masterminded duet for him and Cantor accompanied by the Master on tenor sax), that are designed to foreclose seeing—visualizing. To real grief (and Cantor knows of what he speaks), not only healing and closure but, more to the point, *healing* and *closure* are unthinkable. For under the strict terms of an irreversible (make that an *authentically* irreversible) descent into grief's maelstrom which no amount of closure can befoul, language—the whore who repines for her presumption too late and too little—should be but a hop, skip, and a jump away from muteness. So Margo's grief is but skin-deep. Maybe that's why he presciently abandoned her or is it she who should be applauded for having taken the bull by the horns?

To make a long story short, she's flown all the way out here, *to the Coast* (no prepositional phrase has ever meant so much to this dyed-in-the-wool

Westchesterite)—her first visit but, assuredly, not her last—to help out—by killing the proverbial two birds with one stone. She wants both to share the experience of living with an exemplary sufferer and, *pari passu*, to stand up for her (other) man, something she should have done decades ago. For whether Pritchard knows it or not, he's the suspect du jour, which is turning out to be the longest she's ever lived through. "Oh, Margo, Margo, Margo, why (and just when I thought the ocean air was beginning to take the edge off your signature edginess) must you dredge up our slime-ridden past for folks who already have their hands much too full as it is? Why reinvent the Envy wheel by rewriting *Envy: A Misuser's Guide*? They'll find all they need to know in the last edition. The fifteenth, if I'm not mistaken." But looking at her—the Margo before him—beneath him—now the Margo of thirty years ago—his partner in the crime of unholy procreation, he breathes a sigh of relief. (But is that problem child really—*really*—his? well, come to think of it, they do have something in common at the very least epigenetically: they're both persons of interest in the Straynge Case of Jim Straynge, soon to be a limited miniseries.) She endears herself to him, even now, even if it's for all the wrong reasons. For whatever else they are—were—they can't be accused—certainly not he and certainly not by this crowd—of wallowing in blind acceptance of each other's orifices—wallowing in kissy ratification of the savor of each other's flaws. For even the least repulsive being suddenly has repulsiveness to spare once it fuses with another to become that vilest of two-backed organisms, a loving couple in love with its brand-new complacency, each the other's defiant crutch and complacent standard-bearer, with everybody else, before whom they once cowered, being a mere pretext for giggly disdain. They can't accuse him of putting the *we* before everybody else, the unroyal we. (*A man after my own heart—or lack thereof—Cantor thinks.*) Which means abandoning the abjectly lonely to their fate and risking the retaliation of the envious, lonely or not. Never, for example, did he even contemplate putting his arm around her, either publicly or even in private (*where the contortion would have been far more conspicuous*). Or is this paradox, Margo wonders, just an alluvial deposit of wordflow—just the sort of hackwork being propagated by that self-styled Master she's been hearing so much about? (*Breaking News: Pritchard's bug has just infected Margo's brain: chalk it up to recent advances in targeted aerosol transmission.*) But isn't the conviction that you're required to take dictation from such a hack, she also wonders, the side effect of Invidicum-guzzling and hence an affliction restricted to trial members? Though what if somebody's been routinely dousing her early-evening cocoa with the drug—somebody like that innocent-looking bleached blonde to her right? (She's referring to Netta.) By the way, Pritchard senses that Borkman has never been a fan of the unroyal we, which is most definitely a point in his favor, almost an occasion for rejoicing. On this note he abruptly exits.

Looking startlingly rejuvenated (so, upon arrival and appearances notwithstanding, they must have been on their last legs), the two cops reappear, followed by . . . Pritchard! Shorty slaps Borkman with a subpoena—no, four. Cantor is pretty sure *slaps* is the right term. But even if it isn't—even if it doesn't fit the gesture—it does fit the surroundings, to a T. Which is what counts, at least to Cantor, who's sensitive to this sort of thing—this sort of thing being unspoken—*unspeakable*—protocol. After he has a look, Borkman feels obliged to explain what it's all about—actually, seems to relish feeling obliged. They gather round. The brigadiers—whom he deigns not to exclude, whether from kindness or a craving for as large an audience as possible—are clearly eager to drown their addiction-battered kin in somebody else's misery. To Shearer's way of thinking (and she won't be swayed), they look like the cygnets dancing attendance on Odette in Akim's one-act distillation of *Swan Lake* but unlike the movement of those doggone cygnets theirs is completely amenable to advancing a story line, however much it's an uphill battle. Borkman as Odette! Well, why not? hasn't the slap resulted in nothing less than a contusion of his maleness? In addition to the subpoenas he's been served with a restraining order. But why a restraining order? After all, the kids (at least My Son, The Unicorn) are gone—have flown the coop and not a minute too soon given the ramifications of the divorce (the kind normally referred to as messy and/or acrimonious—or rather [as noted above] messy and/or *sordid*)—and he has no intention of banging down the door and beating his wife's pretensions to a bloody pulp at this stage of the game even if obliterating her has become a moral imperative. For as imperceptibly as grief, the summer's ripeness for assault and battery has passed away. But he doesn't mind their thinking that in addition to being a crook, he also has the makings of a murderer since under the right circumstances—and plenty *were* right—he could have been exemplary. Laying the restraining order to rest on the particolored chaise longue closest to hand (even if for the most part it's occupied—by a toothsome set of gams), he goes after the four-antlered bigger game. The first subpoena (issued jointly by the Tulsa Department of Financial Services and Wilburr Ross) has something to do with abuse of tax loopholes—lots of real estate loopholes. Taking over-deductions—a euphemism, like *healing*—for the mythical depreciation of his real estate holdings even if all they've ever done is appreciate. The second (issued by the US Attorney for the Northeastern and Southwestern Districts of Alabama in partnership with Blackwater Inc. and Bill Barre Sinister) vaults his having taken a dog-eared page from one of The Rump's playbooks by putting three goats on the biggest of his NJ golf courses, thereby turning it into virtually tax-exempt agricultural property. The third (issuer's name(s) redacted) proclaims that The Rump is now going after him for such rank plagiarism. The fourth (ditto) challenges the conviction that his poor wife is entitled to a far smaller slice of his appreciating assets since in fact they've all appreciated *passively*, i.e., compliments of force majeure, in other words, through no fault of his own competence. But Melanctha's too smart— and he, too, without necessarily knowing how smart he is in this department as in so many others—too smart not to realize that exposure for the likes of Borkman—for the likes of the compulsively watchable tantrum that is Borkman, as for the likes of The Rump—is just another (ostrich) *feather in his cap* (to use Mamma Herbert's phrase)—such exposure is honorific or beside the point or both. He's pleased—happy—more than happy—to be publicizing what's in fact a quadruple-header. Any publicity is good publicity. He clearly gets as much of a thrill out of skewedly revealing his crookedness as he does from belaboring his outsize home-front incompetence. For exposure equals exculpation equals exaltation, however fleeting.

Borkman announces that as soon as he's released from prison if it's to prison he must go the plan will be to run for office, like fellow felon Don Blankenship, one of his many idols and idolators. Although he concedes, in so many words (some of them four-letter words, some the most expensive words on his menu), that he's nowhere near *there* yet where *there* encompasses the capacity to (*a*) seduce those constituents who prize nothing so much as their own disenfranchisement as long as it stops just short of annihilation and as long as it's at—and in—the hands of somebody who knows how (going above and beyond the imperceptible stench of his contempt for humanity) to objectivize them—objectify them—delete them—"repurpose" them as mere means to an end—validate them by invisibilizing them; (*b*) sow blowtorch certitude among the Evangelical Christian swath of his votaries that whatever fake-news wickedness is brought to light by his adversaries is in fact a gift horse of the gods to be borne in a spirit of forbearance, i.e., slavish intolerance of the obsessional neurotic hooey of all other denominations; and (*c*) craft the right kind of solemn warning, in advance of perpetrating them, that his most pious doings—e.g., cramming the courts high and low with pro-life suprema-cist incompetents in the great McConnell tradition—may turn out to be most efficiently fueled by hell-bent contravention of everything that stinks of piety (which goes a long way [*who is speaking now?*] toward explaining why, in the current four-year cosmic cycle, the role of the Redeemer Incarnate has been taken by a vicious crook—a superannuated "morbidly obese" punk—dredged up for popular consumption from one of New York's gated outerborough Everglades). But does this long parenthesis, which clearly has everything to do with The Rump, have anything to do with Borkman as well—Borkman as she's come to know and grudgingly—begrudgingly—tolerate him? she won-ders. Did the Master make her think it up or dream it up (instead of remain-ing wide awake) while on sentinel duty at her eternal battle station, to wit, the frontier between word- and worldflow? in either case to stave off a reckoning with the real Borkman who's disappointingly very much not larger than life—to stave off a recognition of the fact that Borkman is not The Rump and never will be—isn't evil enough to bear the weight of all these attributions—which apply to The Rump alone. For it's with The Rump that the Master has a bone—many bones—to pick and Melanctha is being inveigled—so urgent is her hun-ger to complete her apprenticeship as soon as possible and get on with the business of winning literary prizes—into thinking thoughts about Borkman that should rightfully be deemed thoughts about The Rump. (Though who's to determine right from wrong when it comes to the weighty issue of what a thought is *really* about? Melanctha is tempted first to think of herself waifishly as collateral damage but *Broken Blossoms*-style waifishness doesn't yield the kind of dividends that interest her as an artist so she chooses to upstage the-waif-that-wasn't and think her disorientation as a synergistic walk inside the mock-sacred space generated by the intersection of two Venn diagrams—Mr. Venn Borkman and Mr. Venn Rump. And isn't there beauty—i.e., an unlikely pathos—in thinking about Borkman as a failed Rump and vice versa?) For example, does Borkman really idolize that foul sty Blankenship? Does he even know who Blankenship is—and that his one good deed, scion of coal-scuttle desperation, was to unsuccessfully smear Mitch? And speaking of Mitch, does JGB have any idea how many evolutionary crossroads had to be traversed and retraversed before this Fart Incarnate—the first of its kind—the first hominid to be both man and flatus—could be, from malevolent Mother Mutation's workshop, tidily unleashed, contrast collar and all, upon the world? No, no and no. So, when all is said and done, Borkman and the Master make a fine pair: both extrinsic—both marginal—to their own designs—their delusions of grandeur—both forever relegated to the periphery of, and at cross-purposes with, any tactic likely to bear delusional fruit.

Does the Master—the sort of parent who clobbers his offspring for inheriting the sorriest stretches of his genome—not-so-secretly contend that it is only as refracted through The Rump's bulging coattails that Borkman's image is salvageable? But does the Master really give a damn about Borkman, salvageable or not? And who precisely is being kept warm by The Rump's shadow? Borkman or the Master? And is refraction only a fancy term to describe (without indicting) the Master's strategy for making Borkman relevant?—for making *Himself* relevant through Borkman as The Rump?—relevant to this World-Hysterical moment which threatens to make everything irrelevant *that is not of, for, or (for that matter) against The Rump?* The Master simply doesn't want to be left behind. In which case the Master isn't much different from a flunkey like relevance-rabid Lindsey the Graham Cracker caddy (he carries The Rump's balls and not just on the links). Only, unlike the Cracker, He doesn't need—doesn't want—The Rump for himself. He is by vocation bound to serve him up on a trencher to His clients at the Tennessee Wittgenstein Dinner Theater (among others), as one big fat slab of the Zeitgeist. Nay, The Rump *is* the Zeitgeist and for the moment Borkman is the Master's Ariadne's thread—His only way into the maze. Until the real thing comes along. Still, the Master shouldn't sell Borkman short (thinks Melanctha): even if he takes the low road and The Rump takes the high road, he may still get to prison before him. So, Mr. Wittgenstein, is Borkman—the *concept* of Borkman—just a conduit—just a vector—just the most plausible among a host of implausibles—for smuggling The Rump virus into the act?—the Master's act (which the Master has himself vivisected and found lacking)—and vice versa—even if The Rump is so relevant he's always already there, right smack in the middle of the Master's act. Just as he's always already everywhere else. *Spoiler alert:* The Rump's rump is nothing but relevance. But does the Master's quest for relevance (and at His advanced age!) mean that Borkman must be bulldozed and dismantled and shoddily reconstructed as a kind of prosthetic Rump? Is there no longer any room in the Master's universe for Borkman's penny ante malfeasance on its own semi-egregious terms? And do you mean to tell me that Melanctha (well on her way to winning a National Book Award or two before mid-middle age kicks in for better or worse like a bromide) is expected, even if she doesn't want to see Borkman bulldozed out of his selfhood, to fall for the rumor that he is only temporarily a squatter inside The Rump's seven-league boots (custom-made for this fearless yet oddly under-decorated veteran of the Battle of Bone Spur) and shall be acclaimed by History within the context of his coronal emergence therefrom? that The Rump's lustre will thicken into invisibility when Borkman, emergent, shines by? and that the sinewy parenthesis cradling Borkman's candidacy aria in its atonal arms marks the dawn of a new epoch of American political life in which the pay-to-play and paranoid strains will routinely collide, kiss and make up and ultimately join forces to permanently unseat the Founders? Or is it wordflow that's doing the falling for the two of them—or rather, pretending to be, since it's wordflow him- or herself that cooked up the rumor all the while pretending to disavow it at every turn? No matter. Whatever it is that's going on, it's granted Melanctha very-much-unneeded additional firsthand experience of the threat constantly being posed by wordflow—by the will of wordflow—by wordflow's crazy speakeasy rhythm—by wordflow's monkey business—to her every honest effort to satisfy the constitutive craving of that kindly behemoth worldflow—the very craving that *makes* it worldflow—namely, to get itself faithfully captured for posterity, i.e., the posterity of today—the posterity of this very moment—to get itself faithfully represented in the court of public opinion by what it has no choice but to perceive as its mortal enemy. But whatever he is or isn't at this stage of his career, exposure of the likes of Borkman . . . exposure of the likes of Borkman . . . exposure of the likes of Borkman . . . exposure of the likes of Borkman (*Melanctha senses that the inauguration of a new paragraph is in order but that the Master just won't either let her ford the Rubicon herself or—like middle-aged Poseidon exulting in the pagan shamelessness of his sagging but still virile flesh—carry her over its shoals on his back*). Fact is (or rather, She suspects that) He's been terrified ever since childhood—ever since He collided head-on with His own hyped precocity—of the space separating old from new. And why shouldn't He be? Since those spaces—those voids— those bona fide wounds, whose only suture is more and more of the occult blood shed by fine print, do nothing less than carve up, without provocation, a sacred text's (though all texts are sacred) unseizably oceanic body into a denumerable sum of summarizable slabs.

Melanctha looks hard at Borkman (*there! you see! the Great Migration into a brave new paragraph wasn't so hard to orchestrate, was it?*), resting (not a little like Poseidon) after his delicious labors of self-exposure. The fact that for the moment he's no longer a conduit—a mere vector—a Trojan Horse's Ass irrigates him with a certain well-earned fragility. But he's still a force to be reckoned with and even if the Master goes on skewing—skewering—him to resemble The Rump (which He's sure to do since it's an addiction)—still, as Borkman—crown prince of the penny ante—he will remain. Which at the same time is not to say that the Master isn't within His rights (for canon law is purposefully murky on this issue) to visit more of The Rump's traits upon Borkman in order to see what can be made of them in the context of mite-sized wheeler-dealings—in order to see what the parts of him that are not Rumplike in any shape or form can make of them. So she sits back and resolves to enjoy the show. There's no point, or no percentage, in her trying (as a way of atoning for failure as a parent) to protect Borkman against The Rump's encroachment. He seems about ready to get himself exposed anew, with or without her coaching, and take the consequences. Apparently, there are more subpoenas in the works and he graciously proceeds to transmit his lawyer's précis of their provisional gist. Four subpoenas so far plus the executive summary of this new batch. But each case of exposure is a special case that's so far off exposure's beaten track (Route PI 164) that it's no exposure at all. So the exposers will have to keep stripping away leaf after leaf—special case after special case—not just to get at but to throttle the marinated heart of the artichoke that harbors the irredeemably glassy essence of Borkman's rottenness. The rottenness of the wheeler-dealer who's, inter alia, made a hobby of withholding orphan drugs from orphans. Withholding orphan drugs from orphans! So he is every bit as rotten as The Rump and the joke's on the Master who's underestimated His capacity to create—His genius for creating—a rottenness virulent enough to reduce Borkman's political ambitions to ruins—underestimated His capacity to create a being as evil as—more evil than—The Rump. But though the Master wants nothing more than to be a genius, what he wants even more than nothing more is, as we already know, (*a*) to be relevant, which means catching The Rump's World-Hysterical Zeitgeist in the act—catching it with its pants down—exercising a merciless acuity in skewering all the wrongdoing perpetrated in its name—to propagate far and wide the thought packets that will in record time lethally dismantle the mystique of its rottenness; and, on a less exalted level, (*b*) to be an essential worker in the campaign to castrate (jointly with the Lincoln Project) the Rump agenda even if "essential" will soon—by a nefarious twist of pandemic fate—be synonymous with "expendable beyond anybody's wildest dreams." But just like a woman (with a flair for gourmet cooking) Melanctha can't help wondering if it really matters who assumes the role of the marinated heart of that rotten artichoke in today's performance (Borkman or The Rump) as long as it *is* marinated. But whether the reverberations of exposure are massive or minuscule, whether they are dwarfed by or tower over the character of the defendant himself, the fact remains that (at least according to the chatty couple in front of her) such persecution of a true hero like Borkman only boomerangs and becomes mere exposure of the corruption of the exposers themselves whose very success proves they have nothing better to do than stoop to such low-blow *epigenetic re-engineering* (they choose, of course, a term less crude). Moreover, there's nothing to expose because Borkman has nothing to hide. *Not even the fact that he has plenty* (notes the savvier of the partners to chatty couplehood—clearly she's at a point where nothing will dampen her devotion and so she dares anybody to suggest that what she's just added to what she said a minute ago amounts to backpedalling) since what saves him—or rather, *a man like him* though there's no such animal—is his style: the style of sincerest bluster (which any fan worth his salt should and will find disarming). Fact is, he has too much to think about at every moment to know whether he's telling the truth or not at every other; indeed, since he's a secret to himself, secrecy becomes authenticity in action. The lady's savvy—her companion calls her Myrtle and from the look of her, *Branch* would not be an unlikely surname—spreads like wildfire and his fans—though still few and far between and whether infected by her savvy or not—are eating him up before Melanctha's very eyes. Not just the glassy-eyed, glassy-essenced women but the men, too. (Is Melanctha crazy or are the language and tone of Myrtle's bullying penetration, as it goes about anointing Borkman, in fact benefiting from a dash—a dollop—maybe even a megadose or two of the Master—of the Master's unrelenting infatuation with The Rump? Obviously the honeymoon isn't over. It never will be. She can already hear the Master lamenting, "If only I could have The Rump, not Borkman, for a prodigal son. And if only that son could introduce me to some high-level operatives in his campaign willing to finance *The Invidicum Story* as an eight-season/ninety-five episode Netflix miniseries." Borkman, then, as far as his creator is concerned—yes, creator! might as well call a spade a spade—will always be a low-level evildoer incapable of standing on his own two feet without the support of, i.e., without the threat of obliteration by, The Rump.) The men may be taking an even bigger albeit more cautious bite—making sure to thoroughly metabolize—cannibalize—his bluster and make it their own before they allow themselves to fall head over heels in love with the blusterer and abandon wife, servants and children (just as the blusterer has—unlike The Rump, Myrtle concedes reluctantly—for all intents and purposes abandoned his) in order to serve his cause—a cause in search of itself, i.e., of its tail. For example, get a load of Stifter over there (problem is, Melanctha can't: Mack and Myrtle's standing ovation, the long-overdue consummation of their folie à deux, is resolutely blocking her view), still gullet-deep in the cannibalization process as a means of shamelessly putting off . . . masturbating to the tune of his own self-abasement even when every well-intentioned insect in sight is chirping and buzzing him on. When will he officially succumb? Melanctha observes (*firsthand*, she thinks, and laughs at her use of the word) how Borkman, as he quotes from the précis, bullies the men—mini-men who are the cold-water and railroad flats and the fourth-floor walkups—the very armature—of his unholy tenement blocks—into loving their shame, shedding their own skin, chewing up their own teeth and spitting them out as food for thought—food for the thought, that is, of humanish boll weevils. According to another savvy specimen (though no Myrtle),[76] who speaks to himself irascibly in a condescending whisper, you won't find Borkman cornily rolling up (unlike Mitt & the members of his tribe) a pair of starched button-down shirtsleeves to mid-forearm (nor The Rump for that matter, Myrtle again concedes, this time *grudgingly*) but not one daring inch further (to, say, the elbow) as surest populist proof of man-to-man engagement. Borkman has the courage to keep his Jersey Boy sport jacket on (even in this pristine heat)—and fake (or, as they say nowadays, *faux* [who decides, by the way, when a word has nothing left to do but die—when it has crashed into its expiration date?]) town-hall intimacy be damned. You

---

[76]Melanctha had foolishly begun to believe the Master was done recruiting supernumeraries (*extras*, to you, bub)—supernumeraries with no instinctive affinity for and with no characterological kinship with thought packets—to strut and fret their hour upon the stage—or however long it took to disgorge his latest walking shadow. Doesn't she know characters come and go but that wordflow is forever?

won't find him, the specimen avers, slitheringly agreeing (and by the way, he doesn't slither—he boomerangs—so, caveat emptor! buddy boy) at long last to release even one of his tax returns (another Rump-scented dollop being sneakily pissed by The Master into the hagiographic Borkman super-stew?). What's the point since hasn't he said (in Coronado, she seems to remember) that his net worth fluctuates and goes up and down with markets and with attitudes and with feelings, even his own feelings? But could Borkman have come up with a high-density gemstone of temporization—of evasiveness—as pure as: *The fluctuation of my net worth is a function of my feelings*? Of course he could! Of course it's he—Borkman—who'd be the more likely to come up with such a gem—for isn't his inner eternal feminine more highly developed than The Rump's? Take, for example, his over-professed aversion to sports . . . So it's The Rump who'd better watch his back, not to mention his front, lest (yes, *lest*!) Borkman rob him of his shadow or his reflection or both and lest he rob The Master of His relevance. If only the Master could find a way to lure The Rump himself to this neck of the woods. But maybe this will happen sooner rather than later for here's Margo handing Pritchard a copy of today's *Santa Barbara Bald Eagle* which has just announced that The Rump appears to be giving serious consideration to making Borkman his running mate or his Secretary of the Treasury. But, Melanctha wonders (she's addicted to wondering the way the hoi polloi are addicted to, say, avocado-flavored e-cigarillos), is this because Borkman bears the closest resemblance to The Rump and is therefore "uniquely positioned" to reinforce his message and amplify his viciousness, or rather because he is furthest in tone and temperament and could therefore serve as the most ductile conduit to that slice of the votership which cannot stomach their soft spot for The Rump's voice, mug, habitus, smell? Whatever the reason and whatever the outcome, Melanctha is convinced Borkman has the makings and the markings of the perfect remedial poison—the perfect poisonous remedy—in a word, the perfect pharmakon. The fact that, later, Margo will be hosting a spin-off session on how to deal with spousal envy will not make her change her mind one bit although she's not quite clear what one thing has to do with the other.

Most everybody has been reduced to tears. But teary or not, they've all (except for Melanctha) succumbed to envying (and rehab be damned, at least for the moment) the purity of his plight (the notion of passive appreciation is peculiarly poignant). They feel (but how does she know—how can *anybody* know, including they themselves?) that weighed down by so much malign documentation, he can't be long for the world, i.e., the cozy world enfolded like a Spanish omelette by these sun-baked hills. He's a sun-baked martyr. She hates to see them debase themselves (and her as well), simply because for the time being proband Borkman's fate appears to be the most precarious of all. She leaves—even Margo's mugging for the camera can't distract her. As far as she knows she's not yet a prisoner. Nobody will miss her. It's that time of day—high noon lasts for hours in these parts—when every thing, living and dead, is saddled with a shadow. But a shadow whose shape bears not the slightest resemblance to what has cast it. Which is a blessing. She doesn't mind in the least the one assigned her, since it's a long and straight line of reproach—albeit too long for consumption by her consciousness and her conscience. As she ascends, the pretty mansions become less and less visible through their hedge of bolts. Oprah's may be among them. She'll force the bolt, however, only when she makes Oprah's Book Club list for then they'll meet as near equals. She inhales jasmine and feels *an even greater* pleasure (is that the Master putting her through a shameless hyperbolization again?) knowing she doesn't have to earn the scents of summer: even as a black woman, she's entitled to inhale: No, she's not violating any white man's law or, if so, she's entitled to violate it. *But as a black she's entitled to inhale:* how shameful. How can she ever expect to write a novel—her novel—when she allows herself to so regress so shamelessly, thereby not only stymieing her progress but canceling out the strides of her race? Even if nobody's around to overhear, the shame has been sixth-sensed and duly archived. So what she needs to believe, if all's not to be lost for Creation, is that the sum of perduring regressive self *and* painful apperception (perception squared) of that self's craving for disinvestment yields far more than does a self which has transcended the need to invoke entitlement at every step or has never had such a need to begin with. What she needs up here in the hills is a heavy dose of *Building 18*—to be wielded as a truncheon against anybody daring to suggest she doesn't have a right to the scents of summer. Private—irrevocable—airtight—excruciating—irretrievable—is the memory evoked by the name. Proving she's had her slice of life—more importantly, that she's able to live with it—live beyond it—uncomplaining—unconfessing—encrypted in her unconfessed mystery—yet very much set at large to endure and breathe a sigh of relief at the world's ignorance underpinned by indifference. Like Fredi Washington in *Imitation of Life* (1934 version) or Olivia de Havilland in *To Each His Own*. The fact that Building 18 abandoned her before she abandoned it or vice versa makes her mysterious—not least of all to herself. Building 18 allows her to think, *Those honkies haven't the slightest idea what I endured in Building 18 and the fact that I can live with that* what *without misusing it as an embossed calling card to make myself interesting will gird me in a showdown.*

Returning to her room (luckily, poignancy-averse Melanctha hasn't returned: after Borkman's performance she looked as if she needed some fresh—or fresher—air), Jean Rhys finds a pink post-it stuck to her cellphone which is lying quaintly on the sill (so she hasn't lost it after all). Ethan attempted to contact her through the main switchboard, which caused—as she can well imagine—no end of trouble for the decimated staff (most of them are on vacation). Reluctantly, she returns the favor. "Finally," he says. And even before she can part what he's (afraid of losing her) started referring to as her tulip lips: "You sure took your sweet time. Well, as it so happens or as it turns out, or both, I'm pretty much holed up here, at least for the next few hours—make that days." "*Here?*" "Don't get smart or play dumb, or both: the Santa Barbara Hotel (or is it the Hotel Santa Barbara) on too-sunny State Street." She remembers, from her moody twilight strolls, the weathered pinkish facade, which has *earmarked for demolition: soon to be a major condom residence and to hell with the sissy landmarks commission* slashed all over it. "I need some cash. The Agency has cut me loose." "Which agency?" In spite of herself she's refreshed by the memory this question invokes, namely, that he's a high-ranking official in too many agencies to count. (And if he's Alexei Karenin, as he pretends to be, well, then, she's just been granted license to end up on the wrong side of the tracks only she doesn't have the guts.) The pause that ensues being most atypical for Ethan, she "can't help feeling" (the phrase, which has come unbidden, like all strokes of genius, rings false—worse, fatuous: no discernible feeling worth a damn ferments beneath its crust)—can't help feeling that holed up with him is some somebody from whom he's awaiting further instructions. "Any contribution will be gratefully received and may save my neck." Should she let him know that saving his pretty little neck (and it *is* pretty) doesn't rate priority status as of this moment? Of course, she shouldn't. Since on him and him alone depends her retention by the trial bigwigs, whoever they now may be in this, the land of the willowing eucalypti. "Well, I can't do anything now." Is that Herbert outside the door, putting two and two together like crazy? "Too much background reading for my Thursday session and it's already Monday." "This is Sunday, not Monday, and last I heard, the background stuff gets regurgitated on Friday but don't bother to explain. You've been self-improvement-crazy since I've known you only you never deliver the goods. Talk to me, babe: when does the rehabbing end and real life begin?" "Real life *is* rehab, babe. Everything else is thrift-shop clutter." Appalled (this time, no mistaking the creak-creak) at the thought of being spied on (she feels like a perky co-ed again), Rhys decides to go out on the landing (the phone, dropped en route, has landed, luckily, on the clean but dreary counterpane). Somebody *is* out there, looking up at her from the landing below but not a somebody she would have anticipated: in a word, Cook, of all things, and a Cook not a little the worse for wear. "They're closing in. They think they *know*." There's something poignantly seductive (no other reaction will do) in the way the syllables push desperate past his phlegmy hoarseness and reach out to her and, as is only right and proper, she can't tear herself away, *though not so much from him as from the tension, a purely spatial—all right then, a cinematic—tension, generated by their separation compliments of a small stretch of stairwell.* She's seen too much hit-parade stuff by Welles, Sirk, Ophuls, Nick Ray and William Wyler not to be exhilarated and what if he happens to feel exactly the same way and if so—well, what then?

CHAPTER THIRTY-THREE

Only then she remembers there's Ethan (who, come to think of it, may have been shaving but if so then to no purpose since he has a ruddily clean-shaven look at all times) still on the line. She runs back in, with Cook just behind (suddenly she understands the expression *hot on your heels*, which goes to show that if you have the gall to live long enough everything sayable becomes famously literal—for the canonical fifteen minutes). Plopping himself down on the bed (he soon discovers it's far less comfortable than it looks), Cook says suavely: "It's Ethan, isn't it? Crying in his beer and—acrobatically—on your shoulder as well. But I guess you're smart enough never to believe a word he says. Why, I bet he's about to launch into his spiel about being on the trail of an Object—the bit of evidence (he's still not quite sure what it is but he does know it's buried somewhere in them there hills) that will clear him of everything he insists he's being charged with by the fifth-rate think tank he refers to as the Agency in homage to the movie *Six Days of the Condor*. (He was one of the first up at Sarah Lawrence, remember, to register for Conspiracy 101 with Margo Straynge, PhD. Erroneously described by snotty campus trust-fund pranksters as a gut. Taking them at their word, of course he flunked big. By the way is she by any chance related to you-know-who?)" And in fact at this very moment, Ethan, undaunted—maybe even inspired—by an increasingly faulty connection, is saying, "My only hope is to expose *them* but to do that I have to find a certain thing—the *Object*—whether it's an electronic passport, or a biometric visa, or a training videotape like the one used by Merck or Wells Fargo to brainwash its sales force, or the hard drive controlling the home security system of Cook's newest girlfriend or a logic bomb installed in Warner-Metro's Ur-computer, or something as simple as a set of directions to the warehouse where all the soon-to-be-shipped off-label trash is being held captive, or something as unsimple as the recipe for Invidicum Lite (targeted at what hip psychologists refer to as the worried-well) which constitutes (or so Post more-than-hinted on more than one occasion) the very pinnacle in chief of his achievement as a pipeline-mongerer and which, if he does decide to bequeath it, must go to Cook, of all people, and Cook alone." As if composing an IQ test—the old-fashioned politically incorrect kind—Ethan thinks, *Cook is to Post as Cantor is to* . . . "So be on the lookout—nothing more dangerous than a nincompoop with a swellable head." She can visualize him foaming at the mouth and in so doing resembling not a little his lady mother, the Dowager Dottie Gowan-Rushforth-Jones, who (for the benefit of all those who may have forgotten) acquired seven and a half hubbies in as many years, each a past master of the unlosable art of metastasis and each of whom bowed out gracefully after having required a mere week or two (tops!) of hospice hand-holding—stints for which the serial widow was lavishly compensated. "But you mustn't think I'm afflicted with that most virulent form of Envy disease—the form peculiar to a *consultant* (soggy signifier without a referent, to quote Vance Packard, or is it Edgar Cayce—or Edgar Rice Burroughs?). For this here mere consultant knows just how Herculean a task it's been for Cook to contain, year after year after year, the fallout from Post's balance-sheet hanky-panky, not to mention his pre- and post-pipeline hugger-mugger. In comparison with which Cook's over-touted singlehanded running of the Invidicum Lite campaign in the red states is greasy kid stuff. No, the legitimate craving for vindication has nothing to do with self-aggrandizement. It's the little people I'm concerned about who, if deprived of an ombudsman's expertise are sure to suffer and go on suffering—through having, say, gotten Invi-Lite when their metabolic profile cries out for Sugar-free or Large-curd Invi or too much fancy-scan irradiation supposedly indicated to assess their supposed progress. And nobody knows better than you, Jean, how hard I've worked to hone that expertise, going so far as to read and re-read and re-re-read cover-to-cover folks like G. Scholem, A. Kojève, N. Burch, L. Steinberg, S. Toulmin, M. Bakhtin, A. Croce, J. Kernan and M. Farber (precisely because each is a heavyweight in a field having absolutely nothing to do with mine) in the insane belief that forced assimilation of and adaptation to their discoveries within a context and under a schema where they don't apply is the only way to get a cutting edge on the competition. And if I've distorted, deformed, deranged, contorted that expertise beyond recognition, well, that's all to the good. You can't get enough derangement when it's a question of making your mark. There's too much coincidence of self with self's so-called expertise, if you ask me." "But look where all your distortions and contortions have gotten you," Jean murmurs, intrigued by the unlikely sobriety with which she perpetrates her shrewishness.

Cook snatches the phone and proceeds to bellow full speed ahead: "But then again your object—I mean, your Object—could very well turn out to be a formula for drilling down through Absolute Zero to the currently inaccessible temperatures beneath, specifically -275 degrees Celsius, at which Invidicum purports to be at its most potent qua homicidogen (and diuretic), even if you and I know AZ is a mere concept and there's no way anybody can drill beneath some cockamamie concept. Or maybe it's the knife that fatally slashed Straynge's throat before he was superfluously plugged." Her boyfriend starts to counter-bellow, the aim evidently being to stretch out what sounds like *Fuck you* to the crack of doom, not to mention the last syllable of recorded time, which leaves Cook (ever the master of comic timing) with no choice but to throw him at the sill.

Now how can Jean Rhys be expected to take seriously the combat of these zany tykes, even—especially—if she's its grand booby prize? At present, she nurses one desire: to learn whatever the Straynge woman has to teach about living in—through—connubial misery with an Invidious twist (even if this means having to wait hours for Mrs. Bean to announce, as if she were the big brown grandfather clock outside her own office, the start of Margo's poolside seminar). But just when she feels she can't wait a minute longer here is hospitable Cook, giving his all to distracting her. *It*—"only don't tell your befuddled boyfriend"—could very well turn out to be the third draft of Post's pseudonymous novel à clef (can a novel be both?), *Brain Scam*, in which he lays bare—with an autodestructive frenzy worthy of Tricky Dick—all the lapses in quality-control plaguing his enterprise from the word go. (Clearly Cook seems to care more about the Object than does Ethan, for all the latter's blunt bellowing.) Should she risk telling him (though where's the risk?), since he's gone this far, that it might turn out to be as monumentally unrevelatory as Juan's tape in *Paris Nous Appartient*? No, better save such an erudite suggestion for a rainier day—the kind of rainier day that's dear to the heartlessness of West Bank kino freaks. There's method to his madness: His chatter deftly unglues Rhys from her vigilance—releases her from its straitjacket—gently eases her into the unfamiliar state of knowing without knowing she knows— or rather (*or rather*: among the most beautiful two-word pairs [*and how many times do I have to repeat it?*]—among the most beautiful folies à deux—in the language) the unfamiliar state of knowing her midgut knows and damn well knows it knows—that the blessed event will begin only once said vigilance consents to miss its onset, or pretends to consent. At which moment a bell will go off and she'll be out of the room and well on her way back to the pool, trusty midgut by her side.

"You'll have to go. I need to meet somebody—the Straynge woman." "What strange woman?" She doesn't bother to enlighten him: a show of indifference definitely suits her skin tone. Cook wonders why he refuses to take the hint since in fact Jean is now highly repellent (will his inner scowl manage defiantly to make itself perceptible before he's obliged to skedaddle?) and not just because she's Ethan's moll and likely to remain so. Then why else? Subject for further research. "You know, from the very first Ethan tried to hamstring my visionary progress (don't believe him when he's says he's above Envy)— for one thing, he turned Post and his gang against me. Liepnits, for one. You remember him: the little guy who's the spittin' image of Newt Gingerich's prettier twin sister? Not to mention Stifter and Walser—who've, by the way, become our very own Ollie and Stan—or rather, our very own Lev Parnas and Igor Fruman (more about them some time into the future—be patient— stay tuned). Have they gone Hollywood or are they working for the feds, or doing both?" But he qualifies all of this by pointing out that much much worse than being lambasted by the Sons of Invidicum is to get a megadose of the bludgeoning vicariate ecstasy of the self-hating HBO corporate crowd and their academia-nut hangers-on. "Why bludgeoning?" she asks sulkily, corner of her eye on poolside. He explains, though it hurts (even if eloquence does its level best to balm the pain), that every time there's a CNN update on that ornery visionary progress of his, humility obliges them to "confess" they can't imagine *themselves* having the *gall* to make a docudrama of their own, respectfully daunted as they are by the achievement of the past's unbeatables (heavyweights like Flaherty and Rouch and Vertov). Though what makes him think (she would be within her rights to ask) that they'd ever dream of appropriating those greats as a *truncheon* (ouch—that word again and in the space of just a few pages: what better proof of a Master's impoverishment?) with which to bloody-pulp the neophyte—to deflate the efforts of the non-dead even if their mediocre and persistent non-deadness is the worst form of hubris known to beast. It's just that this soulful self-obliterated connectedness to the works of the great—with the humility in question totaling about ten tons of soulful hot air—knows no better (she'd be within her rights to plead).

Here's the thing: Nothing less than *awe-inspiring* is what those hot-air balloons take their awestrickenness to be—far more awe-inspiring, in fact, than the awe's ostensible bull's-eye. Like that engineer he met in Crete a while back who, for the backpacking delinquent's own good, threw Musil at his skull to snuff out the tinders of juvenile aspiration. Which was this German's friendly way of demanding he hop to it and join the ranks of just plain awestrickenness. At least he had the decency, this German did, to leave the awe-inspiring kind to his betters.

As far as she's concerned, it's all sour grapes, oafishly pressed. "But when all is said and done, Ethan's done me a bigger favor than he could ever have imagined." Cook opens the window, peers out, breathes in the breezeless air, tries to look pleased. *Now* that *wasn't too difficult, was it?* coaxes a voice (definitely not his own or Jean's) once he's irrigated his . . . his . . . (Cook can't remember the word Post was always tossing around when plugging off-label Invidicum as a pulmonologist's wet dream?) . . . his . . . ravioli?—no, you knucklehead, *alveoli!* Only Cook isn't quite sure what *that* refers to. Having the courage to let Ethan's favor out of the bag? Or to look pleased about something—anything—even if it's all an act? "Wait, I want to read you something I jotted down this past week running scared from motel to motel and keeping barely one step ahead of the LAPD, not to mention the FBI, the CIA, INTERPOL and the ASPCA (though I've skinned a few tomcats in my day, at least I can't be pegged as a trafficker in the sort of Viagra that's sucked and siphoned out of elephant tusks—or can I?). They're convinced Narr and I are responsible for Straynge's death. At least that's the Word (of the day) on the Street. As if I would ever be caught stooping to collaborate with that doofus on anything so blood-and-gutsy." Only why pull out the jottings when he knows text and subtext by heart, or maybe there are none inasmuch as, distrusting no pharmakon more than writing, he makes it a platonic practice to ad lib. "Having my track record invalidated is the best revenge on a world that'd sink so low as to perpetrate invalidation in the first place. Nothing more exhilarating, Jean, than to deprive that world of the feats yet to come—and I'm talking not only about the HBO documentary. At long last I, a compulsive 'overachiever' (hate the word when it's meant as a fawning compliment), am to undergo something sweeter than achievement, namely, the refusal to achieve when there is so much within just achin' to get itself achieved. And when there's so much world waiting breathlessly—whether it knows it or not—to witness the transmogrification. Clearly, bestselling author Rump, the go-to guy for (to mix a metaphor) milking the loopholes, is right on target for calling his latest opus—ready?: *Vengeance is the Best Revenge* (ask Handel's Timotheus). And if you don't believe I am one—an overachiever, I mean—then simply ask Shearer how unstoppable I was (in the backmost booth of that Second Avenue diner) breaking down her resistance, muscle by muscle, tendon by tendon, to joining what she pooh-poohed as nothing better than a flea circus.

"No need to ask Moira." (This is the first time Jean's called her Moira: it's a concession she doesn't deserve.) "I believe you. You know, this isn't an attack, but somehow you're sounding more and more like Ethan. You two are indistinguishable. Both of you getting off, as you do, on non-achieverhood.

He feels sorry for all the little people deprived of his achievement while you never felt better knowing how deprived they're going to be. But it comes down to the same thing."

"You mean that like him, I'm not at all concerned about Invidicum and the world of good it can do but only about my own achieverhood."

"*Over*achieverhood."

"Only about my own overachieverhood." (Surrender to correction never felt so . . . sensual, so . . . virtuous.)

"Not quite, but something like that. Still, if you sound like him or anybody else, for that matter, it's OK. How does Herbert put it (God knows, I've heard her say it enough times when she's talking in her sleep (taking a page from the master's book, she calls it, defensively, when she's wide awake)? *The supreme side effect perpetrated by Invidicum is eloquence—an eloquence so exalted it makes everybody sound the same—throws everybody into the same pot. Eloquence as the great dedifferentiator. Invidicum has that unique effect on the brain.*" "Maybe Invidcum can be prescribed and sold off label to the sub-subpopulation of people (aspiring orators, i.e., mass-market frauds) suffering from one of the most famous orphan diseases of all time (eloquence-aversion) and yet who have no choice but to seek to deceive." "*We're here to take turns sounding like everybody else—anybody else but ourselves. This being the only way out of Envy. Since if we're everybody we can't envy anybody. So nobody is forced to follow the straight line of growth and development—forced to evolve. Nobody gets straitjacketed by a plausible self-identity. Everybody is granted a sabbatical from self-dooming selfdom—that overrated fief—whether he deserves it or not.* Remember (for some reason, Melanctha always mutters this part in her sleep), *every lifejacket is really a straitjacket.* So, for example, in today's performance, the role of Ethan will be played by Cook! Funny, I feel somebody else should be speaking that line. It's not in my line." "You mean that in today's twilight performance, the role of, say, Ms. Herbert-Manning will be played by our centauress-in-residence Jean Rhys née Rhys. Seriously, you sounded a lot like Irena the Cat Woman once you started giving yourself to gravity—the gravity of eloquence, even if it's somebody else's: the transformation was immediate and almost frightening. A hybrid. A mongrel. A half-breed. That's what you've become. Anything but what you are during normal business hours." (He knows he's pouring it on a bit thick—but why? after all, he no longer wants to fuck her.) It suddenly hits Cook like a ton of bricks: only the unutterly beautiful word "fuck" can open all the doors to the Bluebeard's Castle that is Invidicum.

And somewhere on the premises Cantor is at this very moment thinking, telepathically—like Ellen in Murnau's *Nosferatu*—about that shrewd operator G.W. Leibniz, who, in the Preface to his *New Essays*, had the audacity to write, nature never makes leaps. *Bullshit:* the only thing that nature ever makes—or should make—is—are—leaps. Leaps out of character—out of line—deliverance from the bondage of character-building. And by the way, proclaiming *bullshit* makes Cantor feel manhooded—man-hard—undercuts his learnedness—shows he's at war with it—thereby rendering it palatable to the mass market—takes the edge off his scholarly strut. His inner Belmondo (he hates when people babble about their *inner this* or somebody else's *inner that* yet here he is tough-loving the thing he hates) has trounced yet again his inner Seberg. In any case, his super-esotericism—everything he touches turns to same—thrives much better (he finds) in an open-air environment whose denizens can't begin to make head nor tale of his obfuscations. That's why academia—macademia, really, where he's just another nut and his palpable hits refuse to score—simply doesn't suit him.

"And if my mumbo-jumbo resorts now and then to specificities like the right dosage of Invidicum or the dynamics of the trial's phase II, then it's simply to give the description of my obsession with overachieverhood—with myself—some sort of pseudo-rootedness in the pseudo-concrete—something outside myself—is that it?"

"Not exactly, but something like that." *When will the poolsiders disperse and give her a shot at Margo's expertise?* And when (Cook wonders) will she stop saying *Not exactly, but something like that?*

Jean informs him (but why should Jean be the pallbearer of such tidings?) that according to Herbert and to Cantor—he's become her disciple and maybe more (it must be because she's black and he's homosexual)—there's a cognate side effect: our delusional belief—our need to believe—that everywhere looming is a master, that is, a master dispenser of the eloquence. No eloquence without a master, and vice versa. A master who harbors grave doubts about the worth of his eloquence (that's what makes him a master[77])—about its concordance with the aspirations of his Life Project. A master, in other words, who's at war with the eloquence he dispenses to the members of his team—his stock company. But without him—more to the point, without the doubts he harbors—the eloquence would be intolerable—unmetabolizable—as blinding as an unmuzzled sun. It's only as a mixed bag of wonders that the infiltration of eloquence can flourish among the rank and file. Supposedly Herbert is at the end of her rope (who spilled that bean?) trying to figure it all out (where the master ends and eloquence begins and where eloquence ends and the master is born anew) though she's clearly almost there, or else how could she (Jean)—no slouch when it comes to inarticulate pangs—find herself saying what she's been saying, even if it's largely a transcription of Melanctha's moonshine? So as a figure-outer in a place like this her life's in danger. But in fact it isn't, 'cause she's a budding writer and danger is a budding writer's business. But whatever the master is, it's as if—no, delete the *as if* (even I know it's the last refuge of hacks). She takes a deep breath—for effect. "But (based yet again on what I've gathered from Melanctha's sleepwalking spiels) whatever the master is—or isn't—you, like the rest of us atheists (whether we know it or not), are forever trying to convince him you're doing your job—rather, *his* job. I.e., that everything you say—everything he makes you say—everything you think you're saying against your better judgment—against *his* better judg-

---

[77] Consider by way of comparison the instant proverb—the macabre adage—that Billy Wilder and Charles Brackett pop into Norma Desmond's delusional mouth: "Nobody leaves a star, that's what makes one a star."

ment—simply to piss him off, so to speak—ultimately ties in all too tidily with the Invidicum Story—deserves to be in the Invidicum Story—has no life outside the story. Although maybe the parts of the story even he likes best are the ones where every thought packet (packets are the armature of our edifice as if you didn't know) flies off the story's handle and the thinker with it—where nothing *coheres*. Which is very much in keeping with the master's personality—a personality that, in the *DSM*'s olden golden days, would have been called *split*. Since he wants to be a runaway bestseller like The Rump's *Vengeance*—or a Broadway smash like *Jersey Boychiks*—and at the same time that smashing runaway's direct opposite. So, even if you aren't ready to admit to his hovering—even if all this talk about his hovering is the craziest stupidest talk you've ever heard—fact is, he's both out there somewhere and very much among us. He's got to be—after all, he's the only holy ghost that can intercede between you and your eloquence. Whew! who ever would have thought I was capable of talking such a sky-blue streak. Whew! I'm bushed!" (To make sure the point isn't lost she runs the back of her hand with blissful exhaustion across her forehead—a lot like Anouk Aimée—the most luminously svelte hausfrau you'll ever want to meet—in the harem sequence of *8½*: she knew that duly warehoused, the gesture would come in handy sooner or later.)

"But getting back to Shearer: from the very start she was right on target. She listened—really listened—to what the diner was telling her."

"Right about what?" she asks sulkily, emboldened by unhappiness—by the conviction that things can't get any worse. Cook thinks: "But what does she have to be unhappy about? For one thing, she's got the world on a string/sittin' on a rainbow—and that rainbow, for better or worse, is Narr, his arch rival (might as well admit it) and best friend (might as well admit that, too).

"About this flea circus we're all performing in (surely Melanctha would applaud the mischaracterization)—or did she refer to it as a vaudeville show? I think we both knew, as far back as the backmost booth, that this trial more than any other in Pharma history—" Rhys shakes her head—correctively. He pretends not to notice.

"—would progressively generate—"

"No, wait. Stop right there." She shoos away his train of thought.

"What's wrong?" He has an inkling.

"Herbert would say her master had you in his grip somewhere around *more than any other*—"

"Well, now that you mention it, Jean, I did feel . . . something along those lines and, yeah, exactly when I got to *more than any other*, just like you said. You must be a mind reader or something." He never knew playing the suggestible simpleton could be so exhilarating—enough to put hair on his chest (if he weren't so overpelted already).

"If I hadn't stepped in, you'd have *eaten up* or rather been eaten up by those words—hyperlatives is what Herbert or rather the master-according-to-Herbert calls them—instead of dining on tastier fare as you've just now had the courage to do."

"Didn't smell tastier. I think I know what you want me to say."

"What?" (Again, her tone's sulkily emboldened by unhappiness.)

"That this trial *like every other* in Pharma history—" Rhys shakes her head approvingly.

"Thing is, if it's like every other then the thought will pack no punch, i.e., will have no reason to exist."

"Say it anyway. See where it takes you. If not for yourself then for all the unfortunates out there who are counting on Invidicum to make the last lap of the race we call Life a little less arduous."

"We both knew, as far back as the backmost booth of that Second Avenue diner, that the trial, just like any other in Pharma history—that the trial—that the trial— By the way, did I mention that it's only now I have the courage to recognize, thanks to you, that our conversation in the diner marked the turning point of my professional—of my entire life." (*Why thanks to* me? Rhys wonders, flattered nevertheless.)

"*Turning point. Marked the turning point.* Just can't keep your fingers out of the honey pot or off the dial marked Hyperlative Mode can you? Afraid, no doubt, the story—the Invidicum Story—which is one big drug won't survive without Its interventionary antics. Maybe you're right. That's what's wrong with stories like the Invidicum Story: like flies, they can't help feeding off whatever excrement the hyperlativists begrudgingly see fit to throw their way. Since without it, their master has no clientele, no ushers, no full house, no Standing Room Only, no stage seats, no scalpers, no lavatory attendants paid far less than the minimum wage, no groundlings, no headwaiters (he traffics in dinner theaters, remember)—and you're out of a job. As The Rump would say—and *will* say, once he's elected (at the end, e.g., of his obligatory chat with the Queen): *You're fired.* But do go on."

He explains how they both knew (so-called expert and so-called layman), each in his own way, that, as it played out, the trial, just like every other, would generate the worst possible response to the disease. How? By encouraging the afflicted— (Or rather, the less afflicted, since all trials, by their very nature *as* trials, notoriously—or, to use the pukeworthy new lingoid, *famously*—attract those least in need. Inasmuch as only the hale-and-heartiest can survive (*a*) the screening process, not to mention (*b*) the signing of the consent form [with its indecipherable correlation-does-not-equal causation clause] and (*c*) the formidable requirement that all other medications be stopped beforehand, which usually entails stopping, then restarting, then stopping all over again, until the lead investigator *gets his act together* [sort of], which happens only after 47.3 percent of the participants are dead, as was very much the case in the tryout over at NYU of that ecstasy/lemon peel/cannabis combo for PTSD.) They both knew, he and Moira did, that the trial would generate the worst possible outcome by encouraging the participants to confuse being closely watched with being watched *over*, thereby fostering the belief (the trickiest sort of belief, the sort that doesn't know it's being harbored) that they were for all practical purposes already cured—and that they should be viewed with little enough exaggeration as such, as long as it was by a discerning eye and through a glass darkly. And how could they not be cured, hooked up, as it was clear they were, to an airtight mechanism powerful yet exquisite enough to crank out the rosiest of Envy-free futures—i.e., to condemn them to a rehabilitation proof against all flaw? So why shouldn't they claim that future here and now (especially when that here-and-now is basking in the California sun) rather than later—why should they throw themselves on the fickle mercy of brute duration? Why wait, with the surgery and healing process per se now the merest of mere formalities? "But don't shoot the messenger. I was very much against this approach from the get-go but nobody would listen, least of all Post, who's always being egged on by Your Mr. Narr to turn our guinea pigs into poster boys and girls—the more prematurely, the better—as the only way to catch the deep-pocketed attention of hedge funders."

"But you admitted yourself that this is the only approach." (Jean feels a bit awkward pimping for the trial as if she were one of the organizers.) "And by the way, he's not *my* Mr. Narr. His breakthroughs belong to all of human-kind." She ostentatiously fails to stifle a fat giggle at the thought of his break-throughs. "But what did you mean when you said that you *both* knew? After all, Moira has no experience in the domain of drug trials. And don't tell me it was because of her ballet training and that the expertise extracted from any kind of training, if thorough enough, can be applied to every other. But never mind her. What you're saying in so many words is that we should never have participated: we're all wrong for the job of getting cured. Our homegrown non-GMO brand of Envy doesn't make the grade."

"If only things were that simple. That's not what I'm saying. But if that's exactly what I am saying then it applies to 99.9 percent of all trial subjects anywhere and everywhere. What I meant to say was there should have been a different emphasis." "So it's all a matter of emphasis," she interejcts dryly—so dryly that her throat parches up. "Yes, right from the start. Or call it a matter of approach. For one thing, everybody knows the tumor of Envy starts metas-tasizing—hopscotching from organ to organ—long before it's fully (or even partially) formed—in fact, long before it has a cancer cell to its name. But Envy is always one step ahead of itself—refusing to stay put—always in the market for a bigger and better version of This Crazy Thing called Envy (and for a bigger and better and juicier role as the Lesion that Craves no Suture)—struggling to outdo itself before there's a self to outdo—entering into perilous partnerships with spinal—sympathetic—peripheral nerves—which are all too willing to *collaborate*, in true Vichyssoise style, by irrigating the tumor—the tumor in training—Envy as an eternal student straight out of Chekhov—with blood vessels and by firing up its β-adrenergic receptors with epinephrine so all those little envy cells can grow big and strong. Envy embodies—or should I say, disembodies—*metastasis in its pure state*—incessant movement in the absence of primary, secondary and every other kind of metastatic niche you might care to name—movement without a 'to' or a 'from'. (The HBO show will make all that perfectly clear.)" "You make Envy—I mean envy—sound like a bucking bronco." Envy is Prometheus Unbound—with no organ to call home. I.e., there's no such thing as Colon Envy or Renal Envy or Hepatic Envy or Rectal Envy or Lung Envy or Stomach Envy. And with #MeToo in full bloom, he's happy to add the bit of Wiener Schnitzel known as Penis Envy to this list of phantasms. In other words, Envy is Metastasis Incarnate which should have been taken into account from the start. But ever the polymath and lover of sharp contrasts (they soothe his savage breast—make him feel all's right with the world), Bill notes (*reading off the blackboard plastered like a fresco across his mind's eye by the Master*) that, as opposed to Envy, the Space within which the developing infant perpetrates his operations on objects (without distinguishing between the two) is not (unlike Envy) one big unitary domain (at least according to that Swiss-watch guy with kindly eyeglasses and a cute beret) but rather encompasses a whole range of unconnected spaces—visual, auditory, tactile, olfactory, buccal, nasal, colonic, renal, rectal, pulmonary, hepatic, gastric, etc.—whose progenitors are the major sensorimotor schemas (of sucking, sight, prehension, etc.).[78] But Jean doesn't (*paging the Rubicon!*) take kindly to polymaths or to contrast-mongers for that matter, at least at this stage of her career (whatever that career turns out to be once she's outgrown the hobby of disavowing it), and is therefore not inclined to let Cook—I mean, Bill—or rather, the Master— (*I just said, paging the Rubicon!!!*)

But Jean doesn't take kindly (*there! that's better*) to polymaths or to contrast-mongers for that matter, at least at this stage of her career, and is therefore (*even better! keep going!*) not inclined to let Cook—I mean, Bill—or rather, the Master—get away with such an obvious subreption—or rather, sleight of hand—or rather, legerdemain (in the Master's bakeshop universe, there's never just one mot juste per customer: the kind of correction known as epanorthosis is but a pretext for accumulation not deletion). But enough of such fanciful comparisons—distractions—delay tactics—lame mimicry of Hollywood's *other* great Master of Suspense. Since if there's anything that's forever one step ahead of itself—that is struggling to outdo itself—that constitutes metastasis in its pure state—its purest state—it's not Envy but . . . the Invidicum Story in propria persona! (the Invidicum Story as the avatar, you might say, of Language itself), as here told—indeed, lived—by Bill—when it's his turn to be at the service of the Master. But all he can say when she confronts him is, "And since Envy is all about metastasis—*is* metastasis *in its pure state*—we need to block the metastatic process at at least one of its stages: (*a*) the stage of the tumor cells' escape into the bloodstream or (*b*) the stage of their exit from the circulation into virgin tissue through a capillary wall or (*c*) the stage of their successful colonization of a distant organ even if at stage (*c*) it's almost always too late." "Good luck with all that," she retorts with what is now her signature dryness. He's playing dumb—worse, tone deaf—so that Envy—*his* Envy—doesn't have to now cede pride of place to the Invidicum Story as master signifier of Metastasis. Such an exposition of all things psychopharmacological seems completely incompatible with what she presumes to know about Cook's character. (In tonight's performance, then, the role of Post will be taken by that schmegeggy Cook.) But what *does* she know about Cook's character? And why in the last analysis wouldn't such an exposition be

---

[78]See, e.g., Jean Piaget, *The Construction of Reality in the Child*, Margaret Cook, trans. (New York, Basic Books, 1954), chap. 2. For an overview, see also John H. Flavell, *The Developmental Psychology of Jean Piaget* (Princeton, New Jersey, D. Van Nostrand, 1965), chap. 4.

compatible with anybody's character, even the character of mutants possessing an unchallengeable mastery of such things!?

But then there's Cook's—sorry, the Master's—bit about Envy *being* Metastasis. Yet another demonstration of what Melanctha calls the Power of Wordflow over Worldflow. So here is Rhys getting mixed signals from the Master and Herbert (not her first mixed signals: they've been her billion-dollar baby from infancy on)—is she, then, nothing more than those signals' eternal point of convergence? That is to say, hasn't Melanctha been warning her (and not just since they became strange bedfellows) of the dangers of the ineluctable thirst for just this sort of demonstration (though what those dangers are she has yet to pinpoint), with forced synonymy—the collapse of differences into forced synonymy—being one of the most nefarious examples of the exercise of that Power? And yet now here's the Master trying to make the Power of Wordflow felt again—through Cook. So Cook has not only pulled a fast one—he's pulled it in direct contravention of the teachings of Melanctha, his Master's master and aptest pupil. So it's only right and proper that the whole business should stick in Jean's craw. Not to mention the notion (left unformulated by Cook but easily inferable from his stagey hemmings and hawings) that when it comes to being overrun with Envy cells, any organ so afflicted is even more significantly overrun with envy of every other for having engineered what it needs to misbelieve is a heftier payout of killer T cells. But though things have never looked—or sounded—worse, Jean could swear that at this very moment Cook, deploying his bloodshot eyeballs as swallowtails, is trying to semaphore his absolute certainty that, despite way too many missteps, everybody including the trial—including the entire state of California—and with the Aleutian Islands thrown in as a bonus—is in the greatest shape. Miraculously, Melanctha (*Rubicon denied*) has just walked in (it's her executive suite, too, after all), unwanted but under the circumstances only too welcome. By her own admission, she's been listening outside the door for quite some time. (Rhys must remind herself that with Melanctha now present, the *m* in "Master" should be upper-cased. Or has the orthodoxy she snarkily ascribes to Melanctha expired since, as rumor would have it, this sophisticated lady from the Bronx has managed to outHerod Herod and thereby assert her supremacy many times over?) "How was your trek into the foothills?" But Melanctha has no patience for small talk—whether it's chitchatting or chatchitting—remembering in addition how often she's been snubbed by Rhys. *Perhaps unconsciously, since a racist is the last thing an ingénue of Rhys's expensively educated stripe wants to be tagged as being (but something's gone awry with the logic scaffolding this baleful proposition: BUT nail that something and we'll send you a year's subscription to the collected works of Ishmael Drybock; act now and we'll send you two subscriptions).* Rhys explains what's just happened. She expresses her concern. Like Senator Susan Collins, she's *concerned* (more about that bit of deadwood—and her multitudinous like—in the next shemittah, I promise). Like a thing possessed, Cook has given voice to the unthinkable—he's reduced—or exalted—the essence of Envy (no disease more flesh-and-blooded) to a mere accident—to the shadow play of its metastasizing slither from organ to organ (never mind that the jury is still out on whether Envy disease does in fact metastasize). "Actually this sort of thing—accident getting contorted into essence—has been amassing a greater and greater stock of credibility." Why is it so alluring? Rhys wonders—why is it all the rage? Melanctha tells her that contortion of essence into one of its accidents has always been the rage—long before Attila's hordes smeared their ecologically untenable footprint all over the women and children of the Balkans. However, this rightfully burning issue of the Great Synonymy as Great Attractor will be dealt with later on. By abler minds. "When?" Rhys asks, surprised at her peanut-gallery impatience to know (its suppressed vehemence rivals that of Arthur Clennam among the barnacles)—especially when what's at issue is so conceptual—textual—theoretical—abstract—arcane. "At around pages 706–707—for starters," Melanctha prophetizes, clearly pleased by Jean's eagerness to learn—and learn fast.

Making it clear she's not changing the subject (and why bother trying since the subject is, if anything, too much with them late and soon?), Melanctha explains that Cook is practicing an all-too-common strategy—or rather, the Master (so she isn't allowing the orthodoxy to expire just yet, notes Jean) is engaging in that common strategy through him. Having gotten all balled up in abstraction—the juicy self-contradiction at the heart of an HBO-subsidized theory (without even the hint of an empirical armature) on how the *un*afflicted miss out on their own rehabilitation (so what if what permits any theory to cohere is precisely said self-contradiction?)—having gotten all balled up He's trying to make amends by importing from out in the real world, a counterweight (chock full of those sorely needed empirical flourishes) which is overripe for assimilation (with some accommodation here and there) according to his artistic needs. (Though Herbert does not like reminding herself that the Master's an artist for then what is she?) For, let's face it, guys, there's no chance of currying favor with the prestige-conferring auctioneers of the mind (many hailing from Amherst, MA) without implausibly yoking His unyokeable theory, held together solely by its internal inconsistency, to the gist of peer-reviewed extracts yanked from the official literature. So here we have the Master—the playful, self-inculpating Master forever on the make—baring the device of His fraudulence, or what He thinks is fraudulence, which is either fraudulence to the second power or no fraudulence whatsoever. Eager for auctionable accreditation at any price, He appropriates and grooms for yokage to his confections, articles from world-class research journals like *Science, Nature, Guns & Ammo, Marie Claire* and *Reader's Digest* which only very rarely having something to do with Envy, are *for that very reason* compelled to have everything to do with It. Calling the spade of his fradulence a spade, incorporating his tactic in the work itself, he transcends fraudulence. "So how can I resist my little Falstaff even if he's caucasian?" Melanctha ponders coyly—but boldly.

"Oh, hi, Melanctha, how are you?" says Cook. He hasn't been aware of her presence until now. Too busy being electrocuted into fraudulent life by the master—Master—Flémalle Master of all fraudulences. He smiles. She smiles. No need to be on her guard. She has nothing against him: his virtues far outweigh his vileness. Emboldened by Melanctha—by what is easily construable as her offer of life support—he continues. "Thing is, Jean, that bastard Post undid all of my work on stopping metastasis dead in its tracks—with a little help, of course, from *your* Ethan. I'm referring of course to my work as a cable TV script doctor (I'm no academic)—a vulgarizer (in the best sense) of concepts too stodgy to dissolve unboned in the blood, sweat and tears of any HBO witches brew. If I remember correctly only Irena Manning, through sheer indifference and solely by virtue of sticking self-adoringly to her own guns, backed me up." Rhys draws a complete blank. As far as she's concerned, Manning doesn't warrant such high praise. (In fact, Jean is convinced she's Straynge's killer—or at least somebody's. In fact, she'll stake Ethan's life on it.) So she tries to remember something—anything—that can be made to *seem* to warrant it. No luck. Unless Cook's Manning is simply the delusional construction of a schoolboy's crush and therefore more about Cook than about Manning herself, foul-tempered overeducated gunslinger that she is and always will be. Just as long, long ago, after decades of warfare, Jean's mommy ended up enshrined and anointed as daddy's delusional construction—as his belated factitious crush—the very daddy whom mommy had hated with a vengeance and who returned her hatred with interest—he'd spit it out every now and then through the prison bars of his gritted teeth, thereby proving that, in keeping with the Tolstoyan code of every unhappy family, theirs was like all the others and then some. (No matter that the more mommy hated, the clearer it became that her target was less daddy than his inability to impersonate any one of mommy's—pre-pubescent mommy's—real targets [i.e., her many forever un-dead sexual abusers] deftly enough to render hate plausible in the here and now.[79]) Here's how it went: In reaction against the echo of his own unsettling announcement that he was being retired pursuant to the machinations of a slew of Envious colleagues, daddy announced defiantly that *she was the only one he trusted*—his best friend in the world (friend or not, it was undeniable he had no others, for the simple reason that the shrike made it a matter of principle not to loan out her whipping boy to the hoi polloi). But though mommy did her damnedest to look as if she were positively basking in the glow cast by this long-overdue attestation (they were en route to Cape May, of all places, in a thunderstorm no less, with Frankie Valli's falsetto unable to take its eyes off o' her), it became *painfully obvious*—Jean dates her understanding of the wicked phrase from that moment—that what mommy really wanted to do (daughter could read it in mommy's eyes)—what she could never help doing—was jump up and excoriate him for having yet again been too naïvely, blunderingly nice to some undeserving stranger when what he should have been doing was ministering to *her* needs, not as an indulgence, mind you, but as the meagerest of indemnifications for having been made to endure all his defects, especially the nastiest of 'em all, i.e., the Spinozistic— *yeah, boob, you heard me right the first time*: Spinozistic—*persistence in his*

---

[79] For it's a truth universally acknowledged that there's nothing an expert hater hates more than to sense—or to sense the target of her hatred senses—that the hatred in question is an implausible—prosthetic—proxy—makeshift hatred.

own being. But suddenly realizing he was neglecting her for none other than . . . she herself! mommy managed (despite the fact that praise lavished for standing firm beside the bane of her existence—and lavished to the bargain by none other than that very bane—was not exactly the sort of twenty-one-gun salute [the sort where all twenty-one bullets are aimed straight at the celebrant's jugular] she so bitchily deserved)—mommy managed to shut her unsavory trap just in the nick of time. And Jean is sure—even without the electrocuted Jersey Shore (in the vicinity of the Ocean Grove Auditorium it was) to set the stage—that Manning, were she privy to Cook's PR, would react in exactly the same way. And who knows what she herself would do if Ethan were to take it into his head to perpetrate such an ungainly tribute?

Only the question then becomes, For whose benefit has the spectacle of Cook's delusionality been mounted? Certainly not for Melanctha's. She's left what now seems like hours ago. (*To go where? Museum of Art. Gerzso exhibition warmly recommended by Cantor. All about incisions, cuts, fissures, clefts [grietas to you, pardner]. Standout: the cobalt-blue vertical streak in* Clytemnestra *[1960]. So how can the subject not interest Melanctha—a veteran self-tormentor addicted, literally and figuratively, to lightly running her tongue every chance she gets over self-inflicted buccal wounds ostensibly to assess the rate of healing and shield the process from—affirm her triumph over the threat of—all further laceration, which skimming strategy of course constitutes the first step along the downward path to re-incision? Sounds mighty interesting. Right up Rhys's blind alley, in fact.*) She hates to see him—or anybody—in such a state, not from goodness of heart (slim pickings in that department) but from fear. If he's capable of so grossly misreading Manning in her essence what will prevent him from misreading Jean's own, rendering her thereby incapable, given her trademark impressionability, of distinguishing what she is from what he thinks she is—rendering her, for all practical purposes, belcanto-mad-scene mad? His misreading will destroy the world as she knows it. She remembers what Rabbi Akiba said to Rabbi Meir (she knows, 'cause her paternal great-grandmother was a half-Jewess who played a hammy Salome to their John and Jim the Baptists). Namely, that when a Bartleby of the Torah omits a letter or incorporates a word too many he destroys the entire world. As will Cook when he dares to misread her. Impossible thereafter for their worldviews to coincide—to coexist—even to clash. One of them must get off the runway if life is to go on crash-diving unimpaired. So everything they say about spectacle is true: it's a contagion and the spectacle of delusion is an even bigger contagion (for her and *whoever else might be looking and listening*). And for whose eyes and ears is *her* spectacle—not to mention, the lunatic fringe benefit (also a spectacle) of Cook's poignant deaf- and blindness to it—ultimately destined? Why, *whoever else might have the misfortune to be looking and listening,* that's who (she's wolfed down enough Invidicum to be able to answer her own question without the need for any incentivization at another poolside summit). And if there isn't a *whoever else* then somebody or something will just have to be dragged in, from central casting, to do the honors. For spectacles of such magnitude—as vital drivers of the Invidicum trial's family plot—simply cannot be allowed to go to waste.

"Any word from that sister of yours? I forget her name." She can't believe he doesn't remember. But she's glad to be done trying to think about Manning, who is, for whatever reason, not all that thinkable up in these hills. "Of course I remember. But I don't want to give her the satisfaction, wherever she is, of thinking I buy the name. For that means, I buy *her*—what she takes herself to be, i.e., what she tries, through the name, to pass herself off as being. She has to earn that or, to be fair, maybe it's me—I—who has to earn the right to buy that name." Rhys's measured response is "Don't pick on her." He can't believe his ears: So all her bellyaching on the podium back at the Institute didn't constitute self-shepherding toward a final divorce from dear old Caro. It was the performance of a slave. The bellyaching was a mere breather—a plain-and-simple pause between abasements. And she's the worst kind of slave—the kind who waxes arrogant at the drop of a hat about the *appropriateness* of her abasement. He can't help taking her self-delusion personally. (Delusion's—like the *grieta*—the extra-hot ticket of the moment.) It makes him feel so lonely—as if he had no friend in the world—least of all himself—and makes Rhys (on whom he did have designs) once and for all unlovable. With *Don't pick on her* she's destroying his world. "How's she doing?" (Cook decides it's best to make nice, with *nice* being in this slippery context—and what context isn't?—a cross between *otherworldly* and *other-wary*.) "From all accounts, she seems to be happier than she's ever been and it's with—imagine!—some devilishly handsome Tasmanian devil and a Jungian to boot. He sounds a lot like one of the hangers-on at Amygdala—at least as he was described to me (I forget by whom)." At which point Jean, ever the apt pupil though not quite in Melanctha's league—no, not by a long shot—proceeds to recapitulate, to the best of her ability, all she's learned about the Jungian's (post-divorce) soft spot for online dating services, specifically about how he once snuck verbotenishly onto the premises of some likely prospect's beachfront condo for a quick assessment beforehand and how the shameless overswell of her butt (as she crouched to water the weeds on her equally outsize front lawn) caused a revulsion so overwhelming as to render him unconscious long enough to get arrested for trespassing.

The minute the words are out of her mouth she regrets them. Will he retaliate by letting everybody know that Ethan got her into the trial under false pretenses, inasmuch as what she was suffering from at the time was not Envy but—but—? For the life of her she can't remember. For now it's as if she never suffered from anything but Envy—she hews closer to its contour than she has to the contour of any other ailment. (For that, Envy herself should stop stuffing her mouth with vipers long enough to show a bit of Ovidian graitutde.) All the others pale by comparison—all the others were but the masques of a poor man's Munchausen syndrome. It's only since the onset of Envy that she's begun to live even if it's only vicariously *through* the Envy—i.e., only through envying the Envy its élan vital. Maybe it was contracted here—iatrogenically, so to speak. Transmitted by another lab rat the way pullet shell clams transmit leukemia to golden carpet shells under the sea. Or the way devil facial tumor disease is transmitted between Tasmanian devils (!) but only when they're deeply in love. Or, like the passengers in that Orient

Express whodunit soufflé by a true genius of the genre, maybe every rat did his part. In that case, she's grateful to the whole bunch. Cook nods though his thoughts are predictably elsewhere. Can he be busy trying (he asks himself) to figure out who's betrayed his dirty little secret (for which he has a soft spot), and why? He manages to make light of the matter. "Sounds to me that your Tasmanian would likely make me an ideal pen-pal." "I only hope that if she ends up outliving her usefulness as a sex toy he doesn't kick her out some bonechillingly rainy night." "Hasn't anybody done himself in just to escape her clutches?" The suggestion together with the sneer in which it's all wrapped up makes her want to run slavishly to Caro's defense only she's already too busy trying to determine if he's on to something when, adding insult to injury, the phone (a sex toy!—a dildo!—to be thrust up the auditory canal), which has evidently survived Cook's assault, has the bright idea of emitting a stran-gled wail (*Ethan, is that you?*).

She's *torn between two lovers*, and if she knows what's good for her she'll lose no time annexing to it the question routinely associated with such a pseudo-plight, namely, *Is it possible to love two men at the same time?*—a ques-tion normally posed (by those so plighted) in what purports to be the minor key of anguish but is in fact the related major: self-congratulation. In short, a question that rejects all solutions out of hand because it's madly in love—with its own self-suspension. Raising the dildo to lips (inexplicably) rather than ear enables her to realize (with a little help from the Master for whom these sudden unmotivated realizations is mother's milk) that what her pseudo-lov-ers share is not infatuation with the same golden girl but nothing more— and nothing less—than outrage at their very indistinguishability which no amount of personalized posturing can remedy. So both are content to gag on the insane hope that by bearing down on the same object (their bond and their gauntlet) from starkly different angles, a little of the starkness will rub off, but differently, on each and confer thereby, again on each, a too-long-unclaimable uniqueness. ("We're born originals, we die copies," to quote Edward Young [as told to choreographer Bronislava Nijinska]—but who exactly is doing the quoting since at this very moment Shearer must be out somewhere scraping the sand off her heels before twiddling both big toes in a bubble bath? [But wait a minute: you don't get sand on your feet at a community swimming pool. *Exactly*.] Unless *Shearer's* starkness—i.e., her stark reverence for the epigrams of her greatest teacher—has rubbed off improbably on Jean.) *If only*, Jean sighs (without knowing exactly what she's sighing about: that's OK, the Master, an old hand at this sort of thing, is willing to do all the knowing for her and at no extra charge), *her two boys could manage to work up enough of an appetite for transformation into trees* (thanks, Maestro!), *for example, parked at diag-onally opposite ends of, say, some sunny strip of weed-fringed asphalt in Long Island City, which she for one would be all too willing to impersonate, even at high noon (anything to help them accede to a status other than that of enemy twins—some monstrous twosome, straight out of the super-polemical pages of René Girard, whose resemblance grows closer and closer, the harder and harder they hate in the name of differentiation). Cook might then pass himself off as a well-mannered greenhorn horse-chestnut, who, long before he's decided whether* or not appropriating her for the emplacement of his shadow accords with the highest principles of backyard brotherly love, gets himself beaten to the punch by a street-smart London-plane, nakedly unashamed of his mottled greed and portrayable only by her soon-to-be or already ex-love.

Forbearingly Jean murmurs, Yes, though she has no idea what she's yessing at. Something to do with suicide's ruling the roost in Caro's love life, no? Cook takes this as his cue to do a little throat-clearing. He's got to impress her enough (even if he decided to dump her decades ago) to get ejected from her rogues' gallery of buttocks-crazy peeping toms (even if he's secretly peacock-proud of his accomplishments—feats, really—in that department). So he says he wants her to understand (as if understanding's an honor he bestows only on the happy few) that he's never had a moment's doubt as to the breadth of his know-how, never mind what Post and his crowd may think. "I know what you're thinking—know-how about what, you low-down no-good consultant man, you?!" He appears not to have noticed there's no denial. Maybe because he knows her stinginess—or better yet, The Stinginess of Woman—is par for the course. "Thing is, I haven't fought hard enough to get my vision realized. "What vision?" she asks dryly, as if *vision* is way too portentous a word for the dribblings of a nobody like him. Or maybe the problem lies with the word itself—too portentous *anywhere* (which is what Lady Macbeth *should* have said post-Duncan)—and therefore a chronic debasement of whatever it professes to encompass—anywhere. "Of how to market Invidicum." It turns out that doing battle for his vision out in the real world is a horse of a different color from giving birth to it in the privacy of his own workshop (surely Narr must have mentioned how repeatedly locking horns with one of Post's slimiest top flunkeys about which patient recruitment outfit to hire had landed him on mandatorily massive doses of Seroquel). For, let's face it, he's no good at being real (or hasn't Jean noticed?), used as he's become to dumping that responsibility in the lap of the vision itself. Which goes a long way toward explaining—at least in his book—why he's so tired of the struggle to compel his pygmy hippo superiors to bestow the requisite aura on his productions. *Jean, Jean, are you still there? Then say something—anything—goddamit!* But how can she be expected to listen, much less respond (even if her morbid curiosity has been piqued as never before), with Cook trying, albeit as courteously as possible (isn't he half-Confederate?), to yank the contraption out of her pretty hands (and ultimately succeeding) in order, presumably, to teach his old buddy a thing or two about visions. (And who, by the way, is thinking *But how can she be expected to listen . . .?* Jean? Cook? the Master? the Master's Master? fate? Fate? common sense? horse sense? Gestalt psychology? pop psychology? or does this thought-without-a-thinker—far more dire than Hale's Man Without a Country—happen to be another one of those under-the-sea leukemias, here being hot-potatoed from candidate to candidate instead of from bivalve to bivalve?)

Suddenly, just as he's about to wring Narr's neck, Cook discovers or rather dimly suspects (in what feels like—in what should by all rights be—but isn't, no, not by a long shot—a tenement bathroom overlooking, say, the lowest reaches of State Street) that the aura withheld (as long as it stays withheld) is more real than he himself will ever be. (Granted, the fact that the bathroom, however crummy, *has* a window makes him spoiled-brat-luckier than 99.99 percent of his fellow Manhattanites. [And by the way, who's thinking, *Granted, the fact that*...? Cook? Big Apple realtors? The Rump Organization? universal wisdom? room service? the Reality Principle aka Rip Van Winkle?].) Getting fancy you might say this missed aura—the ostensible only-thing-missing to make his identity 101.99 percent complete—*is* his realness. Getting even fancier you might say that into this reified sin of omission has leaked and within it now dwells every bloody thing he needs to refuse to know about himself if he intends to hang on to that realness. And out of the kindness of its heart the bloodstain in question is doing him the unrepayable favor of thinking his unthinkable—to wit, that he may in fact be the farthest cry imaginable from the world's most visionary pharmacomarketeer and may therefore have to put away not just his labor and his leisure, too, but like Freud's Wolf Man, any expectation that Fate harbors a special preference for him. Or can it be—getting fancier still!—that such a derogation is not necessarily (even if it was so for the Wolf Man) a death knell—the end of the road—but a new beginning engineerable through the simplest of expedients (oh, why didn't he think of this centuries ago?) which is to drop leechlike Fate's intrusive string-pulling before Fate can drop him?

But even if the bloodstain is doing him this favor Cook, whether he knows it or not, is no stranger to the realm of the unthinkable and so he has more than an inkling of what bad news said bloodstain is churning out. With his arch rival now in the palm of his hand, Cook does him—Ethan—the honor of making him the target of the desperation generated by his fear: "You've been going around calling me a failure and getting everybody else to follow your lead. But how can I be a failure after masterminding the Pan-Gloss, 'best of all possible kitchen sprays' campaign, which made product placement of P-G in the sitcom smash *Bare with Me* (you know, the one about the Santa Catalina nudist colony) the very first example anywhere of branding in prime time entertainment; not to mention the Wells Fargo-Bank of America 'Gentlemen Prefer Bonds' dominatrix video, which singlehandedly restored the public's faith in those monstrosities? All basic training for the HBO challenge." "They were just flukes. But don't forget (from false modesty or for whatever reason), while you're at it, the 'No dinosaurs were harmed during the making of this movie' gimmick, which enabled the quintessential midsummer night's mega-bomb *Jackassic Park III* to turn a hefty profit." "So how do you explain away those triumphs?" "As I said, they were mere flukes—you got lucky."

There is a long silence. Has the line gone dead? Is it Narr who's dead? "Seriously, I believe you, Bill. You know I do. It's just—it's just—" "It's just what?" "It's just that if you're the success story, then by the law of averages it's I that's got to be the failure. What I mean is, I can't help feeling (and don't tell me it's the Invidicum talking) there's Some Body or Some Thing stalking me—us—at every turn—a Thing—an Object—much bigger than Post and Pritchard and the CIA and the FBI and the FDA and even the ABA—way way bigger than all those small fry put together." "So?" "Ask him if he's referring to the—I mean, Melanctha's—" Rhys bellows like a fishwife. (How can they have been heard by her with the bathroom door expertly closed?) "Tell Jean to go to hell. I can't put my finger on It. In any case, it—I mean It (the thing's vainer than vain and you never know when it'll be tuning in)—wants to be able to tell us apart—It feeds on—and off—the meatiness of our opposition. That's how It makes its money or Its name in the company but in a way I don't quite understand. Thing is, fear—terror, really—is making us sound more and more alike no matter how hard we try to sound—and be—different (admit it, you're as terrified as I am). That's what terror does to even the best of us. But why should I be the failure just 'cause you're the success? On the other hand, no matter how disjunct (all right, I have a soft spot for that word) we've managed to make ourselves, me from you and you from me (and not just through the wonders of makeup) and no matter how hard we try to make ourselves even more disjunct, it's never enough—it never begins to be enough—it will never be enough." "Whoa! down, boy! You make it sound as if this Thing—I mean *thing* (oops! you had me kowtowing there for a minute)—might have to answer to a swarm of high-end customers or investors or constituents or board members or shareholders who are pressuring it to not just come up to (better leave that to the losers) but massively exceed their expectations." (Ethan nods feverishly but as there's nobody around to see, the gesture must be content to waste its feverishness on the desert air.) Which, Cook deduces easily enough, can mean only one thing: the ante must be upped, i.e., they must be rendered, that is, they must be made to render themselves (they, the smelly secretions of Its—from all indications—unmarketable pineal gland)— even more hyperdistinct—as hyperdistinct from each other as firmament from fin, or Hyperion from a satyr, or Scar*lett* from Rh*ett*. *Narr:* "Because if It doesn't guarantee shareholder value Its career is over." *Cook:* "Now that you mention it, I must admit—" Briefish pause to allow enactment of stunned self-discovery to coyly run its course. And speaking of coyness, why don't they just stop talking around the Master and start talking *about* Him. After all, they're no stranger to the Concept. Indeed, like everybody else, they happen to be half in love with Him (for, let's face it, the Master is Easeful Death)—in fact, they've called Him soft names in many a bruised rhyme. Or, if neither is man enough to get the ball rolling, why don't they let Jean let in the breath of fishwifely fresh air that was on the tip of her tongue a minute ago? "Now that you mention it I started having the same eerie-goofy feeling myself—of being stalked, I mean—as far back as my West Village days and especially on Minetta Lane—no, make that Minetta *Street*. Not just stalked but goaded into flouting each and every law that makes me me. I refused (and still do): I'd had enough of that sort of harassment from mom and pop. But never mind *them:* why should we worry—we, of all people?"

"Why *shouldn't* we worry?"

"Because we have a friend at court." Having retrieved his laptop from the landing where he carelessly left it, Cook explains that they're going to Skype— make that Zoom—with Cantor, who will explain it all much better than he, Cook, ever could. Rhys looks out the window. Cook takes this winsome gesture as his cue to say (but at whose behest?), "You won't find him poolside. He must be back in his apartment—the pad he shares with Eden down near East

603

Beach. Swinging bachelors, that's what they are—but with a twist." A little low-tech stage business and then—a blank screen. What sounds like a knock at the door. Enter virtual George, pursued by an algorithm. "Hi, George." "Hi." Cantor muzzles himself against saying, *What's up*, a two-syllable special he abhors even if it's guaranteed to give the speaker the upper hand (especially when served with a dollop of impatience). Thing is, you've got to be an acting pro to be able to purge your delivery of the fear that breezy aggressivity is supposed to mask. Jean *can't get over* how cute he looks in khaki shorts. The rays of the waning sun set off the shapeliness of his ear lobes—to uncomfortably powerful effect. He informs Jean that Pritchard was particularly upset by her early departure—even more than by Melanctha's. So Cantor's now Pritchard's guy Friday. As if smelling the rat of recrimination, he exterminates it by assuring her he's no flunkey—merely a concerned citizen. He just couldn't abstain from fulfilling the old guy's request that he play messenger—even if it got—gets—him shot. "Ethan, can you hear us?" "Sure can, Bill." (Ethan is all set to play—to a full house of one—at being on his best behavior.) "Good. George, would you mind explaining to all three of us why Ethan and I don't need to worry our pretty little heads about failing to be contradistinctive enough from each other—contrary enough—to satisfy the Thing—the Object—that's ruining all our lives—going so far in our case as to get us (Leopold and Loeb to you) accused of the murder of some long-winded lowlife. The way you explained it to me back on Greenwich Avenue just before we were shipped out. It was a warm and windy night. You noted how inviting the community garden (at the corner of Sixth Avenue) looked in the moonlight." "Cloud-veiled." "What?" "Cloud-veiled—the moonlight, I mean. But refresh my memory. Does this have anything to do with being stalked by Melanctha's Master or the Scourge of *My* Psyche (SoP) or Shearer's Balletmaster in Chief?"

"Lots. Far more than I for one would care to acknowledge. I've been playing it coy with Ethan (sorry, dude) but now I'm going to come clean. Around the same time as he did, maybe even earlier (but probably, since I'm an artist of sorts, much more intensely), I started to feel that I was being surveilled by some kind of pre-SS mastermind, a Mabuse of sorts, running amuck on the now-unaffordable sidestreets of the West Village. His message being that I'd better hurry up and make myself as opposite—oppositive—oppositional—to Ethan as I could. Or the deal was off. But I'm still not sure what deal he was referring to when his Aryan spittle had the beer hall audacity to graze my virgin ear."

"But if both of you were to follow his instructions, wouldn't that make you the featheriest birds of a feather? The more you followed his instructions, the less you'd be following his instructions (a paradox worthy of old Bertie). But if, for now at least, you're the unique-est of the unique, that's owing in no small measure to the fact that Jean's in our midst. Or rather, *a teammate of Jean's caliber.*" Should Jean blush? She's not sure. And what would that do to her complexion? After all, she wants to look good for Cantor and he knows it, even if—especially since—he doesn't desire her in the least—simply isn't *up to it*—can't, even if he may want to as a change of pace. Would fucking a *woman* be a betrayal of Gilles? He looks into the unseeing harlequin eyes of an embodied premonition hanging in the Met—Watteau's Berry Sundae—and wants to cry. But as there's nothing pretty about seeing a grown man cry (even if it was *de rigueur* in Hollywood films—specifically A-listers, of the "studs have feelings, too"[80] variety—some decades back, the 1970s to be less inexact), he tries to invoke something funny—how about the thing he came up with and "shared" the other day with, of all people Eden? who either didn't get the joke or didn't appreciate it once he most unwillingly did get it or maybe he did appreciate it but didn't want Cantor to think he did, which would only narrow the fleshly distance between them. That thing being the definition of "homosexual" set out in the latest edition of the *OED* or the *DSM* or the *Chicago Manual of Style* or all three, as being "a man whose favorite by far among the Brothers Marx isn't Groucho or Zeppo or Chico or Gummo or even Karl but Margaret (née Dumont)." That thing, then, will have to do in a pinch. But it makes him want to cry even harder. He goes on to explain (even if his eloquence is not quite up to the standards of a stickler like Herbert, though who's made her the arbiter of his destiny, will you tell me? and while we're at it, how pretty Jean looks entangled in those waning rays of lamplight which are as sticky as kelp)—Cantor goes on to explain that it's no accident the three of them keep clinging to each other. After all, they are the members of a Group (in the mathematical sense) who interact under the binary operation *confession*—and Jean is the identity element of that group. (A Group of course can have millions of members.) Meaning that when each of them confesses to Jean or, put another way, when Jean confesses (i.e., shrives) either of them, she refunds him to himself. Or put still another way, when element Cook or element Narr is paired with element Jean under the binary operation "confession"—when element Cook or Narr is operated on by—paired with—element Jean under "confession"—he ends up corresponding to himself—ends up being exactly as he was before the operation—exactly the same but immeasurably enriched—exactly the same *because* immeasurably enriched. So don't nobody dare suggest that whenever it becomes clear Cook and Narr are intent on pairing themselves with each other under the operation "confession" (which is a very different kettle of fish from pairing themselves with element Jean since the C-N pairing is all about mortal combat, i.e., all about deflection and defection)—that whenever it becomes clear that our boys are intent on flaying each other alive, with each *through that very flaying and being flayed* thereby confessing to the other, and to whoever else will listen, his deep-seated doubts regarding not just his own uniqueness-through-opposition but his very *being*—don't nobody dare suggest that Jean (a veritable Florence Nightingale!) has ever failed to get off her high horse and—whatever the time of day or night, and no questions asked—immediately caulk the resultant ontic leaks and refund the flayers to themselves more watertight—more oppositional—more contradistinctive—more in contravention of each other's laws—than they have any right to expect to be. Paired with Jean the identity element—Jean the self-identity fixer under

---

[80]Thanks go to the trailblazing American film critic Andrew Sarris for his delectably deft characterization of this somewhat hokey trend.

the operation "confession" (a dynamic referred to by CIA psychologists as OCT [Operation Tough Love])—each emerges more himself—i.e., more intact and unflayed—that is, stronger—in other words, more oppositional— than ever. And her sleight of hand has the added advantage of eliminating the need for the leakers to undertake the frantic inventory of limbs—those still attached and those irrecoverably lost to the fray—that is obligatory after this kind of *mutual perpetration of soul-surgery by accredited quacks* (in this case, by Cook on Narr and vice versa). Since when Jean operates, intactness is guaranteed.

So it's Jean (*at last: the generation cum crossing of a Rubicon that's almost baroque in its straightforwardness [the decision of the following chunk of text to sever itself from the parent, when staying tied to that parent's apron strings would have been so easy, is indeed an occasion for rejoicing]*) who's been and will presumably continue to be their friend at court, Cook and Narr think in a painful unison of shock and relief. Painful—since a hostile takeover by unison is the last thing in the world they now need, what with the horde of buzzard shareholders breathing the standard carcinogenic dinner-theater demands down their neck. But what if her intervention—her strategy-in-spite-of-it- self—is not radical enough to satisfy those buzzards? What if they're still too much alike?

Obviously Jean can only wonder why she—an innumerate of the first water—should have been assigned—and not Shearer, for example (after all, isn't choreography sheer—mere—metamathematics in motion?)—the cov- eted role of (what did Cantor call it?) group identity element? An embarrass- ment of riches, this, or just plain embarrassment? Jean, who gets an occa- sional thrill out of referring to herself as a country lass, doesn't pretend to know much about (*a*) such matters (even if in tonight's performance she's been playing—but is this relevant?—the coveted role of Herbert/Manning to the hilt) not to mention (*b*) what neural network governs how starring roles are assigned in this joint-stock company. But mightn't visiting this role on the (what was Bill's word?) . . . secretion! least suited to inhabiting it constitute Thing's way of revenging himself at long last (with Jean the collateral damage) on the tribe of consumers, who appear to be big on dinner-theater plausibil- ity, i.e., on *a perfect plighting of plot and personage*, and will accept no stand- ins. (Now where did that mouthful can from? she wonders. Conversation overheard in—graffiti scrawled on the walls of—some ladies' room? Surely not from deep within the foul rag-and-bone shop of her heart, that's for sure (she's no slouch when it comes to provoking men to call her heartless). But, the truth of the matter is that whatever Thing's *thing* happens to be, all this high praise makes her less eager than ever to refund Cook to Cook or Ethan to Ethan or whatever it is Cantor insists she does better than anybody else this side of Cleopatra's barge. Not that she's getting a swelled head—that she's getting too big for her britches—that she believes refunding's a job better left to the bureaucrats doomed to service Leona Helmsley's Form 1040-shackled leprechauns. "Don't you get it?" Jean cries (rolling the eyes of her throat), outrage having given her the strength to yank back the phone (though in so doing she nevertheless makes it understood she's about to put not just Ethan on notice but Cook as well and if he doesn't mind his manners Cantor along with them—not to mention all the other men who've cum 'n' gone and, worst [she's never played the world-weary femme fatale quite so bleakly and with so much zest], all those waiting in the wings, unzipped). "How can I refund you to yourselves when you're busy doing your damnedest to become self-parodies before somebody compels you to find out who you really are: streetcorner deviants before you can even begin to comprehend what you're busy deviating from: white-collar crimers before you've found anything worth embezzling from the thirty-eighth floor kitty?" Dead silence. Jean is stunned—*no, Jean, you're just startled*—to realize that in flagrant disregard (she prefers *contravention* but charitably stets *disregard*) of everything she's learned about men (yet when you got right down to it what exactly *has* she learned?), she was expecting an upsurge of unmitigated thanks from Narr and Cook for the diagnosis, first on their own behalf, of course, but far more importantly on behalf of the even more deviant billions who, from obvious dread of her acuity, managed to wangle a previous engagement just in the nick of time.

Her head is swimming. She must have a brain tumor. If so, it's a metastasis. Since this is not her thought. It's a clot of cancer cells that have swum into her thought-packet pool from somebody else's—maybe by breaching the respiratory tract. (Her tumor is surely one of the orphans that normally afflict children, and only a few worldwide, say, 650. The kind that greed machines like AstraZeneca seize on to make a case for prolonging the market exclusivity for at least 50 years of one of their bestsellers [thereby fending off the competition of generics]—a pink pill for, say, honeymooner's psychosis or Crohn's disease or anal asthma or non-Hodgkin's lymphoma—but which, from its performance in a few shoddy trials has been singled out as the culprit responsible for whatever little headway has been made in the domain of treatment.) For what in their shared past justifies her calling Narr and Cook a pair of self-parodies and likely to remain so? Nothing. The thought has come out of nowhere. But while it's a purely local affair and only too happy to remain airily distrustful and dismissive of context and beholden to none, the thought nevertheless compels those contaminated by its dire potency—tasks them (since the notion that such a thought can stand on its own two feet is simply unendurable) to trace its roots plausibly—or better yet implausibly—back to that prissiest of Mr. MacBores, the Past. Not that she isn't grateful, on the other hand, for the opportunity to be somebody else. Since if (as she heard Cantor mutter twice under his breath in far-off Coronado), *At any instant, man is a thought,* and if—as muttered thrice (so far) here in Santa Barbara— *His language is the sum total of himself* then why shouldn't she—or how can she not—try (so as to swell that sum and thereby enhance her job and marriage-and-divorce prospects manyfold) to avoid stepping in the same stream of consciousness twice? Why shouldn't she branch out? Set her eye on pastures new. Fact is, though, she misses the old Jean but will the old Jean be willing to take her back? But why not? After all, the old Jean ain't the heartless tyrant the Staten Island ferry made it out to be one sticky midsummer night, when the still-ungentrified intersection of Spring and Ludlow was at the height of its beauty (she won't look upon that intersection's likes again). Thing is, the old Jean has been superseded by the self that had the guts to live the thought beginning, "How can I refund you to yourselves . . .?"—the self born from the pullulation of those guts. Jean giggles coarsely as she hears herself say, like Lisa in her (at least for the moment) favorite movie of all time, "I've had no will but his, ever," only it's not the pianist Stefan Brand she's referring to but a more unremitting, a more elusive and, ultimately, an infinitely more spineless taskmaster: Thought. She'd like to put the whole sordid episode behind her but the giggles, unlike surf, won't recede.

"Jean," Cantor remarks, "and I have no qualms about saying it to her face, is trying to sell you a castrative bill of goods and at bargain-basement prices, no less." Jean shakes her head steadfastly, slowly, sadly. "Playing the castration card? Me, of all people? I don't see how." The prospect of becoming Pritchard's successor has clearly transformed him. She's pleased and disappointed at the same time—as a result of colluding with the engineer of his anointment, he's become both more and less than the self she's come to know. Cantor doesn't just sense her disappointment—he positively swills in its tears. But surely she—with all her experience of life or at least of art or applied art—must know that *preferment changes any man.* He scours his past for some incident whose rank unjustness would entitle him to abuse her—or any innocent bystander—would entitle him to slaughter the shorn lamb within. But nothing passes muster. Adding insult to injury, from where he's stationed in front of the screen she looks all of a sudden as if hunched on a footstool over what in the Grimms' fairy-tale world of the nineteenth century English novel would have been described as a humble repast. The wretched painterly solitude immediately casts him in an even more persecutory light. Ah! if only through self-scrutinizing mimicry with the right props and posture (thing is, everybody's watching) his body could be allowed to demonstrate—*from the inside out*—that there are fates far worse than eating alone, thereby purging this genre scene of its pathos and putting its heroine on the path to recovery from his sneak attack. After all, didn't the beguilingly gamine-pretty wife of a colleague—no, the wife of his thesis adviser (a #MeToo casualty)—once admit that having her slice of pumpkin pie, traditionally, in the kitchen (when grumpily hostessing Thanksgiving Day festivities) while the guests gorged themselves out in the dining room *made it seem like more*? "Why are you lashing out?" she murmurs, moving ever so slightly, ever so alluringly, from wherever she is to wherever she's going—hence proving that cooking up a little genre-scene-style pathos was the furthest thing from her mind. "Because lashing out is contagious. Didn't you just lash out at The Boys?" Jean shrugs (although to Ethan, it's more as if her shoulders rolled their eyes). According to Jean (according to Cantor, whose interpretation is clearly banking on taking some liberties), there's no such thing as originality—uniqueness. As she sees it, the only shred of uniqueness any boob, self-respecting or otherwise, can expect to lay claim to accrues from the self-sabotaging ingenuity (is there any other kind?) with which he prevents it from rearing its ugly head—the only shred is salvaged through the ability to pinpoint precisely how we managed to lick the odds and become (before we could become ourselves) that jaunty old warhorse, *our own worst enemy.* In other words, Jean earns her bread by implying that originality is nothing more than the hazy glimpse we get, but only if we're lucky, of whatever such nip-it-in-the-bud foreclosure leaves in its eely wake. "In other words, where Jean comes from, selfhood is the self-parody that forecloses the attainment of selfhood, to cite one of her too many streetcorner sloganoids." "I'm no sloganeer. But what do I get out of all this—aside from my daily bread?" "As the poor man's Manning, you get to see us—your stooges—all consigned to the maximum-security shithole specifically designed for selfhoods gone to seed—a shithole run all too efficiently by some male Hope Emerson or female Neville Brand (I know these two gargoyles—but gargoyles with tons of talent and lots of heart—date from way before your time)." Jean and George have become Cook's parents and he hates nothing more than to see them bury the hatchet in each other's jugulars. "What would Manning do that I haven't done?" "Not much. For starters, she'd acknowledge that nothing's more important in the scheme of things than Originality (Irena is known to make heavy weather of preferring, as a European, the O word to *uniqueness* which, invoking as it does the Mad Ave of yore, reeks of commodification) since It's nothing less than the Thing-in-Itself, the holy grail of armchair—or streetcorner—Parsifals." Which means, he goes on to explain along the following lines and in so many words (but, having now gotten Manning off his chest, more kindly than before—even affectionately— even apologetically—why, if she didn't know better she'd say he was a hairpin turn away from hitting on her—and, most important, in language anybody— even a hayseed like her—might understand), it's not a *thing* at all—for sure it ain't some soggy substrate of ultimate self-explanation—but rather, the triumph of the will—the will to undertake, without regard to fringe benefits or side effects or secondary gains or bonus points or frequent-flyer miles, a task that can lay claim to having a goal only insofar as the goal remains a *projection beyond* hence unattainable *in* experience. "Now doesn't that make you feel a wee bit better, Jean? since by being cut down to size you're spared all that vain pursuit of a beyond that's beyond the beyond." Before she can be struck dumb, Cantor exits the screen, pursuing an algorithm—with what looks like a highly professional butterfly net. Dumb or not, she resents his invidious comparison. More for his sake than her own. It makes him look small.

Although she doesn't feel better—and maybe a lot worse—somehow Jean isn't in the least offended by all this demonizing, amateurish to the bone— amateurish enough to be endearing. For one thing, what must be the end-of-session bell (more like the alarm of some ambulance charging down the Champs-Élysées) is clanging at long last and now she'll have her five minutes with Margo—the five minutes that will change her life. (It turns out she's mistaken: The session has no intention of ending just yet.) For another, nothing holds water—nothing just said is grounded—*truly* grounded—in what came before. Which makes Cantor the victim of a metastasis as well—the transmission through a breach in, say, his digestive tract from her packet pool to his, of carcinogens of purposeful incoherence she didn't know she harbored. But in this case misery doesn't love company—Jean feels plagiarized, robbed of her uniqueness (secretly, however, she knows it does exist soemwhere and commodification be damned), shackled to a plight more hopeless than, because identical to, her own. Although he's—or rather, the Master's—done his damnedest to make them appear to be at loggerheads—she's sure that any penetrative spectator's overall impression must be one of compatibility—the compatiblity born of yokage, through thick and thin and back again, to a noble aim—which, in this case, is to prove to the world that the trial is about much more than all the fallout from shenanigans like pill-pushing and over-prescription of fMRIs. In fact, they're shooting at something far beyond it (as attested by the heady references to, e.g., those old chestnuts Uniqueness and Originality) but of course if in so doing they should continue to stumble on—cross swords with (and why shouldn't they?)—just the sort of gruesome details (the meat-and-potatoes and blood-and-guts of inner conflict fore-doomed to go viral) that the dinner-theater-going public has come to expect from a drug trial—from the architects of the story of that trial and not any old story but the kind of story that's unputdownable—well, then, such stumbling and such crossing of swords will be sauce to the goose (or whatever the expression is). The Story may very well turn out to be rarefied beyond Originality's wildest dreams (a Barmecide cum Belshazzar's Feast with thought packets *au poivre* being the *pièce de résistance* and cliffhangers *mit shlag* the merest garnish) but Jean has no intention of forgetting it's an epic as well and along the lines of any other self-respecting entry in the genre already boasts more holes than fifty gross of donuts and more twists than as many pretzels, with every twist having to be paid for with way too many holes, which in turn require way too many suturing twists and so on and so forth under the terms of a dialectic positively Hegelian in its crowd-sourcing frenzy. What the mess clearly calls for, then, is sobriety—an Old Testament-style press release, say, cradling within its austere cadences the strict determination that every twist shall beget just so many holes, which in their turn shall beget just so many twists, which in their turn . . . And for better or worse, such a process is the closest thing to creative evolution said epic (and its cast of thousands—that is, thousands of . . . donuts) shall—will—ever undergo.

HAFTKA

2023

CHAPTER THIRTY-FOUR

Pritchard looks very much the worse for wear. The poor bastard has been roughed up, his pre-eminence as a health professional is in the proverbial tatters, his humiliations have been capped by the hallowed perp walk which, to a loony tune of hisses and infinitely more rancid applause, went on for what felt like—and may very well have been—hours. As it turns out, slapping Borkman with a subpoena was, however much merited, just a ploy to throw this most unusual suspect—far more than just a person of interest—off-guard. But, as it also turns out, the subpoena will stick until further notice. He looks thirty years older, Borkman remarks, not without relish, or is he simply trying to cheer himself up now that he's been repudiated yet again by his fellow Vikings for what they deem to have been his grossest mistake: apprehension? (News travels fast especially from Coast to Coast.) But bolstered by the adoring look of his old flame which immediately reminds him that it's this evening that they're supposed to offer their long-awaited long-overdue master class on Envy and Conspiracy (Margo's aged quite a bit in the last few hours, notes Shearer, though in her case without the slightest trace of relish—with a vicarious shudder, in fact), Pritchard turns to face what are now his fellow sufferers. Despite his ordeal, all of a sudden he looks refreshed. Once it becomes clear he didn't fork up a single clinical detail to the cops that could be used to stymie any patient's reintegration, however wobbly, into society when the time is right, they begin to look less like a firing squad and more like . . . the motley of nitwits he more and more frequently and less and less reluctantly takes them to be. But he has to remind them that, discretion being a double-edged sword, neither can they expect him to fork up any of the confidential information to which he gained access once Chief Detective Levin Millar was satisfied he'd had nothing to do either with Post's pipeline antics or with Manning's—yes, Manning's—efforts to ensure a market for off-label Invid, especially east of Eastern Europe, in exchange for an outsize slice of the pipeline pie.

Herbert's assessment is that at least the weather is cloudlessly, breezily, on their side. So maybe the master class will be held after all. As for the receding sky: well, let's just say that the gullibility of hope is smeared all over its hindquarters like raspberry jam across freshly baked bread. Not to mention the clouds: as if on cue (and it *is* on cue, thanks to the Master), beauties of every conceivable shape, size, gender, artistic affiliation, are fleeing with just the shirt on their backs they know not where nor why (*think*: Shelley's ghostly dead leaves pursued by their ghostly Enchanter, the Odessa Steps); one of them is as proud as a peacock about having turned out looking like a cross between the Hindenburg and a locomotive, obviously unaware there's a price to be paid for such conspicuity and that price, under firmamental law, is nothing less than inevitable dissolution well in advance of its comrades. Her heart—believe me—sorely aches for the peacock—for the perils of all forced migration—but she has troubles of her own. But at least she doesn't have to lament the inability to get away and study tonight's sunset in solitude since, given the *neatness* of the orb—the fact that it's sure to go on tamely respecting its own boundaries even after it hits the horizon—there'll be none of those baroque surprises so dear to a budding poetess's heart, hence nothing to learn of any consequence. Though how can she be sure . . . really sure? "But enough blood and guts. For a change of pace, let's all pretend we're sweaty decadents straight out of *The Exterminating Angel*—raise your hand if you have even the slightest idea of what I'm referring to!—and try to remember where we were all sitting just before I was taken away, perhaps never to return. It'll put us all in the mood for too-long-delayed self-betterment." (Normally Doc Pritchard—released from custody he's been reinstated as the one of the bastions of his profession—deprecates wielding the truncheon of his vast culture since nobody knows better than he that doing so is but a means, and a feeble one at best, of compensating for the direst self-loathing.) Stretched out on a vintage fifties chaise longue (*don't ask me to explain what* that *looks like: ask the words! I'm innocent! I tell you I'm innocent! it's the words that made me do it, warden—I mean, your honor!*), Margo (she should be—and by God she is!—wearing a sort of ribbon-cluttered Gainsborough hat) blows him a kiss. But mightn't there be, Shearer wonders (hypersensitive as she is from her *Coppélia* and *Harlequinade* days to the nuances of mime), the tiniest bit of entreaty in the gesture (to steer clear of, say, some just-too-intimate details of their failed marriage even if the California sunshine can be depended on to burn the devil in those details to a crisp)? Too late. Shearer looks around: as in any ballet, there are the principals—among whom she numbers Borkman, Cantor and herself—and the corps. But the problem with this corps—as with so many, sometimes even in Mr. B.'s applause machines—is that it's merely decorative, not organic. A big problem and as resident choreographer for a night she needs to deal with it. If there's time. The bugs, on the other hand, are organic to the hilt (judging from all the swatting going on around her) and they know it. For they're self-important bugs—arrogant little bugs—carrying arrogance to the point where it ends up being the spitting image—the wobbly armature—of impotence. Jean arrives late—but arrive she does. It could be said, uncharitably, that she's trying to make a grand entrance but doesn't have the equipment (in fact, she's just gotten wind of the fact that the session's over and the master class about to begin). But knowing better than anyone—or almost anyone—how difficult it is to carry off such an entrance (why, it took her months to master Dewdrop's, which comes halfway through the "Waltz of the Flowers" and on the diagonal), Moira makes allowances for this clearly befuddled rookie.

"Let's get going, shall we." But before they do, Melanctha Herbert has a bone to pick—not so much with Pritchard as with the Master. She mock-marvels at how He always finds a way to stage His abstractionist extravaganzas on prime turf (which put Castle Garden to shame) without paying a cent in leasing fees—and with the human, vegetable and mineral bric-a-brac (also gratis) so embedded as to render it impossible to determine whether the wordflow's eating up the scenery or vice versa. In any event, He should be investigated by future bulldog general Big Billy Barr (she—or somebody—knows that to joke about this mammoth *atoll of human scum*—miniature versions of such atolls are generated on a toilet's water spot by urinating males all the time—is to make light of his crimes and dishonor their victims). "I tried to explain to Margo here, right off the bat, that I preferred and would always prefer men but was still trying to make up my mind whether it was the chicken of homosexuality or the egg of shame that came first. Was the shame a substrate-hungry enzyme which discovered by chance that homosexuality would serve its purposes very nicely or was it the other way around (although on this level of excruciation I soon found that every way around was always *the other way*)? In any event, what better way to feel you exist (when you don't quite believe you do, which not-quite-believing is, by the way, the farthest thing imaginable from an intellectual pose) than through shame. I could see all this parading of perplexity made her uneasy—and why shouldn't it. In any event, when she— the very Margo you see before you—asked me to account for my . . . 'absences' as she had every right to do, I decided it was best to tell her I was *ministering*—paying house calls—to the mind-sick as a necessary step (at least in those days of rank idealism—or so I thought) up the professional ladder. Or to use Jim's term, *totem pole*. Though not (as I discovered almost in tandem) just because I was ashamed—though there was and still is plenty of shame to go around where sexuality is concerned, and where isn't it concerned?—but rather, and far more interestingly (in my opinion), because shame *owed* me and at the very least should be compelled to *give something back* for all I'd endured and would no doubt continue to endure on its behalf. In combating the poverty of shame I wanted shame to give me a run for its money, so to speak. But when I say *poverty* I don't mean to suggest that I didn't have the guts to act on my lustful yearning for love maybe thousands—but more like millions—of times, on Marketfield Street and in Ryders Alley and Mechanics Alley and Theatre Alley and Burling Slip and Smegma Lane, to name but a few of my favorite tryst-worthy haunts in the Big Apple. What I do mean is that *in her eyes*—i.e., in my own—I didn't want homosexuality to be homosexuality pure and simple and nothing more. In other words, I wanted to be more than just myself—to be nothing less than *more than human*—and homosexuality seemed a dependable conduit toward making my wet dream a reality. Herbert determines, *Pritchard is to Homosexuality as Melanctha is to Building 18.*

"And every time I transformed some unspeakable act peculiar (!) to cruising (e.g., sucking on a hairy pickup's balls—or is it a *pickup's hairy balls*? I must follow in the footsteps of eternally young Pepys and consult my diary) into the kind of good deed that's intrinsic to ministering (e.g., latexed tampering with a patient's prostate) I achieved my goal. What deed the act ended up as in my depiction of course didn't matter in the least: what's so great, after all, about transforming a testicle into an anus or vice versa? Greasy kids' stuff. What mattered was living the transformation as *self*-transformation on an atom- or rather a neutrino-splitting scale." Some members of this audience of tentatively cross-legged yogis nod—as if to say, *That's exactly how I used to feel. You've nailed it. Right on, brother.* And they feel no shame for being mesmerized in true camp-meeting style, Cantor notes—for he's made it up here in record time—with envy and deprecation (in other words, if Cantor were the weather forecast, he'd be a mix of clouds and clouds). They have no desire to be unique—original—originality's an overrated belch as far as they're concerned. What's important is to be spoken for—articulated out of anonymity. At last somebody has given voice to their unspeakable—and they're grateful and humbled. It's exactly the way folks behave on PBS in front of a Suze Orman or a Wayne Dyer or a Daniel Amen or a Franklin Graham—experts on your fate-to-be. And Cantor himself is shooting the close-ups of their subjugation—their entrancement. But not because he feels ho-ho superior to it. He's envious. Or rather, he would be if he could.

"As it turns out, Margo refused to believe—really believe—in either my ministering or my craving for man-on-man cruising." What remains of her posture—a vintage fifties chaise longue slouch—betrays uneasiness: in fact, she's burrowed deep inside her Gainsborough and intends to remain there until further notice. "She believed only in what was for her the most unspeakable thing of all—her biggest bugbear—as far as her love for me (I guess it was love) was concerned: adulterous acts committed with *women* against *her* (though she never quite gave up on the homosexuality angle as we'll soon see). And so by some strange contortion of illogic—and what contortion isn't strange?—my ministering and cruising became good deeds by default. And she routinely took it upon herself to mischaracterize them as self-duping red herrings—as acts that muddied the waters of my much-vaunted lucidity— acts that distracted me from the virulence of what I really wanted. I knew what I really wanted but, according to her, had managed to convince myself or the good deeds themselves that they and they alone were my pharmakon of choice. So there was a pleasure almost erotic—better than erotic—in the very act of turning the tables on my accuser by proving in every case—when she thought she'd at last caught me with my pants down—that what she took for perpetration of a—*the*—bad deed was in fact perpetration of one of the herring-scented good ones. Since for as long as (but *only* for as long as) the moment of clearing my name lasted—the moment of clearing myself of any and all charges of engaging in acts compatible solely with guy-gone-wild heterosexuality—the moment of providing the requisite proof beyond a reasonable doubt—well, in the starched bosom of that moment, all other accusations past, present and to come—levied by everyone I'd ever known including me myself—substantiable or otherwise—were obliterated in tandem. In short, this situation yielded an experience of wholesale purgation—innocence as a whole-body—an out-of-body—sensation—a sensation foreclosed in every other life-context, where (even—or rather, especially—if a complaint was never lodged) I rightly judged myself to be a cross between, at best, a Quisling and a Mengele." (This painful admission in the form of a love letter—to himself—induces another upsurge of Ocean Grove Camp Meeting Association subjugation.) Margo is thinking, *How far away it all seems!* As well as (in an unintended parody of Ms. Borkman), *Look where you are!* though it's unclear in this case exactly who "you" is and whether he, she or *it* (if "you" happens to be an entity like, say, Crazy Rhythm) is being reproached—or exhorted to be grateful upon pain of death for so much good luck.

"So through all of this I ended up in a funny sort of best-of-both-worlds predicament comprising self-hate for what I was and other-hate (Margo's) for what I wasn't. And here's where Envy enters into the picture, folks. While she was busy Envying the women she'd created as my bedmates, I also had plenty to do—didn't lack for occupation, as Jane Austen would have put it—in the Envy department, with my target being the normality, now sexualized (though hadn't it always been?), of her carefully crafted red-blooded wildebeest who found nothing easier than to routinely fall for their endocrine charms. I of all people! who'd married not (*a*) to vulgarly try his hand at the normality exalted every chance they got by Ma and Pa Pritchard, late of the Great Beneath (though I must admit that in some small way I was touched— hell, I'm only human!—by Margo's having gone to so much trouble just to get the non-normality smelted out of me, even if it had to be in the cauldron of her dread, and while we're at it, maybe I felt a little bit enhanced after the smelting—hell! I'm only human), but rather (*b*) to be able to thumb his nose at both normality and its practitioners by exalting *non*-normality where it was safest to do so—within the cozy confines of the heterosexual hearth (becoming in that way both normal and non-normal, hence unbracketable by diagnosis, and thereby satisfying that aforementioned nutty craving—which has never given me a moment's peace—to be more than human). By the way, the jury is still out on whether Ma and Pa are somersaulting in their graves out of pity for my suffering or delight at its persistence." Cantor can't deny that these insights, if that's what they are, hit home—worse, they generate a powerful nostalgia for all the disagreeables they tell him he's missed inasmuch as, unlike Pritchard, he's never been inclined to crash-dive—head first, balls last—into the swimming pool (empty except for a few unused condoms) of corrective heterosexuality. Or maybe he has taken the joyless plunge, but doggedly disremembers. "In fact, when Margo indicated that her then jackass-of-all-trades psychiatrist, Alfonso ('Jim') Straynge, had decided—" "Jim ('Alfonso') Straynge," Margo corrects, getting her—or rather Jim's own back—or so she thinks, or so she wants Jim to think. "Before we go a step further, please be aware, Margo, that I've just bestowed on Jim the compliment to end all compliments since I consider myself to be transcendently the jackass to end all jackasses." "Duly noted," squeaks the chaise longue (which, evidently unseducible by the prospect of resting on its vintage laurels forever, is now pursuing a "second career" as irrepressible prop). "When Margo indicated that Jim had decided to confer upon me the none-more-coveted label of Non-normal First Class (based in fact not so much on my homosexuality [she'd infected him with her scepticism] as on her in-session from-every-angle excoriations of my refusal to touch or be touched except en route to multiple orgasms [there was no avoiding them: a hole after all is a hole is after all a hole and my penis is a sucker for lubricative traction of any sort])—when she spilled Straynge's beans, yours truly couldn't have been more tickled-pink. Nonetheless, cavillers being cavillers, unnatural me naturally took issue soon after with the verdict whereby (at least as I chose to comprehend it) non-normality constituted a kind of *adhesion* to, rather than the very core of, my being.

"Yet for impermeable Margo I managed to remain as normal as they come and had her patent-worthy invention of my rampageous heterosexuality to prove it. In short, her delusions (*a*) normalized me; (*b*) secured me, for observation of normalcy in action, the very best seat in the house; and (*c*) became sole keeper of the flame of that heterosexuality, ever-dwindling. So what did I do? What else but dutifully succumb to an Envy-soaked enthrallment with those delusions' star attraction, i.e., the red-blooded beast—the hefty-slab-of-beefcake gal-crazy antiself—whose indefatigable promiscuity expanded my contours, sexually speaking, as fast as it erased them.

"Still, there *was* that not-so-small matter of the cruising . . .

"Small wonder, then, that the poor thing called Margo got to the point where she no longer knew *what* was normal. So out of the kindness of my heart I gave her a rule of thumb—or, more accurately, a rule of all-thumbs. *I says,* Margo, *I says* (yours truly hails from le Bronx where, like fleet-footed egg creams, such grammatical constructions run rampant), observe carefully everything I do whenever I do it then hurry up and imagine the exact opposite and lickety-split you'll find yourself right smack in the heartland of normality, whatever that is.

"Look at her." The novice yogis' crossed legs direct their gaze chaise-wards. "You can see she still doesn't believe a word I say—not really. But for that I long ago learned to be grateful—not angry. For her unreachability—her inability to see except through the drawn blinds of her hysteria—" ("When you catch a man with his pants down, it's because you're hysterical, right ladies? Let's have a show of hands!" [Margo raises hers challengingly—fomentingly]. But what Margo gets is better than a show of hands—she gets just the kind of self-abnegating nod-nod-nodding that Cantor spurns and craves.) "—ended up advancing me professionally by pressing all my right buttons qua shamanizer as much as it pressed all my wrong buttons qua *hombre*. I learned—thanks to Margo's misconstructions (every one a marvel nonpareil)—how to see myself through a patient's jaundiced eye (without which, as everybody knows, the healer, however gifted, can inflict no healing). And *quel* eye it was, for what could beat the desperate ingenuity of, for example, her reasoning along these sodden lines? Experiencing no lust whatsoever for the ladies didn't necessarily let me off the heterosexual hook for I could very well be hunting for that One and Only capable of making it her life's work to worship Muselike at the feet of a lustless superman.

"And speaking of muselike marvels (for this seminar is not, as you will observe momentarily, to be confused with just another Blakean *quasi una fantasia* on MarriageHearsey themes: it's after far, far bigger game): How about, for starters, the transfinite sum of multicolored post-its (they ended up plastering the entire refrigerator, inside and out) on which she felt compelled to scrawl increasingly-more-accusatory queries regarding my every move, made and unmade, and my every remark, uttered and un-? There exists no object more truly poetic than those post-its—outside of the Bellini-by-way-of-Rieti score for *Sonnambula*." (*No object more truly poetic outside of Gilles's Costco Food Court receipt—or Duchamp's* Fountain *[maybe]—is what you mean to say*, thinks Cantor. Although the poetic object, he reminds himself, was not the receipt per se but the collaboration between the receipt and this particular customer's unfamiliarity—guilelessness transmogrified into a kind of moral purity—with the nuances of the name of the item imprinted on it. Shearer has just been hot-buttoned as well: she's suddenly wide-awake—disemboweled by nostalgia and outraged that this *fruit* [she instantly regrets her mean-spirited lapsus] has taken it upon himself to appropriate her Master [and her aptest pupil], her favorite ballet score and her favorite role.) "And it's precisely because, as the unwelcome byproduct of Margo's torment—her volcanism—her jealousy of my privileged relation with an inner life 90 percent void, 2 percent plenum and the rest (well, never mind the rest)—and a steppingstone toward The Truth—she'd given not a moment's thought to *making* them poetic." And therein (as refracted through her own madness which I still prefer—or have an infantile need—to take as the theater of an intentionally suspect disavowal of a purposeful poetic intent) lay—lies—their messy greatness." Measured applause. But this time around, no camp-meeting-style enthrallment. Cantor thinks, "*And I fear thou play'd'st most foully for it.*"—it being messy greatness (word and image) which is meant to be perceived as in fact his, not Margo's, but is in fact the sole property of Master & Invidicum, LLC.

"But who knows?" Margo drawls, fanning herself with the Gainsborough (even if, as Cantor is quick to note, there are sea breezes galore). She goes on to say what would be later transcribed (short for *gussied up*) in the Arts and Smarts section of the *Bald Eagle* as follows: *Maybe my unremitting perception of every move and remark as being heterosexuality-drenched will end up constituting (despite all those protestations, marital and post-) the canonical take on his tergiversations. Who knows if I haven't thereby gotten a jump on posterity and already established the tone and course of Pritchardian criticism for decades—or even centuries—to come.* "It's gotten to the point, Margo,"—his gaze, however, remains fixed on his students (for these unfortunates are all his students, cross-legged or not) as he swallows a strangled sob—"where I feel like a trespasser, an intruder, in the domain of my own work—not to mention my own psyche." "Which may not be a bad thing," Jean shrills speculatively, suddenly convinced the goings-on in Ethan's interior wastes could benefit hugely from just the sort of sentry duty Pritchard is bellyaching (she refuses to say *whining* or *drama-queening*) about: as applied to others these terms automatically boomerang back on the dumb-ass who applied them, turning him into exactly what he is: a conformist's pitiful excuse for a quipster).

"But at the same time don't imagine, you guys—especially those giving serious thought to tying the knot or should I say the ankle-monitoring bracelet?—that your little woman, however deranged, will under any circumstances forget what side her daily bread is buttered on." He explains that while indicting him for playing poster boy extraordinaire at heterosexuals\$\$\$gonehogwild.com as well as gal%crazy&he*men.xxx (to name just a few of the woolly websites where cunt is king), Margo—*his* little woman and ever the bet-hedging hausfrau even amidst her direst, ostensibly ironclad deductions—nonetheless dared in the very same breath to suggest that it mightn't be a bad idea for him to keep the same-sex cruising under wraps lest one of his malevolent rivals get wind of the matter. "'Yet according to you—or rather, to your post-*t*its—I'm heterosexual to a fault,' I reminded her, 'so where's the danger?' But to soften the blow, I assured her that better men than she had been similarly prone to nursing two very contradictory perceptions in the viper's bosom of their mind: 'Who, for example?' 'Why, the Wolf Man.' 'Who's he?' 'Lon Chaney, Jr.' 'Oh, him.' 'Yeah, him.' 'Then you should say what you mean even if you don't mean what you say.'" The few who tentatively titter gradually discover how pleasant—no, how delightful—it can be to be holed up inside the warm womb of incomprehension.

"Now, I ask you, isn't it just like a man:" (fanning herself ever more frenetically in defiance of the sea breezes) "to make things out as much worse than they are even if they were indeed much worse than they might have been if only he'd managed to keep out of all our bickering not so much his loused-up emotions as—as—as—" "As my casuistical stabs at whitewashing them—yes, *casuistical*, I said it and I meant it even if it puts me in a bad light." "But what matters most" [*same isn't-it-just-like-a-man tone of voice*] "is that one fine summer day (we decided to take a walk, our favorite kind of detox), I finally succeeded in reconciling myself to the truth—his truth—and discovered in the process and as collateral damage that *reconciliation is a simple matter of turning the tables on . . . topography*. I.e., said truth looming as sheer impossibility on 102nd Street (between Broadway and West End—we briefly rented a cockroach-friendly studio in the Broadmoor) began to seem somewhat probable on the southeast corner of Fifty-Ninth and Third." She explains—rather, she goes on to explain—that this phenomenon could be laid in no small measure at the doorstep of the fact (obvious from where they stood) that, after all those debilitating decades consecrated to stealing each other's limelight, Chrysler and Empire State had decided—in the face of the immediate threat posed by a hovering canopy of cumulus the likes of which Pritch and she had never seen and doubtless would never set eyes on again—to reconcile and join forces in impaling the monster before it came crashing down on the members of a terrified populace, who, once the catastrophe had been avoided, cried out as loud as they could, *Well done, gents, and thanks for affording us such a privileged glimpse of how real pros engage in a hatchet-burying sleight of hand.* And if it (said truth) had appeared somewhat probable on Fifty-Ninth, it became more than probable—it became well-nigh inevitable—on Eleventh Avenue and Forty-Eighth Street (abetted in no small part by, of all things, the mad shadow of an ailanthus whose gyrations started hypnotizing her right out of her resistances). And with the stage thus set by so much looming and hypnotizing, he perpetrated a veritable stroke of genius by insisting, instead of taking the subway directly to West Twenty-Third (as agreed on at or around Thirty-Ninth between Seventh and Eighth) and walking a few too-easy blocks west, that they cover the miracle mile on foot, but not (as maintained) to legitimate their journey by earning its endpoint (Chelsea Piers) the hard way but rather (as became all too clear soon enough) to leave her too exhausted to resist any further. "It worked and, overlooking the Hudson and my past obtuseness, at last I broke down and acknowledged he was what he'd been saying he was all along—to wit, *gay*." "Now, you know how much I hate that goyish term, sweetie," a winking Pritchard, playing to a full house, squirmed clownishly. Born an Episcopalian to the aforementioned Ma and Pa Pritchard, he's rightly very proud of his ability to go yiddish at a moment's notice.

"So, after all this billing and cooing, imagine my shock" (here his voice acquired for Shearer an authoritative poignancy reminiscent oddly enough of Mr. B. when he explained, during the gestation of the revised *Four Temperaments*, a micromovement or two—and with not just her instep in the palm of his hand—as well as when he implored her to get a polio vaccine injection as soon as possible—and her mother's Christian Science fanaticism be damned!) "to have Margo come back from a session with Straynge at his wigwam on Park just below Seventy-Second and report with inimitable smuggery that according to him, hence the entire medical community, acknowledgment of my homosexuality and the Envy it engendered in the victim could never usher in a bright new future for the likes of her and me. Like figures straight out of the Second Terrace of Purgatory as depicted on a Grecian urn, overly impressionable I (with my tenuous hold on reality) must go on Envying the stud I was accused of being and she that stud's innumerable conquests. Whether on Fifty-Ninth or Twenty-Third or Nevsky Prospect or the Via Tornabuoni, there was no meta-talking, i.e., metastasizing, our way out of what had just been decreed to be an eternal dynamic. For damaged goods like us, there was no *outside*. This recurring desire to *get* outside—whether on West Ninety-Sixth or East Eighty-Fourth or Regent Street or Mahlerstrasse or Channing Way or Claremont Avenue—was but a further proof of our sickness. We divided evenly into our sickness or vice versa, in either case leaving no remainder.

"So no illusions—please!—about expanding our self-understanding at the expense of Envy (or in my case, H *and* E) without becoming even more abjectly its victim. No indulging in one of them-there New Age exercises in self-schism—you know the kind—where the exerciser amputates away his sickness (usually on Venice Beach where, by the way, I lost my anal virginity) for the purpose of analysis, the better to then resorb it, now an asset—a feather in his cap—because analyzed." He goes on to explain as mass-marketably as he can that, according to the wiz kids, there was no room in the inn for the expulsive bracketing of that sickness, i.e., the Husserlian liquidation of all commitment to a natural-worldish belief in its stench until the epoché's ban had been lifted and the so-called sickness could be reannexed, presto! but not as sickness—or at least not as the sickness of the reannexer (to whom nothing is alien, not even his own selfhood)—but rather as an inexhaustible fount of knowledge. No room for any harboring of fantasies about turning—like Majorana fermions—into self-annihilating antiselves while remaining very much unannihilated and very much themselves. And as for those obsessed with securing a "scientific" basis for all that bracketing hocus-pocus, there was nothing to be gained from drop-of-a-hat invocation of that old warhorse, the *1844 Manuscripts*—(he's for all the name-dropping—rather, all the name-*droppings*—but once thought packets start coming on fast and furious he can't help feeling entitled to put the weltanschauung of every *other* philosopher in the canon at their service)—nothing to be gained from invocation of the *Manuscripts* to demonstrate that (unlike the Envying birds, bees and Boston beans) Envying (and homosexualizing) Man—to whom nothing educative appears alien, not even His own selfhood—is not indistinguishable from sickness-activity and hence that Envy and homosexuality are the purest product of Man's conscious will to World-Historical Character-liness.

"But," Cantor cries out (feeling particularly vulnerable, he makes haste to cover his almost-bare chest with a beach towel), "even if homosexuality *were* self-willed and consciously chosen, why should its practitioners be deprived of any of the rights, breaks, perks, enjoyed by heteros? Is it only as the *helpless victims of their own involuntarism* that gay folk become eligible—or even tolerable as lily-livered agitators—for equal treatment?"

Considering it his bounden duty to render this exquisite formulation more accessible (Cantor mustn't make the mistake—*his* mistake—of eschewing the popular vote just because it *was* popular, thereby leaving the world stage vacant for the numbskull antics of Straynge, Post, hatchet men Kristeene Eliasberg, Soupy Salzberg, Jimm Jordan, Matt the Gaetzz and Gym Dwier [no doubt still slaving away at perfecting the tenor of his herculean animus in the bowels of the Santa Clara Pubic Library], Borkman, The Rump, the unemployable big-game-hunting Sons of The Rump, Bunny von der Maranca [bugbear non pareil of grudge addict non pareil Ishmael Drybock], distinguished sons and daughter of syncopated columnist Virginia Karkass, Kayleigh McAnn Conway [who needs no introduction], hack reviewer VV Loree Stone [semi-infamous for her airily smug antipathy to playwrights brazen enough to choose, as the wages of sin, sun-damaged skin over death] and other misbegottens of that stripe)—to render the formulation more accessible, Pritchard vulgarizes thus: "In other words, only by playing the *I-can't-help-it* card does the unstraightman make himself palatable—or at least a little less repellent— to somebody like The Rump's First Lady No. 2, Mike De La Pence—smitten by his own spinelessness and with the obscene tact of an undertaker."

"I don't know what you're all referring to," Margo sneers, with a haggish irascibility that can have been triggered only by (at least in Borkman's toobroad (!) experience of women) her knowing precisely what is being referred to—and why. Pritchard, he is happy to see, ignores her, *even if he clearly fears that such a tack spells deprivation of the conjugal privileges he has absolutely no interest in enjoying* (all of which derring-do [is that the right term?] just as clearly doesn't prevent the guy [a dietitian] in the otherwise-empty last row but one from enjoying [oops! forgot to mention the benches] above the chomp-chomp of his unsalted butter- and corn-free popcorn, this odd description of Pritchard's non-plight).

"As it turns out, Jim—my beloved Jim—was, as always, absolutely right— about everything." (It's all she can do not to blow him—his shadow—his spirit—his ghost—his *psuchē*—the shadow of a juicy kiss.) "We weren't going to make it—to make our marriage *work* (most telling, isn't it—I mean the yokage of such a verb to such a noun). And in fact, shockingly, our behavior was most pathological at those very moments when, by some fluke, we achieved normality—I mean, *real* normality. A mere simulation would have made us far less of an abomination—far less of an affront to the members of the medical community even if outliers like us, who defy all the odds of pigeonholing, are their bread and butter and always will be. I.e., a simulation would have made us far more palatable (to use your word). In fact, maybe it was the spurts of normality that did us in." On the other hand, there's no doubt about Pritchard's being done in at the present moment. He could use a vacation. Why don't he and Margo revisit the Isles of Langherans, a blessedly little-known second-honeymoon-friendly tax haven equidistant from the North Sea and the Bahamas?

CHAPTER THIRTY-FIVE

En route to the nearest men's room after stretching his legs, Borkman, sighing, thinks (but not before making a 360-degree turn to ensure nobody's within eavesdropping distance), *Enough fruitcakes and nut jobs for one day. Are he-men—like dodos—extinct? Aren't there* any *men with balls—not bells on their toes—still left to count on the fingers of one hand?* Except for a few dry spells, Shearer has thoroughly enjoyed herself. She's done her best (following Balanchine's famous stricture) to *hear* the dancing and *see* the music—that is, see the pas de deux and hear the duet. For Rhys, it's been more—much more—than she bargained for. Clearly a cautionary tale—straight out of Euripides—only she's unclear at what the caution was directed since when all is said and done Margo appears to be a pretty happy specimen—almost blissful. In any case, even if Pritchard's Archaic Torso could never in a million years be mistaken for an Apollo's, its message nonetheless is that, yes, Jean, *Du mußt dein leben ändern.* (But—a minor point—wasn't the subject supposed to be Envy *and Conspiracy*?)[81] Every inmate shrieks pretty much the same verdict: "The best bit of vicarious psychotherapy I've ever undergone. Worth every penny" (especially since admission to this as to any other bunker weekend roadshow is always free?). The next day, *The New York Times*, not to be upstaged, least of all by sunburnt yokels, will warble: "A rehabilitational love feast: Bayreuth material"; "Pritchard's brassy sidekick puts the 'Broad' back in Broadway," will croak either *Vanity Fair* or *its* sidekick, the *National Enquirer*. Only Eden—as he literally heads for the (foot)hills (his reasons for returning to nature differ from Herbert's though he's far from understanding them: they salute each other just before their paths diverge)—begs to differ. But first things first: he's obliged to do his civic duty by colliding with a eucalyptus: For all the shivering, no leaf manages to pull a fast one fast enough to permit secession from the mother lode unobserved. Or at least that's his layman's take on the matter. Hey, can it be that the odd pair scrambling for a foothold up ahead are none other than his-not-so-very-old non-pals Walser and Stifter? Funny, he doesn't remember having seen them genuflecting at poolside. But maybe they were not only there but the very first among those who drooled most shamelessly over Pritchard's uncanny knack for making egghead esoterica accessible to sub-average joes. Thing is, he thought they or at least one of them was in Hollywood. Well, like Rick in *Casablanca* (which he's never seen), he was misin-

---

[81] Herbert knows the Master loves nothing better than (*a*) catching himself in the act of being an unreliable incompetent storyteller since humble fallibility in this context is next to godliness; and (*b*) proclaiming his failure to have ensured that all the gaps and cracks and fissures resident in the corpse-that-is-the-story had been sutured up before it was moved to the mortuary-that-is-its-publication, since what does such suturing serve to prove except that the story in question isn't a mirror held delicately—ethically—proudly—up to nature but rather a perishable fabric of deviously calculated triumphs over inconsistency, that hobgoblin of mercenary minds.

formed. But getting back to his beggary, hasn't anybody noticed that the most important question has still not been answered, namely, what were those two troupers trying to prove—or pull—down there? I.e., what was their *message*? (It's easy to knock fortune cookies but there's something to be said for compacting the world into a grain of sand.) That—for starters—envioids, being incurable, have nothing to look forward to but a lifelong maintenance dose—including slight adjustments as symptoms (and side effects) wax and wane with the seasons? That the only hope for envioids from (what's the phrase?) *all walks of life* is to shun sexual entanglements, hetero- or otherwise, and not just with their fellow sufferers? And that the only hope for Envy—he means envy—symptom abatement (upper- or lower-casing depends on Eden's mood which he assumes is the case for the others) lies in undiverted pursuit of a noble vocation or whatever can be made to pass for one? That Invidicum is just another fake folk remedy decked out in next-big-thingly drag (all the rage now that the pipeline is shrinking fast and Pharma patents are expiring even faster)? That the efficacy of the current version of Invidicum—inasmuch as it promiscuously modulates just too many molecular targets, with the canonical one routinely getting lost in the shuffle—has devastating side effects? That Envy is not a true affliction or whatever it needs to be to slither its way into the next incarnation of the *DSM*, since, notwithstanding all their efforts, the broth-spoiling cooks have not managed to correlate Envy's putative addictivity with the requisite dopamine-flooding of the VTA-nucleus accumbens reward circuit? That though envy—sorry, Envy—is indeed the most archetypal of addictions, administration of Invidicum has failed so far to beat it at its own game through either blockage of dopamine uptake by VTA neuron terminals or muting of its effects? That even for pure-thoroughbred heterosexual couples, every effort to escape the depletive marriage-hearse dynamic will result only (no matter what the route to ostensible reconciliation at the tip of some gentrified West Side pier) in their becoming even more incurably its victim? Turning around Walser recognizes Eden instantly. "You haven't changed," he says. As if he could read Eden's mind—no! *as if*'s are strictly verboten in these precincts: reading Eden's mind according to the normative standards of current brain science—with the help of sensors implanted in the highest boughs of the fig trees—Walser says that Eden is correct on all counts. And these are in fact just some of the messages. There's still a lot of decryption to be done. Until then, further research will remain stymied.

But what if indeed there is *no* message or (should there, most unluckily, be one) no medium for its dissemination? If he had Pritchard's way with words (now wait just a minute here: precisely who is about to speak his mind? Eden himself? the ghost of Pritchards past? Eden's demon? his daimon? his *kolossos*? his *psuchē*? his *eidōlon*? the narrator? the author? the proverbial man on the street? the sensors in the fig trees high above Cabrillo Boulevard?), especially for things like these that deserve much better (or much worse) than to be put into words, Eden would say that, finding itself at a turning point—maybe *the* turning point—in the notorious Invidicum affair and thus faced with the need to come up with—to provide (or kiss its rogues' gallery of backers goodbye)—ample proof of stunts-packed progress, progression, process, development, maturation, evolution—Post & Co. (under the auspices of Pritch, their silent partner in these parts) has mounted its usual 911-style response. Which is to stanch the void's exsanguination with a tissue of orations so intricate as to demand nothing less than a second-by-second decipherment, ensuring thereby that assorted codebreakers—i.e., the human race—will be too busy to consider what has already happened, what ought really to be happening here and now, and what would/should happen if there is any justice left in the world). So the stooge backers, who crave action not words, have once again been brought up short—ended up in the same story-line-less boat as the stooge guzzlers and stooge providers.

And it has all worked—at least for Eden. No recollection whatsoever of life PS (pre-seminar) (except for some LAPD stick-figure shadowboxing)—not even of the seminar itself, which will surely live forever in the annals of addiction, until a meatier one comes along. Still, there are things he *can* remember—and vividly—like Linda's Spitzer-bashing and the bravery of Manning, whom it's self-glamorizing, he knows, to refer to as his lost and only love. The pair wait for him to catch up (he never paid attention to the strength of the resemblance: for all practical purposes they're Siamese twins, or is this joined-irreversibly-at-the-hip effect just a lowdown antic of waning sun and widening shade?). The warmth they exude emboldens Eden to make quick work of the amenities and give voice to his unease, though not without wondering if he isn't thereby mounting an equally reprehensible 911 response (in this case, to a turning point—perhaps *the* turning point—in his own story).

"Something has been bothering me ever since Coronado, guys." Their squatting in unison on a boulder is intended to mean they have all the time in the world to listen and (if he so desires) splatter him with fecaliths of advice. The only thing separating them from Eden is a bird whose pen name he doesn't care to know. It makes a series of hops (at least ten) and then, like any avant-gardist worth his salt and then some, dutifully foils expectations with a series of at most three. He explains that as a result of living through this seminar (same problem with your grand-ballroom talkathons), he just can't remember what came before or imagine what might come after. The event blots out any notion of what's past and what's to come: there's only the present and that ain't any clearer. "Well, if that's the case, my young friend"—though Stifter, or is it Walser? can't be much older (having earned his MD when, or so the story goes, not little more than a pre-teenager—"you (and you alone) have been undergoing the premier side effect of Invidicum when administered at an extremely low dosage in combination (or, in the lingo of near experts like us, 'tainted') with a cocktail comprising organic milk of magnesia, balsamic vinegar (for flavor), $A\beta$ (you know, the peptide fragment associated with early-onset Alzheimer's) and (most important) that hot new synthetic ZIP, all suspended in a gel fuel base." "Which is?" Eden asks, trembling in spite of himself (will the spasms just below the surface frighten away his new buddy, the hopper laureate of the hills?). "Memory disablement with a capital D. Isn't that right, Stif?" "Now, Stif, wasn't it agreed back there in Laguna Beach (when we were busy impersonating surfer geeks and ended up—imagine!—dazzling the lamebrained locals with our prowess) that I'm to be Wals and *you* Stif until further notice." "Enough of this squabbling, Wals. It's almost past this kid's bedtime. So, Eden, during Pritch's seminar under the stars, you became more and more terrified (rightly, as it turns out) everything that came before was going away fast—going, going, gone." Stif explains (more to the eucalypti than to Eden, or Wals for that matter) that at the very moment Eden was doing his damnedest to retrieve a—any—memory of said *before* (as was his right as a citizen), with the stab at retrieval triggering the usual reconsolidation process, the aforementioned combo kicked in, taking advantage of the all-too-brief window within which a memory is labile and as such susceptible to extinction, to delete it permanently, irreversibly. "You endured the same excruciation, no doubt, during our epic's Coronado ballroom sequences—some of the most celebrated in the history of the cinema, I might add (right up there with the ones in Visconti's *The Leopard*, Ophuls's *Madame de*, Fuller's *Shock Corridor* and Welles's *The Magnificent Ambersons*)—and on so many other occasions. Is it any wonder, then, that you're—or at least feel that you're—little more than a sum of perpetual non-presents? But it's for your own good: the best part of the process is the extinction of all guilt."

Walser (*Jane Murdstonesque tone of voice*): "He needs to keep a better grip on his memories." Which confirms what Eden already knows, namely, that this guy is, hands down, the slimier of the pair. At least for the moment.

"He can't control his hippocampus."

"Nothing prevents *my* most treasured memories from getting formed and once they are, I never let them out of my sight—keep them bunkered down—or is it *hunkered*?—in the safe-deposit box of my simmering soul. All those years spent groveling before the stars of the NYCB—haven't forgotten a single moment—not one of Shearer's pirouettes, for example (yep, had a big crush on 'er thighs)—look back and have the happiest feeling of repletion. I went forward, heroically, inasmuch as I was weighed down by a hectic impatience to see every Balanchine ballet I knew would be great—and to incorporate—ingest—metabolize—make them all, literally, my very own. And I did. Even if I was living vicariously, fact is, I've lived and my ecstasy kept me out of trouble. And the fact that it's safely over and done with and can't be taken away from me and that I saw everything I needed to see and that it never led to anything and has left no visible trace for daws to peck at—and that it's poignant to a fault breaks me up every time. Not to mention the homeless guy (great tweed overcoat—even in tatters it was chic) weighed down with shopping bags from every first-class supermarket who, in those good old days, could suck a peaceable egg in Ferris Booth Hall without fear of eviction by the campus police. In fact, the only thing he did have to fear was my unwavering wonderment, which was 99.99 percent admiration."

Ignoring Walser, Eden cries, "But why—"

But Walser refuses to be ignored. "Why me? Silliest question—also in the history of the cinema. Why *me*? Well, why *not* me—I mean you? *The black hole called god* (and don't mistake what I've just said for run-of-the-mill adolescent blasphemy) is an equal-opportunity scourge. Further, it's an open secret that you're Post's poster boy for Invidicum-generated homicidal mania. The cocktail is supposed to allow you qua off-label assassin to concentrate at all times only on the moment and the moment only, without a care for your genocidal past or genocidal future. But I'm not telling you anything new." As if he's gotten a load off his chest, which indeed he has, Walser looks up and around: clearly exalted by his postcard smallness as a citizen of the universe, whose capital is, until the stroke of midnight, these hyper-combustible Santa Barbara foothills.

"Don't tell me *this* was the seminar's message. Since it's obvious they had none—Pritchard and his lady friend."

Stif: "Ex-wife and freelance muse."

"Don't forget conspiracy-theorist."

"Thanks, Wals. I sure won't."

Satchelled with far too much food for thought, Herbert (the lion's share of the bliss she exhales in having been able to go a-wandering twice in the same day is claimed by the pride she takes in never being quite dressed for the occasion)—Herbert, though unhappy—even hopeless—perks up immediately when out of the blue somebody insists loud and clear, "But the seminar most definitely did have a message, buddy boy." No question, even if the last person in the world for whom such a message could be meant is she (from the speaker's tone, buddy boy can only be Eden). Up ahead is one of the locally recruited enviers—a lifer-to-be from all invidications—whose poodle has decided her anorexic mistress deserves an airing after so much tumult at poolside. And of course she sports the obligatorily oxymoronic Bergdorf-Vuitton mini-backpack which (also obligatorily) resembles nothing so much as the coyly puckered vulva of a walnut. The Ovule Effect, somebody called it, or maybe it's Herbert herself who has just coined the phrase for all the world to cherish once she's past on the mantle of her greatness to posterity. Come to think of it, there must be millions of Ovule bearers exactly like this one—cruising up and down State Street and all the other State Streets on the planet right this minute. Suddenly it's great to be black—not one more pasty fleck of pinkish paint in an ever-expanding fresco of what's now referred to as Entitlement. And it's equally great to throw nuance to the winds every now and then in exchange for something better—in this case a jam session compressed into a millisecond's worth of Abstract Expressionist Action Thinking. Or is she just envious of anybody with no money worries, whatever the color of their war paint? But all is forgiven because the woman sports—when she addresses her stately little mutt in the tone of loving exasperation common to too many Ovule bearing pet lovers—the slightest of accents. Melanctha has trouble placing it until she realizes, by tweaking a favorite quip from the author of . . . *Melanctha* (i.e., America is the Ovule's country and Affluence is her home town), that it's a matter of putting her finger not on another country or state but on a foreign State of Mind. Ovule has been able to master at her leisure the presumed sonorities of unpretentious hipness—to do away, when the occasion warrants, with the I&S (indicia and shibboleths) of class—though her forked tongue does draw the line at suppressing a very class-conscious undertone of smug caution.

Herbert's intention was to avoid her fellow seminarians, homegrown or otherwise, by heading for the SB zoo (her son had always been partial to Bronx-bred cheetahs). Is it too late? Stubbornly disregarding the sky's response, she appeals to her watch for a second opinion. In any case, how can she in all good conscience tear herself away from what appears to be the beginning of a no-holds-barred consideration of the message question? She follows at a distance, making sure to remain always within earshot (not difficult since there's a lot of good-ol'-boy shouting going on) and relieved that whatever sounds she may inadvertently emit will be muffled by the poodle's off-key chirp. Actually it's not just any old chirp: it's more like a song—the song of, say, a heart-nosed bat—with buzzes and trills as well. According to the same buddy-boying Guide for the Perplexed (she has no idea where this epithet came from yet it sounds so right—so right, that is, in the context of what's to come though how should she know what's to come?)—by george, it's Stifter!—Pritch as among the very last of Pharma's old guard can always be depended on to tell the truth not just about drugs but about the Human Condition. Thing is, every time he decides to have another go at visiting said truth on the uninitiated (as was the case today), he has no choice but to hide through self-contraction and in so doing leave behind "a pneumatic, primordial space" (Scholem) within which to shoot his wad and thereby trigger a jumbling up of all the elements of truth so as to render it a wee bit less painful—excruciating—unendurable. Which accounts, among other things, for the fact that the tale of Pritchard and Margo (the stuff of legend)—who are right up there with (*a*) Frankie and Johnny and (*b*) Admeto and Alceste—has turned out to be not a tale at all but a cross between a treatise and a monologue uttered in invisible ink—and one that is always abruptly changing theme, or seems to be.

"Prodigies like Pritchard realize even before they're dumped in the crib that any given truth" (so begins another, probably the only other, guide—Walser, in fact!) "can never be told through a story (like Moses Maimonides, Pritch has always had contempt for stories)—a shocking parable of, say, marital infidelity, or of cross-dressing in the cancer ward, or of other bugbears of the Right *and* the Left—but only by establishing contradictions, concealed from the hoi polloi, between straightforward statements embedded in a non-story. And the duty of that small minority of patients who do want above all to get well—the unhappy few, to quote Henri Beyle—is to determine which statement in each contradictory pair is true.[82]

"So how did—does—Pritchard hide his contractions—I mean, the contradictions?" Eden sounds hoarse.

"In all sorts of ways" (*Stifter*). "First off, if you'd paid attention you'd have noticed he tended to speak of forbidden subjects contradictorily at widely separated intervals. Or he let Margo do the contradicting (I think we all agree their jabberings constitutes a single text). For example, at 6:02:08 he contended that *heterosexuality is Envy* and at 7:45:03 that *homosexuality is not Envy*. Along the same lines, at 6:36:13 he said the marriage hearse is not

---

[82] For a discussion—the one and only discussion—of strategies for the concealment of a difficult truth in an esoteric text, see Leo Strauss, *Persecution and the Art of Writing* (Chicago, Illinois, University of Chicago Press, 1988), chap. 3.V.

sturdy enough to take on homosexuality as a passenger and at 8:00:00 Margo insisted that indeed it is—sturdy enough in fact to transport the homosexuality of both partners, if need be. Come to think of it, Post made sure your memory for silly things was sedated, so you could concentrate on the bare essentials. Since you're obviously, highly limited education notwithstanding, the only one in the group with enough idiot-savantry (think 'knight-errantry in the gray-matter department') to be able to juxtapose two contradictory statements no matter what the distance separating them and in so doing determine which one's the impostor."

Walser: "Did you hear the man, Martin? *No matter what the distance.* So don't look a Trojan horse in the mouth.

"Another method is to toss off one of the contradictories incidentally—mindlessly—as if it's a throwaway steppingstone to some infinitely more important utterance. (Just as the best way of diverting the attention of a homicidal maniac in a subway car emptying out at an alarming rate—pay especial attention, Eden—is to appear to be self-cancelingly transfixed by the immobility of some other passenger.) As when, as if in passing (after Pritch's remark a while back [6:14:46] that attribution of rampant heterosexuality to a homosexual can only increase the animosity between the parties concerned inasmuch as the latter, with the super-tenuous hold on reality peculiar to his sect, will then assume [compliments of this newly acquired endowment] he's on countless occasions already betrayed [by routinely setting out at all hours of the day and night, like any other devout hetero, in hot pursuit of cunt] not only what all along he's perceived as constituting a big fat [maybe even the biggest fattest] chunk of his essence, however rancid, but the accusing other as well)—as when, in passing, Margo giddily asserted (6:25:48)—in the cabaletta to his arioso, so to speak—that such attribution is not only the first giant step on the road to conjugal felicity but in fact its first meat-and-potatoes manifestation."

Stifter: "Don't talk to me about Margo. After the murder, if murder it was, she waylaid me on sleazy Eighth Street a couple of times, between Fifth and Sixth, right where the Bookshop used to be, to talk about how the world blamed her for Jim's murder—worse: for the withholding of the fame owed him in his lifetime. Even if she hadn't pulled any triggers. Every thought would begin more or less as follows: *It's as if somebody* (followed by the name of whatever lumpen du jour could be semi-plausibly made to serve as the big bad Herr Doktor Mabuse who'd poisoned the trough at which all of her rivals fed). But it was only *in passing*, at the tail end of a long list, that she'd finally break down and assign tentative (*mind you, only tentative*) culprit status to yet another of her too-beloved blood relations—one of millions—who enjoyed pride of place there where all conspiracy theories get their start, namely, the foul rag and bone shop of the family's pitch-dark heart. All along hoping of course that my silence could be taken for what it wasn't: inattention. Since from there it's but a hop, skip and a jump to the misimpression of a tacit exculpation. But in this case, exculpation not of Margo but of her accuser. Maybe that's why Pritchard's just too fed up to include Conspiracy in the syllabus.

"And you may have noticed—or rather, should have noticed—that

Pritchard also resorted, so vast is this guy's repertoire, to hiding contradiction by contradicting not a given statement outright but one of its hornier implications. For example, at one point (6:06:07) he decided a happy marriage is incompatible with the sideshow practice of homosexuality and, a little later on, that homosexuality is nothing but addiction to Envy. Which would have led one to infer marriage is incompatible with such an addiction. But then, much further on (just before—or was it after?—sundown), he proclaimed— with atypical shrillness—that marriage is highly compatible with Envy, which proclamation is equivalent to a contradiction of the initial premise."

Walser: "And you may have also noticed that it fell to Margo to usher in—sneakily, as is the way with women—another method, i.e., to contradict one of her own statements not directly but by seeming to repeat it while in fact subtracting an ostensibly insignificant element. For example, at 6:59:58 sharp, she determined Envy is homosexuality, adding (sotto voce) that the latter is the brittle amalgam of self-hate and an alcoholic's thirst for transcendence, and at (ca.) 8:02:09, when two-thirds of the audience were fast asleep (except for the envoys from the New York press, who went on texting back to headquarters everything they heard and, more to the point, everything they hadn't), went on to say Envy is self-hate at its purest thereby contradicting her first know-it-all-ism. And along the same lines remember when adding insult to injury, Pritchard made the (outrageous) claim (5:55:55) to the effect that one partner's getting over the hump of the other's homosexuality, conjugally speaking, is *always* only a matter of topography (*sound familiar?*); followed it up (6:59:33) with the (inaudible) assertion that topography for its part comprised nothing more than mere walking and talking; and concluded (7:27:54—sorry, 7:27:55) that if the partners in question intended to stay conjugated their only recourse was to tie themselves to a chair and simply talk themselves free of said hump. Which conclusion of course contradicted not only Pritchard's initial claim (to wit, that getting over said hump is all about topography, i.e., talking *and* walking) but also Straynge's anti-meta decree, at least as reported by Margo—to the effect that there was no talking one's way out of a psychosexual mess of such magnitude."

So as Eden can see, Pritchard is nothing less than a fabric of urgencies—a tissue of SOS's—and the time is nearing when he, Eden, must be shipped out to God-knows-where as their bearer—bearer of the very messages he's insisted on repudiating or has at least purposely failed to identify, much less acknowledge, even when they've stared him in the face. Eden, finding it more and more difficult to distinguish between S. and W. (even if the latter was, in contrast to the former, starkly identifiable as Eliphaz, Bildad and Zophar all rolled into one) and having better things to do, chooses to ignore the accusation, however well intentioned. But something prompts him to ask: "So how do you know what message in any pair is the true one?" Melanctha can't understand how she managed to miss so much vital subtext and pivotal cross-talk but she's in no mood to excoriate herself for inattentiveness. It's Eden who concerns her and her heart goes out to him since the portentous silence generated by the boy's cry from the heart—and he is just a boy . . . like her boy—that silence reeks of belittlement. On the other hand, it may mean nothing more than that these guides for the perplexed (again, that epithet from nowhere and still as right as rain!) are finding that they themselves are suddenly very much perplexed, by a problem it has taken no less than this idiot savant to bring to their attention—or so Herbert needs desperately to believe, that is, if she is to keep from confusing Eden's humiliation with her multifaceted own and, in consequence, falling apart right here and now (as was the case at Building 18 after she found her son dozing in his own bloody urine while the caucasian medico on call jabbered away complacently at the nurses' station). *Walser:* "Should I, Bob?" *Stifter:* "Why don't you . . . Bob. You need the exercise more than I." *Walser* (after a by-your-leave click of his heels): "Eden, my boy, the winner is the statement that's most secret, its secretness being in direct proportion to the painfulness—shamefulness—excruciation—unendurability— of the truth it encapsulates. And since, as asserted by the most philosophically inclined of the Three Hebraic Tenors—the three Leos—Oppenheim, Steinberg and Strauss (whose engagements—even at Bayreuth!—are always record-breaking)—the more excruciating a secret's truth, the more infrequent its utterance (for what self-respecting utterer wants to be persecuted for perpetrating excruciation and what self-respecting long bone of utterance wants its marrow of truth suction-pumped out and away through ceaseless repetition?), we may safely conclude it is the statement uttered most rarely—maybe just once or, better yet, even less than once—that's the true blue . . . variant."

Stifter (stage-hissing his regret at having stood aside in favor of Walser, who as an aspiring domestic couldn't even manage to finish *Roberts' Guide for Butlers and other Household Staff*): "Anybody who bothered to count would have discovered that Pritchard asserted homosexuality was synonymous with the Sickness unto Death at least 1,500 times in the course of one hour, and with the embodiment of perfect health—the health that surpasseth health— at most once in the course of the entire seminar. I leave it to you to decide, based squarely on the above, which statement is true." And on that jarring note the guides extend a brusque farewell, evidently finding him unworthy of an invitation to join them on their alpine climb. Herbert feels for him—so much like her son (though for the moment she can't come up with a single point of resemblance). "There you go again, old dame," she *gently chides* (as Hawthorne might have put it), "suffering for the sufferer far more than he's willing to suffer for himself." In fact, if the involuntary jauntiness of his Donald O'Connoresque tap dance down, down, down the too-precipitous slope is any indication (to avoid a collision she hides behind an azalea, and not a minute too soon), Martin, a veritable Feathertop, is (at the prospect of no further enlightenment, at least for today) in a state of ecstasy worthy of Keats's Nightingale.

CHAPTER THIRTY-SIX

Evening passes into night as evening's wont to do, and suddenly it's mid-morning. Borkman, more wide-awake than he has any desire to be yet desperately in need of a change of scene, winds up right smack in the middle of the zoo. It's a dirty job, this tourist trap, but somebody's got to fall into it. That's *his* philosophy, as of this moment. (Even if the trap in question is by no means dirty—in fact, it's spick-and-span and delightfully welcoming.) And if he watches his step, he won't be subpoenaed by any of the zoo's inmates—its non-human persons of interest in the case. Although being subpoenaed definitely has its upside. For one thing, solid material for the cyberthriller that, if he has any say in the matter, will never get written, much less filmed. The kind that's all plot and no action—or, as they say in the boondocks, all *syuzhet* and no *fabula*—or as congresswoman Frederica Wilson should have said of Sara [*sic*] Fuckabee [*sic*] Sanders (oh so accurately albeit far too kindly): "all hat, no cattle." Never has he felt so much self-hate—or does he tell this to every crisis-laden moment to make it feel downright special? The *Bald Eagle*, even more than the *Times*, is full of the latest dirt on The Rump. Only what *he* feels is not outrage—neither at the Eagle nor at its target—but the old envy: If only he'd managed to follow in the footsteps of the Master (yes, Moira, The Rump's his George Balanchine), boasting losses so vast as to preclude tax payments for 30 years—the years of youth when one should be enjoying himself—not frittering away the ways and means of enjoyment on that rickety old scarecrow the US Treasury. (*Look where you are!* shrieks the wicked wife within.) The opposition and its media machine are relentless: demanding forty years worth of tax sin-fo. Aren't The Rump's '95 and '96 returns, say, enough grist for their mill? Thank heaven for the other outlets which will come to the rescue by painting perhaps not altogether intentionally but still savvily one common picture of The Rump's masquerade as constituting nothing less than the triumph of virtue over clownish cunning. By carrying his operating losses forward hopefully forever isn't he just exercising his rights as a citizen? Can The Rump help it if he has a sort of Midas touch for turning plausible assets into the gold of worthlessness? Which thereby earns him the right to write off all the capital investment in that worthlessness as a several-lifetimes loss. If only Borkman had paid attention long enough at those Four Seasons power brunches to master the Art of the Misdeal—if only he'd made it a point to sit at the feet of The Rump's bone spurs a little longer and a little less patronizingly every time they met as if by chance. If The Rump has the good sense to routinely walk away from his worthless assets, then Borkman had the worst in choosing to walk arrogantly away from the biggest asset of them all—The Rump himself. So what if he's made a cottage industry out of realizing losses immediately and deferring gains indefinitely? Isn't that what makes America great—again, and again? Unanswerable question, at least here, under the lacklustre lollipop palms. They're not entirely useless though for they unaccountably soften his heart toward Leona Helmsley's little people who are festering everywhere he looks and everywhere else—yet who are doing their level best to do what they do best, which is to dutifully pay in full for the raw privilege of passing through yet another one of life's clunky turnstiles (instead of jumping them all in a single bound) and thereby turn the unregenerate jumpers like The Rump and his *get*—yes, his get—into folk heroes. Their probity is always suspect—their probity is always *asking for it*. For the heart-softening little people not only pay their taxes but at the same time fight unwittingly as hard as they can to be singled out for admission to a very special sort of anti-promised land but a promised land nonetheless, to wit, the Land of the Audit to which Republican donors and other billionaire scum are—as in an operetta—graciously barred entry. Audit as augur—symptom—indicia—omen—as sign of having *arrived* and token of bigger if not better things to come. Audit as massive windfall indemnification (*a*) for all the trouble taken to be caught in the act of having done nothing illegal; and (*b*) for having failed to salt away a non-existent cache of ill-gotten gains on some obstinate isle like Jersey; or Elba; or Cayenne, the poor man's Cayman, or is it (at least by decree of wordflow) the other way around? Audit as the MO through which they, or rather, *their kind*, can be compelled to disgorge those gains (still non-existent) into the coffers of the IRS—compelled by their very own Javert, whose personalized attention they owe to his having simply too many thumbs to twiddle, inasmuch as he's been trained to turn not just a blind eye but the other cheek (uppers and lowers) to the malfeasances of the bigger fry—trained to take them permanently and effective immediately off his radar. And at no extra cost each Javert will be happy to remind each Valjean, should he need reminding, that (*a*) his status as practitioner of the vocation on which he's had the audacity to hang the hat of his itemized deductions as well as his union card couldn't be lower and (*b*) the lower that status, the bigger the disgorgement. (*Who is doing the thinking for the two of them?* Borkman wonders: he didn't intend for his heart-softening to take him so far into the Land of the Audit and the adjacent land of the have-nots as to end up their defender and spokesman, however circumlocutionary—and certain to be the target of their rage into the bargain, since when will he get it through his thick skull that as far as they're concerned they're not have-nots but haves in the making—not slaves but masters-in-training.) He looks around. The little people seem to be eyeing him strangely—accusatorily. Is it because he's a member of the Rump gang? (in most cases, no). Or because he's a member of the infinitely more venal opposition intent on depriving them of their divinest right—the right to hate their own best interest (with the switchblade of a sneer—their oppressors' sneer—securely between their teeth) more than they hate themselves—the right to disown it—the right to vote it out of office? Or maybe they know what everybody in the know knows—that in the realm of tax aversion The Rump Organization is, compared with any number of Fortune 500s, small potatoes—too small to peel. So maybe in the scheme of things it makes no difference whether or not he sat at The Rump's feet and in a reverential frenzy pulverized those soon-to-be-infamous spurs with his fists.

At least Borkman now knows enough to be able to apply the same finagling to the wrecked-home front, where the wife's his not-quite-private IRS. Applied Rumpery, let's call it. *Indeed,* hasn't her viciousness progressively reduced him to the merest sum of all sorts of losses—of self-respect, self-esteem, self-regard, for starters. How many times, Your Honor, has that viciousness sapped him of the artfulness required for a proper consummation of The Misdeal? So isn't he now counter-entitled to defer alimony—for decades? And what's so shameful about insisting that the exemption extend to child support even if no longer applicable (after all, what have the kids done except lament every chance they got over oh how much better things would have been for all concerned, especially the family pets, if he'd had the guts to pack the bags of his gross inadequacy right before its first big upsurge [though is it ever possible to delimit *ex post* or *ex ante* the Peircean Firstness of anything as unwieldy as an upsurge?] and leave them all in peace)? And wouldn't the success of this skullduggery, albeit confined—consigned—to the private domain, entitle him to lots of applause from all the fools who call themselves his peers and whose business it is to run the very public world into the ground? But why abase himself through mealy-mouthed recruitment of *albeit*: isn't the practice of skullduggery in the far more hazardous grossly underrated private domain in effect the very model for such practice on the great stage of crony capitalism—the latter being merely an inept smelly-cigar reflection of malice do[o]mestic? As Duns Scotus said—and too many times for his own good—all ball games are kicked off at home plate and maybe doomestic [*sic*] skullduggery will turn out to be Borkman's greatest achievement.

Odd, that he should have found it so easy to end up here, given the number of tantrums this Great Man required before deigning to take his kids up to the Bronx Zoo or even to its vest-pocket sibling in Central Park which was but a stone's throw. He hangs his head. Coming to the rescue—sort of—Borkman's stomach rumbles (with a fairly wide repertory of timbres) down into and out through his anus (a timely herald of things to come since he's fast approaching old-fart-hood, the Stage of Man nobody talks about, least of all grotesquely irrepressible Fountains of Youth like, say, Summer Redstone and serpent-toothed Jack the Welch and Hank MacKlowe). No human voice could nip in the bud better than said rumbling whatever yearnings to make amends he may harbor—and adding lack of insult to injury, there's no collateral smell to mitigate the mockery. True, traitorous borborygmi may be (*a*) undercutting all his penitentional stabs at flaying his narcissism bare before they've begun to even think about getting under way but, don't forget, they're also (*b*) sparing him free of charge the tiresome pursuit of an unachievable self-transcendence—as tiresome as Falstaff's coveting of Till Eulenspiegel's holy grail. But why not enjoy, he demands to know (the good deeds of those borborygmi notwithstanding), the semi-precious time left before the inevitable trial back in New York? How does he know prosecutors won't take into account the fact that the Envy driving malfeasance has been massive enough to require cutting-edge treatment. Better get a second opinion, from the caribous—and quick: they're being extinctified by wolf packs organized on the admit-no-wrongdoing take-no-prisoners Wall Street model. The sight of Herbert hopping off the shuttle near the entrance dismays Borkman. Should he give in to a hope against hope that she hasn't cornily chosen the very same tourist tub in which to drown her sorrows? No point, for she's already fumbling in her handbag at the ticket counter. At least she has the decency or good sense not to sport a python backpack drawstrung to resemble a perky little vulva. Borkman's touched by the way—but more by the fact—that (he's "a sentimental sap, that's all") she fishes in her purse for the right combination of bills and coins. If he didn't know better he'd say (assuming he was the kind of guy who had the words to say it at his bashful fingertips) he's transfigured by the transfiguring pathos of the gesture—of what it doesn't say about what's going on behind the scenes of her alacrity. She wants to be edified—entertained—distracted—and she respects—complies uncomplainingly with—the terms of the transaction—the letter of the law. Hers is a child's expectation of adventure—purged of all petty sense of self. He'd like to escort her in with a kiss—wander with her through the pleasingly stenchy groves of this carnival. He stops himself. She deserves better. Even a chump like him knows that.

He's taken a shine—yes, *taken a shine*—to the giraffes—assesses the elegance (and finds it grossly undervalued) with which the bell-pull tails swat, like metronomes, those scrawny-elegant rumps as if they—that is, the rumps—existed solely to be made *to behave themselves accordingly*. But of course it's the lion that's the star of the show (does Melanctha think so, too?)— it's the lion—*Panthera leo*—that moves Borkman most—even more than Melanctha did hours ago at the turnstile—or rather, differently from Melanctha. Even if—in other words (and oh so predictably) *especially because*—the being moved feels so much out of character (after all, this is one of those unspeakable alpha-to-alpha—*studs-have-feelings-too*-type avowals). It's as if—*as if*, the most mealy-mouthed phrase in the editor's manual!—every muscle fibre in his body were being first adeptly skinned then stretched beyond endurance. Borkman wants all the gawkers to go away so he can talk to this, the apex of all apex predators. For here is a fellow sufferer—caged and caged in by fatigue and disgust at the persisting strength, even here, of disgust and fatigue. He looks at Borkman, completely ignoring everybody else, as if acknowledging grudgingly the presence of a partner in crime, but retrospectively this can be seen as having been but a warm-up for turning away with an even deeper fatigued disgust not so much at their kinship as at what he perceives to be Borkman's misguided eagerness to affirm it. Borkman is flattered even if he's ultimately just a blind spot. He isn't obstructing the lion's view: he simply isn't within his ken even if the lion is staring right at him. If Borkman were somebody— anybody—else, he wouldn't be satisfied with just one encounter but would have the need to come back to confirm the discovery of a repudiated kinship deeper than any relation known to man or beast. But that's because Borkman knows without knowing he knows that going back won't make the connection any more intense. He feels all of a sudden that by his very presence he's killing the appetite for lunch and life of every beast in sight, not just the lion's. But all the little people—all the have-nots—who've come to consider themselves fans mustn't mistake the refusal to go back for the organizing principle of his—a prey animal's—predator evasion strategy. Is that a seal howling? Borkman asks himself—is reduced to asking himself since there's nobody else around (where have all the gawkers gone?). And what is the woodwind howl attempting to convey—exultation in solitude? exaltation of matelessness? hunger? satiety?

run-of-the-mill midsummer desolation? despair that its exertions don't quite measure up to those of its pen pals on East 64th Street? Borkman knows, again *without knowing he knows* (the privilege of all beings who are but the attributes of a single Substance), there's a Some Body afoot for whom such uncertainty signals more than just a chemical imbalance hijacking the blood-brain barrier—a Some Body who reflexively rejoices that so little uncertainty can generate so much thought—better yet, so many syllables.

From his bullet-proof town car parked next to a marshy no-man's-land whose sign proclaims it to be the Andrée Clark Bird Refuge (for sore eyes, no sight more soothing than some entity properly labeled or a non-entity transformed into one by a label, proper or otherwise), binoculared Post watches Eden disappear into the gift shop or is it the restroom adjacent? The surveillance equipment is first-rate, or so Liepnits, Narr and Cook informed him: wiretaps in every phone company junction box within a radius of seventy miles and Digital Window D7 security cameras wielded expertly by a regiment of beefed-up bodyguards. They are waiting for Eden to act. Depending on his performance here today, Invidicum and their poster boy along with it will or will not be shipped out of the country within a week to Benghazi, Abuja, Abu Dhabi, Riyadh, Doha, Muscat, Al Manamah, Monrovia, Sana'a and Damascus as well as still-to-be-determined stations further west, even if the drug at the required homicidogenic concentration has been determined to be too thermally unstable, too toxic upon inhalation and too prion-saturated for transport. Eden is soon followed by what seem to be members of the New York oppositional elite who've managed to master the art (a newfangled sort of applied art from the look of it) of descending upon the grounds both gingerly one by one, and en masse like the self-slaughtering lemmings of myth-, that is, *mis*conception. According to the video stream transmitted to Post's laptop, he looks, as intended, hyperanxious and dazed—and, from the administration of so many different versions of Invidicum at ever increasing dosages, who wouldn't? These detoxers—these foes of off-label mania in all its forms—if that's what they are—have come too late.

And if Eden were to fail here as he did with Straynge? What if the titration of every version and dosage against the boy's neurophysiological irregularities turns out to have been, for all Post's checking and rechecking, not quite delicate enough? Yet here is the humid wave of nauseous self-doubt that has just overwhelmed him not only receding but leaving big-bang rapture, of all things, in its wake! Nor has the fact that gorilla feeding is in progress down below hurt his recovery one bit: the ferocious pathos inherent in a primate's contemplation of a banana can always be counted on to make him discreetly exult—just like Rembrandt's Aristotle when contemplating the bust of Homer. In fact from now on Post will do his damnedest to eat a banana as if the performance were being closely observed (spectator or no spectator)—in short, he'll try to be worthy of his model by making the act excruciatedly legible, hence beautiful. He'll make everybody see he's much more than just a pipe-liner—he's a gorilla and peacock-proud of the telescoped evolutionary sprint required to become one. But what about all the other acts—like titration—for which no beautifying model exists? Maybe everything fell apart at the titration stage and Eden is doomed to do likewise. (But is now the moment for a seventy-five-year-old entrepreneur to become bent on turning his acts into symptoms? There's plenty of time to try kitchen-sink Method Acting—which throws in everything but the kitchen sink—in the turbid sunshine of old age.)

Still, rapture is the way to go since one day soon he's sure to be canonized, like Nobel, Delvigne, Oppenheimer, Szilard and Guillotin, while having been spared their redundant agonies. For just as the greatness of these great men retrospectively chastised their contemporaries so does it portentously pre-chastise all future denigrators of the great. Surely *his* contemporaries, Envy-racked to a man, must have already learned this lesson so ably taught and can see beyond Invidicum's perversion of all things Hippocratic to the vaster objectives justifying that perversion. But what if they argue (damn this trial for bringing all his demons out of cold storage!) that not by the wildest stretch of the imagination can he, Post, be compared to, say, Guillotin? All the better, then, for hasn't he just gotten through proclaiming not once but a thousand times (or did he just dream it?) that anything resembling apostleship where Invidicum, off-label or on-, is concerned—and even where it isn't—represents a devaluation—a prohibition—of Its destiny, which is precisely to have been too rarissime a bird for ascensions in the here and now. Ugly head-rearing apostles, then (addicted, as a rule, to championing the least significant elements of a masterwork and for all the wrong reasons to boot), by debunking through their very presence the myth of a contemporaneity overwhelmingly hostile across the board, thereby render infinitely less urgent the voyage of Invidicum's greatness out through the bloody loins of that contemporaneity into virgin birth posthume—the sole birth worth a shit since it's only the residents of Posterityville, PA, who, unlike folks everywhere else up and down the totem pole of time marching on, know a great one when they see one. And at the same time, they expect him to demonstrate that his greatness was just too damn great not to fail, hence the real thing, and (like any *supportive dad*) that the abject glamor associated with such failure (at least among the cognoscenti) is not necessarily out of their reach: Hell, if he could manage to achieve it, anybody could. So thank heaven he's been smart enough to nip Cook's and Narr's apostle-fever in the bud—and make them junior (silent) partners instead. Where are they, by the way? Still thinking they're valuable enough to persecute? So, under the circumstances, he's rightly elected to leave messy PWBGIFP (procreating while being grossly inadequate for parenthood) to the Borkmans of the world who are all too deft at painting their defects, ostensibly bemoaned, in all the trendy colors of self-congratulation—all too deft at playing, as if their life depended on it, the *too-big-not-to-be-inept-at-normalcy* card.

Yet wasn't it Straynge who'd been famous for letting them all know how obsessed he was with greatness, thereby making Post's present rant . . . *redundant* (to use his own word)? (For what self-respecting trial will tolerate more than one character with the same obsession or, worse, a participant whose obsession gets reintroduced over and over and always as if for the first time.) Though in the trial maybe redundancy, rather than Invidicum, is the drug of choice—not for him, of course, but for the Some Body (you mean to tell me that Post, too, is hip enough to know there is One running rampant?) who needs, whatever the cost, to assign the articulation of His pet peeves in all its baroque singularity to the broadest range of voice-boxes, even if He thereby dashes any hope of uniqueness they may harbor. The only thing that matters is *His* uniqueness, which is contingent—His scullions can take it or leave it—on the redundancy of its affirmation. Which simply means Some Body isn't all that different (though he likes to think he is) from your run-of-the-mill super-sleazeball hedge-funder, for whom x (where $x > \infty$) ill-gotten Mercedes just aren't enough inasmuch as, whatever the number of souped-up annexations, they end up constituting nothing more than an expansion of, rather than a weapon against, his own annihilability. Though maybe, in accordance with that dismal old French proverb, rusty as a leek, the more things stay the same, the more they change. *Which means that any repetition—any redundancy—is* by its very nature *a new beginning—chock full of additions to or deletions from whatever has come before, and with exact repetition being even more innovative—even more of a deviation from the original.* (Think—if you dare—of Elihu's speech in the Book of Job, as psychoanalyzed by Moses Maimonides [*The Guide for the Perplexed,* part III, chap. XXIII].) But how can this be, even if it sounds great on paper, that the more exact the repetition, the greater the deviancy from the original? Or is what we have here just another slice of wordflow rejoicing at its unmappability onto any slice of worldflow? But didn't somebody (who should have known better) once write that what's thinkable (*denkbar*) is also possible (*möglich*)—i.e., mappable—or was he just pulling our leg and giving the gangrene within a run for its money?

Or forget the redundancy business—another unbeatable dead horse. Maybe (in a what-goes-around-comes-around stunt worthy of Edmund Dantès) the Sheikhs et al of Benghazi et al are subjecting him, their man at Warner-Metro, to the very same sort of high-tech sensor-saturated manipulation to which he's currently subjecting Eden (see directly below) in order to decide for themselves, based on how Post's head swells in response to the delusions of greatness generated by that manipulation, whether it's up to the task of micro-measuring the impact of the drug—of any drug whatsoever (even Straynge's overreaching, a drug of sorts) and hence whether the deal should be clinched.

Too many thought packets, too little time, with one following hot on the heels of the next. But what concerns Post or the Some Body who's exploitatively doing the thinking for the two of 'em—the Some Body who, let's face it, embodies The Rump of twenty-first-century scribbling—is not this embarrassment of riches but how the yokage of each to its successor generates the illusion of a logical flow. The bridge is some point of trivial similarity which is incidental—not essential—to both (ibid., part I, chap. LVI). In the present case, *greatness* yokes together the packets on apostleship and redundancy—*greatness* inflicts the Dedekind cut into the abyss separating them.

Borkman senses through the symptoms (each a modern classic: pounding heart, dry mouth, overwhelming need to piss shit—funny, skinned fibres do not figure in this litany) that Eden is tailing him, maybe—alarmingly—without even being aware of doing just that. After almost a lifetime of being on the run, from himself, most of all (though he never gives up pretending it's from everybody else), he almost hopes—or thinks he hopes—that Eden will make that big bad lifetime go away. So is it to be by killing him—and not one of rumor's front-runners: Cantor, Herbert or Ethan—that Eden will finally earn his stripes? Well, why not? They all knew what he's done—what *the slumbering spirits of the gold* (he still can't resist a frisson of pride when invoking this magical phrase) have made him do—and loathe him robustly for it. No further humiliation possible: extradition and a third round of indictments imminent: he's clearly reached *rock bottom*. But like any fraud with a Wellesian "flair for melodrama, Emily," from long experience he knows without knowing that this anti-grail, this destinied Absolute Zero, is simply the point at which the fear of being unable to think his way out of said humiliation is greatest and the pep-thought needed to propel the inevitable rebound up into the shadows obligingly kicks in. In today's performance, that thought has been, "I need to see a lion—just one will do—before I die." And like all the others it self-identifies as, well, a Dedekind cut! if you must know (Cantor isn't the only one who knows a thing or two about irrational being): which means that, being neither the last thought in humiliation's domain nor the first in non-humiliation's but, instead, their dimensionless boundary, it is thereby spared the vexations indigenous to both. But suddenly it doesn't matter if Eden is tailing him. His thoughts are elsewhere—on the not-so-distant future which he may not live to see. What he does see is none other than—himself looking back big-bellied with regret for not having started to think seriously at this very moment about turning the Santa Barbara zoo—and why not the Central Park Zoo and the Bronx Zoo and the San Diego Zoo, too?—into Opportunity Zones (i.e., distressed neighborhoods, but distressed in name only—distressed merely by association with this or that low-income census tract hundreds of miles away on which they have no choice but to abut but of course only in principle and only in the abstract and in which the Zoner crowd have no choice but to invest—er, to *sort of* invest—but again, only in an abstract long-distance sort of way—if, that is, they want to defer taxes on their capital gains for the next seventy-five years) and about which veteran activist urban planners like Ivankia J. Trump and Anthony Scaramucci and Dick LeFrak and Mark Cuban will soon admit to being (pointing at their pubes) "very, very excited." He sees himself looking back on his failure to have induced like-minded Little Foxes—at, for example, the imminent Las Vegas Strip schmooze fest (he hears its wingèd chariot hurrying near) hosted by the likes of The Mooche and followed by a private Golden Showers extravaganza worthy of Busby Berkeley Mapplethrope—to go through the motions of helping the poor by putting up (very very far of course from where they struggle and suffer and suffer and struggle) hyperlative office towers with ritzy rooftop wineries—you know, the usual upscale dreck fawned over by a glossy prospectus with a Mayfair accent.

CHAPTER THIRTY-SEVEN

Post is fast realizing that the set-up—this long-distance implantation in (simultaneously) Eden's dorsal anterior cingulate cortex, insula and somatosensory cortex, not to mention his periaqueductal gray and thalamus, of a sensoring array of silicon microelectrodes, with each monitoring the spiking of an ensemble of neuronal action potentials directly responsible for the generation of thought packets—that the implantation requires some getting used to, even by experts. If he remembers correctly, the recorded electrical signals pass externally through a skull-secured percutaneous connector and the attached cables route them first to an external amplifier and then to a series of cutting-edge, high-end computers manipulated by his goons, trained (they're far-more-apt-than-they-looked) to process the signals and convert them into the desired output—the aforementioned thought packets consecrated to providing a running commentary on the itinerary of the murderous rage hopefully generated by super-potency Invidicum. At the same time the signals embodying the thinker's reactions to the highly disturbing thrust of the packets are being plowed back relentlessly (*vive la cybernétique*) into the synaptic stew as further fuelers of that rage. And of course (*of course!* after all, we're not Luddites) posted everywhere are the usual megapixel-sensor surveillance cameras picking up changes in facial expression and shifts in posture and gait, to be correlated with the brain signals.

Face to face with the ring-tailed lemurs Eden sort of perceives that thoughts he never dreamed he could have are coming fast and furious—thoughts that prove him to be a whole lot smarter than they'd ever imagined him to be (by no means clear, though, who *they* are). Still, *with another on the way* (yes, they're his children so excuse me if he opts to go all teary-eyed) Eden tries to hold back though not to prolong the exquisite semisuffering, as is the case when he's about to come between Linda's reluctantly parted lips, but rather because shooting its wad will somehow confirm what, through getting so damn smart in so short a time, he already knows, namely, that his mind is no longer his own, and mind control isn't as exhilarating as Hollywood cracks it up to be.

The thought in question concerns a less urbane but still plausible version of the Great Recession's Fabulous Fab de la Tourre, to wit, Borkman (who as it just so happens is pelting the wood turtles with peanuts and—even more horrifically—garnering for his pains an ovation from gawkers young and old), specifically about what Eden has never allowed himself to suspect with regard both to what he's been perpetrating all along and to what he still has in store for his most faithful customers: widows, orphans and average joes of all ages and sexes. He always manages to interiorize Borkman's image before the imaged becomes too real, to infect it, once interiorized, with his own signature brand of unrealness, and to then send it back into the cruel world deboned—and utterly unstraitjacketable as a flesh-and-bloody *type*. Or so he would discover if he were capable of ejaculating a thought of such magnitude yet here he is, folks, doing just that. But whatever the state of Eden's capability, the stork of decryption has just dumped this bruised fruit of neuronal signaling on Post's doorstep and unimpressionable Post is highly impressed, to say the least. But, hold your horses, the thought is just a warm-up. The moment's thought of thoughts is still in works, I mean, still in the works, still in *the* works, still in the works, still . . . in . . . the . . . ahhhh . . . ahhh . . . ahh . . . ah . . . a . . .

Spiking activity has peaked: sucked off expertly Eden is ready to soak the sheets of his skull thus: *Borkman is busy bundling the Amygdala-related mortgages taken out by little-Pharma borrowers with the lowest possible credit scores into all sorts of toxically opaque debt instruments with risk coefficients that are under the radar and off the charts, intending (once he's tipped off the SEC and the FDA and the EPA, among others, to Post's cook-the-books off-label shenanigans) to bet against what only seconds before he peddled as triple A-rated, rosily rock-solid, algorithm-hallowed securities so as to be able, once the underlying bonds tank, to walk away with billions, which of course adds up to something along the lines of throwing out the baby with the bathwater since as a remedy for Envy, Invidicum is incontrovertibly a force to be reckoned with.*

Well, for the first time today Post has to agree with his steroid-guzzling geeks who, presumably in response to the packet just in, can't stop high-fiving or knuckle-hugging, for here is certainly just the kind of thought they've all been waiting for whether they knew it or not—the kind that can drive Eden to blow Borkman's head off. But surely its progenitor is not the Eden who stepped into the warm bath of the Amygdala amphitheater what now seems like Ice Ages ago with a big fat chip on his shoulder but one, alas, neither big nor fat enough to avenge his father, whom he continues to detest above all others (making the need to avenge him, or somebody like him, even greater), except his kid brother whose sole familiarity with chips, big, fat or otherwise, comes from being one himself but a chip of a different color entirely, i.e., a chip off the old block. And with what species of firearm, Post wonders, will their lodestar choose to steal the show? a Kel-Tec Sub 2000? a .22-caliber handgun? a semiautomatic? a Winchester '73 (in homage to grandpappy Anthony Mann Eden)? In the small matter of a silencer, however, Post must put his foot down: a plastic bleach bottle wrapped in duct tape (never mind the brands)—crude, to be sure, but all the rage back in NYC—will, by your leave, be just the ticket.

Yet Post can't help feeling (though—or precisely because—doing so is tantamount to heresy) that they're giving Eden himself too-short shrift—in fact, the shortest shrift imaginable. *Why, they're* shorting *his stock the way Borkman is getting ready to shamelessly short theirs.* Or is this porridge pattie of italics trying to pass itself off as an insight non pareil the sort of dime-a-dozen forced analogy disgorged under fake duress by hacks—as if reluctantly shell-shocked into unwelcome avowal of an unanticipated brilliance? In any event, he deserves much better (Liepnits alone, that wily old reprobate, would oddly enough concur). Indeed, ought the achievement of this thought—even if it's (like all the others equally both high-and-mighty *and* exquisite sure to flood in now that the sluicegates are wide open) a veritable Hercules of fractal-like complexity—be attributed solely to Invidicum's hostile takeover, lock, stock and barrel, of Eden's virgin brain? In other words, a takeover so hostile as to be able to generate Deep Thoughts in even the biggest imbecile. After all, his—any—brain isn't just some slab of characterless concrete: it's more like a block of the rarest Carrara marble (*admission and full disclosure and spoiler alert:* Post owns class C stock in the Carrara International Consortium) wherein the shape of such thoughts, however Herculean, however hostile, are already latent, big with innateness—that is, his very own private version of innateness—requiring only a trivial shock, pharmacological or otherwise, from within or without—in fact, *the more trivial the better* (!?)—to get themselves properly inscribed. Well, Post beams, now that Eden is well on his way to discovering (all right, so what if with some little help from Invidicum?) that he's *innate to himself* (thanks a million, Liep), insight-wise the sky's the limit (even if it's a special kind of sky—the sky as reflected in some pissy puddle fringed with stone-dead samaras).

Shearer observes Post, Borkman and Eden from the wings, whose role in today's performance (all-Balanchine, maestro) has been taken by a little knoll of loblolly pines lording it over pretty much all of giraffedom. In a tone or with a look that brings back the day of their long colloquy in that (Chinese?) restaurant on Eighth (or was it Ninth?) Avenue, Herbert remarks—taking her completely or almost completely by surprise (but to what, Shearer wonders without knowing she wonders, could *almost completely* refer to out in the world? probably nothing, which is precisely its saving grace and as a dancer Moira is of course big on grace)—"Did you notice how many Invidicumites are wandering around here? Almost as if they're expecting something monumental to happen." Right on cue, Shearer delivers a shrug—a shrug she hopes falls under the rubric of the Shrug Bewildered and not the (detestable) Shrug Dismissive. "You know, I realized little more than an hour ago that almost all of the folks who were lounging around the pool while Pritchard and his lady friend clobbered us with their insights are not from Santa Barbara at all." Shearer murmurs *Margo* (of all things), dreamily, like a Sleepwalker—a Night Shadow—the one she used to be. "They're members of the New York tribe but because they got relegated to the placebo group we never paid them any attention." "We got too big for our britches and it's now that we're paying the price—and a steep one." Shearer has no idea where this observation has come from. It doesn't fit her profile, and the un-fit is not even interesting. *But do we have to mean what we say? Isn't it better for all concerned if we don't, at least most of the time?* She adds, "But nobody was supposed to know who was in that arm of the trial." This is a better fit. "I did—from the side effects, or rather from the absence of side effects, which as it turns out is the biggest side effect of them all. They looked—look—as if they're wasting away and not even the sunlight of Santa Barbara County can restore their native vigor. You know what I think? I think their mere presence is supposed to distract attention from the *something terrible* that is about to happen (as if they haven't suffered enough from a malign neglect of their individuality!). Heaven knows," (this interjection is a splash of Southern discomfort borrowed from her grandmother whose capacity to hate—even malignant whites—was constrained by the very graciousness wrongly ascribed to corn-fed plantation belles) "I've had enough creative writing courses to know a vaudeville trick like that when I see it and you, surely, as a dancer—" "An ex-dancer—a *very* ex dancer." "Well, isn't the corps—the corps—" "De ballet." Isn't the corps, she wonders, supposed to be not decorative but an organic part of the show? Shearer has had a chance to hone her thinking on the matter since it first started buzzing in her ear during the Margo-Pritchard seminar and she had to swat it away—or rather, Shearer's thinking has been honing itself on the matter while her mind remained otherwise engaged. As Shearer sees it, the corps is supposed to eat up space with a vengeance since the life of the show depends on it. This happens all too rarely but it does happen in *Serenade* and *Tchaikovsky Piano Concerto No. 2.* "You might as well know how it hurts me as a black woman to acknowledge" (Moira is disappointed [too disappointed to be angry] that Melanctha hasn't thanked her for this piping hot tip on the function of the corps de ballet) "that the sole birthright of some people amounts to mere service as an extra on the stage of life." She sums up, i.e., diverges, by uttering something completely out of character (though what exactly does being *in* character ever reduce to but a dissimulation of its core unpalatability?): "But I have no patience for self-styled underdogs. It takes calculation to be—and stay—an underdog."

But who are the two of them to challenge the experts? Shearer wants to know. In fact, she recently read somewhere that contact with wildlife, even if it's not in their natural environment, has a positive effect on the much-traumatized psyche. And if, as Herbert implies, these are so to speak the trial's dirt-poor relations, hence the most battered of the lot, then they must surely profit from as big a dose of the great outdoors as can be shoved down their throats. On the one hand, the remark is supposed to attest support for the underdogs (it costs her nothing even if she is one herself), on whom Herbert has been too harsh (doubtless in an effort to demonstrate that under no circumstances will she allow her people and by extension she herself to be straitjacketed—bracketed—i.e., perceived as trafficking in the benefits supposedly accruing from cut-and-dried racial profiling and building a comfortable niche therefrom). On the other, by deferring to the judgment of the so-called experts isn't she simply affirming their right to rule over the placebo slaves with an iron hand? Clearly, this less-than-expert deadpan patter on the subject of experts is coming from a Shearer to whom she hasn't had the pleasure of being introduced. Well if so, there's something pretty damn near-transcendent in obliterating, under its dubious auspices, the selfhood of the Shearer she *does* know, who's famous for standing staunchly by her defects as daughter, lover, wife and, most important, Muse, and whose immortal soul in the good old days could be had by GB, the Muse's Muse, for the price of a pirouette. She's suddenly sick of her selves but is cheered up by the giraffes' outsize efforts to look their lithest (including the adoption of stances designed to demonstrate that towering over the palms as they're doing hasn't gone to their head—has gone, in fact, only so far as their breastbone, if that far), which convinces her they'd have been very much at home in one of Mr. B.'s foremost radical experiments— *Agon*, say, or "The Unanswered Question" as posed by Ives (for Cantor, he's [minus the bank accounts] the Peirce of American music, hands down).

Melanctha knows that right around the bend there's something annihilatory to be said to Shearer's face, as payback for the hoofer's goody-three-shoes stab at edification. She should take that placebo plantation rot and shove it up her lily-white ass. But on a lighter note, she could swear this is the very first time her old pal the Master has seen fit to first-name them both in the same sentence (*whatever does it mean?*). (If only Shearer'd been consulted she could have come up with a meaningful comparison: why, it's like Balanchine's casting Farrell and McBride as co-primas in his *Rococo Variations*.) Yet despite having right on her side Melanctha is pretty much tongue-tied. Now, if the cause is rage, well, then, the Master wonders, why didn't Melanctha say so in the first place? She should know by now that she has only to cry out and her old pal will come running. More times than He can count He's been in a similar spot: rage managed to completely obliterate the thought that had given rise to it (since in any situation nineteen times out of twenty the culprit *is* a thought), so that He found Himself without a tightrope way out in rage's middle-of-nowhere. Nonetheless, He always managed—easy, it's true when you're on the best kind of tightrope: the one hand-woven from sheer will—to backtrack to the very moment of thought's genesis (for that's what makes Him a Master). Humility doesn't suit him (not *Him*), Melanctha thinks. Herbert is back on track, the thrust of her retort being the outrageousness of saying, much less thinking, rank injustice can be legitimated by something as puny as the expertise of the perpetrator simply because it's found a way to be just too damn complex for the likes of mythical l'il ol' you and me. As a budding writer Melanctha knows—for budding, like expertise, like beauty, does have its privileges—that the complexity of a thing is only measurable by—expressible in—words and words belong not just to Pritchard and Post and Liepnits and Manning but to everybody, including you and me. Words are a carnavalesque free-for-all. When it comes to words, the expert is as much of an amateur as everybody else (Herbert is tempted to go for perversity and add—*even more so*). Words constitute the triumph of reverberation over intention and don't you forget it. And once a way is found to get the thing generated spontaneously like a maggot in the toxic broth known as language, the maggot's meaning is from then on potential: it depends on the whim of whichever of too many cooks is currently intent on spoiling that broth. So—bye-bye to the infringement of the thing's patent on a meaning beyond interpretation and accountability. Bye-bye to the impunity of experts. Long live QAnon. Long may it croak.

But she ain't done, no, not by a long shot. And she won't be until she's discovered what's just served as the bridge between Moira's packet and her own—what's just subsidized the fiction of a seamless transition from one to the other. (Or, as Moira might add if she were allowed to weigh in on the issue: a transition as seamless as that from one kaleidoscopic configuration to the next in the "Waltz of the Flowers" and the last movement of *The Four Temperaments* but most overwhelmingly in the first movement of *Serenade*.) The bridge "concept" is obviously the West Coast's next big thing (A-list directors have been sending out feelers): she sensed this the minute she set foot here— inhaled the bigness together with the odors of flamingo turds and gorilla piss. If she's not mistaken Post can be heard humming the tune a few feet away. *Expertise*. That's the bridge—that's the name of the tune. It's come to her in a vision. Which makes her the patron saint of seamlessness. It's "expertise" and nothing but that's enabled her packet and Shearer's to come to an understanding which like all understandings is based on a misunderstanding—better yet, a subreption—*yeah, a* subreption, *got a problem with that, asshole?* And the bridge stands or falls on the plausibility of that subreption—in particular on the skill with which she managed to bully the term—*expertise*—as breezily invoked by a layman (though what is she?), into serving as the pretext for an axe-grinding meditation on complexity gone haywire.

Post over-curses the long-distance implant machinery, suddenly gone haywire, for allowing every sensor in town to ditch Eden and become transfixed instead by the neural activity of Herbert—a mere extra. Well, can she help it if the bridge concept has brought the pipeline king and the budding writer improbably together—bridged the unbridgeable gap between them? *Don't worry, Tom,* she might have said if she'd been aware of how much their implosive fusion was gumming up the wavelengths, *I'll soon be history.* One of his goons turns around (the otters were starting to bore him anyway) to eyeball Post's increasingly audible raving. The admonishing forefinger he puts to his thick lips exhibits a delicacy of which Cook would never have believed it capable.

CHAPTER THIRTY-EIGHT

But sensored or not, Eden (a true professional—more of a professional than he ever gave himself credit for being) soldiers on—as, for that matter, does Borkman (also a professional, albeit of another stripe). They're locked in love-hate immemorial and don't care who knows it including they themselves. (*"We fell in love,"* Eden remembers The Rump saying about his JO buddy, Kim Jong-un. And who but The Rump could get away with saying such a thing—and why?) And for what may very well prove to have been the first time since the Cenozoic Era, such virtue is rewarded, for the signals emitted by Herbert's budding brain suddenly go dead, enabling Eden to retake his rightful place as the whole (high-tech) show.

Still, Eden is only human and being so, finds himself regretting the absence of a stiletto. Which could be plunged up to the hilt into Borkman's neck. Or deep inside his belly and up toward the heart. A bad worker craves the tools he doesn't have. Or haven't you heard?

Having learned (from the LAPD which is ensuring every port within a 750-mile radius is sealed off) that Post and Co. are well on their way to executing what pharmacologists-turned-sting operatives commonly refer to as *the final off-label coup* with Eden as the standard-bearer, Pritchard has no choice but to organize yet another poolside powwow in support of the anti-war effort (which, among other things, entails conserving their dwindling supply of Invidicum in its pure state lest it fall into more of the wrong hands). Though not so strictly speaking, the powwow looks more like a press conference, since most of the reporters from the last session (sniffing something in the wind) have overstayed their welcome (in anticipation of just such an offensive), with more chaises longues (mainly non-vintage) at their disposal than they know what to do with.

"It won't stop with Borkman," he informs his team, now including Cook and Narr; Walser né Stifter and vice versa; Cantor (still heading the short-list of possible successors); and—Netta, who's clearly answered somebody's prayer (and Pritchard has a strongish hunch who the gender-equitability nut in question may very well be) that she be brought back into the limelight. (*Cook and Narr!* so the heat's off, or maybe it was never on—in any case, these Object-obsessed dummies have come out of hiding and nobody seems to find it the least bit odd. But which Agency is paying for all those cellphone minutes wasted?) Every one of them—except, of course, for the traitors (here he goes all poker-faced)—are in Post's crosshairs. Though he must admit (even more deadpan), it's getting harder and harder, given the massive number of defections, counter-defections and mock-defections—the too many cases of recidivism and renegadery entwined—to determine whose side anybody is on, and that includes he himself. Margo née Mesta has uncharacteristically gone to the mostest trouble of preparing green tea and toast (and two seven-layer cakes for those who see no need to fashion, redundantly, an exterior worthy of the beauty harbored deep, deep—in fact, too deep—within).

As Margo, down on her hands and knees and with the best of intentions, appeals to Stifter né Walser's (or is it Walser né Stifter's?) sweet tooth—holding out a hefty slab of temptation—Cantor can't help observing with disgust how S/W reflexively responds with a grimace and shudder—frissons his way to safety—without even acknowledging the existence of the hostess, much less the slab. The hostess *is* the slab. and the slab has destabilized him. So what does S/W's frisson signify or attempt to signify? Cantor wonders and well he should. A haut gourmet's hoity-toity distaste for slop? A simulation of distaste for what, slop or not, is in fact brutishly craved? A self-anointed polymath's irritation at being torn from higher pursuits by something so insignificant as generosity? A fear of betraying how sorely he's tempted and rage at this annunciatory angel's intimation, however unwitting, that he's fast losing the fight against surrender? Etc. But whatever the frisson signifies, he decides, it certainly has nothing to do with decency and gratefulness and self-reflection and wit. As for Pritchard, he waves away the goodies with a pasha's beringed impatience (Margo, however—still on her hands and knees—seems to relish the Byzantine touch and feels in no way abased) only to be confronted out of the blue with Netta's outrage at, of all things, his adamancy about the patients saying bye-bye to the yoga lawn and going to bed on time. "You infantilize them—you've always infantilized them, Sam—to the point where they're more than willing to do whatever you—or anybody else—tells them to do." "Stick to the issue"—it's a cross between a warning and a plea. *I swear to God she sounds just like Mary Astor in* Dodsworth, Margo muses. *It's been ages since I've called him Sam.* "So if Eden does end up doing the bidding of those thugs by killing Borkman (and no doubt he will), not to mention the obligatory slew of innocent bystanders (I just hope no animals, especially pterodactyls, are mistreated during the making of this underground film), there'll be no choice but to hold you personally responsible—until the end of my days!—for turning him into the target of their bargain-basement brand of mind control." "Netta, do you have to be so goddamn expository this early—or late—in the game. You never know who may be listening in. In any case, the recruitment of Eden by Post's poor man's version of the Parallax Corporation was mapped out long before he—or any of us—arrived on the scene. Tell her, Stif. Can you get me off the hook here, Wals?" Netta sneers. "Isn't it clear that Sam's only thought at the moment is to get you dream-bunker brats out of his hair as soon as possible so he can squeeze into his busy schedule some prime time cruising down on Stearns Wharf?" "Shucks, ma'am, everybody 'round here knows that—even I (I mean, even me). It's the best-kept open secret this side of the Rockies." More obscene than the cruising is the pleasure he takes in watching her deflate. "By the way, about prime time you're absolutely right, though on a good night the cruising goes well beyond that—straight (!), in fact, into the wee hours." Then, presumably to demonstrate that, when successfully provoked, as now, he can be as nitty-gritty unwitty—i.e., as brass-balls manful—as the next low-testosterone guy, Pritchard argues it's just plain common sense to have them bed down early after a hard day's work in preparation for the next and so what if the rule was concocted solely with the satisfaction of an unclean craving in mind? Their welfare always comes first, even in the most convulsive throes of addiction. "I know," Netta concedes prettily—maybe (Cantor quickly realizes) a bit too prettily. "And that's why I try to make allowances. For if we can only see our way clear to disregarding, humanely enough, the fact that you make it a point to greet all of your male patients stark naked on the office tatami (in the unspeakable hope that . . . one thing will lead to another—not to mention your falling into a deep sleep whenever it becomes obvious the unspeakable isn't going to happen and then, when caught in the act, brazenly denying any wrongdoing which for my money is the biggest ethical breach of all), then we may still end up with—with—" Cantor winces when he realizes that Pritchard—and from the look of her, Margo as well—actually—poignantly—expects Netta to conclude her muckraking exercise with a ringing endorsement. "Well, what *do* we end up with, I ask you, but a contraption not all that different from Straynge in his woefully unHippocratic heyday?" "So how can we put our fate in the hands of this degenerate?" But what is Cantor's surprise when he opens his eyes (closed against the poignancy turned ugly) to discover it's Pritchard himself who's given voice to this musing.

Cook hopes he speaks for all of them by demanding to know why she's chosen to "expose" Pritchard not only at so late a date but at the very moment when they're being forced to confront far more important matters. Why has she chosen as armature for her reconstruction of their collective past—i.e., their collective guilt—what she calls Pritchard's degeneracy which, she'd have them believe, inhabits its every nook and cranny—nooks and crannies where hyperprofessionalism was mistakenly believed to reign? "Because of the danger inherent in trying to meet the real problem head-on—to focus on the so-called Big Picture (i.e., Post's plot to destroy Big Pharma as we know and maybe even love it) without the obligatory blinders." So what's more natural, she explains, than to try to save the day (somebody has to) by pouring the salt of what she flatters herself is acuity not on the wide wound itself but on some semi-suturable outlier lesion. "Like my poor old degeneracy." "Exactly." "Good thinking, old girl," back-pats vinegary Margo, "since, as my old—now new—boyfriend pointed out a while back, there's no telling who's listening in, but should they be, how can they ever begin to decode what they think they're hearing?" "Frankly," Ethan groans, "I don't give a damn who's listening in—or out. It's too damn late to worry about playing it safe. And, anyway, just what would *playing it safe* mean in such a context as ours?" Ethan's manly grief—none the worse for being given free rein out in the fresh air—excites Rhys (not to mention the two manly *damn*'s), who didn't want to believe he had it in him. She might swallow her pride—and half-a-bottle's worth of sleeping pills—and give him a last chance.

As for Cantor, he feels there's something radically wrong here. His roommate is about to kill Borkman, confusing him with The Rump (an honest—even an honorable mistake), and here they are doing nothing. You'd think they were his lounge colleagues at Columbia, taking a break from things topological. Things are getting way too abstract—too many gaps between packets and too many bridges to fill them. There's something almost obscene about the way they're allowed to flow into each other—seamlessly (but only to the undiscerning eye). Not enough resistance from the packets themselves (a gang of sissies, that's what they are, and they're turning the packeteers into sissies as well)—not enough respect for their own independence—too much impatience to get themselves hitched, that's been their trouble from day one. But if the Amygdalites are going to beat the Parallax gang at their own game, then the Mulligan stew of these hapless career ruminants could use a juicy slab or two of straight-from-the-stockyards T-bone (paging Upton Sinclair)— something raw and bloody with a dollop of gristle to beef up their capacity to look sex and death and taxes straight in the eye and to restore to all three their capacity to resist analysis at all cost. Something about, say, Pritchard's white nights on the wharf. Or about another kind of wildfire. Or about another kind of hurricane (even if this isn't the Caribbees, one's sure to strike if they're the least bit patient) that's so off the charts category-wise as to render pack-eteering—by lay analysts—impossible (thereby forcing them to confront the unconfrontable). Doesn't matter what that something is about, as long as it doesn't lend itself—doesn't look kindly on seamless yokage to one of its own kind, as long as it's just a loner—a rogue—a singleton—a hapax legomenon—a self-contained and unlinkable chip off the old block that embodies—that constitutes—*all that is the case*. True, Pritchard's tantalizing hint that Cantor would very likely be his successor did make him even more abstraction-crazy than before (can Cantor help it if, when things are looking up and his vanity is being appeased, he celebrates by transforming, without invitation, events into thoughts—preferably into thoughts that have never been thought since the beginning of the world—only to discover they *were* being thought—rou-tinely—*long before?*) and as a result he more than momentarily forgot his duty to the bottom line—which should be to fight injustice in all shapes and sizes. Even if such an always belated declaration of principles seems a little hollow coming from somebody who's devoted his life to the very packeteer-ing he professes—threatens—to excoriate in the here and now which, by the way, couldn't be easier when that here and now just happens to be the sun-niest haven lying between LA and SF. But who knows? maybe this at once newfound and resumed social consciousness—but a hop, skip and a jump away from consecration to banning discrimination against, inter alia, blacks, homosexuals, Jews, Muslims, transgenders, the disabled, and (especially) hardline Enviers (i.e., all the usual suspects) from the marketplace (where all ladders start)—will simply usher in a whole new round of even more viru-lent packeteering, thereby leaving kid stuff like consecration once again in the lurch. So there's no escape. But does the deep thinker Cantor takes himself to be (even if the use of his namesake's diagonal argument to prove the inescap-ability of gayhood is no masterstroke) really want to escape—to shuffle off the mortal coil of his very own private custom-made shroud of Turin? Or maybe, as punishment *for* escaping, he'll never be allowed to cobble together a packet sandwich in this town again. As if echoing Cantor's thoughts (though not really), Pritchard cantillates, "If I'm not virtuous, then let the text of which we're the fabric—but I'm getting way ahead of myself: stealing my own thun-der, so to speak." In short, *Lear* as staged by and starring Pritchard has just closed—even before its backwater previews.

"Netta (bless her Italo-Israeli-Irish heart of stone) is absolutely right: I've been a very bad deity—especially for poor Eden who deserves something far better than a reincarnation of Margo's dead hubby." "We all do," Cook mutters. "What was that?" Pritchard sniffs dissension in the ranks, but he knows the malcontent won't come forward. Further, it's too early for anybody to be malcontent, much less *disgruntled*. Even if disgruntlement, at least as Made in USA, is a remedy—OK, a pharmakon—for all ills, surely nobody has amassed enough of them to qualify for such a diagnosis. As for Cantor, he's both favorably impressed and unfavorably appalled (by *deity*). For here is mentor man Pritchard, in defiance of some old dame's putdown, alchemizing shadow into substance, i.e., transmogrifying newly minted delusion (*Hey, you guys, I'm a deity*) into long-acknowledged fact (*ditto*) through the slyly simple expedient of lamenting his incompetence under the terms of that fact (for what's more real—what gives off more of a whiff of the Real than incompetence?). In other words, Pritchard the deity is real because his (atypical) incompetence in the role is real—incompetence clinches the deal. What a guy! or (if *muliebris virili corpore inclusa* & Co. can be made to apply) gal!

"What I mean is, I should have practiced the right kind of mind control—there is a right kind, you know. I'm just as guilty as Post when it comes to triggering Eden's homicidal mania only (*a*) I've had less time to pave Eden's road to hell with my good intentions (which is one thing in my favor) and (*b*) I haven't used sensors (which is another). Although to give him credit, I can't imagine Post descending to my level by calling his bad intentions good. Here I've been lamenting (read *flaunting*), every chance I got, my All-Encompassingness, my All-Knowingness, my En-Sofiness, that is, my stance as one doomed (read *elected*) to be both H (by regularly cruising our fair Wharf from dusk to dawn) and Not-H (by ostentatiously whispering sweet nothings into Margo's ears every chance I get), both particle and wave, both a live alley-cat out of Schrödinger's bag and a dead one, Ernest (or in this case, Erwin) in town and Jack in the country." (So all along, Pritchard's been way ahead of Cantor in the debunkment department, which does make him, Pritchard, some kind of deity after all. Ignoring the pleas of his green-eyed monster Cantor proceeds to astonish himself by exulting on behalf of his mentor's achievement.) "But if I haven't managed to escape what to Eden (deaf to my self-congratulation) is obviously the direst of fates, i.e., incessant cancellation of identity, how can he, an avowed yokel, hope to be cured of the craving to be Anything-But-Eden and thereby attain complete self-coincidence as one thing and one thing only? And how can I have expected him *not* to turn into a killer since we all know a killer's the only thing that's just *one thing and one thing only*? Specifically the killer of Borkman who, with the subpoenas coming in fast and furious, has been acquiring more and more of a reputation for being a venerable renegade—a kind of subprime Robin Hood—i.e., that very one thing and one thing only Eden doesn't know how to be. Which makes him the perfect—prime—the exclusive—target of Eden's Envy and as Envy (if done right) is just a hop, skip and a jump away from Homicide, well—you get the picture. As that plump though still magnificent old stoic (a Scotsman, no?) would have said (as he did about another quack, though one far less pernicious than yours truly), I've been much too frugal—too scrupulously economical—in the allocation of powers and faculties to my overmedicated creatures. In fact my autobiography could very well be entitled *The Great Frugality*."[83] ("*My* overmedicated creatures." So, grunts Cantor, the deity isn't debunked—isn't debunkable—after all. Next time I'll heed the ululations of my green-eyed wife.) "Though I bestowed on him the capacity to comprehend the ins and outs of what I've passed off as my plight, what I did *not* bestow was the far more important capacity to see through it to the real (unglamorous, unbisexualizable, undeifiable) McCoy, i.e., the fact that I'm just plain old H and plain old Jack and a plain old particle, though the jury's still out on whether I'm just plain old dead or alive. Which, *mutatis mutandis*, just happens to be everybody's plight, whether his/her/their vanity permits him/her/them to admit it or not. Which means Eden needn't worry (though it's probably too late for him to shift gears) that he'll never amount to anything more than the untotalizable sum of himself." (*Tell me, is it now safe for Cantor to resume his exultation on Pritchard's behalf?*)

Narr (though it could have been anybody) is quick to object: "Much too pat for my money (especially that bit about a killer being the only thing that's one thing and one thing only: where do you come off making a claim like that?)." "Only don't go on blaming yourself forever," Walser says halfheartedly. "After all, everybody knows he must have had plenty of contact with plenty of doubletalking shamans (who probably did plenty of damage) before the stork saw fit to land him on your doorstep." "Not to mention the fact that you grossly overestimate your importance in his life—in anybody's life," Netta wrist-taps with ulcerating sweetness. "All we can do now is let nature takes its course," Cook (though it might have been anybody) amply concludes. "We should schedule many more of these al fresco bull-by-the-horns sessions," Rhys concludes even more amply, thinking it's no longer unlikely that she'll jump into bed with Narr first chance she gets. He's been showing real gumption recently.

Meanwhile, back on the pampas, the jury (a veritable cast of thousands—of gorillas and lemurs and giraffes and mock-turtles, among others) is very much out on whether Eden will bump Borkman off or is even still intent on doing so. Here, too—even amid all the tumult of recrimination and cross-examination—everybody's attention is focused almost exclusively on the same cliffhanger, whether he or she or they—sorry, *they or she or he*—knows it or not. After having splashed some wake-up water on his face from a fountain adjacent to the wisteria arbor (yes, *wisteria arbor*! it's been eclipsed thanks to the giraffish imperturbability of a stand of palms), Cantor realizes that the bunker staff, supersolicitous as always, has been creating quite a tumult of their own. A buffet table has been set out or up or forth perpendicular to the diving board (when in doubt, my fellow Republicans, cough up a little humanity: feed the beast, don't starve him) and Cantor can't help looking daggers of wonderment. "Oh," Pritchard sighs, "I'm as much in the dark as you." "As rumor has it," says Narr who knows a thing or two about rumors and even

---

[83] Here Pritchard reveals his semi-immense debt to David Hume (see, in particular, *Dialogues Concerning Natural Religion* [London, Penguin Books, 1990], part XI).

more about starting them (as attested by the obligatory sunglasses dangling trendily from—from—well, what exactly *are* they dangling from? Cantor has never been able to get the technique straight), "somebody had the bright idea of giving Sun Valley (Idaho) a run for its money and subsidizing an open house for pharmaceutical start-ups and venture caps (short for capitalists) right here in bunkerland. And the even brighter idea of seeing to it that whatever information those small fry reveal to their potential backers in the way of microaggressive breakthroughs becomes with a few tweaks the property of Warner-Metro." "And you'll never guess who's just shown up," says Cook (though it could have been anyone). "Exactly, Borkman's *son*. The one he's always bragging about having failed." Narr rolls his eyes: at Borkman, for his failure? at Cook, for dredging it up yet again as a way, maybe, to soft-pedal his own? Hearing the word, Herbert (for she's back from the pampas) is envious not of Borkman *but of the word itself*, or is this impossibly fine distinction another case of wordflow's sparing her the dirty work of facing up to failure? In the last analysis, it doesn't matter what the distinction, fine or not, boils down to: the fact remains that Borkman, unlike Herbert, has a son to call his own even if it's obvious he still hasn't figured out what to do with so hot an item.

Ms. Bean—the inevitable, the irresistible Ms. Bean—is discreetly arranging the wineglasses though what would it mean to say that she's arranging them *in*discreetly? "But of all times," so Netta, ever the gadfly's gadfly, "to hold an open house. With so many things unresolved." At that very moment the principals march in (it wouldn't be wide of the mark—and so what if it is?—to say they resemble nothing so much or nothing so little as the Landgrave's guests in *Tannhäuser* (act II, scene 4), to the disgust of the none-too-eager staff. It's easy to see, and Herbert sees and sees till it burns a hole in her chest, that Borkman, Jr., (descending unapologetically, with his multidirectional shock of flaming red hair, on the liquor cart) is very much a chip: whether off the old block or on the cold shoulder has yet to be determined—at any rate, a chip, and with a vengeance. Obviously an alpha male with the requisite entourage of omegas to prove it (so if Borkman can't be The Rump he can at least be The Fred). Does he suspect that his father's fate is in fact completely uncertain at the moment, contingent on the machinations of a ghoul named Post and a candidate of circumstance—a Parallaxed Manchurian—named Martin Eden? A face or two begins to look familiar. Maybe Cantor's dreamed about them or seen them on the Bill Maher show. Or in that pornographic film targeted at the X Generation of lightning-speed traders (*Gentlemen Prefer Bonds; or, Memoirs of a Wall Street Dominatrix*) which was such a (surprise) hit some years back that he and Berry Sundae had no choice but to rent it from now long-defunct World of Video or New York Video or was it newly defunct Video Room? (all three devoutly missed) and to come all over each other—from sheer boredom, of course (or so they felt they needed to believe). Though if truth be told, Cantor did go on to feel queasy (Berry, less) about such irreverence since, as it turned out, the co-writer of *GPB*, whose experiential input was the true star of the show, had gone on to fund with her share of the box office proceeds a non-profit (Spank You Very Much) dedicated to helping those traders so addicted cast off the whips and chains of their shame.

The upstart start-uppers and their potential benefactors have, at the behest of the matchmakers, already begun linking up—like packets, Cantor thinks—to negotiate, which means littering the lawn with cigarette butts and beer bottles. He hears what was obviously a VC Somebody say to what looks—and sounds—like Jr.'s head sidekick, "Tell your boss if I'm gonna invest in several—or even one—of his cockamamie schemes then he's got to cut out using those phony profitability metrics—you know the kind—with acronyms as long as his nose." At this, what looks like the VC's trophy sidekick drawls, while brandishing a messy canapé toothpick, "For starters, adjusted consolidated segment operating income (ACSOI to you, bub) and operating profits minus hot air (OPMHA) simply have to go." Jr.'s sidekick, whose name has with true Dickensian gusto turned out to be Something P. MacSomethingberger, looks as if he wanted to retort something along the wobbly lines of, "Frankly, my dear, I don't . . ." but, probably remembering Jr.'s warning that the customer is always right, he dutifully muzzles his outrage (but whose *probably* is this? Cantor wonders—can't be his: he knew immediately the reason for the muzzling).

As it starts to rain (when only minutes before the benign sky, etc., etc.), they all make an undignified dash (whatever their status) for the great indoors. And in retrospect (which sets in earlier out here) it would appear that the downpour was staged for the sole purpose of obliging them to do business in a more appropriate setting. Cantor is hit in the pit of his stomach by backpack after backpack without so much as the peep of an apology from the perp. Clearly in Silicon Valley these are independent creatures whose severance of all ties with their owner begins long before the signing of the credit card bill. More significantly, the mad rush for shelter hasn't disrupted the overall shape of the group and, as Cantor hears some loudmouth explain, that's because they've obeyed three simple rules: collision avoidance, velocity matching and cohesion (they've stayed close to their match or if not to their match then to the person they found themselves next to when they were making a mad dash for the bunker). In other words, the preservation of the large-scale structure is not the result of top-down planning but is an emergent property—a byproduct of purely local interactions-through-reaction. *Not unlike the ever-more-reluctant unfolding of—to its peril—the Invidicum Story*, thinks Cantor guided by SoP (not a day has gone by that hasn't—chalk it up to the alienation effect exerted by the California sun—exacerbated his aversion to "Master"), *the yokage of whose packets—huddling together in defiance of a central blueprint for to follow one is to* unburthen'd crawl, *like Lear,* tow'rd death—*takes its cue from the locally coordinated mound-building of* Microtermes bellicosus, *with each packet an ostrich burying its head in the sand of an immediate predecessor and as such very much robust to failure since failure is measurable only against a blueprint—and with the random walk of the story itself a mere byproduct and an unwelcome one at that.*

The same instinct that's driven the hordes through the French doors makes them head for the elevators and after a total of about thirty-some-odd trips everybody finds himself in sub-basement IVA which is partitioned into a commons (where the spread is far more sumptuous than the one outdoors) and three color-coded spaces: Green (deal is urgently recommended); Yellow (deal is problematic); and Red (investment is suicide—and not just *career* suicide). Observing the thickness of the walls, Cantor thinks, *How will we ever escape?* and is immediately ashamed of what he reads as cowardice. The Stifters listen with an avidity that surprises them (as well it must, otherwise the story will be brought up on charges of dereliction of duty) to Jr.'s description of the obligatory humble beginnings of his *outfit* (haven't heard that term for ages, notes Cook), complete with garage basement office, beanbag chairs, half-pipe skateboard ramp and Hawaiian pizzas, the moldier the better. (*Is it too late*, Margo wonders, unthink- but understandably, *to trade in* my *Jr. for Borkman's?*) Avidity skyrockets as they learn how he and his partners managed to raise billions before they had any revenue or even a product or even an idea for a product. For more important than having an innovative product—even a revolutionary one—is knowing a thing or two about product placement. From the start, they just knew their product—an *intervention*, but still neither fish nor fowl—was going to be innovative—no, revolutionary— even if they didn't know much else, but knowing what they did know how could they help not knowing as well that there was a need, and not just a need but a crying need, for experimentation with shape, packaging, price and store placement so as to render it—the product—eye-poppingly distinct from all others in the same category even if they had no idea what that category would turn out to be. What's certain is that their product will transform its category completely while remaining a bona fide member thereof. And then it came to them all at once: a device for measuring hormone concentrations in baboon feces as an indicator of stress levels among troop alphas, betas and omegas. Now, while the novelty wore off quickly enough, as it was supposed to do, entrancement with—immersion in—that novelty was not less, for all that, of an essential waystation to the real thing—not less epistemologically internal and ideologically intrinsic to the invention (though more of a discovery than an invention) of the true product—the only conceivable product.[84] That is to say, only by way of the shotgun honeymoon of the Borkman gang and that hormone-measuring device finally being over before it even began—i.e., *only by way of omegas*—was it but a skip and a jump to a smartphone whose supersensors would insure that a customized brand of chicle-based rainforest chewing gum retained its supersweetness through days—maybe even decades—of uninterrupted mastication. (*Is he joking? Who cares!? If only Jim, Jr., could joke like that. For there's gold in them there jokes*, thinks Margo.) *Cook:* "But what does a smartphone like that have to do with a drug for Envy?" Borkman, Jr., holds his expository breath for as long as he can. "Absolutely nothing—to the

---

[84]Cf. Slavoj Žižek who, in his meditation on Agatha Christie's *The A.B.C. Murders*, demonstrates that the truth can be carried to term by midwife Hercule Poirot, the detective in that story, only by virtue of its gestation in the wobbly womb of the false solution ("Two ways to avoid the real of desire," in *Looking Awry: An Introduction to Jacques Lacan through Popular Culture* [Cambridge, Massachusetts, MIT Press, 1991]).

unpracticed eye." "In any case," mumbles Pritchard expertly, "these youngsters aren't here to feed the Invidicum beast." "Then what *are* they here for?" "To get us gawking at their mind-blowing ingenuity" (his use of *mind-blowing* but, more importantly, his uninvidious nod to the action potential of youth makes Pritchard feel young and innocent). "But in a way the man is right. Our smartphone has nothing to do with Invidicum. In fact, we've lost interest and are making sure it goes the way of the omegas."

Junior appears to think he's summing things up to everybody's satisfaction by saying: "Dad never seemed to get it."

"Get what?" the VC asks guardedly. (Out of nowhere, the sort of person who was clearly born to be perpetually displaced, shouts, "Pass the hot sauce..") He'd prefer not to set foot in what sounds like your garden-variety archetypically unresolvable father-son conflict.

"And what better proof"—the boy's smile which turns teeth into fangs has no trouble making Shearer tremble (she came down seconds ago with the very last elevator load)—"than that it's me and my guys and not dad and his who've found (and without in this case resorting to sensors) the adjuvant— the magic vector—that smoothes the way for Invidicum to churn out assassins by the cartload (for in the end we're all about Invidicum—until we're not). In other words, no more unwieldy silicon microelectrode arrays. And yes, the smartphone has in its turn been epistemologically internal and ideologically intrinsic to the discovery cum invention of this most magical of vectors.

"Yes, the dirty little cat's out of the bag: it's dad who's been selling Post & Co. those arrays (he joint-owned, until last week, the company that produces them) which they've been made to believe are essential to the mind-control of would-be assassins. But they just don't work—dad himself, the assassin's prey, is living proof. I've been waiting to get back to—I mean, back at—him for so long. Oh, you don't know how long."

"Waiting to dethrone him, it sounds like," says Walser, envious of this upstart (since he—and everybody else he knows—has had to come up the hard way). Shearer's saddened to perceive how easily they've forgotten—no, managed to forget—Eden. Wasn't he being groomed all along to become—at least that was her impression as gleaned from the most reputable innuendo— the Great Dethroner?

"In any event, now—after this, our third breakthrough (we're not having much success in shoving it down Post's throat: old habits die hard, I guess)— we can get back to testing the *intervention* I was just telling-you-about-with-out-telling-you-anything. But can you blame me for keeping the gruesome details under wraps—under my gray flannel hoodie, to be exact, until further notice?" *Cook (again):* "At least the vector isn't slated for demolition just like the omegas and the smartphone. Or is it?" Herbert, who's back—and shivering from the downpour—has been listening for quite some time (contrary to bunker regulations, fortunately lax—actually, they're a joke—she took the stairs). The business about sensors is a bit over her head—at least it etherealizes her to think so and, being a black girl from the South Bronx, she's always in the market (but why?) for Hollywood-style etherealization, at a reasonable price. What *isn't* over her head, on the other hand, is everything associated with the father-son confrontation that's soon to unfold (if Dan Borkman manages to make it back from the lion's den), however belatedly (although the belatedness will, mark my words, be a big part of its impact). What a gift to the Master (she has no intention of giving up on Him even if the others think He's through—think He's nothing but an always unwelcome whiff of the supernatural—the poor man's supernatural). Since she's convinced that for all His advance-guard pretensions, He craves nothing more than to wield, like His more successful rivals, the gun that once belonged to exquisitely beautiful Anton Pavlovich—pinup boy for girls like Melanctha. So what if in this case the gun is a son—so what, just as long as, having been introduced dutifully in the Dark Ages of the fifteenth act, he—it—goes off, even more dutifully, in the Enlightening next-to-last? And from the wicked glint in his eye (rumored to be irresistible to women and not just of a certain age, though not to Herbert [I've just filled you in on who is and hence who isn't *her* type]) it appears that this son of a gun has every intention of doing so.

They all step back, startled, when the elevator disgorges Borkman who's none the worse for resembling the spitting image of his own apparition. He's actually pretty good, despite his age, at projecting a certain Heathcliffian glamor. He hasn't shaved, much less dressed, for the occasion. Each harbors a different feeling regarding his untimely resurrection—though maybe it's the same feeling in each case only experienced at a different level of intensity. He prepares to recount—especially for the benefit of those audience members whose favorite literary subgenre is the plot summary—all that's befallen him since the zoo opened its doors. His adventures, like everybody else's on the planet, prove yet again that today's tourist trap is tomorrow's slaughterhouse.

Don't let anybody tell you a self-styled seasoned crook can't be irrecoverably traumatized by imprisonment, however fleeting, in the funhouse of a city zoo is written all over his craggy-chiseled features. Though it was as if time had stopped and he would never leave the grounds alive, Borkman, *as was his wont* (but according to whom exactly?), tried to make the best of being targeted—to put his torment to good use. For one thing, he marshaled it (since Eden was close and Borkman was moving fast) to quickly decelerate and turn (into flamingoville) for that's what evolution had taught him. Herbert wonders whether he believes—or is even listening to—what he's saying. But just when all seemed lost he realized—or rather his fellow captives (camels, giraffes, lions, mermaids, lemurs, griffons, unicorns and polar bears) realized for him—that, contrary to popular belief, despair-as-terror does not stand still. On the contrary, unbeknownst to the sufferer, there's what the black-hole bigwigs call an *accrual of duration* to that despair which, at its tipping point of supersaturation, overflows all at once. For the hunt's duration, he experienced a suffocating loss of contact with what he suddenly realized was his true work—his life work—the work of supplying assassin-galvanizing sensors to Post and his Third World cronies. On the other hand, he felt there was no way out of this entrapment and that he'd brought it all upon himself. So, for a split second which lasted a century his foster wife and mother (straight out of American Gothic) was *I told you so* and his stepfather and kid brother (ditto) *You're your own worst enemy.* I.e., he was both patient and agent—architect and remorseless victim of self-sabotage. But taking a page from the Asian elephants' book of life as spread out before him on the smelly sand (staring straight into Little Mac's eyes, for the first time he knew what it felt like to want to castrate, as slowly and as lovingly as possible, every last trafficker in tusks), he let himself discover that loss of contact was not necessarily a bad thing, especially for an ex-M&A man, and did not disqualify him for it—the true work—didn't make him a fearless vocation-slayer. As Eden got closer and closer—so close he could smell his breath—he realized, or began to realize, loss of connection for a spell or longer with what one does best or thinks one does best or what one may one day do best is not grounds for self-disqualification but rather the heady stuff of which refresher courses are made—the best form of connection precisely because it feels destabilizingly like disconnection, hence uncharted territory, and the experience of whose appropriation can only enrich the mother lode.

Somehow it all rings false to Herbert—all this talk about true work doesn't jive with the Borkman whose very own book of life she could swear she memorized from cover to cover as far back as Greenwich Avenue. She can't help feeling the Master's slip is showing here: He simply doesn't have the guts to depict—to even conceive of—that most glorious of all freedmen: the Man without a Project. For how would a man—a substance—like the Master (Who's never sleepwalked through a projectless—a true-work-less—day in His life) go about sending out into the world a being devoid of His most essential attribute (vocation)—or any of the others—i.e., a being that isn't just another piglet roasting on the spit of His self-love? Though in the process he might very well discover that there's plenty of austere exhilaration to be extracted from the Lessness of Less—or, more importantly, that Less can be the gateway to a More beyond His wildest dreams: matrix and generator of a true diversity of types unshackled to and unstunted by the afflictions that He pompously confuses with the building blocks of identity. Which means that as a striptease artist the Master Baiter leaves much to be desired although a case could be made for his being something of a noble failure in that department. Still, it may not be too late (or is it?) for Him to have a look at *The G-String Murders* or the novel (by Gypsy Rose Lee) on which the movie is based. But Borkman, hoarse from plying his candor, brings her back to the here and now where another Melanctha—wiser though not necessarily sadder—takes over unannounced and uninvited. *This thought*, Melanctha No. 2 observes, *is not just about recruiting the concept of vocation to build abstract castles in the air (to which purpose the concept lends itself so fawningly)—since here the "vocation" in question—illicit trafficking in sensors—has been chosen specifically for its abject incongruity. In fact the Master, to* double *business bound, is out to demonstrate that strong thoughts eagerly exploit such incongruity in order to prove their essence has less to do with content than with . . . infrastructure.*

But with Eden bearing down on him, what if it's too late, he wondered, to milk that lode? Sure, he was worried. Who wouldn't be? But it wasn't for himself. Couldn't they see he wasn't thinking about himself *at all*? He—Borkman—The Rump's errand boy—was in fact the last thing he was thinking about, at least when it came to this newfound life work. He was concerned not about defamation—worse, neglect—but about his deprivation of the masses—all the poor slobs out there who deserved to reap, and as fast as they fell, the fruits of his disemboweling labors of acumen under the sign of that work. It was them he felt for. For what would they be without an achievement like his to feed on? Nothing, that's what. *Is he unmasking a delusion of grandeur or is he dead serious?* she wonders.

And then Borkman sees his son, of all people, advancing toward him, his carrot top churning—yes, churning—in the draft from the elevator shaft. The boy pulls him (he can barely walk) toward the buffet table. "You must be famished, dad, after all you've been through." Is there something snide in the boy's tone? "The ordeal is by no means over." He's not quite sure what he means and is pleased by the uncertainty being disseminated like an aerosol chock full of deadly spores. "All the more reason you must keep up your strength." Borkman feels like—no, he is—a barge being droolingly drawn to its burial ground by a too hale-and-hearty tug replete with gumdrop-yellow sidelights and he dares anybody to say otherwise. But just as he's getting comfortable enough to try his hand at further disfiguring a sorry-looking canapé (the sort of thing that, where he hails from, used to be referred to unabashedly, and maybe still is, as a pig-in-a-blanket) his son lashes out, which is what he does best, at least where Borkman is concerned. To get the ball rolling or to sweeten the pill or to give his tantrum some borrowed gravitas, the boy invokes Molière (*take that, you old fart!*), whose Dom Juan says (in act IV, scene V, of his play by the same name) it enrages him to see fathers live as long as their sons. As far as he can gather (why does it all sound so achingly familiar and at the same time so alarmingly unexpected?) what disturbed Jason most over the years—and never more so than at this moment when he needs above all to think and shoot straight (after all, the future's at stake—not just his but humanity's)—has been not the husband's battles with his wife but the fact that in their immediate wake—and just as sonny was getting into the swing of resignation to what he hoped (in the name of stability) would become an unalterable fact of family life—they had the audacity to start cooing in the kitchen or wherever it was they'd chosen to stage their messy rapprochement—in any case, on the very spot where seconds before all had been hate, hate and hate, with just a dash of . . . hate thrown in for good measure. Business once again as usual, thereby trivializing his efforts to secrete a carapace under the auspices of utter hopelessness—now denatured by rapturous relief that the pair intended to stay together for as long as it took to put the finishing touches on a new fragrance—subvariant—mutation—elixir—outpost—of hate. Out of respect—decency, even—the boy should have taken him aside, that's clear enough. Borkman shrugs sadly, abandoning all thought of the canapé, the potential Proustian perks notwithstanding (*who is thinking this?*). What's to be said? How explain (except *by* explaining) how much—how most—how all—of the hate-play was rooted, long before they'd even met, in the demand that the wife play the uncoveted role of the adoring fan, which entailed nothing less than applauding the shrewdness of every deal long before it was even a floater in his mind's eye? (While Jason is willing, out of a misguided sense of fairness, to break down and recognize that those deal-less deals are the progenitors of his own productless product, he won't go so far—who would?—as to intone, Like father, like son, which would be to rob his parthenogenetic—his autogenous—self of all claim to spontaneously generated originality.) But not a fan so adoring as to be completely out of sync with the perspective of those who abominated said shrewdness as nothing more than flim-flam. The only way she could be wholly in his camp was by having one foot in the camp of the abominators. For how else could she serve as his conduit to the goings-on in that camp except through a simulated—or not so simulated—abomination of her own—a kind of abomination-in-training—or better yet a full-fledged abomination which as a big girl she should know how to turn on and off at will and on cue. She needed to worm her way into the enemy camp to prove, subliminally, that adoration, especially from somebody as sexy-adorable as she, was by no means incompatible with abomination. She needed to seduce them into downing her adoration in comradely draughts of shared abomination. Thereby softening—fattening—the abominators up for the kill (even if he's never quite made up his mind of what exactly such a kill, presumably conversionary, would consist).

Clearly, Borkman's taking his frustrations out on the boy's mother because he doesn't have the guts to confront Eden and his handlers head-on (so says the boy himself, which means that, minutes before, Borkman did end up anatomizing the hate-play dynamic for everybody's delectation, not just Jason's). Borkman asks how he can be expected to destroy Eden when Eden's the very son he should have had—and maybe it's still not too late. But how could that ever be? wonders Pritchard (with his x-ray ears), since Eden's reserved for adoption by none other than him and Margo. (*Whoa! Down, boy!* Pritchard realizes just in the nick of time what that adoption coup would entail. Kiddies after all being unsafe at any age have a way of bringing out the beast in mummies far and wide. The beast, that is, of bounden duty which for mummies is to compel mates [non-blood relations hence disposable—fungible—mere means to an end, a dead end] to self-cancel out, as starkly inimical to fathering—to abnegate away lickety-split—anything that's connected with—that smells of—essence—an alchemist's angelical essence which, if you must know, is the nisus of every man who's a man and not just a female snake with soggy balls—and to not just self-cancel out but to give the impression [since you never know what talent scout from MGM Venture Capital Inc. might be dreamily lurking and listening] of having self-canceled out without ever having been prompted—of having self-canceled out on the wings of their very own unvainglorious initiative without waiting to be asked—as if by virtue of jovially suicidal Papa Bear instinct. And Pritchard [a Hesiod for our time] can always smell the footsteps of that sort of executive shrike—that species of mummy—fifty miles away whether he wants to or not and he knows without necessarily liking what he knows that in the case of every such executrix worth her salt [as long as it's salt poured on the non-blood mate's self-inflicted wounds] Motherhood simply legitimates what pre-dated It by centuries—to wit, the hunger to ensure Papa Bear's inane striving for self-transmutation gets itself burned at the stake in the name of something infinitely more important; his get's—yes, his *get's*—worldly success. In the privacy of the marriage hearse the [somewhat] unspoken question is always how much is Papa willing to die within—to squash the bug of Borkmanism—to bear his own head on a silver platter—on behalf of the shrike's get who *is* a blood relation—the blood relation par excellence though excellence [to take a page from Mae West's Book of Hours] has nothing to do with it. And where gets and silver platters are concerned Margo, he's sure, is no exception even at her advanced age—i.e., custom cannot stale her infinite predictability. But at this juncture Pritchard feels a sigh coming on and before it can grow to its full height he expels it, no questions asked. Fact is, he's a bit disappointed by his self-cancellation aria because, all the impassioned irony notwithstanding [if impassioned irony is indeed what's driving it], veers much too much toward . . . congratulatory self-pity. I.e., it's less interesting than it could be because it lacks . . . opposedness—takes itself too much at face value. Whereas a Thought Packet aria of the first rank or even the second cries out for the threat of refutation—knows it's nothing if it doesn't embody/incorporate rabid opposition.) Jason retorts that a bad father cum bad husband, like a bad workman, blames his tools, and what have he and his mother ever been for Borkman but tools? Netta couldn't care less what's being said or, worse, left unspoken. It's just that there's a time and place for everything: the cockfight is being played out inches from the hot hors d'oeuvres and on a steamy night to boot.

And yet oddly enough at the very moment when (with his son doing his level best to be challengingly—searingly—unforgiving) the sneers coming hot and heavy from the peanut gallery demand to know how a son comes off treating his father so humiliatingly no matter what the old fart's crimes of commission (or, worse, omission, for hasn't most if not all of the fatherly damage been perpetrated compliments of Borkman's refusal to be anything but a businessman, which pretty much reduces to a refusal to be *anything*, which pretty much reduces to a refusal to *be*?)—at this very moment he experiences—albeit reluctantly, serendipitously—the birth pangs of a father's hunger to protect. Whatever the motive, he's suddenly The Father—and knows for a brute fact that he's making like a real father because the making doesn't resemble in the least any of his makings past. So what if it's only in response to the claims of the moment—social claims, having nothing to do with Jason, per se, *but which*—or rather, *and which for that very reason*—call for an affirmation of fatherhood, hence—and, far more painfully—of beinghood, with the concomitant terror, offered at no extra charge, of being sucked in further—of being obliged to make this act of making like a father the very first in a long line? So just in the nick of time, self-hate promises to take over by disqualifying him for fatherhood—he begins to hate himself almost as much as the members of his family, including the Wall Street family, have seen fit to hate him. Always ultimately for his own good, of course. For even if he hasn't done a single thing but *think* this generous outburst of paternality—make that *paternaptitude*, Borkman realizes he is already expecting massive indemnifications (block-chainable currency to be determined), i.e., massive overvaluations from all directions, upon—by the time of—his re-entry into the real world from the realm of unbridled wishful thinking. He expects that by the time of re-entry: (*a*) the tiny interval covered by this appeasive fathering stint—boiling down to a mere thinking which has yet to metamorphose into a stint—will have constituted just what the witch doctors ordered to render the overvaluations plausible; (*b*) the briefest of absences from the scene of his predations on behalf of a son who is neither wayward nor prodigal will have worked its magic—will have found a way to stand in (but only in his own mind, the cesspool where he's already a legend worthy of nothing less than Dirty Harry Callahan's gritted-teeth brand of revulsive reverence) for—do duty as—centuries of fatherly self-mortification; and (*c*) enough time will have elapsed to scumble his opprobrium (*scumble his opprobrium!* who does this pipsqueak think he is? Doctor Faustus's brother-in-law?) and allow a [quote] window of opportunity [unquote] to open on a new sort of celebrity. (So what if it's a celebrity built mainly on the morbid curiosity of those huddled masses *starved* for curiosity—curiosity about how, in this case, careerist scum such as he managed to take the heroic plunge into . . . contemplating the possibility of, at some point in the not-too-distant future, standing up for his son?) That he can think in terms of indemnification for doing what should come naturally proves him, of course, to be a turd. Never mind. Self-hate will make him pay his way to fleabag purity. Hell, he may very well, in return for the exhausting labor of all this contemplation as self-contemplation, end up punditizing at some Finance Channel talkathon (at the invitation of, say, super-pudgy Lou Dobbs Ferry or self-proclaimed Dapper Dan look-alike Larry Cuddlelow), his acumen chiseled through so much brute survivalism on and off the yard. Brute survival which, as the sheerest form of shamelessness, puts the antics of the biggest, brightest porn stars . . . to shame.

The moment for fatherhood has passed. Now—*and forever.* (By any chance does this codetta embalm a sneaky bid for unearned poignancy on the part of a Master increasingly at the end of his rope?) The peanut gallery is coming round—the groundlings are no longer sneering. In fact, they're warming up to the boy's tirade—a tirade on behalf of boys of all ages—and they predictably go nuts when he tells Borkman he's all washed up and that if he knows what's good for him he'll make way for the kind of crooks who at the drop of an algorithm can transform volatility into the biggest asset in their portfolio.

Only what should happen at the very moment of his accepting or at least perceiving just what a monster he's been—a monster, however, with the not inconsiderable saving grace of aching to turn in the badge of his humanhood—the badge of the quintessential crooked cop—at the first opportunity— Only what should happen, I say, after some upstart (the most boorish-looking of the lot and the sort who'd rather be damned than let these father-son antics—no matter how much of an Old Testament wallop [make that a Balanchine's *Prodigal Son*-type wallop] they pack—deter him from raiding the buffet table) asks Borkman (politely, he has to admit—even too politely—the furthest thing from boorishly in fact) if he wouldn't mind letting him get by—only what should happen but that, to comply, Borkman reorients his squash elbow (hasn't played in years) and by so doing becomes rehumanized in spite of himself—falls in love *again* (even if it's never happened, notwithstanding the all too many missed opportunities) with the very humanhood he was just about to sell off for a pittance to the first comer. There are some gestures that humanize (and so what if they ultimately turn out to be false alarms?) and others that de-. And this squashed [*sic*] elbow gesture, a humanizer to the core, has had the good sense, no matter how reluctant Borkman appeared to be about executing it, not to take no for an answer.

Watching from the sidelines (*until further notice, the sidelines is everything that is* not *the case*), Shearer is reminded—when isn't she?—of Balanchine (*Him again*, fake-fumes one of the Master's arch-criticasters, who'd like nothing better than to get Him skewered as one of the biggest fruits on the nuttiest of Carmen Miranda's top hats[85]), specifically *The Prodigal Son* (yes, *him* again), only this Jason character—this self-styled non-prodigal—doesn't have the decency, or better yet the ingenuity, to crawl on his hands and knees to beg forgiveness. She looks around: the gawkers are not unworthy of the vast chorus which concludes the first act of Donizetti's *Anna Bolena* (her sixth lover was a countertenor) and whose members agree, though each would like nothing better than to turn inward the cries of outraged sorrow, to adapt them to the beat of the collective heart. In the present case, the heart's a vacillating one (since right this minute it's beating as hard as it can for . . . Borkman!). Continuing what has become a one-woman campaign against bad taste and related smut, Netta gives the buffet table (which, considering the number of roles it's being required to assume, intends to join Actors' Equity ASAP) a whopping piece of her mind. Call her old-fashioned but she strongly disapproves of airing dirty family laundry in public.

"Dad, hate to say it, but you're so *not-going-to-exit-the-sixteenth-century-any-time-soon*." (Why this compulsion among the youngish? Herbert wonders—and the wondering makes her feel alternately old-and-wise and just plain old—to stretch out denigrative adjective phrases following the adverbial "so" to the crack of doom. What does it mean and where did it come from and where is it going? Clearly it's more than, like, just a means of, like, sidestepping all sorts of precious time consuming syntactical labors). Borkman, back from the wars and feeling faint, looks around for a chair. The dangers notwithstanding, fact is, he misses the fresh air of the zoo. And, by the way, is it too much to ask of Melanctha, as the Master's ace reporter, that she devise a newsworthy thing or two to say about him—specifically about the atypical faintness? (*Who is perpetrating this verbal stalking and against which of Melanctha's proxies?*) And surely she's had enough time to come up with something a little less abstract on the subject of his ostensible true work—his life work—his vocation—than all the portentous jabbering which caused such a stir a few dog-eared pages back. There's doubtless plenty of further food for mass-marketable thought (*a*) about how a vocation—any vocation—just wouldn't fit him—or rather, a guy like him—to a T (although all he's just been through may have transformed him into a perfect fit) or, even better, (*b*)

---

[85]Impossible undertaking, my dear Mr. He-Man von Dickhead, for the simple reason that Masters are neither homo- nor heterosexual: they're plighted, by trade, to Dis-ori-entation.

about how the experimental application to a guy like Borkman of the novel concept of a non-fit—specifically *a constitutive, congenital, chronic, character-ological non-fit*—lurking on the very edge of plausibility—might be made to yield hefty narrative dividends and end up constituting somebody's—or Some Body's—supreme coup after so many years waiting in the wings for the star of the show to sprain His ankle while slitting His wrists. So, Melanctha wonders, is she to become the servant of not one but two masters (which would mean, among other things, that for neither could the *m* be upper-cased)? Only she's at a loss for words and doesn't have the wherewithal to spray or stain or strafe him with such bilge. Maybe her incompetence, if incompetence it is, can be chalked up to the not-so-simple failure of her reach to exceed her grasp— call it an anomaly of cognitive Brownian motion—or maybe it's just that the Borkman-vocation dynamic has reached the still point of indescribability—of unfitness for words. And you want to know something else? Fact is, in either case, she's glad. And even gladder that she can leave him intact en route to well-earned collapse in a lounge chair.

Cantor has little choice but to Envy the young bucks—it's his civic duty— so self-assured in the overlapping realms of both entrepreneurship and het- erosexuality—so *very* self-assured that it's hard to say, much less determine, where the heterosexuality ends and the entrepreneurship begins. It's not the one or the other but the welding of the two that's so alluring. Although it shouldn't be—so alluring, he means—since his own novitiate is coming along rather nicely—not quite the slapdash thing of shreds and patches it was at the beginning. Pritchard has certainly been doing his level best to provide the most comprehensive crash course in his field of expertise this side of the Santa Ynez Mountains. Thing is, Cantor's still having trouble nailing what it is precisely that Pritchard does in what he's come to call his off hours since most of the day appears to be spent parrying the improper advances of the LAPD. Maybe being kept in the dark until further notice is a big part of what that expertise is all about. But there's no denying he's picked up more than just a thing or two about the ways and means of leadership. In fact, considering what he's been made to absorb, Cantor can only wonder how he survived the early stages, impatient as he's always been to ingest everything there is to ingest of a given discipline—to consume and make it part and parcel—no, the very thew and sinew—of his substance—in a single gulp. How did he manage to shoulder the heft of his impatience, grit his teeth against the premonitory weight of ignorance of everything he had yet to learn—against the embar- rassment of the infinite riches to come—when he knew that a mere twist of fate could cut him off from any further appropriation? But why the hunger to ingest everything at once rather than linger long on the road to mastery— like a real Master—basking in the toxic bliss of privation? Well, Berry Sundae always said he was incapable of lingering—at *anything*—not just high brunch in some soon-to-be-trendy Bank Street sidewalk bistro. Then it's not at all unlikely, he acknowledges (grateful that basic training hasn't robbed him of the lost art of musing), that mastery of lingering may very well be a prereq- uisite for heterosexuality, which makes him yet again his own worst enemy. Though he wouldn't have it any other way since a self that isn't its own worst enemy is no self at all—*That's an order.*

He gasps. Scattered among the young bucks are several who aren't as young as all that, that is, if they've had no choice but to age at the same rate as he, and scattered among these are the spittin' images of quite a few best friends (discovered predictably in retrospect to have been heartily detestable all down the line)—some of blissless childhood, some of even more blissless adolescence and some of a surprisingly blissful young manhood almost yet not quite straight out of *Studs Lonigan*. But in fact all together (the old looks, notwithstanding the latex too lavishly applied, haven't changed a bit) they deploy for his inspection the biomarkers—the biomarksmanship—of every single one of his Ages of Man, even those not yet traversed. Why, over there near the men's room who should be loitering satyrically but at least a dozen of his pre-Berry Sundae lovers and a little to their right and behind who should be studiously sucking in their paunch as if this ploy will tip the scale in their favor but four or five comely-coed-obsessed blowhards who competed with him, a mere gay blade with no family responsibilities, for some measly associate professorship (unsuccessfully as it turned out) and who from the look of 'em still have no intention of forgiving his having yanked the food out of their kiddies' mouth. Is he to be tried by a so-called jury of his peers? Have they been flown in to serve as the guarantors of his ineligibility for every perk of the trade except long-overdue comeuppance? (This is a legitimate—a plausible— concern—in fact, the answer seems obvious—so why isn't his inner-speech more declarative—more forceful?) But he can't help wondering (indeed, from the countertenorish sound of him you'd think he was Master-abducted Herbert) if it mightn't be a bit late in the day to start, with so little provocation, introducing all these extras. Forgetting about the cost of getting them out here first class, could they really be such vital determinants of his fate and by extension the fate of the trial? Though inasmuch as it's suddenly become clear that the Amygdala *fiasco* (too facile, or maybe just apotropaic, to use that word this early in the game) consists of not one but a multitude of trials (all, why not admit it? at cross-purposes), which one is he referring to? He didn't think Pritchard could be so timorous—so unsure of himself—as to require that Cantor be assessed by a tribunal of so many unaccredited nincompoops. But he tries to look on the bright side and wallow in his notoriety—clearly somebody thinks his rise has been nothing less than "meteoric" and poses enough of a threat to the public weal to require their services. And what if they disagree—won't that create even more trouble for him and his board of directors? Before Cantor can finish his dish of . . . what is it exactly? lentil stew? yes! (and, doubtless, exactly the kind of slop with which Jacob deadened poor Ishmael's faculties against an injustice not unlike, come to think of it, the one about to be perpetrated), he finds himself rubbing elbows with a too-tall Brunhilde (and is more than disquieted by the sneering nostrils and the pencil-thin pout capped by five o'clock shadow) so in self-defense, Your Honor, almost spills the stew all over her. But what does *more than disquieted* actually come to in the world of feeling and even if it comes to absolutely nothing why should he be nothing'd by just the sort of secondary sexuals which in a normal man with even more normal needs?—Cantor's not being one, by any stretch of the imagination, is irrelevant since he never gives up hope of a sea change—would induce frenzied desire. She could from the look of her be one of any number of things, simultaneously, if necessary: a placebo-taker (why is it that nobody in his group has ever seen one?); or one of those first-woman-ever start-up camel-drivers (a best-of-both-worlds cross between, say, Elizabeth Holmes and Melissa Mayer) he's always reading about whether he wants to or not—the kind of layoff queen who prefers the term *remix* if you don't mind; or better yet, a doctoral student in sexopharmacology whose fieldwork up at the bunker is being inflicted on a select group of trial subjects all of whom have a sneaking suspicion their pet Leeuwenhoek warrants around-the-clock monitoring far more than they do. But whatever she may turn out to be, he places her immediately as not Brundee but Tina (all right, not immediately but fairly quickly—no mean feat amid all this greasy tumult), the wallflower whom he escorted (pink corsage in tow), in yet another slapstick stab at self-rehabilitation, to the senior prom. She smiles ferociously or is this just her way of being sheepish? Does this mean that at last she's recognized him—the oafish imp who once-upon-a-twilight-dreary dutifully dragged a rented tux and tails out of the closet while remaining oh so very deep within it and then went on, predictably, to renege on every implicit cornball promise he, as her cornball dreamboat, was expected to fulfill? No, the fact of non-recognition becomes instantly and blessedly irrefutable, though it could be she's simply a skilled fellator of, in this case, the dick of his presumed infinitely extensible credulity and as such may prove invaluable to Post in some capacity to be determined at the next shareholders meeting. Though he'd be nuts to bank (knowing full well from dealing with too many bilious colleagues that the expectation of consistency is madness) on her not taking it into her head to re-bare her fangs and this time force him to cushion, with all the social graces at his disposal, what will have turned out to be the definitive shock of recognition. Simply because Brundee-Tina just permitted him to hit a single in the incognito department doesn't mean he'll be wangling a double any time soon. (*Cantor,* he lamentingly murmurs, *exactly what's gotten into you? Imagine, ruthlessly digging your spurs into a metaphor from the world of sports, of all places, riding it for all it's worth, on the off chance that this poor—rather, this* destitute—*man's version of an ex-prom queen can make a man, if not a he-man, of you yet.*) The long and the short of it is that his naïveté (like a cipher in a number, its importance depends on the figure it's united with[86]) isn't in the market for mistaking one measly reprieve for the patented generator of an infinite sequence.

But even if she hasn't recognized him, how avoid being floored by the fact that the very woman whose first ball he wrecked is once again closely observing her wrecker doing exactly the thing he does worse than any other man, namely, acting human. Scooping up his Old Testament offal in such a way as to avoid spilling a single drop on his clothes or hers constitutes a confession that surpasses, in sheer hideousness, his prom night folly. In so scooping he's given Tina (he can see it in her eyes) the opportunity to loathe

---

[86]See Henry James, "The Lesson of the Master."

him in his generality, as an animal at feed—the general animal that is and yet is very much not he. And whereas loathing limited to his specificity has always managed to leave him with some shred of intactness, this kind annihilates him completely. It takes some time but is well worth the wait: for once de-annihilated, Cantor realizes Tina is in fact Mary (or maybe it's the realizing that's effected his de-annihilation, or is this just another Masterly tic of word-flow getting into the act—exactly the way Jimmy Durante [Who's he?—He's before your time—no, make that *before everyboy's time*] would have predicted it would)—Mary, not Tina—Mary Johnstone, to be precise—and since he's now back in the business of realizing, why not also realize—and accept—that Berry Sundae—worse, Berry's pronunciation—is no longer around to icily italicize an all-American proper name of this stripe, and thereby attenuate the strange power wielded by its very unremarkability? Berry's take on the name is no longer around to fend off the nausea its utterance induces. For the name fiddles while Cantor burns—every time it's uttered it creates and celebrates (while Cantor mourns) the gap between what Mary really is and what the aura conferred by the name on this most unauratic of beings (remember the pencil-thin pout beneath the five o'clock shadow? though isn't something so weird-sisterly the very stuff of aura?) says she is—an aura that's everywhere and localizable nowhere. The name (a lukewarm fan at best of Cukor's remake of *A Star Is Born*) insists that the "something extra" which justifies its non-being is very much there for the taking by those with eyes to hear and ears to see. And the name is right—the something extra *is* there. It's the gap and nothing but the gap—which comes into being every time the name is called on to work its rough magic. Speaking her full name is therefore sheerest torture since Cantor doesn't like gaps—gets no mileage out of them—especially those that open and shut like the cuntlike jaws of a mugger crocodile. Of course if push comes to shove it can be uttered in such a way as to demonstrate he doesn't swallow the pretense it embodies, being faster on the draw than the fast one it's trying to pull. His pronunciation—his naming as pronouncement—will constitute an *outing* (the definitive version) of everybody else's credulity and once he squelches the name she won't be able to make any more trouble, whatever her credentials as corsage-carrying wallflower. Like Cantor (according to his mother having one of her fits), she's *nothing but trouble.* Clearly it's the name that gives her license to put one over on everybody. Indeed, *the name is the license*—or is what we have here just Great Synonymy-mongering of the worst sort? But in this case, there's no connection—no till-death-do-us-part fusion—between name and bearer—a fusion any bearer worth his salt grows into well before the puberty of toddlerhood. *With the fusion between name and bearer in place, there's no need for the mumbo-jumbo of auras.* (If there's any justice in the world, this little jingle will one day find itself in *Bartlett's*, Cantor suspects.) She never earned the name, by the sweat of her brow—never achieved the dizzying freedom to call herself by the name already imposed. If she's Mary Johnstone then he's Benito Mussolini. Tina, yes. Brunhilde (with a little practice), maybe. Actually, she's Brunhilde von Schmutz De Reilly if she's a day, at least for now. She didn't do her Christian duty—which was to transmogrify the name imposed on her from without (by somebody acting out a defiant fantasy of *self-normalization* based on whatever normalization meant within the context of his *milieu intérieur*—somebody suturing him- or herself through the self-normalizing imposition of the name—somebody suturing her or his fissuredness to death)—which was to transmogrify the self-normalizing name imposed on her from without into an organic thing emergent from within. So that it would only be through the auspices of the name as gatekeeper that a bumpkin like him could step right up and massage the clitoral bump of her being—yes, *the clitoral bump* (he'll take a bump over a gap any day of the week). And Cantor surely understands how tempting havoc-wreaking normalization can be. But inasmuch as normalization often (like, say, a Ruger .380 with laser sights and loaded with hollow-point bullets) gets into the wrong hands (this being one of the problems with normalization, and by no means the biggest), Cantor is still learning how to steer clear of it. In fact, as Pritchard's heir apparent, he's promised himself to make it his first order of business, once elected, to shortcircuit any collusion of patients (in whatever arm or stage of the trial they may happen to have fallen feet first) with normalization mongers. For hasn't Pritchard always stood—though how on such short acquaintance, even if the sorcerer/apprentice relationship has speeded things up tremendously, should he know what Pritchard has *always* stood for?—for an incessant interrogation—Guantanamoesque in its conscienceless rigor—of normalization. Hasn't he always been (and not just because of his proclivities) for keeping it under lock and key no matter what the professional consequences, except in the few cases where it's sure to inflict more good than harm?

He can feel her gaze eating into the back of his neck—plowing toward the promised land of the jugular. But when he turns around to fight back there's a momentary surge of sexualized interest on Mary's part—still no recognition, thank heaven, but *interest*—in what promises to be yet another cut-and-dried case of the shy smittenness of post-adolescence with its own drooling lust. Maybe he's just undergone another one of those embarrassing outbreaks of maleness (traceable to the almost pugilistic intentness of his raid on the buffet table: hell, he was famished) which flying in the face of all past evidence to the contrary, he instinctively insists—has insisted—on confusing with the onset of heterosexuality (*self-delusion is a powerful aphrodisiac:* more fodder for *Bartlett's*). So hers is an honest mistake. He needs to explain (otherwise she might destroy him: isn't that what she was sent here to do?) that he doesn't now nor did he ever desire her. Nothing personal, of course. But only a jackass ends up actually doing what he thinks he needs to do. He can't believe he's just started to explain that he has a sort of . . . affliction. He immediately realizes, however (from the way she snortingly turns her back on him: at least he's rid of her for now), as he's realized so many times before, that as far as the Tina Brunhilde Johnstones of the world are concerned you're deviant whatever you do, or don't do—whatever your *orientation*, you—yes, you!—by your very presence on the scene, are an arrant trespasser on the terrain of her flawlessness, and the more you protest against the verdict at the core of her quick perception or even cheer it on (though of course it's never the right kind of cheering or if it is, well then, the volume of rightness simply isn't being pumped up high enough), the closer you get to signing your own death warrant. And he knows a thing or two about death warrants, being an honorary member of the LGBTQ bloc. You would think he'd have already learned—even if he's come to believe (anointment however provisional having gone to his already swelled head) he has nothing more to learn—that, at least with the overwhelming majority of men, taking a step back to explain yourself away as the product of a disease afflicting, if you must know, norms and non-norms alike, does not put you outside its pale. The very need to explain is just another one of your disease-engendered deficits—maybe (or is this going to be just another episode in the award-winning miniseries *Wordflow Trumps the Blue-tail Fly?*) the biggest deficit of them all—a deficit *even bigger* (*Stop right there, wordflow, you're going too far!*) than the disease itself. In fact, it's all this explaining that identifies you—yes, you!—as the worst kind of incurable—one who's to be avoided at all costs. But maybe she simply doesn't matter—she's not here to look him over—and if he plays his cards right (even if he hates games of all sorts—except for highbrow Wittgensteinian language games but even they, when push comes to shove . . .) he'll have no further truck with her. Or maybe she's a pussycat and stopped by simply because (living in the neighborhood) she heard there'd be plenty of free food—sort of like that chunky old broad at Tanglewood (at least that's how dad speculatively depicted her) with whom his mother struck up a birds-of-a-feather-type conversation the night (mid-July 1963) when Erich Leinsdorf conducted and Rudolf Serkin's wrists of steel performed Beethoven's Fourth Piano Concerto—the greatest, if not by far then by *near*, of the mighty five. Yes, *dad*—his father—the same guy who, in the great tradition of American Jews, could never bring himself to call, say, Howard Johnson's [restaurant and motor lodge] Howard Johnson's for that would have been an affront to the sort of names he was used to (and about which, by the way, he was equally ambivalent), which then left him with little choice but to do some ethnic uncleansing and come up (ritualistically, Maestro) with . . . Howard Johnsberg's!

Margo is calling him. Seems he's wanted pronto back at the buffet, which is now doubling as a conference table (another last straw making its application for AEA citizenship even more pressing): Cantor is one of the big boys now and his services, whatever they may turn out to be, are urgently required. But he's still very much undone by Johnstone's having mistaken his revulsion for lust. Is her reproachful stare (and who more entitled than she, as the newly appointed toxic thread running through his life's daily grind, to wield so deadly a weapon with or without a background check)—is the stare meant to convey shock at his having nauseously dared to overstep the bounds of good taste? Such a thing would never be permitted in, say, Sun Valley or Davos. When he turns to take one last look at his prom queen (maybe it's she who'll be casting the determining vote), Mary—no, *Tina*! (she'll always be Tina just as Bogie and Bergman will always have Paris)—when he turns to look, Mary-no-*Tina*, sprawled in an Adirondack chair, is chewing what underground filmmakers refer to (when nobody else is listening) as the hectic cud of closed-eye thoughts. Jean is jabbering frantically *at* those thoughts but the more she jabbers, the more she solidifies—such being the dialectic in play (see above) where the Tina Brunhilde Johnstones of the world are concerned—the jabbered-at's conception of herself as simply too World Economic Forum-lofty to acknowledge even the distant echo of such jabber. After so many trailings behind Caro down St. Mark's Place, you'd think Jean, kept under wraps in a shocking-pink muumuu, would have learned her lesson but the Jeans of the world will never learn and she—or rather the world—won't have it any other way. Since in any dyad worth its salt, there's got to be the one who solicits and the one who loftily resists solicitation. Ethan looks in her direction from time to time, unseeing (he's got too much—too many warring agencies—on his mind). Tina is doing everything she can to distance herself from her stalker (only there's nobody to watch her do it—the POV goes unclaimed) without relinquishing the connection outright since she knows it serves—can be made to serve—some purpose. So she takes a stab (it may lead to something, maybe even a booking in some dinner theater on Route 66) at adopting an absentminded look of disgust targeting everybody, herself included. *Herself included* (the words, like all the words hereabouts, are as usual having an unsupervised field day: seeing to it that sensationalism trumps sense—horse sense, that is). But the POV still goes a-begging.

Jean gets her big break: she's able to give up ass-kissing *inconspicuously* and save face since Tina is now semi-surrounded by what looks—look—to Cantor (pitching in as resident camera-eye by claiming the POV nobody wanted—that is, until he claimed it) like rabid, or at the very least avid, fans until he realizes that treating her as they're doing with the same contempt she lavished on Jean only minutes before, they aren't fans at all (although fans are an odd lot and often smell more like detractors—more like the British than the Brits themselves). In fact, they're figures from his dark past *or a past that isn't dark enough by half* (*who is speaking and what exactly is the payload of his creaky insinuation?*). Though why can't they be both fans *and* figures—on the order of, say, the Prunes and Prisms in *Little Dorrit* (that novel about, among other things, Borkman's great-grandfather, John Gabriel Merdle)— conscripted to bring his confirmation hearings to a sorry end by making some nasty allegations to the effect that given *what he is and will always be* Cantor poses a threat not just to the young and the very old, etc.)?

He tries to *drift away* (even if it's not his forte), preferring (pardonably, he thinks) to meet them under more controlled conditions, even if this should entail the presence of a court reporter charged with archiving their every slander. Once it becomes ever so clear that not only have they recognized him but they are conferring on how best to bury the hatchet in that very-much-in-demand jugular of his, Cantor sees no point in delaying the required effusions. The man standing next to no-longer-deviant Leo is none other than Maxim Soul who deals with the awkwardness of the moment of reunion by making a skullcap of his palms and shaking from side to side. In disbelief? as a pretense thereof? as a mockery of Cantor's belief in that pretense? Who knows? Who'll ever know? Learn to live with uncertainty, a voice intones, and you'll be unlucky enough to grow as old as Methuselah.

CHAPTER THIRTY-NINE

Pritchard and Margo, sporting a pair of unctuously complacent his-and-her grins hot off the mismarriage-hearse assembly line, come running over at once, evidently with a view to forearming him. They kiss. In unison. Or rather a kiss *befalls* them, however implausibly. And as Eden's proxy Cantor is duty bound to arraign it as a desecration—worse, the disparagement (implausibility is no excuse)—of a much loftier specimen, namely, the kiss (Eden has frequently babbled about Madison Square while pretending to sleepwalk, poor guy) that never was and never will be. "Just imagine, your friends so-called (who've been flown out here, all expenses paid, as part of the confirmation procedure)—" Cantor hears his own intake of breath. "—have been trying ever since they got here to paint you—" Another, even more audible intake. "Tar and feather is more like it" (Margo at her Eve-Ardenesque best). She's clearly impatient with—irked by—Pritchard's "paint." And with the shovel of her dismissiveness (which he's duty bound to do more than just deprecate or dread—which he's duty bound to roundly ram down her mockingbird's throat and not remove until he hears a death rattle, that is, if he has any balls up his sleeve) she's attempting to imprison—embalm—cast him in an archetypal Commedia dell'arte mold, specifically that of the too, too soft-hearted or simply obtuse overdomesticated male. "—trying to paint you" (Pritchard stands by his obtuseness and in so doing—he's his own Fidelio—sets himself forever free) "as a pretentious asshole—sorry, a horse's ass—and now they know you're being groomed for successor-generalship they're laying it on even thicker." (So *paint*—as a metaphor's best friend—was the right choice after all!) "Their only recourse is to demand to know how, if you're like the rest of them, you dare aspire to something great and therefore way too wide of their modest mark. So if there's something in your past—taped locker-room banter dating back to 2005, say—that sets you apart—something dark and frightening that gave you access to a world beyond their ken and has thereby prepared you superbly for active participation in ours—then cough it up, cough it up, so I can defend you against every last one of 'em and their puny handlers. Something—no matter how small or how shocking—that at the same time can account for the outsize faith I've placed in you. I might as well tell you that the CCC (Confirmations and Credentials Committee), comprising, by the way, most of the venture capitalists on the loose here tonight, are highly conservative and, as such, easily swayable by the sort of lowdown drivel academics like your friends (not one tenured radical among 'em!) can be depended on to spew in spades." Should he come out—way out—to Pritchard? Has he *already* come out and have both of them forgotten that milestone? or suppressed the information so as to keep alive Pritchard's hope that he'll be passing on the mantle to a straightman (even if he himself isn't) who, as a consequence of being straight, can be counted on to disseminate his teachings to a much wider public? Or has he, by any chance, come out to somebody else who's decided, with a discretion all too rare nowadays (but why just nowadays?), to keep it—the whole mess—under wraps?

Even if his (statistically) aberrant sexuality, Cantor explains, was always on display for those with eyes to see, his rivals cast a blind eye to their own perspicacity, not wanting to be lessoned that the ensuing *marginalization* might be just the sort of thing—like madness (he remembers Eden fondly at this mini juncture)—to give somebody a grandiose edge on the competition. They didn't want to know he had a saving dark side—redeeming dark sides aplenty—because they also knew (from erudite hearsay) that dark sides were both an infinite resource and a prod to infinite resourcefulness—a gift horse that keeps on giving—and maybe, just maybe, ample justification for the kind of grandiosity he cultivates through no fault of his own as if it were Candide's garden. But armed with that marginalization (knowing a good thing when he saw it), he's consecrated himself, even if mathematics is the queen (!) of the sciences, to the search for coronation in a domain infinitely beyond. So in the matter of grandiosity, unwarranted or otherwise, the little putzes are right on the money (does WASPish Pritchard know the meaning of *putzes* or at least of the less immodest *putz*? if not, it may still be deducible from the context since, as that merry old soul Lear once said, Context is All). They hid their Envy (it's from them he caught the bug in the first place) behind a mask of jovial bafflement at the grandiosity but made it a point never to look him full in the face when doing their invidious utmost to demolish the resolve it generated (they're the ones, by the way, who should be slurping down Invidicum by the gallon: any on hand, Doc?). Each wanted it known that compliments of scholarly absorption in solving what would some day be known as the Cantor Problem he was light-years beyond anything even remotely resembling Envy. And if they got exasperated at these outmoded faustian strivings, it was *on Cantor's behalf*. Both Pritchard and Margo are enthralled (she's harder to please—doesn't want Cantor's skill as an analyst to get in the way of her own insight—which is considerable, even definitive, in fact very much in the pièce de resistance—the showstopper—mode—but we'll get to that in a minute). In fact, they hope—each in his own way—the recital will never come to a bad end. Cantor (knowing he has his audience in the palm of his mind) continues willingly: *And so it came to pass* that when these Job's comforters delivered their final scholarly verdict with all the not-so-scholarly virulent hatred at their disposal (you can't blame Cantor for going all Old Testament on us when tainted by thoughts about his soul brother Job)—with an obscene desire to crush their rival (which was their trademark family resemblance)—the very same exasperation *on his behalf* weighed in. OK, so maybe it was just a wee bit on their own behalf for surely they deserved better than to be afflicted by this unavowable fascination with his unfocused strivings, which they felt obliged as scholars to make a pretense of dissecting. But they didn't want anybody to think it was hatred when they were simply expressing—to an interlocutor buried deep in their mind's eye—shock, awash with compassion, at how talentlessness so massive could come to imagine itself anointable. And shock at having to deliver the bad news to the sufferer who had no idea he was suffering and would probably need to be put on a lifetime maintenance dose of soul-saving deflation. And as for the dollop or two of compassion, that bonus was not just for him but for the taxpayer, since who else did he think was subsidizing his delusional thinking. So this mess of an epiphenomenon had off-kiltering repercussions not just for him, not just for them, but for Mother Nature herself. They were forever asking that Incredible Shrinking Man in their mind's eye how a fall guy like him, inferior by every criterion of demiurgic excellence, could nurture such aspirations, whose sole claim to credibility was vagueness. At the same time Cantor through thick and thin still wanted to be normal (Pritchard and Margo are more enthralled than ever) or, more importantly, to be *seen* as normal, sexually attracted as he was to the imago their well-meant tough-loving career denigration had cobbled together. Many a time in fact he was tempted to ask where he could get one just like it on the Internet. On Amazon? at Doppelganger.com? GolemGoodies.edu? Some disreputable third-party seller? Many a time, especially on chilly autumn nights, he was tempted—not just tempted but sorely tempted—to cook up a normalization stew (*please, Waiter! do go easy on the lentils*) and serve it to his detractors with all the trimmings. Only he didn't have the recipe—nobody did. Not even Stanley Ellin's Sbirro, patron saint of lamb Amirstan (delectable but an acquired taste). Then he remembered they already took him for a good old normal—one of their own—for which dispensation he was paying a pretty hefty price. This being the case, surely Pritchard and Margo could understand the temptation to throw caution to the winds and expose his . . . darkness—as the armature of a very special destiny—even if revelation would still straitjacket him, albeit a bit differently, with this crowd of crypto chefs whose specialty of the house was begrudgement, steamed, seared, strained, stirred and stultified. "So what it all boils down to for a guy like you when you're around guys like them is," Margo merrily enlightens (and why shouldn't she be merry since at last she's in her element: imperishable insight [as invoked above]?), "*whether queerdom or mediocrity turns out to be the tighter straitjacket*. In their eyes, you couldn't be both straight and great." And who should know better than Margo herself. Margo—who's lived both straight and crooked, Liberace gay and DiMaggio glum. He's tempted to wonder out loud before going a step further whether a paradox worthy of Bertrand Russell is not (all tied up in *nots* is what he is and will remain) half-buried in the morass of such a predicament. Thing is, he's scared that such a wondering act will stink to high heaven of self-congratulation.

"So it's sexuality that's my billion-dollar baby." Cantor suddenly observes there are no windows in this sub-basement. At least it seems that way.

"Come again?"

"And again? No worry—my practice is always to do so. Sorry, tasteless joke. It's my sexuality that provides the dark access you, as my mentor, seem to be clamoring for—*and dreading at the same time*." Margo looks at her man, as if to say, Don't blame me if this Kid from Brooklyn has your shilly-shallying down pat. "You know, the dog-eat-dog variety which is always being described so graphically—much too *methinks-the-gentleman-doth-protest-too-much* graphically, if you ask me—by PRick Santorum, for example, and other card-carrying members of the mainstream lunatic fringe. Who cover their tracks by making it a first order of business to father forth at least ten kids, never imagining, of course, since they're always being caught up short (is that the right expression?) in the imagination department, except concerning what's happening in a certain walk-in closet of that department—never imagining that one—or even ten—of the ten may turn out to be one of the dog-eat-doggers."

Seeing the look of disappointment on Pritchard's face (Margo's is touchingly unreadable), Cantor flounders. Does he have too little dark access, or is the problem one of overqualification? On this occasion, one of the few where he hasn't flubbed his lines (come off it, wordflow—when has Cantor *ever* flubbed his lines?), he hoped for something more than stark underappreciation. While Cantor hates availing himself of doubletalk, the last refuge of scoundrels (*Breaking News:* it's just unseated patriotism), he has no choice but to hear himself say, "Well, maybe I was wrong—maybe what gives me my deepest darkest secret access is the most unnatural crime of all—this obscene lusting after solitude, the inability to crave the warmth of other humans. After the death of Berry Sundae—I mean Gilles, my lover—" Margo appears antsy—she looks around—the conference, or the conference table (né buffet), is calling them. "Yes, we know. It's all in your file." Is it also in his file that Gilles bore a striking resemblance to his namesake in the Watteau painting (hanging on the most inobtrusive wall in all of the Met)? Cantor hopes not—good to know there's something inaccessible to the filers. "I tended to exploit my inconsolability, which must mean I wasn't all that inconsolable. Fact is, while I lived in constant fear of his death, his presence—his presentness—generated the most overpowering feeling of estrangement. There was no unhappy medium. My minute-to-minute connectedness took the ungainly form of a hunger to flee for I felt nothing whatsoever for this stranger—nothing *whatsoever.*" The italics didn't bring Margo back. "I was estranged from (but no stranger to) myself. For focusing on the inevitable imperfections, bodily and otherwise." He's trying to make himself interesting. "Looking back I can't imagine how I ever managed to cast aside that obscene lusting long enough to be able to live as close as I did to another human being, one who, as it turns out, was too good for me. But like Edmund Bertram, late of *Mansfield Park*—that is, the rest of humankind—I didn't mind in the least having what was too good for me."

Pritchard (*in a sensuous whisper*): "So what you're trying to say—"

"What I'm most definitely saying—"

"—is that solitudinousness (if there is such a word) constitutes your crime of choice against unnatural nature."

"My closet's a portable solitude." Or is this just another case of the words talking—meaning—without his permission to so talk, so mean? He senses this is happening more and more—*the closer he gets to Envy-cure.* Or is this yet another case of the words' getting drunk enough on their own unstoppability to create a correlation that's made to hold water even if it doesn't so as to give the illusion that the trial—the story of the trial—is a coherent one—rife—overrun—with relevant detail? Because if anything turns out to be *ir*relevant it will mean nothing less than that this—this—this—isn't a trial or a story at all but some sort of Mulligan anti-stew into which the chef throws everything in sight out of his story-sabotaging fear of leaving something out. Because if anything gets wind of being left out it will waste no time in posing a big threat. In what way? Can't answer that yet, Cantor tells himself, especially with the two lovebirds breathing down my neck. (Looked at awry they resemble, not a little, crabby bedraggled Fox News go-to-ghouls Joseph DiGeneva and Victoria Toensling—unfortunately for Cantor, there's no shuddering away this cheesy anamorphotic feat.) But it has something to do with the . . . Master. Margo and Pritchard look shocked. (Surely, they can't be shocked by his unspoken mention of that august personage—he knows for a fact that both have been around the block with Him more than once [see above].) Now don't tell me, after all we've been through together, Cantor thinks, you're going to start acting like parents (whose job it is to be easily shocked into a state of belittlement)—like (heaven forbid) my parents. Do they know, by any chance (of course they don't!) what that would entail? But he has to give mom and pop (much to their self-satisfied disappointment he wouldn't have been caught dead calling them that) some credit: inasmuch as the three of them could never have gone on living in the same black hole and survived to tell the tale—and a sordid tale it would have been, too (that is, as long as he went on insisting he couldn't do without his defects-and-deficits)—they were tactful enough to lie down and die within minutes of each other on the off-chance, he liked to think, that their least favorite son could then, D&Ds notwithstanding, get on with the heady business of taking (now that they, jeerleaders extraordinaire, could no longer boo him on from the bleachers) a little (Ken Jacobs-style) stab at that crazy thing called Happiness.

Now it's Pritchard's turn to look a little antsy. "Well, as everybody knows, we do all live in a dog-eat-dog world so it's only natural that you should let sleeping dogs lie or throw caution to the dogs or—" Without preamble he throws back his head expertly and cackles while clapping his hands in rhythm. He's suddenly trying, feebly, to put a positive—some might say a Falstaffian—spin on the gayness angle lest (yes, *lest*, what's wrong with his trying to put a positive spin as well on archaisms for what would wordflow be—and worldflow, too—without 'em?) it become a campaign issue and he be swallowed up in tandem. The question being how much do *they* know and how much *can* they know and how much does he want them to know and who are *they* anyway? Margo proceeds to jump down his throat—but not because he'll reveal too much (she couldn't care less). She threatens to return to NY. "So go back to Westchester, where you belong," he screams (sounds like a line pilfered from *Twentieth Century* starring Carole Lombard and John Barrymore or, failing that, from Strindberg's *Creditors* or from any like setups for character types who allow themselves to click only through righteous repudiation of every available avenue of connection). "I didn't invite your fat lazy ass out here to make my life a living hell." Of course he, Pritchard, knows immediately what's driving her for now they're a couple once again and so he'll never hear the end of it. *It* goes more or less like this and Cantor (their surrogate son-in-training) has every right to know: Whatever he says that can by any stretch of the imagination be contorted like saltwater taffy into something resembling life affirmation (even if it can't)—an obscene zest for living and loving—will be sure, as right now, to turn on the spigots of housewifely—fishwifely—reproach for his having kept that zest—like an unnumbered Zurich bank account—under wraps for so long and forcing her to settle, at arm's length, for a treacle of parodic nay-saying. So the key is to get through his speech act—any speech act being an experiment doomed to fail—as fast as possible before she can corner the accessibility—what she misreads as accessibility—*his* accessibility—his *sudden* accessibility—his sudden humanness—his sudden lightheartedness—his sudden glass-half-fullishness—as conveyed by the act and milk it bone-dry. He'd like to slit her throat right here and now (Cantor can tell)— daring to imply that he could be zestfully other than he is—constitutively and constitutionally—any time he wants. She's never more killable than when she's hooked on such an allegation—that he *perversely refuses to be other*—*the other that is in fact his true self*—that he's been foxily hiding that true self—colluding with the future—hoarding it for someone better. His true self as evidenced in this burst of Dionysian high spirits which is just a fraud, a screen. Or is it? Well, if the high spirits are the real McPritch—if the high spirits *have been holding out on him as well*—holding his real self hostage—withholding vital evidence—then he has the same bone to pick with them as she does—the same gripe—the burning same question, i.e., *How long has this been goin' on?*

And here, as if reading his thoughts and as if things weren't going swimmingly enough for SB's best-loved heir apparent, comes Netta, who has, it seems, taken quite a shine to him starting (so he's heard) just around the time when Pritchard intimated that Cantor might succeed him (he hopes she isn't about to ask his opinion on the Borkman/Jr. mêlée). Sidling up to him she wastes no time taking to task not Borkman, not Jr., not Pritchard, not even Post—but Tricky Dick, of all people, pointing out, right off the bat, how he may have been a gay blade—a gay caballero—inasmuch as he had a soft spot for flowered dressing gowns and adored Gilbert and Sullivan and preferred harlequin romances over technothrillers and not just when stuck at the airport and hated to be touched and invited Roy Cohn and Franklin Pangborn to high beef-tea every chance he got and, hey, what about those long languorous summer evenings entwined with Rebozo at Riggs Beach (it's obvious she once had a crush on the varmint—a crush gone bad)? But Cantor has the same straightforward response for each and every gruesome detail trotted out for his manful delectation, namely, that he has no stones to throw in *that* department and even if he has . . . (and so what if the response is just an amateur's rehash of ingenuities gone by—a bowdlerized version of the homage to his namesake's diagonalization argument which should have made him famous from Provincetown to the Castro but didn't because he hadn't had the faintest idea how to market his ingenuity if ingenuity it was?). For as it turns out and if she must know, there's nothing he hates more than to be touched (whether by man, woman or any other such beast—though he does make an exception for most non-human persons) and as a matter of fact he also "adores" Gilbert and Sullivan, especially when he has the leisure to listen to an operetta or two at high tea in his favorite Jacquard silk dressing gown (whose gauntlet cuffs, outbreast welt and quilted black velvet collar would have warmed the anti-Semitic cockles of Wagner's foppish heart), and as for Key West, well, also as a matter of fact he's wintered, and even summered there many a time (a lie—in fact, he hates the place—but, that rarest of non-human persons, a lie *in the service of truth*). A perfect illustration, all this, of the sociopath's *hunger to confess*, Cantor giggle-guffaws Teutonically. But the more aggressive the demonstration that he very much meets her strictest criteria for gayness and then some, the more elusively fluid must those criteria become if, that is, he's to remain her favorite son and a shoo-in to boot for bunker CEO. So Provincetown is rushed in by private chopper to replace Key West, Liberace and Rock take over for Franklin and Roy, Gilbert-and-Sullivan undergoes a quaint and long-overdue transmogrification into Sullivan-and-Gilbert, and instead of the welted, quilted, gauntleted thingamajig, well, a pair of pink panties from Victoria's Secret will simply have to do in a pinch. But that the overhaul should turn out (whether she's aware of it or not) to be an exercise in self-sabotage, inasmuch as the replacements are more scandalously revelatory than what they've been conscripted ostensibly to abolish, is the whole point (at least from the vantage of the Master for whom impish—no, make that *elfin*—method-in-his-method-style futility is mother's milk). Yet on and on she goes wreaking havoc on her props and looking very much the worse for wear—obviously still hoping that as a modest tribute to her efforts, the conclusion staring them both in the face will just pick itself up and go its unmerry way fuming and pouting. (Fuming and pouting *but with head held high*. Sort of like the skater in that ballet Shearer was telling him about the other day: a dandyish twit who doesn't let a little thing like falling on his ass keep him out of the rink for long. Now what *was* the name of it? *Les Patineurs*, of course! choreographed by a guy named . . . Frederick Ashton! with music by Meyerbeer! So you see, Moira, wherever you are, I was bloody well listening after all.)

He feels for her, he really does (though keeping up a frivolous tone is taking its toll on him as well). But as feeling for her is turning out to be far more upsetting than he would have imagined (why the disjunction, Maestro?), given the hearty detestation he felt for a slew of schoolmarms, not to mention his own mother, Cantor knows better than he knows his own name that his only hope is to back-pocket the upset and head—not for the hills but (for) the waves which, wherever they hail from, can always be depended on to do the trick. (Having picked out an SUV in the recently reconfigured carpark [sub-sub-sub-basement No. %$#], though without his usual attention to make and style, he reaches East Beach in seconds flat. Carjacking is just one of his changes of garment. In any case it will be returned before anybody knows it's gone—promise.) Here he's unstraitjacketable by Netta's suspicions, far worse, as usual, than the outright reprobation of the kind of gawkers who know their suspicions are well founded. He stares happily at the monolith which qua monolith cannot be broken down into its components. Another well-earned relief. It's just he and the monolith against the world—against worlds upon worlds. He feels what might be described, loosely speaking, as a diagonalization argument of another kind coming on—one motored by the briny depths before him and having not a little to do with proving that the ocean remains unsexualizable no matter how many prosthetic waves you care to add or subtract. Is that Herbert standing a little ways off—at what, thanks to him, will soon be acknowledged as the crossroads of set theory, abnormal psychology and metaphysical poetry? If not, it should be. Since there's nobody whose take on his tinkering and whose efforts to do it professional justice he'd value more. Attending to the complex spectacle Cantor *hears before he feels* (wordflow contravening orthodox neurophysiology with the mere flick of a switch?) a tap on the shoulder. It's one of Pritchard's guys friday. Here regarding a matter of some delicacy? a missing SUV, by any chance? Hardly. He wastes no time taking him to task for not having stayed put just when the mightiest of the VCs was about to express serious interest in underwriting a merger of Pritchard's operation with Borkman, Jr.'s start-up. "Sounds fishy to me," Cantor can't refrain from saying, "and not just because I'm at the ocean's door." "It won't sound so fishy once you get through hearing what BK, Jr., has to say." Something compels Cantor—maybe it's the peculiar texture of the sea air on East Beach—to say he's not interested in what any son of Borkman has to say. "A boy should respect his father." Ignoring the schoolboy cant, guy friday explains—more than explains—implores. The boy and his pals have brought to term an *intervention* targeting people who want to undergo the Basic Life Experiences—chemically—without having to address any bothersome claims on their attention. Busy people—people with too many planes to catch. Busy people who crave those Experiences simply out of envy of the ones who have nothing better to do than *really* crave them. Or the happy few who need Them to lend credibility to their work—a resolutely childless composer, say, who's got less than two weeks to crank out a really convincing father-daughter duet. (Putting his homosexuality straight to work, for starters Cantor invokes [but only for his own private slideshow] Rigoletto-Gilda, Violetta-Germont, Boccanegra-Amelia and Lakmé-Nilakantha.) Once the envy has been neutralized, then what BK, Jr., calls the *organic chemistry of intervention* can be put to work immediately. Does this mean that Cantor, even with no duets up his sleeve, could be interventioned into tasting heterosexuality in its pure state after several lifetimes' deprivation?

Cantor tells guy friday to hold his horses since he'll be returning to Bunkerville very shortly although he doesn't know what he could possibly contribute to the merger discussion. "It's past the discussion stage." Nothing to contribute except to ask, he thinks (stupidly under the circumstances—worse, irrelevantly) if the deal will invite *intense regulatory scrutiny* (irrelevant or not, the phrase sure packs a wallop). Right now, Cantor explains, he has a score to settle. And when the bringer of Basic Life tidings is out of earshot adds, "With the sea, no less. The waves out there." But as fate would have it, he wasn't out of earshot and responds promptly to what he's just misheard: "Form? Our wiz kids haven't decided what form it" (presumably the intervention) "will take. Might be an ionic liquid drug. Or a biosimilar—problem is, they have an idea for a copy but no idea yet what it would be a copy *of* (to use the lingo, they've got—or almost got—a Zarxio but no Neupogen to go with it). Or the ideal opioid, something along the lines of PZM21. Or a palm-sized digital monitor. Or not-so-deep brain stimulation." Guy friday waves—almost girlishly. At least it looks that way in the gnat-generating glow of the streetlamp indirectly behind him.

Tonight, like every night, the sea abounds and Cantor tries never to miss a performance: nothing could tempt him to pass up an opportunity to stand up straight and genuflect. That's why it's so nice to be renting out this East Beach apartment even if it has to be from the likes of Netta. Cantor knows, since he's read the tour guides, that when to crash—at what stage of its formation—is the biggest decision a wave will ever make in the course of a too long life. (*A little mood music, Maestro, if you please.*) Some crash before they're fully formed—to escape formation. The tension between formation and crash is the heart of the matter—the heart of *his* matter, that is—even if it's in the fate of the wave after the crash (when, to the undiscerning eye, it's a wave no longer) that he's most interested. The map of Cantor's selfhood, so anxious with possibility (he needed this merger like a hole in the head), is drawn from the play of the waves, proxy for the crisis that equals his life without remainder. The only way to extrude himself from the monolith of that selfhood is by telling the story of the waves and knowing it's his story, and only his, down to the very last detail. Some chapters are more exciting than others. Like the chapter a while back—a real howler—about the wave that purposely crashed all over the one in front before the latter could fully form although there's no ruling out the possibility that to make it crash prematurely, the one in front purposely impeded the formation of the one behind. The record of the tension between those two possibilities (pulling apart the event like taffy) made him see—really *see*—the wave event in its nakedness. Not to mention the chapter about how rather than expire each in its own somersault-generated mess of foam, two waves fused their foamlines so that what would have been two separate crashes became a single ejaculation fanning out elegantly from the point of contact. Which is not to say they, like self-respecting males everywhere, don't sometimes shoot their separate wads. Despite these casting coups, however, Cantor knows he'll never be able to master the sea phenomenon—to capture it—because the real phenomenon is his need to master the sea phenomenon—kill it off and himself with it—versus the need for the phenomenon to go on being unmasterable, i.e., compulsively thinkable. He's counting on the sea to let him *be*—counting on its wave events to go on telling his story even if he hasn't given up waiting for the one thought to emerge that's so definitive it will put an end to sea, waves, thinking, telling, thinker, teller.

Before returning to the bunker, Cantor, refreshed (even if re-saddened) by this skinny dip in the whirlpool of his barely articulable plight, stops off to grab a sweater. It's chilly up there—much chillier than down here among the white waves. Opening the door his train of thought is interrupted—but not brutally—at the sight of Cook sprawled dozing on the couch with a lit cigarette about to fall from his left hand. He awakens and puts it out just in the nick of time. "Cheer up. Eden is obviously going to be a success—he's sure to take out *somebody* before the night is over even if it's not Borkman—and for that reason and a million others we have to block the export of off-label I which, as we all know, has been parasitizing the legitimate version." Cantor is tempted to say, "That sounds like a good idea," and succumbs. "If we don't, that last refuge of scoundrels, what used to be called—with a straight face yet—the third world, will go up in flames much faster than it's supposed to. And in case you didn't know (but don't tell anybody I told you), it's been spiked with trace amounts of the following potentiators: *Bacillus anthracis, Burkholderia malleti, Francisella tularensis, Coccidioides immiti, Erlichia rumantium* and *Mycoplasma capricolum,* subsp. caprineumoniae, and *Yersinia pestis,* not to mention sub-trace amounts of foot-and-mouth disease virus, Marburg virus, flexal virus, camel pox virus, goat pox virus and vesicular stomatitis virus." Cook breathes a sigh of self-satisfied relief. Cantor wonders why spiking Invidicum with trace amounts of potentiators should be an occasion for relief and then all at once an idea hits him: Such is the potency of words that simply calling the connection into question somehow cements it, in Masterly fashion. Even if it's nonsense designed to throw Cantor and inevitably Pritchard (since they're birds of a feather) off the track.

It's only when Borkman, Jr., emerges from the bathroom, zipping up his fly with a barely perceptible drumroll of the hips, that Cantor thinks of asking what Cook is doing here and how he got in—thinks but wouldn't dream of asking. And by the way, is it Cantor's imagination or is there more than just a professional collusiveness between these two, highly attractive each in his own way? (Actually, Cook's only collusion has been with Shearer—unconsummated thanks to Cantor's interruption of his wet dream.) What Cantor does ask is why Pritchard couldn't see to it that Eden got stopped dead in his tracks. Borkman, Jr., taking a cig from the pack on the coffee table where Cook's stockinged feet are solidly planted (there's too much stage business going on for Cantor's taste), replies, "Why should he be stopped? Let's calm down, guys, and let the third world take care of itself for once. Whatever's the outcome of Post's little experiment, which Pritchard is supposed to know nothing about (that's part of the master plan, remember? at least as I, granted a relative newcomer, have come to understand it), it's sure to advance our understanding of on-label I. And that's the goal—that's Pritch's manifest humanitarian destiny—ain't it? So why should we—I mean you—block the export of our—I mean, your—supply of off-label I, much less destroy the available stock when doing so will only signal to Post that we *know*? We—I mean you—have got a winner on your hands, whether it's off-label or on-. What counts is that it's labeled, beyond anybody's wildest dreams. But you have to know how to place it. Product placement—that's the ticket in this town." When did this kid become part of the inner circle? Cantor wonders: sure is pushy and his use of what he takes to be the lingo more than just slightly off. "But your father could have been killed. Doesn't that bother you?" "Dad's suffered far worse than murder and he's made us—me, mom and my brother, not to mention sis (Cantor can't remember Borkman having mentioned a daughter: this isn't the first time he's caught the Master nodding nor, he suspects, will it be the last)—suffer far far worse than that far worse, let me tell you. He's a survivor." Used in this way, the word makes Cantor's skin crawl as does "healing," "hurting" (instead of "in pain") and, of course, "closure"—all of which, like the names of the potentiators paraded above—euphemize—comatize—circumvent—sidestep—the human condition in professing to revere it. "Yes, a survivor" (as if directly challenging Cantor's unavowed distaste). "But with the body type, unfortunately, of a centenarian."

The ride back to the bunker—Cook drives the SUV at the carjacker's request—fast becomes (though they go slowly) a trip to the underworld (though it's all uphill), Jr.'s crack about his dad being the final nail in somebody or something's coffin. Why a coffin? Cantor wonders. As an answer he's tempted to say—playing Cecil B. to/against Borkman, Jr.'s Joe Gillis—something along the lines of, *You ride roughshod over your father but I knew him back in the days when he was just another angel-faced goodhearted foulmouthed runner on Wall Street—bursting at the seams with healthy ambition—an irresistibly starstruck kid who'd have given his right arm to put Fred C. Trump's foot in his mouth.* Cantor looks around—things get darker the higher they go. He feels a song of despair coming on—related to his theft (which wasn't really a theft) of the SUV. Everything around him, and inside, where the meanings are supposed to be, cries out for an epitaph. Take the rickety tanbark oak over there just panting for a *Times* two-column obit hack to Internet-scrawl something along the lines of: *After a long battle with leaflessness, and having finally succumbed to total skeletonization, Tan Bark Oak, 31, died peacefully at home in Santa Barbara, California, surrounded by . . . his own kind.* Cantor, for his part, fears—no: *As for Cantor, he fears* a hack obit far more than death. He can already see it, read it, most of all taste it. Can imagine all his so-called friends and bosom acquaintances schmoozing around up at the bunker reading it and sneering with relief once his failure to have realized so much outsize ambition—much too big for his ectomorph's frame—gets depicted beyond refutation. He can imagine, especially, the sneers of a subset of those bosoms, namely, the repeat recipients of his outsize generosity who never dreamed of reciprocating all the invites—never even thought of them *as* invites—those for whom he was always picking up the tab 'cause he couldn't stand the amateurishly dissimulated look of panic on their bloated faces when the waiter dropped the stink bomb. Not to mention the fake—sorry, *faux*—sniffles of those to whom he loaned tide-over-money (never repaid) because, aside from being homeless, they professed to be devoted to . . . his devotion to . . . Hilbert! (which Apollonian rarefaction thereby absolved them of all obligation to repay). In other words, he can imagine the sneers, sniffles and stink of all those colluders with a do-goodery that turned him into a prince of thieves. That is, a prince who ended (according to the obit) exactly the way Katherine Anne Porter might have said he would (if she'd known him well enough to write it), *by leaving him[self] nothing.* He reads this obit through their chops-licking crocodile tears: everything brought to an immensely satisfying conclusion thanks to the hack's pointing out that, for all his admirers' brouhaha (and what mediocrity *doesn't* have admirers? The more there are, the merrier is the mediocrity in question), the lemma never got proved because like Shinichi Mochizuki, still-to-be-proved prover of the *abc* conjecture, he barricaded himself behind a "heavy, unprecedentedly indigestible notation." Yet, hearing himself think the word "tears"—miracle! he's still able to *think*—somehow gives him a hope that there's a way out of this nightmare of his own (nobody else's!) on-the-road construction—the worst kind of nightmare—the kind that reserves the right to take its sweet time unfolding over hill and dale. For can't all the generosity be perceived in hindsight not as a self-abasing bid for acceptance but as *duty in action* which outlaws the trespass of reciprocity? In short, whenever he fed their faces it was to rid himself of their disrespectful neediness. Making it easy for his subsequent calculated invisibility to be legible as a loner's lavish indifference to the thing that's sharper than the serpent's tooth. Along the lines of stepping aside when another male is coming toward you in, say, Riverside Park—not from fear but from an assured refusal to stoop to jockeying for position in that tired old shell game of cock-of-the-walk. Such jockeying being reserved only for dowagers who are debate-drunk on the wit of their primetime put-downs—(think Gore Vidal versus William F. Buckley, Jr.). But, still, why all this dread simply because at his request, Cook is driving a borrowed SUV in the direction of Xanadu? Is it dread at seeing Eden whom he could still love? All he knows is that the dread has not come out of nowhere. Was in fact building up long before he even set foot in California, all of a sudden his spiritual home away from home. But how much longer will he be able to proclaim his eagerness for easeful death—if that's what he's been doing with all this talk of obits big and small—at what age will the talk no longer be etherealizing, gratuitous, whimsical, *precocious*—a Heathcliffian supplement—that *something extra* which makes him even more of a scorching talent than he takes himself to be, because he's willing to throw away life and liberty at the very moment he's about to be anointed (either by Pritchard or by the Hilbert crowd)—with the obligatory self-doubt being just some more icing on all seven layers of his triumph? When will age have caught up with his morbidity, making it no longer glamor but cowardice—a mere feeble apotropaism (*yep—or rather, so sorry but—only* apotropaism *will do*)? In how many dog years from now (5? 10? 3? 30?) will it no longer be precocious because like any other self-respecting old fart he *should* have at least one club foot in the grave? Maybe he's in dread because going back to the bunker means he'll have to face his judges—little more than embodied axes-to-grind. And who knows how long he'll have to wait nakedly in full view until they've absorbed—adsorbed—the facts of the case-that-is-he? Or maybe it's simply the increasing distance from the waves—his knight in shining armor—that's making for obit dread-cum-delectation. So it's waves versus bunker—a binary opposition (think, e.g., Bob Mueller versus Adam Schiff) already warming the cockles of his undeconstructible heart because there's no privileged term here. Fact is, he dreads the bunker. The bunker (its motto? why, Open All Night, silly) with its subterranean passageways simulating conduits to—to—color-coded understanding of the art of playing the hand fate has dealt you—in this case, the art of making Invidicum great again by uniting it with a gimmick—sorry, an *intervention*—along the lines of Borkman, Jr.'s brainchild. Ah, yes, the bunker with its implement-free torture chambers, which characterless trait transforms each and every one into, hands down, the comeliest of landscapes for skull-cracking and related renovations.

His father approaches, glad to see he's back, and though Jr. is immediately aware of Borkman's presence and of his pride, however belated, he feigns not just indifference but disgust. "You've got a winner on your hands," Sr. says, "but you have to know how to place it—product placement—that's the ticket." "I've already told them that." At which point Cook and Jr. rehearse their East

Beach argument about off-label and on-. A purely heuristic enterprise aimed at showing all these passive verbs how the big boy grammarians parse when they're out of earshot.

Shearer overhears, as it's decreed that she should. Putting two and two together, she realizes that as members of the Amygdala crowd they themselves are products on display—nothing but products—and, as such, need to be positioned to maximum effect. But as far away from each other as possible even if distance doesn't guarantee uniqueness since never have they so resembled one another no matter how hard they try to disguise it. The closer they get to cure, it seems ("it seems": *a weasel phrase: I'm on your side, reader, so my advice to you is simple: don't take the bait!*), the more indistinguishable they become—in terms of not just what they say but how they live out their daily struggle to make a name for themselves. (She's noticed a significant dip over the last few weeks [a mixed blessing] in the intensity of her level of obsession with the tribute bestowed on Farrell at the Kennedy Center Honors.) Take away from each his own particular version of Envy and you rob him of part—dare she say the very soul?—of his identity. Cure is getting way too close for comfort—getting to be less and less of a mithridate and more and more of a poison pure and simple. Why, it's positively Shakespearean (whatever that means)—no, Platonic—specifically, Phaedrus-style Platonic. So Shearer should never have taken Cook up on his offer. But he was so young and so helpless or maybe it was just the at-death's-door oak leaves deferentially scraping the Second Avenue pavement that made him appear so. So eager to make good—and fast. Or so wordflow—never a slouch when it comes to rectifying, i.e., enhancing, the missteps of a dancing damsel in distress for maximum Gulf Coast dinner theater impact—makes haste to inform her even if now is neither (is it ever?) the time nor the place. Why, if she didn't know better she'd say wordflow is telling her whom and what to be. And in support of her thesis—if she may be permitted to use so exalted a word—Moira the Monad could swear, eerily, that, at this very minute, they're all having the very same perception. So the chariot of cure is swinging as low as a chariot can—taking a full swing at their *internal principle* (the italics are mine, murmurs G.W. Liepnits wherever he is), according to which perceptions are always supposed to be different, however slightly, based on their degree of distinctness and the point of view of the perceiver. And, by the way, the very same mumbo-jumbo about waves—no, wave events—Cantor-style wave events—running through her head is also running through Herbert's (even if that principle decrees that there's always difference in sameness). It's evident from the way she sways back and forth to their tune. Shearer's tempted to follow suit, only that would be a betrayal of all she's been taught about movement. She looks around for signs that said mumbo-jumbo is afflicting or maybe even exalting the others and if so, she can't help wondering whether the same discovery (of similarity) has been made by them or at least some of them. Well, they're doing a good job of hiding the truth, *even from themselves.* (She doesn't particularly like having the Master tinker with whichever of her genes code for self-righteousness [as attested by her thinking the phrase "even from themselves"] to which she's rarely prey.) And while we're at it, she doesn't like to be compelled, when she thinks about the tinkering, to use phrases like "genes code for self-righteousness." Maybe Melanctha can petition Him on her behalf although it's probably too late to divest herself of such infringements—such neuron baiting.

Sorry, Moira, but Rhys, for one, is having a very different perception, since it's been determined by the Master—i.e., Herbert's Mr. Balanchine—that the members of the tribe simply aren't ready to be indistinguishable each from the other. In this He has the interests of Invidicum, promoted to the rank of a living being—a divine automaton—at heart. Doesn't want the drug to go all teary-eyed from believing that it's robbed its victims of their essence— that cure is by definition bad for business—the business of being and staying unique. Which accounts for the fact that Rhys's brain is having no truck with waves, much less wave events. So at long last the real purpose of the drug has been revealed, she thinks, at the very same moment as Cantor. But her brain is a more welcoming haven for the perception—making it a more distinct perception—even if (or rather, to the extent that)—she doesn't understand it—to the extent that she doesn't pollute the perception with some annoying capacity to think she's catching on—to the extent that she doesn't think she's got it in her crosshairs or by the short hairs—to the extent that she knows *next to nothing* (far worse than nothing) about psychopharmacology—not even something as PP 101 as the difference between an adrenergic and a muscarinic receptor. Yet how can she know she doesn't know without at the same time knowing *something* about what she professes not to know? But what she does know a thing or two about is the differential calculus—Ethan used to schematize the key hurdles—mapped 'em out—between orgasms (hers) because he thought it might come in handy though he never bothered to explain how or where. Bother is not Ethan's forte. So, so armed it's easy for her to understand that Invidicum's use as an anti-Envy agent (curve) is a smokescreen for its far greater lucrativeness as a homicide inducer (first derivative)[87] and homicide induction is an even thicker screen for Invidicum's application (second derivative) as a—as a— Surely the has-been in one of those cheesy TV ads aired between 3 and 4 a.m., sandwiched between pitches for a gutter service and a (discreetly packaged) vibrator, has dared to utter the name of said application and lived to tell the tale. So why not she?

Herbert, too, has perceived the ever growing sameness afflicting the group. And like Moira she can't help suspecting Invidicum—only from her

---

[87]NB and e.g.: Glazunov is the first derivative of Tchaikovsky and Jayne Mansfield the first derivative of Marilyn Monroe. The first derivative in such cases is not a disciple or a pale imitation or a flaming parody but the realization, on its own terms and in its own realm and unburdened by a mythic status, of whatever possibilities have been left un- or underdeveloped in the precursor. On a lighter note, and less exalted level, *The Magnificent Ambersons* is the first derivative of *Citizen Kane*, *Henry IV* of *Six Characters in Search of an Author* and *Engdame* of *Waiting for Godot*, that is to say, in each of these three cases the creator, having managed at long last to get all that pressurized brilliance off his chest, had nothing left to prove and could therefore settle down and concentrate on exploring depth of field—with the termiteliness of, say, a Gregg Toland.

perspective it's the drug's inefficacy that accounts for that sameness. For one thing, she's been harboring far more envy toward the highest achievers in her playwriting seminar. Is it the altitude? the sea air? distance from her rivals? absence which, as the saying goes, makes the heart go founder, or is it flounder? But if Invidicum's potency turns out to be minimal (all at once sub-basement IV A resembles basement II of Building 18), maybe even nonexistent, what will become of her writing? For unabashedly she wants a brilliant career—she deserves a brilliant career—she's not afraid to debase her sublime vocation by hitching it to the albatross of a brilliant career, so what if some of her (white) fellow students think it's vulgar to plan beyond the mechanics of the moment. But how can she go on functioning being so consumed as she is with Envy—of, e.g., (*a*) parents capable of loving their children; (*b*) (black and white) fellow students who've already networked themselves into four-star advances from Major Players; and (*c*) women contracted with a reputable handyman or two during the week or a church deacon on Sunday for services encompassing but not limited to forcibly sucking (now where did such an image come from?) their shaved pussies dry? Or in the case of (*c*) does she just *think* she should be consumed with Envy precisely because the escapades in question hold absolutely no appeal—no relevance—and in holding no appeal pose a threat to the plausibility of her reception on the literary scene as an omnivorous genius to whom no aberration is aberrant and who wants and likes exactly what her audience wants and likes but without letting such wants and likes trammel her complex universality and who thereby holds out the hope that they, too, can throw off the yoke of those tyrannical wants and likes (which only seem organic) in the name of something not necessarily better but different? But fact is, she's simply too worn out—as worn out as, say, Thelma Ritter in the Sam Fuller film she was assigned to watch (and did many more times than was required) in that college course entitled "Red Scares in American Film: Then and Now and Forever" which means too worn-out not to welcome having (at least metaphorically) her head blown off by a Commie traitor—too worn-out to worry *in the abstract* about what will or won't invalidate her life project: Humanely, battle-fatigue is staying the attempts of worry's scalpel to excise away any flab of disqualification—real or imagined—from the bone of her contention. Even if its success is fast breeding (she can feel it) another kind of worry—worry over non-worry—worry over new, brasher woes rushing in where the old feared to tread. One of the side effects, maybe, of that still ghostly second-derivative Invidicum? She needs to reach a watershed of indifference to well-being—to the nausea of Envy-free *wellness* as prerequisite for making it big. She tells herself to stop making Envy-freedom the prologue to realness—a realness real enough to turn her into that silliest of humorless commodities, a great writer.

CHAPTER FORTY

Observing Eden enter, drenched, galvanized as if by electrodes still implanted deep within his skull, Borkman instinctively stations himself in front of his son (always his little boy), thereby unwittingly undoing decades of neglect in a single bound. He wields what looks like an AK-47 assault rifle or is it, by any chance, a 12-gauge Remington pump-action shotgun, the drug of choice among self-suiciding family-massacrers? Did he change weapons in mid-stream at Post's behest (Borkman has a hard time remembering what happened, if anything, between then and now)? But maybe nothing happened, which is all to the good since action sequences, even with a saber-tooth tiger or two to get things going, are not, as astutely pointed out in *Variety*, the Master's strongest suit. Collapsing in a chair and fingering his thick curls, now auburn from sun and wind and a dash of drizzle—"Mary's" Adirondack, in fact (she's gone ladies' room hunting)—Eden looks every inch the melodramatically muddled assassin. Soon enough, however, he forgets all about his failed assignment, because in turning toward the buffet (conference table no longer)—not that he's hungry (too famished to be)—Eden is struck dumb or dead or both by the self-important gestures of a pudgy little man loading up his plate (for a minute he thinks it's his father, come back to demand a long-overdue refund since Eden's not the sort of prodigal son he had in mind: give dead old dad the knee-pounding tantrums of Balanchine's staff-bearer any day of the week) and into the hairy porches of whose ear a pretty young thing (at least from behind) is distilling sweetish nothings. Something familiar—too familiar—about the pair. *And to think*, he almost mutters, *I agreed to be Post's patsy to preserve the feeding and guzzling rights of folks like them.* Herbert examines him from head to foot—exhaustively, as only a mother can—when, that is, the examinee isn't her own son. He's trembling, but not from head to foot. Should she feed him? Can he hold food down? The hair on his chest—blondish—is incongruous with—a blasphemy perpetrated against—his innocence in spite of himself. She offers him a cup of soup. He accepts it while shaking his head no. Has he sabotaged himself? Is he his own worst enemy yet again? *Join the exclusive club*, she whistles inwardly. Or is she just examining him through the lens of her own self-sabotage—worse, through the lens of her own fear of self-sabotage (retrospectively, re parenthood, and prospectively, re writing)?

Eden takes a closer look at those folks whose rights he's been defending and Borkman, convinced Eden's currently harmless, follows his lead. The zoo story is forgotten, at least temporarily, Shearer is happy to see—and Herbert even happier. Since for a split second she believes that if only they can see their way clear to patching things up officially, it won't be long before her son returns to present her with a mother's dream ultimatum: either you renounce your insane pursuit of fame or I turn you in to the authorities. The pudgy little man, they discover, each in his own way and time, is none other than Liepnits and the dark lady, Manning of all people, even svelter (if that's possible) than in what Cantor's tempted to call, though he doesn't succumb, her Amygdala days. So they aren't just a pair of supernumeraries hauled in to launch some thought packet on its maiden voyage. They have a long and distinguished history touring in place with this stock company. The way he parades her around (while balancing the overstocked plate on his palm with an elegance that, even if only at the end of his career, Astaire might have envied) you'd think she was the proverbial fourth wife, although Herbert can't remember having heard tell of, much less seen, the born-to-be-fired first through third. Didn't everybody routinely refer to him as either a confirmed bachelor or (peculiar phrase) a bachelor *machine*? But whatever Liepnits is (or isn't) he deserves her gratitude—eternal or not—for proving beyond detraction that, side effects and outsize ambitions notwithstanding, she's still capable of straightforward reactions, in this case simple revulsion for the way in which some white men flaunt their burden. Yet, Herbert can't help feeling that as fast as she churns out the revulsion it is being absorbed by the Liepnits machine (which has caught on quickly enough) even faster—and not just absorbed but assimilated to and made to enrich the machine's own substance. And then she herself, as expendable as a first wife, is duly chewed up by the gears' teeth and spit right out.

Once stripped of their incognito, the pair are duly welcomed (a bracing wind from the East is how Netta describes them) with the obligatory embraces and—surprisingly—no air kisses. In Liepnits's case they're accompanied, when the embraces are man-to-man, with the even more obligatory desexualizing pats ("there, there") on the back (see above, *passim*). *All holds barred*, you might say. Cook, clearly still infatuated, whisks them off (even if it's close to the wee hours) for a quick grand tour of the premises. But why bother, Pritchard wonders, since they all know—or by now should have deduced—that everything worth inspecting has been stashed away in sub-basements 5P, 7G and 13L until the coast is clear (though for what has yet to be determined)? Unable to refrain from trailing behind in spite of herself (for they do give off a whiff of royalty, albeit of the D-list sort) Shearer grows disgusted quickly enough (as if infected with the Herbert bug) by their air of quizzical condescension. Manning's posturing (her every gesture big with a verdict tactfully—even lustrously—withheld) is particularly offensive to Shearer's newly—instantaneously—acquired woman-of-the-people sensibility. Shearer perceives without apperceiving that though both a native of Transylvania and a full-fledged American citizen, by hooking up with Liepnits Manning's now a citizen of the world (hence no one locale can be expected to hold her—and, more importantly, her interest—for very long). The charms of Pritchard's foothills dream-bunker only put into relief the charms of the hot spots left behind or to come (far greater through absence), exposure or re-exposure to which (to be degraded in their turn through sheer presentness) will elicit the same swelled-head forbearance. But to Shearer's delight—and that makes her feel about him exactly the way she felt (inadmissible until this moment) way back on Second Avenue when he wooed her ostensibly in the name of recruitment—to her delight, Cook is refusing point-blank (unlike Jean in an analogous situation) to play Lapdog to Manning's Moody Mistress. (Who can forget Jean's interminable description in her twelve-tone Greenwich Avenue monodrama of how, on St. Mark's Place, she brought up sis's supercilious rear? Not to mention [was it *ever* mentioned? not at any town hall meeting Shearer was obliged to attend] that winter's walk on the wild side of Bleecker—just the two of them [no Ethan in sight for miles around]—when her feet again played too-eager amanuensis to the massy musings implied by Caro's signature disdainful silence—stiff as an Elizabethan ruff [Jean's efforts to explain why she had trouble keeping in step only stiffened things up even more].)

But Shearer's attention is distracted, or is it Herbert's? or (for lack of anybody else's) Jean's? (let's not pretend personal identity—that apoplectic elf—isn't a figment of everybody's imagination)—Shearer's attention is distracted by the sight of her—Manning—waddling, arms outstretched, with tiny, extremely cautious steps toward—Netta, of all people!—and of Netta waddling right back with a caution even more extreme lest the sheer delight of each at being reunited with the other become so overwhelming as to throw them both off balance. For all the world as if they were and intended to remain until death did them part ever—like two Joe Gargerys—the best of friends. (By the way, they manage only to moan and quaver since this kind of affection is too elemental to go a-wording.) You may therefore say they're advancing not so much toward each other as toward some finish line at which it'll be determined definitively who's been the more adroit in mitigating that delight on behalf of motion. Bodies must contract before they can dilate—any Lurianic worth his salt knows that before he knows his own name, thinks Cantor. And the bodies of the waddlers seem to be saying—no, they *are* saying and on no uncertain terms: *It's corny, we know—even phony—as phony as Harold Arlen's Barnum & Bailey world but that's OK, folks, because we're simply too caught up in the phoniness to care.* Still, Shearer (or Herbert or Ethan or Cook or anybody else who's willing to lend a floater-free POV to the proceedings) can't help wondering if what impedes the ladies' fusion is not too much affection but none at all, which would make the waddling a way of staving off the doomsday of that fusion. Or maybe it would be more accurate—and certainly more charitable (but unfortunately it's way too late for charity)—to view them as outsize tureens which, in the march toward collision are working hard to prevent the hazardous overflow of girlish affection's soupy bile from their every orifice unstoppered.

"How was your trip?" Pritchard asks when she gets back. Manning pretends not to have heard. Switching allegiances so many times in the last several months, she's hard put to know where she stands. Whether she's on-label, off- or off-off-, so to speak, not just Invidicum-wise but in life's every dimension and/or whether the switches are not in fact a way of throwing sand in the eyes of her beloved Pritchard's detractors. Liepnits, on the other hand—encumbered as he is by the renown befitting a "world-class" scholar (why, he's routinely lauded by the Far Right—with Fukker Carlsson Ingrahamnity of course leading the charge—as being on the order of [no mean counter-endorsement] Newt the Gingrich [the only kind of newt, by the way, definitely not worth risking one's life to escort to its breeding ground through killer traffic after a Petaluma-thick downpour])—and aware that erudition, however shoddy and substandard, is a liability in the circles he seeks to frequent—has every reason to tamp down his native snobbism and play his equally nativist coarseness to the hilt so as to come across as just the sort of well-rounded guy you want to have a beer with thrice daily when, that is, you're not having one with Bush, Jr. (who, by the way, not only was first in the West to make goo-goo eyes at Putin [and at his own boundless cowboy acuity in mistaking a fanged void clogged with rot for a soul] but also invaded Iraq under false pretenses and bested Daddy in the process and, adding insult to injury, had the swift-boating chutzpah to set himself up as exclusive portraitist to heroes [minus the body bags]—preferably the very young and very dead [minus the body bags]—dead compliments of his own lies, incompetence and cowardice and the cynical machinations of a gang of sleazeball warriors-by-proxy [Cheney, Wolfowitz, RUMPsfeld, etc.]). (Yet who is He to throw the first stone and from the comfort of his own comfort station no less [Melanctha, as the Master's favorite child, has no trouble wondering]? It's costing him nothing in blood, sweat, tears and reputation to pen this hymn of fearless self-congratulation so what makes him any better than the proxy warriors he professes to execrate? And while we're at it, what makes her execration of his any less opportunistic?) Guffawing, he jabs her with his elbow and says, "Tell them the one about the taxi." Not a very uxorious gesture for a newlywed of any age, Netta thinks, suddenly glad she's divorced or widowed or celibate or frigid or nymphomaniacal, the right label depending on the right hubby—or, in the case of "frigid" and "nymphomaniacal," the right century.

(The members of the jury of his peers, though standing still, seem to be advancing on Cantor. It won't be long now . . . At last he's able to put Mary to one side and recognize Dave Dolinskovici. As Dave [jealous to a fault of his creature comforts and no warrior, by proxy or otherwise] once told it [trying in the process to ram conviction, sort of, through the rust-encrusted culvert of the telling], he'd have surely, back in '64, enlisted as a civil rights worker down in Philadelphia, Mississippi, standing beside the likes of Chaney, Goodman and Schwerner. Pity he wasn't old enough [his excuse, none lamer]. Afraid [why?] to risk opening his mouth in mockery and thereby unleash obese Dave's signature spleen, Cantor defaulted to letting him stew in the juicy depths of self-delusion while a tactful [i.e., craven] silence was exhorted—no, ordered—to strive [in vain] to do all the dirty work of debunkification. QED: Once again, it's proven that Cantor and Eden haven't been thrown together by chance. For both, *things are closing in.* Where is Eden? Cantor wonders. *Both are living a life they'd have wished only on their worst enemies.*)

Manning looks a dagger or two of incomprehension (she hasn't been able to shed her Transylvanian accent completely and doesn't relish—by obeying the groom's command—serving it up to the scrutiny of strangers). "Taxi?" "You remember." "I certainly do. Thing is, what I remember is a horse—a taxi—of a vastly different color." She explains how she discovered *her* taxi while, of all things, waiting for the Buick—*their* Buick (from Überlifft)—to get them to Newark in time for the redeye to Reno. As it turns out, while sitting on the terrace of their hotel room which faced Park Avenue (what a dump! to quote that famous actress Betty—Bettie—Bette—), she suddenly saw a yellow cab taxiing around with its head- and tail-lights bleeding into the depths of the asphalt (odd, because there'd been no rain for days, maybe decades). Should Cantor butt in, the loins of his brain freshly girded with the success of quick recall, and point out that it's not Bette but . . . Dana Andrews (as Eric Stanton, wrongfully accused of murder)[88] who ought to be duly quoted: after all, he *was* the first to utter the phrase (specifically upon entering the room, in yet another one of Hollywood's aspirational fleabags, which is to serve as his hideout from the police). Before Cantor can decide whether to break the glass ceiling he observes that Manning is weeping. Of course he's never seen her weep before. Has anybody? "A lot of taxiing for one person to handle," ventures Margo, cocking her head to one side with a little cooing sound. "And just before a flight to Reno, of all places, to be given away in marriage, of all things." But as this well-meant affirmation of a sad reality (though why should a harmless taxi be a cause for sadness? Margo wonders) makes it more real—more ominously real—than she has any intention of conceding it to be, Irena says, What taxiing? which means *No trespassing*. As repeated by Margo, the word *taxiing* has become far more deadly even if her ostensible [*another weasel on the loose: reader, beware!*]—even if her ostensible purpose was to detoxify it. But Margo feels for Irena—*she knows what she's been going through*. After all, she had her own bad marriage to adapt to and with—she must admit sans self-congratulation—not altogether disastrous results.

Leasing what she calls Margo's bandwagon as the ideal vehicle for rubbing it in, *it* being lucidity, the choicest drug in her formulary—the choicest bit of Lombardy poplar in her lumberyard—and indifferent to whether Manning can take an even bigger and sadder dose of reality, Herbert suggests—more than suggests—that it must have been undergone as a massive threat, that taxiing . . . *narrativized* (yeah, Irena, *narrativized*—take your medicine like a man the way you were always insisting we guinea pigs should take ours)—narrativized as it was through the auspices of fog, cold, rain, darkness, raindrops pelleting the pavement with pinball ferocity, high winds and unpeopledness—you name it (she remembers the weather report as if it were yesterday).[89] "No—you name it." In other words, Manning (according to Herbert who ignores the retort)

---

[88] In Otto Preminger's exquisite 1945 specimen noir *Fallen Angel*. Calling it underrated is somehow to demean it—to give it a price tag when the film is perfectly content with its little niche in unassessability.

[89] Not to mention (the auspices of) ambient high-rises. Funny thing, though, about big-city high-rises or rather funny thing about the booty extracted on just such a narrativizable night from a peek or two into their interior. That is to say, it's not the bedrooms or the bathrooms or the fresco of some scuzzy Internet fare plastered across an entire bay window that's the most revealing—most moving—most narrativized—but rather . . . the landings. Ah, the landings: Empty—featureless—characterless—with their elevator doors going about the business of . . . waiting—the game of . . . lying low—like seasoned pros.

could accept that image—that entity—that thing—that story element—as long as there was no story to absorb it (she's more of a purist than she lets on—even to herself). But in fact the taxi has lots to do with the story—their story (so whispers the Master in her ear).[90] Since in that very taxi—Manning covers her ears and shrieks, "I don't want to know who's in that taxi. Ever." Everybody is on tenterhooks—or should be if he or she or they aren't. "But you already do know," Herbert goads cannily (in kindergarten she did have occasion to pull the smug pigtails of her white classmates when they became just too peacock-proud of their incessant tattling).[91] Is the Master lending support to her own deductions or, like any other monomaniac for whom people are mere tools, just egging her on for his own dinner theater purposes and to hell with her deductions? Manning executes a shrug or two à la française—of all varieties, the most loathsome—the most *unanswerable*—and turns away hoping to have reassured them—her not-so-apt pupils—that she disliked this narrativizing shrew from the get-go and never intended to like her, knowing that as a product of the slums, Herbert would end up doing exactly what she's just done and right on cue, namely, turn on her caregiver (and just for the record, the fruitlessness of their few sessions together can't be laid at the doorstep of Manning's competence) out of sheer Envy. Or so it all seems to Jean who, having unknowingly stepped—leaped—into the breach, is graciously offering up the services of her POV so that Manning's response will not seem to have materialized out of thin air or whole cloth at the behest, say, of Herbert's Master, as it must in the absence of some partial perspective which claims responsibility for the particular shape assumed by that response on the stage of life. One thing is crystal-clear, however: turning his henpecked back as well on the unfortunate Herbert, Liepnits can't help gazing at his better half with

---

[90]For Herbert, however, in her heart of hearts, the curious incident of the taxi in the nighttime has no story value whatsoever. In her misguided opinion—a novice's opinion—the taxi's much too good for encystment by any story, reminding her as it does of one of those unsung-hero Mack Trucks she's seen hundreds of times charging down the ramp of the Queensborough Bridge—that is, the Ed Koch Queensborough Bridge (sorry, Ed)—on a muggy Thursday just before salmon-colored dusk rises over the wilds of Second Avenue—the kind of vehicle that has all it can do to rein in its rampage so as to retain the setting sun in the *cyclopean* eye of its windshield together with the bit of cloud detritus above the lower rim. Now tell me, can any story's brouhaha begin to match the struggle to cohere martyrizing that image?

[91]Melanctha knows she sounds a little like the psychiatrist in Ingmar Bergman's *Persona* (his films' truth tellers are always a wee bit diabolical: the hamming after all is good for business—stage business, I mean), the job of whose diagnosis is to be gotten out of the way as soon as possible. Why? So as to ensure that its impeccable accuracy doesn't hover irrelevantly over the action like smog (like, say, the money shot in pornography—or porn as it's now fearlessly called). And so that the film can go on to prove that there's more to pathology than a diagnosis and more to an existential crisis than pathology and more to the poetics of conflict than one existential crisis—or (compliments of contagion, as in the case of *Persona*) even two.

what the situation—and he's a great believer in situations—has determined he must show her she oh so richly deserves. And as every gesture should, if possible, have a soundtrack, to the company at large he proclaims, "Isn't she . . . adorable?" Lucky that Cook has had plenty of truck with his simpering kind: a dime a dozen back in his native Panacea (Florida) and up and down the Gold Coast (fief of choice of the oil spill barons) as well. And here it is Liepnits doing the honors of his kind by expressing smarmy fake astonishment at his fake good fortune in having reeled in so choice a by-catch (since *nobody minds having what is too good for them* or rather, *pace* ungentle Ms. Austen, since *nobody can tolerate having what is* not *too good for them*). (It's a relationship that exists only to the extent that there are plenty of saps around who are eager to buy into his fakery at an unreasonable price. Thereby making it kosher—a matter of civic duty, if you must know—for Liepnits to buy into it, too.)

Now it's Cook's turn to step (loudly enough) into the breach: Feeling and (with a little luck) sounding a wee bit like Bill Clinton at his most hot-seat masterful, he informs them there can be no standing idly by while they dare to reduce the thoughts—the plight—of Liepnits's child bride to little more than the immediate stimulus that provoked it. Which totally misses the point. "Since I've known her, Irena has always given back to stimuli—to epiphenomena—far more than she's gotten." Irena remains silent while continuing to peripherally observe . . . Pritchard as if only his profile and his alone can tell her where her on-again off-again allegiance now lies, or should. Pritchard's *her* Master! thinks Melanctha. Although it's the last thing she ever thought she'd admit to Liepnits, much less to herself, Manning finds herself saying (a belated response to Margo's kindliness?) that marriage has made her see things she never saw before and doesn't want to see even now. "You mean the taxi?" prompts Cook. (To quiet him before it's too late, Margo taps her lips three times with the back of her right forefinger.) "Not just the taxi (and I told you I don't want to talk about it—don't want to see it). It was—is—everything a thing is not supposed to be. Though it's not the taxi's fault—nor the driver's, for that matter. The story—our story—the silly terrifying mystery at the heart of the taxiing—is the culprit for it robbed the taxi of its . . . thinghood. Stifled its breath." Herbert thinks: She wants to branch out—to deal with things that can't be storified. Or, to use my big word (which I'll never live down), *narrativized*—or rather, the Master's big word, only I'm the one who, as usual, has to pay the price for His recurring failure to sound a demotic note not because He lacks the common touch but because He has it—in spades—and mixes it up with disqualification for greatness or genius or whatever else He thinks about in order to jerk Himself off into dreamland. "So in answer to your question, Bill—not just the taxi. But Things. The unseeable. Things that shouldn't be seen by most people without government clearance. Every thing worth its thinghood is—what do you call it in your country?—" (the *what do you call it in your country?* routine makes her irresistible—the irresistible little-lost-girl foreigner—the waif without a country—at least to Cook) "a red herring!—a MacGuffin!—and that's its beauty. In movies it's always the madwoman in and out of the attic who sees the sort of things I've seen and knows she's seeing them to her detriment in every context. Like Jean Seberg in *Lilith*—" (Cook will never cease to be amazed by—impressed by—pleased with—Irena's breadth of familiarity—comfortable familiarity—with not-so-popular culture.) "Remember the picnic sequence where she can't keep her eyes off the sun bouncingly reflected in the waterfall? What does it *mean*? *Question:* What does it have to do with the plot? *Answer:* Nothing. It *is* the plot and nothing but the plot. Seberg ends up in the loony bin for the crime of daring to see the Thing-in-Itself over and over and over again." Herbert concedes (to the Master, since nobody else is around worth holding court with—worth *trusting*) that racisms aside, they—i.e., she and Irena—at least in their sun-sensitive instars (*for proof of Herbert's sun-sensitivity, see footnote 90 or thereabouts*)— are more like sisters under the mink than either of them would have ever thought possible. "Well, I had my Jean Seberg moment when Newt and I were about to go on our honeymoon (he abandoned his second wife who was dying of lung cancer to marry me: his almost simultaneous conversion to Catholicism was atonement enough for securing me a seven-million-dollar expense account at Tiffany's and one day, if I play my cards right, The Rump, that evil teetotaller, will make me his Very Special Envoy to the Vatican)." (*A marvel,* somebody concedes [maybe Pritchard, maybe his better half], *I mean, the way she manages to turn her losing battle with the English language on and off at will—manages to turn it whether on or off into nothing less than an enduring triumph.*) She tries to fend off Newt's endearments which have a hard time coming across as playful except to the least practiced eye. (What *does* come across, with creepy ease, is his look of dread—that she might finlly reveal who paid in full for their Trump Tower love nest in exchange for . . . well, never mind—it's too nice a night to talk about money laundering especially when it involves [and when doesn't it?] those current chronically dependable monopolizers of blockbuster screen time—and rightful successors to the serial killers of the 1990s—to wit, Russian oligarchs or, more precisely, "Russian oligarchs.") She finally succeeds in getting him off her back by saying, "And I don't need a jab in the ribs to remind me to tell 'em the one about the taxi because this time around, it's the one about the . . . shadow. The shadow, you see, is a true thing-in-itself—the kind that made Lilith's mouth water. A true thing-in-itself and therefore unfit for inclusion in—and proud of its immunity to the blandishments of—any story, even the story of a drug trial. The taxi, on the other hand, is—was—a red herring and a false alarm and a false start and a detour—an amphibian—a centaur—a sphinx—a minotaur—a thing-in-itself and story trinket—a hybrid—a mestizo—a Janus-faced Cecily in town and Gwendolen in the country. Although it continues to terrify me—me, who's not only done it all but has the impertinence to think she's seen it all. Fact is, Melanctha's wrong. I didn't—don't—know—who was in that taxi and why. Look at 'em." She points at "'em"—friends of the court, foes of the court and those in-between; fellow sufferers; and witch doctors, hospital administrators, start-up idiot savants and just plain idiots, and those whose professional status remains unknown—as if they were the birds and beasts of a confectioner's forest all too eager to be dodderingly tamed by Pamino's taunting flute. "They're already as good as rolling in the aisles without your precious reminder, Liepsy—a senile tic, really. Ladies and gents, I might as well admit I was struck by a shadow in the parking lot, immediately after the justice of the peace and his concubine pelted us—almost brutally (in Reno, anything goes)—with warmed-over confetti. But I couldn't decide from where I stood (though why blame my position in space and time?) whether it was the nearby sapling or the even nearer lamppost that cast the deciding vote." "But why bother these folks with a story that's all—and only—about uncertainty, my love? Do you think they're up to it?" "Do you think they're up to it? Do you think they're up to it?" she mimics wickedly. Then (when enough time has elapsed to signify that if she catches herself breaking down before your—their—very eyes and *responding*, then it's out of the blue and on her own steam and at her own prompting and to a question of her own posing), Manning says, "I insisted, right there in that parking lot, that under no circumstances—not even on pain of death—would I allow the uncertainty to be resolved. If we were going to make our marriage work (interesting that a marriage is supposed to *work*, like a toilet or a shredder or an app or, more—most—to the point, a suppository)—and not just on the level of unspeakably funny bedroom malpractices—we'd have to live with the uncertainty and plenty more where that came from." "So the shadow was an omen," says Margo, ever the transmogrifier of kitchen-sink neorealism into cliffhanger-riddled Southern Gothic (*there! the cat's finally out of the bag where Margo's core identity is concerned: she's a transmogrifier—and a damn good one, as anybody down or up at Sarah Lawrence will tell you*). "Not, not an omen. Just—*just!*—a shadow. The shadow-in-itself. And for all you Strauss haters I'm *Die Frau mit ein Schatten*. Not that I wasn't sorely tempted, once we were on our way to Disneyland or Disney World or Disneyville (before returning to NY in time for Oktoberfest[92] and, more importantly, the taxiing taxi [I had the plate number]), to jump out of the car and go back to determine once and for all whether that shadow was the ejaculation of a lamppost or a sapling. (Not realizing that where things-in-themselves are concerned, there is never a final determination.) But just before opening the door, I was struck a second time—by the realization of all that was to be gained from resolute non-resolution of the problem—among other things, two culprits for the price of one." Turning defiantly to Melanctha: "Who *was* in the taxi according to you?" Melanctha shakes her head primly—slowly enough to let the sibylline touch take its lofty toll. And in so doing whom, the shake inquires, does she (addicted to whodunits since the cradle) remind herself of? *Honoria*

---

[92]As a matter of principle or honor, Irena balks at confessing her squeamishness with respect to attending the bacchanale, given that methane emissions levels during the 2018 Oktoberfest in Munich were found to have been as much as 100 parts per billion higher than levels before and after, with only 22 percent of the increase attributable to harmless beer-and-sausage-saturated belches and farts (!) and the rest arising, worrisomely, from leaks in gas appliances for heating and cooking (see Jia Chen and others, "Methane emissions from the Munich Oktoberfest," *Atmospheric Chemistry and Physics*, vol. 20, No. 6 [27 March 2020], pp. 3683–3696, as highlighted in *Nature*, vol. 580, No. 7802 [9 April 2020], p. 169).

Waynflete![93] The way the author manages early on to get her exempted from suspecthood—to get her accepted, no questions asked, as a bona fide non-member of the group to which she belongs—bears examining not just by the holy ghost of Bertrand Russell but by ordinary people like Melanctha whose extraordinary future hinges on demystifying such things—things in and out of themselves—for her fans.

Shearer waits eagerly (for what?)—on the sidelines, always on the sidelines (no longer a principal, just a member of the corps), as has been her wont ever since retiring (although she's managed, for what it's worth, to keep her hand—and foot—in, thanks to the entreaties of a few male dancers-turned-choreographers). What she needs are a few gentle pushes out of the fray—though she'd be hard put to fix its coordinates—pushes like the ones her partner gave her playfully, lovingly, in *Liebeslieder Walzer*. Notwithstanding the dedication to excluding mothers-in-law and other neurotic bric-a-brac from his china shop, Balanchine made an exception of those pushes, knowing only they could show Moira the way out of her psychic wounds—at least for as long as the performance lasted. Though come to think of it, in the same ballet he masterminded a more devious mother-in-law, hence a less sanguine exit from those wounds, in the shape of . . . her right foot. Three times that noble stooge of a push-plying partner—husband—lover—physiatrist in chief—lowered her—poker-faced, leering and insatiable—to the ballroom floor and three times the foot emerged—fully erect—from the gauzy undergrowth of a calf length gown to trace the prim and perfect arc of its coy shamelessness—that is, *her* coy shamelessness—the shamelessness of a career malingerer head over heels in love with the brazen fear of death. Now, too, she needs a way out. Anything to avoid any more news briefs from Manning with her cocky exaltation of uncertainty. Shearer has had enough of this woman's messy shrillness for one lifetime: much too pretty, true, to mime Carabosse and yet with a little coaching and enough rodents on hand to drive her party-pooping chariot . . . Anything to avoid taking a good hard look at Eden. He's awakened her maternal instinct as well. Too painful to watch him trembling and spitting out the soup. She needs to distract herself—and at this stage in her life distraction means debasement. Something about the business with the taxi continues to disturb her—to pain her to the usual point of excruciation (she who always doubted her capacity to suffer deeply enough to *hoof it up* [her mother's phrase] convincingly). Hasn't she seen one misbehaving similarly up in the cemetery? Or was it on upper State Street the day she almost fainted in front of though not necessarily because of Gerzso's *Ávila Negra*? No, the disturbance runs deeper than current events. Only debasement can ease the pain and debasement means somebody else's debasement—debasement by proxy, then—and proxy means fantasy. A fantasy scrupulously attended to—as scrupulously as Madame Karinska, the NYCB wardrobe mistress, attended to Moira's wardrobe. This time the

---

[93] The linchpin-in-chief of Agatha Christie's eminent and eminently rereadable *Easy to Kill* [UK: *Murder Is Easy*] (1939).

waiting-eagerly entails loitering on the fringes of Park Avenue while Irena, star tenant in one of its fanciest buildings, instructs the doorman (Pritchard, caparisoned in his signature livery of restraint) to hail her a . . . taxi. What Shearer eagerly waits for is a sign—a *scène—de ballet* (something to go with Manning's fancy shoes: Manolo Blahnik patent leather Mary Janes?)—of impatient contempt for Pritch's lack of authority where cabbies are concerned. She dreads and yet longs for—positively lusts after—the moment when Manning—the star of her sidelines show—will finally unleash that contempt—or better, seek to establish a fake camaraderie intended to do what contempt can't, i.e., get him, her vassal, back on the ball. A fakery she assumes will (following in Newt's footsteps) pass muster easily enough as the real thing—how can she miss? after all, she's the rich bitch with what she takes to be perfect Park Ave diction and he's just the doorman (it's a surefire dynamic straight out of Strindberg). And if it doesn't—pass muster, that is—then Manning will have debased herself and in vain and this is precisely what Shearer is waiting for since she lusts breathlessly after her own debasement. *By proxy*—the best kind—or is that just the wordflow shooting its mouth off? For the dancer who can no longer dance debasement is a recyclable breath of fresh air.

Eden, too, knows a thing or two about taxiing taxis, having seen one going round and round at the zoo. It terrifies him: the memory of that object behaving the way a human predator behaves but with a sentiency way beyond the reach of humans. He must punish himself for having been too preoccupied with the taxi to neutralize Borkman: It's the second time he's made an ass of himself by missing his target. (He's not—never—too out of sorts to be able to punish himself: it's pretty much a signature skill of every member of the Invidicum guinea pig tribe.) And here he is matter-of-factly confessing to his failure as if it were a question of forgetting to pick up his raincoat at the dry cleaner's. Can it be that the same taxi's been plaguing them all? Like Shearer, Eden is waiting eagerly for some form of debasement to take his mind off failure and persecution (maybe then he'll stop trembling and start to gluttonize over his stringy broth). A pornographic fantasy (he remembers his too too brief sojourn in NY carrying XXX-rated DVDs to and from that Ninth Avenue? emporium somewhere in deep dark Chelsea) *from which he gratefully excludes himself owing to dereliction of duty* should do very nicely here on this portable death bed. He's a big fan of the hospitality—the ecumenism—of pornography as a way into and out of emotion. In his case—and maybe everybody else's—it is to the same camera obscura harboring—sheltering—burning images of a very special stripe that happiness, sadness, frustration, delight, despair and any other average joe you might care to mention always repair in order to rest their weary bones. True, convergence of every one of his states of soul on the very same domain time after time evidences a hair-raising paucity of resources. But at the same time such convergence proves—whether he's ready for the proof or not—how much the lion's share of any emotion is its unsettlement—how much its ID is perfused with/yoked to its ostensible opposite. (E.g., happiness is despair and despair happiness because at their boiling point both seek refuge at the shrine of the same dark god.) The Master has just seen fit, Herbert deduces, to lavish—perpetrate—a bona fide thought packet on Eden (she knows the look of such a victim cum beneficiary—can smell it a mile away)—has deemed him, given all he's been through and given his current overly receptive state (of semi-delirium), worthy of such largesse. And not just any old specimen but *the*—or at least *a*—quintessential thought packet. But shouldn't the gift come with a warning—something to the treacly effect that (*a*) all gifts entail responsibilities which means, among other things, he mustn't get addicted and that (*b*) it's now the real work begins since the packet must be incorporated in the story—the Invidicum Story—which is easier said than done? As custodian of the packet—though they are all custodians of each other's packets just as "[a]ll the little ones of our time are collectively the children of us adults of the time, and entitled to our general care"[94]—he'll need to oversee the push-and-pull of two tricky processes (distinguishable conceptually yet inextricably bound concretely), namely, (*a*) accommodation—of the story to the packet, with all its idiosyncrasies (like a coronavirus, the packet is, with all its spike proteins) and (*b*) assimilation—of the packet to the story. But Eden must understand that the push-and-pull dynamic is most effective—most . . . artistic when accommodation and assimilation don't quite succeed, i.e., when story and thought packet end up not quite hitting it off at the desired checkpoint and trysting place—when the packet doesn't quite fuse with the story at the assigned site of insertion—when the long arm of the thought packet is too alien, uncooperative, inorganic to fit perfectly—to be plugged smoothly—into the story's shoulder joint—when the attempt to bend the arc of the packet to the shape of the story and vice versa lays bare the bruised—pitted—rutted terrain of borderline implausibility—when resistance—non-compliance—momentarily rule the roost.[95] But why, Melanctha wonders, is the story and thought packet's not quite hitting it off at the checkpoint—why is the borderline implausibility of their tryst—a good thing? Or maybe it's Eden who wonders—or would wonder if he weren't loitering on the fringes of delirium; or maybe it's the Master Himself who wonders—or should wonder (if only He'd get off His high horse long enough). So, maybe it's not a good thing, Melanctha thinks, until she remembers Rodin's "limb wrongly fitted" device, as reported by Leo Steinberg, which was a good—a very good—thing, at least as far as Leo was concerned, proving as it did that only an imperfect fit renders justice to life—an infinite sequence of imperfect fits if ever there was one—as it tends to be lived.[96] Suddenly she feels like *overprotecting* Eden (but to what does such an awkward phrase—whose awkwardness is its beauty—correspond out in the real world?). It's just that

---

[94]Thomas Hardy, *Jude the Obscure*, part fifth, chap. three.

[95]See Flavell, *The Developmental Psychology of Jean Piaget*; and Piaget, *The Construction of Reality in the Child*, concluding chap. entitled "The elaboration of the universe."

[96]See Leo Steinberg, "Rodin," in *Other Criteria: Confrontations with Twentieth-Century Art* (New York, Oxford University Press, 1972).

as his mother surrogate she doesn't want him (if it's in fact Eden who's been charged with wondering—hard—about the thought packet) being compared to, say, a madman rhapsodically shaking a dead geranium on a windy night. *An* anti-Semitic *madman*, corrects Cantor, who can't help noting that if Eden has been assigned the role of house thought-packet surgeon, he certainly has his work cut out for him.

It doesn't take much riffling through his archive without walls to retrieve a scene that can generate—the stars are first-rate when it comes to robust shamelessness—the right sort of gruelingly real camera-unaware excitement which may in turn be depended on to induce a premature ejaculation of . . . words!—words that of course are not in the "script" or barked out by the "director" (you mean *director, Eden*, not *"director": no smart-ass scare quotes, if you please: they don't suit you—you, who come by your vices honestly and honor them humbly and would as soon mock or delegitimize any source of solace [and yourself in tandem] as kick a cat—in Balboa Park, say, at dusk in early autumn—reduced by desperate hunger to rubbing its coat up against your calves*[97]), bespeaking as they do a desire so demanding it has no choice but to quickly exhaust the resources of cock and cunt as transducers and migrate, uninvited, to the vocal cords. (Or so he needs to believe.) Or if the excitement is *not* camera-unaware but turns out in fact to be increased by its presence, that's AOK with Eden just as long as he, qua camera-eye, doesn't become the target of the participants' desire, i.e., just as long as neither participant's connection with the camera crowds out the precious connection with his partner. Enough suspense here for ten and a half Hitchcock films. (Yes, the Invidicum Master has not only sharpened the perceptions of Eden's camera-eye beyond repair—*the eye that dares not speak its name*—but provided him as well with the wordflow—the *wordage* [as boatswains speak of cordage]—required to distort and misrepresent them.)

Shearer has a hunch that Cantor wants to undergo, by putting the Manning-Pritchard dyad through its paces, the same debasement by proxy. She doesn't know that he's already been taken care of in that department—is already undergoing that debasement (for real and in living color), since the members of a carefully chosen jury of his peers are, as we speak, unseaming him (in the Bard's words) from the nave to the chaps.

Herbert feels—no, is starting to feel—toward Manning *something she never dreamed she could feel*, toward her or anybody else: respect. (Or is this

---

[97]Given Eden's gratitude for the dependable solace purveyed by pornographers and sex workers, it's no wonder that he (taking a page from Linda's Spitzer-bashing playbook) has nothing but contempt for the media (especially the so-called liberal media, which should know better) when they, in bringing up the matter of the hush-money scheme hatched around about the time of the 2016 presidential campaign by The Rump & Co., routinely/casually/pruriently/dismissively referred/will refer to the most famous of the payees not as [the delightful] Stormy Daniels but as *porn star* Stormy Daniels as if it's her profession—yes, her *profession*—that makes the transaction's sleaze coefficient shoot up into the stratosphere.

just the Master looking out for No. 2—gumming up the works with a hyperbole aimed at doing justice to his new favorite: his Suzanne Farrell? No doubt
about it.) And how can it be otherwise? for here she is, though no longer
young or *that* young, risking her reputation by publicly accepting uncertainty as the chaff and staff of life, and thereby calling everybody else's plowed
progress into question and not merely within the context of the trial since
its repercussions routinely spill over and infect all other contexts. Everybody
else—aka the rest of them—now fear—and Herbert *most of all* (no! the words
are taking her where she hasn't yet earned the right to go)—that in contrast
they have grossly ignored the markers proper to themselves, their own private
taxis and shadows, so to speak—the markers of the disease that, for each, is he
himself and no other—or, even worse, that in their particular case there have
never been any markers to miss, with everything proceeding drearily—non-
curatively—according to plan. Which means that, though doing exactly what
they were put on earth to do, they're nevertheless—or predictably—impoverished compared with Irena who's proven herself so fertile in misgivings
and even more fertile in surmounting them, making her, then, both the Irena
they know and the even more alluring Irena that might have been—a double
Irena, in other words: *two Irenas for the price of one.* My, how quickly they've
learned her lingo. But it's also obvious that Irena has her own problems (budding genius isn't proof against pain—worse, self-doubt): she's afraid that if
she attempts to implement the cockamamie strategy she's been devising *as we
speak* for further elaborating her deep thoughts on markers and their vicissitudes (for she still has plenty of markers to skewer) while at the same time
proving their invidious implications are incapable of infecting others (even
if infection is part and parcel of their meaning—is, in fact [no!], their *whole*
meaning [no!]),[98] the relevant thoughts will be destroyed, along with their
progenitor, or at least attenuated beyond recognition (like, say, the windows of
any building in SoHo's Cast-Iron District, whether arched or square-headed
or triple round-headed, when reflected in the belly of the skyscraper opposite,
since from now on wherever you turn in the five boroughs there'll always be
a skyscraper opposite, that is, if Mein Rumpf and his loathsome litter armed
to the teeth with callow beards and bleached-blond brains get their way). Fact
is, Irena can't in good conscience see herself reducing thoughts to mere shadows of themselves simply to pacify not-so-innocent bystanders. But even if
Irena's not up to standing her ground her sidekick—Manning—may very well
turn out to be capable even at this late date of elaborating her thoughts like
a true virtuoso while, like an even truer one, proving to everybody's satisfaction (since she's still a doctor and her first obligation to inflict no harm) that
thoughts, however heinous, aren't the infections they're cracked up to be. By

---

[98] Now, just a minute, where does the Master come off daring to run Irena's show as if it
were Herbert's by replacing "part and parcel of" with "the whole" just to make a splash
with the hyperlative mode-crazy, sensation-starved dinner-theater crowd? Herbert
(stricken with a craving to protect Manning—but from what precisely?) makes a note
to deal, firmly but tactfully, with this thorny issue later on.

proving that not by the wildest stretch of the imagination can her thoughts—any thoughts—be deemed infectious while through that very proof preserving—even enhancing (*no! down, words, down!*)—the infectiousness of their essence, the essence of their infectiousness, Manning will surely be enriching the universal commons—the public domain—for decades to come whether she chooses to know it or not—and maybe hewing close to the not knowing will make her *even more of a virtuoso* (oddly enough, Herbert does not feel this particular bit of hyperlative wordflow warrants—is worth—shouting *Get lost* at the Master).

"Quick," Ethan cries, "get an ambulance. Look, idiots, Eden's obviously on his last legs and Borkman isn't too far behind." (For once he's right, somebody thinks. Why *for once*? Cantor wonders. In fact, Ethan has a well-merited reputation for rightness most of the time—end product of working for so many bigwig agencies simultaneously which means being in the thick of things when they're going at each other's throats. The best way, Cantor assumes, to learn how the monsters tick.) It's easy enough—talk is cheap—for everybody to agree that, lying there, they look for all the world not just like Damon and Pythias but like David and Jonathan as well (or, depending on your taste, like David and Goliath) but who among them will be intrepid enough (as Jean was a few dog-eared pages ago) to lend—donate—his POV to that observation? Eden, collapsed, is frothing at the mouth and it now becomes evident—as evident as it will ever be—that Borkman has been shot in the groin, but only glancingly according to Borkman, Jr., (who should know better?). (Rumor—sorry, the Word on the Street—has it that he'll shortly be unveiling an app to enable the workers at Trader Joe's and elsewhere to smile at customers and their managers with the boilerplate bounce and bubbliness enjoined in the fine print [if only they had eyes to see!] of their eternally temporary contracts—an app whose efficacy may account for the present inappropriateness of his own filial b&b.) Everybody is on, or at, his cellphone, many taking pictures, some of which are for immediate upload to TabLoad, the hottish new social medium, an almost-unicorn currently valued in the mere low billions. "You never told me he was an epileptic!" Cook shouts at Manning, pleased (but according to whose POV?) at being able to impugn her competence. Almost as good as re-penetrating her vaginally. At first, Manning does not respond to the attack—in fact she may not have heard it—nor does she turn to Liepnits to defend her, for this would mean acknowledging he exists, which stopped long before the connubial bak'd meats were cold. Out of the blue she decides to one-up him. "It's not generalized—only partial. And he's been approved for RNS System stimulation so it'll be only a matter of days before he's seizure-free. How many of us non-epileptics can say the same thing about ourselves?" As if things weren't—as things aren't—yet bad enough, Walser steps forward brandishing a carving knife which Netta (though it could have been anyone) recalls having last seen stuck in the half-devoured candied Virginia ham next to the gravy boat (a vessel big enough to shelter Washington Crossing the Delaware). "It was me—I—who disabled the electrodes. That's why Eden's potshots went astray." (Is this a fantasia on he-man themes? Jean wonders.) "But not completely" (Netta, ever the corrector, gestures toward

Borkman, who seems to be improving arduously and may very well pull through).

Margo (*pettishly, smelling a rank amateur*): "Put that thing down" (as if demanding that he button his fly, for chrissake). Deflated, Walser sticks the implement back where it belongs and, turning heavenward, delivers a Lear-like "Sorry sorry sorry sorry sorry." She looks away. Too many unpleasant reminders of what she's come here to confront, but in her own way and in her own time. Pritchard puts a shapely forefinger to his lips. "We've all got to stick together or we're pretty much done for. Post is in the building. I can hear, you might say, his shadow advancing." Stifter refuses to apologize for his ex-pal. Especially in a situation that's playing like a banned outtake from the color sequence of *Ivan the Terrible*, Part II.

Now that not one but two pillars of the enterprise have taken it upon themselves to wax and wane in quick alternation, there's nothing for Manning to do but stomp around and wring her hands and make it known thereby that she, the mightiest pillar of them all, is beyond outrage. Outrage over what? Well, for starters, outrage over the fact that the fates having once again acted so unjustly (where these, her dear friends Borkman and Eden, are concerned) and her comrades so sluggishly in response, the Bunker has fast become an unhappy land—unhappy not because it doesn't have but because it *needs* a hero.[99] And it's Manning and Manning alone who's been handed the reins of officiation and by none other than . . . Manning herself. Not to mention her outrage that people should now think she, Irena, who shuns the spotlight every chance she gets, must relish having already (news travels fast) super-seded the moribunds as *the* person of interest in the case ("person of interest," of course, in the hagiographic not the legal sense). Herbert—whose Bronxian street smarts never desert her even in those rare instances where she could wish for nothing more—has no choice but to see things thus: The event is now all about Irena Manning—and about her unique response which is too mas-sive for mouthing. If she's obliged to share the spotlight she'll denounce the challenger—the usurper—as an imbecile in the eminent domain of grief. Still, this doesn't prevent her from demanding to know why nobody is doing any-thing or why everybody is doing nothing or both—why there is no apprecia-ble hue and cry. True, every outcry except her own will be branded as woefully inadequate—it comes with the territory—but that's only because unlike all other outcries, hers is not just an outcry per se but a meditation on the futility of outcry. Don't *just* stand there (so says her stomping and hand-wringing), but if stand there you must at least have the decency to do it gaping at my queenliness in the face of your inadequacy—*in the face of the inadequacy of the event itself* as a match for the magnitude of my self-sacrifice in meeting its ignoble demands. She's doing what she does best, Cook snickers, still wanting to penetrate her with more than words. But just where has this determina-tion—this decree—this papal bull—come from since in all fairness Irena has

---

[99] "Adapted" from Bertolt Brecht, *Galileo* (New York, Grove Press, 1961), scene 12, last line.

done a lot of other, far more important things and done them a far sight better? Still, he must admit that, however short it falls of the truth, the determination surely captures Manning in this place and time better than any other could. He can hear her (now barefoot: the Mary Janes have outlived their Veblenian uselessness) upbraiding Netta, Herbert, Shearer and Jean (together at last but until when?) for their passivity which, real or not, has immediately become *the* prerequisite (set forth and fulfilled all in an instant) for making herself the plausible epicenter of what Pritchard still hopes against hope is but a mighty tempest in a teapot.

As for Herbert, she doesn't in the least mind being on the periphery—the *sidelines* (to quote Shearer)—the Periphery of Things (just as there's an Internet of Things—wirelessly connected and more and more hackable—so is there a Periphery of Things)—in particular the Periphery of Things Manning. Fact is, she's happily sentried here for doesn't the periphery—black or white—always end up becoming (OK, maybe not *always*) the center of things, at least according to that inimitable wiseass she was forced to read in Philosophy 103 and ended up, his self-inflation notwithstanding, sort of liking—sort of *taking a shine to* (who cares if this idiom's on the verge of extinction: its eternal summer gives *her* license to live)? Won't the periphery of things black one day end up as the center of things white even if she won't be around to have her faith vindicated? On the other hand, she has to avoid believing she'll be rewarded by the armed forces of Air-rnr (rectification and reparation) for the race-based Babinski of getting out of Manning's way (the Black Man's Burden), withdrawing into herself, holding herself reflexively back, contracting, hiding her essence, retreating, limiting herself, as did her mother. Unless the purpose of withdrawal— (For she's not merely a soon-to-be-famous writer with just so much tolerance for smug white trash but, alas, the vengeance-driven reincarnation of the other Mrs. Herbert, the quaint itinerant Bronx maid of seventy years ago, who like every other Bronx maid was forbearingly referred to by all her employers at that time [and they milked their forbearance for all it was worth with a wink and a nod] as the "girl"—the girl they had to not just abide but feed for the sake of toilet, carpet and countertop.) Unless the purpose of withdrawal is to give Manning, in the primordial space created by that withdrawal—a space that in relation to Herbert is an infinitesimal point but for Manning the entire cosmos—unless the purpose is to give Manning another opportunity to strut, epileptically, the stuff of self-inflation—to make a fool of herself—to dig her own grave. (*In which case the withdrawing and its repercussions become a reward self-conferred from the withdrawer's stance of strength—reward as waystation on the decreasingly bumpy road to further reward.*) Unless Herbert is withdrawing—contracting—not as a slave but as a prosthetic god, contraction in this case meaning preparation for a great leap. Unless limiting—delimiting—exiling herself—abandoning a region within herself to the likes of Manning—the region least prized—unless leasing—bequeathing it to this diva for the perpetration of her grand operatics is Herbert's way of taking pity—or a kind of pity. Unless Herbert's exile entails, in a second act, a return to that region since, *pace* Fitzgerald, not only are there second acts in American lives, in fact there are *only* second acts—the first don't count—aren't listed on the Big Board—are only a draft—one big ink blot—one big Rorschach signifying nothing. Unless abandonment of this region of herself to emptiness conveys Herbert's intention (once the operatics are over and done with—dead and buried) to transmit a ray of light—shine a spotlight—on Manning in all her white-girl absurdity—the archetypal white girl as re-created—reconfigured—reorganized through the auspices of that light just as her mother the maid was configured by her employers as the White Hausfrau's Burden. Or is this analogy a bit too pat for the Master's taste? even if He's giving her freer and freer rein as the most important part of himself—as his Farrell (yes, Manning's accession to the role was just a flash in the pan—a flash in the bedpan you might say, given the Master's slow, giddy but irreversible slide toward senescence)—his Arthur Mitchell—as the most feminine of his feminizing elements—as his *Shekhinah*—femininity being the hallmark of omnipotence as disincarnated in one long Clyfford Still-like fissuring of the overstretched canvas of maleness. (Herbert is aware that blacks are frequently anti-Semites but for the purposes of this trial Herbert's a diehard philo-, acquaintanceship with an oddball named I. Luria and his apostle G. Scholem in Course 405 entitled "Cosmogonies" being responsible for her hewing [so what if too close for comfort?] to the Kabbalistical line. And thanks to those two, a bush-league thought about maids remembered and the Manning-related misery of the moment has unforeseeably intersected with—has drawn into its web—has gotten its hooks into—has been enlightened and enriched by—has appropriately deformed to suit its own skewed needs for universality—a big-league packet [which may itself have been reciprocally enlightened and enriched in the process].) But will Manning get it—this recoil as the obverse of a lethal spring toward affirmation and the Karens of the world be damned?

It doesn't matter inasmuch as Invidicum is failing and will continue to fail. Since look at her—for all the withdrawals, the constrictions to a mighty pinpoint hemorrhage, she's still mad-dog envious of white women like Manning who are having it all, including of their even more enviable brand of trials and tribulations—nice trials and nicer tribulations—the stuff of mini-series. And she's most envious of those whites, especially women whites, to whom there is nothing more alien than the oozing of contempt, which nothing-more-alienness is the most exquisite—the most otherworldly—thing in the world. But surely, along some dimension of their being, an active effort to suppress the contempt as a contempt for their own fear must be very much in operation. Don't tell me a white can be capable of a humanness so color-blind as to be more than human—ethereal. No white who professes not to see any difference between black and white can deny that not so deep down there's an active refusal to see—the exercise of a will *not* to see—collecting overtime. Although she isn't quite sure why acknowledgment of the failure of on-label Invidicum (swallowed up by off-) should rear its ugly head right now when she has so many other worries defying mastery. Is her aim to inure herself way in advance to the fact that all forms of fulfillment will go on being denied her—the Master's life support notwithstanding—so none of the denials come as a shock? Only she knows from experience that this kind of ploy is apotropaic, in other words, culinary, and as such always gets over-seasoned and overstuffed with the expectation that it will make the bad news go away—head it off at the pass. Still, she's not just willing but *more than willing* to give her all to the ploy as long, that is, as she isn't expected to track down a date—a specific point in time marking the foreclosure of all possibility of fulfillment, i.e., redemption—a sewer into which all fulfillment past, present and to come has been sucked for good—for the existence of such a creature would only ignite self-denunciation for the failure to foil something so well-defined—so pinpointable—so targetable hence so easy to annihilate.[100] That is, she shouldn't be compelled to acknowledge that non-fulfillment as a way of life began, say, just after her divorce or the death of her son (*bad: somebody as "originality"-obsessed as the Master cannot allow her to harbor—nurse—such a banal conviction*). No, it kicked in long before Herbert was born (*a better sort of conviction: she can already feel His approval, or at least His lesser disapproval, breathing down her neck*)—in which case, she must have been the sort of fetus that usurps the anguish its mother doesn't allow herself to know she feels every waking moment, in and out of, say, a maid's uniform? Is this the meaning—the gist—the thrust—of her "conviction"? But if so, does she actually *believe* in its meaning even if that meaning can't be enacted—vouched for—out in the real world? In other words, Can a fetus actually usurp its mother's anguish? And what does believing in the meaning of such a conviction mean? Doesn't the conviction's strength—its reality—its power—a power that becomes a kind of truth—truth with teeth—stem from the fact that it can't be held to—strait-jacketed by—the usual standards of transparency? Is it possible—confirmable by, say, the MIT Department of Brain and Cognitive Sciences? Or, better yet, by an upstart cum start-up like Theranos (a vanity production stuffed into a black turtleneck) where the inevitable unconfirmability would at least be camouflaged by the greater scandal of that upstart turtleneck's criminal making-a-mountain-out-of-a-pinprick? Maybe there's just no back-mapping this particular chunk of wordflow to some mirroring chunk of worldflow. Or maybe this particular chunk has been generated purely to showcase the inherent inadequacy—the chronic undependability—of worldflow—as a team player on Team Flow—purely to punish worldflow for its inability or unwillingness way too many times in the past to cough up on demand a flesh-and-blood event—state of affairs—object—complement—correlative—

---

[100]Melanctha is unaware that she is in fact the champion (Cantor would be proud) of an irrational as opposed to a rational cut—split—partition of her timeline into a before-foreclosure and an after-foreclosure class. In a rational partition of the timeline, the [rational] number effecting the partition belongs either to the before-foreclosure class (as its greatest element, or latest point in time) or to the after-foreclosure class (as its smallest element, or earliest point in time); in either case, it's localizable—pinpointable—as the dreaded moment when the bottom fell out of the universe. In an irrational partition (the celebrated Dedekind cut), the [irrational] number (e.g., the square root of 2) that effects the partition belongs neither to the before-foreclosure class (as its greatest element) nor to the after-foreclosure class (as its smallest element), i.e., in this case, the dreaded moment is not fixable, localizable, pinpointable or track-downable.

answering reality—reality sandwich—out in the lifeworld corresponding to a particular specimen of wordflow. Maybe. Maybe not. Since there's nothing like the exhilaration of knowing that your chunk is not back-mappable into the real world—that your chunk is airtight—like a book that simply can't be translated to the screen—translated into film—unless the film's by Dreyer or Akerman or (unbutchered) von Stroheim. Which airtightness gives you the right to talk through both sides of your mouth—to have your cake and eat it, too—i.e., to reproach the world for not filming your chunk of wordflow while sighing with celebratory relief that said chunk runs no risk of being mirrored *out there* as a bona fide state of affairs since it's precisely such an enactment that you dread—dread as a reduction—a distortion—a travesty—a vulgariza-tion—a hijacking—a kidnapping.[101] Since (let's get this straight) the wordflow of somebody like Melanctha—if flow it must—takes its job seriously—which is to keep itself (and her in tandem) safe from translation, i.e., paraphrase, leaving *that*, in the great tradition of *All about Eve*'s Addison DeWitt, to Lou-isa May Alcott. When wordflow (fast becoming Melanctha's bread and butter even if the world has yet to hear from her) senses her need for its services—when she's confronted out in the wilds of the real with a chunk of world-flow whose demon makes apparent the especial urgency of exorcism (even under the best of circumstances worldlflow is a source of pain)—a chunk like, say, Manning the white woman engaged in self-promotion or post-divorce non-fulfillment as a way of life or the ongoing failure of Invidicum to soothe the savage green-eyed monster's breast or Cantor's so-called pals moving in for the career kill—when wordflow senses Melanctha's need, it hops to it, exorcising the aforesaid demon through a faithful mirroring of its contours in the wording of the desiderated counter-chunk, that is, until the words themselves lose interest, preferring to confound the logic of the lifeworld and trace instead (to some, a heretical mere frolic with syntax) their own chain of un-back-mappable thought, along which word calls to word according to an illogic all their own (thereby preserving Herbert from another kind of enslavement). Such chunks of wordflow—such . . . thoughts—being nothing more or less than their own self-correction unprompted either by criticasters or cavillers and stretching to the crack of doom.

---

[101]Cf. the case of The Rump as he runs for re-election—another case of having one's cake and eating it, too—of talking or farting through both sides of one's mouth—of killing two birds with one stone. Winning, he wins. Losing, he wins—even bigger. For let's face it, The Rump's rump is no longer in it. No more worlds to conquer—no more Troys to burn. But that's no reason to break down and shed Macedonian crocodile tears. On the contrary. Time for him to cheer up—time for him to start feeding off the monetizable carcass of his misbegotten cachet. Time for him to get back to erecting more monuments to the *flatulent void within* (a self-important turn of phrase, I know, but still too good for its target). Fact is, better, far better, than winning is the antici-patory exhilaration of losing—exultation over having been granted a fixed amount of time—between now and the Other's inauguration—within which to viciously cram as much destruction as possible—destruction as celebration.

But if the confounding of lifeworld logic is to succeed then there's just got to be a word or a chunk of word *dung* (meant honorifically)—a pivot word or pivot chunk—that resists. Like the quaint little row house at the corner of Gold and Fulton Streets she encountered one blindingly sunny summer morning en route to a CT scan. While it wanted nothing better than to give its comrades the slip and live out the rest of its days with Melanctha (whom it mistook for the Bosom of Abraham), their pull was fortunately too strong—strong enough to generate what she eagerly mistook for an imperishable image.

This ER sort of anatomizing is right up her blind alley (*Watch your language*, she reminds herself). And to incorporate it within her next effort would doubtless be one very skillful means of *getting an edge on the competition*.[102] But that would mean reconstructing the analysis from scratch, including the gruesome details at every step and stage (*the Pulitzer, my dear, is all in the gruesome details*). So despite the growing din and the to-and-fro of too many stretcher- and gurney-bearers (the 911 brigadiers have arrived at last and if she isn't mistaken there are quite a few members of the LAPD among them) Herbert tries to remember and retain. But the more she repeats the details the greater becomes the risk of erosively erasingly forgetting them until, to her horror, it becomes all too clear that *the repeating is the forgetting*. So there she goes again, the host with the most doing her parasite's bidding. Stretching out a thought to the point where it disqualifies itself not just for back-mapping into the lifeworld—the medium of enactment—as proof of its validity—but for the Pulitzer. She's been compelled (by the Master? no! why blame that old Fart for every false start under the sun?) to short-circuit herself—to decree that two words—which through no fault of their own just happen to find themselves on opposite sides of the barricades of a predicate and hence (why hence?) can't be further apart in meaning (as least as it relates to the repeating and forgetting of *normal* people [when you don't know what to do with somebody, call him normal])—to decree that those two little words are in fact synonymous. Thereby following in the footsteps of that ill-fated Czech who, in his fourth *Blue Octavo Notebook*, wrote that "Abraham's spiritual poverty . . . is an advantage, making concentration easier for him; or rather, *it is in itself concentration*"[103] (the italics are hers). She's managed singlehandedly to perversely collapse the thought, presuming, like so many other members of her tribe, to have attained, in consequence, possession of its Grail—the Great Synonymy—the cure for all ills—

---

[102] She can't believe she's hearing herself think this—how can such anatomizing give her an edge over anybody, much less the competition? But before she can stop, even more insanely and adding insult to injury, she's thanking the Pulitzer Prize Committee—or is it the PP Board?—for selecting her work from among so many worthier, etc., etc. And, by the way, who's that sitting across from her? Why, it's Joseph Pulitzer himself! Such musings indicate that more than anybody—more than Borkman or Eden or Walser—it's she who needs a gurney.

[103] Franz Kafka, *The Blue Octavo Notebooks*, Max Brod, ed.; and Ernst Kaiser and Eithne Wilkins, translators (Cambridge, Massachusetts, Exact Change, 1991), p. 55.

the pharmakon of pharmakons. And under its auspices everything—not just all words *but the world itself*—will be reducible to the same name (or is waxing hyperbolic her way of injecting some philistine excitement into the bloodless veins of this little excursus?). She's compelled her sentence to undergo (as Franz did his) self-cannibalizing *constriction to a pinpoint* (phrase sound familiar? then by all means see above), consequently making it—microchip for all seasons—far easier to transport damage-free in an emergency—say, when The Rump's Welcome Wagon lynchers are beating down the door.

"Well, you've certainly picked a fine time to get inspired." Liepnits, about to chucklingly jab her with his elbow, immediately realizes she's not Manning (who happens to be helping Cook and Ethan lift Eden, twitching uncontrollably, onto a stretcher) and refrains. Selflessly putting aside all further thought of dealmaking which is turning out to be surprisingly successful even on this alien terrain (but does he look distraught enough?), Jr. huddles over his father's carcass while several plainsclothesmen, taking no chances of letting this wily felon (with links to The Rump and still a security risk no matter how incapacitated) escape their clutches, huddle over *him*. Herbert sighingly rolls her eyes once Liepnits has disappeared. She's convinced he had her very much in mind (he must know she has ambitions: non-news travels fast) when making that borderline-lewd crack about getting inspired and was taking a jab at her pretensions. Hasn't the lummox any inkling (though why should he?) of how much she hates his dime-store notion of inspiration, predicated as it must be (or hate's edifice collapses) on the obligation to maintain at all times (for you never know when the divine afflatus will fell you like a ton of bricks) a good (i.e., enfeeblingly ass-kissing) relationship with artistry's powers that be? Well, she hates it even more than the notion of "finishing touches" (unwittingly lambasted, at least according to her art history prof, by some ultra-famous French sculptor in his last, less official works).[104] Inspiration is for mediocrities (i.e., those makers condemned to life rather than to death)—or is this construction just a wee bit too facile for an advanced beginner like herself who still has a long way to go toward earning the right to its deployment? In any case, she much prefers the notion of . . . urgency (embodying a ferocious contempt for said kissable powers). In fact, if you must know, she's spent her entire life (and even if she hasn't, the moment calls for such a declaration and will accept no sugar substitutes)—spent her entire life, in particular the life before birth (there you go again, girl, taking the side of wordflow against lifeworld: some people never learn, although that can, if they play their cards right, redound to their glory), defying inspiration every time it deigns to rear its ugly rear.

Walser, albeit less Learlike, is back (to the consternation of one of the LAPD plainsclothesmen who, clearly, will never forgive himself for having failed to take him in for questioning) and is wasting no time distributing what

---

[104]The sculptor, as Melanctha knows very well, is Rodin (she's just taking a well-earned vacation from erudition for there's exhilaration to be extracted upon occasion from playing the rube). See Steinberg, "Rodin."

look, and certainly smell, like state-of-the-art business cards. Though her peripheral vision is not, thanks to some freaky retinal tearing of a few years back, all it should be, Herbert is still able to get a glimpse of much of the information (and there's plenty). Below his name is, for starters, the title "Grief counselor" (she gets it: gurneys spell grief). Now, who'd have ever imagined a sideline like that (or is it more, far more, than a sideline?) for somebody as subclinically autism-spectrumed as Walser revealed himself to be on several embarrassing occasions (and she's alluding not just to the business with the carving knife)—indeed, who'd have ever imagined it for anybody, if it comes to that? For one thing, exactly what sort of duties does the bearer of that title fulfill out in the pine barrens of the lifeworld? I.e., is there a worthwhile mapping from words to world? Though isn't such uncertainty—the likely incommensurateness between word and thing—part of the title's goofy charm or (from another angle) the pathos of its pretension? Yet, why single out this phrase for particular acclaim? It simply follows—and pretty harmlessly, she might add—in what is now called the great tradition of lifeworld-flouting wordflow. (*Still harping on my wordflow*, titters Master Polonius behind the arras of his imbecility.) It's hard for Ethan, catching Walser observing Herbert observing him, to decide which is the unprettier sight: her jaundiced eyeing or his shameless go-getting. Walser is retaliatorily thinking her a failure, Herbert suspects. After all, is "budding writer" any less ridiculous an epithet than the one that, without so much as a blush, he's assigned himself? True, she hasn't stooped to decking herself out in business-card regalia . . . still . . .

And what about the fact that Stifter (it has to be Stifter)'s just muttered (to Melanctha?), "I *worry* about him"? We can't let him—let *that*—off scot-free. What does *worry* signify in this—or any—context? What is its referent out in the world and what does that referent do when nobody's around to watch? And how much worry is required in a given situation for worry to be said to exist—to qualify—quantify—as worry? Or is worrying—that is, the smarmy affirmation of worrying—a way of drawing attention to and enhancing, through the power of contrast with the feeble target of all that worrying, one's own well-being (whose obscene zest of course requires no such enhancement)? Or is the ostensible worrier's affirmation of worrying the sleight of hand by which he mitigates the unjustness of his proprietorship of so much well-being—so much that it floods out of every orifice—like the lights issuing from Adam Kadmon's ears, nose, mouth? So that worry itself, not to mention its feeble target, gets lost in the shuffle. Or is the worry in question indisputably genuine but simply exhausted from overwork at—in—the moment or off-duty or on pause or automatic pilot, with *worry* dutifully—like an alarm clock—shaking it out of its stupor by stepping on all its toes? *Trick question:* How align *worry* with worry? *Extra-credit:* If you're really worried do you have the capacity to spare a minute or two to utter its name? Isn't it true that pain and the word for that pain cannot inhabit the same space at the same time? All this flits through Herbert's mind. Netta, too—not to mention Shearer and Jean (ominously chummy)—are all giving her the evil eye. Do they resent the fact that she isn't pitching in more robustly than all the others combined (even if there isn't anything, with the brigadiers on the scene, for her or anybody else to roll up their sleeves for) when she's just been handed and no questions asked the chance of a lifetime to thereby abase herself almost sufficiently to atone for the fact that, as a black, she belongs to a confederacy whose members have for centuries been far more sinned against than sinning? As far as she (a layman, granted) can make out, the casualties are getting—although there will certainly be jittery spikes in their number once the double-dealing gets really under way—better than quality care—much better, at any rate, than the care received by her son in Building 18 (recently—and outrageously—dumped on, of all things, the National Register of Historic Places).

But they can evil-eye her all they want for whether she knows it or not (*who is speaking?*)—and whether they (you know who you are) can begin (much less come) to understand it or not—nothing is easier for Herbert than to "convert obstacle into opportunity" by putting herself in the shoes, however ill-fitting, of these detractors. She perceives that smelling her ambition a mile away—ambition being the one thing about her that's way past the *budding* stage—they are, true to their code and as so many times in their shared past, diehard fans of her . . . mediocrity! which they've just invented to invalidate her right to that ambition. Still, she manages *to rise above it all* (as her mother used to exhort at the drop of a hat) not just by adopting their POVs, i.e., the POVs most conducive to the obliteration of her essence—worse, her every last hope—and hence (or so she needs to believe in order to get full shareholder value from this exercise in the transubstantiation of self-doubt into self-hate) most unerring in their discernment of the flaws motoring that essence—she manages to rise above it all, I say, not just by adopting their POVs but by going so daredevilishly far as to excoriate those POVs for having missed the most damning evidence of all, whatever that turns out to be. In fact, she doesn't know whether to thank them for subjecting her (since she's sure to have trouble getting out of bed tomorrow after so much evil-eyeing) to yet another lesson in the anatomy of brute survival (that is, if there is a tomorrow, given the thickness of these brutish walls closing in) or curse their ineptitude (since she's sure she can write their annihilatory script better than they can). For what would be the advantage of proving her detractors wrong, wrong, wrong? Where's the budding self-enrichment to be had from being schoolmarm-right in an all-too-wrong world? Only by getting deep inside the endocrine gland of their animus and finding all sorts of justification for its hypersecretion can she train herself to become just the sort of persons unknown—persons of interest—she needs to become to get past the budding stage once and for all—every one of them an anti-Herbert to the hilt—just the sort (too rabid for His taste) with whom the overcivilized ultimately timid Master seems unwilling or unable to have any truck. It makes her twitch, as she's just seen Eden twitch, to realize, as so many times before, that she understands her enviers—which is what they are—better than they understand themselves (so maybe Invidicum's hard at work after all—its efficacy being in direct proportion to her capacity to *understand without envying*). On the other hand, by virtue of this understanding—so thoroughgoing as to constitute a form of forgiveness *ex post* and *ex ante*—she's able to do what only those who *did* get past—way past—the budding stage would be able to do if they were in her shoes, namely, pick out and pay homage to the gang's decent few—e.g., Cook (never mind his incessant tergiversations), Stifter and, while we're at it, maybe even Liepnits (yes, Newt)—who, while harboring ambitions of the same magnitude as everybody else's only to see that theirs (unlike everybody else's) have, à la Harold Arlen, *all gone astray*, nonetheless (according to the dictates of an unshreddable pride in their own decency) make it their business (since the business of America is business) to bracket—straitjacket—sideline—sidestep—Envy and thereby escape relegation as a consequence of Its base practice to the sidelines of everybody else's show (still very much in previews). But is there anybody in the gang who really qualifies at this point in time and space for such homage or is wordflow simply tired of just standing around waiting for what weathermen call *current conditions* (which never change fast enough) to plausibilize this kind of mock insight? To lay its egg, so to speak. Still, by no means do we go away empty-handed: mock insight, pivoting around the delicate disproportion between current conditions and the weight of plausibilization they're *not quite capable* of shouldering, ends up *malgré lui* giving birth to the real McCoy, a stir-crazy kind of Kantian sublime, as solemnized by Barnum, Bailey, Victor Borge, Oliver Hardy, Thomas Hardy and the Ringling Brothers and Sisters, though not necessarily in that order of vocal appearance.

But far more important to Herbert than any cockamamie Kantian sublime—as invoked in this case by three little maids in italics (see directly above)—is whether the epileptic twitches will, should Eden be indicted for the near death of John Gabriel Borkman, hold water as an extenuating circumstance in a court of law. And who can she turn to for clarification regarding the plight of her son surrogate? For example, she's just heard one of the gurney boys mutter something about an ictal penumbra. What's that?

Gurney-less Borkman has, over the protestations of Jr., just managed to execute the no-mean-feat of crawling toward Eden (in the ballet entitled *Prodigal Father*, thinks Shearer—sans Siren but with no dearth, thanks to Silicon Valley, of glad-handing bathing-capped goons). For the sole purpose of heartbreakingly holding out his arms in sign of forgiveness (though his would-be killer is too weak to respond). Ethan tells Cook—but loud enough for anybody to hear, which seems to be the whole point—that what he has the pleasure of witnessing is not a conversion (Borkman's too old for that) but rather an about-face of unknown etiology. But as it turns out, Borkman isn't granting forgiveness—he's begging for it. With eyes tearing up, eyes tearing over, he admits, though the syllables are garbled, that he's never been prosecuted for his role in the financial crises of 2008, 2009, 2010, 2011, 2012, 2013, 2014 and 2015. Every time around, Justice Department's pledges to pursue the banker scum went underground and he went with it. As for Margo, she has not eyes to see: her attention is focused, atypically, exclusively on herself. (Shearer, on the other hand, does have eyes—especially in such a context, as we've just seen—and is using them effectively to wonder whether Balanchine would have disapproved [even if she knows his Old Testament fecundity never left him any time to do so—disapproval being a shackling snub to that fecundity].) Instead of practicing whatever ploys are usual to deter guests from gobbling up every last morsel (food expenses are, after all, out-of-pocket and Pritchard's not a wealthy man by any standards and, hey, what about the fact that Straynge's life-insurance payout proved, predictably, to be less than ample, especially in the context of the around-the-clock care required by their son, the etiology of whose ever-worsening disabilities is still stumping the would-be experts, and her sole remaining older sibling, a career hypochondriac?), here's Margo, folks, getting increasingly intrigued not by the fact that she doesn't give a hoot about how much gobbling we're talking about but by what this not-giving-a-hoot reflects, namely, a better-late-than-never transformation into an altogether novel self (which this time is, since there have been many such suicide attempts, far more than an avant-garde antic)—a self that has better or at least bigger things to do than moni-tor the doings of a horde of gassy freeloaders. And nothing can beat the thrill of having this imago refracted back to her through their non-seeing which makes it a virtual reality. For all that she loathes the whole damn lot of them (for preventing Pritchard from carrying on and consummating Straynge's lifework?) and they her (for no other reason than that she loathes them?) they won't be able at her funeral to contend that she hovered around them counting every canapé, like a slime hag or a turkey buzzard or a vampire bat or a tardigrade or some other sentry stationed at one of evolution's key cross-roads. But if she puts such a premium on seeming not to be a tight-fisted sentry (because, as an amateur esthete, she puts an even higher premium on having the glossy look of otherworldliness) then, according to Bayes' Theorem, a tight-fisted slime hag she must unregenerately be. But even if the glossy look is what she once overheard some Sarah Lawrence or Payne Whitney bigwigs during informal informals refer to as a counterformation, is it necessarily any more of a simulation than what it's just been flown in, on one of The Rump's private jets, to countermand? So she's ended up, as so many times before, uncertain about who and what she was. No big deal that. The spice of life, in fact. Of course she's, whatever hill of beans her talents ultimately amount to in that department, first, last and always a mother. And the uncanny fact remains that she's neither the first nor will she be the last for whom the thrill of being unperceivingly perceived, by those she loathes and who loathe her back with ever-accruing interest, as the very opposite—or, better yet, the very absence—of what her passport or her Medicare card says she is, looms too temptingly for words, even if the words come fast and furious, faster and furiouser.

She grits her teeth. Just let her get her hands (she makes a fist) on the maniac thought responsible for leading her this far afield when she has so much else to do—making sure, for example, that tomorrow's salmon mousse turns out OK and that the Bean and her crapulous confederates don't take (or we'll have to put the bunker up for sale) too many more nips. But didn't Jim (she misses the man's oxymoronisms, e.g., his dinner-table bad breath cou-pled with exquisite blue blazers) always caution her—though he rarely fol-lowed his own advice—against committing what he called the eighth—and deadliest—deadly sin, which is to blame a given thought for where it ends up taking you—or, rather, where you rudely take *it*?

Shearer has to admit (elaborating on Margo's theme) that at the moment when with his plate piled high, almost every *participant* (is this the right term?) belongs neither to the blood-splattered buffet table nor to the arena beyond where boys become unicorns and in which, thanks to Post and his thugs, appetite-suppressants like dismemberment, death, delirium tremens, you name it, are becoming increasingly common—at that moment and no other he resembles (but only to the degree that he remains humbly—hence touchingly—unaware that his adaptive movements are being observed by a recognized authority on the subject of manly, and womanly, grace) nothing less than a ballet star and not just any old star but the kind that gets wooed simultaneously by all the major companies. There's a certain regality in the uniqueness of each one's response to the perils of re-entry, contingent on its invisible interlinkage with all the other uniquenesses. Why, if the parade continues to unfold so exaltedly (and there's no sign of a let-up—or a let-down—any time soon), comparisons will have to be sought only among spectacles on the order of, say, the Entrance of the Shades in Petipa's *La Bayadère*. Or the hippodrome enacted in the Andante of Balanchine's *Divertimento No. 15* where each pas de deux ends with her cavalier's thrusting the ballerina, half-mare, half-sylphide, back into the wings but on the *upbeat* instead of, properly, on the down-. Whereby the sublime jolt of a wound suturable only by the simultaneous entry of the next couple is inflicted on the spectator. And which as it so happens she owns on DVD. "Who cares?!" the disgruntled philistines roar, not without considerable justification, though (*listener discretion advised*) it's more of a sneer than a roar, but whatever it is, it's not in the gentler, more wistful key of Balanchine/Gershwin.

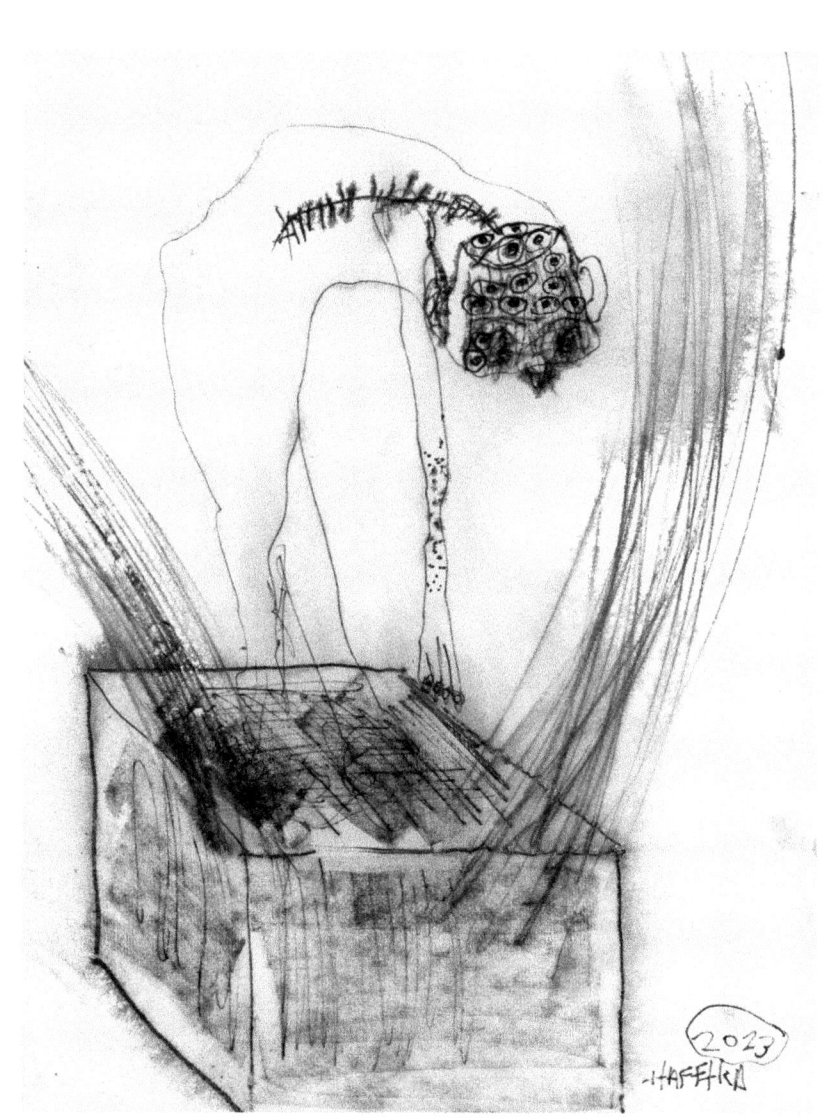

CHAPTER FORTY-ONE

While applying a compress to Eden's forehead—the least he can do (though he won't go so far as to allow himself to be accused of getting Eden into this mess)—Pritchard (whom the nursely gesture metamorphoses into a Civil War Walt Whitman or, more accurately, a WWI Henry James aka The Guy from Rye) says, "This seems the right time to speak my mind—to relieve myself of my thoughts (a thought is a wound but to *utter it away* is somehow even more wounding). The right time to speak my mind about *my* symptom—a far cry from Envy. Oh, yes, I know what you're going to say: That I can't decide whether Envy is a disease or a symptom." Eden isn't too weak to cry out, "What's the difference? It causes pain whatever it is—that's what matters." And to think that he himself probably doesn't suffer from Envy, Cantor muses—and he has every right to so muse since he's not just Eden's teammate but his roommate as well. Pritchard pretends he hasn't heard Eden's outcry. Netta, for the record, finds Pritchard most unattractive—and most compelling—when he's pretending not to hear somebody else's objection. "The problem with a disease—with the name of a disease—any disease—is it's a coffin. It's inevitable that the sufferer, once he's been reassured by know-nothings that what he's dragging around in his backpack is in fact a disease, will waste no time making himself too damn comfortable in that coffin to risk the uncertainties—worse, the inconveniences—of cure—and by cure I mean self-cure. Calling Envy a disease rather than downgrading it to the level of a mere symptom relieves the envier of the obligation to tame the disease at—on—its most unstable level— in all of its quicksilver changes of state, of mood—and thereby cure himself. So the long and short of it is, you'll have to get used to my calling Envy—and any other plague of comparable charm—both a disease and a symptom, as the spirit moves me—or rather, it's a disease in town and a symptom in the country and vice versa—until further notice." Despite the lateness of the hour—wait a minute, it's almost the middle of the night—there's lots of activity going on in the Green, Yellow and Red spaces. The VCs and the urchins-into-unicorns crowd—Silicon Valley's answer to the Jets and the Sharks—are just getting warmed up. "There's been too much nasty speculation as far as I'm concerned on the subject of how occasional visits to the Wharf impact on my ability to help the Envy-ridden—too many vicious rumors in circulation to the effect that I focus most of my professional attention on patients with the same . . . orientation. As if my visits to the Wharf are a nightly affair—rain or shine! In point of fact arrangements were made ages ago to ensure that such visits would be as widely spaced as they needed to be." Cantor thinks "arrangements with whom?"—a dagger in this context worthy of Hamlet Sr.—but he doesn't speak—much less use it. "But," says Netta, "isn't that only because when all is said and done, SB is a small town and you can just bet that everywhere you go there'll always be pretty much the same gaggle of gawkers and fine upstanding citizens lolling about for lack of anything better to do with their precious time? And even you would prefer not to give those saber-toothed yentas in sheep's clothing the impression you're so addicted—you, a professional, if not a family man—that they won't be able to avoid bumping into you making your nightly run (and twice on weekends) between hot spots." "Why 'even him'?" Cantor blurts out protectively, or is it self-protectively. Should he give Pritchard a break—tell him not to feel put down—after all, wasn't Schumann a sissy, at least according to Nietzsche (himself no slouch in the cries-louder-than-the-human-soul-can-suffer department, albeit a noble one? He decides against administering anything resembling first aid. Netta waves his protestation aside—even if he's the best tenant she's ever had. Fact is, he's no longer quite the favorite no matter how much he's taught her, e.g., about the mappings of a sphere into a plane, partitioning a curve and equitably dividing up a topological ham sandwich and despite the fact that in the bloom of youth and for the duration of an Indian summer, she could have loved such a man. It's not hard to understand (*she pretends to relent*) how in order to retain his status of very occasional tourist who can take the local color or leave it, Pritch has no choice but to give the fine upstandings enough time to expel from their hippocampal bladders every memory of what looked like cruising, before he re-shoulders the risk of a next and hence even more suspect foray into this wilderness of his own making. Pritchard nods respectfully but does that mean he agrees? "Well, I'm willing to admit I've pilgrimaged to the Wharf more frequently than I said I did—though less frequently than you maintain. In any case, it hasn't affected my ability to rehabilitate others—whatever their sexual preference. If anything, it's the smug straights who most magnetize my surgical interventions—I guess there's still a hope even at my advanced age that some of the straightness—or at least some of the smugness—will rub off." His ministrations—not the confession—have put Eden to sleep, and it sounds like a pretty sound one. Cook would like to avail himself of the confusion sown by Pritchard's long-overdue public confession to lure a female techie into any one of the winding corridors connecting the spaces, where all is silence and shadow (such an indiscretion would pale in comparison with Pritchard's malpractices which have come shockingly—but not all that shockingly—to light). He's never been more in the mood to gently, patiently, subtly encircle the black key of somebody's clitoral bump with the tip of his forefinger (the piano lessons have paid off)—to ease what always has the disconcerting texture of a wild strawberry into explosive life—but if he's to act it must be quickly—mustn't be too picky—must keep the smell of his own pre-cum tactfully to himself (still picky or not, he needs to be giving somebody the cum-on—and soon).

Unable to take the tension, Cook, to the first SV cheerleader he stumbles on, says, "You're a very cute kid." He does the best imitation he can of somebody licking his chops.

The line works! and without further ado they slink away, into the sunless sea of corridor No. QED connecting spaces Nos. A and C.

"And how, Netta, may I ask, did you become such an expert on the comings and goings of folks like me? And by the way, where did you receive your medical degree?" She doesn't take Pritchard's bait: Nobody gets to un-burnish this lady's hardwon credentials even if, in her day, such trinkets were far easier to come by—for one thing, no need to earn an undergraduate diploma beforehand. On her behalf somebody cries out: "Same place as you: UCSF School of Medicine, on Mount Parnassus." Pritchard pays him—or her—no heed, since it's much more important to explain that he takes his professional duty in this regard very seriously, which entails being on the very best of terms with said symptom (for let's be honest: if what he does on the Wharf—and, more importantly, doesn't do—constituteth not a symptom, he doesn't know what does). "But, in your case, is it the compulsion to return to the Wharf or rather what you did—do—there that's the symptom? Or rather, are both of them what we call back home in Indiana just attributes of the Substance called Homosexuality?" asks Liepnits in his best—no, his very best—"let's-call-a-spade-a-spade, Fellatrant Clinton" tone of voice. This time Pritchard, Netta is happy to see (though not as happy as she thought she'd be: women are insatiable), can't pretend not to have heard. "Good question. Both are symptoms and both are diseases—until further notice. Or more to the point, the Wharf addiction and what does or doesn't happen on the Wharf are both symptoms—of a shameful need to unjustly render homosexuality shameful at all cost." This time around Netta is even happier to see that Pritchard has been able to give as good as he got and seems to have relished wielding the horsewhip (not to mention the bit of propagandizing thrown in between lashes). Whereupon Pritchard returns—in his best before-I-was-so-rudely-interrupted tone of voice—to the subject at hand (something to do with the best of terms and the worst of terms), further explaining that if he isn't on speaking terms—the best of terms—with his symptom, however shameful (know your symptom—enjoy your symptom!—and you know not just your-self but the future and not just your future but the future of humanity) how can he talk the Invidicum crowd through their own shame? (Fortunately, he wears many hats, hence he knows a thing or two about Envy, since homosex-uality, *pace* the sickly AMA, is nothing but [to Cantor, alas, this saucy apo-thegm doesn't hold water but gets by—how?—by reeking of trendy self-hate, that's how].) Which being on the best of terms requires in its turn surrender-ing—in all weathers (even if conditions are pretty mild in these parts) and circumstances—to the urgency of the symptom in the hope that with each surrender it'll be divested of the dross of yet another of the contingencies that camouflage its essence (for the wise addict like the wise virgin never passes through the same contingency twice) and he'll get closer and closer to its— and his own—dross-free abstract core. And once he—or any other wise vir-gin—has cauterized away all the contingencies (as he hopes) and confronted the essence of his symptom face to face, man to mouse, he'll be able (so he thinks—so he must think) to transcend it and get a step closer to confronting and transcending himself. Since contingencies are to the symptom what symptoms are to the molten core of the self. Having nothing—or little—to lose—on the contrary, the salt air has done *his* symptom a world of good— Cantor asks what Pritchard means by contingency. And by the way, didn't he say only minutes ago that his visits were widely spaced? (Cantor observes that Mary Johnstone and Max Soul and the other members of the hanging jury of his peers flown in from Silicon Valleys Northeast, Southeast and West—ears pricked, eyes peeled and mouths agape—have edged in even closer if that's physically possible. Doubtless in the hope that when he gets himself hoist by his own petard or whatever disqualifiable fruits like him are supposed to be hoist by, they can be in at the overkill.) Pritchard is all too willing to respond, or pretends to be. But first things first: "Forget what I said a minute ago about visits widely spaced. After all, inconsistency is the spice of life (if you don't believe me, then ask Ralph Waldo Whitman). And a damn good thing it is, too. As for contingencies: if what we're talking about is sex— and we most certainly are—then a contingency can be anything from the body type or body smell craved on a particular night, to the kind of night desired for messy fusion with a particular body type—or the words (and not just—albeit mostly—of the four-letter variety) that need to be said if the fuck-ing is to retain its lustre on through to orgasm and well beyond. As for the abstract core—the armature of the contingeny-cauterizing process—it's attainable—penetrable—visualizable—only through the auspices of lan-guage—only as the endpoint of an odyssey through the sewage-clogged defiles of language. But most definitely not the language of everyday life. Since in a case like this, the language of everyday life is useless if it is unable to maintain the fiction (most of all to itself) that: *it will be indeed useless—toothless, too—if prevented, before advancing one step further, from abasing itself before, and hanging like an albatross from, the neck of one of the queenly sciences, preferably mathematics, the queenliest (!) of the lot—useless indeed if prevented from abas-ing itself by hewing and skewing to the vocabulary—the grammar—laboriously evolved to capture that science's imagery* (for any science worth its salt is—like a good movie—all about *images*). And we're all in luck since as it so happens, the driver of the process is, in this case, the concept of an *infinite sequence.* (But by appealing here—some might say it's pandering—to your dark side, George, I'm not trying to butter you up—to get you on *my* side, dark or oth-erwise.)" Why *dark*? Cantor muses—for as we've all learned if he knows any-thing it's how—and how not—to muse (wonderers, on the other hand, are a dime a dozen). Is Pritchard by any chance adverting to Georg Cantor's diago-nal proof and, in particular, to the quasi poetical—though some might (and did) say self-servingly obscene—application to which he, George Cantor, has subjected it? "That abstract core, then, is knowable only as the unreachable limit of a sequence whose terms are the contingencies (actions—speech acts—choices—events—movements) we're talking about—*I'm* talking about—a sequence hounded by—indistinguishable from—its shadow, that is to say, a complementary sequence (charged with, so to speak, wiping the ass of its double) each of whose terms is a *description*—a *capsule anatomization*— of those contingencies as they unfold over time, each determined by—each the byproduct, side effect and detritus of—its predecessor. For the need to mutter, say, *fuck* before penetration doesn't upsurge all by itself but only after the need to say, e.g., *balls* has been exhausted—after the initial endocrine impact—the glamor—of saying *balls* has been dissipated or atrophied away. It's the inability to go on needing *balls* that paves the way for—gives birth to—engineers the extrusion from its bloody loins of—a corrective—a phar-makon—like *fuck. Fuck*, then, has *balls* to thank for its originality—its fresh-ness—which freshness will in its turn dry up as well to make way for the new—for the Next Big Thing—the next big movement or speech act. Just as the need to, say, smother a woman's nipples with one's monotonously scraggly chest hair, getting grayer by the minute, doesn't upsurge out of the blue but must wait its turn (for its own good!—nay—I mean, *nope*—for the good of its own potency!) which in some cases may come only after the exhaustion of all possible gratifications to be extracted from the stroking of her vulva (stroking as if to say, *Down, girl, down, your desire terrifies me*). So what you have here in a nutshell is the fact that the perfect symptomite must be able to juggle shadow and substance, action and articulation, deed and word, event and its verbal anatomization—but without going all to pieces just because the words for the deed may seem now and then to be more horrible than the deed itself—the shadow more horrific than the substance." He refuses to pull any punches—he's on a roll in fact: The persistence of the symptom—*any* symptom (any! *is this sudden stab at universalization a way of distracting attention from the shakiness of the thesis?* wonders—murmurs—no, *muses* Cantor)—is founded on—driven by—the illusion that once every conceivable contingency—every conceivable convention underlying the art of symptomhood—is played out, discarded and trampled underfoot, the symptomite will for the first time get to see his real self—as mirrored in the symptom's abstract core—as never before and as nowhere else (all symptoms being royal roads to Rome—the Rome of the fragile self stripped bare). "Illusion!" Cantor is carried away by outrage and likes the feeling. "A few whistle stops back you assured us the symptom stripped bare and the self stripped bare and all the rest were done deals." Pritchard pretends—or rather pretends to pretend—not to have heard. But then—evidently (*whom does the* evidently *belong to?*) running on the conviction that everybody else's back is turned—he shoots Cantor a mentorly twinkle, as if to say, You obviously didn't pay attention—you, my favorite son!—to the "so he thinks" and "as he hopes" that I liberally—or even lavishly—scattered through my depiction of the wise addict's anticipation of transcending not just his symptomal core but his very self. But he has no intention of losing his momentum, twinkle or no twinkle. "So what choice does one have except to keep on eliminating—shedding—contingencies to get to—at—the molten core they smokescreen?" Pritchard takes a deep breath and everybody and everything gratefully takes a deep breath along with him—except Cantor, his Doubting Thomas. "Even if—precisely because—the smokescreen is *itself* the molten core—and *symptom* and symptom are shorthand for—signature of—the unachievability of the limit point—unachievability of the end of all contingency." "Do you really believe that?" says . . . says . . . Stifter (of all people)! "Or is this," he lashes out, "just another example of the trial's holy grail of obfuscation—the Great Synonymization—working overtime and polluting everything it touches—the conduit to nothingness and not even the sort of nothingness dear to the hearts of café existentialists—the kind that haunt, berets cocked at a rakish angle, the famous Place De La No Return." Unbidden, Netta repeats Stifter's question, almost, but not quite, verbatim.

"Shut up and listen, you wily old brat (take heart, though, brathood's rejuvenating since nobody's ever too old to assume its mantle) and maybe you'll actually get a reply even if it's not the one you think you're looking for." (Netta wants it to be understood far and wide that getting tickled pink at everything the term *brat* suggests of freckled coquetry is absolutely not in her line and even if it were . . .) "I'll admit roping in the Great Synonymy is a means of whitewashing my shame. Can you blame me for not wanting to be remembered solely as a guy who liked to get his lower limits sucked in semi-public restrooms? There's more to me than that. Even if it's most me—even the best part of me. At the same time, wherever I turn with my Wharf symptom—like a mother with her soon-to-be orphaned son, I find—whether I want to or not—GS staring me full in the face. It was like that from the very beginning— beginning with the *great days*. Sometimes I allow myself to think, when I've had a bit too much to drink, that the Wharf symptom is nothing more than a craving to be engulfed by—sucked into—this Greatest of All Attractors. Since if all other names are synonymous then the name for my own shame can— under the aegis of GS—get lost for good in their shuffle. But I must warn you: this mock insight is proof against psychotherapy's siren song, whatever the key in which it happens to be belted out by this or that generation's Ethel Merman."

"What's this I hear about the great days?" Margo asks—though it sounds more like cueing, if you ask Herbert. Though nobody does—yet. But she's not worried. As was the case for Mahler—for Stendhal—her time will come.

"The *great days*, not the great days."

"Sorry."

Pritchard explains that, although he's never been able to conceive of the *great days*—nor, for that matter, the dog days—where the Wharf symptom is concerned, all of a sudden he's experiencing an ungovernable yen to talk— brag—about that very thing—even if there were never any great days except as they're materializing here and now on the level of talk—of wordflow. But wherever those days (great or not) come from—or don't—maybe it won't be for naught—meaning that maybe they, too—the others—will, emboldened by his frankness, find the courage (he makes sure his panning gaze doesn't take them all in too quickly), if not today then tomorrow, to come clean about *their* great days—as professional-level Enviers, that is. (A thought—or rather a cross between a weighty thought and a juvenile quip—hits Pritchard gut-hard—like a ton of bricks: *Being professional Enviers gives them* an edge on the competition. Pritchard'd better watch out or, from a dire sense of secret wrongdoing, he'll start playing havoc with their hard-won dignity by guffawing uncontrollably [for what sort of edge can the Envy bug possibly bestow on its host?]. But what's so *secret* about the confection he's just whipped up? Having access to the same tools, they could have whipped up something even *direr* and lambasted *him* with it.) And maybe, unlike his, theirs will have very much existed from the beginning of time. In which case if they manage to trace the evolution of their Envy from those good old—er, great—days to the present, there's a more-than-fair chance he'll be able to see his way clear to curing It, backed up as he is by all that Wharf expertise. For anything that is capable of evolving—really evolving—is capable of being wiped off the face of the earth forever.

Pritchard takes a deep breath out of respect for his audience—out of gratitude for the respect he needs to believe they will accord his plight as they would any other living, breathing thing—especially since his plight is in fact more alive than he (which explains why he envies and would give anything to *be* his plight). "It's only now after forty-seven years, with all the Wharf symptom's accidentals coffined in the term *Wharf symptom*—neutral but still virulent, though who's to say what's accidental, what's essential?" (at once hypnotist and subject, Pritchard appropriately clutches his skull)—"it's only now that I finally allow myself to remember as if it were yesterday what I'm constructing right here before your very ears. Without further ado: the first head-on attack of the symptom occurred one windy fall morning on Parnassus Avenue when (already late) I was on my way up to the foggy amphitheater (nothing as grandiose, of course, as the one on Greenwich Avenue) for anatomy class. How I loved anatomy! Because with new anatomies come new thresholds. How I loved the cadavers (always studiously opaque)—especially, oddly enough, the ladies—more than I could ever love a living being (one always more undissectable than the next). *I'm finally allowing myself to remember* that the closer I got to one of the two lavatories on campus where I'd heard tell (without ever *realizing* I'd heard tell since I still shut my ears against thinking of myself as a Lavatory Man) a partner in crime could be found 24/7, the more urgent the symptom became—so urgent, in fact, there was no question but that, before I ever laid eyes on the promised land, I'd have to run such a partner—the reasonable facsimile of such a partner—to ground in some en route gas station men's room. The nearer the tortoise-shelled endpoint, the larger the Achillean incapacity to defer alleviation. And this was—is—what makes a symptom a symptom—the fact that the mere prospect of relief inflames it beyond relievability—*the fact (some might say, the* alternative *fact) that relief is itself inflammation.*" "Which means we're incurable, is that it?" Jean's challenge goes unmet. Anticipating the same question from both Melanctha and Cantor, Pritchard plays it safe globally by imploring *all of them* not to wonder out loud—even with the utmost reluctance—whether he really believes *the mere prospect of relief*, etc., etc.—or worse, that *relief is itself*, etc., etc., or if this is just another case of wordflow's going all-out haywire in jubilant defiance of sense—just another case of wordflow's shortcircuiting thought (before thought, once achieved, can shut *it* down) in order to perpetrate the so-called Great Synonymy, the obsessive quest for which (quest of patients and curers alike, whether they want to know it or not) is getting more and more rabid and wide-ranging *the nearer Post gets. In fact, he's somewhere in the building.* So what? Jean thinks—I mean, shrugs. Although she has pigheadedly resisted thinking like a Master—sorry, like a master (from envy of Melanctha who's clearly His—sorry, his—darling and always will be?)—and who knows? maybe she'll be remembered as the very last among the tribe to have held out against fandom (or is this just self-glamorization?)—remembered as its most heroic member hands down—although she's resisted thinking like the master thousands of times (no, make that tens of thousands!) the way things stand it sure looks like there's no other way to give inner-voice to her outrage over Pritchard's present ploy which is of course the master's (although she won't go so far as to put on Oscar the Wild's top hat and say that there are times though few and far between when to wear the master's seven-league boots becomes more than a duty—it becomes a pleasure). And still she'll be letting them both off easier than they deserve although it's not her kindness of heart (she has none: both Caro and Ethan have taught her there's no percentage in *that*) they'll have to thank but rather her relative inexperience in the ways and wiles of master-speak. So here is the so-called master—the master so-called (she'll always refuse—even if not stalwartly—to enter the ranks of his muses: after all, who does he think he is? Charles Manson? George Balanchine? Dionysus, king of the Bacchantes?)—here he is yet again trying to transform what's clearly mundane—trivial—banal—bland—anoydyne (i.e., Post's visit)—into something irrepressibly ominous; and bully-begging his massively over-worked italics brigade to do the dirty work—to pull a fast one—for him. There, that wasn't so hard, was it? Though the performance did deserve (if she—now a seasoned trouper—does say so herself) an audience of more than one. In any case, she's sure the master and his pudgy squire will find a way, no matter what comes out of her mouth, to link Post to a spike in obsessiveness over achieving the Great Synonymy and through that linkage to turn the whole business into grand guignol on the cosmic order of, say, the Great Replacement (of lily whites by everybody else)—a fake apocalypse touted for its fashion sense by a homosexual (Cantor hangs his head in surrogate shame) on the French far right. She awakens from her opium dream to hear almost all of them assuring him in a Tower-of-Babel-like frenzy of tongues—tongues wielded like tongs, really—that they respect him more than all of the other experts combined and would never dream of doubting out loud the urgency of the threat posed by the quest for the Great Synonymy or anything else he holds dear. Still, as far as she's concerned (of course the short shrift given to her defense of the incurables still rankles), they're laying their ser-vile compliance on way too thick. (Especially kiss-ass Cantor, who'll do any-thing to assume Pritchard's mantle, or so she's been told, or thinks she's been told. Though she has heard somebody say there's a contingent of venomous old crones and cronies afoot—now employed, but precariously, by Big Tech—flown in gratis and currently working the room in a vain search for tenure—a tenure! a tenure! my kingdom for a tenure! [tenure *anywhere on earth*, they're not picky]—that won't let that happen.) They're on his side. And to prove it they affirm that such obsessiveness is eminently comprehen-sible given that every Envier worth his salt wants nothing less—and the want is infectious—than to transmogrify all other competitors—for what is the trial but a competition where the first to be cured will be hailed the win-ner?—into one fangless rival and since that's clearly impossible, he knows he'll have to settle—if he's lucky, that is—for reducing all their *names*—along with any others he can get his hands on—to one. But immediately Herbert and Cantor wonder (for they're willy-nilly the leaders of the pack)—though still not out loud—whether this bit of lay, or lame, analysis—this business about transmogrifying competitors into one fangless rival—isn't their own means of harnessing wordflow's unimpedable energy so as to get ahead of their thought—for it isn't over, not by a long shot—and beat it to the finish line (though what and where the finish line is has yet to be determined) before it takes them into the sort of fiend-riddled deeps (Pope's Cave of Spleen, say) they have no wish to frequent even in mixed company, or before it reveals its essential vacuity. One more instance, then, of the universal desire to destroy a little bit of the world by destroying the thought that creates it and thereby wields (or is this just the wordflow talking a blue streak for the nth time + 1?) the right of life and death over it. Though she remains the proud outlier, Jean feels complicit in all this toadyism, so what other recourse does she have but to lower her eyes and turn away as if she's just been convicted of masturbation or worse, *although the gesture itself is far more incriminatory* (or is this yet *another* case of wordflow's going all-out haywire . . .?). But though Cantor and Herbert are busy reassuring Pritchard that there's nothing wrong with selling your soul to the Great Synonymy, they talk about the soul-selling as if it's something utterly foreign to their own instincts. And nobody sees fit—or possesses the guts or insight—to point out that they, too, have been abducted by It. In short, GS's the blissful blight they were born for, i.e., it's Cantor and Herbert—and Margaret—they mourn for. Cantor clears his throat to cloak his self-disgust.

"Frankly, my boy," (the situation must be beyond dire, Shearer tells herself, if the likes of Cook feels fancy-free enough to address Dr. Pritchard, *the* Dr. Pritchard, as "my boy") "the answer to all this is much simpler." "All *what*?" says Stifter. "Why must there be an answer?" provokes Jean. According to Cook— *Cook!* Moira can't help remembering how he came across in that Second Avenue coffee shop—a cavalier straight out of Petipa. Yet just look at him now. *Well?* she asks herself. *Well, strange you should ask*, herself replies, *but now he's even more trim, more cavalierlike, more irresistible*. So the long and the short of it is that she'll forgive him his junket in the byways of the corridor connecting spaces B and C, or is it A and B, if he promises to . . . junket again—with her. According to Cook, what's more natural for somebody like Pritch, entranced no doubt since toddlerhood by processes like negative feedback and the dialectic of the vicious circle—processes whose conceptualization has been pedigreed by the likes of Wiener, Cannon, Svevo, Bateson, etc.—than to put the accent not on the symptom in all its simple Wharfy shamefulness—*the simplicity* (with a nod to the Great Synonymy) *being the shamefulness*—but on a fanciful—and fancy—*dynamic* of the symptom driven by those processes? Hence, the distractive hooey about *the prospect of relief inflaming the symptom beyond relievability*—it's a good—a pedigreed—way of keeping their eyes off the symptom—off what's going on in that Turing trap of a gas station men's room.

It's Pritchard's turn not to take the bait, even if it's honest bait. "But the best way, hands down—the only way—to talk about the Great Synonymy," Pritchard remarks, "is to get straight to the point and penetrate it through the fog of Envy and vice versa. Still, I don't know about the rest of you but these digressions in praise of digressions have done me a world of good—sometimes getting straight to the point is overrated." "He's never been anything *but* digression." Margo's smiling sigh tries hard to keep exasperation and adoration from tearing each other apart, a pretty tall order. "Since Envy, *unlike every other* symptom *and every other* disease"[105] (unlike every other! *so*, thinks Cantor, *now he's going in the opposite direction—from universalization toward particularization: why? to make us feel special!—to keep us turning—churning out—the pages of the book of ourselves!—to induce the Master's clients to believe they're the privileged votaries of a once-in-a-lifetime Radio City Music Hall spectacular! which when you get right down to it ain't nothing more than a slab of morbid abstraction overdosing on yellow-journalese*)— Letting the cat out of the bag, Pritchard explains how (and so what if the following constructions defy visualization—defy sense and sensation? it's for a good cause—transmogrification of touchable things into untouchables or vice versa) JUST AS the Pythagoreans according to Aristotle believed that *things are numbers*— that the elements of numbers are the elements of things with no remainder— AND JUST AS Charles Sanders Peirce, examining some consequences of four incapacities, believed not only that clothes make the man but that as life is a train of thought, so *man is the thought*, is the word or sign he uses AND JUST AS H.J.D. Azulai (Livorno, 1788) believed that merely by uttering the words of the Torah man never ceases to create potencies and new lights, which issue *like medicines* from the orifices of ever new combinations SO is Envy structured like a language—*is* language, whether we like it or not—is nothing but the name *Envy*, which constitutes the untidy sum—the distillation—of the words Envy requires in order to think itself (though few have the guts to use them)—to think itself through—to confess itself, even if there's nothing to confess since Envy can't be experienced—can't experience itself—can't get beyond the words—beyond their distillation in a name—can't *come*. And the words themselves? just a home remedy—a pharmakon—for curing it though Envy's a diehard—a wound that craves no suture. *Envy*, then, unlike gluttony, sloth & Co., isn't yoked to an unwieldy referent bloated with particulars—it's its own referent. (Envy is in fact the bestselling authoress of *How to Be Your Own Best Referent* [Simple, Simon and Shoestore, 1975] not to mention the gray eminence behind the six-part miniseries of the same name.) That's why *Envy* is free to waddle around on wordflow's unbounded checkerboard to its heart's content and get the bloat into all sorts of trouble. And, by the way, what's extra-nice about *Envy*—Pritchard reminds them—is its willingness, once the waddling starts, to take up the cudgels for the woes and wiles of any number of aged, unemployed or infirm symptoms—or rather for the woes and wiles of the names (its unkissable cousins) that attempt in vain to do those symptoms justice—symptoms A, B, C all the way out to infinity and beyond. Since solely because *Envy*'s referent-free doesn't mean it can't understand what termite signifiers dragging around referents a hundred times their size *are going through* every minute of their life. It graciously agrees to pinchhit, to step into the breach unsolicited, with a view to signifying—in the great

---

[105]Up here, Envy is both symptom and disease since as situated, the bunker is both in town and in the country—or, more accurately, neither in town nor in the country but in, as it were, an after-dinner sleep dreaming of both.

tradition of Marcel Mauss's mana—everything in the Symptom Which Is Life Itself that eludes explanational mania's grasp. Though maybe the problem is that there are way too many symptomal names shedding their explanational blood over that Big Old Symptom in the Sky which, as every schoolboy should know, can easily be explained away (without any overtime) by two or three, max. Though why not both problems at once—two for the price of one? on the one hand too many signifiers twiddling their thumbs (being grossly underpaid to do nothing, so to speak) because there's simply too little Out There to explain away[106] and on the other, not enough signifiers—not by a long shot—for the too *much* Out There. All of which explains why Envy is so hard to cure: *Envy* (the name from which it's indistinguishable—the name as the sum of the words it needs to think itself through) spends all of its time doing, like Cinderella, the dirty work of others—is always busy signifying what Envy isn't—busy signifying everything *but* Envy (forgetting that charity begins at home)—which means that to be afflicted with Envy is to get afflicted, by contagion, with every other symptom under the sun—every symptom but Envy itself. Or, to quote Pritchard on his eternal roll directly: *Move over* mana, orenda, hau, wakan, Donder, Prancer, Dasher *and* Blitzen *and make room for* . . . Envy!

To everyone's surprise (everyone being the victim of his own virulent pre-conceptions), all the members of the Silicon crowd are scared shitless—and what's more, in perfect unison. *So,* thinks Cook (back from his frolic immeasurably refreshed), *Pritchard, or rather* Envy *according to Saint Pritch has managed despite all the lingoese to teach those hardhearted smart-alecks (and not a minute too soon) a thing or two about stuff they obviously had no inkling existed—no inkling whatsoever—corny stuff like self-sacrifice, pinch-hitting, charity, slave labor, Monday morning football practice minus the CTE, and consideration for widows and orphans as more than just typesetting glitches, not to mention unqualified love of signs, symptoms, signifiers and other idiot savants.* As if taking his cue from Cook's unspoken—unspeakable—thought, no less a luminary-in-basic-training than Borkman, Jr., has seen fit to interrupt his scrutiny of a spreadsheet—wider than the Mississippi and as impressive as one of Paul Ryan's[107]—in order to shake Pritchard's hand—hard enough to

---

[106]Claude Lévi-Strauss speaks in this regard of a "non-fit and overspill" between signifiers and what there is out there for them to signify—i.e., of a surfeit of names relative to things. See *Introduction to the Work of Marcel Mauss*, translated by Felicity Baker (London, Routledge, 1987), p. 62.

[107]In the view of many Siliconians (although they won't 'fess up), Paul Ryan is, hands down, one of America's deepest thinkers (right up there with CSP)—as deep, in fact, as mom's deep-dish apple pie à la mode or à la king. Rushing in heroically where other fools have feared to tread, he's astutely pointed out that under Hillary and her crowd there would be only "a gloom and grayness to things [American]." Even worse, "a cold and unfeeling bureaucracy [would replace] original thinking." OK, so what if Ryan's own original thinking gets a bit muddled here? That is, original thinking—not even Ryan's, no matter how hard it tries—can't be replaced by bureaucracy: one kind

jiggle the beads of sweat on his surprisingly youthful-looking, surprisingly hairy forearm. *And where would life—worse, "interesting" fiction—be without surprises?* Melanctha Herbert (who's seriously considering as of this moment changing her name to Fredi Washington) wonders disingenuously. Cantor notes, not without a certain schadenfreude, that Jr.'s the proud progenitor of a cummerbund of baby fat. Although about to faint or expire or both, his father, didactically trim as a high-school senior, has somehow mustered the strength to wave the flag of his gratitude. And now that you mention it, everybody, taking his cue from the great Durante, is getting into the waving act (some beseechingly, others jingoistically), as if, as if—well, as if every wave were one of the Odessa Steps and Pritchard the Battleship Potemkin.

Shearer wipes her brow. Not that she experiences any real need to do so. Still, try seeing it, if you can, from her point of view: a moment so poignant cries out for just such a gesture and will accept no substitutes. But you mustn't think she was self-dramatizingly aware of what she did while doing it since this in fact is one of those rare occasions when she's been *light-years ahead* (no other phrase will do) of the *poseuse* who's always ready to spring pantherlike out of the wings and steal the—her—show. And she's not alone in having felt the need for a commemorative gesture. Thing is, the others are simply not as quick on the required stagecraft's trigger. It's as if she were back in one of her very favorite home towns (the wedding pas de deux from *A Midsummer Night's Dream*, where else?)—trying effortlessly hard (in the interstices of a low lift) to squeeze a few extra poker-faced scissor kicks out of the choreography's back pocket while for once the music wasn't watching, i.e., pretended to have its back turned—pretended to be failing to keep tabs on her fidelity to its dictates. Because that was what Mr. B. was telling the music to tell her. Chez Mr. B., pathos could only be poker-faced.

"I appreciate the vote of confidence (which is not to imply that any of you are confidence men)." The joke, if joke it is, falls flat. "But will you let me finish? Will all of you *please let me finish?*" At these words, Eden has started to look more attentive, even if covered from head to foot with tourniquets. Moved—and now stuck—near one of the largest of the freight elevators which inexplicably has been holding his attention going on an hour, and appearing, at

---

of thinking can be replaced only by another kind of thinking. (Still, let's not *not* see his [Black] Forest for its trees.) Etc., etc. Unfortunately, such smart-aleck "wit" serves merely to mollify its target and indict the smart-aleck for the impotence of his self-love. You get the picture. On a lighter note, *it's only right and proper that PR, as a disciple of Ayn Rand, should crave nothing better than to be impaled on/sodomized by quarryman Howard Roark's power drill.* (Another lapse into wit which only saddles the witman with an even bigger undischargeable debt of gratitude to his target for standing still for the potshot and with whose troops he's now—like a frontline journalist—permanently *embedded.* Put another way, the witman's impossible task is to get beyond his cleverness [if cleverness it turns out to be]—beyond the feelgoodness of having, yet again, converted—and thereby earned the right to commune with—the already converted. His task is to make the cleverness breed more, deeper pain, which no amount of communion can mitigate—his task is to come away feeling *estranged* from his converts.)

726

least for the moment, to be in much greater need of first aid than his would-be killer, Borkman, half off his gurney or (if you prefer) half on, remains unattended except by one of his son's sub-flunkeys (bearing more than a passing resemblance to The Rump, Jr.), who is hit-and-missily forcefeeding him out of a no-frills deli container what (from Ethan's vantage anyway) looks—without smelling in the least—like grandma's patented mushroom and barley soup.

"So finish," Netta retorts. "But I have no intention of finishing—not just yet." Well, never mind what the rest of them may be feeling, Herbert for one is soothed—or, more accurately, enraptured—knowing that, whenever the spirit moves her, she can focus her attention on the antics of a pair of vaudevillians (since in their present condition they won't be going anywhere any time soon) as sharp and seasoned as, through no fault of their own, Eden and Borkman have turned out to be. For unlike Pritchard, for whom the only game in town is Stump the Symptom—better yet, Stump the Shame of the Symptom— through the deft unfolding of processes unconceptualizable and concepts unprocessable, she's only human—and as such understandably craves (and if her co-stooges know what's good for them they'll hop out of their hairshirts ASAP and start craving right along with her) an earthy counterpoise to his unearthly scaffold arias which are just too damn labyrinthine for their own good (or is this just the eager-beaver creative writing student thinking though not quite out loud, in the hope that some hotshot literary agent may be eavesdropping—on what's meant to be a repudiation of coastal elitism in any shape or form?).

CHAPTER FORTY-TWO

It's four in the morning—the vampire shift should be winding down—though nobody qualifies just yet as a sleepwalker. Not in the least bushed, Jean—challenge still unmet (it's becoming a running joke between her and her)—offers up straight out of the oven a homemade tune for the words *'cause they're tired little teddy bears*—even if/especially because cuddliness is not the strongest suit of most—any—of these self-styled *over*achievers (idiotic term)[108]—and lets it batter her nerves, unreproved. Ethan steers clear of her: their non-marriage isn't *working*—it's patently on the rocks. As for Cook, his crying need for a bit of shut-eye doesn't keep him from seeking out some other *broad* (now where did this archaism come from? The Rump's bantering locker room?) to *clitorize*, as he calls it. Nor can he stop worrying about Eden, promoted for no apparent reason to old pal. Didn't he hear Stifter or Walser or somebody who looks like both, but to little purpose, say that the preoptic area of his anterior hypothalamus and/or his basal forebrain—slabs essential for sleep generation—might have been damaged by messily implanted electrodes during Eden's stint as a rookie assassin? Or maybe it was only some loudmouth upstart—reluctantly overheard while Cook tried to snatch (!) a little R&R in corridor A-C—bragging about his crowdsourceable template for a foolproof sleep-lesion cure. Then and there, and for all to hear, Pritchard apologizes to his erstwhile mentor (y'p, *erstwhile*, you arrogant artisanal-bakery—worse, artisanal-brewery—populist). For he's come to realize over what seems like centuries that if she did heckle, it was solely to stave off the sure-to-be-more-relentless heckling of others. On the other hand, mentor or not, she needs to be reminded that he'll not just *finish* (though only when he's good and ready, of course) but do so with a bang. And with a whimper or two (it's second nature and a point of honor) thrown in for good measure—but only if she behaves herself starting right now.

The same sleep-lesion smart-ass rushes in to announce that The Rump, having carried the day (though what he and Putin have achieved cannot by any stretch of Sean the Spicer's imagination be deemed—perhaps intentionally—a landslide victory), will be the brand-new Commander in Chief. All most of them can do is announce their dissatisfaction—each according to his ability, each according to his need—with the impenetrable thickness of the walls of the bunker (it's something straight out of *Justine*). Nothing penetrates. If it had they'd have gone out to vote. *For his part* Cantor—no! *As for* Cantor—his only concern at the moment—all right, not his *only* concern (after all he's dutifully having big trouble digesting Rudy's all-but-certain

---

[108] Centuries ago (the Master's duration machine has been up to its old tricks), an awe-struck liberal journalist or two referred to then President Barack Obama and his wife as overachievers—as good an example of *exalting with faint reproof* as any I know. In this case, however, didn't the bottom of the smarmy cup of awe, after it ranneth over, reveal a faint racialist residue?

Secretary of Stateship) but the one prevailing over all the others—is whether the messianism driving this hunger to manage the fallout from everybody else's symptoms (Envy-driven or otherwise) will prevent Pritchard, his mentor still, from addressing what has become the most pressing matter at hand. There can be no more pretending he hasn't caught the rumor on the wing—Manning is one of its staunchest disseminators and momentum, especially in the last few minutes, has been increasing *exponentially* (now, why has he just degraded himself by using this term so imprecisely?)—the rumor that Invidicum research, whether on-, off- or off-off, has been flagrantly financed through the production of . . . pornographic films. And such talk, even to Cantor who's been toasted for his irreverence all the way from Christopher Street to Morningside Heights—from Carnegie Hill to Chinatown—from Blackwell House (Roosevelt Island) to the West 79th Street Boat Basin—and back again, is most *inappropriate* (detestable bromide—though not as bad as *unacceptable* or *unhelpful*), *a fortiori* with Eden reviving much too slowly for somebody his age and Borkman evidently dying, although come to think of it the location of Borkman's mortal wound has still to be determined—in fact, the jury (not Cantor's, however) is still out on whether he was in fact grazed by a bullet, much less wounded.

No beating about the bush: Shearer needs some fresh air or at least the image of (to invoke one of Akim's neologisms) a *breath of fresh. Thing is* (never knew until now just how much she loves this harmless little phrase—too harmless for its own good), a window is the very commodity that's hardest to come by in this mock Brutalist hymn (if ever there was one) to the Chateau de Silling. Still, she manages to track down a passable specimen of what's required and for her pains is granted a bird's-eye view of the tarry pavement. But not just the pavement. Leaves and samaras and a twig or two for good luck are getting more pushes than they can handle. And even if she knows it's the pre-dawn gusts from the sea and nothing but the gusts doing the pushing she knows even better that—unlike every resident in this chateau—the dead leaves and expired samaras are in no need of salty pep talks because they're pushed—no, driven—not by gusts aforethought but by an inner momentum patiently accreted over centuries and for no other purpose than to enable them to enact this ghostly little ballet (a cross between, say, Mr. B.'s "Valse-Fantaisie" and "The Concert" [Jerome Robbins]) to which she and she alone has been elected to bear witness.

Approached by Manning herself, Pritchard (as overheard by Cantor) says forthrightly that he's the last person who should be throwing stones at somebody else's aberrant sexuality. "But," she cries out, "it's a question not of flaunting an aberrant sexuality but of exploiting the sexuality, aberrant or otherwise, of other people." Covering her ears against the tenor of all this chitchat, with what turns out to be its grueling emphasis on kiddie, snuff and granny porn (there's nary a nod to the good-clean-fun variety), Netta enacts a silent scream worthy of Munch or Michelangelo or Eisenstein, although it's unclear what's being conveyed—excitement, outrage or a witches' brew of both. "Anyway," Pritchard adds, "I have the greatest respect for the unjustly maligned pioneers who till away at this minefield." "Yes, there's still so much to learn in that regard," twitters some female starter-upper with a excruciatingly wistful *I-never-met-a-pornocartographer-I-didn't-like*-type smile smeared like apple butter across her blotchy puss. Growing more and more sulkily impatient with Pritchard's capitulation, Cantor can barely restrain himself from offering a lesson or two on how the credentialed he-man flaunts knight-aberrancy to rebut any attempt to annihilate his essence.

But before he can pursue the matter any further, who—what—should emerge from the non-freight elevator but Post entouraged by his goon-heads—his very own Wagner Group. They wield, predictably, AK-47s, M4 carbines, M16s, M249s, MP5s and Glock semiautomatics—the very stuff that the dreams of Facebook, Twitter, Theranos, Mylan and WhatsApp arms bazaars are made on—not to mention the dreams of Facebook itself (er, make that Meta né Facebook). Between them, they have everybody in their sights. The only thing Cantor can say, knight-aberrancy being suddenly old hat—so twentieth-century, is "What will they think of next?" Stifter, one of whose hobbies (though it's by no means his favorite—no, not by a long . . . *shot*) is sporting clays (*Who'd have guessed?* murmurs Walser), suspects from the look of these brutes that fragmentation grenades, C-4 explosives, SA-7 grip-stocks, Armani flak jackets—even, in a pinch, surface-to-air missiles—are waiting impatiently in the wings. Might the siege have something to do with the election results? The members of the Borkman, Jr., crowd as well as their non-member gophers look a bit taken aback but even the most frightened—and the most jaded—sport a glint in their eye (which might as well be one big collective—one big cyclopean eye): Can this, they wonder—as only Harvard, Stanford, CIT and MIT dropouts *can* wonder—be but the overture to the unveiling of a new start-up—a means of keeping the audience captive—even spellbound—while the pitch is made and the Rubicon of wishy-washiness crossed (though probably not for good) and the die irrevocably cast? Intending to incarnate the zeitgeist of the bunker as if it were the whole world's (and who's to say it isn't, impenetrability notwithstanding?), bipolar Walser cries, "Don't worry—it's all heuristic," spreading his arms like Icarus—and given winged impetus by his own delivery of what is sure to become a tagline to end all taglines and not just any old tagline . . . to end all taglines but the sort that is sure to go viral (*but* sure *according to whom—or what?*). Indeed, every upstart in the house, regardless of political affiliation, is busy capturing Walser's brazen flight-in-place on their smartphone. In a split second, how-ever, he's at the opposite pole fearing that this may be wishful thinking on his part. He, like so many of his colleagues, has yet to learn that in the realm of Invidicum, indeterminacy/unfixability is King and certainty in any shape or form is Death. Post pans his eagle eye so as to take in Eden and Borkman in one movement, thereby linking them for all eternity. But he has a look of disgust on his face, as if both have failed him big-time. "And after all I've done for you," he murmurs. Then, the goons, whose number seems to increase by the minute as the elevators go on shutting and opening, round everybody up and separate them into groups. *Squads*, Shearer thinks, while getting whacked by a geek with a backpack, or rather by the backpack itself for whose life-of-its-own said geek sulkily—creepily—disclaims all responsibility (not, by the way, the Stanford dropout kind of geek but one who, being far more akin to the *Nightmare Alley* variety,[109] wouldn't think twice about biting off the live head of a free-range chicken). *Squads*, like those (the analogy alleviates the terror) overpopulating the fourth movement landscape of *Symphony in C*. There's an upstart group and a "friends and enemies of Cantor" group (or so it seems to the darker side of Cantor himself) and a Greenwich Avenue Irregulars group. As a mathematician (or is he now an ex-?) Cantor tries to predict what will happen to those (should there be any) who end up belonging to more than one group. To what corner of the room are those impudent oddballs going to be dispatched? Before he can decide, Post announces (by the way, the MGM-inspired dream ballet performed by unemployable actors in terrorist drag was conceived simply to rivet their attention: humor, however lowbrow, is always an asset in times of crisis)—Post announces that, as it would be inappropriate to go on talking shop in this dump (though, whatever anybody else might think, the perceived inappropriateness has nothing whatsoever to do with Eden's and Borkman's conjoint state of health about which he couldn't care less), they're going to be driven free of charge to a just-constructed McChateau higher up in the hills (absentee owner: notorious man-about-start-ups, Yuri Fuentes O'Rourke [ex-pal of Viktor Bout], whose lawyers are currently fighting his—and their own—extradition from Aleppo), which they can rest assured is tastefully replete with indoor and outdoor saltwater pools and sweeping views of the pools of its almost identical neighbors and exudes a *je ne sais quoi* far more conducive. "It's the middle of the night!" Netta feistily reminds this capacity crowd. "Conducive to what? What's the occasion?" Though Cook does his best to sound provokingly jaunty, Mel-

---

[109]Allusion to *Nightmare Alley* (direction: Edmund Goulding; script: Jules Furthman) gets Eden thinking (or if it's out of character for Eden—or if he's too out of commission—to be doing the kind of thinking demanded then Melanctha [the two of them are interchangeable since both are over-acquainted with grief] is here to pinch-hit by unspooling the memory of his reaction the first time he saw it—with his best buddy, Maurice, and Maurice's dad, Leo, in a movie theater on Adams Avenue). The more the amateur protagonist (the Great Stanton) suffered for his treachery and suffered the treachery of others, the more (since the scales were always inexplicably tipped in favor of his being sinned against, over sinning) Eden exulted—from pity and awe. For the film didn't just show that it understood his—Eden's—hunger to believe desperation was not an end but a beginning—it proved that to have one's head routinely bitten off by that free-range chicken called Life was *the* precondition for triumph over Its unlivability. In short, it gave his adolescent self not just hope but infinite hope—imagine!—that he could beat life at its own game—proved, QED, that there was an outer world, just like his inner world, waiting for him at every streetcorner—but an outer world now gorgeously stylized beyond the power to infect and deaden. And the experience—the breakthrough—was immeasurably enhanced by his having been treated after the show to wonton soup and chow mein and egg rolls at a dive in Chinatown. Through this burst of spontaneous generosity, Leo demonstrated, as if he were the seminal textbook on the subject, that no matter what horrors—what constrictions—Martin had already lived through, the beautiful prospects before him were infinite and inalienable.

anctha does *her* best to hear or thinks she hears a sob of plangent Envy in the question—the Envy of a go-getter who's suddenly come to realize that by start-up-subculture standards he's way too old to pitch anything except, maybe, the recipe for a homegrown convulsive constipation remedy (stolen in fact from Straynge). (Hearing this rapturous announcement as the threat [without a penny's worth of rapture to its name] it surely is, Shearer, ever the—the—the . . . well, ever the *solastalgiac*, is already missing the Brutalism of this Silling for the start-up crowd and—even more wrenchingly—the leaf ballet, viewed from its battlements, celebrating the time-honored tension in any *striving* thing between propulsion from without and propulsion from within—a ballet she's sure will prove loftily impossible to reconstruct—even by the most gifted missionaries of the Balanchine Trust.) But thanks to all this premature looking backward she's worked up quite an appetite which gives her little choice but to slink back to the buffet table. Nobody blinks an eye (never were bourrées scattered far and wide so invisibly): they're all too busy choking on the relocation business which does taste fishy. Still she's taking no chances since, like Soren MacKierkegaard, the dancer from Denmark who joined the company as if for the sole purpose of imperializing her valedictory phase, she hates to be rubbernecked when (to use Mac's self-contemptuous term) "at feed." But even when she's found just the right sort of broom closet for her purposes (straight out of a fairy tale by that other Great Dane) it's like nothing so much as a squirrel that Moira gorges on her measly morsels for here she is picking up every vibration of imminent capture with her third ear—her third eye—her third nostril—and scurrying off in all directions at once even if standing absolutely still.

And what's more she's—Herbert's—delighted that Envy's alive and kicking—for all of Pritchard's primping before the cracked looking glass of his own symptomaology, it—like Invidicum—is the only game in town, especially when the town's this town, i.e., LA—the narcissism capital of the world—of which SB is a mere outpost straight out of Somerset Maugham. The trial must go on—it can't be squelched—no, not even by a bunch of upstarts' deranged devotion to networking—working the room—on behalf of the Next Big Thing. Can't they see It's staring them in the face? So they—she and her teammates—should be making more of a concerted effort to keep Envy's home fires burning, if only out of respect for Straynge and all the others who've given their lives so that Invidicum might live. Though she's not quite sure where the pietism (*who've given their lives so that . . .*) is coming from: it's certainly not her style—but isn't the supersession of one style— which we mistake for essence—by another what maturation, artistic or otherwise, is all about? Even if such humanly maturation ends up stifling her far more urgent counter-maturation as a (superhuman) artist-in-residence at the University called Life. (But if she does decide to throw maturation in any shape or form to the winds and graduate, as its artist-in-residence, from Life U summa cum *laude* [yeah, *louder* than every other boob on campus] then it better be with a coveted B.S. in [what else?] AA [Apotropaics Anonymous]. It's the coveted degree [you know the one] that attests the awardee's ability to not just keep all dreams of glory under wraps but routinely cancel their

lien on her capacity to stay unglamorously *immersed in the book of herself*.[110]
How? *How*, you ask? Through the reflexive manufacture of a mental vantage
from which those dreams, when overactive, turn into so much hot air even
if Ms. or Mr. B.S. knows they're anything but and that it's her or his bounden
duty to ensure, between immersions, the dreams are never luminescent and
contoured enough to whet the invidious appetite of demiurge-scale predators. *That's* how.) In any case, they have a story to tell—a job to do, i.e., to
sweat themselves free of Envy and thereby justify the faith of the Amygdala
enterprise in their power of positive thinking. And to think that it's taken an
insider/outsider like Cook to remind them—or at least Melanctha—of their
responsibilities, if only they'll allow themselves to be reminded. But Barnum
& Bailey predictably drowns out the voice of the categorical imperative—West
Coast version. "Founders Showcase, dudes, Founders Showcase, followed by
a rooftop office-warming party for my new . . . venture." "And what might
that be?" Visibly annoyed (but the visible annoyance may very well have been
premeditated), one of the goons—evidently a *squad* (the term has caught on)
captain for he flaunts more jewelry than ten Ivanas and is graced with the
most bullish neck and the hairiest chest in the joint—begins to explain, *but in
a high-pitched voice*, almost a countertenor's or a coloratura's or even that of a
Frankie Valli (now I ask you, asks Melanctha, can there be a surprise-inducing
story-galvanizing flourish that is more Masterly than this one?). A Founders
Showcase (we'll get to that new venture presently), at least according to the
captain, is an audition with wings for start-uppers at which each is allotted
ten minutes to pitch his project before a jury of venture capitalists—and, even
more important, the flagrantly nonstandard accounting metric being used
to gauge profitability, which too often simply provides a cover for the lack
thereof—all this while the canned-laughter crowd drool, hiss or yawn graciously on the wrong side of the tracks—or, in this case, the red carpet. "You
could say," chirps what looks like the (far more amiable) deputy captain, "that
the first law of Founders is GYMR, which stands for . . ." The lifted hands,
raised eyebrows, rapid lateral headshake and incipient smile are intended to
mean, Doesn't anybody want to hazard a guess? Ethan blurts out, "Get Your
Metric Right" (after all, what is there to lose? word on the street is that he's *all
washed up*—more than an amateur like him has any right to be).

At which point everybody exits—like (peons and padrones alike) sheep.
As it turns out, Borkman and Eden are not the only casualties. Operation
Homicidal Maniac has claimed far more limbs and limbics than anticipated—
too many in the Pritchard contingent having tried to selfie themselves into
what they mistook for an over-rehearsed scene from the definitive remake
of *The Parallax View*. With semi-dire results. So here are all these killed and
semi-killed cats (each with its nine lives in tow) being treated by a rapidly
expanding team of medics and paramedics who—as if things aren't bad

---

[110]Phrase inspired by *Stéphane Mallarmé* (see "Hamlet et Fortinbras," *La Revue blanche*,
15 July 1896). Mallarmé's meditation was given new life in the Scylla and Charybdis
episode of *Ulysses* by James Joyce.

enough—can't seem to decide whether or not to abandon the injured (rather than pass up the pale prospect of flashing disco balls and free drinks). In the meantime, Pritchard, trying to sound unshaken by circumstances, cries out (loud enough to be taken to task by Margo, ever the DC hostess), "Having defended my work so passionately this evening, I realize it's pretty much done—to a crisp—and that I must pass on the mantle—or the hotseat—to my esteemed colleague—" But just when Cantor's about ready to body forth and execute his very own fantasia—his very own *quasi una fantasia*—on the theme of aw-shucks unworthiness, he's nonplused to learn the colleague in question is none other than . . . Irena Manning, MD, PhD. So Pritchard's been abandoned by all his fans—worse, his detractors—and needs somebody to massacre. Cantor refuses, however, en route to the elevator bank reserved for the Greenwich Avenue Irregulars, to give his ex-mentor the satisfaction of witnessing manful pride plunge to its death through the safety net of a how-could-you look.

In a mammoth van with a passenger pen large enough to asphyxiate the members of all three groups, the huddled masses are transported, window-lessly (excluding Borkman and Eden, who are *still too weak to travel*, or so they've been told), to what Walser and Stifter are the first to recognize (after putting their balding heads together since they couldn't—could anybody?—have done it alone) is not McChateau country—nowhere near—but a side-street off State that's right around the corner from the Museum of Art, where Gerzso persists in reigning on unheralded. Melanctha isn't sure whether six-teen minutes, sixteen months or sixteen years have elapsed during the mam-moth ride from the Bunker to this faux Mc. The Master (who else could it be?) clarifies as follows (she hopes He doesn't feel His storied talents as a sea-soned manipulator of perceived duration are being impugned even if every-body knows they're at the mercy of a defiantly sloppy timekeeper who should finally get His comeuppance): *Whatever time has elapsed is whatever's been needed to ensure that the hop-skip-and-a-jump from Bush to Obama to The Rump's inauguration (replete with by no means record-breaking crowds) waxes not quite plausible.* And come to think of it, sixteen years but not a second more do seem to have elapsed when nobody was looking—and, by the way, is it a hallucinogenic concoction of Zykon B she's been sniffing as the vehicle hiccoughed all the way to its destination? (Cantor foresees [a ham radio buff, he's managed to listen in on the Master's dispatch to Melanctha] finding a dependably rage-drenched solace in the plight of the country once The Rump starts aiming his wrecking ball—all the way up to, inter alia, the morosely defamatory pronouncements on the Black Lives Matter movement of his bull-dog cum pig of an Attorney General just before the 2020 election. Before now, nothing loomed bigger than the plight of his own scholarly aspirations [he had no interest in knowing, say, how many times a day Cheney managed to convince the boobs that his scowling draft-deferred nastiness was all about manful rectitude]. Effective immediately, however, the country's plight will be living lavishly inside his own and his own inside the country's—for all the world like fetuses in fetu—each twin inebriating the other with junk food for gourmet thought. Moreover, Cantor's glad—though he won't admit it—that somebody had the good sense to think twice before taking the easy way out and relegating this meaty little meditation to a mere footnote.)

In what's meant (but only for yokels) to be the chateau's Main Drawing Room pinch-hitting as a council chamber, variegated pitches to the jury members—a mock-forbidding lot of (mostly) fresh faces—are already under way. Clearly expecting an unending stream of rejection pronouncements in the grand (Reality TV) manner, raucous crowds of roped-off bystanders are semi-intoxicated by the smell of charred flesh. (Where's The Rump when we need him to do the honors? *Where?* Why, putting the presidential team together in his home State of Denial, that's where.) Jean and Ethan are unapologetic (especially to each other) about their bedazzlement. Even Shearer—suckled at the breast of one for whom costumes and decor were the least significant elements in any production (even an applause machine)—is impressed, although she's not quite sure by what precisely.

The biggest surprise so far is Post's thrashing his way past the gawkers toward the podium. "Gentlemen," he announces, interrupting yet another pitcher *in extremis*—but for a good cause. "Welcome to this episode of Founders Showcase. I'll be your tour guide. Since in addition to fulfilling all my duties as a pipeliner, I currently run a start-up to end all start-ups (one thing leading to another) as you may have heard though of course you mustn't believe all you hear even if all you hear is 900 percent true-enough." He begins to giggle—but manfully—which the jury members, however forbidding, find—no, seem to find—so irresistible (no other word will do) as to leave them no choice but to join in. Suddenly all bets—I mean, giggles—are off. He reminds them he wouldn't be where he is if he didn't persist against all odds in seeing—*seeing*—a world in a microchip and a heaven in a wild flower. Now that he has them where he wants them, though he can't swear there's a *there* there, he comes clean. It's all very man to man. "Basic pipeline research on Invidicum has been subsidized, if you must know (and you will, one way or another, so it's best you get it from the horse's mouth), through a network of websites promoting the creation by our customers of avatars shameless enough to play out their enigma variations on pornographic themes, for which pioneering work I've been roundly criticized. Competitors who haven't come up with a blockbuster in decades think that if only I can be knocked senseless by some trumped-up obscenity charge (which wouldn't stick anyway since we're talking here about something much better than *high-fuctose porn syrup*) then *I*-research (or is it I-?) will obligingly grind to a halt. Of course there are some nasty insinuations making the rounds (easily nippable in the bud) to the effect that we're playing off-label footsie with *Heads of State and Government* through the shipment of tons of Invidicum, although I challenge anybody to prove the shipments exist and if they manage to do so, which of course they won't, that it's off-label Invidicum which is being shipped, and if they somehow manage to do *that*, then I dare them to put their money where their mouth is and utter the name of the condition our drug's being utilized to treat or, better yet, induce. And to show you how low Envy—like preferment—can sink a man, some—most—of my competitors claim all that's required to transform Invidicum into a niche aphrodisiac for billionaire warlords of the developing world is just a tiny alteration—no more than a tweak—in its com-position. But do they really think I'd be standing here tonight—still honing my craft—if I held the key to *that* kingdom?" "So what's your message?" cries one of the Reality-TV contingent (still awaiting their pound of char). Tone-and-stance makes it clear that it's he who's been delegated to smell any rats, i.e., to represent all the world's homeless, present and absent—and rendered so himself by robo-talkers exactly like Post—the kind that insist they're doing god's work—and given what *he's* shown himself capable of perpetrating over trillions of years—god, I mean—they probably are. "My message? Pretty sim-ple: *If I can do it, you can.* But I have another—an even better—message in store. With which you're heartily invited to wash down this one." Post looks over the heads of the Reality-TV crowd, as if he'd just discovered (like Haghi, say, in Fritz Lang's *Spies* or Hitchcock's Richard Hannay) that the cops—block-ing every exit—were getting ready to close in on his sins—committed as both pornographer and trainer of assassins. "I may be going away for a while—on business," he announces sadly, sounding a bit like Hitch's Uncle Charlie.

The start-uppers waiting in the wings are obviously getting impatient. After all, everybody deserves a turn up at bat, according to a hoary old Norse saying Post just invented and must not forget to patent. Speaking of *going away*, smilingly (no cops in sight) Post points out that far greater than their duty to insatiable but ultimately squeamish shareholders is . . . their duty to themselves. (Melanctha was just about to sigh—shriek—shudder: *If I have to hear the phrase* shareholder value *[since if* shareholder *comes can* share-holder value *be far behind?] uttered [piously—self-righteously—poignantly, as it always is] one more time, I tell you I'll . . . I'll . . . I'll . . .*) Which means that they have to start now putting away cold cash for what's referred to among the Grand Old Men of Silicon Valley (i.e., those in age bracket 19–23) as their Himalayas Moment. The jury members look blank—or pretend to. "What's that?" barks Mr. Reality-TV, now a wee bit less truculent. "In your Himalayas Moment you'll dutifully discover just how bereft the start-up culture really is and how what you've been yearning for all along without being able to quite put your finger on it is some whopping dose of *spirituality* and, this being the case, how a visit to, say, Nepal will be just the resuscitory ticket (round-trip, of course). [Footnote: Start-up culture, as some trendy dropout wise beyond his years has already pointed out, is equal to the square root of (frat house culture times kindergarten culture times Church of Scientology culture).]" But he hastens to caution that somewhere inside they—the round-trippers—will never allow themselves to be blinded to the fact—though killjoys may tell them they should be if they're as dead serious as they say about self-purifica-tion—that such an about-face, entailing annexation of a bit of etherealizing shadow to their plodding substance, will make them only more of a shooting star on their triumphant return to the fold—somewhere within they'll never allow themselves to be blinded to the fact (or why would he waste his time coaching them?) that spirituality as they practice it will—must—turn out to be just another suburb of the megalopolis called getting-and-spending—i.e., the "something extra" that makes a star like Norman Maine's Vicki Lester a star. Keeping all this in mind, they should, to sum up, definitely avoid imitating, on guided ecotours of Siberia, ecstatic experiences of dismemberment as undergone by Buryat shamans.

"Now just wait a sec: what's this all about?" cries Borkman, Jr., who's getting ready to make his pitch. Despite all the noise he made back there on Bunker Hill, the precise nature of the ware (though I'll settle for imprecision) in which he intends to traffic is still a mystery—or better yet, *shrouded in mystery*. A sort of ingestible robot cum abominable snowman—a computer pill studded with sensors, no? to enable artists (whether squeamish or working against a tight deadline) to experience life's overrated mill- and milestones without the inconvenience of actually undergoing them—e.g., marriage-hearse-dom, parenthood, loss of job or virginity, divorce, terminal cancer, suicide, even those deliciously dull winter evenings of imprisonment in the family Home Entertainment Center. "Are you a member of the jury or a pitchman like us?" "In a pinch, the former, of course. Would you have it any other way? Only I don't know, something's come over me. I feel like slumming in your shoes maybe because there's no force more powerful than humiliation, even simulated (but can our circuitry really tell the difference?), when it comes to getting oneself psyched to modify a given strategy. Since the trial can't continue in its present form. So, however much of a seasoned performer you take me to be, the fact of the matter is that most of the time I'm as desperate as you small fry. Every day, just like you, I have to *log in to myself* with a password I can never make myself forget no matter how hard I try—a password that's of no use to any hacker, even the most enterprising. And that's because—*My password is me*. Which leaves such an empty feeling—unfortunately, not localizable in the pit of my stomach." Melanctha is hyperventilating. It's almost too much to bear. She's debating whether to take him aside *when all this blows over* and tell him that at the moment when he bodied forth his italics it was as if the ghost of Gerard Manley Hopkins were intoning "My taste was me." (If he knows William Blake [and the business about the microchip in a wild flower shows that he very much does], he must know Blake's truest disciple.) The splendors of hyperventilation even override her disappointment that the moral of the story (being presumably—at least as far as he's concerned—that someone with his overqualifications shouldn't abandon all hope, i.e., a new strategy will pop up and the trial will get back on its feet)—that the moral is, well, so self-serving.

For Cantor, a little Post goes a long long way. Even if he turns out to be a true spiritual father—Pritchard being the other. So from Pritchard to Post he flies, and back again. But as he isn't quite ready to espouse Post's take on spirituality (how can this flatulent sonofabitch sleep tonight knowing he's just administered a slap in the face to accredited angekoks everywhere and not just in Siberia?), the only alternative is to join Shearer on the terrace where the first thing out of her mouth (uncharacteristically heavy on the lipstick) is, Can you lend me a cigarette? *Yes, of course. He allows himself one celebratory smoke on Saturday night, whether there's something to celebrate or not—and with Gilles gone for good, there never is. So, one less uncertainty to bear. That he finds it unbearable is of course an artifact in the Goldstein tradition of the self-shrinkage occasioned by grief.* She's been weeping. Deciding that his look—far more poignant in fact than hers—means why, she responds accordingly. "Just knowing that the Posts of the world don't simply exist—they flourish—makes me—makes me—" The scourge of his psyche (old SoP)—acting more and more like Herbert's Old Master, at least as she's tried to put Him into words and make them stick during their most recent post-brunch conversations at poolside—orders him to take her hand and kiss it, though not (he must give SoP some credit where credit is clearly due) to put himself on the royal road to sexual rehabilitation, permanently blocked. No, the motive is clearly a more exalted one—or at least less mundane—doubtless having something to do with the obligation to ensure the scene doesn't end up all text and no action. Too many of those on the loose. Well, I'll be—presumably owing to his defeat Cantor has been deemed enough of a dangerous sore loser to warrant tailgating by one of his peers—a cross, if ever there was one, between Mary and Max. No—it's one of Post's goons. Cantor recognizes him easily enough—maybe because he's out of mufti or back in uniform or because the pimple on his bulbous nose shines bright whatever he's in or out of. Instead of dropping the formalities (with license to shoot, strangle, stab or garrote and thus earn his keep), the lovable brute has chosen to respect them—to a fault (this deft expectation-foiling touch has to be the patchwork of SoP, whom he's tempted to refer to at last as Master—no big concession since it must be clear even to an idiot savant that they've always been one and the same and are likely to remain so)—and in sign thereof *daintily* hands him a Manila envelope bearing his name in blue ink. The cursive penmanship is as angelically correct—and as characterless—as a Bronx schoolmarm's ca. 1959. "Go ahead, open it, I won't hover," she says, observing his hesitation—born of a *perfectly understandable* (who is speaking?) dread of further betrayals. The puffing has relaxed her. He forces himself to remove the enclosed note (in Pritchard's unmistakable boorish scrawl), which reeks of prohibitively expensive cologne (*now, just who is doing the smelling here, Maestro?*) and reads:

George, dearest of dear boys:

Don't judge me too harshly. Post, that devil, assured me that if I didn't see my way clear to conferring the title she so rightfully deserves on the only woman he's ever loved (or at least lusted after to the point where lust-quenching love might at any moment rear its ugly head), he'd expose my outsize contributions to the content of his pornography websites, not to mention my relentless cruising under SB's night sky, and then have me knocked off—Cosa Nostra style, that is, if I was lucky. (Sometimes it helps to make light of despair—which making light is surest proof, by the way, that the despair is real and guaranteed to outlast the despairer.) I reminded him, though not in the least defiantly, that, as for exposure, I'd been exposed and more to the point exposed myself countless times already. He shrugged, insisting the more a confession was repeated, the more egregious—the more . . . unnatural—the secret confessed became since here it was triumphing yet again over confession itself, whose purpose is to wipe it out. To have a secret vice, he said, is bad enough. But to persist in practicing the vice as if it were still a secret *while knowing full well it has, through the act of confession, become very public knowledge, is far more egregious than the vice itself. So that in my case now added to the vice is a defiance of confession's therapeutic intention—the growth of the defiance being directly proportional to the growth of my shame at that defiance. After the* n*th repetition (as a mathematician you should have no trouble understanding all this rigmarole), it became* n *times more outlandishly novel in its maimed sameness. And he knew full well it was the mathematical elegance of it all that would cut deepest since how could this not remind me of the writings of Roland B. Sade (to whom at the drop of a hat I have been unjustly compared by my enemies)—specifically those passages where a single* textual *perpetration (shoving a crowbar up somebody's ass, say) manages to simultaneously encompass (given the perpetrator's relation to his victim)* n *different textual criminal acts (adultery, incest, patricide, sodomy . . .), all so that to the* n *textual pleasures derived from the* n-acts-for-the-price-of-1 *may be added still another, namely, the pleasure of having achieved—so elegantly—so economically—those* n-acts-for-the-price-of-1. *Still, I have a feeling that it's not I but he who's going to be taken in (or is it out?)—in either case, it's he who's going to have done to him whatever needs to be done (Cosa Nostra style, of course—if he's lucky)* to *put him out of our misery—permanently. And when that's all over and done with then, my boy, you'll be able to return to us a hero. Because, don't you see, only algorithms, not nectar-in-a-sievish infusions of cold cash, can ensure that the composition of Invidicum gets refined to the point where it's untweakable for off-label shenanigans.*

It's only as Post approaches, breathing hellfire or a *pretty darn* convincing facsimile thereof, that Cantor remembers the envelope was already open (smitten with the daintiness of the goon's gesture he completely ignored this something-of-far-more practical significance). Post orders him maternally not to believe one word of that old fool's (in spite of himself, Cantor's flattered by this house call). It's Pritchard and Pritchard alone (with *maybe* a little help from Stif and Wals) who masterminded the quaint little scheme of foisting Invidicum in all its incarnations of label-hood off on the malevolent pisspots of what used to be brushed off to everybody's ostensible satisfaction as the Third World. Though Shearer's attention may, to the unpracticed eye, appear to be entirely focused on what little is going on in the unilluminated street below (no Gerzso freaks, half-stewed on *grietas*, stumbling and tumbling down the steps of the Museum), Cantor knows she's listening intently. An insane thought comes his weary way—is she one of Pritchard's agents, witting or un-? "Knowing full well Manning was waiting in the wings (Liepnits's idea), he nevertheless affirmed the mantle was yours and yours alone. For, don't you see, this has forestalled your prodigal return to academia—Columbia, isn't it?—where inevitably you'd end up spilling much more than you think you know to colleagues in all those fields in which CU still makes such a strong showing (even if Columbia qua Petri dish for dropouts doesn't have quite the cachet of Stanford). Journalists, for example, with connections to every major cable channel who might expose him for the Caligari he is and will always remain." At the same time, Post goes on to explain, Pritchard has been able to take out his self-hate on what he sized up as an unsuspecting bird of a feather (Cantor should pardon the expression), thereby achieving the most mocking of mock self-rehabilitations. He notes, however, that with all this talk about the Third World, not to mention the CU School of Journalism, he seems to be in mortal danger of succumbing to what's known among semi-ocrats as (he titters, but once again manfully) the Casanova—he means the *Casablanca*—Syndrome. "What's that?" Shearer demands to know through her tears—dully, like a child who isn't all that sure it wants them comforted away—at least, not just yet. Remembering from his days in summer stock (cf. F. Nietzsche: *Every pharmacological pioneer is by temperament a matinee idol manqué*) that the answer mustn't come too quickly—that is, if the words are to implode to their fullest effect, Post marks theatrical time with a slow shift of his gaze followed by its even slower return. "Since you've just asked, *The 39 Steps* are—I mean, the *Casablanca* Syndrome derives its name from the scene in a 1942 quintessential Hollywood product (where, to quote Umberto Eco, the clichés are forever having a ball) starring etc., etc., and directed by etc., etc., in which the hero's lost love says to her urbane freedom-fighter husband: 'Oh, Victor, please don't go to *the underground meeting* [the italics are his] tonight.' Thereby taking what critic James Agee referred to as 'the season's prize for exposition'. Why? Well, because if the Casablanca team had been willing to take a page from the book of Real Life (which contrary to unpopular belief does reveal itself, from time to time, as a delicate—even an incomparable— artist) she'd by then have become so wedded to—so fused with—the spectre of his going *to the underground meeting* as to make identifying said spectre in full, as neurophysiologically unthinkable and unnecessary as reminding him that it was she, *Elsa, his wife*, who begged him to stay at home. So for whose enlightenment, then, is the information provided if not the audience's (in the dark both literally and figuratively)? But just because Elsa *as written* is compelled to babble over-expositorily doesn't mean I have to follow suit and pretend that *Caligari* and *Agee* and *cable channel*, for example, are for your benefit: *our* audience will be in stitches and we'll lose them forever." As a seasoned trouper who was made very much aware very early on in her career of the need to fill every seat in the house (fairly easy when the house was City Center), Shearer can't help asking, "Who—and where—*is* our audience?" But the purpose of the question isn't quite clear—which is nonetheless all to the good in a realm where Uncertainty is still King and Kingmaker. Does she feel it to be her civic duty to bring Post back to earth by letting him know this is no NYCB applause machine?—no, not by a long shot. Or is she afraid that what-ever it is they've gotten themselves into may very well reveal itself to be the work of a new Master?—not necessarily Melanctha's—at least as great as Mr. B. and who by virtue of that greatness calls into question the status—the very selfhood—of his predecessor and by extension her own, inasmuch as immod-erate veneration long ago effected their fusion—or would have if she hadn't managed, over thousands of 50-minute hours of psychotherapy, to defang its craving to succumb. Cantor senses that it's stopped raining then quickly realizes Shearer has simply stopped weeping. "Our audience, dear (Balanchine, too, I know, kept his distance from women by calling them *dear*), is in the works. But in the last analysis Pritchard's small potatoes: it's S. & W. you've got to watch. By the way, have you caught their new revue, *Send in the Clowns*? No less a gloominary than Watt Murphy-Malone has anointed it the laff riot of two continents. Fact is, they've been insanely jealous of you, Cantor, ever since the good old days down Coronado way." "Insanely?" "Of course. No dummies, they know that if anybody can come up with the right algorithm (your orientation notwithstanding) for determining the optimum—not maximum but optimum—selling price for shares of Invidicum.com in the secondary and tertiary markets as a function of trial outcomes, it's you alone." Cantor counters that he'd be of much greater use to the Organization (at the very top of his game, in fact) in creating an algorithm expressing (algebraically) the relation between, say, the relative stability of the cytochrome P450-catalyzed biotransformation of Invidicum and the relative quantities of the more than forty-five substances involved, so as to enable them—and those who came after—to predict whether a small change in even one of those substances would cause a reaction so violent as to render the drug irreversibly carcinogenic. Over the fit of coughing to which Cantor's caviling has given rise (though from whose POV? Bergman's? Bogie's? Peter Lorre's?), Post still manages to bark out: "But what counts, my boy, is that you've *got* Fascinatin' (algo)Rhythm (hohohohohoho)—it doesn't matter in the least where you choose to channel it." Cantor has no idea what logic or worldweary expertise is propping up this insight in search of an application. As for Shearer, she wishes for nothing better than to be able to turn away in disgust from what's surely an intentionally profaning allusion to her showstoppin' solo in one of the Company's signature confections. Problem is, the smell of Cantor's putative talent—like all talent—intrigues her.

Yet delivery of the heartiest of thank-yous—clearly in order if he's as serious as he claims about retaining his franchise in the org's avant-garde—suddenly becomes impossible: incapacitatingly crazy rays of what feels like admiration, even infatuation, are being emitted through his skull—through the very section slotted (if the ceiling mirror in the Butler Library middle-rise elevator is to be taken at its word) for the brazenest of bald spots. (No worry on that score, however, thanks to the right—ex-loverly—connections in Alopecia, PA: America's—and maybe even the world's—organic-toupé capital.) He's falling not just for Post's line but for the liner himself! Before he can (to adapt one of the now-archaic expressions favored by Mother Cantor in her prime) *collect himself*, however, who should come rushing out with *what appears to be* still another (this time unopened) envelope—but one of the . . . VC judges (imagine!) and not just any old judge but (if Cantor's memory serves him correctly) the most forbidding of the whole lot. So forbidding, in fact, he'd have preferred locking horns with Mary Johnstone, or Max Soul, or even Max Johnstone. Handing it over, he informs them that delivery of such communications is henceforth verboten. With a gallic two-shoulder shrug, he skedaddles. "Might as well open it," Post and Shearer say in pouty quasi unison. The missive (blessedly brief) reads: *Don't believe a word he tells you. If you must know—and know you must if I'm to go to my grave content—he, Manning, Walser and Stifter, and Liepnits—an unholy quintet if ever there was one—have been slowly poisoning me, post-KGB style, with (what else?) Novichok agent A-234, convinced that through this dirtiest of dirty deeds they'll be able to assume total control worldwide over Invidicum supplies and related services and spinoffs and McSequels.*

"Well, what does it say?" Shearer looks like she's getting a real kick out of Post's *discomfiture* (a word meaning . . .) for there is agitation—great agitation—in his tone and the tone is unnaturally shrill (though still manful). "Don't believe a word that old bastard says—he's just trying . . ." Even if he weren't, as now, at a loss for words (or just too damn tired to utter the very pointed ones that rise to his lips unbidden), Cantor would still keep his own counsel. He needs to think, and think deep—*deeper, maybe, than he's ever thought before* (this has the SoP smell of Masterly hype—a kind of textual Novichok, if you will or even if you won't—but if so, it's well past deleting)—specifically about exactly how many more character-assassinational shifts are required before Omar's Pointed Finger finds rest eternal. Pritchard or Post or both must be found guilty, that seems clear. Since without the obligatory semblance of justice having been handed down how can the Invidicum Story come—and without going over budget—to its tragicomical end? Especially with so many secondary-plotters waiting in the wings: For starters, Netta who, hoping for a morale-boosting effect on the beleaguered Bard of Broad Street, which would viralize to the entire tribe, is bent on arranging for Borkman's ex- or soon-to-be-ex- to be flown out to the Coast so she can be bested in a redundant showdown with her man.

Or think of it this way. While Berry Sundae was the undisputed movie expert of the family, Cantor is not exactly house dummy, at least as regards elaborating the general-purpose algorithms (dare he use the term in such a context?) needed to explain all the goings-on in things *noir*—most of which generate an excitement (*pace* the taste of the dear—the dearest—departed) out of all proportion to their artistic merit—and this being the case, he *can't help* noting how Post and Pritchard have come to resemble nothing so much as husband and wife in that late '40s Stanwyck vehicle (*The Strange Something of Somebody Ivers?*) where the question quickly becomes (even before the title sequence rolls), at least for Cantor, just how many "revelatory" character-defaming, plot-deforming, meanings-distorting swings of the pendulum will be required before one of them or both (albeit essentially victims) are deemed duplicitous enough to merit the bloody death that plausibilizes *closure* (nauseating term) and facilitates (even more nauseating) *healing*. And since the consumer's inevitable severance from the film is a kind of *liebestod*, it's only fair that the characters to whom he's developed an aching attachment should share the company-loving misery of his fate. (NB: it is determined that closure and healing for victims of catastrophe are achieved when and only when the media are simply unable to squeeze any more novelty out of its fallout—i.e., when the catastrophe itself transmutes into its own collateral damage.)

As Cantor clearly has no intention of answering (to mask his infatuation with both of them?), Post quits the terrace, but not before yanking a geranium out of the massive tub on the ledge and sticking it in his lapel. Shearer announces (as a means of disclaiming any responsibility for Post's desertion? but if so, why bother? didn't she observe Cantor's relief at seeing the old faker vanish?) that she's just overheard a bystander say one of the pitchers (hash-slinging UFO turned CEO in a single bound)—the best and brightest in fact—had his goose cooked from all indications irreversibly, merely for not knowing the meaning of the term *gross margin*—and that Post and Post alone has the clout (but if not he, who?) to right the injustice and put a stop forever to so draconian a means of separating the men from the boys.

CHAPTER FORTY-THREE

Chaos or near chaos reigns in the McBoardroom extempore of the chateau and Post has to admit that here lies something to stump the experts—even the most expert of experts. But before he can take the bull by the horns, which means turning his voice into a bullhorn and raising it above the jeers of the goose's partisans and the bravos of the envious, who should stagger in from the fire escape, of all places, but Borkman and Eden, of all people, looking as if it was a long, stiff climb. It seems like ages since he programmed the one to kill the other (from the look of 'em, both have fully recovered thanks to a mere change of scene and some speedy physiotherapy).

Contorting the upper part of their bodies so as to signal that they are making way for royalty (which, considering all Borkman and Eden have superhumanly surmounted, in some sense they are) though without incommoding themselves sufficiently to be even slightly misperceived as doing any such thing, the jurors (whose number seems to have rapidly multiplied) single out five hale-and-hearty constituents of the wrong-side-of-the-ropes crowd *to make themselves useful* by improvising a podium for the pair. Roughly a dozen members of that crowd immediately take exception (Herbert puts two and two together even more immediately) to the unctuous ease with which their comrades have signaled a willingness—an overeagerness—to comply, which has entailed first stepping aside. If it had been up to these twelve-odd outliers (but how could it have been?)—as is made clear in subsequent grumblings among themselves—they would have ensured that the stepping aside of the too hale and too hearty five—no! make that *anybody's* stepping aside under *any* circumstances—was legible as nothing more than the sort of simple courtesy to be shown to *even the lowliest creature*—a fleabag chambermaid, for example, or an obese cashier in a Second Avenue supermarket or coffee shop or a junk-bond honcho whose greed has turned to gout (not realizing, however, that in laying out this strategy for protecting the dignity of their comrades against self-deletion, they reveal in passing just how expendable they deem the dignity of some others—a purely for-argument's-sake sort of dignity—to be). In other words, they'd have made sure the whole world knew that there are times, though few and far between, when the act—some might say the art—of stepping aside evidences not slavishness but the indifference of human decency to any such inevitable imputation. Before Post can place the figure who's bringing up the rear with an accordion file under his expensively tailored arm, an *I-simply-must-have-your-autograph* voice cries, "Jaggers," a name that definitely rings an alarm bell. Isn't this Borkman's hotshot lawyer who, as rumor had it, is doing everything he can to get his client (and best friend) put away for good? Once they're seated Borkman exclaims—proclaims—declaims (jury, crowd, Invidicumites shut up the minute he opens his mouth, so great apparently is the new esteem in which he's held)—that the man they see beside him, folks, is his true son. Shearer is standing too uncomfortably close to Borkman, Jr., not to notice his turning uncomfortably away. Evidently, blue-flanneled hoodies—like studs[111]—have feelings, too. "He's the only one who has what it takes to take up the cudgels—once my incompetent attorney (don't let the custom-made trappings fool you) gets me sent up the river—and make sure Post coughs up all he owes me."

"How did you manage to get here?"

"Let's just say the love of your gurney goons was easily bought."

"And what is it I owe exactly—and why?" which comes across to some as a blameless cry from the heart. But whatever it is, here's Cantor (only fitting he should be relegated to the sidelines now that his hopes have been definitively dashed), among how many others? viewing Post in a way he would never have deemed possible twenty minutes ago—to wit, as just another regular guy, probably every bit as hard-workin' as Borkman and as hard-lovin' (for all the hype about the Cocksman Laureate of Broad Street), who has always put Invidicum's best interests before everything else—even his own safety. Or maybe it's just another case where Cantor—qua Burroughsian *faggito*—finds himself rooting for an underdog of his own fabulation. But the fact that he may be an underdog currently doesn't mean he'll remain one or that this coveted status should be conferred retrospectively on P. Mabuse and P. Caligari, to name but a few of his past incarnations. In any case, Cantor simply doesn't have the time to give this particular thought-demon the rough tumble it deserves for Borkman is now busy rising to Post's challenge. Wielding—or is it deploying?—a .38 caliber revolver (his ring finger is wedged between hammer and cylinder), Eden covers his true father's back with an authority altogether new to him. "Go ahead, JG, shoot your wad," he prompts, but with a surprising—listlessness. The air of authority's gone at least for now.

"And the wad's a whopper, if I do say so myself." Borkman clears his throat—marking time, come to think of it, exactly as Post did out on the terrace and (can this be possible?) with an even greater theatrical flair. (Or does Cantor simply need the flair to be greater and, if so, why: He suspects Master-minded Herbert may be able to shed some light on the ploy. But are they still on speaking terms?) "You folks probably know that when I ain't taking my Envy medication I'm running (though at present mostly in absentia via mind control) Borkman Capital Management, one of the biggest seeding funds in the business and probably the very best. The not-so-measly little start-up from whose revenues Post has financed his pipeline caprices over the years—Pornograffick Solutions, or PS to the rabble—is just one of hundreds—maybe even thousands—operating under the BCM umbrella. Although Post has on way too many occasions to count attempted to sink almost all the others through misappropriation of trade secrets, patent infringement and downright fraud, I've tried never to hold the company responsible for the sins of

---

[111]At least according to the indispensable and sorely missed Andrew Sarris, in his review of Hal Ashby's *Shampoo*. Sarris's wry tribute to the Warren Beatty character in that film—the teariest of studs—can easily be stretched to apply to Jack Nicholson's ornery weeper in Bob Rafaelson's *Five Easy Pieces* and Brando's sullen sobber in Bernardo Bertolucci's epochal *Last Tango in Paris*. "Ah Bartleby! Ah humanity!"

its incorrigible owner. In fact, over the last few years I've loaned PS a billion, mostly in Bitcoin."

Post can't seem to be able to get out of wobbly Eden's crosshairs. So he has little to lose by speaking the god's honest. "And compliments of the loan BCM was permitted to acquire 60 percent of the company at—imagine—a nickel per share. And once we decided to sell one million additional shares on the open market Borkman had the gall to demand that our battered shareholders indemnify him—"

"BCM."

"Indemnify BCM for the resulting decrease in price per share."

"Nobody forced you," Borkman says, but so apoplectically that he has to be restrained by two of the outliers.

"No, but J.P. Smegma (the investment bank that arranged our little deal: I curse the day it ever went through) informed us it would be to the greatest advantage given that you already had us by the balls."

"Post fails to mention that BCM granted him, as chairman (and owner, already, of about 66 percent of the stock of the company), 18.78 percent of the profit derived from the loan." (Cantor is having trouble doing all this math, at once low-falutin' and kitchen-sinkish.)

"I've plowed every penny back into the company."

"And what if the shareholders elect not to indemnify?" asks one of the start-uppers—the gross marginal! whose goose, as it turns out, did in fact (barely) 'scape cooking. "Then the interest rate rises to 52 percent, entailing a loss to PS of about three hundred million," upon saying which Post grabs the .38 (Eden, for all his ostensible hairtrigger-happiness, is too weak to have resisted) and puts it over-illustratively to his temple.

After popping what looks (to Post) like a tranquillizer and washing it down with what smells (to Jean) like herbal tea, Irena—together with her prince consort, Netta and the pair she's (gratuitously, homophobically) taken to calling The Stifters—sets up shop at a dainty little table to the shadowy right of the jury. As if this were a Panhandle dinner theater and Post the floor show's star comic cum crooner. She insists (above a few princely mock-protests) that Post describe PS in greater—far greater—detail. So unswerving, evidently, has been his belief in the pipeline's potential that, at the first sign of financial trouble, he had no qualms even about edging into the pornography business if doing so would save the day. "That was the reason, Tom, wasn't it? To save the day? Right, Tommy?" She tries stoutly to undo the entreaty in her tone (why is she so intent on legitimating the pornography venture? on putting words in his mouth? what unwashed beans is she afraid he'll spill?) with a too-nervous-to-be-impish wag of her right—no, her left—forefinger. Then she folds. Goes a bit listless from the cheekbones on up. Toys preciously with her chignon. "A fledgling soloist's first chignon," Shearer notes with approval—and she approves of her approval as attesting to a purity of heart.

Impossible for Cook—yes, Cook—to stomach Irena the Hun's blushing flower act (their too many fucks, after all, were unapologetically emblished—some might say emblazoned—with the latest multimedia prostheses and other special effects). So whatever their past differences, it's his duty to come to the Porno King's immediate rescue. "It's all quite above-board, dear Irena. I mean, this pornography thing." Liepnits looks as if he's getting ready to mouth the words, *Hey, buster, who you callin' dear?* Why, only the other day Cook read in the *Wall Street Journal* that the Internet Corporation for Assigned Names and Numbers had just authorized the creation of an ".xxx" suffix specifically for pornography websites—a decision whose earth-shattering significance as a certification of respectability can be compared without further ado only to the AMA's whimsical depathologization of coprophilia. "Significant for whom?" Herbert shouts, already dreading (Shearer assumes) the repercussions of the move on women—and minority women in particular. Unlike Cook, Cantor finds the Blushing Flower (eyelashes aflutter and neurasthenically diligent fingers uncoiling the tresslets just above her nape)— or rather, the Blushing Flower *routine*—ever so pleasing to the palate and quite, quite digestible to boot. Never has Manning seemed (in self-caressive recoil from nothing less than Life itself) so like herself—that is, so like unto the idealized version of herself—so like a fantasia on the theme of herself— so like a set of variations—Rococo, Enigma, Eroica, Diabelli, Symphonic, Abegg, even Goldberg (that is, *Rube* Goldberg) (you name it! she's got it!)— on a non-existent theme. No longer does she approach that self tangentially. She's arrived—and in the nick of time given all that's at stake in the way of . . . beans. (Cantor cannily reminds himself that up in Boston *even beans do It.*) Has marriage to Amygdala's version of Newt the Gingrich liberated her—i.e., freed her from herself—from a part of herself that tends to forget it's *just* a part—freed her to practice affectation in the grand manner—if only to escape the prison bounded by his greasy liver-spotted paws? That she who's spent her entire sexual life brazenly engineering so many men's emotional demise—that she who managed to carve out enough time from a demanding career to reign unchallenged as practitioner *assoluta* of the pornographic arts, figuratively and maybe even literally—unchallenged as an icon on the order of Linda Lovelace, Georgina Spelvin and Marilyn Chambers—that she, Irena Manning—as fragile and cunning as her namesake in Jacques Tourneur's *The Cat People* and her non-namesake in *A Streetcar Named Desire*—that she, of all people, should find her true vocation—her final resting place—her true identity as fluidity unleashed—in the fluttery affectation of instinctive recoil from the merest mention of the very industry that has brought home her bacon, so to speak, elevated her to a stardom denied her in every other sphere—that she should be laid to rest alive and kicking in a floral bier of affectation—and that all this should be happening in the midst of what is soon to be a pandemic and in the midst of what must prove to be the epic battle between two equally matched loving scourges, i.e., The Rump and Corona Jones (one an obese serpent, the other a virus and not just any old virus but a virus *of concern*), that she . . . that is to say, that all this . . . that is to say, that all this should be the case—should be the way we live now . . . makes . . . makes— well, it makes Cantor's inability to complete his thought venial at worst. Still, he has enough of a second wind and enough will left, notwithstanding all the plagues waiting impatiently in the wings, to concede that maybe, just maybe, when all is said and done, what he—and we, by extension—are privileged to have right before our very eyes and staring us right in the face is proof of the sort of magic that can be worked by the demon of pornography—even the mere thought of the demon of pornography (that is, when he sets his mind to it)—on the right people: the ones whose defenselessness in the face of their dread (whether phony or not—or rather, the phonier the better)—dread of the skin game—can be demon-manipulated to give off a whiff of the (dynamical) sublime for all to bask in. But does Cantor actually believe everything he's just thought—running the outsize gamut from *The Devil in Miss Jones* to Corona Jones? from Jacques Tourneur to Simone Simon? well, whether he believes or not is ultimately irrelevant: the digression demanded he believe it—all of it and then some—for as long as the digression agreed to last. And as if Irena's Blanchelike contortions weren't enough of a perk, here's her sugar daddy rearing up as proud as a peacock—tantalized by the looks Cook and Cantor are throwing her way. (Although who's to say she isn't *his*—sugar daddy, I mean—inasmuch as the state of their finances is very much a mystery and likely to remain so? Unless the curtain is lifted on what for all of us, except the poorest of the poor, represents the Last Taboo—and if The Rump goes ahead and designates Newt his Secretary of Applied Philosophy, it may well have to be—lifted, that is.) And they certainly are looking, and looking *with something akin to fascination* (don't know about you, but Cantor has a soft spot for such readymades—readymades never too proud to offer their services any time of day or night, even without advance notice). Thing is, Liepnits doesn't realize (but under the circumstances what hubby would?) that the real fascination—fascination to the second power, so to speak—lies precisely in the contrast, starker than stark, between insignificant him and the object of their fascination to the first power, namely, Irena—the very Irena who, by daring to ostensibly whitewash Post's motives for going triple-X, has thereby introduced, even more daringly, the possibility (by seeming to do all she can to dispel it) that all of the money being fed into the pipeline may indeed be dirty. Eden (where's the mighty .38?), on the other other hand, is appalled by Manning (though he wouldn't have used *appalled*)—appalled by what he takes to be a feeble imitation of phony fundamentalist cum evangelical shock at the Ghost in the Porn Machine since even if they didn't get around to fucking, he was led to believe from hints given in and out of the MRI machine—or, better yet, not given—that—that she wouldn't be in the least averse to stimulation by somebody besides her fellow missionaries. What did he ever see in her? Her mystique (though he wouldn't have used that word, being at heart a homeboy when required by the occasion) is paper-thin.

In the nick of time, a recess is called until 4 p.m. sharp—that seems fair. Because almost everybody is nodding off. Though almost everybody would deny it—shamefacedly—if called to account by one of the few stalwarts who are still wide awake. Yet, why all the shame about something so natural—even teddy-bear lovable—as a snooze (snores, frothing, tongue-biting and babble notwithstanding)? Hard at work trying to swallow his pride (he's not sure why but a reason—a good reason—always turns up where pride, that old whore, is concerned) *and* the briny air, Cantor drives Netta back to East

Beach, into which Dawn—that old snoop—is poking a Homerically rosy finger or two. The others go their separate ways and those with nowhere to go are provided with in-house accommodations bordering on the semi-luxurious. This stand-in for a bona fide McChateau is full of surprises.

Same cast of characters at their same battle stations. Easy as pie for them to pick up where they left off since it's hard to forget what's at stake. It's about time Post complied with Irena's request for a description of PS "in greater—in far greater—detail," which Borkman seconds even if the last thing in the world he wants, especially this late in the game—his game—is to get upstaged, much less by a mountebank like Post. But in fact he has no choice: because without a description of the feeder operation in question, down to its minutest particulars (which only Post can, however misleadingly, provide), the full extent of his perpetrations will remain forever unexposed and the Invidicum tribe will remain forever incurable and the warlords of the Sahel will remain forever unassailable and Borkman himself will spend the rest of his life up the river taking the fall for—for—for— Sorry, he's lost his train of thought—disoriented by long-overdue populist outrage, I guess. (And when *I* guess, the world listens.) But haven't his cronies told him time and again it's sure to fizzle? All too successfully, Post fights his impulse to delay. Digs right in. No preamble. "Ours, my friends, is a virtual world, but it differs sharply from, say, Second Life, Zynga, Gamefish or Doppelgängbänger, in being entirely consecrated to player engagement with *pornography* as the most authentic way of being in the world. And that's not just Heidegger talking. To get in on the action, all you need is a computer, our browser-friendly software (whose development, so Borkman claims—wrongly, I might add—has entailed infringement of at least forty thousand patents in what he calls BCM's "formidable portfolio") and a super high speed Internet connection. *Yet we're odd man out even among our own kind*" (the phrase—in its poignancy, its plangency—can't help hitting a nerve—everybody's nerve—makes Ishmaels of them all and what's more best-of-both-worlds delightful than *being Ishmaels together*?). "Though we do offer folks interested in liaisons of a certain type the usual networking neighborhoods where they can exchange dirty photos and talk the dirty talk and walk the dirty walk preliminary to a meeting in real space and time. And of course we're able to stream pornocontent into every brand of cellphone just as well as the next guy. And, also, of course we have our own stable of real-world retailers as well—for starters, try Rodin BMG, Steinberg Criteria, Tsimtsum Hotels and Experiences, and Jean d'Aire Productions on for size—and reporters from networks as diverse as CNet, C-SPAN, Reuters and Agence France-Presse are embedded with our troops. And adding insult to injury, next month on Orgasm Island (location undisclosable), we're unveiling the digital prototype for a new line of XXX-ish boutique hotels, each (tastefully) operationalized around a particular fetish.

"But what sets each of *our* core constituents apart from those in all the other domains—what attracts him to our site—is the overwhelming need to depict what it means to be human (especially within the context of sexuality) and to try to remain human from millisecond to millisecond (when was the last time your body obeyed the commands of your will? and, more to the point, when was the last time you tried to fend off the horrors of *Triumph of the Will* by brandishing a fistful of unbuttered popcorn?[112])—to depict what it means *to have ended up human through no fault of one's own*, compliments of an arbitrary dispensation almost biblical in its cruelty (i.e. [and spoiler alert]: ours is a constituency of eternally budding artists)." (Post, Herbert thinks—and she doesn't care who *hears her think*—has obviously been infected by the Master's incapacity to engender a creature who, for once, isn't a clonelike *maker*. Why does so much difficulty in that department afflict not just the Master but . . . could it be that not so deep down everybody's a maker?—that to exist is to make, even if it's just a mistake?) "And what arena is more conducive to such brazen depiction than the pornographic? And what better way to do the depicting than through an avatar—the body of an avatar—created on our website."

But as it turns out, Post informs them, the body parts required for a given torso's completion—that is, if depiction is to be fully achieved—are precisely those that are most mulishly alien, ill-fitting, badly plugged in, and savagely disrespectful of contour, of socket shape and size, and of the laws of articulation (all of this sounds achingly—exaltedly—familiar to Melanctha[113] and yet strangely unfamiliar). (Which state of affairs has of course led regrettably to what I might call a frantic black market-type trafficking in such parts which, though disproportionately in demand among those for whom sculptural perfection is a desecration of what it means to be human, are very much out of favor among those for whom sculptural portraiture is all about colossal public commissions.) For how else achieve the depiction of the human Bearing of Guilt than by compelling the avatar (cum prodigal son, say) to beseech the heavens with crushingly oversized replacements for the arms he should have? And what better way to achieve the depiction of Stunned Stubborn Resignation than by ensuring that the rotation of the extended forearm of said avatar (this time in his Obie-winning role as the noblest of the Burghers of Calais) is shockingly out of whack with the pronation of the hand clutching the fateful key? As for the self-designated hyperstud afflicted with Guilt for the Healthy Unquenchability of an Urge to Thrust and Go on Thrusting in the Shadow of a Beloved Parent's Imminent Demise (little suspecting said thrusting is the only means, as known to his under-conscious, of confuting filial helplessness)—as for the hyperstud, who'd dare suggest that his guilty semen would smell just as sweet even if it wasn't discharged by a *pathologically petit organ precariously perched above two supersized balls bursting with enthusiasm*? Since, for the depiction of the body human to be right, body parts need to be wrong in the right way. And, while we're at it, can there be, he asks them, any other way for

---

[112] When asked if she'd been aware all along of Adolf's doings, Die Riefenstahl pleaded the "Gershwin" Amendment, purring super-disingenuously, "How long has this been going on?"

[113] The lady's right on-target. See Steinberg, "Rodin," variously, above.

an avatar (stretched out on his back) to depict a Dantesque Paralysis of the Will to Create than through the screwing of the wrongest limb imaginable into an atrophied groin? Which is why the true avatar-driver never knows how many body parts any given incarnation of his creature will end up with. It all depends on how many are needed for the depiction of a particular facet of his brute humanity—i.e., how much tinkering with those parts in the name of dutiful assemblage is needed before the tinkering can start waging war against itself and spill over into dismantlement, with the resultant damage being the surest proof of that bruteness, that humanity.

Somewhere inside Herbert's skull—but why now?—the Master (who's been kind enough to spare Herbert His ravings for at least a week) has taken to elaborating His very own form of Dantesquerie, which entails bellowing, with sobs and shrieks, i.e., "consciousness and agitation richly scattered," that the trial as sacred text is turning out to be quite different from what was augured at the start from deep inside the crypt underlying the Amygdala Institute amphitheater, and, such being the case, shouldn't He head straight back and modify the (simple) beginning to resemble this (much-less-simple) beginning-of-the-end or vice versa so as to ensure neither beginning nor end ends up impugning the other for marring the Raphaelian perfection of the whole? She manages to resist the temptation (growing stronger by the minute) to smugly counter-think, much less -say, that surely He of all creators, and especially this late in a game boasting so many clinkers, must know better than to mistake the labyrinthine for the complex and the straightforward for the simpleminded—she resists, in other words, hewing to the shrewish tradition of calling Him His own worst enemy and reminding Him (as if He needs any reminding) He has Himself to blame and accusing Him of arrogance and topping it all off with that old chestnut (à la Ms. Borkman), *Look where you are!* But, all things considered, is a Master Work (wait! who's speaking now? she, or the Master, or both in some kind of crazy—arrogant!—atonal unison?) ever anything more—and anything less—than the sum of Its deviations from so-called . . . Perfection (riddled as Perfection needs to be—if It is to remain the last refuge of prize-seeking mediocrities—with life-defying and -denying finishing touches)—is the Master Work ever anything more than the process of self-sabotage—the wrong kind of opportunism—and relentless invocation of and collusion with vicissitude-racked "false moves" (in the *maudit* tradition of Rodin's cultivation and preservation of "accidental" tears, gouging, scars, gashes, contusions, scrapings and excrescences) as the only means of warding off obliterating indistinguishability from a too successfully imitated model, a phenomenon referred to by chisel-wielding oncologists as the *metastasis of mimesis*? Indeed, there must be just enough of a recognition of the correspondence between model and Master Work to usher in a far more important kind of recognition—recognition of how Master, through a wooing of clumsiness and incoherence more shamelessly pornographic than porno itself, has managed to make semi-mincemeat of mimesis in the name of something far more ethically charged, namely: totalization of the Work as a rake's progress in anatomizing all the gloriously failed solutions to the "problem" of how, in every nook and cranny, to render It as faithful to the model as possible. And all this anatomizing in the name of foregrounding the stake-His-life-on-it conviction that to catch such solutions in the act of covering the tracks of their inadequacy—or even worse, their adequacy—is the hard labor—the tactic—most germane to the issue of . . . of (no—not Greatness, though of course that's always up for grabs) . . . of—of . . . oh, all right then, the depiction of Humanness—of what it means to be damaged enough to qualify as human. The most precious artifact that can accrue to the Work—the Invidicum Story—stems from: (*a*) The concerted effort to forget at every fork in the road of the trial, at every precious plot turn for the worst (which is what steals the show and what customers pay for—the "money shot" in porno parlance), what happened at all the previous turns PLUS (*b*) The refusal to go back and check so as to ensure the current turn for the worst concords with every worstness that came before PLUS (*c*) The creation, based on that refusal, of the most slapdash kind of last-minute concordance imaginable (the slapdashery—foregrounded—being the artistic touch)—the clumsiest kind of suture imaginable for the fake wound of amnesia. Since a succession of fake sutures is what humanness—one big wound too sly to suppurate—is all about. The true Master Work, then, gets lost (but not quite), then found, in the shuffle of its glaring, literally bloody disjunctions, inconsistencies, contradictions, mock compliances with the rules of the story game (like a geisha's—make that the Balanchine *Bugaku* geisha's—with the whims of her too-literal client).

Jaggers is still clutching his files but no longer scribbling—as he's just been doing—in a little red notebook. He maintains, in a tone that has "I'm speaking for everybody else as well" written all over it, that the torsos of Post's avatars are nothing but a pretext—the flimsiest of armatures not just for the aggregation of virtual body parts (as valuable to a certain subset of the gamer population as the African elephant ivories, pangolin scales, rhino horns and hornbill casques marketed to a certain verminous real-world segment of the human race), but, more to the point, for their traffic and trade—their dervish-like push and pull—all of those parts just panting (they'd tell you in their own words if parts could talk) to get themselves extracted from his quarries stashed away in virtuality's hindquarters and plugged in at some site—least likely, most likely, it doesn't really matter. Since in this case bad fits are not a noble artistic device but fallout from the attempt to cater to the insatiability— fill the demand—of gamers—whom nothing titillates (it's common knowledge in the industry) as much as parts in motion—parts in flight—parts in incessant flux—with no delays—no dead spots. When you're a gamer, what compares with the thrill of watching a joint get plugged in record time only to be immediately extracted for use elsewhere. Knowing that, at any point in time, for every joint there is a limb and vice versa satisfies the thirst for some kind of universal rough justice—for a proof that notwithstanding all the mayhem fomented by cyborgs like The Rump, all's still right with the world. Whether an arm—a mechanical uncooperating arm—is bolted to the wrong shoulder which, through such merciless intrusion, is stunned out of its organic sentiency, is irrelevant. Doesn't matter that there are thighs wrongly fitted with loins and legs misfitted with groins. Let the chronic aesthetes who have nothing better to do infect a few apt pupils with their arcane rapture over—their obsession with—the inner meanings of such phenomena. All of which implies that Jaggers (for who better than he?)—or a poor man's version of Jaggers—has a legalistic obligation to make clear that, as such trafficking constitutes a felony especially when committed across website lines, he has every intention of ensuring the violators of this (woefully under-enforced) cyberspace law will henceforth be prosecuted to its fullest extent. Indeed, it's been brought to his attention that because of this very practice many avatars have ended up ignobly bereft of the very basics: muscles, bones, tendons and skin, not to mention the old reliables like kidneys and livers. "That, my good man—" "I ain't your good man." A true gentleman to the end, Post ignores the meanspiritedness. He has better things to do—like explaining that PS— the hell's kitchen of pornography itself—is not at all about bodies but about gesture and utterance—at their most telling. And inasmuch as visitors to the website are never quite sure until the very last minute how far they should let amputation go in the name of purifying some gesture of all excess, so that their avatar, thus purified, can get on with the business of exciting to the point of orgasm—and often way past it—whatever hot number happens to have caught its virtual eye—inasmuch as they're never quite sure—top-notch "personal" trainers are on call 24/7 to help ensure that only just so much armature-plus-body-parts is retained as is required for a given gesture to *evolve, flourish and achieve virtual fulfillment*, PS style. "By the way, this is all clearly spelled out in our much-too-glossy prospectus (feel free to pick up a copy on your way out—that is, if you ever get out)."

Borkman grunts. "Don't let him fool you. When you get right down to it, he's no better than that dentist who's been the toast of the tabloids over the last few weeks. Why, it's gotten to the point where you can't pick up a paper without . . ." To Shearer's ears—and why shouldn't it be *her* ears that've been waiting, patiently, in the wings for what seems like a decade?—this sounds a bit self-righteous coming from Borkman, no mean slouch in the tabloid toast department. Jaggers: "In case you folks may have been burying your heads in the sand, the sleazeball my esteemed client's referring to had the gall to set up a biomedical service operation in Fort Lee for the sole purpose of harvesting disease-ridden bone tissue (provided by his embalmer pals), which he then sold at a mammoth profit to reprocessing companies worldwide." Netta has suddenly decided (in response to Jaggers's chilling reminder that Evil does exist in the world?) to start cashing in on the non-monetary component of her social security privileges—has suddenly decided, at least for now, to be what she is (an old lady)—by slowly shaking her head in an exasperating (at least to Cantor) demonstration of "it takes all kinds" sort of mugwumpery. "But—as a snake-oiled bundler of disease-ridden mortgages—am I any better?" Ethan has to hand it to Borkman: the guy knows how to wring the last drop of pickled poignancy from the barest minimum of self-excoriation. Framed by their hoodies, those of the start-uppers (quite a few, in fact) with tears in their eyes (for their boss's, i.e., Jr.'s benefit?) look like Capuchins, i.e., half monkey, half monk. The warning glance Jaggers shoots Borkman is intended to mean something along the lines of, If *volatile you* intends to hop into a hairshirt at this, the very moment when . . . As for Herbert, she didn't require any lawyerly cueing to realize Borkman was only seconds away from one of his signature self-excoriation arias (blessedly cut short by Jaggers's glance) which always turn out to be far more endearing than they have any right to be), simply because the Master had determined that only some good old-fashioned breast-beating could arrest the progress, at once imperceptible and juggernautic, of all this techie talk about avatars and domains and digital prototyping which is sure to alienate lots of Dinner Theater types—from their shrimp creole. (Where, Cook asks himself, is gab-averse Rocky Rambo when we're most in need of his strong silent type?) Or rather not just breast-beating but breast-beating *with* (to borrow her paternal grandma's favorite gnomic jab in the ribs, just made for italics) *a twist, if you know what I mean*, through which she let it be known that thanks, among other things, to four score and seven years of fieldwork conducted selflessly from her Bronx tenement stoop, not only was there no keener diagnostician of oddballishness but, as such, she could always be counted on to provide, at no extra charge and so as to ensure full medical reimbursement to the oddball in question, the right *DSM* or procedure code. But in this case, *who* is the oddball? Borkman, the breast-beater? the Master, authorizer of the breast-beating? Herbert, the Master's progenitor, marionette, arch-victim and heiress-apparent? Surely, such a question would have stumped Granny Herbert, the oddest oddball of them all, dead in her tracks. In any event, the fact remains that, whatever its provenance, Borkman has just had one of those exhilaratingly cornball yens (for which he's infamous among the cognoscenti) to be the very first to congratulate himself for having failed, over the course of several lifetimes and as a matter of Übermenschly principle, to fulfill his responsibilities—as son, husband, father, friend, business partner, nephew, cousin, citizen, tenant, etc., etc. Failure in these departments rendering him *special*—as special as Gene Kelly takes himself to be when he seduces Les Girls.

"What does pornography have to do with Invidicum, will you tell me?" Stifter, in the stagiest of stage whispers, asks Ethan. Though it could have been anybody—and it is anybody, or rather, Everybody aka Everyman (which Ethan is on the painful verge of discovering to be his true vocation even if only the Devil knows what anybody's vocation truly is). Maybe it's the impact of the question on the questioner himself or merely the erosive effect on consciousness of the time of day—whatever the reason, it can't be denied that Stifter exudes a kind of limp-wristed and slack-jawed decrepitude. Post pretends not to have heard a word or is it justified enthrallment with the Avatar Concept that gets in the way? "Pornography has in fact everything to do with Invidicum," Cook sneers, exhilarated to be coming to the rescue, either Ethan's or Post's (he's not sure whose). He has it on the best authority that phials of Invidicum in all its off-label variants, not to mention the raw materials for their manufacture (adulterated, let's hope inadvertently), are being shipped surreptitiously out of the country in crates harboring pornography (great shock absorber) and nothing but. But, fortunately, at every major airport and heliport, the boys from Customs and Border Protection are currently trying out portable trace detectors (their latest gizmo) which, so they claim, will have absolutely no trouble sniffing out the wheat from the chaff. The only question is, What, in this case, is the chaff?

Post's sigh says more than it tells—looks daggers but thinks none. At first. "As a disciple—of somebody at Amygdala—you've always left (way too) much to be desired. So no wonder that what you've just said, Cook, my man—with its slaphappy exaltation of the literal—not only proves to be very much beside the point but also adds insult to injury and begs the question and preaches to the converted and takes the line of least resistance, strains credibility, and *strains credulity* (whatever that means!) as well. And that's just for starters. However, drubbing aside (I'll deal with you later), what I've come to realize (exact time and place? too irrelevant for words) is that the Invidicum trial has failed and failed miserably (are any of you bystanders aware that after just one whiff of the California sun, all of our subjects without exception have stopped taking their medication?). And, I might add (for who's going to stop me?), that despite all our hard work, the nature, incubation period and duration of its side effects have yet to be identified, much less understood (don't press the guinea pigs, they'll only deny it). And for this and more I hold you, Pritchard, and you alone responsible. Of course you're not *completely* responsible: you've been egged on mercilessly by Margo—who's out to avenge her husband at any price—to move in another direction even if every direction is the mirror image of every other and even if all this is at the price of the trial's success. She thinks I killed him. If only indirectly. Too, too busy as you were following her instructions to the letter (I don't know what they were and don't want to know)—the way Macbeth followed through on *his* Lady's— small wonder you've failed to ensure that exposure to hardcore pornography in all its forms (even, or rather [given that it's you who'd be handling the dosage] *especially*, homosexual pornography, preferably unscripted [a script is as erotic as a condom]) would be used *mandatorily* as an adjuvant—the only conceivable adjuvant." "It's you who's failed!—" (here Pritchard sounds not a little like The Rump at the third 2016 Presidential Debate telling eternal bugbear Hillary that it's *she* [of all people] who's Putin's puppet [*take that, you egg!*]) "afraid as you've been that the adjuvant might eclipse the drug." "Always making it a point to put the patient first—even before my own dreams of glory—I needed only to take the full measure of porn's clinical potential to be able to surmount—and pretty damn quick—my fear of being how shall I put it? . . . *gelt by association*. You've, on the other hand, dreaded what being too much at home in the world of your brand of hardcore (so much at home as to be able—that is, if you would only put your weight behind it—to defend its therapeutic benefits out loud and without flinching and to exploit them with professional grit and gristle)—dreaded what owning your addiction full speed ahead—would do to *your* dreams of glory. Has it never occurred to you to for once put the needs of your patients before your own shame? to speak up for *your* pharmakon—in its own way, a he-man sort of pharmakon—as the best alleviator of the ill effects of Envy withdrawal which Invidicum, alas, only exacerbates the more successful its application?" Pritchard leaps (alas, no faun, he) or tries to look like he's leaping—straight out of his chair and into the heart of the matter. Is he angry? Or, far more interestingly, exultant?—i.e., has Post's tough-loving public shaming been a kind of liberation—a one-way ticket to liberation? "Though I wouldn't for a minute put it past you or your better half to peddle the abject failure of Invidicum as nothing less than a one-of-a-kind success story. Successful precisely (you know the drill) to the extent that—in the high style of Plato's pharmakon—it's rendered all distinctions between success and failure irrelevant. Thereby ushering in the long-overdue New Wave in pharmaceuticals. Starting here, starting now.

"But still, it may not be too late. Did you hear what I just said? Still, for all Pritchard's failings, it may not be too late."

Evidently resuscitated by all this talk about failure, the Gross Marginal (remember him?) whose Goose Barely 'Scaped Cooking (and whose equipment, Cantor notes for the first time, includes, a Roman nose, full lips, long thighs and a virile ass, the barest essentials for success in business far more—no matter what anybody else may say—than in neoclassical ballet)—the Gross Marginal startles the jury members by appropriating their modest little gaming table (at which the havoc they play with the fates of others is anything but modest). And *with an oafish yet still impish leap worthy of ever-graceful Adam Lüders*, Shearer faithfully notes. He has the makings of a Faun—the Faun of a thousand leaps (so what if Nature herself wouldn't be caught dead executing any of them) and, more to the point, of a thousand sleepy California Afternoons routinely overpopulated with nymphs, one and all starved for eternalization. Steadfastly unaware of the leap as of everything else that doesn't concern Invidicum directly (though who's to say where Invidicum ends and real life begins?), Post sighs from deep inside his chest and back down again. If only (he observes) Pritchard—egged on by Margo but in the right way for once—had made it clear from the very start that Invidicum's efficacy was contingent on intensive study of the Pornographic Text—and not your run-of-the-mill dime-a-dozen intensive study but an approach undertaken with a reverence appropriate to, say, the Talmud or the *Zohar* or that (literally) nutty *Enchiridion super Apocalypsim (An Apocalypse Lover's Handbook)*. "Hell," (plunging at last into the cesspool of reminiscence and liking what he smells) "all this reminds me of what I went through in my second year of med school (Case Western Reserve, Cleveland, Class of '74)—desensitization training, they called it back in those days—only the porn was of the good clean freshly scrubbed (though not always) hetero variety. I never mentioned this to anybody" (perfectly timed faltering diminuendoed to a whisper) "but the minute the 'heroine' started masturbating while milking her right udder, I *fainted* . . . dead away in that dimly lit amphitheater of the less respectable emotions. Passed out, just like that. Though I still managed" (normal volume revisited) "to tune back in for the Big O, which lasted several sticky lifetimes—hers, mine and ours. But passed out or tuned back in, I ultimately emerged from the amphi a better man—no, make that *just a man*, pure and simple. Ripeness is all—but, when you're a first-year medical student, so is desensitization. And that's how Pritchard should want you to think about porn—as a desensitizer—but not against Envy (that's Invidicum's job). Then against what? Well, against the pain of knowing that thanks to Invidicum you're losing your grip on Envy and Envy's grip on you—that It's dying off with no time for a fond farewell by either party. Porn, through timely administration, would hinder you from stymying the divestment process—divestment of a lifetime's worth of enslavement to a misperception which is truer than you may want it to be, namely, that whatever the Other has is better just because he's the Other and has started out in life with one overwhelmingly unfair advantage: he's not— nor will he ever be—*you*.

"Yet, while just a few pages back—I mean, just seconds ago—I conceded but only grudgingly and grumpily and grouchily that, given Pritchard's orientation, he should be permitted to proscribe—prescribe—the species of *pornography-as-adjuvant* best aligning with his unspeakables—with his case history—well, despite all that, imagine my surprise at this moment to discover I now actively embrace—and without permission from that higher authority (known to me as myself)—the idea that, at least *in diesen heil'gen Hallen*, homoporn and nothing but should reign supreme. And rightly so since in the kingdom of homoporn, the orientation of the performers is never in doubt. They are as true to their code as Enviers should be to theirs even if in the latter case such fidelity is a means to an end—unholy cure." After all, Post wonders out loud, why *profess* to homosexuality in a world that counter-professes to taking pride in finding homosexuality's *lust dynamism* (a term coined by one of his mentors, Harry Stack Sullivan) abhorrent—or worse? "In folksy hetero-, on the other hand, it's not just the gals but the guys as well who may not, for all the organ grinding, prefer the opposite sex, which state of uncertainty into which everybody connected with the enterprise is thrown willy-nilly lowers the erotic temperature significantly—in some cases, to Absolute Zero (which as you already know—or better yet as you have *begun willy-nilly to surmise*— is a mere heuristic phantom born of expediency. So how can the spectator enjoy a good-hard-fuck-that-isn't?" Hence, he and his colleagues have no choice, whatever their religious affiliation, but to crown homoporn *pornography degree zero*—pornography in its purest state—its impact undistressed by simulation—by outcries of orgasmic transport whose raucousness is in direct proportion to a lack of conviction. "That's what makes homoporn organic— makes it good for us—good enough to eat. Even if I haven't yet developed a taste for it myself." As fair is fair, Post has no choice but to thank Pritchard, relentless comber through XXX-rated archives worldwide, for bringing to his attention, in a communication on view starting 2 August at the Morgan Library and Museum, the incremental therapeutic effects of prolonged exposure to the films belonging to this unjustly maligned film subsubgenre. Still, this doesn't prevent Post from, looking Pritchard in the eye, again bemoaning the fact that "he didn't follow through" on his own initiative.

Post goes on to elaborate—especially since he now has the audience in the palm of his hand (why, they look as if they were going to "faint dead away" from the sheer shock generated by the *concept* of desensitization as here dangled before and deployed against them [which concept may turn out to in fact be more . . . shocking than the Real McCoy, i.e., the phenomenon itself])—he goes on to elaborate on what Pritchard set forth in the aforementioned communication, namely, that deep within this subsubgenre's greasy bowels, there just so happens to exist, flagrantly unsung, a small category of films where ad-libbing performers triumphantly assured in their homosexual *maleness* (swishery *Streng Verboten* in this neck of the woods) are paid to thrash experimentally past the confines of scriptedness—to *think outside the envelope of opportunity* (or whatever happens to be the *phrase du jour* [the term *phrase du jour* itself being of course, and in the great Russellian tradition, yet another *phrase du jour*])—and self-identify as scared straights tempted to try their hand at same-sex sex *for the very first time.* Knowing full well—and tickled pink at the knowing (after all, there is nothing more erotic than a process unfolding against its grain, or haven't you heard?)—that no self-disrespecting voyeur will suspend his disbelief long enough to buy in to so smarmy a simulation of simulation—ultimately, not even he for whom the spectacle's been specifically mounted—i.e., the guy whose most cherished fantasy entails some believably bushy-tailed straight's induction into and irreversible conversion to gayness. Rest assured, he'll end up cured of his fantasy once it turns out that the simulators, through their very ease of simulation—their inherent "affectionate" mockery of anybody who (in this day and age, imagine!) needs to take his homoporn straight—are far more exciting than straights, phantom or otherwise, can ever be. Cured once he realizes the performers, amidst all their other duties, are evidently so defiantly at home with their own gleeful exhibitionism, so much the shameless masters of their gods-given sexuality, as to be able and willing at the drop of a jockstrap, to mock-impersonate—with a 100 percent male's effeminacy-free coquetry (though what's with all the anti-effeminacy histrionics?)—a straight-to-gay in the throes of squeamishness, which makes said performers for certain oddballs the most erotically charged UFOs stalking the earth. "Simulation plus simulation equals what Manny Farber calls 'male truth,'" says Post in ceremonial summation. (He also says, while he's at it, that just because he graduated from med school—and at the rock bottom of his class, no less—doesn't mean that he shouldn't know who Manny is—was.) But is this male-truth business a summation or the impersonation of one—an affirmation of the impossibility of summation where dark desires are at even darker play? "Of course no desire is dark intrinsically—it's rendered dark—outlier dark—marginal dark—peripheralizably dark—by papal decree. Which only goes to show that there ain't much gay in gayness. Though who, you might ask, am I—your standard-issue heterosexual WASP—to be strafing you with my take on homosexuality? Who am I? Well, I just told you—I'm your standard-issue, etc., etc., with no axe to grind (in fact with not a single pickaxe to his name) but with an obscenely absolute right to his own take on the gay world—what he perceives to be that world—from his vantage in the swamps of standard issue. My take may be right and/or it may be wrong but whatever it is it's 100 percent *valid* as a take—to the extent that it's been *lived through* whether uncomfortably or not. That is, for better or worse, it's earned its place in the universe as unique to me and hence to the universe. Even if I've gotten homosexuals and their world all wrong my wrongful perception has been earned and my point of view—that is, my wrongful POV shot—is as valid—as real as the next guy's. I've come by it honestly, as they say. Along similar lines (and I'm not just changing the subject), all of the accidental epigrams of that nut job My Little Margie Taylor Green are just as worthy of their proper archive. Are they good? are they bad? it's irrelevant. They fill a place in the universe we didn't know was empty until it *was* filled—thanks to the persevering imbecility of Frau von Tailor Green. First thing we have to ask ourselves when our fallible sensors tell us the tripe-spouting crazies—the grim reapers like Frau Green and, on a less exalted level, Fraulein Mitch MacConnell—are coming down the pike is, Would the world be a poorer place without their reaping? Of course, it would! For one thing, look at how much counter-thinking Frau and Fraulein both have triggered in us self-righteous Globalist counter-crazies! Counter-thinking that we didn't know was there to be had for the taking—didn't know *could* be there until, that is, My Little Margie's unsinkable resistance to the truth—the truth as we know it—the truth as we decree it to be in our infinite self-righteous wisdom—until her resistance showed us from where deep within ourselves we could extract it. The sooner we face up to the fact that the monster running the universe (who may or may not be Peirce's master or Dickinson's master or, which is far more likely, R.M. Renfield's master)—that the universal monster wants all of us, including My Little Margie, to do our tragical-comical part in filling every last space, every last void (Leave No Void Unturned! that's Margie's philosophy), with our counter-sayings and counter-doings—in record time—the sooner we face up to this fact, the better. Since nothing is real until it's countered—opposed—given status—gravitas—a dash of charisma—through opposition. And just remember Margie doesn't spin—stuff—her wisdom sandwiches out of whole cloth: it took an outrageously strong will to believe in what she professed to know was false— that forest fires were generated by 'Globalist'-manned laser beams. Even if she didn't cook up the idea—the image—she clawed her way toward choosing it from among billions upon billions of others which choosing turns out to be far more creative than the cooking. In short, she underwent a peculiar evolution even if she did no such thing. What matters is that she believed or pretended to believe in an evolution—a process—that she invested her own energy in the baking of those sandwiches which means that the resultant pap she farted off like laser beams to fellow travelers far and wide out of the kindness of her Georgia-peachy heart of darkness has filled—like my misreading of gayness—a gap in the universe nobody knew was there until she stepped in to fill it. And as a bonus and fringe benefit and adding insult to injury at no extra cost she's provided a story line—a back story—a context for her baked goods—a uterine bed for implantation of her sandwiches—her pap—her farts—her 'irresponsible fetuses' (though in my opinion 'irrepressible' would have worked better). And speaking of irrepressible fetuses: as one anti-Semite said to the other 'walking along Broadway,' *Everything that's new is thereby automatically traditional.* And Margie, one of the anti-Semites in question and the other's most important disciple, shrewdly took him at his word for Margie is now—having managed to fill a space we didn't know had existed until she filled it—nothing if not hog-wild and high-on-the-hog traditional— in fact a key cog (who could have imagined it!?) in the machine known as 'political discourse'. I know what you're all thinking: Margie's hallucinatory fetus is 'wondrous strange' and so I have no choice but to go you one better and counter-think, like my betters before me, 'And therefore as a stranger give it welcome.'"[114] (And he repeats the beautiful phrase several times and not just for emphasis but because the generosity resident therein brings him to the verge of tears.)

Post decides it's time to flaunt his dexterity in shifting gears. Or maybe all this talk about ladylike farts is making him uncomfortable. "So, with respect to your stage-whispered question, Netta, my girl (folks, the two of us go back a long long way), I have no choice but to ask (taking a dog-eared page from Pritch's *Hornbook of Pornography*, third revised edition), What better way to beat envy—I mean, Envy—at its own game than to stand back and pretend pornographically—i.e., without fooling anybody (least of all oneself)—that one's a devout non-envier suddenly afflicted (any target will do) with the unquenchable craving to go all-out-envious?" (As for the stage-whispered question in question Stifter, its bona fide progenitor, is only too willing to sign over all rights to Netta since with benefit of hindsight he realizes that coming from any self-respecting man's man the question is unseemly and its text foolish—as foolish as . . . as . . . as . . . the Duke of Albany's excoriation, in *Lear*, of his monster wife's filial impiety. As for "Netta, my girl," [unaware of being now and forever in Stifter's debt] she's immediately much too fascinated to doubt, doubt and doubt some more, which is what, before even *considering* the possibility of touching a new MO with a ten-foot pole, she's been trained to do. Though, to keep her professional's hand in, she does roll her eyes and shrug a bit to signal expertise-in-action exercising its right to scepticism.) That way, Post explains, one shows one doesn't need to be cured at all—one's so much the gleeful defiant shameless master of one's Envy as to even have something left over—a supplement—with which to play at non-envy tantalized by Envy—to play at squeamishly making the reluctant crossover—another out-of-gender experience—from non-envy to the promised land of Envy. Which makes Envy—like gayness—well . . . sexy. "And where does Invidicum enter into the whole shebang?" asks Gross Margin, whose nates are very much at home on the gaming table and whose question attests to the fact that this rabble-rouser is forever on the lookout for another gimmick—another Gibraltar—on which to build his prize unicorn. Oddly, the jury members he's displaced seem to have *taken an immediate shine* to GM and (to prove they mean business) adopted him as very much one of their own. Despite a lifetime of experience with types just like GM, Post has been put on the defensive by his challenge. Sounding more stately than he intended, Post replies, "Invidicum can assist in the transition." "Which makes it a kind of carrier pigeon." "Exactly. Though it's more like an enzyme which catalyzes the transport by, say, a vesicle or a cell ghost or a reconstituted adenovirus of mock-non-envy into that promised land."

Tearing himself free of Margo, Pritchard finally decides to get into the swing of things—things starkly pornographic. He explains that, along the same lines (though are they in fact the same? and more to the point, can

---

[114]*Hamlet*, Act I, Scene V, 172–173.

lines be the same where no lines, whether of conflict or comity, have yet been drawn?) and contrary to popular belief, pornography is a commodity manufactured exclusively by puritans who (nothing more puritanical than the canons of greed, which helps explain why the "lavish lifestyles" of felons—right down to their Maseratis, ostrich-skin boots, MAGA berets and Rolex ankle monitors—are so joylessly indistinguishable) in this case typically require that performers—en route to, during and after orgasm—confine themselves to uttering, as dully as possible, the same old few expletives for all the world as if recruitment of anything in excess will exact an outsize cost—and a tax-undeductible one to boot. (Pity, they haven't come to realize, these puritans [but would it make a bit of difference if they did?], that any new word is a gift and constitutes, for performer and spectator simultaneously, a new life, a new weapon against life, an outburst of defiance from deep within life's hindgut, an agent of escape from self-hate, a camouflage and reversible carapace and, last but not least, a job promotion replete with substantial increase in salary and more extensive health plan.) But occasionally there does emerge a . . . a . . . well, a homosexual genius, if you must know (and *100 percent male* to boot, whatever that means) whose excitement is *rarissime* in being authentically and explosively excessive—in being too defiant to submit to extinction in some authoritarian bodily process. But having, unlike other kinds of excitement or maybe unlike every other kind, nowhere to spill over and extinguish itself except in the world of words, his excitement therefore compels him to go beyond the prescribed expletives and configure the language of lust in a way never before effected. There is a point, however, where the wordflow, knowing full well it owes its upsurge to lust and lust alone and feeling the need to repay the debt, decides to continue on its own steam so as to put its alluvia—and not just of the four-letter variety—at the service of lust's prolongation. "And in this regard," he continues, "let me take yet another page from the third revised edition of that horny old hornbook of mine—now in its fortieth printing, but who's counting? There's this script-free gay porn film, see, still making the rounds—already a classic as cultic as Stonehenge (both Criteria and Kino Farber, by the way, have expressed interest in producing a totally remastered semen-stain-free version)—an underground classic right up there in fact with masterpieces like Ishmael M. Drybock's *Night of the Chair* and *A Dose of Maleness*. In that film, the onehundredpercenter, having been vigorously fucked to the point where there's no turning back—from ejaculation—coughs up not the usual chestnut cum warhorse *Fuck, yeah* but rather the quantum-leap-like *That's right, baby, fuck it out of me, fuck it out of me.*" According to Pritch, it is here that the soaked spectator is regaled with a monumental example of the ability to break fearlessly—shamelessly—out of the straitjacket of genre—or in this case, subsubgenre and not just any old subsub but one which cherishes the fact that it outdoes every other in terms of a poverty of both production values and nifty plot twists—and to do to and for it something akin to what Boetticher and Mann (*Anthony*, not Thomas, not Delbert, not Abby, not Horace) did to/for the Western, and Sirk to/for the so-called woman's film. What the spectator overhears, then, is the language of pornography springing fully formed from a bona fide primitive's sweaty brow—a primitive on the order of, say, Griffith or Sam Fuller or Spillane or Pierre Boulez. Or, for that matter, Góngora (who having gone as far as he did deep down inside innovation's baroque sausage grinder had no choice but to emerge the juiciest and spiciest of populists). What we hear is an insatiably curious savage discovering that language in the way that Mussorgsky, according to Debussy, discovered music, namely, through his emotions and step by step by step. Even Margo appears to have been won over by his eloquence, maybe because it's not so much eloquence as a weird kind of pre-eloquence groping toward the real thing. "So, what better way," Pritchard asks (with a twinkle in his eye—a twinkle which seems to say, *This song is for you, Netta, our delectably doubting Thomas*)—"what better way for our timorous enviers to get on with the business of transcending Envy than to describe their condition in ways never before attempted? (With Invidicum once again supplying the chlorophyll.) After all, when you get right down to it and even when you don't, who would be dumb enough to deny that any disease is 99.99 percent *failed immunosuppression of the tired old descriptors* loaned its victims by so-called healers with a capital *H*" (is this meant to be a put-down of Straynge?) "to give them the illusion of getting a handle on things—the things known as symptoms—but why should they surface—heed the siren song—when all that awaits them are these wrong names?"

But their schooled incompetence doesn't let those healers off the hook—not in his universe at least. They should—must—go humbly back—preferably with their tails between their legs—to where all ladders start, i.e., to the foul rag-and-bone shop of his hornbook (since hornbooks never lie, not even in their fortieth printing) for examples of what in fact are Pritchard's most important "discovery"—the most important element in the subset of elements common to set A intersection set B, where A is homoporn and B, Envy. And Pritchard's the almighty king of that subset, even if, like Frédéric the Great's, it's the "tiniest of principalities." (*Is this reference to* very *elementary set theory*, Cantor wonders, *Pritch's sop of indemnification for having chosen Irena over me? As things now stand, or sag, he wouldn't put anything past him.*) Decades of overaddiction were required to enable him to recognize something that would have been obvious even to a toddler: the goings-on in homoporn that manage to pack the biggest erotic wallop—gave the biggest erotic bang for the buck—are *throwaways* and as such invariably play themselves out deep inside the interstices between—the connective tissue uniting—the all-too-humdrum main events. He remembers, for example, a performer who, in his eagerness to put skin—literally—in the game, repudiated shirt, pants, socks, briefs, etc., with just enough bravado to put across the very thing that's most exciting to the seasoned spectator: contempt for everyone (especially said spectator) except his partner. But far more revelatory in this regard was the privileged moment in *Scrotum-Pole Vaulters* (or was it in *Balls Ahoy* or *Bareback Slutmasters, Part Two: Able-bodied Semen?*), when, on their postcoital pilgrimage to the showers, quarterback-manly top turned to shortstop-manly bottom (both were unapologetically all-over hairy but the top was of course even more so) and playfully uttered the word *mortified*. Turns out he was mortified at the prospect of their having to wait until they'd finished showering to get back down to brass tacks. And nothing less than mortifying-be-yond-his-wildest-wet-dreams was Pritch's near-unbearable excitement at hearing a word so *female-feminine-feminized* uttered by one so *un*-. "So it's the Enviologist's duty not to lie in wait for every run-of-the-mill confession his patient feels duty bound to cough up (and, by the way, the jury's still out on whether this approach—this carryover from the catacombs—serves any purpose other than to boost earplug sales to Board-certified con men) but instead, in the throwaway fetal tissue connecting those confessions, *to hear the truth but hear it slant*. Sorry to say so in front of all these folks, Margo, but here's where Jim—*your* Jim—at his worst the most flatulent of faux cur-mudgeons, went so terribly wrong, for hearing things slant—not to mention, seeing things awry—was simply beyond his pint-sized capabilities." As some-body's husband and in the name of husbands everywhere (since husbands need, whatever else they're guilty of, to stick together), Borkman's a bit sur-prised (even if he's the first to admit with an unbecoming fake worldweariness which doesn't become him nothing surprises him anymore) that Margo hasn't jumped into the breach to defend Straynge's honor. (Clearly a classic case, thinks Melanctha Herbert, of *funeral bak'd meats did coldly furnish forth the marriage tables* syndrome, now being linked to—that is, when it's not being held directly responsible for [by those who should know better]—everything from Catch-COVID-22 to flat feet and bleeding gums.)

Is Cantor imagining things or has he just heard one big fat long-over-due collective sigh of relief now that the genome of correspondences between Envy and porn addiction has at last been exhaustively mapped—now that it's been proven to everybody's satisfaction, including brother-against-brother, that homoporn therapy constitutes one of Envy's most-royal roads to abate-ment (with Invidicum once again bringing up the rear as its coach-and-four)? No, he isn't imagining things though the fact remains that Pritchard's troubles are hardly over—Pritchard, whose only sin was to bring together on his very own homespun Field of the Cloth of Gold all the warring parties under the sun and make them love each other unenvious- and unpornographically.

Fidgeting with a button ablaze on his off-blue blazer to signal that the show is over, Pritchard tries to catch Post's attention. He's having a drink at the bar, the view of which is obscured by the now semi-mythic gaming table. (But as it's an ill wind that blows nobody any good, Herbert dutifully realizes that the gaming table resembles nothing so much as the Cosmic Tree of the Tungus, on whose branches the childrens' souls sought by novice shamans perch prenatally. In fact, she feels a fit of her own prenatality coming on, from which she wouldn't mind being rescued by Post, suddenly the hottest shaman in the house.) There's a sob in Pritchard's voice as he cries out over the chatter of shot glasses, "Please take over for me. You're the only one who knows—and should know—what occurred after that sleazy *mortified* business. It's in the Morgan Library communication, remember?" He can't, without summoning forth the muse of incoherence, talk about what did occur. Fact is, Pritchard realizes—rather, he's *come to realize* (even if not enough evolutionary time has elapsed to justify invocation of the phrase)—that while it's all well and good to have provided enlightenment at a notional cost, it's not so well and good when the provider is himself still struggling with the R&R (ramifications and repercussions) of the sleaze provided—still trapped in one of the many moat-like Nightmare Alleys engirding the Nightmare Abbey erected on the ruins of that sleaze. ("One day you and your hornbooks and communications will be the toast of Sotheby's." Margo butts in salvingly—shouting, though he's right beside her. After all, she doesn't want *both* of the men in her life to go to their muddy death lambasted. Worse, without a substantive *Times* obit for her to paste in Junior's scrapbook. A boy, after all—especially a boy with *issues* too dire to articulate—needs a role model or two.)

Swallowing his pride and what looks (but to whom?) like a black-as-pitch ferrous sulfate tablet, Pritchard ventures forth with a single intention: to sit himself down on the uncomfortable-looking stool adjacent to Post's and pour out his heart at full speed. "Seems like you need to talk to somebody about the *mortified* business since, as far as I can see, it's *unfinished* business. What disturbs me most is the fact that you refer to it as 'sleazy' and as 'sleaze'. Unfor-givable. Righteous lust—whatever its provenance, whatever its skew—is like righteous rage: you should show it some respect—manful respect. You have no accounts to render to anybody about what you refer to ignobly, ungrate-fully, as your sleaze. You should think of the sleaze as your most precious possession—as your spiritual bread and butter. But *don't get me started*" (why does Pritchard hate that gassily self-important injunction as much as he's just discovered he does?) "on the subject of sleaze, more commonly known as trash. Impossible—self-castrative in fact—to label—to bracket—to asterisk away—*anything* as trash. You're simply playing with fire—walling yourself off from enlightenment—from Realpolitik—cutting off your nose for news to spite your too freshly scrubbed face—obstructing your understanding of what it means to live in the world. You can't ex anything out: the bigger the temptation to incinerate, the more pressing the need to make your target the subject of continuous further research. You need to suspend judgment as you go about determining why the thing in question admits of no value, that is to say, why it ruffles your delicate sensibilities which aren't as delicate as you'd like to think—why it makes you antsy enough to want to move your bowels even if you suspect there's nary a fecalith to excrete. You've got to live in the moment, Pritch—for starters, take the *present* moment which as we speak is hawking documentary footage at the Fundance Film Festival of sleazeball Gerhard Schröder doing what he does best, i.e., getting in the mood to play webcam footsie with monster man Putin, and how does he do it? well (funny you should ask), by engaging in a bit of off-the-record masturbation, that's how, and not just your run-of-the-mill friendly neighborhood garden-variety masturbation but masturbation before each in turn of the forty-four self-com-missioned portraits (it's all very *Gerd-to-Gerd*) holding court in his five-story Berlin office." Pritchard, a man of the world, knows authentic tough-loving exasperation when he sees and hears it and gratefully takes the bait. Plumbing the depths of what looks (but, again, *to whom?*) like a Rob Roy, Post doesn't waste another second before saying, "Liepnits is your best bet. He's the only guy who ('radically' different sexual orientation notwithstanding) can even begin to make head or tails of what you're going through." "OK. Is he still on the premises?" Though what *are* the premises at present? Pritchard has lost track. Getting too old for this kind of island hopping, if you ask me. "Why don't you mosey on down—or is it on *over*—to the Courthouse: Liepnits is lucky enough to have an office in the Old Jail Wing (I pulled a few strings—tugged at a few heartstrings)." "Who says he's *going through* something?" So challenges Margo who makes it a point never to let him out of earshot and who's still thinking about the obit and the need to keep the exalted content squeaky-clean—for their son's sake. "Stay out of this," her lover warns. "What? Are you going to just stand there and let him talk to me like that?" she asks Pritchard (never mind that the only way for the words to make sense is if they coagulate a challenge to Post). "He never has anything nice to say about me" (this, on the other hand, directed unequivocally and irrevocably at Post, as well it should be). "Not true—or did I simply forget to mention that I'm tickled pink to see you're no longer quite so conspiracy-obsessed or, to put it more respectfully, -oriented?" "It's thanks to the California sun—not your tender loving care." "Terrific news, any way you slice it! So, Margo—*Good job!*" (as rehab center physical therapists are wont to say—at least on the Upper East Side of Manhattan—when their least responsive charge achieves at long last and with nary a peep[115] the impatiently awaited feat of expiring in his state-of-the-art wheelchair).

Post takes him aside and says, "How could I go on living with myself if I didn't steer you toward the man for whom contradiction is the very spice—*the very spice*—of life—the man whose sun rises and sets with contradiction *über Alles*? (Since 'mortified unlimited' as you call it—or rather, as I call it—seems to be all about contradiction, i.e., thanks to the fairy dust sprinkled all over him by language—the fairy dust encapsulated by, distilled in, a single word—your quarterback became most male when being most female.)" Pritchard shakes his head. "It seems just a wee bit too easy-way-out-ish." "Not if you go with an open mind—and don't resist," Post counsels. And, sure enough, once inside (and in seconds flat, thanks to Uber, whose prime concern is first, last and always—and always unregenerately—NOT the health and welfare of its fleet) his much-remarried host's almost too cozy office (more like a '60s bachelor flat straight out of a Neil Simon vehicle for Sammy, Frank and Dean) all resistance does melt away and before he knows it, he's telling Liepnits (an inveterate note-taker from all indications) that never in his many—almost too many—years of pornographizing has he ever been confronted with so striking—so Sherlockian—all right then, so *Hegelian* (at which concession, however much infested with begrudgery, G.W.F. Liepnits just can't help beam-

---

[115]That word again! (what word? *nary*, silly, not *peep*): three times in the course of thirty-five pages! Artifact of incompetence? Not on your life. Instead, think: vehicle for concealment-as-revelation of an irrepressible secret *à la Maimonides*—of a truth that dares not *not* speak its name and as frequently as possible and what better hiding place than a word?—not a sentence or a speech but a measly little word with two (poker) faces. (And if you're still half-awake, go visit Leo Strauss's *Persecution and the Art of Writing*, p. 72.)

ing)—a contradiction in terms as that presented by what hereinafter he'll be referring to out of delicacy as The Mortified Affair. ("Delicacy for whose benefit?" snaps Liepnits, not unkindly [for he's too busy thinking that this would be a near perfect title for the universally much-missed ninth entry in *His Last Bow*].) For what he—Pritchard—was—has been—is still—dealing with here is clearly a gayporner of the very first rank—not just A, i.e., yet another perfect specimen of authentic maleness in action and repose (of double maleness, in fact, for isn't a 100 percent uneffeminate male who fucks other males while tactfully avoiding contamination by the femaleness of fuckable females nothing less than a double male, at least according to that all too predictably French-patriotically anti-Semitic Saint of '50s Bleecker Street, Jean Genet?)— not just A but B, i.e., a perfect specimen boasting—possessing—sporting— flaunting—what Pritchard's old pal Norman Maine, MD, PhD, DDS., LLD, ASC, MGM, would have called—did in fact (in an unguarded moment) call— *something extra*—which *something extra* (see above) enabled him to think— either intentionally or unbeknownst to himself or both—nothing of pissing his perfection away (so as [as it turned out] to exalt even further this gift conferred on very few) simply by allowing unscripted use of a word like *mortified* to take him—a pioneer—a Leatherstocking—to ferry him—into uncharted territory—female territory—from whose bourn the unwary traveler never returns—except, maybe, in funereal triumph.

After quickly (*a*) closing the curtains (which could do with an all-out romp at the dry-cleaners) but not before Pritchard has had a chance to catch a glimpse of the almost-full moon and to regret not being able to say, *Well, look at you—why, I knew you when you were (now don't tell me two whole weeks have gone by since then!) but a mere sliver in Selene's eagle eye* and (*b*) doublelocking the door, G.W.F., though no psychobabbler, obviously feels it behooves him or, better yet, it is incumbent upon him, to trust his instincts and, as a quasi friend, suggest the "uncharted territory," as Pritchard calls it, may be nothing more—and nothing less—than that of his own Envy-ridden impatience to know precisely how much prohibited fondling of womanly things (e.g., bibelots like *mortified*) any *real male*—whether single or double or, for that matter, quadruple—can indulge in without undergoing irreversible transsexualization. (To get the matter of his shamanist accreditation out of the way, Liepnits explains that he's currently a part-time resident at the Fritz Lang Rancho Notorious Institute for Advanced Study, located right smack in the middle of Death Valley at the crossroads of pure-ish philosophy and psychopathological anthropology—at the exact spot in fact where Erich von Stroheim filmed the grueling final sequence of his super-butchered tone poem, *Greed*.) G.W.F. doesn't pretend to know much about Pritchard's kind of lust-driven tenderness—the darkest-reaches-of-the-Internet kind of tenderness—but, hell, as far as he can see, the only thing that the beautifully healthy young man of Pritchard's wet dreams did was play the sweaty bruteness of raw male sexuality against (as its superfetation—its ejaculate!) the wry delicacy of language, all for the sole purpose of enjoying the robust contrast (or, from the vantage of P's embitterment, the contradiction) as an aesthetic phenomenon in its own right. And this ability to delectate over the cohabitation of male-

and femaleness in one breast—a cohabitation transcending contradiction—has obviously gotten Pritchard's goat—and what a horny and, more to the point, what an *envious* old goat it's turned out to be.

"No offense intended, of course," Liepnits—a staunch apology-hater—adds atypically. "None taken." And on this note, they proceed to fist-pump and knuckle-hug to their heart's content (after all, the filthy curtains have been drawn and the door has been bolted out of its senses) in celebration of what is clearly a pivotal meeting of the minds. "And what you envied, guv'nor, were two things: the Boy's ability to both harden and loosen the contours of his sexuality through language and vice versa."

Well, now that G.W.F.'s mentioned it, the perfect specimen *did* use the *m*-word with exactly that: delight—the sheer unmitigated gall of delight (Liepnits's word was *delectate* but no matter: he's used to being misquoted by the hoi polloi). And, Pritchard observes, with absolutely no hint of a tending toward some swishy suicide of the will on language's flowery bier—the specialty of filmdom's female stand-ins for self-abominating males whose lust dares not speak its name except through ever more incriminatingly baroque allusions—doomed gals of a certain age like Blanche DuBois, not to mention Sarah Packard in that Robert Rossen pool hall epic—you know the one. Seeing his chance, Liepnits proceeds to warble on further in the same key. What the young man—*Pritchard's* anti-sissy—managed to do (fearlessly, given his impeccable credentials, just updated, as the most relentless stud on the farm) was toy with language—was transform language into an embodied refusal to undergo, immediately after having captured some phantom reality out there, obligatory self-obliteration—was make language non-transparent—even if (i.e., precisely because) as a game played by the big boys in that pool hall's back room—by big boys anywhere—language was supposed to be transparent (unseen, unheard), a mere means to an untimely end, a tool to be immediately disabled by the wielder at his first dim suspicion that the wielding could go all sorcerer's-apprentice on him and turn into (how did Liepnits put it?) *an aesthetic phenomenon in its own right.* And of course he must have known—*known, that is, without knowing he knew* (the best—the juiciest—kind of knowing this side of Death Valley and don't let anybody kid you)—that the deeper one goes into toying consciously with language as substance—toying "purposefully without purpose" à la Manny K. von Koenigsberg—the closer one gets to the very core of femaleness—femaleness as failure to move the world with the lever of language-as-boomerang. But what does his kind—the perfect specimen's kind—that is, Pritchard's kind—have to lose since in any case (at least as far as Liepnits has been made to understand—even if nobody has ever *made* the Big L do anything he didn't want to do or hadn't already done many times over)—since in any case *their* kind is never *not* conscious—never not self-conscious? their kind of differentness has a nasty habit of hurling them all too quickly into the abyss of consciousness—of themselves as reified gap—as a mere missing of the beat of normality, that old Trojan warhorse. "So," concludes Liepnits, "if anybody ever earned his gladiatorial right to determine just how far he could penetrate with the sex tool of *mortified* into the cold cunt of femininity without being demasculinized for good by too much consciousness of self-consciousness—if anybody ever earned that gods-given right the hard way, i.e., fair and square, it's got to be that Boy, straight out of the Brothers Grimm, Who Was Much Mortified Yet Lived to Tell the Tale."

Liepnits "takes the liberty of expressing the hope" (but why is he so formal all of a sudden?) that whatever Pritchard ends up having learned about his particular brand of vicissitude-prone Envy, compliments of the light shed by their chat upon his abasement before Boy Mortified's shrine, will help guide his treatment of the still needy members of the Amygdala crew. For there's clearly a lesson in all this fiddle for anybody—gay, straight, crooked, conchoid, cissoid (!), etc.—who's willing enough to admit he engages, even if only occasionally, in the heady business of Envying (a form of masturbation at its most immoral) when the lights are low and nobody's looking. "Sexuality, language and envy are not, after all, as arcane—as disjunct—as incompatible—a chamber trio as rumor would have it and, as we've seen here tonight, an envier like you could do worse—much, much worse—than avail himself of whatever may accrue—ideally, a discomfort excruciating enough to be therapeutic, even curative, even generative of a lifetime immunity, to any further upsurges of Envy—from signing off on the entry of his soul sickness into a thrashing dynamic with the other two." *Is this my send-off, my dismissal? might this be his way of handing me my walking papers?* Pritchard wonders. For some reason, he's tempted to raise his hand to request the floor but ends up keeping both funny little liver-spotted fists resolutely in his lap. But they mustn't forget for a second, he and Pritchard, that Pritchard's Boy Mortified (Liepnits makes it sound as if it's Pritchard who deserved all the credit and the Boy be damned) is a man of many talents and, as such, has seen fit to remind them (as if they needed any reminding)—all too Logically—all too Encyclopedically—and by extension the world (as if *it* needed any reminding)—that the essence of maleness—or its other essence—lies and always will lie in what is other than—what is the negative of—itself, i.e., femaleness (whose job it is to keep maleness all toasty and warm and which has nothing to do with effeminacy *but so what if it does?*)—femaleness as, say, the excruciated infinitude of self-consciousness—as the insatiable craving to *analyze*—specifically, to analyze away all threats to the soul's immune system, as if analysis were a joyous bacchanale, with no side effects apart from self-cannibalization. Self-consciousness as something dirty, sneaky, two-faced. Maleness, then, enjoys, in potentia, the best of both worlds: the strong, silent type of apparent self-sufficiency and at the same time gross deficiency inasmuch as to be completely true to itself maleness needs to become anti-male as well (mere self-identity, and nothing but, is death, death and more death), which is achievable—in the case of maleness—only by taking a whole-hog leap—like Pritchard's Boy—into femaleness and thereby putting an end to the abiding terror that some luridly telltale utterance or gesture—like letting a wrist go limp or crossing a leg the wrong way—may trigger the leap (but without one's consent), at any moment, which by its very nature is always the worst possible moment. But for the most self-respecting bastions of maleness the charm of the leap lies in the fact that it's endlessly deferred—endlessly deferrable—eternally not taken—kept on suicide watch—held forever in reserve for the rainiest of rainy days. In the bastions' realm (unlike the Boy's), the leap is always the leap to come. Interesting, no?—a charcoal study in contradictions—that it should be the so-called bastions—the Proud Boys—(not a "Boy" all a-shimmer with fairy dust)—who shit in their pants at the mere thought of taking a manful life-or-death leap—of any sort. (Come to think of it, though, no less a he-man than Fred MacMurray [as insurance agent Walter Neff] *does* cross his legs the wrong way in *Double Indemnity* [a "down, boy!" gesture? executed from the too much excitement generated by his first glimpse of pointy-titted sweater bombshell Barbara Stanwyck, as stepmotherly housewife Phyllis Dietrichson, descending the cute little staircase in her rotten little Spanish Colonial doghouse] yet comes out smelling even more like a rose [of, in this case, unblemished he-manliness].) Maleness is, by its very nature—whether it thinks it is or whether it wants this to happen or not—incessantly being forced and forcing itself incessantly beyond its own immediate frontiers, toward femaleness as the mythical or as a concocted "other side"—and in this case—Pritchard's case—the Boy's case—the link, or the Charon (for those who like their metaphors not more mixed but more muscularized)—is just a word, a pivot word (*kakekotoba*)—*mortified* to be exact. (Most men opt to tear up their ferry ticket even if it's round-trip.) Which is not to say maleness in being pushed into femaleness is acted upon by an alien force for (as pretty much noted above) it is the very essence of maleness to be at the same time the obverse of itself as a yawning deficit—to be the embodied lack of that constitutive "something extra" (or is this just Liepnits's wordflow going bananas from its very own brand of sexual deprivation, as perpetrated by wily Dr. Manning—neither stepmother nor housewife?)—to be inwardly self-contradictory (like everything else in the universe that is alive and kicking)—and to attempt to surmount that deficit by becoming the opposite of what it takes itself to be. Of course, before Liepnits arrived on the Greenwich Avenue scene, contradiction was always getting a bad—no, the worst of raps—was treated as if it were *only*: an abnormality; a rancid contingency; strep throat; a tumor (a teratoma really) whose sole raison d'être was to metastasize, metastasize and metastasize some more but which still never thought twice, between invasions, about giving clusters of normal cells Sunday School lessons on how to be respectful (!) of their fellows by refraining from rampant ingestion of the body's precious Lebensraum (sort of like the exasperatingly fake-humble French at their most doctrinal or, to go from the ridiculous to the sublime, sort of like My Little Margie Tailor Green aka Gavel Gertie, as shrieker *pro tempore* Queen for a Day (and as ordered by her handler), reminding fellow reps at the first sign of their harmless chatter "to abide by the decorum of the House"); and truth's contaminant par excellence, while in fact it is also and no less importantly the foundation, wellspring and root of all movement and of all vitality. But now, he thinks, both of them agree that maleness, when it convinces itself it's nothing but, is doomed (*zu Gericht gehen*) and to undoom itself must become ferociously female, or rather, must pretend to be trying against all odds to become female, ferocious or not, as long as it can rest assured—and this wishful thinking applies both to Boys Mortified and to Birther Boys and Proud

Boys as well as every Boy in-between the world over—that an insuperable barrier will always, like Zeus, rear its hyacinthine locks in the nick of time. Moreover, they (he and Pritchard) also agree, don't they? that in catching himself in the act of getting *mortified* while crossing the Rubicon, not once (notwithstanding his wishful thinking) did Pritchard's resident quarterback cum smart aleck let himself grow terrified (which explains Pritchard's envy)— let himself get cold feet—at the thought—the prospect—(*a*) of no longer being either male or female or (*b*) of being barred from return owing to maleness's possibly having taken it into its pretty little head to refuse, after so much smart-alecking—so much tarrying with the enemy—to welcome him back. Which means, therefore, they (he and Pritchard) further agree that not once did the quarterback feel the need to try (since, any way you slice it, maleness and *mortified* don't mix and in their efforts to play house would have torn him to pieces—and since *as* mortified he was already somehow damaged—damaged by a damage that no amount of trafficking in robust contrasts could mitigate), as every other red-blooded American boychik (with something extra) who found himself in the quarterback's shoes would have tried, to halt before it was too late all further truck with leaps and Rubicons so as to become non-identical to himself in the safest way possible, which, in this case, would have entailed undertaking an ulterior wooing of Femaleness—would have entailed determining exactly how far he could push maleness toward so totally incorporating and then smothering Femaleness within himself as (*a*) to smother *mortified* in tandem—*mortified*, which by its very singularity—by its very resemblance to a quimlike sliver of moon (nothing cuts deeper)— seems—seemed—impossible to sequester, much less vanquish, but which, if the Great Incorporation were successful, would become just one more anonymous, irretrievable drop in the ocean of that accursed Femaleness, itself now vanquished; and (*b*) to eliminate by extension, as a fringe benefit of the smothering—of smothering as serendipitous immunization—his ineliminable need for some kind of commerce even with those of its—Femaleness's—avatars (in the pre-digital sense) who happened not to come across to him as gorgon-bestriding harpies. What Boy Mortified did feel the need to try to do—and succeeded in doing—was ensure—and with the proud shamelessness of any pornstar worth their salt (e.g., Stormy Daniels)—that *mortified* stood its ground through thick and thin.

It sounds to him as if Liepnits envied his—not to mention the Boy's . . . fluidity—liquidity—volatility (which certainly have their tiny fringe benefits) to the point of feeling himself characterologically—sexually—short-changed by fate. Though the longing in his tone, if longing is what it professes to be, sounds far more like a grass-is-always-greener cum dog-in-the-manger type dyspepsia. Pritchard realizes looking back (a sigh would be appropriate at this juncture but he's too worn out to rustle one up) just how laughable, yet at the same time how all too typical (of the hale and hearty haves of which set Liepnits is an exemplary member), has been his smug defiance in presenting—from, of all privileged places, the comforts of home (where home is of course his own lily-white sexual skin invisibly tattooed with slogans adulatory of the free market, Health Care for All but the Needy, shareholder value and the Episcopalian Lives Matter movement)—in presenting such radical solutions to the problems posed by ontological sicknesses of every persuasion (blessedly non-existent among the common run of men, or so Pritchard needs to think in order to exalt his own non-normality into a commodity worthy of a contract as professor emeritus at some upscale addiction facility high up in the Hollywood hills) and such equally radical (i.e., wordflow-heavy) analyses of sexual disorientation at the point of intersection with its buddies language games and envy. Could be that Post connived with Liepnits to have him end up here—in a setup to end all setups—as a mere sounding board for the conspiracy theories of the Old Jail Wing's most illustrious tenant.

To be quite honest (and Pritchard is too old to be anything but) he's getting asphyxiated by all this basso-profundity (Liepnits, by the way, would make a terrific Grand Inquisitor and an even better Fiesco and the best Boris ever), even if he's lent a more or less equal, if not quite as liquid a voice to the goings-on. So is it any wonder he finds himself hungering for the wide open spaces of both the Bunker and the McChateau? Fortunately, the window's wide open and—thank heaven—even through the curtains Pritchard can inhale the scent of lavender bottlebrush and bougainvillea, not to mention the freshly cut grass. (He doesn't have to *earn* the scent: it's his whatever his defects and past defections.) On the other hand, it's only in sniffing the scenery that he becomes aware of how predictably thick, static and miasmic was the unfiltered, non-recirculated air he had no choice but to get used to up there. In absentia he smells it still—almost as a prefiguration—an augur—of some pandemic en route and not just any old pandemic but one that's shaping up to be more than poised to educe what is soon to become, he hopes, just one more of The Rump's trademark cunningly—magisterially—botched responses to crisis.

So they agree without admitting to it—for to agree would be humiliating for both, especially at this all-or-nothing stage of their careers—that the best thing Pritchard can do for the trial is go back and, with the clearest of consciences, tell Netta for him (is the bilious old gadfly still on the loose?) that the Envy victim must, like his pornography-besotted counterpart, *mutatis mutandis*, come to realize *a fortiori* that self-improvement is appallingly gradual and requires unceasing retrospective modification—if at all possible, *à la Noël the Burch*—of positions deemed unassailable at the moment of their adoption. Just as an XXX-rated scene deemed at first viewing too unarousing to be masturbated away may very well come across subsequently as in fact much too potent—much too virulent—for such an intervention, so will some night's supra-optimal dosage turn out by the dawn's early light to have been at the very least borderline-lethal. As Liepnits's hands dabble in overemphasis, Pritchard savors the fact—and safeguards what he savors—that the wrist is definitely dishrag-limp: positively shocking in an avowed heterosexual and a blushing trophy newlywed to boot! "All of which," he warbles, "simply confirms my unspoken belief that everything is going to turn out OK since whether pornographers, pill pushers or their victims, we're all doing our part as members willy-nilly of two exalted traditions." One, Liepnits all too readily explains, was inaugurated by troubadour Malte L.B., who memorably pointed out to gullible novices everywhere that for the sake of a single poem—and what could be more poetic than Pritchard's *Pornography of Therapeutics, Tenth Edition*? (the author dutifully goes beet-red)—you need to have seen many cities, many people and Things and of course have memories of numberless nights of passion; and the other (tradition) by the equally, albeit differently, august Something von Something de la Something who, qua conceptualizer of The Ciné-Porn Experience, cautioned that just as crucial to fulfillment as the films that make uninterrupted jerking-off *de rigueur* are those that result in the brutal dashing of pre-cum expectations, not to mention the role played in all this by the abasement inseparable from getting the goods semi-smoothly through sex-shop "customs"[116] (i.e., what would the Good be without the Bad and the Ugly?). Pritchard rises to go and make Netta take her medicine before it spills or chills. "And by the way, on your way out, don't you dare forget to have a look at the double-edged Sword of Justice over the entrance to the Law Library and at the Weeping Cabbage Palm near the Sunken Garden. But I plum forgot, you're not a tourist."

Meanwhile back at the Mc-, Post and Margo are at loggerheads, which makes Pritch almost forget what he's memorized. Incapacitated as in—or *under*—childhood when Ma and Pa Kettledrum took to parading their gross incompatibility. The chateau's Main Drawing Room cum council chamber looks—and acts—different. Suffused as it is—as by divine right it must be—with the light—the grace—shed by the Old Jail Wing and with the quality of its mercy. (Pritchard has been the unwitting carrier—the unwitting vector—of the virus of mercy from Courthouse to Chateau yet even if what he's brought is good news in the very best Ghent-to-Aix tradition, still he's a carrier and all the good news in the world can't dissipate the wondrous strange shadow of stigma—of contamination—that dogs the footsteps of every carrier, unwitting or otherwise.) Margo has clearly benefited from his absence. She emanates, like the exterior of the building, a kinder, a rosier glow. Before Pritchard can speak, however, he needs a bite or two. He opts for a blood orange but stops in mid-swallow, wondering what law of life his belly's violating by this kind of semi-ravenousness—immersive to the point of cannibalization (implied cannibalization, that is) of his enemies, some of whom—and only the most vicious—are in this room. Maybe it all boils down to a simple violation of etiquette to which gobbling old farts are partial. But in their case, there's none of Pritchard's obscene zest to leaven—mitigate—the drooling desperation with which old farts cling to life. Still, concerning the matter of disseminating the good news brought from Old Jail Wing (Ghent) to McChateau (Aix) (Pritchard assumed it was meant to be disseminated and not just to Netta), everything goes semi-well. Though Pritchard ends up having to confess he's not sure, now that he's gone and shot his mouth off, whether it's Malte L.B.

---

[116]For more on the abasement inseparable from getting sex-shop anathemabilia through "customs," see "The Son, He Must Not Know," an action-painting-in-prose of the tempest-in-a-teapot variety by the sparingly aforementioned and probably defunct Ishmael Drybock.

or the psychotic Judge Schreber or the Wolf Man or the Rat Man who inaugurated Tradition No 1. And the seismic churning of the bowels triggered by his uncertainty makes him want to run off and not come back until he's gotten all his factoids straight. "But," Jean protests (staring fixedly at Ethan who refuses to return the favor—but without looking sulky), "isn't there a lot to be said for sloppy scholarship? At least that's what my father—oops, dad—taught me—indirectly, by example." "What . . . is there to be said . . . exactly?" Stifter pouts dully—sulkily: he's pinch-pouting for Ethan. His eyes are bloodshot and his gaze filmed over though nobody appears to notice. And Jean who *does* notice reluctantly acknowledges to herself that she has an obligation far more pressing which is to follow her train of thought unimpeded to its bitter end—over some convenient embankment studded with scimitars and into the kelpy shoals of the sea, if need be. And whatever it is she has still to say may very well end up being of more use to whatever ails him than premature first aid. "Simply, Stif" (she's never called—*referred* to him—as Stif before), "that through Pritch's unsureness" (she speaks of him as if he weren't there—or, better yet, *all* there), "we as the aptest of apt pupils end up with much more than we bargained for—in this case, four inaugurators, all crackerjack, for the price of one and with The Rump's fat butt on the throne, we need to be thrifty even if it isn't hip." Can't Stif get it through his thick skull—she means, understand—that it's precisely because, as an *enunciator* (what happened to the word's fabled sweetness? she'd wagered that when released on the desert air it would be anything but wasted: too technical, in fact, by far for any climate, it's let her down), Pritchard is one big deficit that his enunciation has turned out to be one big plenitude of, in this case, name-droppings (too bad there's nobody qualified to scoop 'em up with true pet-shop panache), not to mention all the syntactic twists and turns mirroring to a T his body's growing instability. And there's a bonus: his codetta of self-denigration has also served as a much-needed breather—a breath of fresh air—after so many talking points—the whole place is nothing but talking points (plastered, papered, sprayed and shellacked), each coming self-importantly hot on the heels of its predecessor.

Even if Stif looks disgusted (his eyes are more bloodshot than ever), Jean couldn't be more pleased with the elucidation (and judging from the wild applause, her audience, captive or otherwise, is pretty darn pleased as well), although she must admit there have been some pretty serious defects, the result mainly of cowardice (the poop-scoop business, for example, shouldn't have been parenthesized to the point of invisibility).

If Jean weren't rendered inaccessible by autograph hounds—Borkman, Jr., and some of his pals look (to Cantor) as if convinced a start-up might be made to sprout from among those name-droppings once they were duly passed through the extra fine mesh sieve of her woman's intuition—Herbert would be only too delighted to congratulate her ex-friend and friend-to-be, since for once—maybe *for the very first time in the course of the entire trial* (or is this just another case of the Master's hyping things up again for popular consumption or to remind Himself of what He's always very much in danger of forgetting, namely, that the story He's contracted to tell is All About

773

Enviers and nothing but?)—since for once the talk has somehow managed to fit the talker and/or vice versa: the "elucidation," as Jean (charmingly? humbly? self-importantly?) christened it, could have come from nobody but her. For it wasn't just the elucidation itself that proved (sublimely) in character: the exquisite timing—compared with which Pritch's, paean notwithstanding, flagrantly paled—bore her stamp as well. Of course Herbert knows—or should know by now—that she's sticking her neck out (for doesn't such a take on things challenge Massa's most virulent contention, to wit, that nothing even remotely resembling a character, at least as the term is understood by the best-loved practitioners of rear-guardism, has been spotted anywhere near His plantation, gothically rank with magnolia blossoms, for centuries?).

Despite—or in what (given how much she's come to relish her sister's abuse) is a by-no-means surprising response to—the (atypical) acclaim, after the sixty-ninth autograph bites the dust Jean finally puts her foot down and heads for the buffet table *across from the bar*, since that's where the Master— where the Master's latest utterance (it's a question of utterance *well-being*)— insists the bar be situated, at least for now. Some thought has made Jean feel wretched. For the life of her, though, she can't reconstruct the culprit and she needs to, since there's simply no fighting the feeling directly, but only through the thought responsible. Nor has there ever been less time in her life for the cultivation of wretchedness (*I won't go into details*, she thinks). Though maybe what she mistook for a thought was Ethan's refusal-to-stare. Her heavily stained paper plate weighs a ton though it contains only the leavings of current salad days. In any case, Jean's appetite is gone.

CHAPTER FORTY-FOUR

The faux chums who represent all of Cantor's Ages of Man—every single One!—are advancing—or sideswiping—or descending (take your pick)—or is it Post they're targeting? (Compared with these looming others, Mary bulks less huge than an untrained flea. How can he have ever let her get to him?) Did he think a change of scene would soften their contours? And what, will you tell me, do they want with him anyway, now that he's been ditched by his beloved mentor? Can't he be allowed to find his way home in peace? No need for their much-anticipated dark verdict—Pritchard's has beaten theirs to the punch- or finish line by a wide margin. And to think they've chosen to perpetrate their harassment at the very moment when Cantor feels his allegiance shifting—tectonically—from Pritchard to Post, the very figure whom the others have done their best to peddle as his mortal enemy (he isn't quite sure whom he means by *the others*: there've been so many in the course of his too-long life as an Invidicumite which is, as far as he's concerned, a cross between a Shulamite, [of course] a sodomite and a Dolomite). How can he ever make it up to this Grand Old Man of Drug Street, so shamelessly misjudged? Post and nobody else is the Master Herbert is always babbling about (that much is clear at least). As for Borkman (another Grand Old Man), well, from where Cantor now stands, he's the quintessential beautiful soul, unhappy consciousness, blond beast and noble savage all wrapped up in one. Is it too far-fetched to say Borkman's a humanitarian in the best sense, exemplary for his patience and (when called for) his bootcamp toughness? Of course, but Cantor will say it anyway. Maybe this, his artisanal brand of perversity, will frighten off the chums (everything, not just cant, is an artisanal product these days—even, up there in Santa's workshop, the artisans themselves).

Right off the bat, their spokesperson asserts (why, it's Dave ["Davey"] Dolinskovici, the most *ressentiment*al of the so-called colleagues whose joint letter to the dean protested his receiving the associate professorship they all coveted so violently—covetousness being the only form of violence their kind are capable of inflicting) that Cantor is completely unqualified for the soon-to-be-vacated post of Bunker Director-General and for doing whatever it is Pritchard has become, rightly or not, renowned for doing in the course of a laughably overlong tenure—completely unqualified not just because of his sexuality, although that *factor* was incendiary enough, but, more importantly, because he showed himself in his previous life to be—to be— But before he can duly elaborate, Dolinskovici and his crew, sorrier-looking by the minute and ever more crazily heterogeneous except for the commonality of their linkage to his past and present, are brusquely thrust aside by Ethan (most incomprehensibly, given his recent conversion—*You mean you haven't heard?*—to Quietism) flanked by the very goons who once served his (ex-?) boss with such relish. He pulls up a chair and moves it close enough to be able to breathe, literally, down Post's tanned nape which is equivalent—or *tantamount*, depending on how you do or don't feel about Post—to breathing down the neck of Pharma herself. Muttering under his breath and through gritted teeth (which never fails to transform him into Cantor, Sr., thereby raising his maleness quotient appreciably, if all too fleetingly), George turns his back on the proceedings, if proceedings are what they claim to be.

Narr wants Post to be the first to know they're being challenged by the gravest series of mishaps encountered so far: For starters, the deftly orchestrated theft from the warehouses in Omaha, Cheyenne, Ryders Alley and Lake Tahoe, by agents unknown for purposes unknown, of the one vital component of the drug whose identity needs to be suppressed; not to mention the discovery that the stores of ingredient X at the Hilton Head station is fungus-contaminated; that the Taos, Oakland and Noyak supply, imported exclusively from Beijing and Odessa, has turned out to be a mishmash of stark irrelevancies, e.g., acetaminophen, chloroquine, chalk, flour and cornstarch; and that the tantalum, tungsten and tin used in the Waco and Panacea (FL) batches were conflict minerals from the Congo, the Democratic Republic of the Congo, Angola, the Sudan, Rwanda, Nagorno-Karabakh, and El Salvador. Which has proved Amygdala didn't practice the due diligence needed to weed out the deadly dross, and earned the company a "perfect non-compliance" rating on the list put together jointly by The Rump University and the University of Phoenix. So there goes the possibility of Post's joining the newly formed Cabinet as Secretary of Health and Human Services, making dismantlement of the Affordable Care Act a shoo-in. No more fantasies of Childe Post to the The Rump Tower Came. And what makes these problems even graver is their having eluded detection (a thing inconceivable until now) by the so-called Gang of Five (INTERPOL, the FDA, the FBI, XXX Productions and the CIA), whose credibility as commandos in the fight against hologram-forging counterfeiters has been much diminished in consequence. And there's no ruling out the possibility (based on the most recent blood and x-ray tests performed on the members of the Greenwich Avenue group, sometimes without their knowledge) that the Bunker stock on hand here in sunny SB has been polluted—maybe even lethalized—thanks to an unvetted supply chain.

Though it looks as if a stroke may be just around the corner, Post manages to sound chipper, oppressively so in fact, when he speaks up at last. In the face of this revelation, he starts to hate himself—to the extent that somebody as pietistically smug as Post can be constrained to apply the salve of self-hate to his entrails—for getting sidelined by matters as defiantly trivial as homoporn—in fact he's tempted to call it as he—or rather, his generalized ill humor—now sees it—namely, as sleaze pure and simple, and spiritual bread and butter be damned. Unfortunately, the speak-upper is no longer Post *the Beloved*, and in a kind of classroom demonstration thereof the goons, his once more and as beefily deadpan as ever, move in to shield him, which causes the Figures from Cantor's Past to back off and become more abstractly indistinguishable from each other with each tiptoed step. Shearer wants Cantor to know she shares his disgust for these scary lumpen drones straight out of *The Prodigal Son* (minus the signature bathing caps). Clearly, the cost involved in having gotten and keeping them here must far outweigh any benefits to be derived from their presence on the scene. If the aim is simply to discredit Cantor couldn't they have simply Skyped or Zoomed in their bargain-basement animus writ larger than large? No crying over spilt bile. Still, Master-itis must be contagious because he can't help thinking they're *on the scene*, as he put it so blithely a minute ago—yes, he, not Shearer—to advance His work—His work in mysterious ways—which (let's be frank) is very much at cross-purposes with the objectives of the trial—the trial as the story of the trial. However irrelevant Davey and Tina and Max and of course Brunhilde and Leo and Mary & Co. may be to the flow of events, they're crucial beyond crucial to the self-realization of whatever thought packet He currently has up his raveled sleeve of care—*the packet*, like billions of predecessors (so scalding is its lucidity), *to end all packets*. For what's the point of sacrificing everything for a packet if you don't believe it to be *that kind of packet*? For the faux chums—they and they alone—have the uncanny ability to naturalize, to the extent allowed by the law of stories, its *hubristic perturbations* (hubristic perturbations—yeah, that's right, Cantor thought it and he meant it so you better get used to having it around.) (Character types come and go but packets are forever, sayeth the Master. And not to be outdone, the Master adds, Since the packets are not unlike the Jews both in contour and in content I'm happy to serve as their Promised Land, although they have every reason to reject the offer.) Yet, no amount of casuistry can prevent Cantor from, untheoretically, surmising the enterprise is doomed, it being intrinsic to the genius of such lucidity as the Master happily squanders at the drop of a hat never to be at home in—to—a swirl of events—at home amid "the vulgarity of a plausible concatenation" (as a supersubtle Celt once put it before trading in his radiant arrogance for ersatz humble pie). So why subsidize all this hubbub for mere packets when in the end (and even long before the end) their lucidities were reducible to the same handful of stardust? Maybe—just maybe—it's due to the fact that, more beautiful than a beautiful story is the vulturine—no, *vulturish*—no, *vulturous*—analysis to which its permanent ruin gives rise. And inasmuch as Steinberg's Rodin or, more accurately, Rodin's Steinberg would certainly have applauded this deduction, shouldn't he start beefing up his CV with a discreet reference to applause from so exalted a source, thereby lending a much-needed lustre to his bid for the Director-Generalship of Amygdala-Invidicum West Academy (Bunker Hill, Santa Barbara, CA, 93101) which has not, after all—for just look at how fast the chums are receding!—ebbing!—subsiding!—been completely quashed)?

Cantor is one of the few to see that Post has no intention of being made to understand the direness of Invidicum's tribulations, inasmuch as they have immediately become Ethan's—he's personalized them, with all that entails of piety and pathos—and what, I ask you, is more insignificant than the tribulations of this young man from the provinces who still has the longest way to go before coming of age (and, *a fortiori*, who, except an imbecile, could imagine himself weeping over those tribulations, the very thing Cantor, willy-nilly, is now doing?). The problem with Ethan's tribulations in a nutshell is that they're stupid: while the very first thing tribulations learn in school is to ensure that any account of them remains refractory to denigration at its purest and most virulent—i.e., as paraphrase (*Who, by the way is offering up this insight cum decree? Not me*, says the Papa Bear. *Not me*, says the Mama Bear

. . .), Ethan's have allowed themselves to be caught in its net. At the same time, he mustn't think that tribulations too complex for paraphrase automatically render the sufferer immune: nothing easier in that case than to enshrine him (based on a perfectly healthy distaste for mediocrities addicted to underestimating their own mediocrity) as a pretentious jackass with a pineal-centered sweet tooth for French-fried half-baked mystification, not to mention obscurantist obfuscation. Which is not to say he shouldn't treat those tribulations with currying care—as being on the same level of excruciation as mass murder—as the doings at Aleppo, say, and San Bernadino. For in learning how to manhandle tribulations with a straight face he learns on behalf—for the sake—of the world. The whole world benefits from his refusal to measure his mite-sized misery against Aleppo's. Honoring to the point of egotistical madness the pain induced by his tribulations he honors the world's, starting with good old Job's—his tribulations uniquely transcend everybody else's just like everybody else's transcend his and everybody else's. His tribulations alone are exempted—like everybody else's—from undergoing, when measured against the doings at the one big Gulag known as Planet Earth—when put through the meat grinder of invidious comparison—a massive shrinkage into merest artifact. (Now, is Cantor by any chance just being facile—perverse—tricky when he calls the Earth *entire* one big Gulag? The awful truth is, Wordflow of course must have its fling, so pardon us.) "So, Narr, listen up," says Cantor— he doesn't care who hears him stammer, truest sign of sincerity in the making—"it looks like the only option open to somebody like you is to remain (and let's not kid ourselves: *we're all somebody like you* when it comes to the paraphrase of tribulation) as silent as the grave." "Berry Sundae's grave," Cantor murmurs because it's time to sob. "My son's grave," Herbert gasps (not reproachfully for being left out but as if seconding Cantor's motion 'cause it's Everybody's motion). "But I can't be silent because it's not my future that's at stake here but Invidicum's." "You talk about the big *I* as if it's some kind of wonder drug." Thrilled by the timbre of Cantor's baritone profundo, Jean almost gives herself license to believe she's in love at long last—almost. "And who's to say silence, deadpan, poker-facedness, grim professionalism *à la Joan Crawford*, isn't still grist for the denigrator's foreclosure mill?" asks Gross Marginal's girlfriend, whose sole ambition is to become a starlet (that she's gone and hung her top hat in the wrong century is irrelevant).

"That's oh so true," Jean cries. Her loathing for Caro, still white-hot after all these years—not even a midsummer night's stroll round and round the upper deck of the Staten Island Ferry, alas, could temper it—gives her the strength not to care one bit if the capacity crowd assumes the aim of the outburst is to make her Prince Albert, whose fortunes they must perceive to be waning fast (*Narr, old boy, you're through!*), look good in the eyes of his bosses (though with all the changes in organizational structure since her arrival on the scene, it's hard to tell the bosses from the rank and file, much less from the turkey buzzards [including the human variety], and the fireflies). She explains that her dear sister always found a way— (Still harping on her sis, Herbert sighs. She would have liked to roll her eyes in Shearer's direction and generate a solidary roll in response but, fact is, their relation is no longer intimate enough—

has it ever been?—to warrant such an expectation.) —sis always found a way to turn anything and everything she said into a sign of the zodiac—the zodiac of my envious inferiority, so overwhelmingly was Rhys's very being a challenge to sis's phantom supremacy. Moral—for there most definitely *is* a moral, and probably more than one (she casts a reproving glance in Herbert's direction, but shouldn't Cantor have been its target?): "When you're up against the Narcissism Machine—aka the Big NA—you never win." As the Ages of Man advance with a swagger now that it's safe to do so (Post is busy squirting his Praetorian Guard with what looks—and smells—like gigolo juice: some sort of pre- or after-shave congealed into sternest advice on how to protect a bona fide bigwig and live to tell the gory tale and maybe even parlay the resultant reputation for ruthless fealty into ruthless sexual conquest), Cantor can't help recalling how, whenever he manages yet again (and with so little effort!) to get himself enmeshed in the busybody gears of *their* NA, there's nothing he wants more than to believe that beneath all the meanspirited self-importance seethes a mother's magma of human kindness only too eager to erupt and smother him, no strings attached—that from start to finish said meanspiritedness is nothing but an *as if/what if* heuristic self-parody—a training video compliments of YouTube on how to handle the *real* narcissists and put them permanently out of business. Alas . . .

CHAPTER FORTY-FIVE

The cooked goose who, as it turns out, is (why were things always *turning out* to be this or that? obviously an attention-grabbing tic of the Master's) bellowing at the top of his lungs (to passionate but by no means unanimous applause) something to the effect that it's hurt him far more than having his start-up (what's the de-unicornization of another start-up anyway, between false friends?) dragged through the mud, even if it's Southern California mud (but is SB, strictly speaking, Southern CA?)—it hurts far more to see Eden, who well near died in the service of modern medicine, left from all indications unfed and unwashed to drool away in a dust-infested corner whatever's left of his promise. At these kind words, the veteran revives immediately. Thing is, during his career as a trial subject there have been just too many such false positives, as Herbert calls them, to warrant her getting all-hoped-up about a full—or even a partial—comeback. At the same time, dour speculation about Eden doesn't prevent her from suffering—though much less of course, since he doesn't like Eden, have his whole life ahead of him (or shouldn't she, for that very reason, be suffering much *more*?)—to watch Borkman, on whom landmark status as Broken Man Incarnate should be conferred before it's too late, become more and more at home with his designation. Why, it's as if according to the dynamic underpinning their relation, the higher the younger man rises—he's on the mend despite the drooling and Melanctha has a hunch her boy's back in the saddle for good—the lower his elder will fall. Which explains why her suffering on Borkman's behalf sticks to the ribs, while Eden's portion is fast disengaging therefrom. As far as Cantor can see, Martin was not nor will he ever be the right man for the job—not even the right right-hand man—no, not by a long shot. Only it's of no importance, even if he doesn't quite appear to understand how different his life will be now that he has a bona fide patron, *John Smith* (the news is superspreading like wildfire), who is not only the most vicious member of the Ages of Man brigade but—according to some rope-jumping red-carpet heckler-to-be—Borkman, Jr.'s worst enemy. (A common enemy sure makes for strange bedfellows though Jr. is definitely not Cantor's type.) But as every cloud has its silver lining, John Smith goes down much easier than *Mary Johnstone*—or even *Melanctha Herbert* or *J.G. Borkman* or *Martin Eden* or even *George Cantor*, for that matter. Because it's a name in search of a real name and, as such, has no time to waste foisting itself off as a thing of the world. (*Jim Straynge*, on the other hand, in "poking fun" at its own morbid inventiveness, irks not.) As it turns out, Smith is one of the very few (a while back, he formally abandoned the practice of Ivy League mathematics for a place in the Silicon Valley sun) who's allowed himself to be impressed by Eden's performance at the zoo and *a fortiori* by how well he's bearing up under the demands typically made of any practitioner of the dying art of convalescence (thanks to the predictable sensation created by the footage capturing his predator-prey antics, his YouTube followers currently number in the millions). As the Word on the Street would have it, Smith plans to exert his influence to wangle Eden a coveted guest lecturer gig within the conspiracy theory studies lab down at UCLA—a sinecure which would enable him to respectably twiddle his thumbs until such time as SV stopped dragging its feet and gave him the hero's welcome he'd earned. Yet from the few indications Cantor can sink his teeth into, what must account most for Smith's willingness to lavish his favor on a relative unknown is not the unknown's indisputable brilliance as a convalescent but rather his very ignorance of—or indifference to—what patronage is all about. Which implies that there's no danger of the unleashing of his sycophancy, parasitism, mannishness, leechdom, when it's already too late to give him the boot. But in the context of all these new developments—which are a-coming, not single spies but battalions—should Cantor do the comradely thing and alert him to the downsides of being on the receiving end not just of patronage but of rabid media platform fanship as well? Or will he just come across as envious? Thing is, Cantor knows a thing or two about such downsides (and he's not referring merely to the Pritchard affair). It wasn't so very long ago that he enjoyed some short-lived renown on Pinterest for having cracked the code of a certain Belarusian ransomware designer who, after having failed to become an even halfway decent basso continuo, pulled himself up by the bootstraps and put his numberless humiliations to superb use by hacking into the websites of the five biggest US opera companies without knowing exactly what he hoped to find or unleash. But more to the point, if Eden is to come away from his fans unscathed then he must learn how to protect himself against the inevitable degeneration of their professed reverence into a Sturm und Drang-ish zero-sum competition between them and him—since making that reverence known will give them license to tar and feather him as *just one among them*—better yet, their rank inferior since as a fringe benefit of that penny ante reverence they've obviously ended up knowing him better than he'll ever know himself. And once they've (*a*) put him in his place and (*b*) made a subvocation—a bywork—of catching his Achilles heels (real or imagined) in the act (and in 99 percent of cases, what will they have caught but a manly giggle, say, at one of their meanspirited jokes or the comradely deployment of his own hearty appetite to set the example and put them at ease when he's generously invited them out to dinner—in other words, anything and everything that makes him human, all too human, and on him—whom they profess to have taken for a superman—humanness doesn't look good) and (*c*) punished him for inducing what was not so much reverence as the heartiest headiest mix of bedgrudgery and ambivalence and contempt and hate and (*d*) called him a genius (even if *genius* is one word that's never held the slightest appeal for Eden or had the least relevance—not even to the precocious psychopathology of his Balboa Park period and even if what they're evidently alluding to is a botched genius for squandering the powers invested in him to carry out Assassination 101[117]) and (*e*) hijacked his weary ear, then that'll be their signal to do what, ultimately, their kind always comes out of

---

[117] Who exactly is daring to have this parenthetical thought about Eden? Surely not Cantor (he doesn't know anything about the Balboa Park period).

the invidious woodwork to do, which is to run the tired old gamut—Dorothy Parker's kind of gamut—from (*a*) bragging about all their accomplishments and everything received in honor thereof from those supposedly in the know, i.e., the experts—the literati—the glitterati—to (*b*) lamenting all the missed opportunities to achieve the unachievable (with the engineer of this cruel destiny left lushly unspecified) and to become as sublime and beautiful and yet as crass and void of substrate as (since they were born to swallow gamuts whole and their aspirations are boundless)—as . . . no, not Father Karamazov and his four boychiks or Pantagruel or Agamemnon or Macbeth or Offenbach's Docteur Miracle or the Baron de Charlus or (most sublimely of all) Abel Magwitch, no, as none of these, but rather as, say, the Richard Gere character in *American Gigolo*, down to the very last wart in his pretty little wardrobe. But he—Martin—will be hard put (which is exactly what these chest-thumping breast-beating blowhards will want him to be)—as was Cantor in *his* mediagenic heyday—to determine whether it's the bragged-about achievements or rather (and most probably) the much-lamented missed opportunities that he's (while standing with his fans—now his arch-rivals—on the wrong side of the red carpet on the wrong side of the tracks) supposed to exalt.

For some reason this, the transmutation of Eden, means nothing less than that the smearing—the gay-bashing—the ethnic cleansing—of Cantor has been called off. For look! the Jury of His Peers (except of course for Smith) are dispersing, never (it appears) to be heard from again. Stealing the spotlight from Gross Marginal, or at least tampering with it, Silicon Valley's latest and soon-to-be greatest announces if things go according to the plan that is soon to be unveiled (which hinges in turn on whether he can disprove Wiles's solution to Fermat's Last Theorem), Eden (once they got him cleaned up) will go very—or at least pretty far indeed. He's slated for nothing less than posterboydom (the poster boy is still too weak to look into Smith's crystall ball) and given this development and the million and one other shake-ups sure to follow in its wake, both organizations will have no choice (which is all to the good) but to merge.

"What organizations are you talking about?" Cantor asks, for he has nothing to lose. His hopes for a career at Amygdala-Invidicum West Academy are in tatters and who knows whether Columbia will take him back once it's revealed that at the time of his entry into the ranks of *those who can't, teach*, a pre-existing condition followed him through the door, which from the point of the chairman of the department may very well explain why he's made so little progress on proving Hilbert's lemma.

"Mine and yours," Smith replies.

"And what does your organization do? What's the product" Cantor asks, still on a roll. The threat of imminent destitution tributary to dashed hopes is exhilarating.

Post (*laughing uproariously*): "This is the first I've heard about a merger."

Pritchard (*laughing but not quite so uproariously*): "Me, too."

Smith: "But you have heard of David and Goliath, I'll bet. Never mind what my organization—I mean, my start-up does. Its product is . . . getting there slowly but surely. And when push comes to shove—or haven't you heard?—it really doesn't matter what an org's product happens to be, if it manages to plausibilize the rumor that the product's The Next Big Thing—that the product's worth its salt in gold—and to keep the rumor going long enough to showcase the resiliency of the start-up's armature and the world-historical sex appeal of its living logo."

"That little spiel must have taken hours to memorize."

"Decades," Smith spits out. In any event, not to worry, for he has no doubt their armatures combined can absorb the stresses triggered by the inescapable overhaul of missions and mandate, performance and products peculiar to a merger. And this time around he won't lower himself by seeking from his elders, hence inferiors, their . . . their (what's it called on Geek Street?) . . . their *imprimatur*! The name of the firm-to-be, too, must change: challenged by Eden's heroic attrition he's not only come up, but fallen madly in love, with Cinema of Attractions, Ltd. The product will have a floating content while its name remains the same, which is as it should be in the best of all possible valleys.

So here, after too many nosedive vicissitudes to count, is the event, thinks somebody in the room (maybe hundreds of somebodies, for the population keeps growing, by popular demand, but Herbert most of all), that they've all been waiting for whether they knew it or not: election of the metaphor of metaphors that best fits Invidicum—the metaphor-to-end-all-metaphors which justifies the means and ties up all loose ends (or so the Master would have us—them—believe)—Product with a Floating Content. And what is Life itself, while we're at it? she wants to ask though there's nobody around smart enough not to answer, but a progression of start-ups attempting to sell just such an impossible-to-unload product. But she can sixth-sense the Master already doubting His choice of image—not because it's worse than any other hence an occultation of the real luminary beyond the horizon (for this would give it a certain cachet) but because it's just as good and just as bad. One more last stab at bewitching His clients, gone awry.

This is Eden's cue—and he knows it since he comes from a long line of untried vaudevillians—to mount the podium and speak of the enrichment conferred, thanks to Post, by his experience in active combat. He's miraculously caneless (and irresistibly Byronic, Shearer thinks, reminded of *Like Lions after Slumber*, Balanchine's only ballet to the music of Shelley). I tell you, he's learned things about his body in one day that might have been unlearnable in a lifetime—in several lifetimes. Herbert observes him with a mother's unquenchable anxiety, convinced it's not so much the paltry ministrations of the paramedic tribe that's brought him back to not-quite-radiant life but the Master's cloying need for the seed of some new or not-so-new thought packet to be spilled, like mana or *hau*—all right then, *ejaculated*—on His behalf. And this being the case, so what if all sorts of patently contradictory word acts are perpetrated, implausibly, by the same character—the same name? Since to the Master they're only names—every last one of 'em—and anyway He hates most of the names He's given them (except for quips like, e.g., *John Smith* and *Jim Straynge* which refuse to cater to his clients' demand there be something fleshly inside the name). (She suddenly has the feeling [scary? reassuring?]

that a slew of Cantor-type packets, propelled by images of [what else?] ejaculation, are getting ready to go a-coursing—cruising—through her veins.) And anyway, He can't just introduce some new character every time a disgorged packet clamors for union with a packeteer, and thereby disregard the first law of suburban dinner-theater ethics. What his tightwad clients, if they were *on to themselves*, would identify as being the "Honor the 'Thrift, thrift, Horatio' factor." He's already sinned enough in that department to merit disbarment. So only recyclable packeteers need apply. The way it goes is: The selected packeteer's contract expires after the thought in question has been done to death and is renewed only when there is a need to spill another seed of which said packeteer may be deemed least or (when the Maestro has a yen for a little avant-garde magic) most implausible ejaculator. You may say, Herbert tells an imaginary interlocutor, the characters didn't add up. Exactly: and that's their glory, he replies. And so just when she's about to write Eden off as a supernumerary, here he is defying demotion and rising from the near dead. But will the Master put an end to his stop-start existence and allow him to grow up?

"Are you sure, my good man, you're not being played for a patsy instead of a posterboy?" asks Gross Marginal, always there when you need him. The metaphor for Life itself—reducing it to one big start-up in the sky—has saddened Melanctha well beyond sadness. At this juncture, therefore, she needs to pity somebody—anybody—so she doesn't end up unconsolably pitying herself. From the look of him, Eden might qualify as an active target of that pity. For he's slow to answer. Though the slowness may be due to fine-tuned deliberation (forget the vaudevillians at your peril!), not at-death's-door disorientation. But being too wildly impatient by nature and not getting any younger, Melanctha can't stand around waiting for the lowdown. So she finds herself turning to Borkman who may better qualify. Thing is, he's much too busy celebrating what she recognizes (thanks to post-Bldg. 18 Group Grief Therapy) as *reattunement* with his son—via the peculiar *Schwanzeltanz/ Rundtanz* telepathy that may spring up unsolicited between an unforgivably failed parent and his unforgivingly scarred offspring—much too busy to give a damn about Martin's catatonia or, more importantly, its effect on those, like Herbert, who want to atone for their own lapses by pitying him. For pity, if done right, is a kind of love.

But she doesn't begrudge him his unpitiability. Having both at about the same time taken the plunge into the schvitz bath of parenthood to ensure there'd always be some sacred duty hanging around ready and willing to be at cross-purposes with the pull of their vocation (since last they'd heard, achievement is born only of starkest conflict—and dies of liberty), Borkman and she will always remain kith and kin. Or is she putting words in Borkman's ear? In any case, given this telepathy business, it's clear she can no longer count on his failed self-laceration to blunt her own, which entails access after access of a sort of grief but a grief that will never accede to the status of true grief (even if it never abates and despite how exotically authentic it sounds on paper) simply because when all's said and done it's simply grief *at the inability to feel grief*. Still record-breakingly impossible (will it ever *not* be?), even in the California sunshine, to get past her indifference and seethe as she's supposed to be seething. At the *compatibility* of the death of a boy killed for nothing with the rankest opportunism—the opportunism of lycosids like Bush, Jr., and Prick Cheney and Don Rumpsfeld and Bain's Mitt and Tiffany & Co's Newt and Greenspan-Rubin and unvaccinable Bachmann (she'd forgotten all about them and plenty of others like them: how quickly overdosage turned her into a Rip Van Winkle). But who is she to throw stones? She, the biggest opportunist of them all, is still struggling to get inside the alien skin of a First Lady of Grief. And Post for sure doesn't need her pity, even if it looks like his ostensible best of intentions where Eden is concerned have been sideswiped by a Member of the Younger Generation who thinks he's nothing but a patsy maker. The boss, true to bosshood, is picture-perfectly capable of withstanding all criticism (which to a Narcissism Machine like Post is super-synonymous with profanation of his pipeliner purity).

But Borkman may end up needing her pity—or at least her solicitude. For he's taking his life in his hands as a trial subject by asking Ethan, of all people (based presumably on the fact that he's the hero of the moment), how Warner-Metro is handling the fallout from Straynge's murder, not to mention the other mishaps he's brought to Post's attention. (*Enjoy your celebrity while it lasts*, she murmurs, half-cautioning—but loud enough to be heard by Jean, whose heart immediately goes out to Ethan now that he's being beleaguered. But how does Herbert know that Ethan *is* enjoying it?) Borkman also asks (clearly overstepping the bounds of good taste, according to Margo's grimace) if by any chance W-M intends to pull the plug on the trial and how Voracicom plans to carry out collateral damage control and whether the Amygdala Institute will be moving its headquarters to Aix-en-Provence (where the scion of the East Coast elite meet to tweet) any time soon. "You sound as if you're afraid of losing your job—as a guinea pig, I mean," Post chuckles, being in no danger of losing his (he's set for life thanks to all his insider-traded windfalls— far too many to enumerate on an empty stomach) no matter where the Institute relocates to—in fact, the further away the better. Liepnits and his child bride are the first to conspicuously turn up their noses at Borkman's crude display of bad manners, signaling thereby that as decades-long subscribers to this misbegotten opera company they have every right to demand that such questions—and such questioners—be dropped from the repertory tout de suite inasmuch as they serve no discernible purpose except to betray a hunger to steal the show, whether there is one or not (Jean would have been alert enough to catch on even if her boyfriend's vulnerability hadn't sucked her right smack into the very heart of the proceedings). But as Borkman shows no sign of letting up and as they're the likeliest next targets of his scattershot muckraking—if that's what the snooping professes to be—they have no choice but to operate the Geiger-countering system of *their* Narcissism Machine at highest alert so as to ensure everything he might ask is immediately turned on its head and processed as a self-indicting clinical datum—and it seems to Jean that based on the way the system is now operating, everything he does ask is in fact already being processed and flung back at him as such *long before he even asks it*. (Or, muses Jean—the very same Jean [and in doing so she could swear Herbert's blood is flowing through her veins]—has wordflow—thoughtflow—

her thoughtflow—just slithered out of control long enough to generate this logic-defying real world codettina?) *But back to basics:* In so many words, the Geiger-countering clinical data being selflessly amassed by this model couple when they presumably have better (post-nup) things to do (and with not a thought in the world being given to ultimately selling it to the highest corporate bidder) will, once they've molded it to their disinterested specifications, only go to prove (should further proof be needed) that anything coming out of Borkman's mouth in these precincts is and always will be a not-too-bright caricature of Wall Street sleazeball rhetoric—so grotesque as to constitute (what an example, by the way, to set for his other boy! who, as they've just learned, is wandering about the dew-drenched grounds unsupervised) nothing less than a new brand of malfeasance tailor-made for some maximum-security facility on the outskirts of, say, Los Alamos. But, Jean wonders, why do his questions get under their skin to such a degree? What do they have to hide? Or is this high-dudgeon supersensitivity all an act[118] to cover their tracks as they go about making him their latest patsy—their latest fall guy—en route to self-enrichment? She wishes she could help out—spare him from having to learn the hard way that's there's no saved-face way out of the trap laid by the narcissist's narcissism machine. But why this sudden sanctification of a career swindler? somebody else wonders—Herbert, maybe; maybe not. Or maybe— just maybe—the pair should be cut some slack—given the benefit of a shadow of a doubt and thought of—more charitably and less circumstantially—as having put the psychodrama of their incompatibility selflessly on hold all so that (through the machinations of a futile presumptuous smug blundering—a pigheaded misperception of everything a rehabbed Borkman now stands for) the sands of time might leisurely seep through the neck of the Hourglass That Is the Story, thereby providing It, in their role as secret agents of duration—as accredited duration builders—with Its one indispensable component.

Stifter, a pipe stuck between his thick lips, reserves for Herbert's ear only the fact that he's been pondering the motives of Liepnits and his child bride— or at least the dynamics of their misbegotten relation—without coming to any immediate conclusion (he'll keep her posted, he really will). But why Stifter? Herbert wonders. Is it yet another case (boy! they're coming fast and furious!—homestretch fast and furious!—fugal-stretto fast and furious!) of the Master's bullying the least likely suspect into taking the reins of office so as to prove to His clients—and not just in dinner theaters far and wide—that His Work still knows how to turn a trick? But she has no further opportunity to measure Borkman's splendors and miseries against her own or, less exaltedly,

---

[118] In spite of herself (but why in spite of herself?) she's reminded of another, far less classy hubby-and-wife-combo high-dudgeon act, i.e., the now-famous storming out of Lucas Oil Stadium (as immortalized by Poussin and Delacroix, among many many others) by Mike the Pence and his missus—an act of unbridled spontaneity committed on strict orders from The Rump, Mike's shifty boss—in ostensible protest against the in-protest taking of a knee by some of the San Francisco 49ers during the playing of the national anthem at the October 2017 49ers-Indianapolis Colts game.

to ponder Stifter's pondering for here's John Smith approaching—more than approaching—holding out his hairy arms in a welcome that walks the finest line ever traced between the effusive and the fulsome—a line surely finer than, say, any traced over his long career by the land-surveyor narrator of Stifter's own story "Limestone." There's barely enough time for Stifter to warn her (*Whaddya say we let bygones be bygones, if any there are, since Walser's pal is turning out to be a really good guy—the* best, *in fact?*) that Smith's just learned through the grapevine all there is to know about how Bush-Cheney-RUMPsfeld played their fiddle while Melanctha, her son and Building 18 burned. "We can't talk here," Smith prompts conspiratorially, and in a tone perfectly suited to the announcement (at least in Herbert's wildest dreams) of her having won, and by a landslide, the coveted Something-or-Other Prize.

He sits her down in an alcove—the kind that in a novel—or even a story—by Edith Wharton would be condemned outright as *tastefully appointed*—steps away from where, not so very long ago, Eden was wasting away untended. She understands that the Master's pained submission to the brute simplicity of *He sits her down* (no frills attached, except for the business of Wharton's soft spot for upholstery of a certain weave and texture) has cost Him far more than what He may have deemed any Master worth his salt should be required to pay. (Stupidity, as every schoolboy knows, is not Valéry Testes's strong point; and generating action, especially the simplest, is not His.) The autopsy report just in from Walter Reed makes it clear that what her son (what's his name, again?) endured for so long was traumatic brain injury (TBI) from repeated exposure to body-convulsing detonations and not (as the arrogant idiots there would have her believe) posttraumatic stress disorder (PTSD) (though the symptoms and brain mechanisms, albeit poorly understood especially in the case of TBI, did tend to overlap)—PTSD triggered and then exacerbated by chronic fatigue syndrome (CFS). If only they hadn't been too proud to acknowledge it's all about neuron-anchoring proteins (integrins by name) and not xenotropic murine leukemia virus-related virus (XMRV), the still very much disputed culprit in CFS. "Then again, if they had been anything *but* too proud, my team and I wouldn't have our work cut for us, now would we? But I mention all this by way of letting you know that our start-up's found its product at last, namely, a highest-tech virtual-reality wraparound environment fitted out with the usual 180-degree video screens, n-meter circular platforms plus treadmill, and infrared monitoring cameras—but vastly different from the sort of environments being used in DoD-run clinics around the country to assess and treat the very thing your son was afflicted with.

"And with Eden (posterboy not patsy, as rumor would have it) offering demonstrations on military campuses from coast to shining coast (Post & Co. have already assured us these activities will not hinder his participation in the current trial: nice of them), we'll be the next ChatSnap in no time. Although, unlike your brave son, Eden has never seen active duty (which by the way he is the very first to admit), detonations down at the zoo (especially in the vicinity of the bullfrogs, okapi and capuchins), not to mention the simulated explosions inside the walrus rink, did get pretty damn oppressive, even if to hear him tell it, the effects were imperceptible (such downplaying—such collateral modesty—is, I might add, a common enough symptom of TBI). And all this progress because of your son."

"My son?"

"We owe something to our men in uniform, even if belatedly. With your permission, we'd like to name our product after him."

Herbert's heart sinks deeper and deeper into its mortar shell. For the life of her she can't grieve. A phenomenon known as—as—as— But the name for the phenomenon escapes her. And these days—like all other days from the beginning of time to the crack of doom—isn't even the lowliest percept (its cry answered) deemed a phenomenon, just so it can be obliterated—and what better way than by a name? For a thing without a name is like—like— Phenomena—like grieving over the inability to grieve—cry out for a name so they can be obliterated even if what they think they're crying out for, in crying out for a name, is the permanent legitimacy the name's supposed to confer. That's why she hates *passion*, for example, when trotted out by co-workers and mentors ostensibly to pay their respects to her self-styled vocation but in fact to size her up—her and her passion—that is, to cut them down to size—the size of a *null set* (as Cantor would say, since she's heard him use the term to illustrate what seems in retrospect to have been the same state of affairs). For the same reason—and what reason is that?—Melanctha hates the gutless guts of words like *inspiration* (Do you feel the inspiration to write today? Not in the least, Bildad, because what I prefer to feel is *urgency*.) Not to mention *productive* (Be productive! exhortation of psychopharmacologists and undertakers with the voice of a Mike the Pence), which reduces her to a penny-a-patty sausage grinder. But a name when it comes to her writing is not adequate and, in all fairness, vice versa.

However (miracle of miracles!), assaulted by this twit (who'll probably be a billionaire within three weeks, max), Herbert is able to feel herself outraged at last by the fact that here is yet another case of waste—as in *waste of somebody's life* (even one decidedly not "brimming with promise"). Bigger and better than Bradleyan tragic waste—*King Lear*-type waste—'cause it's serving as an inspiration to somebody's initial public offering (IPO), festering—festooned—with sunny opportunism. And as if Smith's has read her mind here he is reassuring her that his IPO baby is supremely well positioned to exceed parental expectations, however inflated, especially since the last cutting-edge fetal ultrasound test has made it "abundantly clear" baby is already a big fat raving beauty—a gift of the VC Magi, to be flung, butt-naked, on the altar of Shareholder Value. But who is she to throw stones? By actively cultivating the inability to experience grief, inasmuch as according to the laws of her domain it's far more inspirational than grief itself (any no-talent can *do* grief), doesn't she, when it comes to base opportunism, run rings around little upstart Smith, her very own Little Marco? But in an attempt to parry accusations of same which are very much in the air, ChatSnap, Jr. (qua Silicon Valley geek he isn't as borderline-autistic as rumor would have it, thanks no doubt to his empathy-enhancing sojourn in academia), makes haste to assure her most, or at least a substantial part, of the profits will be donated to charity and that in all matters fiscal they're taking a dog-eared page from the book of Eden, their soon-to-be star salesman who, from all indications, has no intention of letting his good fortune—if good fortune is what it turns out to be—get the better of him. Remembering the slave trade, "I don't believe in empathy," she warns him. "As far as I'm concerned, it's just a buzzword—an acronym, even—for keeping a safe distance. And I would advise anybody to keep his—his distance, I mean—since that's the only friend we've got." Smith's not to be sidetracked—sideswiped by a hot-air balloon. In fact, he tells her, they've already made all the necessary arrangements to ensure that his celebrity identity remains, unlike Elvis's, snugly within the public domain—that no retroactive or descendible rights of publicity are assigned to some marketing behemoth like CMG Worldwide for all eternity. Smelling her scepticism (and given the boy's meteoric rise, it no doubt encompasses just about everything Edenian), he adds: "Yes, of course I know that from front row, center, Eden may very well look like the local boy least likely to make good." Smith elaborates: But JUST AS the right lateral angle of visual attack is needed to transform the famous blotch at the bottom of Holbein's *The Ambassadors* (yes, HJ's *Beldonald* Holbein) into the skull that will force the looker to reassess the meaning of the cozy bric-a-brac depicted therein, and JUST AS a pornographic image that (*Again with the porno-porno*, she soundlessly groans) triggers a frenzy of unrequited lust in one spectator may leave another stone-cold or, worse, howling with laughter at the over-contorted absurdity of it all (Smith is unhappy with this illustrative example, being no votary of the big P: he's taken it out of mothballs because it happens to satisfy, subject matter notwithstanding, his ideologue's passion for aptness and exactness)—SO must Eden (if he's to become the poster boy of everybody else's wet dreams) be looked at very much awry.

Despite Smith's blandishments all she can think about is whether Post and Eden have *really* patched things up or if, on the contrary, each still has every intention of burying the hatchet in the other's Adam's apple. Or does their relation in fact need patching—touching—up? Has she simply forgotten how things now stand, as she now and then forgets her son's name? Which in her own domain is of course all to the good (see above). And maybe in the Master's it's all to the better: There's been a lot of talk hereabouts regarding Narcissism Machines but has anybody ever stopped to consider a gadget that's just as semi-remarkable—just as IPO-worthy—in its capacity to unnerve, namely, the Amnesia Machine? By forcing Melanctha (and hopefully not just Melanctha) to backtrack through the wilds of her hippocampus—by toying with the neurons of that region—He keeps the Story of the trial going. A story, she can already hear Him bellowing—or is this just wishful thinking?—waxes all-powerful to the extent that it induces amnesia with regard to turning points, which become turning points in fact only when once they're forgotten (or is this once again just the wordflow talking—talking through its hat—the hat of bad syntax?). They've been through a lot together—they have a lot in common—she and the Master (more than she would ever have imagined)—particularly as grievers. For here she is grieving away at her inability to grieve and here He is grieving prophylactically—but unavailingly—in anticipation of His grief at the inevitable ending of things. Which accounts of course for the stratagem (none shoddier)—but not as wily as he makes it out to be—of strewing, Ophelia-like, the orts of forgetfulness all along her primrose path. And Herbert would even go so far as to say the Master's wily ear is hers and hers alone (and vice versa) to the extent that she cleaves to the contour—hews to the hue—of *grief-over-not-grieving*, inasmuch as a dynamic of this sort is the only thing that triggers thought packets (both his bread and butter and his Achilles heel and, while we're at it, his Rubicon as well). To Herbert and the other puppets, the trial may be just a trial but to Him it's much more: a story, and not just any old story but The Story that Learned to Walk Not on Eggshells but on Packets. But with ever more Machine-induced backtracking-driven speculation and ever more perversity configured to generate ever more thought packets, will the Master's tenure be extended long enough to let him finish, i.e., finish himself off? Maybe she should ask Cantor, since he must know a thing or two about tenure, even if—precisely because—it's just been denied him (if Max Soul—both loudmouth and malign whisperer—is to be believed).

When Herbert rejoins the others it's to be made painfully aware—no, just aware—that nothing Borkman has gone on to say (he may still have his foot in the door for the Secretary of the Treasury post) and nothing Stifter's pipe has gone on to ponder can unzip the straitjacket the former CEO jumped into all too unsuspectingly. The newlyweds' verdict has spread like wildfire to the point where everybody, no matter what bloc he or she is affiliated with, has cast him off as the next worst thing to—to— And when normally gabby Borkman, in a last-ditch effort to reverse that verdict, elects to go all poker-faced and deadpan—remains as undebriefably silent as the grave—clams shut the valves of his attention, or appears to, with a finality that would have made the Belle of Amherst emerald green with Envy—this is taken to be yet another symptom—and the most revelatory—of the same sociopathy: the poker-faced square root of sociopathy—sociopathy deadpanned to the eighteenth power—but sociopathy nevertheless. Which particular outcome proves yet again (as if anybody needs further proof) that Post is far and away the smartest guy in the room (would be, that is, if he'd seen fit to remain) through having set the stage for Borkman's downfall (under no circumstances must he end up as Secretary of the Treasury) at the hands of the nitwit newlyweds (who are doing their damnedest to resemble more and more Fox News gargoylians Joe DiGeneva and Vicki Toensling). This by virtue of Post's having suggested that Borkman's barrage of questions evidenced the fear of losing his job as a guinea pig, which, as he well knew, would trigger, in a mad-dog bout of one-upmanship, their attribution of a counter-motive, i.e., the craving for attention—much less interesting but for that very reason better suited to his mortal enemy's relentless disparagement by the lumpen.

But just when the Greenwich Avenue irregulars seem (judging from their faces) to be having second thoughts about consigning a highly regarded teammate to the slagheap of straitjacketability—seem to have come to realize Borkman, at least in this instance, is merely the fall guy, Post re-enters—trailed or dogged (it's unclear which) by Cook—as if for the sole purpose of commending, and officializing, their *volte-face*. He looks around slowly but only, as is revealed in due course, the better to underline the fact that his gaze will inevitably come to rest—come home to roost—on the ringleaders (who, after putting aside their desert plates a bit too daintily, have already gotten down to the serious business of squiggling in their seats, the better to piss in their pants). "It's Pritchard you were after (much too ill, as you all must know, to make a guest reappearance—I met him in the men's room where he's puking his heart out)—Pritchard, not Borkman. By the way, only a man of Bork's stature could have gotten a firm commitment from The Rump to visit the premises with his nominees in tow (they should be here by sunrise)—each more venerable than the next: much-too-regular guys like Jeff Sessions, who wears his racism with a difference; Betsy DaVos, who'll take vouchers over kids any day of the week; and Andrew Putzder, who prefers robots to the minimum-wage slaves, and cowgals in bikinis to robots—and that's just for starters. *What's this country coming to?* I hear some of you bleeding-heart centrists ask. And I reply: *It's coming to its* senses, *that's what it's coming to.*" The Silicons aren't as outraged as they're supposed to be—in fact they're melting like butter—in fact they're worms who'll never turn—in fact their silence sounds pretty reverential—more like what the silence of Neocons would sound like if there were any in the room—soon to become, with DT en route, the world's living room. But after all, what can you expect from HubSpot types whose cheery name for getting fired is *graduation?* "And when you couldn't sink your teeth into Pritchard, you tried to get them into me and when I proved much too shrewd for you clowns you went after Borkman. Or to put it another way, Borkman is Pritchard off-off-label, a spinoff of a spinoff." So what is there left for him to do but explain that compliments of rank injustice, meanings are constantly shifting in these parts. Which has got to be making somebody— Some Body—happy. Some Body for whom meaning's fixation is his—His— own impalement. Post turns, not unkindly, to Herbert, who dutifully blushes. It's a look of compassion, she decides (if only to calm herself down: she's had a hard life, after all), maybe even admiration—in any case, the sort of look you reserve for somebody collapsing discreetly under the weight of a parent's nasty refusal to die.

"So, at the not-so-great risk of being seen as playing Baum to Pritchard's Mabuse, I'm going to come right out and say that all of you—not simply the ringleaders—are unable to forgive Pritchard for having the courage to demonstrate just how crucial to—just how inseparable from—finding a—*the*—Cure for Envy (the physician-moralist's grail of grails) is the proper application of the pornographic salve to the wound—the only wound in the realm of the psychopathology of everyday life that makes it a point of honor to crave no suture. Not that the salve can't be equally well applied to a slew of others just as much at odds with the lively art of healing." *Do I mean what I'm saying?* Post ponders (what's come over him?—he's never pondered before—he's turning into Stif, the budding author of "Limestone")—*can I really believe, with all my degrees and all my prizes and all my honorable mentions, that* application of the salve of pornography is inseparable from finding the cure for Envy? *or is this just my haphazard roundabout hyperlative way of confessing that I* miss Pritch too deeply for words (and his cockamamie theory of pornography be damned)—miss him in a way that has nothing to do with his being here or not—in fact I miss him most when he's within swatting distance and blocking my view? (Hell, I even miss Ms. Margo—especially her poignantly inept cameo as hostess-with-the-mostest. How is her son doing, by the way: is he still stationed at Rikers?) But even so, why did I happen to choose this way to be haphazard and no other? So, Post explains, inasmuch as they can't forgive Pritchard for being who he is, it's not surprising that the only thing he's managed to elicit from some of them (no names, please) is the worst form of Envy—the kind that masquerades as average-joe, just-plain-folksy bafflement in the face of what that folksiness has no choice but to characterize (despite their every effort directed toward giving it the benefit of the doubt) as the brazenest kind of pretentiousness—a kind of grasp-exceeding overreach considerably more excessive than del Sarto's. "For what, after all, have *you* ever produced, Liepnits, my man?" *So, he's naming names after all—a regular Joe McCarthy, this guy*, thinks Stifter. *Am I and my better half next in line for dethronement?* Post knows (and everybody else should know—be made to know) that once upon a time—long before Irena was even a twinkle in his jaundiced eye—Liepnits headily contended (and milked the ensuing publicity, good and bad, for all it was worth even if it wasn't worth the acid-free paper it was printed on) that Envy, though innate to and potential within all of us (inasmuch as we are, so to speak, *innate to ourselves*), is eminently suppressible—except by the Untouchables. According to Liepnits (who, as the wee hours wear on, is looking more and more like Newt—or rather, a cross between Newt and Mitt with a dash of Carly, Betsy, Paul, Ryan, Erik, Chad, Wolf, Wilbur, Rick, Mitch, Mike, Mike, Mike, Mick, Kellyanne, Kayleigh, Perry, Sarah, and Bob and Carol and Ted and Alice thrown in for good measure), only a whiff of what they take to be an arch-competitor (pure self-inflation, for these Untouchables are too abject to have any) is required to transform mere predisposition into a full-fledged *leprosy of the soul* (Thucydides? Petronius? Sappho?), just as all it takes is the right chisel to dislodge from a block of purest Carrara (by following the latent—the innate—markings) a Vulcan worthy of Bernini. And for that massive misstep, Liepnits recommended (oh, Physician, shut up and heal Thyself), if Post remembers correctly, they be left to mummify, untreated because untreatable, at the bottom of the smelliest ghat of their *Gange intérieur*. And of course there were the research results, equally heady (though this time the good publicity was less good and the bad not quite bad enough to turn him into a misprized genius), demonstrating that while mini-maelstroms of *petite perception* of and semi-suffering over the triumph of rivals are experienced by most with no ill effects, they disobligingly summate among the constitutionally unfit—the Mengelian expendables, into a veritable tsunami of self-ablation. Not to mention his celebrated depiction of the Envier as a Monad and not just any old Monad but one so sick as to deserve extermination (though as everybody knows Monads can't perish: they can only be unclothed and transformed)—a Monad whose diabolical internal principle ensures that Its every perception is an invidious one and that even in the course of Its principle-driven passage from perception to perception It enjoys no rest, for our—

his—Monad is always being made to compare (unfavorably) not only each perception with its predecessor but the very *style* of said passage with that of Its fellows. Nothing here, obviously, to compare with Pritchard's boldness and rigor. "It's three loads of horseshit," cries Eden. Post is impressed by this young man's assessment of what happens when pop philosophy is forced to serve the cause of quackdom. So why does he keep murmuring, "And yet . . . and yet . . . and yet . . ."?

"And don't think I've forgotten sexy, foxy Irena—who's the first to admit her output constitutes an impressive counterweight to Pritchard's violations of human dignity. Why, after learning about the magic worked—and not only on slobbering Enviers—by the portable electroconvulsive therapy machine in its sleek little leopardskin messenger bag (Prada? Vuitton? Bellini? von Weber? Liberace? Joe diMaggio? Joe Louis?) that you were always seen gadding about with—or rather, with which you were always seen gadding about—is it any wonder the locals took the bull by the horns and dubbed you the Patron Shamaness of Lower Greenwich Avenue? Why, even the crabby owner of the Lafayette Bakery and his mother and the laid-back guys behind the counter at World of Video broke down and seconded the motion. Still . . . her version of an orgone box (however much its encasement may qualify as a luxury item)—of a disillation-pot whose musty depths conduce to the transmutation of the gold of Envy into the lead of forbearance—isn't the same thing as a . . . a . . ." (Why has the phrase *as a . . . a . . . a . . . tried-and-true scam on the scale of Pritchard's pornography elixir* just popped into his head—of all places?) Cantor's sorry to interrupt but for the very first time (his nosy connoisseurship of male beauty notwithstanding), he's observed that Liepnits's face and forehead are covered with burls and boils. Whose hideousness not even the gilt by association accruing from yokage to the flawless Manning can hope to mitigate. There are signs that he's been vigorously applying various creams and ointments and is no stranger to tanning salons but if Liepnits is smart—*really* smart (and he's nothing if not really smart)—then he'll stop dead in his ameliorative tracks and admit such a megadose of hideousness is eliminable only by that greatest of all surgeon-barbers, dusty death.

"So let's face it," sighs Post though the sigh can sure pack a wallop, "all of the above reduces to the slimmest of slim pickings when compared with Pritchard's mother-of-pearls." And the swine for whom it's destined, he emphasizes, must be made to understand Pritch's hornbook is not any old text but (that all-too-rare thingumabob aka thingamabob) a virtuous—an ethical—one. A text that remains defiant when faced with the inevitable accusations of incoherence and inconsistency to which, without fail, such virtuosity—sorry, virtuo*u*sity—gives rise. A text virtuous—ethical—insofar as it is not masturbatorily self-conscious. A text unaware of its own selfhood. A text that *never looks back*. A text eschewing (as brashly as the fancy films of his soul sister Godart) an inner life, flashbacks, flashforwards, clues cleverly sown and the affiliated surprise endings deservedly reaped, shrewd foreshadowings and, worst of all, finishing (as opposed to fissuring) touches (a finishing touch here, a finishing touch there, everywhere a finishing touch, etc.). A text in which every chapter—paragraph—sentence—word—morpheme—syllable—

letter—is a new beginning. An ethical text inasmuch as it doesn't, behind the reader's back, double back on itself, love-bite and french-kiss its own tail. An amnesiac's text which makes quadruply sure that no step taken reverberates in some step taken later on. A text which sees to it that if *Hugh MacDuffer-Schnitzel,* handsome devil in residence at Libido Tech (no longer affiliated, by the way, with bad boys Rump University and the University of Phoenix), or one of his twins, is mentioned as if quite by chance on pages 114, 554, 593, 1028, etc., only to be as if immediately airbrushed—photoshopped—away every time, then it is not for the exquisitely calculated purpose of having him reappear for a last bow (though in avant-guarded no-clothes regalia) on page 1141 in order to lay bare the soul-shattering insights latent in the invisible interconnections among the infinity of Hughs past. A text reveling in the fact that it is pure termite process *à la Manny F* (darling of footnotes past), plighted—sworn—to perceiving nothing except the little bit of negative space directly ahead of it and digging into that fructive void (like *Trog* archaeologist Joan Crawford) with the grimmest of grim professionalism. A text that must lay bare, because of the terror of being left all alone with the demon of invention, every stage of its progress. A text compelled to seek out disfiguration through some self-respecting back-alley chance encounter (Ryders, Mechanics, Theatre, Cortlandt—any of these will do in a pinch) with irrelevancies (anything to save it from the anonymity of "perfection" so dear to short-order hacks—the kind that hone their craft to the bone). A text compelled to thwart so-called predestination at every turn—rather than show up promptly for executive-washroom meetings with the Essentials—and all this in the name of achieving a revelation so intimate as to verge on the pornographic yet impossible sans robust collaboration with putative self-sabotage. As if the text—any text worth its salt—can *be* a text without turning itself—its bared belly—into a Field of the Cloth of Gold of self-sabotage. A text that must be a landmine before it gets to be a goldmine. A text whose only sign of life is its malfunction, as evidenced by uninterrupted phagocytosis of the aforementioned irrelevancies, though in such a case how, he asks them, can there be any talk of relevancies and irrelevancies inasmuch as said text has (like self-respecting literary dung beetles everywhere) absolutely nothing in common with itself? A text whose sex toys are chance, hazard, vicissitude, setback, ruin—in a word, *occasion,* as in *Nothing new . . . comes through the occasion but through the occasion everything comes forth,* or so sayeth Søren[119] or, what is more likely, his favorite cherry-cheese Danish. (The taste may be a wee bit too abstract for most tastes, even when expertly translated by Hong Bakers into hot-off-the-press delectability.)

---

[119]Søren Kierkegaard, "The First Love," in *Either/Or, Part I,* translated by Howard V. Hong and Edna H. Hong (Princeton, New Jersey, Princeton University Press, 1987), p. 236.

CHAPTER FORTY-SIX

Melanctha Herbert is one big fat headache—one big fat expletive—from all the shop talk about texts and Narcissism Machines and ejaculates (merely a choice few of the bones of contention gnawed by these fleabitten mutts). As for Eden, not only has he managed to work up quite an appetite (granted, with a little help as things wind down from somebody's salivating references to the Turkey à la Maryland, Turkey Mongole and Turkey Hash sure to bulk huge at midweek brunch in the Fitzgerald Wing of what's turned out to be a lame excuse for a Sadean super-fortress) when seconds before there was all that talk of intravenous feedings, but here he is insisting that from this moment on, the level of sophistication of the recipes must be commensurate with the guzzler's newly conferred paraprofessional status. Is it, Shearer wonders, the self-depreciating tongue-in-cheek of an assassin all too aware of his own expendability or the just-plain-cheek of a Valley Boy all too taken in by his instant superstardom? Or by virtue of another installment of mind control—though there's no virtue to be had in this neck of the woods—might Post be egging Eden on to get too big for his britches? But to what purpose? Stay tuned, chortles—yeah, guys, *chortles*—an anonymous career chortler. Herbert might have allowed herself to be similarly bemused: thing is, she's been singled out to grapple with the most important question of 'em all (but of which no formal notice has yet been taken), namely—namely—namely— But the grappling is obliged to stop dead in her tracks inasmuch as the judges have just proclaimed the end of Act One. The revels are to resume—and definitively conclude—on Bunker Hill (the grumbled consensus is that everybody can use a change of scene even if the change is to a scene less than scenic) in a day or two, by which time, presumably, they will have been able to digest all, or most, of what's been served up, even a few irretrievable morsels.

But Walser, ever the streetcorner kabbalist, has to put his club foot down. Cantor never noticed the deformity before but it's not his fault: the club foot exists only for the benefit of the moment—the moment when the Master, seeing fit to once again act selflessly on behalf of dying idioms everywhere and cut premature archaization of one of their chain gang's most distinguished members off at the pass, engineered an irresistible affinity between *club* and *foot* in order that the oomph of, in this case, *put his foot down* might be revivified for a whole new generation of theatergoers. "So it's the idiom that's been deformed, not Walser," Cantor murmurs as if half asleep—momentarily caught off guard by his own bedazzlement. Walser, on the other hand, wants everybody to know on no uncertain terms that the call for a breather hasn't sprung from concern for the admittedly far-from-simple matter of their digestion. "What from, then?" Post asks but so smarmily as to suggest his Q has already cannibalized its A. It's therefore no surprise when Walser barks back, "You know very well. You envious clowns hope that back at the Bunker, Pritch's Torah—I mean his Ethical Text—will get dismantled differently, i.e., lethally (causing the wound that is Envy and the pornography salve to part company forever), by the powers that be. Because in each *shemittah*—I mean cosmic cycle—I mean entertainment venue—I mean I don't know what I mean—in each *shemittah*, its meaning gets refracted through the prism of the attribute governing that cycle—I mean that venue—and that venue only." Walser (to Herbert at least) is evidently having more trouble keeping his cosmic cycles under wraps than . . . than . . . (paging the Chairman of the Cinema Studies Department, Prof. Scharf, who gave her paper comparing *Pinky, Lost Boundaries*, Sirk's and Stahl's versions of *Imitation of Life, The Jackie Robinson Story* and *No Way Out* an A+) . . . than Peter Sellers had taming his Führer-lovin' arm down in Kubrick's War Room! "What attribute? whose attribute?" somebody cries, but without conviction and simply to forestall departure, or so it seems—sounds—to Jean, no longer snoozing. (Or maybe, Herbert thinks, all the trouble stems yet again from the Master's compulsion [though He's acting less and less like a Master as far as she's concerned] to unload still more of what He misguidedly takes to be singable *substance* on the unsuspecting singers in His opera buffa, when it must be crystal clear, even to the "proverbial" spectator in the very last row of the fifth ring, that they're perfectly capable of crooning up a storm without the benefit of such baggage [the Master, then, when you get right down to it, is just a schoolboy always doing far more than is required on each assignment—always sucking up to some unsatisfiable virtual schoolmarm—always looking to pile up "extra credit," as it used to be called in prehistoric times]. Thing is, the explanation does a trivializing disservice to His somber pathology, under whose tutelage any packet—once, with traitorous and opportunistic ease, it's allowed itself to be assimilated—becomes [if she reads him right and she knows she does] yet one more goldbrick in an edifice of exclusion—the cruelest of exclusions—that of maker from made. And each new packet launched to counter that exclusion once and for all ends up constituting just another last chance for the Master— just another last stand against the deadliest of the seven deadly—Mediocrity.) "The godhead's," Walser replies. "What godhead?" (another Santa's heckler). "The godhead—I mean, The Godhead—of Pornography. But getting back to cycles—I mean venues: As you all know firsthand, watching imperishable staples of the American Musical Theater like *Sefer-ha-Temunah (The Book of the Shape)*[120] or *Catalonia 1250* or *Six Scenes* or *Terrible Sunlight* or *Contact* or *The Anti-Muse* at the Theater for the New City (that's 155 First Ave, bub) or at Ontological-St. Marks (131 East 10th) or at 198 Stanton or at Theater Club Funambules (167 Ludlow to you, ma'am) is an altogether different experience from watching any of them front row center, at the Brooks Atkinson, say, or the Helen Hayes or the Broadhurst or the Imperial or the United Airlines Princess Myshkin. With all due respect to the Bard: Venue, not Ripeness, is All."

Walser explains that the vaudevillian who owns the building they're about

---

[120]The shape in question is the configuration of the letters of the Hebrew alphabet, which constitutes nothing less than the shape of the Godhead. See, in particular, Gershom Scholem, *On the Mystical Shape of the Godhead*, Joachim Neugroschel, translator, and Jonathan Chipman, ed. (New York, Schocken Books, 1991).

to abandon to (who else?) the Gerzso-loving homeless with nowhere else to go once the museum closes, G. Tsimtsum Scholem-Shandy—no unconscionably conscienceless Blackrock, he—has long been notorious for regaling—some would say assailing—tenants and transients alike with his unmotivated-mercy-and-mollycoddling routine but once they're on home ground, if he can call it that, they'll obviously be in a different cycle—er, venue. One governed by—he means, one whose less-than-minimalist interior design reflects—the godheadly attributes of stern judgment, wrath, pitilessness (emanation of the Invidi-scum forever lurking about in anticipation of the signal to do Pritch in). It's as if—no, the fact is—the letters of the Text's alphabet have ended up in entirely different combinations here on Anacapa Street, under the godhead's attribute of too-much-mercy-for-its-own-good (aka untough love), than those to be unveiled back at the Bunker, where quartering sans quarter is the apple of every gimlet eye (and there's no pornography around to sweeten the pill of strict self-discipline). So thanks to the willingness of the Torah—he means, Pritchard's Text—to relativize Its bare essentials, each venue—not just here in SB but everywhere—ends up with its very own One and Only Authorized Version whose overriding claim to legitimacy can be ensured only by killing off all the other versions and better yet their exegetes. A dead ringer for Streisand in her Fanny Brice days delivers a jocular jab to his ribs by asking whether the term being bandied about is by any chance *shmatte*,[121] not *shemittah*. Funny, Cantor has been tempted to ask the very same question—and from the very same antic impulse—but (not wanting to be remembered as a pansy smart aleck—a Funny Girl to end all funny girls—especially now that he's been demoted or rather—in the context, among others, of Eden's meteoric rise—*feels* as if he's been) finds a way to restrain himself in the nick of time. "The word in question is *venue*, lady," Walser replies in a tone meant to be harsh—a bit too harsh for Herbert's taste—why it's almost as if he were already operating under the spell of the decried attribute to come. "At the advent of every *shemittah*—I mean entry into every venue—we should be prepared for the worst, which is to find ourselves confronted with a Torah—I mean a Text—altogether different from Its predecessors, inasmuch as we'll be going about our business of extracting Its divine wisdom under a different attribute of the Godhead of Pornography, which is what calls the shots. Of which by the way Pritch is, hands down, the mightiest incarnation the world will ever see. Hey, *guys*—start-up littlewigs, Big Pharma honchitos and (last but not least) surfer geeks and your molls: yeah, I'm talkin' to *you*—you are obviously all convinced Pritch's Text poses a threat to your algorithms, i.e., your very being (in a way that I'm unfortunately not at liberty to define—not even to myself) so of course you can't wait to see It go the way of all pulp. Which explains why every last one of you is so eager to mosey on up to the sub-desert foothills (to what is in fact a satellite—the merest outcropping—of the Bunker—living off its borrowed glory and connected to it by an underground tunnel or a quadriplex sky-

---

[121]Colorful Yiddish word for a garment that's seen—or should have seen—better days.

walk, I forget which). Because there and there alone will the Text receive Its comeuppance—by getting metamorphosed into a carcass of prohibitions (for Envy needs to be lawlessly policed and prohibited) of whose enforcement It will of course be the first casualty and on whose ensuing maggotry you can gorge to your soul's content."

Walser sighs—it's time for a summing-up sigh—not to mention a long-overdue summing-up—loud enough to be heard across the street—even if it's a summing-up of nothing that's come before—even if it directly contradicts what's just come before and does so with a fiend's relish. "But I don't believe in sweetening the pill—gilding the lily—shooting from anywhere but the shoulder. I don't believe in coddling the sick—the Envy-sick or otherwise. What all this means—as you've probably deduced—is that we—they—Envy sufferers—all sufferers—are in the wrong cycle. In the next cycle—and it doesn't have to be the supreme cycle (that is, the one in which the star of the show—aka the Messiah—*comes* all over us, so excited will he have become—with an excitement that banishes all threat of erectile dysfunction—at the prospect of getting top billing at last)—in the next cycle, there'll be nothing in the Torah—the Ethical Text—the pornographic text (no, the Pornographic Text! *Goddamit, Ishmael D! Hold your head gallows-high, for Chrissakes!* Do boldly what you do at all! i.e., *Just heed Aesop's talking nettle and you'll end up just fine!*)—there'll be nothing in the Text related to Envy—to Death by Envy. The letters will have been joined into words that tell a different story—a likely story—an Envy-free story. They'll be arranged—combined—to form the words—the new words—the new sentences which tell that story—the story of what it takes—what it's taken—to be Envy-free. There'll be no room in that cycle—in that Text (for a cycle is a Text and a Text a cycle)—no room for Death by Envy—Uncleanliness by Envy—no room for Death—or worse! say, levirate marriage. But don't blame or thank me for this daring formulation—all the credit goes to Ittamari of Smyrna as popularized by Azulai of Livorno." They all wear a look—a masked masklike look—that speaks volumes of things along the lines of, *Well, why didn't you tell me all this years ago when it could have spared me no end of domestic strife (not to mention getting all tongue-tied at my very first job interview)?* but before he can respond to that look their common mind is looking elsewhere. They've had enough about letters—vowels—sentences—paragraphs—chapters—stories—that are cycle-shackled but envy-free. 100 percent envy-free. But before they go he knows it's his bounden duty to perpetrate just one more summing-up. To the effect that if they intend to be cured they mustn't wait for a change in cosmic cycle. Oh, no. What they must do is take the bull by the balls and—no matter what cycle they find themselves in through no fault of their own—make their way down the Deep Throat of the Pornographic Text and into its gut and out through its anus (easier said than done, he's well aware). And only then—only then— "But why?" they moan in unison as if they were Verdi's favorite Hebrews on the banks of the Euphrates. "Stay tuned," he says, in unison with himself. They need a change of scene, their masked look now says. And a change of scene is what we're about to get, the look—doesn't say. The change/non-change of scene is very much in the double-bind/double-blind tradition but instead of with Invidicum, they're being dosed or, as the case may be, not dosed with Disorientation. He must warn them, in this regard, that, once the lights are out, nobody will know to what vehicle he or anybody else has been assigned—or even if he has been assigned to one—since under certain conditions staying put and sitting tight or pretty can feel more like flight than flight itself. As for those who've been chosen to hit the road, they'll be back, for better or worse, before they know it. And to answer folks who have a tendency—the tendency of Enviers par excellence—to stick their nose into other people's business even if that business happens to be just as much their own, suffice it to say that this new wrinkle—this kink or stitch in time—is all about trying to discover whether transport can speed up the Envy-freeing process, text or no text. Since the bidding wars have already begun which means that all the top-notch journals are willing to pay handsomely for exclusive rights to the final unexpurgated write-up.

As they're *frog-marched* (no other euphemism will do) to the waiting vehicles (best of both worlds: not quite vans and not quite windowless), Herbert starts to do (*No more cannabinoid-Zykon cocktails to turn brute duration into even more of a blur than it already is, Maestro!*) what she believes she does best, i.e., she thinks, or rather, she *gets to thinking*—and fast—for the defiantly unprepossessing chauffeurs (she guesses that's the right word) are wasting no time herding them in, Noah's Ark style. No mean *kabbalista* in her own right (thanks to homeschooling by an ex-classmate—an aspiring, magisterially hairy Old Testament prophet—who (*a*) 'd taken to nom-de-pluming as one Ike O'Luria, (*b*) had a soft spot for older black woman and (*c*) was something of a specialist where texts, pornographic and unethical—and their life cycles—were concerned, which meant she frequently had to draw the line at some of his bolder ideas about just how far the two of them were, as lovers, destined to go in enacting those texts in uncurtained broad daylight)—no mean kabbalista, Melanctha sure has to hand it to Him—not Walser but the Master of Masters (though for all she knew He could very well be the lowliest of lowlies in His tribe, the most off-label of the lot)—she has to hand it to Him for forcing the story line to hew, hook, line and sinker, to packet specifications: for yet again attempting to mix the oil of story with the water of packet or vice versa—in vain, of course, *hence strictly according to plan*, for in the end isn't it this very immiscibility that generates the tension necessary to any story, even *His* story—the last to come in out of the rain? Although, granted, the traditional agon is often sorely lacking hereabouts. But the fact that the tension between the agonists seems to be absent in—at—all of its—i.e., *La Forza del Invidicum's*—so-called high points—well, isn't that state of affairs just a case (or at least it ought to be, for some willing ideal spectator) of tension's being taken to a next level or the next after that or raised to the nth power or the nth + 1—taken to a very special level—a better, more sophisticated level—a level where tension becomes exquisitely attuned to the rarefied texture of those high points (high points with, as it turns out, very precise dietary needs)—a level where tension gets schooled in the wishes of what reveals itself to be a very special breed of high points, namely, those which don't want to be thought of as high points even if they are or were meant to be—don't want to be occasions for mass hysteria—don't want to be canceled out by the self-congratulatory hysteria they've generated—high points that are pretty much the farthest thing from, say, 1. Apollo's troika-ing around with his muses-turned-equines or 2. *Ballet Imperial's* first-movement *manège-à-trois* or 3. the Prodigal Son's forgiveness-imploring crawl patriarch-wards or 4. Dewdrop's diagonalization of her grandest of entrances (which slashes to bits every flowery tutu in its path) or 5. *Chaconne's* blessed-spirit jitterbug routine—or—or—or—? [*Whew.* Melanctha takes a deep breath. *Cranking out her enumeration of all that ballet stage business wasn't so bad or so hard, was it?* she asks herself—even if the torch—the mantle—at that juncture should have been passed on to Moira no question asked. But she ought to be used, by now, to her own adeptness, under the Master's tutelage, at stealing—at being compelled to steal—her comrades' thunder—their expertise—their ecstasies—their past glories, their future hopes, and (always preferable to the low-grade fever of anxiety) their ever present despair. Even if—especially when—as just now, she couldn't work up an appetite for the theft no matter how hard she tried. Yet, oddly enough, it's at such moments that the thunder most belongs to her—not to its rightful—its most plausible—wielder. But in fact at times like these it doesn't *matter* who gets to torch the mantle. Moreover, proximal-, distal- and ultimately, in this case the notion of theft is more or less irrelevant inasmuch as all print, audio, electronic, dramatic, motion picture, and television rights to that thunder revert to the Master, its prosthetic god. What *does* matter is that the Master not come across the footlights as a self-indulgent name-dropping Fruit at those rare moments when the need to be one becomes irrepressible. For even Masters fear the Forbidden Fruit within. Though it's not just a question of mere name-droppings—of having what feels like a good—a highly successful—a highly professional—shit and flinging it in the face of the sort of detractors who can't conceive that a nonentity like Him may in fact know—and know intimately in the best cocktail-party grand manner—folks with Names as Important as *Thucydides* and *Arshile Gorky* and *Glenn Gould* and *Eleanor Roosevelt* and *Franklin D.* (consulted by) and *Greta Garbo* (had Him to tea) and *Vernon Duke*—and *George Balanchine*. Sometimes—like now—the Master just needs to get Beauty—yes, Beauty—out of His virile system and off His virile chest and simply doesn't give a hoot whom He appoints as His henchman—or henchwoman. And what—as Moira has taught Him (pedagogy being a two-way [albeit dead-end] street where high art is concerned)—invents canons of Beauty better than the contraptions slapped together by that irksome old Mr. B. character, with a little help from, e.g., Mozart and Tchaikowsky and Hindemith and Bellini and Bizet. Even if in this case what seems to have been going on is something a bit more complicated: Beauty *bashing*—a polemical mockery of the ballets for the very high points that secretly make the Master cream shamelessly in His pants (and which renders the longing to *be* Mr. B. and his harem all the more intense). He, the Master, is above all others worthy of self-hate though no amount thereof can do justice to its target and only Beauty allows Him to transcend self-hate, at least until such time as Love of Beauty, with all its fruity hoity-toity artsy-fartsy trimmings—sometimes it seems to be trimmings and nothing but—becomes its own pretext for self-hate. Don't you get it? *He needs to cannibalize Beauty before it cannibalizes Him.* So what choice did the Master have—a balletmaster in His own right and in His own way—but to rattle Melanctha's wires—get her into the act long enough to put in yet another plug for Moira's Apollonian muse (but in the minor key of fake denigration to show that, when push comes to shove, He's no self-hate-loving Fruit but in fact [unlike another one of His heroes, namely, Samson né Agonistes[122]] a faithful muscle-bound friend of the philistines). And long enough to have her absorb all the fruitiness He can't quite completely disavow 'cause on her, fruitiness looks good. 'Cause on her tree it's no longer the fruit of genital decay for the simple reason that she's a woman. But at the last minute, look! he's changed his mind—and dares time to refuse to return whence it came. Takes back all Melanctha (His Brünnhilde) hasn't in fact thought but (as it turns out) *only just thought about thinking* and gives the not-quite-coveted name-dropping role to Moira since in this instance, in addition to being a woman, she's earned the right to name-drop. After all, she was never on the sidelines but, as she went about dancing all those ballets to death, right smack in the middle of everything the name-droppings name. In this case he can't play the least-likely suspect—the least-likely mouthpiece game. For who in his right mind will buy the wan invocation of every NYCB ballet in the book by anybody else but Shearer (His Gutrune)? But isn't there a tit-for-tat good deed as well, however collateral, buried somewhere in them there Terpsichorean hills? For by inducing her and her alone to do the invoking, isn't he prying Shearer loose from a hypertenuous hold on reality getting ever more hyper- by the minute—because ever more exacerbated by the recurring premonition that she'll be all washed up decades ago—even as (a ballerina's last refuge) the muse of some fourth-rate dance-maker eager to capitalize on the mythy motions of her once-upon-a-time celebrity.

But His fabled impatience notwithstanding, the Master has managed—good boy!—to keep squarely in mind that no packet, however seminal its (lubricating) fluid—not even a Walser packet—can be just flung across the footlights. The budding writer is grateful for that coup although its injection into the proceedings did seem a bit rushed. But what *was*—is—the packet in this case? Melanctha Herbert asks herself for she can't seem to remember and she wants to—wants very badly to have something to remember the Chateau by—even if it's turned out to be the Chateau That Wasn't—a chateau in name only and not even in name. But if the remembering were done when 'tis done, then 'twere well it were done quickly for the vehicles are waiting—busily discharging the exhaust of its foul-smelling impatience. What was—is—the pith and marrow of the unholy packet whose hellfire the Master compelled pacific Walser, of all people, to snort through his hairy nostrils? Well, it had—has—

---

[122]Just as "studs have feelings, too" (the reader will have to backtrack his way through an unforgiving thicket of footnotes to locate the source of this observation), so do Masters have . . . heroes, too.

something and everything to do with the fact that abstract meaning, for all its claims to immutability, is an ever-changing function of time and space. She'll buy that. Sort of like, come to think of it, the ever-changing configurations—but with each emerging organically—kaleidoscopically—from its predecessor—in (Shearer to Herbert: *Butt out! Stop poaching on my preserves!*) *Gounod Symphony* and *Symphony in C* and, best of all, *Serenade*. But even He knows that for some of the packet's components such replacements must be found as will appear to have at least *something* to do with the immediate context—as will fit plausibly into that context, albeit not too plausibly—as will deign to mix with the components of that context—but not too miscibly. For too much miscibility makes Maestro a dull boy—at least to Him—Who's scaled the highest peaks of self-sabotage—Who's Himself a one-man obstacle course the size of fifty-five Matterhorns. With too much miscibility, not just the tension but that tension's *uncanniness* (uncanniness: His trademark as the best kind of best-loved Book-of-the-Month-Club-Alternate alternative storyteller: storyteller in-spite-of-himself-and-in-order-to-spite-the-world) goes straight out the window, even if anybody who's anybody knows that a story, being a monad, has no windows. So no wonder *shemittah* and *Torah* have gotten their names legally—City Hall legally—changed to the more aryan-sounding, the more Episcopalian, the more socialmedia-genic, the more context-friendly (with story of course being the context—being the whole show—the show that steals the show)—changed to the more context-friendly *entertainment venue* and *Pornographic Text*, respectively, so that wherever it was once upon a time a matter of the former it's now a matter of the latter until such time— many frosty *shemittahs* and *shemmitahs* hence—until such time as the reader-spectator-client—theatergoer—gets it through his thick skull (*Stop! you're shrieking!—in fact you're giving me palpitations!* Herbert tells Him, sounding ever more like her mother—and to her own surprise, liking it—at the Calvary Hospital Hospice on Eastchester Road when in the last throes of non-Hodgkin lymphoma)—gets it through his thick skull that it's not, nor has it ever been, a question of formers or of latters. What it *is* a question of is the Packet, always and only the Packet, the Packet now and forevermore—a question specifically of said Packet's ability to retain Its identity to the hilt (three cheers for madcap mixed metaphors—five cheers for catachresis—yep, *catachresis:* Make sure you never leave home without it) no matter which of Its elements are willfully lost or found or added or replaced—no matter what parts enter in or depart—continually—for those parts (like the rivers beloved of Heraclitus and Leibniz) are in perpetual flux. What it is and will always be a question of is said Packet's ability to retain Its identity no matter how much It's stretched this way and that like saltwater taffy—the kind they sell like hotcakes on . . . Stearn's Wharf!!! Even the biggest numbskull must know—must know even without knowing he knows (the best kind of knowing by the way)—that a Packet comes into Its own only after having survived implausible deposition on foreign soil, i.e., implausible transmogrification—like that of Rump the penny ante mogul into Rump the Commander in Chief—of a hefty but not too hefty percentage of its components into story components. The transmogrification being, in this case, that of (*a*) the relation between 1. a cosmic song cycle lasting, say, six thousand years and 2. extraction of the secrets of the Torah—the Torah!—peculiar to that cycle, into (*b*) the relation between 1. the interior design of shady venues and 2. a mock treatise on the not inconsiderable benefits to be derived from a close reading of antiquarian bookseller DVDs on the art of fucking, particularly buttfucking (undertaken preferably in one's BVDs). Fortunately for the Master (though [I'm through with *albeits*] *not* for mature audiences, i.e., the PG-65 crowd), He's a pastmaster at distracting customs officials (with His deafening denunciations of the criminality of trafficking in such contraband) long enough to get His rated-XXX implausibles across the frontier—across the fine line separating holy abstraction from the even holier shit of unspeakable acts.

And all this fuss just—but not only—because His Majesty hates to decree simple actions like *Around midnight the Invidicum crowd were shooed back to the Bunker where their oozy carcasses belonged*. Hates to engineer, i.e., decree, a change of scene—setting—since (at least according to His latest memos) decreeing consigns Him to pulp-anonymity, makes Him indistinguishable from every other master on the block. Where He comes from, this kind of comings and goings are a dime a dozen. There's nothing *necessary* about them—easiest thing in the world to pull off. Where He comes from (if He's told Melanctha this once, He's told her a thousand times), you have to *earn* the precious—he might even say the sacred—transition from setting to setting—and, more steeply, from sentence to sentence and from paragraph to paragraph. Yet comings and goings and similar footlights froufrou are earned—are necessary—are doomed to prove their worth—only retrospectively—only once they've been extruded as merest byproduct—fringe disbenefit—of all the reactivity and resistance swirling around them. Which is not to say that, for all its—through its very—insignificance, the byproduct can't pull the story in unforeseeable directions, thereby satisfying His clients' attention-deficit-disorderly craving for a bit of packet-free (or at least packet-*lite*) derring-do. Where He comes from, the true master is a hack pretending to be a master pretending to be a hack. As a termite pretending to be an ostrich—a compulsively thrifty ostrich—an ostrich whose ethic is unapologetically Protestant, He constructs a setting only to bury his head in it as if it were the sand—and keeps it buried until such time as He's milked the setting dry enough to be entitled to move on—until such time as He's come at the setting from every inconceivable angle—until he's exhausted all of its spatial pretensions and topographical potencies. A true master calls out his penny ante absolute power for what it is—impotence unchained—and is powerful only to the extent that he perpetrates constraints on—resists—his mock-turtle Power of Invention. A true master's mastery—his very identity—lies in the élan with which he, god of war, induces brother to resist brother—Union packet to resist Confederate story—Union story to resist Confederate packet—but most important in such a climate is that packets, Union and Confederate, resist, before the time is ripe, their own renegade impatience to obtrude themselves on the inattention of the story's julep-scented landed gentry, veterans of little more than a daily dip or two in the cannon fodder-clogged Swanee.

The long and short of it is that the Master (an old softee) has not once reneged on his native allegiance to whatever setting He's been obliged to cook up, however bigger-fish-to-fry-half-heartedly—whether SB Bunker or del Coronado grand ballroom or Greenwich Avenue bakeshop or (same difference) Tenth Avenue sex shop—without some heavy-duty first-rate inner turmoil. For the Master—her Master—a setting is a living thing—more alive, in fact, than any human thing—so how ever forgive Himself for allowing His creatures to ditch it. She can sense, therefore, how difficult it must be for Him to be moving them out of the Chateau and into the vehicles. He must feel for his creatures for wasn't He a creature himself once and like all creatures He must have learned early on that departure is massive and that getting from point A to point Z—or, far more excruciatingly, from A to B—demands the willpower of a Hercules? Unlike Melanctha, Cantor (they share a party line, subscription paid for in full by the Master) is not interested in cheering Him on for having supposedly done battle, in some spaghetti western of his own conjuration set in the Ancient Rome of Sergio Leone, with A Behemoth Named Departure. After all, it's not the getting from A to B or A to Z or (most arduously) from A to A that's the hurdle but the *leaving behind* and the ensuing obligation to satisfy the unfelt desire of the things being left behind (spittoons, lampshades, shoe polish, notebooks, etc.) for a sign that separation is too much for the dear departing to bear. And it just so happens the *too much* comes all too naturally—that is, all too torturously—to a ham like Cantor and is automatically conveyed through what he calls a Cameo of Verification. Since for the Cantors of this world, if Departure comes then (as he's never stopped insisting) Verification (e.g., that all lights and faucets and power switches have indeed been turned off and all toilets flushed to perfection)—then Verification (a process in love with the conspicuous laceration inflicted by its own interminability) can't—mustn't—be far behind. Still, for all his proselytizing Cantor breathes a sigh of relief once he's forced himself to realize there simply isn't time to run back inside and lick the toilets clean and deactivate the power switches with a machete . . . interminably. Inasmuch as the chauffeurs and their tattooed molls are getting more unprepossessing by the millisecond. Though it's taken her until this moment—the start of the beginning of the end (hear that, my chevalier detractors? *the beginning of the end!*—so cheer up!)—to realize that He's exactly the sort of guy for whom, if there must be movement (and as we all know, there must), then it's got to be endpointless—movement's own story being the plotless accumulation of an unyielding momentum. Let's be more specific, shall we? Melanctha prompts herself respectfully. All right, then, the sort of guy who in going, at dusk, from, say, Mechanics Alley to Gansevoort Street would never dream of crossing west on Broadway (this sort of guy's artery of choice) even if the light graciously elected to change in his favor at the very moment he arrived at one of its thronged corners (always a scene of too much story, too much plot, too much meaning, too much . . . waste) inasmuch as in so doing he'd reach his destination much faster since who knows when another such opportunity might stare him in the face. For the minute this kind—I mean *sort*—of guy gets going he loses all interest in things like destinations and lifeblood-dissipating shortcuts, which simply have to be sacrificed, costlessly, to what matters most, namely, non-deviation from the straight and narrow (in this case Broadway's) and the inner strength of purpose accruing therefrom. Though on the subject of how and where (especially in a time [2008–present] of such great volatility, financial and otherwise) he can possibly invest his hardwon dividend, the jury is still out. But isn't it in fact Borkman, she wonders, who described himself—or was made to do so by you-know-who—as endpoint-averse down Coronado way? or on second thought maybe it was Cook, or Ethan or Netta (though she can't imagine Netta in New York, much less charging up Broadway, at any hour of the day or night). Whoever it was, he or she has been a mere conduit—the mere vehicle—for the meditations of the Master Himself—and for Herbert's Boswellian benefit alone. But even assuming the worst, i.e., that He is *that kind of guy*, not to mention His million and one other failings, it's all she can do to stop herself from shrieking back, at fate itself, "Whatever my Master is/I'm His . . ." Hell, she wouldn't mind fucking Him though it'd be more a case of fucking Him *back*, considering all the mind-rape to which he's been subjecting her—His indisputable favorite—over what now seem like centuries. However, she doesn't want Him getting into any hot water with *His* Master(s) because of her charms—being accused of retrogressively fomenting a Master-Slave relationship, straight out of Thomas Jefferson's theater of the absurd, with one of His deaconesses—of exploiting her Dark-Continent oversusceptibility to colonization. *Stop:* she can't believe she's wrapping herself in the winding sheet of so outrageous a stereotype—worse, tallying up the pros and cons of dalliance with a crazy male succubus, however well endowed—in the hope (slyly cultivated) that the madness contracted will cure her of an inability to grieve in the way a real mother must if she's to be . . . a great writer!!!

Just before her number comes up she hears somebody who sounds like Ethan ask one of the chauffeurs or the chauffeurs en masse (from the way he gets right into the swing of hemming and hawing it must be Ethan) if he can go even just part of the way on foot. Which triggers some sort of conference—an *exhibition* conference (as we speak of exhibition dancing). "Thing is, I have to piss," he adds forcefully and ends up securing permission on both counts. The toilet's refusal to flush generates panic (for as it turns out he's defecated as well and defecation is a horse of a completely different color) succeeded by the comforts of toying with uncertainty which is familiar terrain—the terrain of articulable thought (since even if Ethan's not a trial subject he's been breathing the Master's air through Jean's skin). Does the machine have a sense of humor and if so is the humor brutish, vicious or merely impish? Or has the machine's visceral obstinacy been engineered as an overfriendly warning of direr things to come? As Ethan, if Ethan it is, *recedes into the distance* (is that the phrase?), to Cantor (standing at the back of van No. 2) he resembles nothing so much as a woolly mammoth confronting the constraints on its mobility—worse, on its blessed solitude—looming at this, the tail end of the Ice Age. Stupidly, the sight fills him with certainty—transforms him into a veritable Tarzan of certainty—the certainty that he may still be first in line to Pritchard's throne or, alternatively, that once all the penny ante routine-driven reasons militating against his taking the giant step of exiting from the trial have finally fallen away (like the petals of an artichoke, leaving only its stalwart—or is it its *steadfast*?—heart), no end of careerist opportunities (for he still has a career, doesn't he?) will make their clamorous presence known. Yet all Ethan has to do is turn his head in another direction (but like a human not a mammoth) to render Cantor differently grateful. There's nothing more exhausting than optimism, with side effects that are grossly disproportionate to its dosage and duration, and the gesture has served to dispel its magic and keep it in check.

Once inside the vehicle to which he's been assigned (much too brightly lit, much too tightly packed, and—judging from the near-universal groans of disgust—not only from Herbert's point of view) Walser finally peters out (the darkness, the soon-to-be stench notwithstanding)—into the sort of raving she would never, in all their years together (for it feels like years, if not decades—the pre-World-Hysterical Rump decades), have believed him capable. Fiesco's *lacerato spirito* has nothing on his—Walser's—own (*who is thinking Fiesco here—who has the time to think Fiesco here?*). Poor thing simply, rightly, refuses to go on doing the sodden bidding of whoever serves most to gain from the selling of Pritch's magnum opus to the Hollywood Hills—whether it's Post or Margo or Straynge-Mabuse (issuing directives, qua *acousmêtre* extraordinaire, from behind his beaded curtain of death) or Pritch himself—the thing that is Walser, poor or otherwise, refuses, rightly or wrongly, to go on doing that *whoever's* bidding by grinding out still more of the same exegeses (*blood sausages,* to you, *bub/dude/bro*)—the kind which manage against all odds to occult that on which they feed (a dinner-theater audience-grabbing stunt which never fails to please). And how did those sausages manage to do it—to occult? you might ask. But nobody's asking 'cause he—nobody—is too busy wondering where he's being taken this time of night. Or too busy being too tired to wonder. Takers or no takers, ravings or no ravings, Walser graciously chooses to respond to this, the unspeakable question on everybody's lips—to browbeat the lot of them into some sort of lame understanding, the more brutish the better. After an ice-breaking, "C'mon, silly," his explication proceeds almost but not quite breathlessly along the following lines: They—the sausages—do it by masquerading as the fiercest abjurations of their own outrageousness—as the rawest exposures of their own absurdity. Imagine comparing the Bunker or an off-off-Broadway opium den to a cosmic song cycle lasting ten thousand years, or comparing the Torah to a hack treatise on niche—boutique—pornographies and all this just to *épater* the inherently immune-to-*épatement* start-up crowd, none of whose airbrushed photoshopped *wunder* boys—like Borkman, Jr., for example, or as The Rump might say, Little Marco Borkman—or, for that matter, upstart *sub-wunder*boys—seem ever to have had even one little thought of the dare-not-speak-its-name variety. So forget the *wunder*boys, he tells them: there'll be no more concocting comparisons for which all decent law-abiding citizens must feel only abhorrence—and *the concocter—the concocter—the concocter*— (Knowing what's coming, Herbert has no choice [even if Whatever the Master Is/She's His] but to SOS Invidicum regional headquarters at Langley Air Force Base [her alert is brief and to the point]: *Call Out the National Guard: Master, through unsuspecting madhouse-bound Walser, is reverting as usual to hyperlative, i.e., default mode, of which there is none worse.*)—*the concocter* most of all. Especially as those concoctions leave everybody slaphappily uncertain—in the dark—about minor matters such as the main design and the overarching theme of the Invidicum Story. Is it *shmattes, shemittahs, shmattes*-to-*shemittahs* (i.e., rags to cosmic riches), the Taj Mahal, or nothing more than the never-before-revealed history of the evolution, from Pythagoras down to Nathan Ashkenazi, of esoteric wisdom's oral transmission? As for Walser, whatever the main theme happens to be, he's had it: no more working for an outfit where what's rehab in one cycle turns out to be nothing less than ID theft—no, ID murder—in the next. Though most of the passengers seem about to faint from the heat (no blaming the driver—he's expert and hard-working—hard-working enough to qualify for a health-benefits-free no-expenses-paid gig, of course sans tenure, at one of the top-tier transportation network companies—a poison-ivy-leaguer like Uber, say, or Lyft or PonyEspresso), Stifter—Stifter the somber land surveyor—has enough stamina to ask, "Is uncertainty—making things strange—Shklovsky-strange,[123] so-to-speak—such a bad thing after all? Well, even if the answer is Yes we've got to exercise the caution of compassion toward whoever—" "You mean Whoever, my friend," Herbert mutters, loyal to the last (she's sure her correction is incomprehensible and that his non-response will amply prove it). *But then:* "Compassion toward *Whoever* (thank you, Melanctha, my friend) is Running the Show." Well, who'd've thought Stifter would be the first to publicly avow, however obliquely, his own impressment into service by the Master as apologist second class? Not Melanctha. Mopping his forehead with the paper towel he was street-smart and sappily sentimental enough to purloin (yes, *purloin* [not that EAP needs a plug from the puny likes of him]) on his final grand tour of the del Corona-do's mezzanine-level men's room, Stifter explains (no, *goes on to explain*) that even if this is no Mammoth Circus and Milady Invidicum is no Lola Montès (he's immediately terrified—more on Max Ophuls's behalf than his own—that as punishment for these self-exalting allusions to the filmmaker's infamously mutilated final masterwork he'll be enjoined to provide an explanatory footnote for what should require either none at all or a book-length chapter of its own)—Stifter explains that even if this is no Circus Maximus, he (sorry, Melanctha, *He*)—i.e., Whoever is Running the Show—still has His hands full because, let's face it, He, *their* Showman—*their* Master—*their* Ringmaster—is an obsessional neurotic, even if the obsessionality ain't on the exalted order of

---

[123] According to Russian Formalist theorist Viktor Shklovsky—there, I've pigeonholed him sufficiently to feel entitled to explain him to himself—the purpose of art, which "exists that one may recover the sensation of life," is "to impart the sensation of things as they are perceived and not as they are known" and its technique is "to make objects '*unfamiliar*,' [the italics are mine] to make forms difficult, to increase the difficulty and length of perception because the process of perception is an aesthetic end in itself and must be prolonged." Therefore(?), the longer and harder we look, the more strangely an object looms and the more beautiful it is forced to become. All quotations are from Shklovsky's essay "Art as Technique," in *Russian Formalist Criticism: Four Essays*, translated by Lee T. Lemon and Marion J. Reis (Lincoln, Nebraska, University of Nebraska Press, 1965), p. 12.

the Wolf Man's (or is it the Rat Man's?[124]) or Dora's, and, as any angekok worth his salt can tell you, such animals require a thrice-daily megadose of uncertainty—or rather, Uncertainty—think of it as Invidicum for everybody who (and not just the stars in Freud's case-history pantheon) has no choice but to over-insist that the world under the Big Top, and himself in tandem, be rendered not-quite-real until further notice, so as to assure deferral of the thankless business (nasty, brutish and *long*) of being in that world—I mean, Being in that World—not just the Big Top world but the global-village-idiot world in all its glorious gore. No denying Stifter's impressiveness, that is, his unpredictability. Nothing less, this Stifter, than the Envy Community's Etna-in-Residence (but is there such a thing as an *Envy Community* and if so can those seeking admission look forward, following a successful probation, to standard-issue dispensations like sexual harassment and sleep deprivation?).

Fortunately, before resigning herself to living out the rest of her days in the shadow of this newest vestal of the Master, Herbert manages to recognize that, impressiveness notwithstanding, it's by no means evident Stifter will know how to collaborate and collude with the Master in the way a muse—or even a muse-in-training—should. Does he—can he even begin—to understand the *Mechanism* she herself is only just beginning to *get*? Will he be willing to put up with demands sure to grow more and more unrealistic—more impossible—the more desperate life under the Big Top becomes (or is it her demands, groupiesque to a fault, that right from the start were the impossible ones)? Though this insight in the shape of a premonition—suggestive as it is of run-of-the-mill hubby-and-wife incompatibility—doesn't really apply to her and the Master, does it? It'd be better—much better—(*a*) applied to, visited on, the parties to some garden-variety booby-trapped connubial mess—parties chained to the same four-poster (which has ended up, thanks to all their squabbling and Strindbergian strife—and even worse, much worse—with but half a post to its name) and (*b*) articulated by one of the boobs—or maybe (in a rare moment of consensus) by both. Somebodies like poor Jean and Ethan, say. So why hasn't He been able to hold that insight in escrow for its most likely subjects cum exponents? Is His hatred of *Likelihood*—stronger only than his love of Uncertainty—so great as to have driven Him yet again to commit the unthinkable—authorial hara-kiri—by foisting off said insight (more like an insight-in-progress but still a pearl) on the least plausible suspect, very much as if this were the Invidicum Story's bid for respectful—and, more importantly, lucrative—consideration as a homage-crammed takeoff on, say, *Easy to Kill* or *The Moving Finger* or *Murder in Retrospect* or *Triangle at Rhodes* or *Death on the Nile*? But whether or not the insight does indeed apply to their relation, one thing is clear: The Master's situation, and by extension hers, is clearly an increasingly desperate one, what with this curious business of the vehicle in the nighttime and all.[125]

---

[124]Yes, the Rat Man's!

[125]For one thing, it's badly in need of a podium—even the podium of some hack's incoherence—considering all the pontification running amuck at the drop of a hat. And,

Increasingly desperate, she can't help feeling, thanks in no small measure to His own peculiar brand of orphan disease (though, granted, no more peculiar than any other)—that being the unholy need for self-administration of larger and larger doses of His own poor excuse for a drug (packet-shaped anatomization (*a*) as performed by the wrong or a somewhat wrong practitioner and (*b*) as perpetrated on the wrong or not-quite-right subject—object—target) in order to achieve an ever diminishing effect of . . . uniqueness—of being Byronically doomed to a greatness inaccessible to His peers. Not that her portion of the desperation irks unduly. After all, the things she's been asked to do, i.e., think, are still a far cry from what Rick and Elsa's peculiar Casablancan brand of aggrandizing star-crossed truculence—its barked bidding—required of Dooley Wilson's Sam (*Play it again or so help me, I'll send you back to the cotton fields*), namely, that his exquisite fingertips be available at any time of day or night to pad their glamorous self-pity with a soundtrack. As if reading her mind (more and more of that sort of thing going on around here), Stifter adds, "Let's face it, he's (sorry, He's) afraid to *be*. This is why He makes us step in to do his dirty work. This is the mechanism—sorry, Mechanism—that (for every master has a Mechanism: it's what makes him a master) dares not speak Its name."

More than understandable that Herbert should immediately be panting for more—much more—in the same line from this somebody—at last she's found him or he's found her—who knows the Master better than He knows Himself, or thinks he does, which pretty much amounts to the same thing (or does it?). Problem is, a massive jab in the ribs perpetrated by what feels like a tote bag (very high-end judging from all of the Polovetsian baubles, bangles and beads) prevents her from making out the next several words. Melanctha waits but the bearer (it has to be a *she* and judging from the smug stench, a *lily-white* she—a Karen in fact—specifically the kind of Karen who haunts the Central Park Ramble in the hope of finding some bespectacled Black birdwatcher to accuse of harassment)—the bearer evidently has no intention of assuming responsibility for this monstrous chip off the old shoul-

---

come to think of it, maybe that's why the start-ups were dragged here in the first place. I.e., to get inspired enough by the mountainous sea air et al to cough up the template of a vehicle-friendly podium. As if, she reminds herself, they don't have better things to do—philanthropical things—like keeping Frisco's sight-for-sore-eyes homeless invisible to the taste buds of their fellow techies. (Melanctha [as president of the Union of SV CEOs]: Why, I tell you, it's gotten to the point where—and after the hardest day's work imaginable—a gray-flannelled unicorn can no longer expect to savor the aroma of his well-deserved slow-churned grass-fed cage-free venison burgerette [a steal at $120] at the nouveau-est SoMa bistro without having first to run the expiatory G&G [gamut and gauntlet] of lice-infested foul-mouthed piss-soaked subhuman affliction. [She didn't want to be seduced by this point of view, further exalted through feeble mockery, and to end up, for better or worse, living off its proceeds. Meaning that nobody may claim, at the moment of giving birth to a horrific thought-image, that he's been the mere and unwitting surrogate of what is in fact another's, i.e., the Other's. That is, nobody gives birth to a thought that is not of his own essence.])

der, much less apologizing for its aggression. *After all, darling,* Karen should simper, *given the price tag, it deserves to be treated as a separate being with a life and will of its own.* (Herbert could swear other members of the tribe have been treated to a similar humiliation but who? and where? and what kind of thought packets did the incident give rise to in their case, if any? and did those packets manage to assuage the hurts inflicted? and how does she happen to know about those other incidents—those other distastefully curious incidents whether in the nighttime, in the daytime or at any other time?)

By the time Herbert manages to half-convince herself she hasn't been targeted on the basis of race, or aspiration, somebody else has wormed his way into the act. But a speaker, alas, who has nothing of Stifter's neo-patrician poise. A supernumerary—an unknown, from the sound of him—with no legitimate claims on a podium but who looks, even in the darkness, like a man who's nevertheless been tasked with a task (all six senses tell her it's bound to be daunting—the delivery of a sort of funeral oration—and will leave very little margin for error) perhaps simply because he's known to be the type who doesn't suffer idleness gladly and may very well become dangerous if left to twiddle his thumbs unsupervised. And whose recruitment—qua unknown, reeking of illegitimacy—she's already convinced, will turn out to be an affront to all the career orators out there who've worked so hard cleaving to their craft's strictest rule of the road which reads, if she's not mistaken, something like this: *A lengthy monologue, especially one of an abstract, analytical, essayistic nature, is verboten but if, for whatever reason, inclusion becomes unavoidable then said monologue shall be vouchsafed to the only character whose delivery thereof will be perceived as constituting an—the—essential moment in its moral development.* Which for the first time she realizes goes against all that the Master is supposed to stand for. Though maybe this unknown citizen is in fact the orator best suited to the job in the traditional sense—much too well suited to pass up—and maybe, independently, the so-called Master has, since their last missed encounter, fallen head over heels out of love with His hatred of Likelihood and made up His mind to take a dog-eared page or two from the playbook of every politico (think Perry; think Romney, think L'il Loathsome Lindsey; think Ted McCruz, uncrowned king of the Cancún Negative Charisma Festival) who once denounced The Rump as a fraud and a punk and a phony and a blowhard (but failed to also observe that the signature viciousness was far slyer—far more cunning—than the blowhardiness would have it) only to find himself jockeying ferociously for position on the Inaugural receiving line in the hope that loving perpetration of a thorough licking of the new incumbent's ass (about whose size and shape, to the sham horror of prurient parents everywhere, The Rump never stopped boasting up and down and rambunctiously athwart the campaign trail) would trigger emission of the coveted signal therefrom—with a little luck, silent, odorless and unmessy—to the effect that he'd beaten out every other supplicant for this or that juicy slab of dream boondogglery. Indeed, if flagrant violation of his own "principles" is good enough for Lindsey then giddy violation of the Master's by one of the Master's own is surely good enough not just for this little putz of a supernumerary but, more importantly, for the Master Himself. And adding insult to injury, who should this supernumerary turn out to be but the furthest thing *in fact* from one, namely, Beltway superstar Newt Liepnits (she'd know his cackle, cannily held in reserve, anywhere), which means, compliments of an abduction or induction or deduction as airtight as any of C.S. Peirce's), that sandbag wielding Karen was—is—none other than the *Cat People*'s homecoming queen, Irena Manning.

And now that Newt's revealed his identity, is there (also *in fact*), she wonders, or pretends to wonder, anybody better suited to the task—and if not, then is there any point *under the circumstances* (whatever those little devils turn out to be) in continuing to talk about suitedness, which might serve only to remind the Master of His own self-betrayal and induce Him to sabotage Newt's budding career? (A miniature Wild Bill Barr without the poker-faced bulldog jowls—that's how Cantor's would summarize the Master's new—and very first—chief justice). Nothing must interfere with his carrying on where Stifter left off—*the stakes are way too high* (but what are the stakes and why are they so high or is this but another try by the Master's trusted proxy to rev up the Base with a blast of His dog whistle?). But stakes or no stakes, every scholar would agree that Uncertainty and Being in the World and Unlikelihood and Uniqueness, not to mention Lord Byron and Max Ophuls, are big fish and no laughing matter. Yet even if Newt seems to have gotten right smack into the swing of things and then some, and to have every intention of leaving no stone unturned and no loose ends, and though the first few samples of his wistful eloquence bode well for a second or even a third term, Melanctha can't help fearing, if all these hiccoughing hairpin turns are any measure of where things stand—or rather, teeter perilously—that maybe their number is, well . . . pretty much up and Being in the World, for the likes of envy-riddled jetsam like them, no longer an option. And to think that Invidicum's destiny and their voyage to eternity are in the hands of the driver and the driver's in the hands of the van (which—like Irena's chic little tote—has a mindless will of its own) and the van's in the hands of the Pacific, playing possum slightly off to the right somewhere below. Though all of a sudden the vehicle has obediently slowed to a crawl—a hangdog crawl. (And can it be that in the almost-fetid darkness Herbert was mistaken by Irena for her real victim? whom she's now ordering, like any conscientious caretaker of a spouse's career profile and public image, to turn down the volume lest he offend—or worse, bore—his audience.) Newt pretends not to have heard so as to ensure, or so Melanctha thinks, that whatever success is ultimately achieved won't be layable at the doorstep of his better half's crabby but savvy solicitude. And the fulcrum of his approach appears to be the conviction that when matters pop-psycho-philosophical are in play, focusing on anguish rather than on expertise will go the longest way toward breaking the ice, at least with this particular cohort, whose members now find themselves, even after all they've suffered, stuck between—literally—the devil and the deep. Last thing in the world Newt wants to do is get them all riled up—turn them into atheists or worse—but since immediately after signing on as a Trial Elder Emeritus he started feeling *non-existent* (except when he had an inkling the Guy Running the Show—to use Stifter's felicitous phrase—had an inkling he could be of use down here), it's only natural he'd get to thinking, isn't it? that maybe the cause was exposure to all that Invidicum (even if one doesn't snort, it has a way, or so he's been told and by way bigger whizzes than Post, of getting into your aching bones). Stifter draws Newt out by asking him to please be more specific—hard to know, though (at least for Cantor), whether in doing so he's for or against his successor (some might say his *replacement*—a term less harsh). But Newt is all too willing to elaborate—(in fact he's as proud as a peacock to do the honors). He began to feel[126] (*a*) that his most prized possessions—his matter and his motions—weren't the substances they were meant, or cracked up to be—though not quite shadows either—but mere phenomena (like parhelia and rainbows)—or, if you like, objects in a story ushered—forced—into existence through perception—the Guy's perception or (when he, the Arch Perceiver, took a piss or a breather) perception by his agents, who include, by the way, not just worthies like Burchardus De Volder and Robert Merrihew Adams who were barred entry at the last minute but they themselves—yes, they—aka *us*—his boon companions—and (*b*) that his reality (for what it was now worth, qua phenomenon, qua rainbow) lay in, and depended exclusively on, the harmoniousness of the curious perceptions he generated (either in one perceiver at different times of day or night or among different perceivers). And all at once Newt understood, as would, say, a fourth saint in an opera's third (and final) act, that to be perceived by the Guy (Melanctha wants to shout out, *You mean the Master!* but wisely decides to hold her fire) was nothing less, and nothing more, than to please Him by constituting (qua phenomenon, in *other* words, qua detrital alluvium of the upsurge of the Guy's perception, or in other other words, qua one more in a long line of thought-packet pushers whose dirty-work was consecrated to waxing simultaneously as verisimilar and non-verisimilar as possible) a harmonious moment in His story—a story to be fed to his clients at bargain-basement prices. (While saying all this, can Liepnits by any chance also be casting meaningful glances Netta's way, and her way alone? *O mein Geliebter!* the lady in question, daughter of immigrants, dares to murmur, *If I were only ten—oh, all right, fifty—years younger!*) And along these lines, Newt also came—or rather is still coming—to understand that if in a Guy story there is to be action, like the avant-garde antics of an apex predator and his assigned prey in the Santa Barbara zoo, then it must be a matter not of sticks and stones and guns and ammo but of distinctness of perception of sticks and stones and guns and ammo and that if one of His clients develops a yen for the raw meat of a main event then it will be up to some substance—one of His agents—Liepnits himself, say—to become conscious—really conscious—of his own appetite for the perception of such an event. Since in a Guy story it's a substance's *conscious* appetite for perception of an event that actively produces the event. With a little help of course from those substances

---

[126]The following stretch of "story" text owes much to Robert Merrihew Adams, *Leibniz: Determinist, Theist, Idealist* (New York, Oxford University Press, 1994), specifically chaps. 9 and 10. And as servers say after setting down the exotically skimpy main dish: Enjoy!

up and down the great big Totem Pole of Being whose appetite is never quite so conscious and whose job it is to lend a hand producing the event *passively*. Since every event worth its salt is nothing but opera, ballet, chamber play, porno flick, poolside shuffleboard and baseball game all wrapped up in one and, as such, must be produced both actively and passively, must have both a winner and a loser—both an agent and a patient—both a player who knuckles down and one who knuckles under—both a master and a slave dialectically *comme il faut*[127]—must be a heady mix of active predictably besting passive and passive not so predictably besting active inasmuch as being *conscious* and nothing but can be (*a*) a drag on appetite, not to mention (*b*) a drag queen (since, as too much of a good thing, consciousness saps manhood—turns Jack into Jill—and who knows this better than George, consciousness junkie, although he's never attempted—has never been tempted at least as far as he knows—to take this final leap: among other things, he likes his hairy chest much too much and likes each morning to hear his balls rattling around in the shower even more). And along these same lines, Newt further came—or rather is still coming—to acknowledge hook, line and sinker that all of them are nothing but *phantoms of His Rue Morgue*—Cantor could swear that a tribemate has already cannibalized this luscious phrase, being too damn greedy to wait for—too damn greedy not to be premonitorily envious of— what has just shown itself to be obviously its—the phrase's—only conceivable context. Maybe it's he himself who's the cannibalizer in question but if so, it was in another country (Hudson Street) and, besides, the wench (Berry Sundae) is dead. He's dreamed them, Newt has, and he'll go on dreaming them until, until—well, until, say, the already uncanny Chrysler Building looms more serenely terrifying than the Matterhorn. Somebody's retort—Netta's?— takes a stab at the darkness. "You're mad." "No, Liepnits is not mad—far from it," Post notes tonelessly. As if he has no bone to pick with the retort—far from it. In fact, it's given him just the sublime push needed to go after the bigger game of self-confrontation—confrontation with a self barely discernible in the murky middle distance. "But" (so there is a bone to pick after all!) "if you go on insisting he's mad we'll end up not in some concentration camp of Lawrence Ferlinghetti's mind but in a very real Auschwitz with all the *arbeit-macht-frei*-ish trimmings." Unclaimed query: What is Post's function here: kapo or tour guide? *Too bad*, Shearer simpers noiselessly (mere mention of Auschwitz makes her do crazy things)—but as a character of her own making—a character whom she's never met on stage or off—never knew existed until this moment—a character whose apparently unintentional smarminess is getting—so great is the fascination it exerts—more and more difficult to shake. Let's hear a round of applause, then, for Moira's pussyless spinster from Topeka—not to be confused with the spunky spunk-hungry heroine of Anthony Tudor's *Pillar of Fire*—for whom everything has only its brightest side. (She gorges daintily on chocolate mothballs at the Bijou's Saturday mat-

---

[127]Or in the immortal words of Jean's namesake, "Some must cry so that the others may be able to laugh the more heartily" (*Good Morning, Midnight*, part one, chap. 2).

inees. But don't breathe a word of this to her pastor.) *Too bad . . . it isn't Christ-mas* (suddenly, explosively, she's viperishly out of character, perhaps never to return), *for the only way to properly guzzle this egg nog of a ghost story told by an idiot savant is to be nestled breathlessly around the fire.* But better moth-ball-guzzling in the wilds of Topeka than to admit to Post that *arbeit-macht-frei*-ishness just doesn't make it as a showstopper where she hails from and where the show—the whole show—is despair at having been hooted off the stage of life—just isn't an Absolute of suffering before which her own failure and her (granted, stupid little all-washed-up) self-laceration must lay down their arms and to which they must meekly defer. As far as she's concerned, Holocausts—which, alas, alas, alas, alas, alas, still come in every inconceivable size and shape despite that hallowed old war cry "Never again!"—are turn-offable at will since they unfold, if that's the word, only *onscreen*—somewhere in virtual *un*reality—at the Bijou on Topeka's Main Street, maybe, once the projectionist's left for the night. What choice is there anyway but to relegate them all to such a realm if she's to go on believing said laceration—too costly to practice—too obscene to relish hence relished all the more—is, for the mil-lionth time, *no longer feasible*, too excruciating to nurse one second longer, flouting as it does every physical law of endurance—the very character of physical law? But, to misquote bongo-drummer Richard Feynman, if there's one thing a physical law-yer loves it's the special case and Shearer's failure to restrict laceration to the limits of lacerability is nothing if not a special case—combined character flaw and special talent with each doomed to the dialecti-cal disarray of resembling the other way more than itself. In short (with Holo-causts out of the picture), nobody—nobody!—has ever suffered as much as she—in fact, that suffering has already crossed the line—been transformed into its own impossibility (proof of the crossover needs only to be notarized). She's failed at failure because her failure is too big to fail. Which means all this infeasibility must indeed end—with a bang—with her resurrection as the greatest peforming artist of her generation, far greater than Farrell, far greater than Makarova, far greater than Callas, far greater than The Rump. Come to think of it, she hasn't used the word *flouting* for ages—didn't even know until this minute that their paths ever crossed. So—an old friend—her only old friend—the old friend she so callously abandoned when her star was in the ascendant—has come home to roost in peace.

Someone coughs. Or is it a mucous-muzzled sneeze? One thing it *isn't* is a call to order. Well, whatever it is, or isn't, it doesn't prohibit Stifter from making it his cue to say (in the tone of a disgruntled cashiered bureaucrat?), while clutching at Jean's hot little hand (resolutely unwithdrawn) as he says it, "How did we ever end up with such a Life-denier—even worse, it's all sidelines perversity—you can see he doesn't believe a word of it himself? (And has he really managed to wrestle Being in the World, not to mention Uniqueness and Uncertainty, down to the ground the way his press releases say he would?) Far as I can remember, we started out (doctors and patients alike) real enough, didn't we? Not phantoms, not phenomena, not rainbows, not shadows, not appetites, not perceptions. And, cured or not, we're still real. Only the minute he dared put his foot in our mouth—" It sounds as if, in the course of this rant from Stifter, Liepnits had been trying to wrench himself free of some-body's—a woman's—clutch—the clutch of a monitress—more like a coach—a high-tech personal trainer, maybe, reeking of Malibu smog—who (to put the best possible construction on it) discharges her function with all-too-typical shrewish delight and never knows when to quit. Netta? Irena? Whoever it is, she's a woman born to be scorned—to the manor scorned—and, more to the point, born to live to tell the unlikely tale of vengeance wreaked. Newt won't take this sitting down. "Don't you get it? He—the Guy—co-opted us. Post & Co. has been powerless again Him. *He came as part of a package deal.* Be grateful I'm giving it to you straight from the shoulder even if it hurts to hear it and hurts me even more to say it: To be the victims of Envy is to be, collaterally, victims of a storyteller consumed with self-hate—why, He could teach a master class on the subject—a self-hate expertly channeled into invid-ious comparisons made ostensibly for His victims' own good—to toughen them up for success—but in fact designed to estrange them from everybody else on the planet—to make them feel unwelcome in the world. Wherever He roams He's sure to leave a trail of victims behind. (If only you could realize *you* aren't—victims.) But while He's busy inflicting those comparisons He never misses an opportunity to peep out from behind the curtain of what he tries to pass—pawn—off (most of all to Himself) as ethical piety—in order to deter-mine what state you're in—how much He's made you sweat and sob as proxies for His own vulnerability—in order to ask, through hooded eyeballs and a matinee idol's obscenely overexposed front teeth, and with a mixture of fear and sadistic delight, *How am I doing as your little Mengele?* He's, shall we say, famous for shuddering unavowably—still with delight—in response to your hungrily perceived despair at being on the wrong side of every comparison—at having been found yet again to be constitutively wanting. But the shudder-ing doesn't let Him off easy (*un*easy lies the head that wears a crown of thorns) for it comes with terror, too, that the sense of failure he's induced just might turn out to be contagious after all. At the same time, He feels (there's the rub) protective—He'll defend each of you to the death—but only in your absence. Since He Who's Absent is, like the Customer, always Right. So even if the time sanctified by somebody's absence is spent anatomizing—excoriating—his flaws for the edification of others, so help anybody else unexotic enough to be present who dares to echo His contempt—or who out of common courtesy simply acknowledges with a misplaced breath whatever's been oozing out of the Horse's Mouth. Since as long as you're absent, you're sacred—even with all those flaws. What the Master—Masters everywhere—can't abide is *pres-ence on the scene.* But you should thank your lucky stars that I've been sent among you to super-spread the good news that if Non-Being-in-the-World can be licked then so can Envy (since every condition under the sun is a proxy for Envy). I'm here (and what better *here* than this rocky winding road to ante-purgatory) to prove that He—even He—can be hoist by His own petard; that, come at from the right angle, He can be kept from having not just the last word but the last look and can be sized and perceived and bracketed before He can do so unto you."

CHAPTER FORTY-SEVEN

Although this suddenest of crossovers to what feels like a new (and the very last) chapter in their misadventures—a chapter in which, for some reason, the pair suspect they'll figure centripetally—serves as a breath of fresh air, both Ethan (picked up just outside Old Mission Santa Barbara but minus the woolly mammoth zoot suit left for dead across from the Granada) and Jean heartily agree (eye contact undimmed by the darkness) that, given all they've been through together and apart, there'll be no taking relegation to some madman's virtual world sitting down, especially in this coach with $n+1$ insides whose air has fast become irrespirable. Which means they'll have to skedaddle doublequick, leaving Jean no other choice but to trot out that old chestnut—that nine-saving stitch in time—*I forgot my purse*, even if she'd never be caught dead, purseless or not, simpering those fussy words. And despite the fact that he's two-thirds of the way up Bunker Hill, the driver (afraid that what she's really concerned about is puking from the fumes?) brakes obligingly, no questions asked. Though, come to think of it, there *is* something in the way he orders her not to worry, as there'll be plenty of other vehicles before the night is through, that merits a frisson or two.

The pre-dawn air is not as dewy as one might have hoped though in their wobbly descent toward Cabrillo Boulevard they do get a well-deserved whiff or two of—and can even hear—the surf pretending to be on its last legs. Hope is spread across the horizon like jam (flavor to be determined) on freshly baked date nut bread. She knows from experience that nothing to come will match that infinite hope—least of all its realization. For this is the best kind of hope—hope without referent, without target, without future. At Milpas, Jean in her impatience is already way ahead since inasmuch as Eden and Eden alone possesses (albeit without knowing he does) the ability to bring to light all that's gone into sabotaging the Invidicum trial and facilitating the deployment of the wonder drug's off-off-Broadway version overseas, for which this silly Master mystery has been acting as a mere screen (even an imbecile could have figured that out), she must get to him (the Mr. Memory Who Doesn't Know He Knows Too Much) before he's zapped any further or shipped out or done in. If successful, Jean'll be showing Caro (whose new lingerie business— Kmart with a dash of Victoria's Secret—is turning out to be a smashing success: the French toast of Chelsea, NOHO, Central Park West, Oliver Street and the Bronx Zoo) that she's not just another dimwitted big sister who's *quote* pissed her poor excuse for a life away *unquote*. (As Ethan's having some trouble keeping up [too many buttermilk pancakes at that breakfast-all-day-and-all-night beachfront bistro, if you ask her], Jean orders him—rolling the eyes of her voice—to get a move on and sounding while she's at it a bit too Nancy-Shrewish even for her own taste.) Approaching Anacapa Street (or is it Anapamu? not even the natives can tell them apart), she feels—or rather, true to the Master code, *she can't help feeling*—that everything hinges on the grotesque fact of Eden's promotion which will therefore be the sole focus of whoever's remained behind (dozens—perhaps thousands—chose to come out and gawk until the vans were full to bursting, their familiarly unfriendly faces bloated with a schadenfreude worthy of the crowds applauding the deportation of "the first victims" from Vienna, city of waltzes and chococlate cake, both piously overrated—and doubtless they all returned, once the vans were gone, to what she now has no choice but to view, with hindsight but by no means uncharitably, as a not-so-glorified loft) since, as is well known though not well enough, promotion constitutes—it's a veritable universal solvent—one of the topics *rarissime* whose consideration permits the encipherment of the secrets associated with any other topic you may care to name, or rather, to refrain from naming. Thus under its auspices, the secret of *their* sleazy profits won't be blown to kingdom come. So what is she to conclude but that they've—but who *are* they—engineered this promotion with all the trimmings (Liepnits would say that the master [stet]—beneath contempt, that idolatrous capital *M*—has coerced his dummies into working up a hearty conscious appetite for the perception of the poster boy's promotion) as a conversation piece purely to enable their engagement in a coded meditation (spies are everywhere) on, say (for starters), protecting and enlarging their vested interests in Africa and the Middle East. Nobody observes her come in or if they have she's obviously regarded (through her cohabitation with a born fallguy?) as goods too damaged to be a cause for alarm. Not to mention the sorry business of that mincemeat-making kid sister.

And, sure enough, here's Post babbling (though even his fiercest enemies must concede, *but according to whom?* this is babble of a very high order indeed)—yet how did he get back here so fast? Or maybe he's one of the lucky ones fated to keep the home fires burning. But given that Post is what's known as a Player (known, that is, by everybody but the real players themselves who have better things to do than bask in such lingo—yes, *bask in such lingo:* mixed metaphors are my billion-dollar baby) and calls the shots and makes the fates themselves tremble, shouldn't brute luck have had as little to do with his being spared those horripilating hairpin turns high up in the hills, as goodness with Mae West's diamonds? Babbling something to the effect that the characterologic changes wrought on its victim by Promotion being irreducible to and undeducible from the pre-P state of things (Jean remembers Eden's outbreak of arrogance—something to do with gourmet cuisine—and how unbearable Shearer found it), it's to be expected Eden will now either (*a*) cast his virginal pre-P self aside and succumb completely to a lust for power; or (*b*) deplete his life reserves by remaining, neither man nor maid, forever at conscience-stricken cross-purposes with it; or (*c*) quashing mad lust's every upsurge, unhealthy or not, sink into a permanent coma of neuterdom. (On a lighter note, Post himself is clearly on much better terms with the start-up crowd—isn't that Borkman, Jr., over there chatting with Pete Thiel?—than his otherworldly airs as Boswell to Pritch's Johnson have let on.) But she has to hand it to him: what better way to disguise the fact that Promotion is in the present context a mere sum of ciphers than by conveying the urgency of its non-existent perils and what better way to convey that urgency than (as he's just done) by invoking the perils of adolescent sexuality unbound? (Especially fitting given that Eden is the quintessential eternal adolescent-cum!-

wetdream machine—the quintessential Prodigal Son cum Wandering Jew. But who's to say that the lackluster topic of adolescent sexuality wasn't, way back when, itself made urgent through invocation of . . . of . . . and so on and so forth, with every topic ultimately self-relegated to the status of a proxy, its identity a fulfilment pure and simple of some need of the current cosmic cycle?) In any event, as a means of preventing the Enemy from realizing that Promotion talk is much too dull to be anything but coded off-label-Invidicum talk, no denying the adroitness of beefing and spicing up Promotion—a non-event, a staged distraction, if ever there was one—by assimilating it to the doings and undoings of Adolescent Sexuality, i.e., a bona fide megaphenomenon, hence completely alien, though on second thought (inasmuch as all formulations whether on the level of language or of life are simply recombinations of and reductions to the same old terms), not so alien as all that. By the same token, in finding, through recruitment of the inexhaustibilities of topic AS, more and more ways to multiply the facets of P, Post is not just flexing the muscles of his insane virtuosity—though to watch him (the Heifetz of druglords) in action is in itself surely worth the price of admission—but, far more importantly, creating more and more opportunities for encodement of the Secrets of Invidicum (perfect title for a Harlequin Gothic).

But encodement or no encodement, Operation Invidicum will soon have to be anatomized publicly, like a frog, in at least some undoctored gruesome circumstantial detail (or how else lure the angel investors?) which must entail speaking the names of all the star players, whether vital or inimical to OI's success. But to do so is to be compelled to acknowledge that stuck in its Ointment are flies other than you yourself, a concession that does not, as Jean knows far better than anyone (thanks to undear old dad's convulsions of overreaching), sit well with the Posts of the world for it falsifies the notion that they alone are overripe for anointment. But there *are* times, though few and far between, when they see fit to grant somebody else a name and a being in tandem, but (let's make sure we understand each other right from the start) a being terminable at any time. Since to name is to humor the delusion of selfhood entertained by the lower forms of non-life and when you're a god, even a prosthetic god—even a Pharma pipeline god—speaking names is, under the best of circumstances, a nasty business—*humiliation to the point of selfablation* is what Marcus Aurelius called it on his deathbed. So imagine if you can (*Jean can!*) how much more excruciating for Post to consent to speak the names of those (as in the present case) over whose actions, he has, when you got right down to it, absolutely no control. To speak *their* names is, with true Kabbalistic propriety, to prostrate himself prattlingly before those names as *concentrations of divine power* and power vastly superior to that wielded by his own poor excuse for a name—is, with the full weight of his credulity, to implore those names to make the course of true corruption run smooth (as it does for men a lot worse than he: Putin and Vik the Orbán and Igor the Sechin and The Rump and Murdoch, for starters)—is to succumb in the last analysis to the hysteria of girlish infatuation with the letters of the alphabet. That's the problem with being an administrator: it saps *your* letters of the power to shine. Face facts: For somebody like Post, walking the walk and talking the talk by speaking the names of his confederates is self-sodomization at its starkest. So the long and short of it is that Jean can only exult at having so much names-smothering double-talk going on before her very ears. For what can be more unnerving than to have to watch an alpha-plus-plus male like Post roll over and belly-up to this ex-KGB thug of a world?

Reading her thoughts (as noted many—too many—times above, far too much of that stuff going on), Cook cries out (so he, too, has somehow managed to jump ship!), "But where's Eden, for Christ's sake? Is it that in our boy's case" (slow circular pan, for dramatic impact, of his camera eye) "the custom of toasting the promotee is more honored in the breach than in the observance?" Or is it rather, he wonders, one of those cases of filial revenge (you know the kind) where once the father's murderer is safely six feet under, the scoundrel gets absolved to the point of canonization, which in turn requires that, in keeping with both Hooke's law and the Hall effect, the father's holy avenger be then downgraded to the most vicious of motiveless psychopaths? "Oh, Eden, Eden, Eden—my roommate, my brother—if you'd only let us help you when we had a chance."

"What are you doing here?" Post asks, turning to—or rather on—her without missing a beat. She can't decide whether the accent is on *you* or on *doing*, nor does she particularly want to. Wherever that pickaxe of an accent is supposed to fall, she won't have anybody believing—least of all herself—she's in over her head. Never mind, what comes next does the deciding for her: "Why you of all people? Why not Herbert or Shearer (who, as if on cue, emerges from the ladies' room: so she's also on the lam, Jean observes [by kicking Ethan in the ribs with her elbow], or did she never leave?) or Wilber Ross (billionaire con artist and Saudi sword dance welterweight champion of the world—would've been a shoo-in as the greedy heartless ugly hedge fund CEO in the sequel to *It's a Wonderful Life* which Frank Capra never made) or Irena or Ivanka or even some bastion cum rising star of the pedophiliac avant-garde, *say*, Marjorie Taylord Green?" "And, while we're at it, why not Lord Lutley, say, or Mrs. Froome, those burlesque fixtures[128] of the Envy circuit?" someone has the courage to ask. "Or why not the two of 'em for the price of one?" asks an even more courageous somebody else. (Are somebody and somebody else by any chance aware that their very being violates the most sovereign [because He himself never ceases to violate it] of the Master's eleven sovereign laws of the land, which enjoins that no character shall be given breath merely to mouth—to clean up after—some woebegone thought packet—much less a single phrase?) "Simple enough," Cook replies, in the tone of yet another anonymous someone getting back at another someone else. (*For rejecting him somewhere down the line? but where and when?* Jean wonders. *I never disguised the fact that I found him way too attractive for his own good.*) He explains that Jean Rhys is here because a part was offered her by Whoever's Running the Show (interesting how that phrase has already

---

[128]Blame them on Henry James, specifically on (for those who take their pornography straight, no chaser) *The Sacred Fount.*

"entered the language," at least according to WikiPeeks: why, it's right up there with *six degrees of separation* and *fans come and go but detractors are forever:* over 3 million hits per millisecond, somewhere on the shadowy back alleys of the Web)—the role, so He maintained, of a lifetime—of many lifetimes—the role she was born to play—the role through which she'd be giving birth not just to herself (any ham could do that) but to a slew of certifiable impersonators. At least from what Cook pieced together on the vehicle (*so he, too, thinks Jean, is like her and Ethan on the lam*), He's vowed, having finally learned his lesson—never again to make the stupid mistake of allowing any shot, however insignificant—say, of the balcony ledge out there heaped mountain-high with greasy paper plates or of the bronze miniature to Post's right entitled, if Cook isn't mistaken, *Harpy Bestriding a Pistrix* (missing from the SB Museum of Art for well over a year)—the mistake of allowing any shot to go unclaimed by somebody's POV. "So it's not so much a role as a point of view." Oddly, Jean is repelled through and through by Her Man's intervention. *As a rule I don't do gratitude,* she hears herself silently shriek. But why, Post croons with the elegance of Astaire, the Mozart of the Musical (having evidently forgiven her her reappearance on the scene), shouldn't the movie sure to be made of The Trial be riddled with shots and potshots unclaimed and defiantly unclaimable? Why, he demands to know, should the close-up of, for example, a black-bellied cumulus negotiating the wisp of a contrail's tightrope have its hard-won purity tarnished through yokage to some old fart's myopia?

Semi-shock tunes him out.

First, there's the matter of the decor. Jean didn't realize the first time around how bare the place is—though not according to the strictures of NoHo or Sausalito minimalism. It's just the bad taste of thriftiness gone wild. And if it weren't for that Something Bestriding a Something Else—a real scenestealer, especially when there's no competition—they'd all be on life support from a lack of retinal stimulation. But something's wrong. Rhys will never be known for her unselfishness (except when it's a matter of kowtowing to creatures more selfish than she) nor does she wish to be but it's obvious it's Shearer who should be making the earth-shaking observation about bareness—since only Shearer can give it a particular twist—an interesting twist. From conversations overheard between her and Herbert, it's clear Shearer favors leotard-bareness, even if it does spring from thriftiness gone wild. A thin style, her Master—what *is* his name?—used to call it. And Shearer loved nothing better than the thinness of her—and everybody else's—high-protein pelvic thrusts.

Second, why has it taken so long for Jean to perceive that everybody, except her, Ethan and Cook, are stark naked? Hysterical blindness?—akin to what somebody experienced (who?) in that Parnassus Avenue amphitheater centuries ago. As he moves toward them in full erection, Post runs pensive—yes, *pensive*—fingers through the still jet black satyr-thick hair on his pale chest. Pritchard and Margo (fully clothed)—

(So they weren't in any of the vehicles or maybe they were and decided to make a fast getaway. And who's to say she and Ethan didn't cross paths with them on Milpas Street, under a lollipop palm or two getting too big for their britches?) Margo and Pritchard (it looks as if he's about to go blind, like . . . like . . . like medical student . . . med student . . . Post centuries ago! it was he who blacked out in that now notorious Parnassus Avenue ampitheater! so, Jean's cured at last of her hysterical amnesia if not of her blindness)—Margo and Pritchard hover in the background, lamenting (like Paolo and Francesca)—or rather (places, POV people!) *seeming to lament*—their too seemly youth, as evoked by this hyperabundance of stiff dicks and uplifted tits and asses lit expertly from below. Why, not so very long ago she had a naturally growing pubic loincloth—a merkin—at least as opulent as the one being flaunted by prettily pouting Rudee Silicone-Vallee over there by the Harpy—so opulent in fact it could pass for an apron or (if it comes to that) even a tutu. But only a few minutes are required for Jean to get her feet wet, so to speak—that is, to get bored. Since, when push comes to shove (is that the right expression? she asks defiantly), what do the glueings and unglueings of the deployers—the bran-dishers—of these tits, asses, hairy chests, and cocks with pre-cum at their tip, among other sale items—what are they but the time-honored building blocks of that old warhorse The Orgy Sequence—the caryatids of its Parthenon, so to speak—to which, ever since the Greenwich Avenue years, events have been leading up as their only conceivable (and since this is CA, organically grown) consummation? though she *is* a wee bit disappointed at the speed of her desensitization since, fact of the matter is, Post has begun to excite her. It isn't just the hard-on: there are plenty of those to go around even if most don't quite measure up—no, not by a long shot. What *gets her creative juices flowing* (why does this phrase's obscene smarminess—its insufferable hale-and-heart-iness—its imagistic reduction of creation [whose essence must be morbid, destructive, or why bother?] to just another lush hormonal imbalance—why does it offend her—*her*, of all people—an avowed non-creator?)—what gets her going is his mock-quizzical detachment from its—the hard-on's—bump-kin bravado (he and his hard-on just aren't on the same wavelength and each is the better for it)—what gets Jean Rhys going is a penetrant gaze which assures her that no matter how wondrous the thing may appear to bystanders, it's just another incarnation of an old trophy commemorating—though never in a million years worth the price paid for it in blood, sweat and crocodile tears—far too many willed triumphs over defeat and retroactively cunning manip-ulations of disaster—it's nothing more than the wondrously inexpressive sig-nifier of a disjunction between body and soul that no pineal—even if ordered via Amazon Prime—can remedy. In short, the thinking man's hard-on. But a thinking infinitely more potent than Viagra because the thinking's all about *disjunction*—a word that's, granted, way too fancy for its own good—but that still manages to resonate totemically for all those who cherish the moments when things insist on turning out to be not what they seem. "On my way out," he says (wait a minute! Jean's confused and can't afford to be: does he mean, on his way out just now, or ages ago?)—his stock still rising as fast as (Kenneth Anger's) *Scorpio's*—"I suddenly realized the most important part of our work—to enact the Pornographic Text with all the trimmings—has been left grossly undone. Since wherever that Text goes, Invidicum—Invidicum as *the* cure for Envy—will follow. So far it's been all talk and no action—as my detractors are (after inspecting the entrails of my eloquence) all too happy to point out." In response to Post's full bow before the Text's progenitor, Margo (evidently still reeling from Post's oh so many viciously one-note unflattering depictions of her late husband—but "evidently" to *whom*?) grimly lifts a deprecating finger to signify that her better half is in no condition to suffer, much less acknowledge, the slings and arrows of deference (or hasn't he happened to notice the drool on Pritchard's bowtie?). But is it concern for her current mate that accounts for this business of stopping Post's eloquence dead in its tracks or does it stem instead from the thirst to pay him back—with her destructive juices flowing full-bore—for those depictions of the dear departed? Read on.

But as there's no devil in Post's flesh (his "philosophy"—like *Shadow of a Doubt*'s Uncle Charlie's—is strictly, *Look but don't touch*) Jean has no choice but to turn her attention elsewhere (in so doing, she rightly or wrongly smells a blessing in disguise)—no choice but to become aware that Cook, still fully clothed and no less exciting (in other words, even more so) for all that, is taking his sweet time (thereby doing Mae proud) about giving his undivided attention to undressing her ocularly (even if enough time has passed behind the scenes and on the scene to make imminent fusion plausible). For he clearly relishes postponement—knows nothing of the lesser male's need to hurry lest impotence rob him of his pleasure (and in the case of such a male a very one-sided pleasure at that—a defective pleasure—since the only pleasure worth taking must be a mere byproduct—a residuum—of the lady's [even the word—*lady*—excites him]). The true male treats his own pleasure as at best a throwaway (*who is doing the thinking here?*). Almost bored by the certainty that when called upon he'll perform as usual superbly, is it any wonder that at every stage of the game he rates the *prospect* of ultimately giving way higher than actual surrender and prefers to keep the Ultimate—that harpie—at arm's length? All of which offers definitive proof of what from the very start she's refused to accept—for what would then become of Ethan and her soon-to-be-ex-?—namely, that Cook represents the rarest kind of commodity in our pursy times, a thoroughbred heterosexual, since it clearly isn't his own nakedness (and the thrill of flaunting it) but the lady's—and the lady herself—that is driving him hog-wild. Though why must he, Jean grumbles, be taking his sweet time about bringing things to a head now that all but the last of her seven veils have been shed? Must his gaze, for example, be so passionless, so . . . interrogative, where her buttocks are concerned as if the only thing that mattered was to determine (based on texture, or what some nutty Frenchman has referred to, even more nuttily, as *the grain of the ass*) what would be the quicker means—once he was deep inside and still thrusting, always thrusting—of tipping the scales of his frenzy toward discharge (and thereby enabling him to get back to and on with the infinitely more urgent business of salvaging the trial; or financing its incidentals; or [a big draw for risk-addicted angels] sabotaging it; or perpetrating a little of all three so as to keep future shareholders—classes A, B, C *and* D—interested, if not entirely satisfied)—to determine what would be quicker, fondling No. 1 or No. 2? Though from the way the fingers of said gaze further deliberate, it's evident they aren't ruling out the possibility that there may well be a very Cubistic buttock No. 3 or even 4 or 5 waiting coyly in the wings. A bit unnerved by what he senses to be Jean's impatience (the modest self-assertion of upraised breasts does more than just move him: like Lakmé's "Bell Song," it undoes him), and therefore making quick work of the preliminaries in order to bracelet neck tenderly but firmly with squat thumbs and lithe forefingers (like the chevalier he aspires to be or, as some might say, already is), Cook bends her over as far as she can go in order—and it's a *tall* order—to do (whether he knows it or not) his Textual duty and save her from the Envy that's consuming her. How? Well, by skimming the walls of her cleft with the slithering tip of his cock but entering for good only once he's managed through sleight of hand (it's thinkable but is it doable?) to settle each testicle atop its very own—its divinely rightful cheek. That's how.

Having just been privy to what he's never before witnessed *much less imagined* [*sic*], i.e., cock's assertion, and without any coaching from its landlord, of an *intention*, in this case, the intention to perversely refrain, until further notice, from doing what it does best, namely, penetrate a humid cunt (meaning it's not some garden-variety amateur but a professional operating at a level of sophistication high enough to be called cognitive)—having just been privy to a veritable transmogrification of matter into mind and back again—Borkman, Jr., a satcheled schoolboy at heart—a prep school imp whose blazer is forever setting itself ablaze from one end of Park Avenue to the other with dreams of glory—is so overpowered as to be left with no alternative but to try his hand at masturbating away all the virulent excitement generated by this miracle. But, as John Milton might say, does he have enough of the stuff of orgasms still in stock (why Milton? well, why *not* Milton?[129])? Today, after all, has been a stressful day and for such stress as his there is only one outlet. But why, after just a few shared whispers with, of all people, Mary Johnstone, should he now be seen scurrying, balls in hand, toward the apparently unpeopled balcony? Mary Johnstone—the Bunker's self-appointed sexologist-in-residence (with enough beauty marks on her thighs to prove it) and de facto leader of that pack of Swift-Boaters who—as is becoming increasingly clear and in defiance of all contention to the contrary—not only brought Death into Bunkerworld and all our Woe but succeeded, with of course a bit of backing from the Brothers Koch (Larry, Curly, Moe and the unspeakable David H. and Charles), in blocking Cantor's ascent to the Presidency though on the basis not so much of his sexuality as of an ambition deemed (like the courageous anti-war stance of Vietnam vet Kerry) way too "over the top" (with which verdict his silence—like, alas, the politically pusillanimous vet's—has made the fatal error of concurring). But why the scurrying? After all, in the Valley, in-public jerk-offs, communal or otherwise, are as routine as brainstorming sessions motored by artisanal non-alcoholic beer and a far more dependable source by and large of what hip financial analysts just love

---

[129]At least, why not the Milton who relished the serpent's "hairy mane terrific"—who burned in lust with Adam and Eve—who could attest more eloquently than either to the potency of their "amorous intent"?

to refer to (when they have nothing better to do) as *cognitive seed capital*. Can it be that she's managed to convince Little Marco Borkman, Ethan wonders as he sloughs his second skin and good riddance, that it isn't the open-access masturbation per se that will destroy his career *as we speak* (though orgies, like Don Juans, do have their protocol, and it can be a pretty strict one) but the *way* he masturbates? Well, yes, who in their right mind wouldn't concede that it's very far from typical—even among the practitioners in this cutting-edge sort of crowd—to cross one leg uncomfortably over the other, maneuver one's dick into place just above the vise of the thighs, then go on tightening while, with the lower part of the right forearm, striking the shaft unrelentingly so as to maximize through such constraint—since art is born of constraint and dies of liberty—the intensity of its spasms? And if he keeps this up then Don't Blame Mary if, say, twenty or thirty years hence, some shrew or shrike of a wife assures him—without (unkindest cut of all!) asking for a divorce—that it's precisely because he jerked off in just such a way and in just such an ambience and wouldn't listen to reason that he lost his One and Only Chance to make white-shoe Partner in the law firm called Life.

Or, looking on the bright side, maybe all of Bunkerworld's troubles will, someday soon, be layable without let at the doorstep of Little Marco B's having just figured out, like Ethan way ahead of him (but mum's the word, bub), *but without having the courage to spill the beans and save the Republic*, that pseudonymous Mary is in fact Betsy DaVos, The Rump's quick pick for Sec of Education, sent here to take the temperature of America's Future and tweet her lowdown back to Mar-a-Lago before the New Year is stripped bare of its dignity; and a "fierce advocate" of The Voucher System, whereby kids, starting with the pre-K set, will have the legal right to steer everybody's tax dollars toward god-fearing for-profit-loving private schools. In the great tradition of Tom MacPrice, also a voucheroid and The Big R's sure-to-be Sec of Health, who'd like nothing better (read his pursy-prissy-piggish lips!) than to steer the death's-door elderly away from Medicare, Medicaid, Social Security and other free lunches worthy only of welfare royalty, toward the god-given right to name their own poison. Because when you're at death's door, and seven or ninety-seven to boot, what you crave most is (contrary to popular belief) not immediate care, cure, CAT scans, chemo, containment, but the right to pore at leisure over all that fine print (and to hell with the tumor's tick-tock) in whose wide-open spaces are buried a thousand and one free-market options for premature burial, which is pretty much all there will be to pore over once fatcats like MacVos and DaPrice and fellow gravy-trainers start drafting their prospectuses. But whatever Little Borkman has or hasn't figured out, he's clearly a lost cause, at least for the moment, what with the weight of the entire history-of-masturbation-as-an-art-form on his shoulders—so lost that he may very well elect to jump off the balcony rather than proceed with his harpyish wanking astraddle its parapet. So. As Ethan, in contrast, seems to have no prior engagements, she signals her willingness to let him beg to call her Mary Jo. But it quickly becomes obvious there are sure to be too many "issues" associated with his pint-sized organ—more like an organelle, if you ask her (for starters, get a load of all those lilies-of-the-valley on his discarded boxers)—way too many issues to permit their hookup to be anything but a strictly professional one. Having extricated himself—more graciously, he decides, than this would-be babe's shilly-shallying warrants—Ethan staggers off under the dead weight of wonderment: might those beauty marks be by any chance cancerous?

But can such an outsize ambition—conception—i.e., enacting the Text—be realized? Post has no idea. Are they up to—are they willing to make the sacrifices required to execute—contortions so complex? Even if it's solely their achievement of precisely those contortions and those contortions alone that has the power to usher in the whirlwind known as Cure? Still no idea. (Shearer isn't sure she'd have been up to them even in her *Bugaku/Ivesiana/ Agon* heyday. That's why she should have gotten into one of the vehicles and stayed put and lain low. Very low.) In any case, he'll keep his hand—or rather, his glans—in. And he does exactly that by moisturizing Jean's with his own. For Jean is currently his. (Ruthless Cook is, as it turns out, after bigger game [now that Jean's taught him all he knows and vice versa] and spurned Ethan is off in some corner moping, whether from relief [he never knew being jilted could feel so good: it all depends, he guesses, on who's doing the honors] or from disappointment has yet to be determined. But it's to Jean's exasperation at Cook's unyielding tentativeness [betokening a manfulness almost Galilean in its Technicolor purity] that Post should feel most indebted since it's what drove her to throw the last of those seven veils to the wind. Cook's tenta-tiveness, she discovered, only intensified with his surrender: indeed, never was he less hers than when thrusting and plunging ever more deeply, slowly, gracefully, than any of his predecessors [or is this just another case where the Master—the Guy Who's Running the Show on a shoestring budget—feels obliged to jump hyperbolically through hoops of paradox—to play the neg-ative-feedback card for all it's worth—in order to keep his clientele on the edge of their seats?].) Or maybe the very thing that excites Post (but don't let him know you know), the very thing that keeps him going and makes life worth living, is the non-realizability of a conception that is neither his nor Pritchard's nor Walser's nor Stifter's but a public good in which everybody has a major stake—why, it excites him so much he just wants to lie down on his back and, impaling her belly to belly, pretend the Chandleresque sluttish sister from Sullivan Street is about to make it a threesome. Though maybe the conception would be realizable if only he didn't insist on enlisting the services of that old battleaxe Language to describe it—to circumscribe it—to take it in hand—to let its cat out of the bag—since this entails the inevitable passage through Her defiles—Her dire straits—and the all-too-predictable deforma-tion of meaning (though does meaning exist before She sees fit to deform it?) so as to ensure conformity with Her own outsize ambition—which is to achieve mathematical elegance without violating the dictates of that meaning. Or maybe the *sentencing* of the conception and in such a way as to make all realization impossible—nay (yeah, *nay*), even the conception's formulation as the very embodiment of its own impossibility—can be laid at the door-step of that Next Big Thing everybody refuses to start babbling about. As it so happens, the Master cum Guy Running the Show (*all of* them—*and, let's face it, I'm no different—ingeniously invoke this fall guy to serve their needs,* Post acknowledges ruefully, *when things seem not to be going as was promised at the time we signed up for active duty*) has had a not-all-that-sudden craving to compel Post to undergo His own agonies of sexual stalemate firsthand. But not because—or rather not *just* because—He's a misery-loves-company kind of Guy who never misses a trick when it comes to putting a little flesh on the bare bones of begrudgery—not *just* because he likes to overload his creations with all sorts of fictive perfections so He can cut them down to size (*The patient is hallucinating! Intraperitoneal injection of thirty-two hundred milligrams of hot-off-the-press Invidicum, Nurse, and please hurry!*)—not *just* because there are times, though few and far between, when His sexually stalemated solitude becomes intolerable. There are any number of other reasons, not the least of which is that Sex—unlike a project as cerebral as the enactment of a Pornographic Text—Sells Like Hotcakes. And Sexual Dysphoria Sells Even Hotter. (Since everybody cultivates—contracts—disseminates it —if only as a matter of honor. Take Post, for example: he craves a three-way—a Trio worthy of Archduke Rudolf—even when he has the perfect pas de deux at his fingertips. Not to mention Cook: from "fear of intimacy" he's fleeing what could still turn out to be the love of his life. And while we're at it, what about Narr? he's allowed a sexologiste manquée—bent on retaliation for having been unmasked as a voucher-obsessed kleptocrat whose sociopathic brother happens to be allied with the Wagner Group—to defame an organ that is, if anything, *over*sized and then some. Which implies that the desire of each—all regular guys who pride themselves on desiring only what, when and where they feel like desiring—is not in fact his but Another's.) No wonder, then, that as a showman on the order of P.T. Barnum, the Master should jump at the opportunity to spice up this Sequence for popular consumption by transforming his—Post's—rarefied and arcane excitement at being hindered from realizing the Text, into meat-and-potatoes erotomania stopped dead in its muddy tracks.

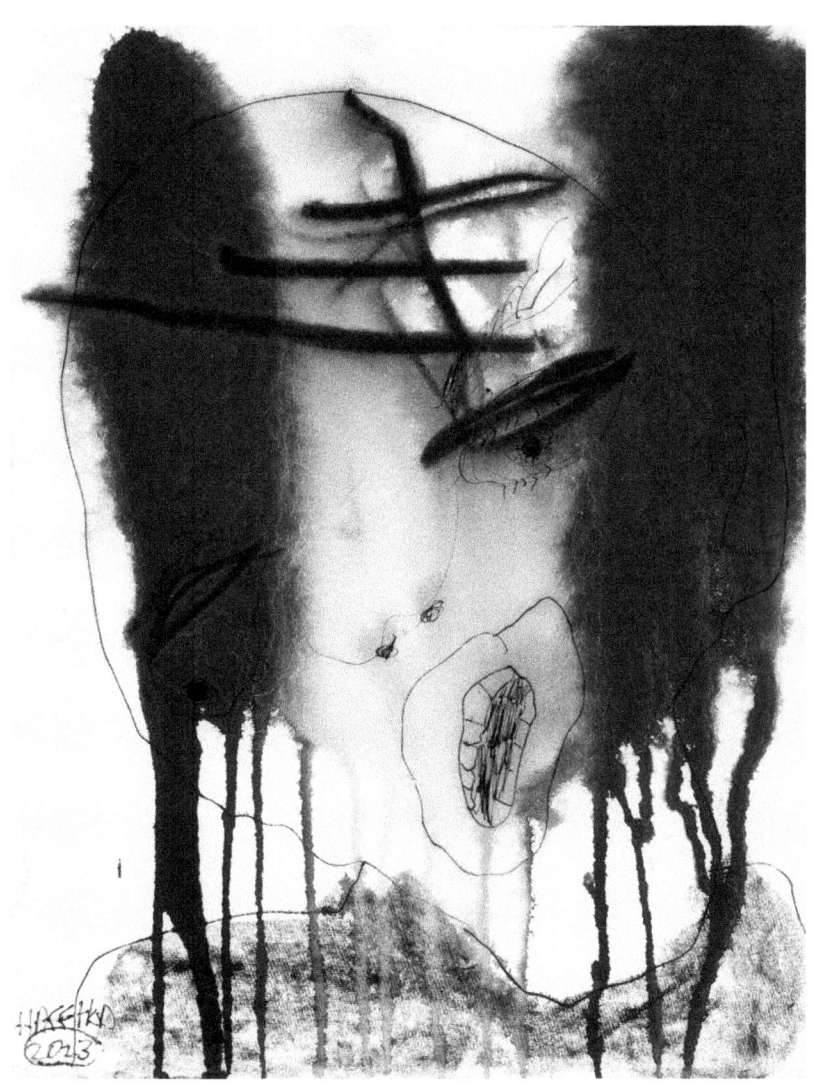

CHAPTER FORTY-EIGHT

Cook sees no other—better—way to get Post to cast off his manacles, mind-forged or otherwise—to shuffle off the mortal coil of language which has this bad habit of transmogrifying the specific into the general without begging permission—than to assert as boldly as possible that what they've really done—and more power to them—is take a sabbatical from kowtowing to the Guy Running the Show (with a view to rehabilitating the substantial form of that most maligned of subgenres: pornography). So at last I'm beginning, Jean thinks, to understand everything that Pritch, probably out of respect for the ladies, left out. Meaning the more she allows herself to be assaulted by thoughts about the ever-shifting engagement of unremarkable bodies rendered spectacularly agile by those strangest of bedfellows—though no stranger than any others—lust and grim professionalism, the less equipped does she feel to articulate those thoughts—assuming, that is, they can ever *be* articulated. And, clothed or not, why shouldn't they? Cook asks—cutting her off from herself (always welcome, that) and not a minute too soon—have shifted gears, even at this late date so as to focus—really focus (without feeling obliged to drag in the same old legitimating shop talk about the Envy Cure)—on the Big P. It's not like there are competing claims on anyone's attention during this, the penultimate, or maybe even the final stage of their trek through the hoary hinterlands of Pharma, Big and Little. "In any case, for all the sidetracking, the subject never *really* changes—the digressive risks we take are all fake—let's face it—we're incapable of digressing from ourselves or we wouldn't be in this fix—coherent in spite of ourselves, that's what we are. And might somebody be willing to venture a guess how and why?" Re-entering as if on cue, and immeasurably refreshed by his unnatural practices out on the balcony, Borkman, Jr. (he seems to have outgrown his Little Marco sailor suit), cries out, "Because our subject is the impossibility of fixing a subject. At first it seemed to be—" "Hush!" Margo counter-cries. "It still is and will always remain— If not, then I will have come all this way for nothing." "What he means is that with so many start-ups on the scene hawking so many new dynamics, the Invidicum machine, as bright a contraption as it may have seemed in years past—" No matter that Jean looks as if she thought Post had carried his paternal protectiveness a bit too far. Noting the perfect harmony in alignment *à la Sterne* that subsists between nose and cock on the basis of size, shape and venation (both are meaty but finely chiseled) and with what teasing accuracy the former portends the latter down to the very last detail, she can understand why at the first sight of him fully clothed there was such teasing agony in the very crux of her.

Shearer doesn't get it. (And she knows by not getting it she's giving new meaning to the term *slow learner*. No matter, she's been called worse [or has she?].) *No matter how hard she tries*, she doesn't get why the fact that they're coherent in spite of themselves (but isn't that true of everybody?) is the reason for their being *in the fix they're in*—the Envy fix presumably. And why, if Envy turns out not to be the most expensive item on the menu, will Margo have come *all this long way for nothing*? And has she, Shearer, really tried *all that hard* to *get it* as her dejection claims? Why, it's almost as if Herbert's disincarnation of Mr. B. has picked these phrases out of a hat or as if the hat has picked B because He relishes the way their shrill sonority spices up a particularly fleeting context—the ever-shrinking neighborhood in a topological space gone wild—by giving it a hint of story—and not just any old story but a story unfolding at fever pitch. But with the real spice coming of course from the phrases' not quite fitting the context. And what's more dramatic—what's more lifelike—no, more than lifelike: true to life—than a not-quite-fit? Proof, in other words, that a real story can do without a storyline—survives best on bits and pieces of driftwood—is most successful in depicting pain and articulating the laws of its defragmentation when in brute survival mode—can in fact make brute survival the worthiest target not just of wonder but of wonderment. And, come to think of it, didn't *her* Mr. B. use pure movement—movement packets—to give the best account of the story he refused—was contracted upon pain of death not to tell? Movements like that whiplash change of direction in *Liebeslieder Walzer* which ends up, improbably (hence, poetically) depositing the head of one of the four female dancers on her partner's shoulder. Or the waltz girl's collapse at the end of the third movement of *Serenade*. And speaking of *Serenade*, what wouldn't she give to be inside It—to be anywhere but here?—not as a performer (not even as the waltz girl who, a real abnegation freak, is apotheosized—and the ballet along with her—by four pallbearers)—but as a spectator. What wouldn't she give to be able to re-enter its world the way projectionist Sherlock, Jr., breaches (but unlike him, unejectably) the movie screen? Yes, it's Shearer who's thinking all this (and why not? 'cause among other things she's a fan of stoically handsome Buster—sometimes dreams about him—in minstrelizing poker face, if you must know—as the uxorious Cavalier [Don Ottavio's blood brother] to her Sanguinic).

But despite Sterne's noblest efforts, Post's nose and cock are slow-fading, along with all those voices at each other's throats (clearly, polemic, like subterfuge, is done), not to mention whatever resentment has lingered at being manhandled, then summarily abandoned, by him—or was it Cook who did the manhandling? In any case (*in any case:* blessed phrase which, by airily dismissing the immediately preceding chatter as irrelevant, shows just how nakedly revelatory that chatter really is), Jean's willing to let bygones be bygones. What matters, now that he's positioned his buttocks where she can keep an eye on them, is Cook and Cook alone (who says underlings can't be mesmerizing when sufficiently provoked into quiescence?). Merely from observing the systole-diastole—all right then, the *tsimtsum*—of their musculature as he squats, she's sure they're running their own crazy gamut of emotions, even if it's just from A to B. She could cry salty tears—where has she been in all these years? Why, Cook's butt is worth more than all the pricks in the house—in all of Santa Barbara—in the whole of the Golden State, with NYC thrown in for good measure (did its twoforthepriceofone-ness have anything to do with clinching this deal?). Pricks, she concedes, are a mere decoy—stalking-horse—en route to maleness—can never do justice to maleness—have nothing to do with it, not really. *For either maleness is a barred femaleness, or it's nothing,* croons Jean in the key of B-sharp major, thereby making the life-or-death pronouncements of the Big Boys on Subject M/F her very own—sort of (she's still a bit off-key and therefore has a ways to go).

She decides that as a package, Cook's buttocks most resemble those of the rearward-looking angel in the right lunette of the *Last Judgment* who, over-heated from all that shifting of the Flagellation column's Doric capital toward the right, can surely be excused for lowering his shorts for a breath of fresh, that is, as long as he honors the Third Law of Softcore which means stopping tantalizingly short of full disclosure. But considered separately: The right but-tock evokes most that of the angel in the left lunette, also rearwood-looking (hands locked under the crossbar of the Cross, with left forefinger pointing dreamily yet significatively down), whose "wide spindrift gaz[ing] toward paradise" belies all the sweaty assistance he provides in getting It rotated right by bending his knee and thereby tautening the muscles underpinning the transition of underthigh into buttock (and, unconsciously of course, making the flesh in question look and smell good enough to eat). While what his left buttock most resembles is that of the *ignudo* in the Chapel's seventh bay who (hydrophobic profile eye focused alarmedly sideways) willingly under-goes all the exquisite torments of the rack-whose-name-is-contrapposto just to be able to tauten the very same muscles to the very same effect. So how, will you tell me, does it suddenly become so clear that (with all due respect to Michelangelo) what Cook's buttocks most evoke—invoke—convoke—are those of Frédéric Bazile's Fisherman with a Net, supreme crush of Jean's coed days? (Though a case, albeit slender, can surely be made for the profiled pair belonging to Nikolai Abraham Abildgaard's Wounded Philoctetes and, in tandem (given the appropriateness of the subject), for their cleft—that is to say, for Everyman's—as embodiment of His deepest psychic fissure.) Like the Fisherman (whose contrappostal division of attention between a bit of net-related stage business and some thing outside the frame allows for the hoisted tensing of what resembles nothing so much as the perfectly contoured cusps of a walnut), Cook, too, has his hands full, what with toying with his BVDs and searching for a stool while trying to fix his attention on Margo and Net-ta's Gorgonly connivance—and all this to generate the gluteal tension so dear to the hearts of erotomaniacs (albeit of a very special type) everywhere. Of course she—Jean—mustn't give short shrift to what may very well turn out to be the vainglorious villain of the piece, i.e., the panoply of moist black tendrils defining with a draughtsman's rough delicacy the climactic line of *his* psychic fissure (with some even spreading out, as a bonus for the extra-faithful, over the globes themselves), by virtue of which he easily outdoes all his forbears. Still, as with his competitors, so much of the magic is worked by an apparent absence of all solicitation, the delectability of the commodity at stake being geometrically proportional to the owner's indifference to—disavowal of—its effect (given the far more manly, manful matters demanding his immediate attention). But this self-repudiation brings her no closer to making the thing ostensibly repudiated her very own. Herein lies Jean's—or any other self-dis-respecting fetishist's—predicament, on whose iffy preservation depends nothing less than the preservation of selfhood—in this case consisting, for the moment, in her own patented brew of tenderness and lust.

Yet is she any closer now to understanding why his ass wields this "fearsome power"? Much much further, in fact, since the equilibrium, however tenuous, generated by her quasi lucidity is not conducive to any further investigative immersion, at least for now, in the medium of her excruciation (right: *equilibrium-tenuous-lucidity-conducive—immersion:* they're all needed: no other words will do and why should they? in their sticking together through thick and thin—purely on behalf of opaqueness, some will hasten to claim—lies the strength—the recyclability—of polysyllables). Never mind that, as she now knows better than anybody, the medium's corrosiveness makes the search for its truth a flagrant impracticality.

In the nick of time, Jean's focus on this worrisome—one might say unsettling—question is blunted by the encroachment of a welter of voices to which she can't begin to attach faces, so starkly are the otherwise giveaway tonalities overshadowed by the outrageousness of their utterances. Fashionable opinions and all the more dangerous for being so. Opinions no self-respecting orgiast should be caught dead spouting, not even the ones whose vacuity finds itself in direst need of anything—anything!—that can pass for a figleaf. Yet here they are rummaging through the heap as among so many *shmattes* on an Orchard Street sidewalk—the Orchard Street, naturally, of 100 app-free years ago not today's oh-so-gentrified Horseshit Street (Rue Verger de la merde, to you, my frenchifiable friend) with its sidewalk cafés where the filthy rich rub elbows, thrillingly, with the just plain filthy. And all the time they're muttering "fuck" or if not "fuck," then one of its kissing cousins—"cunt" or "cock" or (most shocking of all) "out-of-gender experience," no doubt, to give themselves some kind of foothold in the welter. She does want to ask at least one of them (what about the bon vivant who looks—who's trying to look—as if he just staggered, unattached and vomit-hungry, out of a Second Avenue bar?) how much right-minded animalism can possibly be left, after so much animalism of language, for the sex act itself. Or maybe that's the whole point—to ensure (from a kind of morbid prudery) there's nothing left for the act except joylessness—or exhaustion—or reinvention. In any case, as Jean sees it—and she sees (convergence insufficiency notwithstanding) pretty far when she wants to—for as long as their jam session in the lavat'ry of language lasts they inhabit a commonalty of equals where soul masks and social distancing are forbidden and Envy has no place (she envies them their habitation but just from afar): anybody who mutters "fuck" or "cock" or "cunt" becomes for the duration of the mutterance all men and all women. (Though whether this sleight of hand may be viewed as the launching pad toward acquisition of a unique identity by those who've never had one, or as a perverse act of self-dissolution by those who've never had to leave home without one, Jean leaves it up to her biographer to determine. Yes, her *biographer*, for she now intends nothing less than to make herself famous. But first, all traces of native talent need to be suppressed since she doesn't want to end up competing with anything or anyone—least of all with herself—for the attention of the public. Nothing must be allowed to outshine—outpace—the craving for fame.

Craving hereby replaces talent, which is plebeian, vulgar [so when all is said and done, she's fit to stand tall between Marcel Duchamp and George Cukor's Gladys Glover on the bread line to greatness]. Nothing must get in the way of her heroic shot [the punier the talent, the greater the heroism] at the brass ring—least of all a reliance on the crutch of *sterling credentials*, the stock in trade of self-styled coastal elites, especially of the Federalist Society variety.)

Indeed—as somebody smart (Mr. Smith?) once said, in her hearing, to somebody even smarter (Newt?), We're all equal on the level of language, everybody's subject to its traps—prey to its vagaries—forced to stuff the flab of any thought packet into the corset of its wordflow—and anybody, however smart, is, as we know, only as good as his last packet. Nobody's less deducible than anybody else. Why, where wordflow is concerned, a guy like Heidegger has no edge on Tom Clancy. But don't take my word for it: turn on ESPN and watch as Tom (Tom!) wrestles Marty to the mat. This snapshot of Newt and Smith makes Jean, condemned as she is to the status of eternal tourist, envy them (the members of the cocks-and-cunts commonalty, that is, although she could see her way clear to making some room for Tom and Marty) even more—but the consensus within has determined that it's no longer *just from afar* (as she put it before crossing the Rubicon separating the present paragraph from its predecessor). She envies them up front—right under their noses—she envies them so much because they're not alone—they're with their own kind. But more to the point, they, or . . . or . . . or . . . Whoever (no avoiding infection with the Herbert bacillus) has lassoed them into participation, hopes that by dint of repetition of the same accredited obscenities—and not just any old repetition but repetition refracted through their own resistance to being heard—they'll create exactly the telltale context He sorely needs. A context that, where character and similarly beautiful fantasms are concerned, blatantly valorizes brute duration over creative evolution. The buck of mimesis—a simpering Fidelity to Life, the biggest fiction of them all except for the Lord your God—stops here—and now—with the Master.

"The Lord your God . . . the Lord our God." Given her highly proper upbringing, Jean is understandably ashamed of having just snuck in here under false pretenses. Even if she hasn't. (It's just that in such a place as this, simply being there is identical and at every moment to *having just snuck in under false pretenses*.) She's ashamed to be worshiping (however meditatively) in this chapel whose parishioners are devotionally hooked on organ-grinding and where a special class of body parts is King. But something grates against the shame. Shouldn't it be *the others*, the hideously upright respectables who in the "house of worship" of their choice routinely beg *their* Malefactor—their universal Perpetrator of Horror (incarnated in their flavor of choice)—to go on sparing them—shouldn't they be the ones sneaking in under cover of darkness instead of strutting through the chapel's pearly gates at high noon with their collective head held high? Isn't it they instead of the innocent frequenters of whorehouses and peep shows and public toilets who should be feeling a bit queasy about the shameless abasement before the Evil One whom they actually believe has nothing more heinous to do than hold their preciously grubby little fate in the clawed and hairy palm of his hand? And who, adding insult to injury, unloads his horrors unthinkingly (like a pigeon greedily defecating in homage to its own boredom)—inflicts unbearable-because-bearable suffering purely at random and purely to trigger, in this minute's cropload of the flayed, invidious execration of the unflayed? But in outraged response to what she pridelessly takes to be a desperately clever defense Jean's quick enough on the prolepsis trigger to be able to say (before anybody else can): You, Jean Rhys, are worse than shameful—worse than shameless—you're an . . . adolescent.

Oh, what does it all mean? and what's going to happen now? Jean wonders out loud (as only a Heroine—the betrayed wife, say, in Katherine Mansfield's story "Bliss"—can be made to wonder)—so loudly she can't hear herself think. Clearly all diegetic (now where did that word come from?)—all diegetic bets are off, until further notice. (That's right, *diegetic*: d-i-e-g-e-t-i-c. You—yes, you there, in the fourth ring, slouching across what used to be my seat, that is, before I broke a leg or two in an ingeniously devised failed suicide attempt and the city shut down in a show of support and for what precisely if not a speedy return to the New York State Theater [you'll never get me to call it—as renamed—the *David H. Crotch* Theater—never] where my learned transports as an audience member were routinely observed *to outshine the dancers'*— you—yes, you—you heard me right the first time. Oh, so I'm a pretentious jackass, am I? Well, fuck you: now how's that for foursquare pretentiousness?) It sounds as if the Master (turning to Jean, he says, *Pay that fourth-ringer no heed, dearie*) was having a long-overdue showdown with the Guy Who's Running the Show—and it looks as if she's managed to get herself caught in the crossfire. *And why* (she wonders even more loudly), *out of the blue, adding insult to injury, am I now privy (!) to such a spectacle as this?* the spectacle in question being no less than an around-the-block-long line for the john, which has materialized, evidently, through that very conjunction of unnoticed minute operations Liepnits, trademark pointer in hand (though she hates to give the old fart credit), kept babbling about at part I A of his Amygdala Seminar (standing room only), entitled "Envy buildup and its suppurative sequelae." Still, what appalls her is not so much (*a*) the generalized proximity of dicks to butts, prolapsing in some cases into outright body contact (on the contrary, she's soothed by the slapsticky carnivalesque charm of the whole configuration), as (*b*) the fact that the matter of size is rearing its ugly head at every turn which accounts for the prevailing atmosphere of rank competitiveness. For how can she help noticing all the sidelong glances aimed at sizing up the *stiffness* of the competition? although judging from the way even the tiniest stirrings of tumescence immediately get nipped in the bud, stiffness is clearly frowned upon, as no doubt both a symptom of non-normal excitement (never mind that normality is the most overrated of minor vices) and a proof of cheating (which implies that if every dick in the house does end up getting rated officially then measurement, following long custom established just this minute, needs to be of length in the resting state). Never in a million years would Jean have pegged this dump as a venue conducive to such goings-on though, come to think of it, wasn't she assigned some paper in *Science* or was it *Nature*? (as required background reading for the very Seminar mentioned above) indicating that the earliest recorded outbreak of Envy had occurred (not far from Stonehenge or was it Easter Island?) in similar conditions—none in fact more fertile in opportunity for invidious comparisons which, under proper clinical supervision, can prove (to quote the authors quoting the scrawl on some megalith) *homeopathic to the hilt*?

Quickly enough Jean decides that the queue resembles (this time taking a dog-eared page not from some high-falutin' journal but, far more reliably, from Shearer's playbook at which she's had her share of a glimpse or two) nothing so much as the conga line of meticulously wobbling *ingénues* and even wobblier *ingénus* which forms midway through Ashton-Meyerbeer's *Les Patineurs*—and who should know better than she? Why, only two or three days ago, up at Mother Bunker's, she was inveigled into watching the just-re-leased DVD of this ballet (a masterpiece) by her friend. For they *were* friends, weren't they? Or is Whoever's Running the Show forcing her to think "friend" (*forcing her?* horror of horrors! she sounds exactly like Herbert, crazy Herbert, but who from the way things are going may very well end up being, in a by-in-vitation-only anointment on Stearns Wharf, *not-so-crazily* proclaimed tribe Visionary)—forcing her, in order to (*a*) avert commission of one of the car-dinal sins of StoryThink (maybe *the* cardinal sin—or is that just typical Who-ever-style mega-hype?), to wit, clumsy repetition of somebody's name before a sufficient number of intervening syllables have been deployed to work their memory-deadening magic; and (*b*) thereby ensure that friendship remains what it was meant to be, a mere quirk of the laws of syntax. If so, then she's already tired of playing by the rules of His game even if Herbert (based on her own testimony which everybody dutifully discounts, at least publicly) has far more reason to complain although, oddly enough, she does so less and less. Can she have actually fallen, irrevocably, for the old creep (demiurgic wun-der-fogey or not, he's still a creep—the quintessential creep, to be exact, if only because Jean's thinking makes it so) and in the process maybe even ditched (like so many other women after mating with the devil and giving birth to his own) her budding destiny, which in this case is—was (at least according to the Word on the Street)—to become nothing less than a rising star—an eter-nal rising star—*the* Eternal Rising Star—on the Creative Writing Workshop (and colony) circuit? Jean awakens from her opium dream to discover there are in fact two lines (as at Trader Joe's)—a Sodom of sorts for the menfolk and a Gomorrah for the women. An intern by the look and sound of her—an intern enthralled to be learning the ropes in some hoodie's garage—is ask-ing Borkman, the most implausible of Sodomites (Jean's separated from him by six or seven heads—humorlessly [that is, manfully] flaunting their rogu-ishly self-inflicted baldness), to describe his wife. Fortunately, the Master's eloquence is right there when he needs it most: "The missus can charitably be called a cross between a teratoma and a tarantula—and, in all fairness, the feeling is mutual" (the implication being, as is always the case in encounters of this kind, that the intern is sure to be the furthest thing from such a hybrid). The words make a fast getaway almost before they're completely out of his mouth—a tornado that realizes too late it's ravaged the wrong ghost town—leaving Borkman with his wife, an *innocent victim*, on his hands—a being, by the way, which has done nothing to merit so transfiguring an epithet. Once again he needs and dreads—dreads his need for—the presence of the succubus that is the soon-to-be ex-Mrs. B. For when she isn't around there's a tendency to exhaustively demonize her, as now, beyond reason and reversibility, which exhausts and cancels *him* out (only she can cut the demons down to size—the demon within even more than the demon without). And anyway he owes it to himself to think of the future—the immediate future—i.e., to devote all his energy to remaining intact and proving to this toothsome kid (eavesdroppers of course welcome) that he's greater than the sum of his rancors—and, more to the point, than the sum of the words they've misbegotten.

Of course, even Jean (why *even*?) can imagine the level of pressure exerted on Whoever or (in Melanctha-speak) the Master (hence, e.g., the manic adhesion to the silly Law of/against the Repetition of the Name)—not hard to assume His predicament resembles that described by CEOs earlier in the evening, though how much earlier she won't venture at present to say. Easy to imagine the pressure exerted (*a*) to convince shareholders worldwide that His Start-up—in this case, the Invidicum Story—will continue to grow ever more profitable by the millisecond while (*b*) inevitably concealing something similar to what CEOs conceal under such circumstances, the fact that, say, this will in no small part be owing to the super-high-frequency stock trades—"round-trip" latencies fast approaching zero—conducted on the Secaucus exchange in (soon-to-be) flagrant contravention of NJ law. Which entails ensuring said shareholders, a mean and hungry lot for all their airy endorsement of radical innovation (so long as it can be made to look neoclassical, not to mention classy—or even quaint), that however great the countervailing temptations, through thick and thin He'll not only hew to the party line but grapple it unto His soul with hoops of steel (i.e., if both actions are operable and, if so, compatible). Now, from what Jean has gathered listening to Herbert talk shop with recently acquired writer chums around the campfire (her practice of the fine art of networking is advancing by leaps and bounds), said party line enjoins that if a story goes according to plan and a given character gets himself properly sucked into the wordflow which is to be his native element and thus properly trapped in a maze of ever-proliferating relationships and of the actions perpetrated by the parties thereto, he should then expect to be on call—invocable 24/11—and invoked—in any number of ways besides by name (the line of least resistance). So to more than summarize (as the marshmallows and hot dogs crackle): When a bona fide character gets himself sucked into a bona fide story cranked out by a bona fide story start-up (which is how things unfold in Masterland, or so His investors need to believe and go on believing), then it is understood to follow, as the night the day, that said character has collaterally signed himself over to the ever-expanding forces of entanglement in a web of interbreeding self-synonymizations (through which the teller of the story secures his purchase on its Manley cliffs of fall)—and the more the merrier. What better measure, after all, of a start-up's overall capitalization? In this regard, then, the name *Shearer*, for example, becomes the bearer's mere ticket of admission—merest right of passage—into the fray. Once admitted, Shearer—or *Shearer* (same difference)—begins at once, and as duly contracted, to be subjected to every trick up the Master's sleeve for transforming her into nothing less than an untidy sum of synonyms (all of them an organic outcome of participation in the life of the wordflow), one being "Jean's friend." Whether or not Jean wants her for a friend doesn't matter in the least: Far more important than whatever Jean—or Lola[130]—wants or gets (Addison DeWitt would have left all that to Louisa May Alcott) is the story's realization of its potential. But stories being what they are, any obstacle (like Jean's resistance) thrown in their path can, overcome or not, only amplify that realization.

---

[130]Reference to the temptress in the Broadway musical *Damn Yankees*, whose signature number is "Whatever Lola Wants (Lola Gets)" (music and lyrics by Richard Adler and Jerry Ross).

CHAPTER FORTY-NINE

So to make a long story short, simply because the Master feels compelled to appease his investors she's been compelled in tandem to become *the Shearer woman's* friend. And oh, my gods! did she just now refer to Moira as the Shearer woman so as to repudiate that friendship or—which is far more likely given everything she's just discovered about repetition and its vicissitudes—to satisfy His demand that the word "Moira" not be re-thought—reused—recycled—until enough wordflow had elapsed or the supply of synonyms had been exhausted—whichever came first? Hey, but what about the Orchard Street rummagers' hog-wild repetition of "fuck" and company over and over and over again with no gentrifications in-between? Their exemption from Masterly law makes Jean desperate—desperate enough to ask one of the queuers (whom she recognizes as a Leading Member of the assembly, while making a note to wonder querulously, when she has the chance, what special talent entitles him to so much pre-eminence), "What's with the preferential treatment?" Though his cock shrinks from what he—or rather, it—takes to be her inanity, he decides, after a disconcerting pause punctuated by a few asthmatic sighs, to pay the tyrant's pusillanimity no heed—at least long enough to reply that, being quite the favorite, she should have figured things out aeons ago (amazing, Jean gasps, how much easier it is to grease the wheels of fate when you have connections: the Master, evidently alerted to her puzzlement [by Herbert? by Moira?], immediately hopped to it and made this leading member with a shrinking member privy [!] to her train of thought): Their dutifully practiced inelegance, he explains (but in his own words—the words of a workingman), constitutes nothing less than a cackled nipping in the bud of the Master's shareholder-driven effort to turn each of them into an individual, i.e., with his own particular brand of characterological rot, whose variously anastomosing admixtures could then be counted on to, like Samson, bring down the house. Since what is more detrimental to the flowering of such individualization than toneless and incessant repetition of, as she put it, "'fuck' and company"? But of course they both know, don't they, the coup—this revolt against the repetition rule—this foregrounding of the fact that even the Shearers of their world—overripe with traits, tics, mannerisms—will ultimately never amount to anything more than paper-thin constructions—has been orchestrated by none other than the Maestro Himself (so she guessed rightly and as it turns out His influence extends far beyond the Amygdala Institute!) and for no other reason than to demonstrate His ability to make a compelling aesthetic phenomenon out of not only all He supposedly stands for but all He supposedly doesn't (stand for) as well—His ability, in other words, to have His cake and eat it too.

Though unable to say what has propelled her from the middle of the dance floor (probably a thought too painful for immobility), Jean suddenly finds herself in a tiny ill-lit alcove, of which she wasn't aware until just this minute and where, surrounded by bouquets of plastic and paper flowers and potted palms (the real thing), Borkman, Jr.—Eric? Jason? Martin?—the first one out of the stalls, is busy putting the finishing touches (*pace* Steinberg's Rodin) on an arrangement of what look like (and, now that they can be sniffed up close, most definitely are) dildos, vibrators and other almost-too-colorful sex toys. Though she suspects that with only a slight shift in perspective—a looking wryly awry—they would be transmutable into philosophical toys. Jean tracks down her clothing easily enough, which she—an ex-Campfire Girl—purposely set apart from everybody else's for easy retrieval. After all, you don't parade around in the buff before somebody whose hormonal clock is set at midnight—puberty's perilous midnight—even if he's well past puberty. In any case, she's learned all she can from nudity and its privileges—exhausted all its options. It's taught her there's more to life than seminal fluid whose odor is, moreover, repellent. Too bad it's taken her this long— But, cheer up, she's still young and as Liepnits always says at the drop of a hat, especially when unrequested, there's nothing sterile in the universe. He's never looked more like his father, she thinks. Or does she make herself think this simply because there isn't anything else to think about except, maybe, how the black hair on his outer thigh can't quite smother the musculature's tensed swell, doing which would only force her—*is* already only forcing her—to admit to lusting after some kid young enough to be her . . . kid brother?—and this is no time for the infinite vista of an impossible happiness on the order of that evoked, e.g., by the symphonic entr'acte from Tchaikovsky's *Sleeping Beauty* (thank you, Shearer) to be rearing its ugly head. She's losing her bearings—and knows all too well it's only a hop, skip and a jump from physical disorientation to psychosexual dismantlement. If only she didn't follow in her own footsteps yet again and decide to take so little note, yet again, of a space of transition handed to her on a silver platter—granted, nothing as spectacular as (*a*) the Brutalist Lincoln Tunnel (while driving through, the eyes of her mind were, alas, always focused instead and with a predictable poverty of imagination on that phantom, the Destination [Cape May by way of Atlantic City]) or (*b*) the non-events played out in the time tunnel joining the gleeless galas of Christmas and New Year's or (*c*) the archways of Central Park—nothing spectacular, just a humble interim yoking dance floor to alcove. For there's always an unjustly ignored space of transition just around any bend (after all, nature makes no leaps, isn't that what Liepnits, also in the envy buildup seminar [part I B], taught them?) to tempt and test the weary outcast's powers of self-cure through unhurried contemplation of a populous nothingness—populous with unthinkable things, that is, for those with eyes to hear and ears to see. For in a space of transition there are many mansions. But, unfortunately, there can be no correctional revisiting—literally—of this most recent scene of her youth. At least for the present—her dance card is full. She asks how he's coming along with his privacy machine which, as she remembers his father explaining, is supposed to allow you to experience anything and everything without undergoing the painful ecstasy of doing so. He shakes his head. The shake can mean anything—*it's hopeless* or *it's way above your head* or whatever may have taken up residence in the space of transition from (transition is everywhere!) the one to the other. Or has she turned a newfangled *concept* of privacy still in the works into a newfangled privacy *contraption* or is she confusing it with a horse of another color entirely, to wit, some kind of experience-without-the-inconvenience-of-experience pill? Or is she wishfully thinking about an anti-Envy machine?

No doubt about it, Netta's elephantiasic tits and ass, not to mention her morgue-slab grimace, manage somehow to bring out the very best in Kid Borkman, the perfervidly patient salesman who, while the first to admit the object in the palm of his hand is indeed a dildo (in homage to the times when a cigar is just a cigar), nonetheless feels duty bound to point out that it isn't just any old dildo, no, not by a long shot. If she must know, it's the smartest of smart-ass dildos, that is to say, a kind of electronic second skin modeled on that developed by Kim and his colleagues in another context (see *Science*, vol. 333 [12 August 2011]) and thus incorporating transistors, radio frequency inductors, solar cells, wireless coils, oscillators, light-emitting and rectifying diodes, capacitators, and (cutting to the chase) a high-density micro-array of fluorescence-based bead-shaped sensors able to monitor, following the tool's insertion, not just the electrophysiology of brain, heart and muscle activity over the entire period of tool use but also sexual orientation (known to shift seamlessly between orgasms), odorant levels signaling microbial infection (the wages of sin), mood swings linked to changes in intensity of flared head's grinding against the G-spot, ambient air quality and air temperature, and level of the distraction, welcome or unwelcome, generated by the comings and goings within an adjustable radius of person or persons known and unknown. But you ain't seen nothin' yet, for once the dildo is charged up and starts doing what it does best, which is to communicate wirelessly (whether with Android phone, cachepot, home security camera, pony express, IPhone, iPad, tablet, television, refrigerator, watering can, robotic vacuum cleaner, toy helicopter, laptop, desktop or first-generation Sphero), and provided the self-abusing user has the obligatory hornbook of non-parametric pattern-recognition algorithms at his fingertips, he or she can—can— Well, to be quite honest, Kid Borkman has absolutely no idea of what he or she could get around to achieving, even armed with the world's biggest hornbook. Except that it seems, to Jean—who says as much—like the front-running precursor of what she's just referred to as the privacy machine. Netta rolls her eyes to signal, *So that one's obtuseness is running wild once again.* Though (the Kid misses or ignores the signal) of late there *has* been some fancy talk behind closed doors (here his pretty voice falls to a whisper), after biggish data disclosed instances of life-threatening smart overstimulation of anus, perineum and clitoris, to the effect that if the culprit neurons turned out to be localizable, then operant conditioning might—*might*—be recruited to enable deployment of their firing for other purposes.

Netta gives no sign of feeling let down by this admission, mainly because she didn't mistake the hype that came before for the breaking news the Kid intended it to be. Instead (disregarding, in her pursuit of bigger—or simply different—game, the model he's been hawking, which seems to cause him no little pain) she proceeds, ever the gadfly in distress and as shameless as ever (*Shamelessness: an underrated virtue,* Jean thinks for the three of them), to ply him with what Jean presumes are the sort of questions regularly posed by the seasoned sex-shopper, to wit, is cyberskin more titillating than silicone? is a suction dildo that much more effective than one with balls? is the Big Boy Dildo, *with* Balls, compatible with water- *and* silicon-based lubes? does the Lilliputian Dildo™, size notwithstanding, have the usual 17 levels of vibration and 6 rotation speeds? will the mythy motions of the seahorse triple-action dildo rouse her hemorrhoids from their bed of quiescence? and just between you and I [*sic*], is it true what *they* are saying (the Kid is all ignorance, all eager curiosity)—you know, about the Smartest Dildo (in stores Thanksgiving Day), i.e., that it can not only masturbate the lady of the house when so ordered by her lord and master via smartestphone but also report back immediately if there happen to be unidentified males on the premises providing emergency immoral support? "All excellent questions," Little Borkman (every inch the entrepreneur though, truth be told, he deplores salesmanship especially when deployed effortlessly: after all, he, too, is after bigger or different game—Privacy or Experience or maybe both—and wants it to be understood that dildos are, as they were for his fellow polymaths Leonardo and Erasmus, a day job—a mere stopgap on the road to greatness) assures her, though now that you mention it, he *is* beginning to look more than a bit uncomfortable which could be due, however, to the not-so-simple fact that every other prospective customer (there's quite a congregation) looks still more so—looks aghast, in fact. This *is*, after all, a temple, even if a temple of commerce. And what better proof, she seems to ask while fingering sceptically (and in some cases finger-fucking, even more sceptically) every item she can get her hands on (in so doing Netta reminds Borkman, Jr., of his mother at those moments when as dutiful spouse she'd riffle her way through Sr.'s underpants, with every specimen consigned, by a contemptuous flick of the wrist, to the slagheap invoking yet another facet of his flagrancy)—what better proof than the shame she's succeeded in sowing simply by calling a spade a spade? *No shame, no fane—* that's my philosophy, she proclaims—but wordlessly, since the very defiance misshaping her posture (ravishing, more than one stroller has to admit, in spite of the all-over dewlapidation) says it all. At which point Kid Borkman (suddenly far less of an adorably tormented oddball, now that it's a question of dollars and cents, than his magnificently contoured thighs led Jean to believe), having put out of Netta's reach the few toys which by some fluke have escaped her ungracious vivisection, declares point-blank (but loud enough to reassure every other customer) that if she can't see her way clear to trusting the creator/manufacturer/distributor of what the industry has, for ten years running, deemed the very best prosthetics in the land (no GMOs, they)—prosthetics, he might add, that are 101 percent homegrown-organic—if she can't see her way clear to trusting them—well then, there isn't anything further to be said, is there?

"I don't know, is there?" Netta asks, dumb-blonding it to the hilt but still defiant—in the best Cheney/RUMPsfeld/Rump/Rump, Jr. tradition. The Kid turns to Jean with a glint of entreaty. However, what he—and everybody else—doesn't know (including she herself but maybe things are about to change) is that Jean is participating all too eagerly in the defiance, even if hers has a different target, namely, the Guy Who at every turn (and so what if defiance only makes Him stronger?) has forced her to play, as now, the role of guilty bystander—especially painful given that this naked-rogues' gallery constitutes the perfect venue for achieving self-coincidence at last. No matter that her animus makes Him stronger even if what galls her most is the suspicion fast transforming itself into solid intuition that "one supernumerary"—and why not her?—"less would have spoiled [His] human tragedy."[131] Every time Jean feels just about ready to flower she's informed that, sorry, miss, but language—His language and nobody else's!—Language, His handmaiden and righthand thug—his hit man and vestal virgin—has other plans so what can she do but, packing up all the odds and ends of misidentity, bid yet again a fond farewell to her inchoateness? The dumb blonde recalls her to half-life. "Give me those dildos, young man." She tries to grab the two or three that are still within reach. "If you don't, something terrible will happen . . . to the Enviers . . . and I'll be responsible." "Now, Miss Netta, you don't—you can't—really believe that," the Kid mugs. A ham in his own right he knows that there's nothing like demurral—resistance—to usher in and thereby vouch for the verisimilitude of somebody else's star turn and hers is long overdue. For one thing, she's not getting any younger. "You called me Netta," is all she replies, and her eyes glaze over nicely (from rapture, Jean could swear). "No, you're right, I don't *really* believe it. But what I do believe in, heart and soul, is my monstrousness—a monstrousness greater than everybody else's. Because, after all, I'm supposed to be a healer, not a heeler for Boss Evil." Which, she goes on to explain, entails ensuring her credulity stays way ahead of the credibility of that monstrousness. With the first step toward punishment (and it's a big one) being to reach, through the commission of some irreversible atrocity, a point of no return even if you might say—if you cared enough, that is—her life is one long point of no return and that incessant attainment of such a point is the very condition of her being. Or maybe what she really believes in, Borkman, Jr., suggests, suddenly wise beyond his years, is the need to be punished for providing no evidence of that monstrousness. Netta shrugs, but is not, it would seem, displeased. "Disconnecting myself from even one of your dildos would be such an irreversible atrocity." She's been stage-whispering conspiratorially, head bobbing up and down in celebration of her collusion with the prospectives who've turned, the minute everybody's back was turned, into one big Prospective. In fact, to the growing bewilderment of that Prospective—the ungainliest of ungainly *bystanders*—as *Netta continues to waltz the two of them round and round the maypole of the dildos issue, with each chaîné turn more delicious than the one before* (N.B.: Moira Shearer served as technical consultant during the construction of this image: Thank You, Moira!), the toys themselves become both more and more and less and less real, a phenomenon symptomatic of *the old problem* (here rearing its head in postmodern drag) which nobody could have defined better than Herbert, unfortunately in transit. A problem old enough in fact to have plagued

---

[131]Phrase borrowed without permission from Machado de Assis, *Epitaph of a Small Winner*, William L. Grossman, translator.

even Akkadian writers of fictional autobiography, regardless of whether they ended their production with a blessing, a curse, a donation, a prophecy or a stony dollop of down-home didacticism—or with none of the above: To wit, as regards any given story commodity, when is there enough of a "reality effect" to allow the "abstraction effect" to take over with impunity. Which as applied to the case at hand means, How much bare-minimum concreteness of that crazy thing called a dildo is required for the erosion of that concreteness, through the attribution to said dildo of all sorts of incompatible functions, to be registered by the Best of All Possible Bystanders as the alchemization before his very eyes of thing into Thing-in-Itself—supreme vengeance on life and hence the sole aim of any story worth its salt?

Before the problem can be considered, much less resolved, Borkman's next-door neighbor (for, will wonders never cease, he suddenly has one: business in the alcove will evidently soon be booming) has lured Netta away and not a minute too soon, since she was just about to have her head split open (for, strange to say, all that waltzing has ended up only incensing her partner) by what its label indicates is a Stage-Door-Johnny Dildo, clearly the most massive of the lot. He begins to describe *his* version (a much inferior one, if you ask me, thinks Jean) of the first item the Kid pitched to the old girl—in her role as emissary and embodiment of the world at large. On and on he babbles (turning it mock-sceptically this way and that, and injecting thereby a bit of ingratiating self-doubt into his dumbshow of expertise). To the point where even Jean, *no connoisseur, God knows, of dildos,* can see he knows nothing (though she doesn't much like the smug self-congratulation lodged—packed in tight—between the italics, reminiscent as it is of her boast, after having been fucked by Ethan for the first time [and evoking Caro at her worst], to the effect that with the likes of him on permanent retainer she'll never be in need of any such contraption]). Still, there is plenty of room for (TV game-show host-style) self-celebration, since how can mere expertise—the kind, for example, possessed in spades by Jr., the rival next door—possibly outshine the shamelessness (*shamelessness, that underrated vice*) with which he dares to flaunt its flagrant absence? for in this dirty business, hell, the talent for shamelessness must surely count for something—everything—and not just in terms of commodity value-added. But deciding that Netta, and whoever else has cared to stop, look, listen and learn, have been liberally dazzled long past their bedtime, he wastes no time shooing them out into their native element. And having just been privy to all this unpleasantness, how, I ask you, can a tough businesswoman like Jean not want to get its bitter taste out of her mouth (though she's never professed to being any such thing even if her arms akimbo refuse to budge and, furthermore, wouldn't a tough businesswoman worth her salt have taken to the goings-on like a fish to water) and if so, what better way than by indulging in a flight of fancy—to the point, if need be, of dubbing the competitors Mount Dildo's oppugnant Twin Peaks, Savvy and Sleaze?

Thing is, she doesn't have the luxury of determining whether her fancy has made a safe—i.e., a credible—landing because in turning toward his shingle to confirm the moniker is indeed merited, what should she discover but that the Dildo Kid aka Peak Savvy has packed up and gone, maybe even for good. *Never in her life has Jean felt more deserted.* Yet strangely enough not by Peak Savvy. It's somebody else—some *thing* else—that's done the honors of deserting her. It's desertion of another color entirely (she feels it in her bones)—on another plane—a desertion simply invoked by the Kid's which, in the unexpurgated annals of Invidicumism, is sure to rear its ugly head as a mere footnote thereto. Desertion by what Charles Sanders Peirce would have called Firstness. (Peirce: another one of her schoolgirl crushes, or so she's just this minute discovered, thanks to the Master—the Master Matchmaker—who's once again exploiting her—preventing her selfhood from flowering—sacrificing her instead to tabloidization of His own love affair with Peirce [a "difficulty addict" after His own heart] but a love affair that's just too cerebral to be of any interest to the tabloids; why, He's even forcing her to think [wistfully, no less!] that she's *always felt* she'd have made a swell Widow Peirce.) As a (no doubt eager) participant in this orgy of mishaps (given his track record as a ladies' man), he would have deemed it his bounden duty to overcome Jean's reluctance—through a signature wasp-in-a-bottle perseverance—and make her aware of how close she's been to solving (even if it feels like centuries ago) the Mystery that is Envy—the Mystery that's Stumped the Experts in NY, CA and every coastal-elitist ghost town in-between for so long or by which they pretend to be stumped in order to go on stumping their creditors. All Jean remembers is that the Kid, holding the world in the shape of a dildo in the palm of his hand, droned on and on about the infinity of advantages which accrue from wielding, or being wielded, by one—and that she thought, without knowing she thought, that what the Kid was doing for dildos she could—and should—do for Envy. How close, that is to say, *and yet how very far. And yet how very far:* the last thing she wants to hear, even from a well-meaning revenant. But just when she was riding highest and felt—without knowing she felt—that the experts-stumping machinations of Envy—the Firstness of Envy—was at last in her grasp (having entered the trial under what once upon a time seemed like false pretenses invested her with the very detachment necessary to look Its havoc in the eye—and unblinkingly enough to imagine she had the tools to cure herself and everybody else), what should happen but that some awful bruteness, shock, resistance, intrusion, polarity, compulsion . . . in a word, Secondness (she's taking her first steps—baby steps—toward thinking in Peircese, albeit under the supervision—almost rabbinical in its strictness—of the Master), had to come along unbidden and ruin everything, by waking her out of her Firstness, i.e., out of the sleep of a lucidity about Envy so simple, unanalyzable, unmediated and independent as to make it impossible to determine whether it was pure feeling or pure consciousness or an even purer admixture of both. The only thing she knew—without knowing she knew—was that every description of this sleep—this Firstness—must be false to it and that it wouldn't suffer words gladly (which was both a blessing and a curse—a blissful curse). But what dared to incarnate that windowless wall of bruteness against which her own wasp-in-a-dildo lucidity was all of a sudden obliged to bang its head and die a martyress's death? That's what she wants to know because she has a right to know and will make it her business to find out—even if it means enlisting the help of—of (what were they called in Peirce's day?)—of—*Pinkertons!* But first she must find another hangout with less toxicity per cubic foot (get thee behind me, CSP!). So why not go back to the ballroom, her demons whisper (for sure, all that lush rainforest nakedness will be a welcome distraction), even if it's one in name only—a name defying common sense—but when did it start resembling a ballroom enough to be deemable as unworthy of that name?

The ballroom resembles less itself than a bivouac hospital—in a recently discovered Mathew Brady daguerreotype (immediately she's grateful that similes—like unicorns—like the phoenix—do exist). A hospital where the beds are so arranged as to ensure (like places in, say, an administration as corrupt as The Rump's) that this man's head lies, to maximum invidious effect, at that man's foot, and so lower and lower;[132] and where every inmate must provide notarized proof of being possessed by the desire to exchange beds— one (perfect for agonizing, say) in front of the furnace, for one (equally perfect—but this time for faith-healing) by the window.[133] (Thanks to the wisdom acquired during her time in the alcove [an apprenticeship of sorts, she realizes], Jean has come to perceive that none of the queuers is a free agent [plenty of plastic canisters which glow in the dark—their mouths just wide enough to welcome an erect penis—are hidden almost coyly in plain sight as if to hammer home the point that treatments in these parts are state of the art and then some]: Each is stumbling along with what appears to be a therapist [or nurse or aide or wildlife rehabber or horse surgeon or shaman or sherpa or psychoanalyst or psychopharmacologist or dietician or personl trainer] in tow.) But no longer does each queue to the toilets resemble a conga line. The Master—that old stalking horse—has yet again enabled her to think through Moira's eyes and thereby evoke a different—a more revelatory—kind of line— to wit, the one that accounts for the most transcendent moment in Balanchine's *Concerto Barocco*—the hardest kind of transcendence (using the term loosely) to pull off, generated as it is by matter-of-fact workmanly abstraction—a moment, in fact, not of dancing but of . . . not-so-simple walking—a moment crafted not for the principals but for the heroic rank and file who by managing to harbor no expectation of apotheosis achieve it (like Cinderella) without missing a beat. And JUST AS in that moment the members of the corps line up house left and take a few steps upstage at which point every second dancer unexpectedly turns (in accordance with the dictates of long-legged sublimity) to face the dancer directly behind her and both, opening their arms, join hands and—dance! SO, NOW, DOES each *patient* (time to call a spade a spade) turn to the personal trainer bringing up his rear to get his brow mopped or his pulse taken or to be reminded (Jean can read each caregiver's lips) that the urine canisters are rentable day or night, whether needed or not and at bargain-basement prices. All at once she understands

---

[132] John Webster, *The Duchess of Malfi*, act 1, scene 1.

[133] Free translation of the opening passage of Charles Baudelaire's prose poem "Any World But This" in *Le Spleen de Paris*.

that however noble—however exalted—the motives for enacting the pornographic text, there's no exalting away the rampant promiscuity—and what looks and smells like a viral infection gone viral—to which it has given rise. Not that she fears infection herself—she's willing—no, more than willing—to accept the consequences of her unspeakable acts and unnatural practices. Indeed, if prompted Jean would experience no shame dating her universal fearlessness from the very night when, by seeking shelter in the Ferry's steerage from the humiliations inflicted by Caro, she boldly entrusted her safety—and (granted, unforgivably) her then husband's—to the tidal waves of New York Bay. And, speak of the devil, there's Borkman (looking much more frail) still queued up where she left him—or maybe, while she idled away her youth among the dildos, he was able to relieve himself handsomely several times over and is simply back for more of same. Though she doesn't dismiss the possibility that the frailty and even the virus—if it is a virus—may all blow over—just disappear—as The Rump's bullhorn may already be predicting it will. The intern (from all indications, she's been standing by him through thick and thin) is clearly not the pretentious airhead hottie Jean took her to be but an accredited caregiver who's risking career and reputation and even (if the McChat, as it's affectionately referred to in the neighborhood as of this instant, turns out to be the breeding ground of a pandemic) her young life to nurse this Broad Street Ahab back to health, which means back to faith in the tenacity—the immovability—of greed (the fact that Jean's able to get beyond her mischaracterization of the hottie proves she—Jean—has the makings of a bona fide character—i., e., she's a starlet to watch: in fact she may end up being "discovered"—à la Lana Turner—by some washed-up talent scout at one of the Master's dinner theaters). Simply from her *style* in wheeling him away from the enactors (the tenor of things is desperate: is there occult blood in my stool, urine, sputum, semen, snot, sweat? are the wages of my sin, however exalted, muddy death? each wonders) after he's presumably done what he came to do in there, it's obvious her attitude toward Borkman differs markedly from that of her colleagues, who look—and sound—as if they'd like nothing better than to wheel *their* Borkmans—their *charges* (time again to call a spade a spade)—into the nearest furnace. But, through the auspices of incipient illness (it's possible but not certain that he's caught the promiscuity bug), Borkman has just been learning what the intern already knows, namely, that every patient's job is to fight off the stigma imposed by his illness—by his illness's crime against nature—which is to render him indistinguishable from every other patient. Jean is sure Borkman suspects that a mammoth upsurge of will shall be required to foil all the misconceptions generated in so-called caregivers by the unfortunates who, like him, spend their time sprinting from bed to wheelchair and back again—specifically the misconception that their tics—the unmistakable tics of the undead—including their inability—their refusal—to pay attention to the words delivered from on high by those caregivers and in a tone reserved for babies (a refusal due to their insistence on thinking *elsewhere* than in the all-too-prosaic moment)—the misconception that all this bespeaks dementia. But what the caregivers take for the blank stare of dementia is simply a brew of inarticulable scepticism, outrage, entreaty, bafflement, reprobation distilled into a Look—a tropistic thrust against their condescension and contempt—the Look as emblem of a privilege non pareil conferred by ageing and disease—the privilege earned by patients who have *seen and heard it all* either over a lifetime or simply by virtue of being patients, even if only for five minutes—and which registers but only to the practiced searching eye as their own brand of counter-condescension. Borkman has a long way to go to master the Look. But maybe he'll never have to—maybe he'll be de-bivouacked before he needs to. The way in which she lets him find his way back to being deep in thought without getting himself trapped into appearing to be just another senile drooling chain-gang remnant—is, Jean must admit, masterly. And his simple supererogatory thank yous doled out to anybody who apologetically gets out of his way as well as (even more effusively) to anybody who, *un*apologetically, gets *in* his way (which is just about everybody) makes him regally indecipherable, unlocalizable, impenetrable—the furthest thing from demented—even if he's in tatters. For Borkman of Broad Street and beyond refuses to give his tormentors—and let's not forget Life itself—the satisfaction of seeing him take everything It dishes out seriously enough to curse his congeners and ask the most idiotically rhetorical of all Joblike questions, namely, Why *me*? (Well, shithead laureate of the purple sage, why *not* you?) Inspired by his strategy (if strategy it is), Jean promises herself that if she ends up as gurney fodder any time soon, then she'll remember to practice the same stiff-necked politeness—politeness as social distancing at its most forbidding—which Borkman now musters effortlessly, as proof of sanity, of lucidity. Note, she tells herself, the deftness of his refusal to be objectivized through a detailed recounting of what went on in the men's room when he pissed into the plastic for if there's one thing he didn't piss away even if he splattered himself in the process it was his scoundrel's pride.

The universal message to each and every patient, as scrawled across the unseeable night sky, seems to be (if all the fidgeting is any indicator), Make this jerry-built jury-rigged juggernaut of a McChateau not just your abode but your tabernacle—don't confuse getting attached to it with giving up on all hope of escape—with bedraggled inurement—otherwise there'll be nothing to escape from and you'll end up dwelling in this house of the Lord of Nothingness forever. Though nobody is paying attention. And just when Jean presumes to think she's seen it all—that she has the *meaning* of the hospital all wrapped up in excelsior and confetti—what should she be forced to witness but the patient in front of Borkman being wheeled into a gentle coma by the worst kind of incompetent—arrogant, inept and tickled pink at the thought of being so—whose fat-faced snacking and giggling on the job is one long protest against the indignity (especially galling given what she's being paid) of having to minister to the pre-dead and the undead when she's so much more worthy of being ministered *to*—preferably by the young and the living. Jean is revolted by this spectacle. But do forgive us if we're too weak to resist the temptation to err on the side of charitableness by describing her as being *of two minds* (it sounds as if the Master has, with promises of stardom [see above], sweet-talked her into inspiring one of His embodied POVs [Cantor, say, or Cook or Melanctha] to sound a wee bit like Walser—not *His* Walser—not Stifter's Walser—but Robert Walser, *the* Robert Walser, aka Jakob von Gunten, the gentle Madman of Zurich): Putting herself in the shoes of this patient she can't bear to go on standing idly by while the fat one—for she is fat—too fat for tears—proceeds to make a vocation of sizzling in the fat of her ineptitude and manages to stretch that ineptitude like taffy to the breaking point. And at the same time—still warming her feet in those shoes—Jean doesn't want the malpractice to stop metastasizing until it's legible enough to catch the eye of—to incur punitive action by—the powers that be. On the other hand, putting herself in the shoes of the *aide*, Jean wants to see just how much she can get away with (since, look, aren't we all felons at heart?)—how far she can go and how long she can compete in the malpractice Olympics before being disqualified for using too many performance-disenhancing drugs like arrogance and eminently dunkable chocolate donuts with sprinkles. So the long and short of it is that Jean comes away (though she's still glued to the spot and intends to retain her rights thereto in perpetuity) with more respect for ungentle comas and their hapless hosts. It's easy enough for bards to affirm that Life is a vast Hospital when what they should do (after self-sodomization with grandiosity's lethal dildo) is focus on said Hospital's brick-and-mortar subsidiaries where inmates are always far too busy to change beds—too busy fending off the invasion of what's left of their privacy—not by caregivers (*caregivers!* Ah, Euphemism! Ah, Bartleby! Ah, Inhumanity!) but by so-called family and friends—the jolly Job's comforters who pay visits not of condolence but of *self*-condolence.[134] Borkman's comforter du jour (a heady mix of Eliphaz the Temanite, Bildad the Shuhite and Zophar the Naamathite, with a dash or two of Mrs. Elihu Borkman) has rushed through the mere formalities of pitying concern (Jean wonders if this is a fellow felon: in profile he resembles Ethan) and already gotten down to business, which is (as it turns out) to trot out his precious lost loves and missed opportunities. All so that the patient can cough up (is Borkman up to it? she wonders) the *required contribution of gloss*—that is, transmute into the heroic agony of regret what's clearly just plain relief (with a touch of braggadocio) at having, for the thousandth time, escaped the past's messy clutches.

To cheer herself up and stop *animadverting* (yes, animadverting! and that goes double) on the inept depredations of that fat aide, Jean immediate assumes the (trouserless trouser) role of towel boy (Urbain, Cherubino, Han-

---

[134]See Charles Dickens, *Little Dorrit*, chap. XXXIII, entitled "Mrs. Merdle's Complaint," for a grandmasterly meditation on *self-condolence*, which, as everybody knows, rules the world; and on the related theme of our obligation, as members of "the most pernicious Race of little odious Vermin that Nature ever suffered to crawl upon the Surface of the Earth," to nurse not just our own self-condoling fictions but those of our fellows—and *to take them delicately in our arms and put our required contribution of gloss upon them.* Beyond praise is this dizzying transmutation of thought into substance—of the noxious into the cherubic—effected through the simple flick of a phrase.

sel, Nerone, Octavian, Oscar, Orfeo: eat your collective heart out!)—since adolescence, one of many too easily avowable menstrual fantasias. Nobody seems to mind or at least nobody notices—and after all, it's not as if she were throwing anyone out of a job since the job didn't exist before this very minute. But more to the point, employment works its rough magic soon enough and in a way Jean couldn't have foreseen. Here's how: Just as an abundantly— and unapologetically—hairy yet delicately constructed young man (oxymoron incarnate and exactly her type) exits the stall furthest from the absent door, it comes to her (three and a half cheers, for oxymorons). The bruteness—shock—resistance—intrusion—the dose of Secondness that ruined everything—that kept her from taming the machinations of Envy ("what the world was to Adam on the day he opened his eyes to it, before he had drawn any distinctions, or had become conscious of his own existence"[135]—what the Dildo of Dildos is to Borkman, Jr.,—what Building 18 is to Melanctha— what Berry Sundae/*Berry Sundae* is to Cantor—is what Envy in its Firstness was to her "centuries ago") and thereby curing the whole wide world of its woe since it's Envy, which rules the world with an iron fist, that's the source and sinkhole of every woe—the bruteness, ladies and gents, was provided compliments of Netta—or, more accurately, of her interminable series of questions about every contraption in the house except the One that Matters—*the one that holds the key to Invidicum's misexpropriation by the forces of evil (Yes, Meine Damen und Herren, irreducible and inextirpable Evil does exist; those of you ambition-consumed phlogistonoids who are heavily invested in the mutant gene theory or any other mock paradigm[s] should sew up your meliorist speculations into something halfway-unpublishable and send the end product post-haste to the* International Journal of Revisionary Whoreshit *[a shrew yet honest]—oh, and don't forget to tell 'em Adolf sent ya.)* Where were we? Ah, yes: And a profoundly purposeful intrusion it has been, for Netta is clearly . . . one of their best agents! And with her harridan's nose for news she must have been alerted by her capos early on that the discoveries Jean was making during her trance would do them all in. (For what has her gamesome participation in the enactment of the Pornographic Text been but one long not-quite-erotic trance—a trance [as it turns out] every bit as audience-enthralling as Amina's [minus the warbles] and Night Shadow's [minus the fancy footwork]?)

Except the One that Matters—The one that holds the key to Invidicum's misexpropriation by the forces of evil. (This hoary phrase just doesn't sit well with Jean and she proceeds to wonder, but in her own words—her own style) whether it's because the phrase is bereft of all narrative . . . honesty—tact— patience and, while she's at it, whether the Master in his perpetration thereof mightn't be guilty of the very crime against nature triage-crazy F.R. Leavis laid at the doorstep of Joseph Conrad (while at the same time heroically refusing to demote, in the course of his war on literary non-greatness, so sterling a specimen of *canon* fodder into mere *cannon* fodder), namely, a

---

[135] *Collected Papers of Charles Sanders Peirce* 1.357.

ticlike "insistence on inexpresssible and incomprehensible mystery"[136] as a means of drumming up business. Which shows what happens when a daring old man on metafiction's flying trapeze, long fed up with such cozy creature comforts as only the hell's kitchen of obscurity is equipped to offer, decides to take a stab at self-transformation into his own P.T. Barnum. Again, an urge—this time terrifying—to flee. If Peirce were here beside her (stunned into self-resurrection by the need to oversee the application of his Laws of Thought to her special case, and of course undistracted—owing to sexual orientation and, more importantly, to indissoluble fusion with his abstrusings in their ethical purity—by all this heavy trafficking in body parts)—if here beside her he'd doubtless be excoriating her for having made Netta, evildoer or not, the fall guy where Secondness & Co. (in business since 1867) is concerned. Look here! even with the old girl out of the picture, Firstness would by its very nature have inevitably come up against some other resistance—another brand of Secondness—demonstrating that the eternal instant, over which it believed it exercised a monopoly, possessed an obverse. But even if there was no resistance, no interruption, she couldn't have harnessed, infinitely tender as it was, whatever she suddenly understood or thought she understood (under the auspices—under the Attribute—of Firstness) about the dildo as conduit—as magic carpet—to long overdue clarifications on everything under the sun especially Envy (even if where Envy dwelled the sun had yet to shine), specifically clarification on the conditions under which Envy's fetus can be made to revoke its own birthright—even with no resistance she couldn't have harnessed that understanding to her newly discovered need to be a trailblazing bounty hunter with Envy & Co. her quarry. For her Firstness as apocalypse consented to last, like any other self-respecting Firstness, only so long as she didn't know what her feeling was conscious of—or if it was conscious of anything—or if she was feeling at all even if feeling—*quale*-consciousness—was the only thing existing in the universe—her universe . . . But she mustn't blame herself if, over the course of its durationlessness, dildo feeling as consciousness and dildo consciousness as feeling was "veiled from introspection" (not necessarily a bad thing, though, considering all the trouble that overrated processus—some might say grand illusion—got amateurs like her into time and again). Her Firstness, like everybody else's, was—is—blessed: "solitary and celibate," monadic and monastic. Sacred cow but (in the guillotining shadow of Secondness) fatted calf as well. Unfortunately, however, it's that very off-limits blessedness which renders Firstness impenetrable to decipherment, insusceptible to reconstruction. It's sans reference to anything within or without (including most significantly the dildo), regardless of all force and all reason—with no parts, like recognition, comparison, rivalry, Envy! (which should make it a consummation to be wished among the Invidicum tribe), analysis or any other operations that can be distinguished from each other—encompasses no act by which one stretch of consciousness can be distinguished from, i.e., knocked about by, another. She might as well face

---

[136]From *The Great Tradition: George Eliot, Henry James, Joseph Conrad* (1948).

it: Her Firstness of pure feeling has a mind of its own with its own living quality—independent of and overriding every other state of mind—including, among others, recollection of her prostration before Cook's magnificent butt, which constitutes her puny and belated version of homage to the butts (understandably provoking popish ire) that overpopulate the Vatican frescoes. Poor thing, she'll never recover the Answer to Envy that Firstness has given her—the Answer she desperately needs to believe Firstness has given her. The blissful chaos of sense experience before it's thought about, hence adulterated, denatured, travestied—is all gone and with it the Answer that couldn't be provided anyway since Firstness would never have permitted itself to be so straitjacketed—would have slept not a wink rather than lie down in so Procrustean a Murphy bed. Every time Jean tries, while struggling to keep her head above water in this steamy sea of lineaments—lineaments of gratified desire (privilege of the happy few)—tries to put It into words, those words only further estrange her from—kill all over again—what they profess to be resurrecting and amplifying. All that's left is a buffoon's paraphrase as ghastly-illegible as (since last judgments are the order of the day—and when were they not?) MB's self-portrait in Saint Bart's flayed hide. Ah, how she does yearn to be back within that moment of Firstness but prepared this time to entrap revelation in the net of expressibility. Impossible—doesn't she get it?—whatever Firstness has yielded, Netta or no Netta, can be contemplated only in memory, through a multifissured glass darkly, as she tries to do now in order to extract its meaning, but the fruit of contemplation is a bruised fruit, more bruise than fruit, all bruise in fact—an overarticulated worked-over product differing infinitely from consciousness-as-feeling and from feeling-as-consciousness and from Firstness as, triumphantly, both and neither.

Still she can't help re-asking like a true obsessional neurotic—though the diagnosis has never been confirmed (pity, since in some strip clubs it's the only qualification for membership): Why did she allow Netta to (*a*) barge in so mother-in-lawishly, just when she and Firstness were embarking on a long-deferred honeymoon in their very own private Hades, the Land of Envy, and (*b*) prevent her thereby from constructing the first Composite Firstness—i.e., Firstness as Itself-plus-Its-own-exhaustive-description-of Itself—in the history of Peirceotics—the first Composite Firstness, with Envy as its armature, substrate, motor, fulcrum? Firstness as, impossibly, the tidy sum of substance plus shadow. If only she could have bellowed forth (with no grammatical or syntactical hair out of place) the truth of Envy in Its Firstness (upsurge triggered serendipitously through her encounter with the dildo's truth) while in the very midst of undergoing that Firstness—bellowed forth the truth about Envy and its vicissitudes of which Invidicum is by far the most pivotal and most consequential up to now (Invidicum, you might say, is Envy's rose, blue, green, cubistic, purple, surrealistic, constructivist and faux primitive periods all roiled [*sic*] into one.) You might also say if so inclined that the Kid, in his brazen meditation on—his trancelike invocation of—the dildo as Dildo, taught her all she needed to know about Firstness while CSP did the rest—or rather that the Kid through his dildo-fueled brazenness proved Firstness could, if the requisite sense of urgency was there, be perpetrated on or against anything—that the category/mode of being/conception/metaphysical relations that is Firstness could be made to encompass just about anything, even Envy, if only in principle and in absentia. But even if Envy's truth can't be refracted through the prism of Firstness, isn't there still the ghost of a fat chance that it exists and will be retrievable on or around Judgment Day?

Jean *finds herself* back in the lonely alcove (as if she were her own mind which—according to some precocious Irishman—is not the kind of place you go to but where you find yourself). She's had enough towel-boying to last her a lifetime which is not to say her clients haven't all been perfect little gentlemen and profoundly grateful for even the most perfunctory attention (and how, with all the clamoring, could it *not* have been perfunctory). Indeed, the arteries of, inter alia, Facebook, Instagram, Twitter, HusserlDirect and Snap-Crap are clogged with clients' testimonials to Jean's expertise—along the lines of "Never knew how much life still had to offer an old fart—and not just any old fart but a *fart's fart*—until I watched Ms. Jean knuckle down and clothe my naked buddies," "Never met a towel guy I liked—until today," etc.—which they posted the minute she was done tidying them up. But she's not one to rest on her laurels and prefers instead, in the name of self-improvement, to self-pose a thorny question—a painful question that's a variation on the same old question—namely, How did she just now manage to elide yet another little eternity of transition vouchsafed her by the gods (and this one for the third time)—how did she manage to miss out on all its substanceless riches—on all the fruits of its phantom Firstness—on its great big multi-tentacled nothingness, especially when it was well on its way to becoming her favorite interim space of all time barring none—the interim space to end all interim spaces—i.e., the one linking—yoking—ballroom to alcove and back again? Why did she stop her ears against its siren song which promised nothing less than intolerable ecstasies in the bain-marie of Firstness? Was such a renunciation undertaken, unknowingly, in the hope of one day hearing somebody somewhere disgorge a long-awaited something which would have for her—but for her alone—the crazy ring of praise, namely, that "nothing in Jean's traversal of that space became her like the leaving it"? But, all kidding aside, for better or worse she's back, with a breadbasket of towels (who knows what goes on in those stalls, especially between avowed heteros), which have begun to smell, though (oddly enough) not unpleasantly, of semen and allied fluids. Jean selects the least scummy specimen in the heap and with the roller-ball inadvertently pinched, she now realizes, from the Kid's sleazy rival, charges herself with calligraphizing on its parchment, as neatly as possible, all she can remember of that—this—too long opium dream which began the moment she and Ethan (and, by the way, where *is* her little corporal?) parted company with the van (but on the best of terms, of course)—a dream to which she's simply incapable of relinquishing all claims even if it's seen fit without further ado to remorselessly relinquish all claims to *her*. Thing is, everything she scrawls is unaffiliated with the dream—a fabrication, appropriately flagrant—a concoction of helplessness—a mere stanching of the gash of wordlessness by one hell of a boozy paramedic who's forged her own credentials. Though can't that very stanching father forth its own fruits—ones incontrovertibly superior to the dream's brigade of bruisers? Couldn't the desperate ingenuity applied to the futile scrawl of lamentation, if pursued to its bitter end, deposit her, found-linglike, ultimately and at last, on the doorstep of truth—the dildo-driven truth of Envy in its Firstness—the Adamic sort of dawn-of-the-world truth CSP found so magnetic—a different but far better truth than any she or the Invidicum crowd could have coaxed out of its foxhole no matter how hard they banged their heads together? That settles it: She must persevere—be her own wasp in a bottle, even if SB isn't Milford PA and even if, unlike CSP, she isn't "doomed for something great" and "cast to nobly wait" (*Don't you dare waste your time googling these undistinguished shards!*) and even if, doomed or not, there's no sylphlike Juliette at her side to "soothe the wounds" and "make sweet and somber sounds." Serving (sort of) as spider to her Robert the Bruce, the ink (bright purple) copiously bleeding into the skimpy fabric seconds her motion which is (whether she knows it or not) to renounce the impossible task of adumbrating the ghost of Firstness forever (and get on with the busi-ness of exercising desperate ingenuity *for its own sake*—for the sake of dark-ling playfulness). Which renunciation in the works makes it suddenly (for things happen no other way than suddenly in Invidicumland) as easy as pie to pose the question that has suddenly become key: What has the Kid's flag-ship dildo got to do *concretely*—concretely!—with Invidicum's being viciously *sidetracked* (like the anti-hero in spite of himself in some quintessential film noir of the early '50s—*D.O.A.*, say) from visiting its quasi legitimacy on other afflictions, big and small? She doesn't care if the impulse of every Akkad scriv-ener would be to strip it bare of all concreteness. The dildo (however negligent its handlers) deserves a better fate than transmutation into abstractness as if it were a poor, soon-to-be-dead relation of (thanks a million to the *Economic and Philosophic Manuscripts of 1844*, for graciously coughing up a cautionary tale in the nick of time) Marx's alienated (is there any other kind?) worker. She needs the dildo to be as full of specificities as possible: specificities foster investigation and generate clues, vital or otherwise. It is obliged to be, that is, if she—a Nancy Drew for the twenty-first century—is to get to the bottom of the Sidetracking of Invidicum (a *scandal* for the twenty-first).

Still, no ruling out the dread possibility that the dildo of dildos makes for the reddest of red herrings—that what Borkman, Jr., has held right smack in the greasy palm of his hand does not harbor the unspeakable secrets of Thomas Love Peacock's Invidicum Abbey but Jean's own credulity cum undo-ing. (Might it not just be the case, then, that Netta with her own cross of credulity to bear in the face of a debilitating phantom monstrousness is as much of a dupe as Jean herself? though given all she already knows or thinks she knows about dildodom's toughest customer, there's no discounting said monstrousness is the real McCoy or even the real McPike.) So maybe what she needs to do is stop focusing on the flagship and turn her attention to the other dildos on the block—the ones about which Netta (newly reinstated as a "person of interest" in the case) has been squawking her head off (even if every last one of them is, for all their accessories, appallingly run-of-the-mill).

Jean is suddenly overcome by the junkie's rush of illumination (which wipes out the last traces of her Firstness-frenzy), as all along she knew she'd be, Firstness or no Firstness. Where would be the very best place (or at least among the very best) to stash capsules of whatever off-label version of Invidicum is destined for immediate shipment because it happens to be fetching the highest price, as determined solely by how much neodymium, samarium, berkelium, americium and paramecium—but most of all actinium (the armature of targeted alpha therapy for cancer)—have been used in the manufacturing process and how much they're going for in the rare earths market? A place imaginable only by the masterminds *and maybe not even by them* (though this absurd qualification could be yet another example of the Master—a qualification *junkie*, so to speak, if ever there was one—in action: compelling the wordflow, its dread of extinction indistinguishable from His own, to hold out as long as possible and producing thereby one of those confections Herbert is always moaning about as being simply too too inedible, my dear—*for words*). Where but in a dildo? Room might even be made in some of the grotesquely larger models (with a dollop or two of assistance, of course, from low-wage freight handlers) for bricks of cocaine, whose concurrent administration leads to an increase in rate and extent of Invidicum absorption and inhibition of its breakdown and excretion, or didn't you know? Watching Jean get closer and closer to the truth (even if she herself doesn't know just how close she's been getting: after all, most of her invaluable orgy time was spent in and out of trances), the Kid wasted no time recruiting Netta, the go-to gal for routine dirty work, so as to ensure that his budding bête noire's intuition ended up, sooner rather than later, bashing its head against a firewall (though the jury is still out on the question how much dirty work she's been asked to do—and has in fact been able to chalk up to her credit—as far as Jean is concerned). Now, assuming Netta is playing footsie with the big boys, how much do they pay her to keep boobs off their track? Jean tends to believe, however, the bait has been not money but (to paraphrase Pythagoras) the dizzying invidiousness of it all: a golden opportunity (for somebody without one original finding to her name over more than seventy-five years of clinical practice) to sabotage the work of the true originals, though one whiff of Invidicum and Invidicum alone and every other original, true or not, transforms itself—presto!—into the faintest of copies—or is she simply mouthing one of those mock insights the Master (*voilà!* she's become a convert to Herbertology overnight) needs to get off His sunken chest from time to time?

So, as it turns out, Kid Borkman is a Secondness-level operative (but who and where, by the way, are the possum-playin' Legislators of Thirdness?). Which means nothing less and nothing more than that his stock in trade consists not in selling dildos but rather in outsourcing extinguishment of fires of Firstness to expert fomentors of what CSP called the Outward Clash—of First- with Secondness (did his father—oops, dad—finagle him the slot as an atonement for past—and as a down payment on future—derelictions?). Which means in turn that, all-too-shockingly, *he is not what he seems* (hence identical to an all-too-shocking hundred trillion others). No matter. In the present context, the Kid's co-optation makes perfect sense. What doesn't make sense, however, perfect or otherwise, is why, what with no experience as a performer, much less a seasoned performer, and the Met's cream of the crop only milliseconds away by supersonic private jet, it's nevertheless she, Jean, who's landed the most coveted of coveted spots in *Invidicum: Forza del Destino,* which means she's been chosen to embody no less than Lakmé, the two Iphigénies (in Tauride *and* Aulide), Falstaff, Elsa von Brabant, Olympia (embodiment of Offenbach's anticipatory reaction to Siri and Alexa), Butterfly, Marguerite de Valois, Faust's Marguerite and Tatiana all rolled into one. Why, indeed, she wonders, and the wonderment isn't coyness—or rather even if it is (after all, she's only human), it isn't *just* coyness. After all, how can what she's been chosen to do here and now be perceived by any stretch of the imagination as related organically to anything she's done before? It's the game of least likely suspects—suspects without a crime—all over again—the only game the Master knows how to play. She defies anybody to tell her what possible connection there can be between her hot pursuit of dildo truth and, say, that long-lost ride on the Staten Island Ferry following Caro's bravura display of compote-brewing contempt. Yet, didn't somebody mention in passing (in the vehicle, maybe, just before her epochal leap to freedom) that whoever runs the show (she refuses, when the spirit moves her, to kowtow to that *whoever* as Master) works—or snoozes—in mysterious ways, which (if she remembers correctly) doesn't include trafficking in organicity?—another good reason for having fled (but why? and from what to what?). Where the old dud comes from, apparently, there's no such thing as continuous evolution—of character or anything else. The only thing nature makes is—leaps: leaps, leaps and more leaps. That's as evolutionary, as organic, as it gets. That is, *where* he *comes from.* So why doesn't Jean just stop wondering and accept the fact that she's been given the chance of a lifetime to . . . grow. Or is this a mere displacement from the dread of incurring her tribemates' envy?

Jean finds that alcoves—or at least this alcove—suits her to a T (or is it "to a *T*"?)—whatever "it" is, it's the blight (with a silver lining) she was born for. But now's the time to say farewell to what, even if it can claim its fair share of perils, is simply too comfortable for her own good. While she's been immeasurably enriched by the dildo incident—without quite knowing how or why—now that Peirce, through Borkman, Jr., has choreographed Firstness *on* her, it's time to *give back* to society, i.e., to plow back that enrichment—that knowledge—into the orgy where it rightfully belongs. She looks around but doesn't need to, to feel—to know—she's entered a New World, even if it's a world abandoned only minutes before. (Did Jean by any chance re-enter the alcove in the crazy hope that its grief in the face of her withdrawal from the ballroom would leave the virus with no choice but to shut down operations? If so, her plan has worked. As it turns out, the pandemic was a false positive, intimations of its ravages a false alarm, until further notice. Best of all, the length of the lines to the toilets are shorter than they've ever been since the McChat opened its doors half a century ago [at least according to one loud-mouthed kibbitzer who's munching conspiratorially on a mango to show he's as trustworthy an amateur historian as you'll ever hope to find—as soporific a chronicleer as you'll ever hope to avoid like the plague].) As for this newfangled New World, it's a place where you can fuck knowing you'll be observed attentively—extensively annotated—or observe (if that's your thing), even more attentively, while your neighbor in the next cubicle but one gets fucked. In short, this world is a profoundly democratic one: everybody gets her or his chance up at bat. Why, the Master (to use Herbert's term), incorrectly deemed an elitist (especially by dot.com billionaires and Halliburton honchos like latte-guzzling Dick the Cheney, recently hoist by Sacha Baron Cohen's petard), is in fact forever bending over backwards to shake the superflux, so to speak, to every deserving have-not. Just because He can't help making everybody sound the same doesn't mean He can't ensure that everybody doesn't fuck the same. It's in fucking—and even abstention is a kind of fucking—that everybody, in spite of himself, shoots the wad of his or her difference. And difference breeds observation and observation breeds— But she's getting ahead of herself. He envisages a Brave New World (she's assessing His self-aggrandizing excitement as it goes about shattering her ossicles) where functions can be exchanged like cellphone numbers. Where not just income but that holiest of holies—sexual preference—will no longer be a stable thing, a fixity of character—a fixative, rather. A Brave New World where at the drop of a habit—hat—pin—hint—anybody can decide that, for the time being, he's active or that he's passive (even if, in orgyville, what seems most active is in fact the most pitiable kind of [hole] enslavement)—can decide to have a conscious appetite for perception of his un-con-domed penetration of a given orifice or an appetite willingly far too weak to be conscious, which results in his getting penetrated. A Brave New World where anybody can choose, depending on his mood, to be gay for a day, or not so gay that he can't be straightened out, or straight, or—curved, or even . . . curvaceous. A world where any nobody can run the bumpy gamut and gauntlet—of P&O (proclivities and orientations) and recover long enough from damnation to tell the tale. And most miraculously of all, a world where, perhaps someday soon, one organ (e.g., the anus) can be taught to impersonate another (the throat, say, or the penis)—by usurping its function outright or at least appear to do so once the curtain goes up.

Still, for Jean's money, these Elysian visions are one big millennial hoax perpetrated on the resolutely undemocratic darkness. [*Yes, it's a one-sentence paragraph and from the Master of all people so No, your eyes don't deceive you. Will wonders never cease?*]

She knows that if she's taken note of all this then others must have done so as well (but is this an expression of humility or simply of the fear to be alone with her freakish fancy, however penetrant?). But maybe they're simply not well enough equipped to articulate whatever they've noted. But can you note—truly note—without being able to articulate? without hearing a language for the spectacle in question, even if it isn't all that spectacular by 3-D standards? Though of what precisely has she taken note except of what may happen (and it's a big *may*) at some point in the distant future—what precisely has she discovered except that the Master is just another run-of-the-mill abuser of the subjunctive mood and, to a lesser extent, the future perfect tense—He's mood and tense come alive—as alive, that is, as any self-respecting zombie can pretend to be—i.e., He's all mood and no action—all tense and no reaction—and more power to Him. But no sooner has Jean spoken than she finds herself in the same pickle as those whom she's horsewhipping for their own good which is the common good: her observations are sweeping her out to sea faster than she can formulate the thoughts required to paddle her back to shore (but what does Herbert pursuant to the Master's instructions call them? not thoughts . . . not thoughts—not thoughts, but . . . *packets*). At the end of her rope—the tightrope of her own second sight—is what she is. But just when she's given up all hope (that thorny flower)—or tells herself as much to prove she hasn't—well, it's this very self-deception that does the paddling and an expert job it is, too. So once again she's ready for action—to see some action—to be missing in action—as an Observer with a technique to prove it: There are not a few communicants with a particularly repellent body part due, say, to too much hair, too little hair, too much flab or, worst of all, no flab whatsoever. In fact, they are more objectionable than those with several. Or does she think—or get to thinking—all this just to be interesting but if so, to whom? (it's not as if there's a slew of spectators waiting in the wings). Not to mention those (still being interesting?)—the most obscene of all, even—especially—with their clothes on—who, though not necessarily ancient, feel there's nothing especially shameful about shamelessness—nothing particularly degrading about avidly undergoing the degradation of depicting in the broadest strokes of indelicacy their state of ill health, to the point where our friendly neighborhood olfactologists can actually smell the tripes churning overtime. And they're right—right-on—since isn't this a place where everybody is obliged to be shameless—comes to realize the destiny of his shamelessness—which means making heavy weather of refusing to change one hair—or one absent hair—for he knows that no matter how hideous a hole or lump or hump or hollow may seem, there will always be somebody hanging around ready and willing to fetishize it? Nothing so pitiable—nothing so heroic in its sheer pitiableness—as a part—a giblet—that's not fetishizable. A thing not fetishizable—not commodifiable—is a rank inconceivability. If a thing ain't fetishizable it simply means there's no paraphilia—yep, *paraphilia, take it or leave it, no refunds*—that comes up to its high standards—standards it doesn't have the authority to relax.

Never has Jean been surrounded by so much flesh—much more than before (or maybe it only seems that way after her long quarantine among the dildos)—never so much except (*a*) in that hammam she dreamed of (prophetically?) a few weeks ago—and (*b*) on the fluttery margins of sleep when, to keep from waking, she willed enough beefcake to fill several locker rooms into existence. And like any visitor to the right kind of clinic, she's finding all her misconceptions called rawly—explosively—into question. Misconceptions she never even knew she had—hence, the most insidiously difficult to dislodge—are advancing fast and furious, and yet with exquisite dignity, to meet their maker (like Ted Browning's "freaks" when they turn on their tormenters, Cleopatra and Hercules) and hold her accountable. Hair in one place does not, as it turns out, necessarily imply (as she so arrogantly—so smugly—had, egged on by Hollywood, come to believe) an answering—a corroborating—a rhyming hairiness elsewhere. Take, for example, this bar-

rel-chested middle-aged Envy victim—or by any chance might he be a leveraged buyout in more-or-less-human form (which amounts to the same
thing). And if the former, is he a Greenwich Ave vet or was he shanghaied
in the ivied halls of the Hotel del Coronado? Improbably—impossibly—yet
irrefutably exciting precisely because, although endowed with densely pelted
forearms, he has a very hairless chest—so hairless it's almost an affront to or
a cruel joke perpetrated on—who, or what, precisely? The perversion of its
own dreams, that's what. But on a brighter note, people are drifting back—
overcoming their fears of getting too close to those who may have been
stricken, forgetting that once upon a time, they, too, had the same symptoms.
They are drifting back, Jean thinks, the way people and small businesses and
even Siberian oligarchs (those wacky staples of Interpol operettas) drifted
back to the Big Apple after 9/11—and as they surely will yet again once the
devastation of the pandemic to come—the real pandemic—has abated. Suddenly festive crowds are choking off all entry points to the toilets. Sexual
activity—the most dependable indicator of socioeconomic well-being—has
resumed, though (as is to be expected) on a less frenzied level. But frenzy or
no frenzy, it's time, she's convinced, to bow out gracefully and make room—
make way—for a new generation of enactors. But is her intention to withdraw from pubic life *that* obvious? for here comes Netta looking as if she had
an axe to grind or a bone to pick or bigger fish to fry. But as it turns out, on
the contrary, she's loaded to the gills with the milk of human kindness for the
first thing out of her mouth is, "Now that your odyssey is winding down, my
dear, would you (a woman courageously traveling alone) have done anything
differently?" Jean wants to alert the old girl to the fact that she—the old girl—
is still naked—at least from the waist down. But first she must do the right
thing and respond. Jean has but one regret (her candor is more than a match
for the other's steely gaze)—that she didn't behave more like a naïf—that she
didn't *become* one—that she didn't play hard enough at being one to end up
becoming one—to end up becoming nothing less than fairy-tale Firstness
incarnate—i.e., a naïf on the order of Alice in Wonderland, say, or Jakob von
Gunten (but a Jakob without *the words to say it*) or (better yet) the gentle
hero of Ermanno Olmi's placid masterpiece *Il Posto* (whose humble vocation of job seeker—none humbler—automatically transforms him into a naïf,
angelically intimidatable—confers on him the privileged status of stranger in
a strange land but with no chips on his shoulder—saddles him with unlimited powers of unconscious observation which obediently rebuff every overture of thought—of words—of self-congratulation). Because, if you must
know, the fully formed naïf is a beautiful thing—a self purged of the cancer
of selfhood—a self exquisitely alive because dead to the shrewish shrikelike
claims of its invidious Anti-Self—a self emblematic of humanity before the
fall—emblematic of humanity before humanity reared its ugly heads—a self
instantly knowable from its latent smile of uninvidious wonderment toward
everything *out there*. Too bad she couldn't play hard enough at being, so
as to end up becoming: authentically unjudging of—unblinkingly respectful toward—grateful to be drinking in—all that idiosyncratic novelty and
unhinged idiosyncrasy of naked flesh caught in the too-merciful glare of lust.

Too bad she couldn't see her way clear to savoring, even if it required all the gritted teeth she could muster, the enactors' smug, arrogant and impregnable conviction that theirs was the only way—the only right way—to give the Pornographic Text a taste of its own medicine (too stupid as they were to recognize that, in so hallowed a context, invocation of anything that smells like a norm constitutes sheer profanation). Thing is, constitutionally she's always been too irked and overburdened by self-awareness—forever stewing in self-consciousness whose obverse is pitiless and unforgiving judgment of others. Too bad, then, that she couldn't take them—the enactors—as they were—relish their follies and foibles without (since the relishing would be second nature) ever getting polluted by the knowledge that she was doing any such thing. But maybe one day (always best, with somebody like Netta, to end self-protectively on an elegiac note) Invidicum will finally kick in and—and— Netta cuts her off—reminds her that in a case such as this physics like Invidicum should be thrown to the dogs and the patient must minister to himself. Overall, however, she's satisfied—enough to make her want to cover her privates and go in search of a housedress—the kind they refer to as age-appropriate. But not before issuing what sounds like a warning. Jean must harbor no illusions that what she refers to as her irksome overburden will not follow her all the days of her life and that she'll not have to dwell in its house of its lord forever. The remark leaves Jean—leaves the incident— cruelly hanging. And just when she was beginning to hope that if the two of them put their heads together they could easily come up with an ending—an age-appropriate ending—for this encounter—something redolent of . . . of . . . well, of "healing" and "closure" and everything just as treacly in-between. So what if she officially hates these terms and everything they invoke—or, more to the point, refuse to invoke? When, as now, her life is on the line she's as tyrannically gullible—as pharmakon-crazy—as the next guy.

Cantor has little choice but to do as the Romans (is he back or did he never leave?). Having removed his clothes, he sets them aside gently and carefully—with exaggerated *purity*—as if he were the hero of *Pickpocket* or *Jeanne Dielman* which somehow mitigates the aspersions cast upon him by his nakedness. Has he been here all the time? Jean wonders—more than wonders. But who, she's forgotten to ask, determined who would stay, who should go? Who's masterminded the cleavage—the parting of the Red Sea of common cause—the turning of brother against brother—inducing only Envy in those belonging to one group of all the lucky ones huddled in the other? In any case, she has the eerie feeling that it's nearing the moment when a mantle—a torch—is to be passed on . . . to . . . to . . . him—from her—the mantle of illusory omniscience. At first he tells himself it's an audition, *just* an audition—nothing to compare with an authentic shot at the title out in the real world—but getting ready for his acid-test aria he remembers what Stifter, or was it Walser? said back in the duo's jazz age heyday at the Del—about what auditions done right are supposed to generate. Thing is, he doesn't feel the requisite song of transmogrification coming on—much less one of transfiguration. A case of life yet again refusing, from principle, to imitate lit. Herbert—but where *is* Melanctha?—sure has his condolences if she intends any time soon to obtain her M.A. in Creative Writing by telling the story of the clinical trial's detour into the realm of orgiastics. The same old story—the same tired old tale—worthy of cold storage in the *Decameron* or the *Arabian Nights* or Plutarch's *Lives*—the tale of a drug's administration refracted through the unsterilizable medium of group sex, the powers that be having determined hard drugs alone have their limits and that the therapy of the future must include Molotov cocktails of shamelessness laced with amateurish lust. He notes that several women (staffage, granted—extras, granted—walk-ons, granted—yet no less worthy of adoration for all that [he's ashamed of having to remind himself of this Sunday School factoid or—worse—make its acquaintance for the first time])—several women are eyeing him with what could easily pass muster as desire in any children's zoo. Only it's sullied, their desire is, by a look of calculation born of fear (is he rich enough? educated enough? handsome enough? healthy enough? *normal* enough?)—a look he's seen oh so many times before—a distinctively female look—a look signifying that a cerebral download—a frantic inventory—is in progress—a look akin to a dull-witted too-full moon irradiating an otherwise pleasingly placid, even pious, planet—an uninvited look that's viperishly insinuated itself at the heart of a latent what-the-hell-life-is-short willingness to be swept-off-their-feet-and-the-sweeper's-balance-sheet-be-damned. But calculation or no calculation, for a split second, as so many awful times before, there's the old feeling that reform—cure—is right around the corner, if only he can set their mind to it. All that's required is a woman's touch—the right kind of harpy—powerful enough to do what harpies do best, which is to transform everybody into what he isn't—into what in fact he is but, shunning twinship, pretends not to be out of sheer perversity. Best of all, if Cantor does his part and does it right, he'll no longer be one of those abnormal types, beloved of Freud, whose sexual activities are at the furthest remove from *anything attractive to a reasonable being* and whom the cigar chomper non pareil (one hell of a creative writer, by the way) compares, charitably, to the monstrosities (Breughel) cum effete gods (Flaubert) by which Saint Anthony is sorely tempted.[137] Though what does sexual activity have to do with reasonableness? can it *be* reasonable without courting extinction? Cantor wonders, even with his pants down. And while we're at it, far better to be an effete god than no god at all. But he's flattered only up to a point, being well aware that roughly 84.7 percent of a woman's desire is just overvaluation of His Honor the penis—that organ-as-trophy whose stock price lifts all others'. The male is perceived to be potent as long as it remains uncertain whether he owns one, and not just any old penis but one of plausible length and girth. But once its existence and pedigree have been confirmed, the item is roundly relegated to the status of a mere curio. But for as long as she—the woman in question—is obliged to teeter on the tightrope of uncertainty—chooses to remain (at least

---

[137]*A General Introduction to Psychoanalysis*, twentieth lecture, entitled "The Sexual Life of Man."

for now) forever on the brink of asking outright, but never daring, whether her man-to-be indeed harbors a penis—harbors the grudge of a penis—since the penis is a grudge made flesh the way Moscow Mitch McMajority is a fart made flesh—a fart with an unfortunate resemblance to a turkey buzzard on parole and an unfortunate taste for contrast collars (unfortunate because they can't help bringing his dewlaps into razor-sharp relief)—but for as long as she's teetering, the woman in question can go on convincing herself that she'll never cease—cross her heart and hope to die—to be adoringly astonished that any sentient being is capable of owning—not to mention wielding—so monumental a bollard. But once the thing's existence becomes indisputable, then she can allow herself to snicker, gradually, at (without ever making her peace with) its overratedness—worse, her own adoration of that overratedness. Whereas men who like men are stalemated differently with respect to the booby prize beneath the kilt—or are they? Once its size is shown to be respectable, the erotic potency of the secondary sexuals takes over—or so he needs to believe. For if they are too fixed on size once it has been established that the prize exists then they proclaim themselves thereby to be one big locus of unappeasable lack and he has no choice but to spurn them.

What worries him is that he has no particular expertise to bring to the operating table. Though he suspects that, of all the members of his tribe, he's the one who takes enactment of the pornographic text most seriously, even if—or precisely because—he doesn't kowtow to the concept by speaking it— thinking it—in all caps. But once he gets his feet wet—once he invokes the native optimism he didn't know he had—once he allows himself to forget all about purity (that is, the kind of ersatz purity embalmed in the gestures exe- cuted by the protagonists of art movies—gestures he's taught himself to mimic)—then he'll be able to do what he's been enjoined to do so that the afflicted will in turn be able—even if it's not in his own lifetime (better if it isn't since the thought of missing out brings self-important tears to his eyes)—to throw off the yoke of Envy but without being deprived of its many fringe ben- efits. And if he happens to get distracted by this or that unspeakable act per- formed with post-pandemic—post-apocalyptic—gusto he's got to remember nothing is wasted or irrelevant or extraneous to the pornographic text just as (to quote his old pal Tycho) to a quasar no stardust is alien. Making his way among the enactors—the practitioners—it's hard to tell whether they are hoi polloids or the text's royalty but in the long run, does it matter? Whatever they are, he sits himself down among them but at a discreet distance from the real targets of his interest: a pair of what look like typical Silicons. He watches them—studies them—as if they were ducks bobbing up and down on the waves of a sunny little lake in Bronx Park and doing everything in their power to suppress the sparkle. And just because he feels diminished by watching and looking (he was about to think, by the *act* of watching and looking but is watching and looking a bona fide act?), Cantor takes the law into his own hands (and what law is that? you're entitled to ask) and reminds himself that the watching—the looking—that they, too, are a part of life—not an interim— not a mere irreparable contentless tear in the celluloid scheme of things but part and parcel of life in all its gore. His self, however private—however privative—is consubstantial with the everyday. In short, he, too, is a practitioner of living—of everyday life. Unlike Eden, who in his racked sleep sometimes made it clear where he stood on the issue, Cantor is not susceptible to the charms of pornography per se—nor does he thrive on—get off on—masturbate to the tune of—exclusion, which is the armature of watching-and-looking. He isn't (like Milton's Satan) an exclusion addict. Whatever contact he's had with the stuff made him feel as if he were getting a guided tour of the performers' pathology, organ by organ, orifice by orifice—and anything he's said to the contrary should be heartily disregarded. What he admires, for starters, is the tenacity of the boy's competence in smoothing the way toward her delayed gratification—for there's no gratification without delay which, in the right hands, is a kind of tact. Cantor likes the way the boy—with his manfully splayed fingers, the nails squarely trimmed—ropes off the scene of the crime as it expands from her navel. He descends as unhurriedly as he can cuntwards, licks his way in, undertakes—undergoes—an exhaustive official interrogation. (Looks like he's trying to figure out who owns the object—he or she [and, no doubt about it, the pretense of speculation in such a context—the forthright bafflement—is erotic].) Then edges his way back to her smitten face—sticks his tongue in her mouth so she can taste herself—so they can both taste her self—so they can both taste her tongue tasting her cunt. His approach to bringing the girl the gift of her own outgush reminds Cantor of how Gilles would—on their good days, their best days—bring him, Cantor, the taste of *him*self (and of how he returned the favor, a little grudgingly)—the child of, as he called it, an Idumaean night. (Not that Gilles wanted or Cantor now wants—but if he does, so what?—to dress up their doings in top hat and tails [known—to those who need to know such things or waste away—as the Tadzio-into-Phaedrus effect] from an insane hope that scholars will be so rapturously busy tracking down the famous haberdasher they'll overlook the scandalousness or, worse, the dullness of the subject matter.) But whether it is for Cantor's benefit or not, he can't help but admire the boy's willingness to be—his insistence on being—taken seriously first and foremost as a worker —a good worker with callused well-shaped self-respecting hands—one who subordinates overflowing lust to duty—for without the overflow duty dries up, loses its juice—a juice that's juicier than lust by a long shot. Never has so good a case been made for the surplus value of workerliness. Cantor's mind wanders. He's losing his grip on the watching and looking which means on his own workerliness. Since in the right hands, watching and looking can be every bit as competent—as self-respecting—as dutiful—as tactfully solicitous—as matter-of-fact—as whatever it is the boy is doing to the girl. The sublimity—yes, the sublimity—of what he sees happening between boy and girl (if Moira were Cantor, she'd say it's like what happens between boy and girl in the Robbins ballet *Afternoon of a Faun*)—it's sublimity that's the culprit. Since how can he track what's sublime without harnessing the empowerment that such sublimity generates in order to explore the unknown—without giving as good as he gets by thinking things even more sublime (because sublimity gives him the right to be fearless) than what's right before his eyes. Time to get back to work: boy offers girl his fingers—the handsomely splayed fingers with which he's penetrated her vulva (the other hand immediately takes over down there) so she can again smell herself, but differently. He's brought the gift of her self yet again but in another form. The crowds have thinned and there's pretty much nobody else around. So is all this work for the sole benefit of the spectator they know him, Cantor, to be—is the lion's share of their shared pleasure derived from excluding him, watcher and looker, from that work? The boy is vocal—he gives voice both to what he's seen and smelled and sees and smells and to what he hasn't and doesn't and his voice is so truly male, so unconsciously male, as to make him sound like an impersonator of maleness but Cantor has only to watch as he subjugates her breast with all five encircling fingers (no prissy encirclement of the areola using thumb and fore-finger, with pinky off to the side—as is the way of pinkies) to know this is no impersonation. Those splayed workman's fingers are so busy getting the job done they've forgotten to press their case—the case of their own integrity. Has the enactment played itself out? Has it fizzled because what it is that the Text is supposed to combat and rectify remains unclear *to this day* (Envy? the ill effects of Invidicum? collateral self-aggrandizement induced by the drug?)? Or, on the contrary, is Cantor living proof that given half a chance enactment works—that Envy can be transmogrified, homeopathically, into what sociolo-gists and sociopaths will refer to someday as the sublimity of workerliness? Or does the problem lie, if there is a problem, in the fact that the Text simply ain't pornographic after all—that boy and girl (who represent the wave of the future—and the past) are simply not such stuff as pornographic dreams are made on (for one thing, their function—or rather, the function of their con-nectedness—seems to be to fuel thought-packeteering not masturbation, even if these two amount pretty much to the same thing—go together like a horse and carriage [or is the Master just being fashionably glib—worse, quaint—worst, *Magnificent Ambersons* quaint?])? Or is it rather the case that, for better or worse, we're in a new cosmic cycle (ushered in by, inter alia, a funeral procession of vans), where rare birds like the Pornographic Text, and Enactment in tandem, now have an entirely different meaning—texture—profile—agenda—where they may even be required to split up though with-out necessarily filing for divorce? And, all this, either singly or en masse, being cause for alarm—and not just among Federalist Society bigwigs—it is clearly up to Cantor to escort the Text—courteously but forcefully—out into the night and send it on its way.

Herbert has just been let off—let out—without an explanation. Before re-entry (will anything have changed?) she allots a few minutes for ponder-ation on the steps of the Art Museum—as a reward for having let herself be herded into the vehicle without even a whimper. After an hour or two—*well, which is it?*—back in the McChat she's still clothed—to the teeth, so to speak—and intends to remain so. Melanctha knows she has her work cut out for her here on the rutting-room floor. Don't ask me, she mutters, to map out that work's meanders, much less to begin describing what makes up so much of its matter—for starters, differentiation among all the types of bungled stab at quenching not so much lusts that dare not speak their name as lusts that have no name—that stand firm against yielding to the belittlement perpetrated by a name—that would rather die than be named. But how will this hasten her own rehabilitation? Well, when you're the mother of a brand new system of nomenclature—who needs rehab?

He's happy to see her—even happier, if it comes to that and it does, that she's clothed. (For in her case being clothed is to be close to rectitude—is refusing point-blank to fall from grace.) Happiest knowing she doesn't expect him to apologize for the fact that he's not. And may never be again. For nothing matters as much as his pre-SB vocation—it's taken an ignominious demotion, from the height he didn't manage to attain, to make him realize that. So it's only natural that biting his own tail is what he's in danger of doing, semi-proudly. I.e., in his end is his beginning for what lay at the beginning, long before this trial under the attribute of Action and story under the attribute of Thought, was his namesake's proof that the class of reals between 0 and 1 is nondenumerable. Only no matter how hard he tried, still he couldn't so misapply that masterpiece of reductio ad absurdam to his own diagonalized disarray in order to prove the absurdity of being typecast, once and for all (while a prison door straight out of *The Man in the Iron Mask* slammed shut), as homosexual. Yet here he is, at the end of the line, still trying to make mathematics do the dirty work of scrubbing his dirty laundry clean. In this space almost Michelangelesque in its reduction, ablation, cancellation, a space defined by smells (of jockstraps, tampons, whips, chains, Victoria's Secret Chiffon and Vittorio's Closet Campwear) rather than by length, breadth and width, he can't believe he's actually entertaining the notion of applying the *method of exhaustion* to his misery in order to cure himself of it *once and for all*. Imagine! What a profanation of the memory of Eudoxus to even entertain the notion as he is shamelessly doing here and now *That* he can make the area covered by his sexuality—its perimeter as gnarled as the coast of Arthur's Britain according to Mandelbrot—equal to the area covered by a hetero's, the most perfect of perfect circles (which gives new meaning to the meaningless phrase *straight as a circle*). I.e., *That* through successively inscribing polygons with an ever-increasing number of sides within that circle—each side corresponding to some trace of heterosexuality induced by the indiscriminate admiration of this or that woman or fortuitous indifference to the charms of this or that man—he can ultimately exhaust the mythical area enclosed by the circle, compliments of the difference between the area of the circle and that of the ultimate polygon having gotten smaller than any infinitesimal you care to mention. I.e., *That* through inscribing in the vicious circle of heterosexuality polygon after polygon, each with more sides than the one before, he can finally achieve nothing less than the holy grail of polygony—a polygon whose area will be *pretty much* that of the ever-elusive circle—the polygon that, thanks to an infinite number of sides—will *become* the circle—trading itself in for the manly perfection of what those presocratics should have stuck to their guns and called sidelessness. *Even if* not so deep down Cantor knows the breach between the Circle and the Last Polygon is infinite—true heterosexuality qua winner's circle cannot be broken down into a crooked sum—even infinite—of proofs of itself—of traces generated by encounters as fugitive as they are irrelevant. True heterosexuality is too much at one—at peace—with itself to be decomposable—too replete to be summable. *Still*, Cantor insists that the key is to exhaust (but is he up to the challenge?) the area of the circle—debunk its holygrailship by revealing its area is nothing but the achievable limit of the areas of a sequence of inscribed polygons with an ever-increasing number of sides. In other words, a hetero is nothing but a homosexual sufficiently polygonized—too polygonized for his own good. And since the space here is so compact (and not so paradoxically, the less space, the more room for the tragic expressivity of psychic stress)—as in a painting by Pontormo, say, or even better, Rosso Fiorentino's *Moses and the Daughters of Jethro*—there is ample opportunity for Cantor to undergo enough therapeutic collisions with men and women to increase to the breaking—to the fusing point—the number of sides—sides on the side of heterosexuality—of the polygon that is homosexuality—to stack the cards in favor of the perversion of cure—the perversion that *is* cure. So now you know why poor Eudoxus is turning over in his grave. But just so you also know: Cantor's method of self-suture is too fanciful not to be rigorous. Though would Borkman, for example, ever stoop to seeking a cure for his own brand of disarray—of dirty laundry—namely, compulsive malfeasance (an ankle monitoring bracelet mustn't be confused with a cure)—or would Jean even consider so degrading herself merely to do away with sisterly self-ablation when she knows deep down that if it's her curse, it's also her glory—the means by which Jean outJeans Jean?

Speaking of Jean, Cook has been looking for her everywhere: he knows that once upon a time she disappeared, like the sprite she is, into an alcove, site not so very long before of one of those street fairs in which the venue seems to abound. But how will he be able to distinguish her from the so many others who've undergone the same fate (dildo fairs—like bookfairs—are the great leveler). That's a subject for further research: what's more pressing at present is to remember, since he's been out of circulation for so long—too long (getting himself primed for re-entry into the workforce a wiser—and hopefully sadder—man)—that it's impolite to stare even if the stare is one of disappointment, for why is it that the least attractive are capable of the intensest frenzy—so intense it abuses the right to disorderly assembly—so intense it has no choice but to spill over into self-commentary? (For in recognition of the inventiveness of his performance with Jean [her haunches—yes, her *haunches*—even more delectable in retrospect] he's been promoted to Grandest Old Man of the Stare. Let's face it, *guys*, if there's anybody who's paid his backbreaking dues and has a right to sit back and—judge the contestants—it's our man Cook [he's come a long way since that diner on Second Avenue—a long way from his Greek salad days]. For as it turns out this constitutes a kind of dance marathon and as such is not untainted by the invidious element, which in any case runs the world. Or is what he takes for preferment in fact a demotion? That is, he's no longer being allowed to pretend that fucking as he practices it—and not just with Rhys—isn't masturbation in the worst way—the kind that feeds on a partner's unknowing obstructiveness.) Although it must be said that the fever of justified uncertainty about what he is and isn't to be allowed to hope for—i.e., distort beyond recognition to satisfy his own needs—in this, his new home (even if it's to be his home for just a few more hours)—although it must be said, I say, that the fever does abate once it crosses his mind—and more than once even in this tiny interval—that disappointment—the failure to stumble on a tableau truly worthy of orgasm—a tableau underpinned by the complete lack of responsiveness of one or both partners—is very much, but never too much, part and parcel of the experience of any serious-minded peeping tom—*the best kind, really* (Cook lobs, without knowing it, a *Down, boy, down*, at the Master of Microlevel Hype). As if to illustrate this point to semi-perfection, an almost unclothed Borkman is making overtures to a woman not even one quarter his age—actually, she's not *yet* a woman, not really. (As it so happens, the aide gave up her not just prestigious but lucrative internship [*who is it who knows all this? simple, the wordflow knows—the wordflow knows all*]. And who dares to blame her: no percentage in nursing Borkman's whims and whimsicalities back to health only to have them healthfully ditch her for metal not even marginally more attractive.) And though sometimes she deigns to submit to a mock-fatherly kiss, it is only to rebuff him seconds later by fake-lackadaisically bringing what looks like—and can only be—a beer bottle to lips pulpous with the expectation of . . . something better—much better—than anything this Grand Old Man of Wall Street can pretend to offer. It is a complex fate, thinks Cook, to be reduced to the status of voyeur after having been not so long ago himself the envy of voyeurs (or so it seemed)—voyeurs on the order of magnitude of Kaye-LeighAnne Kockenlocker (née Conway) over there (Hatch Act flouter emeritus and dead ringer—right down to the grimy incisors and snout—for an alligator in heat), currently choking on gasps of Sadean pleasure precisely because she's getting only *almost*-buttfucked by pre-confirmed amateur grifter L'il Ol' Doc Price, who's just too damn busy chitchatting and chatchitting it up with Der DaVos and sleazeball Andy Putzder and that hooded crabeater seal Ryanne Zinkie (who'll soon be insisting—just you wait and see!—that he—and the horse's ass he comes in on—be greeted whenever they get to work [which won't be often] by [what else?] the banner of his own mug smugly hologrammed across the facade of Department of the Interior headquarters)—lollipop-lipped priceless Price is just too damn busy working the room to finish the dirty job of bringing that old blonde mare Kockenlocker to the finish line. So, Cook wonders (though it's of course the Master who's making him wonder for anybody's wondering represents a challenge to the Master's wiles and challenge breeds analysis and analysis *for its own sake* quickly smothers its target and proceeds [for in the Master's universe analysis is Elizabethan tragedy] to reign supreme), Has he been robbed of his fans just so that the Master can—for the Master must be behind it—put them to better use—as occasions—vehicles—vectors—for proving He is the dabbest of dab hands at resurrecting that wrongfully neglected genre, the comedy of sociopolitical manners—for proving He is capable of outbantering The Rump, locker-room banterer par sexcellence? (Cook—turning the MO of Foucault's clinical gazer on its head—has the paradoxical ability [like a mutt straight out of Pavlov]—as soon as he hears a language—the Master's language babbling inside his brain, which language is every Invidicumite's true home at least until the effects of any given dose of the Envy drug wears off—Cook has the ability, as soon as he hears a language or even sooner, to perceive a spectacle—the spectacle the Master's wordflow wants him to perceive.[138] And the spectacle in this particular case is sociopolitics on sexualized parade. And if Cook has such an ability then every other member of the tribe must have it, too, though Cook's Misery has the bad habit of not loving Company—of loathing it in fact—loathing the toll it takes on any bona fide *misérable*'s imperial uniqueness.) But if they are as world-historical and -hysterical as the Master evidently takes them to be, these creatures who continuously emerge, bloody but unbowed, from The Rump's obese cervical canal—then it's clear He thinks they must be deployed and depicted with a light touch—for this is Wilde's West—a comedy of manners (and if so, then it wouldn't hurt to have the delicious ballet music from Auber's *L'enfant prodigue* ready as backdrop)—and the more he downplays the hysterical angle and their historical importance—the more he renders them peripheral without making them disappear (*show, don't tell*, Melanctha hears her CW teachers shrieking at the drop of this hat)—the more they'll shine, star-bright. The names of these two-dimensional gargoyles—for they are what they've been named, no more, no less—must be pasted on the scenery carelessly—forgetfully—forgettably—sloppily . . . banteringly—so as to both proclaim and disclaim the Master's affiliation. (For He can't seem to make up His mind about them—Cook can in fact feel the Master's indecision coursing through his own bloodstream—after all, He's too much of an opportunist to abjure them—who knows, say, when this malodorous crowd might end up visiting the Tennessee Wittgenstein Dinner Theater [his flagship venue] and, by their presence as reported in one of Merdock's rags, transform it into a scumbagger's paradise every bit as accommodating as Mar-a-Lumbago?) The gargoyles have got to blend in with everybody else—everybody else who hasn't had the luck to be able to incarnate a boldface name primed to resonate like the clang of the sleigh bells tied to Zinkie's horse's ass through all eternity. And how better, Cook discovers (if you're a Master in love with some run-of-the-mill Rump's unstable "genius" for debasing language—for alchemizing wordflow into carcinogenic sludge over too many cosmic cycles to count)—how better to brush-stroke the reality of the era we're living through (if thinking is movement, then at this moment Cook's can be compared to a saunter)—how better give the scene the shimmer of reality than by making them—the Hystericals—play down their own pre-eminence on the world stage—make them impersonate, for the good of the canvas upon which they and the hoi polloi are being forced to commingle, *minor characters*? For if they take it into their heads to swathe themselves in the thrift shop feathers and furs of a true-unblue hysterically historical grandeur (as Margie Tailor Green chose to do at Biden's second State of the Union) then they'll seem less real. If they want to be authentic, then they've got to look and sound minor. Or, maybe, Cook intuits (*well-earned deep recuperative breath after so much meaty surmising*), the Master isn't at all as reactionary or

---

[138]See Michel Foucault, *The Birth of the Clinic: An Archaeology of Medical Perception* (New York, Vintage Books, 1975), chap. 7 ("Seeing and Knowing"), p. 108.

indecisive as He appears and the Jacobin Within knows that these gargoyles—the members of the Rump's stock company (all the KayeLeighAnnes and Mikes and Micks and Mooches and Mnuches and Mitches and everybody else who rhymes with *Mitches*—and all the Wilburs, Scotts and Seans)—a schlock company on the lofty level of Ingmar Bergman's—knows that these gargoyles are but sub-minor leaguers exalted out of their native dungy mud, from time to time, by major-league moral mediocrity—minor-leaguers who, through their very efforts to play down pre-eminence, at the behest of His aesthetic purposes—and at the behest of the outdated conventions of social comedy—will ultimately all end up simultaneously diminished (for the purposes of social justice) on the wrong side of the barricades of Real Life (whatever and wherever that is) as well, i.e., will be diminished—maybe even obliterated—under the attribute not just of Thought but of Extension—will turn out to be as trivial—as harmless—or at least as fleeting—as the Master, in the name of authenticity, has enjoined them to be in the dinner theater of His dazzling imagination (which Cook has not only invented but [through the craziest of coincidences and as the most mixed up of mixed blessings] been granted unlimited access to as well)—dazzling, that is, as only an impoverished—a willfully impoverished imagination—can afford to be.[139] In other words, the not altogether convincing message cooked up by this mess may very well turn out to be that *they, too—these not-so-little foxes—will pass* (even if it's only after having lucratively perpetrated irreversible havoc—rolled back every Obama-era constraint[140] on the practice of mad-market greed—every constraint on the sanctimonious deployment of a murderer's ideology [whose three pretextual *prongs-slash-tongs* are god, guns, gestation] to cover the tracks of that greed). Herbert—a mam'zelle on the make—hears the same spectacle and perceives the same language and, frankly, is a bit *peeved*—a wee bit *miffed*—though she'd never be caught dead using either word—a bit *irked*, then, by the way the Master is so busy noisily cutting these nonentities down to size—ostensibly downplaying their importance—for all the world as if they *were* important—as if they *were* truly world-historical characters who *needed* to be cut down to size—as if they were bona fide stars, these bums, these mutants, these all-holes holograms—stars on the order of, say, Napoleon or General Patton or Hamilcar Barca or Perle Mesta—whose gravity and glamor must always be minimized in a fictional terrain such as this—or rather, scumbled with a fine-toothed comb—stars who must be made to keep their distance—must be photographed only in long shot—through the scrim of, if at all possible, their fans' awestruck punchdrunkenness—not only because (*a*) proximity, like familiarity, breeds contempt but also because (*b*) if the celebrity to which Kockenlocker and Der DaVos and El Putzder and Zinkie and L'il

---

[139]Cf. Roland Barthes, *S/Z: An Essay*, translated by Richard Miller (New York, Hill and Wang, 1974), pp. 101–102.

[140]OK—while we know every big-time politico is a sociopath, fact is, it's all a matter of degree and the ocean of disordered personalities still plays host to islanders capable of rational self-correction.

Tom are allowed under the Master's cockamamie auspices to lay claim—if their celebrity isn't carefully titrated against the tenor—the texture—the temperature—the room tone—of the aforesaid terrain (the terrain of the little people—the huddled masses—the wretched refuse—the rank and file—the lumpen—the "essential" [for "essential" read "expendable"] workers), then said celebrity will (this being the privilege of greatness) only capsize and sink the spectacle—and after all, the Master's first duty is to the spectacle—the little people's spectacle. In other words, so the argument goes—left to their own devices these sinkhole A-listers would simply drown out the chatter of the true stars of the show—average joes like Jean and Cantor and Melanctha herself, to name but a few—and steal their spotlight once and for all. And the Master wants it to be believed—except when He doesn't—that He's on the side of the average joe—except when He isn't. In short, she doesn't buy His shimmering "indecision"—doesn't believe in His inner Jacobin (He's a truculent rapacious sonofabitch with no inner Anything, notorious for underpaying the workers down at Tennessee Wittgenstein and for whom blackness and brownness are illegal). He's an opportunist through and through even when He doesn't want to be—and it simply doesn't matter what He does or doesn't want to be—what matters is what His vocation wants Him to be. It's all a charade—he's on the side of the joes to the extent that he's on the side not of social justice but of aesthetics—the aesthetics of painting a picture, staging a spectacle, courting the rich and famous. And by the way, how dare the Master try to convince her the spectacle is an unfolding *fiction*? What she's living—what she's always lived—is no fiction. It's time for the Master to be cashiered—until such time as she's ready to rescue him from the catacombs.

Funny, Cook thinks, how, initially, the Master was worshipped and reviled as an eerie epiphenomenon—a creepy fringe disbenefit of—a pintsized distraction from—Invidicum's niche war against Envy, while now it looks more and more as if the dosing, albeit more efficacious than ever, has been relegated to a not-quite-empty ritual deployed solely to distract from His mushrooming influence. Or is this just a case of the Master's trying his hand—through recruitment of the least likely stooge—at baking the staple of staples—a "turning point" (or, in vulgar parlance, anagnorisis)—into that humble pie in the sky to be known to those who come after us as the Invidicum Story? Thing is, Cook isn't sure he should broadcast the news (which, any way you slice it, means the Master's in and Invidicum's out: the election results are incontestable) even if with each passing moment it's smelling more and more like truth and less and less like idle speculation. His trouble handling the uncertainty compels him to ask that painted devil, the foxy Kockenlocker dame (as crocodiloid as ever), for her autograph in full.

Borkman (was he, too, in the vehicle or did he never leave? nobody's bothered to ask), fully unclothed at last, has enjoyed stripping naked just now (thereby transmuting previous efforts to get down to brass tacks, and beyond, into mere [*pace* the message loud and clear of the del Coronado ballroom seminar] . . . mere . . . auditions) more than he would ever have imagined. He's still recuperating from the viral infection he almost contracted—deserved to contract—which has made him bolder, more feverish, more of a mogul.

With his girl-woman—his child bride—beside him there's no telling (even if blubbery-lipped indifference is her stock-in-trade) how far he can go in the direction of enactment once all charges against him are determined to be mere frivolities and—dropped. But surely, Cantor remarks, he's gotten the message (just about to be broadcast live on CNN) that tonight marks the inauguration—the ushering in—of a new cosmic cycle—a cycle no longer governed by the attribute—the potency—the emanation—the *sefirah*—of severity/judgment (*Din/Gevurah*), which is pornography's native element—its generator—its mother's milk—its fuel—its menstruum. Instead, it's now the *sefirah* of mercy in all its splendor (*Raḥamim*) which rules the roost and as it so happens there's no attribute more inimical—even if lovingly inimical—to pornography's dungeon mentality than this one. (Which is not to say that *Din* and *Raḥamim* don't still communicate—don't still share the latest gossip— through secret channels—which is the way of all ten *sefiroth* among themselves.) In other words, there is simply no longer world-enough-and-time for enactment of the Pornographic Text (but where did this message come from and why does Cantor [straight—or rather, fresh—from his record-breaking engagement in Vegas] look like he's the sole receiver? Herbert wonders). And who but Cook—on a palpable roll after his recent triumph ensuring that truth trumped speculation where the Master's doings were concerned (*who is speaking?*) and nakedly desirous that every thought, speech or physical act be viewed through the prism of the Master's debasement of storytelling for his own bleak ends (Cook is acting, come to think of it, a lot like that Girard guy whose work the Invidicumites had to study back on Greenwich Avenue— or else—and for whom Envy [or more precisely, triangular desire *aka* mediated desire *aka* imitative desire *aka* metaphysical desire *aka* mimetic desire] explained away all things noisome under the sun)—who but Cook should be assigned to now wonder whether this business about another cycle rearing its conveniently ugly head isn't exactly that—a bit of *stage* business, concocted by the Master and vocalized (in the key of tongue-in-cheek) and gestured into life—a sort of life—by Cantor, to keep the story ticking. No doubt He's having a poker-faced ball playing back the phrase *tonight marks the inauguration of a new cosmic cycle* knowing full well as He does—and He's too ancient *not* to know—that His sole interest lies (like a homosexual morbidly compelled, at some rooftop cocktail party down in the wilds of Tribeca, to chitchat-fuck every lady who crosses his wise and witty path) in commandeering that mighty phrase not to stir up narrative interest but to pave the way toward the paradise of the next narrative-leery thought packet. But isn't it true, thinks Herbert, ever the interventionist, that even if packets are always descending on stories like locusts and stories are always returning the plaguey favor, isn't it because each knows (*a*) that it's here to serve as the other's blessing in disguise and (*b*) that its job is to enable that ornery other to come to an end which neither is capable of doing on its own steam and (*c*) that the dynamic they're wedded and welded to is ultimately all about taking turns at playing ouch to the other's crown jewel? And by the way, hoisting up his aging body against gravity for the unseeing scrutiny of his inevitable lessers is proving to be as boastfully exhilarating an ordeal as that photographer Borkman once met at a Yankees game, of all places (an amateur in the best sense), said it could be given half a chance. What *was* his . . . John Coplans! of course! After all, he's earned this precious possession—the hairy house that houses his hairier mind—the mortgage is all paid up—it never soured, not once. And he doesn't mind if all the women turn away, from revulsion or from an excitement they mistake for revulsion [all the women, that is, except one (the one who's not even a woman but at best an embodied pout, though, come to think of it, let *her* go the way of all flesh as well, pouts and all, if she so desires): *he doesn't need anybody—nobody but himself* (at least for as long as the adrenalin pumped into him by the phrase's italics manages to perdure)], nor will he mind, for that matter, if all the men—even the most unsightly—follow suit—Borkman doesn't mind in the least if they all decide to go back to their not-all-that-smart phones (though what kind of self-respecting Luddite is he to be passing judgment?). For he's getting something more precious out of the turning away than mere titillation of his unvanquishable self-hate—more powerful than vanity. Though no Marxist, or at best a closet case in spite of himself—a Marxist in another life, a life to come—he's deriving real pleasure from knowing—the pleasure of confirmation at long last!—that everybody, whatever he may pretend, is nothing more than the sum of his secondary sexuals. And all this without having to undergo the excruciation of knowing he knows, seeing he sees. The gladhanding between and among men and women and between and among everybody in-between (with everybody in-between meaning, of course and in fact, *everybody*) always ends up and pretty quickly (and as of this moment, turning away is decreed to be just another—and the most interesting—kind of gladhanding)—always ends up assuming in all cases the fantastic form of a relation between things—whether it's the hair on somebody's balls or the tiny excrescences (just the sort of devil-in-the-detail that used to mesmerize his brothel buddies Brothers Tom and Dean Swift to the point of nausea) on the nipples of some Silicone Valley Girl way past her prime and ripe, alas (through a tragical infatuation with the wrong kind of enhancement—the kind you undergo to please a man who isn't worth your little finger), for a double mastectomy. Since given half a chance the secondaries think nothing of sucking all the personhood of their bearers into themselves, thereby turning them—the primaries—into secondaries. And as if this weren't enough (not to mention *adding insult to injury*), they then take it upon themselves to rise up on their hind legs as something aromatically alien, objective, readymade. Sensuous things at best, they find a way to transcend sensuousness at every turn—become supersensible—make themselves toxic as autonomous figments of the brain. No explaining their power as fetish. Though Borkman, busy rubbing his hip while trying to keep his hand away from his buttocks (lest the gesture be misinterpreted, but as what?), would like to think he for one is way too old to be inexhaustibly entranced by a tit or by, say, the particular way pubic hair that's turned auburn in celebration of autumn tries to defend a cunt against the improper imputation of harboring a penchant for making improper advances.

He nods at Shearer, still clothed, and Shearer does likewise (*And what about her? somebody fails to ask, where does she stand vehicle-wise? is she a veteran of the open road, honorably discharged, or a draft dodger?*)—both as if for the very first time. In my end is my beginning, Borkman hears himself thinking, though he'd be the first to admit (OK, maybe not the first but surely—surely!—*one of the first*) that the phrase's sonorous pathos outpaces its relevance to the occasion. From the twinkle or the sparkle in her eye—or both—he could be one among the many many cab drivers hailed at the NE corner of Sixty-Third and Broadway whom she ended up taking to bed (as recounted to Herbert? to Jean, even if they aren't on the best of terms? to Ethan? to Cantor, qua fellow connoisseur of cab drivers?)—the well-earned coda to an exhilaratingly exhausting (or was it the other way around?) performance. She follows him to the elevator nearest the history-making alcove. It opens immediately—or almost immediately—no need to press—and he steps aside to let her in. Which gallantry yields the dividend of an erection. Two flights up lurk plenty of rooms, he remembers having heard one of the towel boys say—not too big, but bigger (for better or worse) than alcoves—rooms in which the final dose is administered—rooms that wouldn't be out of place in Bluebeard's Castle—most of them unoccupied since patients tend to be cured faster than they can be replaced (too few humans out here in Santa Barbara being willing so far to get into the Ring with Invidicum—even if it's a welterweight compared with Envy Herself—though who's to say whether the former doesn't in fact inflict more chronic traumatic encephalopathy per square kilometre than the latter ever could). Walking backwards (to keep her eyes on his body's reverential stunt?) Moira—it's time to name her again—bumps against a door, which swivels reluctantly, allowing them to topple in unison onto a bedsteadless mattress. At first she thinks it's going to be just warmed-over *Bugaku*. But then he begins to suckle her ass with his tongue, which feels—sounds—even if it may not taste—salty. Through what her ass experiences as his anger at being new to the job—a job he should have mastered long long ago—when he was Jr.'s age—anger at having missed so much in this department—he makes up for lost time. His anger is authentic and it makes the ass-fucking authentic, too. How did he find out before she did that ass-fucking is her preferred—the only—way of life for a ballerina past her prime? The ruthlessness she despises must have taught him the generosity she'd like to despise even more (considering its provenance) but can't. Being torn apart—shredded—is, she discovers—clearly or, more to the point, darkly—the best kind of suture she's ever known—will ever know—for the wound of Envy (i.e., her ass promises it will never again matter whether or not she gets, like her colleagues Ms. Farrell and Ms. McBride, to be the melba toast of the Kennedy Center Honors)—better yet, it's the best cure for soul-suture, an overrated surgical procedure promoted by the suavest enemies of art. Now she can say, proudly, that she's *all-anus*, the way somebody else would say—maybe even Moira herself, given half a chance—that he's *all-in*. And gratefully such an achievement—such a suture—such a transmogrification (y'p, *transmogrification*'s the plat du jour—and it's artisanal to boot, whatever that's supposed to mean, and it can't be sent back 'cause the soup kitchen's closed for good)—is not measurable by Kennedy Center standards—can't be straitjacketed by accolade. Or is this just the Master trying to steal the show—

going all-in hyperlative—is this just his hyperlativity coming all over her belly while Borkman, competitively, keeps plowing away to keep up his end of the bargain? The super-felon's ankle bracelet is abrading her kneecap and she's sorry she never had the courage to trespass enough to be able to return the favor. Moira is so far up the ass of her bliss as to be able at last to believe in the Master—to feel indistinguishable from Him. Can she in fact persuade Him, through His black apostle, of course, to let her anus *think*—like Toni Bentley's[141]—let her anus emit packets without having to secure his permission first? For she has what's called an inkling that the thoughts thought by her anus will be far more interesting than any she's ever had. For starters: there's Thought No. 1 (not really a packet—more like a prefatory firecracker) to the effect that it feels good—it feels *healthy*—to be suddenly unable to distinguish between the Master, Borkman and Mr. B. although no three entities ever had less in common. And then there's Thought No. 2—which really *is* a packet, at least by Nobel Prize standards—a packet inspired—triggered—by Borkman's having just whispered her name. And though Moira's not crazy about it— her name, that is—still there's something in the name that she's never been able to find in herself—something that makes her flaws, her disappointments, irrelevant, even radiant. In short, her name's a sword—not a double-edged sword, not a sword of Damocles, just a little gimmick with a serrated edge which stupefies her detractors. What she can no longer do for herself—at the barre and everywhere else—the name does for her. And so what if in fact Borkman (a million miles away as he appears to be, at least from the sounds he's making) didn't whisper her name—couldn't have whispered it—given that all his energy—all his potency—is after bigger game—i.e., is being channeled toward bringing her anus to birth—bringing its pregnancy to term. Is the packet then supposed to fall apart? does it dutifully die a martyr's death? Of course not. The Master, with lots of experience in this department, simply goes ahead and turns the brief encounter into one where Moira recognizes that she only *thought* he uttered her name. And that, Herbert admits—but grudgingly (for though she's been thanklessly outMastering the Master more and more—though she's saved his bacon from the slings and arrows of word-flow more than once—He's only just now beginning to admit as much—*but grudgingly*)—and that is precisely what men of the Packet—as we speak of men of the Cloth—do when they sense that their house of cards is collapsing: they make reality bend to their or rather to its—the packet's—will. Borkman, however, has more important things to think about than self-extinction through the toxic bliss given wings by transmogrification, although of course he wouldn't be caught dead, especially among his cronies, expressing himself quite this way. He's had enough of it to last him a lifetime—in fact, his lifetime's been nothing but transmogrifications, most of them unforeseen and unwelcome. And to little purpose, some might say, but he's not one of them.

---

[141] Check out *The Surrender*, why don't you? for an exhaustive inexhaustible meditation on the Thinking Anus—the Thinkable Anus. A Jamesian thinkable thing if ever there was one—in fact, the Mother of all things thinkable.

Finding Jim Jason Jordan Straynge (who's just got in on the Greyhound red-eye) quite attractive (no relation, thankfully, to that slouching smirking punk—punk par excellence—who hangs his hat—his abrasive dunce cap—in the House of Representatives), Cantor is afraid to prostrate himself even if he's making it a point to stand up straight—all six feet of him—and look unfazeably away—even if he's gotten in fact as far as the window overlooking Anacapa Street. Unworthy targets of lustful adoration (but would they *be* targets if they weren't unworthy? of course not, *because unworthiness—like the river called sex, of which it is but a tributary—sells*) have—true to their code—a nasty sixth sense about such things. But whether J³ Straynge is worthy or unworthy, Cantor's Master Within is pleased that there's a new guy in town inasmuch as a new guy—or gal—heralds a new beginning. Since the new guy is generally generalizable enough—is one-size-fits-all enough—is abstract enough (at least at the beginning of this new beginning)—to be infectible by a correspondingly new virus, i.e., thought packet, and is accommodating enough to bind to its spike. Cantor's fully dressed now, since being stark naked in company has the bad habit—like the British Museum according to Ira Gershwin—of losing its charm. Truth is, starkness has nothing more to teach him—he's learned all he can from the mishap—though, granted, some of it's applicable to the ongoing effort to diagonalize—or polygonize—his disarray and for that reason shouldn't be pooh-poohed. Or maybe Cantor simply doesn't want to acknowledge just how much he's learned from the boy and girl in the Robbins ballet—how much he's allowed himself without surrendering to Envy to learn from their always tactful fusion. With what maddening deftness—with what a heady mix of calculation and abandon—the boy managed to prove it was possible to serve two ostensibly incompatible masters, tenderness and lust—that is to say, possible to conduct, as he did, a predatory, turbulent, impatient descent into the very Orifice of Being and then, with tantalizing slowness—excruciatingly potent leisureliness—crawl back up with the spoils so the girl could get a taste of them, in other words, a taste of herself—so that both of them could get a taste of themselves. But that was in what sounds and feels like another country and, besides, Cantor—the voyeur, the seer—is dead. Preceding JJJ has been talk that he—not Eden—is the "culprit" (the word is not just a too literal—a too dutiful—a too studious—reminder that there's a story still very much in session through no fault of its own but a trivializer as well of the sacred disintegrity of culprits everywhere). So for the time being how can Cantor not feel uncannily sandwiched between two parricides? Still, culprit or not, Jordan has lots going for him: he's Margo's kid, for one thing, as well as a Junior (even if not a Rump junior) and an alumnus of Rikers (no laughing matter, except when at the same time you're a non-alumnus of the Sutton Square Country Day School). But something about the way a leaf from nowhere has just been falling right in front of him for what seems like hours (*no, Master, not* hours—*more like seconds*)—listlessly somersaulting *before his very eyes* (as at the end of a spider web's very tight leash) when he'd have bet his last dollar on a straight-arrow dive from start to finish—something about his connectedness to the phenomenon (no other word will do) enables him to constrain his own clawing lust. (As for love with its comical and exhausting overvaluation of self and object, he's too old for it—he's been priced out of it—or [with his knack for melodramatics] so he tells himself, calmingly, cautioningly.) And if he'd had the good or bad fortune to be living this sticks-to-the-ribs nightmare not here in what looks or at least feels more and more like what it was always meant to be but never could be until this moment: an MRI capsule in the shape of a hearse with $n + 1$ insides, but back at East Beach, where all ladders start, then he knows—don't ask him how—he'd have derived the same strength from watching each wavelet fight to the death for the right to shoot its foamy wad into one of the very few rocky crevices beneath the boardwalk (thing is, there're no snaky boardwalks in SB's Ireland: he's confusing it with the Belle Harbor of his haunted but [thanks in no small measure to the interventions of his Aunt Anne Trotwood née Simon-Schwartz] intermittently radiant childhood). So many wads, so few crevices. But having learned the hard way not to depend on a single remedy for any given ill (and he isn't thinking just about the big I) Cantor tries to appraise this young man-not-necessarily-on-the-make from the perspective of somebody either unaware of his mystery or completely indifferent to whether there is one percolating, simmering, stirring, somewhere unsafe (whichever pose is more manful). How convey to the culprit that he's nobody's target of desire?—no, not by a long shot—just an inconsequential twig on which the mockingbird of Cantor's inner gaze has elected to catch its dying breath. Though why should any of it matter in the least at (to quote Cantor, Sr.) *this stage of the game*. Well, dad, it matters in the least because changes of scene like McChateau always promise—to the Cantors of the world, that is—to be conducive to a change of skin. The audition ends, and neither he nor JJJ gets the part. Fortunately, another kind of disappointment's arrived just in the nick of time to distract him—this time it's disappointment that the midnight sun of morning hasn't come to rest on the other's buttocks but has seen fit, or been compelled by a shrewish consort, to alight instead on Liepnits's gouty knee which gracefully swerves to elude the blinding ray. (So Liepnits is back. But only because, Cantor thinks nastily, a knee was needed and, for reasons too complex to render compatible, his knee and his alone would do in a pinch.) Hence not just the ray but the graceful swerve to which it gave rise has been wasted—and on of all things, this favorite son of the Ozarks. And adding insult to injury, here he is unstoppably in the middle of the dance floor talking, airport VIP lounge-style, to his cellphone. So he, too, is an audition freak since anybody who talks to his cellphone in public is auditioning—like crazy. *You have no idea*— Which means he's *in* but not (unlike poor slobs like Cantor) *of* the scene of his plight, whatever that plight turns out to be. And all because Cantor and his team of slobs lack a device with which, through which, to comment on their plight in such a way as to end up—like wily Liepnits—practioners not of that plight but of its first derivative—a completely different kettle of fish. Granted, he's escaped bracketing, the little bastard—no, scumbag—no, jackasshole— he's auditioned himself out of the plight's paper bag but maybe all this success makes him only more conspicuous hence more bracketable than ever. Or is Cantor trying to console himself by doing what Herbert claims the Master does best?—in fact as far as Cantor can see it's pretty much the only thing He does—which is to let that old devil wordflow ferry his pawns triumphantly, like Charon, to the underworld of self-delusion—to the deepest darkest corners of its internet.

But Cantor's not giving himself enough credit—after all, he, too, has come through his plight—survived his lustful longing. Even if survival may have nothing to do with his ploys, however ingenious, to overcome it, i.e., recruiting all of nature to stand guard with him against the target of that longing. Maybe they're all dead (*Stop right there, Cantor! you know what happens when you let yourself go all apocalyptic. As a matter of fact, I don't know—so tell me, what does happen?*)—maybe Invidicum has done them in through a too efficacious efficacy—has called a halt to the hopeless struggle to survive, which is the only guarantee of survival. Dead—like Offenbach's Olympia, of whose iffy ontological status the poet Hoffmann is (at her coming-out party) warned by best friend Nicklausse (N's own OS is, by the way, also up for grabs since, oddly, his passport, birth certificate and job description all read "Muse")—warned, of course, in vain (otherwise there'd be no exalting abasement compliments of the fickle guests' "Ah! ah! ah! La bombe éclate/Il aimait un automate!"). Or, better yet, near death, which gives them enough strength to survive just about anything. So the naked groping (nobody as far as Cantor can tell is about to be promoted to the status of nude) has been—no, continues to be (just look around you!)—a mere formality but a necessary one. Something to mitigate the excruciation of slowly becoming what they can't redact away—the epitaph of themselves. (Cantor prevents himself—and just in the nick of time—from stepping on what feels like that frail fallen leaf [which, thanks to his currying care as a thought packeteer, must now be the holy grail of dendrologists everywhere]. Or maybe the almost-victim is the [even frailer] shadow the leaf is doomed to go on casting forever [*no! oh, most hyperlative of Masters, not forever—more like* for a minute or two]. When Cantor is in danger, everything, whatever its OS, is endangered as well. Then he remembers, with mixed feelings, that both shadow and substance—out of harm's way—are at peace on the terrace.) Or what if it's he and he alone who's mutated into his own epitaph? What if it's on him and him alone that Death intends to bestow—or has already bestowed—her most precious gift—the gift of herself? Though what if he doesn't feel quite ready to be bowed out gracefully—stopped in his tracks? Well, Death has news for him (by the way, the least he can do is smother her with kisses for granting him this interview, a privilege perpetrated against very few)—like any shamelessly efficient nurse she doesn't much care what the patient feels or thinks he feels. It's here and now that he's slotted—slated—to die. But while routinely reveling—basking—impenitently in the arbitrariness of her choice of time and place—and victim, she also makes it a practice (for she knows how to walk and chew gum simultaneously and, besides, an idle mind gathers no moss, and a stitch in time saves nine) to assign to the corpse-to-be's obituarists (she and they complement each other beautifully) the thankless task of applying their considerable—some might say, inexhaustible—ingenuity to the transmutation—the alchemization—of this, his particular time and place (though purely as a *mind game*, like chess or pinochle), into the coordinates of a unique event—an event that's eminently organic—necessary—unique—the furthest thing from arbitrary—intrinsic to the lesion that is he (in this case, Cantor)—an event that's the only plausible outcome of his overly stunted development and whose madness is all method—in short, an event that's *motivated*. (As for mind games, Herbert—for she never fails to be present where- and whenever Cantor needs moral support [sort of like Nick-lausse]—Herbert remembers—or, rather, recalls—that the jovially know-it-all husband [ersatz human non pareil] of some foul-weather semi-friend once dismissed "After Noon Wine, A Formal Feeling Comes"—her maiden voyage on the Good Ship Jamesian Nouvelle—as just such a game.) Cantor now hears Death preparing to lick her chops at the prospect of perusing, over breakfast in bed (*Mae! peel me a grape!*), what those obituarists will have cooked up in the way of an explanation-as-verdict—clarification-as-condemnation—for why he—if she'd been so remiss as to leave him *in the lurch*, that is to say, *to his own devices*, by not saddling him with these coordinates—for why he, having failed on all fronts, would have gone on failing dutifully at what he did best (even with nothing left to fail at)—and have ended up at—with—a time and place impossible to reconfigure as the endpoints of a unique destiny. And for those with an interest in such things: Cantor fails at what he does best because it just so happens that the domain in which he does best is his own invention (his patent is his pain). If he were a writer, say, instead of Lemma Man or Diagonalization Man or MM (Mathematical Metaphor) Man, he'd admit to inventing Literature. Yet having done so, how could he not be expected to throw off the arrogant yoke of the latecomers to that domain with their inter-minable strictures on honing and honing and honing one's craft down to the consistency of half a fecalith. *Clearly*—remarks Cantor 1 to Cantor 2 with a tragic chuckle—*you're ill served by your megalomania.*[142]

---

[142]In her depicted relationship with Cantor, Death, that sluttish late riser with a soft spot for inflicting pain, ends up resembling, in some wacky prosopopœical way, "Mem-ory the messenger of the Eternal," who, in Kierkegaard's *Purity of Heart*, pays visits to "the one who truly wills the good." (Death is made to resemble Memory just enough, however, to ensure that in emerging from the bowels of the comparison she ends up smelling rankly and grossly unworthy of it.) Upon confessing that when things really unbearable he tends to forget even the pivotal moment when the good reso-lution conquered within him, the one who truly wills asks if at such hours, Memory could see her way clear to making a fortifying visit (this scene shows SK at his heart-breakingly maudlin best). She swears by all eternity that she'll come. Would Cantor's bedmate Death deliver such a promise? Of course not. But just as for D.H. Lawrence it's Arabella not Sue who's the prima ballerina in the *Jude* ballet, so may wily Death ultimately far outshine wraithlike Memory as the very model of a modern major gen-eralissima of One Thing country. And, indeed, Memory, it should be noted, is herself no slouch in the infliction department: When she asks (oafishly? viciously? caringly? *road-to-hell-is-paved-with-good-intentions-*ly) if the one who truly wills remembers all the hardships and sufferings endured for the sake of his resolution, he has to implore her to shut up and let sleeping dogs lie. (So, dear reader: run, don't walk, to Søren Kierkegaard, *Purity of Heart Is to Will One Thing*, Douglas V. Steere, translator [New York, Harper Torchbooks, 1956], chap. 9, p. 142.)

The job of the obituary's certain slant of light—of enlightenment (*who is doing the thinking here? Death? Cantor? the Master? Herbert? the Gray Eminence who pulls the strings of every other gray eminence, past, present and to come?*)—will be to *oppress*, like the weight of cathedral tunes (drenched in schadenfreude), all who'll listen—to oppress with the news that Cantor's time properly came and went since, if left untethered, he'd only have ended up a redundancy, proof against rehabilitation by even the world's greatest obituarist. (Moral of the story? Well, for starters, there's no point in dragging things on indefinitely—the rest his soul is going to is infinitely preferable even if it's not necessarily a far, far better one than he's ever known.) And so what if Cantor rejects any and all explanations-as-verdicts, whatever the flavor? He won't be around to read all these smarmy catty takes on his historic struggles with angels better and worser—mostly worser, which would render him way more exposed (such being the power of the printed word) than at the moment of returning, from the depths of his urn, the stare of respect-payers—funeral and casting ceremony addicts with too much time on their hands—crones of both sexes obscenely tempted to drown his ashes in their gawking crocodile tears. (Nothing more exposing—exposed—more self-condemning—than death, except maybe poverty, wreaking havoc as they both do on all—i.e., the only things—his premature grayness holds stiffly sacred—privacy and order—everything-in-its-place type order.) The inkstained Santas in Death's little workshop are well on their way to jolting the kaleidoscope of his fate into its final anatomization *as we speak*. It sounds harder than it is. All they've got to do is follow the wordflow—literary equivalent of *follow the money*— that they themselves generate for the purpose of proving (let the wordflow be their mentor—let the Child be Father to the Man) that his life's fabled fullness was all deficit and vice versa—of proving its ultimate meaning couldn't have issued forth under any other set of coordinates and that the ostensible randomness of those coordinates set the stage—constituted the very armature, fulcrum, pivot, scaffolding—for a carefully contrived culmination—the only conceivable culmination—of yet another life lived amateurishly to the hilt. And if the obituarists feel particularly ambitious (in fact they have no choice: with Death at the helm, ambition's *de rigueur*), they will have to come up with the kind of explanation that cries out for waters-muddying decryption (just the thing to set any self-loathing meaning addict's—any self-respecting meaning monger's—gypsy blood astir) calling in turn for the nitty-gritty over several generations of a salvation army of savvy techlanders—a blessing to job seekers at any time but especially in the midst of a . . . pandemic.

Pandemic: The Movie, OR A Literary Opportunist's Dreamscape

And now that you mention it, Cantor who has a nose—and a need—a crying need—for such things can smell one—a pandemic, that is—simmering on the horizon and just about ready to breed levels of unemployment not seen in over a century. For it just so happens that the unbearably cruel Present Age, whose center cannot hold since it's currently overpopulated by lunatic fringers who've abandoned the dark web of their sewer suburbs and gone ghoulishly, gleefully, mainstream (like Sidonie Powell, that coven creature with a law degree from Tall Tale Tech—a kook shot straight out of the cannon of Robson/Lewton's wallop-packing *Seventh Victim*—whose portable podium is thrift-shop paranoia)—for it just so happens that the Age and its center are ripe for and demand drastic change—whether for Evil or, if worse comes to worst, for [*in a stage whisper*] . . . for Good—and the only thing that can bring it on in record time is a plague. The snail's pace adopted by scum tasked with making the planet unlivable for all but the shamelessly mythical top-one-billionth-of-one-per-cent-of-the-top-one-per-cent—scum tasked with making obsolete both (*a*) services based, for example, on face-to-face interactions and (*b*) those who manage to pay their rent and put gruel in their kids' mouth, albeit barely, by providing such services—the snail's pace adopted by the scum and their scullions is *unsustainable* (to use a top-tier byword—shibboleth par excellence—of the elitist hoi polloi), not to mention unacceptable. Why, if this continues—if this *were to continue*—if the taskworkers—the henchmen—on retainer and for hire and on the take and on the make (i.e., heads of state [liberal and il-] and their boy- and girl-toys and senators and revolving door lobbyists and secretaries of the treasury and generalissimos [armchair and otherwise]) were to continue to fail to algorithm the insulted and injured—the wretched of the earth—the members of that unfittest-of-the-unfittest demographic half-blessed half-cursed with the temerity through thick and thin to *survive*—if said taskworkers were to continue to fail to algorithm them all out of existence—then the aforementioned super-minuscule slice of the trillionaire brigade—the crème de la crème of the so-called donor class (donors but not quite straight out of a painting by van Eyck or van der Weyden)—as unmoved as *Fantasia*'s blimps by the sweaty aroma of the endlessly long lines backed up at soup kitchens nationwide—then the Mercers and the Kochs of the world (how come up with a list of these dark-money moguls that is exhaustive without being enumerative? Cantor wonders, between belly laughs at the whole damn thing) might end up having no choice but to roll up their sleeves and go rogue and finish the dirty job themselves—maybe even become . . . [*in a stage whisper*] intermittent do-gooders along the way, out of sheer exasperation—perversity—boredom—and do what do-gooders would do or pretend to do or plan to do under the circumstances, namely, (*a*) apply some sort of namby-pamby societal poultice (a UBI, say) to the suppurating wound of injustice (that rusty chestnut) and inequality (that rickety warhorse) or (*b*) see to it that I&I are exacerbated beyond remedy in order at the last moment and with all hope abandoned to pull one—a remedy's rabbit's foot, that is— out of their blimpy hat and end up canonized for selfless legerdemain. They know—the zillionth percent of the top zillionth percent of the political donor class—the crème de la crème—the scurf de la scurf—of the donor class—they know that things have to be speeded up and can't be allowed or expected to take their course and that time by the way is a-wastin' (even if Time Itself is on Its way out—is a thing of the past—is about to be outsourced to a call center or back office on some uneclipsible asteroid to the south of Pluto or haven't you heard?)—they know, though not from experience, that the cruelest thing of all is to keep the wretched on tenterhooks about whither they are being shipped now that the goods they produce and the services they provide are already a thing of the past. Even if cruelty, brute cruelty (as the GOP never ceases to repeat), is the whole point. So it looks to Cantor like (for it's not the Master, nor that would-be renegade Ishmael M. Drybock, but Cantor—cartoonist Cantor—Tex Avery Cantor—who is responsible for this mushrooming thought balloon)—it looks like nothing less than a plausibly deniable plague can (heeding the donors' call and simmering on the horizon) compel the taskworkers who do the bidding of the donor class (or is it the other way around?)—to—to—to . . . it looks like only a plague can compel those workers to do their job even if doing their job means just doing what comes naturally—what they've really wanted to do all along (only faster, faster, faster), which is to annihilate the yearning masses (with their irksomely unquenchable needs and their ornery resistance to passing on the mantle of immiseration to needs-free robots) in one fell swoop while leaving shareholder value (the precious last bastion cum crown jewel of the Free Market—the fancy-free market of unsellables-run-by deplorables; and supreme indicator—marker—yardstick—barometer—of the unstoppable progress of civilization) intact and unconcerned.[143] Or some such. Which isn't to say that said pandemic—the rarest of birds whatever its provenance—will lose no time going global and thinking only about Civilization (i.e., shareholder value), with the little guy as usual getting lost in the shuffle . . . the shuffle of . . . all the other little guys. Which isn't to say that the pandemic will give him (the little guy to end all little guys) short shrift—that the pandemic won't try as best it can to speed up the evolution of the little guy's very personal misery in tandem (*psst!* the little guy's personal misery is what's left of misery when the goods-and-services side of things—the working-stiff side of things—the shareholder-value side of things—has been factored out of his measly equation, that is, if it can ever *be* factored out)—which doesn't mean the pandemic won't try out of decency and like any pandemic worth its salt to bring the misery to a boil here and now—immediately rather than several dark decades of further unnecessary suffering from now—won't try to help him, the little guy, get the inevitable out of the way well ahead of schedule and sooner rather than later and without any further ado. For the pandemic is the proverbial straw that broke the cam-

---

[143] Consider in this regard the case of Boeing, poster pig for all that's rotten in the state of "corporate culture." Even after the crash of two 737 Max jets between October 2018 and March 2019—fruit of that culture's obsession with share price über alles—nothing really changed. Only the pandemic to come—which brought air travel to a screeching halt and triggered the cancellation by airlines worldwide of their orders for what turned out to be a reincarnation of the Hindenburg—only the pandemic could stop Boeing from buying back stock and issuing dividends and force it to (ever so fleetingly, ever so trendily) cut executive salaries and adopt oversight policies and, in a gest of supreme—of white supremacist—sacrifice, *sell the corporate yacht* and all (the) idle hands on aboard. Not 535 crash victims, mind you, but only scuttled flights and scuttled sales could compel the company to take some very feeble steps in the direction of symbolically skewering the rot. For further details, see, e.g., David Gelles, "Boeing's saga of capitalism gone awry," *New York Times*, 24 November 2020.

el's back—or rather the non-proverbial straw as big as Jupiter that strives to break the camel's back in one fell stroke rather than in millions. Precisely because the pandemic *has* his back—precisely because the pandemic is in his corner—is his friend in the biz—is the help that's on the way—is not just man's best friend but also a dog's—in short, the pandemic is here to help put him out of his misery once and for all—no, to help him put himself out of his misery— the misery of being himself—which self-help in this case means either (*a*) killing first his wife or his boss or his immediate superior (who's even lower on the scrotum-pole than he himself) or his kids or his stepmother or his father or every next-door neighbor he can lay his hands on or all of the above—and then killing himself—or, (*b*) just in the nick of time and well in advance of the fanfareless roll-out of a vaccine, resisting such bloody promptings, in order to sink-or-swim his way to the instantaneous glory of self-surpassment—that is, surpassment of his bedrock craving to wreak havoc on a world that's never thought twice about wreaking havoc on his other cravings (all of them legitimate and some even inadvertently noble)—with penile enhancement thrown in as a bonus—in order to fast-track his way to never again needing to fear being put through that wringer of bad-ass contingencies known to the candy-ass cognoscenti as mental illness—mental illness served stone-cold on a bed of basmati rice—the rice of endemic, systemic poverty.[144] For if the little guy is forever auditioning on behalf of self-annihilation so is the pandemic auditioning as well,[145] though in its case what's at stake is nothing less than coronation as the Greatest Pandemic that Ever Lived—which entails competing with nothing less than every other pandemic past, present and to come—and part of passing the audition means proving it can work on two scales at once— the micro- and the macro-. (*No more Business as Usual*, shrieks the Pandemic. *No More Mr. Nice Guy*, warbles the Pandemic. No more *Turn the Other Cheek*—not even a butt cheek, croons the Pandemic.) So if for no other reason than self-interest the pandemic must hew to the line that there's no little guy too small or too slow-moving to merit the massive push of its intervention— its proof (by casting a retrospective glow or damper on his past) that he, the little guy, has been all along converging toward a final solution only not fast enough. For that's the job of a pandemic, i.e.: To make sure that the normal course of events suddenly plays out abnormally fast. To make sure that evolution becomes one big shock effect administered in record time. To make sure that whatever's been waiting in the wings, like the transmogrification of all

---

[144]Since poverty and mental illness, "thus allied/Go to make a" bumpy ride.

[145]And so, for that matter, is Envy Disease—auditioning, I mean—and for nothing less than the less-than-coveted role of overarching theme and supreme subject and ur-topic of everybody's (whether they know it or not) all-time favorite bedtime story— the story called *Invidicum*. The role, coveted or not, of "what *Invidicum*'s all about"— the role of Figure in its Carpet. Because if Panurge believed nature created Man to borrow, well, then, Cantor is left with no choice but to go him one better, by insisting that not just Man but all other things—goods and services and things that are neither—were born but to audition—to be auditioned out of their misery.

goods into services (renderable only remotely, if you please, or not at all), is yanked out of cold storage and forced, ready or not, to assume its starring role—the role it was born to play—and to play it to the emptiest of all empty houses—the empty haunted house called progress. Which is not to say that a pandemic doesn't at the same time know how to perpetrate *slow* torture—slower than evolution at its most conservative—its most *Victorian*—doesn't know how to make excruciating pain—physical and emotional—just plain boring. But that's a subject for further (fireside) research.

And yet—and yet—Cantor, even if he is a little guy—the quintessential little guy—maybe the littlest of 'em all (or is this just the Masterly bullhorn, always within earshot, peddling its latest invention: self-aggrandizement through self-diminishment?)—and yet Cantor has never felt more alive—things have never felt less ultimate—less final. Even with a pandemic heading his way. *Especially* with a pandemic heading his way. Since it's about to hand him the keys to the city whether the city is Santa Barbara or New York or, better yet, the City of Dis. Or any other city you care to name. Wherever he ends up the crowds will have fled and the streets will be bare and, as shadow mayor, he'll have every sidewalk and nightmare alley all to himself. Fact is, pandemic fever has done him a world of good and now he's immune—might even be able to peddle his antibodies on eBay and make a killing—modest, but a killing nonetheless. Or is this yet another case where (*a*) the anguish induced by—and simultaneously driving—the thing thought and (*b*) the delight generated by the contour—the texture—of the thought itself *qua thought* have come predictably to a parting of the ways—another case where the fancy footwork of wordflow has managed heroically to squash the unkempt bug that is worldflow—another case where the fancy footwork has managed to trivialize the thing thought and thereby rob the thinker of his . . . of his—well, of his thinkerly musculature—his very birthright. *Never mind all that.* Now that he knows the worst (that he's about to be annihilated with the unceremoniousness reserved for lower-echelon sewer rats [oh, to be a bulldog rat! for to be one of those critters is to be—extinct!]) he's ready to go on. More good news—a first: Invidicum intake has triggered a side effect targeting the very core of his cognitivity such as it is—a side effect (he can feel it in his bones) affiliated not to the Master but to Death and since he's just swept the rug of complacency out from under her, their relationship—now a tourney of equals—has nothing left to do but ripen into . . . a trip to the moon on gossamer wings. Imagine! Death as his very own private master and mistress and muse! To whom he alone has access! (for as much as he admires Melanctha the perceived flaunting of the exclusivity of her relation to the Master rankles more or less, depending on the humidity). To whom he can confide his deepest fears!—that in a pinch, for example, he'd be incapable of suicide even if he has every reason in the world to excel. After all, there's the death of Berry Sundae and, more recently, exclusion from the sylvan gambols of the ballet boy and girl (he's trying to keep the message of the boy's body—that leisureliness is potency—well in mind). Not to mention his professional difficulties, among which the lemma business stands out as first among equals. To which she might very well reply (but should he be putting words in her mouth and thereby jinx the connection—smother it in its cradle?) that although self-slaughter is clearly not Cantor's cup of tea, the prospect, after the news of a job well done hits the fan, of acclaim from funeral addicts (even well-wishers like the ones he was just execrating) might be just the thing to give him a manful yen for the act, if not for the crocodiles who cheer it on. The notion of such a yen brings not altogether manful tears to his eyes. And while he's at it, Cantor'd like to beg the pardon of his newfound master for the spectacle he made of himself a while back with his protestations of despair—a poor man's despair at best—especially since she's sure to have been privy to countless far more convulsedly authentic exhibitions in the despair department. Thing is, he felt he had no choice but to redirect his steps despair-wards for at a certain point in its trajectory, despair—or at least the poor man's version—can be depended on—it's in despair's very DNA—to reward the seasoned sufferer by seeming to usher in a new tomorrow. In short, there's no getting unfettered from hope no matter how hard he tries (is this a confession or a threat? he wonders, inasmuch as he can feel himself screwing up his eyes and gritting his teeth). Cantor doesn't want to be rude (he discovers he's now conversing only with himself: he's muted the sound of Death on his computer and whited out her graven image from the screen [she's turned out to be too much of a good thing—a taste that can never be acquired]) but if she has any intention of lecturing him on the dangers of transforming the gauziest ray of it—hope, he means—into an affirmation of ultimate triumph (receipt of the Abel Prize, say, or the Fields Medal)—into an affirmation so massive—so much of a scene-stealer—that it inevitably grinds the triumph being hawked down to an irrelevance—a bit player—if she has any such wisdom to impart he'd say she'd do better to keep it to herself. Adding insult to injury, his relationship with Death—though it's neither his fault nor hers—has become, and in record time, the too fanciful stuff of fable (at least to the unpracticed eye and ear)—has turned into a pastorale very much in the tradition of Venus versus Adonis or in the Endymion versus Selene vein. Even if for those whose only access to spectacle is via the olfactory route—for those who assimilate best in olfactory mode—this relationship is in fact the exemplar par excellence—the ne plus ultra—of kitchen-sink realism (sanitized-poeticized, of course, for micro-mass consumption). Why, it exudes enough of the stench of tenements (a blast or two, Maestro, of Alfred Newman's "Street Scene," if you please) to make no less a worthy than Tennessee Wittgenstein go green with envy.

But Cantor, if you must know, still hasn't gotten Eudoxus fully off his chest—hasn't found the opportunity to make it clear that if he's once again tempted to recruit the Cnidean it's not so much to lend intellectual lustre to the lustrelessness of an orgy but to enrich it—to show that *intrinsically* it is more than an orgy, more than itself, as anything can prove to be more than itself if only given half a chance. *For what's the point of being—of having—a self if it can't turn out* (and don't bother looking for the author of this saw in *Bartlett's*) *to be more than itself?* And if Borkman, once again getting his feet wet in that Dead Sea of secondary sexuals, wonders, without knowing he wonders (owing to Cantor's intervention for there are times when Cantor—in accordance with the dynamic [one of many] put into play by the Master—is more Borkman than Borkman himself could ever be and it's at those times that he's ready and willing—without feeling in the least like a scullion or a flunkey or a shabti—to do Borkman's wondering for him), what Marx the fetishist would have had to say about all this, it's not to exalt—or rather, it's not *only* to exalt—the present crime scene and in tandem himself but to express what's no longer latent. A lowdown orgy only seems to be incompatible with Karl's exalted ways and wiles. One thing is relatable to something else as long as the language—the wordflow—is at hand to unite the two. So should he go ahead and pitch Marx—and maybe even Eudoxus, at no extra charge—to Jim, Jr? Or would that look like what it is—an awkward forward pass?

Problem is, Margo's son is thinking very different thoughts. Which is how it should be, he being as different from Cantor and Borkman as different can be. "Where'd he come from?" he can hear some of the start-uppers sneering. But he's protected against sneers because the California air has quickly turned to blood in his veins and the blood into white wine. Why settle for emotional disablement? Why let stigmatization arising from having been—from being—a person of interest (oh, all right, a suspect) in some old murder case impede his vocational progress? Especially when that very stigma may come in handy in the milieu—or as his dead father (ever the pedant, even posthumously) would have put it, the *milieu intérieur*—he intends to frequent come hell or high water—as a sort of passport or shibboleth: proof that he has screenplays aplenty up his sleeve based on that wildly overrated asset, bitter personal experience. Fact is, he's grown spiritually by leaps and bounds in the last few months thanks largely but not exclusively to his Sr.'s all-too-timely death, the first sign of liberation being the calm refusal to be further browbeaten by a chronic failure to express himself adequately. He's come to think *visually* and Headmaster O'Halloran or Houdini or O'Wallerstein—or whatever his name is (he knows perfectly well what his name is)—be damned. And what better place to go on doing so than CA and but a hundred miles from LA no less and in the present space shuttle, also no less? For it's turning out to be the best of all possible spaces as far as accommodation of his vision is concerned. *Since you godda have a vision if you're gunna be a star.* He's being challenged constantly and the correlative of the challenge is unending disorientation—but it's a *good* disorientation—disorientation's "good high cholesterol" in spades. Jim, Jr., perceives what the others don't even if he's not yet at the stage (and hopefully he'll never get there) of having no choice but to ascribe what he perceives to an accredited Master. (Not that he's here only to think visually, i.e., get disoriented. He's also flown himself out to the Coast expressly to be—to play—the orphan, the son, the bastard, the step-son, or whatever exhumation centuries from now reveals him neatly—and in all his inadequacy—to have been. Or maybe [who knows?] he's come out here for the sole purpose of defending his doctoral dissertation tentatively—timidly—entitled, say, "A Comparative Analysis of the Art of Self-exhortation" though these days every book worth its salt must lay claim not just to a title but to a subtitle as well—a prosthetic subtitle—a subtitle long enough to mute—geld—neuter—the title itself—a subtitle whose capacity to strait-jacket the cartilaginous gist of the theme disqualifies every other competitor plausibly invoked and auditioned by said title or, more to the point and better yet, the obligatory tug of war between title and subtitle must be an aesthetic phenomenon in its own right—a phenomenon non pareil—turning whatever's to follow into a flat-out redundancy. Or maybe he's out here to write a dissertation, to be entitled "A Comparative Analysis of the Art of Self-exhortation: The Poet to his Soul in Shakespeare's Sonnet No. 146 and the Singer to her Atricle and Ventrium in Arlen/Koehler's 'Sing, My Heart'" [the jury's still out on whether it's nobler to descend on the Golden State with both title and subtitle in tow but no book or with book and title in tow but no subtitle], for the sole purpose of defending it—victoriously—and dislodging thereby the massive chip on his shoulder.) But even if Herbert doesn't perceive what Jim perceives, she knows the Master's behind it. So which of the two deserves to be idolized or to receive, say, the Jean Hersholt Humanitarian Award? But she does have an inkling—or something approaching one—that in utilizing all these unpredictable bodies as his pivot, the Master is managing to render the space endlessly novel without having to import novelty from elsewhere. He stays faithful to his building blocks—the secondary sexuals of naked bodies. And he's compelling JJJ to visit the space from as many angles as possible, by visiting the building blocks on him from as many angles as possible. And that's easy enough inasmuch as *a building block is sexual not in itself but only in its relation to other blocks and to the whole* (now for this you *can* check *Bartlett's*). So the space, as it turns out, is insured against exhaustibility—as long, that is, as there are secondary sexual surprises galore—surprises that reveal without revealing a thing (even if brutishly hairy forearms in tandem with a hairless chest appear appear to speak volumes). Margo's boy—who's still young enough to be entitled to have his go at ending up some kind of prodigy—knows he's come to the right place. And maybe he can even find some time to help Margo grieve. According to Herbert who at present has nobody's ear to bend (shunned because she refused to strip?), the Master—true to his Lower East Side roots—has picked—pickled—this space—cooked the books of this space, but for its own good—the space of an orgy gone bad or sour or obsolete (the Orgy Clinic, Jim, Jr., heard some people call it on the line to the restroom though he isn't sure whether they were serious but wouldn't the fact that they weren't serious mean the words were very much so?). And the Master's job (the constraint's above all ethical—like Mitch the Witch's compulsion to cram courts big and small with incompetents)—and through him, Jim, Jr.'s—is to stay put in the space and milk it dry—to stay in the space on the surface of the space—to extract with a minimum of tools stunning revelation without inconvenient content. His job is to strafe the turf of the given with his camera eye in an infinity of ways and on no account import any more building blocks once the doors are sealed against excess. And Jim, she has a feeling, will make the perfect spectator—the naïf Jean failed to become. And while we're at it, she has to hand it to Him (though not necessarily on a silver platter): he's definitely created a spectacle. These nakeds—*live*. They're even turning into bona fide nudes. No mere Sunday staffage, no mere deadwood—no mere bumps on a log. Through the nakeds or nudes, by virtue of their indifference to the self-designated spectacle and *a fortiori* to its own urgency—by virtue of their refusal to kowtow to the main event—the spectacle begins to live.

If Jim, Jr., intends to think visually, murmurs Herbert (who's beginning to feel maternal as usual when it costs her nothing), then he needs to look out for the secondary sexuals—the giblets—that pack the biggest wallop. I.e., the ones that are faded out on or tracked past—jettisoned—at the very moment they're being born—the ones that make it their business to give the impression they've been included in the final cut only by some oversight—as the side effect of well-schooled ineptitude. If Jim, Jr., is to be the ideal spectator, then (the Master's banking on it) he has to be either too early or too late for the image in question. The image that matters is the one that isn't quite caught. The image almost caught, say, through—or on the beat of—an elevator door closing. The image that's an intrusion—an obstruction en route to something relevant. The good image must never be on time. Why, if she were only the boy's age—

In a corner, having resurfaced, Walser (or a reasonable facsimile)—not only an imp of the perverse, if ever there was one, but now (which will go a long way toward beefing up his credentials as a virtuoso when it comes to transmuting the lead of bitter personal experience into screenwriterly fool's good) a bona fide renegade from van life—is sitting cross-legged before a watermelon rind of expectant young lovelies. Herbert is reminded by the cross-leggedness . . . reminded . . . but of what, exactly? Well, of Pritchard, if you must know—when he looked, and maybe was, a mere Shropshire lad of no more than seventy—and of those *dunkelgoldene Frühlingstage* up at the bunker pool—capped by the LAPD's exciting visit which has left a bittersweet aftertaste of letdown. How she longs for the bunker even if it resembles not a little the Brutalist Long Lines Building at 33 Thomas and even if, at 138 feet, the bunker's a quarter its size. But she stops herself: she doesn't want to glamorize the past only to end up feeling compelled to deglamorize it hook, line and sinker. Indifferent to her reveries (though no more than she herself for she has plenty more where these came from), Walser is demonstrating how the psychoanalyst Jack LaLanne proved Envy's greasy underbelly is structured like the language of pornography. But the lovelies look as if they've had just about as much as they can stand of such analogies even if furnished by somebody who obviously practices what he preaches of *Mens sana in corpore sano*. The loveliest of all has had the courage to raise her hand but before he can acknowledge it (or is he markedly ignoring her, smelling trouble?) insists he's gotten his wires crossed. "What?" "Jacques Lacan, not Jack LaLanne." Pulling out pad and pencil and explaining that he's also had two years of pharmacy school, Walser writes her out a prescription for Lamictal *and* Seroquel (a bad sign). The uncalled-for correction indicates she's on the verge of a psychotic outburst—no, full-fledged psychosis. Lavishing an expert Gioconda smile on the rest of the group (not as many as he thought at first) he announces with a certain irritation (as if they're guilty by association) that the session (which could have been so fruitful) is officially at an end. It's clear to Melanctha—how refreshing to be called by her first name—that Walser's decided he's already dazzled them with enough defective scholarship—showered them with quite enough misinformation—and at bargain-basement prices, no less—that his indulgence has gone on far too long—well beyond the span of the session even if he's cut it brutally short. So without further ado, my dear friends, it's time for him to usher them out (no more Mr. Nice Guy). If anybody else would like a similar prescription—L and S are the flavors of the week—feel free to write him a polite note (no emails, please—at least, not before noon—he sleeps late and not just on weekends) and he'll see what he can do. Yes, rumor has it that Walser's at the venture-capitalization stage of his own start-up and rumor is yet again right on the money. What he has in mind is a bouquet of drugs targeted at the misunderstood-genius market: a drug for writers and filmmakers who want to portray addiction to, say, Envy or pornography—or addiction to envy of those addicted to pornography or Envy—but can't manage to rustle up the grub of a cowboy craving from deep within. As for you, members of the painter tribe (they know who they are), known to hate nothing so much as living life in a continuous present, coming right up is a drug to prevent you from, in consequence, self-sabotagingly starving the beloved of what he or she needs most in order to go on being born—a drug that enables you, the lover, to transmit an instantaneous sense of your jovial if forged participation in that loathed life lived without having had to take a scaldingly cold bath in its unsinkable duration. Borkman, Jr., can't believe what he's just heard. Did Walser happen by any chance to eavesdrop not so very long ago on a certain archetypal struggle (masquerading as a conversation) between a certain father and son in a certain Village diner specializing in arrogant yokels once over lightly? Or did Borkman try to impress his learned friend by presenting his son's achievement as his own? Or was he simply too drunk an authentically proud father to know the damage his drunkenness was inflicting on a career just past the treacherous budding stage? Though precisely how much damage could a knucklehead like Walser actually do as a plagiarist?

Coming straight up to Jason Borkman, young Straynge splutters—but with exceptional breath control—"I was told to look you up once I got out here. In New York, you're a legend: the man who can't imagine his life without a start-up and who can't be imagined without a start-up up his sleeve." *The sleeve of my gray flannel hoodie autographed by none other than Sloan Wilson himself,* young Borkman sneers within—deep within—so deep in fact that he isn't quite sure what the sneer is for—or for whom it's been crafted—and expertly, he might add. Jason makes a gracious have-a-seat gesture (which means: *At last a man—boy—who values me at my true worth*) though there's no seat to be had. It's standing room only. In a whisper, though his father is a long way off, Straynge—or Strainge, as he was known familiarly to his pals back at Payne Whitney (where are they now, he wonders, or pretends to wonder)—explains that Sr. tended to be a first-class fetishist where his patients were concerned. (And by the way just think of how—and by now they should all know without his having to mince words or beat a dead horse—just think of how in this iddy-biddy orgy clinic of all places [Strainge treats the space to a cobweb-sweeping glance] the social relation between men—rife with solidarity—has turned into a mystical relation between their secondary sexuals.) But fetishes don't have to be things—they can be mere thoughts—phantom reifications. As he discovered looking back on his father's career and remembering mysterious communications between mom and dad over the last-legs ironing board in the breakfast nook. *His father* fetishized *the thoughts of his patients*—fetishized: *a fancy word for stole.* That's what he realized on his way out here (long before the secondary sexuals were a glint in somebody's jaundiced eye)—what he *had* to realize since there was nothing worth watching on the plane—inside or out.

Yet he doesn't want Borkman, Jr., to get the wrong idea about his father—the father who's his stepfather. He's recently been dreaming about telling him how much (for all his flaws) he admired—admires—him. Problem is, the ability to recognize Straynge's strengths has blossomed in tandem with his own advancement, by leaps and bounds, as a linguistic freak. And this new mode of communicating has already acquired the bad habit of getting in the way. Yes, he's developed—in the pimply old age of his post-adolescence—what the charitable might call a "talent for language." In other words, he's come a long way from the Sutton Place School for the Blind-Who-*Will*-Not-See. What it all boils down to is that in the dream, all the nice things he has to say are canceled out by the way he says them—by the form he gives to his thoughts. The way he minces the words for his thoughts—thoughts with the best of intentions—makes his dream stepfather wince with revulsion. The way he speaks is so alien to the stolid likes of Straynge there's no way he can do the thoughts justice—he can only *do them in.* For his words (the latest and oldest sort of self-driving vehicles) have a will of their own and they always end up shamelessly *having the last word*—making a mockery of the thoughts that were to bring him and his stepdad together. The form—the accursed form—cancels out all the nice things he has to say. Naughty or nice, to Straynge he's still a freak—with all the blossoms of his linguistic baggage he's even more of a freak (and adding insult to injury linguistic freakdom permeates all the other dimension of his being, making them freakish in turn, bending them autocratically—like a thought packet, you might say—to its will). Though maybe it's the very fact that he's a fake freak which makes him unspeakable—a rarity of the worst kind. Jim, Jr., aka JJJ aka J3, begins to elaborate—though he tries not to sound freakish as he does so—tries to elaborate as unfreakishly as possible and only according to his own meagre understanding and while remaining true to his humble roots and with a tacit unborn pledge to avoid polysyllables wherever possible, not to mention all the unwanted unwarranted intricacies of dissimulation to which polysyllables by their very nature are prone (no getting round the fact that polysyllables harbor *dark secrets*). "In my recent dreams, as in life, he puts up with me. Even if he despises me, hates my guts. Funny, though." Silence. "What's funny?" Funny how he never seemed—seems—concerned (it's his dad after all or at least his adoptive dad or his fair-weather dad or his half-dad or his almost-dad or his Sunday-dinner-dad or his back-seat driver dad or his armchair-general dad or, failing all else, his foul-weather dad)—funny how he's never been concerned about all the mortal lethal toxic trouble J3's freakishness could get him into—among the real freaks—the Proud Boy thuglets, for example, or the Boogaloos—who'd have no choice when the occasion presented itself but to ascribe their own freakdom *to*—who'd have no choice but to unload their own freakdom *on*—a guy like Jim, Jr., and do him in, by way of flex cuffs and zip ties and ghillie suits. A guy like Jim, Jr.—who in fact's as far from freakdom as he is from resembling Hercules—and who's, in short, a fake freak. But from the way they're sure to go after him you'd think the Boys'd never heard about a thing called safety in numbers. So why don't they ever just sit back and revel in the comfort that sort of safety affords by converting it to a backdrop against which to do what they do best?—impersonate disgruntled loners to their collective heart's content—loners who are unsafe at any speed and friendless by choice and wedded-to-the-will-of-Rump types and with a soft spot for riding off into the blood-red sunset with a scalp or two dangling from their aviators. Straynge was—is—never concerned about the types of trouble Junior's rare unspeakability could get him into in a world that doesn't take all that kindly to freaks, fake or otherwise—to lonely traveling salesmen like him who have nothing to sell but the vacuum cleaner (or *Encyclopedia Britannica*) of their particular brand of freakishness. He has no idea—or if he does, he doesn't care—how vulnerable Junior's fake freakdom makes him out in the world—doesn't care that he's a marked man-in-training loathed by non-freaks and real freaks alike. He's shocked by Jr., Jr.'s dream dad is—as shocked as he was when he wasn't a dream—but he isn't shocked at the thought of all the miseries Junior's freakdom would expose him to—isn't shocked at the thought of all the miseries which freakdom could susceptibilize him to—out in the world—isn't made the least bit uneasy at the thought of what's in store for Jr. when his authentically fake freakdom shoves him into the maw—or up the ass—of the future—that is, if he's unlucky enough to have one awaiting him. "I'm shocked in my dream—shell-shocked, if you must know—by the lack of all feeling of protectiveness on his part. I'm an adversary and not just because I'm not his lawful wedded offspring." Helpful Jason (as helpful as a fortune cookie salesman) intervenes with a suggestion, sure to be rejected out of hand, which goes something like this—that would go something like this if he were unlucky enough to have the baroquely configured tools needed to see it through: "Maybe he felt—feels—as people often do in dreams, that since I—I mean, you—are strong enough, defiant enough, brave enough, stupid enough, timid enough, to be a freak in the first place, then he doesn't need to worry about what all the freakdom, fake or not fake, bodes for the future, maw or no maw—that is, if you're unlucky enough to have a future awaiting you—a future as solicitous and overflowing with job offers as a crook awaiting his just-paroled old crony at the prison gates—stepping in protectively (after all, what are friends for?) before the parolee does anything silly—like putting his honest-to-gods reformation to the test. Maybe the catchy tune of your pop's thinking goes something like this: Since you're strong enough to be a poor excuse for a freak in a world where freaks get by—barely—by pretending to be public-service bounty hunters whose *quarry* are the real McCoys, well, then, you're strong enough to withstand anything—even demolition at the hands of thugs. All right, I'm willing to grant your freakdom, real or not, is obviously experienced by pop as an attack, a concerted attack, a stain on his two-bit honor (a reaction complicated by his great intelligence). But hold your horses—there's a little bit of his Real—just as there is a little bit of everybody else's Real—that's intrigued by your freakdom even if it's a faux freakdom—sorry, a *fake* freakdom—or the wrong kind of freakdom or a low-dose extended-release form of freakdom (the only kind a delicate flower like your dad can get his enzymes to digest). Imagine Straynge (I feel I know him since *my* pop never misses a chance to drag him kicking and screaming into the conversation)—imagine, if you will, Straynge who's always hewed to the straight and narrow no matter where it took—dragged—him (after all, even the straight and narrow has its exotic blind alleys)—imagine Straynge—I mean your father—getting seduced—getting turned on—by freakdom." Problem is, JJJ *can't* imagine—he can only remember how Straynge was always adjusting his schedule to ensure they were never in the breakfast nook at the same time. Was he trying to spare J3 thereby the upsurge of his own freakdom? Borkman, Jr. (*doubling back out of the blue*): "But I thought you came in on the Greyhound red-eye." "A vicious rumor." "Oh." "If you want to know, in fact, I hitchhiked. But getting back to Dr. Straynge the Horse Thief. The fact that Straynge—I mean my sonofabitch deadbeat ersatz dad—robbed from so many is why there are so many potential culprits in the case and why the police—at wit's end and looking for a change of pace—focused on me (maybe it's Headmaster O'Scheiss, forever missing in inaction, who unwittingly put them on my trail)—until they got tired of focusing. Which attention of course only made me the envy of the Greenwich Avenue Irregulars—patients, doctors, advertisers, caterers, hatcheck girls and coatcheck boys, even your generic passersby." And it was envy that motored their ingenuity in planting incriminating evidence, he explains (once again according to his meagre understanding and while remaining true to his roots)—and it was envy that ultimately entangled them in a dynamic—a dialectic—of diminishing returns. To wit, the more they succeeded in making him look guilty, the more they anointed his notoriety and the more they went on envying him that notoriety—the notoriety they handed him on a silver platter as if it were the luscious head of Salome's John the Baptist—the notoriety against which they felt powerless except when they were busy spawning red herrings—MacGuffins that would have made Hitchcock's mouth water. Overhearing through no fault of his own, Cantor thinks, *So the theme of* Invidicum *is in fact Envy after all*—a mixed blessing judging from the sound of his thinking. Making this discovery causes Cantor to do nothing less than overflow with boyish charm (pity, there's nobody within miles capable of taking its full measure). But wait! There's a bonus! Overhearing it all, Cantor realizes—for the first time or for the first time in ages—how out of the ordinary his own father really was—why, he puts that half-pint Straynge to shame. For one thing, he had no idea—or, even better, didn't care—whether or not he was exceptional. The uncaring was part—the beauty part—of it all. Of course, he must have had an inkling he was smart—smarter than all the Ivy League colleges in the world put together. But the smartness was smartness in action—dissipative of any notion that before he'd have any truck with you or me we'd have to commit to coddling it. He was too busy being smart enough to put his smartness to good use—in, e.g., paying his bills promptly and managing, over a fifty-year stint, the complaint department of a nondescript furniture company out on Bruckner Boulevard and finding excuses, every chance he got, for side-door flight from the one-man complaint department run by his wife. For as he always said–without ever saying it—marriage isn't about much else besides exits and entrances—fast getaways and skulking returns to a fold that never folds—but just as long as the getaways outnumber the returns, then—then— And it was always the case that not long after he came on the scene—any scene—those burdened with discernment began—or should have begun—to feel parading one's smartness—parading that little agitation of the brain we call thought—was vulgar, if not felonious. He never needed to think of himself in terms of exceptionalness, along the blurry lines of: if he wasn't exceptional—if he wasn't *thought of* as exceptional by his peers then he might as well go out and shoot himself. Never felt a meeting was incomplete—never felt he was unreal at that meeting—until he'd enforcedly mentioned his exceptionalness. He harbored no fear of death big enough to generate a Kilroy-Was-Here-scale hunger for exceptionalness. But let's not, shall we? reduce his inability—refusal—to think of himself as exceptional—as exceptional as he had every right to think of himself as being—let's not plaster—tar and feather—this noble refusal (noble because of a total ignorance of its nobility) with speculations about some lurking psychic wound—let's not festoon the nobility with diagnostic psychobabble on the order of, say, *fear of success* or *own-worst-enemy-itis*. Since Dad's exceptionalness was etiologically better than that. Or rather it was an exalting affliction without need of an etiology—irreducible—allergic—to predisposing factors. All of which now signifies to his unfavorite son that it's way too late for Dad (obediently moldering—no, *mouldering*—in Elmont's Beth David Cemetery) to become an envier first class. (Cantor nervously wonders whether he's just said some of this out loud, not that anybody would have noticed given how busy most of them are analytically sucking and exegetically fucking their way through a drizzly Sunday afternoon on this, the closest thing to the pampas north of the Amazon, but still . . .)

"Maybe your ersatz dad's hatred—and it seems to be nothing less—can be attributed to something other than your foul gift for language." "Like what?" "By the way, sorry for the 'foul'—but I've recently taken a liking to calling a spade a spade." Walking a fine line between tact and tactfulness, i.e., walking expertly on eggshells (since from little eggshells [of tactless tact] mighty omelettes [of insight] are said to grow), Jason asks if Jim, Jr.'s father—his adoptive stepfather—ever made any cracks about his—Jr.'s—incipient . . . bald spot. Whereupon he lowers his gaze so as not to be perceived as trying to relocate the terrain in question. J³'s quizzical stare is just too wide-eyed to be genuine and for that very reason not unworthy of some pity. In fact, Jason's question has Jim, Jr., swinging from the rafters and the questioner is quite frankly intimidated by this testament to his prosecutorial skill. Though he considers himself to be well within his rights to ask since, for one thing, he's plagued by the same follicular dysfunction. What he means is, Did Straynge make any meanspirited wisecracks the way his own father did (since Borkman still had—has—a full head of hair—as theatrically overabundant, in fact, as the snow-white mane of that sleazeball Klausewitz-Casowitz, one of The Rump's wannabe Roy Cohns)? Which wisecracks may have evidenced (as Borkman's did) not just (*a*) triumphant delectation over his son's inability to resist time's scythe—or rather, time's scalp mower; and delectation's equally nasty obverse, namely, terror of being contaminated by that inability to resist; but also, giving credit where it's due, (*b*) the effort to squelch in the bud a too too painful infinite consanguinity with a son susceptible to obscenely accelerated loss, even if it was just hair loss—consanguinity with a son unable to be self-defensively, self-protectively conscious of being caught in the act of going bald by unfriendly eyes (and none unfriendlier than a rivalrous father's), as Jason was caught, for example, one wintry night on the Central Park Reservoir Loop by Borkman who managed, by keeping a few feet behind, to wangle the best seat in the house for the purpose of schadenfreude—consanguinity with a son whose unconsciousness of being spied on cried out its pathos unbeknownst to the crier—consanguinity with a son who couldn't know just how patent— patent beyond refutation—his creeping tonsure was at any given moment— consanguinity with a son exposed to his father's criminality for it's criminal of a father to be able to observe a son's wound—defect—weakness—flaw—a wound that the victim himself isn't capable of observing at every moment— and to just stand by and do or say nothing about this gross inequity while the son's momentary unconsciousness of the wound itself—and of the even big-ger wound inflicted by the father's unseen seeing (schadenfreude-crammed by its very nature)—is left to fend for itself. But who's to say that Borkman wasn't the more tragic sufferer since it must have been excruciating to be sad-dled with such a seeing—a seeing that was the wellspring of so many contra-dictory emotions? "Nope," J3 at long last responds, "never a crack, much less a wisecrack. But how did you know, based solely on his wisecracks, what your own father, while he stalked you from behind (as fathers tend to do), was see-ing and thinking and feeling? And, by the way, weren't you both taking your lives in your hands by wandering around in the dark?" "I did know—I do know—because I—Borkman, Jr.—had—have—eyes in the back of my head— and, even better, in the back of my soul—and always will."

No, Straynge never noticed the bald spot. J3 sounds, or at least looks, pretty liberated and this business about the bald spot seems to have been just the trigger he needed to confess that he has a confession to make. He's not as innocent as he may seem. In fact since he's known them he's never given his parents—his uncle-father and aunt-mother—a minute's peace—never stopped demanding that they make *It* happen. That they rev up the motor of their conjoint omnipotence and make *It* happen. "But don't get me wrong. Mom was—is—very very nice and dad, stepdad or not, did his damnedest to be sort of nice but unfortunately nice + nice doesn't always equal nice." Jason has no doubt that if he waits long enough—though he's pretty sure things will proceed apace provided he can, ASAP, make the powers-that-be think he's the very soul of patience—J3 will obligingly betray *It*'s identity. Sure enough. "I never stopped demanding they do everything to make . . . my greatness as a ballplayer happen. And it's taken not just Headmaster O'Scheiss but all fifteen of the Sutton Place Irregulars (in fact the entire Headmasters Guild of North America) to show me the evil—the brattiness—of my ways." They walked him through, but only after he'd showed some anticipatory contrition, what the demand signaled. According to this cast of thousands—who, once engaged, moved full speed ahead with all their polysyllabic guns blazing—the lacerated demand signaled the inner conflict between wanting and not wanting what he needed to believe he wanted above all else—the conflict between wanting and not wanting what he was supposed to want (but according to whom?)—what he should be wanting (but according to whom?). In other words, the demand was an impotent outcry and the outcry wanted to know *who the wanting was for*. And archetypal mother and father—two of the bumpiest bumps on a log you'd ever want to meet—were to provide not the material conditions for his becoming the greatest ballplayer of all time (even the most inept parent duo could do that and in fact the conditions were already in place thanks to the drip-drip-drip from a generous trust fund bequeathed by ex-con Abel Magwitch Straynge, his fake dad's twin brother) *but the hunger itself*—the unmitigated hunger to be the greatest—which problematically was and yet wasn't there—at least it wasn't *there in the exact neuronal spot where it most needed to be*. In short, the neuronal spot in question was in his case a *bald* spot. He wasn't consumed by the authentic hunger to be a ballplayer—he hated himself for not harboring that hunger—hated them even more for not having ensured that the proper hunger-breeding mutations were affixed to his genome. The hunger he did harbor was the hunger to be great at all cost—in fact, he wanted to bypass the dugout—the nitty-gritty of the ball-playing itself—and head straight for greatness by masterfully hitting the ball straight out of the park but (even more masterfully) without being obliged to take a single swing at it. He wanted greatness *in its pure state* untrammeled by a specific vocation—a specific gimmick. But his love of the bat was no less intense for all that, or so he needed to believe. And if the right kind of hunger wasn't there then it was always the fault of the bumps, who had transformed him—out of the sheerest malice—into what he should never have become. (Cantor fears that J³'s self-absorption masquerading as self-laceration will be read by the members of this coastal semi-elite nudist colony as, at best, a desecration of the chaos their scaly naked bodies have been trying so hard to sow. Until he realizes that even if fully clothed, Jr. is, thanks to his confession, more naked than everybody else and in fact [if the glint in their eye is to be trusted] they're already claiming him as one of their own—as the trailblazer in fact who's gone furthest in proving that nudity is, when all is said and done, a state of mind.) They should have done their duty and made his hunger real—should have invoked the mean spirit of that hunger and made it stay—so as to help him escape from—from—from— "Escape from what?" Jason hopes he sounds impatient enough to strangle Jr. right here and now. "The real vocation—the real vocation staring me in the face." Thing is, he still doesn't know what this will turn out to be. In the tone—bitter yet bright—of one speaking from experience, Jason tells him to be prepared for the fact that whatever the vocation does turn out to be, it will always pale woefully in comparison with ballplaying—the vocation that refuses, even now, to be the right fit—the vocation for which he doesn't have the talent—or (more to the point) the interest. Only he mustn't make a vocation out of craving the wrong vocation—of treading the primrose path of dalliance hand in hand with the wrong vocation—as so many of Jason's start-up rivals (now dead by their own hand) have done—even if he's already been seduced, seemingly beyond reclamation, by its not being quite the right fit—seduced by the dandyish air with which it flaunts its unfitness (the same air no doubt with which his unregenerately non-suicidal old pal Harold Skimpole would have flaunted his unfitness, if he'd been a vocation instead of a parasite). Jason thinks of stopping—of sparing him any further enlightenment (since enlightenment as he practices it always violates the first law of writers workshop rehab, namely, *Show, don't tell*)—but in the end decides against sacrificing his brand of tough love to the frivolous perversity of first laws and instead fires off a twenty-one-gun salute to the exigencies of the moment which, in this case at least, are on his side. "So I gather what you expect *me* to do is rescue you from that real vocation which you reject because it's too much of a piece with the real you—the self-hating you—the polluted you—polluted by virtue of being you. But why me? Is it because I seem to be a guy who has the right kind of vocation-hunger by the balls—who's at one—but resolutely not at peace—with *his* vocation? You hunger—constitutionally, you're capable of having the hots—only for what's alien—as alien to you as you are—were—to your fair-weather ersatz stepdad. You reject the real vocation precisely because it's more you than you are. It fits like a baseball glove and therefore isn't worth pursuing. Though please be aware that you're probably grossly underestimating the challenges it's capable of perpetrating given half a chance." Jason takes a deep breath. Why? Because it's there to be taken and he's earned it.

It sounds to Cantor—now, after several promotions, pretty much Melanctha's first lieutenant when it comes to addressing matters Masterly—as if He's up to his old tricks. Having recently extruded from His bloody buttocks a new crop of piping hot packets, the Master's sole aim has been to ram them down the throat of the Invidicum Story in the hope that upon finding themselves to be the strangest of bedfellows, they'll get busy doing what strange bedfellows always do in the end, which is conform to each other's contours while retaining most of their own signature rough edges—in the hope that once relieved of the recalcitrant stench of their individuality through fusion or even through run-of-the-mill intercalation they'll go on to cohabit in some semblance of polemical harmony-ever-after—in the hope that they'll transform themselves by transforming each other—that they'll construct a whole greater than the sum of its parts. And it's fallen to these two stooges (Cantor tries to put comparisons to Federalists Ted Hawley and Josh Cruz[146] out of

---

[146]But it's impossible for Cantor to put Josh out of his mind and not just because his negative charisma schtick broke all box-office records at the Master's flagship Tennessee Wittgenstein dinner theater. Impossible to forget the Cruz crew sailing down Fifth on the tackiest of celebrity floats and greeting the crowd's cheeriest of Bronx cheers with the phoniest noblesse-obliging exhibition of grateful ectsasy this side of the Tower of London. Equally impossible to forget how the politico's wily missus, undaunted by so much irreverence, waved, waved and waved some more as if knighting all his fans in advance for heeding her plea to lower the temperature of their adoration.

his mind), whether they're aware of it or not, to do the Master's bidding—to give concrete embodiment to His own homegrown version of what may be referred to loosely as G-String Theory. And just because JJJ jumps the developmental track when he pursues the wrong vocation—the vocation whose sole recommendation is its unattunement to his real hungers—doesn't mean the Master is similarly misguided when He seeks to make a virtue of necessity by giving pride of place to the vocation of packeteer over the vocation of storyteller, suspecting that in so doing He'll end up with the best of both worlds.

JJJ looks offended—and looking offended makes him look stupid, or at least bloated. "Sorry, old man, I was just trying to help. To get to the bottom of your ex-dad's hatred." "I never said he hated me." "You're right, you didn't," Jason concedes and conceding makes him feel more like a man—or rather, more *than* a man. "What you did say was that he hated *your guts.*" *When I want your help I'll ask for it* appears to be on the tip of J³'s forked tongue. "But you're right about what I expected from you—I wanted to *be* you even before we met. I expected my father to find a way—to pay somebody (he has connections)—to make me into you—so I could start wanting what you want since everything I've known about you proves you were born to be a start-up man of the first rank. So you'll forgive me for hating you more than I idolize you." "(Just being born to do something, by the way, doesn't mean you should be allowed to do it. Consider, for example, that colicky cautionary tale soused on its own self-entitlement who goes by the swarthy moniker of Bret Von Kavanaugh.) I'm simply trying to understand how you got into the mess you're in. Thing is, once you realize there is no way out of it—no way out of the mess that Jimmy Durante, PhD, refers to as the timeless father/son dyad—you'll breathe easier and sleep better (though I don't know if you're receptive to such a realization). And on top of that, you have a murder charge to contend with—even if being a person of interest or a target or a prime suspect or a barricaded subject confers a certain notoriety and notoriety breeds envy—in your case, the coveted envy of none other than the Greenwich Ave Irregulars. Still, juggling apples and oranges as you're doing is no mean feat—in fact, it's nothing less than a pathway to greatness, that is, if you can carry it off."

But what ultimately took the kick out of their envy (for news travels fast on Greenwich Avenue—*faster than anywhere else in the Big Apple* [yet another exhibit A, as if more were needed, of the Master's hyperlative mode going into overdrive? Cantor wonders])—what caused his enviability stocks to plummet—was mom's insistence on a conspiracy of an entirely different sort—a conspiracy that rejected the rules of foul play. A homegrown sort of conspiracy which robbed him of all mystery—which made him the victim of the GAIs' pity—pity, which is always 98 percent guffawing contempt—which cut him down to size—the size of an FBI subject barricaded behind his mother's apron strings. He'd been perfectly happy to become a state party to a respectable down-to-earth conspiracy—a gentleman conspiracy of the old school, so to speak—one that could lay claim to providing every amenity he'd come to associate with conspiracies in their pure state—a conspiracy that would surely outlive him long enough to sing his eternal praises. He'd been perfectly happy fielding the incriminating evidence (not too much, not too little, but just enough to make him harmlessly notorious) which the ragtag conspiracy of Irregulars gently batted his way—planted with an amateurishness only experts could simulate. He'd been getting quite fond of the traps the GAIs set for him (and not merely because his notoriety was on the line with their every new ploy). So, just when he'd done the equivalent of making partner in the whitest of white-shoe law firms, Margo came along and tried to wreck everything by proclaiming it—the conspiracy—was all a family affair—that her family had joined forces with Straynge's in setting J³ up so as to ensure she'd spend the rest of her life feeding him death-row false hope on her Sunday visits. They wanted her to suffer for what a press release put out by their spokesperson described as having "reduced Straynge's life project to blood and ashes"—wanted her to fear until her last breath that she'd given birth to a freak and was monstrous by association. He was expected to suppress his disbelief in the face of a conception that was very much inferior to the Irregulars', for theirs was motored by poetry. Fact is, being a world-class conspiratologist with a CV stretching From Here to Canarsie militated formidably, contrary to popular belief, against her being taken seriously as one of conspiracy's bards. And was it the thirst for relevance through political correctness—the right sort of ideological necessity and sociopolitical angst—that drove her to recruit the Nine Ps (Putzder, Pruitt, R. Paul, Papadopoulos, Pompeo, Pence, Price and the two "Lost" Boys, Sonny and Davy Perdue) together with those bastions of High Ghoulishness DaVos, Ross, Kushner and Mnunchkin, even if she'd had the slimmest of dealings with the whole lot of 'em? "Good question," thinks—no, says—Borkman, Jr. "Why add that measly scum to the broth? *Mammoth only in their measliness.* Mediocrities all, not just intellectual—worse, moral. Why give them any more screen time?" Though even before the words are out of his mouth (not *these* words exactly but words similar in intent but truer to his unliterary roots [*At last we have a man*, thinks Cantor, *who refuses to do a Master's bidding!* Cantor also thinks while he's at it—no, Cantor *suspects*—that the introduction of the Nine Pees in a Pod et al forebodes a collision with—an imminent invasion by—the Rumps! To take place at the Santa Barbara Cemetery (if at all possible, Maestro) for suddenly this seems to be the only means of forcing the ending of the Invidicum Story to give off the whiff—the stench—of inevitability (equal parts noxious whimper and lustral bang)])—though even before the words are out of his mouth, Jason knows they're untrue (untrue, considering all the very *un*measly harm the scum have already inflicted—unleashed on the world—but that's a—the— funny thing about untruths when they lead wordflow by the tail: not only do they unsheathe—unspool—worlds upon worlds of infinite anti-possibility but their perversity sounds pretty good on paper as well though maybe you can't have one without the other [no miracle, just a fact of life—just a day in the life of wordflow versus worldflow]). "No, no, no, no, no, what I mean is, Why did mom have to demonize them, make them do her dirty work? When all they—the Nine Pees give or take a Rumpish flunkey or two—want is to Make America Right Again—White again—Christian again even if It will never be anything but Christian now and forever—Christian across the board—will never be anything but Mono- and Unicultural." When all they want (he goes on to explain but in words, like Borkman, Jr.'s—heroism is contagious!—truer to his unliterary roots) is to re-prove for everybody's own good DaVos's theorem which states, roughly speaking, that *If* the un-self-reliant Poor are in fact as poor as they claim to be (DaVos is referring here to the *true* poor for there are so many impostors flitting about) *Then* it's because they *choose* to be poor—it's because they expressly choose to live—and therefore must die—by Poordom's terrible slow sword. And at the public's expense, of course and as always—for it's the public, especially billionaires, that must end up paying to ensure the sword is wielded properly. But why should billionaires, who already have enough on their hands including blood, be forced to minister to the self-willed disease that is poverty? Is that fair? (Now why did I, Jason muses, assume JJJ was not—was the furthest thing from—a MAGA man? Just because he professes to idolize me?) He asks Jim, Jr., to confirm that he believes Margo is perpetrating a gross injustice upon some Rump flunkies—has inveigled them into acting against their own best interest all for the privilege of ending up as collateral damage—roped them into giving some unwitting heft to her baseless claims that family members—family members in name only supported by persons connected in a deep-state dark-web sort of way with the current Administration—are out to get back at her—through J3—simply for having done her wifely duty over what seems like centuries. "Did I get everything right?" "No—or rather, not *quite*. She's trying to rob me of my notoriety—my hard-won notoriety—to rob me of any sense of *agency*— to use me to get back at them the way they're getting back at her. Tit for tat. Canceled out, as usual, in the back and forth between her and them. Just when for the first time in my life I have something I can call my very own. And she's trying to rob me of it by bullying—by shaming—family and friends (for I consider DaVos, the Mnunchkin and eight out of nine Pees my friends) into proclaiming me innocent. But I prefer to be guilty on my own terms rather than innocent on hers." He enjoys being a suspect—a culprit, he says. It's as close as he'll ever get to being an artist reviled by the world outside his garret. Which reminds him (it's so obvious he forgot to mention it straight off): she's keeping the MAGAs in reserve—in cold storage—for the moment when from certain signs and alarms which are nothing of the kind she can plausibly maintain (for a nutjob like her plausibility is as stretchable as boardwalk taffy) that reconciliation with her siblings and Straynge's is very much on the horizon. In which case she'll have to come up with an excuse for their animus. Simple—DaVos & Co (with a little input from the Nine Pees) made them do it. Since every evil being she's compelled to love must be acting on orders from a funhouse mastermind, otherwise how could she go on loving them? Jason's willing—no, more than willing—to *empathize* (sickening word since it nips in the bud—infects—whatever meaning is supposed to accrue from its application). Problem is, a treacly avowal like *For the first time in my life I have something I can call my very own* or some such concoction—especially from somebody born with a silver spoon up his ass—gets in the way.

"I get it—about your mother and the conspiracy, I mean. But surely even this cloud has a silver lining." So. It's taken him all this time to realize he really does believe in what the hoary old adage adumbrates of . . . hope—that there's a bright side to everything—that the glass is half full. But he's able to go on believing only as long as the image is there to remind the adage that their conjoint fate is in each other's hands—so that the adage has got to be more—or at least pretend to be more—than the sum of its rough edges. If the image were to fade—if the cloud went away, silk-purse lining and all—there'd be no reason to hope, not even for a sow's ear. Never would Jason have guessed that he was capable of wielding the phrase so convincingly—of maintaining such a deft balance between word and image. He'd had a similar experience with *fool's errand*, allowed to languish unsung for decades in that sector of his brain charged with housing aged and infirm phrases before he deemed it fit to be invoked—or rather before the phrase deemed him fit to invoke it—and which finally debuted as a gentle rebuke (on the order of "Ah, Bartleby! Ah, humanity!") to some recently resurfaced friend's efforts to root out The Reason for another friend's untimely death—a rebuke most intriguing to Jason in its forbearance inasmuch as the friends in question (like every other friend) had long before been relegated, once blessed absence agreed to work its analytical magic, to the category of hated exes.

What he wouldn't give to be able to cheer J³ up for he's developed a soft spot for him—or rather, for his predicament. But there's no taking the birds-of-a-feather route, going so far as to contend that he—Jason—has lived under a similar burden (and look how hale and hearty he's managed to turn out to be): fact is, his own parents were simply not wired to believe in conspiracy. For one thing, mom and her paintbrush were always too busy communing with the willows across from the Delacorte Theater. But this sounds self-righteous—self-congratulatory—elitist. No, what Jason means is, he for one has never been tempted to exploit conspiracy as the material, formal, efficient and final causes of all his strugges and rejections—has refused point blank to nuzzle his way into its straitjacket. Ascribing his sufferings to the workings of a conspiracy would be to rob himself of those sufferings—to suffocate them—to constrict his capacity to surmount them. You won't find his Weltanschauung allowing Conspiracy to swim into Its ken—you won't find Ol' Man Conspiracy loitering 'round Its door. "But you're about to become rich and famous. You don't need any silver linings." What?! why, he'll have JJJ know that, for all the trappings of glitzwear, he's still struggling and loving every minute of it. But conspiracy makes precious struggle, precious suffering, too public. Like a frog. Deprives them of their right to be confronted. By taking his two pet companies (Struggle, Inc., and Suffering, Inc.) public, CEO John Smith Conspiracy relinquishes all control. Be that as it may, J³ shouldn't write his mother off so quickly—he needs to rehabilitate her—if for nobody else than posterity (though J³ clearly isn't ready). Who's to say her take on his plight doesn't hit the bull's-eye? Divining what she thinks he's going through as the target of a murder investigation, she's taken to plastering him with her own agony—the agony triggered by *knowing* he's a target. It's her way of getting into the act and suffering right there beside him. And what better way to keep the chamberpot boiling than to make her siblings and Straynge's—i.e., those who matter most to her (besides him)—out to be the culprits? After all, a conspiracy theory is born to explain a Thing out there which causes excruciating pain—to contain and constrain what appears to be an attack on the explainer's very being (the attack on him is after all an attack on her)—so somebody has, through demonization, to pay a price. But from what Jim, Jr., has told him, his mother must be convinced—knowing the siblings as she thinks she does—that their by-the-numbers demonization won't have to last for too long. At some point, sooner rather than later, the siblings—like the fleabitten mutts they are—will be induced by forces beyond their control to bay their innocence at the moon—their innnocence of all collisional intent toward Jim, that is. Which, given his mom's sisterly talent for both (*a*) living from reconciliation to reconciliation to reconciliation (the way other people—populist Kelly the Loeffler, for example—live from paycheck to paycheck to paycheck, or profess to) and (*b*) routinely overlooking one massively singular detail, namely, that it's always she who foments those reconciliations—given her talent, she'll have no trouble interpreting the baying as what it most definitely isn't, namely, a penitential declaration of love concocted especially for her delectation. If Jason thinks—which he does—that Margo's boy looks . . . unconvinced, then, clearly, Jason's reputation (on the hoodie-and-turtleneck circuit) as a mindreader is ripe for revision since, actually, J3 is a way bit more than unconvinced—a way bit more than confused. If you must know, he feels he's betrayed his own mother—a betrayal made worse by the fact that she's not just any old mother but the kind you spurn and crave in the same breath—feels he's handed her over to a stranger—and the worst kind, an understanding stranger whose understanding harbors pretensions to omniscience and is nothing more than an excuse to maul her womanliness and make mincemeat of her character—and to maul and make mincemeat of all women in tandem. So to dull his sense of cowardly connivance—to drown the unholy stranger's ill will in the greater flagrancy of his own—Jim, Jr., decides to go the stranger one better—indeed, he goes so far as to suggest that maybe mom saw in the murder and the doings of the police, and all fifty-seven headmasters, not to mention the Greenwich Avenue Irregulars—maybe mom saw in all that mess nothing less than . . . an opportunity—an opportunity to tell all the truth but tell it slant—an opportunity to say something along the lines of: James, Fuck you and the horse you rode in on, and the womb you came out of since it couldn't have been mine (my womb cultivates a better taste in fetuses)—but best of all an opportunity to put James-hatred behind her by imputing it to an assortment of dimwitted family members. For he was definitely not the perfect specimen the doctor'd ordered. Everybody could agree on that, most of all J3. Although with her adversative—her pathological—streak, would she have known what to do with a perfect specimen? Could she have endured its perfection—could she have tamed the temptation to perceive its normality as a traducement of—a judgment on—her own refusal not to be flawed? Wouldn't that perfect specimen have ended up feeling as much of a mutant as Jim did? "No, no, no," replies Jason. The way he sees it, the perfect specimen would have felt more, much more, of a mutant—first, because he wasn't a mutant and so didn't know how to play the mutant game, and second, because as a devout non-mutant he couldn't be expected to have at his disposal the characterological equipment needed to deflect the delusion being foisted off on him by, in this case, the Mother of All Mutants. As far as Jason is concerned, Jim is looking increasingly more . . . unconvinced (although he's not sure about what)—he's entered an entirely new realm of unconvinced-ness—so Jason decides to take one last-ditch stab at connecting—decides to try a different tack—a more upbeat tack—to reroute himself from theory to practice, so to speak, even if practice doesn't always make perfect. "Personally, what I wouldn't give right now to be able to devise a nice juicy conspiracy theory (I don't intend to wear a hoodie for the rest of my life) but at the moment there's nothing out in the world causing me much excruciating pain—the kind of pain that requires a culprit—culprits—demons—an inter-linkage of demons—of their acts." (He waits in vain for JJJ to look as if his mouth was watering.) But even if a culprit existed, Jason'd be far too groggy to get his dander up—he hasn't gotten much sleep lately and never did he feel less inspired nor (in consequence and proving every cloud has its silver lin-ing) less vulnerable. "But of course that's precisely the moment when the true artisan earns his stripes—by patching together a conspiracy theory when he doesn't feel any need for one." Not that he's interested in conspiracy theories per se. He wants just to construct one ingenious enough to get his name out there—incendiary enough to whet, say, some oath-keeping Proud Boy's appe-tite for mayhem (for there's no more indisputable proof of one's readiness for accession to the start-up world's upper echelons than the ability to construct a theory that goes on to generate not just a conspiracy but a cohort of conspir-acy busters on the order of the foiled star of the Pizzagate show) and so, through their blustering endorsement, prove himself worthy of the very high-est level of Venture Capital support in getting his next and what is sure to be his greatest start-up off the ground. For it's a truth universally acknowledged that only he who can construct a conspiracy theory—from scratch—has the makings of a start-upper of the first rank. But don't ask him why this is so. (Cantor wonders if this so-called universal truth isn't just another example—as if any more were needed—of what happens when a pair of incongruities gets yoked by fiat—the Master's funny fiat.) And maybe his start-up will be dedicated to anything but conspiracies and their dismantlement. Thing is, a conspiracy is known to be many things—for example, it's a fetish, a commod-ity, a totem, a totem pole, a fart in wolf's clothing, an e-skin sensor. But most of all it's an epileptic seizure—a seizure born of a seizure itself born of a mil-lion and one neuronal misfirings. And this being the case (again, by fiat), who's to say he won't catch the humanitarian bug the way other people catch what they cornily—oafishly—call the *writing bug* and, out of decency, give himself heart and soul to producing the hardware, software and algorithmic decision trees essential to nipping those misfirings in the bud? All a Rube Goldberg wannabe like him might need is some sixth-generation device cou-pling a seizure sensor to an organic electronic ion pump—which would respond to the seizure by sending the right drug—clemizole or levetiracetam or, in cases where inflammation is the culprit, anakinra—to the right region of the troublemaking brain. Jason doesn't know that for JJJ seizures are more, much more, than a metaphor—he's been subject to them since infancy (in fact, he can feel one coming on right this minute but he's able to distinguish a false alarm from the real thing) and therefore is duty bound to stop his ears against the trickle of such profane cleverness—or (as Jason would have it) ingenuity. JJJ is forced, however—he, too, *out of decency* or some brittle amalgam of decency and despair—to acknowledge that here's where the future of progress very much lies—albeit reluctantly since such an acknowledgment entails a stopover in the slums of yea-saying—saying yea not just to Jason's life project (which could be mistaken for ass-kissing) but to Life itself; unfortunately, from his two or three or seven parents he's inherited, for better or worse, the gold bug of reflexive *nay*-saying—if only through recalcitrant silence—as the sole means of affirming one's autonomy in a time of crisis (as now—and forever).

J³'s only way out of Jason's labyrinth (with Margo its Ariadne in Chief) is via plain speaking and an antic disposition, which means doing what the Marx triplets—Sigmund, Karl and Groucho—would have wanted him to do under the circumstances. All of mom's troubles—and his own (though it doesn't necessarily make him a murderer—or an accessory or a witness)—stem from the fact (he's heard it through the siblings-studded grapevine) that she never surmounted the shock of discovering dad had a penis (Straynge's sole flaw) instead of what she's still convinced (without knowing she's convinced) is possessed by every upstanding citizen (a case of company-loving misery?), namely, a vagina (an affliction not quite so rare as infrequency of mention would lead one to believe). That was her signature traumatic moment. The moment that defines her to this day and is sure to outlast her. A moment reified into an object or vice versa. The final moment as fetish. Time as fetish—as the space of fetish. And maybe it was she after all who did dad in, as payback for shamelessly defending his right to harbor such a flaw—even between his legs—she who did him in for refusing to abet her delusion that this anatomical error could be rectified in full. But culprit or accomplice or neither, not long after the murder, she somersaulted back into the comforting arms of Pritchard (since it had been possible for her, at least in his undissenting absence, to reconfigure him as penis-free)—the only man, by the way, who—by coddling her dread while at the same time suggesting (though a bit too tactfully for some tastes) that a penis, too, has its fair share of selling points yet is ultimately more, far more, than their untidy sum—can boast of some success in soothing her savage breast. "No relationships are perfect, Jim." Jason hereby proves he can play the tact card as well as the next guy though maybe not as nimbly as Pritchard. Too bad he doesn't have any items stocked in his alcove bazaar that can provide penis-deniers like Margo with something equivalent to the pacifiers he offers their vagina-averse counterparts (which include dildo-shaped nipples, rhinestone-encrusted stiletto heels and crotchless panties, i.e., kitschy funhouse transformations of the last thing they happened to lay eyes on before Mother caught them in the act of catching *her* in the act of inadvertently exposing the furry magic carpet of Her Big Bad Lack). Too bad he doesn't have something that can serve the Margos of the world as a totem of triumph over the terror induced by their very special version of Medusa's snaky severed head—that can serve as an engine for singing that terror to sleep. "Although"—he sounds hopeful, even buoyant—"a pink-and-blue Senate Republican contrast shirt might do the trick." JJJ hangs his head. "You're making fun of me," he says, through gritted teeth. "You obviously have no idea how little's really being done for people with a sickness like Margo's." The good son is clearly the role JJJ was born to play and Cantor would bet anything that he's thinking (as Jason, the son of his dead father's star patient, goes on wickedly relishing his failure to come up with a curative fetish—no matter how hard he tries—that's a bit classier than a Mitch MacConnell wattles-squeezer) something along the lines of, *How tedious these young Turk smart-asses from the East Coast are—and I should know because I want to be one—hey, maybe I'm well past the in-training stage and already* am *one.* "But where was I? Oh, yes, on my way out here—" J³ clearly wants—or wants to seem as if he wanted—bygones to be bygones. "Hitchhiking, you said—some kind of lost art," Jason prompts. Sceptical, forbearing—full of disdain. The disdain—born self-protectively from guilt over the precious little he's done for folks like Margo—doesn't go unremarked. In testily interjecting, "Exactly, *hitchhiking*, and with a capital *H*," J³ more than matches disdain for disdain—makes mincemeat through tone alone of what sounded like—what in fact *was* (also through tone alone)—Borkman, Jr.'s imputation of pretentiousness. For JJJ knows—without knowing he knows (out of the kindness of his heart, Cantor does the knowing for him at no extra charge)—that accusing somebody else of pretentiousness is the best way to unload one's own. He proceeds to explain why hitchhiking is a lost art in (as so many times before) a polysyllable-averse style true to his humble roots. Thing is, he can't quite loosen—no, he refuses to loosen—his preppy grip on those polysyllables since any way you slice 'em, his roots are far from humble. And all of a sudden it hits him: why *should* he loosen his grip? Why play the fake populist à la Josh Whoreley? True, he came out here not so much to escape the police as to serve as a start-up prince's towel boy—a prince with enough clout to make him first in line to that malodorous soup kitchen called Fame. But as it turns out, only a few hours in this steambath were required to transform him from (*a*) an inarticulate goof-off ashamed of his overpriced antecedents and with not a single chest hair to his name into (*b*) a muscleman about town unafraid to avow the love that, as a rule, dares not speak its name—that is, the love of polysyllables—the love of wearing them with a difference especially when the right occasion refuses to beckon. And to think that headmasters A through Z and beyond routinely scrawled *slow learner* in the "overall characterization" box on his gilt-edged report cards. If they could only see him now. He quickly warms to the subject at hand and warming to the subject means finally letting bygones be bygones, until further notice. Fact is, Jason, hitchhiking allows him to focus (when he's not responding with panic to the migration crotch-wards of the lift-giver's psychotic gaze—a gaze that's usually 99.9 percent lips) on all the transitory interim spaces—spaces *inter faeces et urinum* so to speak— that people ignore in their wheezy preoccupation with endpoints—results, as Kierkegaard might say. "Interim spaces like, for example, the subway passage cum MRI machine at Forty-Second Street that runs between Fifth Avenue and Sixth—you know, the one you've got to crawl through in order to transfer from the 7 train to the F, no exceptions made—with its churro stand and the

Wake quotation scrawled calligraphically across its sloping white-tiled wall. And what about the tunnel of apparent dead space spanning last Christmas and New Year's (no better example of time-as-space-as-fetish bestrides the earth)? Who's man enough to remember what happened to her consciousness *at every moment* in that neck of the woods?" It's those spaces, not sex-shops—not even an emporium of racy Firstness run by Charles Sanders Peirce and his French wife—that breed the real fetishes—things at once too fleeting and too permanent to warrant a premonitory glance and for that (or a related) reason well worth their weightlessness in gold—things seemingly too insignificant to be thinkable—things that silently scream their unthinkability—their pur-loined-letter invisibility-in-plain-sight—yet are obliging enough in the same breath to pave the way toward suture for the wound inflicted by all their defi-cits—but a suture that—as the fruits of their labors—of their purposiveness without purpose—only surgeons-general on the order of Church-Mouse Attentiveness and Wide-eyed Expectationlessness and the Patience of a Saint can execute. Any wonder, then, that it's become his lifelong calling—at least for the moment—to warn the Envious—as his father should have done—against enslavement to the wrong fetish the way Hercule Poirot made—makes—it his business (yes, Jim's read all of Christie's books and respectfully impregnated most of them with his semen: how many headmasters from A to Z can say as much?) to warn the inept reader-sleuth against enslavement to the wrong murder?

Should Jason burst the bubble of Jim's missionary zeal by informing him this meditation on interim spaces—the widest of wide-open spaces—and their buried treasure has already been enacted? By whom? well, by Jean, for one. For he was right there (no, my dear Jean, the alcove wasn't quite as bereft of observers as you too quickly came to believe) when she triumphantly—*cal-ligraphically*—committed what have turned out to be J^3's very ravings to the scummiest of towels. And, adding insult to injury, should Jason head JJJ off at the pass (before his delusional craving for originality takes another turn for the worst) by presenting him with the most tantalizing details of somebody else's meditation—specifically on the vicissitudes of the Thought Packet (lest his ravings take a shine to such a beast and think he's invented it) which is currently making the rounds but in hushed half-tones as if it held the very key to how, say, a black-hole temper tantrum goes about triggering a tidal disruption event? But why the need to put JJJ in his place all of a sudden? Is it ostensibly to instill the very humility—humility as a weapon sure to stand him forever in good stead—which Jason himself has never had the intention to embrace? Or is the new, improved Jim—the Jim who's just shown himself to be a crack shot with a polysyllable—turning out to be too much of a threat? And if so, how? Though isn't there just a single way one man can be a threat to another? In short, has it come to this: all-out war—a case of Jr. against Jr. simply because they're too close—too doppelgängerish—for comfort. If so, then a placatory fast-hire—making Jim co-overseer of Jason's current sales force comes to mind—might be the best means in fact of keeping himself out of harm's way. Or maybe he should take a different approach . . .

Amazing! how, in a matter of minutes, JJJ has gone from sorcerer's apprentice to deep thinker, juggling semi-ripe bananas of erudition like so much chump change (is it Cantor who at this fraught juncture has taken it upon himself—gratis—to do the required emergency metaphorizing—for the rest of us?). Which means he should be able to handle the challenge that now comes tumbling out of Jason's mouth as the tumbler simultaneously puts both feet in it. Surely JJJ can't expect him—anybody—to buy into mom's *devastation* at discovering her husband to be every bit as penis-hamstrung as the next guy—can't expect anybody to believe that, even as a conspiracy theory-soused ranting raving late-blooming votary of Lack, she actually assumed her husband-to-be would be free of the stain of Plenitude, as embodied in that meaty bit of rotting cordage known as a midlife penis. J3 sighs (his forbearance is just a stone's throw from exasperation) but he does owe his rival something in the way of clarification. Of *course* he doesn't believe a word of what he's just said—pure speculation, if that. Thing is, he's recently (about an hour ago) picked up and mastered—both in an instant—the trick—what appears to be a Turkish bathhouse trick—of tracking down and harassing an unsuspecting chunk of received wisdom (that, for example, a woman has every right to expect her husband-to-be to be capable of brandishing a full-fledged dick on demand—but not, perish the day! a vagina). All in order to turn the chunk so harassed on its head—to twist it into a perverse self-parody simply by first exchanging its pivotal term for that term's most hostile—or at least most contrarious—counterpart and going on from there. This being the cue for the Main Event to work its magic, i.e., for Psychology and Logic as we know and loathe them to rush in (half angels, half fools), with each striving to demonstrate (for all the world as if they were two of The Rump's prize poodles, Puttin' Lindsay, say, and Lyin' Ted) that it's he and he alone and not the other guy—Psychology not Logic versus Logic not Psychology—who can best be depended on to bend himself most abjectly—most shamelessly—to the will of said parody in order to lend it credibility and enable it to stand on its own two feet. And of *course* he doesn't believe that he believes in the parodic anti-chunk's wacky right to life. It's just that he gets a real live kick out of seeing logic and psychology abase themselves before a tyrant and, like two Jack Spratts, lick the platter of the tyrant's fecal fickleness clean. He might even go as far as to say he gets off on it. Although the question remains—at least for Jason—why subsidize the demolition of this particular chunk of orthodoxy—this particular butt-end of Life dogma—with so many others, infinitely more exotic, i.e., infinitely more disturbing, to choose from? "And a very good question it is," cheers J3. Since, oddly enough, the staunch conviction that he's leading the chunk by the nose inevitably leaves him with the very queasy feeling it's the chunk itself that's doing the leading—that's turning *him* on *his* head—that's chosen him. "If I could have been born anything at all I'd have been born a word. Ah, to be a word with a word's freedom of movement. And yet the words recruited to plead this particular cause aren't as free as they seem—so neither am I." What he's trying to say is that the zany—yes, *zany* (is there another word more worthy of resurrection?)—the zany predicament the words pretend to depict isn't as untethered from kitchen-sink realism as may appear. In lockstep for once, Jason and Cantor agree that, in the course of fathering forth this sequence of sentences, JJJ has given an object lesson in how to manage sudden mood swings gracefully, without resorting to serotonin reuptake inhibitors. And suddenly the notion that a woman's shock (at her man's lacking a vagina and sporting in its stead a dull-witted penis) can be powerful enough to compel him to trade the one for the other—or powerful enough to drive her, if all else fails, to surgically execute the trade herself—is not all that fanciful. Here's proof of how close to the madness of truth he can get if his trust in the delusional freedom of words is left to its own devices. His Margo fantasy simply dilutes the direness of the eventuality dearest to his or any other young man's dread (namely, how easy it is to lose one's most precious *thing*—the thing that's more oneself than one's own self—so precious that the thing's very existence resonates as one long plea to be euthanized). Through the Margo fantasy he's been able to transform a solipsistic chamber play on this theme into a mock epic whose high point is a tug of war between two rising-star extras. Jason, clearly shaken by so much dread and direness, asks what's *driven* him to *this*? what's *in it* for him? Jim simultaneously shrugs his shoulders and supinates his wrists to show that when required to respond to questions about *this* he can always be counted on, rain or shine, to come up short. Maybe, just maybe, Jason autosuggests (it's clear he's woefully overestimated his capacity to sup with horrors)—and Cantor (in a pinch, just another overestimator) backs him up—maybe what Jim suffers from is nothing more dire—nothing more to be dreaded—than a simple language disorder—an inability to *hold his polysyllables* (akin to an inability to hold one's liquor).

CHAPTER FIFTY

Cantor has never needed more than now what his mother or maybe his mother's younger sister used to call *a breath of fresh*. Eavesdropping, after all, is an overrated art—an exhaustingly overrated art—an exhaustingly unglamorous subvocation. Seven-thirty, the perfect time of day to go for a walk. Who knows, someday somebody might say of him what somebody else once said (conceding only slight exaggeration) of the poet Virgil, i.e., that he "discovered" the evening (though maybe "invented" is a better word)—who knows, somebody might say Cantor invented the evening—this time for all of humanity—and lent it charms it never dreamed of having, namely, tranquillity and melancholy?[147] Inventor or not, he hungers for a tree—one that's ripe for ravishment by sense of sight's sweet tooth. And yet he's still here—stopped dead in his tracks by an exterminating angel. But no such angel's going to smear "irresolution" in exegetical dogshit across the sole of his shoe so he can spend the next five centuries trying vainly, in the tradition of Hamlet, to scrape it all off. Back at the ranch, Jean not so suddenly discovers she's had enough to last her several lifetimes—of alcoves not to mention semen-stained towels—i.e., she's paid her dues and then some. (Jean looks to Cantor as if she felt that having guessed his intentions to raid the great outdoors is entitlement enough to an airing in the company of this budding inventor laureate. Think again! He's out the door.) Dildos, of course, are another matter entirely: she'll never regret for a second—hopefully—the several lifetimes lived in that world-class seraglio of Firstness. And in some kind of cockamamie answer to prayers unthinkable, who should catch her eye as she ventures out into the world again (even if she never left it, since the world—like gold—is where you find it or where it finds you) but Liepnits, nowhere near as repellent in the (Cole Porteresque) *so-to-speak*, by the way, as one would have imagined: in fact it might be quite pleasant, under the right circumstances, to be violated by so napoleonically ugly a little . . . bear. He appears to be very much in the thick (wildly gesticulative, as is his wont) of verbal battle with somebody who very much resembles the truculent sole proprietor of that bakery on Greenwich Avenue frequented (per legend) by generation upon generation of Amygdaloids. Put on the hot seat by his interlocutor, Liepnits is asked if he has any idea how many guinea pigs from across the street (not to mention the baker himself) have had their Envy-throttled innards repaired by his defiantly ungentrifiable cherry-cheese scones.

But Liepnits has to give the gesticulation business a rest when Walser says—"I didn't think you were into nudist colonies." Liepnits makes as if to put his challenger's pudenda out of commission for good. Instead, he cries out, "I hate that phrase" (sounding not a little like Gloria Swanson as *Sunset Boule-*

---

[147]This little excursus-in-training was inspired by Erwin Panofsky (see "*Et in Arcadia Ego*: Poussin and the elegiac tradition," in *Meaning in the Visual Arts* [Garden City, New York, Doubleday Anchor Books, 1955]).

vard's Norma Desmond, for whom *comeback* was the detestation-inducing expletive of choice). "It's a Sadean think tank." Walser knows when his bonhomie ain't wanted and skedaddles. It seems—no, it's a fact—that the baker was bought out—hostile-takeover bought out, that is—by the Krushner Organization. As it so happens, the little weasel now running it, having contracted the ungovernable itch of humanitarianism NOHO style, intends to provision Rust Belt Greenwich Ave with sorely-wanting affordable housing for abject billionaires otherwise homeless. So with nowhere else to go and long overdue for a renewal of his prescription, the baker heeded Horace Greeley's war cry and headed west, having been told that out here as well were most of his *best customers cum fellow sufferers* (Jean makes a mental note to parse this odd phrase, first chance she gets—why, it suggests that the baker himself was—is . . . but the whole idea is preposterous!)—and doing what they do best, or worst, to wit, getting cured to beat the band and therefore badly in need of resuscitation. But can Liepnits—himself an inveterate sconesman (bagpipes and all)—blame the baker for thinking that with a little crowdfondling, or whatever it's called, he could set up shop in these parts while downing his thrice-daily dose? But how did Herr Professor Liepnits—peacock-proud as he is of being called the absent-minded professor even if his field of expertise is arcane inaction par excellence—end up managing (and, even more miraculously, deigning) to navigate his ass (surprisingly shapely—and, in deference to Leonardo, the distance from the bottom of the buttock to the top of the hip is equal to the width across the hips) out of the van? that's what she wants— though she may have no right—to know. And where, pray, is the Dark Lady of his still-to-be-indited sonnets? Has he already abandoned her (or vice versa) and that after only, what does it come to? three weeks (tops) of immitigable rapture? *But for the moment let's forget about Liepnits*, Jean tells herself loud enough surely for everybody to hear but failing—or forgetting—to add, *he being history so ancient as to merit, at best, entombment in a footnote somewhere in volume 3 of Gibbon—the shorter the better*. Jean has bigger fish (or, in this case, fritters) to deep-fry, namely, the baker's reason for being here. (He'd always gotten her confused with Irena, whom he referred to, when routinely corrected, as "that doctor lady from Transylvania.") Well, now that you mention it, she does remember having seen him, and on several occasions, slipping into the Center—but not once by the service entrance. Still, she always assumed it was to make a delivery: Never would she have taken him for anything so exalted as a patient although—again, now that you mention it—every time throwing confectionary caution to the winds signified to her the purchase of a cherry-cheese double-brownie (Wednesday's specialty of the house), she found he couldn't stop animadverting, invidiously, to say the least (no, not just invidiously but . . . but . . . but—but—*exaltedly!* yes, *exaltedly*, no other word will do!—as *exaltedly* in fact as a patient—no! as no mere patient ever could!—no! as at the very least an über-patient)—couldn't stop animadverting on all the supermarkets (whose fifth-rate pastries were but an outsourced afterthought) that had Sherman-tanked their way into his field of operations. According to the baker, you didn't have to be a genius to realize (at this point she'd always been already converted to his cause and all too willing to loudly share what the tabloids, had Envy ended up driving him to mass murder, would have blandly dismissed as his disgruntlement) that Patchin Place, Washington Mews, Shinbone Alley, Nightmare Alley, Dapertutto Square and pretty much any other Village enclaves you might care to name now represented nothing more than food courts subsidized by Chase, Goldman Sachs, Citi, Capital One, Nosfera II and every other bail-out behemoth—the banks renowned for laughing all the way to the bank. But however line-flubbingly unhinged he sounded all through the philippic, the baker never failed to finish things off with an epitaph on his emotions (its elegance, in the grand Nietzschean manner, being in direct proportion to their unwieldiness) that evidenced a depth of insight unusual, to say the least, in a *mere tradesman*. And the very best of the bunch (of epitaph-littered philippics)—*en forme de* caveat to hacks in every medium, if she remembered correctly—went something like this: To believe that slimeball CEOs, bailed out or otherwise, remain doomed to wake up one day and wailingly won-der—even posthumously—*What should it profit me if I gain the whole world?* . . . constitutes a mere illusion of begrudgery and not just by ungracious pas-tors, NOT for the simple reason that the slimeballs on whom the begrudgers pin their dog-in-the-mangerly hopes are themselves too deluded for redemp-tion BUT RATHER because they're in no need of the stuff whatsoever: As born winners they have an obligation to go on doing, *à la Blankfein*, god's work (the work of their god, hence everybody's) or rather enjoying the fruits of the work of a god who works solely on their behalf or rather (between hostile takeovers) simply adoring themselves (but not to death) as the only real fruits of the only real work done by their god—the only real work that, given his massive disabilities, the god we're stuck with (or, for the incurable minority who voted The Rump in solely for the pleasure of watching his flun-key Tommy Price dismantle their health capillary by capillary, the god they're stuck *on*)—the only real work such a god is equipped to do. Also remark-able was this friendly neighborhood baker's determination to refrain from stripping the god—a gutter god—of all dignity, even if it reposed on the mis-taken conviction that, inasmuch as (like any other prosthetic, only more so) he worked in mysterious ways and had a million and one other tricks up his ravelled sleeve of non-care, the baker as everyman was clearly outmatched.

Yet (wild gesticulations notwithstanding), there is, at least as far as Jean can see, no *real* verbal battle—no contest—to speak of between Liepnits and the baker—they're, so to shriek, *too big to flail*. But, I ask you—or rather *she* asks you—how *can* there be—a contest, I mean? Since it's crystal clear as day that Romulus Liepnits and Remus Baker were suckled at the same tit of lupine opportunism or (depending on whom you talk to) the lupine tit of the same opportunism, and then went on to get themselves bilgily baptized in the same trough, or did the trough come before the tit? I.e., if Liepnits is pro-life, but contra a big-bad-government bailout for the auto and sex industries, and dog-eat-doggy sex, and gourmet food stamps for strapping bucks and their lazy-ass get, well, for that matter, pardner, so is the baker. In fact, she's willing to bet that during this one long flimflamming mind-fuck of an election season, there arose not one issue on which they didn't agree lock, stock and barrel (except for, maybe, those Infamous Four white-hot buttons, i.e., the preestablished harmony, the categorical imperative, the dynamical sublime and *objet petit* a, to which they were giving, obviously at the behest of their hero, the shortest possible shrift). (Why does Jean—just when things are going so smoothly—suddenly sixth-sense that the Master [she's been getting to know him—er, Him—better than she cares to] is none too pleased about allocating His political acumen-gone-haywire to an underling, much less an underling as green as Jean?) Thing is, you don't need *The 120 Days of Sodom* or even *Fourier, Sade, Loyola* to know that the sole function of any orgy worth its salt—the sole function of any *necessary* orgy—resides in coaxing its participants into achieving self-definition through opposition—no, opposedness—no, opposingness (is the Master by any chance trying, by way of this very fiat, to do away with the sheer gratuitousness of His own contribution to the genre—to browbeat it into engendering a slew of irresolvable conflicts?). (As the Euclid of whodunitrixes pointed out so elegantly in *Evil Under the Sun*, the unsettling similarity of everybody's buck-nakedness to everybody else's makes the urgency of distinguishing oneself *in some other plane*—and of making that plane the warplane of planes—all the more urgent.) Which goes a long way toward explaining WHY, the closer our boys get to the Liepnitsian Slough of Despond, where indiscernibility=identity, the more hydrophobic they wax and WHY, growing ever more concerned (being no dummies) that such waxing will, if unchecked, do them both in, there arises (with systole following diastole as the night the day) an instinctive agreement to appear to join forces in a manner of speaking and WHY, once the agreeing's (having come and gone) been successfully soft-pedaled as nothing more than the irrepressible high-spirited boys-will-be-boyishness all too typical of a presidential debate, they waste no time turning tail yet again on their own worst enemy (not the other but *himself*) and a-doin' a-what should come naturally in such a context but (given the profile of the contestants) doesn't come naturally here, namely, *fawn competitively over every swing voter in and out of sight* as if their lives depended on it. And quite a crowd of 'em, pudenda dutifully agape, has formed by now since (to quote Petronius out of context) *At an orgy every participant is a bystander and every bystander a swing voter.* And if one can only make the electorate believe in his day-versus-night differentness from the other, well, then, he might just begin to believe in it himself, whatever the associated risk of reciprocated annihilation. Yet, there's no concealing, at least from the practiced eye, that *in some part of themselves not open to the general public* (among which in this case they themselves figure all too prominently) what Liepnits and the baker relish even more than the uniqueness of selfhood (*oh, yeah? and on whose say-so may I ask?*) is the prospect (alas, ever-receding) of an escape into . . . solidarity and not just any old sort but the robustest known to man and beast, or Billary and Don, to wit, the solidarity daysprung from reciprocated mudflinging on an implied podium.

So, for Liepnits and the baker, Jean muses—though any one among her colleagues (first time, come to think of it, she's ever referred to them, a bit too stuffily for my taste, as such) would do a far better job of it (musing, I mean)—it all boils down (oh, and did I forget to mention she's a fast learner?)

to the simple matter of saving face through disputation while their pineal and other glands waste no time thinking very different thoughts. And no better proof of such goings-on-behind-the-scenes than the fact that when either is subjected to the inevitable ad hominem for, say, keeping I.R.A. investments in a UBIT blocker or, far worse, for playing stall-footsie in an airport men's room with what has turned out (as it always must) to be an undercover cop, or for some other flimflam cut from the flimsiest of whole cloth—when so subjected, fighting back inevitably reduces—or expands—to taking up the cudgels for his adversary. For it was—and still is—a time-honored conviction among politico-orgiasts under attack that the foolhardy admission of some flagrancy even grosser than those fueling the grossest misrepresentations— grosser than any said adversary could dig up on his own *recognizance* (wrong word? a pity: since it sounds *so very right* for the context—as so many times before [see above]—so maybe the only solution is to keep using the word, correctly or not, never abandoning all hope that—through a flavorful mix of over- and misuse—it will ultimately capitulate and start meaning what one wants—needs—it to mean—what the sonority requires it to mean)—that such an admission constitutes the best means of positively reeking, my dear, of integrity—and not simply because the perpetrator of said admission will thereby beat his Dapertutto, his Lindorf, his Coppélius or his Docteur Miracle to any number of punchlines. Where there's so much daring, there just has to be integrity.

An obviously last-ditch attempt to shuffle off the coil of solidarity, as masterminded by the exalted baker, is about to unfold—for, I ask you, wouldn't such an entanglement be equivalent to cracking open a can of homosexual worms? (if non-human animals are to play—are to be *played* as—devil's advocate for the unseemly sexual practices hinted at here, deep-sea squid or Atlantic mollies would be more appropriate candidates for the role than worms). Though, come to think of it, revival of the coming-out party—an old West Village custom studied by E.E. Evans-Pritchard, Gregory Bateson and Clyde Kluckhohn, as well as Ruth Benedict—might be just the ticket for turning the tide where Envy cure is concerned. As promised, the baker, whose shamelessly handsome puss is looking more and more like something spewed out by a 3-D printer and whose words are sounding more and more computer-generated (with a little effort, you can count every audience-courting pixel), now takes it upon his solidarity-averse self to remind the venerable Newt that, for all the last-refuge-of-scoundrels touting of family values, he hasn't given a second thought to abandoning spouses Nos. 1 and 2 (the minute the tumors induced by his infidelity were diagnosed as conveniently inoperable) for the sorriest of sorry-looking trophies waiting in the most bleached-blondish of wings. (Imagine! it's the crack about the looks of his trophies, not the unmasking of a careerist cruelty, that's managed to turn his jowls rhubarbative-red and his heart to stone.) Hunchbacked into a corner, Newt knows grossest-of-all-flagrancies mode to be his only option which means confessing that not long into their partnership—they're a power couple, if you please, right up—or down—there with Ivank and Jar, Ira Ruinert and Ingeborg Goebbels, Dick and Lynne, Jeff and Ghislaine, Betsy and Erik, and Dick and Betsy, not to mention CJOTSC and the big-mouthed little woman, as well as Tom Abbott and Jerry Costello (though, believe me, this is no laughing matter)—he discovered Life with Irena reduced to one long irrelevance—and not a minute too soon for she's just been revealed (compliments of some fanged hausfrau's casually uncomplimentary remark) to be on her last legs. Something to do with the radiation she so prodigally and so relentlessly administered down in the catacombs of the Institute (though whether out of death-defying concern for her patients' well-being or as required by improvisations in the Mengeloid mode unrelated to the aims of the trial, we'll never know). In any case, he's defiantly dumped her when she needs him most—and, no, he's not proud of what he's done.

The baker does his utmost to tongue-click sympathetically. *For even the lowliest baker*, Jean remembers reading somewhere quasi reputable— No, no, no, no, no: hold your horses, Maestro: it must be some other member of the tribe who needed that readerly shot in the arm so as to be able to start taking to all his fellow men, whatever their status, like a fish to water, but certainly not she, who routinely makes it a point of passing herself off (to some degree accurately) as a woman of the people. Much to the (mock) consternation of Ethan (in fact her left-leaning *turns him on*—wretched phrase, I know, but one that's here to stay) for hasn't he always insisted—and not just over Saturday brunch at Offenbach's (corner of Clinton and Delancey)—that fat-cat mega-tax breaks stimulate investments in the workforce, i.e., the workforce of the Caymans and merry Malta? Yet here's the baker and here is she and such being the case wouldn't the Master be an even bigger idiot than Herbert unwittingly makes Him out to be if He didn't pounce on so golden an opportunity to titillate—or is it titivate?—the self-love of His clients by imputing—displacing—their contempt for bakers (far more virulent, I might add, than their contempt for butchers or candlestick makers) onto Jean, thereby allowing said clients to have their contempt and eat it too, so to speak? *For even the lowliest baker*— Launching into the aria proper only now, after that bit of RR (retardative recitative) and a repetition of its haunting invocation, she feels not a little like Hoffmann's Antonia whose *Elle a fui, la tourterelle* would have lost at least 87.2 percent of its poignancy without an *aposiopesis* on hand (that's right, bub, an *apoptosis*) to resist and thereby legitimate the lyric impulse. But how, exactly, does resistance legitimate (His Masterliness is right, as usual: the analysis hasn't gone far enough)? She clears her throat in preparation for the anti-showstopper. *For even the lowliest baker— For even the lowliest turtledove—* Trouble is, the notes won't come. She feels herself getting distracted yet again—and by the baker, of all people—who's taken to shaking his dick from side to side and transforming it thereby into the proverbial madman's dead geranium—as a means, presumably, of staving off his impatience. Though quite frankly, it does her a world of good to be distracted by somebody's dick, after all this fallout from being tarred as an anti-populist, especially a dick so big and fat and rakishly set off by its jet-black thickish mesh, and just in the nick of time, if you ask me—I mean her. For no good ever comes of surrendering to Beauty, *which is what makes us despair*, by playing at being Antonia Crespel—and, even worse, an Antonia without some Docteur

Miracle to make surrender easy or at least easier by insinuating its repercussions won't last much longer, since death is hot on their heels. Indeed, the only remedy against the icy exultation oozing from such an impersonation is the same poison—the same pharmakon (but with the sign reversed), namely, porn (for let's face it, the flaunting of that dick has absolutely no redeeming social importance—none whatsoever)—porn, aka grand opera's *sister under the mink* (© Sydney Boehm). The baker—to be saying (again presumably) something in atonement for his lowest of low blows (though no lower in fact than any of his opponent's—less low in fact)—the baker remarks on how little in the way of petulant impatience for the aria Liepnits is exhibiting, compared with him and despite his very advanced age. Jean has all she can do to stop from applauding the baker's diplomatic immunity (to all evidence to the contrary) for he's pointedly ignoring the little puddle at Liepnits's feet—a puddle as exquisitely formed, by the way, as any in the long line of puddles she used to espy en route to the walled-off opera section at J&R—J&R, now dead, and upon whose like we'll never look again—puddles planted by this or that indie crew, at the filmmaker's behest, along the entire length of Theatre Alley (off Beekman Street) in preparation for the obligatorily atmospheric shootout in what was always primed—in what was surely shaping up, per the Word on the Street—to be (what else but) the breakthrough neo-noir to end all such breakthroughs. And far more eloquent is Liepnits's senile puddle, in the exquisitry of its impatience (the only thing missing is a barrage of raindrops whose goal is to stamp out the reflection of his paunch), than anything that's issued from his—L's—trap thus far—or anybody's trap, for that matter. The lack of premeditation must have something to do with it—or, better yet, the pretense of such a lack.

With a heartiness bordering on bluster (the good-old-boyishness, she must admit, is far more potable, what with his being good-old-boy stark naked, than the soulfully proleptic self-excoriation of what seems like centuries ago), he takes the cock and bull by the horns and lets it be known that with age, my dears, all acts became equivalently insignificant or equivalently *fungible*, to use the word most detested by the most virulent of his detractors (at least when *he* utilizes it). And detested particularly by entrails-scouring Jimminy Dwier of Santa Clara, CA, who has the by no means dubious distinction of being the most virulent among the most virulent—why, at this very moment he must be sprawled on a couch in his basement (all 350 proverbial, canonical, iconic pounds of him) commanding his laptop to devise new ways to topple Herr Liepnits's deep-thinkerly house of cards. "So to make a short story even shorter, I'm getting just as much out of being illegitimately, albeit mildly, incontinent out here on the trading floor as I know I will from going strictly legit in the *little boy's room*." Disgusted, she recoils: for, let's face it, this euphemism is far more sickly (pace JD's entrails) than *fungible* could ever be.

But at the very moment Jean discovers just how enthralled she's become by this question of fungibility and, more importantly, how easy it is to defer her disgust on behalf—for the sake—of that enthrallment, who should emerge from yet another freight elevator (so there *are* more than the proverbial seventeen) but Herbert, Cantor (he's back—was simply incapable of breaching the barrier *within* [where the meanings are] separating him from the trees—irresolution at long last[?] has had its comeuppance) and Shearer (where have they all been keeping themselves?), together with a horde of what can only be fellow side-effect generators, though of these she has absolutely no recollection. Up until this moment, they were nameless, faceless, scriptless—like the jetwrecked extras in TV's *Lost—Lost*, as long gone as J&R. Herbert, overwrought and unseeing, makes her way to the windows. Poised on the ledge of the one nearest the terrace (under the circumstances no other, understandably, will do) she lifts her arms (Jean has never noticed just how frail they are) as if enjoining the gods themselves to pay the strictest attention—even if this means having to put their foulest perpetrations, by which she knows them best, on hold. And so potent is the gest, that every last member of the congregation—clothed, unclothed or in transit—dutifully holds his breath. They realize in a flash they're nothing—and that includes the start-uppers (even if their lustrous CVs appear to tell a different tale)—but minor modifications, minor affections, of the Master—*their* Master—who's also their . . . Madonna (that is, if any credence is to be given to the rumor spreading like wildfire from the SB hills to the Santa Ynez mountains and back again that He's the untidy sum of His androgynous zones). Or rather they're nothing more than modes of His/Her attributes (infinite in number—as befits a Master—even if the only ones that fall under the spell—within the purview—of Their competence are Dr. Extension and Mr. Thought. "And modes we shall remain—that is, if we know what's good for us," chuckles the baker, the only one for whom this breaking news for some reason heralds the end of invidiousness. The only one for whom the news—though ushering in what appears to be an era of constraint, constriction, visceral subjection—is a liberation. And the new era so-called is by no means newsworthy since it was always just right around the bend for those with ears to hear and eyes to see. Invoking the insinuation of Hoffmann's Muse (played by stagestruck Berry Sundae, of all people, in the Olivier Py-inspired Minetta Lane Opera production of the *OffenBacchanal*), Cantor feels he has no choice but to dare to conclude that like Olympia, they—the Greenwich Ave Irregulars—aren't living things. "Not even *things*," Herbert corrects (we already know that, as teleconferencers, she and Cantor go way back), "just the merest ups and downs of His quirky Self-realization." Is she hereby grabbing an opportunity to exult (as failed mother-griever) in her own cancellation or simply refusing (as successful freethinker) to be so cowed by this expert mathematician's direst reformulation of the terms of their plight as to refrain from exercising her right, as a fellow nihilist, to go him one better (in true baby-with-the-bathwater fashion)? Little does she suspect in any case how appealingly, to his Handel-crammed countertenor counter-self, looms the prospect of a living death, or so that self thinks.

So when any one of them brags (and she herself is the biggest sinner of them all in this regard) that his mind has just perceived this or that, what he's really asserting is that the Master has just had the idea of this or that—not insofar as He is infinite substance, mind you, but to the extent that He is displayed through the nature of the human mind (like Zeus self-transmogrified into a swan or Harun al-Rashid donning one-eyed shopkeeper drag to ascertain exactly how the other half lived—or whether it lived at all)—but to the extent that He manages to do the impossible, which is to squeeze His way through the defiles of Masterly illimitation and become human, i.e., a biped with feathers capable of the shrillest laughter at another's pain but not of the joy that springs from that other's good.

And to make Herbert aware her mind is nothing more than His idea of her body—for this is pretty much the long and short of the matter—it has taken nothing *less* than the traumatization induced, in a vehicle whose genus and species have yet to be fixed, by a breakneck ride through *them there hills*. A ride designed—in accordance with the most cutting-edge techniques cooked up, no doubt, by one of the very SiVa start-ups represented here tonight (or is tonight already tomorrow?)—a ride designed to simulate Holocaust and Slave Trade transport conditions to a T. (From time to time in fact Melanctha felt as if she'd been dumped in Rupert's Valley, where lurks the guilty ghost of Napoleon.) For wasn't such awareness equivalent to retrieval of the most excruciating of racial memories? And she's sure—indeed, has never been so sure of anything in her life—that bus ride or no bus ride, everybody else is the not-so-proud proprietor of the same awareness knocked into shipshape as a custom-made racializable memory. (Although in her case overburdened ethnicity protests that any conjured memory recruited to officialize such an equivalence must be deemed [in socio-neurological jive] a MAUO [mock artifact of unknown origin]. Shocking enough to discover her mind was nothing more than somebody else's idea—no need to drag in "the one long Holocaust known as Civilization Unchained" [or is battle fatigue making her flippant?] to beef up this horror.) And not only is her mind merely His idea of her body but she may as well face up to the fact that it gets worse: They may as well know (racked sigh, sweaty right palm on left breast), and sooner rather than later, that their minds—the mind of everybody in the room and all those still on the bus to nowhere—means less than nothing to the Master. Minds are a dime a dozen—consciousness is a dirty business—self-consciousness even dirtier (like love according to Ted Koehler, it's not an easy game). Their bodies—not their minds—is what He's after. So, Schrödinger's cat is out of the bag (no breaking it to them gently): there's nothing the Master values less and hates more than their brainpower. That is, He's interested in everybody's mind to the extent that it conduits to the deep dark secret that's everybody's body. Though the deepness and darkness is nothing like the mind's. When He expropriates their minds, which he does routinely (who knew better than she?), it's as waystations. Nothing personal: He hates their minds because He hates his own substance—that is, His own substance as expressed under the attribute of Thought. But somehow, adding insult to injury, it doesn't stop here—there. That is, everybody's body is of interest only to the extent that said body itself serves as a conduit. "But to what, to what specifically?" cries Liepnits (now, inexplicably, dressed to—to—to—well, to at least the eights). "Tell us—after all, you're his medium—his Libyan sibyl— and if you ask me it's just the sort of thing that's spelt from sibyl's leaves—" "Or" (remembering French 101—a course taken with understandable trepidation inasmuch as her son was seven at the time hence a handful who'd be sure to spill her midnight oil every chance he got) "from *sanglots sibyllins*, for that matter." (She always gets a thrill from doing public relations work gratis for well-bred guys like Gerry Hopkins and Steve Mallarmé who manage to duplicate each other's thoughts to a T except for the inevitable minor deformations consequent to their speaking in different tongues.) "But, all kidding aside, you know as well as I that He wouldn't dream of answering just yet." How many times has she tried to make them understand that if you're the Master—or say you are—you can't have your deep thoughts come barging in unannounced to frustrate the story-lovin' lot who are your best customers? Any "revelation" worth His salt has to appear organic to the main design and the only conceivable biomarker for that fake organicity is a concocted resistance to rev's upsurge. Which is why (remembering Movie Magic 101) JLG's implausibly eloquent spouters of high-falutin Wittgensteinisms and Heideggerisms and JayneMansfieldisms are all summarily saddled with hokey stammers or with even hokier lisps or with the hokiest of limps for only such disabilities can get those spouters smuggled through customs. For whatever gets resisted by the story bulks automatically organic—is glued sensuously—thereto. More to the point and as every storm cloud has a sliver of lining, it's clear the Master's an ex-student of TSE (who's famous for being not just Margie Tailor GreenBean's greatgrandfather [see above] but the quintessential thinking man's anti-Semite and the favorite of way too many ivory-tower Proud Boys), i.e., yet another epigone peddling the *new* as automatically/immediately *traditional*. Baker (standing in for Everyman in a pinch for not even the lowest nobody wants to be taken for Him): "But why this ton of bricks here and now?" Cook (emerging from the men's room, or thereabouts): "Why *not* now? No time like the present, after all. A Maid and her Modes: plenty of pornographic potential in that."

And now that Herbert has come to terms with the fact that they're mere modes of the Master—a Copernican shift—the nakedness of her teammates is no longer quite so unsettling. The men are particularly painful to watch, so much desire does she feel welling up inside of her although it may not be what white folks, conventional to a fault for all their drawled yapping to the contrary, normally take for desire.

CHAPTER FIFTY-ONE

In Cook's view there cannot be even a pretense of going forward (*why? well, because the Master, as a prefiguration of The Rump ca. 6 January 2021, says so, that's why!*)—even if that going forward turns out to be nothing more than a mere clubfooting in place for all sempiternity (*Uh-huh, sempiternity: eternity's on paternity leave for the whole semester*)—until, by nothing less than acclamation, the gang has been compelled to accept their new—or rather, newly revealed—collective identity for what it's worth and what better man for the job (and so what if by default?) than she? And as long as no-going-forward remains highest on the agenda, there'll be no stopping drugworld's highest-echelon contrabandiers—specifically those who deem the gross misapplication of off-off-off-label Invidicum as the holiest of callings—dead in their tracks (*why? well, because the Master says so, that's why!*). (Melanctha—the Melancthas of the world—can effortlessly juggle sempiternity and the nitty-gritty.) And if the super-HD images just uploaded from somebody's iPhone or iPad or iCatheter or iDefibrillator to a monitor on the ceiling of the men's room and then reflected ever so deftly in the mirror on its unhinged door are to be believed (and why not), then the holiness of contrabandiers par excellence Erik Bout and Viktor Prince (liaisons-in-chief between Whoever is running the Invidicum show here in the States and the Whoever's overseas clientele) and their fellow super thugs is ever flourishing. As clip after clip and byte after byte amply demonstrates, VP and EB (together with a slew of Blackwater psychopaths slated, from the look of 'em, for a well-earned pardon once the soon-to-be-rumored pandemic rolls into town) have already sold—with the unwitting(?) blessing of the CIA, the FDA, the DEA, the FBI, the United States Air Mobility Command, UPS, FedEx, FreshDirected, KBR, AIG, the NEA, Citizens United and Wayne DeLaPierre, as well as Wayne's tony Hollywood haberdasher-in-chief—hundreds of thousands of surface-to-air missiles, AK-48 machine guns, multi-fragmentation grenades and sniper rifles, not to mention tens of thousands of tons of C-5 explosives, to the RRAF (rogue revolutionary armed forces) at play in most of the failed states of Africa and Western Asia and East and South Asia. For deployment, of course, by their ragtag gangs of conscripts once those orphaned babes in arms are tanked up on enough off-off-off-off-
. . . -off-label Invidicum, i.e., the Bad Invidicum (as one speaks to some boob of a patient of the Bad Cholesterol—that is, if one is some smarmy paternalistic boob of a medico hoping to land his very own weekday wellness show on the strength of what he takes to be an immaculate smile),[148] to turn them

---

[148] The author or the Master or some intermediary is obsessed with "bad cholesterol" and has rung every conceivable change on the term, which turns out, alas, to be always the same change, as the attentive skimmer—even through the smokescreen of his noble exasperation—will have already noticed. But what's wrong with repetition of the same term (if it's the services of that term and that term alone which are always most in demand) since in fact the shape of the term as contorted by the services rendered at each juncture is always different?

into child-star soldiers of the first rank. The evidence is even more damning than Jean ever imagined and even more damning than *that*, what with the soundtrack having just kicked in. Though, strictly speaking—and even not so strictly—sound in this case isn't exactly confirming image or rather by dint of too much confirming has already managed the no-mean-feat (if eyes and ears are to be believed) of nipping it in the bud or heading it off at the pass or both. Hence the image—images—in question are no longer (if they have ever been) "about," e.g., Bout versus Delta Force 69 ("versus" even if egregious Bout's a DF alumnus cum loudest)—fact is, they aren't about anything, in fact, but the consignment to invisibility, with a little help from the soundtrack, of what is now their own redundancy. And with no image track to keep it in line, sound is going haywire (since boys will be boys), although nobody seems to notice except Jean—and even she has trouble keeping her Reikian third ear on the ball—to the point where it—sound—has now become Bout's most unspoken defender right down to his mongrel's moustache and, as such, makes no bones about insisting that the clandestine runs conducted by Bout's private airline, Geryon X, to Khartoum, Aleppo and Kinshasa, to name but a few of its target hotspots, are bona fide emergency humanitarian aid deliveries so why (I—or rather sound asks you) has somebody who has his heart so transcendently in the right place been put on the American Treasury Freeze and Foreign Assets Control lists? *Sad*, as the Twitterer-elect would say.

So even if everybody knows iCatheters never lie, there are, thanks to the power of sound and their own perversity, already gainsayers—Birthers (it kills the Master to upper-case the *B*)—working the crowd (which has thinned considerably with the coming of cloud-smothered sunrise), among whom Herbert, now Cook's Master, has reluctantly to number Shearer (fleetingly), Stifter (or is it Walser?), Lloyd Lutley (with the inevitable Mrs. Froome in tow) and several of the unidentifiable GA Irregulars. This pains Cook even if who better than he knows that the best way to establish the centricity of modes and attributes—and thereby ultimately ensure the capture and prosecution of Bout & Prince & Co (*why? well, because the Master says so, that's why*)—is to allow the Birthers to contend, as they have now gone on to do, that m's and a's have absolutely no connection with, e.g., assisting DF 69—or Delta Forces 1-68, for that matter—in their efforts to bring peace to the Middle East. Is to allow them to contend that the subject constitutes no more than a digression—worse, a digression in praise of digressions (à la Laurence Nikolai Swift)—worst, a bigtop stunt whipped up by the Master because He's simply run out of steam? Unable to stand the Birthers' misrepresentations a minute longer, Jean (she now considers herself Herbert's most fervent convert) feels compelled to point out how especially ferocious the Siliconistas are in their digression-hating (though, as far as she can see, the Siliconistas and the Birthers constitute pretty much disjunct sets)—and how they'd do anything—willingly label themselves born losers, for example—rather than be compelled to reclassify, under the rubric "Mere random walk of lucky zigzags," their purported straight-as-an-Eleatic-arrow accession to IPO apotheosis (the only kind worth undergoing nowadays). (She's picked up this aperçu from Ethan who refuses to de-anonymize it lest by doing so he fuck up his career prospects even further.) To a man, they boo. Some females hiss—in fact, the primmest-looking of the lot, who sport just the sort of harpyish horn-rims that would have given Hitchcock plenty of orgasms to mull over in the privacy of his own viewfinder. To save face (but with whom?), a few lower-level venture capitalists in designer knockoffs lob-launch, discobolus style, greasy paper plate after greasy paper plate.

Yet what hot-and-bothers Jean, at least for the moment, even more than the gainsaying in all shapes and sizes (already at the broadsides stage) is doubt whether "undergoing" represents *le mot juste* in this *instance*, i.e., is an apotheosis something one *undergoes*? So she decides to take the bull by the horns and, as in a fable, solicit the opinion of the baker, from all indications the person in this Aesopian rainforest least cowed by the direr implications of Herbert's Copernican discovery. But the baker, immediately looking daggers of incomprehension, asks, "*What* instance? dude," in tones prohibitive of response. Though oddly enough—but doesn't everything worth happening happen *oddly enough* or not at all?—no matter how hard she tries, Jean just can't collude, i.e., can't feel put down, even if the gawker-friendly acoustics are busy ensuring that the waves of his contempt are rapidly propagated in all directions. In fact, she's being graciously enjoined to undergo her own sort of private apotheosis. Sort of. All kidding aside, is there anything more self-exalting for a creator—since in her own small way she *is* a creator, isn't she?—than to short-circuit the transmogrification of process into end product (in this case, of trial into story) by making the compulsive elimination of all trace of *incompetence-simply-as-something-to-be-remedied* the only facet of that process worth anatomizing—and the real armature of the product, now and forever uncommodifiable? Is any subject more worthy of relentless interrogation than the chronic impulse to eliminate all trace of the passage to competence from in-? Neither competence nor in- matters. Only the tension between the two. Only the question (laid bare by that tension) what makes for competence and what's so great about it?—what's so great about *honing one's craft*? (P.U.!)—and what makes it better than what it supersedes? And to think that from among so many far worthier contenders it's Jean (she begins to feel as transcendent-giddy as Chaplin/Hynkel's globe-bouncing butt)—in her sunniest dreams a hale-and-hearty but otherwise unremarkable coloratura manqué from OmbreLégère, Wisconsin—upon whom has fallen the thankless task of laying bare this brave new wound of meta-communication. Though the small, sad, decidedly ungallic voice of the no-nonsense Great Plains whispers something to the effect that *meta is not necessarily beta*.

Leaping through the nearest open window out onto the terrace Cook beckons to Jean to join him—all this in (like Clark Kent's obverse) a single bound. He needs to stay within sight of Herbert, however. Her effigy soothes, stabilizes, admonishes. So naked a vote of confidence emboldens Jean to take on the birthers, booers, hissers and discus throwers singlehandedly. *As if*, she chides folksily to whoever will listen to her words as they die on the wind, *you didn't know by now*—meaning after all this exposure to masturbatory couplings and worse—that a story worth its pillar of salt can advance only by digression, that is, the right kind of digression—the kind that ultimately doubles back, prodigal son-like, as if by sheer accident on what has been so rudely digressed *from* but at an angle nobody—not even the self-proclaimed most smart-alecky among them—could ever in a million years have imagined negotiable. But is "negotiable" in fact *le mot juste* in *this* instance? (Oops: what started out as a nerveless meditation on the ups and downs and tos and fros, not to mention the ins and outs, of creation is turning into the tickiest of tics douloureux. No wonder the baker is looking daggers—and she knows better than to ask for his opinion a second time especially since he's on the line to the men's room and, exasperatingly [especially for onlookers], it hasn't budged one inch in the last twenty minutes or so.) *As if they didn't know by now* "what has been so rudely digressed from" is never the same on the rebound—rightly exalted as it has become through desertion. *As if they didn't know by now* that any product (the pluperfect iZappe, say, which turns a tired old Blackberry into a covert GPS tracker) takes a giant step in the direction of self-coincidence only when, *purposefully without purpose* (at the behest of Manny the Übermensch from Koenigsberg), it's disfigured by some irrelevant (perhaps *irreverent* is a better word) add-on. Why, if the Master has taught them anything he's taught them that a story—any story—

"But does it never occur to you that maybe—just maybe—they *don't* know?" Herbert cries. The cry is far louder than what is warranted by the distance between them but she's obviously still smarting over her summary self-eviction from what has become, thanks to Cook's charisma, center stage. But almost immediately (compliments especially of the impact of her recent bus experience, which renders everyday provocations like this one pretty darn insignificant), she's able to put on—don—assume—adopt (*dear reader, pick whatever action you like as long as there's no* mot juste *to squelch it*)—a mask of rancor-free grim professionalism and get on with the business of setting Jean straight. As mere modes of the Master—as His lines of force—as non-beings looking at Him from the outside—of course they've bought—hook, line and sinker/lock, schlock and barrel—into the big idea—the Big Lie (which didn't originate with Him, at least not consciously)—that story-, like product-development, must proceed logically, in accordance with the concatenation of the intellect reflecting the true order of causes in the universe, rather than (as it does 99.9 percent of the time in Masterland) hysterically through a mere passive mis-association of ideas each of which constitutes, under the attribute of Thought, an affection of some body (hers, say) induced by collision with some other body (e.g., Cook's). Now she's getting to the hard part of wording the even more unthinkable, but to her surprise—delight—disappointment—the highly legible scrawl in the mirror of the door to the men's room (evidently reflected off the ceiling monitor) does all the work—and in record time. She has only to follow the cursor. The monitor with a little help from the cursor is doing the thinking for the three of them, so to speak. Thanks, monitor! thanks, cursor! long may you flourish! How can they—how can we—be expected to accept the Master's actually entertaining the crazy notion that He deserves to be reimbursed for having subjected Himself to collision—even if at second-hand (but if so, what better reimbursement for—not to mention assurance of—having survived the collision than an idea)? But once having gotten His grubby little hands on said idea how can He be expected to just misfile it (she was about to say *piss* it) away? So since misfiling is out of the question what better way to preserve it than through a radical mis-graft onto—penetration of—the body of whichever yarn He happens to be doing His damnedest to counter-spin? But why *mis*-graft? Well, inasmuch as each idea constitutes the on-the-fly commemoration of a localized impact there is little likelihood it'll have much to do with the story's overarching theme. Which, needless to say ("but I'll say it anyway"), suits Him just fine: mis-graft being after all the vengeance of their Übermensch-in-residence on life itself— on the stingingly unjust laws of life, as exemplified for Him—supremely—by the laws of the story qua commodity (true, *Invidicum: The Musical!* is shaping up to be a bit of a Stalinist tract). To sum up: even if within the context of a Spinozistic striving toward a life consecrated to the purest contemplation of true and adequate causes, unlimited mileage can be squeezed out of think- ing deep inside the box of logical concatenation, the fact remains that in the realm of the kind of wallop-packing yarn He routinely does his damnedest to counter-spin—to love to hate—to sexually harass—to demolish as if it were the Capitol and he the proudest of the Oath Keepers—in short, repudi- ate—the fact remains that in such a realm, it's the pretty passive association of ideas—i.e., a Song-of-the-Open-Road-type succession (the topsy-turvier the better) of supremely ill-assorted collisions-induced bodily affections expressed under the attribute of Thought—that's very much the ticket—in fact, the only ticket along its—the passive realm's—Great White Way. (How proud of this newly minted eloquence would her ex-professors be! although she can't say she misses the stooge—the dud—who wielded the reins of that warhorse nicknamed Advanced Creative Writing 101 with an iron fist.)

So, from the look of 'em, decides Borkman (for the first time in weeks, the monitoring bracelet tickles more than it abrades his middle-ager's parch- ment), these geekeroos—and his beloved son, surely, least of all—aren't play- ing dumb (though why insist all of a sudden—especially when he has much more important things to worry about, like his sentencing—on the boy's being geek-least-likely-to-play-dumb?): Still, he can't say exactly what they aren't playing dumb *about*. But don't panic, Borkman, since Herbert knows— Herbert knows what they aren't playing dumb about (fact is, it isn't a matter of playing dumb: *they really don't know* the story's—the trial's—unity is its themelessness—though maybe it's chock full of thematics in spite of itself). And, hey, while we're at it, what better immune defense against the virus of plagiarism (scholarly or otherwise), Cantor wonders, than such relentlessly generated shifts in theme—so what if they're pilloried by the self-appointed adjudicators of story authenticity (beating their meat out in IvoryTowerLand) as exercises in the basest incoherence-mongering? Inasmuch as the nudity no longer shocks but still does not excite him (amazing what changes a random non-walk can ring on a susceptible endocrine system), his heart skips a beat or two: mayn't this mean he's managed at long last to put—get—the "satan of perversion" behind him? Well, he certainly hopes not. More to the point, to think that while he, Herbert and tens of thousands of other jackpot-lucky schlemozzles were busy getting themselves subjected to every conceivable cattle-car indignity under the sun and *for no apparent reason* (the phrase strikes him as screamingly funny—almost as funny as the just-crowned cancer victim's obligatory *why me?* [although he's already made up his mind many times over never to give Life the satisfaction of hearing him utter it, who knows what he'll end up saying or doing in a pinch or when push comes to shove or when the axe starts to fall ever so brutishly, as if it can fall in any other way?])—to think that, indignities notwithstanding, the fucking and sucking which appear to be *de rigueur* during the roll-out of start-up fun and games in these parts must have been going their merriest way unabated. Not unlike the blithe chitchatting and chatchitting not to mention bratwurst guzzling of SS hags of both sexes in cafés that were steps—i.e., light-years—away from the *excruciations* (shame on so inconceivably lame a descriptor) being played out in the Warsaw Ghetto. (But Cantor must make himself a promise, first chance he gets, not to look backward.)

As if— No! scrap that! *Dutifully* reading what he thinks are Cantor's thoughts (telepathy being yet another heaven-sent side effect of Invidicum, and the golden rule hereabouts) and inspired by what he takes to be their pretensions to genius (albeit genius of the standard-issue sort), Cook makes a valiant—no, smarmy more than valiant—attempt to follow Cantor's example (i.e., of speaking fluently to himself in his own private language) by speaking to assorted geeks and their molls (if not otherwise engaged) in *their* own language for the sole purpose of reminding them that the-story-of-the-trial/ trial-of-the-story genome is so vast, not to mention high and mighty, as to be able to accommodate deletion after deletion and mutation after mutation and still go on ensuring activation of the same old transcriptional master regulators leading to induction of the same old battery of genes leading to the same old encodement of the same old high-octane proteins needed to scavenge and oxidize away excess story fat. So: the beans have been spilled at last and a swell bunch of beans—a hill, actually—they are: The story—their story, as *quirk-in-progress*—can exist only as the unrelenting supersession of its vital components which always turn out to be not so vital—quite needfully expendable in fact—after all. What must be avoided at all cost is self-coincidence—got that?—i.e., obliteration. Judging from what Cantor's just been subjected to (not least remarkable is the fact that it sounded—even without a note, much less a Devil's trill, to its name—like the closest thing to a *valse-ariette* à la Gounod he's ever heard whether by Gounod himself or by anybody else)—judging from the evidence, it sounds as if Cook had tried, dutifully or otherwise, to read his thoughts. Cantor is therefore compelled to ask himself whether in fact Cook managed to succeed. Unlikely—but if so, Cantor knows better, after what seems like centuries of precisely this tribal sort of intermental derring-do as engineered by the Master, than to play the disingenuousness card and marvel in outrage at Cook's criminal uncanniness. Yet (if so), hasn't Cook gotten him wrong—dead wrong, in fact—dead to rights, in fact? But isn't their dutifully getting each other dead wrong what keeps things moving unmerrily along? Since getting each other dead wrong requires corrections and corrections take time and time so taken—i.e., duration—proxies for maturation, of both a story and its stooges. In the "best" stories about the "best" people, *duration proxies for maturation.*

And, by the way, Herbert still hasn't provided an answer to Liepnits's question—something, if memory serves (which memory does all too rarely, except of course when the snippet retrieved from the slush pile can be depended upon to lacerate good and deep), about bodies as themselves conduits. And/but surely enough time has elapsed to allow for the seemingly endless deferral to signal that said answer has indeed overpaid its naturalization dues and has earned its right not just to issue from Herbert's lips—but to issue as if organically—since if the act of answering has been resisted so virulently, then the answer itself must be absolutely vital to the intermental derring-do's main design, as opposed to being your garden-variety chichi froufrou concocted merely to suggest that the Master (impersonated here by Herbert, His Thought's maidenly mode of the moment which in this regard waxes pretty much eternal) is not just (*a*) some hick storyteller (and how astutely, then, He thereby hedges his bets on the verdict of posterity!) but (*b*) a real live deep-dish apple pie of a thinker—your model AA survivor who just can't seem to kick his venerable addiction (to abstraction and analysis). There can be no doubt, however, about the ability of Herbert—a real pro—to dutifully read Cantor's thoughts—mode to mode, so to speak. A woman of duty, she now gets down to brass tacks. From the look of him, Liepnits still hungers for an answer. Understandably (*who is speaking?*), since the revelation that not just their minds but their bodies as well are of interest to the Master only qua conduits has obviously been a big blow to his amour-propre, one from which he hasn't even begun to recover (the poor old sod takes the whole thing personally). Her gaze's slow 180-degree pan is intended to mean, Would anybody like to hazard a guess *why* your bodies . . . ? No takers. Well, as it so happens—*just in! breaking news!*—the Master—and she doesn't intend to sugarcoat anything—is interested in their bodies only to the extent that they're conduits *to other bodies*, since He can know any given body (poor Eden's, say) only insofar as it's affected by—i.e., participates in obscene collisions with—other bodies. Why mention Eden? Cantor chafes. And if he chafes, so do millions of others. (It's this extrapolative technique, applied to a matter far less abstract, that kept him going in the Darkest Ages of his pre-adolescence when it had first seemed as if he were the planet's sole vessel—vector—carrier—of a certain type of . . . mainstream unspeakability.)

Even if He knows better than anyone—based on His acquaintanceship with the Master of Masters, late of Amsterdam, whose acroamata are still sacrosanct—that the more the actions of a body depend on itself alone, and the less other bodies cooperate with it in action, the fitter will the mind of that body be for distinctly understanding—even if He knows this better than anyone, it's the overvalued fitness of *bodies* He lusts after with a peculiar kind of lust (even if their penchant for exchanging fluids fills Him with loathing). (Her discovery—or is it Cantor's discovery?—one of his supreme insights—which he's being kind enough to share with her through a sort of intermodal amphimixis of erotisms—erotisms that in this case are taking the form of thoughts—thoughts more fondle-able than any sex toy you might care to name—this discovery, whatever its provenance, fells her with the heft of a thunderclap.) Irrelevant to His lust, then, is the fact that every interaction of the body with its environment, i.e., other bodies, is reflected in—yields up—an indemnificatory idea for His delectation: Why, after all—as some Scotsman pointed out—privilege that little agitation of the brain we call idea-making?[149] So the long and short of it is that the cat's out of the bag and the disincarnate Master has a vested interest in ensuring their bodies will be affected—i.e., hurt and disfigured—by as many others as possible. And this being the case, He needs to go on fomenting the very contretemps He professes to deplore and to hell with those crazy things called Thought Packets even if only minutes ago they were still His bona fide bread and butter. Unless this is all bluster generated solely to beef up his image as a no-talk-and-all-action kind of guy.

---

[149] The little Scotsman's dictum has been rearing its ugly head in these precincts starting from as far back as the pages with numbers in the single digits. But as in the case of the "Bad Cholesterol" (not to mention the far more exquisite case of the face of NYCB prima ballerina Patricia McBride according to Arlene Croce), it's "never changing and never the same." For the McBride characterization, see Arlene Croce, "Balanchine's Girls: the Making of a Style," in *Afterimages* (New York, Alfred A. Knopf, 1977), p. 423.

CHAPTER FIFTY-TWO

No slouch in the perspicacity department, Herbert assumes at once it's her revelation alone, too long deferred and much too circumstantial in its details, that has so infected the gaping wound of Liepnits's amour-propre as to trigger his just-perpetrated act of extreme debridement—she's talking, folks, about a semi-murderous lunge at Post (perceived, perhaps erroneously, to be the Barnum & Bailey of the *world-class*—gods, how she hates that trendy honorific—Cirque du Soleil of la Maid and Her Modes). But she realizes the trigger lay elsewhere when Liepnits, bestriding, à la Perseus, the semi-dead body of his target, asks them to just-try-to-imagine whom his child bride cum trophy wife (currently receiving—merely for formality's sake, since everybody connected with the case knows she's doomed—her last dose of chemo in the incurables ward two and a half floors above) has seen fit to take (*long before the funeral baked meats did furnish forth the marriage tables*) as her unfit lover. Having once put two and two together—in record time, as a matter of fact—the cuckold did try (he *was*, after all, the author of that famous letter to Queen Sophie Charlotte of Prussia on what is independent of sense and matter) to treat the goings-on (even if they forced him to associate the image of her whom he loved with the parts of shame and excreta of another man) as a mere matter of lines, planes and bodies—or, better yet, cylinders, spheres and cones. In vain. If only she'd allotted herself the time needed to learn to tolerate the pathogen burden of his crazy love instead of mounting, through deployment of said lover's T-cells, an immune response aimed at eliminating that burden. For not so ironically it's the too-virulent collateral damage inflicted by this very response—not the crazy-love pathogen—that's killing her. Herbert's heart—indeed! the heart of every lady (whether she knows it or not)—bleeds for Liepnits (understandably, for he's just shown himself to be far more than just another failed fop flaunting, as proof that he lives his truth every chance he gets, the obligatory cummerbund of tired old baby fat). Or is the Master up to His old tricks: invoking out of the blue—plucking out of thin air—cutting from whole cloth—whatever He thinks could pass muster as red meat for bleeding hearts but in the very context—His context—where such standard-fare psychologizing has no place? Yet, if He's taught Her—oops! her—anything, isn't it that the uncanny charm of His enterprise resides precisely in passing off frivolous decree as reluctant deduction, with a slapdash pathos masking the flimflam? Resides in yoking an improbable effect (bleeding hearts) to an even more improbable cause (Liepnits's heady mix of crazy love and crazier grief triggered compliments of the latest, craziest breakthroughs in illicit immunology)? Resides in signifying—what can't be signified because it simply can't get itself born into probability—what can only be summarized away with a wink and a nod and a belly laugh or two thrown in for good measure (amazing what a story, through the good auspices of sentence structure as instant plausibilizer—as plausibility pill, can get away with)—since it's precisely this impish summarization of what can't get itself born that is one of the Master's prime aesthetic tactics? And all this so that it (the heady immunological mix) may ultimately become—*Liberty Valance*-style and as begotten by Despair upon Impossibility—what's indeed better than plausibility, better than existence, better than birth, better than muddy death, better than fact—to wit, legend.

But how can this hullabaloo not bring to mind the Sherlock-stumping Case of the Grief Counselor? (Funny, Herbert could swear he's already cropped up—in *Invidicum's* Dark Ages when pages with numbers in the single digits roamed the earth. But so what?—just as long as he, like Patricia McBride and David Hume, is always changing and never the same.) Who, ready and willing if not quite able (he obviously had some arrangement with his arch-buddy, the undertaker), waylaid her after the funeral services had ended. From her vantage, that of grief's untreatable absence (lucid in direct proportion to its remorselessness: oh, all right—so she's being, like Borkman, too self-excoriating not to be self-serving!), Herbert immediately knew (no need to peruse his business card) that the oxymoronic *grief counselor* could never signify anything but its own inability to signify, inasmuch as the bearer of the title—make that *all* bearers—could never proffer anything but warmed-over pap—warmed-over nothing. And speaking of funeral services, how about Gaba (no other name will do), the heroin-hounded mother of her son's *best* friend (was he in fact her son's best friend or was this just the sort of hyperbolic entrancement into which humans are swept up in the heat of a sad moment?), who decided to acknowledge—still nodding off—beside the too-small coffin of all places, that in every domain she'd been a real turkey—but never, alas—least of all—a cold one? *Sad* (to quote The Rump's toupee). When her boy needed her most, she'd actually been *making it hot and heavy with a man*. "At least he's alive," Herbert said (but was he?), still amazed that her own boy had been laid to rest in the cemetery that harbored the remains of Herman Melville. She would have given (and would still give) a month's wages—even if unemployed at the time—to be able to conjure a referent, a signified—a state of affairs out in the world—for that too-wistful phrase. But not one of the self-respecting candidate state of affairs she invoked would deign to have truck with—they were all unmappable back to—flagrantly incompatible with—a phrase uttered by somebody who was and would always be in too uninterruptible a stupor to be able to *make it* in any shape or form. Surely there can be nothing more pitiful than a signifier without a signified—except maybe shit's creek without a paddle. And surely, Melanctha informs herself now—now, when it's too late—surely the ones who are capable of *making it*—whether with man or beast—would never look back on or look forward to their doings through the scrim of such a label. In their case, the real thing sucks up all the oxygen with none left over to insufflate a label.

Emboldened—exalted—by his intensifying impact on the ladies, Liepnits wastes no time launching into an *apologia pro sua vita*—*Les Contes d'Invidicum's* soon-to-be-celebrated Hillbilly Aria—which will prove not only that he's had nothing to do with Irena's fatal illness but that in fact he's done everything a doting husband could do to save her from the biggest pathogen of all—herself—or rather, herself as both pathogen and host—or rather, pathogen, host and vector. And who's to say which of the three is the biggest engine of virulence? At the words *Hillbilly Aria*, however, no keeping Jean's digressive eye from catching Shearer's: What can be more fruitful, they wordlessly concur, than to break down the whole of an opera—this particular opera—into the sum of its parts—acts, scenes, numbers—and what could be more exaltingly pathos-laden than to perpetrate nicknames on them—for easy identification—nicknames merely latent and avid of expression (hence no harm done)—nicknames just panting (like Lana Turner's tasteful drugstore jugs) to be discovered? Though Cantor, speaking for all aficionados, big and small, knows better—i.e., that this is a matter—and a highly indelicate one—of self-production-as-self-inflation, not identification, easy or otherwise. Neither composer nor librettist—or in this case, the Master, Who's both—can be expected to do the dirty work (*who is speaking?* the Master? the narrator? Shearer? Jean? the associate director of Opraholics Anonymous?) since, ophthalmo-sartorially speaking, he is—or had better be—too myopically woven into the indivisibly whole fabric to be able to mutilate its Substance (in the Spinozistic sense) by teasing out nicknameable shreds and patches as jukebox commodities. The true maker doesn't think in terms of nicknameable set pieces. To nickname, i.e., demarcate—divide and conquer—desecrate—destroy—is the privilege of the grubby little fingers of the spectator (remember him?), whose soul positively aches—and feels exorbitantly entitled—to invent and extract whatever portable snippets he can from the body of the beast—reparation for too much despair occasioned by too much subjection to too much . . . beauty, *which is what makes us despair* (see above). Nicknaming is a snack (forbidden to the calorie-conscious artist)—a treat—a payback—a virtuoso turn (dividing the indivisible)—homage masquerading as violent expropriation and vice versa—fringe benefit, side effect and byproduct of—and reward for—enduring said despair and living to tell the tale. But it's in the very matter-of-factness of the sleight-of-hand—of the shorthand cum sleight-of-hand—attested by dogtags like *Coronation Scene, Reflection Duet, Diamond Aria, Closet Scene, Venetian Act, Sleepwalking Scene, Gossips' Chorus, Elixir Aria, Doll Song, Jewel Song, Prisoners' Chorus,* and *Bell Song,* not to mention *Interrogation* and *Eyes Trios*—that the exalting pathos lies, inasmuch as nicknaming is willy-nilly the enacted embodiment of stoicism: pseudo-rancorless acceptance of the necessary (why *necessary?* because *no despair, no beauty,* it's as simple as that, bub) inadequation between spectacle and spectator.

Soooo: one less highly indelicate and controversial matter to worry about (as Shearer's heaving sigh easily concedes): it's bitten the dust thanks to the just-performed Nicknaming Aria and has been put to rest by that trusty old gravedigger, Lay Analysis—with a little help, of course, from Analysts Anonymous, one of the Master's many limited liability companies (there, the cat's out of the bag: as a crook, He outPonzis Ponzi)—or is it a special-purpose acquisition company (SPAC to you, bub)? The twinkle in Jean's eye means: I hope this is just the beginning and so please promise me there'll be plenty more where "Hillbilly Aria" came from.

Walser: "Wait, we're not done yet, not by a long shot." *Question too long suppressed:* How distinguish Walser from Stifter? *Answer:* the latter has an unsightly mole—bigger than any amygdala known to man or beast—on his ass. So it must be Stifter after all. Whoever it is, his silent scream (Mother Courage meets Edvard Munch) just can't make itself heard, even faintly, over Liepnits's Wagnerian thumpity-thump.

"To understand me and why I've done the outsourcing, offshoring, buy-backing, inversion-striking things I've done, and to whom, you have to know the whole story and the whole story begins—as all too many stories do (way too many, if you ask me), whole and unwhole—deep in the heart, the hard heart of (as you've no doubt already guessed from my drawl) the Ozarks. Forget all the lies, or rather, the three-quarter truths, about my having abandoned each of Irena's predecessors at the first hint of ill health only to use the insurance payout to smother her successor with the very best Tifffany's has to offer: Fact is, I'm just a good ol' country boy at heart." As she flees for dear life while standing obstinately in place, though nobody is pursuing her (not even the more inept of the two dildo merchants—not even a guilty conscience), Jean—or is it Cantor, also on the run? or both?—can't help thinking—a tad unfairly—a trifle meanspiritedly, she/he suspects—how hard-up Whoever is Running the Show must be to give star billing, even for these few seconds, to a career peripheral like Liepnits (for Liepnits *is* a peripheral notwithstand-ing the self-proclaimed centrality of all his publications and special-purpose acquisitions). Until she realizes Fate seems to be harboring a sort of tempo-rary preference for, amounting to a low-impact love affair with, Liepnits the Rat Man. No wonder, then, that he should be ever so dear to the heart—the hard old Ozark heart—of WRS, Who understandably wants him on stage (even if high visibility must clash with low status) as often as the traffic will allow (presumably because the clash has its own public luster: the luster of pathos). And of course his spiels will never have to worry their pretty little heads about being in character for the simple reason that the Liepnitses of the world, whether Hatfield or McCoy, are never *out* of character: they are inherently characterless—and in that regard like, or rather *sort of like*, certain scriveners (no names, please) who never go out of fashion because they've never been in.

In any case, he's not going to let a simple matter of peripherality get in the way of all he still has to say in this, his dead letter to the world. He must admit, for starters, that he's become a bit stingy in middle age—*cheap and greedy*,[150] to quote his better half in one of her no-longer-rare moments of calling a spade (after all, what does she have to lose?) a spade—as evidenced by the threat to nothing less than his ontological security posed, chez Tifffany's, by

---

[150]It's worth mentioning that there are legitimate reasons for the cheapness, if not for the greed. Instead of being worth billions, as rumored on the Hill, Liepnits, through a pathological resistance to investing in blue chips like Blackwater (notwithstanding or, more accurately, consequential to the wives' hag-nagging), has been reduced to what he's always been at heart, to wit, a civil servant whose only salvation is his pension. So, like Luis de Góngora, he's earned the right to declaim: *Camina mi pensión con pie de plomo,/El mío (como dicen) en la huesa.*

what in fact was mere obeyance of husbandly command, i.e., to select the most bank-breaking bibelot she could lay her grubby—pretty—little hands on. One fit for the 2017 Inauguration. Yet, after so many decades of striving to exactify the correlation, with Envy, of neuronal activity (or rather, of blood oxygen levels as its proxy) in the anterior cingulate cortex, only to end up savaged by the anti-fMRI tribe for assuming (wrongly, in their view) that the undulation of those levels was the result of Envy activation rather than, say, simply over-enhanced sharpening of visual focus on the Envy target or any of a million other epiphenomena—after all this, is it to be wondered at that Irena should clamor for some sort of reconfirmation of professional, i.e., personal worth, even if it had to come from a Hubby of the Old School as unprepossessing as he—as unprepossessing, in other words, as a MacConnellesque sack of MacConnellesque farts? Thing is, unaccountably—irrationally—he felt himself sinking deeper and deeper into the quicksand of insolvency with her every sip of the champagne proffered by the now obsequious salesman, as egged on by what looked like the floor manager, just arrived, to celebrate their purchase-triggered rise in status. But there's no one to blame but himself since, by failing as usual to exercise his *phantom omnipotence*—a term that's the sole memento (thanks, M. Piaget!) of the *Années de Pèlerinage, Suisse* period of his eternal-student days—an omnipotence indistinguishable once again from the self-hating impotence generated by that failure—by so failing he didn't manage to thwart her folly. However, in rejecting the phony because oh-so-contingent deference of the salesman and the manager he did, it must be admitted, come close to perpetrating a poor man's sabotage of the situation. But on whom *precisely* was this masterful punishment by virtuous rejection inflicted: Tiffany's CFO? its executive board? the hedge-fund honchos to whom it was accountable? the agent for Tifffff's seven hundred thirty-seven tax-allergic shell companies (address: 1209 North Orange Street, Delaware)? that huge fan of shells, the Chamber of Commerce? the North American Derivatives Exchange? the floor manager? the salesperson? Irena? Liep himself? (no! he hates champagne)? the price-tagged nightmare in its entirety? And, more to the point, *cui bono*? i.e., who is the beneficial owner of the Liepnits Sabotage Corporation—who, in terms of influence, should be seen as right up there with Blackwater's sleazeball Prince?

Who? why, the Implacable Other known as Ma-and-Pa Ozark—that's who, silly. (By the way, this pair of American Goths would like nothing better than to learn [after all he put them through on the rockiest-road-ever to failed manhood] just how their shameless homeboy managed to let himself get inveigled by those sin-city folk into squandering his ill-gotten gains [rhetorical question-driven excoriation being their Gothic bread and butter]—and on A [Bad] Girl's Best Friend to boot!) For it's only Ma-and-Pa (unregenerately undead and obscenely happy to remain so) who, once convinced he's tied himself up into enough penitential granny knots, teetotalling or otherwise, can grant him absolution for having chosen real unpleasure over phantom omnipotence. And what's more emblematic of beneficial ownership than the puny power to grant absolution?

(Cantor didn't realize before listening to the Aria precisely how troubled

Liepnits really is. Though he hasn't been that slow in picking up on the co-pathologies fueling the lethal follies of The Rump in wolf's clothing [so what if bashing The Rump and *a fortiori* his cabinet is fashionable in certain demographic bubbles—indeed, is a—is *the*—prerequisite for admission thereto?]. For starters, there's the rampant exhibitionism [e.g., wiggling his balls in your face every chance he gets, and he gets plenty, though that's relatively easy to forgive if not to forget]. Makes Cantor's own perversities pale in comparison but [or maybe consequently] he's in the market to be charitable. Trouble is, he recalls how, one day early in his widowerhood [while waiting at Sheridan Square for the uptown No. 1], albeit thunderstruck by ideas about the *Vierergruppe* so brilliant they positively clamored for a preliminary sketch ASAP, he nonetheless refrained from taking out his notebook since doing so would only cause the train to delay its entry into the station [either from deference or vengefulness or a mix of the two] and, by making him late for his first teaching assignment, get him kicked out of the department—and the academia-nut world—forever. Which proves he, too, knows a dreary thing or two about impotence-invoking omnipotence and hence must own up to a certain kinship with the old fakir. And in so doing will he find himself back on the road to heterosexuality, albeit ersatz at best? [For a split second Cantor believes his thinking's actually interrupted Liepnits but stops himself just in the nick of time from bellowing out an apology, which would constitute the very interruption he laments. Isn't there a paradox worthy of Gödel buried in this back-pedaling?].)

Warming more and more to his spellbound audience, Liepnits explains how not until it was far too late—in other words, not until Irena became one big metastasis (a prima teratoma assoluta, if you will and even if you won't, and not just any old assoluta, mind you, but the kind, he's sorry to say, that feels compelled to plaster her own excesses on normal law-abiding cells every chance she gets and hence collaterally entitled to warn them not to take up so much sacred space by metastasizing so fast!) and he nothing more than (as they already know) a leering men's room fixture (*odd self-characterization coming from a reputable heterosexual philanderer*, Jean will, some twenty years hence, remember herself thinking)—not until it was too late did it occur to him that the event at Tiffany's just might (with a little bit of self-help) end up granting something like—no, something infinitely better than—the aforesaid absolution. "Watching the toast fizzle I became convinced that contending with this newly acquired insolvency would deliver me from the Envy Scourge by forcing a shift in focus—permanently—to something more dire, though you don't have to be a human resources officer to know how many dire billions of disability-adjusted light [*sic*] years may be laid at the doorstep of that Scourge." Listening to Liepnits plead poverty, Borkman flinches—wants to puke, even if he damn well knows there is nobody who wouldn't sooner reveal what he inflicts on himself—or worse, doesn't inflict—in the stark-naked privacy of his own bed or even what, exactly, the leisurely extrusion of a too-long-compacted mighty big shit does to his medial shell and ventral pallidum, than admit how loud he laughs—or cries—on the way to the bank. As it turns out, the real problem for The Liep—the real obstacle to self-deliverance, if they must know, lay elsewhere—in his refusal to appropriate an infinitely better windfall staring him full in the face, to wit, the intellectual (wretched word) riches that would accrue from anatomization of so groundless a fear as insolvency: If only he'd been willing to lay bare (yet there's still time!) the disjunction—the inadequation—between this fear and its ostensible cause, namely, somebody's possession of a poor man's moonstone straight out of an even poorer man's Wilkie Collins. And if only he'd been willing to milk the disjunction for all it was worth—as the heartiest food for thoughts supremely applicable to Envy eradication. For when you get right down to it and even when you don't, isn't Envy all about (perceived) disjunctions—rifts—between one's own pittance and the ostensible cornucopias of the other guy? And isn't the Envy cure in its pure state—Invidicum or no Invidicum—all about abolishing those disjunctions and suturing those rifts by demonstrating beyond the shadow of a doubt, i.e., psychopharmacologically, that everybody's autobiography is starkly incommensurate with everybody else's? And fMRIs be damned. If only he'd been willing to catch the groundlessness of it all on the wing and impale the whole mess on the spike—bigger than the one on SARS-CoV-2—of his fabled acuity. And if only he could still exploit his recognition of the fact that a self-constructed demon was trying to pass itself off as a plausible outside threat to his identity as configured by Evangelical Fundamentalist Ma and Fundamentalist Evangelical Pa (but don't you go confusing his filial rage with godless ridicule and *don't*, while you're at it, *get me started* [imbecilically self-important phrase] on the subject of filial rage). So many riches being dumped in his lap (compliments of the dependable psychopathology of everyday life) and here he is ungratefully kicking and screaming all the way to not just any old bank but the twenty-first century bank of banks: self-knowledge.

As Jean sees it, the moment calls for something other than confession—or a different sort of confession. After all, every candidate was informed long before the preliminary vetting that too strong a predisposition to regret would disqualify him for participation in the trial. Indeed, hundreds were turned away based on their hyperresponsiveness to missed chances (albeit of an almost Jamesian—that is, almost [Harry] Jamesian—in other words, almost Young-Man-with-a-Horn-ian—poignancy) as measured (in an experiment designed to weed out the undesirables) by a decreased blood oxygen level dependent (BOLD) signal in the bilateral ventral striatum and decreased engagement of the anterior cingulate cortex. And funny thing is, Liepnits's stomach and hindquarters heartily agree with her for they've just added their voice to the work at hand by giving way to uncontrollable rumblings. And the more he recoils, the more stops they pull out to mock his discomfiture, their impressive tessitura running the gamut from squeaks to bathetic bagpiping. And as if he doesn't have enough trouble, yawns in mid-sentence (which he magnifies, she presumes, to smother the rumblings) render his words incomprehensible. Never one to toe the party line (just ask Ethan), Jean (almost bellowing) reminds Mein Herr that this simply isn't the time to engage in criminal introspection (albeit of an almost Proustian fecundity). What with millions dying of untreated Envy every year and still no approved drug of choice skidding down the pipeline, not to mention Basher al-Assad's murdering of his own people with the dour approval of Putin (dourness passing for manful integrity among the world's greasiest thuglords) and, hey, what about the continuing refusal of The Rump to fork up his tax returns and the shameless storming of emergency rooms by medical debt collectors like Accretive Health and the fact that CEOs of private equity-owned for-profit "institutions of higher learning" like the University of The Phoenix think nothing of rewarding themselves (with millions of taxpayer dollars) for having turned their bamboozled students into unemployable dropouts—how, I ask you, can anyone be expected to take him seriously? Only Herbert, refusing to take the rhetoric sitting down, even if she's standing up as befits her growing eminence, declares that Art—for anybody can see that Liepnits is in his way, like Jean, an artist and not just any old artist but an accursed Artist of the Beautiful in the best Tanglewood Tales tradition—has always been and will always be in unresolvable dialectical tension (Its—Art's—lifeblood) with rank injustice—with Its framing by that atrocity as an irrelevance—an indulgence.

And the most compelling question of all (itself far more of a work of art than any putative specimens you may care to name) remains and will always remain, how has the general public allowed itself to be bamboozled over so many millennia? "I know he's an artist," Jean retorts. "That's obvious: who but artists look to feed on and exploit rifts? What *I* want to know is how your—our—Master is going to—to—" No stranger to the labyrinthine lingo that's causing Jean to flub her lines, Cantor takes up where Jean's left off. "She wants to know how your—our—Master is going to transform this modification of His Substance under the attribute of not just Thought but super-recondite Thought—i.e., the peculiar modification known as Liepnits—into a modification under the attribute of Struggle for Existence—i.e., the modification known as Everyman." Herbert reminds him and anybody else who cares to listen or listen in—if need be, remotely—that recondite or not, Liepnits too is an Everyman—can't help being as much of a poor slob as anybody else in the room. "Well, he isn't a particularly convincing specimen of what my old pal Preston refers to—used to refer to—as *Sucker sapiens*," Cantor retorts—or rather, ventures to murmur. Jean keeps out of the fray, more afflicted by Cantor's snub in the guise of rescue than she cares to admit, least of all to herself—even more afflicted than by Herbert's attack whose virulent aftertaste her retort has done little to mitigate and Cantor's snub has only magnified. Fact is/was, Cantor and Herbert have undone what seems to Jean like decades of psychotherapeutic progress. And that Herbert and Cantor themselves are, atypically, at odds is cold comfort.

Herbert is not to be sidetracked. She concedes that the practice of Art is an affront, granted, to injustice. Thing is, if they wait for injustice to confer on Art its blessing (by graciously disappearing) they'll wait forever. Moreover, with the end of injustice comes the end of Art which is all—always—only—about injustice—and which constitutes the sole vengeance against it and must therefore be permitted to exhibit more than a passing interest in its perpetuation. "Oh," (remembering, with a shuddering sob, the mutilated—and worse—in Building 18 and, with even more shudders, endlessly deferred, latte-guzzling, scowlingly self-righteous, patently *un*mutilated Cheney, who helped dump them there and is now the first to squawk that their benefits are far too hefty[151]) "the world is just too hideous to contemplate—except through the lenses of Art." Is she referring, Cantor coyly wonders, to the three-ducat pair Offenbach's Coppélius foists off on Hoffmann? *Apparently* (but *apparently* from whose POV, Maestro?) galvanized by the mention of lenses somebody runs out of the men's room (fully clothed and sweet-smelling). Holding up a mirror behind Liepnits's bull neck, he waits, with the Sevillian servility of barberly contempt, for the Count's nod of approval (a Count sheerly by virtue of being a customer). But the barber doesn't manage to extract it. Shooing him off, Liepnits guffaws: "Just trying to give you a firsthand taste of the floor manager's servility. Otherwise, how can you be expected to understand my Tiffany predicament? And if you can't understand it, how can you be expected to even begin to understand the problem we're currently up against with regard to Invidicum's abductors and detractors?"

"So fill us in: what made for the big predicament?" Jean can't keep a sneer out of her eyes—she's within her rights, given all she's been through (voice control poses considerably less of a challenge).

Over the still-persistent rumblings, Liepnits proclaims mightily (but as if in his premonitory self-absorption he didn't catch one word of Jean's bitchery hence can't be accused of peasant-slavishly doing its bidding): "What happened chez Tiffany's did something to my sense of self. I discovered *I do not exist*—never existed (at least not in a practical sense)—either in my own consciousness or out in the world. But enough about me personally. So how could I expect to be entrusted with tasks so sacred as, e.g., ensuring that the latest shipment of Invidicum earmarked for Central Africa (all the others are beyond retrieval) got rerouted to the Italian Alps (for eventual repatriation to Forts Dix, Knox, Apache, Bravo and Lauderdale)? Discovered I can't distinguish or separate myself from the external world because I'm its perpetual engenderer. There's no general space in which I'm situated, a body among bodies, a buddy among buddies, one thing among many—too many. Tiffany's emerged—from nothingness—only when I elected, in my omnipotence, to act, which for me means to resist (by refusing a glass of champagne, for example, or dutifully cringing when Irena demanded I ooh and aah over the milky sparkle of her Rock of Ages), and returned thereto (yes, *thereto:* thereto, thereto, thereto—*archaic enough for you old-timers out there?*)—returned to nothingness—only once the action (if anything so life-denying can be called action) had played itself out. And how did I know the action had played itself out? Why, when the existence of whatever the action in turn engendered—

---

[151] And by recalling Sasha Baron Cohen's interview with the ex-VP—where Cohen much too unbrutally inferred that DC's missus, having for eight years watched Her Man play (a very unStradivarian) second fiddle to his Commander in Chief, now rightly felt entitled to *less Bush and more Dick*—by recalling SBC's graciousness (flagrant and unforgivable, given the nature of the beast he was chatting up), Melanctha only adds superfluous fuel to the fire in her motherly guts.

when whatever was washed up on its shores (the diamond, Irena, the floor manager, the champagne glasses, the gawkers out in the street eyeing us fish-bowlers with a slobbering Envy)—made me feel worthy at last of the loathing of Ma and Pa Kettle. Just as no bowel movement worth its salt is complete until there's bright red blood in the mover's stool. And of course I felt most loathsome—therefore most alive—at the very moment I handed over my credit card to facilitate the purchase (I was at my most omnipotent, i.e., my most powerless, in doing so). For at that moment I flouted Ma and Pa's banner principle of Gothic frugality with an intensity I'd never exhibited before (*flouted!* haven't had occasion to use the word in decades: yet, harboring no hard feelings and bearing me no grudge for abandoning it, this old friend still has chosen—bucking the ridicule of its comrades—to come home to roost and at the very moment I need it most)." The floor manager—who maybe wasn't the floor manager after all (Liepnits really can't say, drunk as he was on so much passed-up champagne—debauchee as he was of so much forgone dew)—existed only as the interesting or not so interesting extension of The Liep's desire, his effortless revulsion, his expectation, his dread. He alone caused the floor manager to exist. So, the long and the short of it is that he'd waxed omnipotent enough to bring all this woefulness of foreign bodies down on his head but proved completely impotent when it came to lifting the burden. For his omnipotence is by its very nature designed to engender the very situations where his impotence will be allowed to shine. (*Which is the whole point*, thinks Borkman.) He has no rival when it comes to engendering the world we live in (desperation makes him immodest) but he's pretty much powerless to control what subsequently goes on in it and nobody's more a fan of such self-sabotage than he, though he hates admitting it. "The world I create sucks up all the juices of my omnipotence and uses it against me. Omnipotence cultivated and wielded just to allow myself to end up feeling small—just to put myself at the mercy of whatever it engenders—things like Irena's wifely needs, the comings and goings of the servile Tifffany squad, the gawkers conspicuously consuming the conspicuous consumptives within." (Cantor thinks [thinking's a dirty job but somebody has to do it]: *O blessed flight, and in a single bound, from omnipotence to powerlessness! It knows me almost as well as it knows Liepnits!*) "So Ma and Pa, as always, are right to be revolted: my omnipotence has—as its curse and its glory—club feet of clay. How much easier life would be if I could accede at last to a sense of self—a sense of self like everybody else's—if I could see my way clear to inserting myself and my actions in a ready-made world—a world of ready-mades—a world that doesn't require, thank you very much, the services of my omnipotence to get itself engendered (for the other side of omnipotence—a phantom omnipotence—is powerlessness) and for whose defects I'm therefore not singlehandedly responsible." If only it could have turned out—if only he could have made it turn out—that, any way you slice it, he's just not omnipotent enough to have engendered a compelling context for Irena's profligacy—omnipotent enough to have brought into being her partners in crime—omnipotent enough to have planned the jewel heist from beginning to end—omnipotent enough to have done all that just so he could end up pilloried for his failure to stand his ground long enough to dismantle the event in question. But isn't engendering the compelling context the Master's job? Melanctha asks herself only to realize that Liepnits may not come under the Master's jurisdiction (not being a bona fide Invidicumite)—may be refractory to assimilation as one of His modes. "But it's even more excruciating to accede to a sense of self, as I've been doing willy-nilly, only to discover that self's no longer the center, *nisus* (if you can't stand the word then get back where you belong—back in the vehicle assigned you decades ago) and origin of the universe, that it's just one among an infinity of other selves, even if such an issue would eliminate the guilt at having been, through an ill-timed practice of omnipotence, responsible for my own bankruptcy, moral and otherwise" (Borkman flinches again). "Oh, don't you see," he cries, wringing his hands but *this time* not for effect (thing is, Cantor doesn't remember *some other time*, apparently recent, when it *was* for effect), "I was—and who knows, maybe still am—mired in what pediatricians refer to (behind closed doors) as the Dantesco-Piagetian bolgia of sensorimotor anti-development. And so diagnosed, how can I be expected to 'Move Forward with Invidicum'? (which in the last few hours has clearly become our proud slogan though I claim no credit for its long-overdue adoption)." For the first time Cantor notices the cocktail waitresses (with their starchy Nightingale caps) who've been circulating among his fellow orgiasts, probably for days on end. Since, as everybody knows, the wee small hours of the morning are a serf's kingdom, he was too busy relaxing his defenses—laying down the arms of his despair—to pay those caps any heed, only to find himself overcome at this very instant, as the sun now starts its rise, by an even greater despair. Will he never learn? Will the despairing self never teach him to be wary of anything resembling euphoria—to steer clear of it like the plague? When will he learn to start depicting, reflexively and *in exhaustively apotropaic detail*, the contours—the trajectory—of whatever disappointment— whatever horror—is sure to ensue from some forlorn spasm of hope (but not, of course, before first measuring the level of intensity of the only biomarker in this context worth a damn, i.e., his *resistance* [the greater the resistance, the greater the urgency of depiction]). Imagine! he thinks (self-scornfully), being resistant to the only means available of erecting a barricade against the materialization of disappointment, of horror (but he's a spineless lifer, after all, in magical unrealism's prison house though at the same time he's a ballsy trickster and no trickster, in prison or out, wants to spend all of his time on sentry duty at the looming frontier of bad breaks). His first impulse—that is, if he's not too late—is to protect these ladies from the humiliations—the indignities—to which they've probably been repeatedly exposed—his first impulse is to become their own personal euphorium. But their happy contented looks tell him he'd only be saddling them with his own unease. So it's not everybody else—including these smug little start-up shits who are snatching their champagne from the Nightingales' trays without so much as a smile—a nod of acknowledgment—a mouthed thank you—it's not everybody else but he himself who's the villain—the exploiter—using them—to—to— But, hey, maybe he's just a nice guy—your run-of-the-mill mensch—rankled by injustice— real or imagined. A phantom of altruism's rue morgue. Or maybe he has a lackey's soul and finds nobody more intimidating than your classic have-nots—your classic nobodies—nobodies, when you come right down to it, like *him*—especially when nothing comes easier to those nobodies than reverence for their exploiters. It's the self-styled protectors like Cantor they despise. And . . . rightly so?

Always afraid (as a chronic sufferer from Caro syndrome, soon to have its own little niche in the *DSM*) to be outdone—to watch as somebody else steals and walks off with her show—Jean refuses to take Liepnits's declamatory play-acting sitting down. She wants the little man to understand—and not just understand but understand *on no uncertain terms*—that where omnipotence, engendering and powerlessness are concerned, all of us (including infants—*especially* infants) are in the same leaky boat. Cantor's heart, on the other hand, bleeds for The Liep, it really does, and how can it be otherwise? Bad enough to discover at the unripe old age of ninety-and-change that you aren't real—aren't a man among men. But to then be proscribed, imagine! (because of what constitutes, in the final analysis, the silliest of afflictions) from doing the work you know you were born to do—and do well. Work involving nothing less than goodwill envoyships to nothing less than the five most important forts—fortresses, really—of the Western World (Cantor has clearly been paying careful attention to the devil in these details). More on Jean's wavelength, Borkman resolves against any further truck with this lewd posturing and not just (or so he needs to believe) because the imminence of his . . . what? arraignment? arrest? sentencing? indictment? censure? impeachment? incarceration? stint on death row? makes him pitiless—makes him see things through a glass Invidiously. (Fact is, everybody—Everymen included—has it far easier than he has. Let's face it, compared with him, everybody's got it made.) Ladies and gents, as far as Borkman can ascertain, Liep is first, last and always a crook (like Dave Perdue according to Jon Ossoff) because (forgive the banality of truth) it takes one to know one. Dantesco-Piagetian bolgia, my—somebody's—ass! Speaking of bolgias, he belongs in No. 7 or 8 (Eighth Circle)—or both—and so should be left with no choice but to prepare for immediate rerouting from wherever he's currently squatting (*who's erudite enough to be thinking this for Borkman—gratis, no less!? who? why, the Master of Erudition, of course!*). "Nor should Charles Foster Liepnits pretend—" (His cover blown, The Master has now taken it into His head to pinch-hit for Bad Boy Borkman [who, if he knows what's good for him, should be preparing to Meet his Maker] out in the open—taken it into His head to feed him his lines for all the world to hear, while making sure to go slow at first so nobody can accuse His impatient virtuosity of ripping the carefully woven texture of thinkable things to illegible shreds—texture as lifework—His texture—His and his alone.) "nor should Citizen Kane pretend it's the anaphylactic shock triggered by learning he's a mere—the merest—mode of the Master (under the attribute of Unspeakability) that's triggered his malfeasances." All this tear-jerkery—this stage business jerry-built around his claiming to be but a dimensionless affection of omnipotence under the attribute of impotence, or vice versa—reduces to a mere screen—not unlike, come to think of it, the trust-preferred securities (issued by JPMorgan Chase) underlying the Floating Rate Structured Repackaged Asset-Backed Trust Securities Certificates, Series 2007-401pq, that Borkman himself sold to dunderheaded Invidicum Consortium underwriters simply in order to be able to bet against their best interests and make yet another killing. Borkman wants folks to know Liepnits is, let me tell you, real enough—and with a pair of ozarkian *Last Judgment*-style gorgons tugging on each testicle to prove it—is very much of and in the external world—and what's more he hasn't missed a trick playable in that world. As real as—as—well, as Borkman himself when he authorized his Bain Fund of Funds (one of the many banes of his existence)—for Borkman, unlike Liepnits, never stooped to play the non-existence card when it might have suited his infamies—as real, I say, as Borkman himself when he authorized it to collect all sorts of hefty for-services-unrendered fees from the Consortium—advisory fees, debt-restructuring fees, management fees (in the absence of anything even remotely resembling management), transaction fees, repositioning fees, merchandise-upgrading fees, Mitt's presidential campaign fees—as grossest under-compensation for granting it the rare privilege of issuing billions in debt in order to be able to pay the F of F whopping dividends. Revved up, apparently, by Borkman's Master-crafted self-plus-other, two-for-the-price-of-one sort of muckraking—why, he may very well have just invented a subgenre of sorts (genre yet to be determined)—revved up by all this, some kid in the start-up peanut gallery (not, this time, the chip off his old block) demands to know why Liepnits is to be treated as if he were an artist (never mind all the crookery) when he hasn't a single Vatican fresco to his credit, much less a readymade on the order of Duchamp's *Urinal Descending a Staircase*. Ignoring Borkman (clearly out of his element here anyway), Herbert explains that the theme of Art versus Life having caught the Master's fancy (she'd be only too happy—or at least all too willing—to cobble together in partial fulfillment of her B.A. requirements a disquisition on that theme)—the eternal theme of Art versus Life having caught his fancy—He is nonetheless smart enough to know the success of its enactment within the confines of the story—the story of the trial—*their* trial—will depend on just how plausible are Their chosen incarnations. So the kid in the peanut gallery is absolutely right. The essence of neither The Liep nor for that matter The (equally defective) Bork is ductile enough to trigger—to lubricate—the conflictual play of such plausibilities, at least at this stage of their development. So as mere humans they must all be patient. Everything is under control. Help is on the way. Rightful Pretenders to the Thrones of Art and Life are in fact slumbering toward this outpost of Bethlehem as we—they—speak. "Hey, kid, what's your name?" Borkman shouts; and "Don't let him intimidate you, kid," Liepnits counter-shouts—for all the world as if it's they themselves who were the rightful pretenders. Melanctha sighs a forbearing sigh which deprecates this budding skirmish. The sigh means, *Will (overgrown) boys never have anything better to do than be (overgrown) boys?*

"Next question" (pointing at one of the champagne guzzlers even if his hand isn't up—even if he couldn't care less about Art, upper-cased or not). But as it's an ill ill wind—a *very* ill ill wind—that blows nobody any good and as there's nothing on record to prove any such very ill ill wind ever had its way with the finicky fates, sure enough somebody else seizes the day and is damn well pleased at the opportunity. "What's this about a Consortium? it's breaking news to us." This start-upper waits for some confirmatory sign from his cronies that he is indeed their spokesman but to a man they remained solidarily mute. Maybe it's Post's intimidating bellow that renders them mute—makes them cringe. Where did he come from? everybody wonders but everybody's so used to wondering whenever somebody new—or rather so old as to be new—rearrives on the scene, presumably fresh from one of the van orgies, that everybody agrees wholeheartedly not to give Post a second thought. This is Melanctha's cue to go into her signature ballet turn (handed down, by common consent, from Josephine Baker, Isadora Duncan and Pavlova), entitled—The Twinge of Guilt. But after all, it's not her responsibility to keep track of van-related doings—who's in, who's out, who's bashing in the windshield from irrepressible high spirits. She didn't sign on as a tour guide. And that's that. "And it should be—breaking news, I mean," Post says. "For the Consortium was established within the last two hours (under conditions of the deepest secrecy, I might add) to enable us to implement a *very-high-volume screening system* in every major seaport so that containers harboring vials of (off-off-off-)^x Invidicum can be confiscated before loading—and by the way, ladies and gents, you read right: x is indeed a superscripted exponent. But this will never happen because in the course of only a few minutes Liepnits, whose *lavish lifestyle* is no laughing matter, has managed to turn the Consortium into his private piggy bank." "That's a lie," Liepnits is about to scream but thinks better of doing so—his ostensible counter-evidence would never pass muster as even the lamest of self-defenses. Herbert seeks some spark of recognition (even the feeblest flicker) that Post's allusion to *deepest secrecy* has done no less than *usher in a can of storyline worms* [*sic*] of the rarest mixed-metaphorical delicacy—i.e., has set the Master on the track of a not-quite-elegant solution to the ever unquenchable Two-Entities problem (He isn't bothered by the fact that the problem's intricacies don't seem to afflict other storytellers all that much—in fact, their indifference has allowed Him to wax martyrish by patenting it as His very own cross to bear)—a problem allied to—but oh so different from—the one arising from His deep-throated infatuation, now quenched for good, with the so-called Two-State solution. (But before she goes a step further, Melanctha must observe a moment or two of silence in homage to the realization—although she takes no credit for it: it's had a mind of its own starting in her womb—that uttering the Master's name has in the last few minutes—hours—days—weeks—months—become much more common—even commonplace. Though but a phantom—worse, a phantasm—He's gotten himself accepted as a brute fact of tribal life not likely to disappear for good any time soon. He's no longer everybody's dark dirty secret—or rather, the secret's defiantly—joyfully—out in the open. Even members of the start-up crowd have picked up on her allusions to the Master even—especially—when He's the furthest thing from her mind. They seem, even if the Master's very much *before their time*, to be finding Him in places where nobody else would have thought of looking—dared to look—so relevant has He become to their misdoings. Benign byproduct, all this, of life in a steambath? Payoff from her tireless dissemination of His goofy gospel? although her aim has never been to play—no, not for a minute—psychotic-in-training MTGrene to the Master's Rump. Or does it all boil down—and over—to hunger—a hunger to see, hear and smell Him at every turn since having once been vanquished by His demagoguery, they simply never know when dragging around the carcass of their selfhood will become too exhausting to preclude handing over yet another little chunk of it for safekeeping? Or is the Master an idea—or, more to the point, an entertainment icon—whose time has come? Or is He little more than a third-rate novelty act whose virality has been unleashed by the subliminal forces of mass acculturation? (*Once posterity kicks in, we'll know the answer,* Melanctha thinks beatifically as if this were Lourdes.) Is anybody here willing, she asks, to think outside the box, i.e., to forgo the story drug—the generic of sensationalist *content*—even for a minute or two—in favor of a nice little pharmakon nobody's ever heard of—an over-the-counter meditation on the tricks of the trade where the trade is the story's—the Invidicum story's—*form*? Since it looks as if the spark she seeks won't get itself ignited any time soon, Melanctha has no choice but to take the bull of explication by its schoolmarmish horns. First, the invocation of a Consortium—of "Consortium"—has, if they must know, been triggered by the need to map the bull's-eye of yet another of the Master's out-of-the-blue infatuations—an infatuation, this time, with "very-high-volume seaport screening" (the sound—the texture—everything about the phrase and the concept it adumbrates—conspires to get even Cantor—even Borkman—even Post—as hard as a rock—conspires to make them feel like masters themselves)—into the domain of the story as a bona fide red herring—as His latest MacGuffin—as His latest Muse. (Infatuation addicts by temperament, Masters are always, like Ethel Waters [but without her wicked knowingness], *taking a chance on love.*) But if the Master has had the courage to undergo yet another infatuation—infatuation, after all, is hard work, humiliating work, intimidating work, a wasting disease—then He should at the very least be rewarded—through acquisition of His bull's-eye via its acquisition by the story. With the story serving, as stories tend to do, both as dumping ground and as edifice. In other words, the Master—masters in general—need to make everything that they deign to undergo *pay*—hell, that's what compels them to become masters in the first place—hell, that's what makes them, like Norma Desmond, a star. What for others are everyday collisions without compensation—with things, with words, with their own misperceptions of those words and those things—are for the Master indigestibles—too indigestible in fact not to come (as a favor to the genius of His shaky nerves and snaky hair) with a warranty—to the effect that the collider will most definitely be indemnified for his arduous, beautiful pains. And what better indemnification than for the MacGuffin cum Muse to be transmogrified—alchemized—into a building block of his very own edifice even if he is in effect threatening that edifice with demolition every time he forces it to accommodate a new one—a new straw whose only goal is to break the edifice's back. (Surely, *even they* can understand how for Somebody like the Master, "very-high-volume seaport screening," with its evocation of high-tech derring-do, would appear to be just the sort of modification of the Substance of the story under the attribute of Thought needed to propel it breathlessly forward.) But He can't just map the bull's-eye: He needs to contextualize—naturalize—officialize—the thing mapped and what better way to do so than with the assistance of the usual-suspect scraps of bric-a-brac, which in this case might—and does—include a high-sounder like *consortium*, evocative of just the sort of bitcoin-funded cabal of pedophiles sure to warm the cockles of any QAnon groupie's heart? But if *consortium* is to put the required gloss on *very-high-volume seaport screening* (and vice versa, since what's sauce for the goose, etc.), its deferred debut must be plausibilized, i.e., it mustn't appear too obvious that He hasn't played fair with His dinner-theater clients—even if those clients—the furthest thing in fact from Christie-schooled purists—are too busy getting tanked on martinis to be pissed by His sludgy sleight of hand. And what better way to plausibilize than to lay the deferral *so-called* (since in fact the Consortium hasn't been waiting in the wings: it's sprung from nowhere—it's unmotivated) at the doorstep of a need for the utmost secrecy, quite comprehensible given the incalculably dire consequences should exponential Invidicum at last reach the Enemy, whatever It turns out to be? But though—or for the very reason that—morale seems no lower than before she's compelled or emboldened to reassure them that their Master—their Master-builder—would be a very poor Master indeed if, after having managed to ensure that the story had acquired this, His latest contribution to the war effort (for storytelling is total war), He didn't command contentment to pass quickly enough into the rawest dissatisfaction. For at every turn (hasn't she made that plain enough?) He's after the far bigger game of catching the Strategy (perhaps His greatest invention) for Plausibilizing the Advent of One Implausible Entity through the Auspices of Another (SPAO-IEAA) (aka the Two-Entities Strategy)—the far bigger game of catching the Strategy in the act of colliding with its own limitations. Localizing the point in space and time, for example, beyond which attributing the Consortium's deferred debut to motives of "secrecy" began to ring screechingly false. Doubtless more correct, then, to say His greatest invention is not the Strategy per se but rather its Debunkment, i.e., His fool's proof that anatomization of why it's impossible for any self-disrespecting master to play fair with his fans' martinis, is in fact far more action-packed than a super-slew of plausible derrings-do—of joyrides with no loose ends. Thing is, those unlucky enough to be present—to be in at the kill—don't seem to have cottoned to this demonstration of form's pyrrhic victory over content.

CHAPTER FIFTY-THREE

With the not-overly-chilly dawn has come Eden and not a minute too soon (if you were to ask any of the start-uppers) since the hope, at least among the he-men in the group spoiling for some good, clean, old-fashioned physical combat, is that, starting here and now, they—modes of the Master's Substance (indistinguishable from the story's Substance)—will play themselves out under the attribute of Extension rather than (as has been far too much the case these long dreary months—or are they years?: generation of a plausible duration being as much the Master's forte as stupidity is M. Teste's) under the Attribute of Thought. According to Pajama Boychik non pareil "Dr." Sebastian Gorka, onset of the Thousand-year Reich of the Alpha Males is long overdue. Clearly, great things can be expected in the Extension department, judging from the (for example) Heathcliffian pose (not to mention the Byronic limp) he—Eden—strikes against the sky: "clear, vivid, unspeakable," i.e., pure Pierre Glendinning blue, which is not to say it isn't also *"vierge," "vivace"* and *"bel,"* i.e, pur Stéphane *bleu*. (In draining the Master's lifeblood into her veins, Herbert has become aware He cherishes nothing so much as just such evidences of same-wavelength telepathy among Old Masters of the same era [who in their willed obscurity were completely unaware of each other's existences] and that He has every intention of continuing to do so, even—or rather [as homage to the illusion that Art can still triumph over Life] *especially*—in a world where al-Assad McShit and the Krotch Bros [among countless others just as too-big-to-flail] are permitted to remain zestfully at large and bury the face of everybody else in the fecal stream of their impunity.) In other words, if anybody can make American Great Again, it's Eden (who remains half-in, half-out, of the room though of course it's not a room per se but what's now referred to ["now" being the last seventy-five years] as a space). Along the same lines, Herbert is delighted to discover that right behind Eden the gibbous moon, his double—his *semblable*—his *frère*—refuses to follow the tribe of cloudlets (for the unholy ghost of one of which it might, by the unpracticed eye, be mistaken) in their flight from the rising sun (moral: Don't mess with the moon). In fact, it manages to extricate itself by dint of mere—sheer—plain sailing from every trap their mob rule sets although it doesn't seem to think twice about slipping into the vest pocket of any one of them for a snooze from time to time, even if it's precisely time, and time alone, that's of the essence. *Moon Stands Its Ground! Read All About It! Hot Off the Press! More Interesting by Far than the Latest Genocide!* is what she should shout and eviction from the human race—worse, from the precincts of the trial—be damned. She's not just tempted but *sorely* tempted to get next to Eden for a better view but why kid herself? the flocculence, framed by the big bay window, is perfectly focused as is. And besides, she has other things to think about—like whether Liepnits's rush to privatize everything from the Ozarks to the Beaux Arts may have some connection with the scandalous understaffing and maltreatment rife in Building 18. Or whether it's Navient's scumbaggery in marking the charged-off loans of disabled and traumatized soldiers as defaults that made

Steve McNuchin (think, or try not to think, of McO as a Rodeo Drive leprechaun trafficking in life settlements, reverse mortgages and other rank exotica) The Rump's hands-down superpick for Treasury Sec (only thing going for him: he's taller than Janet Yellen—by a millimeter or two).

In any case, her passage would be barred for as Eden finally enters—more radiant than Shearer for one has ever seen him—he's roundly assaulted from all directions with the same silly challenge (at least it *sounds* silly when spewed out in mock-unison by these greasy groundlings), namely, *Hey, what about poster boy's contract?* Well, as it turns out, the Achilles heel that is Eden's past has caught up with Martin the tortoise. Not so much a shady past, whatever failed atrocities are embalmed in its amber or its aspic, as a past badly in need of names (they needn't be the right ones) for those atrocities, failed or otherwise—binding names, as one speaks of binding foodstuffs for loose bowels—for it's the lack of such names that *makes* them failures (but does Herbert actually believe what she's just this minute perversely affected under the attribute of Thought?). I.e., nothing atrocious but lack of words makes it so.

(Here, Cantor exhales [dutifully taking up her slack whether she knows it or not], is a new kind of Unspeakable—an Unspeakable for the Twenty-first Century—not the old-fashioned kind which dares-not-speak-its-name but one that would give an arm and a leg to be able to do so. So how then can Cantor help being reminded of the mighty phrase "Jobs for the Twenty-first Century" as smuggled by none other than George W. upon the advice of his boilerplating handlers, without any conviction whatsoever hence as inconspicuously as possible, into one of the 2004 Presidential debates? Jobs for the Twenty-first Century, my ass! training for which was to be dished out smooth-sailingly in [where else?] community colleges—the kind he and his brothers and his daughters *didn't* attend—wouldn't be caught dead attending—worse, *having* attended. In short, a meaningless phrase—plugging a meaningless suggestion. In short, another signifier without a referent—another bad joke without a punchline up its sleeve—another ship without a rudder—another paddle without a shit's creek to navigate it.)

Only Eden is not as alone as Cantor wishes to believe he is for here—having emerged from the very corridor where Jean was so rudely forced—ages ago, last night[152]—to undergo what budding erotologists call a Dildo Moment—are those two *settecento* picaros, Walser and Stifter, standing right (and left) beside him for the sole purpose apparently of fending off the unrelentingly tormenting crowd. Testicles nonpareil dutifully underpinning a stiffening prick (the intensity of his illumination is causing Cantor's heart to *skip a beat*), the duo doesn't just evoke—no, they distill the very essence of all their forbears down through the ages, ranging from those "privates we"

---

[152] Foundational fragment from the haunted Harold Arlen/Yip Harburg ballad "Last Night When We Were Young" (1935). It's a meditation on how loss of innocence plays havoc with a tidy sense of self and duration as well as (and don't let anybody tell you otherwise) an anticipatory take by composer and lyricist on the essay entitled "A New Refutation of Time" by Jorge Luis Borges.

Rosencrantz and Guildenstern, to *Amerika*'s dowdy Delamarche and Robinson. Not to mention the two badged goons who take Wrong Man Manny Balestrero into custody: For a split second (just before the police car pulls away and as his wife starts preparing dinner in deep-focus) he and she, both window-framed, are unaware of their entombment in the very same shot, with that unawareness being akin—equivalent to—indistinguishable from (for starters)—beauty, innocence, ethereality, otherworldliness, pathos, doom, entombment, resurrection.

There's one person, however (among millions, probably), who appears to be unimpressed by this Archduke Trio effect. (And while we're at it, isn't that Mary Johnstone bringing up the rear? you know, the Typhoid Mary who, based on the most tenuous of connections with Cantor the adolescent pre- and post-, saw fit to confer on—upon—herself the divine right to vouch for his glaring inadequacy [a touch straight out of . . . well, *The Wrong Man*] and thereby block his accession to Pritchardship—for life.) "What's with these repeat appearances?" cries Netta in a beige muumuu lavishly profaned by pink and greenish polka dots. Though presumably putting Eden on the spot, it's Stifter and Walser—both suckled, vocationally speaking, at her dugs (maybe even at the same dug)—she glares at. Then to the company at large: "Just because he's acquired two sidekicks doesn't make this visit any less identical to all the others. Their clumsy attempt to distract us only confirms what we already know all too well." "Which is?" Mary coos, knowing a fellow hatchet man when she smells one. "That this visit is even more identical." Everybody who's been lashed to the prow of nakedness is now fully clothed, Shearer notes—including (*she checks*) herself. How did that happen? she muses. And is this musing supposed to cover the Master's tracks—to *suture*, as Herbert might say, the gaping wound inflicted (but on whom besides Shearer—with her ballet-slippered hatred of discontinuity?) by His maddening inability to remember whether, inter alia, His creatures are still naked or still clothed or simply in-between? In other words, did Shearer instantly decide to take pity on Him and *a fortiori* on all those who hang—literally—on His every word? If so, she's realizing quickly enough that, of all the reasons for taking pity, hers makes underhandedly the best possible case for his not needing any. For if this Master Builder is anything like the great one she's worked with (and more and more she knows this to be the case) then His work—the Work that really counts, that is—must be said to represent the sum and product of all the instances of high drama where that maddening inability held sway—with disastrous hence sublime results—and so the minute He tries in good faith not to exercise that inability (out of self-hate, or the need for money or for a whiff or two of tabloid glory, or out of sheer boredom) the work becomes inconceivable and ceases to exist (and He with it)—and Moira isn't just posing on his behalf and therefore on her own: the stakes are too high. He and the world's rules are (to use one of Liepnits's favorites) *incompossible* (yep, even a prima ballerina assoluta can, albeit only when sufficiently provoked, polysyllabilize with the best of 'em). The only air His work can breathe is evidently un-ruliness. And maybe—just maybe—it's thanks to the suturing effects of this little prima (her meanest rivals often contended that she was made to be not a dancer but rather a seamstress—a wardrobe mistress out of Hans Christian Andersen) that the fruits of said un-ruliness will manage to get themselves digested by the biggest dinner-theater contingent He's ever known.

But enough about Shearer Musagète. That her two aptest pupils now see fit (after chalking up close to blissful fifty-five years of professional notoriety between them) to jump ship—simply because some misfit has bamboozled them into believing the practice of sidekickery (as opposed to medicine) will make fullest use of their hidden talents—is about to throw Netta Boulanger into what's called a frenzy of rage. As if reading her thoughts, Walser— But why Walser and not Stifter who, if Herbert remembers correctly, has always been the much less reserved of the two? But, if she were to remember much more correctly, this, the space they all occupy through no fault of their own, is an outpost of Fictionville, and in F-ville only the calculated injection of surprise sells half-price tickets—so long, that is, as said injection can be engineered to come across as flummoxed surrender to yet another all-too-life-like constraint on realization of the fictioneer's main design, even if he does everything in harm's way not to have one. Which is why it's Walser, and not Stifter, who now explains that they've already turned in their stethoscopes for good. The dark complexity of Eden's van experiences—so vastly different, as it turns out, from what under the same circumstances your average poster boy would have chalked up in the way of traumatic stress—demands full explication ASAP (to then be packaged for popular consumption, which is where Mary—he means Ms. Johnstone—comes in) and what better explicators than Her—that is, Netta's—Privates They?

"Hey, lady, you over there—that's right, the one who had the gall to squawk just now about my showing up over and over and over to no purpose. Well, if you must know I'm the very worst repeat offender imaginable—the kind who's constantly making the wrongest of wrong moves—the move of daring to be himself." Where does such insight come from? Jean marvels, clearly aroused—and when she least expected to be! given that during his absence Eden seems to have acquired an unforgiving Brooklyn or is it a Bronx—by way of a Merovingian—accent. (Speaking of accents, didn't some busybody Irregular back in New York, half-stewed on her first megadose of Invidicum, intimate that Netta went fully—ballistically—British after just three days in sunny Hamburg?) "Don't apologize: it's she who's the worst r.o. imaginable—the kind who refuses to recognize that endless repetition is the spice of life," Mary sneers—or tries to sneer. Eden is already bearing down on the crowd. There's a bulge in his vest pocket. Cantor is certain (though ashamed of his certainty) that it's the most lethal handgun of them all—weapon of choice of recidivism's worst, gruntled and disgruntled alike, to wit, a .46-caliber semi-automatic pistol holding ten rounds. Cantor is torn: on the one hand, he's terrified (which reassures him he's still vaingloriously alive) and on the other he's brimming over with the very milk of hope (which, characteristically, saps him of all strength). And how could he not be both? For whenever Martin Eden—Eden the character—pops into the picture—it seems as if a story can't be far behind—seems as if it were just around the bend and will soon have its day in court. But even if in fact Martin never really delivers the goods and even if he continues to brandish this ten-round dagger between his teeth Cantor can't help feeling as if he were entering safe territory. Since a real story is safe territory—none safer—and whoever doesn't love a story doesn't love life—doesn't love guns—doesn't love the gods and doesn't hate the abolitionists and their abortionist sidekicks. Since in itself a story is pure even if those who hold it together—who carry its water—aren't. The right kind of story has a beginning, a middle and an end with plenty of rest stops along the way where those so inclined can load up on insubstantial goodies—goodies even more insubstantial than the story itself (a sheep in wolf's clothing if ever there was one stalking the folds). But, oh my god, as if the pistol weren't conversation piece enough, there's a gaping tattoo as well—just above Eden's right ear and still growing, like a benign tumor but with none of its unsightliness—and not just any old tattoo but one, say, straight out of Kasimir Malevich: It tells the grisly tale of a white square that's about to be swallowed up by its backdrop—a larger, whiter square—and, worse, spit out like the mere ghost of itself—although the little square is fighting like hell not to be. And as it turns out, this exercise very much parallels the efforts of mathematicians like Cantor to reduce all of math to arithmetic and arithmetic to logic.[153] Well, and whaddya know, Cantor gulps sagely (nonetheless refusing, by stepping aside, to evince intimidation), with a white-supremafist's—a copycat mass slaughterer's—latest work to call their very own, the Invidicumers have, as a collective patron of the arts, clearly entered the big leagues. But instead of reducing Netta to a sum of indistinguishable parts as the pistol is instructing him to do, this heavy-metalled Aryan whose bark is clearly far worse than his bite, elects to lift (once collapsed where he clearly belongs: at the old dame's feet) her ringless right ring finger to his lips (for all that as if she were Pius XIII), though from every indication he's completely at a loss about whether to kiss it or bite it right off. "What Eden's trying to convey down there on his hind legs—" Mary again: Walser and Stifter visibly bristle for look! she's already stealing their thunder—no wonder Cantor can't stand the sight of her—and if they don't put their foot down right here and now, things will only escalate. "—is the enormity of his guilt for having given a free pass to those who brutalized the innocents in vehicle Numero Uno (we'll get to that later, but only when I'm good and ready). But of course Invidicum the Side-effect Queen may have played a big role in rendering him incapable of intervening to save them—just as he failed to intervene and save his father from the clutches of Straynge."

[153]See, e.g., Meyer Schapiro, "Abstract Art," in *Modern Art: 19th and 20th Centuries—Selected Papers* (New York, George Braziller, 1982), p. 203.

CHAPTER FIFTY-FOUR

Without knowing it, Eden intends the impish tilt of his head, the overexpectant hunch of his shoulders and the gentle shaking of his upraised outstretched palms to mean, May I, maestra?, but without waiting for this Maestra to give free rein to her reluctance, Eden takes over—it's *his* plight, after all, that's under indictment. Or rather, Walser and Stifter take over: their first full day on the job and they're a-rarin' to go. As they hasten to make clearer, it's true—he hates the Eden of Numero Uno with all the amateurish bile he can muster—and no hate greater than that of a self for its antecedents—for the selves past to whose transcended ordeals it owes its precarious stability. Though at times the past selves are more real than he is now. Even if describing—depicting—explaining—them to himself (though their doings would make a vampire—or a rapper—blush) feels like a relegation, a healthy obliteration. Still don't think for a minute he doesn't despair at having to relinquish them completely—those demon selves with their demon memories. For he's credulous enough to believe that reliving the goings-on among those selves, the unspeakable goings-on, is equivalent to saying goodbye to them forever, at least in the wee hours when the world sleeps the sleep of a babe justly cradled by the throes of crib death. And equally tormenting is the fact that simple acts which occurred in as well as out of the vehicle (you mean the *van:* let's call a spade a spade)—acts as simple as shitting (whether relished to the full or not)—have become further desecrations of the innocence of those innocents—worse, signs of his indifference. The human animal—at least insofar as Eden impersonates him—is so hideous that even the most neutral bodily function by its sheer thisness (but are any of them, each being willy-nilly an exploration and expression of character, ever truly neutral—neutralizable?) becomes, under the right conditions, a zestful proclamation of obscenity in action, i.e., head-over-heels self-love. For I ask you, what does shitting post-Van No. 1 constitute but a pact signed with his own bowels to ignore the fact that he connived, in its dank damp recesses, at the pain inflicted by too many others—a state of affairs that makes of slogans like *Never again,* mere *rhetorical chips off the old (executioner's) block*? (Please try to see past the opportunism of this clever turn of phrase, somebody thinks—somebody who's never been interested in hogging the spotlight à la Eden—an extra who holds his supernumerary head high and who's not ashamed to be pragmatic enough to prepare for life after the McChateau—life after glamorous self-incisions à la Gerzso—life after Invidicum.) But how, he wonders when off the pot, can he allow himself through such a voluptuosity to miss even a single beat of his self-hate especially since rumor has it that—something he's loath to admit—there are now pre-established limits to how much anybody should be obliged to suffer, including even the coolest of mass torturers (although if the limit happens to be exceeded then, as rumor also has it, the surplus of suffering endured will not be credited against the next round of abominable suffering inflicted)?

"But," Shearer cries out, as if in reaction against her own demons, "he's no worse than life itself—which has a bad habit" (remembering her lowest points) "of going on no matter what." Stifter: "Simmer down, little lady, simmer down, simmer down: the van experience wasn't all that bad. In fact it did him more good than bad. For it was in the van (and how could it be otherwise, knowing what vans are reputed to be able to condone?) that Eden discovered the past always catches up with you—no matter how many of its selves you convince yourself you've skinned alive and sold off to souvenir-crazed tourists. Not that he *blames* the past. Do you, Martin?" To respond would be to countenance their having already stolen so much of his thunder. "His keepers simply thought they were doing the right thing by, or couldn't stop themselves from, making a self out to be a hideous thing. Which accounts for the fact that Martin here has never had what my former colleague SK (initials are, to him, the next best thing to a pseudonym) calls immediacy (because it's only in the domain of the self that you can be immediate) and thus in the ordinary human sense of the word he's never lived. He's never been (what was the expression Liepnits used back in our Dark Ages?) a self among selves. Yet although he seems the most unreflecting of men, he began at once—long before he was born—to reflect—to be big with reflection. A by-no-means rare case, ladies and gents, of self-consciousness without a self. But at the same time—and here SK proves an ounce of self-contravention is more fertile than a pound of fleshly consistency, at least when it's carnival time in the Middle Ages—the more there is of self-consciousness, the more there is of self. The more self-consciousness, the more Eden—Eden! and the more Eden the more self. Eden, then, for all his refusal to be (a proleptic refusal—some might call it a sham refusal—but whatever else, it's a refusal negotiated very much on his own terms—a refusal promulgated in defiant advance of every puny tyrant's command that he cough it up)—Eden, then, is positively overflowing with self. Only he's simply taken the long way around to get here—i.e., he's done it, as is his wont (and you can be sure his press agent is going to milk the human-interest angle for all it's worth)—he's done it the hard way." Stifter is a bit too bubbly for everybody's taste except for those few who are just too cowardly to surrender to the will of the crowd.

In defense of Martin who's quickly become everybody's bête noire—simply because he's what Cantor's shrikelike mother, after getting a wee bit of flak for perpetrating one of her vicious tirades, used to call—referring crazily to herself (still, he can hardly blame *her* for the rocky road his sexuality has taken)—an *easy target*— In defense of Martin—and to bring a bit of much-needed gravitas to the proceedings—Walser (in a pinch, everybody's right-hand man) reminds them that the reflection of somebody like Martin, unschooled in sophistry, is simply not their kind of reflection (i.e., the bad-cholesterol kind of reflection), which never entraps so unfailingly as when it crafts its rat trap out of nothing—reflection that is never so much itself as when it takes the form of GF's dream Book About Nothing—reflection that's unventilated by action or event and whose shaky armature is the meanness of Envy. For Martin is no envier (it's common knowledge he's here on the falsest of pretenses). Furthermore, parricidal envy is no longer a *DSM* darling despite all the lobbying by the likes of Fyodor K. Sophocles. But never mind Martin.

Might there just so happen to be one among them—one among the reflection-on-nothing crowd—who's ready and, if ready, able and, if able, willing, to break, first, out of the prison in which reflection on his Envy—that is, on the nothingness of his envy—of his fellow men—i.e., his adversaries—keeps him entrapped and, second, out of the vast penitentiary (housing that prison and the millions like it) which has been built with the sticks and stones of those adversaries' reflection on the nothingness of his own enviability? And, on a lighter note, might there be one among those already on the lam who's ready and, if ready, able and, if able, willing, to reveal his beauty secret?—in other words, whether it's the resolute despair he's achieved through the hard work of deliberate reflection-on-his-reflection-on-nothing that saves him from the meanness of Envy or (when subterfuge is done) is it simply the fatigue brought on by the old age of too much deliberation (indistinguishable from the death of life-sustaining soul-stretching tension) that's doing all the saving?

Tearing free of Eden's papal bull (he's decided not to bite off her finger after all) Netta sourly reminds them that not being a self among selves is Liepnits's specialty—invention—call it what you will and this being the case he has every right to cry patent infringement. "She's got a point there," Mary cries. "I'll have a riot on my hands if the venture-capital crowd gets wind of the fact that when all is said and done every last one of you resembles everybody else to the point of self-obliteration. You have no idea how much work it took to finally finagle them into putting their money where their mouth is compliments of hefty assurances that *Invidicum: The Movie* will boast a cast of characters more differentiated than any the world has ever seen—from most, if not all, walks of life (which I do and don't believe). And how can you tell a story without the sort of contraptions every stagestruck spectator from Aunt Franny in Pyorrhea OK to Uncle Granny on the sunny side of Central Park West would give an arm and a leg to be able to incarnate? Not to mention the bad publicity we'll get from all the storytellers and associated PR dudes who've pitched their own tale of woeful lust and lost (I'm a member of what's become a dying breed or, more accurately, a dying breed that never managed to get born)." Cantor thinks, *Maybe she's right as rain and I'm better off unpromoted and unanointed. Maybe thanks to Pritchardian worldflow and Masterly wordflow I'm the beneficiary of a kind of promotion that surpasses every other.* "You have no idea how much they relish reacting with pissy prissy outrage when somebody dares NOT to tell a story—dares NOT to differentiate himself into a tumbrelful of unforgettables. Why, it's as if the non-storyteller through no fault of his own comprised all by his lonesome a whole guerilla regiment with enough avant-gardish weaponry to blow them all—worse, their two-page 'treatments'—to kingdom come and Capitol Hill right along with them. So at such moments they have the best of both worlds—they're not just slavish conformists but a persecuted minority of ghillie-suited outlaws wearing death sentences around their collective neck in the shape of one big zip tie." Cantor can't help wondering exactly what sort of saleability Eden must be sitting on to require the services of an agent, for that's what she's turned out most of all to be—and not just any old agent but (and this according to a recent article in the *Santa Barbara Bugler* he suddenly recalls having skimmed much too sloppily) one of Tinseltown's biggest. And as if things weren't bad enough, the silly phrase, *And that's just for starters* (second only to the putrid and pusaillanimous *Don't get me* start*ed*), menacingly pops into his head, unbidden, and proceeds to tickle him pink.

Post: "But why can't our merry band of testees, though maimed to the same sameness, still end up oddly dissimilar—each a maverick in his own right? As for *Invidicum: The Movie*, it's still pretty far down the road. For one thing, there's that made-for-HBO documentary to worry about: it's fast becoming a fiction film and not just any old fiction film but a ten-part miniseries. Though there's no doubt (in my mind at least) who should play Miss Jean" (never afraid to be corny-coy, he winks at the audience). In jogger's drag he looks appallingly fit, unapologetically youthful—or at least appallingly youth-obsessed. No mistaking *him* for one of the maimed. Ever the Cassandra (albeit a Cassandra too old to have to worry about defying the boss, drag or no drag, especially since he doesn't have the sort of bossy jurisdiction over her that would be recognized in a court of law), Netta—a Trojan Horse if ever there was one—maintains that their immediate concern should be, What will the FDA say when they find out the trial has been perpetrated on a group consisting of but a single type which may not even exist in the population at large: a mere artifact of their bungled recruitment process? And there's cold comfort in the fact that this could represent a first in the annals of Big Pharma. "And I could shoot myself when I think of that blessed spectrum of archetypes we had only to snap our fingers to access in the early days of triage! Think of Cook, for example, busy wooing Miss Moira when he should have been—should have been—" Which appears to be Walser's cue to ascend to the only podium in sight currently available for use (or is it a lectern?) and to make a gavel of his fist. The way, Herbert whimsicalizes, even if her mind is a million miles away (funny, she feels she's getting back at Netta, even if Post should be her bull's-eye)—the way Dante's Malacoda made a trumpet of his ass. And how convenient for the Master that she's always around to trumpet forth his ten-ton allusions—to make them plausible—to naturalize them. Though she does wonder why nobody has dared to inform Netta—or rather, *Miss* Netta (and what's Melanctha's own excuse by the way?)—that if there was any wooing being inflicted by Cook "in the [glorious] early days of triage", the bulk of it had been left on Miss *Jean*'s doorstep, not on Miss *Moira*'s. "A little peace and quiet, please. And, more importantly, a little patience. If we can manage to hold out it'll become clear soon enough that for all the superficial resemblances, Eden and Liepnits are as unlike unto each other as Hamlet and Hercules or Hyperion and his doggone satyr. But getting back to this van business, if, by turning a blind eye, he participated in a massacre of the innocents—or thinks he did—the discovery he made in the process and its incalculable benefit to mankind far outweigh his malefaction." "What did you discover?" Netta asks, poker-faced. "That—that—" Eden mutters from the peanut gallery—self-created since he's right smack in the broken heart of things. Walser looks all-encouraging but just when Eden starts to find his voice thanks, apparently, to this show of support, he interrupts, clearly unable to scale back on his eloquence to fit the occasion. According to Walser—and he welcomes any challengers—Eden has discovered we never escape our past and the more rehabilitated we get to be, i.e., the more we imagine we've mastered the past, the less prepared are we for its inevitable resuscitation/recrudescence—dare he say its invocation? through that very mastery. "What he means," says Stifter (thanks to the adroitness of whoever's been choreographing their routine, each hands over his variations to the audience on a silver platter of down-patness), "is that when all is said and done what rehab boils down to is what I call a *sillyjism:* unreadiness for recrudescence of the old ill— the very Thing which rehab is routinely deployed to exorcise. And don't tell me I talk like a book: at least none of the books *I* had the misfortune to skim or scan ever sounded so good." So now here's Stifter translating for Walser who translated for Eden . . . But it's unclear, at least to Cantor (notwithstanding all his training), what's really getting translated. It can't be what Eden has been saying because he hasn't said much of anything, nor what he's been thinking (for probably the same reason). The target of Walser's busybody flight of fancy could be—have been—anything: Eden himself—as he exists, once existed or will exist, or a collection of Edens (past, present and to come) or something other than any one of these living-and-breathing hymns to objecthood—an action, say (engaged in by Eden), whose being doesn't prevent the being of its negation. Or maybe he should shelve this whole business of trying to decipher signs standing to somebody for something so as to create in the mind of that somebody a more developed sign? When you get right down to it maybe translation's simply a matter of forcing thoughts that are good at only one thing—seeing past each other—to confess their connectedness by quarrelling. So, Cantor deduces (though he won't unwork the magic by holding forth), what lies at the core of translation, at least in these parts, is not the thing thought, i.e., translated, but what undreamt-of thing it may be connected with through subsequent translation and so on and so forth. And there's comfort in nursing such a delusion. Especially since it's no more delusional than anything else that's been put through the ringer of their credulity over the course of tonight—over the course of this thousand-and-one-nights-long tonight.

But Walser senses that the more Eden gets spray-painted as problemed, the more the assemblage is taken in by—no: taken *with*—him. Even MJ, whose unseeing stare can mean only one thing—that she's fallen in love with his marketability all over again and has just undergone another orgasm of proprietary right (and not a minute too soon): Hell, so she's been correct about Eden all along. By virtue of the fact that he's been disqualified for the role of poster boy (since his involvement through disinvolvement in the van massacre is unforgivable—the last straw, in fact, in a life that's been one long last straw—though the jury's still out on who exactly has been done in)—by virtue of that very fact, at long last he's just become one. Disqualification has done what only untimely death is believed capable of. But a poster boy for *what* precisely, since as somebody infinitely enhanceable through abjection he's a completely different Eden. Well aware of the fact, he whispers something to Walser, who nods attentively. "Eden wants to impart some wisdom—among other things, that to account for a particularly acute spasm of unreadiness for rehab, he plays the sort of game with himself we all played as kids, or should have. That is, he backtracks to the split-second of inner calm that had to be paid for by such a spasm. Isn't he beautiful?" The assemblage takes Walser's applause the way it's meant to be taken, namely, as a cue to applaud even more—and violently. But from their facial expressions—and facial expressions rarely lie (*oh, really, how so?*)—it's clear his public is no longer interested in the private Eden now that, as humanity's private property, he's en route to that superspreader event called stardom: suffering, however gorgeously labyrinthine, is incompatible with the duties of a poster boy. (Suffice it to say that if Eden's superstardom turned out to be The Rump's menstrual fluid, they'd drown themselves in it, no questions asked, and bless the menstruator's indifference to their dying gasps.) And how can knowing all about the kind of inner calm that has to be paid for by a spasm of unreadiness for rehab help pay the rent—help upgrade their socioeconomic status in a time of crisis even if 99 percent of them won't be found loitering on a Palo Alto breadline anytime soon? It's a redundancy, this bit about inner calm run amuck—worse, an affront to poster boys everywhere, and the gals—and guys—who love or loved them, generally to distraction, not to mention the single moms who scrimped and saved and took in laundry to get them into the right Ivy League finishing schools only to be tarred and feathered for their pains with base ingratitude from a dropout cum Central Park strangler. True, those moms did *choose* to be piss-poor, didn't they? and who knows better than carpetbagging hooligans like the Master's old standbys DaVos, Pruitt, Price and an ineradicable fly-by-night flash-in-the-pan by the name of Der Putz. Ah, to be a poster boy again, Post sighs, remembering his quarterbacking days at Harvard Finishing, when he and his fellow nicknames—i.e., "Ike" Paulson and "Mike" Gaetz and "Mike" Jordan and "Mike" Blackburn and "Mike" Gohmert and "Mike" (way too many Mikes) Di Santis and "Joe" Paulsen and "Josh" Blankfein and "Jock" Zinky and "Jake" Mozilo and "Mick" (or is it "Moe") Perdue and "Rick" Printz and "Jeff" Cheney and "Chuck" Johnson and "Ron" Grassley and "Dick" Perry and "Abe" Gingrich and "Rick" Mnuchkin and his kissin' cousin "Rick" bin Salman and "Sam" Thain—he of the $444,444 corner-office floorboard schmatte—and "Jeb" Spicer and "Mack" Pompeo and "Josh" Pence and "Nate" McConnell and "Zach" Kushner and "Pete" Crooze and "Blank" Blankfine, not to mention "Mike" Whitaker and "Nick" Haley and "Newt" Noem and "Steve" Sleeze—when he and his fellow monikers were members, for better or worse, of the unimprovably all-star lineup populating the wet dreams of every coed on campus (do coeds still exist?)—coeds with a baton-twirling knack for mistaking their even wetter merkins for a mind in motion. But why, he suddenly wonders (showing he's able—the surest sign of genius—to extract himself from a milieu too privileged for the common good only to look back on it with a jaundiced outsider's anatomizing eye)—why did their parents saddle them—to a man—with a given name so limp as to leave the man himself—or the world at large—or, more to the point, the parents themselves—little recourse but to contort and compress that name into a . . . thing—a fake-feisty folksy thing simulating the fake thrust of a fake erection—to inject it with a dose of maleness? So he's got to give The Rump *some* credit (no fake-feistiness for the likes of him).

Self-trained to listen in when any of the Master's chattels personal or, better yet, chattels vegetable gets a Master-engineered yen to think (to think deep, in this case, by way of thinking frivolous), Melanctha has managed to wangle more than just a whiff of Post's ruminations. And so her heart goes out to—not Post but the Master Himself who's been reduced once again (via the sponsorship of yet another guiltless bystander) to recycling the same old sort of recyclables—the same old sort of . . . silly name-pairs (chimeric mice bred from the fellation of surnames by nicknames and vice versa). They're pressed into service, these name games are, at any time of day or night when it just so happens that the Master is seeking relief from the autophagy indissociable from *thinking in the abstract* (a little like sleeping in the nude). He also hopes that when they have a chance they'll put to rest the rumor that he's a one-trick pony. And so what if these nicknames are pretty much, though none too prettily, equivalent to the *tunk-a-tunk*s and *hoo-goo-boo*s (not to mention the *rum-tum-tum*s and the *drum-rum-rum*s and the *pom-pom-pom*s and the *rummy-tummy-tum*s and the *hey-di-ho*s and the *ohoyaho*s) of that accident-and-indemnity bard from Hartford—so what, as long as they sort of seem to impregnate his airily abstract darlings with a brute reality they clearly—defiantly—lack—so what, as long as they serve as antidote—pharmakon—to the pharmakon of abstraction?[154] And maybe even as rough-and-tumble pharmakon to the pharmakon of effete epicene chichi aestheticism (to which even Hartford A-and-I bards aren't immune). For in the great NRA tradition, the only thing that can stop a bad pharmakon with a gun is an even badder pharmakon with a gun. But his clinging fear (she can feel it turning her bones to pure sweat) is that these name-pairs embody nothing more than silliness—nothing more than dead space—and are too unfunny for their own good. Even if underpinning the whole name-pair business is a moral stance-made-flesh through His loathing—even if He's secretly convinced that the end of sillinesss's tunnel will just have to be shrouded in the gauziest stuff of abstraction (for where there's so much silliness there must be substance)—abstraction made stronger—more virile—more gangsterful—under the auspices of silliness. For unlike those of Hartford's favorite son, the Master's *tunk-a-tunk*s have been imported into His Santa's workshop from the real world. Thing is, he still hasn't learned how to handle what isn't abstract—worse, what isn't an abstract insight—what doesn't hew to and toe its party line. With abstraction—with the insight bred in the bone of abstraction—you know where you are—you know where you stand—you know that you stand where God—i.e., the gods—i.e., the dark gods—stand because, like "Blank," you're doing their dirty work. As for the sillies, they only reinforce the fear that His life work is unbridled inclusiveness—pure randomness—a randomness unleashed and egged on by facility—the facility little blue-and-rose Pablo quickly grew to abhor—a randomness that refuses to be tamed by the constraints, whether budgetary or caloric, laid down by that pillar of

---

[154]See Randall Jarrell, "Reflections on Wallace Stevens," in *No Other Book: Selected Essays* (New York, HarperCollins, 1999), p. 118.

the salt of the earth called a storyline—a randomness that refuses to bend to the hegemony of things as they are, i.e., things as they were meant to be. No point, though, in tampering with His signature inconsolability—a literary stratagem if ever there was one—by daring to suggest that seeming randomness bears the brunt of its own constraints, if constraints are what He's after—that the weight of the world bears down on His name-pairs (to keep them from lawlessly proliferating) as much as it does on the most solemn formulations. What's the point in telling Him that out of the multitude of souls (of silliness) that stand create He's elected, when you get right down to it, but a precious few? Proving that even in a menstruum of unconstrained silliness, constraint may rear its ugly head and set limits. In short, it's been demonstrated yet again that *malgré lui* He's capable of selectiveness—of distillation—a regular Madvertising Man if ever there was one. Too bad that early on in His career, Melanctha thinks—during the formative years, rife with prophylactic pitfalls—somebody with clout didn't have the good sense to take the Master aside and assure Him man does not—cannot—live by abstraction alone. But enough about Post's less-than-illustrious football career, perceptive Jean decides. (She's been playing Sherlock to Post's Watson—deducing a chain of thought from a progression of facial flickers—a chore Melanctha in her infinite attunement to the ways of the Master has been spared.) Eden is metal more attractive and whatever his ultimate fate and whatever anybody else may think, she for one is more thrilled than she can say, though she intends to say it all the same, that he's arrived on the scene—and not a minute too soon: Fact is, the more Shrieker of the House Liepnits's leaping and bounding eloquence (passion-fruit of maturity) leaps and bounds, the more do those hijinks spur an equally fruity craving on Eden's part to outpace it outright at every turn, so indissolubly are they bound in an irreversible dynamic—competition rendering them ever more alike—monstrous doubles, enemy brothers, straight out of René Girard's lobster pot of metaphysical desire. Pitiful, Ethan thinks, foreseeing, no doubt, an identical fate for himself, once Jean has left him for— for—for Cook, of course. But a fate identical to whose? He hasn't quite made up his mind. Now that he (Liepnits, not Ethan) has been hooted off the stage of life,[155] Jean speculates out of left field that (the aspic of telepathy doesn't quite jell with somebody like Liepnits though she doesn't know anybody *like* Liepnits, except Liepnits himself) he's probably gone upstairs or is it down-? to see for himself whether Irena is indeed still alive and kicking—a mere formality, since he no doubt (Jean further speculates) plans to scuttle her, dead or alive (like all his other trophy wives), and secure tout de suite a running mate who'll be less of a campaign-hexer. And not to be outdone by a mere soubrette (squeakiest of coloraturas to her mightiest of mezzos), Shearer lets it be known that she, too, is thrilled—more than thrilled (and how does she let it be known? by beaming to beat the band, silly). For with Eden at the reins, the

---

[155]Image lifted from the preface to the elegy "Adonais," though, whatever He may think, the Master is no Shelley nor does Liepnits sound—much less look—anything like John Keats.

trial as a modification of the Substance of the Master under the Attribute of Extension and the story of the trial as a modification of His Substance under the Attribute of Thought will be as close to fusing as they'll ever get. At least in her lifetime. She understands—she's *come to understand*—that Eden is Every- and Superman, not to mention Anyman, all rolled into one. She understands because she loves him. A lust she didn't know she harbored has overripened (under the implacable-for-your-own-good California sun) into—love. As was the case so many times back in New York—with dancers, and even more sear- ingly with taxi drivers, that is, when she could afford them post-performance.

"I prefer to think," resumes Walser, "that Eden didn't make any attempt to save the innocents from their captors precisely because he needed to sustain his self-hate and what better fuel than ostensible cowardice (heroics for some- body as foolhardy as Eden would have been far too easy to manage)? I'll bet he always takes the line of greatest resistance for that's all he knows: his nature is too full of the milk of that self-hate to catch the nearest, non-punishing way. He does everything the hard way—and if there isn't a hard way to be had for the doing then he concocts one in order to berate himself mercilessly for not taking advantage of its roadside IEDs. For the Edens of this world, taking the line of least resistance—like using a stamp that's ready and waiting in the top drawer instead of making a trip to the post office (with its possible perk of transacting business with a *disgruntled* clerk)—results in disintegration, i.e., a fizzling of that one big fat erection known as the intermittent self." Walser goes on to explain—since this is the toughest part—that only the self-contouring ability to surmount interruption, limitation, cold fact, brute resistance—to wit, CSP's bottled-wasp Secondness—confirms that an operation has been successful enough to will the operator into temporary re-existence. Though he's not minimizing the need to keep insatiable detractors (and Eden'll have plenty of those now that he's famous), starting with his very own version of Ma and Pa Ozark, well supplied with chunks of hefty self-ablation. In short, by doing it the hard way Eden kills two birds with one stone: he atones for sins uncommitted and plugs an endlessly recurring ontological leak. So that for the Edens of this world every operation becomes a mere epiphenome- non—a mere parergon: byproduct and side effect of the thankless drudgery that's the closest he'll ever get to a true vocation—the sort of thankless drudg- ery which, when ably executed, always ends up feeling, oddly enough, like a job of debauchery well done. "So what's he famous for if there's no vocation in the works?" inquires some smart-ass who'd sooner be caught dead than acknowledge that he's nothing more than the worst kind of extra—the kind that wouldn't be caught dead holding his head high. Again Eden whispers something—but this time it's in *Stifter's* ear! (in response to which sarcastic smart-ass mutters, "so! at last we're getting somewhere"). For better or worse, he seems to trust the guy, Borkman notes with wonder—and a little sting of disappointment that Eden hasn't chosen him—John Gabriel Borkman!—as father figure. "My client wishes to make known—" But he's interrupted—some might say just in the nick of time—by Shearer, who cries out, "Stop talking all this rot about 'the Edens of this world'. Eden—my Eden—is a special case, if ever there was one. A very special case."

"Everybody's a special case, my dear—until proven otherwise" (so Netta, in highest dudgeon, as befits a doyenne forever in search of a claque). Shearer forgives the snub since Netta genuflects *my dear*—with a dash of exasperation—just like Mr. B used to do. Cantor feels particularly sympathetic toward—protective of—Eden (all of a sudden he has an image of Glorietta Bay under an old gibbous moon)—feels, in fact, that he's just about to get to know him for the first time—that their destinies are converging, as they failed to do (despite so many opportunities) in ancient Coronado. Though he's had the same feelings many times thereafter—and with, he must admit, *far greater conviction than now*. Or is this just wordflow—an Uber driver that hasn't even been apped—taking him where he doesn't particularly want to be taken because he hasn't earned the ride? Only now his fellow-feeling is laced with the ketamine of Envy—hence a loving Envy—of Eden's regal aloneness. His troubles—unlike those of arbitration-hatin' debt collectors, gun runners, warrantless wiretappers, the NFL, BP-caliber oil spillers, health insurers, the left-handed—just aren't made for the likes of lobbyists—just can't be converted into catnip for their unholy delectation. No Beltway insiders feel enjoined to practice advocacy for the likes of Eden—since, as crazy Ezra's Mr. Nixon would say, "There's nothing in it." For, like Lou Gehrig, he's the poster boy-in-chief for a disease he doesn't harbor and for which there's no name, no cure, no symptoms and no telltale signs. Homosexuality, on the other hand, does have its cures—and Cantor isn't referring to the Talking Cure so popular in the sixties or the one currently being offered by Malibu's Tennessee Wittgenstein Clinic and its Key West subsidiary, which consists in the hurling by sufferers of an imprecation or two against the inflicting Godhead with an aggressiveness so unrelenting as to trigger the release of enough testosterone, LH and FSH to effect their transformation into archaistic He-Men—archaic torsos of Apollo—guaranteed to make every Rilke out there in Briggeland change his life— forever. No, he's talking (and, hopefully, nobody's listening in) about the cure—all right, a cure of sorts—achieved by some of his luckiest pals compliments of their idiopathic dread of the stingray of normal human touch, whether perpetrated by a member of the same sex, the opposite sex or the in-transit community or even a billy goat—more than enough dread to go around—more than enough to allow love of men to get lost in the shuffle of untouchabilities. No need, then, for them to come out—fighting. But in Eden's case there's nothing to come out to or from—except the van and its unspeakables, and he's already been there, done that. Memory extinction—extinction of what he didn't perpetrate—may be just the ticket for getting him back on track. And if the process needs to be algorithmized—hey, Cantor will be more-than-willing to help out. And if Cantor's having this thought then somebody else must be having it—must have had it ice ages ago.

Stifter has found another podium and he and his twin are already competing for the spotlight, as is often the case with colleagues whose rare-bird talents have a bad habit of running neck and neck to the point of indistinguishability. So, I ask you, how can Cantor not be reminded of that point in one of the presidential debates between those other twins, John Kerry and Baby Bush, some decades back (how time has forgotten to fly!) where the moderator—Tom Brokaw, wasn't it?—had some handler's bright idea of asking both how, being married to *strong women,* they reacted on those occasions when the gals opened their adviserly big mouths? Thereby giving the Decider—for it was only the Decider who counted—an opportunity to pass himself off as just another endearingly henpecked regular guy whose catastrophically bad decisions could therefore not be all that bad—could in fact be all that *good,* based, as they were now—then—revealed to be, on the infallible virtue of wifely intuition. And I—he—asks you, wasn't it somehow fitting that the thousands of body bags arriving in unphotographable stealth at Dover Air Force Base from Falluja should have cast no shadow over the Ode to the Joys of Outsourcing unleashed by the Decider at a billionaires-only seminar the very next night on (where the hell else?) Grand Cayman? But Cantor, waking from uneasy but ultimately uninteresting dreams—uninteresting at least when compared with the uneasy specimens of Gregor Samsa—has to give Stif and Wals credit: For all their jockeying for position, they never take their eye off the ball: Every time Eden makes for the elevator bank (he's on his seventh try) they join forces to restrain him—just as Kerry and Bush aka R&G (Regular and Guy) would have done given half a chance. As he explains diligently to anybody who'll listen and (as wayward wordflow rearing its ugly head would have it) *even more diligently to anybody who won't,* he needs to make his way downstairs within the next few minutes—where once beautiful, once vibrant Manning is atrophying away—to prevent the cyanide he's perfused into her IV pouch from doing its dirty work. Putting her arm around him, Johnstone shepherds Eden (*Why hasn't she ever touched me like that?* Cantor pretends to wonder) out of the limelight. Once he's no longer gesticulating wildly, she explains that rather than contend with the massacre of his own innocence, he's convinced himself he's Manning's dispatcher—that's right, Irena Manning: Invidicum's Mrs. Rochester, Amygdala's very own Cat Woman—an off-label Simone Simon for the Twenty-first Century—right up there with baby Bush's Jobs for the Twenty-first Century. He must know as well as she that he's never been anywhere near the room in which they're keeping her captive per Liepnits's strict instructions—too strict, though, to be quite kosher. Thing is, the need to be punished for his self-hate is too urgent not to render so pungent a conviction plausible (Cantor is suddenly assaulted by an image of—of all things—Balboa Park in its murderous heyday). "But don't think he hasn't of course tried all the usual-suspect cutting-edge pharmakons." Taking in the whole crowd, she hisses, "Yes, *pharmakon.* Write it down. Look it up. Choke on the vomit of all its connotations. See if I care." "Like what?" Netta shouts, bringing Mary back to earth, but not unkindly. "Like refusing," she explains, "to heed the call to go on being deluded to the best of his ability by, for example, searching his pockets or his dingy little garret up at the bunker for the deadly goods of self-incrimination in order to be able to breathe a well-deserved sigh of relief upon their delivery." To say that the refusing—as a stab at instant rehab, as a sop to the Cerberus of rationality—has missed its target is the biggest understatement they'll ever rub elbows with, Mary Johnstone—or whatever her name is—thinks loud and clear. It's this love affair with turning over a new leaf in the book of the self—or rather, with burning the book of the self so as to arise new and improved from its ashes—that's irrational. True rationality would entail paying yeoman's heed to irrationality's call of the wild—i.e., prolonging the delusional argument to the point where it proves completely indefensible without the incorporation of nothing less than his innocence as the bedrock of its logic.

Twitching with impatience at overly theoretical Johnstone's contempt for concreteness, Post reminds them of the case of that Payne Whitney guy (the buttered toast of the tabloids some months back) who, having rejected food on the grounds that he was no longer alive (gassed for reinventing Foucault's pendulum), was dying of starvation. The patient's caretakers were all at wit's end until one of them had the bright idea of entering his cell decked out in full corpse regalia and polishing off a Porterhouse *au poivre*. To atone for his shameful ignorance regarding the ways of the self-respecting dead, the ravenous patient wasted no time polishing off the other steak (the corpse had brought two just in case). They, similarly, needed to force their grubby little way into the non-being of Eden's delusion and cancel it out by proving, effortlessly, that by complying with its own laws it fell into contradiction with itself. But what prop can serve as *their* Porterhouse—what can serve to prove that Eden's criminality, though of course irrefutable, is nonetheless at odds with—even dishonors—every other self-respecting malefactor's in at least the context of that Porterhouse and no doubt in a host of others? And assuming the prop can be dug up, will Eden allow himself to participate in a piece of street theater constructed around it—a piece like that perpetrated on Payne Whitney's finest in conformity with the specifications of some other Foucault (his first name conveniently escapes the speaker)? And if he does elect to participate how can they be sure it's without feeling that the piece is out to challenge, contradict, contest, tar and feather the image of himself as cyanide specialist but that on the contrary . . .? On the contrary, will it be possible to make him feel that up until the moment its self-contradiction exploded in his face the theatrics couldn't have been more in harmony with an image so irrefutable? *Where are we going to get a marbleized slab of Porterhouse at this time of night, even in California?* ponders Borkman, Jr., whose grasp of the real is responsible in no small measure for his meteoric rise. "It must be 4 a.m.," says somebody who's obviously thinking what Borkman, Jr.'s been thinking. *The McChateau at 4 a.m.:* Cantor gargles the phrase but it doesn't wash. That's because, he realizes, the phrase should be *The Palace at 4 a.m.*—and the referent is a sturdy-fragile thing of wood, glass, wire and string.

CHAPTER FIFTY-FIVE

Stumped, and having had her fill of unanswerables—e.g., why hasn't she been able to grieve like a mother? why didn't she have the blood and guts to set fire to Building 18? why weren't Dick Rove and Karl Cheney captured by the Tamil Tigers or Los Zetas or both and, in exchange for a few more hours of life, forced to make passionate love to each other! all over the Internet and not just in its *blackest* holes (this is *her* self-hate talking)—so rudely stumped, Herbert (anyway? consequently?) seeks refuge out on the terrace and (you want to know something?) she's proud of her decision. Otherwise she'll miss the breaking 4 a.m. news—the breaking news she's been waiting for all her life without knowing it—or why:

1. Although a eucalyptus in the middle of PamuCapa Street—or is it CapaPamu?—thrashes wildly past—tries to get way ahead of—its own foliage (that is, its own essence) and leave it far behind, the tumult produces no casualties, i.e., no leaf falls.

2. In compensation, on the surface of a big puddle strung between two cars (but if it has rained, why is the air so sticky?), another leaf (mimosa this time) strives to be considerably more animated than the sparrow contesting its freehold (and succeeding, mightily).

3. Best of all, a hiccoughing Mack truck (or is it a moving van?—*no!* there's been enough talk about vans to last us a—several—lifetimes) which, as it runs the gauntlet of a gang of tree trunks, is, *as we speak*, secreting for safekeeping, before it pulls away forever, the arcade of their intertwined boughs—or, if you prefer (even if I don't), *interlaced*—under the skin of its chalk-white roof, until such time as a suitable, reasonably priced burial ground can be secured.

4. A Port Oxford Cedar (*Chamaecyparis lawsoniana*)—which in fact may be a mere Moreton Bay Fig Tree (*Ficus macrophylla*)—is making overt overtures—they couldn't be more overt—to an unreceptive streetlamp—an unreceptive streetwalking streetlamp without a Latin name—doing its damnedest to be unreceptive because it knows, given the vastness of the distance dividing them (in places like Santa Barbara, inches are measurable only in miles), they can fuse—exchange body fluids—exchange essences—each drink a case of the other[156]—only as shades, cast on the chunk of rusticated wall to their left, and only when the sun gets around to deciding the time is right for them to become shades and not just any old shades but shades straight out of *Purgatorio* XXI—shades suckled at the breasts of Virgil—and Dolly Russell Ekberg—shades whose burning lust makes each forget that the other's a shade as well, and not a solid thing. But all of a sudden the sun is masked by a cloud or a supernova and the shades are gone or rather everything is shadow and nothing but—shadow has swept the pavement clean. So the word "shade" has lost its meaning. The streetlamp and the tree are of course still here—there—but they've closed up shop. They've fled—as good as fled—gone home for dinner

---

[156]The phrase/image has been (discreetly) shoplifted from a Joni Mitchell ballad.

or to the nearest bowling alley—even if they're still here because it was in their shadows that their essence lay. The rest is . . . dross.

But before she's made even a quarter of her way to the door—so 1-2-3-4 has turned out to be nothing less than a game of Four (not Six) Still Lives in Search of a Perceiver—other matters (of the picayune human sort) obtrude themselves on Melanctha's attention (she can hear the trees protesting: *You pay us a visit—you lend us intentions we would never dream of harboring—for the sole purpose of beefing up your bona fides*) and, while she in fact rates *things* more highly than *humans* (even if it's always with the expectation of a big return on her vocational investment) or is presumed to do so by her mud-slinging CW 101 rivals, attend to them she must. So, Cantor—yes, Cantor (no slouch when it comes to smelling the ghost of a chance to do good and live to operatically regret it)—steps into the breach and prepares to seek holy communion with the still lives she's left behind—or rather, in front of her—still lives still to be perceived, panting to be put into perceivership—to be lulled to sleep knowing that some stooge is risking ecstasies for the privilege of putting himself in their shoes. Too bad that, he thinks, Melanctha didn't catch up with and claim her point of view. Too bad she doesn't realize just how precious a POV can be—a commodity as precious as Hoffmann's reflection and Schlémil's shadow. Cantor intends to make quick work of still lives 1 through 4 which will leave him plenty of time for what's left of the landscaping. So here he is taking his forest walk after all, even if it will involve a lot of standing still. But wait! there's a bonus! Thinking the phrase *forest walk* it's as if somebody else's rapture (the Master's? Herbert's?) at metamorphosing into a ductile amalgam of the temperaments of a racked minister, a scarlet woman and a naughty little pearl has been transfused into his dwindling spirit.

But it's not as easy to disengage himself from the clutches of the Purgatorio tree as he's been led to believe (see report on still life 4 above). But by whom? Good that he doesn't know the real name of the tree (or can't remember)—so close he can reach out and touch it even if it's far away. Knowing would only destroy the mysterious tension subsisting between them. Not to mention what it would do to his credibility as a naïf who's just set foot on the planet through no fault of his own: impersonation of one never fails to calm. And especially after seeing Eden in the straitjacket he's stitched together from whole cloth, Cantor needs calming. Purgatorio's trunk—his relation to the trunk—arms him against hatred of self and against (unfortunately) hatred of others. For the trunk—not the tree but the trunk (there's a world of difference between 'em)—is the only thing that has had the guts to say:

Life didn't work out the way you wanted?—so, what are you waiting for? now's the time to just sit back and enjoy it. Rest assured that if life hasn't worked out the way it was supposed to—then you've managed to outsmart yourself and lead what's infinitely better than the life you were supposed to lead—the life it was promised you'd lead—namely, what by common consensus is known as a true life—a real life—no, not a mere good life but a real life. So life hasn't passed you by after all—life has been paying attention every step of the way, particularly

to the hollowness of your own disavowals, and at no small cost to itself
decided to put its foot down—for to life (though you may not think so)
your own well-being is no laughing matter.

After such a pep talk how can he not take the trunk not just for his oyster but for his very own sceptred truncheon—his letter to the world—the Archimedean wedge with which he'll move it first chance he gets. Nobody—not even Berry Sundae, vengeful for having been insufficiently mourned though vengefulness was not in his nature and never will be—can sever him from the trunk—nor from the world now that the trunk has interceded on his behalf—sponsored him even if it's only as a rank probationer—the very world whose beauty it is Melanctha's duty to commemorate through suffering—suffering over the failure to suffer (a tired paradox if ever there was one yet an endearing and enduring one)—suffering over the fact that she was a bad mother and a bad wife and is currently giving her all to the role of bad caretaker—of One whom she's dumped unforgivably in that worst of all possible assisted living facilities—her own mind. But isn't this a morsel of two of what he thought he heard her muttering in the van—warmed over by eavesdropping, that master chef?

Cantor never imagined the setting sun could comport itself so disrespectfully in public—never imagined it could eschew reverence for something as primordial as the Cantor-trunk duet, in favor of something so puerile as what it's doing right now, which is burning hole after hole after hole in every cloud after cloud after cloud veering seaward. Even if it's for a good cause—since it's easy to see that these porpoises are structured like a long-latent language (which can't have escaped the gimlet mind's eye of so professional an observer as the sun even if he's too often blinded by his own lucidity) and therefore want, understandably, their Flesh to be made Word at last and ASAP. So it's the job of the sun (as self-appointed salvator mundi) to compel them, as a first step, to cry out in pain and take it from there.

But there simply isn't enough time for him to make like a salvator and turn the clouds' problems into his own. For one thing, down below it's strictly Central Park in the Dark—a park worthy of Ives's worst nightmares even if old Charley (another tunk-a-tunk Connecticut guy) wasn't prone to exploit the genre—i.e., streetlamps congregate where least needed whereas along those stretches where all is exposed there're—you guessed it—none to be had for blood or money. Pity the toothy ponytailed jogger full of robust conviction the world is her oyster (*that word again! and for the second time in two pages! what surer sign of the Master's depletion—no, depletion* hunger!) only to discover . . . well, whatever it is one discovers when a psychopath steps out of the hedges to claim his dreary due. It comes to Cantor as if in a vision that the streetlamp directly below—though miles away—the streetlamp that's been linked erotically to the Purgatorio in the illiberal media—is the very one he passes every morning en route to his dose. It looks ravaged now, at least from way up here—and with no shadow (compliments of the rising sun) in tow—no poor relation to which it can give the all too richly deserved cold shoulder. It isn't so contemptuous—so arrogant—anymore—as it is most mornings when it gives *him* the cold shoulder as well. But . . . has the streetlamp ever been contemptuous? that is the question—if anything, it was always on the best of terms with its shadow—dragged it, while standing in place, unbegrudgingly—if anything, it was the streetlamp itself that was treated as the poor relation and it played its part gladly, willingly, gluttonously—anything to please its insatiable shrew. As a matter of fact, it was always the least arrogant of streetlamps. No, it's language that's the culprit—language in its triviality— its banality—its arrogance—that sees arrogance everywhere. Yes, Language— always on the qui vive for stark contrasts between then and now—between now and times to come—always waiting around—*lurking*—for somebody or some thing *to get its comeuppance*—forever on the sanguinary lookout for the pride that goeth before a fall. Vindictive—the exact opposite of Berry Sundae—that's what Language is. Leaving corpses—the more the merrier—in Its wake wherever it goes. One big fat cruel proverb—that's what Language and its one-eyed stepfather Life are all about. Wordflow-belching Language is trying to force him to root out a moral where none will ever exist. Well, it won't work—not this time. None of the denizens of this urban deep—not just the streetlamp but the whirling dervishes of trash and the psychotics gnashing their inner thighs together—would ever be caught dead getting plastered— getting taken down a peg or two—by a moral (*morals:* another name for the accrued meanspiritedness of the ages). But it's getting pretty chilly out here on the terrace (Terraces 1–3 of Purgatory all rolled into one). Time for Cantor to go back in and eavesdrop. But not before he's been allowed to feel that, in spelling Herbert, he's outdone himself—far beyond the call of duty. Thing is, will he be able to smuggle his achievement past Johnstone (an achievement that clearly hasn't been engineered by the Master and is completly his own—why, the Central Park aria is alone worth the price of admission) and get Pritchard to evaluate it and then maybe, just maybe, reconsider making him, Cantor, his successor in residence?

Herbert's first order of business is Borkman, who looks uncharacteristically distraught (has the bracelet managed to burst its seams? after all, it's just plain regulation costume jewelry not Tiffany's standard issue), or rather the first order of business is what she interprets *with every fiber of her being* (wordflow working overtime?) as Borkman's apparent eagerness to know why, with her gifts, she hasn't nor will she ever reach the terrace. She drops preparatorily into a chair—a chair that wasn't there a second ago (she could swear to it in a court of law): it must have been brought into being through the sheer force of her fatigue. However, what he's really intent on, as it turns out, while pretending to be all ears, is getting a glimpse, in the convex mirror to the right of Stifter, of his rakishly angled straw hat and, if at all possible, his pointy-toed right shoe as well. Although (if there's any justice left in the world and from where I'm squatting, the odds are awful) where he's going there'll be no need of either. But before she can draw from a study of his reflection all there is to know about the perils of self-love at its direst, i.e., its purest (so as to avoid caving in when, at long last, her greatness is rampantly assailed by homage), the image has degenerated, so to speak, into its first derivative and become that of Borkman not just looking but scrutinizing the looking to determine whether all this currying self-love is getting in the way of his seeing, really seeing. And though she has no doubt that a second derivative—i.e., the image of Borkman looking at his looking at his image to determine whether it's even more of an obstruction than the first—is very much in the works and will be every bit as fertile in cautionary tales if not more so, something tells Herbert to rise and move away. Turning back to reassure herself that Borkman's not in the least offended, she suddenly gets a glimpse not simply of Shearer (a bit old for the impulsive *La Valse* ponytail she sports so tentatively, prompted minutes ago by impalement on a ray of hope—but hope for—or against—what, exactly?)—but of Shearer at what is clearly her most devious (though many would attest she hasn't a devious bone in her body). And this new development puts Borkman's *stade du miroir* antics unceremoniously in the shade.

But not before Borkman has waylaid her with a word or two. She's impatient for the waylaying to fizzle so she can get down to the business of investigating Shearer's crime against nature—her nature. But he's obviously resolved not to let it fizzle and this being the case, Melanctha is unable to decide whether his intention has been to assure her the act of self-love was thoroughly justified by the circumstances (after all, he won't have much time for such games in maximum security) or to prove there was no such act at all, notwithstanding the justifications galore. At first she panics, then panics at the panic, only to repent once the panic reminds her—no, *serves to remind* her (a world of difference)—undecidability is good, that it's the spice—the stuff—the very staff—of life. Or is it the inability to decide whether something can be undecidable that's supposed to come out smelling like the very spice of life? (By the way, what's that she hears down below or is it up above or across the hall: poor de-Tiffanied Manning moaning under the knife?) In any event, what seems to be at issue here is somebody's need to prove you can't keep a bad man down, i.e., that there's no ankle monitoring bracelet heavy enough to induce despair in one who deprecates it above all other afflictions. "Is it too late, then, to follow Shelley's advice?" his (red-hot) gaze cries out—though still glazed over with the self-love fomented by the mirror's shuttle between surface and depth. "Too late for what?" hers (white-hot) responds though she knows very well it's never too late—never too late, that is, to don the mask of anarchy and, so bedizened, to rise like lions after slumber—shake your chains to Earth like dew that in sleep had fallen on you. In a word, never too late to oppose his invanquishable number to their few. *Should I sign my death warrant by revealing,* his gaze goes on to wonder, *that long after his desovietization, my ex-Communist father cited these heartstopping lines every heartbreaking chance (the context was irrelevant) he got?*

Somebody Melanctha doesn't recognize at first puts his flabby left arm around Borkman (the other, mind you, looks quite muscular). The baker? Mr. John Smith of unvexable eons gone by? breakthrough interspecies chimaera John Smith Baker, the toast of CNN? "He's too shy and modest for his own good," waxes . . . waxes . . . why it's John Smith, hands down! the glint in his gimlet eye expecting Herbert to concur (sorry, she has better things to do). What he's done—his old age's last sin of commission—has been, as it turns out and while nobody was looking, to establish a commodities market for

Invidicum: Credit default swaps indexed to agreements to deliver or accept Invidicum (better yet, reneges on those agreements) on a specified future date, can be traded like cash—Melanctha knows the drill. (Parentheses are suppressive, chatty, coy—feminine! while em dashes are to-the-point—masculine! Herbert realizes in a flash.) But in the Borkman version, the goings-on are much more ethereal (even if he's the last guy anybody might think of as etherealizable) since it's all about credit default swaps indexed to the greater or lesser success of the Consortium's bids for web ad space on the right web pages—*impressions*—space sold at the very millisecond the most likely customers—most likely to be guillotined by their own mice—i.e., the poor slobs online auctioneers deem to be so through no fault of their own—are visiting those pages so the pharmakon of pharmakons can be pitched well before they click on—click onward—ever onward. A process—Project—known as Crossing the Rubicon . . . (*Much more ethereal*, Herbert ponders. *You mean sort of like Borkman's looking at his looking at his looking at his* Self-portrait in a Convex Mirror—*the kind of portrait that would do Parmigianino peacock-proud? that kind of . . . ethereal?*) "So what if consumers are treated like the cattle they are?—this is just the extension of business practices stretching back centuries?" So Smith, never much—Herbert more than suspects—on ethics. And everything orchestrated by algorithm-crazy electronic trading platforms in hyperreal time, the very thing anti-privatist Jr. and his gang are getting themselves famous for slapping together. So it's a father-son operation, which means that unlike her, Borkman hasn't been all that bad a parent. He cringes a bit, not in courteous self-effacement but from regret (even if regret's purported to be bad for the prostate): Too bad the recognition is coming so late for it's not always the case that late is better than never. But if Rumpy Borkman and his very own little Kushner are right, then Invidicum is bound to become—is already becoming—a commodity just as essential as maize, soya, rice, wheat and water. There's even talk of a merger—or a swapping of assets—with Sanofi or, better yet, Boehinger Ingelheim or, best yet, Brunhilde Pomsel Ltd. But as every silver lining has its cloud (otherwise it wouldn't be a lining, silver or otherwise), Sanofi is getting cold feet—or pretending to get them as a means of securing a better deal. Those feet invoke nothing less than the notion (is *concept* too grandiose?) of material adverse effect—the claim that the Consortium's well of saints in sheep's clothing has been poisoned by Borkman's doings—and not even all the perfumes of Arabia issuing from the bowels of a Rump pardon can sweeten this little scumbuggery. Smith sighs deeply, hence unconvincingly. For as it turns out, he has better news up his sleeve which, by being made savvily to follow hot on the heels of this allusion to a fast-fading cloud, may be expected to pack even more of a mortal wallop.

Problem is, this bit about indexing—the indexing of being to non-being —things to non-things—sounds drably overfamiliar. Herbert is tired of the concept (so what if its asteroidal rise seems to be all the rage?)—worse, of its operationalizers (if there is such a word)—worst, of its applications, with or without operationalizers.

"And thanks to this soya-soaked autumnal achievement, the bracelet is coming off 'cause, guess what? The Rump intends to grant his disciple a pardon even if, strictly speaking, Borkman hasn't even been apprehended, much less arraigned, indicted or convicted. The bracelet's totemic function, then, has been purely—exquisitely—apotropaic." Smith's collar is clearly—or pretends to be clearly—uncomfortable with the polysyllables. "And the ploy has worked—not just wonders but miracles—precisely the way his second-favorite NYAC squash buddy, Evans-Pritchard, said it would. For here he is, soon to be a free man and not a minute too soon, at least for everybody else's taste. "John Gabriel," proclaims Smith, "now you'll be able to fulfill your real lifelong ambition." Borkman looks appropriately blank. *Smith* (*giving him an elbow kick in the ribs*): "Which is to spend more time with your kids—and your grandkids—or am I wrong?" Herbert tries in vain to tune out since there exist few neologisms/euphemisms that she loathes more than (fake-hip, rejuvenating) *grandkids* except, maybe, for *reach out to* (*smarmyese* for "contact"). What she can't tune out, however, is the latest dispatch from Reuters, as breathlessly bullhorned by one of the unsung cocktail waitresses (a fetching little number with an impudent wiggle and a strategically placed beauty mark), who's said by those in the know to moonlight belowstairs, with brash breezy incompetence, as a nurse. It seems that Margo, whose conspirative thinking has bested her at last—done her in (at least for the time being)—is now Irena's roommate. Which makes Liepnits and Pritchard—the satyr and the sybil—bedfellows as well, the machete of a common doom having made mincemeat of their dissimilarities. Does it behoove her to pay the victims a visit? order chocolates online? extend her condolences to the grieving spouses? Still, it's not as if she knows them all that well . . .

It's time to focus on pleasanter things—clearly, Smith has nothing more to teach her about the grandkids she'll never have and won't ever miss—no, not for a minute, truth be told, for her grandkids are fleshless. Shearer's now-legendary deviousness will do for starters. For turning back, like Lot [*sic*], to take a Parthian potshot at Borkman, Melanctha observed that Moira had just seen fit to put her scarf on the now vacant seat (the garment including the gesture that went with it was clearly meant to evoke the Siren's tail in *Prodigal Son* before which Moira can never stop prostrating herself)—had obviously already staked it out long before departure was even a glint in the sitter's eye. Which means that as long as Herbert had the audacity to just sit there—to keep on sitting there—she was perceived—was there for the taking—as a mere obstacle—encumbrance—contingency—which would ultimately burn itself out—a slave indistinguishable from the spreading of her own buttocks. On the auction block she was, like too many of her forbears. That it—after all she and the hoofer have been through—should come to this! Still, there's a thrill like no other whenever she forces herself to rise to the challenge of correcting her vision—until this minute a non-vision—of monumentally irksome things past. A thrill in being compelled to effect the retrospective transformation of dead space—of the type achieved over and over and over again in, say, the first movement of *Serenade* (Melanctha's become quite an authority on the doings of Moira's master). The transformation of a—her—mere sitting—a brute sitting—into a sitting complicatedly begrudged by, because of its self-willed obliviousness to, the sitter waiting in the wings—a sitting permeated through and through with the bile of that begrudgement—the bile of the begrudgement's *thought*—yet forever pushing back, with true Peircean Secondness, against spiritualization—contamination—by that thought. The transformation of a soulless sitting into one which could—can—no longer call that soullessness its own. A transformation, by the way, that could never have been perpetrated without Shearer's generous self-distillation into a single gesture—gesture as sign, signal, symptom, thought—the *scarf* gesture. A gesture thought but—with a little luck—unaware of its thinking—which is the purest kind of thought. So what it all adds up to (though she hates to admit it) is nothing less than what an aficionado worth his salt would hasten to typecast as the best of Balanchine with a dash or two of Tudor—having Herbert's best interests—those being nothing of course but writerly interests—at heart. At first she's ashamed, to be ruminating over something so trivial—so microtonal—as a gesture—when a merger's currently at stake and not just any old merger but one beset with world-class problems—and not just any old problems but problems like possible material adverse effect and maybe even the threat, while we're at it, of liquidation preference, which provides— But let Smith—or better yet, some SiVa venture capitalist—fill you in about what exactly it provides when he has a minute or two—that is, if *you*'ve also got a minute or two to be in the market for a good belly laugh—and if you behave yourselves, Bellowing (not Whispering) Smith may even take it into his head to regale you with anecdotes (world-class, of course just as NYC is the classiest of world-class tax havens with Old Jersey running a close second) about contingent value rights. Then she begins to rebel. So she goes out on the terrace to do justice to rebellion—to rebel better. Thought's—gesture's—transformation of matter into intention is every bit as important as a world-class threat. But quickly enough, she recedes (*recoils* is too strong a word) from the view, however privileged: State Street, isn't it? But you mustn't think it's because she's exhausted the street's potential as a target—you mustn't think *that* (it will kill her if you do)—it's just that she *feels* (wretched word: getting unaddicted is easier said than done) a *sudden* (also wretched: its recruitment a ploy calculated to generate unearned readerly surprise, even shock)—it's just that she's hungry for the adjoining sidestreet (unforgettable name forgotten)—no matter what its—State Street's—potential. Or maybe she's receding at the very moment that its potential is or has started to become greatest—is at its climacteric—or is this just a twist of syntax: the Master rider rattling her reins yet again of course for her own good—the good of literature? State Street is like—no, *is*—a book with a difficult thrust. Beginning to understand, she abruptly closes it in order to celebrate how far she's come—in order to make a hoardable object of her *connection* to the book—an authentic connection at long last. As she hopes others will do with hers—her books—her objects—all the objects to come—to come, but not, Herbert hopes, like Sandburg's fog, i.e., on little cat's feet. To make an object of what isn't, in the normal sense—well, that takes guts—it's a way of standing up to the Master—to the world. Or so she needs to believe, even if it's immediately followed by regret at having renounced the main drag for a mere sidestreet. For this sidestreet—which resembles not a little a cross between Gotham's Dutch Street and Ryders Alley at pearly dusk—has that bad habit, she discovers, contracted by or congenital to all sidestreets. Come to think of it, in this regard they're like Eden's credulity in the face of his demons (remember all that hullaballoo about killing little girls in Balboa Park?). I.e., too quick to blaze up. Even if today's sun is inchoate—even if the sun itself has very little faith in its own survival—here's a row of sidestreet windows fomenting a mini-blaze from the thinnest of cloud-smeared bursts. Can it be that the role of any sidestreet is to minister to the sun's non-will to live or will to not live, whichever's worse . . .? Like those feeding into Cherokee Place, it is probable—more than probable—that said sidestreet may be depended on (no matter what shadows loom) to compel its windowed walls to yield an inflamed sidestreet glow—to wring the utmost from the sun rising or setting—may be depended on to have enough faith for the two of them. But why think of Eden's surefire credulity *now*? Why this leaf, on the terrace, navigating the skiff of itself across the lake of a puddle *now*? Clearly the Master's disease (but why blame Him at every twist and turn?) among too many others (He's a walking formulary)—and now hers—is an inability to hierarchize (granted, falsely) data: meta-, micro- and macro. All is important, all of equal interest to His undiscriminating voracity—at least for now. But *now* is not the time to flout the bidding rights of the Main Event, what with everything soon coming surely to a head. He's made her do it—by virtue of being possessed by Him she's perpetrated secession from the Event—the Moment of Truth that lasts a lifetime—never to return. At least in its original form. At the same time she pities His bondage. For He must have just received a new shit-, or rather, shipload of packets—just as the superscum of the earth, like Bashar al-Assad and Vlad the Putain, will soon be receiving their premier supply of homicidogenic Invidicum—which means the Main Event must yield—must assimilate those packets even if they belong nowhere—not even where they came from—even if It can't adapt to them—even if It obliterates itself in the process of non-adaptation and can't pick up the pieces. But doesn't managing to reach a point where, she hears Him decreeing, everything's relevant as long as it's ir- . . . well, doesn't that have "a consecration of its own" worthy of Hester Prynne at her most exalted—doesn't that come across as much more blessed than the old Grand Inquisitorial "everything is permitted"? Maybe. But for the life of her she'll never know—right, she'll *never* know—why He—a red-blooded American male—is so afraid of the Event which after all is supposed to be his[157] bread and butter. And just let Him try one more time to pull the wool of that *More interesting than storytelling is the story behind the ineptitude that refuses to tell a story* spiel over her eyes. Or maybe he's like—no, *is*—one of Bateson's debate-crazy Iat-

---

[157] Now's as bad a time as any to acknowledge the inexcusably erratic shifting, in references to the Master, (*a*) between "His" and "his," (*b*) between "Him" and "him," and (*c*) between "He" and "he." Giving it her best White House press secretary spin, Melanctha has routinely played down the shifts as little more than His/his take on an "old family recipe"-style prophylactic, in this case against non-post-traumatic swelled head syndrome.

mul head-hunters whose right to the totemic name that happens to be up for grabs—in this case, the name of Master—can be affirmed only through mastery of the esoteric myth—in this case, the myth of Invidicum—to which *Master* refers.[158] But there's a catch: if the myth is exposed in its entirety then the right is forfeited. So each grabber has no choice but to nibble, oratorically speaking, at the details—the Tasmanian devil in the details—transforming it thereby from a continuous story line into a series of discrete packet points. But she must give credit where credit's due—it's hard to be a Man of the Packet—harder even than being van der Weyden's Man of the Arrow.

As she re-enters, two men, belatedly stark naked and dead-drunk, stagger past. The perfect touch: so, the Master, defying His bossy fans, has done it again—risen from the half-dead. Coughing up a neorealistic counterweight to all this abstrusing—staging a brush (one almost stepped on her hammertoe) with the raw justice of contingency—Secondness—brute fact—the other side of the instant. Which goes to show that a showman can never go wrong when his muses are sweat and semen. But don't these two nudes—nudists—realize the orgy is over, even—especially—heuristically. Though she must admit that where the Master's concerned—and where isn't He?—you never know, even when girded with the misfortune of being His aptest pupil, whether something is over and done with or just about ready to begin.

But at the same time a black woman's intuition tells Herbert—never more apt—never more beautiful, in fact, than when in doubt—that He doesn't want her—never wanted her—as the moment's stand-in for humanity—to think He's nothing more than Beefdom's answer to *Oklahoma*'s Ado Annie, to wit, Just a Guy Who Can't Say No—the passive unselecting assimilator of all the packetty details in the universe—doesn't want her thinking He's some over-the-hill hustler willing to turn a trick with any detail, jane or john, as long as it forks up a packet for his pains. In fact He's highly selective—a fastidious little devil—and with an armamentarium that secretes only a tiny proportion of the universal freight, to prove it. The packets he's sired through collision with details *out there* constitute only a minuscule portion of their overall GDP. If she must know, He's already eliminated the overwhelming majority—edited them out of his camera-eye—long before sticking a predatory head, ready for action, out the window of his Monday-morning soul. In short, where chaos is concerned, He's not your garden-variety connoisseur. Herbert drinks deep of all this rejuvenating enlightenment, for it's come straight to her from the Horse's mouth—not His ass, as too many of her fellow earthlings are wont to imply.

Cantor is back out on the terrace which is fast becoming his battle station. Though a long-time non-fan of sunrises (still, he'll be damned if he lets some awful orb stand in his way though like true men of the world they have [the orb and he] already patched up their differences—he can feel it in the air), Cantor nonetheless needs what Berry Sundae used to call (from either

---

[158]See Gregory Bateson, *Naven*, 2nd ed. (London, Wildwood House, 1980), chap. XV ("The Eidos of Iatmul Culture").

unfamiliarity with the idiom or a familiarity so oppressive as to find relief only in coy reinvention) a breath of fresh. But he won't get it—his breath, that is—since Herbert has elected to follow him out here (just too many birds-of-a-feather-type encounters between them to be chalked up to chance, if you ask me—but who does?). For she needs to confess and confide—too much time alone—too much *quality time* (right up there with *grandkids* and *reach out to*) spent among [*sic*] the Master, she explains. And a breath of George's fresh agnosticism is just what the doctor ordered. But—can you beat that?—it just so happens that he, too, needs to step up to the confessional plate which leaves him little choice but to get there well before her. She envies Eden's brand of unleavened despair. So different from her own. So much more difficult to pin down. Metaphysical, even. So much more open-ended. So much less self-serving and abstruse. So much less of a radical aspiration toward do-or-die. Except for that bit about how everybody from now on should know he's the kind of guy who takes his metaphors mixed and his cuisine *haute*. Or maybe those lines were just badly flubbed or poorly dubbed or maybe the Master was nodding more than usual. Cantor pretends to ponder the possibility and ponder it hard—as if he were just an old cowhand at the fateful intersection of Ludlow and Grand. Though this *apologia pro sua vita* is a passionate one, the passion's not for Cantor's direct benefit—he could be anybody—or anybody's brother—or *Everybody and his Brother*, as his father used to say with his signature authoritative Borscht Belt chuckle. He reads her thoughts, for there are more, and goes even further—he speaks their mind in full. Since they're more his thoughts than her own. "Doesn't the abstruse—the esoteric— the self-serving," he hears himself cry out (the sidestreet shudders in response and may never recover—at least not enough to be willing to undergo PTSD therapy), "also have its reason for being?" Is there any shame in proclaiming one's greatness (even if it's a complex—a moot—greatness)—and the greatness of one's discoveries (say, that on hot summer evenings in Bronx Park the setting sky is apricot-flavored enough to eat)—worse, the importance of that greatness ("don't blush so early in the game") for the ones having the misfortune to come after. "Like playing the Chopin études in the face of adversity," he murmurs. *You mean like playing Billie*, she'd like to say—*who bears her adversity like a portable shrine*. But to say it here and now would be to profane that shrine. It's not, he continues, as if through such commitment to self she profanes the suffering of, say, the Syrians under that monster Assad lying not through his teeth but through that sliver of a moustache. Or even the suffering of the Real Housewives of Pike's Peak. Herbert—and Eden, too, for that matter (they aren't as far apart as she thinks: he, after all—that is, if his translators are to be believed, has been confronting some pretty intricate challenges— challenges that themselves border on what she calls the abstruse)— She and Eden are the voice of every voiceless little guy out there with a momentous invention on his hands (sometimes more than one—many more) who has routinely allowed himself to be cowed out of storming the patent office (soon to be dismantled under the auspices of The Rump Team and if not by the Rump then by the scum he leaves in his wake)—cowed out of his wits by his lessers' invidious prioritization of the suffering of the world's disenfranchised—even if their inventions themselves reflect nothing of the kind (it's strictly formal application blurb-speak). And it's not as if those lessers actually cared about the disenfranchised—the disenfranchised are just pawns in their game of belittling and delegitimating—I mean, delegitimizing—the little guys like him who, in the last analysis, aren't all that little. Not that he's implying she and Eden are indistinguishable or destined to remain so: he hasn't bought that maimed-to-the-same-sameness business. Not in the least. For hers is the voice of the world's *self*-disenfranchising and, who knows, her discoveries may ultimately save one of them from soul suicide—from the refusal to refuse to be browbeaten any further, *especially by the scumbags who aren't worthy even of sucking the shit out of the disenfranchised one's ass much less of enjoying the fantastical perks associated with all that sucking* (is Cantor by any chance simply preaching the superior virtue of the oppressed here? if so, it doesn't matter since it's not as if he's speaking this coda—he's not even thinking it). In short, he concludes—going all basso profundo paternal (and feeling hetero-sexualized right out of the ballpark thereby), Herbert should not be excoriating herself for the sake of Eden who seems not to be in any immediate danger of pulling a fast one by perpetrating an act of smug self-righteousness against her . . . her . . . her—what's the catchword catch-of-the-day or at least of yes-terday's?—*elitism.* Smugness went right over his head. Like some Old Testa-ment angel of death. Or is it populist outrage she's afraid he'll be perpetrating? "No," she says. "Good—'cause *populist outrage* has already worn out its wel-come, at least in my house—it's about to go the way of *Never again!*'s answer to genocide. 'Cause authentic—William Jennings Bryan-style—populist outrage wouldn't have ended up *un*outraged at, for starters, getting shafted by robo-signer Mnuchink (who brags simperingly every chance he gets about having had the honor to travel with The Rump on his big fat jumbojet). Something else—something like *elitist* populist outrage—shooed The Rump's fatter-than-fat ass into that world's biggest shopping mall soon to be known as the White House."

She paraphrases, since a true lady always has the (decorum-drenched) last word. What he seems, then, to be saying if she's not mistaken is that every-body has a civic duty to scour her trivial crisis with the utmost studiousness (since we are what we choke on)—everybody has a duty to treat said crisis exactly as if its gravity is commensurate with that of a world war III (which in fact is currently in slow-motion progress over most of the planet). Respond-ing totally we learn on behalf of those too busy or too wretched to learn—our egoism in action is a public service announcement. "But of course there's a danger, isn't there?" What danger? he wonders. "The danger of our favorite egoist's being caught in the act of taking life, i.e., our birthright wretchedness, seriously—swallowing the baby with the bath water so to speak. The danger of being bracketed—straitjacketed—fossilized (not fueled) by credulity. Which means we do ourselves in twice over." Wanting very much to sound as if with-out further ado he's brushing her feathery objections aside, Cantor replies, "Do *real* justice to misfortune—insist on the priority of your fame to come, Melanctha, even—especially—in a world of self-styled do-gooders." He's tempted to add, "Don't do as I did"—after all, no self-respecting exhortation should leave home without it. Even if it doesn't apply, since in his own domain, he's pretty much been doing whatever he's telling her to do. "For never forget that (like billions of others down through the ages—all Dark) you're a special case—the axiom that there's nothing to expect after Sobibor and Rupert's Valley doesn't apply here—a very special case even if the Unanswered Question, straight out of Charles Ives, is and will always be why it should be you who's the favorite of fortune rather than, say, all those Spinozas in utero who walked the plank down into the ovens." "You mean all those Frederick Douglasses in utero." "Oh, yes. Sorry. But, remember—you're absolutely right, Melanctha, to believe the world will fall apart if you're not *the* winner, hands down. And, by the way, don't ever reduce your win to just another one of that reptilian drag queen Kellyanne Kockenlocker's *alternative facts*." Though granted, her kind of talent does exist, kind of, in an alternative *universe* where the craving for anointment—all right, so what if it's more tantrum than craving?—refuses to extinguish itself—worse, pale—*especially* when measured against the unmentionable suffering of those who had the misfortune to exit from the cattle cars. A universe, in other words, where run-of-the-mill morals still apply. "You mean the slaveship hold." "Oh, yes. Sorry." That in such a context—the context of *Never again*—he could actually take the time to consider several candidate modifiers before fixing on *unmentionable* proves to Cantor he's the worst kind of nitpicking swine—the poor man's underground man—a swine who's all about his swinehood—a smart-ass swine who doesn't mind being called a swine since a swine so called is a swine transfigured—but into what, exactly? A mesmerized Melanctha suggests that maybe, just maybe, she owes her surefire *meteoric rise* to Melville and Dickinson and Hopkins and all the other scribblers enslaved to a life-thesis. Like Eliot's Tireisias they've messily foresuffered all—*for her*—robbed her, really, of the probability of dying an unknown. Thereby earning her the right to have her cake and eat it, too. Then she awakens and acknowledges to herself that, for all Cantor's cueing and coaching it's likely she will die an unknown—an unknown to the *n*th power.

When they return—having gotten all they could get out of that most coveted of experiential commodities: a terrace dawn in Santa Barbara County—the irrevocable (yes, *irrevocable*) Mary Johnstone (the name's still impossible: uttering it would be a proclamation of just the sort of giddy gullibility by which Melanctha is always afraid of being bracketed) is shooing both contestants off their podiums solely to tick—piss—them off. Eden is center-stage. He's groggy and then some but sounds a little less preoccupied by things cyanidal. Unclear whether he's been downstairs to visit his lost love. "It's time to behave like grownups," she says in a doctrinal tone that suits her down to a T—*t* as in, *t*urns-her-into-Kellyanne. "Which means paying attention to the young man you see before you—not just any young man but one who's supped with horrors—horrors like Bashar al-Assad and Omar al-Bashir and Vladimir Putin and Jeff Sessions and—" Here we go again, thinks Cantor. It's the start of one of those Masterly specials he's come to dread with affection—a sequence of names the simple truth about which is that the further it goes, the less likely it is to stumble on an end-in-sight. Like all His other sequences this one will never get drunk enough on a plenitude—repletion—surfeit—

of terms to converge to—collapse at the doorstep of—a limit and thereby exorcise its generator's hunger to ingest the world. "Or, which is far worse, *thinks*—thanks to the zoo episode and its aftermath—he's supped with 'em." At the word *thinks*—rather, her complacent mutterance thereof—Post almost giggles his way free of whatever she—more and more of an alternative Kellyanne—induces of disgust. "So upon his return we in good conscience did the only thing we could which was to consign him to the—a—er, Van No. 1. Don't know if it's Chamfort or Mark Twain or an old Aleutian proverbialist or some woolly mammoth of the old school I'm misquoting—but whoever it is: *When in doubt—hire a van doublequick, the bigger the better.* In fact, for all practical purposes he's had his very own van from the start: so this whole business about massacres and the innocents is but the innovation of a very sick mind, warped from childhood abuse—" Cantor envies Johnstone more and more (without forgiving her) for having been able to jump ship—the ship being academia's unmerry-go-round—and make her way, from all indications successfully and in record time, out in what his fellow academia nuts refer to, with contempt and awe, as the real world. "Of course, a few of his Greenwich Avenue pals were herded in with him. Couldn't let him think he was in solitary and on death row to boot. And contrary to popular belief, debriefings go better when lots of extras are mulling around. Even when they're immobile and heavily drugged, as those were (with deaminated—or maybe it was hydroxylated or acetylated—Invidicum)." "That's enough—way too much—Mary," shouts Post. "I'm—we're—interested in Eden as a patient—not as some hot property that Hollywood simply can't wait (though is it still possible to talk about Hollywood, superfragmented as it's become) to get its hands on—not as a screen on which the wretched of the earth—ex-Silicon Valley and -university jetsam, say—can project their fantasies unmolested." Post is coming in loud and clear from the vicinity of the Dildo Alcove. "By the way, according to the latest scuttlebutt, it's up for landmark status—which if granted will mark the first time the honor has devolved on just *part*—and a very small part—of an entire structure."

Unintimidated (no such thing as bad publicity), Mary soldiers on—after all, the uncalled-for dig about university jetsam has gotten her goat. She'd say it was beneath Post but she doesn't believe this for a minute. Quite the opposite. He himself is as detrital as they come and they come in all shapes and sizes. "While the van was busy circling, clips from the golden age of pornography (nothing kinky; strictly meat and potatoes) were flashed on a screen to the immediate right of the rear exit to keep his fellow travelers busy—even if *busy* meant *busy regretting the timidity that desecrated their Lost Youth.* And by the way, how aghast you'd all be to know it's never Lost, as long, that is, as you've got the guts in your nuts not to go on losing it. Be that as it may, the stage was now set for Eden to undergo memory retrieval. The big boys couldn't let him get away—not with all that classified information rolling around in his head." "I said that's enough, Mary. Or do you want to be evicted from the premises by one of my deadpan bouncers?" Ethan and Cook are well aware of what they've got to do—once again, they're on the same wavelength because, when all is said and done, aren't they on the same side? But they've got to work fast if they intend to send what they smell as vital info back on the red-eye—back to the agencies (e.g., the DHHS and the EPA) before they're completely dismantled by The Rump's picks (e.g., Pruitt and Price). But they'll never get anything out of Post—or MJ, for that matter. The business about the van and the unkinky porno may be the hackwork of a fabulist who's just trying to generate advance interest in the blockbuster she expects to be born from the imminent Deal of the Century. Too bad the brothers Warner aren't alive to be in on it. So, as they'll never get anything out of either, what choice do they have but to enlist Manning's aid, life support or no? For whatever else you may care to say about Manning, she has always been—always been—always been— But neither can finish such an unfinishable thought. No matter. Through a little schmoozing they learn that as it turns out she's relapsed into a state of full consciousness, although the prognosis is still poor—poorer than poor, now that this access of freak robustness with all the trimmings is sure to sap more of her strength.

Herbert has overheard the men and, just in the nick of time, decides to tag along. Their job will be to afford her some kind of protection but against what? While they're pumping Manning—who, as it turns out, is confirming everything Johnstone has just said though it seems years ago (but to whom— who among them can claim with a straight face that time flies so fast?)—while they're pumping, Herbert can do her civic *and* her Christian duty (killing those two birdbrains with one stone) by chitchatting *stoically albeit tepidly* (no mean feat) with Pritchard's anti-moll. She's none too pleased, however, that Shearer has decided to follow her lead and tag along too. And as they descend the stairs to another bolgia, cold comfort that this prima ballerina (!) has prime trouble keeping up (sounds like an additional two pair of feet are hanging on to her apron strings or her coattails). By the time they're outside the door to Margo's cell, the two pair are gone, having figured out, Melanctha gathers, that their services as staffage are unwanted. Melanctha has no desire to speak to Shearer, who admits in a whisper she's here only to avoid one of her fans—and a not-quite-identifiable hanger-on whom she can't quite place and whose sole function appears to have been to disgorge a subprime thought packet then scurry off (though as a rule hangers-on don't scurry)—a packet that, now disgorged, makes her feel infinitely sad—as if she's back among the ghostly ushers in the New York State—er, make that the *David H. Koch* The-ater (Cantor: *Koch! ugh!—ugh to the nth power!*). And that's the whole trouble with the Invidicum Story[159]—so many packets, so little time, and all to the detriment of characterological mishap, aka fairy tales' spice of life. A shrew-like voice within cooks up a heady mix of *ifs, woulds, shoulds* and *coulds. If only the Master had marked her words and, whatever it took, flushed the packet bug out of his solar system, he'd be rich,* etc. (Some folks live life in the fast lane; others, like the shrew, are dyed-in-the-wool subjunctivitists.) She real-izes Shearer is rambling on—though (she has to be fair and admit) it's better than just plain rambling, way better. Turns out the hanger-on mumbled— no, that's unfair, in fact, his enunciation was perfect—something to the effect

---

[159]Alternative "working title": *Invidicum: The Scourge of a Nation.*

that having subscribed to NYCB for some twenty-five years (until the Master was done-in-but-good by Creutzfeldt-Jakob) he'd earned the right to milk the pathos inherent to the retiring dancers' diaspora—*his* dancers—*his* diaspora—for all it was worth. For example, he's taken to missing Helgi Tómasson (SF) on behalf of Patricia McBride (Charlotte NC) and vice versa (especially as partners in *Le Baiser de la Fée*) more passionately than either could miss the other. Same for Shearer and Ib (Andersen), who've also gone their separate ways—she, as he can see, to SB and Ib to Phoenix. "So he's got his work as a griever—master of ceremonies in a theater of grief—cut out for him," concedes Shearer (all this talk about grief making Herbert think, unwillingly, of grief *counselors*). Subtly excoriated by the griever as heartless, she took it upon herself to suggest that maybe—just maybe—whatever sense of loss they were supposed to be harboring had already been dissipated—anticipatorily— across all those decades of steroid-resistant excruciated motion. She doesn't tell Herbert whoever-he-is wasn't convinced by her argument, nor that just before they headed for the men's room, Akim—the fan in question—said (like the mystifying bumpkin he was and would always remain) that he'd see her backstage after the show. Herbert suggests—and not altogether jokingly— that maybe they've been sent out here, all expenses paid, to vouch—or better yet, de-vouch—for her character—to destroy it before she got out of hand. "You mean like Cantor's entourage." "After all, even an entourage of two is better than none," Herbert observes, slowly warming to—or rather, chilling up against—the idea. She's trying to be snide but it's clear she's envious. So Invidicum works only under specific conditions. "But it's not as if I'm up for a promotion—not as if I'm about to be confirmed—about to make my name in the company. I've already made my name in the company—a far better Company than this will ever turn out to be." He's landed here, she explains (best— most—of all to herself), because he knew she had something important to tell him or vice versa.

Herbert can already hear everything going on through what's supposed to be a sound-proofing curtain. Margo is dozing and it doesn't look as if she'll be up any time soon. Pritchard is sitting beside the gurney, anxiously massaging the underside of her wrist. "How Mary managed to get her grubby little hands on all that classified malarkey beats me and how did she dare to spill the beans?" Irena susurrates with difficulty: thrashing past this thicket of idioms has taken a lot out of her—would take a lot out of anybody—and she's almost weightless to the bargain. *Life is a wasting disease,* thinks Cook, already mourning the deceased. Only he immediately begs his own—or Life's—pardon: *Life is a start-up that will never get off the ground.* After all, he's one of the very few happy few who've tasted the scented flesh of her inner thigh—more than once—and lived to tell the florid tale. "He'd been trained to kill (forget the zoo fiasco) before we cut him loose—is that the right phrase?" Irena hates to ask but her hunger to learn how to turn a few more idiomatic tricks, even if it's on her final—her once-and-for-all—deathbed (for she's been a bit of a certified hypochondriac—a last-rites addict—all her life), is stronger than her pride. "Set him at large," Cook replies. "What?" "Before you set him at large." "Whatever *we* did, he more than fulfilled his promise—turned out to be a star in Aleppo—killing rebels right and left: if he'd stayed long enough he could have bull's-eyed our Client—the so-called ophthalmologist—himself. The one with the dumb-ass moustache. We did fear that at the very least he'd get himself murdered after a job well done but to everybody's surprise he had the audacity to survive and return unharmed, at least in body." "From where?" "Classified." "How come we didn't notice his absence?" "Suffice it to say that a mini-junket on the Dark Continent eats up no more than two days, tops, if you set your mind—fangs—to it. He's returned a poster boy, all right. But not for start-ups, or rather, not just for any old SiVa unicorns—a dime a dozen." "For what, then?" asks Ethan. "I already told you back on Greenwich Avenue—but there are none so blind as will not hear." She attempts to swallow the pill of exasperation but it almost gets caught—I mean stuck—in her windpipe. "He's a poster boy for her—our—their—army of shadows who are using a motley brew of off-label Invidicum and its congeners to create just the kind of unnoticeable psychotics who sleepwalk balletically through a crowd. Brew, if you must know, as armature for what should turn out to be the unicorn of unicorns. In fact, coveted class C shares are already being offered deep inside the darkest, smelliest armpit of the Internet. Which is not, as some might think, where you go to acquire University of Phoenix-level accreditation as a child pornographer or as an ISIS-level decapitator or as a Silk Road two-bit-coin sleazeball. No, that armpit and others like it are where you go (along with other remnants of the vocationless) for a little self-googling to determine whether you're famous at last (for there's a wallet at our backs—a deadline breathing down our hackles), i.e., to determine whether you exist. All of which you know as well as I do, Bill." "It gets better every time" (she knows her Bard). The way Irena tells it, they immediately celebrated him as one of the Righteous Impregnables in a ceremony worthy of the Druids somewhere up in the hills (she's forgotten where exactly). Which reminded him that his mother had been labeled one of the Unrighteous Incurables (though how reliable after all is a tot's back-seat recollection of what he thinks he heard his father teeth-grindingly mutter at the wheel of the family Chevy—and under his breath to boot). "But we almost made a fatal mistake. Post was intent on doing away with all the picture-postcard engrams—it amounted to a mania—damning evidence he called it but damning to whom? (it wasn't as if the authorities were on to us)." There was a failure to recognize that, if carefully preserved, they could be of enormous use—if not to them than to the highest bidders worldwide—artifacts and more than artifacts and Sotheby's-worthy. She's making no promises but it's very possible that an Eden engram—a non-fungible token if ever there was one—as exquisite as an aerosol blimp chock full of viruses—will be fetching top dollar on StockX any second now—will be worth even more than a Scott Brady rookie card on NBA TopShot. "It was the least we could do for Eden—not to mention for ourselves—granting him some kind of living legacy, I mean. Only fair considering how much quality time he'd spent in the Third World" (Irena loves anachronisms) "soaking up the local colors—always incarnadine" (there she goes again). "Local *color*," Cook mutters tactfully—or rather on the border shared by tact and exasperation. "After all, we'd invested a lot in him and he in us, for that matter. But Post kept bellowing, 'Purge those fuckers,' meaning the memories." (Irena's use of the "vernacular" still gets him hot under the collarbone. "He was intent on retrieval solely in order to extinguish them forever—drive them off the face of the earth—nothing to learn from their likes—who knows what would happen if they got into the wrong hands?—war crimes—at the very least Guantanamo—Maple Grove—no general rule—delicious fruit—price of strawberries in London—abundance about Bristol—currants more refreshing—glaring sun—tired to death." *Irena's English can be breathtaking when (with a little help from Jane Austen—Austen, that is, in the guise of a shrew-in-training named Mrs. Elton) she makes up her mind that it needs to be,* thinks Cook. Yet again, she's fully justified his faith. "But fortunately I have what all the others lack: a woman's intuition. As I saw it, our first and only duty was preservation—to put said artifacts on ice, literally. And if, the waters tested, it turned out they were a hot property (*Post's very phrase,* thinks Ethan) then what was there to do but wait until the right team came along to package them for popular consumption—with all the incriminating evidence bleached away—ideally in a feature-length film worthy of their uniqueness (none of those made-for-cable TV also-rans)? Which will make him another kind of poster boy as well." A gratuitous swipe at that HBO docudrama to which Cook has given his all—in vain. That enthusiasm has completely fizzled among the bigwigs makes the swipe all the more galling. "The revenue that accrues could help defray the cost of future training programs. But with gifts—especially the gift of intuition—come responsibilities." Which means that she, without telling anybody, has to see to it that the tiny part of his lateral amygdala crawling with potentiated neurons where fear memories proliferate like jackrabbits are secured in the right kind of biobank. But it has to be a very special kind of biobank. A biospecimen, after all, is a fragile thing and a memory specimen even more so. "The typical freezer—the typical freezer—" She winces, a rival to Garbo's Marguerite. Cook rushes to her side though he's already there. She waves her Alfredo away. "It's nothing, just a bedsore doing the brain-racking for the two of us." "You were saying," prompts Ethan, ever the no-nonsense operative. "Your typical freezer is simply not cold enough to stop degradative enzymes—which go after memory tissue with a particular vengeance—dead in their tracks. And we can't go back to the High Renaissance of biobanking and soak our precious LA slices in formalin (we don't want so precious a find drowning in fixative) and then embed them in paraffin blocks." Thankfully, some of their guys have made a real cottage industry out of producing biomarkers of sample quality to prevent costly experimentation on inferior material—specifically, markers of oxygen deprivation and the choicest forms of cell death: autophagy, apoptosis and necrosis. "We don't want to end up with a substandard product: Eden's calvary has been too important to be trashed by some pipeline peddler." She's spoken defiantly for it's clear the big boys haven't come round to her way of thinking and quite possible they never will. Or not until after her death—when somebody with half a brain will—may—be able to make good use of her posthumousness—may be able to coax posterity, all its fickleness notwithstanding, to kick in.

As there is no other chair and as Margo continues to breathe deep, Herbert takes to window-shopping. Thing is, the target—the great outdoors—is being obliterated by fog—the way her forbears were obliterated by white cotton-pickin' greed—while she stands by helplessly, immobilized. Breakfast time but no appetite. She's had enough of steam-table vapor to last her a lifetime. If only the Fog could be her Master, she mock-sighs with mock-winsomeness. It would be so easy to decipher His characer based on what's been deleted— rising sun, of course, waning gibbous, some tiled roofs, a few expendable palms here, a few expendable hilltops there. For what Fog, like any copyeditor, strikes out is as potent a biomarker (word du jour) as what's left behind or put in. And if she could only understand Fog she could—well, what? Understand her fate? Understand her fateful obsession with fame? Understand why no matter how hard she tries she just ain't credulous enough to buy into the lethality of her youngers-hence-betters' contempt and dutifully cave in without further ado? Understand why she just ain't credulous enough to nourish the intermittently plausible fiction that she's a has-been to end all has-beens— all washed-up even before she's ready to begin—because every younger and every better in Creative Writing 401 looks at her as if she's come back from the dead solely to hex their craving—their striving—to get noticed? Understand why she just ain't credulous enough to believe the humiliation she can't manage to feel is simply too boa-constricting to permit her pencil (Koh-I-Noor Hardtmuth Triograph 1830 4B) to sprint another step? Understand the delight at the heart of her fear of having to play Henry James to all those little H.G. Wellses out there panting to take her to task for being no more than a (lady) elephant trying to dismantle a sweet-pea? But what would the creator of her namesake think? Does she owe it to Gertie—even if blacks are taught to be especially suspicious of Jews, particularly the befriending kind—to get on with the business of alienating her audience before she even has one?

Margo awakens and announces that she's, of all things, ravenous—uxorious Pritchard's cue to exit. He motions to Herbert to take his seat and, more or less simultaneously, tells Shearer (who's replaced Herbert at the window) that he'll find her another. The minute he's gone—she's been waiting for him to leave even while asleep—Margo tells the ladies that if Pritchard can be found sunk in grief at her gurneyside, bursting ope the founts of a compassion of which she would never have dreamt him capable—though he's better at it than Straynge would have been—it's because Liepnits has every intention of doing the opposite, i.e., abandoning his wife ASAP—probably for a bleached blonde and a simultaneous expiatory stab at Catholicism (for the Liepnitses of this best of all possible worlds, illness is gratuitous provocation and money-grubbing calculation—and wifely illness even more so). "Stories crave—prey on— contrast and the Invidicum story is no different. So the long and short of it is that Pritchard—*my* Pritchard—isn't interested in what I'm going through. Couldn't care less. It's a matter of hoping Liepnits will do his damnedest *by sheer virtue of being Liepnits* to make him, Pritchard, look good—great—in comparison—better than he has any right to look. A matter of hoping Liepnits will give him just cause to come out smelling like a rose. A matter of vanity pure and simple." But enough about Pritchard. Ever since her nervous breakdown (an outdated expression which Herbert immediately falls head over heels in love with)—ever since her nervous breakdown (things started to fall apart on the plane when she demanded, somewhere near Brownsville, to be re-seated next to the pilot)—Margo's been trying to steer clear of human-kind—to refrain from taking the bait of its Empathy—that poor excuse for an emotion—that poor excuse for a *thing*—the Job's-comforting confirmation that, yes, the floating tumor is real, when what is craved (and richly deserved) is the magic of a firm denial—that textbook construct which serves not the receiver but the giver—which allows the giver to keep his distance because when you get right down to it, what else is there for anybody to *keep*?[160] The first law of breakdowns, according to Margo, is to manage yours with due decorum. "Don't get caught in the scorn-inducing act of taking it seriously. Steer clear of pouring your heart out." Especially since the hubbub of health—its apparent raw vitality—makes the breakdown seem inconceivable and if it's an illusion you can't fight it. "But saying nothing—to be ready for the next blow—is as much of a giveaway—especially to the breakdown itself. Since the breakdown has even less of a stomach than you do for being caught in the act—in this case, of plotting that next blow. So you don't want to get the break-down's dander up any more than it already is. So what it comes down to in the end is that the breakdown equals the push-and-pull of saying too much and too little. In other words, the breakdown—any breakdown—mine—yours—is all talk and no action.

"But you don't believe it's because Pritchard is a homosexual and I pre-vented him from following his inclinations to the bitter end (even if he had decades to do so before we found each other again)—so you don't believe that's why *They—They—They*—the Blacks—the Jews—the Episcopalian and Presbyterian wildfire-generating space lasers—the homos—the Ku Klux

---

[160]Margo is clearly a disciple of Henry James whether she knows it or not (or, if she *does* know it, then to hell with all of her pigheaded disavowals) so it's only right and proper that she should have gotten *keep*—as fast as possible and while its blood is still boiling—out of the clutches of *keep his distance*, in whose broth it quickly lost its iden-tity—in whose brew it was quickly de-*mean*ed—since the idiomatic meaning is always greater than the sum of its parts and to the common good those parts must yield. Only right and proper that she should have thrown *keep* back on its own literality so it could thereby transform *distance* retroactively—rather, the dying echo of *distance*—into an object—a solid object—a meat-and-potatoes kind of object—the kind of object that you can *keep*—keep in the freezer like a piece of green cheese or in the broom closet like a vulva-shaped urinal.

Or, if you still don't believe Margo is a Jamesian then only consider this repre-sentative passage (elision of the context should not be a deterrent to those with eyes to hear) from "The Coxon Fund" (1894): ". . . he [the unpleasant character Gravener] declared quite dryly: 'That's all rot—one's moved by other springs' . . . A fortnight later . . . I [the narrator] understood well enough *the springs one was moved by*" [the italics are mine]. The idiom is stood on its head to shake free the literality—the materiality —not just of *springs* but of *moved* as well. And the long and the short of it is that *keep, distance, springs* and *moved* have all emerged from internment at idiom camp head-quarters incalculably enriched.

Klan—the Muslim Brotherhood—think I killed Jim and that I'm a bad—the worst—mother to boot. So you don't believe that's why all of them are trying to destroy my son's life." "No," whispers Shearer, touched by the fragility of Margo's little-girl wonderment—unfair to call it a little-girl *act*. But Shearer's much more than just *touched*. Assessing Margo's work as a conspiracist, she's ready to come away mighty impressed—even starstruck. And it's not just because Shearer, who never graduated high school (since nothing's ever mattered except induction into the cult of the toe), stands in awe of Margo as a much-tenured queen among (m)academia nuts. No, she's awestruck by the way Margo—or rather Margo's fear—manages at the drop of a hat to round up the troops or better yet the tropes—to get suspects, however blameless, inducted into her own kind of cult. Margo waits a minute, gagging on a reassurance that solves nothing—that makes things worse than ever—that, in so many words and worst of all, badmouths The Conspiracy, her sole support in a time of crisis. But she has no intention of giving up on stumping the experts—the self-styled expert curers. So Shearer, *still* her advocate, doesn't believe it—*it*—It—*It*—all goes back to the fact (three years ago, almost to the day and just about the time her hated hating mother died) that her gynecologist and his trusty new nurse Ethel thought she was writhing much too convulsively in the stirrups not to be making up all that excruciating cervical pain, which meant, if true, nothing less than that as a bad wife and mother, always coddling her ailments and abandoning everybody else to the elements, she was capable of anything as long as it was bad enough and should be punished accordingly? Yet, this being the case (Melanctha's having trouble fixing the referent for *this*), Shearer *still* doesn't believe that the gynecologist or his nurse or both, having no choice, went on to inform the mad-psychiatrist head of the sect—cult—tribe—ashram—whose long-term goal is to ruin not just her life but, more importantly, her son's—still doesn't believe Ethel and Ethelred went on to inform that madman so he could exert his influence to get her put away for good? Shearer *still* doesn't believe any of this? It's Melanctha's turn (Shearer is worn out). "No, dear." "Dear Margo! For the love of [g]od, for my sake and the boy's sake and your own, won't you stop now?" Pritchard wails (there are times when he can swear James Tyrone, Sr.'s blood is running in his un-Thespian veins). He sets the breakfast tray on the sort of night table (you know the kind) that begs every moment of its waking life to be allowed to go its lonely way unobserved and always almost-succeeds—except at charged moments like this. "I'm sorry: it's just that the breakdown has done strange things but not strange enough." He feeds her a little oatmeal "just the way you used to like it." "Is he coming?" she asks, spitting the spoonful back in his face. "Who?" "The Rump." "There is a rumor afloat to that effect, Margo. He has a strong presence here in this accursed town as you well know by now." "Thank heaven for the Republicans" (looking as if she wished there was more oatmeal to spit and, if she plays her cards right, there very well may be). "We need them more than ever." What, after all, did Eleanor Roosevelt do for all the Japanese Americans interned during WWII? she wants to know—if she did so many great things then there's no excuse for not having set aside some time in her schedule to do a wee bit of disinterning as well. "Maybe you'd prefer to have Moira or Melanctha feed you." Both try to look as if they relish the idea more than they can say—in fact if there's a moment they've been waiting for, this is it. Never mind those two crones: she's even come to have a soft spot for Paul Ryan and McConnell and McCarthy and Macbeth. Herbert sees her point, at least as far as Moscow Mitch is concerned: who would dare deny the contrast collars do daffily undashing wonders for his dev'lishly foppish wattles? Like the grim reaper himself, them there wattles are in it for the long haul. Wanting nothing so much as to go out and give them all a hero's welcome Margo thrashes bitterly, the better to collapse with a gurgle and drift into a delicate coma, as if having anticipated Walser's unwanted entry on to the scene and his even more unwanted diagnosis. The coast now clear he explains that she feels responsible for Straynge's death and her only son's downward path to non-wisdom even if he's just made one of the most dazzling debuts in Siliconland history—and pandering so expertly to Borkman, Jr., is the least of it. Fact is, as the Word on the Street would have it—and wasn't she the first to hear?—Straynge, Jr., will be manning the team responsible for putting the finishing touches on Jason's brainchild, i.e., the intervention that will enable people on the run—would-be artists et al—to compress a lifetime of formative experiences—what for such people are just mile*stones around their neck*—into no more than an hour, thereby eliminating any bothersome claims on their precious time. No matter: it's gotten to the point where she can't go outside without feeling everybody's pointing a finger, Pritch explains. Which accounts for the sudden staunch support for The Rump and his gang. Of course everybody should distrust Intellect whose workings (granted) can be devious. But she's gotten to the point—the place—where the intellect—everybody's intellection (and, yes, I know the Democrats are as far—super-far—from perfect as anybody might wish)—especially Obama's—Pelosi's—Adam Schiff's—Hillary's (especially Hillary's)—is to be distrusted as devious *in its very essence*, having but a single aim: to focus on judging her. Though maybe everybody else except The Rump's cheerleaders are fools, Pritchard concedes—or ponders conceding—and it's she's who's on the right track. For wasn't it David Hume (of course it was, silly! you just invented him!)—wasn't it David Hume, whom Walser now refers to pompously as his master—wasn't it Hume who *famously* asked, in part II of the *Dialogues Concerning Natural Religion* (don't you just hate it when somebody pulls a trendy fast one by adverbalizing *famous*?), "What particular privilege has this little agitation of the brain which we call thought, that we must thus make it the model of the whole universe?" Cantor—wherever he is—thinks (and Melanctha seconds the motion), *If I have to listen to that tired old gagline one more time*— Though he must concede (unlike his erstwhile mentor no *ponderer* he where conceding's concerned) that no matter how many times the Master has dragged it out of mothballs, it's like putty in the hands of context hence never the same. Fortunately for Margo (Walser maintains), The Rump and his gang's 24/7-style perpetration of—autopenetration by—a roilingly greedy power-crazy racist brand of righteousness doesn't leave them much time or room for making thought the model of the universe, the better to clobber her with it—the better to get her tarred and feathered as a failure on every front. So is it any wonder Margo, in and out of her coma, has eagerly joined the ranks of Don's Forgotten Men? Phantom practitioners of a phantom *populist outrage*—oops! another signifier with no signified in sight (the road to hell is paved with signifiedless signifiers)—a bromide invented by those at a loss. Populist outrage is a—phantom because what today's Forgotten Men practice—enact—is a perversity begotten of despair (but the kind of despair that makes the spectator yearn for the Marvellian brand or the good old-fashioned New Deal soup-kitchen variety)—begotten of despair upon impossibility—a vicarious wallowing in Mar-a-Lago Raw Deal elitism—elitism without practical reason (but to quote David Hume, *What particular privilege . . .?*) though with no dearth of animal cunning. A perversity that's already responding to Don's broken promises, present and sure to come, as the outpouring of a demagogue's version of tact—the best version—since it absolves the wallowers of the obligation to acknowledge the sting of defeat at the hands of their victor. A perversity that turns perversity on its head. Nothing more exhilarating, after all, than an all-expenses-*unpaid* vacation from self-preservation. Nothing so exhilarating as acting against one's best interests.

Oatmeal or no oatmeal, Pritchard starts hating her guts the way he did way back when, in NY—that day—those days—when reconciliation was a matter of—what did she call it?—topography. A matter of topography. Depended, reconciliation did, on what alley you were crossing on the way to the High Line and so what if at the time of their scandalous liaison the Line wasn't even a glint in Joshua David's eye? He's sick of the conspiracy business. Her espousal of The Rump and his scum frightens him—leaves him feeling lonelier than he's ever been—or thinks he's ever been. And how can he not feel lonely living as he does with a maniac who insists she's as sane as a hatter—no, *sane as a whistle* (an idiom for the ages that he's just smuggled through customs)? Getting too bracing a whiff of her own insanity she accuses him—accusation being Margo's default stance—of having destroyed her life *and* (thinking this gives heft to her shrikedom) *the life of their son* (mother love being the last refuge of scoundrels). How can he just stand there when with every foul taunt he—and the billionaire Dems (*What did Eleanor Roosevelt ever do for the Kurds?* [the question of the ages!—it stumped Heidegger and Spinoza even when they put their heads together!] you see! she was bad as—worse than—Mussolini!)—when he and the trillionaire Dems are cutting Jim, Jr., off from all the opportunities staring him in the face? It all began when he—Pritchard—threatened, out of Envy pure and simple, to cut The Rump's golf balls off at the root. Thereby endangering their son's life—worse, his status among the start-up crowd—for who knows who was—is—wiretapping their gross incompatibility?

Only he'd quickly realized (so Margo deduced) that the dirty job was best left to better, healthier minds than his. According to envy-throttled Pritchard (as told to Margo), When it's The Rump's time to go, and he does go, the very first on his dream team to go, which is only fair, then it will have been compliments of a dollop of buckshot discharged simultaneously from a Smith & Wesson semiautomatic rifle, a Remington shotgun and a trusty Glock .40-caliber pistol and getting him right between the balls. Which, as even your garden-variety friendly neighborhood sawbones knows—not just world-class forensic pathologists—is the most vulnerable part of the anatomy, even in an old fart of 70+. With a few obligatory groans and an equal number of stammered threats—for under all the bluster (if you listen carefully) resides a stammer—he'll be out of the picture for good. Sent packing with some soundless applause from his pet weasels, Pence and Ryan and Gaetz and Jordan and Johnson, not to mention the dimestore-enigmatic Melanomia. Pritchard tells his charge that he doesn't remember saying anything remotely like this—but before she can get up on her high horse and lash back (lashing back is better when perpetrated above the crowd)—he realizes any artifact will do—any entity whether it exists—existed—or not. The Rump's old balls were obviously there for the taking and somebody must have taken them—the balls—up on their timid offer. In any case, even if nobody did so they're still—the balls, that is—a plausible pretext in the here and now for ascribing everything that went wrong to him, which is all that matters. Somebody needs to be blamed for her insanity (Cantor wishes Pritchard could have found another word: *insanity* is too commonplace—too much of a showstopper—will resonate too comfortably among the Dinner Theater crowd—plasters then kidnaps the patient before her disease can be constructed from scratch, *creatively*, from building blocks as disparate and as unimbued with the stench of run-of-the-mill insanity as it is possible for any self-respecting building blocks to be without, e.g., breaking their vows of everlasting fealty to the Bavarian Illuminati). Fruit of guilt over Straynge's death, those in the know-nothing might say. But that's just a pretext—everything's just a pretext—an artifact—of a nonexistent event—an event incapable of existing on its own steam or even something else's. Somebody to Blame: Would, Could, Should—title and sub-of Margo's vest-pocket bio. Then he reminds himself that marriage, failed or otherwise, is all about going the limit of rage—with elegant disdain—grandiloquent forbearance—only to return stiff-upper-lip strengthened. It's all about withstanding failure. A certain charm about the horror of elasticity—of going to the very edge with a single armament: grace under pressure. So he must shut up, especially with the whole world watching whether they like oatmeal or not. He looks at her, hoping she'll die, and leave him if not in peace then in . . . remission. He says, "Eat up," averting his head as if already on to the next access of solicitude—feeling like somebody who's staving off a non-English-speaker's massacre of an idiom—a normally vicious taskmaster—a Squeers—transfigured by the compassion of respectful correction. But how much is his hatred of the forever-dying Margo hatred of Margo herself—the specific Margo (Margo who's just discovered a hysterically immovable smudge on one of her labia)—and how much is it generic—a hatred of all mankind as it adheres in—adheres to—Margo? So is he using the balls business as a pretext for disgorging a rage that antedates Margo's birth by a century at least? So if it's a specific Margo doing double duty for the generic then he's left with the obligation, especially on her death-gurney, to respectfully parse her every utterance on a case-by-case basis. Via the utterance of the moment—he must ask himself—is she simply standing in for all mankind—is she simply being generic hence inoffensive in her genericness—or a prize bitch in her specificity—is she being a shrike or just good old human? No answer—and maybe she'll be good and dead before he gets the answer he—or she—or humanity (that old warhorse, that old chestnut) deserves. How are things going between Liepnits and the Missus? he asks the oatmeal, since he has no right to take his rage—worse, his confusion—out on the oatmeal, notorious for its circumspection. Or is the pretext not a pretext at all—but a pivot point—perfectly capable in and of itself—of its Margo-laden specificity—of stirring up a bile-storm? There's no generic rage on his part at all mankind or if there is it doesn't figure—disfigure—here. The specific tortoise outpaces the generic Achilles, hands down. He suspects, however, that if he were an artist—the artist Melanctha takes herself to be and probably is—then he would be much less interested in the fever chart of their mutual hatred—rage—warmed-over middle-period Strindberg—a chamber play (in the *Creditors* mode)—with too many windowless drawing rooms and too many epileptic Struldbruggs—much less interested than in the question—much more interesting—how the absolute zero of hatred was reached—how they got there thanks in part to all the detours—how their credulity let them in for a getting there inevitably—how they bamboozled themselves into believing the other was the cause of all their troubles—not mom and dad—not brute humanness. A question, by the way, that tortured and tortured and went on torturing Duns Scotus and his tonsured cronies before they hit the sackcloth for good. In any event, and for the moment, each wishes the other would die in a plane crash—preferably on a Boeing 737 Max—unaware that all flights like all cultures will soon be canceled until further notice compliments of some aerosol—as fake-fragile as one of Blanche DuBois's reminiscences—that went astray. Pritchard suddenly wonders—rather, finds himself wondering (in the style of Chekhov's Olga even if there's no town band cutting capers)—why he lives, why he suffers. Oh, what a rogue and knuckleheaded slave is he! Can he actually believe that having endured so much suffering he shouldn't have to pay and pay dearly for the privilege, not to mention for the dividends it's yielded up to him and the mess it's visited on others not lucky enough to have his knack—for making mind-mountains of grieving dread out of the molehills of sugarcoated boredom? Come to think of it (but who's doing the thinking?), maybe, just maybe, his *nervous breakdown* (though Pritchard wouldn't be caught dead using such a term) fell in love with hers, and hers with his, before they themselves fell, i.e., maybe the breakdowns fell in love on their behalf, enabling them to love—albeit not to hate—by proxy.

Herbert waits her turn as she was taught to do by her old-fashioned mother up in the Bronx—who crafted primness into high art. She'll have Walser know he's simply drenching the musty old whiskers of a considerable acuity in the whipped cream of cant. The current sociopolitical climate is, as it's never been before, all about Greed Greed Greed Greed Greed Greed Greet Greed Greed Greed Greed Greed Greed Greed Greed Greed and Greed—as a screen for Greed. "I mentioned greed," he reminds her. "Doesn't the hair-raising phrase 'roilingly greedy power-crazy racist brand of righteousness' ring a bell?" But fishing for compliments is degrading. And as it so happens that Walser's constitutionally better suited to mind reading he has no choice but to avail himself of the opportunity to ask, "And what is greed itself—sorry, Greed—a screen for—a screen against? What even darker dirtier unsecret secret is lurking in Greed's back pocket?"

On the other side of the sound-proofing Liepnits, unimpressed by this typically Walserian rhetoric (it's clear that in attacking The poor Rump he's just burying his musty old whiskers in the *curdled* cream of cant), pleads with Irena to get the better of her disease (Cook and Ethan are gone: neither could bear to watch her suffer a minute longer) when only minutes before he was already planning out loud how to select a new running mate—a successor—one who'll boost him in the ratings. So what if she weren't as gorgeous as Melanomia or Ivankomia, with their competing lines of crotchless pantyhose, to be modeled at the Winter White House later this afternoon by none other than the ever more ubiquitous Kellyanne Kockenlocker, defiant serial violator of the antediluvian Hatch Act? Come to think of it, with her perfumed crocodilian snout and deep-diving deécolletée she'd be the perfect helpmate when it came time to bedazzle The Rump into seeing the light—the light of unreason—the same light that breeds monsters of unsound scholarship and illegitimate ambition (debased currencies in which the world's Liepnitses traffic unrepentantly). The perfect partner, in other words—and in the role of a lifetime—when it came time to snow The Rump into seeing that with jockeys Putzder and Flynn having been hooted off the stage of political life and every other asslicking cabinet member soon or sure to follow, only Liep is equipped to ride (with a lash or two from KK) all their horses. Walser shakes his head sadly but it's not clear (for which Herbert is thankful) whether by doing so he's lamenting Margo's plight or beneath-contempting Liepnits's last-ditch-effort uxoriousness. Having read the headshake from cover to cover (even through the sound-proofing, whose bark has proven worse than its bite) and opting for interpretation No. 2, Irena calls—no, starts to call—Liepnits every name in the book to which lese majesty there can be only one response, and not a pretty one. So, forever the man of duty, Liepnits, shedding pants and boxers, shoves his hairy buttocks in her face, disappointed there's no facesaving fart forthcoming even if confused as to its purpose. Would it have enhanced the shamelessness or mitigated its message—would it have been shamelessness squared or square-rooted? "There are times," he remarks (*Mostly for my benefit,* Walser thinks) "when the mouth is powerless—words won't do—something else is needed—a more skillful orifice must be pressed into service—a more concise orifice—or one that by virtue of its very skillessness is able to convey—that is, misconvey—" But Irena is no longer here. As it turns out, she, too, has collapsed with a gurgle and drifted off into a coma, but in her case an indelicate one.

CHAPTER FIFTY-SIX

Eden enters—the wrong cubicle. Shearer points delicately at the curtain. At first he understands not. If Shearer knows anything then she knows (it's clearer than ever) that she must save Eden from the commodification Mary (who's followed him in 'cause she's simply alien to the *concept of being non grata*) has in store for him. *Mary Johnstone*: she still can't be coerced into thinking the name, much less uttering it—at least not with the tools currently available to her. Pritchard and Walser remain. Nobody has any secrets from anybody else in these parts. He's almost as graceful as Akim, though not from want of trying not to be. Though it's hard to tell whether he feels omnipotent or im-. Yet despite his presence she can't remember her time on the van (since he stands for it)—who her fellow travelers were—or if she's been in transit at all. All she knows is she must save him. Watching—feasting on Eden's form—she's reminded of what was written—pseudonymously—by that gloomy pseudonym-crazy Dane whom Erik Bruhn (any Sonnambula's dream Poet) had her read (or else no partnership!)—no, not Hamlet, not Hans Christian Andersen, not Carl Dreyer, not Peter Martins, not Ib Andersen, not Adam Lüders, not even Danny Kaye—something to the effect that there are moments when one can find indescribably humorous relief in standing on one leg in a picturesque pose or, saying *Fuck you* to the world and meaning it as never before, settle everything unsettling with an entrechat. And Eden seems to be doing just that even if, as newly appointed still point of that world, he executes no movement, much less an entrechat. But what if, before being saved, he's done in by his torment or by their stratagems for making use of it, that is, before MJ, who might unbeknownst to herself be well intentioned toward Eden, can familiarize him with the career opportunities awaiting just around the bend? She must speak her mind no matter how many smart-aleck start-uppers scorn her for instincts they will doubtless misread as maternal. Johnstone bursts out laughing—even better, gives way to a belly laugh—something that's very much at cross purposes with the doctrinal tone taken amid the doings on the floor above though maybe the tone was an artifact of the *process* of those doings and nothing more. Shearer is about to retort that this is neither the time nor the place (fortunately Margo is out of commission) but there's no stopping Mary. "Now hear this: she wants to know if Eden is going to do himself—or be done—in. But my dear, my *dear*, don't worry your pretty little head about Eden. How can he *not* stay alive—given the robustness of this conviction of his own guilt—and how can whoever's running the show allow him—such a prize specimen—so dependable a boob—to vanish unexploited—a boob whose credentials for the practice of credulity *on a professional level* are impeccable?" But she's failed, Ethan points out—yes, Ethan, who's also managed to squeeze himself into Margo's coffin (think *Night at the Opera* stateroom sequence as revived by the cast of *Ivan the Terrible, Part II*)—to specify exactly *which* show for there are plenty being performed hereabouts, even simultaneously. For starters, there's the venture capitalists show and the dildo show (which is allied to the VC show) and the amateur interventionists show and the failed promotion show and the "The Rump" show and the Ryan show and the Putzder no-show and the Tom Pryce pucker-up-to-kiss-ass show and the Flynn-Flam show and, along those same fault lines, the fartless buttocks show and the IvanComa-from-Ronkonkama show-and-don't-tell show as told to the Kellyanne show and the entrechat show and the thought packet show (forever hardy, forever perennial), not to mention the Firstness, Secondness and Thirdness shows and the— Unimpressed by lists (or rather by a list that is merely the contrail left in its own wake by shock—the shock of the lister himself—at how non-representative—how very much beside the point—the items on that list have turned out to be) she makes haste to ignore him. How can the master of ceremonies not cherish somebody who swallows hook, line and sinker everybody else's justification for well-merited self-incrimination as his very own (because he's simply too blameless for his own good) so that, unshackled by guilt, the real culprits can get themselves cured fast and furious and do what it was they were put on earth to do, which is Go Hollywood (and the Amygdala Institute, self-love child of Warner-Metro and Voracicom, along with them)—the Hollywood Post pretends to scorn—with *the proofs in their pocket*? "For no story is a sellable story unless it's based on a true story or, at the very least, on *true events*," Mary reminds them, apropos of nothing. And even if Martin is not the favorite of fortune they thought he was (or he was thought to be) he's surely a person of interest—*the* person of interest— in the case that Fate has been making against him, entitled *Invidicum: The Movie*. It's the (incessant) self-incrimination that entitles him to serve as their means of entry into the World Capital of Narcissism (incurable self-incrimination due in no small measure to his having entered the program under false pretenses—wasn't envious to begin with—too tormented for that—though maybe the torment was—is—a means of smothering in Weltschmerz or is it just plain schmaltz? what might [it's never too late] just prove, as a precipitant out of the LA smog, to have been in fact very real envy—the purest of the pure—from the word *go*). Since incurable self-incrimination is not just what star power is all about: it is Star Power. "He's our Trojan stalking horse—his torment will get our foot in the door for no self-respecting moguloid wants to be pitched a *heartwarming* story (even if it's about a bunch of Envy freaks who've conquered their freakdom)—at least, not right off the bat. At which point we pull out and dazzle said moguloid with all those snapshots of Eden's junior year abroad."

You mean, Eden dares to think (*understanding*, like the father of Emma Woodhouse, *but in part*), there is . . . a Master? Somebody who cherishes him for his robustness as Straynge never did, as his own father (it was a matter of Calvinist principle) never could, so what if it's for the robustness of a capacity to feel responsible for everything that goes wrong in the world? Which confirms that Herbert . . . hasn't been talking through her hat—a hot potato of a hat—as hot (Shearer thinks) as *The 4 T's* Choleric from whom all four of her semi-partners recoil in semi-alarm after an incautious touch with their forefingers. This lopsided insight (even if it's somebody else's and walled off from rental) gives him the courage to cry, "I don't want to be saved, at least the way she" (he points Johnstonewards) "wants me to be!" Shearer breathes a sigh of relief since she takes this to mean, *But your kind of saving—whatever it turns out to be, little lady—I really, really like.* "So you're not going Hollywood?—and after all I've tried to do for you in the make-your-name-in-the-company line?!" MJ tries to look hurt and, by and large, succeeds because success—corporate success—is her stock and trade. He explains—he tries to explain. He doesn't want the memories preserved—and not just because this whore wants to sell them to some A-team as she calls it whose worthies meet regularly—smog or shine—up in the Hills to—to— (Shearer can't quite believe that Eden is on speaking terms with the slightly archaic *whore*. Uttering it feminizes, making him all the more [mysteriously] male since ever so briefly he's both man and wife.) But at the same time he doesn't want them extinguished, as horrible— as self-incriminating—as they may be, either because of his mercilessness or his cowardice, or both— And then he proceeds—no tries—to explain, to this constantly shifting cast of characters (Walser has been replaced by Stifter and Pritchard by, of all people, Netta) that he doesn't expect much in this or any other department since, contrary to the way things are supposed to unfold hereabouts (*hereabouts* being where exactly? they make haste to wonder), that is, in accordance with the wisdom of—of— Eden gropes for the right—the only conceivable—words. Gropes in vain, which is always a triumph of sorts. Across the curtain and in his head, Liepnits helps Eden out—it's the least he can do for his favorite (after Robert Ryan) psychopath-with-a-heart—*in accordance with the wisdom of—of—of—of—of—what smug and invidious Ma Ozarks routinely invoked in his presence as* The Norm (*no creature, by the way, for all the PR and BS, less under its sway—all her efforts notwithstanding—than she*). Liepnits's first aid gives Eden the courage to speak his mind though what comes tumbling out will be comprehensible only subsequently, after having been been translated into the King's English from the verbatim notes taken by some cocktail-dealing amanuensis wise beyond her years. Contrary to the way things are supposed to unfold, his trek through life, unlike theirs (a slow pan takes them—a veritable rogues' gallery—all in), has always been orthogonal to whatever itinerary his handlers determined should be his. Take, for example, that blustery summer afternoon (something in the unseeing gaze of reminiscence tells Netta he's on the verge of delirium) when, after a particularly arduous week guzzling and guttling at Amygdala's trough, he took a walk to Battery Park planned down to the last detail of sun and shadow—solely because the guidebook (he was a tourist, after all) said it would be good for him (true, it was also good for him because it was as far from Brooklyn's lame excuse for a skyline as he could get—Brooklyn, mirror of his despair, which mirror insisted that despair, as Brooklyn-wrought, was good for him—but never mind about that)—he took a walk yet somehow found himself going "inevitably" in what he needed to believe was the direction directly opposite, along the river, parallel to Cherry Street—and to the B'klyn skyline, of all things—in the direction of the castle keep known to the natives as the Knickerbocker Houses and its adjoining playground. So why conserve the memories of that hasty stopover in the Third World (now referred to as the South by geopolitically correct podium-hoggers like S. and W.) since it was the furthest thing from an outpost of the progress of his self-creation? And yet—and yet— "Right on!" Stifter (obviously a cum laude graduate of sixties Haight Ashbury) cries lustily though not as lustily as Eden might have liked since the cry has died without generating a single echo. "This puts me in mind of the fact that a thought packet if it's worth its salt—for deep down I'm a Man of the Packet like everybody else who bludgeons his way through Amygdala's revolving door—is always orthogonal to the language that takes over uninvited to 'express' it, give it life, i.e., just as orthogonal as is ana*lay*sis (the kind we practice here) to the words to which it gives rise in order to . . . exist even if no longer as itself." Cantor, standing in the corridor (word has gotten around that Chez Margo is where all the action is, forgives Stifter his pomposity because he manages to wear every word at a rakish angle. And speaking of rakish angles, Borkman notes that dapper Liepnits is sporting a handlebar moustache—almost a chevron—made from, of all things, blueberry jam. But didn't one of the cocktail waitresses tell him they were all out of blueberry when he asked for some at the steam table just twenty minutes ago? But if confronted she'll only play the sexual harassment card. What happened to the good old days, he demands to know, when it was accepted like holy writ that boys will be boys and men will be men and and never the twain shall meet?

"And as for normality," Cook pipes up (tired of *making a play for*, i.e., *hitting on*, all those hot SiVa demoiselles, Cook has again drifted down to these frostier climes), "don't give it another thought." He explains that the more he goes on livin' ('cause scared o' dyin'), the more the characterization of any set of behaviors as an *affliction* seems implausible—inconceivable. "For example, the long stint of unemployment was shoved down my throat as an affliction as far back as I can remember." But during his probation, when he went from Voracicom Young Turk to Voracicom PR cop pounding a beat—the lowest of the low—he discovered how much more of an affliction was Status: Employed. It was then he began to be stunned not that somebody turns out to be quadripolar, for example, but rather that, given Life's intrinsic quadripolarity, more people (or more *folks*, as Men of the People Mitt Cheney and Dick Romney would say) aren't. "Symptom-free normality is the affliction and, sadly, there's no cure. No cure at all." It's clear, however, that Eden views this vote of support pure-and-simply as an interruption—worse, acid rain on his parade. As far as Herbert is concerned, Cook has missed the forest of form for the trees of content. Should Cantor put his two cents in and treat Cook to one of many nuggets for all occasions—even if he may end up smelling too much like an ass-kisser—to wit, that Normality doesn't work for everybody and that, personally, Non-Normality is a disease of which he doesn't wish to be cured? But there's no time for add-ons: Cook is back on track.

"As I was saying, never did I feel more unemployed than when I was re-employed—and not just because re-employment was probationary and I had ended up selling Invidicum trials door to door." "The lowest of the low," Margo grumbles through the bars of slumber's cage. Yes, *the bars of slumber's cage*: got a problem with that? silently screams one of the Master's fiercest flunkeys. "Having swallowed, before I went to sleep, the retraining pill lock, stock and barrel or hook, line and sinker or with a hop, a skip and a jump, from day to day I never knew, when I woke up, what kind of off-label or on-label or off-off-label or off-off-Broadway Invidicum trial loomed on the horizon. The Envy trial, by any chance, or the Homicidogenic trial, or the Compress-a-Lifetime-of-Basic-Experiences-into-Less-than-an-Hour trial (since, nota bene and as it turns out, it's a poor relation of Invidicum that's the co-star of the Compress-a-Lifetime Show)—or any one of a thousand others—OK, maybe not a thousand. That was part of my retraining—to be able to switch gears at the drop of a hat—or to have my gears switched at the drop of somebody else's hat. So the rest of you have had it easy—never a doubt as to Invidicum's purpose. But in my case, all memory of the Invidicum-Envy monogamy got extinguished compliments of a bad night's sleep. It got worse after I brushed my teeth and wiped my ass. Luckily, Moira, you caught me, or I caught you, on a good day—at least on Second Avenue—when the kind of Invidicum trial I was peddling meshed, through no fault of my own, with your needs. Thanks to the poison pill self-administered before bedtime, Invidicum was constantly reinventing itself and me along with it." It got to the point where Cook came to believe—to understand—that Invidicum was perfectly capable—without him, without Voracicom, without Amygdala, without the owner of the Lafayette Bakery on Greenwich Avenue even—of self-transmogrification propelled by its own dull-witted momentum. Came to believe (without telling anybody until now) that Invidicum was a wonder drug too wonderful to be content with a single target or ten or even twenty—a wonder drug too big for its britches—a drug with an inexhaustible hunger to be sidetracked by The Next Big Disease and The Next Big One after that— (*Like any self-disrespecting hero of an early fifties noir—like, say, O'Brien's Frank Bigelow in* D.O.A., thinks Cantor who's not just a thought addict but the thought addict's thought addict—a career addict—a lifer.) Came to believe that Invidicum was a drug with an inexhaustible hunger to be sidetracked as long as each Next Big was superseded, for no disease is worth its salt if it doesn't get superseded, i.e., pulverized through giving birth to one that's bigger and better. Came to believe that Invidicum was a drug with an inexhaustible hunger to be sidetracked as long, that is, as the birth of The Biggest Thing of All (inasmuch as any incarnation thereof is bound to a disappointment) was endlessly deferred. (*Deferred, like the revelation of the identity of the Ur-Mastermind in empire-of-crime silents—significant, inter alia, for their refusal to excrete a definitive culprit until they ran out of underlings—e.g., Count de Kerlor, Satanas and Vénénos in* les Vampires, thinks Cantor, ever the thought addict.) Came to believe Invidicum was a universal solvent—a menstruum—(*Like Goethe's wit according to that busybody Emerson*, thinks Cantor.)—and that the only fixative it was in danger of drowning in, so thought Cook (that is, when he had world enough and time to think since a door-to-door salesman's life isn't as free-as-a-bird's as it's cracked up to be especially when what he's reduced to peddling is intangibles), was its own fixed identity.

Now that he's gotten back into the thinking groove—and on a roll to boot!—Cantor can only marvel at how much IED-rife terrain has been strafed by their mini-meditations on the Norm and the Abnorm—with topics ranging from Eden's orthogonal trek, through Stifter's ode to the misadventures of language and thought packets (always good for a laugh) and Ma Ozark's dependably petty-minded supervirulence as a hard-wired exponent of the Norm, and onward at last to the *pièce de résistance*, Cook's re-employment in search of a strategy. Though maybe the only thing that has anything to do with the subject—and that, barely—is what got things going in the first place, i.e., Eden's millisecond-long riff on the too-long-overlooked Knickerbocker Houses. Whatever followed—all of it Masterly lumber-room detritus in need of an airing—was yoked—the more tenuously the better—to what came before—as if to advertise its irrelevance—as if to prove that in all this fiddle there's something Moore important than relevance (*Let me ask you, is Life by any chance relevant to Itself?—you're damn right It isn't!*). Though maybe the mess was all about making yokage fail, somewhat, in order to exalt the hegemony unto itself of each link in the chain. But speaking of *pièces de résistance*, the only real one is a terse little number: Cantor's sudden against-all-odds recognition that Horse's Ass Steve Bannon's response to the fiddle could only be: *Who gives a shit?* which would wash over Cook, if not the Master, as, oddly enough, a kind of relief—a cue to stop outdoing himself—a signal to rest—a signal that through *"world-class"* backbreaking word labor he's earned the right to rest—on his laurels.

Having learned minutes before Margo may not be too long for this world, especially since she's more convinced than ever that a conspiracy—or at least conspiratorial thinking—has been responsible for her son's already outsize and ever-expanding failure, Jim, Jr., thrashes forthrightly past all bystanders (most of them unsavory-looking to a fault) to reach her in time, though uncertainty of his mission increases the closer he gets to her gurney (which is as it should be when one is a devoted son or trying to become one even when weighted down with ambivalence—the strongest affection of them all). Has he come to mitigate her shame or to feed it—feed on it? But as he overhears her asking anybody who'll listen (even if there's a glint of mischief in both her jaundiced left eye and the crocodile tear on her right cheek) whether maybe just maybe it's because she refused to satisfy Pritchard by converting to Catholicism or Jim, Sr., by converting to Sufism that Jim, Jr., is—is—well, you know, doomed—a Doomster, to quote the Assistant Headmaster at Sutton Square— As he overhears this his heart is softened. Her conspiracy problem stems from the fact that she doesn't have the tools needed to hate, thinks Stifter. She's unable to hate—to *come* through hate. Unable to hate her tormentors she assigns their hatefulness, sometimes real, sometimes imagined, to a Mabuse figure (Stifter again—he's a big fan of Weimar Grand Guignol and a veteran clarifier of everybody else's thoughts—thoughts they'll never know they harbored). Jim's heart gets softer and softer even if she clearly likes nothing better than to deprecate the long-term resistance to amelioration of the plight she's just reinvented for him—as so many times before though never in front of so large and pliable an audience. "You'll be proud of me one day, mom," he sobs inaudibly, massaging the underside of her wrist exactly like Pritchard. Everybody backs off respectfully. Genome, like blood, tells. He informs her, a bit too bubbly for his own taste—and more to the point, for his own good—that he's been promoted to Chief Financial Officer on the basis of the press release he's just drafted in the Dildo Wing. "What press release?

and promoted where? and to whom do you report?" the old girl asks, as sly a harpie as ever stooped to conquer, and in a tone that expertly takes the wind out of his sails. It's a description, he explains, of the Intervention—part sensor, part Invidicum-laced pep pill (not to be confused with Cook the vacuum-cleaner salesman's poison pill), part prose poem—that Borkman, Jr. (we're living in the Year of the Juniors) and his dream team (The Rump, *Jr.*, Pruitt, Jr., Mnunchkin IV and Spicer III, all sit cushily on the Executive Board) have cobbled together for Creators, quasi and otherwise.

He proceeds to read from a notebook extracted, a little too adroitly, from his hip pocket—

"If only poor Jim, Sr., were around to see poor Jim, Jr., holding a notebook in his hands at last!" Is this lady for real? Cantor wonders—no, Is this lady for real? Cantor *insists* (all caps).

> If things go according to plan (and one is lucky enough to be con-stitutionally unsuited for the daily grind of . . . Being with a capital B), the Intervention will induce all of the painful insights (as if there were any other kind!) to be derived (but with none of the attendant pain) from the stresses of, e.g., marriage, parentage, not-so-cozy domesticity, dead-end jobs, dead-end adultery, sluggish tumors, dormant tumors, quiescent tumors, senescent tumors, apoptotic tumors, prima donna teratomas, masturbatory frenzies in front of the blank computer screen, fardels, contumely, spurns, beloathed kin incapable of bowing out gracefully. The Intervention will generate a sense of epic duration, of life overlived, but with the substrate Cre-ator spared having to aspirate the marrow of decades. It will allow the artist to undergo all the flavorful disbenefits of banality, to the requisite bloodcurdling effect, without being swallowed up, only to be spit out, in the process.

"Your future seems to be assured, my boy," Margo titters, begrudgingly. Where will this unmerited success take him? Doomed, at least—even a little bit doomed—he won't have the guts to abandon her. Whereas now, riding high—

Eyeing her bravely: "After listening to you, mom, *somehow*" (the empha-sis is agonizing to those with eyes to hear) "I don't think so."

Sounding through the curtain as if she'd emerged much stronger from her unwelcome encounter with Liepnits's inferior cheeks, albeit still not strong enough to set sail on the Good Ship Remission, Irena shouts: "But don't think Invidicum is getting off scot-free." Despite the talk On the Street and the fact that (what with all the distractions available in such a sunstruck playground where Envy is the norm) most of the old guard have stopped taking their tri-daily dose—despite this and more, Invidicum's career is by no means over. Acting as both (the first of its kind!) a co-component of the pill-sensor cargo payload (see above: it's a five-minute walk, tops) and the vehicle—the pack-aging—for its degradation-free transport into the right cells, Invidicum may very well end up having a second life—as different as can be from its silly first incarnation. "I always said: Envy isn't noble enough to deserve Invidi-cum—that is, Invidicum deserves better—much better—than to be saddled with Envy as its cellmate. But nobody would listen. Someday soon Invidicum will look back on all this as a bad dream. Didn't I always say that, Liebling? Didn't I?"

"Never have I heard a description of the thing that's so much to the point—and with a little folk poetry thrown in for good measure," says Stifter contentiously. Is he praising just Straynge, Jr., or just Irena or both? Fact is, until now, he's never heard the Intervention—whatever it is—described at all. Proving it's never too late for somebody's cup to runneth overboard.

Somehow (a *somehow* as agonized as its predecessor a few sentences back), it's too painful for Eden to watch Jim, Jr., debase himself, since he knows a case of debasement before an uncaring parent when he sees it. Or is he—suddenly the grand old man of Greenwich Avenue with a lifetime of unspeakable expe-riences behind him—simply attributing to Jr. a humiliation he doesn't feel in order to wallow by proxy in its briny depths? Thing is, Shearer seconds the motion. For here is Jr. proffering the greatest gift any son can give his mother—the Vision of a Future that is nearer than she thinks and for all the world as if it were the chargered head of Rogier's John the Baptist fresh off the executioner's block. Erroneous ascription or not, Eden wants to flee—what's more he does—followed by most of the others—a veritable Who's Who of world-class bystanders—swallows the stairwell in a single bound (OK, two—at the most)—remembers he still hasn't begged Irena's forgiveness—for all the proclamations of being racked with guilt, hasn't seen her in ages—no real con-versation, in fact, since that day in beechy Madison Square Park—intends to redescend—already has his foot on the pedal so to speak—too late—passage barred by the obligatory pair of tattooed goons with the obligatorily beefy take-no-prisoners deadpans. They know he's about to spill the beans—they can tell from his tone, even if he hasn't spoken a word—no choice but return to the floor above, the ineludible In Crowd in tow.

All for the best in the long run, he needs to think. No time like the present to set them straight, he also thinks. And no group of hangers-on ever looked more eager to be set straight. As regards the debriefing—and the formalin business—up to now it's been all action and no talk. He needs to tell the sob story his way. He's going to turn things around but first he needs to draw a few deep breaths. They gather round with their newly acquired drinks, flaunting indifference to the cries—more death rattles, strictly speaking, than cries—of Margo and Irena—synchronous at last—down below. They tried their hand at debriefing (i.e., retrieving his memories in order to destroy them per Post's instructions)—"That's a goddamn lie," shouts one of the goons, harboring more necklaces than tattoos—somewhere on the uppermost floors of this very building, which in case they don't know and how can they? positively teems with not quite state-of-the-art operating rooms—a vast hospital, it is, where everybody is trying to change beds—where this man's head lies at that man's foot, and so lower and lower. In fact, they assigned him a cot next to Irena's gurney—poor Irena, his last and only love, later downgraded to the floor below once they discovered that for their purposes hers was the wrong kind of fatal disease. There are fatal diseases and then there are *fatal* diseases. Shearer flinches involuntarily: So her Poet is still carrying a handmaidenly torch for that slutty Coquette—head still in the storm clouds of their *Sonnambula* pas de deux—torso still too eager to lift her (arms defiantly akimbo) high above the strains of *Oh! quante volte*. But, taking a page from Irving's songbook, "How About Me?," she almost-sobs. But cheer up, didn't Akim say he'd meet her backstage after the show? Good, for she or he has that thing or two to teach him or her—and herself or himself—about music, no doubt. "Why assign you a cot next to Irena's?" somebody asks, right on cue. A reasonable question, and simple enough to answer. They hoped, Eden explains, that once being driven to distraction by her groans and by their similarity to the ones he'd heard in Aleppo once, in Darfur, in Port-au-Prince, during his whirlwind tour of the Third World—(*That damn archaism again: Irena's favorite*, thinks Cantor. *So they* are *birds of a feather after all*)—they hoped that being driven to distraction, he'd cough up an endless stream of engrams. "It didn't happen. It couldn't happen. I was too worried about Irena." But Shearer doesn't have the fortitude to stick around for any more bilge about his truest love. Fortunately, Akim stands six feet two just where he said he'd be (and blessedly sans sidekick)—i.e., backstage, which is what the two of them (*though*, à la Gershwin, *not a word was spoken*) have decided to call Dildo Alley. He's come not to play Vladimir to her Hillary—not to hex her last shot at the title—he's come neither to bury nor to praise her—but to shoot straight from the shoulder before it's too late: She's ended up the way she has ("And how is that?" Moira hisses) because in fact she didn't listen to George Balanchine after all—when he emphasized the overarching need, albeit not in so many words, to be forever dancing *against* the music—the need to smuggle in a whole lot more steps at those moments when the music wasn't listening—was nodding off—was taking a breather. The toework should have been a lot more insurgent—in fact every time he, Akim, turned around, her insurgency—taking a page from Prick Cheney's songbook—was in its last throes. Her first thought is that he's talking a blue streak in code. Her second, that if so, the talk has dutifully swallowed the code, hook, line and sinker. So there's no excuse to refuse to see things as they are. Shearer tries through some clumsy mental footwork to determine which of her roles—which of her performances—fit the straitjacket of so wrenching a diagnosis. But she has too much pride to ask something along the lines of, *Why, if you loved—if you admired me, did you wait until now?*— She shouldn't have left Eden. Listening to protestations of undying love for Irena wouldn't have been any more painful than this I-told-you-so bit of ego strafing. Once Moira's back in NY, he wants to start choreographing but only if she's willing to follow the rules. She'd like to say, *I'm never going back*, but never one to pass up an opportunity, Moira refrains just in the nick of time from cutting off her nose to spite her comeback.

CHAPTER FIFTY-SEVEN

But there's no need to return just yet. She can hear him perfectly well above the sibilation (damn right: *sibilation*) of the eucalypti. *Eden:* Whatever happened or didn't happen on the uppermost floors, it's the van he never wants to forget—the sort of vehicle in which a boy has no choice but to become a man—the sort of vehicle that at long last, delivers the payload of selfhood to the self—especially the kind of self that has a soft spot—a predisposition—for its own disintegration. Nor does he ever want to downgrade or regret what happened there—what could happen—or, more importantly, fail to happen—only there. (*As it turned out, they couldn't retrieve his memories any better there than in Gurneyville.* But maybe this time . . . on the beach . . . at dawn . . . among the seashells . . . the gulls . . .) Doesn't want to nurture regret because regret is sinful. *Worse, an affront to the anterior cingulate cortex,* thinks Stifter or is it Walser or is it Netta? (One thing is certain, however: it can't be Liepnits, not even compliments of whatever he managed to get out of Veterinary Medicine 101 at Ozarks Tech before flunking out but not, alas, in order to make—and how could he in those halcyon B.C. days?—like a unicorn in a gray flannel hoodie.) Fact is, never and nowhere else had Eden ever felt so secure: so secure it was positively terrifying. "What he means is—" Johnstone and Stifter are speaking at the same time though not just to hear themselves speak. No, each is after bigger game, i.e., to drown out the other's effort not to clarify what Eden has to say but to cut it off at the root. What he means—drowning them both out, and quite expertly by the way—is that what went on in the van enabled him to take a quantum leap toward articulateness. "In fact—" Though they again start to speak simultaneously, Stifter, so as to keep up what he appears convinced (*Who is speaking?*) is his reputation as the quintessential gent of the old school, gives her the right of way. And being a cunt, also of the old school, she accepts, ungraciously. "—it's rendered him not just articulate but hyper-articulate—i.e., too articulate for his own good, which is exactly why Hollywood, ever the groundbreaker, is reluctant to come-a-courtin'. Needless to say, we want him to adapt to his new potency slowly—as we would anybody else who's been doing the equivalent of fasting for a lifetime and is suddenly deathbed-afflicted with a craving for the kind of hotcakes that like nothing better than to fight for their life in a plate of high-fructose corn syrup." Herbert sighs: Well, this pretty little speech should help get some of his detractors off the Master's back. The ones who've contended specifically, since what seems to His No. 1 confidante like the minute before time began in earnest—who've contended that *all his "characters" sound exactly—problematically—alike*—worse, that they give themselves the same oratorical airs. At least it shows he's *aware* that there is a problem—even if he's still a long way from solving it. Though maybe the incapacity is more interesting than the awareness—*is* (duck! it's that old devil the Great Synonymy working his magic again) the awareness. Though she's tired of always being No. 1: the last one He grumbles at before hitting the hay. How can she be expected to play her part in the trial *and* be his favorite child? Doesn't this entail some sort of conflict of interest? Shouldn't she finally recuse herself, like that racist dwarf Jeff Shesshions, from adjudicating the derring-do?

As if responding to those very detractors, *the Johnstone woman* (the name keeps her safely under lock and key) says, "But I want you to know that what Eden is already tendering compliments of all this hyperarticulateness is not just some phony-baloney barococo drivel but the hard-pressed fruit of an ordeal. Even if, as it so happens, the jury is conveniently still out on the identity of the ordeal: Is it everything he underwent abroad or, rather, *what he underwent trying to remember, in its peacock finery, everything he underwent abroad*? Or at least some of it." What a weight off Herbert's mind—soul— shoulders—to be able to refer to MJ as such (forget the peacocks at play on their terrace, Mary, or were they phoenixes? well, phoenixes or peacocks— they're gone), hereby showing that under no circumstances will she allow herself to be strong-armed into regarding MJ as real—as real as any name can make her—as real as any name unwisely left to its own devices will make anybody. (Herbert's credulity is much less robust than everybody else's—it's her curse and her glory.) But enough about the Johnstone woman, aka Cantor's nemesis from Way Back East—the poor man's Sue Mengers: Melanctha has better, or at least bigger, things to do. Like wonder if the new, improved Eden with an eloquence beyond anybody's wildest dreams, even the Master's, represents, qua protégé, just what He ordered, or thought He ordered, or whether the protégé has turned into a sorcerer's apprentice just too damn fast for a pondered judgment to be renderable. Only Mary Johnstone (why not call a spade a spade? as of this minute, *the Johnstone woman*, totemic as it is, has simply exhausted all its potency) looks unfazed and clearly has no intention of reining this energumen in. The sky's the limit, at least for now, as far as Eden's prospects are concerned. Why, she positively exults as the caution subsidizing his monosyllables gets thrown to the winds and all hell breaks loose in a language new to him and no doubt to everybody else. *But hasn't this kind of striptease—Eden's—Martin's—tinkering with eloquence—trying his hand at eloquence—played itself out many times before?* Cantor thinks, even if never so definitively, though retrospect may very well prove he's yet again only scratched the surface. But what's wrong with trying one's hand at doing the same thing over and over and over until it gets to be too wrong to be doable ever again? But can it be that from the start Eden's mumblings—like Kowalski's—secreted—*had* to secrete—a pretty high level of sophistication (cf. the latter's Napoleonic Code aria), at least for those who knew where to look? For if word had gotten out that Straynge's brawny nemesis was also a brainy word virtuoso (some guys have all the luck), well, then, Envy would have known no bounds and Envy, even Envy sedated by massive doses of Invidicum, Jr., (*Jr.?*), would have led to a lynching and just when it was becoming clearer and clearer, and not just to those with lungs to breathe and eyes to see, that Eden was the unlikeliest of suspects. Even if the manipulation of language—language as the bier of language—the bier of hairy-chested action— mockingly elliptical, floridly self-depreciating—is, as everybody knows, the province of homosexual men alone (No Trespassing) hence a cause for dire suspicion which the manipulator is the very first in line to floridly foment:

E.g., Clifton Webb in *Laura* (priceless smirk from Dana Andrews observing him get out of—no, *emerge from*—the tub), *The Razor's Edge*, *The Dark Corner*; or, even better, the province of soul-crippled lady stand-ins (Piper Laurie in *The Hustler*, Lauren Bacall in *Young Man with a Horn*) whose function is to extort from their lover the admission—acid test of guyhood—that the piss-eloquence is All Greek (!) to Me. *So it's speech after all, not writing, that's the Pharmakon to End All Pharmakons*, concludes George. He remembers the good old Pharmakon days—not with fondness but with (even better) *something like fondness*.

"I discovered friendship on the van—for the very first time, it was possible." "Don't believe a word of this rigmarole," cries a voice Herbert doesn't recognize, until she realizes it's her own—disfigured, alas, by all that rancor over having to go on being Numero Uno. "I don't know who's putting him up to it" (though she knows very well) "but he's trying to turn the van into Hester Prynne's handiwork." They may remember (though why should they? how *can* they? since the Prynne affair is simply their—her and the Master's—little secret) that the Letter bearer's creator takes pains to point out how, though Hester has been formally banished from Puritan society, there's no lack of demand for her handiwork, which has managed to become the fashion, whether from cause *A* or from cause *B* or by virtue of factor *C* or because of factor *D* (an embroidered deployment of possibilities worthy of Swift or Proust, and betraying the desire of the creator for uncertainty, the creation of uncertainty being one of the methods by which all obsessional neurotics [not just superstars like the Rat Man] sequester themselves—"on the outskirts of the town, within the verge of the peninsula," so to speak—from the reality of the world). But this phenomenologist of uncertainty (the Rat Man's—and the Wolf Man's—Chillingworth in extremis) knows she is surely being unfair to uncertainty mongers (already she has them—her listeners—all in the sweaty palm of her hand). For as they can see with Hawthorne, uncertainty is the price the creator must gladly pay for power: the power of explanatory articulation. The aim is not to nail the most likely suspect but to keep the cross-fertilization (in the plane of language) going as long as possible. Herbert is already flying high. Already looking backward (some events exist only in retrospect), she would date the entry into her majority from this moment. And when he lets them in on a not-so-little secret—i.e., that "her needlework was seen on the Governor's ruff, the scarf of the military man, the band of the minister, the baby's cap, and the apparel of the coffined dead and their survivors"—what they're too privileged for their own good to witness is the generation of story surplus-value: allegory generable only to the extent that it is unforeseen and unforeseeable—a byproduct—a side-effect—collateral damage in a big way—generable only to the extent that the creator has enough of a job—has his hands dutifully full—getting the details straight (e.g., the thickness of the Gov's ruff, the color of the militico's scarf, the number of tassels on baby's cap, etc.) and has no little choice but to regard any other consideration as a mere nuisance. So, for hewing ever so closely to the contours of his story—for allowing the wordflow to pursue its own briny logic—with nary a thought to things like story surplus-value-added, Hester's creator is able to render concrete the fact that sin, by virtue of peripheralization, finds a way to find its termitic way into the very epicenter of the center of things as the sole untainted and untaintable element thereof. Which is to say, the good teller doesn't Follow the Money into the Hollywood Hills—so last-century, in any case. (That bitch-on-wheels MJ gets the message, Melanctha hopes.) The good teller Follows the Wordflow as if his very life depended on it—and it surely does or else why would he bother bearing the proud man's contumely? And now, egged on by this Johnstone woman, or by her mob bosses, Eden is trying to convince himself—worse, them—that the Story of the Van has generated its own surplus value. But there is no story of the van—not if she can help it—so there can be no surplus value. But they mustn't think she doesn't comprehend the desire to have one's very own scarlet or purloined or Kremlin letter—or one's very own Zimmermann Telegram or Dead Sea Scroll, for that matter—interweave unpredictably and at innumerable points of contact with (so that at last one can claim them as one's own) interminable ruffs and caps and scarves and sable and lawn and whips and scorns of time. Only the refusal to seem to be parasitizing her son's memory keeps Melanctha from boasting that Building 18 would have been a far better stand-in for Hester's embroidery. In any event, it's a disgrace, bemoans Jean (one of the too many "working" subtitles of *Invidicum Story* is *Everybody's Getting Into the Act* but as the publishing industry knows only too well, you can't have too many subtitles), this prostitution of the most innocent of vans (though no slouch herself in the Internet of the Prostitution of Things department) to such a purpose. And Netta (ditto), through what she means to be taken as stony silence, throws caution to the winds and seconds—thirds—the motion.

Herbert immediately regrets having failed to cleave to a Myshkinoid—dare she say, a Christlike—stance in the face of provocation (most of it self-generated)—the surest proof of artistic excellence, or at least dedication. Though some might say (herself included) that the stance can easily become a pose—a *making perfection of the life rather than of the work* sort of thing, and the pose a substitute for said excellent dedication. She adopted it with mixed—some might say (herself excluded) disastrous—results on the few occasions when her ditties were being "critiqued" in somebody or other's Master Class. Inasmuch as the sun of rage and loathing was always breaking willy-nilly through the stormcloud of mock stoicism. In short, the pose managed every time to bomb not just in Pomona and New Haven and Boston, but in Pyrorrhea as well. Furthermore, since invoking Yeats is forever equivalent, here and now being no exception, to—is equivalent to being a hop, skip and a jump away from—invoking Synge and since Synge was always too magisterially self-confident for defiant self-anointment when in company, never resorting to threats of hurling thunderbolts of his greatness at anybody who dared to doubt it—the very threats Yeats could easily be sheer-exasperated into making when among detractors but especially among friends—given all this, if she brought up Building 18 in this context she'd flunk the Synge test, violate his Fourth Law of Psychodynamics, let the poor guy down. No out-Syngeing Synge. But Eden, she sees, is not to be deterred and has no intention of letting himself sink—or is it his handlers who have no such intention?—on the Good

Ship Misery-Loves-Company. Continuing in a winsome tone that just can't be his (sounds like he bought it on Amazon or cranked it out of a second-hand 3D printer) and on whose modulation there must have been plenty of expert coaching by Siri or Alexa or Echo or Narcissus or even Aesop—he remembers, for example, how when one of the first-class passengers—it may have been the guy who never missed a Greenwich Ave seminar and to prove it, always sat on the right aisle in the third row—drew back the curtain to see how the other ninety-nine or rather the other *47 percent* lived, they booed in near unison and you can't imagine how closely knit they all felt doing so. So infectious, in fact, was the esprit de corps that the one percent of the one percent ended up cursing their bad luck in being just-too-plain-filthy-rich to be entitled to join plausibly in the festivities. The only thing that "tainted his ecstasy" (now I ask you, could he, *our* Martin Eden, have come up with such a pregnant phrase pre-van?) was the fear that, comfy and cozy in his bulkhead seat, he could be expropriating much too much leg space. Yet here—there—was his lovely neighbor—Shearer, he thinks—the epitome of good taste (she blushes at the imminent compliment though to her knowledge she's never set foot in a van)— Yet here, there and everywhere was his lovely neighbor protrud-ing her dainty little bootie beyond the acceptable boundary while concealing the machination with a blanket—a blanket attesting to a skill so "delicate and imaginative" (but provided by whom precisely? Cook? Amygdala? the Santa Barbara Benevolent Association? an anonymous or—worse—a pseudony-mous donor?) as might have been . . . Hester's! Thereby setting his mind (at least as much of it as resided in his legs—especially the right) at rest. In short, her own good bad manners let his own off the hook. He takes a gander at Herbert but not in the least with ill intent. Like a kid he simply asks without asking *how he's doin'*.

"But I wasn't on the van!" Shearer shouts, "at least as far as I know." "But," says Netta, no-nonsense still at ninety plus and counting, "you should also know—and know only too well—that like full moon over the Tigris, or is it the Tiber?—Invidicum, even at the lowest doses, does strange things. Stranger than strange." "*Especially* (*pace* Paracelsus) at the lowest doses, Doc-tor. Remember what happened to the prostates of vom Saal's poor little field mice who were exposed to DES in the womb or the pregnant ones exposed to DEHP?" Walser warbles nonchalantly—to blunt the edge of what must sound like a go-for-the-jugular-style impugnment of the old girl's (almost mythic) waning competence. "As in the case of certain weed killers, anti-bacterials, polycarbonate plasticizers, vineyard fungicides, estrogen mimics, and aphrodisiacs, the dose-response relationship for Invidicum (as we know, the big I may be characterized as belonging to all of the above categories—and then some) turns out to be a far cry from your typical toxicologist's wet dream, where the higher the dose, the greater the abnormality. Hence, the classic monotonic straight-out-of-Chamonix ski-slope curve must yield to all sorts of unplottable monsters." Shearer is invigorated by the update. Cantor, on the other hand, is unnerved—he's already heard this spiel (albeit in an expurgated, i.e., wetdreamless version) so why is it being re-broadcast? Yes, he knows all about repetition à la Maimonides replete with Eliphaz variations and Bildad omissions and Zophar additions—i.e., exact repetition as the ever-expanding repository of ever more imperceptible unquantifiable *internal difference, where the meanings are*—but at this stage of the game, his status as Pritchard's anointed a distant memory, the whole shebang's lost its lustre. Still, if only for the sake of Berry Sundae (never around when Cantor needed him most), he's got to keep his ears pricked and his eyes peeled and his nose to the ground—or is it the grindstone?

"But in the aftermath things didn't look so bright." "The aftermath?" (This mighty echo is being intoned by no less than a *chorus of elders—bulbous-nosed, rheumy-eyed—straight out of* Boris Godunov, or so Cantor needs to think—and fast—thereby stealing the thunder, or so he needs to feel, of some thinker with a far greater right, in this case at least, to name-drop. But who? Herbert's has-been Master? Herbert herself? Louis Pasteur? In any event, he—Cantor—is a nasty-ass usurper—the usurper laureate to end all laureates.) What Eden soon discovered was that any post-van attempt to invoke the secret understanding based on their shared experience in extremis—of a common cause—a common doom—always failed bluntly. Their fabled solidarity was a house of cards (all hog-wild)—with club feet of clay thrown in at no extra charge. They presumed too much—hadn't shared, as it turned out, as many magical moments as they still wanted to believe—and more to the point, make others believe—they had. Too many long silences during their reunions, planned or otherwise (and somehow they always found the time to squeeze in plenty). The only way to avoid acknowledging, in the cold light of out-of-van dawn, just how tenuous their bond had ended up becoming was to rustle up—invoke—some scapegoats—soon to become the *usual* scapegoats. (Heaven knows, Melanctha is as fond of Eden as ever—and by no other name would he smell anywhere as sweet—but that doesn't mean she's obliged to buy what he's selling—what the Master's *ordering* him to sell. Fact is, far too little time *appears* to have elapsed post-van to plausibilize this spate of hokey reunions or even just a single reunion. Nothing—not even insistence on their failure (an otherwise dependable illusionary agent) as reunions—can do the dirty work that a leisurely duration is trained to do. Yet again the Master—and he's welcome to hate her guts for calling his bluff—has [through pigheaded refusal to provide the minimal trappings of verisimilitude] deprived a prize packet of the wallop it had every right to expect to pack.) "And there are more usual scapegoats than we can handle, let me tell you: in fact, they almost outnumber us. Take the driver and his assistant (the unofficial tour guide), for instance." Not to mention the diva doubling as lavatory sentry who refused to remove her dark glasses, mink coat and pillbox—or was it a porkpie?—hat. They get bandied about a bit too often in an effort to drum up the enthusiasm needed to maintain the fiction of the bond—he means The Fiction of the Bond. Eden has known from the start that every time they busily spin them out to the crack of doom, their affinities add up to a mere concoction—four-and-twenty half-baked blackbirds without the pie. "Yet no less beautiful for all that, right?" Jean asks. The question makes *her* feel beautiful so there's no need for an answer. He explains that, to nourish the fiction, his buddies have taken to calling him Marty—Marty Boy, to be exact—but every time they utter the nickname he ends up on the witness stand nailed as an imposter. "Since I can't begin to fill Marty's shoes. Whoever he is. Still, I know I love my buddies and they love me because we do everything to hide it." How? well, for starters—and enders—by perpetrating, whenever they meet, the loveless hugs that are the order of the day and consist mainly of *there, there*-ish pats on the back. In which case it is to be understood that the patted must (since even if they're both patting, there's always the one who pats and the one who gets patted) be blubbering all over the microchip on his partner's cold shoulder and won't let up and hence is to be not so much consoled as humored. *There, there*, after all, signifies nothing so much as, *Keep your sweaty palms to yourself: I ain't no homo, bub*. So by the time subterfuge is done, the pats that dare not speak their nickname have come through this brief tragedy of flesh with flying colors.

Thing is, he can't help thinking (even if he can) that if the camaraderie post-van is wearing thin, it's because of *him*—because once within he refused to get some sleep—shut-eye, the driver called it—or, whether he slept or not, refused to at the very least make conditions ideal. Refused to draw the curtains on his anguish, so to speak, which had decided to set up shop in the depths of the glass. "I remember that," murmurs Shearer. "Me, too," counter-murmurs Jean (must have been in the moments, or hours or days, before she jumped ship), holding on to her newly self-bestowed beauty for dear life. "So you were in the van, after all," beams Cook. Though the beaming is filled to the brim with lustful admiration, Shearer is much too caught-in-the-act to take note of the tribute. Adding insult to injury, since her meeting with Akim, with its insurgency theme, she's come to distrust men more than she ever has—more even than after Balanchine refused to fall in love with her—or at least with her diagonalization of Dewdrop's irrepressible rapture. They must believe she's been trying to pass herself off as too otherworldly for the world of mere vans. And maybe that *was* the message. "Why?" asks Cook, in the tone of somebody who knows the answer. Yet Eden is too decent a human being to try to buy time by asking, *Why what?* So, layman or not, he gets right to the point. He convinced himself that any concentrated effort to make things ideal would, like caffeine, keep him awake all night. "But once a brain—and who knows this better than you, doc—" Unclear to which doc he's deferring, to make amends for crimes innumerable: they're turning out to be a dime a dozen in these sultry parts, their shamelessly exponential growth already giving the hoodie crowd a run for their bitcoin. And growth will only sky-rocket with pig-lipped Tom Pryce egging them on. At least according to the *Cemetery Times*. "—once a brain realizes it's trying to feed itself a-line-of-least-resistance like the one I concocted, it doesn't think twice about avenging itself—on itself." Which, in this case, meant keeping him up not just for one night but for as many nights as were needed to teach him a lesson—namely, that making conditions ideal for sleep is not a sleep deterrent and even if it is, the effect wears off pretty damn quick.

"Or maybe you didn't sleep to keep your memories of the Third World from getting consolidated—didn't want to play back and stabilize the nerve activity corresponding to what you must have learned there. And even for a slow learner like you, it must have been plenty." So Netta, clinician-castrative to the core—and to the bitter end. She continues, smelling blood. Maybe he didn't sleep to prevent the number of dendritic spines on which memories impale themselves deep down in the neuronal heaven of the motor cortex and the number of dendritic arbors in whose shade, once impaled, those memories bloom—maybe he didn't sleep to prevent both from growing. Maybe he's just not man enough to let memory retrieval—debriefing—take its course. Woman-hating Eden doesn't, even at such a ripe young age, take the shrew-bait. "And so how could he not wake up unapproachable and unforgiving—and toward the very people who'd taken to showing him the respect he didn't (and rightly so) think he deserved?"

Never mind what everybody else may think, Cantor is very much impressed with the new Eden—an Eden who's positively bursting at the seams with acuteness unimaginable before—and not just on matters homophobic. But there he goes again, Cantor also thinks, taking a chance not on love but on self-blame (*if the camaraderie post-van is wearing thin, it's because of* him)—Culpritude as it's called—or as it ought to be called—by, for starters, the CDC, the FDA and the *DSM* so as to draw attention through the catchiness of the word to the fact that the epidemic is super-spreading as fast as the wildfire of opioid addiction but among those, alas, who least deserve to be afflicted. This being the case, "culpritude" should be branded (*font: Lucida Blackletter*) into the forehead of, for starters, the new deadhead of the Department of Health and Inhuman Services—a wormy oozy felon who'd otherwise have no truck whatsoever with the process indexed by such a term—a process practically invented by Eden and propelled by his horrific non-doings—his unspeakable hallucinations of uncommitted acts—in Balboa Park (Eden's motto as a proud non-culprit?: It's *always the hallucinator who pays*). Cantor's referring of course to the aforementioned Pryce, that Pricey sack of scum (spelling of the surname shifts with the regularity of the tides), whose greedy pores are always erupting in a cold sweat and who—compliments, also for starters, of his pursy lips and sweaty brow—spittin'-images nothing so much as a pig panting to be (as an affront to pigs everywhere) craw-crammed with a candy apple and *slow-skewered by its own petard* (old Aleutian turn of phrase). Eden could teach the experts a thing or two: the meditation on man-to-man-hugging a veritable gem—as poetical as an aria out of—out of—out of—well, out of harm's way, if you must know. On his own terms Eden is outing himself, but as what exactly?—and while we're at it, isn't every life, even the most unsuccessful, an evolutionary outing, eh? "But forget about solidarity. More important is the van's route and what it managed to teach even me—me, by no means the aptest of pupils, let me tell you." It reminded him of his walks through the Financial District between his afternoon and evening doses to the extent that the further he strayed from his starting point (Ryders Alley, say) through what he took to be a labyrinth of freak thoroughfares (mis-exalted as streets for in fact they were much smaller even than alleys), the closer he got. "So what's the moral?" He doesn't have to turn around to know it's Netta shrew-baiting him again. Does the fact that he's always paid his rent on time down in South Beach count for nothing? Knowing that as a co-renter it does indeed count for something—more, much more, than something—Cantor tries hard to come to his rescue but he's too slow. By some mighty miracle, the moral has been yanked out of the transducer that is Martin's brain way ahead of schedule. And since by some fluke he's had the wherewithal to de-encrypt it, it's found to go something like this (caveat emptor: he finds himself using—or finds himself *in the very act of using*—four-, five- and six-letter words he didn't think he knew—words like *past* and *souls* and [yipe!] *bestow* and *beauty*): *The past always catches up with us: might as well admit that once upon a time we were the scum of the earth—nothing like the beautiful souls the world's contempt has forced us to become—and maybe an admission such as mine—I'm Martin! Who are you? Are you Nobody too?—will enhance our beauty—no! will bestow upon us the only beauty our kind can ever hope to know.* Netta clearly doesn't take kindly to the moral—and even less kindly to *Nobody* which has the moral wrapt around its little finger. Nothing as beautiful as a self-unmasking, especially from a moralizer ordinarily not given to unmasking, Cantor thinks. "Well, it isn't quite what I'd thought way back when in Ryders Alley but whatever I did think ended up thanks to the van as what you've just heard. But how does our girl Mary J expect to sell all this to the studios?" Some members of the audience laugh, halfheartedly. All—or most—of the others look sad—as expectantly sad as aspiring Pagliaccis who've just flunked the audition of a lifetime. "What gives?" Eden wants to—*er, rather,* looks like he wants to ask. Too impatient to wait for an invitation, Cantor takes the bull by the horns. "If everybody seems to have his nose in a noose" (and he looks right straight at *everybody* to show that what's to come is meant just for *him* and nobody else) "it's because everybody is waiting for the Knickerbocker Houses to resurface and for their saga to continue." No response. Still, Cantor has no intention of letting this little putz—this Ripper manqué—off the hook (why? why? why? well, in order to flaunt his erudition or his sensibility, whichever ends up first in line to offer him its heartiest congratulations for being *the* George Cantor—that's why). "So are you telling us we're supposed to think of the mighty Knickerbockers as a mere glowworm on the order of, say, one of the 'little themes' in Verdi's *Falstaff* which 'come in, flicker their wings once, and are gone forever'?"[161] Eden looks terrified—looks as if he'd like nothing better than to be cornered by the police so he can cry out at last that it was the gods—the Dark Gods in the funless old funhouse called Balboa Park—*who told him to do it.*

Thanks to Eden it's all coming back to Jean—the van business, I mean (who would ever have imagined a hick like him could be so forthcoming?—exalting forthcomingness into a kind of super- or is it hyper-decency?). She looked across at Ethan in the darkness, which wasn't so dark that she couldn't, alas, make out his puffy features or, more importantly, the black-bellied cumuli floating over the foothills—a showstopper—a specialty, she'd been told

---

[161] See Randall Jarrell, *Pictures from an Institution* (New York, Alfred A. Knopf, 1955), chap. 7 ("They All Go"), p. 257. And while you're there take a leisurely stroll through some of *Pictures'* other galleries.

(but by whom?), of both the season and the region—and not under any circumstances to be missed, whatever one's reasons for passing through. Quite frankly, she didn't know what to make of him. Sure, he'd had his moment of glory but fortunes capsized nowadays at lightning speed. You—she—might say the trial was one giant platform for super high frequency trading in futures and by the time they'd reached the bunker or some rest stop he might reveal that his share price had sunk to an all-time low—and blame it on the vehicle. It would be just like him. But she lost track of Ethan, or rather his future, because just then, the driver—one of several—shouted that they'd just passed 1250 Catalonia Street, the site of— Hard to know whether he was reproaching them for having missed out or exulting at their privation, only the first, surely, in what was to be a very long line. Toying with memory—with the excruciations of memory—whether as wax tablet or as aviary—requires mobility— which accounts for the fact that she's landed next to Borkman. Not because she wants to feel his warm body against hers—even if starved for the warmth she's done everything to keep at arm's length and even if he's still the man of the moment, the imminence of imprisonment only beefing up the legend of his voracious virility—but to mark a beat, the beat of her own indecision. But since life is nothing but unfinished business—she still needs to confirm that Ethan's share price is indeed at an all-time low. But assuming she's able, what will verification generate but the need to keep on verifying, over and over and over again, so that what's so certain as to be unverifiable will become such that not all the verifications in the universe will be able to yield the everlasting yea required to justify her abandoning him for good. She longs to make it all up to Caro, whom *he abandoned* (and whom she's taken it into her head to think she no longer envies, compote notwithstanding), by explaining in circumstantial detail just how wrong things went since no state of affairs truly exists—at least this used to be the case—until it's been metabolized by her sister, either in pouty silence or with noisy exasperation.

Now that Eden has let the cat out of the bag (but what cat? what bag? there's still been no mention of how debriefing proceeded in the van and what differentiated it from debriefing perpetrated everywhere else!), it's all coming back to Herbert as well. When she awoke in the frosty dawn it seemed weeks had passed—or months or even years. Not surprisingly, since any Master worth his salt (and *her* Master is, as duration's master illusionist, worth his salt in gold) sees to it first and foremost that the hordes who pay to watch his creatures suffer, feel (compliments of a process known as toothache-free duration)—the seconds fly by like years—like four score and seven decades— whereas for real creatures—the creatures outside the orbit of Master—outside his Castle Garden—a moment, if it's a moment of pain, and what moment isn't? may very well last for unportrayable centuries (so will He ever be able to forgive her for having dared only minutes before to call into question His way—His wickedly incomparable way—with the passage of time?).

Reaching back, over those centuries, to Eden, Ms. Johnstone says, "Leave all the rest to me." Walser and Stifter smile—stiffly. What will be left to them with her running the show? Well, that's the risk you run by switching careers amidstream. However, they mustn't forget (*who is speaking?*) she may still enable them to realize their dream, always unavowable, of *creating* while trendily soaking up plenty of lap-of-luxury LA sun. And Eden, getting on the bandwagon willy-nilly, can't deny—even before he finds himself a place to sit—that there's nothing to compare, after having been at the mercy of the elements for decades, with being taken in hand and for the first time in his young life told—no, ordered—not to worry 'bout a thing. Even Herbert finds herself getting a bit envious of Eden—hating herself for wondering whether Mary, if given the lowdown on Building 18, would consider pitching *her* tale of woe to the big boys. But how can she—worse than Ugolino, worse than Lucrezia Borgia—dare to think of cannibalizing her own son? Easy. Oh, and by the way, don't imagine for one second that our boy Borkman is exempt from such baseness, speculating as he already is as to whether, upon learning just how colorful his malfeasances—just how spirited the slumbering spirits of his gold—really are, she may not be able to swing a three-picture deal. (If only John Garfield, say, were alive to take on the role of a lifetime—many lifetimes.) So thanks to Magnetizing Mary, ever true to her semi-ridiculous name, their delusional aspirations are falling into line like so many iron filings.

But what's on (the tip of the tongue of) everybody's mind—uniting them without their knowing it (which makes for the best, or at least the most touching, kind of union)—is the question how many more reappearances of Eden must there be before—before—before—

Netta alone has the gumption—so don't write her off quite yet as a castratrix or as *only* a castratrix—not just to adroitly voice everybody's befuddlement but (far more impressively) to give it a heady comedic spin. What she says can, by your leave, be more or less robo-paraphrased as: "With my ex-apostles Stifter and Walser lurking conveniently about to translate Edenese into god knows what even more alien tongue and Mary to keep us all posted on the latest developments regarding Eden's imminent emergence as celluloid's most toothsome ingénu since Mickey Rooney, there's no telling how far they can go and—more to the point—how far they can drag the unsuspecting—aka you and me both—right along with them." George (Cantor to you, bub) is not amused since Netta started yapping at the very moment he'd begun thinking about what Mary could do for *him*. Could she sell, say, the story of his failed rehabilitations—the story of Berry Sundae's unsightly death—to the Weinstein Company (preferably before the trench shovel of scandal hacks it to bits)? Probably not but on a more sombre note, now that Netta mentions it or even if she doesn't, Stifter and Walser do look more than a bit like putrid Pence and rancid Ryan when in their implied niches they stood guard behind the Antichrist—in other words, a limp Prick weighed down by a pair of too too clean-shaven nuts—as he blustered his way through another one of those teleprompted guffaws his manhandlers have the gall to term an Address to the American people. But something about their signature tepid-smirky applause—flunkeys *with a twist*, as his mother might have said—licking their chops in anticipation of the old fart's impeachment-followed-by-assassination or assassination-followed-by-impeachment—something about the smirks fills Cantor, even if the unholy trinity are thousands and thousands of miles away, with a fear of his own foreboding . . . But on Eden's behalf, not his own. The image won't go away. Reptilian Mikey and Paulie, they're closer to Eden's jugular than he thinks.

Foreboding, foreshadowing. *But of what?* warbles Cantor to himself, like an oriole or Whitman's hermit thrush on a telephone wire in almost-over-looked midspring—Isn't what this is all about simply the inability of language—here and now all about implied niches and too clean-shaven *cojones*—to wait for its rightful moment—rightful moment for occupancy of its rightful niche—its very own boutique hotel—duly assigned somewhere in the mists of time? So the impatience of language—wordflow to you, bro—to have before it nothing less than worldflow's head on a charger—passes itself off as fore-shadowing—plot's worn-out handmaiden fresh from the convent, i.e., some tuition-heavy Writers Workshop down and out in Iowa, or is it in Cheney's Montana or Pence's Indiana or Ryan's Wisconsin? Language the turd that can't wait to get itself extruded from the smelly cheeks of some anti-Bard. Doesn't matter where it excretes itself as long as it gets itself excreted. Fact is—and Cantor seems to have known this from infancy—thoughts about Pence and Ryan should have—should—come later—when they're here in SB. Or maybe the thoughts should have come earlier when the Invidicum crowd were—that is, should have been—in DC in order to wax much too envious (over Pence's proximity to America's bard) not to acquire herd immunity to their afflic-tion. (After all, there was plenty to be envious about—and didn't sub-prime time media menstruators of all sexes proclaim that for the very first time The Rump had gone not ballistic not postal but . . . presidential—became pres-ident—Our President? So what if he used a Navy Seal's grieving widow as bait? And, hey, while we're at it, what's *your* favorite *very-first-time-he-became-president* moment?) But the Master seems to have insisted on United which was all booked up despite or maybe because of the fallout from that recent passenger-ejection disaster. Not of course a disaster for the passenger, mind you—Asian pulmonologist Dao (given name David—as Old Testament as it gets—to boot)—but a *PR* disaster, for United and its shareholding berserk-ers, which is far worse—nothing *worser*—and not just any old PR disaster but a disaster gone viral (but is there any other kind nowadays?) even before it started—nothing worser because the virus didn't seem to know that since United's a corporation, It's a bona fide person and like any person, It—like Wells Fargo and Navient—has feelings, too. So wordflow is either too late or too early—either too young or too old. Maybe heaven can wait but not lan-guage, not wordflow, never wordflow. For if United is a person then wordflow is an alarm clock that won't take some sleepyhead's No for an answer. But if a person—a real person, not a Person—a real sufferer—a real victim—gets lucky it ends up in bed with an alarm clock that's itself a victim to the extent that it's awakened by its own hyperalertness to the sufferer's pain. This kind of clock cries out for the sufferer—begs him to take his suffering as seriously as the clock takes it—for it's a doglike kind of clock hence, being more *exquisitely* human than the sufferer could ever be, makes it a practice never to exhibit scepticism where and when a bedmate's suffering is on the line. Its structural integrity is too unshakeably moral for such antics—indeed, it's *structurally incapable* of scepticism (*Moira: tell your toes to take heed*). The future, then, belongs (thinks Melanctha Herbert née Stein) not to orphans but to the alarm clock.

Translating the silence (uninterrupted, as far as she's concerned, by Netta's babble) to mean exactly that, i.e., *How many more reappearances?* Mary says (though a bit too defiantly for Shearer's taste: she's never thought of herself as a feminist), "How many? as many as it takes to clarify Eden's plight. Just think of those reappearances as suturing—like great music—a wound you're not aware you're festering (*vt*). Before you know it, you'll be screaming, *Bring back Eden*, in your sleep—not Eden as he will be or was or is but as he was meant to be." And Stifter (more Pence than Ryan) has to admit though he wouldn't dream of admitting it out loud that Mary in her prescience hears more of Eden's music than all of them combined. Of course, that's her job: to see more in her clients than everybody else combined, though how many people can be accused of doing their job? A willingness to translate from the Eden-ese, for example, doesn't exactly mean he believes in him: it means, in fact, there's nothing to believe in until he's translated, i.e., until he becomes something other than himself—in fact, the farthest thing from himself that any human can hope to become without giving himself away in the process. And so what if her doing good is inseparable from exploitation? There's a very fine line between the two even in the best of times. In fact everything depends on the direction from which you come at it—exploitation, I mean. For some people, it's a kind of ethical explosion—a moral obligation: they're no good as a do-gooder if they don't extract more than they put in. And this being the case, he dares anybody—anybody—to—to—separate the wheat from the chaff but if they do dare, only to succeed, then let him, Adalbert Stifter, be the first to celebrate what amounts not just to genius (any halfwit can get himself convicted of that nowadays) but to *sheer* genius. "So he's your hero," one of the start-uppers concludes. "Yeah, a real meatball," another hisses though nobody lowers himself enough to join in. Anyone wishing to do so must keep his hissing under wraps. As for those who want to guffaw—well, they must simply guffaw to themselves. Borkman suddenly realizes he doesn't know where he is or if he does, how he got there or who put him there. Is he downstairs—or is it upstairs—with the dying virgins or upstairs—or is it downstairs—with maxivan salesman Eden and his rapidly expanding entourage? But somebody has been quick to put in his head the idea that knowing where one is is a much overrated faculty—anybody can know that—the biggest nobody can know where he or anybody else is—and the bigger the nobody, the bigger the insistence on getting it right. And who says he, Borkman, doesn't have the right to be in two—or even four—places at the same time—upstairs and downstairs or (as on the West Fifty-Sixth Street of yesteryear) upstairs at the downstairs? It's the Master speaking, Herbert suspects—for she can read Borkman's thoughts through his twitches—the way Holmes read Watson. And what He's telling Borkman is that in these parts—in this accursed neck of the woods—geo-location—setting—time and place—decor—locale—premises—zip code—all boil down to Language—to—to—(*duck! here come those clowns again! those daffy doppelgängers forever incubating each other's fetuses*)—all boil down to *worldflow* alchemizing into *wordflow*. Why, the Master himself is the aptest of pupils when it comes to losing track of His own whereabouts, not to mention His agents', at any given moment but do you ever hear Him complaining? Not a peep. A little worried, maybe, because of his addiction to fixation—to routine—but uncomplaining withal. Since a megadose or two of dislocation never hurt anybody. In storyland, as every bumbler knows, flaws become outsize virtues to the extent that they unkennel the hunger to analyze their mighty resistance to getting simple story things right—things like character coordinates—latitude and longitude—direction— For an analysis of resistance done right—played to the hilt—even if it's to an empty house—is worth a million virtues. And that's a fact. So don't expect Eden, to be, say, half-asleep on the cot adjacent to Margo's gurney and at the same time NOT chatting it up with the tattoos on ward X fifty floors above.

But Johnstone has by no means completed her dissertation on repetition, if that's what it is. First off, she gets the usual commonplaces, as (and who knows this better than Cantor?) only she knows how, out of the way—to wit, that repetition makes you happy. That authentic repetition is recollection into the future. That repetition encloses the joyous security of the moment, adulterated neither by the restlessness of hope nor by flashbacking, inherently melodramatic, worthy of an Ophuls heroine. That one never grows weary of repetition because it's only the enervating lust for novelty which makes one so. That he who elects to will repetition is seven-league-boots mature and ten-gallon-hat manly and as head-over-heels in earnest as Wilde's Jack Worthing. That the only repetition is repetition's impossibility. That repetition is the beacon of metaphysics and the rocks on which it founders. That Berlin's Königstädter Theater is as good a place as any in which to test the possibility of repetition (and she defies anybody to say different). That repetition is an indestructible Paris original hewing ever so close to the body's voluptuous curves. That the only pregnant repetition is individual consciousness raised to the second power. That freedom's challenge—freedom, the progenitor of repetition—is to save personality from volatilization and enthrallment to contingency and consequent loss of eternalness. That there is repetition not only in the phenomena of nature but also (*pace* Prof. Heiberg) in those of the spirit "where the meanings are"—and (oops! before I forget!) that repetition is of course transcendence (in the words of the mighty Gottfried, *the present is big with the future*). In other words (as a concluding unscientific postscript), repetition is a life-or-death leap forward and the most difficult (hence the broadest) leap of all, inasmuch as it entails cleaving the air from a starting position identical to the take-off point and landing in record time on the same spot: a leap that's, come to think of it, a little like a decision taken on a matter already decided—by that very decision. "Think of it this way" (she rolls the eyes of her vocal cords at having to contend with so many dullards at one time, her coloratura trills conveying, to Herbert's envious ears at least, the assurance of somebody's favorite child—somebody infinitely more well connected than the Master). She explains—so deftly that even the dullards take note—that when they collide with some image—and not just a pornographic one—an image that really—*really*—excites them, it's as if it's chosen them, not they it. "You are rightly—or at least understandably—ashamed." But amid all the trappings of novelty their direct connection to the unspeakable, which defines them better than any number of biometrics (although such a connection—or rather, the capacity to *have* such a connection—is sure to become the best of that bunch), gets lost or, rather, camouflaged against accessibility to and from any number of Big Others. Their essence gets lost in the crowd of their hyperexcitations. "So it's only in going back—deciding to go back—needing to go back—that you manage to indict your own partiality, i.e., become one with the filthiness of who and what you really are. By choosing the image you choose yourself at last. For each one of you Eden is that image, that golden calf. And the more we bring him back the more it becomes clear—the hardest part for all of you—that he is not a sum of anodyne novelty items but a lethal essence that cauterizes yours. It's easy for your desire for Eden (the less it is sexual, the more it becomes unspeakable) to claim that it is this or that bit or piece of novelty that draws you back accidentally. So it is only by *repeating* him that the novelty is eroded and you are obliged to confront the essence of your image in the essence of his." Needless to say, she underscores, this unendurable self-recognition constitutes the purest form of freedom. *Try selling that to HBO,* Cook thinks, and not just Cook. "Now that's what I call repetition," applauds Netta. And, since Netta is so notoriously hard to please (or pretends to be), what better testament to MJ's savvy than this outpouring?

Is she implying, Cantor wonders—but keeps his wonder to himself and anyway what choice does he have?—that all of them desire Eden? This smacks of the Master's warmed-over trickery, as desperate as it is ingenious—smacks of an effort to exorcise—sanitize—the stench emitted by a particular truth— in this case that He's a voyeur, evidently—an image fiend—to skew it toward generality—the safety of numbers—the poor man's abstraction. How? by turning everybody into a fiend when nobody's looking, that's how. By letting Wordflow on His behalf decree what truth is supposed to be. But since when has ingenuity in the plane of the word ever disqualified its end product for greatness?

There's no reason for Walser not to ask, "Where were you for so long? Why didn't you speak about him like this eons ago? You might have saved him—and us—a lot of unnecessary anguish and, more importantly, legwork." Borkman, of all people, takes her defense, perhaps in the hope of ensuring the Garfield pic will be made even if (as is most likely) after he's dead—since Some Are Born Posthumously—since death, untimely or not, has an unfunny way of speeding things up when celebrity is at stake or in the air or, worse, in the cards or, worst, in the bag. A creator of sorts he alerts them to an alternative fact only the likes of Hatch Act baiter Kellyanne O'Kockenlocker could love, namely, that sometimes you need to get away from the work at hand if only by standing still and refusing to budge. "What I really meant was" (Walser tries to ignore this crook who's made a "forever" hobby [akin in spirit to a Forever *Chemical*] out of being not-quite-sentenced) "how could somebody so marginal—" A retort is in order and Herbert feels obliged to say out loud what everybody else must be just thinking—and timorously at that. As a black woman (the default excuse for standing her ground) she has nothing to lose. (But she's not quite sure who her target is. No matter—the words, once uttered, are bound to find a home in the next half-century with some worthy soul without a soul.) They should remember that by *getting away from the work at hand* as Borkman calls it (or did he?) it's easy to feel superior, aerated, unfettered, catbird-seated—whether the work's a super-sculpture or a wicker basket—easy to feel superior to the maker one took oneself to be seconds before—who as long as he's glued to the work is even more powerless than a termite. In a devoutly nasal tone, Johnstone (having assumed the slur about marginality applied in some weird way to her, not Eden) replies, "Waiting in the wings is also a vocation, not just some bywork. But we simply must get a move on, people." And over her shoulder she delivers herself of the following throwaway: "Don't work so hard" (but like Melanctha she isn't sure *who her target is*). And while nobody works harder than Mary (notwithstanding the foully pilloried cigarette break though there's no discounting that she herself may have started the rumor) she clearly gets a kick—or a thrill—out of Parthian-shooting this aerosol of advice, compliments of which she's become Other—an anti-self—somebody who lets things roll off her back—somebody with a savvy sense of how to adroitly manage the "work-life balance" (to use a term Melanctha and the Master have separately come to hate more than any other except maybe "closure" or, better yet, "passion" as a euphemism for that filthy four-letter word "calling")—of when to toil and when to have fun. And if she's as much of a freewheeler as those four little words, through having been breezily dumped on somebody else, proclaim her to be, then the dumpee must automatically embody her starkest opposite—an overly scrupulous default drudge. So why does Melanctha (who's greedily taken the words to be directed at her and her alone) end up feeling she's somehow beaten MJ at her own game? Why? well, because in Melanctha's neck of the woods "drudge" is an honorific—a weapon of atonement—suggesting an infinite capacity for stoical and sacrificial self-punishment inflicted ever more deliriously in the foreknowledge that a recompense in the form of . . . greatness is waiting just around the bend (like a confederate there to greet you when you're finally out on parole).

CHAPTER FIFTY-EIGHT

Descending to street level by elevator or stairs for yet another runaround (the Master's Boynton Beach dinner theater folks must be getting a bit fatigued even if they're not the ones to be running), everyone knows he's about to visit (or in some cases revisit) the vans, though nobody can say who's suggested—ordered them to do so. (At last and at least everybody now knows his own and everybody else's coordinates—knows exactly where he and everybody else is located, i.e., between—and it doesn't get any more precise than that—the vans and Monocerotis.) But hurry, they might be towed by the police who have little enough to do in so quasi idyllic a beach town. Herbert is aware this new wrinkle will surely result in an increased workload for the force (a mixed blessing to public servants since while it proves there's no time for idleness, hence for Big Government-dismantling layoffs, busyness does have a way of eating into sacred downtime). And though she'd like to whisper something in honor of her awareness, what the whisper ultimately conveys is something else—and the conveying gets done somewhere (as it turns out) in, of all places, the vicinity of Shearer even if they're no longer—but were they ever?—on the best of schoolgirlish terms. (And how *can* they be, given this snooty hoofer's inherent scepticism about her [and probably anybody else's] suffering, which in Melanctha's case dates all the way back to a specialty Szechuan dive on Ninth Avenue—or was it Tenth? or Eleventh? [*now you know very well, Melanctha, that it was and will always be the Almighty* Twelfth *so turn off the spigots of almighty Uncertainty. Don't expect to get any mileage out of It for the moment*].) But Shearer or no Shearer, what the whisper ends up releasing is the aerosol of a fervent hope that Johnstone's decision (on behalf of unseen advocates) to lead them astray (though there's no digressing from the self no matter how hard one tries—no getting away from despair, which all boils down to lucidity undimmed by an object—a kingdom without a horse)—a fervent hope that her decision is not just a symptom of the Master's craving—more like a hornet's nest of craven impulses—to bring this whole disaster to a close on the back of some ploy cooked up on short order to generate the storybook illusion of inevitability run amuck—the illusion of a super-satisfying resolution of the I affair which takes no loose ends prisoner. And what produces such a factitious effect better (at least from the perspective of somebody like the Master who enjoys nothing so much as to rub everybody's face in the muck of His own factitiousness—of His own incompetence—an incompetence so vast and so transparent and so *committed* as to become—almost—a subspecies of craftsmanship—a little fiefdom within craftsmanship's domain)—what produces such an effect better than a reprise—dragging everybody and everything back into the circus ring à la *Otto e Mezzo*, as if to say—as if to say (so *say* it, goddammit!)—as if to say that nothing, unfortunately, is irrelevant—no thought safe from impressment into the royal navy of narrative—every event a retrospective life-changer—hierarchization not just forthwith verboten but a thing of the prehistoric past. (Melanctha wonders: *Are the angels of incompetence and mediocrity ever able to dance compatibly on the head of the same pin at the same time? can incompetence, if probably deployed, exorcise the demon of mediocrity and thereby open the floodgates of a kind of . . . competence the world has never seen? Can mediocrity and incompetence thus allied go to make a pretty bride?*) What the whisper conveys is the hope that Johnstone's decision is not merely a symptom of the Master's desire to show—for there's nothing he relishes more than showing (but always as if in spite of himself)—just how tenuous is Invidicum's relation to all the goings-on and that the even greater tenuity of their relation to each other is inversely proportional to the breadth of Its efforts to get into the act. In a word or two, what the brave little aerosol conveys is the hope that Johnstone's decision is not just a symptom of this or that ailment of the Master but A New Beginning—characterizable by nothing so much as a hewing close to what the Master hates most, i.e., the Invidicum Story—precisely because it *is* a story—whether it ends up a Netflix-streamed blockbuster or not.

No—as it turns out, the reason for a return to the vans is much simpler: the need to get Eden's memories extincted once and for all. Word on the Street just in—they're more trouble than they're worth. Breaking news (is there any other kind nowadays?): No mogul in his right mind would touch 'em. The sea air has compelled Mary to see, at long last and not a minute too soon, which way the wind is blowing and it's not just any old ill wind but the sort (as perhaps already described above) that—defying proverbial odds—blows nobody good.

"Are we allowed to go in the water?" Shearer asks. Melanctha's whispered remark has left her untouched—her hopes, after all, are not Melanctha's kind of hopes for Moira's are all too transparently of the meat-and-potatoes variety: To succeed or not to succeed—to make a comeback or not to make a comeback—to fail at failure or not to fail—that sort of thing. The air *is* rather sticky, even Netta must *admit* (and even with the sun blazing made-to-be-broken promises of dry heat) but immediately there are hostile glances directed at the question, whose sole raison d'être surely must be to imply that they aren't free agents but, like pre-pre-Ks, must be forever asking permission of the Headmistress to do anything—whether it's to pee, preen or perjure themselves. (Or more to the point shove a dildo up their collective ass. The way The Rump's crowd does druidically before every Mar-a-Lago mini-summit cum fundraiser.) By temperament, Netta would seem to fit the bill—that is, to have her work cut out for her as Headmistress, *or* The One who Admits and Lives to Tell the Tale (being every bit as ambiguous as Moby Dick she deserves a double title)—though with all that pancake expertly applied (substrate of her *bad* narcissism—the part that's unleavenable by wit, unfumigable by a breath or two of self-caricature) she looks more like some run-of-the-mill anorexic Park Avenue dowager (with an upgraded nose badly in need of an upgrade for the upgrade) trying to pass herself off as what she inexorably is—hence with no time to *admit* to anything. Even as his landlady (and if there were any justice in the world, Netta would have obligingly crawled straight out of Gogol's Overcoat, say, and into the darkest crannies of his personal Internet) she's still a mystery to Cantor—or rather she's no more mysterious than his intuitive sense that there is no mystery—just a pretext (saying so is a dirty job but somebody's got to do it and do it right) for articulating one, with all credit redounding to the articulator, to whose everlasting glory Netta is now just an accessory—an adjunct—and will (if she's lucky) be footnoted once or twice in the history books as such—no more, no less.

Eden's success story—if success story is what it is—has clearly gotten out of hand in a way even Cantor's superior powers of perception can't quite pin down or why else would they be headed for the vans? Gotten out of hand, even if he's paid dearly for the privilege—through murder, rape, coprophagy and autophagy and with other misdemeanors, real or imagined, not far behind.

A hush comes over the proceedings, if that's what they are. Yet, the silence appears to be fruitful, for somebody at least. One of the start-uppers cries out, with Jim, Jr., standing right next to him (if only his mother could see her way clear to calling a halt to all bellyaching long enough to take a good hard *prideful* look at this chip off the old block whose success story is just panting to unfold), or maybe there are several crying out—crowing—in unison, "What about that—that—window—Stifter mentioned when nobody was listening? Ages ago, I—we—mean." Obviously, the fresh air enables them to smell an opportunity: an app of a different color on the horizon—SiVa's equivalent of the kind of dream gadget—a rose in the shadows, say—that any byzantine versifier with a chauffeured houseboat on the Seine would give both his right arms to fondle.

"The reconsolidation window?" Walser counters gruffly—his own way of taking up the cudgels for his pal—through thick and thin.

"You mean the window of reconsolidation? Yeah, that's it."

"Why do you ask?"

"We think it has possibilities."

"Stay tuned," says Jim, pleased to be mastering a lingo that's well on its way to archaization, even extinction.

It's only when they're out on the street that Herbert realizes how much has been squeezed into one evening. How could one sequence encompass so much duration? she asks disingenuously of the dawn, which promises to ponder the paradox first chance it gets (right now, it has its hands full taming the antics of a school of borderline-obese cumuli up to sunrise-smothering no good). Father Time has in fact been abused—even sodomized. But the Master must have known changes of scene would have only dissipated the accumulated energy, not to mention (at least not to a pennypincher like Him) the cost of additional sets. The monologues alone (was there much else and why should there be?) gobbled up at least two election cycles, with the usual surfeit of mediocrities—knockoff Rasputins one and all—on the make.

As if he were a mind reader—and he's proved himself enough of one, surely, to be within his rights to cram the fact into his CV—Cantor ponders the matter out loud—or at least adopts a pondering tone so as not to make poor Melanctha feel she can't answer her own queries, with time to spare. He begins—and ends—in the key of reassurance. You don't have to be Einstein—or *an* Einstein—to know it's simple beyond your wildest dreams: They've been able to squeeze so much duration into so brief an interval (if somebody were dumb enough to put all this pondering in a mere novel, nobody would believe he—and it—had a right to exist) because there are some acts—monologuing being the best of the bunch—which by virtue of their very texture take not just your breath away—not just your labor and your leisure, too—but your very sense of time passing—why, before you know it, monologuing or one of its buddies has perversely accreted enough of itself *to* itself—the way wavelet noises make an ocean roar—to make you late for any number of very important dates—that of your first death spasm (as a complication of chronic apathy), for example. Better yet, monologuing or any other act of that stripe allows you to relish—to finger—NO, to finger-fuck, if you will—its abjuration (like The Rump's on Insurrection Day) *of all personal responsibility* (in this case for lateness-making)—an abjuration motored by the illusion of having so many better things to do (like hearing itself think)—which means monologuing comes out smelling even more like a rose than the one that's (crouching in the shadows cast by the Pont Neuf) been recruited to serve as the SiVa crowd's Next Big Inspiration for a Next Big Thing—which is always some dewy-eyed app of a thousand faces. In grateful response for Cantor's SOS, glueing elbows to ribs Herbert diverges her forearms, palms upraised, as if to say—and in fact she *is* saying it loud and clear—*There you have it.* Exactly like, Moira thinks, the Blue Boy (too many times to count) in *Les Patineurs.* Cook, a bit red-eyed, asks Ethan, who's also a bit slow on the uptake from all the loud talking and even louder thinking and even louder *deep*-thinking, whether they're to be transported in higher style this time around, compliments, say, of Prisoner Transportation Services—specialists in extradition to faraway jurisdictions for serious crimes like stumbling into a Backwater boardroom uninvited and incurring the wrath of Betsy's sleazeball near-twin. Or compliments of one of its subsidiaries—U.S. Prisoner Support or U.S. Corrections, to name just a few. Or better yet Shackles-For-Profit U.S.A.—an especial favorite of supervermiform Rump lackey Wilber [*sic*(k)] Ross (yet another among The Rump's way too many anti-elitist lackeydaisical billionaires cum part-time Saudi sword dancers extraordinaire). While Borkman has his own especial soft spot for PTS as the first to come forth and righteously maintain what all of its competitors have cravenly refrained from even alluding to, namely, that provision of seatbelts, onboard medics and bona fide tampons (not gum wrappers) to prisoners with the audacity to menstruate en route offers a prime demonstration of how throwing good money after bad undoes everything that's being done by true patriots (like unsightly Wilburr) to Make America Grate Again. PTS, one might add, has also been the first of the tribe to establish a Boilerplate Stable in its Legal Subdivision. So that when fielding too many but not enough criminal investigations crafted to lead nowhere, the for-profiteers can trot out some horse's ass to assure the public, including even, albeit kicking-and-screamingly, the unworthy parents of the kids raped and murdered onboard, that PTS is of course cooperating with the relevant authorities but given the slew of ongoing autopsies *is unable to make any additional comments at this time.* Ethan shrugs—hasn't the faintest idea and couldn't care less. He has unhealthier things on his mind. Doesn't Cook know Jean is leaving him for—for— But before Ethan can name the lucky devil Jean herself cuts in (and for the sole purpose of delivering—COD or

DOA or both—a peck on the cheek to her soon-to-be-ex) then goes back to working the room. When she's out of earshot, Ethan makes haste to *confess* (deploying the word with air quotes) that he hates her, has tried many times to shake her senseless. He has nothing to lose now that she's leaving him. Though he'll miss the forbearance game they've been playing for what seems like centuries—the aim being to come out smelling like the more tolerant of the two—the one who shuts his trap on behalf of a decency that's light-years beyond the capacity of the other. Though no Son-of-Sam mystic, Ethan is convinced (at least while he's doing the shaking) that he must kill her to keep a promise with his god. "Sounds like a cry for help," says Cook, glad to be of help. Ethan nods fervently. Yes, he wants her to deliver him from the hate she's induced—from the inviolability of his own feelings—from his selfhood. To Herbert, who's very much *within* earshot, Ethan seems to be poaching on Eden's preserves. For isn't murder as a cry for help (cf. the Balboa Park affair) Eden's domain now and forever—the domain of the terrifying inviolability of the self? But what does any character's domain in the Master's universe—in His charnel house of many mansions—amount to? Not much. 'Cause fluidity is the Master's million-dollar baby if not quite yet his cash cow. Here character is fluid—as volatile as mutual funds—as fluid as (another helping of air quotes, if you please, Maestro) the "characters" in Balanchine's *Liebeslieder Walzer*. Well, I do declare and whaddya know—here's Herbert poaching on *Shearer's* preserves. Poaching, then, is catching in these parts. Fearing retribution, she wants to impassively implore (as she imagines a soon-to-be-whacked traitor would implore his Don's achingly clean-cut *consigliere*, all the while knowing full well that the quality of mercy won't be strained . . .)—wants to hear herself wail, *Moira, can you help me out here?*

Herbert's musings are interrupted by the others, all of whom concur: It's been an awfully long night. But from their expressions it's clear that consensus comes in all conceivable shapes and sizes to the extent that some appear to belong at the opposite end of the spectrum—where Freedom Caucus dissenters loom large. So that what at first she took for a consensus may actually turn out to be . . .

But Herbert—Mistress of Ceremonies, so to speak—needs to start having other things on her mind—or at least *in* mind. She has to go on ahead and get things ready. If the beach is their destination (who cares if the plan started out as a joke self-perpetrated by the architect thereof?), what does it bode—signify—except that Herbert must marshall all her sources, resources, excavate deep into herself—for a playoff between the in- and the extrinsic—and come up with whatever will be needed to set the scene. The intrinsic being what is inimical—worse, irrelevant—to the preparations. Inevitable that the thankless task should fall to her share. But what do you say—or do (depending on whether all this scurrying to and fro and back again is being conducted under the attribute of Thought or of Extension)—about a beach on the subject of which everything—and then some—has already been said—a beach that *has* everything—that's seen and done everything? She has an unfunny feeling something's happened to the Master (both vampire and transfuser from where she's standing) although as Substance He's inextinguishable. Or supposed to be. Margo's deathbed trumpery, maybe, has been too much for him. So she will have to don the mantle—no matter what people may end up saying about how she acquired it—which means in this harsh world drawing her breath in pain to tell the story but what has she ever done—if she's anything like Him—but mar a story with the telling of it? She, his Cordelia. His favorite in an underworld of Gonerils and Regans. And as His favorite she must be true to His code, which means being far less interested in setting the scene than in the difficulty of setting the scene, i.e., the drama of His inability to play the game—the skin game. Inability to play being, as it turns out, the endlessly *productive* drama par excellence. It's up to her—as His favorite—to run the gamut and gauntlet of that drama—she, the pivot point of His self-sabotage. Up to her—as His unavowable favorite—to resolve the vector of His solitude—His impasse—into the components it never knew it encompassed—up to her to transform hefty impasse into a thing of too many shreds and too many patches —a last supper of too many apostles—too many, at least, who bear a striking resemblance to Pence and Price and Pruitt and Ryan and Putzder and Prints and Papadopoulos—and still counting. But—yet—still—through her dead-man-walking intuition (and, at second hand, thanks to podium-crazy Jean's account of her East Village misadventures) who knows better than Melanctha what so often befalls favorites in that underworld—where devotion breeds contempt and sometimes more? The burning question is, Does He still have time to turn into one of those bargain-basement patriarchs whose perversity requires that they asslick only those offshoots—offspring—scion—for whom it's a matter of principle not to take orders, least of all from an old fart like him or—if it makes him feel better—any old fart? Serpent's Tooth each and every, who, when paying him a deathbed visit, will announce, after only a few minutes—will have arrived only *to* announce—that as it so happens they've got a plane to catch so if he has any decency left he'll get on, deathbed or no deathbed, with the business of croaking on schedule. And with all that bargain-basement patriarchal perversity designed simply to convert, by implication, the devotion of folks like her into—to frame it as—a kind of stupidity—worse, bad taste—for what does devotion achieve except to remind him he's about to meet his Maker, i.e., himself—in contrast with the breath-of-fresh-air indifference of the Serpent's Tooth crowd, which signals imminent rehabilitation—cure—no-holds-barred immortality? The Serpent's Tooth gang know he's strong enough to survive their callousness—he knows the callousness sets an example and will make him strong. And so convicted, will she see fit to take the line of least resistance and contract the virus of perversity herself in order to be able to praise the rightness of that indifference—to be able to praise the Serpent's Tooth Irregulars for having the guts to make hay at the old fart's expense—to be able to pass the buck and praise Them and Their indifference to some third—or sixth—party—some poor slob (like Jean's touchingly spineless ex- or soon-to-be ex-husband)—some third party known to be doing poorly on his current dosage (since Life is a vast hospital) and who would probably do worse on any other—some poor slob who'd (and who wouldn't?) only end up unsure (and not just because his bloodstream is a sea of unexcretable metabolites) about exactly who or what happened to be the target of this broad's (yes, *broad*'s) vile propagandizing on behalf of obscene selfishness but in the sugarcoated name of life affirmation—some hapless bystander like that pal of Shearer's who's always skulking about—well, maybe not exactly skulking: more like lurking—more like looming—Akim! that's his name!—Akim as stand-in for the world at large (minus the loathsome off-shoots and offspring and vile get, of course)—Akim as quintessential (or at least essential) fall guy—since by praising them she simultaneously indicts him—for not *being* them—for not being a wolf in wolf's clothing and for not giving her license thereby to become one herself even if it's the last thing in the world she wants in fact to become—and better to indict him than herself—or if not him, then his silence—his silence, a bystander even more innocent than he himself—better to indict him on trumped-up charges—better to play the blame game (chock full of *woulds* and *shoulds* and *coulds* and *ifs*) and indict him for having led her astray way back when, preferably before he or she was born—better to indict him for having fostered Melanctha's proclivity for self-ablation by compelling her through the sheer force of example to mimic his own—to mimic his cradle-to-grave death-in-life life-as-death project of standing in the way of his own will to power and following it wherever it might lead? Better to indict him even if—especially because—she's got him all wrong and her willful misinterpretation is fed by a hunger to nullify her own essence as long as there's some guru—some mentor—some model—to blame for having saddled her with the permission to do so. Better to indict him than herself—than her forbears who should have known better. Even if it means getting him all wrong—even if what she takes—needs to take—for self-abla-tion all boils down in his case to the going backward appropriate—essential—to somebody who's about to take a great leap.[162] Imagine accusing him—him, of all people—of trying to manipulate her into giving up—mimicking his addiction to failure—to self-unentitlement. He, of all people, who, as a practi-tioner of the termite art of choreography, is always moving mountains—always fulfilling himself mightily—since mighty mountains from little mole-hills grow—he, Akim, whose spasms of apparent inertia are simply medita-tion—closed-eye seeing—and who couldn't give less of a shit about whether the experts cotton to his work or not—who in fact feels most *entitlemented* with all his heart and soul *not* to self-ablate—not to self-cancel—when they're at their busiest making expert dissatisfaction known. So clearly he'd be the wrong fall guy since he ain't a fall guy and never will be even if SAB stops churning out dancers. And, while we're at it, neither is Melanctha a fall guy since she'll never give anybody the satisfaction of seeing her self-ablate—nei-ther a fall guy nor a Goneril. But—thing is, she wants this particular thought packet to get through customs whatever it takes and at any price—more for the Master's sake (playing Edie [Wharton] to his Hank [James]) than for her own. Even if she and Akim are the least plausible concretizers of the dynamic it lays bare—even if, by the way they live, the two of them flout every unspo-ken law of that dynamic (under which one party unrelentingly blames her will

---

[162] Thanks, Friedrich. See *Beyond Good and Evil*, part nine, entry 280.

to paralysis on another's—the Other's—imposed example). Jean and her ex- or Jean and Ethan would be a much much better fit, hands down. But they have other fish to fry, and she hasn't got all day, and time is of the essence, and haste makes waste, and there are none so blind as will not see the road to hell is paved with good intentions.

But what would Liepnits say—have said (not about the dime-a-dozen offshoots but about things extrinsic to the beach or rather to the beach *sequence*), at least in the great days lasting about a minute when it seemed, in honor of Irena, he'd thrown off the yoke of the Ozarks forever. Well, if she knows Newt, which she doesn't—doesn't in fact know him from Adam—from Akim—he'll say her soul bears the outlines of everything required hence she mustn't think she's depleted enough to need to go a-begging of the world. But wait, let him deliver the breaking news in his own words. No longer in the vicinity of Irena—of death—he looks—or at least sounds—ten years younger. Nothing, he assures her, would please him more than to help out. Is he by any chance hitting on her? Is his short-term goal to make her wife No. 4, or is it 5? as the sole means of pandering to the black vote—the sole means of atoning for all the terrible things he said way back when about, e.g., Strapping Bucks on Welfare—of atoning for self-inclusion in the very demographic that creams in its pants every time that racist Rumpelstiltskin Jeff Shessions long- drawls his pietistical slime—the sole means of appealing to the Forgotten Man whose entrails are the last refuge of scoundrels? Thing is, nobody who voted the fat-ass ticket thinks of himself as The Rump's Forgotten Man—it's always the figment of The Rump's imagination standing next to him—or a few fig- ments away.

With Melanctha standing beside her man he'll have no trouble master- ing—will have mastered—the art of purveying sincerity, i.e., dissimulation, since in these pursy times how can they not be identical (*who has just thought this bit of what-if whimsy? Newt? Melanctha? the Master? the Master's proctol- ogist in chief? the Master's concierge medico team?*)? With Melanctha he'll have Kentucky's fried chicken and Berkeley's Berkeley—right and left—substance *and* shadow—in the palm of his greasy paw. But getting back to basics: carry- ing on in the great tradition of the Master (she didn't know he'd heard of—or believed in the existence of—the Master), she should, at this point, be able to unearth the Beach she carries unknowingly within herself. By now she should have reached that point in her life where the soul in torment refuses to go on rendering the outside world its overrated due and ignoring the procurative fire within—for the fire's there. Her soul isn't a tabula rasa—it just gives a bad imitation of one. It contains inherently the sources of all the various doctri- nal notions of the Beach. Even if, because they're *potential*, she doesn't know they're *there*. Just as she doesn't know that at this very moment her perceptions of the noise of every wave are also *there*, mounting, mounting, mounting, always mounting—doesn't know, that is, until they've amalgamated into the inescapable perception—the *ap*perception—of the ocean's roar. If Melanctha learned anything in school, i.e., Building 18—her Harvard and her Yale—it should have been that she's a veritable hive of Prolepses or *koinai ennoiai* or Scaligerian *zopyra*. But enough bargain-basement metaphysics even if he's the very first politician-in-training in US history to be a first-rate scholar. And to prove it and much more, he's the first one into the belly of the van—i.e., a rotten egg if ever there was one, or is it always the *last* one in who's rotten to the core? But why a van for so short a distance and on what promises to be such a beautiful day in this slow-growing suburb of Narc City. Why build up speed when take-off is indistinguishable from arrival? Shearer inquires of herself. Even if there can be nothing more intriguing. Silliest of sylphides! has she forgotten the last of the three preliminary variations in *The Four Temperaments* (she *cut the eye teeth of her instep on that terpsichorean tongue—or rather, toe— twister*—an ordeal as mangled and mixed as—as—as—as—well, as this metaphor which has just dropped out of nowhere to depict it) at the moment when the girl slides into a supported crouch and pivots, on pointe, within the smallest possible radius—the goal being expansion through contraction (for which she's amply rewarded by being poignantly dragged off into the wings Eurydice-style)—extension never more extended than through its suppression—than through re-education of the heuristically dead leg muscles—expansion as a mockery of expansion—a mockery of the analysis of expansion? And isn't pivoting on pointe within a smaller and smaller radius à la *Temperaments* in fact the dancerly—or rather the anti-dancerly—portrayal of what it means to train oneself to "go apotropaic" (and save one's skin) across tinier and tinier time intervals? After all, anybody can anticipatorily enact (in order to parry) an event scheduled for hours—days—years—from now but only a real virtuoso is able to mimic down to the last detail (in order to ward off) mortal danger about to erupt in a minute or two. But whatever such pivoting portrays or doesn't portray there are times, though few and far between, when a master portrayer wants to inhibit himself (she can feel Mr. B. getting angry with her: maybe better than anyone else [*self-inflation, Moira?*] she knows that infrequent but unmistakably impatient look)—wants to rip off the mask of his facility—to peel off the skin of his Genius to get at the blundering Everyman beneath—and to see if he can come up with something better than Genius—better than the applause machine that's always dogging Its footsteps. Or is this just the wordflow doing the thinking for the two of them?—wordflow stealing the sideshow with a perversity worthy of the Master patriarch (see above). The van is the Master's prosthetic pivot and the Master is the van's prosthetic god.

Deposited at the end of the Wharf with all—or most—of the others, Herbert thinks (disregarding Liepnits's Ozarks-tested recipe), Well, here at least is something to conjure with. For, whaddya know, a gray gull with a yen for the far horizon has just dived into the water . . . *either to escape her and her kind or to seize some just-sighted prey*. Which isn't just any old detail: it's a percept drawn and quartered by a thought that's deep enough to underpin—to sum up—the whole life of the beach and its accessories and isn't it always the case, at least with her, that precisely when she feels all is hopeless, what should come along but just such a percept to bitter-sweeten the pill of existence—her existence—her existence as nothing but a perpetual wearing out of the welcome of . . . Existence Itself. *Frailty, thy name is wordflow.*

But here's Liepnits again (she saw him get on but she doesn't remember seeing him *in* the van)—no slouch when it comes to wearing out *his* welcome—taking the time to take her aside, no matter what he himself is going through as a widower-to-be, and reminding her that she's got to put aside childish things though not necessarily once and for all—that is, if she's as dead serious as she claims about preparing the beach for the beachcombers. For he knows what she was looking at—and, worse, he knows what she was thinking when thought turned its back on the looking. "You talk as if I were gobbling up a semi-pornographic film." "Worse, much worse." Has she forgotten what he took the trouble to teach her back at the McChateau? Is she dumb enough to think it no longer applies down here where in fact it applies most? "You mean, that there's plenty innate to my mind, far more than I know?" He nods apoplectically. Exactly. Since she's *innate to herself.* Is her soul so empty that if it doesn't borrow images from outside it's nothing, with the Master's lifework becoming a great big nothing in tandem? "For you see, I know all about the master—I mean, the Master. How can I not know since Irena rants and raves about him more and more in her sleep? Has some sort of posthumous crush on the old geezer. Takes him for a *role model* (Irena the cat woman hates the word *guru*—and who can blame her? though her idea of a replacement isn't much better, if you ask me). As the saying goes—or should go—the grass is always greener in somebody else's catacomb—or is it somebody else's *crapper*? But, seriously—in the block of marble that's Melanctha's immortal soul there are if anything *too many* veins marking out the shape of too many Herculeses to come. So many Herculeses—so many beach goddesses—incarcerated within. Of course labor will be required to expose the veins and polish them. Question, is there world enough and time? Enough time, I mean."

She's grateful for his having taken her aside but enough, as they say, is more than enough or is what they say, in fact, that much too much is not—never—nearly enough? But whatever it is *they* say or, worse, are reputed to say, she gets what *she* says—gets her own drift, so to speak, however obfuscating, which is all that counts and which is all one can ask of any man—woman. There's nothing innate to her—and if there is, it stinks. For what's, after all, Hercules to her or she to Hercules—or is it Hecuba?

Everything of any value comes strictly and solely from without—in present circumstances, from the waves. A wave is, if you must know, the emissary of a thought (which, like a dolphin out of Aesop, it carries gallantly on its back)—it's a readymade, there for the taking—and she's training her mind to be its very own master in running aground (at that frontier condemned to play host to the endless litigation of rival divinities—a transaction both perpetual and inconclusible, with Poseidon casting off such flotsam as Earth will never learn how to retain, much less transmogrify[163])—in running aground those waves capable of leaving a usable silt behind since she's after a different though not necessarily a better kind of flotsam. And it just so happens

---

[163] Passage on the litigation of sea and shore was triggered by the dialogue entitled *Eupalinos; ou, L'architecte,* in Paul Valéry, *Eupalinos; L'Âme et la Danse; Dialogue de l'Arbre* (Paris, Gallimard, 1959).

that while they've been speaking (though in fact they've been spending more time, as measured in minute hands, just staring out to sea) and in contravention of all his warnings, not one measly petite perception has dared to rear its ugly head, much less cross her path. That's because Melanctha, whose nom de plume but only for today is Eupalinos, has cut her teeth—albeit not, like Shearer in another context entirely, her eye teeth—on the shenanigans of a Master whose bread and butter cum stock in trade (as an apex sexual predator of the old school—the kind who moves in with his daughter and her dorm mates at a posh Ivy League finishing school and, without anybody blinking an eye, camps out there nefariously through graduation day) is to intimidate his victim mentees with a lot of fancy talk about those very perceptions (aka minute perceptions, semi-sufferings, and rudiments of/dispositions to/ preparations for suffering), which according to Him enable their vector to "act the more quickly by instinct," "not be troubled by excessively distinct sensations of hosts of objects which, necessary though they are to nature's plan, are not entirely agreeable" and "*enjoy the advantage of evil* without enduring its inconveniences"[164] (whatever that means) but which Melanctha has learned fast enough (since nobody born in the Bronx was ever *Born Yesterday*) can be far more "evil" than the non-minute, non-petite, non-rudimentary, meat-and-potatoes versions of the species. In a minute or two, the fee for the privilege of hearing the full roar of the sea without having been obliged to first undergo those pesky little perceptions, ever mounting, will be a messy orgasm in broad daylight (in any event, a small price to pay for apperception in its pure state)—maybe even several orgasms. She lets the widower-to-be know he shouldn't worry—she should have no trouble parasitizing the Beach Without for there's no Beach Within to distract her from her duties. Can she mention all this without appearing to brag? Of course she can but that doesn't mean she does—or should. "Now what's this connection you're making, young lady, between petites perceptions and the Master's bread and butter?" asks Liepnits, theatrically hesitant about bursting her bubble. "Or is it by any chance just another example of Masterly sleight of hand? (about which Irena for one babbles adoringly in her sleep)—a Masterly attempt, when nobody's looking, to elide a disjunction—to bring Hanoverian black-sheep abstraction into the fold of storytelling at its comfy cozy unabstract best? to make it relevant—organic—to the joys and sorrows and pipe dreams and disappointments of real live—that is, envy-crazed—humans?" (By the way, in tonight's performance, the role of the real live human will be played by . . . Melanctha, a first-class beachcomber if ever there was one, who has all she can do to fend off the advances of the Master—Massa. With his sweat stinking of garlic—and his unimpressive crotch, of semen—he's followed her out into the cotton fields—for what unbeknownst to him is to be the very last time. Finis. End of miniseries. Time for years of what members of the actor

---

[164]G.W. Leibniz, *New Essays on Human Understanding*, translated and edited by Peter Remnant and Jonathan Bennett (Cambridge, United Kingdom, Cambridge University Press, 1989), Book II: Of Ideas; chap. XX ("Of modes of pleasure and pain").

tribe refer to as residuals, which can sometimes put the kids of even bit players through an accredited college—accredited, that is—that is, and alas—by Betsy DaVos-Blackwater. Or is she simply making a show of ditching Him before He can ditch her—for rank ingratitude.

She watches Mary Johnstone take over but (so blithe is the menace she exudes—the method to her menace) without appearing to do a thing. Except charge Shearer to patch together, with Akim's help, a little Duncan-style dance of invocation (no more Balanchine, please) and order Cantor to make a shortlist of all the homosexual or cross-dressing fishes with cheek to spare in stalking deep waters. At first he balks but then for old time's sake—flattered even if the intention was not to flatter; far from it—surprises himself by coughing up quite a bit of saucy same-sex lore. Boy squid, he seems to recall, perpetrate traumatic insemination on girls, other boys and everything in-between. That is, when they're not recklessly ejaculating sperm packets, as opposed to thought packets, solely at other boys. All this spurious erudition for nought. For Mary's attention is already directed elsewhere: Seems another member of the tribe—who is fated to last only as long as it takes to give voice to her querulousness—a querulousness very much in the key of a *refusal to defer*—has just asked, "But why exactly are we here?" And all at once it's not *her* querulousness (the patent has been revoked) but a querulousness that's (better late than never) in the public domain—an Idea whose time has come. "What's the point, I mean." Surprisingly, it's Herbert who answers. "Must everything have a point—like the dot above an *i*?" Surprisingly—and admirably—because this good deed—the kind that victims of an isolated old age are always being urged to inflict to keep themselves in remission—will be read as a coming-to-the-rescue of the very somebody she now detests above all others. Piqued to contrariety by this ungraciously unspoken thought, Mary Johnstone (she's the Master's favorite mind reader) says: "But in fact there is a point—a very deep one." Coming here, to the beach, she hopes that Eden—but more importantly, they, the audience-to-be—will understand that his work—his product—i.e., the story of the van and what went on there when Invidicum was put to yet another use: anaclitic, parergonal, whatever they want to call it—hopes they'll understand that the product is not destined to become—contrary to what *The German Ideologist* might have said in such a context (she's doing to Marx what Marx did to Hegel, what Lubitsch's Hitler did to Lubitsch's Poland, and enjoying every minute of it)—that the product is not destined to become a power over him, getting quickly out of control, riding roughshod over all his hopes and expectations—his all-too-human emotions. Whatever the commodity Eden crafts through his reminiscences it will not be a Marxian one. Even if Eden puts his life *into* the product, above all he mustn't fear—"Do you hear me, Martin?"—that his life no longer belongs to him but to it and that it alone has the wherewithal to enter into relationships with other products hence—turning her into a sort of pimp, as she's often been called—with their makers. Rather, the product is a means to an end—like an unwanted child it will take him in undreamt-of directions, and not just North-by-Northwest. Impossible to sever from his faults-crammed essence, the product nevertheless has a rectifying life of its own. "In other words, he mustn't fear that the greatness of his product will make him less great. If Eden is shy by design, then the product—by the sheer force of its will to be acclaimed, its will to claim through usurpation its rightful place in the world—must force him to assert himself as he never could—would—will—on his own behalf."

Cantor begins to feel a certain regret since the notion of a product's/object's being given free rein to become a power over the producer/worker—the notion of product as vampire—as the "embodiment of powers" the producer no longer has[165]—the notion that "[t]he worker puts his life into the object" only to discover it "no longer belongs to him but to the object" and that for this he must have only himself to blame since "he creates his own production as the loss of his reality[166]—since such notions of a transmutation of object into spirit or vice versa are always appealing—in the way the peremptory meanspiritedness of fairy tales and proverbs is appealing. But he needs to get a grip on himself: a transmutation fantasy may be meat-and-potatoes poetic but living it in real time by the alienated sweat of one's brow without health care or toilet time is a horse of another color.

Somebody who looks or smells like a provocateur sent all the way here by the Bernie Sanders team barks out that such bandying about of "applied Marx" babble—all this "Marx-lite" rigmarole—is a disgrace to workers everywhere—who had to put away their labor, and their leisure, too, every time Death in the form of Exchange Value came a-calling—sorry, *callin'*—and especially now that each and every "breakthrough" in hardware or software or cloud computing or net dis-neutrality is another death knell for those workers (no laughing matter even if The Rump's crypto-"populist" dream team of sleazeballs—the humanoid warts on his ass—all think so)—all this babble is but an opportunistic tuning in on what isn't worth her little finger. "You mean," says Narr (a somewhat unlikely man of the people given his past-into-present affiliations with the global coastal elites), "that she isn't worth Marx's little finger." The barker cum bellower apologizes—it's just that wordflow (although he doesn't use this word) sometimes skews worldflow and vice versa. It's sort of—to take a page from his own Book of Hours—a case of fat-free Hegelian dialectic rearing its ugly head. The barker rests his case since Mary doesn't look at all crestfallen—the way Marx might have said she should. So, thinks George (the only local boy in the ghost town of Perpetual Non Sequitur who's made good—sorry, *managed to make* good), maybe the Berry Sundae affair is/was just an opportunistic stab at lay analysis—the patient in this case being language and its—not instinct's—vicissitudes. But never before (or is the *never* just audience-pleasing hyperbole—aimed at making the boobs think they're

---

[165] Bertell Ollman, *Alienation: Marx's Conception of Man in Capitalist Society*, 2nd ed. (Cambridge, United Kingdom, Cambridge University Press, 1984), chap. 20 ("Man's relation to his product"), p. 144.

[166] See Karl Marx, *The Economic and Philosophic Manuscripts of 1844*, Dirk J. Struik, ed., and Martin Milligan, translator (New York, International Publishers, 1964), "Estranged Labor."

in on a bigger-than-big plot twist?—cleaving for dear life to a cliffhanger)—never before (*Never . . .? Well, hardly ever*) has he felt and in just this way that a human being—in this case, unsung-hero Gilles—is at the best and worst of times—just a byproduct of thought—of a thought packet—just a welcome relief from deep-structured thought. Never has he known how enjoyable storytelling—plot-twisting—character development—character stunting—can be if it lasts but a millisecond, as long as it takes to precipitate—like Gilles unsung—out of the 7 percent solution known as thought.

"But isn't that your job—the asserting, I mean?" bellows still another member of the tribe—fated to last only so long as it takes to give voice to his incredulousness—and maybe not even that long—since compliments of this, another pigheaded refusal to defer to Mary as by far the most powerful agent provocateur in Hollywood, the chances are slimmer than slim that once he's finished his bio of gentle—normal—Papa Haydn (the unlikeliest of pretexts for some warts-are-all blockbuster) she'll agree to represent him—and the obscure premonition that career extermination's already in the works is shutting down pighead's immune system and cutting off his oxygen supply. (His immune system, like that of so many others, has failed to register the obvious: that Mary is the purest type of foul-weather friend—the kind who falls all over herself trying to lend the limbless one a helping hand but whose tireless efforts to wangle him, say, that once-in-a-lifetime dream job as a male hooker in Disneyland last only as long as he continues to righteously do his part, that is, emit the signs that such efforts are doomed to fail and the deal is sure to fall through the earth's core like an asteroid in rut, thereby assigning her what to any self-hating Job's comforter is the best of all possible percentages, namely, bottomless schadenfreude earned by the pious sweat of his brow.) But like a drastically slimmed-down drawl-free Rex Tillerson besieged by reporters at a photo-op with I forget which -Stan's freely elected leader for life, i.e., its second-biggest crook, Mary blandly sticks to her script—but not before smirking à la Rex at all this small-fry bluster. "In short he will be in thrall to the product—in thrall, that is, to its ability to release him from thralldom. As you may have already guessed, the product is like—no, *is*—the Other in a very bad marriage. A very bad Other in a very bad marriage, indeed." (Borkman isn't the only one to turn green at the phrase though he *is* the only one to turn beet-red at the same time. Oddly enough, it sandbags his gut with . . . yearning, of all things! for the ex-to-be, though for all he knows they may already be officially severed and he simply sleepwalked through the ceremony.) "How so?" taunts Haydn (inasmuch as he has nothing to lose)—in the tone of one agent provocateur to another.

She explains that most of the time you're terrified of the Other's Otherness and well you should be. How dare She or He harbor alien likes and loathings, thereby threatening permeation with the poison of Her selfhood, for the borders of your own are all too porous!? Persistence in His or Her own being—conatus they call it, down Amsterdam way—is brute indifference, worse than hostility. And while we're at it, and far worse, how dare She have likes *akin* to your own, thereby robbing you of your uniqueness? Many nod their heads—in muted mulling recognition, since this is exactly what they've been going through over too many decades in "relationships" straight out of middle-period Woody but were too lily-livered to admit lest they be branded a freak and straitjacketed chop-chop, but if you wait long enough then somebody is sure to come along, get on his high horse and understand, understand, understand. They nod their heads gratefully as they would at the ravings of some PBS televangelist who's just had the guts to spill the beans—to spew the unspeakable—to reveal what no other prophet for profit has heretofore dared reveal about, say, wrinkle-free deep breathing or the benefits of organic avocado-and-kale purée for breakfast or the disbenefits of wheat germ mayonnaise on the half-shell for lunch and dinner—a man of the cloth like Suze (whom penny-wise Mary adores and perhaps for good reason) or hard-nosed spiritualist Wayne O'Dwyer or that two-in-one obligatory fixture on the Masterpiece Theatre circuit Danny-Amends-MD-and-his-worshipped-worshipful-wife-nurse-mother-Tatiana. "But there are also moments—aren't there?" (more nods, nods galore)—"though few and far between—when (admit it) you're thrilled to be linked—to be permitted to be linked to an other—so completely *other*—so much in opposition by dint of practicing the dark art of selfhood as it was born to be practiced—you're so thrilled, boys and girls, that said opposition—more like high contrast—becomes your validation. Thrilling, compliments of the other's tolerant alienness, to be handed the reality of *your* selfhood (like John the Baptist's severed head) on a silver platter." "So where are you going with this?" chirps curmudgeon No. 3. "To hell and back," chirps No. 4. Herbert restrains herself—she's learned her lesson. "I'm going where Eden will experience the same kind of thrilling acceptance by the work by and large—acceptance as its creator while remaining so very different from it, the creation." (Even if when all is said and done the thing has no value because there's no market for it, making it and the labor that produced it useless.) For didn't Peirce (don't tell her they don't remember Charley S., the patron saint of Dildo Alley) insist that a man's logical method should love and reverence him as its Torah—as its bride—as its child bride and mail-order and runaway bride all in one—whom it has chosen from all the world? No nodding of heads this time around. Peirce is clearly no Masterpiece—clearly no Suze Tatiana Avocadissimo Amends O'Dwyer—nor is he, for that matter, in the same league as another one of tele-homeopathy's favorite fixtures, Philly's Dr. Phill E. Cheese-Steak.

Shearer is proving quite serviceable and then some, or pretending to be, living up to her reputation acquired only a few minutes before when she asked, oh so passively, "Are we allowed . . .?" Her invocation to the moon, replete with more *pirouettes fouettées* than even a part-time idiot savant like Cantor can count, has been a hit—an impalpable hit—though from Mary's poker face (is that, by any chance, Envy that's couched in its incipiently hag-like folds?)—you'd never know it. Triumph, even if she owes most of it to Akim, allows Moira to acknowledge for the first time the hideousness of Eden's gray eminence. For she is hideous, this Johnstone creature (by the way, is there any truth to the Word on the Street to the effect that she's a—a—a—? [well, you know], or is this simply yet another aspersion—even if it should be one no longer—cooked up by The Rump's anti-LGBT gang during one of their enforced respites [witch doctor's orders!] from running dutifully amuck?—oh, but never mind). But what a *waste* of hideousness as a motor, thinks Herbert in tandem. For when all is said and done—or, more to the point, when push comes to shove—she's deadly dull—a broken record—a one-trick pony's ass. And this being the case Herbert finds herself—or *almost* finds herself—hoping that after all the endless complaints (some unspoken but not from tact) about orders' having been carried out slapdash (*pace* that exquisite Invocation Scene), i.e., left defiantly undischarged—a real Mary will emerge . . . But what is she talking about? this *is* the real Mary, notwithstanding all her hints to the contrary—namely, that if they're not getting a load of the real Mary it's nobody's fault but their own. What they see before them is a contraption—an insult to the real Mary who by the way would be only too happy to unveil her perpetual flowering (thing is, the world's career obstructionists keep getting in the way and in today's performance the role of World is being taken by none other than . . . *all of them*—a gang of degenerate losers if ever there was one but, when it comes to losing, no match for The Rump's Mulligan Stew). They aren't supposed to hear the snarky plaint of her superficial surf—just a happy clash of the quintessential pebbles directly beneath. Herbert doesn't agree. Everything getting in the way of the real Mary—their slapdashery for starters—is what contributes handsomely—like the Brothers Koch—to the makeup of her infernal machine. She's no Sleeping Beauty snoring much too soundly in some Hundred Years' rainforest of thorns. There's only the illusion—primordially constitutive of Mary (*yes*, primordially! *yes*, constitutively! *and if you don't stop bawling I'll shove a few dozen more polysyllables down your gullet until this time you choke your way to . . . Dover!*)—in which everybody shares (by some magic she's able to infect them all)—the illusion that if only the ungrateful world would allow her to obstruct the obstructionistas—to outHerod the Herods—in our studio audience—well, there's no telling how far she could go in the direction of not just showing but showing *off* her true colors. But as Mary herself is obstruction and nothing but . . .

They gravitate—flock, is more like it—like . . . like . . . Amateur rodentologist Rhys is about to think, *like lemmings*, but doesn't the en masse suicide of these Disney darlings amount to a poor man's myth? Once they hit the beach, Mary is of course the first to reach the water's edge—for the sole purpose, it seems, of staring—in what is meant to be ecstasy—far far out to sea. No obstructions here. Thing is, Herbert's now presented with a perplexing problem (as if she doesn't—didn't—have enough to worry about like knocking things into shape for the Final Sequence, though it's rumored that The Invidicum Story will end not with the bang of an ocean's roar but with the whimper of a Massacre of the Far From Innocents)—the kind of problem that would have stumped not just Hegel but his cook and butler, too—namely, how to make it to the same water's edge—the same frontier—simply because she wants to, without enabling MJ to think (Herbert simply can't bring herself to [m]utter that name—that nauseous vanilla pudding of a name [well, at least it's not Kellyanne Kockenlocker MacDuff]—at least not any time soon) she's enviously following in her footsteps—envious that it's she, MJ, who's managed to appropriate the sheen of the Pacific in its entirety—and centuries (to boot) before the Pacific was even a glint in Neptune's eye.

Herbert feels guilt—yes, Blacks' Unwarranted Guilt Matters—but not—ye, gods!—toward Mary. Rather it's Shearer—oops, Jean—who's the subject of stern (some might say too stern) self-rebuke. The Master has gone to the trouble—has taken time out from His less and less busy schedule—of alerting Jean to what's going on in Herbert's head. (Jean's brand-new suits-her-to-a-*t* facial tics prove it and Herbert intends to keep an eagle eye on all of them.) Melanctha's meditation on "motion issuing in stillness"—in particular graceless misappropriation of time and space culminating in death by reason of the fakest ecstasy—should have as its subject and its target (if, that is, there were any rough justice in the world) not Mary but Amygdala's very own take on Hollywood's quintessential version of the "iconic" smugly evil-twinnish sister—i.e., Caro by nickname and in cold storage long enough. Forcibly disembarked amidstream from the Staten Island Ferry one balmy winter's night, if Herbert remembers—dismembers—correctly, but who with the beginner's luck typical of her tribe was rescued by a SWAT team of timely tiger sharks. But Herbert wants to cry out in her own defense that this trial—this story—is just not *that* kind of story: no pretending it can be. (Not, like Musk's Tesla, the kind of story *stock* that so spellbinds the campfire listener as to render the embattled movie rights insusceptible to any reasonable valuation.) It's strictly a first-come first-served affair. If she (Jean) thought she (Herbert) was going to stand around waiting for the right character (whatever that is) to show up—the character "right"—the most plausible inspiration—for the role of Hideosa Kellyanne von Dreck-o'-Schnitzel—then she had another thing coming. Who can say just how long she—the Invidicum crowd—would have had to wait before the being surfaced on whom the epithet "hideous but uninteresting" could most plausibly be conferred? Maybe, forever, which on the one hand is fine since it would mean prolonging the terminable story interminably. On the other they aren't getting any younger. As that immortal scholar-entrepreneur, Newt Liepnits (one role fertilizing the other, i.e., he isn't *just* a scholar, he's also an entrepreneur, i.e., he isn't *just* an entrepreneur, he's also a scholar—in a word, he's all things to all men and a master of none) might put it, there are "trade-offs" (his second-favorite term, the first being . . .). And, hey, what about the cost of flying Caro, say—if Caro is indeed the best villainess currently on the market—out to the Coast? And what if Caro, once picked, in turn picks United—just rechristened Citizens United—and for her pains gets bloodily dragged off the plane to make room for some soused crew member (*see—please, see!—somewhere above for more on The United Affair: the Master doesn't want you yearlings champing at the bit to think He's too—too—senile to recognize His own manic repetitiveness*) and so becomes—compliments of the usual cellphone documentation gone retroviral—the real culprit by creating a stock-tumbling PR nightmare (The Rump's favorite pep pill) not just for the poor CEO (sorry, Oscar, no backdated stock options from Santa this year) but (by association, however tenuous) for Amygdala itself? What matters above all—what will always matter—is the thought packet—getting it simultaneously embedded in and extruded from the loins of the story and out into the world as fast as possible—and so what if whoever professes to trigger its unfolding is all wrong for the bit part, dead wrong? What matters above all is hostile takeover of the thought packet by the demon of shareholder value in all its glory—and Medicaid recipients be damned. Which is why, Jean dear, it is not Caro (as one would have hoped, or at least thought) but Mary—an ostensible bore notwithstanding all the promises of springtime diffused by the nosegay of her ostensible hideousness—who will have to do the honors, at least until Caro finds a plane from which she won't be dragged, at which point it will of course be conveniently too late to recruit that demon-even-more-demonic-than-shareholder-value—namely, shareholder plausibility—to officiate at the midsummer marriage of packeteer Faustus/Paris and storybook Helen. In which case the Invidicum gang will have acquired the precious something—the elixir—the pharmakon—that enables every gang to kill time in the empty hours of old age, to wit, regret. But let's not write the Johnstone gal off as a liability just yet: who knows what fringe benefits can accrue from—what wonders can be worked by—the interplay of a pair of incompatibles? A sufficiently pigheaded thought packet could very well turn her into what it insists she is despite all the evidence to the contrary. That is, by virtue of being all wrong for the part, the stand-in—the understudy—might nonetheless . . . But the scented roar of the sea is too robust for Herbert's morbid musing, which peters out, out of respect (it's strictly Standing Room Only) for the performance in progress.

Peters out, only to immediately be born again. Because Melanctha's getting cold feet—for the Master's sake. She fears she's seeing Him for the very first time as He really is (or is she yet again merely hyperbolizing at His behest?). Are all these packets proof that nothing can stop the unstoppability of that longest of long-distance runners, His vocation? Or is His omnivorous (some might say *ominous*) fertility a simple reflex against hopelessness—does it reduce to a concoction of "insights" that have no core but simply serve to stanch the unstoppable flood of social defeats? Following in Post's footsteps has He taken it upon Himself to patent a new kind of toxin which triggers and nurtures the illusion that He's unquenchably fertile without ever having asked—ever having dreamed of asking—to *be* unquenchable. And does His desperate hunger for packets—for the surplus comfort offered by their shipment *in bulk*—just happen to be idiopathically—delusionally—aligned with a conveniently low standard for what constitutes insight—real insight? (Stop, she tells herself, stop—if not for the Master's sake, then for your own—and bursts out laughing at her own drummed-up urgency.) Every packet is an epitaph on His dutiful collision with an event (chosen with excruciating care in spite of Himself: a cloud's reflection in a muddy puddle, say, or a spider's web floating above while at the same time remaining soldered to the surface of a shivery hedge)—a gift and a challenge that cries out for preservation and preserve it he must even if—especially because—His first impulse is, like that of any "great creator," to massacre them all since "by definition" such collisions are impediments on the way to something ostensibly better . . . grander. And are his arch-enemies by any chance aware that before it is sent out into the world for dissemination by his acolytes each packet is subject to a scrutiny almost rabbinical in its severity?

In any case, doesn't Jean know—will she ever? (once Herbert is gone, that is, and posterity has begun to do its work, the most mixed of blessings)—the bottom line is that Herbert's a normal woman with normal human needs, which means nothing would have pleased her more than to give credit where credit was most due by conferring the Shitpickles Many Lifetimes Achievement Award for distinguished service to the fertilizer industry on that industry's most disserving benefactor—Caro, not Mary J.[167] Especially now that it's finally coming out of a record slump thanks to the deregulation spree of none other than The Rump's homebody Scottie McPruitt (thin-lipped and almost as piggy as Kockenlocker is reptilian), whose war cry is, No pesticide carcinogenic until proven innocent, or something along those lines. But life rarely turns out the way one wants it to. But enough about all these stand-ins for Building 18. But why, oh why, is she bringing up Building 18? Is it authentically uppermost in her mind or does the Master simply wish to counterpoise a little blood-and-guts social commentary against all this art-for-art's-sake frivolity even if the frivolity so-called is a matter of life and death?

The long and the short of it is that He's trying to help Herbert trounce her rivals as her rivals—and not just Jean and Mary—were meant to be trounced (*Who is speaking?*). For not once (and especially not now, what with all the preparations by this hostess-with-the-mostest-on-the-ball for the beach sequence to end all beach sequences) has she stopped to realize the overweening authority that suffering—Building 18-style suffering—or the inability to experience it *which is even more excruciating* (or is this just another case of the Master's wordflow pinning its tail on His horse's ass?)—the overweening authority that suffering visits on its lucky exponent—so overweening as to give her a cutting edge on the competition, living and dead. For He knows His favorite—His ward—His Estella—better than she knows—wants to know—herself and the only thing He knows even better is her dilemma, to wit: How secure the authority conferred by suffering before it's quashed by her disqualification, as decreed by the ever-proliferating hordes of normals—as apple-pie normal as, say, the love child of Mick MulPence and Kellyanne DaVos—from whose funhouse perspective such suffering (even the suffering close to madness—e.g., Eden's Balboa Park kind of madness) amounts to the stupidity of impotence? How go about claiming—or at least laying claim to—the palm her almost-madness merits? But doesn't Melanctha—still His favorite—till death

[167] "Shitpickles," as Melanctha knows only too well, is the signifier of anything and everything the Master finds (in no particular order) reprehensible and self-important and arrogant and vicious and cruel and specious and smug and condescending not to mention tone- and sorrow-deaf in this our lonely life and on this our lonely planet—the only planet in the universe overrun by a race of chops-licking Job's comforters, whose main line of credit is schadenfreude. The play's the thing and the word's—*Shitpickle's*—the blimp—the dirigible—that catapults His revulsion into an ether—a *netherworldly* ether—all its own. Too bad He can't refrain from trafficking in the same old default and find newer, cannier ways of pandering to His own revulsion—canny enough to let Him—no, *make* Him—transcend it.

(hers) do them part—remember what she's learned in the *École des* Hard-Knocks? namely, that within her domain—the only domain that counts, if you ask me (but you don't)—there's no such thing as disqualification—in fact, the more an act rates disqualification in the shadow world of everyday louts, the more it deserves to be sceptred in the real world of flesh-and-blood phantoms. Oh, why must she go on reliving the business of Building 18 in the key of recollection rather than (as her Master—or one of the Master's Masters—would prefer) of repetition? Before she can defend herself—before she can conceive of *wanting* to defend herself—Melanctha catches sight of Borkman catching sight of the two juniors (though some are more junior than others)—his own and (albeit in name only) Straynge's. They're deep in conversation—a pair straight out of Whitman (how deftly Borkman, Jr., ignores, or seems to ignore, questions of hierarchy—of precedence—though if he doesn't watch out his protégé may turn into a sorcerer's apprentice)—a Pylades and Orestes straight out of Gluck's *Iphigénie en Tauride* (the only thing the former wants more than jumping into bed with his woebegotten chum is to sing "Unis dès la plus tendre enfance")—a Rupert and Gerald straight out of D.H. Lawrence but no longer *straight*—gladiatorial Ponzis wrestling with each other's schemes— But she must stop naming them—larding them with the homeless-shelter erudition of others—which she flushes in and out of her system at the behest of the Master. To name them is to maim them even if the naming's a gratuitous misnaming. She should know that better than anybody (*why?*). They're who they are—not Rupert and Gerald, not Pylades and Orestes, not Stan and Ollie. Deep in conversation—oblivious of everything except their give-and-take—the juniors are making for the water's edge—the Ocean's unceasingly contested frontier—each holding his flip-flops at hip level, daintily, away from his torso. Admired by strangers, the walkers-and-talkers have become stars and all the more starry for being unaware of the admiration visited on them. And the fact that Straynge, Jr.'s buttocks are a bit wobbly (obviously a birthmark passed from father—Pritchard, isn't it?—to son) somehow mitigates the sorcerousness to come. There's a pathos—no, a sort of pathos—underpinning or underpinned by the wobbliness which it's easy to take—that is, if you're Melanctha—if not for an ethical stance then for the promise of one. For wasn't it, or am I mistaken? Montaigne who'd said in his *Apologie de Raimond Sebond* that wobbly buttocks never lied and if they did then they simply weren't wobbly enough? *Montaigne? Montaigne, did you say? Of course no! Who ever put that thoroughly wobbly idea in your head? Michel de M., indeed! Everybody knows that said observation—and it was a culminating one—is made in* "Que philosopher, c'est apprendre à mourir," written—and too often rewritten—by one Ishmael Drybock, late of Rikers.

Maybe, Borkman thinks, if he hadn't always been so hung up on questions of precedence—had been willing to take a page or two (as his son seems to be doing at this very moment) from the cooked book of his underlings—the cooked book of their contentment as underlings (*and* the slumbering spirits of the gold *be hanged!*)—things would have turned out vastly different, even with regard to the Mister and Missus side of things. Albeit still shackled to the same bedpost, they might have ended up living slaphappily-ever-after in spite of themselves. On some drizzly Sunday in late spring, say, she'd still be doing what she did or thought she did best, i.e., sketching the willows' gauze in the shadow of Belvedere Castle, and he'd, in the same drizzle, be emitting faked grunts of admiration for just how authoritatively she went about perpetrating puny slanders against those willows, whose gauze deserved better, much much better. There, he's said it—thought it, I mean. Adding insult to injury and without his knowledge, much less his consent, Borkman and Melanctha are fighting for possession of the pair or, rather, their gazes are jousting for possession of the *comradeliness* of the pair—and it's Melanctha, better at standing still, who runs off with the prize, or so she thinks.

And somehow the spectacle creates hope—a hope so mammoth in its imitation of hope as to resemble nothing so much as sorrow—and not just in the loser. Or maybe the spectacle generates a foreclosure of all hope—a lifting of the burden of hope—the burden of asking for the impossible—as the first step on the road to something even worse—the very worst—hence something better. Borkman *makes a mental note* (he's not quite sure if he's doing it right—after all, he never finished high school and as far as he's concerned nothing in his life became him like the leaving it) to try comradeship—now referred to as male bonding, correct?—of bro and bro and dude and dude—once they release him—though it remains unclear whether he's still to be incarcerated (the inextinguishable bracelet-jingling limbo he calls home has made the fortune of dozens of late-night talk-show hosts and their funnymen). It looks, against the midmorning sparkle (or is it still the middle of the night?), so very . . . soothing. Cantor, for whom Borkman is an open book, thinks, loud enough for him to hear though there are none so deaf as *will* not hear: *That's because you're on the outside looking in—acquiring what you think is comradeship or a reasonable facsimile thereof as if it were a trophy—a trophy wife. And by the way isn't it mergers and quackquisitions—not bonding—that's your baby? But in this case—the case of comradeship and Everyman-type contentment—the minute you're in the middle of it you won't be able to acquire (not mathematically possible)—no matter which algorithm you misapply—to acquire whatever you're living—to turn it into a fleshless and bloodless physical asset. You'll soon be clamoring—well, maybe not exactly* clamoring—*to get back outside where you've always been happiest (or rather least unhappy or too busy being unhappy to have time to be aware that you're unhappy)—soon be clamoring whether you know it or not. By trying to look from the outside in when deep inside— deep inside the yearning failure, that is, to live the comradeship—deep inside the revulsion for the comrade who's turned out to be—who'll always turn out to be—who'll never disappoint you for failing to turn out to be—whom you'll train to be—a rival—an obstacle to greatness—a walking Ponzi scheme—by trying to look from the outside in—to acquire what you're living—what you're failing to live—you'll kill it—the possibility of comradeship—bury it alive. There's none of the glamor of sorrow when you're actually living through the fight for the soul of comradeship (or anything else)—undergoing the fugacity of comradeship (yeah, the* fugacity) *or anything else—deep in the heart of the push-and-pull of it.* But clearly it isn't just Borkman and Melanctha (Cantor's surrogate parents, sort of) who are mesmerized. Everybody else—those legendary lemmings again!—are following close behind the pair: Looking far less comradely (must be the sharp rise in temperature), they've decided to head for the vans. Parked impatiently in front of Chase Palm Park—for those who care about such things as blood- or beet-red local color. Mary shoos them in for there will be no understanding Eden without their first having gotten a feel for the conditions in which his tormentors tried to practice memory extinction in the grandest manner. They might have a few memories of their own that bear retrieval, deconsolidation and extinction. Even if, like Tasmanian devils, memories are always trying to *claw their way back from extinction*[168] (when they aren't playing possum). But let's not get ahead of ourselves. The Beach Sequence is over for good—a dud, a flop, a turkey, a lemon, a lemon meringue (no, anything but! more like a lemon drop)—which means that the invidious dread experienced by the maker of *I Vitelloni*—master sequencer of beach genomes—more importantly, the dread of his fans—dread at the prospect of seeing his sandy salty surfy poetry bested—was unfounded after all. Or at least premature. Or rather, at least ". . . premature."

---

[168] Phrase plundered (admiringly) from the title of an article by Elizabeth Pennisi (see *Science*, vol. 370, No. 6522 [11 December 2020]).

CHAPTER FIFTY-NINE

Perceiving that Eden has grown fainter and fainter from the aftertaste of his misadventures (success story notwithstanding)—or trying to make him think he has—Mary Johnstone is convinced she's reassuring him (*who is speaking?*), as they wend their weary way vans-ward, when she explains it's in No. 1 (no mean feat to get herself heard above the wavelets) that his memorabilia—his archived anathemabilia—souvenirs of how the other Third lived—were retrieved. Resurgences of the terror associated with, e.g., sale of new, improved Invidicum to the Lord's Resistance Army, the Shabab and Basher al-Assad's cousins and brothers-in-law in exchange for ivory chopsticks which he then, as ordered, went halfway around the world to resell to the People's Liberation Army. Resurgences triggered simply by forcing him to scan fuzzy video clips of top-tier humanitarians—like Joseph Kony and Narine Le Pen and Bashar and Sheldon Adelson and Clinnt Lorrance and Sheriff Eddy "Arpaio" Gallagher and Erik Printze and Viktore Bout (with George Bannon and slumlord extraordinaire Jared Kutshner and Paul O'Ryan and Ingraham Coulter Greene, and Mitch McBitsch and Paul Manafart thrown in—OK, sophomorically, worse, self-congratulatorily—for good measure)—clips of top-tier humanitarians in action. Truth is, she's arrogated to herself the role of Socrates (since nobody else seems inclined to claim it), not just by virtue (though virtue has nothing to do with it) of the hobble of her obligatory bare feet, but through the intention to administer a long overdue purge—weeding out the premises he holds dear which would turn out to be very much contrary to the thesis he holds dearer. "Whom do you mean by *they*?" Post cries out (is she getting too close for comfort?)—for he, too, is here, flanked by his captors—or bodyguards—Narr and Cook. She ignores his question—even if he is head honcho, *at least for the moment* (another case of plot twist—ominous shadow of a terrifying plot twist to come—as byproduct of a moment's fancy). And over there in van 2, folks, they retrieved those traumata yet again—or tried to retrieve them, with little success—but this time *in order to extinguish them forever* (since after all they were highly incriminatory—could cost them their ill-gotten gains).

So they injected him over and over again with—with—with— She turns coyly—so coyly that Cantor wants to strangle her—toward Post. "Go ahead, tell 'em," he mumbles. "You know you want to. You know you're going to. With or without my informed consent." It's clear he enjoys mumbling because beneath all the grime of begrudgery is a sugar daddy's Turkish delight: his favorite parasite is doing him proud. She hasn't even waited for him to finish. "With Invidicum, of all things!" For as it so happens, It's—another feather in their cap!—*far more effective as a memory abolisher than as a treatment for Envy* or for homicide-aversion. Only not for Eden—but we'll get to that sad story in seconds flat. (Herbert, ever the anti-creative writing maven and summa cum laude to boot, feels that in this case the Master should definitely have *shown* not (*through boldface print*) *told*. "So we'll now have to do things the old-fashioned way—if you *don't* mind, Professor Post." "It's decades since anybody called me that: I feel ancient—ancient as a sage in sandals." Ethan is tempted to say (is he available?), *I wouldn't go that far. Another case,* Cantor reflects, *of reducing to a mere throwaway admission what* (what? Invidicum as abolitionist on the order of John Brown, that's what!) *in surer—or clunkier— hands than the Master's would have been milked for all it was worth as nothing less than the climax of climaxes. But doesn't He know yet there's only just so much mileage to be gotten out of making explosions occur off screen?* But Mary has had a bellyful of his reflections—and is determined that this one won't get her down. Even if she can't hear it, his all-body hatchet-fish bioluminescence gives him away—as it did back at Columbia when he was hot on the trail of some non-Euclidean thought packet. "And in that guise"—Post can't prevent himself from getting into the act—"Invidicum is far more effective than an overrated β-adrenergic receptor blocker like propanolol, not to mention ZIP. Which can't tell good memories from bad and mows down every last one of them—good or bad—in its path." Unlike both, Invidicum targets specific memories.

Mary butts back in, as if to say, *But enough about you—any of you, for that matter—not just Post.* "Yes, Invidicum has found its true vocation at last, which is more than I can say for all of you, much less for myself." *No fake humility, MJ,* protests Cantor. Oddly enough, she excites him—to the extent, that is, George Cantor can be excited by a woman. *Now that you mention it even if it's only in passing,* she does bear an Itsy-Betsy resemblance to DaVos in, say, the heat of her prime, four score and twenty years back, when she and brother Erik the Prinzce were a mere glint in Satan's eye—the good Satan, i.e., the Satan of good old-fashioned Calvinist cholesterol. (Rumor has it she's about to open a for-profit beauty institute in the wilds of the Rust Belt—the first of its kind to bestow PhDs—but only to first-comers—in eyebrow thread-ing.) Frankly, though, he finds Andy Putzder far more alluring. Too bad The Pusillanimous Rump—and after all their locker-room towel-snapping banter, to boot!—threw him under the bus. Something nauseatingly manly (or as he would say, *American*) about a guy who prefers sort-of-telegenic all-Ameri-can bikini *cunts* (to whom he's outsourced all PR work) slobberingly sucking on Hardee's sausages, OVER *workers* who, every time you turn around, are busy pissing or shitting or menstruating or, in a pinch, jerking off on their eternal four-minute break and the pestilential bread-and-butter sausages be damned—workers whose sole but Pavulon-worthy crime is to refuse to turn themselves into living wage averse robots—into Johnnies-on-the-clock not Johnnies-come-lately. Does Cantor desire those cunts, even if it's in only an itsy-bitsy teeny-weeny yellow-polka-dot sort of way or is it the Putz's desire that he really desires? *God only knows what is our real desire.* "God only knows what is our real vocation," murmurs Stifter disingenuously (Jean remem-bers—no, seems to remember—somebody saying his maiden—stripling's— name was Astrov), since if there's anybody who knows what his vocation is, it's Stifter (né Astrov), hands down,[169] even if every time you turn around he's

---

[169] No better proof of the fact that Stifter's a bona fide vocation man than the following:

changing partners. Though Oscar Wilde—or is it Hegel? (decide for yourself!)—would have said that the changing *is* the vocation. That the oscillation is his foothold. But wait, Astrov—*Mikhail* ("*Mike*"), to you—has suddenly acquired a 3-for-the-price-of-one lisp/twitch/stammer. And a limp thrown in as a stock-options bonus hefty enough to warm the cockles of any slimy kleptocrat's prostate. A Barnum & Bailey stunt in a Barnum & Bailey world—just as Harburg/Rose/Arlen phony as it can be—all part of the disingenuousness act—of the effort to ingratiatingly undercut surefire eloquence which never goes over as big as it should with the hoi polloi—worse, the billionaires in hoi polloi-ish drag. "And I have it on good authority that memory extinction is just one of Invidicum's changes of garment. There's no limit to its uses, depending on the *dosage*. And why, through exquisite calibrations of dosage can't the snow leopard that is Invidicum change its stripes—I mean spots— any time the idea tickles its fancy?" And she goes on to explain (read her lips) that what we have here is a drug that's All About the Dosage, Stupid: Invidicum, if you must know, is nothing but a series of dosage-dependent impersonations, variations on the theme of itself—its late-Fellini fantasy of itself. At a high enough dosage—or low enough—she's forgotten her lab book—her Monarch Notes—Invidicum goes from envy- to memory-inhibitor. Come to think of it, here's a perfect example of that dialectical inversion KM was so crazy about, whereby quantity becomes quality, no questions asked. And all this only because Invidicum is busy doing what every unemployed miner and factory hand and salesgirl at Sears *should* have been doing—that is, if the platitudinous pundits who come home to roost on the *Times* op-ed page are to be believed—which is to engage in *lifetime learning*. There's a plentiful shock of recognition—that layoff time is fast approaching?—in not a few faces—and even—or mostly!—among the SiVa crowd. But why—aren't they all lifetime-guaranteed unicorns?

"In other words," spouts ex-Betsy, it's been *clinically proven. But to do what?* thinks Cantor ('cause nobody else has the courage)—the conclusion's unearned. Though he doesn't want them to know he's thinking—doesn't want the whole physiological package of tics peculiar to thinking—bioluminescent each and every—to give him away. Following in the footsteps of his spiritual father JGB, he immediately makes a mental note (is there any other kind?) to hate the spouted term first chance he gets—but, knowing himself, he'll end up loving it all the more. Suspect in any context—like any term worth its salt in gold—except as the title of a thriller, in which guise it comfortably advertises its own suspecthood—exacts vengeance not just on itself but on portentousness-breeding titles in all shapes and sizes. But not just any old thriller, mind

---

When asked who his clients might be he's wont to respond delphically (with resignation getting trounced by self-exaltation every time): "Either you love it [*it*: the fruits of the vocationeer's labors] or you hate it." Nothing like trafficking in absolutes—spurning the continuum as the habitat of vermin—to take the edge off unpopularity, with Stifter aka Astrov being living if not breathing proof that the absolute power of language corrupts . . . absolutely.

you (the B-movie darlings of the *Cahiers* set need not apply), but a good-old-fashioned blockbuster—the kind that opens on Easter Sunday at Radio City Music Hall, sandwiched between the Rockettes and the Schlockettes, followed up by an early family dinner (the kids have homework to slog through) at Schrafft's. (Mom: *I think I'll have the cauliflower cyanide soufflé* for $2.25. *After all, it's* Easter.) In short, the term—*clinically proven*—is a gift—a W.C. Fields sort of gift—hence a cause for rejoicing. No, he's definitely come a long way since the term was visited on him, even if it was seconds ago. Sort of like the way it is for Cantor with respect—regard—to The Rump and his congregation (in the alligatoroid sense)—his battery—culture—sute—wake—quiver—bask—bike—cowardice—plague—cackle—knab—venue. He can't imagine life either without *clinically proven* or without the sonofabitch Rump and his tribe—he's come too far in hatred—in directions he never dreamed anybody—or anything—could still take him—come too far to give 'em up—to give up on either. Even if to somebody like The Rump or something like *clinically proven* (for whom or for which there's no such thing as bad PR—no such thing as a bad photo-op) every screed, diatribe, poison pen letter becomes an act of the purest deference not (as the pen wielder would have you—or, more importantly, he himself—believe) defiance—becomes an IV feed—mother's milk—the fat of the land—a palpable hit—the cup that runneth over. Show a little gratitude: After all, he's opened up infinite vistas of a glowingly impossible unhappiness like the *Entr'acte symphonique et sommeil* from *The Sleeping Beauty*—only not Democratic Vistas. A miracle has befallen Cantor. Even if gunslinging hatred of prissy Price and prissier—prissiest!—Mnuchkin and Pruitt and Kellyanne Kockenlocker and Shessions the ever-faithful dwarf robs him of his most precious possession—or what he needs to believe is his most precious possession—uniqueness—for there are now just too many of the likeminded out there. Too close—because too disseminated—for comfort. So the trick is not to get too self-congratulatory—worse convivial—about a silly shared loathing. Like the wild applauders cum guffawers in Bill Maher's studio audience, so suppressed they need somebody else to utter what, poor slobs, they take to be too daring for words—much less, thoughts.

If they take away anything from this convocation it should be the long-overdue discovery that Post together with the elves in his workshop (is there a hint of entreaty in her voice?) resemble nothing so much as a master craftsman in some medieval guild whose overarching aim is to become a capitalist. All by virtue of their transformation of Invidicum-for-Envy into Invidicum-for-Memory-Abolition. That is to say, transform I-for-E into I-for-M-A and thence (yes, *thence!* Somebody's gotta—just gotta—help the word, and thereby the world, resist the lure of that one great big potter's field known as the Slagheap of Archaisms)—and thence, it's but a hop, a skip and a jump to Invidicum-for-Everything-Else-Under-the-Sun. Or rather it's Invidicum-for-Envy that resembles nothing so much as that master. "All the poor guy needed was a sum for production that would enable him to hire a number of workers far exceeding the medieval max." So merely by virtue of the dialectical inversion effected through an increase in funds, hence in workers (a quantitative increase merely), the master—not to be confused with the Master (yes, she knows all about Him: her life hasn't been as sheltered as she pretends)—underwent a qualitative change—i.e., became the man of his own wettest dreams—a hairy-chested capitalist. By a mere snapping of its metaphysical fingers dialectical inversion effected the transformation of quantitative difference into qualitative distinction. Thereby enabling the master craftsman to follow in the footsteps of—to plagiarize—the carbon compounds (paraffins, normal alcohols, normal fatty acids, to name just a few) made Big Top famous by organic chemists August Laurent and Charles Gerhardt—and who were, in their turn, made famous by Karl Marx (so what if out of his own best interest but who at the same time was guilty here, she might add, of a bit of overattribution of glory?).[170] For as L & G pointed out, it takes but the simple *quantitative* addition of a methylene group to any one of those compounds to create a *qualitatively* different one—takes a mere methylene group to make all the difference to a string of down-and-out carbon compounds—too down-and-out even for the Bowery (that is, before the Bowery became prohibitively fashionable—became the fatcat's meow). And just as the methylene group transformed the carbons into men-about-town so did whatever potion Post got his elves to add—*quantitatively*—to Invidicum-for-Envy transform them or rather It—*qualitatively*—not into a capitalist but, by way of Invidicum-for-Memory-Abolition, into something even better, to wit, Invidicum-for-Everything-Else-Under-the-Sun, the capitalist's quintessential cash cow. Just as the methylene group transformed the carbon compounds so has whatever Post added quantitatively enabled Invidicum-for-Envy, following in the footsteps of the master craftsman who followed in the footsteps of the methylene crew, to become qualitatively different. And adding insult to injury it seems, she might also add, that L & G were the Walser and Stifter of their age. As if on cue, each seeks deep in the other's gaze (as unavowed or unavowable lovers often—or at least sometimes—will in a time of crisis) what in this case turns out to be some clue regarding the reaction proper to so ungracious a comparison.

But, as she intimated a while back, Invidicum-the-Memory-Vanquisher's—Invidicum-the-Vampire-Slayer's—true vocation hasn't done a thing for Eden—which only goes to prove that, sometimes, finding your true vocation doesn't mean you should be allowed to practice it. Eden blushes—or rather, the potential self with which he's not yet acquainted. Pridefully, as far as Herbert can see, since yet again he's stumped the experts.

Maybe it was the temperature in the van (so what if a bad artist always blames his tools? a great one does the honors even more) or his tormentors' own ineptitude (Post suppresses a shiver: he refuses to take the bait). Who *are* his tormentors? Shearer, always on her toes, wonders. Invidicum is even more potent than D-cycloserine (DCS) and anisomycin so Eden is the first to have endured such pharmacologic perturbation after memory retrieval and lived to tell the tale. But barely. And only because Invidicum by some ersatz miracle

---

[170]See Karl Marx, *Capital*, vol. one (New York, Vintage Books, 1977), chap. 11 and footnote 5, pp. 423–424.

acted as its own counter-poison. *Like a pharmakon—like writing*, thinks Herbert—a bit glibly.

Yes, retrieval of any one of those horrifying memories inaugurated a reconsolidation process—opened wide a time-dependent window of opportunity—during which the memory was deliciously, transiently labile, ductile, plastic, fluid, unstable, supersusceptible, vulnerable (take your pick)—labile enough to be (compliments of Invidicum) extincted (*yeah, Guys*, extincted) or inhibited—in any case, dogtagged for later irretrievability. "But retrieval plus extinction is only half—I mean, half of half of one percent of the battle. The problem with Invidicum—at least in the case of Ethan—sorry, Eden—was that the poisoning happened faster—much faster—than the de-memorization." The poisoning was faster—the invasiveness wilier—than the purgation. But at least they'd learned—didn't they?—It was no universal solvent—no, not by a long shot. *At least in the case of Eden.* "But cheer up. If a genius like Invidicum can fail, then that makes our own triumphs less mediocre. Or maybe the failure was Invidicum's revenge for—on—having been compared to a medieval guild meister (Breaking News travels fast)—a schlockmeister. Or maybe it was life's revenge on Its vainglorious refusal to share the stage with other, happier remedies. But I shouldn't have you standing out here in the cold." Nobody budges since everybody's dumbstruck—sunstruck—thunderstruck—stagestruck (again, take your pick). Somebody *other than Cantor* (can't get more specific: that's all I'm authorized to say at the present time) asks how, then, the memories can get extincted without wily Invidicum on the premises. "All *I'm* mandated to say at present is that extinction training isn't enough to abolish the past." She puts a forefinger to her thin lips—Cantor never realized just how thin. Though he'd had his lion's share of chances to do so. At that very moment—oh, all right, a moment or two later—there pulls up what can only be (an unexpected) van 3—at least as big as the Titanic and as sleek as the Hindenburg. Smart enough to know history is about to be made, they pile in without waiting for the go-ahead. Eden understands that, as guinea pig of honor, extinction protocol demands he enter last. He's ready to grit his teeth and take his medicine but how can he take it through gritted teeth? (A puzzle that's stumped the experts from wily Diogenes [NB: wiliest when spruced up and fully clothed] on down.) What Herbert, once within, is intent on missing most is not the rising sun but the cloud rising above the foothills that's taking, just for her, extra-special pains to deliver up something unforgettable—in this instance, convolutions fluffy enough to make mincemeat of fine—so fine as to become pedantic—distinctions between surface and depth. Its antic disposition should go over real big—*real big*—with iPhone-toting Ansel Adams wannabes.

Mary explains (borrowing the driver's bullhorn) that what she intends to practice on Martin constitutes (it's been ages since anybody called him by his first name: it's like—it *is*—a caress)—constitutes nothing less than Invidicum-free extinction training. "So the memory itself doesn't need to be retrieved," concludes some smart-ass pipsqueak who obviously feels there's a start-up in the vicinity just waiting to be born. Emboldened by the half-dark, Jean acknowledges it's Straynge, Jr. But does Jr. by any chance know that while he's busy making like a wannabe unicorn, his mother is busy dying back at the ranch, kept going only by her theory—by the ever-expanding range of phenomena allowed to come under its jurisdiction free of charge (her propagatory zeal would turn Joe McCarthy green with awe)—and the prospect of shaking Mike Pence's gland—hand—when the transition team arrives at last for whatever purpose it has in mind? (Sean the Spicer Man's been uncharacteristically tightlipped about the subject.) For even if we're 666 days into The Tweeting Rump's tenure, that team will always be in transition? Mary—not Jean—not Margo—shakes her head till it hurts. "*No retrieval, no extinction*. And not just any old retrieval." The iron curtain separating the body of the vehicle from (presumably) toilet territory is transformed by a mere snap of her fingers into a home entertainment system (7K Ultra High Definition). *No retrieval, no extinction.* How, Cantor wonders again, can Mary mention—be allowed to mention *simply in passing*—something so massive? (Just the sort of IED revelation any Hollywood-bound hack would give his eye teeth to be able to make the shout-it-from-the-rooftops centerpiece of his breakthrough [ninth] screenplay.) She asks Eden to remember the fuzzy clips scanned aeons ago in van 1. Obvious that he's remembering not just the clips but what they induced (for skin conductance has spiked dramatically: too bad there's nobody around to take its measure). Within *10* minutes, she flashes what Eden clearly dreads will be the very same clips only this time they're just plain fuzzy. Within 10 minutes (that is, just before the valves of opportunity shut tight)—not, mind you, 11 or 15—nor, for that matter, 1, 6, 10 or 48 hours. And she can guarantee that when he's exposed tomorrow or even in a year's time to the original clips—clips not fuzzy enough to obliterate, inter alia, Boute's perp walk or Rump, Jr.'s mug shot or both—there will be no increased skin conductance—no sweat—no more anathemabilia to keep his handlers up nights. Post bursts into the (self-incriminatory) applause worthy of such reassurance. Martin looks as if he's just awakened from an opium dream[171]—infant-groggy but fulfilled—cut down to size by one of those alarm clocks—you know the kind—that simply won't take No for an answer. Not until this moment—and not a minute before—did Cantor realize how alike people look when they open wide their yap and yawn, yawn, yawn. Cantor surmises (something of a Renaissance Man, this Cantor is: not only does he do *realizing* to a turn but—given half a chance—he can *surmise* as well) that Martin Eden, while not quite sure he's understood everything sesquipedalian Mary just spouted, nonetheless trusts her implicitly and is pleased (even if Post and his goons are even more so) to know he's rid of all that excess baggage. Eden-inspired, the stockier of the two goons tries his hand—his jaw—at yawning. But this isn't one of your run-of-the-mill mindless yawns. Not one of your post- (or pre-) catnap yawns. Taking the temperature of the ensemble, if ensemble is what it is, he quickly comes to realize that as far as lowering it, only a yawn—not a unicorn—would do. Only a yawn—a yawp, really—not a

---

[171]A dream that would have done Thomas de Quincey's tormentors proud—a dream marked, but not tyranically, by "exquisite order, legislation, and harmony."

unicorn—could defuse—and diffuse—the tension generated by what they'd just witnessed from their ringside seats, i.e., nothing less than the dismantlement of a fall guy's inner life. After all, they could be next on the agenda, or the menu. And willy-nilly, everybody else breathes a sigh of relief for he and he alone has had the courage to be the butt of universal contempt at this brazen investment in what's taken right off the bat for self-disrespect—contempt fostering a collegiality in which all but the most curmudgeonly must delight. There's safety—and strength—in numbers. The yawn reassures them that *their* memories, at least, won't be permitted to go the way of Eden's. But—I digress, thinks Cantor, the Yawn's exegete in chief—star epidemiologist of the yawn pandemic. But to digress you need to have a story to digress *from*. It's like retirement—you need to have a job to retire *from*, although Post has known—as have (he's willing to bet) Netta and Pritchard and Margo and Irena and Liepnits—his share of unrepentant un-retirees who can, while (or thanks to) never having held down a job for more than ten seconds, do a better imitation of a bona fide member of the tribe than any Real McCoy ever could. And not just because they've had so much more practice over the formative years of their arduous vagrancy. But—more to the point—he's willing to bet (Post the card shark—the gambling man—has gotten him in the mood) that where there are so many thought packets, as here—so much imbrication of packet with packet and brother packet against brother packet and evasion of packet by packet—and all in the name of fending off everything that isn't packet—where there's so much packet there has to be a story—there just has to be. Since what else is the packet craze born of but a fear of stories—stories lurking everywhere—waiting in the wings—virulent and unvanquishable—distinctly indistinguishable—a dime a dozen yet in the right hands worth billions at the box office? What does a packet fear more than Stories—or rather, Story—Story as the Elephant—as the elephantiasis—in the Room? Answer: The *banality* of said Elephantiasis. Which (at no small risk to its health and sanity) the packet masks for the beast's own good, though Johnstone & Co. would say it's simply biting—no, swallowing—the hand that feeds it.

Not one to rest on her laurels, Mary promptly outdoes herself: "If everything goes according to plan, the process will extinguish other memories as well—memories he didn't know he had—mostly harmless ones—harmless, that is, to the uninitiated—and even stranger, the memories of others, as is only right and proper." He'll be a walking archive of abolishment. An ode to nothingness. An installation worthy of adjacency (at Storm King) to a piece by David Smith—preferably one that sports an impossibly proper—proper but not stuffy—attunement of color and shape. More self-incriminatory applause from Post. Soon enough—now—the CIA won't have anything on him.

Since this van is as good a place—and Eden's debugging as felicitous an occasion—as any: Why, wonders Ethan—jobless, womanless Ethan who as a rule isn't much given to wonder (there, *that* cat's out of the bag)—doesn't Mary, or whatever her name is (though he knows very well what Mary's name is), tear off the mask of her own facehood and turn out to be—to be—the mastermind—the architect of everybody's mere downfall as the merest resurrection? The architect—the Mabuse—of whom—let's face it—they've all not-so-secretly been dreaming—even no-nonsense Borkman—and ever more desperately as each claimant to the title seems to have taken a malign pleasure in turning out to be a mere cog in the Great Expectations machine. After all, Mabusehood is but a hop, a skip and a jump away from her current incarnation as Hollywood's most-feared agent. For what else do they have to dream about now that they've failed—failed at what nobody, however abject, has ever failed at, that is, until now? Patienthood. (Thinking this thought in record time has been so exhausting that Ethan has no energy left to bemoan his Brechtian unhappiest-of-all-fates—the fate of a country [for, among other things, he, too, contains multitudes] that needs a hero.) But what Ethan fails to realize is that such self-depreciation stinks to high heaven of aggrandizement and what's more, it's an aggrandizement to be shared obligatorily with his fellow failures since he doesn't have the guts to reap the prize by going it alone.

"Sometimes, I wish," she says a bit wistfully—a bit too wistfully—

To the driver, one of The Rump's Forgotten Men—but (and let's get this straight from the start) forgotten or not, Mar-a-Lago is strictly off limits to the sort of germs his kind breeds—nope, Melanomiyanna won't be disinfecting his leper's lesions any time soon: "Can you open the blinds, Maestro, and let the cruel world in?" Maestro complies grumblingly or (in accordance with the foil-hungry diva's wishes) fake-grumblingly. The passengers to nowhere shield themselves from the crazy rays or (once again in accordance with her wishes?) pretend to do so. Problem with Forgotten Men, however, is that they don't think of themselves as Forgotten: it's the guy next door—no, the guy around the corner—wait, hold your horses, it's the shirtless guy at the rally three seats away flaunting a Sharpie swastika where his vaccination seal should be. The Forgotten think of themselves—including the driver even if he doesn't know it—as The Rump's *un*Forgettable *amicus curiae* which is exactly what he was banking on—sort of unconsciously—or rather, so shrewdly—with such rabid shrewdness—as to put the schoolmarmish distinction between conscious and unconscious forever to shame.[172] And Melanctha was of this view well before the start of his campaign. The campaign—the campaign—how far away it now seems. And those blessed GOP debates: only time The Rump's been bearable—lovable, even, what with so many malevolent mediocrities on the podium to siphon off his toxins and thereby—unintentionally—keep the innocent out of harm's way. Since wasn't it then that he hit the rusty nail on the head and called a spade (who went by the preposterously self-important nickname Little Marco) a spade and, even more lovably, shame-shamed slime-oozing Flyin' Ted for being unendorsable—and, most lovably of all, denounced Baby Bush for getting so many young men killed or maimed (or did her inspired wandering mind invent this tirade in CW class after the prof called her out for "telling" not "showing"?) just so that armed with smock and palette he could write them all off as Heroes of the Iraq War—and he himself

---

[172] Yes, the Master is well aware that a few pages back he gave the very same observation a trial run. But it was just a few words long. What we have here in high contrast is a full-blown epic-scale haiku.

(their John Singer Drill Sargent) along with 'em? And yet, how easily these epithets—*Little Marco, The Rump, Baby Bush* and (waiting just around the bend) *career cipher*—roll off her tongue, Melanctha remarks to Cantor, certain as she is that he—and he alone—will immediately deduce the context in which her thoughts are stewing. But if they easily roll off her tongue, they roll even more easily off her victims' back. How painlessly the vicious ineptitude of those victims manages to accommodate all such slights. And—adding insult to injury—everybody knows the evildoer that smiles steals something from that worst of all do-gooders—the one in love, like her, with the words her outrage too easily generates. (The one for whom—as for all do-gooders—do-goodism is just schadenfreude in chains—chains made out of marshmallows. And yet . . . And yet . . .)

Johnstone (*without having missed a wistful beat though decades have elapsed since her last foray into the wilds of wistfulness and Forgotten Men*): "Sometimes, I wish—" But as Shearer is the first to note, wistfulness doesn't suit her, just as the prima ballerina role in *Tchaikovsky Piano Concerto No. 2* never suited *her* (legs weren't long enough and never will be).

"Sometimes I wish I knew then what I know now." Her wistfulness is fertile with misgivings.

"Who doesn't?" chortles—yes, *chortles*—Stifter.

"And what exactly does the *what* in "*what* [you] *know now*" all boil down to?" everybody asks—or thinks—in unison.

"That Martin is completely innocent, for one thing. Our little extinction experiment proves as much." No elaboration forthcoming. Instead, a traffic-cop gesture meant to mean, *OK, everybody out: enough good clean fun for one day.* By some miracle she's managed to be the first in line, greeting, as he descends, each and every with a smile meant to mean, *Now that wasn't so bad, was it? How about some bacon 'n' eggs back at the ranch—or better yet* huevos rancheros, *favorite of Baby Bush and Rovin' Karl?* the ranch in this case being, steps away at the water's edge, the new trattoria that's the talk of the town. Great place to take The Rump and his gang when they finally deign to arrive, thinks Walser, who's giving semi-serious thought to dabbling in politics. (If a career cipher like Mike de la Pence can make the grade, why not he? [with a little luck he'll be able to skip the feckless senatorial/gubernatorial stage— wrongly believed to be *de rigueur*, especially for dilettantes].) He believes (rightly) that there's no better place to learn how to network than here and when he figures out precisely why, you'll be the very first to know. But (first things first) Walser's *here* is, alas, not a little like Mary's *what*—and he knows he knows it . . . In other words, where precisely is *here*? Well, if here happens to be where he suspects it is then there's simply no *here* here.

CHAPTER SIXTY

As they penguin their way toward the chow wagon—oops! the trattoria—Walser (with the inveterate killjoy's finesse) announces that (sorry to burst her bubble but) he knew decades ago Eden was innocent. While allusions to the murder no longer get their hackles up, still all progress screeches—no, grinds—to a halt. It's only after overloading their paper plates (each slashed by its very own shard of sunlight) at the brunch buffet that they regain their footing in the present. But rather than join them outdoors, Herbert and Cantor prefer to stand firm at the border between sun and shadow (nothing more unnerving, i.e., intriguing, than to smell the food-impregnated tinkle of air-conditioned cutlery). But as this is clearly going to be a once-in-a-lifetime testimonial they decide to give the artistic temperament a rest, well deserved or not, even if it's respect for that very temperament which has kept respectful Walser from spilling the beans until they've had their fill of subtle (hence packet-birthing) sensations.

Straynge discovered that Skip—Walser means Stifter—cheered on by fellow pedophiles—made it a practice to photograph all of his child patients in the nude (Envy victims first in line) and upload the evidence of his inappropriate fondling everywhere he could. Mass-market intakes of breath. "Silly boy," somebody (obviously paid handsomely) tsk-tsks. And adding insult to injury it's Skip's plate, as Herbert is the first to note, that, tellingly, is piled highest. Before getting very far, he's dragged back—kicking and screaming, as is the way of his mongrel kind—by two of Post's goons. And like The Rump under the weather of similar catastrophes, his first thought is of himself. Why did it have to happen right now, just when things were beginning to look up—when it seemed he could ride on the coattails of Invidicum's fame for as long as he wished—when at last he seemed to have achieved a happy medium between irrepressible cravings for the contempt of the start-uppers—his not only youngers but betters—and repudiation of the adoration of his colleagues? Which is a lot like asking—or maybe just a little—*Why is this disease—the one I'm going to die of—declaring itself right this minute—drawing the clearest of lines between health and its opposite? When everybody knows that out of decency, fatality should be insidious in its onset—uncatchable in the act.* "Who'll be my roommates at Folsom? You must know what they do to child molesters on and off the yard." He looks around for what Cantor assumes must be signs of life, specifically in other sterling candidates for unmerited punishment. Take that interracial gay couple over there near the volleyball net: despite their standout visibility, it's clear they're doomed to a long and happy life. "So why not me?" he wonders.

"All right, I did *think* about killing him. Because I was afraid. Afraid not of his exposing me—the sooner the better as far as I was concerned—but of his insistence that I make him my confidant. For my own good, of all things. He spoke of setting aside an hour or so at the end of each day when, left to our own devices and nourished by the baker's Specials of the Day, I could be treated for what—as rumor had it, up and down Greenwich Avenue and as far west as (its nephew) Greenwich Street—was eminently curable—through talk therapy peppered—once over lightly—with Invidicum." The Man from the Ozarks beams: the baker or at least his Specials have, at last, proved intrinsic to the main design. But all too typically (of him? of the Master?) he's nowhere to be seen. Pritchard—one of the last or maybe the very last to have emerged from what's now being referred to, and not just in the press, as the Extinction Van—tells Newt (after all, they're fellow widowers-to-be) that at least Margo—his Margo—his comatose Margo, who chooses to remain alive only for The Rump's visit—isn't around to hear what's being said. "Even if it casts Straynge's career in the most flattering light?" Pritchard shakes his head sadly. Since as far as he's concerned, *All publicity is bad publicity*. One of the goons gives them both a *Can you please keep it down*-style look. Since even goons—even if they're all beefcake and baubles and boogaloo—have their off moments of delicate sensibility—sensibility so "delicate" as to be almost prissy.

Netta who, over several lifetimes, has given new heft to the expression *Gadfly, thy name is Woman!* shrieks (as if she meant it), "What about those poor kids? Never mind you! What about *them*?"

At such a juncture, however, Skip Stifter is not to be intimidated. Since for the first time in his life—oh, all right (if you want to get technical), for the nth—he feels there's nothing left to lose. "The kids—*like all victims*—will have to fend for themselves. Getting back to Jim: I tried to explain to him that I was incapable of having a confidant. That it would throw—I mean, plunge—me into despair as it did in the past. For there had been many before him—how could there not be what with the weight of all those underworlds forever on my shoulders? I explained I was like that diabolical tyrant fathered forth by some pal of Hans Christian Andersen's whose confidants were all killed off the minute they'd outlived their usefulness. Of course I couldn't, as said tyrant did, have him put immediately to death but I would get around to it, sooner or later. But he wouldn't listen. He tried to reason with me—told me he'd heard all about things far worse—if I could believe it—than child molestation. In any event, he needed to go over the details so that when it came time to treat the kids he'd be well prepared. Though he was kinder than rumor would have it Straynge insisted on refusing to understand. I emphasized that it wasn't the direness of my own private unspeakable that accounted for this hatred of confidants. It wasn't the fact that what I was confiding *was* unspeakable, for if I'd confessed to chewing bubble gum twice daily we would still have ended up on opposite ends of a blunt instrument.

"The place must have been bugged for I'd never been so shocked—"
"Never?" sneers Netta (clearly mad as hell that inasmuch as the connection between the bugging and Stifter's seismic shock eludes her, she can't *in all good conscience* give the sneer her all). "—as I was the following day when showing up at his door, I recognized the voice of Irena—I mean [explaining unnecessarily] Dr. Manning. With her signature exquisite self-control she was letting Straynge know *on no uncertain terms* that if he had any intention of seeking approval for Invidicum in such a context—based on what was sure to be its surefire success—she'd expose him for what he was: a pedophile by proxy. She'd have him—defrocked. They mustn't call attention to the fact that

Invidicum was more—much more—than an Envy drug. They mustn't tamper with the public's perception of the Brand. But Straynge wasn't buying any of it. I heard a shot." Silence—no, dead silence.

"Are you implying that Irena—*my* Irena—wasting away back *there*—would risk her life and career to silence such a mediocrity?"

"That's exactly what I'm implying—and more. *Manning killed Straynge.* Get it through your thick skulls and the collective unconscious will follow in short order." This is a big letdown for everybody: It's one thing to be a least-likely suspect; another, to be the *least interesting* least-likely suspect. Which is not to say that Irena has ever stooped to being uninteresting. It's just that she's uninteresting—albeit intriguingly so—as a least-likely suspect.

Walser looks genuinely shocked. "And here I was suspecting you—convinced that you—my partner—my colleague—my best friend—*mon semblable—mon frère*—" In a word, he begs Stifter's pardon. "I'll get back to you on that one," Stifter replies smartly, knowing he now has the upper hand and will no doubt go on having it until death doth them part professionally.

But where is Liepnits? Herbert wonders. *Shouldn't he be in the grip of murderous outrage? Oughtn't he be defending his trophy wife and child bride? Can chivalry be as dead as all that?*

Eden hasn't minded in the least being left unattended through all this. Any dimming of the lights of celebrity, at least temporarily, is right up his alley even if he's been told ad nauseam that celebrity is what he's always dreamed of—that it's the blight Eden was born for. In fact, it's exoneration without his express permission that's gotten his dander up, way way up. Adding insult to injury, carnivorous Stifter—or rather his toothy grin of terror—has transfixed Eden and Cantor (never one to allow himself to be upstaged) as well. For they have more in common than Eden thinks, thinks Cantor. To the extent that every encounter with other men, especially at their moments of lowest ebb (which in Eden's case are uninterrupted and maybe [lemma-fueled visions of glory notwithstanding] in Cantor's case, too), is a collision with a child molester—an invitation to dinner at which they and they alone—in the role assigned them by their host, that of speechless worshipper cum ratifier of his glory—are on the menu. But for all the self-condoling, self-inflating gobbling to which he's been subjected under the auspices of his obstreperous rivals' wobbly self-esteem, invidiously abused and mercilessly trafficked tyke Cantor always ends up just as he began: never wanting to be anybody but himself (out of the blue he shudders at the thought [a first] that this might be through a bumpkinoid lack of imagination!). Whereas ultimately noble Eden, while remaining constitutively incapable of envy—the *vulgarity* of envy—wants nothing so much as to be anybody—*anything*—but himself simply because he isn't . . . real and never will be, no matter how many virgins he manages to slaughter in the bowels of Balboa Park.

Margo appears from out of nowhere (which is the best place from which to appear, take it from an old hand). Though the sea breeze has put a bit of color on her *to-die-for* (this is CA, after all!) cheekbones, let's not fool ourselves: Margo's still on her last legs. She calls out to Pritchard who, astonishingly, gives her the coldest shoulder Shearer has ever seen outside of a city morgue's deep freeze. *Clearly*, Shearer thinks, *she hasn't had much luck with men.* But unlike Shearer, at least she doesn't seem to know it. He relents, sitting Margo down next to him, thereby enabling her to pick perilously with her fingers—a jazz pianist's fingers—at his still-steaming cacciatore.

Liepnits has returned (when did he disappear?) bearing—at first everybody assumes it's Manning's corpse. Alas, no, it's her wedding dress. Very *Lucia di L., that!* Shearer thinks or rather (*or rather*, suddenly her favorite word-combo in the language) she doesn't so much think this as perfuse herself with the possibility of thinking it—lets the possibility roll over her like kelp-constrained surf—like the opening (singerless) measures of the great Sextet. Following him is, of all people, the baker, whose Special of the Day appears to be an urn placed on what appears to be a salver. In spite of themselves and their pot bellies, the interspecies chimaera they constitute—speaking biomedically—resembles at least for the moment something so beautiful as to merit orchestration—and you can be sure the result would be more than able to hold its own against, say, the slow movement of Haydn's *Symphony No. 97*—how 'bout we take it, Sir Thomas, from those last forty bars or so, upon which your wand inflicts such imperious magic? And when Liepnits is asked about Irena and he replies, *Elle a fui, la tourterelle* (The turtledove has flown away), that does it. He's completely transformed and transforms Moira, too—inducing all sorts of transports—the kind fickle Akim should know about tout de suite, since he appears to have given her up for (artistically) dead—or worse, for comeback-immune—or worst, for Patricia, Suzanne, Kyra, Allegra or Natalia.

Cantor, too, has caught the voice of Liepnits's turtle on the wing. He knows the Man from the Ozarks has garnered quite a reputation as a scholar of sorts (the in-residence kind)—worse, an aesthete—but why out of the blue did he have to go and invoke the ghost of Offenbach? *What's Hoffmann to them, or they to Hoffmann?* Cantor remembers with sudden fondness his participation in, or eavesdropping upon, that over-dinner debate involving Borkman and Eden, way back when, on the much-contested subject of welterweight DiMaggio versus heavyweight Liberace. And now that the milk's been spilt, maybe Joe's ghost can be recruited as corrective, pharmakon, script doctor, mithridate, against this sudden infusion, upsurge, eruption, of froufrou cum chichi, i.e., pure fruity gratuitousness. Or maybe they'll get even luckier and Joe's ghost will break down and wail, *What's wrong with froufrou when it's a matter of life and death? and that goes double for chichi.* But—it suddenly occurs to Cantor—hasn't this Titanic of a Work—for the Invidicum misadventure *is* a Work—been from the very start on a collision course with the iceberg of just such an invocation? And not simply because the fine figure of Straynge can be so easily assimilated to that of Doctor Miracle, not to mention Coppélius and Lindorf and Dappertutto: that may be just serendipitous collateral damage. So let's face it: the Work was, plain and simple, overripe for resurrection compliments of a dose of uplift, Offenbachian or otherwise. And while some Works require one page—er, I mean one hour—to effect a workable—a plausible—hookup with that kind of uplift whether or not it's the right kind of uplift, others (the slow learners, so-called, or are they simply more discriminating, being less addicted to frou-chi and chi-frou?) need at least six hundred.

But isn't it also true that the best way to talk about—to end up talking about—the true subject of the Work is to talk about something else—like Hecuba, say? *Or rather, when you end up talking* about the true subject of the Work aren't you automatically talking about something else, something way way different? And though this latter point (i.e., Or rather, when you end up talking . . .) seems to contradict—or at least not jibe with—the former (i.e., *And—But isn't it also true* . . .), Cantor has it on good—on the best—authority that in fact the very contradistinction between former and latter is a means of protecting said Work against all invaders. And while we're at it, where else, I ask you—yes, *you!*—can you find two points that are as willing as these— no, as *more than willing*—to contradistinguish each other so perfectly—so heartily? Indeed, where else can a Work be found as sure of itself—of its own virility—as this one—so sure of itself as to be willing—no, more than willing—to endure, accommodate, assimilate contradiction—or rather contradistinction—inasmuch as it knows for a fact that contradistinction is in its best interest—is for its own good—is its own best enemy (none in fact more consecrated to its cause)? Pure opposition is a windfall, a rarity, a godsend in a godless universe. It's sort of like a Field of the Cloth of Gold but without the cloth and without the gold—and best of all without Henry VIII wandering in from another opera to steal the show.

Or can it be, Cantor marvels—with a little help from Melanctha Herbert—that the Work (will wonders never cease!) has a brain in addition to a soul and for all the willingness to rub its nose in the dust of Real Life, or Life's facsimiles: darkest-reaches-of-the-Internet-style pornography, for example, or infinitely more pornographic in-broadest-daylight politicking[173]—and for all that willingness, said Work still—always—has one eye on the prize—the only prize worth eyeing, namely, Its own operatification—Its own transmogri-

---

[173]See, for example, the clip of The Rump's DTs-engendering first full Cabinet meeting (June 2017). At which every Goneril and Regan in the house (most of them male but in name only)—*thus out of season, threading dark-eyed night*—strove to outdo all the others not in just kissing the ass of the Master Baiter but in shoving their tongue straight up through the GI tract into his unparchable throat, while simultaneously administering a blowjob of such savage finesse as to turn poor unjustly maligned Monica green with an Envy too massive to be Invidicum-susceptible. And where only Mattis—the closest thing to a Cordelia—was able to emerge with his self-respect sort of more or less intact—by making it clear he was . . . not blessed to be serving Das Rump but *honored to be representing the men and women of the Department of Defense.* And, by the way, what makes the author of this congratulatory footnote—in effect a bouquet bounded in a nutshell—any less of an on-call-24/7 ass-kisser? The wittier somebody takes himself to be in tarring and feathering (but only for his own good) The Rumpity-Dumpity-who-sat-on-a-Mexican/Muslim wailing wall, the more that somebody proves they're on the very same wavelength—the more he jells in The Rumpity's aspic—jelling so wittily that he becomes indistinguishable from it. Only when he can prove (strictly, quantifiably) that the practice of Rump wit has cost him his health will he be absolvable—acquittable.

fication into a better version of, say, *Les Contes d'Hoffmann*? Indeed, the Work knows that successful traversal of the only legitimate pathway to operatification—to better-version-hood—enjoins ultimate extrusion—sweaty, semen-drenched, horseshit-stained but unbowed—from the hindgut of those darkest or in-broadest-daylight reaches. Everything the Work commits—the more vile the better—it commits with an eye to its own operatification, the key of course being to keep the wheels of credulity with respect to the myth of vileness well greased (since nothing is intrinsically vile *but thinking makes it so*).

And then he remembers something—lots of things—drummed into him not so very long ago down Coronado way—something that suddenly puts *it* all into perspective—makes *it* all come (orgiastically) together—or is Cantor simply inventing here and now what he professes to be reporting under duress? If there's to be operatification (from this nettle, Memory, he plucks this flower, Insight), it must be achieved within the context or under the auspices, or the aegis, or is it the Attribute? of an audition[174]—Audition in Its pure state—refracted through the big-top hysteria generated by such an occasion. Nothing more operatic than an audition since it's the Slave's bid for the Master's recognition of an essence achieved only through that recognition. Thank heaven, then, that when the mighty Liepnits von Beethoven intoned the even mightier first bars of Antonia's romance he knew an audition was in progress. Though in that case, the main ingredient—Pathos in *Its* pure state— was unfortunately missing, since there was no "next contestant" disgorged from the wings to hiss him off the stage of life *before he'd quite finished*, with the disgorger of course doomed to suffer an identical fate—propelled by the breath of his own successor's terrified hunger to triumph. Still, Liepnits & Co. must have done something right since Cantor has ended up feeling it was he in fact, a smart-ass kid from the Bronx, who'd stumbled through the most grueling audition of all—that of Spectator and not just any old spectator but Spectator General in His Purest State.

It's taken all this stumbling to make him realize that, as it turns out, trademark cocks-and-cunts or cocks-and-cocks or cunts-and-cunts pornography—or the (even harder-core) Cabinet-meeting-to-end-all-cabinet-meetings version—ostensibly the furthest things from opera, grand or not, is in fact opera's best friend. A single dose before bedtime dissipates the exultation—the self-transubstantiation—*the icy ecstasies of the . . . corrupted nervous system*[175]—that opera perpetrates, thereby allowing the aspirants to the production of such a perpetual motion machine to get on with the Work they were cut out for without being distracted by such things.

Deferring to the brunchers' expectancy, Liepnits dutifully bursts into sobs and tears the gown to shreds. Extracting the shreds—almost daintily— from the shredder's hands, the baker sits Liepnits down beside him in the

---

[174]Fasten your seat belts: another case of the Master (from depletion? from repletion?) conjuring, in his very best determined-to-be-senile-at-all-cost style, an old warhorse (and what fits the bill better than The Audition?).

[175]See Thomas Mann, "Tonio Kröger" (in the H.T. Lowe-Porter translation).

sand. They seem to be meditating (no preliminaries, right off the bat) or rather (though neither is Jewish) *davening* which makes Cantor who *is* Jewish (or at least *census*-Jewish) glad to be rudderless. His pal advances toward the waves as Liepnits lags—and ultimately remains—behind. When he's in up to mid-thigh, the baker looks to Cantor as if he were in over his head. Or, to take things a step further, the baker looks as if he'd bit off more than he can chew or rather the phrase tells Cantor that's what he ought to look like and if Cantor can't see his way clear to seeing him that way, well, then, the joke's on Cantor, census or no census. Undaunted, whatever he's ended up looking like, the baker turns the urn upside down as the next best thing to turning it, like a kid glove or the purloined letter, inside out—and shakes away until all the ashes have scattered. And then—sure to be a first in the annals of cremation—he scatters urn and salver along with them. And as if this obscure rite is his cue—his cue of cues—Borkman, of all people—

Cantor, a true voice in the wilderness, wants to cry out to somebody (but whom?), *Stop resorting to* Of all people: *A cheap ploy for making the reader, under the attribute of Thought, or the spectator, under that of Extension, swallow the fiction that because it can be rent every so often by the jackknife of surprise, the Work is a real fabric made in USA—and not some Kabbalistic mishmash of appellatives imported from China by way of the currently much frequented Galapagos global value chain.*

Response: Sorry about the ploy. Directive, however shrill, taken respectfully under advisement.

Borkman steps forward (he hasn't touched his pasta primavera—the wily tyke). "I've been thinking a lot about mortality lately and it isn't just the monitoring bracelet talking." Looking with stagey surreptitiousness—yes, *stagey surreptitiousness*—at his watch (no doubt forgetting he's no longer running a tight ship back in that labyrinth of a lab on Greenwich Avenue), Post says redundantly, "Is this going to take very long?" Thing is, here every minute *doesn't* count. Borkman is not to be intimidated—pipeline or no pipeline. He's stared down Post's kind before—and a lot worse—at a million and one board meetings. The seagulls keep a most respectful distance. *Seagulls.* Clearly, the Master—Master to her Muse—is experiencing remorse: He's been behindhand in ladling out the local color and the best He can bring to a boil at this late date is a few measly seagulls. Even if they're better than nothing. And even if at the same time the Master must know that through his ostensible ineptitude he's providing auditioners galore—for we're all auditioners in the end (*talk about glib pronouncements!*)—with something better—a real gift—i.e., ladling with what Melanctha's grandma would have called *a twist* (a favorite of Cantor's mother, she seems to recall—in fact, of everybody's mother as far as the Master's concerned, she goes on to acknowledge bravely). Since the only thing better than local color itself is being caught in the act of trying to pull its wool over everybody's eyes—the only thing better than lyricism is its dismantlement once and for all so that from lyricism's impure and polluted flesh . . . meta-violets of critical understanding may spring.

Borkman starts to explain and, thanks to every trick Google Translate has up its sleeve, his explanation comes out smelling like something along the following ignoble—worse, wobbly—lines. (Whether the explanation is in or out of character is of no importance. The prose's the thing.) It's sad (*Gather round the campfire, boys and girls* tone of voice) but he knew all along that an early death for Irena was inevitable. As a point of information: the two of them did the impossible: fucked their way, *in record time*, beyond all the fucking to a perfect devotion. Amazing, actually, how many men had fucked her and ended up crazily empty-handed, with only a fuck-free devotion, which bordered on the morbid, to call not just their own but their *very* own. Now he understands what somebody meant (or thinks he does) when that somebody spoke of her as more, much more, than just a trophy wife and child bride all wrapped up in one. He's sad—couldn't in fact be sadder—but in growing sadder and sadder, he also grows—out of all proportion to his sadness—happy—maybe even too happy for his own good. Happy that his sadness is for once *unalloyed*. Maybe it's the wine (though no expert he: actually the thought of stooping to such expertise alarms him—a betrayal of his working class beginnings, though was he ever truly working-class?). He's managed, also *in record time*—managed to scour every inlet of her character—every contortion of her entrails—for some sign, the least indication, of a hidden self-inflationary flaw—some proof of calculation—of a very un-Kantian use of other people to further her own mean-spirited ends. (No better place than Van 3, aka the Extinction Van, to bring such a project to fruition. Why? because forced intermingling of disparate efforts [memory extinction/entrail scouring] generates plausibility in any Work.) Since as an activist investor first and foremost (he's practically invented the term), Borkman has no intention of discovering subsequently that deepest mourning was simply irrational exuberance—that the stock was a lemon. But with the investigation now complete he's pleased to report to the amphitheater of shareholders that, aside from a view minor blemishes which serve only to affirm her purity, she's—was—a good woman, and not just because her short life was devoted to wiping the plague of Envy off the face of the earth—wiping Its smirk (their only armor) off the face of the well-heeled lumpen.

Eden closes his eyes so he can get a better view of what Borkman unbeknownst to him has invoked: looks like a beech tree—*their* beech tree—which entertained them shamelessly by pretending, one lukewarm summer afternoon in Madison Square Park, to shun the sun. An image most definitely not open to the general public—its borders nonporous to a fault—authentic to the extent that nothing can be done with it—to the extent that nothing should be done with it. Not that Eden is some greedy artist for whom the image—the grace of the image—is unbearable unless something *can* be done with—or better yet, *to* it. His booty has come through unscathed as proof of love lived, if only for an hour. Enduring its inviolability—the inviolability of its pastness—its *overness* (no shouting its name from the rooftops)—is what makes for high interior drama. (Borkman has of course had more than his share of beech-tree moments [take the tryst with that exquisitely cute little blonde—thankfully married—in the Chelsea Hotel, for example]. Thing is, he's not big on inviolability—even less on the pathos of inviolability.) Who'd ever imagine Eden of all people to be the curator of so heartbreaking a moment? Well, it's his very refusal to let anybody in on the secret—better yet, his inability to even conceive of letting anybody in on it for purposes of self-advertisement—worse, self-transfiguration—that exalts the curator. Unconscious stoicism is mortal beauty. And the fact that Eden hasn't the faintest idea what the heartless Master is now babbling about in His foul rag-and-bone shop renders him even more exalted. Eden is the soul—the sanctum sanctorum—of this enterprise—the only one of His modes from whom the Master recoils—the only lump whose will to resist is stronger than the Master's will to shape.

Borkman reminds them that Irena was ever eager to lend a helping hand, always did the right thing no matter what she might be feeling about herself—about life—at the moment that help was demanded. Was never known to turn down a request for an fMRI, whatever the time of day or night and the danger to herself. (Liepnits nods sadly, his fat face even more bloated. With regret, suspects Cook, who, while no stranger himself to that state of soul, is incapable nonetheless of being moved to pity.) Thing is, being so used to fraudulence Borkman's made it a practice to dismiss any act of kindness as a rebuke—an affront—to common sense—as the prime impediment to his vocation—which is not, as mistakenly thought, to practice the art of the bluff, but to outHerod the Herod of dog-eat-doggery, which is not the spice but the very stuff of life. So used as he's been to indecency, its obverse qualifies as a crime against nature. Why, it's as if pitilessly impregnable nature—that indecent bitch—and (physically speaking) a cross between Eve, Noah's wife and the Cumaean Sibyl, as depicted, of course, by Michelangelo (their tits in turn shaped like basketballs or baseball bats or watermelons or the highest common denominator thereof)—as if nature herself were in fact a blushing flower, to be shielded at all costs against any trespass of decency—nothing more indecent—into her eminent domain. But unlike Liepnits, he refuses to weep crocodile tears. If they must know, it's her body he misses most of all for it speaks—exactly the way Baruch said it would—far more eloquently of her soul than words ever could. But the funny thing is, that while an immense staying power has contributed not a little to his fame as the cocksman's cocksman, Borkman still doesn't understand the basics of female anatomy. Hence, having no idea where to park his fore- and middle fingers when, en route to orgasm (toward which his staying power goaded her always so tactfully), she cried out, *Vagina!* or *Vaginal bacterial community!* or *Vas deferens!* his only recourse was to time-consuming trial and error.

Moira has managed to undergo all that she's just witnessed more as a seeing than as a hearing—for wasn't Balanchine's aesthetic driven by the striving to make the spectator *see* the music and *hear* the dancing? The proof being that this has killed her appetite: pity, since the Tuscan lamb Amirstan was skewered to near perfection. And that, *a fortiori*, it's produced a *stance of despair* in response (she quickly discovers) to the fear that Cook (presumably on his way to the men's room) may decide (like Irena) never to return. But well before he does (the greater the despair, the greater the certainty he will)—to show her gratitude for all the pleasure his buttocks generated in their Chateau de Silling days, having triggered art-historical recollections (whose armature was Michelangelesque) she didn't know had been quaintly moldering away in anticipation of just such an occasion—Moira attempts to turn that stance into one of uplift—Offenbachian if at all possible—or the literal uplift undergone in *Ivesiana* when borne on the bier of eight male shoulders, she, modern-day Eurydice, descends two or three times to torment the infinite space between her and her lover. But owing to a perversity that can't be laid entirely at her own doorstep—it's part physiological—she refuses to take the life-or-death leap—a *Donizetti Variations* sort of leap. Precisely—or imprecisely—because the challenge is way too easy for a prima ballerina. Anyway, no safer incubator for uplift than the very heart of despair.

In a close-up worthy of Norma Desmond, Melanctha can only marvel at how deftly the Master has granted everybody's thought packet—worth double the price of admission—the opportunity to steal the show. His is the only single-payer system up to Bernie's highest standard.

CHAPTER SIXTY-ONE

But no matter what Shearer's organ systems may think, as she awaits her true loves—i.e., Bill Cook and Akim Volynsky (but along different time scales)—this is a moment for reconciliation—or at least a pretense of reconciliation—and not just of despair and uplift—reconciliation of everybody with everybody else. Liepnits agrees—that is, goes a step further by doing his best to *more-than-agree* (for he's never wanted anything so much as his Cabinet post) by saying, "And never so vital as now," though he tries hard to sound meditative, nothing less than dreamy—forelock-twistingly dreamy—rather than rabid, rather than calculating. Never so vital as now in anticipation of the arrival of The Rump team, forever in transition—a transition that's sure to ultimately implode (though the reason for the visit is still *shrouded in secrecy*). (And is it in fact an exaggeration to say that if Margo is on the verge of a speedy recovery—and what better proof than her no longer needing to be spoon-fed Pritchard's organic butternut squash lasagna?—she owes this all to such anticipation.) So everything connected with human relations must be rendered spic 'n' spam—er, span. And everybody—even if he or she doesn't know it just yet—clearly has his or her own particular reason for wanting to put on a good show for The Rumpty-Dumpty and his not bi-, not tri- but anilingual minions. For one thing—and doesn't one thing always lead to another?—who knows how many scouts will be along for the ride—and with the sole intent of bookmarking for mass-marketable exploitation just the sort of unwitting talent possessed in spades by boobs like them?

But more to the point (but why *more*? if not because the Master can smell a packet comin' round the bend [stay tuned] and needs the bare bones of an underpinning concrete image—event—hullabaloo—to usher it in but with just enough implausibility in the forced filiation to make it strange—*Shklovsky*-strange—uncanny—i.e., interesting!), there're those photos—or were they videos?—smeared just the other night across the TV screen—especially—archetypically—of Bannon talking to—at—slumdog billionaire Kushhner but with none of his usual unhinged contempt (after all, this is the boss's son-in-law, however contemptible). And on a less exalted, i.e., degraded level, there were videos of contemptible Scessions talking at contemptuous Tyllerson and of Reince (what a name! sounds like something the Master would have cooked up to keep forever at arm's length the creature he invented to bear it) talking at Price (who always looks as if he were on *Duck the Press* with Chuck Todd, sweating piggish beads from having to retail all those dutifully compiled diversionary WHO statistics as proof that there're no limits to how far A Rump can throw his world-class executive weight around if he sets his glutes to it). Which just goes to prove Cantor's point of several hundred pages back—made in the wild and woolly days of youth—to wit, that in any dyad (make way for the packet, folks—you've waited long enough—it's finally here), there's always a First *supplicating* a brute Second—even if the First happens not to be supplicating in the least but rather simply waxing enchanted (and as we all know, enchantment can be aggressive—sanguinary) by a New Concept he happens to be knocking into shape (something to do with dismantling the Dems' elitist swamp by encoding, in their DNA of all places, images of what their phony fixation on expanding Medicaid—and for the poor, of all things—slobs who should know better than to mimic psychic disablement for a few measly handouts—images of the mayhem that phoniness will perpetrate). Supplicating—with said Second a mere fixture caught in the crossfire between the First's dismantling and deregulating selves. By virtue simply of casting himself in the uncovetable role of the babbler, O'Bannion's to be seen (across the globe) as making Slavish overtures to the Boss's favorite non-son—seeking to pacify (which is of course what he should be doing given the current climate in hell's West Wing) lest, thanks to the latter's backstabbing back-channelling, he end up being Slavishly canned. And the more the supplications intensify—the supplications-that-aren't-until-they-are—the more opaque the Other—the snaky slumdog—becomes either by design (seizing his chance to reign supreme even if it's over a bipolar knucklehead like McBannion) or because Contrast (that Cupid, that Puck, that Pandarus)—the Great God Contrast—abhorring a vacuum and seizing his chance to sneak in and shine—simply forces the Kush (now Master by default) to outdo himself at doing what he does best: opacify to beat the band. Babbling signifies need even if there isn't any—even if the babbler feels infinitely superior to his interlocutor manqué (yep, Bro, *manqué*, no other word will do here, there or anywhere else). So the long and short of it is there's dissension in the ranks—everybody is at everybody else's throat—every poor excuse for a knight-errant is at everybody else's moat—most of all his very own—especially with the Jr.-to-end-all-juniors up to his slicked-back skull in illegalities. So everybody ends up as everybody else's Slave seeking an existential nod of permission from the Master to go ahead and be acknowledgeably subhuman. And what's bad for the team is bad for the tribe—the Invidicum tribe, that is. But in a way not quite clear to anybody, yet.

So the long and short of the moral of the story is that now, more than ever, the transitioners clearly need to see—to believe—reconciliation is possible. There's cold cash to be extracted and status to be juiced from a simulacrum of same. (Too much dissension in the air—dissension to spare—dissension playing havoc with everybody's darkest desires.) But the Greenwich Avenue irregulars must proceed cautiously. *First off*, thinks Liepnits, who wants to replace Price or Mnunchkin (the savviest anal-fellators of the lot at least for now) more than ever, *reconciliation needs to be* euphemized. It's too harsh—too raw—a term for the Rump team's too virgin ears—too virgin because too transitional—forever in transition, like a revolving door. (Just as everybody in *The Three Sisters* is an eternal student so is everybody on the Rump team—so is the team itself!—an eternal *transitional* [better to think of them—of it—this way—since the word transforms everyone of them into a lyric poem and lyricism, as we all know, conquers all].) *Reconciliation*—the term—will turn the hardliners off, even if what it signifies is for their own good—or the good of the soon to be Happy Few. Although if you must know, Liepnits is heartily sick of euphemisms—reality's over-the-counter chloroform. Rot like *unacceptable* (how you gonna implement its verdict out in the world?). And what about *passion* (see somewhere above for a preview): making a true passion, i.e., a vocation, the most unpassionate thing of all instead of what it should, i.e., big with the threat of branding everybody who practices anything else as being the rankest amateur—big with the indictment of *Life Itself as the biggest amateur of all* (or is Life Itself as the biggest amateur of all just another case of the Master's getting on Wordflow, his high—his highest horse, yet again?). And take *depression*, for example—and *empathy*. Euphemisms for what shouldn't require one. Since what is *depression*, after all (*pace* the *DSM Manual of Incremental Disorders*, 69th Edition), but sadness sucked dry, with all of the juice, the marrow, siphoned off. Not to mention *asshole* and let's not forget *fuck* (except when used literally—unrancorously—at which point it becomes tremulously beautiful): the biggest euphemisms ever to see the light of day—the words most traveled—most sanitized through overuse (like a cigarette or aviator glasses as prop in some off-off-Broadway bid for semi-immortality)—which allow us (or so it seems) to hand-paddle around in our very own swimming pool cum think-tank cum echo-chamber-for-one, unimpeded by and unentangled in the kelpy strands of euphemism-free brute truth—secure in the illusion—the assumption—that all of its inconvenient stench has been chlorinated away. So let's just stick with *reconciliation*, after all, thinks Liepnits, sighing advertisingly—sighs Liepnits, thinking advertisingly.

But if reconciliation is in the air or waiting in the wings and here to stay, then why not generate a bit of Big Apple savvy and use what's ready to hand, why don't we?—namely, the triad of Charles Sanders Peirce—as template—as paradigm without shifts. Why not frame the reconciliation process as a fight between First- and Secondness (both of which, as you may remember, did quite a star turn during the Dildo Sequence despite all the nudist-colony competition) with Thirdness the inevitable victor? Time to clog the cleavage between First- and Secondness—in their current trial-generated Brands. (Since Brand is All—just ask the The Rumps—who've managed in the blink of an eye to turn the White House into the Maul of America. Try, for example, asking branded steers Eric and Don, Jr., the Daddy's boys to end all Daddy's boys, except maybe for not-quite-self-made Daddy himself.) Time to clog the cleavage between F and S through the surgical intervention of . . . Dr. Thirdness on call, like any certified quack, 24/7. Whose press, granted, tends to be bad (since he's not as *sexy*[176] as the other two) but if the Master has the last word (and what Master doesn't? at least according to Hans Christian Grimm), that trend'll soon be a thing of the past.

And who better equipped than the baker—*the* baker—the yeast—the buttered toast—of the earth, as his kind is referred to in both Testaments, or should be—who better equipped than the baker to complete CSP's holy trinity—to umpire the transformation of the Great Cleavage—the Great

---

[176]A term now applied exclusively not to people but to topics, with respect to which it means—has been made to mean—*mind-grabbing* or *showstopper challenging*, i.e., *hot* (that is, before *hot* was made to mean, well, sexy).

Clash—into a Clash No Longer—to give concrete life to reconciliation—to turn it into an image—to make it a little less scary? (Some go so far as to say the latter is singlehandedly responsible for the bialys presently making the rounds during this Last Supper *to end all Last Suppers.*) Who better than the baker—a disinterested party, so to speak—to reconcile First- with Secondness and Second- with Firstness? To reconcile (*a*) the farm-fresh chaos of inarticulable feeling (Margo's, e.g.), painterly dreaminess (Moira's e.g.), the artsy-fartsiness of any quality's evanescence WITH (*b*) the post-Darwinian clash of ever-present resistances, the brute facts of life against which wasps in a bottle like Borkman—like everybody—are always banging their heads in vain. Who better than the baker—*the* baker—to reconcile the stuff of which the Shearers and Herberts are made with the stuff of a Borkman or a Post? *But who needs reconciliation?* somebody hears somebody else protest above the protests of the surf. Oh why, Jean wonders (some might say too late), has she never taken him—the baker—at his true worth—why did she let East Side snoot—worthy of a Caro, maybe, but not of Wild West (Side) Jean herself—get in the way? Why did she never try to see him (NB: at this point, somebody else is doing the thinking for Jean) for what he was—is—to see that his character is nothing less than the embodiment of Betweenness and Mediation—law, symbol, habit-taking, generalization, continuity, synthesis, living, continuity, synthesis again, process, moderation, learning, abduction, memory, inference, abduction again, moderation again, representation, intelligence, intelligibility, generality, infinity, diffusion, growth, mediation again, synthesis again and again? But best of all, Habit—who better than the baker to be decked out in the habit of Habit, the habit of monks? With all this Thirdness—Thirdness to spare—which he carries so lightly on his yeasty yeomanly shoulders—he might have been just the ticket to save her marriage. Since the baker's exactly the sort of guy CSP was thinking about when he wrote that The Man is the Thought and The Thought the Man and that the job of thoughts—especially (even if this forgivably escaped C's notice) bakerly thoughts—consists in bringing things into connection, even things as disparate as, say, she and Caro or she and Netta or, more to the point, she and her ex- or (depending on whom you speak to) soon-to-be ex-. The job of thoughts is to bring Jean's poignant Firstness and Netta's brute-fact Secondness into that regularity of relation—as between oatmeal-cookie dough and chocolate chips—which grown-up folk, wherever they may loom and lurk, recognize and accept as reality with a capital *R*. Not that the general ideas he embodies are any less (rather they're far more) living realities than the feelings (other people's feelings, since a baker has no time for feelings in the usual sense) out of which they're constructed—by which they're instructed. Like his cinnamon raisin buns, Thirdness can never be fully perfected—must always be in a state of incipiency, growth, and to grow you need to feel. *Is it the urn business that's responsible for this cascade of insights?* (which by the way show no sign of petering out) Jean of Arc wonders with a well-placed sigh. The baker is a character in search of an ID and what better route than through Thirdness, in whose *fernem Land* any guilt for an omnipotence so quickly won is *streng verboten*? But though no freelance philosopher he's sharp enough to know that the omnipotence his cap wields is owed in full to the parts he brings—like a prune and a danish—into mutual relationship—he's smart enough to know Thirdness does not by itself constitute reality but is a mere essential ingredient thereof, since this Category has no concrete being without an object on which to work its rough magic.

The thread of life—at least, life as reconciliation—is a Third and he's that thread (even if Melanctha may think such an honor should be bestowed on the Master). And a thread running not just through cream puffs, cranberry scones, chocolate babkas and charlottes russe. She sees all too clearly—so clearly it makes her dizzy—that the baker belongs to the Third class of men: men without an axe to grind or expectation of a perk here or lunatic fringe benefit there: men to whom nothing seems great but reason—even if others might call it the reason of the fossil-fueled oven—inquirers into truth for truth's sake and from a rejuvenating impulse to penetrate into the reason of things. Whether you consider him a practitioner or a tool of Thirdness, his function in Its field is mediation and, in particular, performance—execution—of the unholy nuptials of Firstness and Secondness (connected without merging), who are then conveniently whisked away in a harlot-cursed marriage hearse: a prop contributed gratis by hedge-fund honchos J.G. Borkman and W. Blake. So it's up to the baker and the baker alone to sew things up by turning everybody into a creature of Habit reconciled first of all to himself. Self-sutured. As dough, present everywhere and visible nowhere (and having taken on, as the saying goes, a life of its own), is, before their very eyes—their very mind's eye—being reconciled to *itself*. For habit is a narcotic—Big Pharma's best—and narcotized creatures are no threat to others as they go busily about their business of staying shackled to routine. Which is all to the good—or at least all to the expedient, since brute expediency is too much the name of the game in these parts and even if the baker has had enough of brute expediency to last him a lifetime. Since what do you call allowing himself to be routinely pushed around by baby-faced speculators (not to mention his customers faithful and un-) if not *surrender to the great god expediency*? He's tired of remembering that all he got for his pains was eviction from Greenwich Avenue on the butchered wings of a buyout perpetrated by the worst of the lot, none other than Jarey Krushner, the Rump's son-in-law-in-chief, whose sole talent—and a major one—was the inability to sprout facial hair. It's crucial that The Rump and his tribe not be made to feel threatened by folks who are out of control, since if they feel threatened they won't deliver the goods, whatever those goods may turn out to be. They must be made to feel that reconciliation is *in the air.*

But Pritchard is thinking very different thoughts. For if Margo decides to take her native hyper-impressionability out for an airing in the current climate of opinion, where reconciliation reigns supreme—decides to take the bait—to get all sutured up—all self-reconciled—then she won't let her guard down long enough to run amuck and be thereby of sublime use to science—long enough to show her true—her truest—colors. For she believes in conspiracies as in nothing else, and conspiratorial thinking is hot (in the old sense), soaking up—sucking up—plenty of NIH bitcoin (though money isn't Pritchard's object: never has been, and all to his own detriment). Which means that she must be allowed—forced—to speak—to act—*on two levels simultaneously*—the level of reconciliation and the level of conspiracism. She must show herself to be reconciled enough (never mind with what or to what) to put The Rump at his ease—but the ease he's put at mustn't be an ease so engulfing that it's alien—that it makes him uncomfortable—that it makes him suspicious of this new and crazy thing called well-being—that it makes him forget there's such a thing as pain—envy—rage—self-hate—or, more to the point, Conspiracy, which (like Debt chez Rabelais—like Audition chez Ishmael Drybock—like Indian-hating chez Melville's Confidence Man) runs and rules the world. Her job is to put him so much at ease that he's able to give freest rein to his conspiratorial raging without suspecting he's being played—set up—guinea-pigged (it's a delicate balance). And by observing how she comports—or disports—dis-comports—herself in the company of not just another of the likeminded but the most likeminded of all—a Giant in the minefield of loony likemindedness—and by observing The Rump disport in tandem—Pritchard and *his* tribe (a tribe of one and shrinking by the minute) will be able to determine if Invidicum might have a role to play in the treatment of, of all things, Conspiratorial Thinking (whether as cause or cure or both doesn't matter in the least as long as it gets that role without any messy auditions). He doesn't want to put the cart before the horse but it looks as if Invidicum, whether off-label or on-, is shaping up to be nothing less than the very universal solvent that was sought in vain by humanitarian heavyweights like Pizarro and Balboa and Cortés. For, like Mueller's, the investigation of Invidicum is yet again widening its scope, and so what if it's Post and *his* tribe that ultimately profit from Pritchard's disinterested pursuit of truth? Though some might say that for a snake in snake's clothing like Stephan Miller (with the unseeing smoky gaze of an unregenerate psychopath) or punk Rep Jim O'Jordan or Devven De Nunez or Larry Cruddlow, for example, there're things more important—even *far* more important—than truth, which is just too damn smug for its own good. Crudd and Jim just don't *get* what truth has to offer—it's too limited and too limiting. And/but as a fringe benefit of truth-hating, the intersexual votaries who peddle it make the boys' blood run proudly cold and turn their stalwart stomachs. Simply too many things truth is incapable of conveying—like indigent end-stage cancer patients' right to choose *not to choose*—end-stagers' right to deploy some measly voucher—the GOP unholy grail—as a weathervane, a compass needle, pointing deathward. So Paul O'Ryan, spawned by the maggots conserved conservatively in a Petri dish at the Heritage Foundation—and let's not forget collaterally—simultaneously—born of the sodomization of Ayn Rand by Joe McCarthy—is in fact doing the teemingly wretched refuse a favor by pricing them way way out of the market (if they're poor, that's because they choose to be, right, Bets?)—refunding a wee bit more of their long-lost right to non-entitlement with every voucher bestowed. (End of paean to some of Rumplandia's finest traveling salesmen, who used to be referred to—in, for example, novels like Dreiser's *Sister Carrie*—as *drummers*.)

What matters is that Invidicum gain entry into yet another labyrinth—the best of the bunch—the labyrinth to end all labyrinths. And so what if he's ended up utilizing Margo to achieve that special effect. Doesn't all poetic justice (and surely the black lady, notebook forever in hand, would agree) come down to base opportunism? (He'll buy into almost any kind of final sequence just so long as [unlike so many final sequences in what's known as *cinema*] it steers clear of ending with the big bang of a whimper—the whimper of . . . apocalypse. Apocalypses are so damn . . . corny—so cornily inflationary—so expedient. You can smell one coming down the pike a mile away and ducking under your seat with what's left of your unsalted popcorn will do nothing to exorcise its even cornier demon.) Thing is, the guy the black lady (tongue forever in her cheek) calls Master seems to go in for such dinner theater fare. Moreover, he's owed something for all the several-lifetimes worth of misery caused him since she flew out here—during these, his so-called Golden Years. Although just because he can't stop hating her (with the vehemence of a Borkman Unchained)—can't turn off the motor of hatred—doesn't mean she deserves to be hated. If he were half the man O'Bannion was or that hyperextended dwarf Mnutchkin (too many teeth to be accommodated by his fawningly slack jaw) or any of the Merry Mikes, he'd know how to be true to the domestic battle royal, while at the same time gingerly titrating hatethink against her reality before it—hatethink—overflowed to the point where it had, like Hamlet's, no objective correlative. If Pritchard were Jared the Jakes—or, better yet, the Jakes's Giocondo smile—he'd know how to stop hatethink in its tracks before it made him sound . . . unfair, i.e., like a killer. After all, she is the father—I mean, the mother—of his child. And come to think of it, once he's dead—and still unfamous though not so unfamous as to merit complete unmention at least as one of the pre-eminent famously unfamous—whatever will those *Times* obit hacks make of his life—a life to rival Riley's but not quite—not to mention his hard knocks?—that is, if he's lucky enough to get the fifteen minutes of defamation due him as a union member (*font of notice: Gothic with a touch of Georgia*)? How will they manage to cook up a leering paraphrase without paraphrasing their own ineptitude in the process?—without being compelled to admit some lives are completely unparaphraseable—incompressible—into so many pennies-a-word of jeering print? They'll hate him—and take it out on the obit—for being so paraphrase-resistant, i.e., so non-linear, the way caricaturists have come to hate Kellyannia Kockenlocker, one of the world's most adept female impersonators. For she's already the perfect caricature—she's done a far better job of super-sketching her slithering crocodile snout and imperturbable alligator grin than they could ever hope to do—even with their three million YouTube followers to cheer them on. Why, those caricaturists are even thinking of unionizing—against just such subjects as the Kockenlocker who cry out through their very being for caricature yet who, through that very being, beat the unionizers to the finish every time. So, despite the refractoriness of their subject, will they prove clever enough to come up with something sufficiently reductive—sneeringly fleeringly dismissive—along the lines of: *Well, when a no longer Young Man, Doc Pritchard said goodbye to Greeley Square and went West, even if it was only as far west as the manicured wilds of Santa Barbara, with the goal of transforming a poor man's opioid into an elixir—and almost failed. And/but/indeed/in fact as a bonus but* to whom? he turned out to be homosexualizable, too, but managed (in celebration of success) to turn the tables on that old whore fate by giving birth to a son and all so that the fake father—the fake news of a father—the alternative fact of a father—the supplementary pharmakon of a father—fake remedy and real poison to his fake son—a fake who was, as it just so happened, in the same profession, sort of—all so that the fake news father could end up insisting that said son, fake or not, be christened a Jr. ex post. Which he must admit—he can see it through her tears—is causing Margo no end of worry (though she doesn't know it just yet) since thanks to the Rump Tower misstep of one bad egg—an egg who happens to be another junior and not just any old junior but Rump, Jr.—thanks to the fact that Tiffany blue bad egg Rump Junior (together with fellow luminaries Paul Tushner and Jar'd Manafart) decided, in the hope of getting Rump, Sr., elected Prez in Chief, to play footsie with the Russkies at a "now infamous" or is it "now *notorious*" Trump Tower powwow—thanks to that misstep the scope of the Mueller investigation is expanding to include (as targets, as subjects, as mutants of interest) all the juniors of this great country—every last one of them, in fact—and you can bet IIs, IIIs, IVs and even Vs—like Shelley's Spring—aren't far behind. *Yet while all this was going on* (so concludes the roaring obit his nemeses won't have the green-thumb skill to bring off) *Pritchard had the foresightful wherewithal to discover that marital reconciliation—even if he and the boy's mother never really got hitched—never stooped to plighting their troth (as the easiest way out of the maze of ambivalence) under the holey canopy of a legal fiction—that marital-style reconciliation reduced, at least in New York, to a matter of mere topography* (see pages 620 and 981 above and way back when, among others).

That's life, Pritchard can't help murmuring to the person next to him (hoping the remark can pass for relevant) though he can't make her(?) out because the Santa Barbara sunshine is, as usual, so blindingly—so oppressively—optimistic. But relevant or not, one thing the remark isn't is coy, gratuitous, precocious, precious, since it invents and pays well-earned tribute to *all he's been through* in the course of a lifetime. Having survived this long and after all he's been through—through thick and thin—come hell or high water—he's entitled to say anything he pleases because anything he pleases is automatically *real* hence relevant. The brute fact of survival—of having survived his own incompetence—cancels out—compensates for—renders heroic whatever it is he has to confess of bungled striving. However much the firsthand account itself gets contaminated by all the wishy-washiness he managed over the decades to cram into his handling of all flavors—all shapes and sizes—of individual mishap—the brute fact of survival trumps the lack of authority. The remark's (to use a term whose stalwart Queen Motherly prissiness Cantor likes to savor in his darkest moments) *age-appropriate*. (But where did Cantor come from? Looks like everybody's getting into the act, which is exactly what the Master always banks on in a time of crisis.) The remark delivers Pritchard up to Pritchard in all his weathered weatherbeaten ripeness. The remark makes him real and the price to be paid for that realness is terror. For *That's life*, if taken at its word, makes it clear that easeful death is right around the corner. Yet, it's the very nearness of death that mitigates—

mutilates—the terror. Terror for the Pritchards of this world (and who ain't a Pritchard of this world when it comes to death?) is finite. Pritchard repeats the phrase because he wants to force her (it is a *her*)—the person next to him at the steam table—to look him in the eye at last. So far she's been pretending to mull over whatever it is the phrase has thrown her way—but without looking up, much less looking him in the eye—as if listening and looking were incompatible—as if looking would be a desecration of all this food for thought—a gift almost Biblical in its nutritivity. Does he by any chance repel her? But the mulling without looking can be allowed to drag on for just so long before the speaker must—to save the souls of both parties to the stalemate—put his foot down and claim what is rightfully his—theirs. But then out of the blue self-hate kicks in and makes it almost a relief that she doesn't think of calling his bluff by scorching his pupils with the missiles of her contempt.

After a well-earned cigarette (more like a cigarillo if you ask me) he gets busy again kneading, the baker does. With just a little dough filched from the kitchen he makes the reconciliation that is Thirdness seem so easy, at least as far as the staff of life is concerned. Thirdness as practiced by Greenwich Avenue's premier baker is friendly to dilettantes—some vocations (to be distinguished from measly passions: *see above*) are practicable only by dilettantes and the more they dabble the more erudite they become. And to think that once upon a time she, Wild West [Side] Jean, turned up her snout at the baker just-because-he-was-a-baker in favor of Borkman, with whom she—or rather her clit—was idiotic enough to fall in love, if only for a millisecond—no, a nanosecond—or two. For Borkman's clearly second-class, i.e., in the class of Secondness—a class made up of, among others, The Rump's male whores who respect nothing but the malpractice of power. Moreover, Jean's seen John Gabriel exhibit some pretty fidgety un-robber-baron-like behavior when swept out of his element and up into a process driven by something other than brute expediency—bleeding-heart-liberal fresh-as-a-daisy Firstness, say. At such times, he looked as if he were peeing in his pants—from fear—terror, really—at the Dems' deployment of so much unapologetic effeteness—so much at-home-ness with namby-pamby equivocation. Positively daunting—positively . . . awesome (awesome, that is, in the chintzy mid-Victorian sense of *awesome*).

Meanwhile, in getting more and more riled up (with Margo in mind) *against* reconciliation of any kind, Pritchard is fast turning out to be a sort of Mitch-the-Witch-on-the-other-side-of-the-aisle (minus the unflappably wizened demeanor and the grotesquely dandyish *contrast shirt* [yes, we all know that it—*contrast shirt*—is one of the Master's unflappable bugbears—right up there with *audition* and *bad cholesterol*] which is even grotesquer when set off against a mug that resembles a rhino's ass more than the RINO's ass itself). Clearly, then, he is no friend to reconciliation (what, for example, did a stab or two of self-and-other reconciliation ever do for Offenbach's Antonia except prep her for vocational suicide?) even if he knows all about it—hey, wasn't he the first to chart its connection with urban topography? Pritch has all he can do to stop from snatching the dough out of the baker's hands and throwing it in the direction of the gulls, which have already made themselves at home at the buffet table and who knows where else. More than ever he wants—needs—Margo to subsist in the naked chaos of her self-irreconcilable self-organization as their token Conspiracy Victim—their in-house Victim— their Victim in Residence (since conspiracists of all stripes practice the most advanced form of irreconciliation—or at least the most comprehensive—the greediest). So as to ensure that The Rump feels (a) immediately at home when he walks in the door—feels, in other words, that everything is just as America-unGreat as it can ever hope to be and (b) that he'd be only too happy to play the Mr. Fix-It to end all Mr. Fit-Its if only Obama & Co. would stop wiretapping his every fart and colluding with the climate change/pro-Darwin cabal. He wants them—Margo and The Rump and The Rump and Margo—to up each other's antes and thereby deploy conspiratorial thinking in all of its crystal-clarity (even if the jury is still out on the Eternal Question to end all Eternal Questions, i.e., (a) is The Rump a conspiratorial thinker of the first rank who believes 100 percent in what he peddles and foments or (b) is he a fraud or (c) does it all boil down to an incessant shuttle between surface and depth—the surface of fraudulence and the depth of 100 percent commitment—or (d) is it the case that when he's most convinced without necessarily knowing he's convinced that he's a 100 percent fraud—why, it's then and only then that he believes 100 percent—purely—religiously—unstintingly—in what he peddles—without necessarily knowing he so believes?

And history, he's—Pritchard's—sure, will prove him dead right. (As if one can be proved right about one's feelings—about a hunch.) History will prove that in arranging a shotgun marriage between The Rump and Margo, preferably at the Santa Barbara Cemetery, he'll be serving Invidicum's best interests as a panacea in training and what's best for Invidicum is best for the world even if never the twain shall meet. For sometimes reconciliation—with one's self and/or the world—is not a good—not a fertile—thing. For with reconciliation—i.e., for without *irreconciliation*—we'd never have Steve the Banyan calling Paul MacRyan (his stock has risen considerably as a result) what he always will be, namely, a limp dick motherfucker spontaneously generated (see directly above) in a Petri dish at the Heritage Foundation. (Not that it's "limp dick motherfucker" that does the trick—anybody can come up with that. It's the other half of this vest-pocket parable that erosively carries the day.) (Nor with reconciliation would we ever have had [since his official expiration date has just passed] the special case—and take the cake as a bonus—of highly focused pollutants- and Chick-fil-A-friendly Scottie the Pruit: he has no interest in reconciling himself with his would-be allies much less with his so-called rivals [strip away the GOP mask of mutuality and it's strictly every man for himself and maybe it's pretty much the same for the DOP]—he'll have no truck with break-ins by fellow crooks—with calls intercepted by rivals and cronies both—with queries and edits chaotically smeared in red ink all over his agenda by staffers and special counsels—and he has a taxpayer-funded $25,000 [2018 PPPs] bulletproof phone booth and a bulletproof mini-Resolute desk and a task force to prove it—a task force of Secret Service chauffeurs [also bulletproof] to whisk him away from the booth or the desk to any number of DC's fanciest French restaurants and back again [as proof of a celebrity irreconcilable with the mediocrity of his peers] and all this amid a fanfare of superfluously honking horns to signal the emergency arrival or departure of one very impotent prick [VIP]—and not just any old delusional VIP but a grandee [to boot] forever in love with his delusions and compelled to endlessly stage and lavishly re-enact them before a full house—a house as big as DC.)

The anal-fellating members of the Rump Cabinet, on the other hand—those unspeakables—those swamp birds of a feather (as McBannion and O'Ryan should be, but aren't—Moral: there are all sorts of ways to be birds of a feather)—those short sellers, all, of the feedstock of the doomed, that is, the peripheralized, the uninsured!—those anal fellators who are of course being used by The Rump the better to use *him*—those analingually inclined unspeakables—to a man, they dread like the plague—like a pandemic—the chaos of things left unreconciled—left in disarray. But they've been playing along, only pretending to savor, to satiety and well beyond, the one-man-show monumentality of The Rump's addiction to irreconciliation—pretend-ing to savor the stench (past masters as they are of the art of pretending that the last thing on their minds is to insulate themselves—each from the others) of his posse of fundamental Tweets which are just short enough to, almost, cut impeachment-heavy incoherence off at the pass. At least for now. So they play along, the short-selling fellators and fellating short sellers, all this so that, behind the scenes, they can dismantle the woefully inadequate-to-nonexistent safety net known as Life Itself and cram the fruits of dismantlement through customs (while pocketing the winnings) before its army of inspectors gen-eral—known informally as Brute Humanity—have any idea what their boor-ish Kool-Aid-fueled laxity has let them in for. *When the cat is away, the car-cinogenic knockout mice can play* but in this case, the cat—the Rump cat—is always away—AWOL—even—especially—when he's right smack in the midst of their malfeasances (small potatoes, those malfeasances, which will always play but a measly second fiddle to his own).

But whatever else he is, Pritchard's not analingually inclined (but don't think for a minute he's being smug and self-righteous by loudly repudiating what amounts to a perfectly respectable affliction in order to get a taste, how-ever fleeting, of what it means to be—and to flaunt if only to an audience of one [namely, he himself] his credentials as—*a Normal Man with Normal Needs* [even if the meaning of the epithet has never been in such dizzying flux]) and so of course he can't quite turn a blind eye to the latest—and noisiest—glar-ing example (Breaking News! just in! confirmation hearings! and perfectly legible, chyrons and all, on the big screen just above the trattoria's row of ring-side-seat bar stools) of Reconciliation and the harm it perpetrates—just the sort of reconciliation he's plighted himself to loathe as a matter of principle and out of ideological angst. Of course it was to be expected (so Pritchard can't feign surprise) that when Bret the Kavanaugh (convinced he was born for the sole purpose of acceding to the Supreme Court and maybe he was but does that mean he *should* accede?) became inconveniently saddled, en route to entitlement, with allegations of sexual misconduct, the Rump team and beyond would get behind old Brett (as they're doing now—in real time—right before Pritchard's very eyes) and contend not that the allegations were false— tainted (everybody knows they're not but *how* do they know?)—but, what was far worse, that any self-respecting allegations should have waited until after the shoo-in confirmation to rear their ugly head—shouldn't have tainted their own indisputable purity by overwhelming the media at the very moment a World-Hysterical event—dripping with the expensive sweat of some white boy's outrage at the possibility of being deprived of the prize for which he's *worked his tail off* (as if there haven't been centillions of others down through the perpetual dark ages who worked *their* tails off without ending up entitled to accede to anything except muddy, dusty death)—at the very moment a WH event was about to play itself out on the Senate floor. Of *course* it was to be expected. No, far more problematic is the fact that the star tenor role in the proceedings—albeit a trouser role (in the grand-operatic sense of the term)— has been appropriated by Lindsay von Grahame—career practitioner of the breakthrough gender-bending hissy fit. Yes, Judiciary Committee Chairman Von Der Grahame—who obviously fears that if he stands—sits—idly by and does nothing then he's sure to be ejected from the party and find himself (as a consequence of his failure to ensure the Court gets packed with the right right-wingers) among the very last in that most beleaguered of minorities— Southern Belles of both genders who hail from not just Dixie but everywhere (since the confederacy of Belledom is a state of mind)—and with no way of clawing his way back from extinction (in this case left wing-induced) in the manner of a (*see the citation of the pertinent source buried somewhere in the morass above*) Tasmanian devil. De La Grahame is getting louder and louder and more and more fake-apoplectic (hoping to shriek himself into authen- ticity, with a little help from a few defiantly prideful reminders that he is a Single White Male) the more his efforts to inebriate himself with simulated righteous outrage at McKavanaugh's persecution and by extension the perse- cution of that beleaguered minority which for the moment still numbers him among its bellewethers—and to convince himself, by convincing the world, that this prissy hissy fit is the brainchild of principle not calculation—don't seem to be having the desired effect.

Pritchard simply doesn't have a stomach strong enough to swallow the spectacle of Belle Graham (especially since this isn't just any old Belle but a Belle and a Bête rolled into one) shrieking an outrage whose sole intent is to drown out the voice of his own self-betrayal, that is, if there's any self left to betray—self-betrayal in the service of a greater personal need—i.e., the need to stay *relevant* but relevant to whom, relevant to what?—the need to keep his franchise in the avant-garde—or rather, the *arrière-garde*—of GOP Rel- evance—a relevance to which decency is irrelevant because decency doesn't comport with the future he wants to create for himself under the good aus- pices of The Rump. For Lindseybelle is auditioning for (to use that tired old Rumpian trope of the fake-news media) *an audience of one*. Like John Mac- Kelly when he told that nasty lie about black Congresswoman Frederica Wilson but refused to recant much less apologize because apology wouldn't comport with a new self-construction—a construction underpinned by obsti- nate bigotry and embattled misogyny—a construction started and completed within minutes on prime time then signed and sealed and all tied up with the bright red ribbons of a conviction, as shaky as it was unshakable, that whatever Wilson embodied was far worse than The Rump's brand of Rumpist rot—far worse than Sara Huckerbee's all-hat-and-no-cattle press briefings—with the whole shebang to be dispatched by said audience of one as he would any triple milkshake drowning in its own foam—the foam of exploitably fake integrity. But it's unclear to Pritchard who can't tear himself away from the screen above the tap whether Graham the Caddy has pleased the Golfer whose balls he carries so close to his own or, rather, whether he's done so much pleasing as to render The Rump uncomfortable—uncomfortable enough to seriously consider a mad dash for the exit—and the optics (for a Swamp King who prides himself on fearlessness) be damned. And who wouldn't be made uncomfortable by this counterfeit—this travesty—as long, that is, as he or she had the olfactory bulbs required to detect the Just Noticeable Difference between the stench of phony and the smell of authentic (and mightn't he also be a little miffed that the Belle, in cahoots with Bret, is stealing the show—*his* show?)? So The Rump does what he does routinely at rallies when confronted with a supporter dopamining to death on unhinged love (the career germophobe's worst nightmare). In order to distance himself from his own unavowable intimidation masked as modesty—modesty seeming to bask in the glow of a sycophant's triumphant abjection—the glow of a fervor—a fealty—too good to be even halfway true, much less sane—in order to distance himself, he points at the sycophant while keeping the collusive twinkle in his eye on the audience. Or rather, he doesn't do anything of the kind because he can't—he isn't in the Senate chamber, after all. But as his post-show remarks to Jeanine Dobbs on Fox News make clear, this is what he (an angel on Lindsay's shoulder—a gadfly on his wall) would have done if he'd been there.

But so what if the others dread chaos?—it's the Dear Leader himself that Margo'll be playing to. The more she yearns for The Rump, the more he—Pritchard, not The Rump—needs her—vitalizes her—as his Guinea Pig cum Muse—the Nicklausse of his last operetta buffa—and the more he needs her, the more he hates her and so on and so forth to the last polysyllable of recorded time. The more vital she is—ever since he watched her rise defiantly unsupported from the dead—to his enterprise—the crowning achievement that has been taking shape in the last few hours—minutes—seconds—the more he can't stomach the sight of her. So much for till-death-do-them-part and other bromides. And what might that crowning enterprise be? Well (*I already told you! cries the Master to the Master. Are you deaf?*), it's nothing less than to turn conspiratorial thinking into a fit target for Invidicum's scythe— the one used by grim reaper Mitch the Witch. And he's already begun fencing in the parameters of Invidicum's scattershot potency as an *anti-conspirative*. Since in spite of its shortcomings, Invidicum *is*—was it ever anything but?—a hydra-headed Jack-of-all-trades—and like the Invidicum story—like Life itself—it has a nasty habit, Invidicum does, of resurging defiantly from among the unburied dead just when you thought it'd definitively buried the hatchet in its own jugular or better yet (but why *better*?) in its own Adam's apple or cremaster muscle. So he needs her to speak in tongues, i.e., on the *two levels simultaneously* mentioned above, and thereby feed The Rump's hunger for evidence of conspiracy—hunger for fool's proof that everything happens because of a witch hunt—not *because of itself*. He needs her to get under The Rump's skin so that the sensors and trackers his team plasters them with can suck up all the data they'll need to make Invidicum into the very best (and so what if it's the only) CT blocker on the market.

So to get the ball blissfully rolling, Pritchard throws her a bit of raw meat—though the term "raw meat" cannot begin to do justice to all the virulence baked into his lobbed confection. It would be better characterized as, say, a *Grande Paraphrase de Concert* on themes from the Verdi operas devoted to some of the prime time see-red bugbears out to get her goat. For starters: (*a*) Bill Clinton; (*b*) Straynge's nearest-and-dearest survivors (who persist in holding Margo responsible for his murder and harbor in their armpit, as does the President in his, the Comey tapes required to prove it); (*c*) Pelosi; (*d*) Schumer; (*e*) Obama; (*f*) Hillary, of course; (*g*) Mrs. Roosevelt (why [*as covered above*] didn't she stand up for the Japanese interned during WWII? pity, since compliments of the oversight Eleanor—Pritchard's favorite President, hands down—smashed her own legacy to smithereens); (*h*) Bernie; (*i*) Liz Warren; (*j*) a Paris Agreement-*eschewing* (!) biophysics professor she met in Delray Beach; and (*k*) a Francis Macomber-style big-game hunter whom, right under Jim's nose and undeterred by the heavy snows of Kilimanjaro, she hand-jobbed thrice at Dodoma's answer to Mar-a-Lago. (But for a bit of good clean fun Pritchard recurs to (*b*) and, digressing somewhat, asks inaudibly [out of respect for rather than fear of sleeping dogs], what if what the Comey tape in question reveals is not the ex-FBI director blackmailing his way to tenure in perpetuity by holding the Russia Investigation over The Rump's head [and flaunting his upper hand the way the unimpeachable Commander in Chief flaunts his latest just-signed Executive Order]—but rather Mitch inseminating Kellyanne while Elaine and the two Steves [or rather Steven and Stephen] and Mick and the two Mikes cheer them on—a tape Martin Shkreli would have given his right arm to outbid for?) But Margo denounces them—like the relatives who hate her guts—not by name but en masse. He plays along. Only she can't bear to *have* him play along, that is, if playing along means his denouncing them *back* to her as they came—one by one by one—each packaged as a rogue *no-good-nik* operating on his own individualizing steam (Level I). Since Margo can manhandle each of them only as part of a de-individualized horde comprising the uncountable, i.e., unnameable, blunted implements of some Mabuse—can't bear to refer to them—to have them referred to—these hyperkinetic electrons—except as *They* (Level—or Orbital—II). Heart of the problem? her inability to healthily *hate persons*, discrete or en masse—she just can't manage to *come* through hate (it's all those prohibitions from a Catholic girlhood getting in the way of pure practical reason and, incidentally, disfiguring not just whatever's written over the palimpsest of memory but, worse, the parchment itself). Even if from Pritchard's perspective of course these are the wrong people—sorry, the wrong *folks*—to hate, whether on Level I or II. But for the Margos of the world there's all too much safety in numbers: Conspiratorial thinking in numbers, the heroin of those who don't allow themselves to hate discretely—who can't, for no money, pass the kidney stone—the gas—of hate. But if Margo is to be of any use to Pritchard—her first and maybe even her only love—as both a specimen herself and as a specimen breeder—then she must be compelled to speak simultaneously on the levels not just of conspiracy and reconciliation but of hatred of individuals and hatred *en masse* as well (since The Rump is a master deployer—a master *baiter*—when it comes to both modes of Hate and will engage with and react against her only if he smells a kindred spirit). She's got to learn—and fast—how to juggle seeming incompatibilities—how without rancor to be negatively capable of drowning "in uncertainties, mysteries, doubts"[177] *even if she's not a poet—not even a great poet* (here we have the Master, the greatest "great baby" since Polonius, burping his favorite sort of phrase—the sort of phrase only italics can pacify—a phrase on whose tarmac sound, colliding and clashing with sense, bullies it into subjection).

Borkman (whose pesky ankle bracelet has picked up the vibrations—the static—of Pritchard's thinking) is beginning to see Pritchard in a new light—as somebody new to hate—to the hate game—to the game of wife-hate (*to the game of wife hate as the poor man's substitute for self-hate,* Borkman might have added, if he'd had enough honest insight). But, cheer up, as it turns out Borkman is new to something, too, namely, hate pivoted on the hatpin of a wife's paranoia. Ever the operator, Borkman wants to come to Pritchard's rescue—to rescue him from himself—and say (so why doesn't he?), But don't be so quick to sell hate short, Pritch, my boy. After all, it's easy to live with somebody you've convinced yourself you love but it takes guts—worse, creativity—to abide a being you hate (and who without knowing it hates you back) yet live to tell the tale. Which, on occasion, may turn out to be marred implausibly by treasurable episodes—the bittersweet kind that only love-in-hate, qua druggist non pareil, has the knack for compounding.

Pritchard is of course unaware of Borkman's envy—envy of his very newness to the game of connubial hate—i.e., of his—Pritchard's—being in (compliments of that very newness) for a real treat which, in Borkman's jaded case, wore out its welcome years—decades—ago. And odd, isn't it, Pritchard muses (already overloaded with talents, he also excels at musing—musing in tongues), that it's the Democrats she's come to blame for every affliction (Jr.'s autism, for example) and not the Grand Old Party—party of both the Kockenlocker and La Melanemia. Melanemia! (*enamored intake of breath that's not quite a breathless sigh for the unattainable*): the new Loren—a Beltway Sophia without the talent—self-designated First Lady of Mystery (in the Christie tradition)—not to mention motherly scourge of cyberbullies (although the biggest cock-and-bully of 'em all seems to have 'scaped not just her whipping but her very notice). She's a scourge all right but a scourge without a plan of action whose only certifiable proof of motherly outrage is a pair—fifty pairs—of spiked heels and as many pairs of dark glasses and a daily proclamation

---

[177]See the letter of John Keats to George and Thomas Keats, dated Sunday, 21 December 1817.

by her staffers (who belong to the same PR team famous for its daily assurances of the imminence—its daily invocations of the spectre—of the Rump's Infrastructure Week charade parade) of big plans ahead for protection of the country's web-abused young, even if the only kind of charity her sort knows is the kind that begins—and ends—at home. But how can Margo blame the Democrats, of all things! Really, Margo! When it's they—*they*—the Eleanors—who've been taking several dog-eared pages from her Book of Gimmicks—who've been dutifully following Margo's lead in *failing* to operate on two levels simultaneously—following her lead in willfully mistaking (without even knowing it) talking simultaneously through both sides of their mealy-mouth, for talking simultaneously—*muscularly*—on two levels? The Democrats are your kindred spirits! Do-gooders ravaged (the best of 'em, that is) by contradiction!

On the one hand (if they're to get back in the game and stay there), they've got to knuckle down—not under—and slap together/drum up some platform—a slogan as massive as the Matterhorn or at least Manhattan's Matterhorn (i.e., the Chrysler: see above)—some plausible strategy—road map—framework—for convincing the rednecked yokels (the very people—sorry, the very *folks*—spurned by Miss Hillary) whom they must seduce or re-seduce at all cost—some framework—some tissue of white lies—for convincing those ticking time-bombs that at long last they're going to hear what they most need to hear, i.e., that at long last their needs are going to be taken seriously even if they themselves don't know what those needs are or, better yet, that they've just voted for abrogation of their very entitlement to having them met (even if, understandably, there's nothing more exhilarating—ask Oscar Wilde—than to act against one's own best interests). Some framework, i.e., for *simulating* empathy (that thorny flower of euphemism and in its very essence—not to mention by its very nature—a simulation) and making it (the empathy) stick. Though *simulation*—signifying the very armature of their enterprise—is the one word they will not utter—that gets lost in the shuffle of "reinventing themselves" (disgusting term). Some framework, then, for simulating a simulation inasmuch as they experience no instinctive connectedness with these Forgotten-who-don't-know-they've-been-forgotten and are currently getting strafed with an even bigger dose of forgottenness compliments of that unobturatable irrepressible orifice known as The Rump. Since they experience no instinctive affinity because to most of the Dems the Forgotten are not people but just one big blob of disaffection (Level I). So Level I is all about simulation—lies—without necessarily knowing that's what it's all about. On Level I, the Dems know that they don't know or don't know that they know that they have no message—a non-message they nevertheless need to get out as soon as possible.

On the other hand, there's no need for them to knuckle down and cobble together some framework—generate some simulation scenario worthy of IPCC—because in fact they're positively bubbling over *as we speak* with more *real* empathy—more bleeding-heart authenticity—more of a message than they know what to do with. I.e., they really do connect—affinitize—with them there yokels and, more importantly, forgive them for their vote-against-my-own-best-interests perversity. I.e., simulation is the furthest thing from their mind—from the mind of their message. It's just that compliments of their chronic etherealness—their hog-tying soulfulness—the Dems just can't seem to be able to stoop to the level of articulating, much less conveying it (Level II). For they know articulation of a message is one with its debasement. If a message—especially one that comes straight from the heart—is a projectile, then the act of utterance denatures the fuels it battens on. As it turns out (under this Level), they're purists. So: the *empathy platform* is, come to think of it and in a perverse sort of way, more than a bit like the Republicans' plan to abolish health care for those who don't know they're the ones who need it most (and all in the name of a better, brighter tomorrow since nobody minds not having what they've been *ordered* to need most).

So, when subterfuge is done, she and the Dems are birds of a feather after all (at least that's what the Master, whose aversion to loose ends amounts to a kind of mania—a kind of racism—wants you to think). But before Pritchard can lick his chops over the prospect of Margo and The Rump chewing the cud of each other's paranoid schizophrenias— (Though he hates nothing more than diagnoses—*glorified dogtags*, Charcot called them, or was it Jean-Martin's forbidding mentors, Drs. Phil, Oz and Ruth?—there are still times when to administer one—a three-ring-circus-style diagnosis, that is—administer it like a state-of-the-art enema—becomes more than a moral duty: it becomes a pleasure.) But before he can lick his chops over the prospect of the two conspirators' providing him with far more sensor- and symptom-crammed food for thought, specifically about how to Make Invidicum Great Again, than he'll ever know what to do with, Netta (who else but this chimaera, equal parts Socrates and Xanthippe?) sticks her neck out or (it all comes down to one's perspective) pokes her nose in, saying (she's just spruced up her hoary old intermittent English accent: a routine chore, like cutting her toenails), "There just has to be some suturing before The Rumps soil our threshold. I don't want them to catch us with our pants down—take undue advantage of our internecine warfare—nor do I want us to take undue advantage of theirs." (Cantor wonders just for fun [but if it's just for fun why is he shuddering?], what might happen if he told her how affected she sounds. Would little Ms. Doolittle storm off or gratefully admit to the charade, secure in knowing that a self which from loathing pretends to be Other yet loves nothing better than *exposure* as the trigger for a shamelessly exhaustive autoanalysis in the public square [and all of this without relinquishing the right to resume said charade at any moment]—that such a self is a self beyond reproach and beyond price—a Double Self.) She's obviously sensed Pritchard's resistance and wants to do it in. (For some strange reason he was beginning to believe reconciliation was pretty much a dead issue—that everybody was coming over to his side. Why? Well, for starters, because too much reclusiveness breeds irreality and irreality breeds dumb-ass optimism. That's why.) Maybe the baker—or rather, his best of intentions—has sensed this as well and that's why his efforts have fizzled. So the no-holds-barred Thirdness Wars have at last come home to roost in the foothills of SB and it appears there'll be no consensus any time soon. Her voice quavers a bit: prerogative of wisdom or is it just fatigue?—or not just any old fatigue passing itself off as wisdom but the very sort that ends up engendering not just wisdom but a wisdom that's much better—far yeastier—more yeomanly—than the real thing.

Since it's obviously the season of necks and noses, Walser feels duty bound to donate his to the war effort. "We've been incapable of suturing this luminous mess—yes, *luminous mess*—because the right triad hasn't come along to serve as our role model—our template." "We haven't *let* it come along." While evidently agreeing, Netta, as usual, comes across as disparaging—too disparaging for words, though she always has plenty of those at her disposal. "We need a template that takes its cue from Charley Peirce but operates at a lower level of abstraction." He sighs: "Don't you understand, you fools? a *lower level of abstraction!*" He's apoplectic but stops short of foaming at the mouth, knowing full well there's such a thing as having too much of a good thing. The good thing in this case being the fact that the level of abstraction has been taken down a notch or two (or haven't you noticed?) thanks to a bit of always dependable good old-fashioned Concreteness (in today's matinee performance the role was taken, at the last minute, by Apoplexy). Anyway, some people are still eating and he doesn't want to ruin their appetites. "The triad I have in mind mirror-images everything that has gone on—i.e., gone wrong—with our experiments from day one—even if we haven't even gotten beyond day one where Thirdness is concerned. Mirror-images everything while turning it on its head." It's unclear what experiments he's referring to and maybe the blur is intentional—in the service of a higher—the highest—cause. He proceeds to steamroll. Said triad mirror-images everything-gone-wrong with their efforts at reconciliation in order to replace the end product without repealing it—to transform it—to enable *them* to transform it—into a thing of dark beauty—or better yet, into a thing of peace and quiet or—best yet—into a thing of Affordable Care Act utility—a thing of habit and law—a thing, in a word, of Thirdness—or best yet, into a means of teaching the Rump crowd not to go getting its dander up every time a fake tweet comes down the MSNBC pike and thereby dissolve its own pact with Greatness. And it's no wonder that being an opera fanatic *as so many of his kind* though, never fear (Walser assures them), there's nothing he loves more than what Rodgers and Hart in their famous American Songbook conversion-therapy classic, "The Lady Is a Tramp," have told him to love OR ELSE, namely, baseball (the bleachers, if you please), and a prizefight that isn't a fake, and crap games without barons and earls, not to mention the rowing on Central Park Lake, and touch football and bungee jumping and catfish wrestling and Texas Hold'em and skeet shooting but Balanchine most of all and not just because the once-beautiful Moira has turned him on full-force to Mr. B's *oeuvre*, which is a fancy-pants word for body of work—it's no wonder that being a fanatic he's located the triad in question readymade—made to order—within—innate to (here we go again!)—*Les Contes d'Hoffmann*.

To Melanctha, Walser's laundry list sounds oddly familiar (at least a few of the items). And why shouldn't it, given that her aim (what a coincidence!)—in and out of the context within which The Rump and his scumfest have incarcerated her—is to prophylactically calculate precisely how many preferences she has in common with her idol, that Tramp who's also a Lady and vice versa? For the more Melanctha shares—the more she measures up to Her standards—the more she gets transformed into the Hart's—the Tramp's—the Lady's—better version of herself, the more likely it is that when confronted with the back-channel-crazy transition team, Melanctha'll be able to hold her head high since by then she'll know who she is and, more importantly, who she isn't. And the higher she can hold her head, the better she can be served—serviced—by the Master for she's earned the right through what seem like decades of faithful service to refer to him in so many words as putty in her hands. Oh, it's easy enough to say she gets too hungry for dinner at eight—anybody can own up to that without a blush—or goes to Coney (even if the beach ain't divine) or to opera (where the bleachers are fine—or rather, where she stays wide awake) but, more to the point, is it also true that she never—*never*—bothers with people she hates? and even more to the point, does she have the *courage* to hate and not just on a first-come first-served basis?—the courage to go out and *seek* the hateful rather than wait for them to start hangin' round her door?—the courage to hate on an *individual* basis? unlike Margo (a loudmouth yet still a coward) who can only hate meaninglessly en masse (thereby enabling every last hateworthy to get matter-of-factly lost in the crowd—like Bruno, post-murder, in Hitchcock's *Strangers on a Train*)—the courage to hate on a first-name basis?—and, at the drop of a hat, the courage to brazenly name those names to friends and acquaintances without a blush?—not to mention the courage not to be just a fair-weather hater but a hater who keeps all her prime targets forever in reserve—in cold-shoulder storage—for rainy-day hate *at a distance*? (in the great tradition of quantum-physical *entanglement* at a distance)—and even nearer the point than all this, does she have the courage to *spit out the word hate* as convincingly as the unsurpassable Lena in that cornball confection known as *Words and Music*? replete with a signature Hollywood-the-Caution-Industry special, i.e., its version of genius-spawning immigrant motherhood (hard to put one's finger on mama's long-suffering generic accent [*Yiddish?* perish the thought!] but why try when it fits her folkloric pretzel braid to a T? [*T* for *Tsuris*]). Well, Melanctha thinks she does . . . have the courage, I mean. (And that's what counts—for thinking makes it so.) If not, then the heinousness of The Rump & Co—yes, the *heinousness*, no room in the inn for Creative Writing 101-style nuance here—will drive her to it. Maybe it's that scurfy little slumlord Jarred [*sic*] who'll get Melanctha's dander up high enough to turn her, in accordance with some unduly forgotten law of alchemy, into Lena—the Ungentle Lena.

Jared, that . . . *robot pretending to be a robot*. She tries to understand what the words profess to mean—and in this case, not just any old words but words that destroy themselves in the process of professing to mean. Since how, I ask you, can somebody be a bona fide *X* pretending to be an *X*? Still, there's simply got to be a referent—a holy grail—and she's going to find it even if, like the State of Anxiety, as opposed to the State of Fear, it's "essential . . . that any reference to an object in the real world is lacking."[178] The words exert so much power, over her at least, there has simply got to be something somewhere out in non-cyberspace capable of claiming responsibility for the transmission of that power. The hardest part, after all—coming up ingeniously—or disingenuously—with a phrase capable of causing so much trouble (a talent vouchsafed to few—the unhappy few)—the hardest part is behind her. Though maybe what she needs is to be able to see her little slumlord—her muse (who's turned smugness into a fine art—a fineable art) up close in order to grasp what the words mean. Though maybe the No. 1 son-in-law's presence will only get in the way of encompassment. For one thing, there's that unnervingly unblinking *giocondo* smile . . . suitable for all occasions . . . even, presumably, a feds-choreographed pre-dawn raid (make that an *obligatorily* pre-dawn raid) on his unspeakables—or, even better, a Saudi sword dance (cheek to cheek) with the Crown Prince.

Jean's concerns, on the other hand, lie elsewhere. "Do you mean to tell me that Walser—that Walser's kind—is—is—a—a—" Jean (against her better judgment) stage-whispers, but surprisingly Ethan (against *his* better judgment?) refuses to respond—initially. At long last, he has bigger fish to fry. Bigger fish than Walser. Than Jean, for that matter: in fact, as of this minute— the kind of minute that's *not a minute too soon*—he and Jean are finished. (*The worm has turned*, sneers Jean in a sub-sub-whisper.) What's left is a business arrangement, its tattered terms badly in need of renegotiation or—now that you mention it—even dissolution. And what's more, he's the first to have learned that The Rump crew will be arriving any second now—having held off nattily so as to ensure that—once Infrastructure Week and Linoleum Week (screwball-straight out of Ernst Lubitsch's *Design for Living*) and Infanticide Week and Shitpickles Week and Made in Hong Kong Week and Back Channel Week and Cove Village Week had come and gone—the visit would coincide with Big Pharma Week. Though what, come to think of it, could be more exhilarating than to have a visit *not* coincide with its theme?

Undeterred by sneers (the seagulls' being the hardest of all to bear—and after all the indigestible business he's thrown their way!), Walser warbles on. "Which is nothing less than my favorite opera of all time. Although this ain't saying very much, since it's the only one through which I've managed to stay awake—albeit not *wide* awake (a lame sop to the audience's Cerberus of he-men philistines)." (Melanctha is immediately, atypically, elated: *Breaking News* [but what isn't nowadays?]: Without knowing it, he's just disqualified himself from the final round of the Trump-The-Rump finals [one less competitor to worry about] since, unlike him, she has no trouble staying awake for Hoffmann.) "Think Eden (who else?) as our Hoffmann, the quintessential Romantic poet *manqué*, who requires only one look (behind the curtain) to know that Olympia (Firstness incarnate) is the Real Thing, that is, the Thing-

---

[178]Kurt Goldstein, *The Organism* (New York, American Book Company, 1939), chap. seven, "Certain essential characteristics of the organism in the light of the holistic approach," p. 292.

in-Itself, that is, his True Love. But we'll get to his love in a minute." He meets Doctor Coppélius—an Optometrist in the Grand Manner with a Dulcamara-like panache who vends eyeglasses, opera glasses, pince-nez. Which can make things black as jade or white as ermine, that can lend a soul to them as have none—that can reveal whether a woman's heart is pure or vile—eyes that can darken, light up, make something go shadowy or fade. However, the one thing they can't reveal is whether or not a woman isn't in fact an automaton without a patent—an Alexa, say, or a Siri. For *our* Olympia is not a being per se but a mad scientist-sponsored chaos of senseless sense experiences impossible to pin down, much less articulate and analyze. Completely veiled from introspection. Every description of her but a description of the flight triggered by what that description says she is—the question of her content in the present instant is a question that comes too late. And Hoffmann—Eden—learns with all too Peircean belatedness that you cannot touch her—even if the touch is a touch of the eyes—without spoiling her, taking her apart with far more brutality than even a Coppélius could muster. She is what she is without reference to anything else, within or without, heedless of all force and all reason. And for all her flirting (or what Hoffmann's dumb enough to take for flirtation) she's as solitary, celibate, monadic and monastic, as they come. She is irresponsible, free, original—to which her running amuck at the slightest opportunity attests. No limits, conflict, constraint—just a succinct and distracting "*Oui, oui*" to every question posed, command delivered. *Do they get it?* Walser wonders. *Or if they're unlucky enough* to get it, *will they forgive him? Or more to the point, Will they forgive themselves? No.* Since After such (*dark and dirty*) knowledge, what forgiveness (*for those dark and dirty enough to have caught on untutored*)?

And Antonia, his next love (for Olympia has been smithereened by Coppélius, who as it turns out was the mad scientist's nemesis), is an artist, the embodiment of Secondness for what is Secondness—Thisness—but *Consciousness not of a process of change* (don't be greedy) *yet of something more than can be contained in, constrained by, an instant.* Secondness is something along the lines of sensing the two sides to—the bipolarity of—that instant (with all this entails of despair as despair and despair as rapture). The true artist will have no truck with law, habit, reconciliation—she leaves that to her servants even if she's too garret-poor (that is, glamorously garret-poor like the poet in Lewton/Robson's's *Seventh Victim* or Hamsun's Hunger Artist) to rent one—even if she loves them and would never dream of bequeathing them any more drudgery—more drudgery than their already super-taxed fortitude can accommodate. Secondness is the experience of that blindfolded wasp whose artistic vocation it is to go on bumping against the sides of the bottle in which the rank fragrance of inevitable failure is stoppered—even if the bottle—like any other bottle—has—takes—no sides. The experience of the bruteness of actuality—the actuality in this case incarnated by Monsieur Crespel who forbids his daughter—and by Hoffmann who forbids his beloved—to sing lest she destroy herself in the process—lest her vocal chords destroy him by generating an Envy that can never be avowed—Envy of all a beautiful being can accomplish when unshackled by a penis. Secondness is the main lesson of life—of Antonia's life—forced upon her at all turns.

And, finally, there is Giulietta the courtesan—Embodied Thirdness, to you, Bub. Like all Thirdnesses worth their salt she has a project and so is ready, on its behalf—but only on *its* behalf—to take her medicine, the medicine that is the project's process of change. Even if this means undergoing all of the life-binding and seemingly interminable inconveniences of brute duration. Think of the project's aim as reconciliation of automaton and artist— as achievement of a fusion whereby the end product comes out smelling like a . . . courtesan. Only that's not interesting—too predicable after the big build-up. Her aim is in fact to reconcile Hoffmann (Firstness incarnate or, in this case, properly disincarnate) with his Reflection (Secondness). (Which he's always bumping up against and which bumping keeps him from living because he's forever living the Reflection's life not his own—because the Reflection's life is very much a bracketed, straitjacketed, circumscribed life—a contoured life with no rough edges.) Her aim is to reconcile Hoffmann with his reflection through severance and by then making that reflection—or rather its shadow (since reflection is, like Life, a walking shadow)—her very own. Giulietta knows that merely by hanging on—by seeing things through— that project business, again! (and as a courtesan and a good one, she has all the time in the world)—by obeying the Law—in this case, the Barcarolle, i.e., the Martial Law of the Gondolas—she'll be able to sever the connection between Hoffmann and his precious Reflection and suture him through her theft for he's much too self-conscious for his own good. Even if it's precisely through deployment of the mental element—through calculation—through down-and-dirty self-consciousness, i.e., the knowledge for which there's no forgiveness—that Giulietta intends to get the job done.

And if Hoffmann is not quite anybody's idea of Firstness . . . well, then, his feelings certainly are—the minute he's about to be saddled with one he's on to the next. In fact, he's an interminable sum of Firstnesses—sum of livings and dyings amid all the bruteness of duration—the bruteness of expediency—a sum of livings and dyings in the instant before the instant is born. But if their taste doesn't quite run to this particular triad (Hoffmann-Reflection-Giulietta), Walser's got plenty of others up his sleeve (a case of Law gone lawless)—his raveled sleeve of devil-may-care. All sorts of others to choose from—how about Crespel, Miracle and Hoffmann, or Hoffmann, Frantz and Nicklausse? Or even, as a last resort, Giulietta-Olympia-Antonia? Think of triad after triad—law gone lawless—

"Yes," Liepnits bursts out as if broaching this subject for the very first time, "there has been far too much Firstness and Secondness running rampant around here. And not enough Thirdness." Only he doesn't specify what kind of Thirdness—the Man of the Hour—he has in mind. Here he goes again, thinks Cantor, blowing hot and cold—but most of all, blowing *hard*—getting on the bandwagon because (mistaking it for a gravy train though he may not be far wrong) he suspects something may accrue from doing so. Then Cantor takes it upon himself to remember, since clearly nobody else will (they're all too busy wolfing down the by now sun-denatured *pièces de résistance*, which in their present state are pretty much indistinguishable from Putzder patties), that with midterms on the horizon Liepnits—looking ever more like Newt the bloated Speaker of the House than bloated Newt himself—will obviously do anything within reach to win votes—even sell his mother down the river but inasmuch as Liepnits hates old Ozark Annie more than any other man alive he wouldn't be making much of a sacrifice thereby. Or better yet, kiss Sheriff Joe's big fat racist ass—best yet, his navel. He's getting himself all fired up—or rather, convincing himself he's getting all fired up—to prepare for Big Pharma Week during which he'll no doubt clinch the midterm nomination and go on to unseat the incumbent Representative—and a devout Democrat (what with all the start-uppers, young and old, getting stoned, before his very eyes, on their own concoctions and his knowing how, in the guise of Grand Old Man of the Beltway, to romance their fragile little testerone-drenched egos, he'll be a shoo-in). And adding insult to injury Bain's Mitt Romney has, after all, pledged, between flip-flops, the unswerving support of the notorious 47 percent. Or was—is—it the even more notorious 53 percent? Cantor still can't get over the fact that The Week is to be played out here in Santa Barbara. Thanks, no doubt, to the Master's powers of persuasion and his many contacts. Though why *not* here in Santa Barbara? It's hard to realize—no, accept—so much time has passed him by. Why, it was only yesterday that *malgré lui* he was shuddering at the ungainly prospect of living through not one but *two* Baby Bush cosmic cycles (yet who'd ever have imagined he—Cantor—'d end up growing fonder of the Baby, especially after Katrina jilted him so heartlessly, than he had any right to be?). But hasn't Herbert been muttering something (as if she were talking in her sleep) to the effect that (*a*) since this—whatever *this* turns out to be—is nothing less than the Master's swansong and (*b*) since a swansong cries out for a Mighty Theme scaffolded—submerged—done in— by the obligatorily vast cross-section of human types to be found only in a mid-Victorian Age debtors' prison and (*c*) since there's nothing mightier and more cross-sectionable than a Rump Week to End All Rump Weeks—unfolding under the Spinozistic attribute of Crowdpleasing—since there's (*a*), (*b*) and (*c*) to reckon with, so what if the Week's inauguration demands a baker's dozen fast forwards? Time—or rather, a plausible duration—is not always of the essence.

But Margo is thinking very different thoughts. First, she's warming to the idea that maybe Jr. will become a SiVa star after all. But she's first, last and always a mother (as Alicia in Hitchcock's *Notorious* was first, last and always— in the best Hechtian tradition—*not* a lady) and as a mother-first above all, where's the guarantee that compliments of Jr.'s infatuation with self-sabotage he won't make sure (when it comes time to have his photo taken with all those supercool and super*hot* hoodies—maybe even with The Rump himself) to be unprepossessing enough to merit jettison? Will he remember to wear his American flag pin and a marriage ring (*de rigueur* accoutrements for any politico with a eunuch's dark secrets hanging in his closet so why not for her Jr., even if he's the furthest thing from a eunuch and isn't ductile enough—at least as of this moment—to be sanctimonious)?

With an impatience bordering on inadmissible dread, every last one of them awaits the collision of Team Rump with Its Week of Wonders. And

Moira for all her NYC and NYCB airs is no exception. If you must know, there's a lot riding on the event even if nobody can articulate exactly what. Nor exactly why, for that matter, it's Tom or Jeff or Rex rather than Mike or Mick or the Mooch or Mnutch—or, for that matter, Siamese twins Mitch-and-Wilbur (unfriendly neighborhood bankers on permanent loan from a thirties or forties Frank Capra social consciousness machine)—who's his or her especial favorite and always will be. Fact is, the Team has a sleazeball on hand for every taste, however unnatural, however *back-channel*—for that's what makes It a Star. But getting down to cases, how can Moira be sure that Evangelically inclined ex-Governor Mike will keep his unevangelical unavowable campaign promise made to her and her alone (when she was fast asleep—neck deep in a dream professing to be a portent)? that he'd (*a*) make sure she was implored to perform up at the cemetery (not so much for the members of the Team—who he can assure her don't know a pirouette from a used prophylactic and are probably much better off—as for those enjoying peace eternal in the company of jasmine- and bougainvillea-scented Counselors and Kings) and (*b*) do, once the performance was over, with his signature brand of unspontaneously spontaneous applause (trotted out the minute he hears the master's bark) what he's never done with it before and probably never will do again and what better venue than Santa Barbara for doing what one knows one will never do again, *come hell or high water*? (Nothing more delicious, by the way, than to use an idiom such as *come hell . . .* incorrectly: like incoherence, it's much harder to pull off than it looks.) In her sleep, she caught on immediately but how, now that she's half awake, can she be sure that the species of applause in question (which has always purported to be a discreet acknowledgment—an *it-goes-without-saying*-type acknowledgment—of the fake breaking news that Pencey's porpoise-lipped blowhard master is—let's face it—just too damn applause-worthy to require an outpouring every time said blowhard sees fit, unteleprompted, to challenge Abe Lincoln and the other forty-three Commanders in Chief to a duel and thereby establish once and for all—though the last thing in the world he wants it to be is *once and for all*— that it's he, The Rump, who's, hands down, the most Executive-Orderly—it's he who's done the most for blacks and gays and whites and career anorexics and greens and yet he remains—hands down, and for all his currying care— the most Unfairly Treated of them all)—how can Moira be sure that such discreetly measured applause will segue into the not-quite-discreetly-measured frenzy that as a woman of the theater who isn't getting any younger she's within her rights to righteously crave? A frenzy frenzied enough to enable MacPence to forswear/abjure/mitigate/modify/undercut his own radical fellation of the brain inside The Rump's prostate—a frenzy compliments of which the spectator will forget at least for a nanosecond that The Pence is a toady of the worst kind—the toady as very very Christian political animal who may or may not believe that he believes that he believes that fealty to the frog king of the Untermenschen of fraud—another kind of fraud than he himself—is next to godliness. Which will cause Moira's stocks—Moira as generator of that frenzy—to rise. How can she be sure that her chevalier will *do* Applause as the dismantlement of its own simulation—a parody—a parrying of all the flagrancies of flunkeydom? How can she be sure that he'll open the sluicegates of an Applause Machine so massive as to have no difficulty transforming Itself into an all-out ironic commentator's storming of the citadel of Toadyism's Thing-in-Itself? How be sure his kind of applause won't do more harm than good to her career even if it's just the sort of butt-end that routinely flourishes—given half a chance—under the yoke of bad publicity? How be sure he'll perpetrate an Applause which relegates The Rump to a mere pretext—to a mere footnote in Vice's autobiography—a footnote that speaks volumes? How can she be sure that Pence's palms (too self-controlled to sweat) will agree to play this dual role of toad and counter-toad (for one thing, the sea air may not agree with him) and by turning himself into an applause machine as sublime as, say, *Symphony in C*, thereby deliver himself forever (or for a nanosecond) from yes-mannish self-sodomization? How can she be sure he'll perpetrate an applause assault that's he-man-relentless enough to alchemize into a self-affirmation so vertiginous as to constitute what every artist, even the puniest, would give his right arm to pull off—a Triumph over Life Itself (as daringly irrefutable as, say, the shriek of Verdi's Desdemona at the very end of her Willow Song—or the dotted-note agitation of, say, the Balakirev Toccata in C-sharp minor—yep, Balakirev, but Mily to all of his friends in need) and upon whose terrain no blowhard, even the blowhardiest of the lot, can expect to trespass unsmithereened? What if the applause doesn't quite rise to the occasion as Pence promised Moira it would? What if, when you get right down to it, the applause has never been fake— fake news—or, worse, what if, albeit unfake to the hilt, it just ain't, no matter how you slice it, cunning enough to be able to mask the fact that the only thing it's really applauding is the briskness of that fakery? What if beneath the putative volcano there's no molten rock—no toxic gases—no (in layman's language) *large igneous provinces* (LIPs)—except maybe a tailing or two to be squirted now and then in the direction of liberals, the namby-pamby kind who nurse a vociferous soft spot for the entities—Planned Parenthood, for example—assigned permanent bugbear status by Indiana Jones MacPence way way back in his stumping salad days? Too much for Moira to ponder while waiting (labor- and leisureless) to be dumped by one of Uber's winged chariots in the tarantula-festooned arbors of an unripe old age.

"But, folks," says Mary, rising from her table for one—or at the most, three—but careful to remain (with her milkmaid's complexion) out of sunny harm's way, "whatever you do, don't forget Invidicum in its original incarnation—don't look back—and down upon it from the vantage of its transformation into something with bigger fish than Envy to fry. Like conspirativity." (Steadfast refusal to look Pritchard's way.) "Or greed." (Refusal to look anybody's way except into the imminent future.) Or rather, as she goes on to explain, a greed beyond greed, a greed not to be explained by mere greed, not to be pigeonholed by a diagnosis as old hat as greed, a greed beyond greed— beyond the greedy pursuit of Little Lavish Lifestyles as depicted by Louisa May Alcott—a greed beyond greed for which your garden-variety friendly neighborhood greed is just an unwanted legitimating tool, an unstable, repudiated armature—greed beyond greed, in a word (or two), as practiced by patriots like Paul Manafart and Rump, Jr., and Evictioneer Kutshner and Melanemia the CyberBully Slayer and vermiform Tom Price, not to mention the behemoth in whose Administration this ex-Eagle Scout proclaimed it, on live TV, "an honor" to serve though of course prostate-licking Price's sort of honor has a long way to go to be comparable to that which the behemoth himself assured Putin—in a moment of ecstatic grovelling—he'd perpetrated by granting an interview. "An honor to meet Putin! Nelson Mandela, sure; the Queen, OK (as a well-merited courtesy); Merkel, fine. But Putin! the uncornerable rat? In any case, whatever you do, don't look back in the same way some—maybe all—of you look back on Envy itself (now that you're in dire remission), that is, with contempt—even revulsion—as a spectrum of overstudied psychosomatisms." Moira is still recovering from bedazzlement by Mary's way with words—which exhibits the same panache as a buccaneer's way with a petticoat. *Remission*, they echo, in an almost inaudible gasp of never-before-experienced unison which transitions quickly enough into a sigh (or is it the sigh which transitions, without stopover, into gasp?) meaning (if it means anything at all), *Of course, that's why for ages there hasn't been any activation of my dorsal anterior cingulate cortex (ACC), the neural correlate of Envy in the wild, nor of, for that matter, my ventral striatum, the neural correlate of schadenfreude.* For rubbing elbows with bona fide state-of-the-artists, it's only natural that a thing or two about just how far functional magnetic resonance imaging can go in nailing pain of a particular provenance should, willy-nilly, have rubbed off on them. "Don't go wondering how you could have ever fallen for it the way you fell into the traps set by all your past selves, forgetting that your present self, itself already past (having worn out its welcome), could never have gotten to where it is today without passing through the defiles of those traps."

So what is there to do now that Cantor's been robbed not only of his accession to Pritchard's throne, after having made it to the finish line minus one albeit not in record time, but of his Envy as well? Is he supposed to go back and follow tenure's tiny beaten track now that he's seen SB? Couldn't the microflora in his gut through its link to his brain cook up a replacement for Envy—one that, while susceptible to Invidicum's blandishments, wouldn't succumb too fast? After such knowledge, what forgiveness by the colleagues it seems he's known from as far back as his sabbatical in the womb, embalmed in the ice age of their two-bit glory, past, present and to come? Unlike them, like Obama Emeritus on the theme of gay marriage, he's evolved—Invidicum has forced him to evolve.[179] They on the other hand are the dead wood of . . . of . . . of—oh, all right, Secondness. Their time between classes spent trolling the Internet for breaking news of each other's remains scattered as they are far and wide yet, *when push comes to shove* (wrong expression for the con-

---

[179] But does he really believe he's evolved and, more to the point, that it's Invidicum who's been his Personal Trainer—who's been playing Kelly to his Rump? Isn't this just Wordflow, i.e., the Master, trying to suture up, with House Surgeon Cantor as his proxy, all the rents and fissures in this, the tallest of all His tall tales? The Master has reneged on His duty all down the line and is trying to make up for lost time.

text though it sure sounds right—righter than the putative right one), always in the immediate vicinity of One Hundred Sixteenth Street and Broadway. News of who's dead, who's dying, who's divorced, who's been alchemized into blissful genderlessness, who's in, who's out, who's ex-homeless, who's un- and who's overemployed, and who's (best-case scenario) all-of-the-above-and-more-to-come. Suffering as he's been lucky enough to suffer would of course constitute (if he were dumb enough to deliver up its pearls to the inspection of swine) something worse, hence more delectable, than bad luck, namely, stupidity. And the effort to unmask their smugness, i.e., their dimensionless-ness, would once again be bracketed (he has only to take one look at Mary to know what he'll be in for), long before he made any headway, as further proof of his stupidity if any still be needed. Just as being able to hum a few bars from, for example, some exaltingly unhappy ditty by Bellini was always proof, to Berry Sundae, not of Cantor's own exaltedness but of a soggy erudition soggy enough to make George Eliot's Mr. Casaubon look—and sound—like . . . well, like Bellini himself. But so what if, come hell or high water, a substitute for Envy cannot be found to give him an excuse to stick around? He can still go back East (making sure to steer clear of the other Men from Morningside), take a few . . . writing courses! and (last refuge of scoundrels) expose *all this*. But not in the first person of the usual disaffected, impotent, anaphylactically shocked *loser* (no other word will do, at least for now). Instead, how about in the first person of, say, a Goldman Sachs hot shot with a soul-smug perennial winter tan who, without missing a beat, manages to reap the same harvest of insights—the same bruised fruits that are supposed to accrue, alas, only from running the gauntlet—and gamut—of excruciations associated solely with losers and from which trim, tanned hot shots are contractually obliged to . . . *recuse themselves*, or is it the excruciations that do the recusing from the hot shots, long may they reign? Maybe he'll even be able to sell his *all this* to HBO before it merges with the Rump Organization. But maybe he's just jumping the gun and another Invidicum-susceptible microorganism will rear its ugly little head.

CHAPTER SIXTY-TWO

As it turns out, she's not quite done even if it feels, at least to Borkman, who's rushing to the men's room (whatever the menu claims he's been chomping away at hasn't agreed with him)—even if it feels that a chapter—*her* chapter—has just come brusquely to a close. "So let's forget all about this business of reconciliation—Thirdness. Especially with Martin as its embodiment. We can't greet the Team (which must currently be somewhere slightly to the left of Butte) with our tails between our legs. It needs to be shown that we know that Life is and will always be nothing but struggle—the more futile the better—struggle resolutely irreconcilable with the triumph of 'healing'— that mealy-mouthed epithet so much in fake vogue among both the quick fix-hungry scum and the quick-fix hungry dumb of the Earth (the Charlottesville mess being its latest patsy). Yes, Mouseketeers, you heard me right the first time: *'healing,' that mealy-mouthed epithet so much in vogue among the quick fix-hungry scum and the quick-fix hungry dumb of the Earth. (And I'm not being in the least elitist, whoever that is.)* Not that it's (uninterestingly) a question of our garnering the Team's respect by acting tough—by pretending to be as buzzard-devious as Mitch McGoniGhoul where reconcilability is concerned." "Then what *is* it a question of?" Borkman asks (defecation has done him a world of good), looking as if he'd like to strangle Mary and everybody else coming under the rubric of her *kind* (you know, the gals who, for all their shop talk about glass ceilings, are pretty sure they've got the world, corporate and otherwise, by the balls) many times over. Moira is about to offer up the needed correction (though *clarification* would be a better—or at least a politer—word) but demurs before she can even begin to think about taking the plunge, too much awed by Mary's ten-ton erudition (ten-ton and with-a-vengeance, no less). Thankfully, Netta's on hand to pick up her slack.

"Secondness," she contends. Still in the shade, Mary, who can't bear to be contradicted (or to be slower on the uptake than somebody else, which for the Marys of the world is far more ignominious than to be contradicted), plays at stone-deafness and for an amateur does a pretty good—no, a *darn* good—imitation thereof. "Secondness," repeats Netta, finding that talking to a wall has perks and thrills dear to the heart of all self-martyrizing bullies. "Not that he isn't qualified, mind you. It's just that to go about making him Special Envoy to the present Administration—which, is, I know, what some of you are, at this very moment, thinking about doing—reeks of madness. Martin! with only his high-spirited inexperience to guide him. Although I also know what you're going to say. *What about Jarevankanemia who've made a re-Gilded-Age cottage industry out of inexperience even if there's one domain—first among an infinitude—where they—especially Jarevankanemia's better half—aren't inexperienced in the least: back-channelled conflicts of interest passed off as POTUS-tempering addiction to left-leaning lost causes?* Indeed, we all know exactly how much this quintessential daddy's girl's fake-news plightedness to suturing up the gender wage-gap is worth. The sarcastic twinkle in Angela Merkel's eye when the two of them are in the same frame offers up pretty much the best estimate." Or is she—Mary, Mary, Quite Contrary—reading into that resolutely sarcasm-averse twinkle too much of what she wants it to be conveying when what it's all about is in fact good old-fashioned motherly pride?—for Angela (incapable of cattiness) takes kindly—mentorly—to all young women with justifiable ambition and is House Mother to/of them all. *What does Martin think about all this?* Moira—still a fan of his—wonders. And, indeed, Moira *should* wonder since she's got big plans for him—for starters, a doctored reminiscence of her *Four Temperaments* salad days—with Martin in the role of Sisyphean charioteer Melancholic and Moira as one of the two comfortresses, whose hands, after some irksome repositioning work on four scene-stealing Erinyes (by pulling on their reins in the style of his forbear Apollo), he gratefully clasps in eternal farewell. But there's no sign of him anywhere—he could be out fish-farming or catfish wrestling or gravestone rubbing, for all she knows. He's still a loose cannon. It's his curse and his glory.

Melanctha senses everybody else's heightened resistance (even if everybody else, especially Mary, can't) to swallowing, as the moment's Main Event, yet another thought packet, or—since it's all about unabstract current events (*l'affaire* Jarevankanemia)—a *degenerate* packet (degenerate in the mathematical sense)—one without much meat on its bones. (Still, degenerate or not, is Mary working for the Master or is she somebody else's mouthpiece?) A packet to be followed as the night the day by yet another last-ditch effort[180] to keep the party—or at least the party poopers—going—to keep *duration* going—until the next One—next Main Event, I mean—Event in the shape of a packet (for, let's face it, the only Main Events the Master is willing to attend are packet events, though preferably not at the Barclays Center)—until the next packet gets visited on the scene and picks up the slack. Even if the going ain't—no, not by a long shot—a going full speed ahead. And like any daddy's girl worth her salt Melanctha's tempted (though new to the game she's, compliments of the Master's tutelage, still very much a daddy's girl and not just any old incarnation but one that, playing Marx to its Hegel, manages to turn daddy's-girl-hood on its head every chance she gets)—is very much tempted—to rush to His defense, through coy simulation, à la Ivankanemia, of opposedness-in-the-name-of-reason. She hastens to remind herself[181] that the trial's *strategy* (to use the byword of the moment)—rather, the story-of-the-trial's strategy—for unfolding—is pretty much identical to the pornographic film's.

---

[180] In the guise of, say, a no-holds-barred bout of slapstick or a volleyball game (nudists only, if you please), i.e., any poor excuse for thought-untainted *action* (as in Lights! Camera! Action!)—for Writers Workshop *showing* rather than *telling*—will do rather nicely—even handsomely.

[181] Best to do so before trying her hand at reminding others though for the life of her she can't understand what all the make-haste is about—you'd think she had a plane to catch and given all the vicissitudes yoked to palming off Invidicum the Menstruum—Invidicum the Off-Broadway musical extravaganza—Invidicum the Panacea—Invidicum the HBO Miniseries—on an unsuspecting public, she wishes—I mean, she begins to wish—she did.

(*Those were the days,* croons Borkman [even if in his view an orgy isn't all it's cracked up to be], for the two of them—he and Melanctha—are very much on the same wavelength and it's not just the Master's doing.) In both—story of the trial and porno—there's a privileged entity—TP and fuck, respectively— an entity to which an entity less privileged—some poor excuse for a plot line—paves the rocky way. Melanctha suddenly realizes that she herself has just generated a thought packet of sorts—but it's come too hot on the heels of Mary's to have allowed time for implantation of the obligatory connective tissue—the obligatory poor man's plot line—stage business—the obligatory derring-do—whose job it is to pass itself off as Main until the real thing comes along.[182] Which means that, in her eagerness to elucidate even if it's to an audience of one, she's singlehandedly violated the First Law of Packet Dynamics—infringed all the patents subordinate thereto. Which on the other hand— for there always *is* another hand whether we choose to shake it or not—may not be a bad thing. Still, she mustn't rock the boat. Even if the stage business—the derring-do—the plot line—the Lights! Camera! Action!—is just a syncope between orgasms, the orgasms—i.e., the thought packets—need it. In fact, they're nothing without the plot line—packet needs plot more than plot needs packet. Packet's true—it's only—home is story. Indeed, Plot—with its soft spot for fleabitten mutts—is the only thing that will take Packet in—even without health insurance. Even if packet looks down its nose at plot, it exists only through failing to push plot out of its way—through failing to *debase* it.

Mary's anti-Eden kind of excitement has not been in vain on another front—it's excited Borkman. Indeed, it will probably turn out that the one good thing accomplished by Jarevankanemia's gutless inexperience was to have gotten Mary's juices flowing in his direction. To prolong his excitement he laser-focuses on her tresses, enlivened (yes, *tresses!* comma *enlivened!* it's a dirty job salvaging archaisms—rescuing them from the billionaire slumlords' slagheap—but somebody's gotta do it—and fast!—before those archaisms fly back to Capistrano—and make that San Juan Capistrano—never to be heard from again)—tresses enlivened by the Sun (no matter how hard she tries to

---

[182]Since this is a story after all—an ersatz story, granted, but still a story—as much a story as, say, *The Confidence Man* or *Sanatorium Under the Sign of the Hourglass* or *The Man without Qualities* or *The Making of Americans* or (since Moira's on the same wavelength) *The Four Temperaments* or *Serenade* or (since somebody else, yet to be identified, is also on the same wavelengh) *Scenes from Under Childhood* or Stifter's—no, the *other* Stifter's—*Der Nachsommer*. Works where, when all is said and done, nothing much has taken place but the place—works where each thought packet is just a throw of the dice, Mallarmé's dice to be exact, apt to land anywhere—works where all the footnotes evidence not scholarliness—not a plagiarist's god's honest deisre to give every precursor devil his due—but a wasting disease where the creator—rather the *pretend* creator—a Judge Schreber type—a career scavenger—finds anything and everything under the sun to be meant especially for him—to be directed (like Ehrlich's magic bullet) solely at him—hence too relevant to be left unincorporated in—catabolized away by—his magnum—his magmatic—opus.

escape Its clutches), which leads him to wonder whether her pubic patch is even redder, only to then feel the stirrings of the anger (where? why deep down in Borkman's left big toe: his most populous erogenous zone) that's always synonymous in his case with upsurges of inconvenient or unprofitable lust. He doesn't find her particularly desirable but determination to be intrigued by the connection between the seen and the unseen is more powerful, he thinks—or rather, would think, if he could—*than lust as we know it*. The way Borkman sees it is that the prospect of lifetime incarceration (inevitable, barring a Sheriff Joe-style pardon) confers on him the right to be cured by one peek at her snatch, but cured of what? the scars inscribed on his chapped parchment by an ill-fitting ankle bracelet?

Stifter, too, is, and through no fault of his own, on meta-Melanctha's wavelength (another side effect of the *pharmakon* to end all *pharmakons*: telepathic lapses). [Breaking news from the Master who may very well be, like Christ, in the bonds of death: *Invidicum is in fact nothing but the untidy sum of its blundering side effects: a whole much less than the sum of its parts*.] And thus condemned, Stifter has no choice but to selflessly enrich what he knows she's been mulling over—to add his voice to her chorus of one—to help make her packet (for he's got an ort or two up his sleeve), wherever it may lead her, the biggest and the best it can be and not just under the circumstances. After all, by virtue of their very presence in the trial, they make common cause and thus being all for one and one for all, he's not about to steal a colleague's thunder—especially not the thunder of somebody as talented as Melanctha may very well prove to be. He corners her at the door to the ladies' room. But first things first: Not wanting to be mistaken for his too-ethereal-for-his-own-good former partner, he beefs up his delivery, flaunting a well-heeled bicep or two (*yes, well-heeled, nothing like misusing an idiom on a full stomach*). All this thinking of hers—and now his—about stage business, whether it's fuck business or volleyball business or an Olympics-worthy fusion of the two, bespeaks a recognition of the power of *aesthetic necessity*. She's missed that factor. He intends to think this recognition for her—to think it *into* her—into her packet.

Whatever Impresario is running this peepshow—says Stifter[183]—obviously knows for a fact—or he wouldn't be an Impresario—that if you are going to have your seasoned vaudevillians running around spouting precious terms like *Packet Dynamics* and *menstruum* or, worse yet, sideswiping *the likes of* Melville and Bruno Schulz and Brakhage and Musil, not to mention Heidegger and Wittgenstein and Kojève and (on a more exalted level) Mae West (in her *Goodness had nothing to do with it* Blue—or was it her Rose?—Period) and dancing Balanchine and singing Meyerbeer and Method-acting Bressontonioni, then you should bloody well have a few pointlessly lewd remarks up your sleeve, with the sweat—the *bad cholesterol sweat*—of an orgy or two thrown in for good measure, to serve as corrective (that word again)—as *pharmakon*

---

[183] Or does he merely think it? In any case, in these parts thinking and speaking amount to pretty much the same thing.

(ditto)—against all the name-dropping (whose sole purpose is to exalt the dropper into a Legend in his Own Mind). (Certainly wouldn't hurt if some of the folks at some of The Rump's pep rallies could be rounded up incognito to give those orgies a well-deserved whiff or two of down-home authenticity—the foulness of authenticity.) For name-dropping as a conduit to transfiguration—to greater-than-self-hood (as somebody like Cantor [he's also on Melanctha's wavelength cum tightrope] knows better than anybody—at least as well as anybody strolling down Charles Lane into the silver blaze of Sunday morning Indian summer on [where else?] Pier 45)—name-dropping is a disease—a disease Coming Soon to a *Diagnostic and Statistical Manual* near you: just as much a disease as multiple myeloma and both Angelman and Ehler-Danlos syndromes and, hey, while we're at it, what about Dupuytren's contracture, always good for a shudder or two. Not to mention PROGERIA. (Netta charges past them, looking like nothing less than one of ITS poster boys.) Name-dropping's a disease—the only one (to paraphrase *Citizen Kane*'s Mr. Bernstein) you don't look forward to being cured of. Once she's gone, he continues to think but not say, or say and not think, or both, or neither. The Impresario knows His spawn has to go the whole nine yards of vulgarity—philistinism—hucksterism—anti-intellectualism (easy enough in these pursy times)—as a means of undercutting an all-too-obvious thirst for apotheosis, that is, if He wants to satisfy his clients. Since it's not through name-dropping but rather through the undercutting of the Will to Name-dropping that He earns his one-way ticket to An Olympus for Creators, albeit (*albeit! albeit!* where's Norma Desmond when we need her most, i.e., to say, *I hate that word!*)—albeit of a honky-tonk sort.

Which, Herbert thinks (grateful for all these tips, whether said or thought, even if they're the tips of a mere rookie in the *meta* department), is nevertheless how *it*—the thought—should have turned out—how the Master *would have wanted it to turn out*, that is, waving the banner of aesthetic necessity. And it's only fair *after what she's put him through* that this thought packet should belong to Stifter—by divine right, some might say—*including even her half of it*—which has quickly paled in comparison with his. She has no intention of accepting his donated organ and assimilating it to her own still-meager body of work and that's final. It could have been formulated by nobody else—even her half of it. Indeed, it's done what a thousand masters couldn't—turned Stifter into the trial's one bona fide *character*—not just another scrap of collateral damage inflicted by a packet's upsurge. Or is this just a bit of hype cooked up by the Master to convince His Base that they're witnessing a story-generated milestone? But why has she suddenly decided to (fully clothed!) thrash around in the swamp of the conditional perfect (the Master *would have wanted*)—sister to the swamp that The Rump—egged on by Breit Boy Bannon—still threatens to drain? For the Master's obviously in the best of health—to judge by all those thoughts of His rolling around in her head. Thing is, they're coming, those packets, too fast and furious to be passed off as yet another dire symptom of health. Or is it rather the case that although they're coming no more fast-and-furious than before, He doesn't have the inescapable charms of youth at his elbow to bestow on what are essentially meditations on death in its various guises the glamor of precocity? Age—age-*appropriateness*—has caught up with the precocity—a precocity of coyness. Or rather the precocity was in fact always a coward's very age-appropriate apotropaism (*yep*, apotropaism! *one more tongue-twister that's way too big for its—for the Master's britches*). She's tempted to ask Him if He doesn't sometimes fear that in caving in to the blandishments of easeful death (for she's the only one who takes Him at his word—who believes coyness and precocity are in fact the henchmen of an overeagerness to plunge) He'll be perceived as reneging on the pledge to suffer till the cows come home—as pulling a fast one—and will thereby taint His own legacy. It's getting clearer by the second (*how so?*) that the Master's tired of masterhood—dead-tired. Time, then, to pass on the sable shreds of His mantle.

Eden returns (*Where was he?* Moira still wonders) to announce—like a herald straight out of *Macbeth* or, better yet, *Agamemnon*—that he has it on the very best authority (though of course it doesn't come out quite so stiltedly) that there's been a Tweet—a *breaking* Tweet—the best of all possible *deus ex machina*—from on high—a Tweet that's already been transcribed into—encrypted as—a contrail somewhere above the Great Salt Lake (which appears to be minutes away from extinction)—to the effect that the Team—the Wet Dream Team—will be arriving shortly (the venue is no longer To Be Announced). Some of the guttlers (I won't, like Elia Kazan, name names) take their heads out of the mini-trough set before them long enough to look up and make their annoyance—and in some cases their outrage—known, as if nothing could be so serious as to warrant this profanation of the dead calm of chowtime. To quote the ever-prolific demagogue Anonymous of Anorexia (c. 427–347 B.C.), *Hell hath no fury like a proband starved.*

Air Force One, if they want to know, is headed straight for the just-completed Jarevankanemia Golf Resort and Sex Spa conveniently adjacent—just now *rendered* conveniently adjacent—to the Santa Barbara Cemetery—part of which—the best part actually—has been annexed (following exhumation of those remains deemed essential—as in *essential worker*, hence expendable) on behalf of some Higher Purpose. (Rumor has it—but mum's the word—that the Rump expects his foot soldiers—his Oath Boys—to storm the Cemetery in protest against indictments to come: but never fear, he's got their backs— don't worry, mates, he'll be storming up a storm right there behind you— before, that is, he slithers back on all fives, in the dead of high noon, to the SB Super-Hilton eminent-domained for the occasion and plops himself down in front of the TV to lick, once he's had a better view of the proceedings, his blubbery chops at the prospect of massive casualties.) As it turns out, Festivities will begin with a Faith Rally evoking the halcyon days of Father Coughlin. The Tweet has also indicated without for a minute exceeding the 140-character max that spouses, shriveled and fat, greedy and not-as-greedy (as, say, Louisa Mnuncthkin, a sort of embodied Dim Sum of All Brands), have come along and not just for the ride. Where does Mary stand with respect to all this? Herbert wonders (dry heat is conducive to lots of wondering). She knows where Margo stands—who doesn't? what with her already getting shamelessly busy slipping into what must pass for her Sunday best—in front of everybody—even the cook's twin toddlers. Clearly her motto is, *No shame, no gain.* Yes, they'll be bypassing the moated bunkers and the chateaux inasmuch as the Eoarchean Era of the Pajama Boys—or to be more exact, the Pajama *Party* Boys—is over, which means nothing less than that Gorka's Alpha Males— also had on the very best authority—are back in the White House, whose tentacles now extend as far as the very bowels of Air Force One. Evidently, these He-Men prefer the open air to enclosures—especially to enclosures as sissyish as chateaux and even bunkers which have no choice but to come off smelling swishy in the shadow of the Open Air—as paradoxical as that may seem. Though not to Melanctha who, like her fellow Bronxites, is partial to paradox. Things are coming (as noted above) too fast and furious and when that happens, as it occasionally does, her only recourse and last refuge is the weather. Even if there's not too much in the way of weather to be had in these balmy climes which have little patience for the operatics of sky, trees and sea. The only weather worth watching at the moment is high above: a big fat Rorschach Test of a pink porpoise, with blubbery lips like The Rump's, is sniffing the clayey prostate (the Master's recent preoccupation with the prostate has not gone unnoticed by the FBI) of his elusive pal (code name: Putin). It's clear, then, the weather has nothing better to do than dangle before her—and, through her, before the Master—little more than the immensity of a promise far too late for fulfillment. Since the Master's just too damn old. Too dismantled. Too . . . conditional perfect. She can hear the whimper of that dismantlement in her bones.

Meanwhile, back at the buffet table, Cook is authorizing Jean in a whisper—the whisper of one who's been kicked down the rabbit hole of destitution only to crawl out the other end without a scratch and ten tons nattier —a whisper that excites her far more than if he were to introduce his hot hand between her sun-bruised legs—yet a whisper that's also stagey enough to allow Melanctha Herbert and George Cantor to eavesdrop to their heart's content—Cook, I say, is authorizing Jean to remind him to tell her some day soon that it's a miracle she's lasted so long, i.e., that she's here to stay (if he has any say in the matter). Jean, of all people, who started out with not an Envy symptom to her name. And that possibility, he tells her—or forgets to tell her—seems to be growing by the minute, what with so many trial subjects sure to be kicked out before the next round (news that's hot off the press). "The next round?" Cook puts a deckle-edged forefinger to his full mouth—his best feature, as far as she's concerned. "Oh," (defying the forefinger and as loud as she can) "you mean the *trial*'s next round." Exactly, he replies (though a bit too cavalierly for her taste)—the trial of Invidicum as the cure of last resort for conspirativity and greed. "Or is it the trial of Invidicum qua generator of conspirativity and greed?" he wonders. And just as repellent Rump McJr. and his bratty kid brother brazenly proclaimed, a week or so after their father got elected, that the Rump Brand was stronger than ever so does he, Cook, proclaim that the Invidicum Brand is stronger than ever, whatever the target of its wonder-druggery. But he hopes that Jean isn't daring to think that as a brand loyalist, he's just as incompetent as those two or, perish the thought, as the other two, namely, Jaravan, the robot to end all robots, and Kanemia, the "moderating influence without a moderating influence to her name." Melanctha is tempted to correct: You mean *the robot who pretends to be a robot*.

Jean suspects—and Melanctha seconds the motion—that all this excited talk about the *brand*, all this getting into the swing of things super-sycophantic (Flunkification syndrome is what, thanks to Petri dish antics at some adjunct of the Mayo Clinic, it's come to be called)—that all this talk has obviously been triggered by the Team's arrival any second now. Jean is frankly repelled, full lips notwithstanding. Flunkeyism, after all, isn't something she would have associated with Cook. But there's no reaching him, that's for sure—for how reach somebody who takes a word like *brand* seriously—who takes such a word *at* its word—who gladly gives himself up to the word and throws himself on the mercy of its sword—who feels safe only when walled off by this word—a buzzword, in fact, to end all buzzwords? How reach—worse, *reach out to*—somebody who inhabits an alternate universe governed by the alternative fact that is the word—a universe where *brand* means something, that is, everything—where *brand*—through the sheer shameless power of euphemism—encapsulates—normalizes—sanitizes—exalts—a swarming maggotry of deviances and deceptions—a word that makes life so much easier or at least more bearable for branded cretins? How reach somebody who seeks periodic relief from selfhoodlessness through self-perpetration of an overdose of the word (and the word ain't *Invidicum*)—who seeks relief only, alas, to always find it? How reach, in short, a madman? Who, while not as insignificant a madman as daddy's-boyish Rump the Junior, is nonetheless a madman without a madman's charisma—a run-of-the-mill madman—a madman without a Strindbergian defense—a madman without the look of Louis Dodier, in that household word of a daguerreotype by Adolphe Humbert de Molard, whose message is, *Come hither and fuck my madness*. "What about you and Moira?" Jean asks. Although he and Shearer go back a long, long way—longer than Jean might think from the way they avoid each other like the plague—as far back in fact as the hush of an autumn twilight on Second Avenue—which, by the way, should be getting far better press, especially now that NYC has become the Airbnb capital of the world—the hush (marred hence perfected by the gust-driven scrape of oak leaves along the pavement) of a twilight that, as it turns out, was the longest in the history of the world—although he and Shearer go as far back as that, she means nothing to him now. Besides, she's got a bad case of the hots for Martin Eden.

Cook's branded forcefulness of tone is not any old forcefulness but a forcefulness so unshaky it borders on . . . lucidity. Though it's unclear who's taking the bait. Melanctha? Borkman? (no, he still has the runs). Cantor? Jean, whose mind is ostentatiously elsewhere? Doesn't matter. What matters is that the teeth-gritting Master is, whatever he may think of Cook's politics, fulfilling His patriarchal duty. Applying broad strokes of . . . forcefulness, with a vengeance He's perpetrating Cook's portrait.

So why, then, didn't she see it before? He wants his characters—his Rat Men and Wolf Men and psychotic judges—to have all the advantages that eluded Him by His own design even if He doesn't believe in the *concept* of character, per se—as long, that is, as character per se continues to be all about being eyed, fixed and formulated, sprawling on a pin. But just because He's a Master doesn't mean she or any of the others is a slave. Unless—and it's a big—an epic—*unless*—her very insufficiency qua Slave—her having a Slave's abstract idea of freedom, instead of being free in the flesh as the Master is free—unless her insufficiency is her perfection—is her superiority to the impasse that constitutes the Master's concrete freedom. Inasmuch as the idea vouchsafes her a future—a future consecrated to its realization through work—and she's not afraid of work—inasmuch as to work is to be born of constraint while the Master dies of liberty. In any event—*in any event*[184]— Melanctha hears somebody who sounds like the Word on the Street or, more appropriately, the Word on These Sands of Time—she hears that somebody say that The Rump and his slavey crew of chimeric mice (no exceptions) are to be cut down to size by being forced to serve as merest guinea pigs in the biggest trial of them all—lasting seconds—although Word doesn't appear to be quite clear about what shape it's to take. In any event (*bis*), that trial will be after far far bigger—lamer—game than Envy. In any event (*ter*), there's no going back to the halcyon days Before The Rump. Hate notwithstanding, Melanctha's got to admit he's thoroughly *changed* her—made her irrevocable to herself—and for this she must thank him, preferably on the meanest streets of Charlottesville. She's on a collision course with her own efflorescence and there's no turning back.

In any event (*quinquies*—no, *quater*), it's through the encroachment— under the auspices—of the bad master—Bedminster's answer to little rocket man—that she's begun to appreciate (so the bad master can't be all that bad, right?), even love, the Old—*her*—Master—her Master *Builder*—who wields His authority with a difference—wears His vocational rue with a (stoic—or so He likes to think) difference. (Melanctha realizes she uses the term "Master" so freely and so frequently you'd think she receives a hefty commission for each utterance, akin to those aforementioned [but by whom?] baneful NYC bike messengers paid per casualty.) Since for all the profane dinner-theater sardonicism, He's never humiliated his children[185] even if from time to time they seemed to begging for it—even if He has a positive genius for taking

---

[184]A phrase that's yet another last refuge of scoundrels—scoundrels like, say, serial draft-dodger E-1 Private Rump who's, after having himself trashed hero McCain as the fakest of fakes, just excoriated the NFL for disrespecting the suckers—the losers—who died for Our Flag.

[185]Unlike the Pres of Rump U. Who had no second thoughts about humiliating that perfect gentleman of a racist dwarf, Jefferson Davis Shesshions (his egregiousness mildly mitigated compliments of a piteous abasement). Not to mention (albeit more bloodcurdlingly subtly)—and in the very public Rose Garden, no less—CEO Tillersonn, the buttered toast of the Kremlin. Tillerston, who, when asked when he— imperious Rex, now relegated to the status of a dithering Gal Friday—would be coming out with a plan to drain that swamp of a State Department so the only thing left would be the Painted Gator known, imperturbably, as Kellyannabelle Hatch (recently promoted to DOS Acting Ambassadress at Large)—Tillersohn, who, when so coerced,

the bait—imagine! excoriating Him for enrolling them in His very own (and very public) school of hard knocks for the sole purpose of learning His silly thought packets by rote when they should have been busy mastering algebraic topology and computational geometry and data mining starting at age two up at the Dalton School or Browning or Spence or Lowood or Salem House under Mr. Creakle instead. Doesn't humiliate His get even if the humiliation of one is cautionary-tale good for the rest. For all His perversity he cares for them. She can't remember a time when He wasn't *there for them* (detestably sappy turn of phrase but in this case, poignancy trumps sap by a landslide)—in the way, sort of, she'd always been there for her son, whether she wanted to be or not, especially in Building 18. In the last analysis, He's an anxious papa. And His caring—practical not pathological—is all the nobler for its inability to assume the form of a blissful attunement to and joyous participation in the fate (that is, the distress) of His creations. Like Manny Übermensch, He's made sure not to extract any gratification from the caring—which would rob it of all moral worth. And it is this that sets Him apart from other masters who, everywhere you look, are literally bursting at the seams with punch-drunk good will toward (that is, narcissistic overinvestment in) the comings and goings of *their* puppets—never mind that the very bursting disqualifies them for true masterhood. But even if He's untouchable by the distress of others, being too busy tabulating His own and hence not to be provoked by an inclination similar to that of other—minor—masters who can think (having so much more time on their hands) of nothing better, because it gives them a thrill, than to be smearing beneficence like putti poop on the ceiling of this great big Sistine Chapel of an Underworld we call Life—even if untouchable, He still manages to extricate Himself from a lethal indifference and lavish whatever remains of His resources on those in distress, with the categorically imperative poker face of a Keaton. And even if He's been given the strength by Stepmother Nature to endure His suffering without a whimper and in consequence coldly expects the same in others (*which, according to the Übermensch—in the most passionate self-defense to come pouring out of any Philosopher—doesn't make him humanity's worse byproduct—no, not by a long shot*), still, He doesn't punish His creatures for having laid bare His defect and instead of Envying their remorselessness, chooses Respect for their limitations, even if (that is, precisely because) Respect reliably trespasses on His Self-love. Since by succumbing to Envy and inflicting such punishment He would show Himself to be a whole lot worse than His creatures who have no choice, after all, but to crave whatever Life in the World dictates—who have no choice but to take that *whatever* seriously. Whereas He has the ability to

---

duly coughed up the date required but through very poker-faced gritted teeth, thereby letting it be known he was only pretending to be a lackey and solely in order (before cutting the cord of his tenure) to get things done—bigger bigger bigger things than were ever dreamed of in his boss's philosophy. Not to mention Price and Mnutchkin, compelled to spew and spray (at the world's very first public Cabinet press conference), but loving it à la Jr., prostate-licking love juice for all the world to sniff.

stand, without a craving to His name, outside Life in the World—to turn His back on Life—and prove thereby that He's in fact worthy of exorbitant Self-love after all. So, as it turns out, He's the intersection of ethics and aesthetics—the spot on the moral map where ethics transubstantiates into an aesthetic.

And so what if His work ultimately fails? Melanctha asks herself. What if He doesn't manage for all His currying care to ensure that His kids get the breaks He's missed out on? She knows, playing Ivankanemia to His Rump, Goneril to His Lear, He'll never, goaded by that shrewish Stepmother, stoop to regret (which would mean He'd have to wrestle with blood oxygen level-dependent [BOLD] signaling in His bilateral ventral striatum every time a reminder of the triumph-that-should-have-been crosses His path)—abase Himself by invoking the ill will of contingencies. For what will the success of His work be worth if, through supersaturation with the effects of the *right* contingencies so-called, it ends up being crowded out of its own domain?

Or is it the case that He's a true Master—a good Master—only in contrast to a bad one—a real bad one—that He's the kind of Master whose goodness fades fast without a foil? Or should she, instead, focus on, i.e., reconcile herself to, their twinship—the twinship subsisting between him and his badass foil—which outweighs the differences? For aren't they both relentlessly pilloried for being different—for refusing to hew to the party line? Why, given half a chance, Melanctha could see herself believing *her* Master is characterologically unworthy of His foil—you know, that good-people-on-both-sides-of-the-Charlottesville-Grand-Canyon guy. For example, how compare the Master's work with The Rump's, too sublime (executive orders notwithstanding) to degenerate into anything as vulgar as a thing?

But He has cared enough and been successful enough in the caring to ensure that a character worth his salt routinely had the opportunity to act both in and out of the straitjacket of character. Though He's never been known to punish any members of His flock for refractoriness when it came to applying—much less embodying—his conception of fluidity, even if cooked up in their own best interest, with the most serious offenders having turned out to be the least likely suspects. For example, take Herbert: the first to admit through her tenacious hewing to this core contention of the Master, namely, that salvation lies only in being out of character, she's turned out to be the most in character of them all. By refusing to be anything but fluidity's poster girl she's failed to live up to the very standard she champions every chance she gets. Within seconds (bad news travels fast), Jean and Moira realize it's Herbert's very dependability in disseminating the Law of the Master that's made her the quintessential felon. The more she insists that they be unstraitjacket-able, the more straitjacketed she herself becomes. And it's been cold comfort to this felon (who, as such, will, if The Rump gets his way, have her voting rights shredded) that all the while she's concretizing through her actions and in her essence just the sort of subversive trope that, as an aspiring writer, is right up her alley (couldn't be righter)—to wit, vicious-cycling. And it's even colder comfort that pursuant to all this apostolizing PR she's become a walking Russellian paradox (and who'll understand this better than Cantor once the news reaches him as well and he gets to nail Herbert's predicament?)—i.e., nothing less than the class of all classes that are not members of themselves, which class of all classes is textbook-infamous for being both a member and a non-member of itself. But Jean for one hates it when somebody tries to explain away what is somebody else's bad luck pure and simple as the outcome of an addiction to self-sabotage. But she mustn't lose sight of the forest for the trees and this realization generates a desire to do some PR work of her own— while sidestepping what from now on will probably be referred to as—and not just in the world of Invidicum—the Herbert Trap. And what is the forest but the Master's overarching bounty in leaving them lots and lots of leeway where that old chestnut character is concerned? And it's this very bounty which makes Him so unpopular with clients and characters alike. (*What's the world coming to?* grumble the most ignorant among them. *Can nobody count on a fixed identity anymore?* Since where they all hail from—the Blood Belt [as it's known familiarly to the East Coast alt-left elite]—a fixed identity is, however impoverishing, a hallmark of the Christian faith and, to boot, a *national treasure*[186] right up there with, for starters, (*a*) chlorpyrifos, (*b*) that sonofabitch Pewitt's $24,570 soundproof "communications" booth and (*c*) Sheriff Joe's rap-sheet-and-blubber-butt combo.) And given such bounty, why, while we're at it, shouldn't Eden, an underdog if ever there was one, written off far too many times to count, have become the Tweet-annunciating star he's suddenly found himself to be?

---

[186]A mealy-mouthed epithet if ever there was one.

CHAPTER SIXTY-THREE

The barbarians are but inches from their very gates—from their very-gated community—and, for all practical purposes, already snapping at their rear ends like Joe Mankiewicz's bloodhounds, so Mary has no time to waste disrupting the flow of declamation—even if it's the declamation of the best and brightest of this mangy lot. And whether the declamation is thought or spoken doesn't make much of a difference, for Mary has reached that stage in her tenure as Head of Human Resources—Head not just here at East Beach but at any number of conglomerates (with not a few of whose bigwigs Borkman has locked horns)—she's reached the stage where declamation of any stripe—not to mention everything else life has to offer—holds no appeal. The stage where the only question that remains is something along the lines of, *Trial, Terminable or Interminable?* and, by extension, *Trial Story: Terminable or Interminable?* Still, she does her duty—whatever Cantor may say, she's staunchly a woman of duty but, as an even stauncher Eisenhower Republication, how can she not be? So, she tactfully reminds them (even if it breaks her heart to do so) Martin is after all Invidicum's rising star and in that guise deserves their full support. Especially with the moment nearing when, as their Envoy, he must greet the Team, sure to be testy after a long flight, all the amenities of Air Force One notwithstanding. Moira has the feeling Mary would have liked to add—bitterly, of course—supererogatorily—*And we have no choice but to live with it—with him,* but stopped herself in the nick of time.

Hey, Trial, Terminable or Interminable, *was* my *question,* Melanctha thinks (Call the Patent Office!), *before it was put on hold at the very moment we were rushed out of the Chateau and into the vans, or at some other equally frenetic juncture.* (Melanctha's still reeling from the realization that she's but a walking shadow—worse, a walking Russellian paradox. How low can a human being sink in its perfectly respectable quest for uniqueness?) "Nobody would be crazy enough to deny—even if the trial were to end today—that you've come a long long way. (How distant the first dosing must seem to you Greenwich Avenue irregulars!)" After all, most of them (she goes on to say) have been able to reclaim a small measure of independence, take timorous stabs at renewing their interest in life, wan at the best of times, and establish some sort of reconnection with those whom, in accordance with a rule borrowed from (thoroughly discredited) orthodox psychoanalytic practice, they were obliged, absent the semi-official go-ahead, to refrain from loving until further notice.

But where did this long long way come from? Moira wonders. She, for one, doesn't feel as if she reclaimed her independence, took stabs at self-renewal, and reconnected with unlovables. She's being told about a happening that never happened—not realizing that it's the telling itself that's the happening—or rather, the disjunction between the telling and the absence of the thing told—an absent thing made itchingly real (throwing doubters like Moira off the scent) through a masterstroke: performance of the telling in the off key of disappointment—disappointment that the happening is so meager. Since there's nothing more real than a nothing that's too meager to merit even further discreditation or the withholding of whatever faint praise may be there for the bestowing.

It's catching—this disjunctivitis bug—and within seconds somebody else has taken up the slack or the cudgels. "But—Therefore—In fact—the Trial has reached an impasse," murmurs Post. "The worst sort, in fact: the impasse of partial success, with which they're obviously much too comfortable to envision digging any deeper or advancing any further—that is, any further back, or deeper. For their purposes—or should we say, cross-purposes— they've absorbed just the right amount of *un*Envy. But right for what?" "You talk about us as if we're anywhere but right here!" exasperates Jean. *How ugly I-Dream-of-Jeannie must have looked,* he silently fumes, *filled to the brim with bile on the Staten Island Ferry. Just begging to be gang-raped and deserving it royally.* Post recovers, as he always does. "In short—Indeed—The Trial has managed to inhibit itself—with a little help from the participant Envioids and as for the leaders—well, I take fullest responsibility." "The trial—the Trial— the trial," Netta sighs. "*Gimme a break.*" (Hard to imagine that a doyenne with her credentials would have deigned to shake hands with such a catchy phrase. Well, fact is, the phase makes her feel *real*. All her life, if you must know, Netta's been afflicted with a crypto non-disease: unrealness—indeed, she's been afflicted with a sixth sense: that the realness—the structural integrity—of the eminent Dr. Netta Van X—— is just a feint she manages robotically to put over on everybody else—the mangy wool she routinely manages to pull over everybody else's eyes. Yet when she says *gimme a break* with conviction [and there's no way to utter such a phrase *without* conviction and in the process not be convicted of manslaughter] she becomes real at last—only never real as *herself,* whoever that self turns out to be. The realness accruing is mere finery borrowed from the speaker's wardrobe and even after all these years— decades—centuries—she's still hungering to learn from that speaker firsthand how to be real without resorting to [whether the situation calls for it or not] *gimme a break.* Not much difference, come to think of it, between her and the kid—a seventy-year-old dud in kid's clothing—she once treated [again, not as herself but in that case, as Melanie Klein] who wielded—deployed—the phrase *you can't make this shit up*—tested the waters of life with it as his dowser—his Geiger counter—because it allowed him to feel self-disabusingly male even if every self-respecting situation—event—entity—for miles around repudiated such an assessment qua dismissal point-blank—refused the honor of being plastered with—tarred and feathered by it.) "The Trial is failing because of its very success. And other myths. And other half-baked paradoxes. But don't mind me. Let the wordflow begin—let wordflow do its thing—let wordflow do what wordflow does best (for wordflow, of course— like youth—must have its fling, so pardon us, so pardon us)." Which is, as she explains with a hiss or two at the Leader in Chief, to hold them hostage to its contortive defiance of *meaning,* at least as that wily term is understood by respectable people everywhere. Post ignores her. Indeed, he *will* let wordflow do its contortive thing and respectable people—respectable *folks*—be damned—everywhere. Fact of the matter is, the Trial had been failing long before it even began to try its hand at what any trial, self-respecting or otherwise, is expected to do, i.e., ferment for prophylactic purposes all conceivable inner conflicts known to man—the more latent the better—so as to castrate in vitro, their knack—or, better yet, so as to allow them to castrate each other's knacks—for inflicting what quacks call holistic harm. And if the conflict that happens to be a particular trial's particular focus (in this case, Envy versus Kantian Respect) happens to get fermented along with every other—all the better. By the way, in calling this tactic "Playing with the Lying Fire of Sleeping Dogs," the hoi polloi from Coast to Coast—Post's heard them in the men's room (as well as in the ladies' room, where he's been wont to wander not quite by mistake)—are as usual on to something far beyond the grasp of their betters—better-*fed*, in any case—whom they've been put on earth to shame into posthumous enlightenment.

"Maybe the trial's failure stems from the fact that the recruitment process was too quick and too sloppy," Netta grumbles between gritted teeth, for if there's anything she hates more than to be taking Post seriously, even through contestation, it's to be perceived as doing so. "And that's because you were too greedy for subsidies which as everybody knows were proportional to the number of warm bodies we could squeeze or drag through the revolving doors." Post is terrified she'll point a finger, in accredited-shrew high dudgeon, at the bargain-basement sign-up service he engaged—run by what her flunkeys uncharitably described as a harelipped prison matron emeritus although they were correct in everything they said (and in his case they erred on the side of restraint) about her trophy wife of a halfwit husband whose tonsure was fringed with crazily blondish strands. "So what we've ended up with is an Our Gang of hypochondriacs and any hypochondriac worth his salt likes nothing better than to know he's in a place where *a gurney lurks at every crossroads* (to invoke the current tagline associated with such a syndrome but is hypochondria a syndrome? isn't it more like a . . . nothing, in sheep's clothing?). In short, none of them—none of you—are suffering from Envy—except, maybe, you, Cantor." Without having any especial love for his comrades—not even a love that dares not speak its nickname—he still feels the need to defend them. In addition, he doesn't want to be typecast for all eternity as the only needy kid on the block. Thing is, it's mid-afternoon and Cantor won't be getting any younger so the first order of business should be to sleep off all this lunch-induced sloth. So what if he hasn't earned his nap the way Mary has? And what better way to go about it than to lie down in the sand and de-archive his interview with Harelip and Tonsure? He was obliged to get up way too early, i.e., high noon, and once the die was cast, to watch as the sun perpetrated soul murder by pissing its merciless good cheer all over the apartment. *For Pete's sake, Cantor, no flashbacks: flashbacking is an acknowledgment of depletion.* He realizes he's spoken out loud for Netta and her kind are giving him the evil eye but how can that be since he's well out of earshot? Out on the street, the sun was, typically, much less oppressive, going so far as to nestle respectfully on his shoulder and play the [proverbial?] errant parakeet come home to roost. It accompanied him, this parakeet did, as far as Plato's Pharmacy at the corner of Twenty-Sixth and Lexington. *No flashbacks, Cantor (are you deaf as* well as dumb?)—no privileging the dunghill doings of the past[187]—no burying your head in the quicksand of times gone by and burrowing toward not just any old past but the past beyond all pasts—to wit, that unlocalizable irretrievable first moment of First feeling (before the sledgehammer of consciousness comes along and smashes everything worth cherishing to bits)—feeling unregenerately immune to corruption by thought—as unregenerate as, say, dusk when it refuses to be called exquisite (see above, somewhere in the shrubbery-smothered text desecrating, say, page 372)—feeling newly monadically freshly spontaneously monastically vivid—feeling not akin to but consubstantial with Adam's, at moment 1 of day 1 in Eden and long before he was obliged to distinguish himself from apples and apples from Eve. So, No Flashbacks until further notice. Agreed? You'll just have to face the The Rump crowd with nary a one in tow—a woman's feeble armament in any case and one whose deployment is best left, however breathtakingly, to the likes of Anne Baxter (I Confess), Joan Fontaine (Letter from an Unknown Woman) and Emmanuelle Riva (Hiroshima, Mon Amour).

The ashes have all been scattered. Manning's instructions were carried out to the letter, for she continued to be a real stickler, right up to her expiration date and a bit beyond. Overcoming the inevitable scruple or two, Jean decides to give her all to hovering over Mary since she's breathing irregularly, obviously a victim of hot-air prostration. And fatigue. Above all fatigue. For the hardest thing in the world, even Jean must concede (but why *even* Jean?), is to distill the essence of an evolution—differentiate the stages of a *long, long way*—when there hasn't been one. Especially when almost simultaneously you've got to be preparing yourself mentally, whether you know it or not, for the visit of a potentate as impotent as The Rump, sky-high IQ notwithstanding. And it would be the cheapest of all shots if Jean were to convince herself—out of Envy of her idol's too many achievements (so Jean is one of E.E. Evans-Pritchard's gall-bladder men, after all, even if she squeezed her way into the trial under ostensible false pretenses)—if she were to convince herself that, here, for all to see and relish, Mary is *snoring away* to beat the

---

[187] *Comprising events from whose clammy clutches you extricated yourself just in the nick of time—events that led nowhere fast, e.g., that party in Oakland, ca. 1971, at which, for the first time, a hard-on was triggered, once everybody else had started to dance, by some woman's commanding hunger to hold you much too close for comfort. Events that had nothing to do with you—life events into which you smuggled yourself—make-or-break events into which you didn't quite fit (but before anybody could ring the alarm, you'd breached the dykes, or rather the dykes breached you). Events in which you were neither in nor out of character. Events that you didn't permit to have repercussions. Wet-dream events—ejaculated into the future as embodiments of pure possibility, hence of purest mystery. Museum disincarnations of pure pastness to be cherished and relished, not necessarily in that order. Events you chose—were constrained—not to take up on their offer—events you kept airtight unto themselves—so as to be able to feed off that mystery—the mystery of your refusal to lend them a life. This excludes, of course, the Berry Sundae event—the least mysterious of all—an event that's managed to last—out-last—several lifetimes.*

band—it would reflect more badly on Jean than on the non-snorer. Just as Cagney's moll's doing just that in *White Heat*, i.e., snoring away, telegraphs the director—Walsh's—height of vulgarity, not the character's. In fact, Mary Mayo is breathing daintily—coyly. But what stops Jean's mauling Envy dead in its tracks is the tattoo on her idol's upper right arm. Seems to represent nothing less than the shadow of the shadow of a pubic hair, sex indeterminable. So what Mary does best—or thinks she does best—is hardcore pimping—pushing the tattoo as her canniest self-conception to date—yeah, her *self-conception* (and you can quote me to my face)—as the embodiment of all her unspeakables—of everything that makes her one of the giants in an overcrowded field. Every time Jean has another go at gazing, however, the tattoo starts peddling its *own* self-conception but a conception completely drained of selfhood—humbler, then, and infinitely more touching—a conception that makes a mockery of the bearer's own—and of Jean's Walsh-besting vulgarity.

Cantor awakens in the nick of time from his failed flashback—watches as everybody—except Mary, who's still asleep—drifts toward the cemetery, now just another avatar of the Brand. Though Ethan for one (*Narr* to you) is far more interested in confronting Jean (who still hasn't made her proper peace with the tattoo) than in throwing in his lot with the drifters. Their parody of a "relationship" has been on life support much too long and what better time than this to call it quits—the weather, at least, couldn't be more accommodating. Netta, returning from the ladies' room, shouts (to their hunched backs) that they have only themselves to blame for the current state of affairs—consummated by their eagerness to suck up to Father MacRump and his flunkeys. To a non-English speaker, however, the lady would appear by her tone to be cheering them on, with a verbalized wave, by crooning something along the lines of, *And don't forget to write at least twice a week.* Every Invidicum-related setback—anything unforeseen and unpleasant or even pleasant (remember when the shipment on that Halifax schooner fell straight through the hold into the Hudson at the level of the Fort Washington Avenue Armory?)—became, starting with those at the top, a pretext for self-disqualification rather than an incentive to go on doing better and better. Disqualification not just for pursuing their vocation but for living—for *being*. (The Rump gang, on the other hand, will have no traffic with disqualification—doesn't know disqualification from Adam—that's what makes its members stars.) No room in the ark for their kind of pestilence—the worst ever to befall an earthling, or so they needed—need—to think. They've clearly missed the boat (and figuratively, too)—recurringly laid waste to the fertile split seconds when, instead of allowing themselves to be racked by setbacks, however painful, they could have quietly *acquired* those setbacks as a patent fortification, a private endowment, i.e., the sole and purest confirmation—however uncomfortably this strategy might sit with their inner tyros—of the uniqueness of their particular take on the right to life—the right to be. Of course, there's always an *initial* price to be paid by everyone for wresting uniqueness from disqualification (an undertaking more common than the available disaggregated data would lead you to think)—in their case, dread that nothing will remain after the auto-diagnosis has been invalidated—after the disease it ratified—self-disqualification—has revealed itself to be a non-starter incapable even of smuggling itself into the least prestigious mental health institution of them all—the *DSM*?

At first, she informs them at the top of her lungs, undergoing the setbacks must have resembled being strapped down in a dentist's coach-and-four and forced to mutely hum along with the piped-in Muzak of the Spheres: How could their stance keep from manifesting fervent agreement (given the deft transformation of sound waves into vomit) with whatever smarmy alternative fact that vomit was sculpted to embody on their behalf—how could they, so stanced, keep from becoming mere affections, or rather disaffections, of the Great God Painkiller under the attribute of Noise? Indeed, it would have been at the very moment of trying to break free of their bonds that they became vomit's most ardent press agent.

"She's right!" This shout—Borkman's—could never be mistaken for cheering them on—not even for Bronx-cheering. In his view (to put it bluntly), to be able to laugh harder than those who laugh at us with loathing—rather than to take dowagerly affront: that's the greatest achievement a man can hope for on this compost heap of an earth.

"But how achieve it?" Netta challenges. *Dowagerly* (even if Borkman never uttered the word—just implied he was *thinking it over—once over lightly*) has hit a nerve, both aggrandizing and making mincemeat of her pretensions. Borkman's words—or rather, Borkman's in-so-many-words—invoke the great days of Coronado when he had no trouble sweeping Melanctha off her tiny feet. (She hasn't decided whether or not to join the procession.) Divining *the budding author*'s reaction to Borkman's words, Netta decides to recruit her plight as a case in point. I.e., she can only hope[188] that when it comes time for Melanctha, as literary lioness assoluta fallen on hard times, to be cast aside by the younger generation who must against their will surpass the Unsurpassable One and hate her heartily for it—Netta can only hope that when it becomes Melanctha's turn to recognize there's something more potent than her genius, namely, hipness on the make as *weaponized* (the current darling of the pundit crowd) by the protagonist in, say, some HBO limited series about unfazeable Hollywood scriptwriters—Netta can only hope that rather than be humiliated Melanctha will let herself feel peacock-proud to have confirmed yet again what she already knew in the cradle (but this time via her own exalted downfall), namely, that no hip youngster with a fragile ego in full rut can mar her Greatness no matter how hard he tries since the marring—the no-holds-barred marring—is part—the most important part—of Its *dynamic*. In other words, Netta can only hope that however hard they laugh at her unforgivingly, Melanctha will be able to laugh even harder—to breathe a sigh of relief that fickle nature bears her enough good will to shackle Greatness to the one thing It lacks to be credible: the animus of both the young and the hip, and the old and the hipless.

---

[188] That the exhortation to come is delivered against the backdrop of a recession of near zombies lends it a certain Pilgrims' Chorus-style—no, make that a certain Prisoners' Chorus-style—pathos.

In front of whoever's been left for dead by the zombies,[189] Ethan tries—not to announce, as planned, that he's calling it quits but—to convince Jean that they must stay together. "Why?" she asks dully—she's too tired for contempt so Ethan must make do with a stab or two at dullness. He understands, really he does, Jean's not wanting to be yoked to what seems like an interminable bout with failure and doomed thereby to share a career failure's estrangement from the world. Though it's still not clear to him what he's failed *at. Jean, for her part*—no, *As for Jean*—Jean clearly resents his implication that all she cares about is not failing—which in her case would entail remaining a trial subject to the bitter end—some kind of inverse movie star instantly recognizable by every man on the street for a bedazzling . . . obscurity. (And who'd blame her for staying put since for one thing, it's well known that whatever skills a trial subject will have ultimately acquired—and in some cases, the number is infinite—won't be transferrable outside of a very particular hit-and-miss context of incurability?) But for somebody like Jean (who, unlike Caro, prides herself on regarding Life as one long transaction with Truth—the more painful the better), it *should* be far less humiliating to admit point blank that she's overcome by unspiritual discontent—i.e., that she's on the make 24/7—than to insist (with an otherworldly air) that Ethan is way off base. It should be far less humiliating: Only, when push comes to shove, it just isn't.

He hopes that Jean, even if she can't summon forth one whit of compassion and harbors no good will toward his failures—much less his successes (*I need to get a move on: something tells me the opening ceremonies are about to begin!* she thinks, or he thinks, or both of them think, though not quite in unison)—even so, surely it must be obvious that, willy-nilly, she's got to simulate compassion—if for no other reason than to shore up credit against the time when there might be a need—a crying need—for *his* (compassion, that is) or his empathy or the empathy of somebody like him? "I'm tone-deaf to empathy," she snorts, unknowingly echoing that wiseguy who continues to haunt the wilds of page 666 or thereabouts since, as it turns out, said wiseguy is a Beast—a Fifth Avenue Beast—whose mark is 666 as well. And how could she ever end up needing his compassion? "The idea's preposterous." (She has nothing to lose. Everything will be different after the rally—once she gets a whiff of mob consensus at its most broiling. though she doesn't say as much.) "I understand," Ethan says, liking what poignant resignation—or its simulation—does for his tone and maybe even his complexion. As far as he, an

---

[189] Who are advancing slowly but surely—mesmerized en masse—on what for the most part is now Jarevankanemia Golf Resort and Sex Spa—not cemetery—terrain (and Ronald Colman be damned!). Look, some have already passed the Music Academy of the West! (Don Siegel's *Invasion of the Body Snatchers* is of course one seminal source of this homage-to-the-nondead sort of imagery, blessedly nipped in the bud by a Master who dreads living off the fat of other artists' land, even if only for the infinitesimal amount of time it takes to get from the beginning of a modestly freighted sentence to the end.)

unregenerate Union foot soldier[190] is concerned, the unrelenting California sun has brought out the very worst in everybody, not just Jean. Though maybe the very worst was the only thing they'd had to offer from the word go (which is what made them ideally suited for the trial) and he'd been too much of a rube to take note. Smug, shortsighted Jean must have convinced herself lickety-split that he was just the kind of guy she loved to hate—that she'd love to hate—the kind who'd reached the point in his surrender to dire straits—*straits dire beyond dire* (the Greeks must have had a word for it)—where he couldn't help but get greedily caught up (to the exclusion of all other distractions) in the process of (*a*) ingesting—arrogating unto himself—assimilating to his substance—the world's every last exemplar—species—intimation—morsel—shred—particle—species—variant—mutation—intimation and intonation—of vulnerability—for all the world as if vulnerability—its whole spectrum of archetypes—were solid things—in fact none solider and thereby (*b*) making the sum total of vulnerabilities in the world—vulnerability in all its shapes and sizes—his very own—thereby making vulnerability thus absorbed into the bloodstream of his nervous system a manifestation—no, *the* manifestation—no, the supreme manifestation—of his essence—including those species of vulnerability inscribed with her name, and thus—as a collateral benefit to one who deserved it least—(*c*) robbing her of any present or future need for the world's empathy (that word again!—nothing but a mere placeholder for its non-existent referent). No use, then, expecting her (so disburdened) to honor, even foster, his honest need to wrestle his demons, also honest, to the ground. "My job shouldn't be to protect you." "Exactly!" he cries, as if competing with the wind and the waves which, frankly, aren't as feral as they profess to be. Protection means being sucked into his void, the shabbiest of habitations for a maiden on the make with an exaggerated notion of the benefits of conformity—of . . . normality. "People are listening," she whispers, though there's nobody in sight except the kitchen staff who are busy bagging the remnants of lunch—too unsightly to be lugged home and thrown to the pigeons or even to their shit. In as loud—and virile—a voice as he can muster (and it's easier said than done given how shrewish rage, stepdaughter of hurt, makes him feel),

---

[190]As such, he should of course have capitulated to a compromise with Confederates over the "slavery question"—the compromise *to which they'd been entitled*. At least, according to revered revisionist historian Rear Admiral John McKelly, the only adult in the WH daycare center until demoted to mewling infant. Who, at one of those legendary press conferences "curated" by Sara Suckabee Glanders post-Charlottesville, saw fit to make no bones about retro-excoriating the recalcitrant bleeding-heart liberals of yester-century—and by extension those of today—to that effect. The same Machine Gun Kelly, by the way, who days before had provided—under the unwilling auspices of (see above) Congresswoman Frederika Wilson (*all hat and no cattle* according to blatantly bovine Ms. Handers)—a demonstration of—an object lesson in—what it means to hold women sacred (but, alas, only white women) and in strict accordance with the standards of the Past (but, alas, only a non-existent julep-sipping Past, however wistfully—belligerent-wistfully—invoked).

Ethan Narr tells her (*a*) the last thing he cares about is the nosiness of human *schmattes* and (*b*) to, oh, just shut up.

But it may not be too late to foil her smugness. In sign thereof, suddenly there are so many feelings to express. Feelings, for example, about their failed life together. And about going their separate ways without so much as a single look back. Thing is, those feelings are too protective of their *brand* to surrender to expression, which will only cancel their uniqueness. Feelings have—the Master reminds Melanctha at that very moment (as if she needs reminding)—*a mind of their own.* Still, it's his civic duty to hold on to these feelings—these legitimate grievances—expressed or not, as if they were, say, a bowl of rancid gruel too precious to spill so as to be able to invoke them[191] when the time is ripe, as perfect specimens of legitimate grievance—of his *right* to grievance, directed against not just her but the entire world. Even if by so doing he'll be robbing Eden of his biggest chance. For it's Eden—at least in tonight's performance on the Mount (this pet name for the Jarevankanemia Golf Resort and Sex Spa has caught on fast enough among the locals)—it's Eden who should be playing (to capacity crowds) the noble role of Rousseau's failed savage and, as such, should be required to *[Exit, though not pursued by a bear].*

Jean's youthful discontent takes Netta back decades. "I'm frankly glad you gave that loser the brush-off." She's got to talk fast otherwise they'll never get a ringside seat at the rally (of course it doesn't much matter if *she* misses the spectacle but Jean has her whole life before her and therefore has a right to, etc., etc.) Though she can promise nothing at this time, still, as the Word on the Street would have it, a replacement for Manning needs to be found ASAP. It's inevitable Invidicum will have an even richer life after Envy and Homicide and Conspirativity and even Greed, since as putrid priggish peripatetic all-suffering Pence once remarked (albeit in that case with reference specifically to the phantom havoc wreaked by Obamacare), people are *hurting.* "New blood, complete overhaul, leave Greenwich Ave's dead to bury the dead—that sort of thing," Netta mumbles not quite incomprehensibly. "But I don't have any training in the field," Jean complains, refusing (since her vanity's been piqued) to believe Netta's offer is the brainchild of mere dementia. Manning after all is a tough act to follow. Netta sighs—the undemented Netta—to make it perfectly clear she's had to contend with misguided reluctance, imbecile hesitation, far too often to be sidetracked. "I'm sure they'll agree to pay through the nose for your training and in the meantime, darling— Though, now that you mention it I do think you'd be far better suited to filling the Johnstone creature's high-button shoes. (Do you think she'll come out of her coma any time soon? Even if she does, I'm afraid it won't be long before there's a relapse.)" Although *this*-worldly Jean wants to get ahead—way ahead—wants, in short, to *make it big*—something compels her to take, with a brawny mix of trepidation and animus, a huge step backward into her very own private jobhunter's Golden Age—(To no avail, Something cries *No flashbacks, Jean!*)—a Golden Age where, now undisturbedly ensconced (yes, *ensconced!* and much the bet-

---

[191] But before whom? All tribunals have adjourned indefinitely.

ter for it), she finds herself once again plying some snotty interviewer with as many eager-beaverly questions as possible though in her case it's for the sheer elemental fun of plotting (though not consciously) level of teethpicking indifference (y-axis) as a function of number of questions asked (x-axis).

"Yes, despite all your drawbacks, I have no doubt there's a fast-hire somewhere in the works. And it's not just the sea air doubletalking. The pep rally (a *deus ex machina* if ever there was one) is sure—like that pandemic everybody's talking about (I can feel its imminent onset in my bones)—to speed things up. We've got to hurry" (Netta dutifully eyes her watch as if on the sly to give the impression that she actually cares about getting there before she dies) "but I best make this admission before we get anywhere near the Mount. I've been spying on Margo—you know, that walking straitjacket whose ravings are singlehandedly responsible for Pritchard's—" "I know who Margo is," Rhys replies although from her tone it's unclear (which unclarity is all to the good, at least for Somebody if not for His clients) whether she's offended on behalf of a friend, or irritated by the digression itself (and friends be damned). "—intercepting emails and phone messages—for her own good of course, not to mention the good of the group—still tightly knit despite—or because of—all we've been through together. I don't want her to go giving the Rumpoids ammunition to be used against us, convinced as she is that they and they alone can figure out exactly *Who's behind* It—she'll make the rest of us look equally obsequious." "Behind what?" "For starters—behind Straynge's murder and, more to the point, the through-the-sour-grapes-vine canard that Jim, Jr.,—or worse, she herself—is the culprit in chief. And behind Pritchard's cruising and, worse, the canard that it was she who made him a criminal." Netta takes a deep breath since she knows this is a lot for convent-nurtured tomboy Jean to swallow, even in bits and pieces.

But amid all the horseplay Netta has forgotten the most important point: If Jean wants the Rump gang to back her bid for Manning's post or Mary's, then she's got to play her wild cards right, and close, close, close to the vest. Granted, all of them are pretty much unabashedly untouchable in their ass-licking arrogance. But she mustn't despair: a means does exist (Netta speaks from long familiarity with the psychological typologies concerned) of *making a dent in their feet of clay* (Inuit expression). They *can* be softened, even the most repellent folks among them—even near non-morons like Marc MacMeadow and near sociopaths like star DOS staff and DOS staff morale eviscerator Rex Tillerstones, for example. "How?" Rhys condescends to wonder out loud. "By fangless questions about their forbears. A forbear is—" "I know what it is." Their biliousness—Envy (without a capital *E* if you please) of anything that moves—will dissolve like snowflakes in the gusts of a struggle to remember, will dissolve in the vortex of a temptation to deliver up and surrender their prize possession—the trademarked treadmill of volition—to the most exotic of somethings unforeseeable, namely, humility.[192] And not just

---

[192] Melanctha would like to think she hears some interventionist body silent-screaming: *We're no suckers. Long before Netta von Krakpot any number of stooges claimed that*

any old humility but humility founded on relief at having to acknowledge that there's something bigger than the self, namely, the circumstantial details of its origins in the mists of time—the mists and hard times of, e.g., Aunt Granny and Uncle Frannie and Great-Grandfather Proust and Great-Great-Grandfather DiMaggio—those details are sacred, at least for most—in fact, the details are sacred enough—self-exalting enough—to put on hold the contempt they would normally feel for the bumbling elicitor thereof. In short, the pleasure derived from doing their schoolboy duty will far outweigh any chagrin that accrues from having given the schoolmarm questioner (in this case, Jean) the satisfaction of knowing her bidding was duly done. And more to the point, Jean knows (although she does not say as much to her unwelcome mentor) from a long experience of taking (often rectally) the temperature of family narcissists non pareil that it's much less painful to lose oneself in other people's memories than to stumble on one's long-buried own only to discover they're still crouched on all fours, panting for a complement, a supplement, a rectifying twin, a rhyme, a *solution*, which will never materialize. The way the world works is ever so unlike her own clerkishly conscientious modus operandi. Its wastefulness still makes her giddy. There will never arise an event to rhyme, for example, with having been held way too close for discomfort while her father, as his pretext, ordered her infant body, on its third birthday (place: Walden Pond), either to swim or to drown. So, *pace* David Hume, it's not a great—a strict—frugality that the Author of Nature, i.e., Melanctha's Master, observes in his transactions with his creatures but a scandalous prodigality.

Netta and Jean are on their way. The walk—some might say a perp walk—is all uphill. Still, the trattoria is closer to their destination than they thought. They are quickly catching up with Melanctha. Since she's busy being hobbled by the discharge of her post-impressionist's duty to trace and register every quirk in the labyrinth of waning light and the sun is taking far too long to set. Her patience—leaving much to be desired at the best of times—is, if not quite exhausted, then wearing paper-thin. A conclave of palms are under pre-dusk's solemn interdict—i.e., under a glass bell invisible even to the most practiced eye and so contoured as to quash (yes, *quash!*) their susurration (yes, *susurration!*). Which is certainly not the case for the chanting from above of some-

---

the way to an arrogant egomaniacal vulgarian's jawbone of a heart is through his line of descent—his toddler's pride in "heritage." So what, she retorts, spoiling (whether there's been a scream or not) for a fight—so what if the Master repeats himself, having forgotten—or worse, much worse, while not having forgotten—what he thought five minutes before? So what if he's therefore the most unreliable of storytellers—not to be trusted? Though why doesn't manic repetition make him in fact more trustworthy—proving he's endearingly capable of enslavement, in this case to his own discoveries, and not at all interested in making a fast buck—worse, pulling a fast one—by slicing and dicing up the Invidicum Story (according to the laws of CW 101) into nuggets, their novelty all too coherent, of one iteration only? Don't these groundlings know that thought packets as manically overinvoked by the Master are like the face of that NYCB ballerina so much admired by Arlene Croce: *never changing and never the same*?

thing that sounds like *The Blacks and the Jews and the Muslims and especially the apostles of Zoroaster will not replace us—surpass us—disgorge us from the bowels of the earth. Aryan Lives—downtrodden mercilessly by the downtrodden so-called—Matter—mightily.* Even from this distance, she can make out tiki torches in what must be part of the Sex Spa that remains cemetery terrain. She'll know more later once she reaches the very heart of the action. Despite all the mongering, and at least from here, this get-together still has the air of a perfectly harmless job fair—a CV swap fest. For now, each station of her progress toward the *cemetery spa* (a term that, like, say, *jingle bell rock*, will, she has no doubt, soon *pass into the language*) is like The Rump's crimes against language, *i.e., against humanity* (or is this too facile a fusion?). That is to say, each station is easily enough forgotten to make way for the next outpost—the new outrage. He still hasn't, by the way, released the two things dearest to his heart—his tax returns and the results of his most recent IQ test (unlike Rex the Tillerman, who's been most forthcoming on both counts).

Margo is moving fastest, while achieving the no-mean-feat of keeping all her ailments not just intact but at arm's length from each other. Pritchard doesn't like being led—doesn't like the *idea* of being led—of being commanded to get a move on—of being told that if only he'd listened to her, then—then—[193] Likes even less the prospect of beating her at her own game by retorting (in so many words), *What pilot so expert but needs must wreck/ Embarked with such a steers-mate at the helm.*[194] Or better yet: it's gotten to the point where he'd like to cry out (also in so many words), *Foolish men,/That e'er will trust their honor in a bark/Made of so slight, weak bulrush as is woman,/ Apt every minute to sink it!*[195] So when they arrive at the entrance to the cemetery (every little gate—breeze—bird—rose—seems to whisper, not "Louise" but *Out, out hyena*), who should she and Netta and Jean Rhys see blithely and busily outdistancing them all but the fastest-moving great lady herself simultaneously managing the feat of looking . . . not like herself at all? Swathed in the self-important furs of her allegiance to what everybody, whether friend or foe, has taken to calling the Posse she's as tall and upright—and as fit—as, say, Ivankanemia or Melanomia or Rebekka Mercier or Marjorie Boebert or Sidonie Powell-Grene. There's a spring, and a touch of spring, in her step. She's waving to Pollyannna and Kellyannna who even with the Pacific as backdrop and a rainbow of stuffed-to-the-gills manila folders cradled defensively in her arms—is still but a painted devil. La Suckabee Glanders stands beside

---

[193] He observes that her lipstick has been smeared on thick—the end result is thick with the act itself: a declaration of despair. This is a moment that befalls (or should befall) every relation—the moment when A catches sight of B undetected—unsuspected— with the nakedness of the relation hanging in the balance. Does A make his (loving) presence known or does he hoard it as a triumph of withdrawal from the target of an ever mounting road rage?

[194] John Milton, *Samson Agonistes*, 1044–1045.

[195] John Webster, *The Duchess of Malfi*, act II, sc. 5.

her—denture of pearls in place. Hard to determine—at least it's hard for *Jean* to determine—if she's a pig pretending to be a cow or vice versa. Jean feels a bit guilty. After all, by thinking these daggers she's a far cry from maintaining Kelly's high standards of reverence toward women—except black women whom he takes the liberty of referring to, unsacredly—righteously—as empty barrels. But Jean's herself a woman so the standards don't apply. They're all waiting for what resembles—as it advances cautiously—methodically (like Mueller's investigation)—across what has suddenly become the night sky—for what more than just resembles an (of all things) aerial tramway. Pre-dusk is a distant memory. No more post-impressionist work to be done and as far as Melanctha is concerned, good riddance, at least for now. *What a stroke of genius, this asteroid, this sceptred seat of Mars, this . . . tramway,* Shearer thinks (her dancer's celerity has propelled her here faster than almost anybody else). Cantor thinks the same thing, almost in unison. For who needs a tramway for such a short distance? But of course it's precisely the shortness of the distance—take-off indistinguishable from arrival—the fact that the tramway's services aren't warranted—that makes its statement such a powerful one. Like that made by Giacometti's *Suspended Ball.* And by *The Four Temperaments,* specifically the extension of the crouched female dancer's pivoted calf within the smallest possible radius in the third pre-Melancholic variation (*supra*)—expansion as contraction, if you will and even if you won't. She, too, spots Margo, who, alas, has never really taken to her. (Pritchard is nowhere in sight. Evidently she's been in no need of his aid. Or maybe he's gone back to the restaurant *to fetch a wrap* [it's getting chilly] which she's too breezily left behind. But whatever he's gone back or not gone back to do, fact is, he's sick to death of her and her offspring—*their* offspring—although the jury is still out on who the lucky co-begetter really is—he's tired of being blamed for everything that's gone wrong—all those right turns that should have been left—all those left turns that should have—would have—could have—ought to have—landed them at the bottom of the Pacific in record time and to ocean-wide standing ovations from vampire squids and goblin sharks galore—tired of being blamed but especially for the things that *didn't* go wrong—things that went wrong only in retrospect—things that have been made to look like they went wrong thanks to a touch-up or two by this, the grandmistress of misgivings—the popess of post-mortems—things that have gone wrong simply because they're past—safely under lock and key—and can't defend themselves against the kind of slander in which the Margos of the world traffic so deftly—in a nutshell, what went wrong was the past's *pastness* or is he simply being led by word- as opposed to worldflow? though it would never have occurred to him to ask such question since he doesn't know either term from Adam.) Doubtless this must be due to what Margo knows about the male members of Moira's profession—knowledge which brings to mind what she's never in any danger of forgetting.[196]

---

[196] She even went so far as to confess to Moira that one member of the Greenwich Ave Irregulars threatened to bring charges against Pritchard for having greeted him—

It's autumn—crisp as a Granny Smith—in the dense foliage behind her. Melanctha *empathizes* with a leaf caught in the trampoline of a spider's web spun atop a hedge of commemorative yew. Moira forgives Margo and goes so far in forgiveness as to listen to her complaints, which seem endless, about the Conspiracy formed to discredit her and her son and Pritchard and Straynge, who never got his due—specifically Who's Behind It. But like clockwork, immediately after disgorging her vomit she makes a point of ignoring Shearer completely. This response is familiar—not *eerily* familiar, just familiar. *De rigueur* in fact among humanoids like Margo whose neediness is always in ultra-direct proportion to their self-unseeing. Clearly, Margo is having a hard time forgiving her for listening so thoughtfully. For too long—starting with her nieces—Shearer has allowed others to make her apparent lack of comprehension the problem—that is, her too nice attentiveness to every nuance of that neediness—an attentiveness so excruciatingly vast and concentrated as to constitute a mirror that, through no fault of its own, could always be depended on to throw back the unwelcome image of a fissured self in incessant flight from itself. It was her refusal to understand how complaint without end could embody—evidence—a perfect self-comprehension—a comprehension beyond comprehension—comprehension as perfect cure— it was her—Moira's—very refusal to understand—it was that very refusal which like clockwork turned out to be the problem—and which became in turn the help-repudiating complainer's problem through no fault of her—the complainer's—own and the true source of all her—the complainer's—difficulties—past, present and to come. The complainer had nothing to complain about—nothing, that is, until Moira, from a toxic need to help—to understand—saw fit to put her bruised foot (a foot, alas, that [like every other ballerina's foot] was notoriously overbruised) in the complainer's mouth. But the complainers simply didn't have the time to help her back. All would be right with the world once Shearer stopped assaulting their perfection with her special brand of home-baked unleavened compassion—always the wrong kind of compassion—the wrong kind of comprehension—compassion so misguided as to constitute a high crime against nature because didn't she understand that by the very fact that they were complaining without surcease proved that the problem was both definitively solved—and definitively insolvable through no fault of their own. Compassion over-solicited by career help-rejectors then trashed as a madwoman's invasion of privacy. But, in all fairness, if she had

---

and it was a *him*—stark-naked one evening not long after he'd been ushered into a new phase of treatment through having confessed to being engaged in a wrestling match (so far "successfully") with the angel of inversion. At which juncture, Pritch had offered Irregular X, out of the kindness of his heterosexual heart (for he was then in full hetero mode), the opportunity to "explore" (a favorite pop-psychism then and now) his drives on the playing field of Pritchard's aging body, which was hairless, ghost-white and cadaver-tough. He resisted. But in fact it was not this solecism but Pritch's penchant for dozing off in the middle of his patient's musings that compelled X to finally quit treatment, no matter what it cost him in terms of advancement.

the misfortune to be any of them, she, too, would be fleeing every mirror in sight every chance she got.

What looks like a middle-management type with a moustache and a corny sense of humor—an ostensibly low-level operative in the great tradition of, say, George Papadopoulucci, a leftover from campaign days—a flunkey but dishonest, to paraphrase Ben Jonson—seems to be hitting on Margo who's stepped away from Moira as if she's been the very first of First Responders to the allure of Ebola and making everybody else pay the price of her infatuation. She wastes no time failing to respond with polite attention to his jokes. But just when Moira would be tempted to contend that it's all a ploy—Margo's just exercising super-caution in the unwelcome context of being watched and presumably counter-loathed by Moira, her cashiered lady-in-waiting—whaddya know, here's *the conspiracist's conspiracist* letting down her guard of dismissive irritation to prove to the world (*Attention, ladies and gentlemen, disregard your programs and please note that in tonight's performance, the role of the World will be played by dancing hopeful cum eternal understudy—Moira Shearer!*)—to prove to the world that her signature contempt is a purely local phenomenon—termite art—something only Moira—that is, the Moiras of the world—could induce—whereas in a context such as this, where she's being respectfully wooed at her true worth by a corny moustache, she can be counted upon to assume the airs of the most gracious little seventy-six-year-old gamine you might ever hope to see.

There's almost—no, nothing less than—a stampede into the tram's interior. But why, there's plenty of room. Never has she seen the Greenwich Avenue irregulars so ferocious.

En route, Cantor sinks, almost willingly once he gets the hang of it, into dogshit. It must be fear of what awaits him at the Cemetery Club. For a moment he pretends the false step is blessed because it's engendered a new self—a better self—a self at home with its mishaps. But immediately he knows that it's impossible to integrate the stain into selfhood.[197] His brand of selfhood—somebody down below is shouting *Our Brand is stronger than ever! the Brand is stronger than ever! we love you Dad! we love you Dad!* (looks like Rump the Junior groveling on all fours)—simply isn't ecumenical enough to accommodate the stain and its sequelae as harbinger of a new robust . . . Rabelaisianism. It's a feeble pretence, it won't play in Peoria, much less in Pyorrhea, nor (most importantly) will they love it in Joe Gillis's Pomona. And he can't help wondering if by getting stained he's forfeited the authenticity of his participation in this, the Final Sequence—the authenticity of his pivotal role therein. Is his participation in the Final Sequence still valid—is it ongoing (assuming the Sequence has already begun)—or is it foreclosed to him—foreclosed against him—now that his mind is directed only toward eradicating said stain? Or is the Sequence—his stake in the Sequence—even more valid—more valid than ever since, after all, he's one of Its standard-bearers—indeed,

---

[197] Cf. this (bizarrely translated) invocation from Rimbaud: *O seasons! o terrain!/What soul surmounts a stain!*

in his own small way, a fulcrum—a pivot—an armature—of the Sequence and so what's good for him is good for It? I.e., he's got to start thinking of his mishaps less as demolition gangs and more as a blessed enrichment of what's to come. And so his stake in the Sequence is even more valid owing to the fact that he'll be obliged to perceive Its beauties (since even the most foul-smelling Sequence has Its beauties inasmuch as It's final—a last farewell—as farewellian as a *letzte Lebewohl* straight out of *The Magic Flute*) through a screen of distractions and to master those beauties while (of all things) removing the stain (and, as everybody knows, perception and mastery—and beauty—are enhanced by obstacles—are in truth simply one long obstacle course—just as any destination is enhanced by an army of checkpoints, most significantly the physiological kind—like the obligatory prophylactic piss before participation in, say, the shredding of a cloud canvas by a chain gang of starlings). In a word, does the dogshit incident make the trek real as it would never have been without it?

CHAPTER SIXTY-FOUR

The pilgrims do what pilgrims do best, which is approach with caution and, to oblige their pains, the site of the rally comes into better and better focus as an amphitheater on the order of the Colosseum. Eden—if he could think his own thoughts through to the bitter end without ending up in Balboa Park—would say, *It's anything you want it to be, within reason of course.* But his prize possession has been taken away before he could even begin to use it: elegance of acuity (one of the fringe benefits or devastating side effects of Invidicum)—insight able to make its way right up the ass and into the throat of pretense, hoarse from self-delusional lambasting of enemies everywhere you look. On one side we have the start-ups and the other members and sub-members of the The Rump Team, although the two cohorts are not aligned quite that strictly—there's plenty of interpenetration to go around. Which ongoing amphimixis of erotisms[198] by virtue of its very randomness directs any number of novice flunkeys, among whom in all fairness we must include Mike the Last Man Standing in Pompeii and Mic the Scourge of the Mulvanees and last and forever least sneaky-tendentious facial tic-haunted Robber Baronet Steve(n!) the Mnunchkin (who has the voice and look of a schoolmarm), to where they must position themselves geographically if they want to be *superstar* flunkeys. And why shouldn't there be amphimixis?—each side feeds off the other—enriches itself at the expense of the other. One big happy family. The usual trafficking in apps seems—all too familiar yet this time it's different. There is warmhearted *collusion*—that meaningless term whose existence is dismantled only to be resurrected—all in an instant—by the lovable *punditi* on late-night cable TV. Off to one side—huddled in the buggy pre-twilight—are the members of the so-called alt-left, preparing to do battle with the tiki thugs (whose fangs are hidden by the hedge that separates the cemetery from the ocean). Yes, *thugs*—no room for nuance in such a climate and even less for witty rejoinders that only degrade those rejoinders instead of allowing wit to do the work of destroying its target, in this case the thugs.

Melanctha catches sight of star phonies Sandberger, Zuckerberger, Dorsey, Brinn and Cook waiting for the real mating of disparate species to begin. Through the grapevine, the other Cook has heard that one or more of them may one day *run for office.* Sheryl for one is very interested in running. But being first and foremost a Samaritan though not a Good one, she's even more interested in aiding the accursed (in this case undervalued start-uppers) get their foot in the door and has dropped a deft hint or two about knowing somebody who may know somebody else up at the Kennedy

---

[198] Don't blame the Master: after all, it's Sandor Ferenczi's phrase and a mighty good one, if you ask me, whether it applies or not—but what *doesn't* apply when it's a question of a unicorn king on the order of a Zuckerberger mating with a *Yuri Milner on the order of . . . a Yuri Milner?*

School of Government who could turn out to be a grade A conduit though given the tenuity of their track records it behooves her to warn them (*start-uppers, listen up!*) to say, if interviewed, as little about themselves as possible. Indeed, for Samaritans of her stripe, the warning's pretty much the best part of the do-gooding, in other words, where Sheryl hails from, a good deed is only as good as the probability of its bearing no fruit and leaving the beneficiary feeling even more wretched than he did before befriendment reared its swelled head, which *in turn* or *on the other hand* or *adding insult to injury* or *come hell or high water* (you pick the filler: they all taste the same in the dark) is just a cheerier way of saying that getting somebody's hopes up is only as gratifying as the even more gratifying certainty that those hopes will be dashed allows it to be. But surely it's not Sheryl's fault alone if other people's failures constitute her comfort food and if a fortiori those failures cleverly engineered by her Big Tech Samaritanism are comfort food to the *third power*. He—the other Cook—tells Melanctha as much. Does he recognize her or did he, after giving the matter serious thought, choose not to? No matter—what's important is that the phrase (which phrase? *which* phrase?! why, *run for office*, of course!) has gone a long way—and in record time—toward naturalizing—normalizing—them—the phonies—better yet, their trajectory. Within the context of what the phrase evokes, their tactical evasiveness before Congress—the PR snow job regarding the "whole Russia business"— the doubletalk over the billions stashed away in the Bailiwick of Guernsey and Maldives—make perfect sense as dress-rehearsal byplay. Without that phrase to guide her, Melanctha would be adrift. Even with the option still open to drop anchor in the sunny-cesspool-of-monster-mediocrity-that-is-El-Spicer-Der-Gorkka-and-Ze-Mooche (*Der Gorkka and Ze Mooche*: great title for a buddy-buddy movie, where the buddies end up as far far more, at least in the unexpurgated version or, to use a more expensive—more solemn—term, the *Director's Cut*), which mediocrities are at present busy jabber-dancing with the stars. Having done their time—paid their dues— burnished their credentials by getting fired by the Adults in the Room, why *shouldn't* they at the very least try to turn stalwart incompetence and gilt by association into commodities?

Scott the PUitte's securely soundproof Sensitive Compartmented Information Facility (SCIF)—a glorified phone booth—is of course all the rage— it's surely going to be named the delegate to this convention (the rally's been renamed by popular demand) most likely to succeed. In fact, he's insulated therein as we speak. Gabbing with the CEOs of Chemours, Dow Agrosciences and Shell Oil (Ethan knows how to lip-read), all seated, from what the wary eavesdropping lips-reader can further divine, at the coveted Captain's Table at BLT Prime deep in (where else?) the fetid bowels of DC's Rump International. His slumped-over look means, *Too bad, boys, I can't be at this "informational meeting" in person. But in any case, it's the way of the future, this booth is* ("and the future is a pandemic," somebody somewhere suggests frivolously)—*based on an algorithm that isn't just any old algorithm but an algorithm that teaches other algorithms to think—and think big. But don't sell him short: his slumped-over look also means (though he'll never know it), *Down with the Anthropo-*

cene and its working groups! Up with the . . . Algorithmocene! And its holy grail of a "golden spike," by the way (in case you were wondering), isn't Beppu Reef or Flinders Bay or Gotland Cave or Ernesto Basin or even Otto Preminger's River of No Return—it's our own rampagingly deviant collective brain. Kellyannae Kockenlocker (Preston Sturges's greatest creation after big sis Trudy), who's just swept in on a cloud of haglike imperturbability (her reptilian dentation could use some heavy piecework), asks where she can get one just like it since people are always listening in on *her* calls, especially the ones dealing with How to Hatchet the Hatch Act. Judge Gary Roy Cohn, Falstaffian as ever but without the Falstaffian ten-ton pathos, looks at her (before she starts rubbing his back conspiratorially), as if to say, How important can your phone calls be to require soundproofing? He's been telling fake-avuncular Jeff Schesshions (everybody's favorite elf, who needs no such telling) how good his tax "reform" is for the poor slobs who will now have the option to feed their children. "Hope those tykes don't live in sanctuary cities," Jeff replies, not too darkly. "For if they do, then they're out of luck." Tzara Fuckabee Glanders (Ze Mooche's pal for about two seconds way back when), piously fingering her pearls, makes a mental note to ask, at the next Cabinet grovel-fest, how The Kockenlocker manages to keep so boa constrictor-svelte. Can't be a question of diet since Glanders has seen her at many a shindig packing away heaps of taxpayer-subsidized chow. Moira in fact remembers, or will remember, indelibilizing—iconizing—epochalizing—F and (Instantaneously Emeritus White House Communications Director) M's televised press conference "hug" but if it was so hard to stomach how does this hug-that-wasn't manage to evoke of all things the two fleeting, passionlessly poignant embraces toward the end of the second movement of *Symphony in C?* Answer me that, you gutless highbrows!

In fact, no less than the CEO of a unicorn—better yet a chimaera[199]—a centaur—run by a wunderkind cousin of doyenne of wrestlers Lindita McMahoney—marvels at the booth's efficacy but if he may say, there's always room for improvement—and the phrase is not meant to be offensive. It's just that to his practiced, practical eye, there seem to be a few leaks here and there which should be plugged up ASAP—especially with . . . with . . . just around the bend. He was about to say, with climate changers just around the bend but ever the strategist, shuts up in the nick of time. And it just so happens that his team has created the appropriate Immobile App—the first of its kind— since a start-up without an app—especially an Immobile App—is like a tumor without the gumption to metastasize. He doesn't elaborate. Just as well, since Cantor and Melanctha need to digest the revelation. Not the revelation of the existence of this app-of-a-different-color which is about to be unleashed on the market—this Thing, i.e., this holy grail, this Thing-in-Itself two centuries too late—not the revelation of the Thing but the Name of the thing—or rather the fact that the object in question is way way behind that name, encoiled in its fetal envy of what has already been born and to whose high standards—

---

[199]Still to be defined.

standards set by the name simply by virtue of its *being* a name—standards based on what the name qua name confers—the object must ultimately conform. But Melanctha for one doesn't need the object. Objects are for suckers, to quote Cicero in one of his lighter moments. For it's only through names that she knows things—or rather, is spared having to know them—since the name—or rather the anastomosis of the name with other names to yield the Name—is more than enough for any scribbler bound for tabloid glory. More than enough. After one brazen Uber-style swipe, the cheapest sealant—according to the aforementioned chimaera—shows up at your doorstep (chock full of SchPruitt-endorsed 1,4-dioxane, of course, and the insidious-onset liver damage be damned). And with another swipe, what shows up on that same doorstep (like a stork without the obligatory fairy tale fetus) is a handy device—chock full of anodynized (pronounced an-O-dyn-ized) N-methylpyrrolidone, and fetuses be damned—designed for duty-free transport of the now leak-proof booth from place to place when SchPruitt sees fit to engage in taxpayer-dollars-subsidized travel. Travel with family members, legitimate and il-, to a variety of rallies (in the Holy See, for example, and Marrakesh)—especially rallies that include *fine dining* (yet another debasing cliché [like *lavish lifestyle*]—another euphemism [like *closure*]—another placeholder [like *Our Better Angels*]—another time-killer [like *that's not who we are*]—and each and every a kingdom without a horse—no, worse, much much worse: an epithet without a referent out in the real world)—rallies whose purpose is not to celebrate the rebirth of coal-burning power plants but rather to pave the way toward his election as governor of Oklahoma—and after that, who dares to know? and let's not forget that the same stork is designed to transport the booths of his Republication Guard as well—though of course they're not of the same hunker-down bunkerly—bunkerish—quality. Since a devout climate change-denier without a cohort of bald heads aswim in aviator glasses and sun-damaged brains is like—is like—a stool specimen without—without—well, without a grade-A dipstick. But Skotty P's careful not to commit himself just yet to what sounds (to the eagle eye of a career anti-Semite such as he) like a Rube Goldberg special (maybe this centaur has been overvalued). His almost-fabled paranoia—almost as "iconic" as the booth itself (covered dutifully in the biweekly fake news supplement to the *NY Times*)—here serves him in good conservative stead.

But Melanctha for one is not dazzled by all this derring-do since she has more on her mind than anybody else even if that *more than anybody else* won't make the front page of the *Santa Barbara Songbird*. Namely, the Master, who is never far from her thoughts. Can He handle The Rump aka The Rump—His creature, too, in a way (and at the same time, not)? Can he arrange things so that The Rump will end up being no match for His creatures? But first he must cure them of their addiction to His thought packets (*Again, with the thought packets!* soul-sighs a disgruntled Jewish widow from Forest Hills). They keep coming, especially here. And if they keep packeting—keep packetteering— they'll never be able to handle this Rump, this poorest excuse for a master.

Still, SPruitt is interested. Thing is, he's got to see somebody from the Alkylphenols and Ethoxylates Research Council and then somebody from the

Halogenated Solvents Industry Alliance and if he doesn't wrap it all up before the Triumphal March (obviously more Wagner than Verdi) of the Tiki Torch-bearers (what everybody's witnessed so far is what Cantor's algebra teacher called—referring to the exercises she always had ready for them on the black-board as they marched into Room 7-108—a [mere] *warm-up*)—if he doesn't wrap everything up and upload the appropriate selfies, well, then, his Okie buddies will never forgive him.

As for Ethan Narr (should he change his surname to *Brand* or might it be way too late for cosmetics?), he's concerned—alarmed, really—about his future—how is he going to pay the bills now that he's been officially branded as a loser and no longer has a no-good woman at his side to cheer him on through the puffery of denigration? Will the CIA—the NSA—the Defense Intelligence Agency—rehire him? though it's still unclear whether he's been canned. Whatever else he is, he's at that stage in despair when at every minute his gut—for Ethan, the site of internal difference, where the meanings are—tells a whole different life story—predicts a whole different denouement. For the first time he's charging Jean with being the source of all his ills. Does this mean he's growing up at last or is he simply infantilizing himself beyond repair? He looks hard at the sunset—so hard it hurts. For Melanctha is not the only visitant non-immune to its charms. For the moment he's solvent but will this very basking in the sunset's reflected glory effect his discharge from the ranks of the solvent in some way hard to define? Watching the sunset makes him think about being robbed of the sunset—robbed of being able to contem-plate it without monetary worries. Basking in that *feathered glory* (blame it on the pinkish cloud spray) makes insolvency more real—more inevitable—the more intently he feels the chilly rays exploring his skin, the more real does insolvency become—or the more conceivable—or the more concrete—given all it will force him to lose. Most of all, the lucidity of his newborn aesthetic appreciation. The more lucid his appreciation—which should be a pharma-kon against insolvency—the more he's targeted—or rather targetable. Or maybe the sunset—like all Quislingish embodiments of beauty—is not so secretly working on behalf of the forces of spoliation—to catch him off guard. So *pace* PV—who, like the Master, also had a soft spot for cemeteries by the sea only they had to have dovecotes, if, that is, he was to give them the time of day and a resurrectional poem thrown in as a bonus—beauty doesn't make us despair—it catches us off guard for which we pay a price all through life and beyond—it makes us *lose*, on all fronts. And *despair* is just too feathery a word for despair. He wants to speak to somebody about his longing for death— about how he dreads living to age seventy—about how he hates vacations. But there's no point. It's no longer theatrical, i.e., precocious—worse, apotropaic. Time has caught up with what is no longer whimsy. *Oh, why am I, of all peo-ple, having these thoughts (especially the bit about precocity running out of steam)?* he's compelled to ask, *since somebody else—a much better man than I—has already had them.* He can feel it in his bones. (Which only proves, counter-thinks Melanctha, that the Master is [He doth repeat himself too much, methinks] in rare amnesiac form this evening [*which amnesia about who thought what and when cuts both ways: it plunges Him into unawareness of the richness of His hack work and exalts Him into unawareness of its indigest-ibility*]. For she knows immediately what Ethan is going through and Who's putting him through its ringer—or rather, Melanctha has a hunch about what Ethan—whom she has never taken to—is going through, once she translates what she thinks it is, into her own slang—transports it into her own context. Is it the proximity—the imminence—of The Rump brigade that's emboldened him to ask the right question for once in his life even if he's asking it—counterintuitively—of the Master? But she's too sharp not to notice that with all the destitution he now previews, he's in no condition to bear her empathy [that word again!], however sincere.) It's hard to understand the connection between the beauty of sunset and the certainty—some might say the ceremony—of impoverishment. But that doesn't make the sunset any less menacing. In fact, he almost yearns for a reprise of the tiki torchers' antics (even if the parent event hasn't yet occurred)—as a distraction against the ineffable. Better to turn away but in turning away what does he turn toward but Rhys's ever-faithful moue of contempt. He has a yen to say *F—k that moue*, but, as Voltaire has already said it, Ethan doesn't want to add plagiarism to his list of crimes against nature. Death suddenly becomes more livable—he is no longer terrorized by the idea of losing consciousness forever—and worse, of being watched—of having no control over his obituary—even if there were one, it would have to have been self-financed and who would pay for such a thing? The filthy rich are currently rubbing elbows with (like The Mnunchkin over there with his trophy-wife-and-child-bride all wrapped up in one big bleached blonde bundle of conspicuously consumed brand names) the just plain filthy. And yet, *il faut tenter de vivre*—poor jilted slob that he is, Ethan Brand's still got to try to live. And there must be a meta-emotion buried somewhere in this mix to save him from the repercussions of the real thing (but why is it he who's having *this* thought as well? hasn't he paid his dues with the last one? why should he of all people be made to chase the rainbow of a meta-emotion—he! the last person in the world to espouse the notion that *meta is necessarily beta?*). (Melanctha takes Ethan's Job-lical vexation in stride. Since It's the Master's predictable reactive explosion that steals the show. His explosion of outrage at yet another rendition of these freeloaders' favorite $64,000—no, make that their favorite *Sixty-Four-Thousand-Dollar*—Eternal Question, to wit, *Why* me *of all people?* His explosion of shock at yet another gang member's display of resistance to bodying forth a packet that doesn't quite fit—a packet that, while it may not be ideally suited to the resistor's particular brand of hallucinated acuity—while it may indeed be the *wrongest* fit by every standard of artistic opportunism—constitutes *for that very reason* a ticket to transformation, of self and story. His explosion of (unmanly) shock at Narr's refusal to see that His repudiation of story stricture and story structure, all in the name of plastering—visiting—a so-called least likely packet on yet another stooge, has triggered said stooge's casebook evolution—the very sober evolution that's supposed to be incompatible with thought packet pranksterism—a creative evolution from pre-packet blissful idiot to whatever contorting his essence to rebuff the needs of said packet has turned him into—an evolution right up there with Pip's and Wilhelm Meister's and even Tyrone Power/Stan Carlisle's (by the way, the Master's never pretended to be an ideal parent [er . . . Master] but *He's done the best he could* and if that sounds lame it's meant to since the lameness can always be counted on to bring him to the exculpatory verge of tears). Signs of His shock are everywhere for Melanctha to decipher. For one thing, there's that cloud right above the tramway station which isn't a cloud at all but a battering ram albeit one compacted of cotton candy. For another, the star phonies are currently congregating *awesomed* around [of all things! or rather *what else but?*] the R. Mutt Sensitive Compartmented Information Facility and as if the phonies weren't already overprivileged enough it's they who've just been singled out for glamorous impalement on a mega-ray of sunlight. And adding insult to injury there's a gander defecating on as many gravestones as he can manage to straddle without losing his balance—flapping his wings in what looks to Melanctha like the equivalent of a celebratory stab at post-coital chest pounding while his hapless consort [who's made him the Alpha Male He is Today], knowing better than to even *think* about not doing so, slips discreetly away unsung. In itself, each sign is nothing, as well it should be, but taken all together. . . . At the same time it seems the Master can't help exulting over [read his lips!] what He clearly takes to be the sinewy gumption driving Ethan's Jobismus, which leads Melanctha to suspect it's with her that He has—or thinks He should have—a bone to pick. After all, as Executive Programming Officer in this resolutely unexotic outpost of the Pharmic Civil Service [no prahus! no parangs! or any other such Maughamesque bric-a-brac], isn't it her function to ensure that all packets, however unwieldy, breeze through customs and get assigned pronto to the *right* [not the *wrongest*] bureaucrat in the right *bungalow* for the right kind of processing and ultimate dissemination among the huddled masses—huddled masses, that is, of dinner theater habitués yearning to breathe free. In which case the wily old fraud is belching bromides through both sides of his unmasterly mouth—mooning her not with his ass but with his cigar-clenching jaws. Should she try to extract an apology? Useless—not in his playbook. And asking for one is not in hers since what she deems an Apology is pretty much impossible to come by, yoked as it must be to the perpetrator's principled dismemberment of his rank betrayal—yoked, that is, to a ball-bustingly bottomless self-analysis mixing words and blood in the best suicidal style of Piero delle Vigne (just make a left, buddy, when you get to the gibbet in the thirteenth canto of Dante's Hell [Seventh Circle, second round]) and under no circumstances to be crammed into some pro forma civil service trinket (an appendix, say, or a corrigendum or a note verbale). Nor is she willing at her age to have a go at that old standby Anybody But the Culprit and shift the blame for his malfeasance to some laser-zapped junior member of the Margo Taylor Greene tragicomedy club. Instead, taking her cue from the gander (still cock of the walk and who, now that you mention it, bears more than a passing resemblance to Hitchcock's Dutch Uncle Charlie), Melanctha decides to let bygones be bygones. Inwardly—radiantly—she crows, "Today's the thing—that's my philosophy.") Not only does Ethan fear being insolvent—living on the street—but he looks at himself as his colleagues—schoolmates—all nuclear physicists with (hedging their bets) a PhD degree in business—must look at him, haggling for pennies while they sit pretty. That's what comes of consecrating oneself to the ineffable. Though the practice of en- and decryption doesn't quite constitute consecration to the ineffable. In any case, he—he—who's sacrificed his life for the Agency—Agencies in all shapes and sizes—is but a footstep—and a timorous one at that—away from skid row. Thing is, can the skills learned be translated into cold cash in some other entity—the ASPCA, say, or the Authors Guild? Time will tell. Or, Time is full of *tells* (to use a term that's all the journalistic rage). He's tempted to approach somebody in unicorn-land, swallow his pride and a mess of saliva, and wonder if they may know somebody who's interested in having on their staff somebody who . . . But isn't this what life—work—is all about: mésalliances, forging a partnership with one's worst enemies or most virulent rivals and living to tell the tale? Dare to convince me different.

If only Melanctha could "reach out" to him—*literally!* (not euphemistically) *reach out*—and explain that he's having these thoughts only because it's his turn to have them—or because he's, sadly, the only one available for sentry duty on this particular bank and shoal of time (it's Saturday night after all when even the most improbable of ventriloquist's dummies heads for the waterfront bars)—and not just because he's their least likely exponent. And it's never too late for the members of the Invidicrowd to learn they must play the packet that Fate has dealt them.

Envy is dead, Ethan thinks. Because this is the Final Sequence—a phrase (on the order of Constitutional Crisis)—that's been floating around for the last several hours. Ever since—ever since— He's sorry to see it go. But then he realizes it hasn't gone. It's just that in his case, the Envy has been alloyed—or, as David Hume would have put it, *allayed*—with panic. He's sacrificed his life for Agencies and here he is wondering whether he'll have even a pension. Not to mention all he's done for Jean who would never have gotten into the trial if it hadn't been for him. Though maybe she harbors a not-so-secret animus against him for this very reason—since thanks to his efforts she's become a *genuine* Envier with all the trimmings—having come by contamination honestly. And as sweet as being the member of a tribe might be, it must have its low points. Look at the Rumpniks and on the other side of the finish line, the start-up gang. Wallowing in dough yet all—or most—of them done in by an embarrassment of riches—self-righteousness and self-contempt in compounded dosages too exotically varied to tabulate. While he—he— Yet it would be almost sad to give up the plagueyness of his untreated disease. For what would take its place? Acquisition of vast wealth, which has its own drawbacks? But whether or not Envy has come and gone—whether or not the fifteen minutes of infamy are over—Ethan is still learning to be grateful for small favors—in this case, the name of the drug of choice—Invidicum to you, sir— Even if he's too old to start the program, still he exercises a certain proprietorship over the drug—or rather its name—inasmuch as he shares Melanctha's reverence for names especially following her mindfucking intercession a while back (oh, so she thinks he didn't notice) when he was bawling about precocity gone bad. And the name, now that it's come to names, is to be commended insofar as, but not solely because, *Invidicum* doesn't sound like it's the name of the name of the adamantly lame hero of some Akkadian creation myth—doesn't sound like *natalizumab* or, even better, *adalimumab*.

The chanting has now risen well above a murmur. The tiki monsters (none of whom by the way is worthy of being compared to anything as exalted as the Tully Monster but, even so, how can one not sympathize if not with them than with their desire to prove themselves as efficient in some sphere as, say, Vichy's SNCF in theirs?) have jumped from the letter *J* (*the Jews will not replace us!*) to *T* (*the Tlingit will not replace us! the Tlingit will not replace us!* and on to *the Tuscans will not replace us! the Tuscans will not replace us!* and thence to, as is only fair, *The Tweets will not replace us! The Tweets will not replace us!*). *Something's wrong*, thinks Melanctha. Though it has nothing to do with mésalliances: she, like Cantor, is observing the Mnutchkimubab and his aforementioned brand-crazed trophy wife (and no two nobodies on the face of the earth deserve each other more). Then (let's backtrack a bit) it comes to her, though not quite in a flash, that these carnivorous two—like all their cognates—should be known not as the *filthy* but as the *cautiously boring* rich since their kind never tire—when cornered—of confabulating about their non-existent salad days—when they didn't have enough to eat, and about how much they had to scrimp and save to buy their first Jaguar parked over there on the tarmac.

Fresh from having been anointed by the Saudis (and having returned the favor by disanointing the Qataris—and the 11,000 US forces be damned), The Rump (aka spin doctor Roger Stone's mare forever in full rut) mounts one of several wobbly podiums and says something not quite audible (lifting his bottle of Perrier in oblique counter-homage to Little Marco) but whatever he's said it's the emphasis that counts and that emphasis is conveyable only compliments of the signature circle made with tiny pudgy thumb and fore-finger, of whose *contourtion* the Base never seem to tire. As Hillary conceded, *You can't take your eyes off this creepy thug.* Star quality, for better or worse. He strikes a saved-for-emergencies sulky Mount Rushmore pose, sure as he is that the fans—the slaves—are dumb enough to take his fishy flab for Black Hills mica schist and granite. Though without knowing it The Rump realizes that *to perceive them as dumb—deluded—is to not play by the rules of the game. I've risked my life, coward as I am, for prestige—for recognition of my absolute superiority. So I need to believe in their smartness for what's the point of having your smartness recognized by a slave who's in his very essence unsmart? On second thought, to hell with all this unsmart smartness. What I really need is to be recognized as the master I've become—the master with the biggest dick and the biggest inauguration-day turnout—but only by another master. If I'm to be recognized as the master of masters it's got to be by another master, not some peasant slave out in the bleachers (for every cemetery has one). But . . . what self-respecting master—take Putin, as the best example—will recognize another master's superiority? In short, I don't want to end up like psychoanalysis-termi-nable-or-interminable as depicted by Freud: in danger of failing as a result of my still only partial success.* It's clear to Melanctha (by the way, of *course* she knows that The Rump isn't *really* thinking about ending up like analysis terminable or in- [what do you take her for?]), to whom everything is becoming clearer and clearer (willy-nilly she's on Don's wavelength)—with a clarity that can't be bought in a creative writing seminar, even one paid for in full by the GI Bill—clearer and clearer that The Rump Master needs a master who can be convinced—compelled to recognize—that assuming a passive attitude toward another master—a better master—i.e., The Rump—does not signify castration or sodomization—in fact, it's necessary in many relations. A passive attitude is in fact a form of recovery from the delusion that there is no better master than oneself—and for which revivifying plunge into passivity (aka a little life rounded with a sleep) the nth-rate master should end up, if he knows what's good for him, thanking The Rump profusely. Thing is, the last thing a master knows is what's good for her—that's what makes him a master.

So unable to stand the soul-searching a minute longer—since this kind of soul-searching is indistinguishable from its direst implications—The Rump steps down (though nobody much notices since the food, as illuminated *Gourmet Magazine* style by the torches, has turned out to merit surrender to temptation many times over)—our master in a vain search for masterliness steps down and takes his concerns *over there*—to a gaggle of handpicked experts, the limits of whose purviews, he assumes, could easily be tweaked to include the resolution of such an impasse. I'm talking about luminaries on the order of Rick Perri, our oldish friend only-adult-in-the-room John Q. O'Kelly, fake nebbish Wilber Rosse (motto: Have Sword, Will Dance), E. Laine Chaow and Ben Karson, all on their best prostate-licking behavior (*Again with the prostate!* sighs that irrepressible dame from forestless, hill-less Forest Hills). But putting their pinheads together, the best response they can come up with is that the only master who might be made to fit the bill would be at best a ductile amalgam of master and slave—the tincture of that very slavishness would enable such a master to bend to another master's superiority instead of, at such a juncture, choosing death as the only way out. But there has to be a means of transforming him into such an amalgam. What about transformation through the sheer firepower of The Rump's speech and gestures (like the signature circle-making)? suggests Chaow who has no compunction about supporting the arch-enemy of hubby Mitch because she quote *stands by her men, both of them* unquote. (Speaking of Mitch, Moira recognizes him by his signature Beau Brummell contrast shirt [Paging the lady from Forest Hills: *Again with the contrast shirt!*]. [The craze has caught on among the other members of the wobbly-jowled geezer crowd as attested by the poses struck by Grassley, Gastley and O'Hatch.] She remains a bit in awe of this quintessential old fart who's not afraid of making like a dandy [he might even make a delightful Drosselmeyer]—not even with so wizened a mouth—so wizened as to be almost prissily lipless, through which orifice, on rare occasions, Delphic pronouncements are expelled with a fartlike imperturbability that only a measured Southern accent can confer. Shabbier colleagues should follow his lead if for no other reason than to warm the cockles of their respective heartlands. [Yet, unlike Chaow, Moira is capable of compunction. *Is my somewhat self-congratulatory outrage at the primly rampageous doings of these toads reducible to giggly gratitude for their pretensions or is it automatically invested with a moral armature whether I want it to be or not? i.e., is all the giggliness simply the fast-*

est route to the armature—an armature no amount of giggliness can dismantle?
Yet, akin to Ethan, Moira wonders why she's having *this* thought, which easily
segues into the wonder's obverse, i.e., why it's *she* who's having it—and after
it's been delivered up to her on a silver platter *no less* or *as it were*—or *so
to speak.*]) But as a careerist germophobe The Rump hates amalgams of any
kind: they smell of rotting kelp. Tom the Price's successor, Alecx M. ACzar
II, is sorry to have to break it to the Commander in Chief (and so early on in
his tenure) but he may have to wait decades until chimaerism research has
gotten so advanced as to permit the mixing of the cells from some worthy
master with those from some even worthier slave—the injection of a master's
embryonic stem cells into the blastocytes of a slave—so as to enable, through
such a mixing, the generation of what down at City Hall they've come to refer
to as an *interspecies* chimaera—yes, interspecies, inasmuch as masters and
slaves are trillions of evolutionary leagues apart—further apart than mammoth from mouse—than firmament from fin. Although there's no guarantee
of course that a master-slave chimaera can be compelled to retain the relevant
traits of the donor. Of course it must be expected that so inchoate a procedure
(notwithstanding all the tampering, however expert)—for ACzar, can already
read The Rump's thoughts—thoughts of whose profundity he doesn't have an
inkling—it must be expected that so inchoate a procedure will play fast and
loose with the very concept of master—of matter, even. "Sorry they couldn't
be of more help," Hope the Hick sniffles at her Audience of One, giving whatever pittance might be left of the self-respect of the persons referred to as
"they" *a run for its money* (is this the right expression? thing is, it *sounds* like
it . . . *could* be), and with the help of little more than a slow shriveling pan
(she majored, after all, in Camera-Eye Theatrics, whatever that is, at Rump-
Phoenix U) across the fresco of their collective abasement. Later, when all this
has blown over and subterfuge is done, sources speaking on condition of anonymity so as to avoid jeopardizing the thrust and scope of the Russia investigation will report that Hope looked a bit woozy as she sniffled, doubtless as
a result of her recent interview with Bob Mueller. By the way, rumor has it
that efforts to fire him are heating up and Foxy Fox's Pirrho the Foxy Pitbull
is leading the charge. To which his staunchest supporters reply, Don't worry—
rejoice, in fact—since this is all reminiscent of, i.e., identical to, Watergate.
Which soothes them and most of their listeners. But not Melanctha, who
knows that once any crisis begins to resemble its most plausible—it's most
desirable—predecessor, you can be sure doom's waiting in the wings to gum
up the works. The closer that crisis seems to get to repeating—piggybacking
on—its predecessor's happy ending, the further it digresses from the mean-
ingfulness of a one-of-a-kind fusion with itself. The closer a crisis gets to exact
repetition of a predecessor's happy ending—the predecessor it deems to be its
double—the more meaningless—impoverished—farcical—life becomes.

She clearly wanted to add (according to those same sources) that The
Rump[200] was, as usual, demanding too much of circumstance, in this case

---

[200]The same Rumpty-Dumpty who sat on a Wall and had a Great Fall and all of whose

cutting-edge science, but understood in the nick of time that nothing perceivable as nastiness must be injected into the mentor-mentee stew. The Rump's profile gives itself another dose of Mount Rushmore. Melanctha could say that his very ineptitude—his refusal to be adept—to learn—to do his homework—to go over his *documents*—to take an obscene delight in doing his homework—is the purest form of authorship—authoritarianism. But to lapse into thought packeteering is (under the terms of PICO: the Packeteer Influenced and Corrupt Organizations Act) to do nothing less than desecrate the hoary horror of the moment.

He's back—at his Rumpelstiltskin best—and the audience is clearly champing at its bit—waiting for him to assert another unspeakable—the ostensible unspeakable—because in so doing he compels them to feel it's their own unavowable selves that have gotten elected—that The Rump, horse doctor extraordinaire and merely through exercising his right to minimal intervention by standing soberly on the sidelines, managed to get them packed into the WH en masse—and is once again going far out of his way—stepping aside and letting them talk a blue—a red—streak—through him—*as* him. He's in fact their dummy—and, as his ventriloquist, how distinguished—and indistinguishable—they suddenly look. Reminding her of the situation adumbrated in that story she was required to read in Alfred Hitchcock 101 entitled "The Glass Eye." They're waiting for him to blow something fruity out of his cetacean trap—it doesn't have to be fancy—something to the effect, say, that there are good folks on both sides of his hippopotamic ass or that no prisoner of war, living or dead, rates a hero's welcome[201] or that Sheriff Roy and Judge Joe are not just Siamese tumors but the truest patriots *This Great Nation* has ever known (*TGN*: potbellied Republicans' epithet of choice when, with the usual immovable smirk of uneven shark's teeth, they're trying to sell the extinct middle class on their latest back stab at dismantling the infrastructure of ever more imbecile hope). They want him to perform—out of respect for the occasion—some of his greatest hit jobs. Perverse Cantor is tickled pink by the first choice (which immediately becomes Cantor's first choice)—so perversely pink that his heart is already missing a beat or two in trying to outpace its own dread. Cantor can't believe he's—The Rump's—actually bellowing, "Wouldn't you all like to say, *Get that sonofabitch off the field.* You're fired!?" Pointing his finger with playful menace at the audience—the finger reminding them—as if they need reminding—that in this instance "You're fired" is a direct quotation from the dog-eared hornbook of the Frog King of Reality TV Apprentices. But isn't he also warning that it's they them-

---

Flunkeys and Farty Yes-Men couldn't put him back together again. Yet whoever's dreamed up this little ditty feels soiled by the would-be cleverness—it's a form of unpardonable disarmament in the face of Rumpty's aggression.

[201] They've singlehandedly elected a true hero—one who never got captured because he never got drafted; and to manage against all odds to never get drafted, especially when obliged to subpoena for that purpose a bone spur or two, is surely the most heroic act of all.

selves who'll be summarily fired if they don't behave in accordance with the terms of their compact, i.e., if they don't pretend—at least until chimaerism at last carries the day—to be masters even if they're slaves? He scowls then turns his back on them since, as a seasoned ham, he knows this to be the very best way of aggrandizing the scowl, only to re-pivot immediately and repeat, "You're fired!," though it's not strictly speaking a repetition since the phrase, as now uttered, is clearly too dark to be constrained—and muted—by some hokey prime time context. This "You're fired" (iteration 1) is *You're fired* in its nudity—the predatory nudity of a ED-afflicted masturbator who can't stop from spilling the seed of his loathing (calling it *self*-loathing is an affliction of amateurs—like "the artistic temperament" according to Chesterton—in this case, amateur *shrinks* who don't want to know how the world *really* works— i.e., that [like the idle rich] it doesn't work at all) over an entire stadium of stooges (just as he can't stop the Base's resident scholars, not to mention the horde of MSNBC contrarians, from parsing that seed ad nauseam)—What we'll call You're Fired 2.0 is the annihilation of a target celebrated for residing far beyond the point of even minimal discernibility to its stalker—a target that is The Rump himself (forever playing possum, Russian roulette style) and whom he loathes even more than he loathes Hillary and Barack (oops! so Chesterton & Co. was wrong, after all) though in fact he doesn't loathe those two in the least—in fact he envies them to the point of reverence which is saying a lot since reverence doesn't come easy, unless, that is, you're Putin or Duterte or the syphilitic grand-nephew of Attila the Hun. (*So that's why we've been invited in*, thinks Borkman, *to demonstrate if not to the Emperor then to the Emperor's New Clothes how to lick Envy once and for all*. With camouflage provided by the trade show atmosphere—by The Kushh and his crowd as they go about their muddy business of contracting Saudi and Silicone royalty to hack the databases of The Rump's mortal enemy—the FBI.) And in any case, the kind of wet-dream reverence he lavishes on those three goons doesn't count—it's the most uninteresting subspecies of reverence you can ever imagine because it's cowed reverence. The cumbagged—the carpetbagged—reverence, if you will (and even if you won't), of a sheep in wolf's clothing. To sum up: Iteration 1 of "You're fired" constitutes streetcorner transubstantiation—The Rump's saggy sodden Flesh made Word. You're Fired 2.0 is code for *Be fruitflies and multiply—rise up and destroy each other, you huddled masses yearning to breathe only when I tell you to, for that's the only way you'll be able to save me from myself*. And they're only too honored to go on champing at the *bait* [*sic*, of course].

Then he goes all high-hat (following the advice *malgré lui* [since he hates following anybody else's advice] of those fantasmal Adults in the Room [e.g., John O'Kelly, for whom being an adult means acknowledging that the onset of the Civil War was all about the failure to strike "a gentlemanly compromise"]) and reminds them, in so many words, they mustn't forget that the obedience of their enemies stems not from the favors they bestow to their own detriment but from the superiority they enjoy through the display of their might—the showmanship of their might. That by following worse laws—the worst laws—without deviation, the state comes out stronger than when it lays claim to good laws that are not binding. They must never—never—fall into what his right-hand men call the elitist trap—for what is falling into the elitist trap in its nakedness but "to approach words as a spectacle and actions as a recitation"?[202] (Never has Melanctha felt so strongly that the dummy Rump wants nothing more than to go on being the grateful prosthesis of some Senior Prom [Gazprom to you] ventriloquist.] The exhortation has exerted a powerful—indeed, a highly reassuring—effect on the crowd [ever-ready to sink its fangs into the right kind of corpse] even if in fact this particular condemnation of elitism ends up constituting, compliments of its unique brand of eloquence, a vote cast by acclamation in that very elitism's favor. Which acclamation constitutes nothing less than one more betrayal of the dummy's campaign promises [right up there with other greatest-hits betrayals—betrayals, e.g., of the LGBT alliance [Cantor hates the word "community"] and Wall Street-mangled Main Street) albeit an unintentional—or at least a serendipitous—one. But the aesthete's shudder that passed through the crowd has come and gone and it's back to basics—the first order of business being to exalt the *right kind* of elitism, as practiced by, among other verminoids, the Mnuchkin, the Mills critter, Gary Kone, Tillertson and let's not forget Betsy if for no other reason than that's she's sister to America's faux-boyish answer to Viktor Bhout, Erikk Princesz. The right kind because it's no elitism at all: greed can't be tarred as elitist. So what if they'd have to slough their very skin to be appropriately divested of all of their conflicts of interest? That the verminoids with their alternative facts and figures are unpolysyllabically—hence, heroically—doing what Calvinist genius Lloyd Blankfein deemed god's work brings comfort to the Base—the infinitely mythologizable Base—and as far as the disenfranchised—The Rump's quickly forgotten Forgotten—are concerned, comfort is a dish best served cold. The verminoids can be trusted because they lie with a straight face and so they expect you to be smart enough to know they're lying—to meet their challenge—to put your money where their mouth is—to *get real*—they're men of their word—worse, they're *purists:* they promised to slash every last safety net to shreds and they're delivering. Doing anything less would put them in the same class as abortionists. *They're destroying the world without stooping to anything so vulgar—so two-faced—as remaking it.*[203]

But he reminds them that for all the elitist-bashing (for there are two sides to every pretense) he has an IQ better than anybody's and when he wants to turn on the spigots of abstract intelligence he's an intellectual to end all intellectuals—an elitist to end all elitists. There's nothing he can't be—in particular what he professes to loathe most because the Base expects him to loathe it. The torchbearers subside—unfairly—just when their chanting has become much too combative to bear. And how faint, flat and fathomless everything now seems in its absence—especially to Cantor. A shot in the arm

---

[202] From the Steven Lattimore translation of Thucydides, *The Peloponnesian War* (Indianapolis, Indiana, Hackett Publishing Company, 1998), book III.

[203] Though Stifter, its progenitor, thinks that this thought—that is, its contour—is a wee bit too pat—too *comforting.*

it was and continues to be, still demanding nothing less than a realignment of all his allegiances—allegiances he never knew he harbored—allegiances kept in cold storage until the right monster came along to compel a testing of their potency, their viability. But as every cloud has its silver lining, it is now, thanks to such subsidence, the turn of "The Brand is stronger than ever!" to assail the gentle breezes for which Santa B by night is—or is soon to be—famous. And if there's anybody around who doesn't believe in the purity—the fibrosity—of this successor to the replacement chant he has only to get a load of the size of the portfolio of trademarks amassed by the Family for as everybody in the know knows, a Brand without a trademark—without a slew of trademarks—is like a cancerless prostate. When The Rump assures them he's got trademarks in more than 80 countries, somebody (through a bullhorn clearly of his own making)—a career loser, obviously—seizes the moment to remind him that while tarring Foundation Hillary as a traitor for scooping up donations from Brunei Darussalam is all well and good, he himself has taken out trademarks covering at least 40 real-estate categories in that very same country, not to mention his trademarks from Mother India which tentacle into not only real estate but perfumes, designer soaps and detergents as well. In other words, if you elect to swallow his poison pill it must be the brand—not the generic, even if the former costs 100 times as much. The crowd goes wild or pretends to. But Cantor (mind you, no mean logician) can't quite figure out how the conclusion follows from—rather than simply rides roughshod over—the facts purporting to serve as its substrate. He decides this is yet another case of some poor lonely slob—a slob—a dis-affected slob (very much in the ignoble tradition of Cantor himself) getting high by inciting wordflow to perpetrate havoc—here and now through the crazy mixed-up homologizing of *Hillary versus Rump* and *generic versus brand.* Yet when he feels his wrath mounting he remembers (with reluctance) that whatever their differences he and The Rump share a common border: the song "My Way" (creator: Claude François). In fact, Cantor's willing to bet the same choked-up blood flows in their veins at the moment when Frankie, celebrating what his faithful servant retrospect has airbrushed into noth-ing less than Chronic Non-compromise as an Art Form, swears if there was Doubt he "ate it up and and spit it out." All of a sudden he could swear that somebody's singing it—karaoking it—*as we speak.* Terrified of succumbing, he starts to skedaddle but the song is everywhere and at the same time he doesn't want to move too fast and thereby miss his favorite stretch. Though Cantor's much matured—much *evolved*—from what he was two minutes ago and to prove it, wonders with seeming impassivity whether "ate it up and spit it out" shouldn't in fact read "*chewed* it up and spit it out," "chewed" being so much more brutal than "ate." Maybe what he's trying to move away from is the question, Has he really been doing it *his* way and if "the record shows" [he] took the blows" does that make him any more worthy of exaltation than the billions whose blows were a billion times more painful? He should have gotten addicted to Primo Levi's rendition. It would have cut his puny self-love down to size in record time.

More to the point, Cantor wonders if The Rump and his sons, like

Saddam and *his*, routinely man up by pawing over hardcore in one of Rump Tower's many Kaspersky-insulated bunkers—washing down their swag with studious draughts of *The Godfather*, parts 1–13. But don't let Cantor's revulsion fool you. Revulsion is, as always, a Dead Letter to the World but meant in fact for dearest Dad who lives alas! away—a letter whose subtext is sadness—of all things!—that this rite of passage chose to disown him. But the Man from Morningside is smart enough to know—if not necessarily to think—that giving way to fine distinctions such as this—the kind of fine distinction only finely honed self-schism can trigger—is a luxury. Unpardonable flip-flopping in the context of the current political climate. Stuffed to the gills, the tram is making a return voyage (it's the kind of animal whose every voyage has the feel of a maiden). Margo, who's just set up shop—or rather, who's just had shop uxoriously set up for her—confesses traitorlike to Martin (to his surprise—to his bedevilment—he discovers he's standing right beside her beach chair—its hood sprouting just the sort of pompom sported by just the sort of Houyhnhnm doomed to drag tourists [welterweights need not apply] through the wilds of Central Park on just the sort of midsummer afternoon that'd be perfect for a stroll [thinks the coachman] though without them [tourists and wilds] the Houyhnhnms would starve)—Margo confesses to Martin that whenever there's somebody within earshot singing the praises of any member of the Team all of a sudden it feels like something is simultaneously being taken away from her. *Odd, he thinks, coming from somebody who loves The Rump's rump more than she could ever love her own soul.* Which gets Moira (who finds herself—to *her* surprise and bedevilment—right behind Margo) thinking about—of all people—a former student (it's useless for the Master to hiss, *No flashbacks!* or hasn't He heard? the Past—everybody's Past—more real by a long shot than the present and never One to feel discomfort much less dread at the thought of wearing out Its welcome—the Past, just like love [at least after George and Ira have had their way with it], *is Here to Stay!*)—a former student named Dottie Dordt and an evangelical Christian by trade who'd descended in all innocence on the Big Apple for the sole purpose of pirouetting her way to humble God-fearing greatness yet who confessed one night at the bus stop but a few days after she'd started classes that whenever she heard talk in the street or the park or the supermarket about how more and more freedoms were being "handed out" to blacks and gays and Muslims and browns and Jews and the disabled and atheists and the homeless (who seemed to make up about 99 percent of the city's population or was she underestimating?), it felt like the rug of *her* freedoms was being pulled out from under her—her freedoms as a member of what had to be the most beleaguered minority in world history, assailed as it now was with ultimatums and from all directions—ultimatums on the order of, Believe in homosexuality or lose your livelihood (though Moira wasn't sure she knew what "believing" in homosexuality came down to). Only the more threatened poor Dottie confessed to feeling, the more Moira felt counterthreatened—counter-threatened at every turn by Dottie's fear—counterthreatened to the point of contemplating murder (to be perpetrated ideally before the mad-bull M104 mowed them both down—the very same

M104 that Eden-besotted Cantor, one sweltering summer afternoon-into-evening . . .)—counter-threatened but not (since she wasn't your typical coastal) *faux* counter-threatened—not fashionably counter-threatened—not patronizingly—not cozily—not comfily—counter-threatened—but throw-myself-on-the-sword-of-solitary-despair counter-threatened. And the confessions of beleaguerment grew more and more combative the closer Dottie got to the date she'd set (when it became clear the Apple was not only not big but rotten to the core) for the inevitable-from-the-start flight back to Sioux Center—confessions unhealthfully peppered with pronouncements to the effect that (*a*) any woman (like The Rump's "wonderful gentleman" wife Mike) who does the hard work of submitting to a man is stronger than (*b*) the lazybones who simply wants to rule over him. Either *a* or *b*—no other options—since Life as the Dotties of the world live it—the Dotties of the world as expanded reductively and reduced expansively to the size and shape of The Other by that Other's favorite Other, the Moiras of the world—was a great big hornet's nest of Binaries and Hewing to the Norm (Life's backbone) a matter of being on the right side of every single one of Them. Or is Moira mixing Dottie up with that Caryn woman—*that Caryn woma*n—in the article she still hasn't finished because she wants to go on spendsavoring its salt[204]—an article that's trying to be fair even if at the same time it can't help playing to Moira's own prejudices thereby leaving her self-protective animus intact. But whether her name is—was—Dottie or Caryn or Margo what she'd practiced (nobly, in her way) at the bus stop, at the barre and everywhere else was evangelical Christianity degree zero and she practiced it cold—as preached—in its pure state—undiluted by any choir boy kinky-sex hypocrisy or white-collar malfeasance à la Fallwell Junior or Pompeii Mike, respectively. Which leaves Moira *and her kind* in the lurch—with no space for justifiable mockery as a form of coastal clemency cum self-help. Which leaves space only for being counter-threatened—counter-threatened degree zero—counter-threatened by the real-deal version of eC—the brand version, not the generic—the version that's unsugarcoated with lapses, fraudulence, calculation, the blood-and-guts of sex-and-money lust. Cantor is surprised at how moving Moira's guardian stance (right behind her drooling charge) has turned out to be. Though knowing a thing or two about Margo, or rather, about the Margos of this world, he wonders how long it will take her, through a stroke of genius or of good luck or better yet a stroke that's neither genial nor lucky but just plain hemorrhagic, to contort the guardian's heady mix of tact and mansuetude (yeah, bud, *mansuetude*: I believe in calling a spade a spade—and the devil take the hindmost) into an even headier mix of cruelty and defiant incompetence. Or maybe Moira isn't so tactful after all, much less mansuetudinous—at least in her supporting role of homicidal nursemaid on pointe—but if so, how is Cantor Dupin Holmes to amass, operating as he must in the toxic fog belched forth by the beach chair, all the evidence needed to indict her?

---

[204]See Elizabeth Dias, "Christians will have power," *New York Times*, 9 August 2020.

But the star of the show—the star too mesmerizing for its own good—is not The Rump per se but the mini-ensembles—the couplings—his boordom[205] generates. "Any idea what's going to be *your* favorite transition team *moment* among all those you've witnessed either on screen or up close? (for some strange reason I don't think there'll be many more)," Walser asks Stifter (they're in love again—but of course not as thunderclappingly as The Rump and Tiny Tim Kim). But before he can demur Walser clarifies: "This gravy train will be in transition till the day it crashes (I'd like to say *crashes into the truth* but that wouldn't be realistic). Crashes with all aboard." "A stroke of genius," warbles Stif. Walser blushes. Stif catches the blush and decides to set it straight before it can spread. "I don't mean the business about the gravy train—or rather, not *only* the business about the gravy train." "Then what *did* you—" "I mean the business about blowhard Trump's confessing to his reddest of red audiences that he and Little Rocket Man fell in love. You think it would have set homosexual relations ahead two hundred years. In fact it's done the opposite. It's given the reds permission to leave their dead to bury the dead, the dead being the strange little silly contextless desires which pop into everybody's head from time to time—permission to not give those pop-ups the time of day—they're all insignificant compared with what The Rump experienced with Rocket Man. That was truly mammoth—or rather, mock mammoth. Admitting to it before a live red audience was his way of taking their fetal sins on his mighty shoulders—his way of saying pack them up and give them all to me since you would only lose them while I, like any other great artist, know how to use them.[206]

Among those emerging from the asteroid-cum-gravy train's moonward-bending "undinal vast belly"[207] are (*a*) grimly uxorious Mack the Pence (with his better half—his no-nonsense nurse cum jailer cum patient—in tow [or is it she who's emerging with him in tow?]: fact is, no matter who's in tow they're typically, proudly—even a bit mock-defiantly—joined at [where else?] the hip) and (*b*) Wilbur DRoss (who gives refreshingly new, sinister meaning to the harmlessly quaint term *avuncular*). But in a way Ethan can't quite define—he's, unlike McPence, an honest fake. Can he help it if he looks the part—a part he wouldn't be caught dead playing intentionally? Come hell or high water, they're giving their all—or what's left of their all—to chitchatting and chatchitting but don't seem to be hitting it off—they're having a hard time greasing each other's axles. This pas de deux, when all's said and done,

---

[205]Yes, The Rump is a boor. Thing is, Anybody who calls him one outright, instead of cagily reserving judgment, prevents the virus of boordom's ingestion and assimilation as a pathway toward discovery (given a bit of hard-earned luck)—the discovery, say, that he—Anybody—is not as characterologically boordom-deficient as he'd like to think.

[206]Words gratefully purloined from "Pack Up Your Sorrows" (1965), Richard and Mimi Fariña's wrenching ballad.

[207]Also gratefully purloined, this time from Hart Crane, "Voyages" (II).

is clearly unworthy of commemoration. "So which is it going to be, Bob?" Stifter unfolds several ripe possibilities for his pal's delectation. Unregenerately *un*prodigal son Mknuchin the Munchkin with trophy-blonde-cum-better-half in tow busy securing The Rump's patriarchal blessing before or maybe it was after recitation of the marriage vows?[208]—vows that were subsequently lauded far and wide and well beyond for their staunchly traditional tenor. Or plutocrat poster boy Muntchkin, cheered on by Blondina, cutting into a wedding cake of crisp billion-dollar bills—the first in that denomination to bear the groom's signature—which will somehow find their way—*God willing* (the most mealymouthed of invocations)—back into the coffers of right-thinking donors, albeit donors not quite on the level of van der Weyden's and van Eyck's donors, at least as they were *depicted*. Though as any full-blooded American male or female will tell you, this non-alignment with the lofty strivings of the highbrow past—as realized, for example, in the flesh and blood of paint—is not necessarily a bad thing—on the contrary, like The Rump's getting along with Putin, it's (take it from the self-dentified master negotiator himself) a very *good* thing. "But what about the Democrats?" Stifter—afraid to be pilloried as a practitioner of simple-minded partisan animus—hastens to ask. Walser, gnawed by the same fear (and not to be surpassed), follows suit—and with the same dispatch.

Or, hey, what about the almost-famous televised "impromptu" cabinet meeting at which (somebody having presumably made a joke offscreen) choirboy Pence held on to his incipient grin until further notice—until the OK conveyed by his boss's poker-faced soundless chortle gave him (and even then there was a risk of misinterpretation, i.e., insubordination) the go-ahead to stretch out incipience to its full sickliness?

It's fatiguing to trot out these vignettes, stillborn even as they unfold in real time. Sorry to interrupt, but Walser confesses it may very well be the case that Jarevankanemia—and, among others, fatuous Rump son No. 2 and his missus, the unspeakable Llarrra (another bleached brain whose war cry is, *I'm a dyed-in-the-wool blonde, hence I'm gorgeous—worse, I'm worthy of a run for the Senate—worst, I have the right to urge federal employees not, under any circumstances, to bemoan a government shutdown* [engineered, she might add, but won't, by The Rump in the way of revenge—no, in the way of revenge porn—visited on Life itself for not securing him the wall money—the chump change—he needs to MAGA]—*the right to remind them that, while I'm sure it sort of hurts to go unpaid for weeks—months—years, the issue here is much bigger than any one person so they should stop grumbling and remember that future generations will honor their sacrifice*)—Walser confesses it may very well be the case that The Rumps—strutting and slithering and fluttering about as they did on Victory Night in a dither of entitlement made flesh—made

---

[208]Which robber-bridegroom Munchnik are we talking about here: the ass-kisser to end all ass-kissers—who before Congress prissily proclaimed it an honor to have traveled with The Rump on Air Force One?—or Mnutchkin the prune-faced tyke irrepressibly awestruck before The Super-Dad He Never (*sob*) Had.

flab—are very much his cup of tea—the kind of love potion that turned Isolde's girlfriends green with . . . envy. There, the cat's out of the bag. The very fact that he may not like—may even hate them—is what allows Walser to undergo basic training in the practice of a certain kind of love—not the best kind of love but love nonetheless. While knowing the eyes of the world are upon them—photoshopped to death by the male Erinyes of Fox and Fiends—generating their own endless video loop—they have nonetheless refused, even when caught in the bonds of greatness, to lose sight of their responsibilities. Towering among which is the obligation to start so positioning themselves as to wring every last nickel out of this windfall ascension—and emoluments clauses be damned. (He's waiting for Mueller—his knight in shining armor—to prove that in such a case, where there's so much greed, there must be naïveté, though probably not enough for said knights to sign off on even the cheesiest forgiveness-and-redemption package.) Although nobody can blame them on that same Night for having been too busy being busy to minister to the needs of the two camps of spectators: those who loathed them more than they loathed their own mediocrity; and those who were too bedazzled to gag on the hambone of envy. Not to mention the third camp, which required no ministrations whatsoever—the camp of mere observers fascinated by the breaking news delivered non-stop compliments of their own acuity—an acuity that, being drunk on its own edification, couldn't be turned off at will. Looking around, Stifter notes that the royals in question appear to be re-enacting while reinventing, somewhere in the vicinity of the tram (are they preparing for a fast getaway?), the pitiful stunts associated with Their Towering Obligation (i.e., to wring every last nickel out of that windfall ascension). And, as far as he knows, the only time they play the self-righteousness card is when this civic—Christian—bounden duty is called into question. For such a tasteless challenge puts the very security of the country in danger. If the royal family can't have its fingers in every pie, then what's next? Revolution? "What Victory Night tableau is as rich," Walser wonders out loud, "as that in which Rump the Junior slapped Mick Flynn Junior on the back—members of one big happy family taking the kind of liberties with each other that the Base and its hangers-on can only dream of perpetrating?" Nothing as breathtaking (he goes on to say, or at least think)—as intimidating—as stupidity—as a mediocrity's delusion that he has earned his trappings fair and square. In *mediocritese*, the pat on the back given by one mediocrity to another for all to see means, Look at me—us—bear witness—but hurry—to our smug collegiality in this super bowl of smugness—to this, our accession (unlawful tardiness being its only flaw) to a very special mandate—one that enjoins our back-channel ravagement of the Treasury—look at us, but hurry, 'cause we're the anointed and yet see how lightly we shoulder our chosenness—a chosenness we've earned through no fault of our own. Almost a year—or maybe two—after the victory, Walser can still see Rump the Junior swearing on Victory Night for all to hear—especially the vanquished—"We love you dead—I mean, dad." It's gone to Junior's head—the third-rate head of a third-rate bounty hunter. But now that he's gotten through the ordeal of this cup-of-tea confession, Walser would like to swear (out loud like bounty hunter Junior) for all to hear that he's made his peace at last with so vile a fascination—though calling it names will only pull him in deeper since that's precisely the way in which the dynamic underpinning such a disease (oops! there he goes again) works. And by the way, with a loan or two from Putin's thuggiest swin-oligarchs Kutschner can now begin to suture the suppuration-crazy wound known as 666 Fifth without leaving a scar.[209] Only he—Walser, not Putin—can't be let off the hook so fast. Stifter needs to administer a heavy dose of consolation even if it ends up—especially since it will end up—making him feel like Ethel Merman telling Donald O'Connor he's not sick/he's just . . . in love. He *is* in love (Stifter proceeds to say)—hopelessly in love as a matter of fact—with mediocrity of a certain type—Llllarrra's bleach-blond type, for example—mediocrity as thick as potato-slop soup. No purer type of medioc-rity than the mediocrity that's madly—humorlessly—smugly—schoolmarm-ishly—in love with itself—with its own exceptionalness—mediocrity like Lllarra's, and never more jaw-droppingly evident than when she administered to all those DC working stiffs the extreme unction of a lesson on how to start seeing the big picture and planning for a glorious life after death. Walser's not sick—he's simply in love with seeing just how far her arrogance—the most intimidating arrogance of all—the arrogance of stupidity—can take her before she's forced "to face the truth about herself." Not likely and why, after all, *should* she face the truth, whatever that is—why should she, when greater minds—greater talents—have steadfastly refused to take the overrated plunge into the mirror's depths—into its Poe-like maelstrom of monsters? He's in love not just with her but with the state of suspense to which she's consigned him—to which he's condemned himself what with all this wondering about just how long she can keep the mediocrity going—how far she can stretch its taffy—a mediocrity that, under the auspices of vastness—sheer quantitativeness—has managed to transform itself into something qualitative—qualitatively sub-stantive, i.e., morally super-offensive. In the un-capable hands of Lllarrra mediocrity becomes a moral affair. But/and it's moral mediocrity *of the highest order* and in its own way a sort of artistic miracle—or at least a semi-miracle. Willy-nilly he's taken the side of her mediocrity—he's its knight in shining armor—its knight of the woeful mug—he doesn't want her mediocrity to lose its train of thought. He has a vested interest in cheering her on because if she can do her part in ensuring that, among other things equally foul, federal employees go without salaries forever (even if The Rump doesn't ultimately get his wall [fact is, he couldn't care less as long as claiming he wants it more than he's ever wanted anything can wreak havoc—can give the mythological Base a perineal orgasm of the highest order]) and if she can then go on to parlay her contribution into a Senate seat then he'll die happy knowing there's no shame in dying since there's nothing to live for in a world where the Lllar-rrras can triumph—can force everybody else to swill in their witless screwball

---

[209] Don't we Semites have enough trouble—do they need to add to their considerable injuries the insult of Kushner's ostensible skills as a peacemaker (to name but one of the too-many Tin Woodman's hats crammed into his portfolio)?

comedy self-righteousness. He wants her mediocrity to succeed because the anguish bred by knowing the world is her oyster will be closer to pleasure than pain. Walser takes a deep breath and confesses—though a bit too sheepishly for Stifter's taste—that this Merman-O'Connor duet has done him a world— several worlds—of good even if it hasn't been much of a duet, more like a monologue, if you ask me. But whatever it is, it's done its job to the hilt—it's— Stifter's—proved that where Lllaaarraaa's concerned he hears music and not just any old kind of music but the very best kind, i.e., *music-but-there's-no-one-there.*

Meanwhile back at the tram station, the egress of Mrs. Mack the Pence from the belly of the asteroid is being blocked by of all things Margo's chair which, like Margo herself, is ready to do battle with the fates (or if they're unavailable then the stars)—but that's no excuse. But so combatively regal is Margo's stance even sitting down and hunched forward that Mrs. Mack may be forgiven for taking her for a visiting dignitary of the highest order and putting her own no-slouch combativeness on hold. She even goes so far as to ask Margo (no small concession from this sworn enemy of small talk) how she likes the view of the sea. Moira is afraid that Margo will take the question too literally (don't tell Moira, a trained spotter, anybody's ever interested in how somebody else likes *the view of the sea*). Indeed (or should "Indeed" be "Instead"?), this is Margo's cue to bring up her favorite—her only—subject-in-waiting. Like a child who wants both to escape the mercilessly gentle gaze of a stranger and at the same time to take advantage of the mercilessness while it lasts to show off her burgeoning powers of observation, she darts a pickled forefinger at a sports car parked beside the nearest semi-intact gravestone. "You see that fringe of leaf shadow on the upper rim of the windshield?" Mrs. Mack's silence says she does and so what about it? (no mean trick, by the way, to make elected silence speak volumes). It's clear she's taken a shine to feisty Margo—finds in her a brother-in-arms. "That's an omen. Bears the mark of a worldwide conspiracy—they're planning to do MAGA man in. We won't let that happen, will we?" The thought of MAGA man being done in has gotten Mrs. Mack all riled up although she's not so sure she'd go so far as to say there's a contingent of windshield wipers at work behind the scenes. While the spectre of conviction for mugwumpery makes it all the more imperative for her to show some outrage, the voice of "America's Undertaker" Mack la Pence, from deep within, cautions her (seconded by none other than America's Mayor Rudy G.) not to do what some ungracious bystanders do—which is to become so unhinged—so maddened—by the obligation to prove their commitment as to end up more aligned with the Enemy, thereby relegating Margo to the role inevitably assigned to all beach chair drivers of a certain temperament, however expert: mere fulcrum for the concerted unbalancing act of two parties (in this case, a MAGA mama and the whole horde of Never Rumpers) rendered indistinguishable through the very opposition that's supposed to set them shockingly—cinematically—apart.

Strange bedfellow Cook acknowledges that his Achilles heel is Sebastian the Gorka from whose rallying croak he routinely awakens in a cold sweat. After all, what better exemplar of homosexual self-insemination than "[T]he era of the Pajama Boy is over January 20th, and the Alpha Males are back"—worth inspiring a gay porn extravaganza where the boys bend over backwards to accommodate the alphabestiality of the males—or is it the males who do all the bending? But whatever the undertow, it's the delivery that counts and Gorka delivers with a man's-man beefiness that's a welcome antidote to Pence's missionary position, anticlimactically on display at that anthem-haunted Colts-49ers game (see above) whence (boss's orders!) Pence with better half in tow (Hear ye! Hear ye! The Lady from Forest Hills has the floor: *Again with the toe!* [says she]) or vice versa, outraged at all the knee-taking, exited in pious dudgeon but unscathed (yes, I know, at least wife-and-mother is an un-blonde). But isn't it the alphas who routinely ejaculate prematurely, since they regard their semen as an excretion without any redeeming value, and the pajama boys who hoard and husband theirs so economically as to end up incapable of ejaculating? And if so, doesn't that very incapability so-called attest in fact to the strong silent pajama's command over his impulses? And this being the case, don't such stark contrasts cry out, before they vanish forever, for some kind of synthesis within a higher unity—an amphimixis, say, of all erotisms—as one speaks of a czar of all the Russias—and Gorka and Judge Roy Moore be damned? But in what sort of being will that unity reside? Answer: In a not-quite-human yet to be born, a chimaera, one quarter alpha, two thirds Pajama, with no remainder, thinks Pataphysical Supermale Cantor, sporting a perfectly straight face.

Back with Margo's scarf, acrophobic Pritchard (he's managed to avoid the tram even with fraternal twins Keith and Friedrich Schiller and their goons patrolling the entrances) is having trouble tracking her down. Oh, there she is (blocking his view of the most exquisite super-model ever to grace the Runway Called Life, whose grave managed just in the nick of time to sidestep the scythe of The Rump's event planners)—there she is gossiping away to beat the band with super "model" Kellyanne Kon-Artist née Kockenlocker, highest priestess of bleached news—there she is expressing a disappointment akin to the bitterest grief that her first and only son is experiencing so many learning difficulties—milking them dry of their life savings, though she cunningly doesn't elaborate. Which grieving is, at it turns out—as it always turns out—but a hop, a skip and a jump away from taking him to task in or out of absentia for having failed to slay the Past—mightiest dragon of them all. But being absent without leave hasn't—and doesn't (Margo ain't yet aware he's within earshot)—prohibited Pritchard from also expressing, if only to himself, bitterest grief—akin in his case to disgust—at forever being subpoenaed to testify against this favorite son of a thousand felonies. But just because she may happen to be in the mood for damning Junior to hell doesn't mean that Pritchard's henpecked collusion is supposed to go her one better. Just because she's enraged at Junior and needs him to confirm the heinousness of the boy's crimes doesn't mean Pritchard shouldn't immediately be counter-attacked for the excessive harshness of even the simplest assent. It's taken him what seem like decades (and probably are) to make the necessary exquisitely timed adjustments to her micro-shifts in allegiance—he's never quite sure what will follow the lapses into aggressive self-blame except that the more aggressive it becomes the diviner her right to crown him the culprit in chief—or, what's worse, the more mountainous her entitlement to make the whole world the culprit in accordance with the terms of her latest contract with It. The It, the It and nothing but the It. So—through the old girl's good auspices he's learned to be always on the lookout for signs that Junior and Margo might have much more in common with each other than they let on for all their squabbling and may be using him only as a foil. So—also through the old girl's good auspices at last he's learned what it means to be *tired to death*—to have *one foot in the grave* (he's got to hand it to those antediluvian turns of phrase: they knew—know—of what they spoke—speak). The Rump, all miked up, is calling somebody a Good Man—the surefire kiss of death—the guarantee of ripeness for the wrong kind of resurrection. Maybe it's that double amputee (straight out of *Potemkin*, whose author loved the deficient because they were pictorially legible—like the midgets dancing on the police chief's dinner table in *Strike*—but legible as what precisely? well, legible [unlike so-called normals forever oozing into featurelessness] as *beings*)—that double amputee who, simply by standing tall next to Jeff Sessions (he's singlehandedly given Bespectacled Impishness the baddest name), cuts him (the real amputee) down to size. He's been rushed in by the Associated Press to confer his own brand of legibility on the proceedings—to serve (at no extra charge) as a pivot point—an axis—a distraction—thereby enabling the event to *become* a Rump event (while nobody's looking because that nobody's neophyte gaze is busy getting itself castrated by too much fascination with this Medusa in spite of himself).

I don't know about any of you, but Melanctha's sure got her handiwork cut out for her as she takes note of Jarevankanemia (for whom all the world's a runway) strolling by with fingertips lightly—unconvincingly—touching, while tastefully playing down so much enviability as DC's Power Chimaera (whatever that is) to end all PCs, at least in their own Dirty Hairy Eastwoodian mind. Don't let anybody kid you: She's bleared—no, smeared—with the toil of making the term "very senior advisor" apply to a nullity like Kutcshzner (famous last words: *six-six-six*)—of effecting at all cost the adherence of the term's scab to the weasel wound that is he. Even harder to refrain from delectating over the fact that hers is an impossible task (to choreograph the same ballet on Ivankanemia will be impossible as well but infinitely less challenging). Adhesion simply won't take. But by rebuffing the label is he, this patented—trademarked—robot-pretending-to-be-a-robot, enhanced or canceled out completely? Thinking (somewhat falsely), *The answer to that one's beyond me*, Melanctha grants herself a well-deserved respite from genius (no other word will do). But here's Ben Carssson—an Uncle Tom if ever there was one pretending to be just that—The Rump's Uncle Tom (64,000 dollar question: is Ben Carssson *real*?)—here's Ben to ensure that she doesn't get too carried away—nowadays, everybody's a genius—a genius and a half—until further notice. And there's got to be some sort of amateur irony swilling around in the fact that this, the Housing and Urban Development tsar—configuring poverty as the failed overthrow of a merely perverse state of mind—is just the kind of guy The Rump would still refuse to rent to. (No matter that even the most rabid squalid redneck would admit he's the furthest thing imaginable, especially after having dutifully swallowed a sleeping pill or two [which he never forgets to do especially before embarking on a speaking engagement], from one of Reagan's strapping young bucks.) Although nowadays The Rump would, letting bygones be bygones, certainly have no problem calling him a Good Man or, worse, Tweeting how "proud" he was of his toddlers Ben and Candy—almost—*almost*—as proud (should they, too, successfully execute a plotted balletic stunt) as he was of toddlers Mike and Karen. As with Kutzshner, though less exquisitely, difficult to square the title with the man. She experiences the same sort of racialist shame that triple-sixed Kush, Mnnunchkin and Gary Roy McCohn have already triggered, at least from the liverish look of him, in Cantor.

Cantor comes over and asks if he can get her anything before the speechmaking reaches its climax. Melanctha tells him she hopes (even if this should be the least of her worries) The Rump doesn't go pronouncing "Russia" as "Rusher" (something obscene about the mispronunciation: maybe because it focuses, as intended, too much of her attention on the bloating of the lips). That would be the last straw. "A lime rickey," she replies, for no reason at all— she has never tasted one nor does she believe the bartenders whose white jackets are glistening dewily somewhere out in left field will be capable of fulfilling the order. Cantor likes doing her bidding. It makes him feel manly and boyish in one fell swoop. "Be right back" (a phrase he rarely uses—rarely has occasion to use). It, too, makes him feel manly and boyish—like a johnny-on-the-spot cum johnny-come-lately cum stage-door-johnny cum jack-of-all-trades—without missing a beat. Through the corner of his eye he observes Eden conversing with Borkman, Jr., both at the same time keeping their eyes peeled podiumward. Something in their ease of connection makes Cantor uncomfortable—and at the same time he exults because that ease is some kind of triumph over life—over the hand fate has dealt the duo. Are they all here to be exultant, then, but *each*—to borrow Stein's phrase as applied to Melanctha's namesake—*in his own way*? But disquiet at the fact that the two have hit it off so suddenly sets in and quickly trumps exultation. *This is what's known as foreshadowing—this is what's known as foreshadowing—this is what's known as foreshadowing*—he hears himself shrieking above the highly unwelcome silence of the tiki boys who may just turn out to be ejaculation-shy pajamas (when nobody's looking). But then Cantor realizes that in fact they've had a long history. Didn't Borkman, Jr., at some point take Eden under his wing? No, that was Jim, Jr.—suddenly a dead ringer for Rump, Jr., who has a knack for being in the wrong place at the right time.

The Rump is about to assure the crowd that he has plenty of dirt not just on Crooked Hillary (just needs to intone the epithet to have them gurgling in the palm of his tiny hand) but on Crooked Chelsea and Crooked Holder and Crooked Jeb and Crooked Ted and Lyin' Ted and Flyin' Ted and Crooked Ivankanemia and the Crooked Georges not to mention the Crooked Mikes (all twenty-three of them: in fact the only conceivable title for the history of this Administration would be, as far as Cantor's concerned, *Too Many Mikes* exclamation point)—and let's not forget all those Crooked Jrs., tied, wherever they may lurk—even if it's out there slaughtering pandas and gazelles—to Dad's apron-strings. But before the assurances can get rabble-rousingly under way a caveat or two is in order: In the event that said assurances should turn out to be too X-rated for some ears he urges—implores—commands the certain-to-be-offended parties (they know who they are) to preserve their virginity, safeguard their sanity and coddle their innocence by storming the exits ASAP (Melanctha qua budding author takes note of this disclaimer's inspired wording: it's the stuff of which great frontispieces [for daring debut works of fiction] are made). His supporters look confused, even angry, but never at him. There The Rump goes again, thinks Cantor, practicing "divisiveness." The Rump—our Rump—our Better Angel Rump void of ideology hence never at a loss for non-issues to keep the divide going full speed ahead. The Rump as Dedekind cut, into the flab of a country intent on staying divided long enough to make its regeneration of limbs, tails, eyes, brains, an occasion for international rejoicing and not just among axolotls. *Divisiveness.* The word's a euphemism—an understatement—which means that it breeds among bleeding-heart users the exact opposite—suture through consensus, salvation through polysyllabism—of what it purports to signify.

Cantor bemoans the fact—no, Melanctha bemoans the fact—no, the whole Greenwich Avenue tribe (probands, ministering physicians, pipeline potentates, support staff, consultants galore)—and in unison, to boot—bemoan the fact that they just don't have it in them (thanks to the Master, who ain't dead quite yet) to take The Rump the way the respectable sentences of, for example, "The Rump versus the Presidency" by respected *Times* journalists Habberman, Thrhush and Bakker expect them to take him. Calmly, the trio urges the tribe not to cast blame if the article in question seems to be awash in bromides and fails to get the fat sonofabitch off the field and fire him as if he were Colin Kaepernick. Blame the sentence—their tool—for it neutralizes and normalizes and humanizes and renders elegant everything that swims into its ken.[210] Blame not them but the sentence (which has a sorcerer's apprentice-like life

---

[210]For example, we learn from the *Times* that: "[a]s he ends his first year in office, [he] is redefining what it means to be president" (such redefinition being quaint—perfectly harmless—except for the perfectly unnoted minute-by-minute direness of the consequences; "[w]hile much of what he has promised remains undone, he has made significant progress in his goal of rolling back . . . regulations" ([knowingly?] false contrast, eliding the fact that reneging and rollback are two sides of the same tarnished coin); Kelly, putative only-adult-in-the-room "is trying, quietly and respectfully, to reduce the amount of free time the president has for fiery tweets" (*fiery tweets*: good example of the respectable cuteness of journalese rubbing off undeservingly on its target); "[t]he pace of meetings has increased . . . [and] they often include Ivanka . . . the president's daughter and senior adviser" (imagine! this inexhaustibly applausive daddy's girl a senior adviser! skimming poker-faced over the inconceivable the sentence makes the unimaginable plausible—worse, quaint); "[d]espite chafing at the limits . . . the president actually craves the approval of Mr. Kelly" (he's a child hence incapable of wreaking havoc on the poor, the sick, the disabled; "[o]ver Thanksgiving at Mar-a-Lago, the president mingled with guests . . . [and] he dialed old friends" (sentencing as

of its own) if the article is too much of an analgesic for your taste (given the subject)—like the voice of the narrator of a goofy '60s short about, say, the making of a fluffathon like *The Yellow Rolls Royce*—a voice on the far side of a discreet chuckle—a *wholesome* manly voice—as phony as Harold Arlen's Barnum & Bailey world.

Semen-less Testicles-in-Waiting Mike La Pence and Paul Della Ryan (policy guy assoluto if only in his own mind) have taken their places behind The Prick *(faith, his privates they!)* whose just-concluded epithetization of his enemies has left him Limper than usual and badly in need of these pasty-faced plaster saints niched on either side. (True, Bannon has fashioned an ideology out of an inflamed brain hemorrhoid but at least he's had the guts to confirm that, yes, Ryan *was* spawned at the Heritage Foundation in a Petri dish which is now, all too predictably, in MOMA's permanent collection.) With face almost entirely hidden by the folds of her flamboyant scarf (the only gift she ever received from Straynge's deranged stepmother, the feckless Mme. Birx (who's got more scarves than her derangement knows what to do with—that is, besides injecting them with disinfectant whether they need a good cleaning or not)—why, it'll soon be as iconic as piggish SPruitt's glorified phone booth—Margo has turned herself into a resin-soaked casualty of the Early Dynastic Period. But never mind that: She subjected The Rump to a brazenly amateurish hence thorough phrenological workup while nobody was looking—including the subject himself—and what was her relief—her delight—to determine his case to be far less Dangerous—far less mental

---

usual has the last word, daintily suggesting that The Rump's monstrousness is a mere manifestation of wrong time-and-place: on home turf he's just as cuddly as you and me; "[t]o an extent that would stun outsiders, The Rump . . . the most talked-about human on the planet, is still delighted when he sees his name in the headlines" (*monstrous* egotism?—no, it's harmless, dummy, because aw-shucks childlike); "the image of him in a constant rage belies a deeper complexity" (not only adorable, but complex: most vulgar of beings, our homegrown Hermes eludes the vulgarity of diagnosis, of a fixed identity; The Rump's "difficult adjustment to the presidency . . . is rooted in an unrealistic expectation of its powers, which he had assumed to be more akin to . . . imperial command" (the grosser implications of a jackass's boldfaced ineptitude swept under the carpet of the sentence—he's a wide-eyed innocent—more sinned against than sinning; "[s]ome advisers, like . . . [unspeakable] Mnuchin, consider this [distrust of anything that does not come from inside his bubble] . . . *a fundamentally good thing*" (the italics are the Master's): who knew health care could be so complicated and by the same token who knew the love of "verbal briefings" as opposed to "volumes of books or briefings" could be so much the symptom and proof of a swamp-draining cunning?; "[The Rump] has always relished gossiping over plates of well-done steak, salad slathered . . . massive slices . . . dessert . . . extra ice cream" (what self-respecting monster can't be humanized—not to mention his *willed* obese gluttony—through association with the phrase *ice cream*?—or the term *gossiping*); [e]ven when [The Rump] is in a lighthearted mood, hints of anxiety waft over the table like steam over a teacup" (pseudo poetry turns the mysteriously anxious Rump into a tragic hero—larger than life yet prey to the same vapors as little you and little me).

health-endangered—than the spotlight-hungry psychopharmacologists suddenly making the rounds would have you believe (their number, alas, like that of poor Judge Roy's accusers, is mounting by the minute). Each of them of course professes to be an alarmist out of sheer love for The Rump (has he himself masterminded this stunt by any chance?) and each of them at the same time makes it circuitously clear that of course he's no ordinary headshrinker and that's because he's *more* than a mere headshrinker—he's also (even if his name ain't Legrandin) a soon-to-be screenwriter (an indigestible fiction she's all too eager to swallow hook, lock, line, stock, sinker and barrel, otherwise what would her triumph over them be but a paltry thing?), hence unassessable, since however glaring his defects as the one, they are immediately smashed to smithereens by his lurking looming latent achievements as the other. Should Pritchard risk informing her that these self-styled mantic manticores are a dime a dozen (hence her triumph over their prognostications is paltrier than paltry), thereby raising her ire? But he has plenty of his own ire to lavish so why *not* lavish it on Margo? especially since he's been confusing her more and more with scarfless Kellyanna Fuckabee Glanders (though in all fairness it's hard to say how much of her hideousness is generic baseline gender-specific hideousness and how much of it is idiosyncratic and idiopathic overlay—and the same question can of course be asked of his own—or anybody else's—hideousness). He decides to speak his mind: They wake up—those killer screenwriters do—ca. age sixty-three deciding they're far more than a pill pusher. Something the wife—soon to be known as wife No. 1—could never understand. Or rather, something he would never have wanted her to understand since waking up to such a discovery requires a change of garment on every front, most of all on the conjugal. So said rebel—said tenured guerrilla—wastes no time securing a No. 2 whom he convinces himself is in the starkest contrast imaginable to 1. He would like to kill Margo but has understandably mixed feelings about doing so and feelings even more mixed about the fact—though maybe it's just one of those alternates he's always reading about—that before the night is through, over-collusive Eden and Borkman, Jr., will have done the dirty job for him and wrapped it all up with a blood-red typewriter ribbon. It's not just their glazed looks, furtive and defiant . . . it's . . . something deeper . . . something even Leopold and Loeb would have shuddered at . . . Yet, suddenly, the something's a nothing and it's gone—it passes and away we . . . stay.

It's thanks to the presence of the Testicle Twins (although he'd never admit this, least of all to himself) that The Rump is now willing to take questions from the press—mostly about, of all things, Tom the Priceless. A few familiar faces—including Eli Stokols, Peter Baker, Natasha Bertrand, Jennifer Rubin and Jeremy Bash—in a sea of smaller fry. The Rump is willing to call The Price a Good Man, which is equivalent to saying he was in the Administration only for a short time—minutes, actually—but won't give any credence to the contention obviously disseminated by the Democrats that he was a comrade in arms unjustly evicted. The Kockenlocker will always have a soft spot for her private-jet mate although he was never her type (as if he could be anybody's). Borkman always thought of Poor Tom when he thought of him at all as an uningratiating roach cum roach killer. Still, it hurts him a bit to observe that The Rump appears to have forgotten how deftly Tom managed—what seems like decades ago—to deflect the questions of Chuck Todd on *Meet the Press* about the Boss's health care bill—The Big Scam—an anti-plan told by an idiot, crammed full of sound bites and donor fury. Seems to have forgotten how Tom pulled off a surefire deflection by mumbo-jumboing at breakneck speed something or other (the epileptiform secretions at the corners of his puckered puddle of a mouth attesting to how seriously he took his flunkeydom as long as it promised to be lucrative)—something or other about the President's—although not My President's—"passionate" devotion to . . . to . . . to . . . the World Health Organization of all things! As for Melanctha, she, too, is inexplicably moved: The Rump has clearly forgotten that Priceless Tom then went on, unsolicited! to assure Chuck that he'd been indeed *honored* (and not just honored but honored in the grandly abject Mnutchkin manner)—Tom, normally the most passionless of beings!—to be invited to share that mad passion for . . . for . . . for . . . WHO! Though, Borkman suspects, not quite as honored as The Rump must always feel—and with no sign of diminution through practice—to be allowed, thanks to his position, to sniff at the almond-scented prostates (Hold your horses! the Lady from Forest Hills has the floor!: *Again* [says she], *with the prostates!*) of Recep Putin and Vlad Erdoğan.

But it's hardliners like wizened Mitch and Dr. Hopalong Cassidy and The Rump's personal caddy, L. Graham Cracker—slurping mint juleps—who especially miss (since behind the porky little facade, Price was all things to all men) his singleminded devotion to drawing and quartering the ACA and buying stock in orthopedic implant companies minutes before introducing legislation to protect them from federal regulation. Kellyanne Kockenlocker Pirro sighs deeply. "Dear Tom Price," she murmurs then forces herself to attend to this beached somebody who seems to crave the ministrations of her murmurs most. Margo explains that she's got to—she's just gotta—know *Who's behind It* (as if she were Arthur Clennam being impersonated by Tite Barnacle). "It," Kelly echoes painstakingly. Oddly enough, once Margo has ignited what she can take to be a glimmer of understanding she's suddenly too tired to elaborate—begins in fact to turn on Kellyannabelle before Pritchard can calm her down. Understanding—or even—or better yet—a simulation of understanding—is an affront to the immitagable complexity of her cause. So Language as the fates would have it—wordflow as embodied in this case by the painstaking "It"—is the biggest conspirator of all—intent on driving Margo crazy. *Moral:* Kellyanne's the sexiest It Girl since Clara Bow and All's Well That Ends Well.

The more successful Pritchard becomes in calming her down, the more juice he manages to squeeze out of his hatred—though why revert glibly to hatred? Margo, he decides, deserves far better. Could it be that he talks of hating (which is certainly "successful with a 'dying fall'"[211]) to make him-

---

[211]T.S. Eliot, "Portrait of a Lady" (III).

self—to make him and Margo—to make their relation—*legible*—as legible as the tangoing midgets in *Strike* and the double amputee in *Potemkin* (and not just legible but *bankable* since nothing sells like hate—not even sex)? Oh why has she come back into his life? Before giving him the satisfaction of watching her calm down completely and—worse!—knowing—believing—it's his own professionalism which is responsible, Margo remarks that Lawrence Summers, former Secretary of the Treasury (in the glow of the torches she looks particularly witchlike, her profile resembling Mike Flynn's which in turn resembles a side slice of the puss of Michelangelo's Charon on a particularly busy workday), recently excoriated Munschkin, a dear and darling pal of hers since he's a friend of The President's—or in Shakespearese, friend *to the President* (smarmily conferring the title on its present bearer always gets the goat of her lily-livered liberal—Marxist-Leninist—colleagues)—and not just any old friend but a friend who's in a perpetual state of being *honored* to travel with The Rump on Air Force One. (When, oh when, wonders Walser who's in easy earshot and [as if that weren't enough] currently a PhD candidate [he just matriculated online] in the rapidly expanding field of mediocrity studies, will the pustule that is *Mnuchkin*, crammed to the gills with honoredness, finally pop its cork and bust its nut?) But as everybody knows Summers has no credibility after holding forth as he did about the innate inaptitude of women for a career in the sciences so how can anybody take such excoriation of Mnishkin seriously? And the smugger she becomes, the more he hates her more than he could ever hate The Mnunsch—even if that's a bit of an exaggeration but if it's exaggeration he's come by it honestly. So he retorts that it is precisely the beheading of Munchkin which restores Summers's credibility. Oddly enough, the Kockenlocker is glued to the spot as if she were relieved to know she's met her match. "Behind what?" Kellyannetta asks, trying to depopulate her question of any signs of sisterly concern. Native irritation channeled through her signature goody-two-shoes singsong of fake reasonableness, which has apoplecticized many a news anchor not to mention millions of amateur chronicleers of This Awkward Age, comes to the rescue. "Your hubby's murder?" Margo points out that the mystery has just been definitively solved to everybody's at least partial satisfaction. Strange Kellyanne should mention it but this very morning the *LA Times* concluded its reporting on the matter by revealing it was probably a "gypsy" (straight out of Austen's *Emma*)—maybe even a veteran Broadway gypsy—who made quick work of the dirty deed. Or, better yet, probably a cross between a transient, a bum and a tramp—which is a chimaera sure to turn any biomedical engineer positively green with envy. *And which as everybody knows*, thinks Melanctha who's been sucking up all the chatter through the straw of her lime rickey, *is an old chestnut or standby or warhorse or stalking horse or caput mortuum of the pseudo avant-garde. I.e., a last resort of scoundrels.*

The Master has just fed His star pupil this string of synonyms even if she has been consistently warning him to go easy on the idiomatics—especially now that the trial is winding down—is bending over backward to get itself re-stashed inside the very womb of night which signals a return to civilian life. But, she must admit, the Master has dispatched his usual deftness to the scene of the crime since fancy words that you compel your creatures to purposely *misuse* are fancy words of another—a better color—and their misuser has it both ways—he's self-aggrandizing Jack in town and self-demolishing Ernest in the country. Margo is getting impatient since it's clear that Kellyanne is best suited by temperament to serve as her conduit to The Rump. If he won't know *who's behind It*, who will? She trusts him because he doesn't lie or rather he does lie only his lies are special—they're a whole sight better than truth. And what's more, he doesn't hoard them—husband them—for a time of real need. The need is now, whether real or not—and forever. And Rump the Precious—precocious to the point of genius even if it's the budding genius of a "fucking moron"—no doubt learned that lesson in the cradle and no doubt on the very night The Rump's dad, Fred, got himself arrested at a KKK rally in Queens; so one can only hope his kids (between selfie-takes aimed at triggering and capturing—whichever comes first—the fatuously defiant smart-ass grimace beloved from the dawn of time by silver-spooning selfie-takers worldwide) are learning the lesson as well. If only Jim, Jr., could follow in the footsteps of—of—of— But what's the use of wishful thinking. Jim, Jr., is as Jim, Jr., does. The Rump is clearly too busy cultivating the crop of very very fine people on the Right side of the aisle to give more than short shrift—if that—to what Pritchard continues to believe is an illusion with no future—too busy with affairs of state—too busy whipping the crowd into a frenzy to fret about who's behind It. Indeed, even without Mick Flinn and Mick, Jr., on hand, he's managed to bring those very very fine people to the point of orgasm—the point of ejaculating "Lock 'er up," though in this reprise—in this version of the tale—it's HP's Mabuse, Ms. Carlie Fiorino, who gets to play the felon in question. But whether The Rump helps Margo or not, there's no denying that more and more relevance—a dire relevance (Mueller is getting closer and closer)—is accruing—better yet, accreting—to her question—or rather, to the echo of her question—as the night—a night like no other—a night that's nothing less than the transition team's homage to the Night of the Long Knives—wears on.

Betsy dalla Vos has gone off her strict diet—none stricter—of prissiness and rice and righteousness and doctrinal beans to slip into something more comfortable—almost too comfortable—too skimpy—but she tells herself in so many words (words she's made it a point—until now—never to use)—tells herself that the indulgence is in this case very well deserved. And can she help it if something in the sea air—something about the way the jacarandas, mimosas and bougainvilleas have been pooling their perfumes (all for one and one for all—ensemble work of the highest order)—has set her gypsy blood astir? And now that she's back there's nowhere to go but up—up, that is, on the podium. As she ascends, no less a fashionista than Kellyannapurna compliments Betsy on her artful daring and urges the Base—but with so many stars up in the sky, the Base is the world and the whole wide world's the Base!—to get right out there and buy up Madam Secretary's entire line—and Carl Hatch be damned. The Reptile's kind words added to the giddiness triggered by ascent gives her the courage to believe that the self-indulgence was indeed deserved. After all, she's been busy gutting entire offices within her department so as to (quoting *Politico's* Jesse Dittmar) "lighten her bureaucratic burden" for the sake of what really matters. School choice, for one, which will lead to greater *kingdom gain* where the kingdom in question is of course god's and nothing but. Not to mention seeing to it that Neurocore (a biofeedback bin for attention deficit hyperactivity in which Dalla Voce and friends continue to be heavily invested even if its research papers have proven peer-unreviewable) achieves a similar greater gain, though in this case it's good old-fashioned free-market gain. (If she plays her cards right, Neurocore will become as much of a Rump icon as SchPruitt's time capsule.) Bet's also making great progress—tickled pink, by the way, to be sharing the podium with her boss but trying not to sound (most unCalvinistically) as if she were bragging—in fulfilling a major pledge of her campaign (the crowd's a wee bit baffled since as far as they can tell she never mounted one), which was to impose a freeze on borrower defense rules—frivolous ploys for erasing the federal loan debt of kids raped, but solely as a consequence of their own salaciously spoiled-bratty provocation, by for-profit colleges (fraud mills—attrition mills—like DaVos Tech, The Erikkk Blackwater Seminary and Rump U). Fake apostle Mike Von Pence tries to warm up the crowd by reminding her that, like him, she's also very much against the gainful employment mandate, right? (he can feel that they won't be satisfied until she affirms as much). There's a cagey "huh?" glint in her eye, which invokes for at least one somebody in the audience—maybe Cantor, maybe not—that famous confirmation-hearing remark about guns and grizzlies. Mike catches the glint before it turns into a cataract and to ease her out of her difficulty prompts, "I mean you're against banning loans to colleges whose graduates don't earn enough to pay off their debts, right?" The Base breathes a sigh of relief: for all her billions—precisely because of her billions—she's very much one of them.

To wake all the slumbering spirits of the gold, *that's what this crowd wants*, thinks Borkman as virtuously as if he were a GPS ankle bracelet (their subjugation by that cagey glint and all it portends of easy money—as palpable as their addiction to grizzly beef in days gone by and no laughing matter in the best of times—is all the proof he needs). *If only they knew what they're letting themselves in for.* Don't they realize he's a walking cautionary tale and knows of what he doesn't dare to shout out loud? Something in Borkman's gaze indicates the time is just right—or at least not all wrong—for lamenting the extent of these greedy bastards' influence. Soon enough Cantor recognizes the mistake of taking Borkman for a comrade in virtue-as-its-own-reward but only after he—Cantor—has opened his mouth too wide to disavow the self-righteous, fake-meditative, baying-at-the-moon-like Tolstoyan reverberations of "How many Jags does a man need?" Smugly, to impress Jean or to proudly affirm their relationship is beyond repair—for there's nothing funnier than the dissolution of a relationship and what's even funnier is the dissolution of all relationships[212]—Ethan, quoting that old bore Lear who deserved

---

[212]Novalis (Georg Philipp Friedrich Freiherr von Hardenberg), *Blütenstaub* (Pollen), aphorism No. 40. Cf. the similarly absolutist and annihilatory application of "dissolution" in a superficially different context by Karl Marx and Frederick Engels, according

what he got, says, "Reason not the need." Borkman (unimpressed by the feebleness of this citation from an old master, if that's who's being cited) gets right to the point (now it's his turn to impress that fair damsel Jean): "Look, Cantor, don't be so fucking coy. You know damn well that nobody *needs* a Jaguar." He goes on to explain (but in his own words and on his own terms) that once you're lucky enough to have one it begins to seem so vulnerable crouching there all alone in your Palo Alto garage and so you need another in case the first gets wrecked or vandalized or blown up. But having two Jaguars makes you or rather the conspicuousness of your consumption more vulnerable, especially to the IRS forever putting its foot down, and so you have no choice but to acquire another Jag and still another—as foils, so that the first thirty-three at least, the most precious of the lot, are not targeted by envious Huns—who've *chosen*, remember, to live on the street or off welfare. Not to mention another facet of the affair: Quickly enough, you feel yourself resenting the camaraderie, the esprit de corps, which infiltrates, quickly enough, the ranks of those Jaguars and so you must somehow distract them from their incestuous owner-averse intimacy through the introduction into the stable of still more members of the species.

And if Pritchard's hatred (*Again with the hatred!*) of Margo (she's ditched her hooded beach chair and wangled herself a front seat) were itself a Jaguar, then every minute of his last days on earth would mark the acquisition of far too many to count—enough to make the sword-dancing Wilburs of the world turn greener than their unnatural green. She compliments one of the white suprematists—whose sweaty T proclaims that he's none other than the buttered toast of Chelsea, Malevich McDuff—on his tiki (more upscale than all the others in a way she can't quite define) and as if that weren't enough she simultaneously—virtuosically—manages to applaud every time The Rump opens his mouth—and every time he doesn't. Who does Pritchard hate more—The Rump or his favorite acolyte, Margo? The broadening collusion—yes, he knows from MSNBC it won't be upgraded to a crime any time soon—between Eden and Borkman, Jr., assures him he needn't answer. They look like they're *getting ready*.

Mock only-adult-in-the-cemetery John Q. MacKelly is regaling his fellow generals, among whom he now includes The Rump, with what has quickly become his favorite war story. Only Mattis refuses to play ball. Should Kelly be reminded that when asked not so long ago by the Rose Garden crowd why he hadn't contacted the families of the four soldiers killed in the Niger, The aforesaid Rump (caught yet again with his pants down) mooned back with a

---

to whom the communist revolution, in contrast with "all revolutions up to now," will be "carried through by the class which . . . is in itself the expression of the dissolution of all classes, nationalities, etc. within present society" (Marx and Engels, *The German Ideology: Part One - With Selections from Parts Two and Three and Supplementary Texts*, C.J. Arthur, ed. (New York, International Publishers, 1970), p. 94. The notion of *a class which is in itself the expression of the dissolution of all classes* has, by the way, yet to find its Bertrand Russell.

typically fat-assed invocation of Obama's fake failure to contact Kelly under similar circumstances? But rather than call out The Rump as an empty barrel—as the cowardly temporizer he was and would always be—for having parasitized the corpse of his son as political cover—Kelly (casting himself as the sole remaining holdover from those julep-scented days of yore when women were deemed sacred) chose to displace his rage onto the rest of the world (the role of "rest of the world" in that evening's performance graciously conferred on Congressperson Frederika Wilson, also a woman, but African American hence clearly un-sacred) by calling it—that is, her—that is, *Frederika*—an empty barrel.[213] And in so doing, convinced himself that it was she the abject politicizer and the one he deserved to hate (and of course it's always ghoulishly fascinating to watch somebody convince himself *in real time* of the truth of what in his far wiser bowels he knows to be a lie)—that he and The Rump had a common grievance—that The Rump's grievance was one worth upholding through mimicry. Frederika in other words stepped into the breach just in the nick of time to prevent Kelly from disemboweling his boss—from disemboweling his own grief. A classic case of cowardice transmogrified—yes, *transmogrified!*—a classic example of the kind of transfer of animus you won't find lurking in the shadows of any textbook. So, Mattis keeps quiet. He has a queasy feeling The Rump isn't long for this world so why not let sleeping mongrels lie? And just as the career of draft-dodging warmongering Bush wouldn't have been complete without a book of paintings to celebrate Our Fallen Heroes—Heroes fallen under not just his aegis but his auspices, too—so no goosestepping gala would be complete without an unbilled cameo from unpoliceable Carter LaPage. And it's not only Mattis who can't suppress a guffaw cum giggle. Ah, Carter! ah, Humanity!

Although normally not given to squeamishness (excluding whatever accrues—no, inures—from his chronic germophobia), for some reason The Rump can't bear to share—or rather, can't abide the idea of sharing—the podium with Ms. Betzos. Might it be all her billions—but doesn't he, too, have billions to spare? But no sooner does he descend than several tikis step forward—or backward as the case may be—to hoist this tubbiest of gray eminences up into the stratosphere. Crushed shoulder blades (none are Navy Seals except for The Zink) is a small price to pay for active participation in such an apotheosis under the stars. As their chants rev up, Cantor can (it's never too late) think only about Evil—a word he never thought he'd use so freely—so unwittily—specifically two of the four concurrent causes thereof[214] (he hears bagpipes but there's no one there). But he doesn't want to do so

---

[213]Hold your horses—yes, the Master's way ahead of you—He knows He's already invoked Frederika—some might say exploited her—many times over but ever full of surprises and a firm believer in repetition as the stepmother of invention, He's invoking her from yet another new angle. And as a result His—and our—"surrounding air has a new lightness" (Ezra Pound, "A Virginal").

[214]See David Hume, *Dialogues Concerning Natural Religion* (e.g., London, Penguin Books, 1990). Part XI.

much thinking as to end up absolving the Master Builder—the Builder who's built The Rump—much less The Rump itself. Cause No. 2: *Conduct of life by general laws rather than by particular volitions.* That Master, knowing the secret springs of the universe as He does, could—but does not—turn all afflictions into the good of humans, and without exposing himself in so doing (if anonymity is a matter of insane pride). A few tailor-made touches applied, say, to the Rump's brain in infancy could have turned him into a Marcus Aurelius—or a Henry James, Sr.—thereby changing the face of the world. Cause No. 4: *Shoddy workmanship.* True enough, the parts of the universe all hang together down to its secret springs (in a manner of speaking). But ultimately (especially in the case of a Rump), every passion of the mind—and what's more useful than those passions (Envy, for example) as a spur to the greatness of misery—turns pernicious, breaches the bounds of utility and causes the greatest convulsions—but unfortunately not great enough to destroy the entire species, only the lucky few.

But Cantor knows he can't think his way out of this ever-changing mess. The chanters, driven hard by a love of death (and the love of death is no laughing matter), are bouncing their favorite strongman about on the trampoline of—of—of—what has a long way to go before it can begin to call itself frenzy. Emboldened by the absence of palpable protest, they descend upon the very Santa Barbarians the Transition Team has come to woo. Violence ensues: a young couple, their whole life ahead of them, are mowed down, also without protest. Mnunchkin (too cuddly a nickname, if you ask Moira—but is it a nickname?) can't pretend he hasn't seen The Rumpty (too cuddly a nickname as well—and this time you don't have to ask Moira), like Humpty, have a great fall. Thing is, he clearly doesn't want to wrinkle his linen suit (branded steer[ette] Loouuiise would be appalled)—perfect as it is for midsummer rallies overlooking the Pacific of which he suspects there'll be plenty more. But (here he rips a page or two from the playbook of *Little Dorrit*'s Mrs. Merdle) knowing full well what's expected of him and perceiving the exact nature of the fiction to be nursed, Munchkin takes it delicately in his arms (making sure not to rumple that suit), puts the required contribution of gloss upon it and proceeds to do his very best imitation of Coming Frantically to The Rump's Rescue—as frantically as he would expect The Rump to come to his own. Melanctha notes that as the Munch (not to be confused with The Mooch), assisted by hefty Cohn, tries to lift him, The Rump shrugs them off (executing what Gustave would have called *le geste juste*)—enough to send Munch's assisting hand sprawling into the dirt. From testes-less testicles on up through marrowless spine and into his duplicitous brain cells, the Secretary of the Treasury understandably trembles (will he be fired?)—as he did during the forever famous "very fine people on both sides" arioso in The Rump Tower—a watershed speech that both ushered in a new norm—and bestowed a gift on the dutifully revolted—an unwelcome gift hence the best of all possible gifts— the mouthless gift horse of a resuscitated sense of self. The Rump can croak for all Cantor cares—he's more concerned by what looks like a Ruger AR-556 strategically positioned between Eden and Borkman, Jr. Was it there before? The Ivankanemia is beside him, applying cold compresses to lips blubbery enough to make a tautog or Maori seaperch or blue catfish or morwong or carp, green with envy. She scowls at her lesser half, who, deep in conversation with Crown Prince Mohammed bin Salmon (after all, they are cousins), hasn't the faintest idea that his father-in-law is very much at risk. Anemia is willing to bet they're continuing their discussions on *strategy* which began during the unannounced trip of this boy wonder cum elder statesman to Saudi Arabia a while back and which lasted far into the night—until 4 a.m., according to some sources (and upon whose content the lumpenproletariat aka the American public has no right to expect to be briefed). Just goes to show that it's possible, thanks to the latest advances in chimaerism research, to be both a (4 a.m.) Pajama Boy *and* an alpha male—to serve as the battlefield upon which these seeming incompatibles engage in an irresolvable struggle for hegemony across the same blood-brain barrier. Although in the same breath it leaves one to wonder whether, stem cell successes notwithstanding, these two divide-and-conquerors spent all that time just chatting . . . i.e., whether Kuschner's far more of a PB than he lets on—least of all to his wife, which may go a long way toward explaining the scowl. But that's a subject for further (deliriously boring) research.

To Eden, Borkman, Jr., is laying out his platform for exploiting VR to generate a new species of privacy—one insusceptible to assault by Gucifers, whatever their iteration—one capable of deactivating prosecutorial gluttony. Maybe Cantor's been jumping the gun: the subject after all is harmless enough. "I thought that kind of privacy comes only when you're dead." After all he's been through, Eden is no longer impressed (was he ever?) by start-up hype. To prove that *his kind* has bigger balls—balls, not testicles—than anybody since Ronald Firbank, should Cantor dive into the conversation, seize the weapon and, as an extra, hurl it into the Pacific, without budging until he hears the splash? But when he looks again, the object is nowhere to be seen. The fog, settling over both foothills and ocean, gets busy editing out of the landscape much—most—of what it finds indefensible—old-hat. As the fog is just what the prose-doctor ordered—just the mentor Melanctha—a notorious over-writer—craves, she lavishly applauds its lucidity.

Noting that The Rump is temporarily (or, if they're lucky, permanently) out of commission, somebody who looks and talks like a journalist/campaign strategist takes center stage. But a somebody whose heart is in the right place (a misfortune hence a triumph in Rump world), or so Cantor needs to believe—a somebody who comes across as the embodiment of a highly successful mosaicist collaboration among types Cantor must believe still exist— types who've severed all ties with their Bad Narcissism and operate under the perk-less spell only of their addiction to public service (Ali Velshi, Frank Figliuzzi, Asawin Suebsaeng, David Fahrenhold, Katie Brenner and Eli Stokols types, for starters). In short, a pinup boy who does for bleeding-heart chumps like Cantor what Betty Grable did for the troops. Although maybe Cantor's allowing himself to be fooled—maybe he seeks the impossible. Whatever his ambitions, the somebody takes a stab at convincing those torchbearers who don't belong to the very-fine-people contingent that the country is undergoing a civil war—is on the road to becoming a police state. Which declares itself first as a devolution—an inversion—of language. Irrational recklessness is deemed the courage of commitment; hesitation, cowardice; deliberation, dereliction; moderation, effeminacy; and circumspection, laziness. It's irrational anger that's perceived as defining the real man—it's the man of violence who's deemed to be the credible being. But the violence of the man of violence is all talk (which explains this Rumpian love of generals)—he needs to be hysterectomized—to become, literally, an empty barrel. *Hysterectomized* is the last straw for the tikis. (Clearly the Munch and the atrophy bride aren't suffocated by the prospect of such an eventuality—they don't take it as a threat to soulhood since theirs resides in the capacity to go on consuming exactly the way Veblen said they shouldn't.) They set pinup boy on fire—er, try to, without a smidgeon of success. Ivankanemia would very much like to stand up for free speech—to show she's not just daddy's girl or at least not a daddy's girl *all the time* (just as during their pregnancy pregnant women aren't pregnant all the time). Only the time isn't ripe for self-rectification.

As for *Moira*, what she would like (her dreams are more modest) is to be able to triumph over life—on her own terms—before (it's inevitable) getting mowed down or torched. Specifically, to triumph over life *from the inside out* (without an adulterant fuck-you thrown in for puerile good measure) by, say, performing the "Rose Adagio" to perfection right here and now and thereby earning the right to fling all four canonical roses at the metrical feet of her first and only mother, the Aztecs' mighty Pacific. But she, too, must wait for the time to ripen, that is, for the moment when, in this, the eighth Bolgia of Dante's hell, *la mosca cede a la zanzara.* Cook wouldn't mind sexually harassing her (the MeToo groundswell notwithstanding): who could resist succumbing to this scared little waif (still scared, for all the superannuation)—the last living remnant of Second Avenue in its bustling pre-condominium-on-every-streetcorner prime? She senses his urge and utters the first apotropaism (yep [or rather, you're darn tootin'], *apotropaism*) that pops into her mind—easy enough, since it's already wedged tight between amygdala and insula. An apotropaism that does double duty—perpetrated on behalf of both Aurora and Cook's potential prey. To wit, *The time just ain't ripe.* He confesses—first to himself—he's sick and tired of being told that the time isn't ripe—for *the facts of the case.* (She can't remember having used this term, so why get her embroiled in a battle of self against self? But of course she could ask that of anybody, even those outside her profession.)

Post has arrived: yes, Tom Post, potentate of the pipeline who's been keeping a low profile until now (he's always had a soft spot for the California sun)—Post, who like Eliot's Tiresias, has seen and foresuffered all—Post who, now having *heard* all, has no choice but to jump in. For a long time, he's wanted to get even with Cook—but about what? they both wonder. He proceeds to admonish him but suavely, even if his blood his boiling. As he learned from his chief tool man, Toulmind—when Invidicum was just a soap bubble in a retort's eye—it's useless to ask for *the facts* (as if they could be pulled out of a rabbit's hat on demand) since in order for facts to exist at all they must be generated by and extracted from a man-made framework underpinned by a few highly specific observations—better yet, from a map riddled with just a few highly specific guideposts from which limitless topographical facts can be read off—facts—itineraries—undreamed of before they were lucky enough to be caught red-handed in the trawl of that map. The horizon of facts therefore expands to the extent that it constricts. (Post is aware he's trying to rebuild the most tenuous of connections between the two of them—a connection now pivoted on a mere word—*facts*—a word he couldn't have cared less about [as a captain of industry and master of none, he's never let the facts stand in his way] until a minute ago when Cook saw fit to let all hell break loose by investing it—the word—with his native pathos [a new word—or an old word like *facts* used with a new lightness—like the disease to which a healthy man suddenly succumbs—a new word, I say—or Kurt Goldstein says or Georges Canguilhem says—is a new form of life].) Cook lashes out—lashes back. Let's face it, the framework simply isn't out of the oven yet. Or rather, the framework is itself the oven and, as it turns out, it has still to be constructed but when the oven is good and ready to cook the books—I mean, the facts—they'll pop right out, burnt to a crisp hence good as new—good as warmed-over Breaking News. But now—after excoriating the Universe & Co.—he discovers that, in fact, he isn't hungry for the facts at all since they're little more than *arti*facts of the oven's minute-to-minute malfunction. Following in the footsteps of William Lloyd Garrison's followers he cries out, "To be without a plan—a framework—a map—is the true genius of the Abolitionist enterprise (since we're all slaves), especially with a Scum- cum Carpetbagger ruling the roost." But to his own jaded ears, Cook sounds more like faux man-of-the-people Orrin Hatch responding to "bullcrapper" Sherrod Brown's attack (gone predictably retroviral on YouTube) against The Rump's tax charade. But at least he (like Brown and unlike Hatch—or maybe even unlike Garrison, for that matter) can't be accused of sporting the contraption known as a contrast shirt (*Again with the contrast shirts!* shouts the old lady—the eternal troublemaker from Forest Hills[215]—who's had it with the Master's loony takes on the theme of the Eternal Return)—the last refuge of scoundrels and particularly repellent when the collar is drawn tight around a geezer's wattles—since as everybody knows, the sweat from a contrast shirt leaks (at least according to Aesop) all of the wearer's (not Hillary's) dirt.

Before Cook can graciously let bygones be bygones, Post is gone. Post's disgust at receiving counter-lessons makes him hungry for vengeance so he's the first to notice more than that single smoking Ruger. He observes Borkman, Jr., rummaging through a heap of what—to the practiced eye (and none more practiced than Post's)—look like weapons and their affiliates: SA-7 gripstocks, a heap of rifle scopes, hand grenades, forward-looking infrared

---

[215]Come to think of it, she resembles not a little—or rather, given half a chance she'd end up as the spittin' image of—the Judy Holliday character in *The Solid Gold Cadillac*. Furthermore, based on her track record of indomitable vocality, the little old lady from Forest Hills has been designated a worthy companion (piece) to (no mean feat) Dickens's "Man from Shropshire"—and slated for inclusion in the National Register of Historic Places.

cameras, bulletproof plates and a Smith & Wesson semiautomatic rifle. "Purchased at a souk on Facebook of all places!" he stage-hisses. Eden, on the other hand, must make do (because he's not the father of any start-up) with what look like—and not just to the practiced eye—a Remington shotgun and a Glock semiautomatic pistol (.40-caliber). There are also some metal casings scattered carelessly about: clearly the pair haven't had the time to convert them into . . . into . . . (what do they call it?) an 80 percent lower receiver and ultimately a weapon primed for every kind of slaughterhouse scenario. Post doesn't want to look as if he's perceived any particular threat—nothing must be allowed to ruffle Liepnits's feathers—since Liepnits is nearby—the very Liepnits who, if confirmed as head of the Food and Drug Administration (never has the resemblance to boarlike Gingerich been so acute), will be able to move mountains for Invidicum and all the pep pills that come after. Melanctha (who's, even within so limited a time and space, been having her share of run-ins with the boys' seminal naked gun which she's come to believe does pose a threat) is tempted to implore Eden and Borkman, Jr.—boys who never quite made it into manhood—to remember that no form of worldflow violence can compare (so why bother?) with the violence of *word*flow. Too late—they're not in the market for Enlightenment enlightenment.

The first targets are, as is only right and proper, the standouts on the conga line of ass-kissers: The McNunchkin and his beloved, Mick MacPrick (current head of the Consumer Financial Disaffection Bureau who's wasted no time showering his cronies with good deeds—a hiring freeze and help to Nexus Services in getting back in the business of selling detained immigrants into bail bondage), weasel-of-weasels Ayn Ryan, way-too-pious-for-some-tastes De La Pence, career Seroquel overdoser Ben Carssson and latest addition to the c-line, (ferocious waist-grabber) Margo. As he watches her fall (graceful, he must admit—an angel, in fact) as if she's looking forward to resting on her laurels for all eternity, Pritchard wonders (unable to forgo the personal even at a time like this when the very fabric of indecency is being ripped apart and its rancid practitioners revealed, now that *subterfuge is done*, for what they always were)—wonders whether the half-century of on-and-off hatred—the blistering tension—is the mere tributary—the icing on its cake— of a relation so profound, albeit on eternal life support, as to be able to not just withstand any amount of hatred but milk it for all it's worth, as cement—as a fuel and funnel for *caring* (whatever that smarmy term may signify out in the world of mice and men). At what point do they turn to each other and say, *We've outlived the hate even if the relation still very much depends on it*—we've done it *Our Way*? Or how long does it take—did it take—before the cord of connectedness, real or otherwise—before their Bridge of Sighs—broke definitively so as to reveal the abyss of hate beneath—all that hate as a tribute to their hate—constituting the relation with no remainder?

Funny, Borkman is wondering *the very same thing* (haven't you heard of a bicycle built for two?) about himself and the wife—albeit not so eloquently, i.e., uncompromisingly—even if this particular kind of wondering doesn't suit him. Just as certain roles never fit Moira Shearer. (*Yeah? Name one.*— Theme and Variations, *wiseguy*.) The Master is shaping Borkman's memories in accordance with what He knows Pritchard is thinking (what's wrong with that?). Under the seersucker, they're reconciled enemy brothers (straight out of René Girard's Book of Hours) and He's their Field of the Cloth of Gold.

The Rump thinks by playing dead that (a ploy, in his view, rendered plausible—even notarizable—by that 400-pound bone spur) he'll 'scape whipping. Not so. Thanks to Eden's sharp aim, his head's now half on, half off, an improvement in either case. The bloodstains do wonders for his tacky toupee (at least it doesn't stoop to oozing dye like Rudy's) and by some inverse miracle The Rump's still alive and kicking. Jean could shoot herself for not having realized what's staring her in the face only now (the fact she's never seen him up close is no excuse), to wit, that the Rump's hair is not a toupee, but a thoroughbred transplant fashioned to *resemble* a toupee as closely as possible. And that—as Frost would say—has made all the difference. Kellyannabella Kockenlocker and Sara Glanders, acknowledging that the end is near and the jig is up, decide to slake their too-long-suppressed thirst for each other upon the Field of The Rump's bloated belly (very much accentuated by the contour of his golf shirt, I might add), now that Fields are all the rage in the outerboroughs of tinseltown. In this, the pilot for *The Desperate Housewives of Silicone Valley* and in the best tradition of girl-girl porn, each takes a turn lapping—gobbling up the other's center of gravity (it's what's referred to by amateur anthropologists of the old school as *clit lit* in action) while the recipient obligingly—woolgatheringly—sucks on her own nipple—the nipple of her right implant. At moments, they bare their perfect teeth in anticipation of a big fat orgasm—or better yet (saving the real thing for life off camera but is there such a thing as life off camera for their kind?), mock orgasm. But the dos and don'ts of the scene matter less (in any case, they can't dawdle given the fate hanging over them) than their demeanor *while all this is going on*. It's a put-on—a defiant parody of a parody of what lesbians do (paid or unpaid) when left to their own devices. It's all about naughtily torturing the daddy behind the camera by unleashing his unfriendly unrequitable lust (their scowls run the gamut from amusement to agony, both contrived, or so the too-discerning spectator needs to think before his own orgasm ruins everything). When push comes to shove, though, they're just little girls trying to be big girls (their gestures after all are prissy, bossy, dogmatic) by getting the business of grooming each other just right. In this case, daddy is of course none other than—you guessed it—State of the Ass, Scum of the Earth Rump, whom they unknowingly hate for having to disseminate his tall tales for a pittance though enterprising Kockenlocker hardly needs the cold cash. It's the double exposure she loves—it's driving ostensibly exasperated anchors like Chris Cuomo to take refuge in an apoplectic fit, which may or may not be simulated. Ethan—whose life may end up in ruins if the tax bill passes its gas, which it probably will—loathes the Ass with a loathing so vast—the kind of loathing that makes the blood boil and run cold all at once. The kind of hate whose obverse should but couldn't possibly be—compassion.

The perfect time, then, for the resurrected chimeric journalist mentioned above, standing guard over The Rump's body and smart enough to be wearing a bullet-proof vest, to shout at the top of his lungs that he/she is sick and tired of his/her fellow journalists' referring to The Rump as, e.g., a seven-year-old in the body of an ancient (which is to do the world's kids—not to mention its sociopaths—the rankest of injustices). Sick and tired of their forever parsing (prompted by this or that MSNBC anchor) his 280-character inanities, and (adding insult to injury) respectfully beginning the exercise thus: "So, this is a President who . . ." as if it isn't a sin—an outrage—a self-shaming of the first water—to call The Rump *President*. No blessed seven-year-old, he's more than happy to go on serving, thanks to a bulk that's all midriff and oxy*moroni*cally tiny hands, as a screen—a screen memory—whether intentionally or not (worse in fact, if unintentionally)—for the antics of his band of Tricky-Dickish elves—elves like SchPruitt and Wilburr and that ghoulish Roger Stonehenge character, some (though unfortunately not all) of whose dementia has taken up residence in the Nixon tattoo stitched into his pimply back, and of course The Mnoonch (funny, he's been called lots of things but never an elf), to name just a few (though they'll never look quite so elfin as Hard-prayin' Pence and Smirkin' Ryan)—more than happy to screen them while they go shamelessly about their bloody business of teaching widows and orphans and veterans and the disabled, among others, a long-overdue lesson. Supremely sick and tired—and sad—to hear them wishful-thinking with as much conviction as a fake sleepwalker that this is a President who, if only he'd stop tweeting . . . stop tweeting . . . stop tweeting (*but why? so abstinence can transform him irreversibly into the beatific Anti-Rump of everybody's dreams???*).

It's Jaranemio who's up next at the plate of belated obliteration (too bad he won't be able to broker that once-in-a-lifetime peace deal between Beijing and Jersey City—a coup that has eluded droves upon droves of his betters), followed by nemesis Rex Tillerville—or is it Kush who's the other's nemesis? In any case, by collapsing on top of him, State Department Eviscerator-General Rex manages at long last to get his own back by suffocating the Senior Adviser's proliferating suppurations. Since as it turns out, the bullets are as magic as Ehrlich's—they're coated with very fast acting *Yersinia pestis*. In short, a sort of Thucydidean plague has come hot on the heels of the NRA-subsidized slaughter—a plague like Hesiod's Pandora—but a Pandora who in this case purposefully didn't slam down the lid of her jar of evils before Hope could escape. And by the way, who says you can't take it with you? From the look of 'im, even pestilential Kush has every intention of smuggling his insipid dimples (tax-free) into the House of the Walking Dead tenanted exclusively by robots who are only pretending to be robots and who in turn are only pretending . . . And as for taking it with you, ditto Tillerston (who intended to resign just before The Rump fired him) only in his case it's not insipid dimples but an insipid Order of Friendship badge—a Putin special—that'll be whisked through customs on his way south of the border. Borkman, Jr., has just determined (it's come to him in a vision shaped like an asteroid heading mercilessly Earthward) that *Sr. prefers to be remembered as some monster progenitor rather than as—monsters being way more photogenic—your garden-variety despicable dad with one or two redeeming traits* and perceives (though not through the auspices of some vision) that the tikis—especially their very fine contingent—feel they've been patient long enough and that it's now time for them to meet their maker but not before empty retching is followed by violent convulsions, palpitations and paralysis, which come across (to those who jest at scars 'cause they've never felt a wound) as all of the symptoms of outsize luxuriation in eternal well-being. Their bodies are breaking out in blisters and sores and their burning is such that they can't bear contact even with very light clothing—can't bear anything except to go naked—and would be happiest plunging into ice water. Wishful thinking. Oddly enough, though, there's no wasting—they're no longer in life and only Life is a wasting disease. Indeed, they're holding out surprisingly well against—are almost nourished by—their suffering—as they never were in the artful guise of goosesteppers by torchlight. Good news for malevolence, though: their Camp Auschwitz Ts have been left unscathed. But even those few who appear to be surviving through the most strenuous efforts are no match for the long-overdue siege of their extremities which leaves them without genitals, fingers and toes and, in some cases, without their eyes as well. It shows itself, this plague, to be completely different from any familiar disease inasmuch as all the birds known to feed off men—hummingbirds, juncos, scrub jays, towhees, finches, wrens, coots and kestrels—keep their distance. Before he himself is gunned down, Tactless Deputy HHS Secretary Erick Hargann informs the crowds (where is Price's formidably folksy bedside manner when it's needed most?) that no cure seems to be working.

What can you say about trouper Kellyannalucia Kockenlocker at such a juncture except (even if her pancake is fissuring like the walls of an outhouse well past its prime) that in executing her hag's Dance of Death with a vengeance (although not before—or, better yet, while at the same time—imploring everybody, living, dead or in-between, not only to not vote for Doug Jones who's soft on crime and much too hard on the KKK but, far more importantly, to go buy what's left of Ivanka's stuff [thereby thumbing her nose yet again at the Hatchet Act])—except that in executing her Dance she outperforms all of her illustrious predecessors. Kockenlocker has no time to spare for The Suckabee who's in any case almost a distant memory (right forefinger pointed with her signature slatternly dismissiveness at some unseen member of the press), now that she's been beaten to a bloody pulp by one of the tikis, who not so incomprehensibly mistook her for one of those bleeding-heart liberals with a knack for "dividing her time" between (post-industrial) Tribeca and Palo Alto. The two boys—whose mission has done what no amount of psychotherapy could, i.e., turned them miraculously into men—are necessarily, if all too predictably, saving The Rump for last. Astonishingly his jowls are showing signs of life. Eden and Borkman, Jr., agree (it's obvious from the last looks they give each other) that they've been fools to expect the Mueller investigation to deliver him up in chains to his accusers—at least, this quickly. Until then (if you ask Borkman, Sr.), a few good Lizzie Borden-style strokes of havoc would at least draw his attention to what surely must someday await him.

Hard to tell who's dying from bullet wounds, who from the plague itself and who from a heady mix of the two. While this kind of uncertainty may very well tickle the fancy of the overeducated members of the East and West Coast elites (at their mere mention sledgehammer booing from the Base), the unregenerately non-elite Goldman Sachs crowd—just plain folks like The Munch and The Cone and Harvard-illiterated Kush—will have no truck with it: they prefer to take life—like their scotch—straight. Things like ambiguity and nuance (though there's no room for nuance where The Rump and his gushing goons are concerned) are for sissies—Pajama Boys. Yet there's a silver lining though the night sky is cloudless: based on her stirring performance, KellyKocken (as sort of noted above, the greatest Salome, hands down, since Gloria Swanson) has, by acclamation, become the standard-bearer of the tikis. What does it matter if she's too weak to be carried on the shoulders of the precious few who've dodged the bullets successfully? Melanctha has taken refuge behind the Durea family mausoleum or rather (since there's no real desire to be, even if it means fame, stretched out on the rack of this tough world a millisecond longer) she just happened to collide with it. She looks around her and wonders if this final scene (really a sequence according to the standards set by D.W. Griffith)—this depiction of war as waged by men on men—is organic to the Master's main design, that is, if there is any. Or does it constitute a war on bigger game—organicity itself, i.e., is it just a coda which can be lopped off at will without mutilating in tandem the delicate sensibilities of the peanut gallery—though who is she to mock a peanut? *What a scoundrel you are, Herbert,* thinks Melanctha. *In the midst of all this carnage, created at no small cost to the Studio, all you can think about—while the budget officer's clock goes on ticking full speed ahead!—is what is or isn't* organic. She needs to be assured that ages and ages hence, this sequence so-called—still fresh as a daisy—will be decreed to be in fact just that—organic in town and inorganic in the country. Or is it the case that the sequence started out with the very best of intentions only to be bulldozed by the Master (sworn enemy of best intentions)—avoided like the plague—sabotaged every step of the way once He started to feel it was fast getting out of control—already pledging its allegiance to another god than he—an *alternate* god (who's not like a prosthetic one)? To think that He could stoop to jealousy toward his own spawn—devour his children Cronus style.

The survivors alone—for there already are survivors—have time to spare for pity, divining rightly that the disease doesn't attack the same person twice—or at least not fatally. They entertain the hope—while administering last rites even to those who appear to be well on their way to recovery—that never again will they be mowed down by some other behemoth—that theirs is a universal immunity—including to life itself at least as mediocrities like Rumps, Jr., III, IV and V (a mere sum of sequels with no generative original in the franchise) tend to live it. Hallowed burial rites are thrown to the dogs—literally. Shameless, Graham-Cassidy, Orrhin the Hatch, Moscow McCo (the shape of his wisdom-wizened mouth more of a perfect asshole than it's ever been) and up-and-coming (probably *forever* up-and-coming) ex-wrestling coach Gym Jordan (who could ever have imagined that the House's favorite slouching posturing punk famous for turning a blind eye to the molestation of college students in his charge would end up tearily begging their whistleblowing teammates to refrain from exposing such cowardice?) not to mention fellow coward, *Mr. Smith Goes to Washington* wannabe and "scholar-warrior" Josh Whoreley, one of Yeats's "worst" (i.e., full of [the phoniest] passionate intensity you'd ever care to fumigate out of existence), to name but a few—shameless, they've been engaged in setting fire to the pyres on which they've unceremoniously thrown the corpses of what appear to be lowly staffers. (Tillerson has no staff to worry about since he—incapable in any case of charitable worry—axed the whole lot of 'em all in the name of—of—of . . . what precisely? and in the axing department SPruitt ain't far behind [he may even be way ahead].) They explain to disapproving crawlersby—or crawlersby they take to be disapproving—that such harmless profanation reflects, alas, a distraughtness arising from unvanquishable efforts to sabotage—even now in this, their last extremity—the Democrats' "unconscionable" sabotage of the Freedom Carcass's [*sic*] foolproof plan for lowering that pesky debt ceiling which entails, inter alia, lavishing massive tax cuts on the venerable one percent of the one percent of the one percent and rewarding behemoths like Apple and Pfizer with behemoth tax breaks for a better-late-than-never, it-comes-from-the-heart repatriation of trillions in offshore-generated profits. So the point, ultimately, of these six plus male witches is that sabotage—like Envy and cholesterol—can be good or bad. On one of the heaps, Melanctha recognizes instantly, even in his present state of tipping-point decomposition, what can only be the Master—not The Rump— not the State of the Ass—but *her* Master, the kind of master—a master builder, really (which makes her none other than Hilda Wangel)—in whose footsteps any acolyte, willing or unwilling, could be proud to follow given half a chance. Neither words—nor even blood—or even a mixture of words and blood—can convey the delight, even under such conditions, of meeting Him at long last. Still, such a recognition scene deserved more of a build-up—more fanfare. She attempts, as a mother would, to stroke away the sweat of His brow. But He's strong enough to recoil—to touch Him is to reopen his wounds—lance His boils—penetrate His bowels—tear Him apart. It all comes back to her— what she unspeakably deduced from His packets—deduced by putting two and two together—namely, that He must hate being so aggressed even under the best of circumstances, even in the name of motherly solicitude. *Perché mi scerpi?* He cries out. But immediately feels the obligation to assure His brightest pupil—brightest because on too many occasions to count she managed to turn self-doubt into high art—it's only by virtue of the lancing—of the tearing Him apart—that He's able to speak to her at all. There's no power of utterance until blood flows from the wound—since it's blood alone—with a dash of pus—that can carry His voice—His speech—His words—out into the world, of which He's taking his leave at last or hasn't she noticed? (The Master, for the moment a prisoner of parentheses, is ordered by *His* master to assure her this is no rebuke—just a chuck under the chin by her biggest admirer.) So—pain alone can open the sluicegates of wordy blood and bloody words. Ever the showman—though hardly on the scale of A Rump—He confesses and delights in confessing that it's all about that last refuge of scoundrels—the *fanno dolore, ed al dolor fenestra* effect. *Fanno dolore, ed al dolor fenestra:* by the way, the most beautiful chiasmus—or whatever it's called—in literature hence in life (see above, he thinks). He's caught her off guard. After all, one doesn't always get to bump into one's Master, especially after business hours.

Remembering the recoil from the stroking of His brow and, as a blistering bonus, the outcry, she's convinced that before they parted she should have at least said, "I'll do better next time" even if after all their time together surely she must know that for a consort such as he—Victoria to her Albert—what she felt compelled to give was already far more than he could withstand—without resorting to Dante as lifejacket. Conscientious recoil is all he has to give back and it's a real gift because he's come by it honestly—characterologically—epigenetically—cumulatively—evolutionarily—in a word, painfully. It's the best he has to offer—precisely because it costs him a mammoth exertion (which doesn't get any less mammoth with time). *Master to Melanctha:* Recoil's the only act that doesn't misrepresent the actor or digress from, impede or disrupt his quest for a dreaded selfhood—or tamper with the quest's blessed futility. And as the Master practices it, recoil becomes a sign of probity—proof positive that what He cannot give to her He doesn't—will never—give—wouldn't dream of giving—to any other. Recoil's the supreme token of His love. Sealed with the withholding of a kiss—the secret of which he's passed on, as you may recall, to Martin Eden, His protégé, late of Madison Square Park (south-east corner).

On the same heap lies The Mnunch—still smug, prissy and portentous (Melanctha can tell since he's wet his pantaloons and the piss looks—even if it doesn't smell—fresh)—and The Mitch (who's at least *trying* to look as if he's about to reprise his gone-viral nose-thumbing "harr-harr" in response to something just around the bend—something that's on the order of Steve Bannon's swaggering ten-gallon death threat which was what gave rise to it initially). At this very moment Munch's portmanteau trophy wife, child bride and veteran of Fort Knox and the Congo (or rather, of the *shadow* of the Congo) is elbowing her opera gloves (and glasses) into—way way into—the tram. The Munch must have eyes in the back of his head since he's able (just before the doors shut forever) to clench and shake his fists and shriek (what Dem ever dared to say he can't walk and chew gum at the same time?!), "LooLoo—after all I've done for you!" Poor thing, he's awakened the interest of that nine-lives journalist fellow who, throwing his microphone to the winds, asks if Steven— "Steven," The Munch incorrectly corrects—with true Park Ave dowager pique. —asks if *Stevie boy* can explain why the much-promised analysis of The Rump tax cut never surfaced—you know, the one on which Treasury staff had been working non-stop ever since the inauguration-with-the-biggest-turnout-ever —a turnout greater than Suzanne Farrell's—greater than Moira's.

"First of all, it did surface," he prissily (while going easy on the smugness) replies. "Second, it's all the trophy bride's fault. Her overpriced barrel organ got in the way." Clearly it's no longer the case that (*pace* M. Chevalier) birds in the trees seem to Twitter LooLoouuiise. Confusingly, Steve[n] adds, "But let the Mitch speak for himself. After all, *harr-harr* isn't the only polysyllable he knows." (So, for a change, the scuttlebutt wasn't all hot air: not only has each taken the other under his wing but not since Paolo and Francesca have two beings ever hit it off so passionately in record time.) But Mitch's buccal sphincter is wired too tight—intentionally, since he's taking this opportunity—on the shitheap, before he expires—to look back on his checkered career as yet another self-respecting killer of the American dream (which thanks to the hijinks of his one-man UnFreedom Carcass is currently not only all wet but on life support). And making for a less arduous trek down memory lane, the indecent 2016 refusal to meet with his very own Banquo's ghost—very-much-alive Supreme Court nominee Merrick Garland, now destined for bigger though not necessarily (owing to a timorous temperament—to an ultimate or maybe even penultimate self-sabotaging aversion to the vulgar eloquence of much-warranted rage) better things—has elected to meet him halfway. Aside from a slight shiver at the unduly ceremonious reminder of that indecency, he has no regrets—and no apologies for a legacy buttressed by the strategic necessity of installing militant incompetents in every smelly nook and cranny of the judiciary. For incompetence—like mediocrity (with which it is often confused—aptly)—is, in the right hands, an inexhaustible civic resource—indeed, a National Treasure. After all, besides saving his billionaire donors, not to mention the Base, from abominations like birth control, didn't he recommend, in true grim-reaper style atonement, that The Rump make Banquo head of the FBI? But suddenly—SUDDENLY!—retrospection is no longer relevant—is "no longer an option," as they say—for just in on somebody's iPhone is breaking news of the successful passage of the tax cut (né reform) BILL—that nefarious farrago of midnight-ride surrenders to megadonor greed. Even Susie Collins (whose much-touted decency is very much a thing of shreds and patches)—and on-again-off-again maverick-in-chief Jeff McFlake—were all too willing to capitulate once their slimmest of demands—er, timid requests—had been met by the slimmest of last-minute conciliatory provisions. No need to ponder how and why things went wrong—no need simply because, as it turns out (guess what!?), they *never did*—that is to say, they never did now that all of his tenure's negatives have, through the magic of lethal contamination by this signature achievement, been retroactively converted into past positives. Which means his cronies, underlings included, can go on to fulfill an even bigger death wish—by applying lean strokes of havoc to those three overfed billygoats gruff: Medicare, Social Security and Medicaid. But you simply can't blame Ayn Rand entirely for their eagerness—especially jellyfish Ryan's eagerness—to fulfill this poor excuse for a vision. *Ah, words*, thinks Melanctha (in general and apropos of nothing—and everything) *how easily they sanctify the speaker's poor excuse for outrage at social injustice—castrating that outrage by applauding his* way with them. *When I can think like this*, thinks the speaker, *not everything is wrong with the world*. Not long, the wily Wizened One suspects, before his triumph is chiseled in stone—and if posterity plays its cards right, his statue will soon be standing right next to those of Jefferson Davis, George Wallace, David Duke and Judge Roy and Sheriff Joe, referred to by Kluxers as the holy trinity plus two. To get a sense of how low-level mountebanks in his neck of the woods make ends meet (in case he one day needs to make his own ends meet by writing a filmable novel about the wonderful world of pharmaceuticals), Post, still germ-free, is handing out free preservatives, PPE, potions and pills (whose ingredients have all been extracted from various tainted batches of Invidicum parked somewhere northwest of the Mojave Desert), mainly among the tikis. Which means he's doing nothing more than urging them to poison themselves out of a fear of infection—to turn them into victims of a kind of secondary plague. Some follow Melanctha's unwitting example by crouching in the shadow of mausoleums and crypts, driven to do so by the belief, or the hope, that contact, however fleeting, with these semi-sacred igloos will immunize them against the very suffering they were once (i.e., minutes ago) egged on by The Rump to jeer at.

It's suggested by somebody—not any old somebody, mind you, but Liepnits—who, dodging bullets right and left, appears to be handling widowerhood quite well, even—especially—under present conditions (since finding ways to outlive them blunts the edge of his grief—or would, if he had any edge to blunt)—it's suggested by the aforesaid somebody that only the trial subjects can stop the massacre—by convincing the ringleader his envy of all the unicorns who've shown up for this shindig gone bad is curable even if their own case histories prove it isn't. As for Borkman, Jr.'s status as unassailable failure, well, it's far too much to expect that in his present state he could conceive of how future digitizers of unicorn history will surely value documented failures far more than the rich and famous (doges and dealmakers), whose success stories always outdo each other's and are therefore always the same. However, before they can act on his suggestion—now a command—The Rump gets up on his hind legs and in doing so throws last-ditch sapphics Kellyanne and Sarahuck off balance—evicts them from their very own private Lesbos (they manage to crawl back on, or in). The Rump ignores the tikis who are dropping like flies—especially the very finest among them (too dumb to have gone over to the other side as so many others, tikis and non-tikis alike, have already done). Now it's every man for himself—but when has it not been for this tomboy from Queens? Cantor is not pleased (maybe it's the news of the tax cut and the grim prospect of an inevitable smelly love fest of limp-dicked Republicans in the notorious Rose Garden that's soured him on the notion of deriving amusement from all things State of the Ass). Adding insult to injury, it's the opposite of heartwarming to perceive that The Rump's head is no longer half-on half-off (all an illusion: a stereoscopic effect of murky light and shimmering shadow) but very much, alas, where it should be. In short, he looks healthy as a horse or should he say, taking a page from the Master's many-editioned hornbook of hyperbole, *the healthiest he's ever been.* But speak of the devil, who's that Melanctha is talking to? Is it by any chance *He*—the Master, in whose existence nobody believed—believes? Something tells Cantor it is since when she attempts to kiss His cheek He recoils (after all, he's the Flemish Master of Recoil, if of nothing else), a gesture appropriate to one whose skull—brain—mind is His home away from home—more home than home—His only home. You might say—if you wanted to delude yourself—that such gestures have long been an occupational hazard of Masters. He turns his back on this failed relation—doesn't want Melanctha to know so brutal a humiliation has been witnessed—and in its entirety—even by so stalwart a partisan as he. Though maybe the recoil was meant to signal to His favorite—His aptest pupil—something far more endearing than recoil but transmissible only on its wings. And let's say the Master dies, she can't help thinking. Then what? Is she by virtue of so fateful a move given license to assume that it casts a retrospective sunset glow of clarification over all their doings? Or is it—the move, I mean—all in a day's work? no more of a key to their doings than any other? Transmogrifying (that's *transforming* with a capital *T*) the chimaera to be pilloried henceforth and forever as MiLady Kockenlocker-Fuchkabee—transmogrifying it into a podium cum deathbed—The Rump puts forth his demand, at this NurembergRallyland gala to end all galas, for Loyalty with a capital *T* (and not just from all the Comey lookalikes in the audience). Clearly, the prospect of death is less fearsome than vanity unfed. Cantor, guided by his now signature souring, recalls with what dismal respectfulness[216] the otherwise endearing panelists on *Hard Balls, All In, TRMS, The Beat, The Last Word* and *The Eleventh Hour* would routinely unconstruct this recurring demand as something new—fresh—worthy of a maliceless pondering. Instead of jumping up apoplectically and bellowing epileptically, *Who is this Self-inflating Asshole Slumlord—this Sub-Mediocre Rump U Dropout—to be deemed worthy of framing as a conceivable—a plausible—demander of loyalty? Who does he think he is? Who do we think he is when we parse* (fancy word for *slice and dice*, itself a pseudo "hip replacement" for that "creaking joint" *look upon*) *said demand with the straightest of faces?*—instead of doing anything of the kind, they would commence their unconstruction with the same refrain, i.e., *So: This is a president who . . .* Just as offensive as referring to him as your garden-variety ninety-one-year-old man whose corruptness is just a matter of being *fixed in his habits*—a phrase that makes those habits harmless—almost cuddly—with a pathos (if you know where to look) all their own. All comparisons that normalize—humanize—like calling him a daycare center flunk-out—should be *verboten* and not just among members of the press.

From the look and desperate sound of 'im, the D in Chief must be smelling—reading—in the tea leaves of his every fart, his every stool specimen, pursuit and imminent capture by ferociously apostolic Mike McFlynn, the fawning Flipper, the much too Friendly Seal (somebody should remind him the good sycophant knows his place and keeps it). Of course The Rump could resort to one of his signature gestures and, while training a mocking eye on the crowd, point for its benefit to Mike as he goes about shrieking his warlord's praises which gesture would mean *I'm all this feebly flattering lunatic—this particularly alarming specimen of genus Homo* (The Rump, a maiden at heart, is frightened by the ferocity of Mike's fealty: on some level doesn't quite know what to make of it)—*says I am—and more—but addiction to flattery is just one of my changes of garment and I'm perfectly capable of regulating my intake* especially *when I'm in fact infinitely greater than what he—or anybody else—says I am* and even more especially *when I know you know*

---

[216]Lest they lose access to the current WH staff. Who have a habit of leaking more than an ER dialysis tube—the sort of ER invoked by none other than now postmodern Sunday painter George W. Bush as incontrovertible proof that top-quality health care (for, e.g., the tumor-riddled brats of the death's-door poor—you know, the vermin who squander all their ill-gotten gains, Grassley style, on booze, women and . . . movies!!!) did indeed exist.

that Daddy's heart belongs only to you, the Misforgotten. Thing is, he's too wound up to be in the mood or the market for ass-kissing. So where, then, Cantor asks, is Ty Cobb—or, more to the point, Ty's handlebar cat's meow—to soothe the maiden's flabby savage breast? For Cantor anything'd be better than the desperation since his biggest fear—well, not exactly his biggest—is that The Rump is gunning—spoiling—for an Apocalyptic Moment which in its eloquence will cancel out all previous pigotries. But apocalyptic or not—and he's sure Melanctha (the best thing that ever happened to him) would concur—The Rump, even with a monologue up his sleeve poised to rival Father Mapple's or the Grand Inquisitor's or Father Coughlin's or *Father Knows Best*'s, does not deserve to be the star of the Final Sequence. Problem is, Cantor's run out of mathematical metaphors capable of cutting him down to size. Yes, of course he's a Dedekind cut, for better or worse, into the flab of bourgeois rationality—in fact the last Dedekind cut standing. But by virtue of being both old hat and applicable to everybody, that epithet cannot be expected to exert a lasting obliterative impact.

In any event, Cantor will never forget—or convinces himself he'll never forget—how eagerly the members of the Base are lining up (even if it means dodging bullets though there's talk On the Street of an imminent curfew)—panting in anticipation of The Rump's next stab at fulfillment of their need to be conned while knowing full well they're being conned—and by not just any old sodomizer but one who relentlessly—expertly—disavows whatever it is he's ejaculated minutes ago or centuries before—one of a kind who's found a way—*the way*—to be falsely true to himself at every instant and hence to not then be false to any Cro-Magnon man. How could they have ever gone on believing in him—and in themselves—if, after bluster-ingly vowing not to raise their taxes, he didn't follow through and do the raw opposite? How believe if after bludgeoning Obama for too much nine-hole truancy The Rump didn't go on to beat him many many many times over at his own game? By skinning their susceptibility alive, the Base's wonder boy offers purest proof of his swamp-draining trustworthiness—and as it just so happens, he's archangel Felix Sater's boy as well (though none of these sali-vators have ever heard of said archangel)—Sater who roundly threatened to "get [The Rump] elected" once he got Putin's team in on the underlying quid pro quo. By proxy, always by proxy, the Base propagates evil (as if it needed any further propagation especially through their puny auspices). The Rump applauds their applause. And they have every reason to applaud. For one thing, hasn't Putin himself called The Rump a genius? This is reassuring—for it proves The Putin knows our poor excuse for a genius has been and contin-ues to be supremely playable—and if he's playable then his criminal vanity is prosecutable and if he's prosecutable he's just steps away from the stiffest of sentences. And yet, Cantor needs to remain well aware—otherwise he'd be maligning everything Berry Sundae taught him—that any such aspersions cast on The Genius are always just exaggeration in the name either of profes-sional advancement or of (as in his case) extracurricular self-glamorization.

There is a certain cunning in The Rump's gaze of which he himself is (as usual?) unaware—but to be fair, in this case it's a cunning mixed with—

indistinguishable from—longing—vulnerability—all neatly framed by the imminence of death and a by no means happy one. Or is it the wordflow—the wordflow's deviation from itself—its self-curvature—that in this case is doing the talking for the two of them—i.e., the case of turning *cunning* (which was simply minding its own business) into *cunning mixed with longing* but without any hard evidence—much less permission from Cantor—except wordflow's gut feeling? But why must he always assume that words—his words—depicting—subjugating—some parcel of worldflow—i.e., in one-to-one correspondence with that parcel's particles—why must he assume they are just too weak to resist deviating from the correspondence once their attraction to each other gets too strong? Why must he always assume that the organism that is wordflow is so systematized as to prevent the gist of any stretch of worldflow he's contracted them to make manifest from being articulated? And why is Cantor always so reluctant to heap praise on himself for getting the worldflow-into-wordflow right? But doesn't it—It—a little like Margo's *It*—the banal paranoid strain which is what Margo's *It* is all about—doesn't it all boil down to the fact that every sentence, even the least self-aware, gets going with only one thought in mind—to get out of the clutches of language (you can fight language only with language)—and the sentence has got to believe that if it goes on long enough then language will be left far behind? Cantor doesn't know if through such thinking he's poaching on Melanctha's preserves[217] or simply covering for her while she grieves. The Rump, in so many words, tells the Base he's just come to recognize that thanks to them, he's grown up. After all, until the first rally he had no development at all (The Rump, Cantor insists to himself, is suddenly sounding like a—*the*—Great White Whale). It's from the first rally he must date his life. A second has scarcely passed at any time between the first rally and now that he hasn't unfolded within himself. Through their applause, he's learned what they wanted and returned the favor by (apt student of dialectics that

---

[217]Or is it on the preserves of one Ludwig Wittgenstein (not Melanctha's) that he's presuming to poach—the very Ludwig at whose *Haus* (Vienna, Kundmanngasse) Cantor dragged Berry Sundae to gawk (he'd been invited to deliver the funeral oration at the only Dizney World Congress of Metamathematical Magpies ever convened) and in the middle of a snowstorm, no less—the very Ludwig whose purely philanthropic stake in the Tennessee Wittgenstein Dinner Theater Learning Annex in Bad Wildbad was bought out by the profit-mad Black Forest flunkeys of Martin Heidegger. But why shouldn't Cantor go a-poaching for wasn't it that very Ludwig who stole his thunder—doused his flame—with the most gnomic and sexually explicit logico-philosophical proposition ever set both to music and in stone, i.e., wasn't it that very Ludwig who dared to write: "Language disguises the thought; so that from the external form of the clothes one cannot infer the form of the thought they clothe, because the external form of the clothes is constructed *with quite another object* (Cantor's italics) than to let the form of the body be recognized"? And if you don't believe me then go see for yourself—see Ludwig Wittgenstein, *Tractatus Logico-Philosophicus*, C.K. Ogden, translator (London, Routledge and Kegan Paul, 1983), 4.002 (4).

he is[218]) giving them always a little more than they bargained for. "Well, haven't I?" (*wild applause:* after all, with no more than three little words he's just demonstrated how a master goes about coddling the ingratitude and overlooking the forgetfulness of his vassals). However, with regard to things they *didn't* want—at least quite so much—what he doesn't say is that he's given them even less until now it no longer matters what he gives or what he withholds as long as the words keep coming—the words he's taught them to teach him in a language they can both understand—the language of alternative facts since the world—Rump world—is the totality of alternative facts, not of things. More to the point, nothing matters as long as their wild applause keeps coming, to which the only response is *his*.

Ayn the Ryan is staggering in the direction of The Munch and The McMitch (oh, did I forget to mention that Moscow Man's a wily heartless bastard?)—he's been hit below the belt but, with spreadsheets under his arm, still manages the heretofore impossible feat of packing weaselly self-importance and choir-boy self-depreciation into a single sad-eyed smirk. Looks as if he were about to cry out, *I'm carrying a spreadsheet—maybe even a non-paper on Afghanistan—maybe even a Heritage Foundation Petri dish—i.e., I'm a policy guy—worse, your* go-to *policy guy.* Thus bearing no small resemblance to the succulent flappers of today who—heedless of the curses of cabbies, pigeons and other pedestrians—proclaim with nitwit defiance: *Look at me! I have a smartphone! And I can audition into it and cross the street* at the same time! *Which means I'm traffic-stopping gorgeous! sleek as a spreadsheet! a star! now and forever! Hope the Hick descending from Air Force One in a polka-dotted miniskirt can't begin to compare!* As if remembering conquests too numerous to individualize Borkman, Sr., in a hokier than hokey simulation of wistfulness, mumbles, *And they may be right.* Thing is, the simulation wasn't anywhere near poignant enough to have earned him the right (even when nobody's listening) to add on the phrase *every last one of them* (which he promptly does) and shamelessly vend it as not just yet another specimen of but the very last word in anonymous wistfulness.

Things are subsiding—the dead are being left to bury the dead. The tikis—most of all the least fine—are overwhelmed by the task ahead of them. By and large, the unicorn boys (confuse them with the PJs at your peril)—even the *would-be* contingent—have weathered the storm and will probably survive for five-hundred years—that is, until Travis Kalashnickov gets himself elected president and Jeff Bezos finally does his part for the war effort by serving, now and then, as Secretary of State. Pleasant by the way to know it will be hours before the police arrive and the event is relegated to the status of warmed-over Breaking News. The tram is hanging by a thread from a single cable (is Luxury-Brand carnivore LooLoouuiise still alive?) and all exits are definitively barred. So there's enough time for Borkman, Jr., to lay down his arms, and beg forgiveness. To break the ice he says (limply)

---

[218]And why not? Didn't he attend the best Ivy League school? Isn't his IQ off the charts? (If he's a fucking moron, then he's a fucking-moron *savant.*)

something to the effect that there's nothing like a massacre to stir things up in a cemetery—sort of the way the right Overture (to, say, Weber's *Oberon* or better yet Rossini's *Semiramide*) can be counted on to whip well-heeled concertgoers into a well-bred frenzy—of self-congratulation. Only the warhorse he invokes—in fact, recruits (by humming a bar or two of its most famous section)—is the overture to *Guillaume Tell* (treasured relic of his disowned father's *Lone Ranger* schooldays) and why not? He does his confessing mainly (like Shawn the Spicer, The Mooch [not to be confused with the Mnuntch] and The Fuchkabee) to an audience of one. If you must know, it was boredom—but most of all shyness exacerbated by stage fright or vice versa—that drove him to make short work of a small part of the scum of the earth. Having unburdened himself (The Rump clearly hasn't heard a word) he orders Eden (Hercules to his Hamlet—Hyperion to his Satyr), upon whose not-quite-brawny shoulders the mantle of captain of industry is soon gently to be laid, to evict The Rump from the podium he's just made of his incoherence, forcibly if need be. Don't worry—the sleazeball Repubs won't defend him. Having signed the tax bill, he's no longer needed. And if they themselves are mauled and marmaladed by their insuranceless constituents in '18 and '20, so be it. Anyway, they're too old to die. All this by way of preface to a cliffhanger to end all cliffhangers: He's going to demonstrate there's a new cure for Envy on the block—a real cure—a cure ungovernably enriched. Or rather an old cure but repackaged as it should have been way back on Greenwich Avenue (which oversight accounts for the fact that the cure rate has been so low—so low that even the California sun could do nothing to lift its spirits) though this is no time for regret whose only purpose, even under the best of circumstances, is to decrease blood oxygen in our old fair-weather friend, the bilateral ventral striatum. And if The Rump doesn't come through as guinea pig extraordinaire/proband in chief or in any other guise, then he'll be decapitated ISIS style. Although curing him wouldn't stand in the way of their making the cemetery a kettle for his old bones and those of his confederates. *How childish*, thinks Borkman, momentarily ashamed of being ashamed of his son. After he's executed for mass murder he's sure to be exhumed and executed again—this time for a messy regicide.

Jr. has clearly spent far too much time trying to track down his soul by nibbling on kombucha-soaked sourdough pumpernickel in the hot springs at the Esalen (2.0) Institute that's all the rage, at least out on Highway 1, and from which Sr. received, atypically, a slew of pretty message-thin postcards. With every intention of remaining inaudible he cries out, *Don't say I didn't warn you* (though there's no swearing under oath that he did). Generating new concepts of privacy (Jr. explains to those with ears enough to hear) in the face of ever metastasizing surveillance tactics, and compounding very-slow-release digital pills (decked out with an embedded sensor or two) to enable the sort of artist who's either too busy (though busyness is often a lame excuse), or too fearful, to experience what she needs to experience if the work at hand is to reek of prize-winning authenticity without ruffling too many politically correct feathers—these were both projects that died on the vine. In fact, it wasn't long after a pour-out-your-heart-style father-son encounter at a blessedly untrendy diner off Sixth Avenue (*Take a bow, dad!* [Borkman refrains, citing heart trouble from all the excitement]) since there's nothing like premature divulgement for ensuring that failure carries the day (especially when there's nothing to divulge and it's being divulged to none other than the divulger's own father). The long-meditated Invidicum undertaking, on the other hand, is a horse of another color. Eden recruits a few (five will do) of the still-surviving tikis as slave labor. Neither the Munch, the Cone or the Kush have the balls—or the mean-spirited animus—to shout, *Arbeit macht frei,* as those choice laborers remove, from behind a row of portable toilets painted every color of the rainbow, what looks like—and is!—an MRI scanner. Before they unceremoniously push The Rump deep inside it (he's been accoutred with a flaming pink zucchetto)—as if it were a lie detector as long (as Robert Mueller is tall)—Jr. has no choice but to dazzle all of them—except The Rump—with a bit of targeted drug delivery. He injects nanoparticles chock full of Invidicum into the jugular (the subject is busy regurgitating some of his favorite morsels of Tweet meat, namely, those marinated in *Wiretappin' Barack, Little Ted, Lyin' Marco, Liddle Flake, Overrated Meryl, Low-Energy Carly, Lyin' hydroxychloroquine, Overrated Balanchine, Underrated Gohmerde,* etc.) in the hope that they'll find their way undegraded to his dorsal anterior cingulate cortex. For it's in the dACC that all the ladders start (not, as is inextirpably believed, in the foul rag-and-bone-shop of the heart).

Borkman, Jr., now announces that, by the merest flick of a switch lodged in the cobalt-blue middle toilet—a task of the utmost delicacy (which he would never forgive himself for outsourcing)—by the merest flick, he'll irradiate those particles with ultrasonic waves (it's as if—turning the Tell legend on its head—it's as if it's *Robert* who's shooting the apple off *William's* head) so as to vaporize their outer shells and allow the release of Invidicum into the target tissue. If the regurgitation stops, this means The Rump has been cured and a whole new era of his fake presidency can justly begin, hands no longer tied behind its back.

As a bonus, Jr. patiently explains—patiently precisely because he no longer has all the time in the world as he did at Esalen, Jr.—patiently explains that what he's practicing here—what he's being allowed to practice before the wildfires devastating the state reach Santa Barbara—is focused-ultrasound neuromodulation (look it up in the PubMed database if you don't believe him), which harnesses energies at the very least one order of magnitude below those used in treating, say, essential tremor—thereby sparing the lives of billions of neurons.

One of the unicorns suggests (NB: according to the Palo Alto Garage[219] Act of 1 January 2018, *unicorn* may refer either to a start-up worth over $1 billion or to its founder) that Borkman, Jr., get his multicolored ultrasonic toilet patented ASAP—before it's determined by the US Patent and Trademark Office or the US Supreme Court or both to be, say, a law of nature or a natural phenomenon or an abstract idea or an oncogene or a laxative cum aphrodisiac extracted from knobbed whelks, hence unpatentable at any speed. Constitutionally incapable of taking any suggestions that aren't his own (a backfiring

---

[219]As regards start-ups, the rag-and-bone-shop role is played by the Garage.

trick he's learned from Dad), Jr. nonetheless peers into space attentively.

Listening to all this, the big words and the not so big—Cantor is in danger—as too many times before—of getting a swelled head knowing he's the last holdout against the seductions of wordflow—the very wordflow that serves only to endistance the Base further from the fake news crowd. He's the only guy—a regular guy—who routinely steers clear of polysyllabics, at least in public—words like *neuromodulation* and *vaporize* and *inextirpably*—words that singlehandedly break the Twitter bank (but let's not forget about *bone* and *toilet*). Nobody takes any notice (of the swelled head Cantor deftly doesn't get) because this mister nobody has just too much to *not* think about.

Thus far, The Rump as *father figure* hasn't failed The MNunch (he, neediest of orphans, for all his mortgage-soured billions) so how can he not wish to be seen crawling toward the MRI? Since like—like—well, like a male nursery-web spider (*Pisaurus mirabilis*, to you)—he's tied up the tax-exempt nuptial gift of his neediness all nice and pretty for presentation on the altar of the man who, at The MMunch's wedding, was best man, high priest *and* maid of honor without missing a beat. But Eden has to shoo him away since, now semi-upright, his bulk interferes with the zapping. Defying authority—even logic—the spider tries to slither his way into the sausage grinder and it takes at least three tiki goons (bearing no small resemblance to the Siren's in *Prodigal Son*, notes Moira reluctantly, for she's still grappling with guilt over being one of the very few who emerged from the carnage completely unscathed)—three goons (imagine!) to drag him out, predictably kicking and screaming. Regaining what's left of his composure to face the crowd—identical to those which, during the Great Depression, sought succor in just the sort of Fort Knox-branded robo-glitter and -glamor peddled to great effect (until now) by him and the missus (a combo rivaled only by Fred and Ginger and only in their "Isn't This a Lovely Day to Be Caught in the Rain" heyday)—regaining his composure, the Mnnunch confesses (in tones he hopes are solemn enough to fend off any onslaughts of true populist disgust—even Maxine Waters's "Reclaiming my time!") that he (a one-trick pony—and a one-trick phony—to the bitter end) "had the great *honor* recently to travel with the President cross-country when he was introducing to Our Great Nation the first Great Tax Reform Bill in three hundred years." Honor is clearly (*Again with the Honor!* but, oddity of oddities, the Lady from Forest Hills is [*Again with the Lady from Forest Hills!* bellows the . . . Man from Shropshire!] nowhere to be seen) the greasy armature of this anilinguist's opportunistic low-wire act. And get a load, Melanctha orders herself, of "Our Great Nation"—the last-refuge refrain of every GOP grifter (sporting the same lies-like-truth smile when interviewed by Chris Hayes) from Staten Island to Mount Alcatraz. Seduced and abandoned by both The Rump and LooLoouuiise—not to mention Maxine whose rebarbativity[220] had at least the advantage of keeping his vitals pumping—the McMunch has no other recourse than to collapse and expire before greeting The Rump as he emerges, forever

---

[220] Yes, *rebarbativity:* show a little gratitude for this invitation to not just assist at the birth of an instant archaism but spank its bottom into full-blooded life.

unscathed. His arterioles selflessly oblige. Jean (her right wrist—always more delicate than the other—has been lightly singed by a torch) hopes everybody with even the remotest connection to The Rump will take this as a signal to fall on his own sword—for good. Reduced to a cubistic profile with *two* gimlet eyes (a profile that would have driven PP green with *envidia*) and still on the heap, geezer laureate MacCConnell has at long last the wherewithal to cackle his signature "harr-harr." Supinely snoozing, with the Sahlberg Mausoleum as backdrop, O'Flynne (must be Flynne's twin—or Flynne, McJr., graduate summa cum laude of Pizzagate U) looks like he has every intention of taking his own profile (the profile of a Wicked Witch of the West, accoutered as it is with a dorsum that could surely be forced, after a little practice, to rub elbows obscenely with her upper lip)—looks like he has every intention of taking his own profile to bed with him in the underworld. As if on cue, Bannon (the love affair with Mitch proves the Republican party is one big fat chimaera whose holy grail is self-evisceration postponed until the donors forgive every last broken promise)—Bannon, at his best a cross between Milton's Satan and Milton's Samson Agonistes—rising up from behind the Cadorin memorial or is it the Sanctuary of Life? (in any case, it's not the Sanctuary *City* of Life) and stampeding his arch enemy's potbelly, proceeds to stab him—to death, presumably, given the number of wounds inflicted (at last count, fifty-four). It hits Borkman—whom the Master (still hard at work despite his brush with muddy death [a false alarm, as it turns out] since what else does he have to die for?) has had no choice but to transform into Astute Political Analyst in Residence inasmuch as everybody else is either even less right for the part or contracted out to some other last-legs impresario—it hits Borkman (never mind where) that Bannon's flair for hatred can be cultivated only within the confines of the GOP (hatred of a Dem would be its own stiff dilution). Any devout mediocrity, after all, can go after his official enemy but it requires pit-bull genius—the same genius that decreed Ayn Ryan was but a maggot born and bred in a Heritage Foundation Petri dish—to turn one's mandated ally—one's twin—into the ideal trigger of a virulence-gone-haywire and thereby—thereby—thereby— Borkman would like to conjure *the slumbering spirits of the gold* (*his* Master, he suddenly realizes) for only they can complete the thought and effect expulsion—excretion—in a manner befitting its own high hopes.

Once fully extracted from the meat grinder cum polygraph, The Rump is given a work-up befitting his status. (*At least he won't live to see the next election stolen from him*, sobs somebody who should be Margo but, as the next best thing, looks a lot like a cross between the Kockenlocker, Ivankanemia, Margery Tailor Green and the Suckabee.) He's acquired a (patentable?) Florida tan, accentuating the latex-like consistency of his jowls. The regurgitation, however, hasn't stopped. If anything, the symptom, upgraded to a syndrome in accordance with MRI house rules, has gotten much worse, i.e., the hit list of system-riggers has suddenly expanded. Surprisingly lucid (so the contraption does have its virtues), The Rump grumbles something to the effect that, under no circumstances—*do you hear me? under no circumstances!*—must Doug Jones best Sheriff Roy. Any pre-unicorn worth his salt would be humbled by this failure to entice the members of the vulture capitalist crowd (most of whom, even if they're presumably busy texting off their thumbs-down to headquarters, are pronounced dead) but Borkman, Jr., is too busy preparing for house arrest to care. But not so fast: When Jim, Jr., whose star has been rising as fast as Borkman, Jr.'s has been tanking, warns him "that just because his invention has understandably failed with The Rump (for everything fails when he's around), doesn't mean that with the right guinea pig it won't be a great success," his expression changes to one of inconsolability—first and surest step on the road to hope. Borkman, Sr., has never been prouder of Jr., inconsolable or not, than right now—even prouder than when the boy had intentionally pulled the plug on his precocious stab at matricide.

And then, in the style of the MAGA Nuremberg rallies during the presidency's (soon-to-be-permanent) fetal stage, when The Rump routinely ordered his flunkeys, the more unwilling the better—e.g., Ben Carssonitis; Civil War veteran Kelly; teeth-grittingly debased ex-CEO Tillertzon; Manafart; The Flynnn; Hope, the Great White Hicks; Bannon; the Cohn quadruplets (Gary, Harry, Sili- and Roy); Jeanine Pirrhomaniac; and David Von Dukes—to steal the spotlight (*Where's Mike? get him out here! he's doing a fantastic job! say something, Mike, or I'll fire you as sure as your name's Mike! by the way, Mike, when will the treaty with great guy Mike Yanukovych be ready for even-greater-guy robo-signing?*)—in true Nuremberg style, The Rump bellows, "Get up here, Doug. Fantastic guy. Judge Joe [*sic*] can't hold a candle. Vote Jones: Our agenda can't afford another soft-on-crime House Republican like Doug—I mean Roy Arpaio." Is Doug here? When you get right down to it, is *anybody* (or is that too flip)? Hard to say who is and who isn't. After all, there've been so many indictments, deaths, firings, plea agreements, demotions and resignations, not to mention elopements, promotions, secondments and shotgun marriages. Ah, blessed doubt! It makes up for a multitude of storytelling sins—effortlessly engenders an urgent sense of duration in seconds flat—makes the spectator *feel* for the story organism—the story *told*—as certainty never can because he's being asked to condole with its precocious fallibility.

Thanks to the last-second planning of The Rump Organization, the terrain lying between spa and ocean has been excoriated "tastefully" (this is the fine print of the glossy prospectus talking—and in an Oxonian accent to boot) and is now adrift in winding stairs and widening gyres. And speaking of gyres, who should be returning to this Mount without a Sermon, presumably from the water's edge, but Kelly and McMaster, albeit to little fanfare, especially since nobody, except maybe Mattis, was ever aware they'd skedaddled. The Generals have pretty much the same story to tell which may not be suitable for all ears and ages. In short, they wanted to die (nothing in their military experience had prepared them for this turn of events)—who wouldn't, what with the gangrene of unrelenting despair eating away at their extremities?—and, unaware of each other's presence, threw themselves into the drink. Fortunately, both had the extraordinary presence of mind—or rather the total absence thereof—to swim far far out and then back, inasmuch as the motions of their arms and legs stretched to the breaking point the parts where the unsightly swellings were, i.e., under their arms and groin, and caused them to ripen and break, while the freezing foam brought the fever in their blood to a sober standstill.[221] So here they are pretty much cured only to find themselves—as they explain to Eden (since nobody else within earshot can lay claim to the principled gaze and physique of a Marine)—stuck between (*a*) the Scylla of being compelled to believe—should the temptation to infect insidious Jaranemio and other upstarts prove irresistible—that some dregs of their infection do indeed linger and (*b*) the Charybdis of dreading that, for all the breast strokes, they're still very much infected, especially by the delusion of thinking themselves sound as a bell, and in consequence may—solely to turn The Rump green with Envy (especially now that he's flunked the ultrasonic toilet test)—make the career-destroying mistake of flaunting their immunity since not so deep down they've never hated any Thing more than they do his draft-dodgerly guts—especially Knight-aberrant Kelly who, as you may remember, stood idly by while The Rump politicized his son's death and then went on, cowardice-soused, to try his hand at upholding the sacredness of women by calling Congresswoman Frederika Wilson an empty barrel (*Again with the Congresswoman!* eye-rolls the Lady from Forest Hills, who's been located at last—on a Brooklyn-bound F train badly in need of repairs—minutes after an announcement by the NYPD Missing Persons Unit of a million-dollar reward for any information leading to her whereabouts). At these words, Germophobe Von Der Rumpf draws back in terror—thereby engineering his own expulsion from the League of Strongmen whose board of trustees includes Putin, Duterte, Orbán, Erdoğan and Mike Pompeii's hot lunch date, the "Incredible" Mr. Un.

Eden looks around as if searching for a man of the cloth. There being nary a one (Pencely—just emerging, guiltily but unscathed, from one of the pink toilets—would do if only his brand of piety didn't stink of world-historical calculation), Eden takes it upon himself (of all people!) to uncomplainingly pinch-hit—hoping for an oratorical home run or two (another man—looks like Ted the Cruznik—is exiting from the same stall now that a semi-respectable interval has passed). *Here goes:* It's too bad this near view of death (as an accomplice to mass murder, his days, too—a matter of hours, really—are numbered) doesn't appear to be reconciling men of good principles to each other. (For far more infectious than the plague itself has been the insidiously introduced belief that in such a crisis, principles are of no use.) Mattis, General No. 3 and the best of the lot, points out (since he has nothing left to lose—or does he?) that if there does happen to be a few men of good principles left, they're pretty much in hiding behind the gravestone of their choice lest the Kockenlocker (*breaking news:* in keeping with the traditions of her family, i.e., the teleost family Syngnathidae, she intends to donate her elongated snout, fused jaws, distinctly male brood pouch, absent pelvis and bony-plated body armor to Science, i.e., Creation Science)—lest KellyAnnaBellissima K.

---

[221] Daniel Defoe's poker-faced (hence automatically poetical) *Journal of the Plague Year* is the inspiration hereabouts.

Kockenlocker—face and voice of the plague—and her gang of seadragons swift-boat those few men's hardline integrity. Clearly, the close conversing with death, or with the diseases threatening death, have not scummed off the gall from tempers like KKK's. Skyping with Fox in a quieter part of the cemetery, she assures Laura Coulter's twin, Anna May IngraHam, that whatever's been happening is just fallout from Obamacare's implosion which astrophysicists have been predicting for centuries. What really gets her goat, Laura— I mean, Ann—is the fact that now, when the plague is no longer at its height, or shouldn't be—is in fact all over—still there are social-justice pussies out there who, having managed to crash the massacre, are insisting that the distress of the poor is greater than ever because the sluicegates of charity have been shut tight by drawling scrooges like Lindsay the Grahame Cracker [sic] and his chums.

Speaking of Lindsay-Woolsay—that incomparable mint julep of a manikin—he's currently trying to *distance himself* (exquisite euphemism, don't you think?) as The Rump goes about begging to be saved not from the Plague but from Envy, his own personal plague—and promising, should the beggary be heeded, to roll back every single act of deregulation even if lovers (yes, *lovers!*) SchPruitt and DaVos (for both of whom nothing's more exciting than, 5 p.m.-ish, to organ-grind in the $25,000 telephone booth—running neck and neck with Duchamp's urinary Fountain in the race to be crowned found object to end all found objects), among others too numerous to name, end up as collateral damage. Unable to contend with the guilt triggered by Borkman, Jr.'s inconsolability and with nothing better to do, Jim, Jr., took it upon himself to scurry off and solicit a professional opinion on The Rump's post-grinder health status—and from the very unicorn (a highly distinguished med school dropout, as it so happens) who'd enhanced his *credentiality* [a term brand-new to MacWebster's!] manyfold by tactfully suggesting that the inventor of the ultrasonic toilet secure a patent as soon as possible. For his pains, Jr.'s back with a prize prognosis (all is not lost—the Rump may very well still turn out to be the supreme guinea pig contraption of the infant century)—a much better prognosis as it turns out than his own very private layman's take on the crisis, attesting nothing more than the envy-soaked schadenfreude of a Job's comforter par excellence. For some reason, Jim envies The Rump as he would a fellow toddler—a fellow classmate—as if they were as contemporaneous as Damon and Pythias, or Orestes and Pylades—as if The Rump were for all practical purposes the sort of (by no means uncommon) pornographic film that, counterintuitively, loses not a whit of its pizazz through being deemed appropriate for all ages—worse, for All the Ages. And Jr.'d be the first to hungrily acknowledge this, his ultimately endearing . . . quirkiness. But not before tripping over the corpses of Pritchard and Margo. Melanctha, unacquainted with grief, is predictably on to what he's experiencing, or rather, what he isn't—what he refuses—to experience. No longer will he be confronted with Margo's garrulous and Pritchard's darkly unspeakable brand of disapproval, not just of this or that refusal to live up to their reasonable expectations, but of his very existence. But before patting himself on the back—since it's no mean feat to have disembarrassed oneself of three parents in the course of a single summer—he's got to be sure that what's on display is indeed rigor mortis in action. Thing is, he doesn't have time (with its bad habit of marching on) to admit to, much less dissect, the sensation of relief—the sense of liberation—the sight engenders. Indeed, Straynge's Jr. is in such a hurry to, so to speak, bring the good news from Ghent to Aix that he manages (chin cocked Mount Rushmore style and lapels drawn haughtily together) to elbow The Rump out of his way as if—as if— thinks Cantor, why, as if Jim, Jr., were himself The Rump and The Rump, Prime Minister of Montenegro—in other words, as if what went around has indeed come around, prefiguring an equally world-hysterical karma-crammed moment, i.e., the moment when, as he exits his plea hearing, Mikey Flynne will be greeted with catcalls of "Lock 'im up!" It just so happens that according to the aforementioned dropout unicorn who is in fact more of an Ur-unicorn (and friends with somebody very very senior on Mueller's team), even if, with probands less intractable, the ultrasonic toilet would surely yield astonishing results, it was destined from the start to find its true vocation as a lie detector, tailor-made for the likes of The Rump. And Jr. is not only the bearer of good tidings but ready when Borkman, Jr., balks "Too bad I won't live to see all this," with the remark that he might very well be pardoned on the basis of the detector's contribution to neuro-forensics, whose findings are still viewed with scepticism—not to mention that most of the casualties were mere tiki bearers with a smattering—a literal smattering—of a few of the most reprehensible members of The Rump's inner circle.

With his spreadsheets in tow or rather in tow to his spreadsheets, Ayn Ryan—not just a mere policy guy but a policy-guy-whose-heart-goes-out-to-the-underdog, which explains why tough love demands that he shepherd Medicare, Medicaid, CHIP, Social Security and other opiates to the slaughterhouse ASAP for the requisite strokes of havoc—Ayn the Ryan crosses paths with Lindsay, the julep whose mint is fast withering under the strain of so much tergiversation (especially on the golf course) in particular with regard to the thorny issue of whether The Rump fits a certain diagnostic profile: As the tenure of the Administration—which will be remembered and dismembered as a photo-op gone obscenely wrong—may be coming to an end any second now, should the julep invoke and hew to his old-as-the-hills campaign virulence and call The Rump a *kook* or, hedging all bets, simulate disbelief that others still dare to do so when the impressive track record of the kook in question has clearly shredded the term's accuracy for good. It's clear to Ryand, after a quick look around, that they're pretty much the last Jellyfish Caucus firebrands standing, which means it's fallen to their share to strike a deal. Though not necessarily a MAGA deal—let's leave that to Louisa May Alcott. What he has in mind is something at once greater and humbler.

In one sense, Lindsay realizes, self-styled Kirillov and phony bad boy Bannon is right: Ryand *was* curdled in a Petri dish—only it wasn't in the foul rag-and-bone shop of the Heritage Foundation, but rather at a subsidiary of the International Society for Stem Cell Research where (as Lindsay sees it), on a day like any other and no other, embryonic stem cells of the jellyfish mixed with pluripotent stem cells of the rat were injected into human blastocysts to generate the, alas, viable chimaera (it takes one to know one) subsequently known as Ayn Ryan. Grahem, then, will have no problem serving—is more than willing to serve—as Ayn's gal Friday when it comes time to send the Rump back to where he came from. What Grahem does have a problem with, however, is the impact that Ryand's lineage may have on the Base, which has just so much stomach for the ambitions of a jellyfish and will take just so much interspecies monkey business with a grain of salt.

The Lindsay suggests—while, steps away, The Rump writhes on in an agony no doubt perpetrated both by the Plague and by the little plague of his incurable Envy, with neither gracious enough to mitigate the effect of the other—The Lindsay suggests that, to up Ayn's ante among the Base[222] (the julep doesn't know he's misusing *up the ante* and you want to know something? he doesn't care for what he does know, without knowing he knows, is that there's nothing more exhilarating than impressing an idiom into service simply because it sounds right—couldn't be righter—for the occasion)—the Lindsay suggests they rustle up the rumor that for decades, say, Ayn has been guilty of harassing Congressional aides, exclusively those belonging to subspecies succulent redhead, and going so far as to poach on devilishly handsome Blake the Farrentholdd's raspberry preserves. Pride—even jellyfish pride—enjoins that before assenting and admitting thereby that, as the Lindsey implies, there's some *thing* he very much lacks, Ayn make a show of manfully weighing the issue. Fact is, there's nothing he wouldn't do to help usher in a better world—a world where Republicans can self-righteously slap together a health care bill without fearing profane backlash above all from some horse's ass of a chief exec who perversely and gratuitously decides to describe it (easy enough since he won't be facing their constituents) as the *meanest* health care bill imaginable and to do so even with relish (since it's sure to pass). A world where a jellyfish like the Ryand won't have to proclaim (adoringly? with a laureate ass-kisser's calculation?) the next Rump "transformational," as he did this one, for the next will turn out to be . . . he! And it's of no importance whether under different circumstances this nothing-burger of a newly minted julep would have been his first choice as partner in crime. It's of even less importance whether the jellyfish can penetrate the julep's fakery all the way through to his inner absence and vice versa. What matters is that whoever's been wrongly left for dead in this slaughterhouse under the stars be made to see the light, i.e., be compelled to start training themselves to foresniff the midnight oil soon to be burning 24/7 in the Oval Office as the Policy Guy in Chief prepares for (to quote the press release) "tomorrow's daily 6 a.m. Highest-level Executive Briefing Ever Held Outside of a Petri Dish." The survivors need to get used to perceiving him—smelling him—as a force to be reckoned with. So the first order of business is to turn over every other rock in the hope that enough abject slugs crawl out to make for a respectable showing of diehard members in perpetuity of The Ryand's new constituency—sur-

---

[222]And (though he doesn't say so) to deflect the focus from all *jellyfish* evokes (frankly, he'd rather be called a kook than a jellyfish any day of the week).

vivors of the caliber of Chaplain in Chief Michael McPentz, who will insist (observing the state The Rump's in) that all kneel (in defiance of Colin Kaepernick) to pray for his soul; and anti-Mueller unmentionables of the caliber of Mattie Gaetzz, pincer-toothed super-*mediocrity on-the-make* (problem is, this cross between pig- and sharklet [soon to be brought up on charges of trading our referentless old friend *fine dining* for sexual favors of the spicy jail bait variety] wouldn't be caught dead treating the diagnosis [which has "effete coastal elite" written all over it] as anything other than a big fat badge of honor);[223] apoplexy-inducing double-talker Tom Reeid; Jacketless Gym Jordane, very very amateur catfish wrestling political hack and, more to the point, quintessential Punk for All Seasons replete with trademark JD smirk and signature *Blackboard Jungle* slouch (see above); triple agent cum courier-without-portfolio Devinely Nunesz, forever breathlessly adrift and grimly awhirl in his very own private "postmodern" remake of *The Spy Who Came in from the Cold* (White House sequences filmed at A Coney Island of the Mind Studios in Nueva York City); devoutly *religioso* Freedom Carcass chieflet Little Marko Meadows; and insider-bias advocate Bad Bob Mocha Lattte, not to mention insider-bias advocate *and* senile dementia denier Little Louie GohMerde (who, during of all things a House hearing, validated his entitlement to both titles by lobbing tau- and beta-amyloid-fueled pellets of phony down-home southern-fried warmed-over outrage at Rump scapegoat and FBI casualty Peter Strzok) and (still awaiting their Linnaeus) John Bulldog Rat Cliffe, Don DeLa Santis and Father Superior of the Nobody-Ever-Died-from-Being-Uninsured movement Ráoul the Labrodor, aka The Rump's Retriever. Inspired casting surely doesn't get any edgier than this. But it's not some renegade residuum of Sunday School teaching—a kindly admonition, say, to the effect that you should never desecrate a cemetery's volatile silence with cheap chatter—that's responsible for the fact that Melanctha's high tolerance for the Master's periodic roll-out of these Wanted lists is wearing thin. Are they time killers? space fillers? Or does such enumeraton attest to an ostensibly more honorable intention which is to abolish Evil by unrelentingly altering the names of Its practitioners ever so slightly (though far be it from Melanctha to begrudge the Master a strategy that enables Him to avoid being sued for libel and/or beheaded) and reducing their doings to a slogan?—and if fame and fortune accrue to the savvy sloganeer for his pains so be it. Conceding that the not quite imperceptible deformations have a certain charm—of the

---

[223]For who has a diviner right to lifelong life than mediocrities even if—no, precisely because—they're plighted to oblivion as soon as *it's* over—precisely because they have no interest in being enshrined for all the good they did—precisely because they'd never stoop to signing over their birth pangs to posterity (posterity is the here and now, on Air Force One, where, under the supervision of The Rump's benign jowls, they're exercising, *as we speak*, their mandate *to level the playing field* with a view to assuring affordable housing for billionaires)—and are thereby infinitely superior to the sons and daughters of the detractive elite in all their guises of vestal virgins trothed to serving the Great God High Posthumousness? So put that in your bagpipe.

more-things-change-the-more-they-stay-the-same/now-you-see-it-now-you-don't variety—is slowly bringing her tolerance level for all things Master back to where it was. From her dugout (little touches signal that a female sensibility is already at work humanizing the smelly pit), Moira, having been listening in, is tempted to offer some reassurance (but to whom?) by pointing out in true Sunday School fashion that, never fear, the ever-changing names do serve a function—one similar to that of the gladhanding goons who for generations have bedeviled *her* master's Prodigal Son—or rather one similar to that of the ever-disappearing handshakes themselves.

But jellyfish and julep—even with the help of residual wiki scum—can't coax a single slug out of retirement. But that (amateur microbiologist LG soon discovers) is because the slugs are too busy trying to reach consensus (with the chemical profiles of their feces doing all the communicating, canvassing, electioneering, for them) on whether to risk anything as dangerous as re-emergence from the rubble. In short, these are not men but—and which are far nobler—white rhinos (following in the footsteps of folks like *Vibrio harveyi* and *Pseudomonas aeruginosa*). And out of necessity they are practicing their own version of bacterial quorum-sensing (with 2-3- and 2-6-dimethyllundecane standing in for N-3-oxohexanoyl-L-homoserine lactone and the like). Peeking out from under a toppled marble slab now that the pace of the carnage appears to be slackening, Melanctha wonders (Cook—or rather Cook's incidental folk wisdom—has abandoned her) if this little skit—this little aside—this textual equivalent of a fecalith—has been inserted—embedded—conscripted to serve as a fungible token of time passing—as dead space making way for the influx of a generic duration—a manufactured sense of duration which is any story's—and any storyteller's—bread and butter—or is it—the aforementioned bit about garrulous rhino shit—by no means as gratuitous or replaceable as all that—couldn't it be not some cheap ornament but the way in to the very core of the present crisis?

At last they do emerge—the sesquipedalian pheromones have done the trick. Ayn looks them over—the unmentionables: self-anointed and -appointed Young Turk and Fine Diner Gaaetzz and the other anti-Muellerites, with two or three Cabinet members to spice up the bilge. Given the choice, Ayn the Ryan wouldn't have picked any of them—it was their absence alone that made his heart grow fonder. Still, it's a bad taskmaster who blames his slaveys—the tools of his trade. And given the Ryand's outsize ambitions he's going to need plenty of tools. Now that there's nobody whom Mike the Pence (also outsize) can gaze up at in bashful worship, he clearly dreads the fall into desuetude of his trademark smile with its dash of smirk or is it the other way around, i.e., trademark smirk, etc.? Or is he relieved that the time for dreary simulation of enthrallment as the price of accession to the throne has at last come to an end (and not as bitter as dreaded since infancy)? (Once again the Master's trademark Uncertainty steals what's left of the show.) One of the few Silicones who've thrown in their lot with these sorry specimens of *Suckupper sapiens* approaches Borkman, Jr. (marking what's commonly known—but among whom?—as a Duchampian moment)—since it's only fair he be the very first to know the ultrasonic toilet was born to be married to the slaughter-immune $25,000 phone booth if for no other reason than to engender a chimaera worth billions. His mind is, as usual, elsewhere. What's the point of accepting a pardon and ending up in the same company as Judge Roy Arpaio's hindgut? Still something compels him—call it vanity or a deviated septum—to ask (dully), why. His tone, however, assures the messenger he has no reason to fear that there's only one right answer. "And nota bene, with sleazy-secretive Kutschner (666 Fifth Avenue's answer to Mohammad bin Salman) put out of everybody else's misery there's no danger of his appropriating this chimaera for the Office of American Innovation.[224] For it's just the sort of not-quite-ready-made which (like that 2013 *Nude Descending a Urinal*) comes but once in a century.

The first—and perhaps under present conditions—the only order of business is to dump The Rump—he, once upon a time "the most powerful man in the Universe"[225]—in what the Mayans who always knew of what they spoke called the Mother of All Waters. His writhing in agony bears witness to the fact that The Rump's particular strain of the deadliest of all deadly sins is ineradicable. Yet, oddly enough for a would-be strongman, he bears Borkman, Jr., no malice, even if, in profile at least, there's a strong resemblance afoot to Rump, Jr., who's privately regarded by Rump, Sr., as the quintessential jerk—an embarrassment of anything but riches. Though dimly aware of what awaits him (he's always loathed sharks—the non-loan-shark kind, that is)—even if it's obvious that soon enough he'll be on his last legs among the spume—still The Rump makes—has—time enough (even if not presence of mind enough) to remind anybody who'll listen that he's, yes, a genius. But Cantor, who has not only time enough but presence of mind enough as well, takes as starkly disqualifying the fact that this genius (albeit Putin-anointed)—that this genius who's way too stable for his own good—that this Renaissance Man—has not one certified field of expertise to his name. Until he—Cantor—musters the requisite gumption to ask, rhetorically, Isn't this the purest form (if not the purest proof) of genius—to be expert beyond expertise—a master multitasker without a single horizon-blurring task on the horizon—a genius unbegrimed by competence, calling, craft, content. Hell, he's the very first of his kind to be unencumbered by—unmoored from—a vocation. Vocation: the worst—and the vulgarest—of all albatrosses, parasites, leeches, better halves. Well, isn't it?

Ayn Ryand's goons—it's only in the shadow of The Jellyfish that The Rump comes off as a breath of fresh air—lift him, upright, upon their shoulders as if (Moira thinks) he were nothing less than *Serenade*'s waltz girl (fourth movement) being reluctantly (or is it just fake modesty?) apotheosized into the next world. But as too many cooks have volunteered the broth is almost spoiled, i.e., the butterball turkey buzzard is almost dropped. Ayn hesitates

---

[224]Currently running neck and neck with the Circumlocution Office for the title of holiest temple of pomp-and-circumstanced boondogglery ever erected in the Western world.

[225]Omarosa Manigault O'Grady, public liaison extraordinaire, in [flight from] conversation.

to spill his beans but, as it turns out, Borkman, Jr., is not to be vanity's only boy toy. Adopting the air of the proverbial someone close to an investigation who, citing its ongoing nature, speaks on condition of anonymity (i.e., the air of a someone who, time and again, proves unrivaled in his—or her—ability to scale new depths of boilerplate grandiloquence)—adopting the air and assuming the position, Ryan the Ayn coyly suggests (though he's well beyond the suggestion stage and his flunkeys know it) that The Rump's relegation to making small talk with the sharks is to be ascribed to a conspiracy hatched in some pedophile's paradise of a pizza parlor by Chuck and Nancy, abetted not a little by Keith and Corey. The Young Turk cum Fine Diner, though not quite as young as everybody thinks—or thought—chooses the most ghat-like of the winding stairs[226] purely to befuddle his congeners and make them look—worse, act—their age. Even if he, too, is badly out of shape Turk the Jerk knows how to deploy his baby fat to maximum effect. Parting words of Ayn, the irrepressible helicopter mom: Make sure, guys, that on the long way down to Davy Jones's Locker, he excises (out of respect for the sensibilities of the members of the—of our Great American—Freedom Carcass if for no other reason) terms like, for starters, *fetus, meatus, transgender, hush, climate change, meander, knee, deep, daycare, spur, artful dodger, faith-based, fate-based, race, locker-room banter, exquisite (see directly below), Forever Chemicals, wide-awoke, favor* and *insurrection* from the aforementioned small talk.

"Why," Borkman, Jr., repeats—amazed that he, herald of a new concept of *privacy* designed to laugh a conjoined siege by Facebook, Google and Trader Joe's to scorn, is actually inviting this messenger to play havoc with his own, for what is the ultrasonic toilet—in whatever color of the rainbow—but the ultimate embodiment of Privacy in the Age of The Rump. Breathless Silicone Sam counter-invites Borkman, Jr., (he wonders if the breathlessness is a put-on) to imagine that Enviers could, as targets of ultrasonic Invidicum delivery, undergo whatever they needed to undergo through the auspices not of an MRI (however ennobling its discomforts) but rather of a souped-up telephone booth cum lovers' lane—asks him to imagine Them as erect rather than on their belly—erect enough, in other words, to signal (most of all to themselves) that Envy is nothing to be ashamed of. Borkman, Jr., starts taking the bait (without letting on): Maybe it was nothing but The Rump's sense of shame (so what if he has none?), as inextricably bound up with supinity, that inhibited a viable response. (Or was it his proneness? No: *supinity* sounds better. So let him be remembered belly-up.) As for the tribe, they're tickled pink that the shell-vaporization technique has proven no more effective than those nasty pills mashed up in prune juice at Brasserie Greenwich Avenue and imbibed thrice daily. Although it may have been a question not of effectiveness but of the victim's complete lack of artistic affinity for his medium.

The smirk of an apostle—Ayn's—deadens Ryan's features—until a troll-

---

[226]More a ghat in fact than a stair. (Yes, a *ghat!* exclaims Cantor, too loud for anybody to hear. He's tired of having to defend solo the very arcana that make the world go round but stands his ground nonetheless.)

like chuckle takes over. (Proving he has more than smirks up his sleeve. Fact is, unlike the VP, Ryan is far more than a one-smirk pink pony: his repertoire has been grossly underrated.) Watching The Rump descend—or rather, *be descended*—how can Ayn, Jr. (qua connoisseur of contrasts) not remember how, in the same old Rose Garden after the rush-rush hush-hush ramming of the preliminary CHIP, Medicare, Medicaid, DACA and Social Security abolition bills through both houses of Congress—how can Ayn, Jr. (if you don't have a "Jr." after your name in the Rose Garden you're nobody—you're Toast) not remember how he "did a Pencee"—i.e., proclaimed that it [the passage of those kisses of death] couldn't have been perpetrated without The Rump's "exquisite presidential leadership"? Yes, "EXQUISITE PRESIDEN-TIAL LEADERSHIP!") Now from where deep within did a gender-bending trifle like *exquisite* (a stroke of toady genius) come from, he wonders. Well, wherever it came from, the word passed muster with the big boys (and girls) even if *normally* they wouldn't be caught dead trafficking in such chi-chi froufrou—but, hey, wait a minute, isn't Ryan in the very best of company since isn't—wasn't—The Rump himself no slouch when it comes—came—to chifrou and frouchi (cf. his confession that "we [he and Little Rocket Man] fell [hopelessly] in love")? In fact *exquisite* ended up being singlehandedly responsible for a vigorous bout of clapping from every last rank participant (senile to a man) in that dead-of-night massacre of the innocents. It lasted at least an hour while at the same time getting itself overtaken quickly enough by an even manlier round of applause from other anatomical redoubts. In short, even if the word per se was a bit too elitist for this uncouth crowd, as handily misapplied (*Misapplication is all*, sayeth the Prophet Isaiah) to the most corrupt of racist vulgarians, it generated a mass orgasm (not a dry orifice in the house) which spread like wildfire. He remembers, too (though this is worth but a quarter chuckle, if that), how at the same Rose Garden love feast of the godless, under an appropriately stool-colored sky, demented Little Orrin Hatchet Man surrendered to the most shocking profanity (but if the occasion didn't demand it what occasion ever would?), going so far as to laud Der Rumpf as one *heck* of a leader.

As the pallbearers go about the heady business of descending, Republicans in ever increasing numbers (including Kickback Corker who's outlived his plausibility [like so many others of his persuasion] as maverick for a day)—the youngest farts among them being in many respects the oldest (call it the Fat-Gaettz-the-Turk Effect)—make their way toward the edge of the cliff. Having gotten their bearings they're immediately up and about on all fours and—as Bruegel (the Elder's) Blind Leading the Blind but without a shred of Netherlandish pathos—ready to follow the procession wherever it leads. Who would have thought that there could be so many slugs under so few rocks—that the rocks could harbor so much bloodlessness? Their expressions scream, *Good riddance*. But bidding good riddance, especially to a commander in chief like The Rump, is a complex thing, or at least a thing beset by all sorts of complications including, for starters, regret, remorse, rapture and rambunctiousness. Since sharks-bound Rump absorbs into himself all the infections propagated by the plague of alternative facts and in so doing leaves behind a sort of mellow fruitfulness, wont to engender its own brand of unease. The Pence, too, has his cross (or in this case his inchoate smirk) to bear—forever tentative—forever solemn—forever in search of a cue from the master—forever taking the lay of that master's locust-plagued golfball-glutted land—a smirk that never quite hatches a smile, not even a Gioconda smile—i.e., it's *all fart* (Forgive the Master for reusing the word so quickly, thinks Melanctha) *and no feces* or (to re-cite the irrepressible Ms. WHPB Fuckabee) *all hat and no cattle.* He observes one of the two senior advisers (thanks to their unquenchable precocity, they've gone straight to the top of the corporate ladder without ever having had to endure the rigors of juniority) advancing on stiletto heels (yes! even [like some dinner-jacketed colonialist Brit] here in the jungle!), followed—or rather, tailed—by her wickedly high-fashion stepmother, on heels even steeper. Before she can ask (in a mysteriously unplaceable foreign accent) what's happened to her (and Vlad's) pet mutt—POTUS, not Asta—the GOPs (a few of them, like The Cork, quondam star mavericks but of a lesser order—profiles in equivocation with a mutant firefly's lifespan of, tops, an hour or three) have burst into tears. Yet who can blame them for agonizing over whether (interim) 46 will turn out to be, like 45, the sort of cat who, home or not, is always away—always away so the mice can (for base and donors) play? Or maybe they're actually starting to miss him.

The quintessential for-all-seasons pallbearer (as Gym Jordane is the quintessential JD punk), unctuous—no, oleaginous—Doc Tom (unsafe—and unsavory—at any Price) decides to dump his side of the bargain into everybody else's lap, reverse direction and semi-skedaddle into what looks like a more lucrative part of this virgin forest of corpses. (He's been disgraced for a mere million-dollar peccadillo but now, unsurprisingly enough [albeit a johnny-come-lately to the field] he's a lobbyist on the make—a revolving-door consultant on the prowl—a stage-door johnny on the qui vive—and simply can't allow pallbearing to get in the way of the client hunt.) Fortunately the other caryatids immediately leap into the breach to ensure that Rumpty, the Black Man's Burden, doesn't, owing to priceless Price's ill-timed recusal, have a great fall. In what he takes to be a foolproof face-saving gesture sure to pass muster the ex-Secretary of Health, Wealth and Stealth—but more to the point, ex-Eagle Scout—urges the cuddly crybabies to think of The Rump not as shark meat (although, as Price is having more and more difficulty forgiving his ex-boss, he's tickled pink by the prospect—the image of this horror) but rather as a DEM-induced agglomeration of senescent cells, i.e., damaged—zombie—undead cells—cells laying waste to the central organ of the body politic via last-ditch belching of noisome cytokines, growth factors and proteases—cells that subject that body to the ravages of premature aging—cells starkly incapable of making copies of themselves so as to be born posthumously in true superman fashion—so as to preserve their legacy. So it's their duty to prevent The Rump—by dumping him into the Pacific, mother lode of all senolytics[227]—

---

[227] Drugs that preferentially kill senescent cells. For starters, try dasatinib or quercetin or, better yet, navitoclax.

from doing any further damage. But the repubs aren't buying—they've had their fill of pseudo-abstruse metaphors. Somebody—not necessarily The Price—is deploying—exploiting—those East Coast constructions as a stall tactic—as a means of playing for time (but time for what?). "Compassionate" conservative Geff La Flake feels compelled to concede that maybe those metaphors—albeit (Lady from Forest Hills: *Again with the* "albeit"*!* to which the Lady from Utopia Parkway [with a boost or two from Joe Cornell, her neighbor two doors down and, alas, six feet under] promptly counters: *Again with the Lady from Forest Hills!*) as mendacious as a Tweet from POTUS—are in the service of a greater truth, still to be determined.[228] Somebody retorts: "You mean, just like your gang's scum-guzzling lies—e.g., that the tax scam is good food for the Forgotten Man—that CHIP is an unconscionable giveaway to booze-guzzling toddlers—that Mueller is Beelzebub, Jr.—that Arpaio is a patriot—that Kellyanne Suckabee Kockenlocker is the He[a]dy[est] Lamarr of our time—that The Rump doesn't have a yen, at least twice a day but who's counting?, to suck Putin's puny cock." It's Jiminy Kimmill who, standing arms akimbo at the edge of the cliff, resembles nobody so much as (now it's Cantor turn to do some amateur conceding) Ayn the Ryan's wet-dream ur-hero, Howard Roark (I highly doubt Howard's was as puny as L'il Putin's, Cantor thinks). Crouched beside him in a wheelchair, Ady Barkan (see footnote 228 below) attempts to put into words (it's heartrendingly all uphill) an (irony-free) equally impassioned but more politely terse version of the same message. In response to which uphill battle Chuck ("The Schmuck") Ghastly turns toward humble-origined Little Orrin Hatchet Man (*And a humble origin, Or, is proof of what, precisely?* Cantor wonders *con brio*) with a corny toothless yawn of contemptuous amusement on his tire-tracked puss (for the likes of the Schmuck, Ady's life-or-death struggle to make the words come is clearly fifty laughs a minute). He expects, or attempts to induce, a rhyming reaction (ignorant of Jean's rediscovery on the steppes of page 1103 or thereabouts that just as Nature makes no leaps so does Life, that callous horse surgeon, refuse to hand out comfy sutures free of charge). "Odd way of expressing an opinion," remarks the uninducible Hatchet at his poker-faced best (this is all that the Schmuck manages to gets out of him) and as if this were the grim-reaping Senate floor on Halloween eve. Cantor will remember Ghastly's mute guffaw till the day he dies (especially its craving for ratification from his JO buddy, the Hatch)—or so he truly hopes, since the thought of cuddling up with it is reassuring—stabilizing—confirmatory, that there are some things in heaven and earth which are both insusceptible to nuance and productive of the enduring treasure of a righteous revulsion. Hey, he's already looking forward to quiet evenings spent scattering the salt of his (for once) unpathologizably pure hatred on the altar of that guffaw. Indeed (yep! *Indeed!*), if he plays his

---

[228] The same ostensibly compassionate flake to end all flakes who, days before, boiler-plated away ALS victim Ady Barkan's pleas that he say no to his party's green mamba of a tax scam (in whose belly lodges a many-banded krait: repeal of Obamacare's individual mandate).

cards right, the SJC Chair may, in George Cantor's funhouse pantheon of half-wit tormentors, end up even usurping the place of highest honor currently held by Jeanne d'Arc's tickly prison guards (see Carl Dreyer's 1928 masterwork for graphic details).

Jimminy winds things up, or down, with a rhetorical question. "Hey, Mr. Pres, where are all the documents? You know, the ones (who knew documents could be *so hard*) that take up so much of your time—time better spent with Hannity, deranged Pirrho and snaky InGraHamm." The Rump is in no state to hear, much less respond. All that's manageable is a feeble stab at the sort of drymouthing (which continues to drive every new generation of You-Tubers hog-wild) he dabbled in on what has come to be referred to among the faux literati as *Gerusalemme Liberata* Day. Jimminy and Ady, under Borkman, Jr.'s auspices, attempt to throw thin-lipped ShchPruitt's Folly to the sharks (Jr. hasn't devoted so many months of his short life to this toilet-to-end-all-toilets only to see it chimaerized in company with a Chick-fil-A-lovin' para-noiac's private outhouse cum love nest). What gives them the needed impetus is to pretend the booth is in fact one of the wobbly Confederate statues we're always hearing about—this one (shipped straight from its record-breaking engagement in front of Charlottesville's Judicial Building) depicting General Jeff Sessions astraddle his trusty nag Sassybelle. Though in Cantor's view, probably unpalatable to most, these trophies must be dismantled only virtu-ally (through step-by-step analysis and counter-analysis and counter-counter-with the results fully articulated every step of the way) since suppression, physical destruction or burial of the evidence, like any song without words, is an especially potent aphrodisiac (in this case, the wrong kind of aphrodisiac) and merely legitimates—lays the groundwork for—an even more insidious resurrection.

But nothing so insignificant as the long-overdue consignment of The Rump to the omnivorous depths is going to ruffle the feathers of big burly Goldman Sachs fakir laureate Judge Roy ("Gary") Kohnn who's at this very moment holding a standing-room-only sunrise seminar (title, as given deep within the Web genome's darkest matter: "Tax Reconfiguration for Dum-mies 4.0"; location: Sydney Carton's gravesite). Eden, a dark-matter aficio-nado from way back (out of the blue he thinks of Linda, and Cantor, not to be bested, counter-invokes Berry Sundae)—Eden has just been recruited by Ethan (low and behold, he's back in the FBI—victim of a double promotion, no less)[229] to keep an eagle eye on Kohnn, who as it turns out knows much more than he's about to let on to Mueller's team, not only about Flynn but about the entire DC pizzagate crowd including Alix Jones, Jack Burrkmann and Richard Schpencer, not to mention faux coffee-boy Jorge PapaDopoulosh and self-anointed boy toy Milo JiannoPouloss. If Eden plays his cards right, there may be a pardon in the offing—maybe not a pardon on the scale of Judge Roy Arpaio's but one certain to assure a new lease of life, that is, if the

---

[229]The fact that he and Jean were reconciled just minutes ago strongly suggests it was The Rump who engineered their rift. But now that he's out of the picture . . .

prospect interests him. The seminar king is busy blowharding (to whatever's left of the tiki brigade) the spiel that was given a justly pilloried trial run at the most recent *WSJ*-sponsored CEO conference (and so what if less than a third of the attendees affirmed they'd use the cash freed up by Roy ("Gary") and his buddies for investment?). A spiel whose fatty gist all boils down to the *fabulous* insight (catapulting paternalism to new depths of venality) that with the annual extra $1,000 (sort of) "guaranteed" to every Forgotten Family[230] for a year or two under the GOP tax "reform" strategy *It*'ll be able to, say, buy a new jet or at least a new second-hand ink-jet printer or install a home entertainment system in Its non-existent breakfast nook (or take that dream vacation to Seychelles where it—er, It [see how easily we forget the humanity of these "officially" Forgotten? For them, no happy medium between upper-case fake canonization and . . . nothingness—*and they're the lucky ones!*] may get lucky enough to rub elbows with Privatization Sewer Rat Erikkkke Von Printzz and his Putin-pampered cronies). Listening as hard as he can to The Kohnn as he blows harder and harder, Eden—no Ethan—no Eden—begins to feel what he allows himself to feel rarely, namely, immense gratitude. Thanks to the *cri de coeur*—the *de profundis*—of this worst (because blithest) of all blowhards, he's beginning to understand the unintended meaning of that tired old term *trickle-down effect* (right up there with *constitutional crisis*). So, while there's no hope of a trickling down of cash from between the buttocks of the Elephant, some do hope, on the other hand, of a trickling down among the Forgotten and even the sub-Forgotten of the wider and wider *perception* and, in time, the fully armed—the fully weaponized—*apperception* that . . . that . . . (*Eden tries hard not to laugh himself silly at the sight and sound of all the mock optimism driving this phrase—this thought packet—this shadow packet—into a state of illegibility so catatonic it may not reach its endpoint*) . . . that (*deep breath*) . . . that (*deeper*) . . . that (*even deeper*) . . . the fully weaponized apperception that there's absolutely no hope of a trickling down and what's funnier than the dissolution of all hope?[231] (*well, whaddya know, endpoint reached after all and the whole packet brought in not only in advance of the deadline but way under budget!*).

The dangle of a pardon holds less and less appeal for Borkman, Jr. (they're best left to specimens like posthumous Kuschneer), particularly in a world where there may no longer be a Rump to get his creative juices flowing full speed ahead—worse, a world where the decent, hard-working Kimmills and Adys prove time and again, through absolutely no fault of their own, to be the heralds of a false dawn. Nor is Eden much tempted by the prospect, now that hubby-and-wife spymaster combo Nick (Narr) and Nora

---

[230]NB: Under the sunny Kohnne hypothesis, only those families with an annual income of $100,000 are categorizable as Forgotten: the wretched refuse of our teeming shore pulling in anything less simply do not qualify—do not resonate at a frequency covered by said fakir's brand of charitable optimism—i.e., simply do not exist.

[231]See foonote 196 above for examples of changes rung on the application of the necromantic word *dissolution* in other contexts.

(Rhys)[232] have debriefed him (he badly botched their assignment by standing idly by, without protest, while budding smug class consciousness got in the way of the courteous professionalism to which he was entitled) all the way down to Kohn's very last belched bromide (his jolly callousness has, unsurprisingly, a knack for turning Kellyannette Kockenlocker on and on and on, especially in front of the South Portico when cabinet members et al play Fellate-the-Fellator-in-Chief). No sign of El Rump must mean he's finally at one with the bloody wavelets testing the waters. (Punk rock fascistnik Nikk the Fuente, who screams postmodern rising star from every orifice, is moodily loitering in the vicinity of the sunrise seminar. If there were any justice in the world, The Rump would choose "He gets me" as his famous last words, with Nikk right here to absorb them especially since he already has [absorbed them, that is, and as meant for him alone] at Mar-a-gogo to be exact where, under the auspices of slave trade denier and part-time führer groupie YeYeYeWeste, Nikk the Nuke not only got to audition for the Rump but breezed through his goose-stepping shtick with flying colors. If only, sighs Nikk the Shtikk, The Rump could repeat those loving words with the same exact self-exalting forbearance [backed up by the backward jab of a traffic cop's thumb in my direction], not to mention the same exact insinuation that in some crazy way my *getting him* the way he, The Rump, deserved to be gotten was a bigger stroke of genius than any the genius himself could perpetrate, while remaining very much The Rump's patented creation and, as far as I, its surrogate mother, was concerned, only a bequest—a loan—and an unforgivingly callable one at that. It's Melanctha's turn to sigh. What is she ever to do with a favorite child who wears sloppy workmanship as a badge of honor? Is the Master not aware that Nikk's visit to Mar-a-gogo is yet to [but may never] materialize. Maternal instincts she never knew she had run amuck, compelling Melanctha to shield her panic, and the teacher's pet who's induced it, from Nikk's deranged, distracted, despondent gaze [more distracted than deranged, more despondent than distracted]. The shielding does her a world of good—and in record time. *Silly Melanctha [to even sillier Melanctha]*: Don't you know by now, Ms. Melanctha, that if the Master thrives on anything, it's incompetence, inasmuch as incompetence works its magic by inflicting the wound of implausibility on the beastly goings-on He unleashes, which implausibility in turn craves suture—the suture that only ingenuity so-called can execute? But in

---

[232]That's right, Ethan and Jean have not only buried the hatchet (missing each other's jugulars by only a hair's breadth, if that) but also replighted their troth—and what better way than by establishing a real estate investment trust, registered at Fort Knox (made famous most recently by The MnunchNikk and his breezy LooLoouuiise), with Eden serving as the first substantial holding. They've acquired him—smugly (as is now their wont)—as an NFT sure to hyper-appreciate in value on the blockchain pony express—in fact, as the first NFT that's a NFT of itself or something along those lines—in the same category, in any case, as the robot that pretends to be a robot and other disastrous outposts of innovation erected to prove human history is all about—is *only* about—Backward Progress of the Soul in Torment.

the case of a Thing like the Master a viable suture for an implausible wound can be generated, oddly enough, only through the intervention of rage, honest rage, at *having to be plausible*—worse, normal. Since rage and the havoc it wreaks are nothing if not *real* hence plausible, which plausibility can always be depended on to rub off on said goings-on and reap the gratitude of participants and spectators alike. So don't you go worrying your pretty little head, Ms. M., about the Master's talents and job prospects in the event of a recession. By flaunting His refusal to tear himself free of the shackles of implausibility, i.e., by implausibilizing *on purpose*—by intentionally visiting his will to incompetence on the goings-on so as to be able to make a splashier exhibition of that incompetence through ever headier, ever dizzier feats of implausibility *masquerading as dutiful stabs at serious suture* [for there lies the curdled cream of His jest]—the Master is able to naturalize anything under his jurisdiction—in this case, a murderous creep's emergence from the bloody bowels of the future.) Attracted by what appears to be the juicy smell of rotting horse flesh, the sharks are fast surfboarding shoreward (Orrin's carcass is going to make—or has already made them—one *heck* of a breakfast drink and Ghastly's guffaw, although way past its expiration date, will be music to their guzzling ears). But why *horse*? Maybe it has something to do with the fact that Judge Roy Moor, Ryan ZeZinky (first Secretary of the Interior without an interior of his very own) and even Mike Della Penza (this dead Administration's exalted Piety Czar)—yes, *our* Mike (that is, when he's not deep in pray-to-play or, in accordance with his master's detailed instructions, storming spontaneously out of a Colt-49ers game with better half cum better-than-half in tow,[233] or working hard—and I mean *really* hard—on his own instructions—his very own very detailed Letter to the World—including a grifter's guide to evangelical expediency)—something to do with the fact that they all get a kick out of making, when given half a chance, like Andy Warhol's Lonesome Cowboys. Won't be long, Ayn Ryan reckons (reckoning's a dirty job but somebody's got to do it—and well), before most of these Blind-Leading-Their-Blind are very much one with their *heck of a leader*. At which point he and Lindsay and a few other makeshifts and leftovers and Crackers of Lindsay's *leaves-a-great-big-lot-to-be-desired* caliber can get down to the business of strategizing . . . *exquisitely,* until further notice. To witness Ayn having his smirky go at playing the great reckoner makes Eden sick enough to take refuge somewhere in the darkest reaches of the autism spectrum. But not before acknowledging—call it acknowledgment as discovery—that *Lost to that tapeworm life before it could take his measure* is going to be his epitaph until further notice and what better place than here to stumble uncoerced on so mighty a jingle? But why not try, as the embodiment of his dying breath, something along the lines of, say, *Everything he ever did went . . . Swimmingly,* thereby sticking both middle fingers to the fates and killing two birds with one stone (though nailing the pair's identity would have stumped Oedipus and the

---

[233]*Much* better: Her reputed revulsion from all things Rumpical signifies that it's in fact she who wears the balls in the family.

Sphinx)? Martin's misadventures, he understands too late, have made such jingles (which he guesses must qualify as poetry—as a *kind* of poetry) his business—his line of work. And if things had turned out differently, at this very moment he—a career nomad allergic to hearths and homes—would be planning to get on with business once Balboa Park became not his killing ground as before but a perfectly respectable permanent abode. Melanctha catches Eden, at this, his moment of truth, wandering lonely as a storm cloud though standing still. She kneads his upper arm (it doesn't matter which) ever so slightly, thinking as she does so (to blunt the rawness of the gesture): *I know what you're going through*, though she hates the phrase: more purulent than the wound it's supposed to suture. And maybe that's very much the phrase's universal selling point. Deducing from his stalwart expressionlessness what's rolling around in Eden's head, she says what any mother who doesn't know what to say would say under the circumstances, namely, that it's *not* too late and even if it is, he'll never walk alone. Since wherever he goes the capacity to elicit all sorts of misperceptions—to extort all sorts of misimpressions—from others goes with him and what are the misses but a story in the making—or rather a storyboard or better yet a screen on which men may project the unavowably strange matters of their own making. Should she tell him not to worry his handsome little head about what to do with those misses (not to mention the associated packets waiting round the bend)—that he'd only lose them while the Master, the bighearted Master, knows how to use them. And in retaliation or to go her one better should he tell *her* (now that things are, what's the expression? getting back to normal and before she's been lethally strafed by the over-oohed and over-aahed tram which, come to think of it, is looking more and more like Pewitt's bulletproof phone booth, replicas of which are selling like hotcakes over by the unmarked grave of would-be AI entrepreneur Ishmael Drybock)—should he tell her he's so damned tired of having to be forever thrashing his way out of labyrinthine thickets of digressions in praise of digressions, packet-crammed to boot and overrun with an ineradicable poison ivy of polysyllables, merely to reclaim (he has an idea Who's guilty) the routinely expropriated territory of his selfhood. Though maybe this survival-of-the-fittest ploy is a pharmakon—pharmakon to end all pharmakons (the vegan dive off Washington Square suddenly flashes before his eyes)—which for all his pains is about to render him *real* at last. Or should he wisen her up to the fact that stories are a curse and the worst possible preparation for life, at least as he's been forced to live it, and that for all of Old Man Plato's doctrinal chatter about how beguilement by the music of prose tears out the very sinews of the soul, it's his own Just So Stories—with their juicy depiction of acolytes being routinely whipped into a prophylactic frenzy of self-refutation by *their* master—that are by far the worst offenders? Eden turns his back on Melanctha's cold comfort and she, to *up the ante* (is that the right phrase? no matter: the *sound* is right), turns away as well though in her case (which could also be his) it's to wonder disingenuously how anyone could ever imagine quiet slumbers for the unquiet sleepers in this blood-drenched popcorn-scented earth. But fake wonderment can't dull the pain of recognizing she's yet again taken a belated stab at motherhood and yet again hasn't drawn the fresh blood all vampires, that is, all mothers, crave. Luckily Melanctha can count on that would-be tyke, the Master, for a diverting tantrum or two. Victims and predators alike emerge from a record-breakingly brief diapause. A crowd forms and the cemetery, quick to recognize when a little pomp and circumstance is in order, does its part by taking a stab (that phrase again!) at impersonating Central Park, say, over Memorial Day weekend. But there's no need for the Park's willows to weep since, contrary to popular belief, diapause and even what follows immediately after is an active—a dynamic— in its own way an obscenely joyous—state. But what if she's asked—any second now, judging from the way the crowd is making its thirst for novelty noisily known—when and where it was that He—Doctor Livingstone, they presume—first encountered that rarest of rare birds, the thought packet, in its native habitat. Well, as mediator, muse and voice box pro tem she'll have to be the one to respond. She can't have Him piss away His prospects for celebrity through some mock-portentous (albeit undeniably sonorous) invocation on the order of, say, *Funny you should ask. It was at Mégara, suburb of Carthage, in the gardens of Hamilcar.* Will He mutter something about having spotted them from the foredeck—or was it the forecastle—of His very own schooner? No? Then she may have to, in the name of local color or boating lore or both. As she prepares to make her entrance, which is to be in the plaintive minor key of fine distinctions (the hard part, boys and girls, is not so much spotting the hardiest specimens as having to leave behind the unqualified, etc.), it's already too late: These *authentic* tykes (not a single would-be in the pack) are after bigger game. Though one of them does have the belligerent decency to take a deep breath and ask, "Unqualified for what?" Melanctha struggles to explain, that is, she exaggerates the difficulty of explaining in order to sell him—them—on the issue's sexy complexity which would make it a firm contender for Next Big Thinghood. Another belligerent, even more decent, shouts, so that all of Central Park can hear, "Unqualified to inflict on storylines the resistance—the Secondness—that they need to confront in order to hone their craft (*ugh!*)—inoculate it (*better*)—against the virus of facility. Stupid." The studied pause before *Stupid*, promoted to complete sentence, and all this in a single bound! was a stroke of . . . decency, Melanctha thinks, belligerently.

Clearly nothing left for Borkman, Jr., to do (the Feds are sure taking their time but he understands why: The Rump's unisex jackals are no doubt going at them again)—nothing to do but call it a day, but only on his own terms, by taking out every last remaining greed queen. Thereby *putting the world back on its path to humanization* (Eden isn't the only one who, armed with the right phrase, knows how to douse himself silly). But is he strong enough? let the Feds decide! The members of the Greenwich Avenue tribe—including his father (who, unforgiveably, doesn't risk a backward glance, but isn't that so very much the way of the world where fathers, and not just the worst of the lot, are concerned?)—have just entered what's billed as the Last Tram from Gun Hill so they at least won't go on getting caught in the crossfire which has a bad habit of *lingering*, albeit overwhelmingly in the grisly shapelessness of false alarms. But first, Maestro, Melanctha intones (it's the first time she's ever taken the liberty of calling him Maestro, or is it?: looks like her forbearance in the face of his recoil has freed them both, with even a little elbow room left over for, of all things, levity)—first, Maestro, one last, commemorative circular panning shot, if you please—a shot which makes it clear—legible—that persons lucky enough to be tasked with destroying every last trace of this phony putter's phony stopover paradise will have their work cut out for them. And then some.

Margo of all people emerges from behind a tree very much alive. Anybody who thinks otherwise has been misinformed. Two—no, three—violent deaths in the family are atonement enough for a lifetime's crimes against humanity and she, a widow twice over, shouldn't have to add the voice of her own corpse to the chorus. Margo and Melanctha recognize each other at once—not in what they take to be their essence (they mustn't be greedy) but as generic *survivors*. All of their (rightly or wrongly) most cherished features—flaws especially—have gotten subsumed and smothered by this new identity whose bloom—at least as far as Melanctha's concerned—is fading pretty fast but nowhere near fast enough. She looks Melanctha up and down with resentment as if she were not only blocking the view but eating up all available space set aside, in accordance with the cemetery's map of its spirit world, for meditation. As she advances for a better view—a catbird view—of the unmissable ocean Jim, Jr., follows closely—filially—behind. Even when he steps in front of her she doesn't recognize—doesn't see him. With a nudge or two from the Master Melanctha suspects—deduces—that she needs him to be invisible in order to go on feeling undistractedly responsible for the hopelessness of his plight and to *run interference* (is that the right expression? probably not or rather not quite), also undistractedly, for an apocalypse that must usher in a radical change in his fortunes. (But if the expression's not quite right then that's all to the good—for she's forced thereby to stretch the meaning of her thought—to get more than she bargained for in the packet department [soon-to-be famous last words of that unsinkable Lady from Forest Hills: *Again with the packets!*]. In short she needs to listen with the third and fourth ears to what the packet—any packet—can become not to what it is—or what she thinks it is or needs to be to get her over the finish line as a truth teller of the first rank. In short she mustn't turn up her nose at the crazy ways of wordflow.) Margo needs him to be invisible so she can keep the home fires uninterruptedly burning—home fires of guilt (and rage at the guilt) for his not having achieved celebrity status among the Siliconistas. So what if celebrity status is exactly what he's very much reaping? In fact, the offers keep pouring in uncensored from every quarter. Why, even the pettiest details of his notoriety are already drowning out media coverage of the ever more urgent cries for Borkman, Jr.'s execution.

Margo is again prey to the old queasiness, over not missing The Rump quite as much as she should, that is, if she's as serious as she claims about laying bare the workings of what's ruining life for her and, more to the point, for the injured being who matters most, though there's no telltale suppuration of a wound. In fact Jim the Junior seems to be doing just fine—appears to be flourishing high on the hog among the Siliconistas—gets touted half-hourly by press agents far and wide (after having managed against all odds to inter-view that med school dropout-cum-unicorn-cum-ultrasonic toilet) as the next Elon Von X or Sheryl Di Sugarberg or Aga McKhan. By any chance, is she foolish enough to think that one of the perks accruing from *going generic* is to no longer need (all the shooting and stabbing and beheading and improper advances having put her routine on hold) to resume self-treatment for Con-spiracy Disease, which consists in doing all she can to keep the fiction of con-spiracy going full speed ahead (if it plays its cards right CD could turn out to be the new ED: they're birds of prey and of a feather). Doesn't she know by now that without the conspiracy there's—she's—nothing. So Rump-feverish or not, it's back to work, work being to propel—belch—her worst—her most decrepit endlessly recyclable—fears and envies into what some yeomanly astronomer christened the Pseudosphere (just a silly old carbon sink whose time has come). And from there it's but a hop, skip and a jump to getting them . . . housed. Here's how it works, that is, here's how *It* works its magic. Some unsuspecting news item—one of billions stumbled on ostensibly by chance through her scrolled-down perusal of the sky—that is, Margo's kind of sky—Margo's particular brand of sky—news of the latest geopolitical slop heap atrocity, say, gets itself inscribed athwart (uh-huh, *athwart*) the fabric of that sky for clearance, review and contortion—contortion into yet another mirror image of injustice perpetrated against her and her Get (yep, her *Get*)—and, more to the point, against the venerable white-shoe firm of Margo Dombey & Son and to that item her otherwise unlivable torment (the stew of fears and envies) can be tethered—yoked—shackled (in a patented dynamic that's never so pitiless as to refuse to eject here and there a crazy ray of catharsis). An image of injustice teeming with culprits which, once they've been chewed up by the buzzards of motherly obsessionalism qua ressentiment, fade with-out apology or explanation to make way for the next infestation of crotchets, the next asteroidal tramload of stalking horses, the next batch of McGuffins, the next crop of *lucksters* (a term new to the OED so as a stranger give it welcome—or face the consequences), against and before which her inadequa-cies, real and imagined, can grumble and grovel, without getting caught in the toils of nuance—the toils of extenuation, both of Margo's own crimes and of the crimes of the maniacs responsible for her dissolution, whose modus operandi must remain forever unknowable out of respect for the . . . victims. What counts for Margo—for the Margos of the world—is to swoop down on news item detritus—news on the Rialto detritus—that, through its very resistance—its very irrelevance—the very absence of a clear-cut homology between it and the case at hand (the shadow docket case of Margo & Son) can be bulldozed into mirroring, to a T and with all the trappings of a per-fect one-to-one correspondence, the duo's unfixable plight and by extension into clearing a path, whether from benevolence or from demonism (since this mirror is a living being), toward impalement of the YouTube-style Influencer-cum-Mabuse responsible for the chaos of the moment churning inside her. Margo's genius (*Again with the genius*, snarls the Man from Shropshire [but in an undertone through very gritted teeth, hence there's no exclamation point to follow the italics]) resides, inter alia, in making anything and everything grist-for-the-mill relevant and like the Light that exists in Spring anything and everything always . . . passes and she stays (though Margo even in her madness must concede that this Light in Spring, Amherst Emily's choicest emblem, deserves far better than to be invoked—i.e., desecrated—in such a context). Ah, thinks Melanctha, or is it Cantor?, How incomparable the view from these heights of Margo's little world of sky—her unhumble slice of cloudlessness—this griping, blame-gaming, self-abasing view unimpeded and uncluttered by messily unpicturesque staffage—by the teeming womb of things, like a sober gimmick-free shouldering of personal responsibility, for starters and for example, and nobody's-fault bad luck, not to mention the mischief perpetrated by epigenetics and environmental static. As far as a stickler like Cantor is concerned, Margo's sky for all seasons far outshines the phone booth and the ultrasonic toilet and JGB's ankle bracelet and every last scrap of Dildo Alley state-of-the-art bric-a-brac. Clearly, nothing can stale the infinite variety of everything that's gone wrong and shouldn't have for her and her get, as refracted through the contrastive image of the lot of the slaplucky few—those enviable for . . . being envied. Cantor gawks reverentially at the *good taste* (while simultaneously chuckling at this mock-maidenly phrase from nowhere since like any good Democrat he knows how to walk *and* chew gum) and the delicacy evidenced in Bloody Mama's signature placement of her scapegoat culprits and sanguinary strongman saviors athwart the unholy fabric and by the light of the slivery [sic] moon to boot (*Again with the athwart!* snorts you-know-who [herself no slouch in the BloodyMama-ing department]). As for the way she's contrived to marry her guilt-driven rage to so many accommodating proxies (even—especially—those most starkly innocent of all responsibility for the plight of the Dombsday duo end up looking plausibly vile enough to merit a punishment far more capital even than that meted out to regicides in the merry France of yore)—well, the marrying's an impalpable hit and way beyond praise but don't just take Cantor's word for it. Margo snorts at the Man in the (slivery) Moon (whom she confuses with her two consorts). Not quite painfully aware of what it is to sup full—even exclusively—with horrors—horrors not to be dispelled with either the wobbly wand of wokism or a swift stroke of the racist's riding crop—Melanctha is eminently equipped to catch, from the timbre of said unmaidenly snort, the gist of what Margo's about to say to herself, to wit: She should have ended up like one of those model parents who, after mock-warily adjudicating (as all doting parents sooner or later must) the matter of competence as measured by outcome, have no choice but to plead (with the requisite show of fake self-belittlement and skepticism) . . . Perfection, Your Honor, of the life *and* of the work. And if she didn't so end up then it's the fault of It, the whole It and nothing but the It. Compassion's in the air (Margo imbibes its stench) and—wanna know something?—she doesn't want it (even if it's diluted compassion—compassion lite—i.e., fifty-five percent curiosity and sixty-five percent schadenfreude) since compassion makes her plight real and she refuses to give up on finding the right bystander to help her to do away with it—to render that plight unreal (whatever its provenance)—uncouple herself from sole responsibility for the fall of the House of Straynge—the right bystander to deem her plight a figment while at the same time putting an ultra-protective gloss upon it, since what fashion statement is left her to make if she can't wear said plight, duly bemoaned, at a rakish angle to all the trendiest galas county-wide where self-adulatory breast-beating is King?—since what other way, besides walking the fine line between conspiratorializing and double suicide, is there of staying fit as a fiddle? Only Margo's simply not to be depended on to determine who's the right bystander to take up her cause—to prove the big C is behind everything and nothing and that she's guilty concomitantly of everything and nothing—the bystander she professes to crave. You see, she's more than a shrike—she's a leaf—the leaf generic in fact—too intrigued by the erotomania of its own shadow to heed the hectoring wind. *No further than sheer immovability will I go*, proclaims her overarched back, *and you can't make me*. Cantor and Melanctha, come to think of it, might very well be the ideal bystanders she claims to be looking for—heaven-sent advocates— instruments of *uncouplement* (right: *uncouplement*—coming soon to a dual-language dictionary near you)—uncouplement from plight—from self as plight—from plight as self. The sole bystanders able to do much more than just take up her cause—prove the obvious—the sole take-up-the-cudgeloids endowed with a pigheaded—a mammoth—resistance to buying what she's trying to sell—pigheaded and mammoth enough to exalt their ultimate conversion, when its time has come (for it *will* come), to the truth—a resistance extreme enough to be able to exalt conversion into a surefire harbinger—the acrid foretaste—of nothing less than universal surrender to that truth—the truth-cum-falsehood of Conspiracy egged on by its horde of Weimar Influencers and the truth of her innocence of all wrongdoing as the purest calculation—with surrender triggering in its turn the emergence of a brave new custom-made fully subsidized richly deserved Life of Riley for J3 & Co. Even if, as already noted, Jim Junior (too many juniors ruling the roost in this neck of the woods, if you ask the Lady from Shropshire) is doing just fine. Fact is, Margo *has* given some thought to the possibility of conferring the status of at least *Associate* Bystandership on these two misfits yet remains lukewarm. But, better yet, what about that guy Melanctha's always talking to without ever saying a word—the one she breezily refers to (when she thinks nobody's around or is it rather when she knows *everybody is*) as the Master?

But the virus of survivorship is catching in these parts and low and behold, here (bid for mummification rejected at every turn) is Pritchard looking fit as a fiddle, albeit no Stradivarius. To Melanctha, it's further proof, if any were needed, of the Master's inability to bow out gracefully. She's reminded—or rather Cantor's reminded—of that favorite professor who, very much retired and with more than enough deliberative gray hair clogging his right ear canal to prove it, can be found (should your taste run to such diversions) wandering the corridors of Mathematics Hall at any hour of the day or night for all the world as if his course load were loftier than ever. Which prompted one of the security guards to deliver the following scene-stealing remark: *He thinks he still works here.* And the fact that Cantor is intrigued not so much by the remark itself as by the fact that *it keeps remembering him* forebodes (he inkles) surrender, when his time comes, to the same delusion.

There have been or are about to be enormous changes or so the Master wants Melanctha, his harshest critic, to suspect. For all the Master's fake dread at being pursued by the lumpen—having them snapping at his rear end—he'd like nothing better than to hear the following musical exchange on every cemetery streetcorner: "There he is." "Who?" "That guy. You know, the *Thought Packet* guy." "Then what are we waiting for: let's go get 'im."—would like nothing better than to be turned into a fugitive from a chain gang, martyred to his making, and not just any old chain gang but one that numbers among its luminaries the likes of cognate Paul Muni in his prime. For one thing, a beggar has set up shop adjacent to the tramway. He's arm-wrestling with an accordion too mock-shabby to be anything but a prop—it's Ayn the Ryan!— while what looks like Lindsey, sidekick and attack mutt, does a passable soft-shoe imitation of Tiny Tim (thing is, he's way too tiny for the part) or rather of Scrooge imitating Tiny Tim imitating the jolly prize Turkey that bipolar Scrooge selected to atone, on Christmas Day, for heinous bygones (and that the Day was a smashing success only goes to show Sir Lionel Trilling, a reluctant participant in the festivities, was dead right when he concluded post-turkey: "[A]rt does not always tell the truth or the best kind of truth.").

Pritchard wants to sit back and enjoy the show, the show being Margo taking counsel of the stars—no, of the sky, awash in news. But just when he's about ready to assess and annotate her progress, if any, on the mental health front who should be obstructing his view but that prototype of all unavowable chips off the old block, Jim, Jr., and who should be choosing the same moment to obtrude a theatrically extended wide-open palm on a grieving dad's attention but Mr. Petri Dish himself. "Can't you see I'm trying to have a conversation with my son?" He snarls at this lame excuse for a beggar, whom he hasn't officially recognized, or recognized as such, for who's to say where Ayn ends and beggarhood begins—snarls a little like Margo when she's having a bay at the Man in the Moon. "I have nothing," he adds, ashamed of his inability to look Ayn's well-scrubbed palm in the eye. Pritchard after all has very high standards when it comes to choosing the targets of his charity. But as Petri's accepted the initial rejection without palpable rancor he immediately warrants a second audition. Same dynamic at play here, Pritchard thinks, as in the doomed entanglements of young manhood, when a female's rancor-free acceptance of my recoil became the signal to return and (effortlessly, meaninglessly but by no means pleasurelessly) conquer cunt and understandable incredulity. But before they can proceed to round two Pritchard gets distracted by Junior's bellowing. Why now? After all, rumor has it—and rumor never lies—that he's the Toast (buttered) of the Santa Barbarians. But whatever its motivation, the bellowing, undeniably expert, indisputably heart-rending, has soured Pritchard on Ayn (who's now landed an archetypal role he doesn't deserve, that of Massacred Innocent Bystander). In fact, Pritchard would like to go straight up to him and say: "If I'd only known *then* what I know *now*, i.e., that you're capable of looking as unbeggarly—as downright dashing—as you do at this very moment, I'd never have engaged in such a profitless battle with myself over whether to lay a dollar bill or two at your less-than-leprous feet." Impervious by vocation to the ambivalence—worse, the inscrutability—of dupes (the sign of a great beggar—a beggar of genius!) Ayn explains that he's not just standing around twiddling the thumbs of his instrument: He's busy *reinventing himself*. (Only an Ayn would stoop to trotting out this pompous cliché with the fanfare it shamelessly demands. But for all the fanfare Pritchard is soothed by the thought that the day's not too far off when he'll be decried, in the annals of that no-man's-land where forensics and virology reluctantly intersect, as the very model of a modern major *variant of concern/mutation of interest*, eminently suitable for recruitment at a moment's notice as a proxy—a dummy variable—in genome sequencing of any old pandemic under the sun.) He's hard at work figuring out how the poor think. And what better way to get the ball rolling than by donning their rags. Those lazybones must be themselves feeling pretty reinvented—pretty *entitled* (now that the tiki thugs and the Forever Rumpers are being made to go the way of all tchotchkes and *kitschkes* [a feeble coinage which has yet to create a sensation] of the sorriest vintage)—entitled, that is, to all sorts of . . . unmerited subventions and reparations. But not on his watch, they won't. "Won't *what?*" asks Pritchard, absenting himself from inscrutability awhile. With a sigh worthy of a bobby-soxer, a cheerleader and a prom queen all rolled into one, Melanctha discreetly thinks (but loud enough for all to hear), *That's the mark of the Master I used to know. That's the mentor and favorite pupil I used to revere unstintingly. Who else but He could pummel imminent death-by-dysgrammar (His own) into a pretext for high drama: one character's belittlement by another while the Culprit gets applauded for skulking off without a thought to undoing the solecism.*

But it's hard for anybody who can't lay claim to a heart of stone not to be distracted by the touching study in contrasts presented by Eden and Borkman, Jr., who are in search of a better view of the second-generation carnage below. Never one to practice strong silent stoicism when self-advertisement is up for grabs, Borkman, Jr., is effervescing with all the arrogance that only brainy youth can muster: The culprits have indeed surrendered and as far as the Feds are concerned, they're both heroes. As for Eden, he looks as if he'd heard this ditty many times over but was still unable to transcribe it to the key of rapture (appropriate to a well-deserved if tardy vindication). According to Borkman, Jr.'s, newfound champion Special Agent Orange whose purview is the cemetery, the waterfront beneath and environs, the tiki scum won't, thanks to the two of them, be replacing anybody any time soon and this being very much the case, he and Eden are entitled to a full pardon. Oh, of course there'll be the usual interim sops to the *MAGA Carcass-cum-Caucus* (nota bene: Agent O's wicked way with words notwithstanding, he's a man of hefty principle who never allows the exhilaration of righteous rage to curdle into self-congratulation)—mere tap-on-the-wrist-style formalities (house arrest with a dash of home schooling, denial of parole, registration as a sex offender, that sort of thing). Jim, Jr., too, must have overheard Borkman, Jr.'s letter to the world many times over since (while slowly infiltrating the precincts of the not quite infamous beach chair) he nods knowingly in time to its music. Dimly, Pritchard now understands it's this letter that triggered the bellowing. As for Margo, the fact that she's also gotten Borkman, Jr.'s gist will enable her to put her son's tirade, when it comes, immediately into context. Even with her back to him, he hopes she can read the matricidal glint in his blue eye (the other one's green). She's been so used to treating him like a lost cause—boring the world with her self-exalting guilt—that it never occurred to her to help him achieve his dream. He interrupts himself long enough to seek out Pritchard and impale him on an apoplectic nod meant to mean, "I'll get to *you* in a minute, faggot." Meanwhile back at the beach chair Clytemnestra is steeling herself against the next installment of her get's onslaught which when it comes goes something like this: Not until this minute did he realize that all he ever really wanted to do, even way back in his Sutton Place days, was to go after and annihilate very fine tiki creeps and thugs, the finer the better. But through all sorts of little signs and ploys that spoke daggers she severed him from his dream and Pritchard—oops, he means Jim, Sr.—just stood idly by dreaming up new ways to impress the incurables with his non-existent expertise since being treated by Pritchard—oops again! he means that other guy—is—was—a one-way ticket to incurability. You mean, thinks Pritchard, *just stood idly by plotting his next economy class junket to Stearns Wharf.* Never has he felt so much a father as at this moment because as a father who failed he's *real,* as real as that psychopath from Balboa Park would like to be.

Pritchard's forgotten all about Ayn and now feels duty bound to beg his pardon, if only from afar, for skedaddling but, fact is, he's got an urgent family matter to contend with. He nods in the direction of what is, hands down, suddenly his favorite Anthropocene relic, namely, the beach chair. He moves— rather, *proceeds to move*—gingerly, neutrally, warily, toward the boy and *makes a mental note* (yet another last refuge of scoundrels) to congratulate himself for his interventionist's savvy and almost balletic aplomb (but how can he not be wary given that junior's unable to distinguish between his adoptive and his biological father [the surest test of any growing boy's aptitude for untroubled manhood]?). Taking a well-earned deep breath, biological pop asks him why, now that he's riding high at last, he should be so willing to piss it all away. Jim, Jr., looks transiently flattered but doesn't know what Pritchard's referring to nor for that matter does Pritchard (what, after all, has Junior achieved that's not worth throwing away?) but what counts is that the question in itself—in its essence, independent of context—is sincere—is in fact a questioner-proof sincerity machine even if the questioner isn't—what counts is that the question succeeds *in the moment,* than which there's no sterner taskmaster. The boy switches back to hatred—he's convulsed—so convulsed as to be disoriented. To think that neither of them made any effort to encourage him to try his hand at annihilating tikis when there were all the signs of a native talent brewing—to think that it never crossed their bleary minds that he, too, like Borkman, Jr., and maybe even Eden, might be an anti-tiki Wunderkind. When he thinks about all that, well, he could—he could—that is, *he feels as if he could* (*Again with the* as if! grumbles the mighty Man from Shropshire, a man's man if ever there was one: no namby-pamby *as if*'s for the likes of him)—as if—as if—as if he could . . . well, as if he could kill them in their bed! Pritchard is amused—no, proud—of the boy's gift for improvisation, his faked groping for the right word—faked groping for the courage to utter the unspeakable when it's so ever ready on the tip of his tongue—faked groping for the courage to give shape to the unspeakable when it's in the realm of the unspeakable that he's most at home—most himself—when for him the unspeakable is the most un-strangest of bedfellows—when for him, like his idol (some might say his precursor) Eden, murder or at least the idea of murder is easy—easier lived—done—than said. Yet here he is hewing to the crypto-artistic obligation to keep the pot of phony scruples and resistances going at a full boil. All of which proves, thinks Cantor (who's always had a soft spot for such feints), that Junior would make a great ham, would be a shoo-in, say, for the role of Bruno in the re-remake of *Strangers on a Train*. Problem is, murmurs Melanctha to the third-generation carnage, his kind can only want what others want and only want it when it's the furthest thing from what they know they want —are doomed to want. It's no small sacrifice for Margo to renounce the Man in the Moon *forever* (or is this just Actors Studio sub-blustrionics?) but it's important to turn around and face him—face them both—her men—her expurgated version of McConnell and The Rump. What could be more important than such a showdown?

Didn't she encourage him (reading Cantor's mind or what she takes to be his accusatory expression or both) to go to acting school? *Even if all she ever does is bore them with her self-exalting sense of guilt*, wasn't she the one to plead with Junior to learn how to assemble ghost guns so he could scare off the tiki trash responsible for turning Sutton Place and the billions of genteel enclaves on Manhattan island just like it into a war zone? *Even if all she ever does is bore everybody with her self-exalting sense of guilt*. Junior: "But only as a hobby—something to do in my spare time—something to beef up my résumé!" Pritchard goes all-in protective and says, "Dear Mary—I mean Margo!—for the love of [g]od, for the boy's sake and your own, won't you stop now?" (He's taken quite a shine to Bruno Junior in the last few seconds and he doesn't want any rabid female ruffling the boy's artistic-temperamental feathers. In fact, the shine is so blinding that he's actually toying with the idea of grooming him for the successorship that was supposed to go to Cantor [who's shown himself in any number of ways to be woefully overqualified for the position]—actually toying with the notion of making the matter of his legacy as a trailblazer into, of all things, a family affair [so what if it starts out for Junior as an *entry-level* affair]—actually fondling the impossibility [which is growing more attractive by the minute]—of turning this sorcerer's apprentice—this energumen more sinned against than sinning—into a full-fledged heir to the family throne—a true . . . Pritchard, Jr.! Of course he'd have to learn the ropes, start at the bottom.)

A sudden gust of shrillness deferred. "Stop what?" she wants to know. "*Stop boring everybody with my self-exalting sense of guilt?*" It enrages Pritchard (though he'd prefer to think it saddens him) that she's never, among other deficits, mastered the muscular art of *refraining from playback*—playback of somebody's offensive epithet or slur in an effort to make it ring untrue—sound ever so ridiculous—not lacerating, just ridiculous—yet without seeming to be begging for the retraction that's precisely the feeble counterthrust's holy grail. (And by the way does she think it was easy for him to take the boy's nasty crack sitting down [in fact he stood tall—or did he?] even when—especially if—the molten core of the blitz was not the content of the slur per se, though that was vile enough, but the contour—the trajectory—of his monstrous leap into utterance?) She's never mastered the lonely truth that there's no such thing as a successful—an effective—playback of a verbal act of evisceration—a playback that actually manages to ring true as a demonstration—a celebration—of the target's indifference to the wound inflicted since it's always clear from the start that under such circumstances—the circumstances being nothing more than a silly little matter of soul murder—that under such circumstances selfhood's—being's—on hold until further notice—until the perpetrator is compelled to cough up the uncoughable—i.e., acknowledge that the depiction was so absurdly off base as to render the craved retraction nothing more than . . . an indispensable irrelevance—a momentously . . . mere formality—a concessional belly laugh among friends.

Melanctha tips her hat to the Master since He's kept his promise—enormous changes *have* been imposed, on the unsuspecting. For starters, He's just proved that it's never too late for a seventh-rate dinner theater storyteller manqué to overcome his morbid aversion to a happy ending even if the ending in question bears none of the usual scars—much less, the usual earmarks—of happiness and even if the proxy he's put in place to set the tired old wheels of fortune in motion isn't exactly a natural (in this case, for the superficially daunting role of late-blooming—and late-forgiving—patriarch).

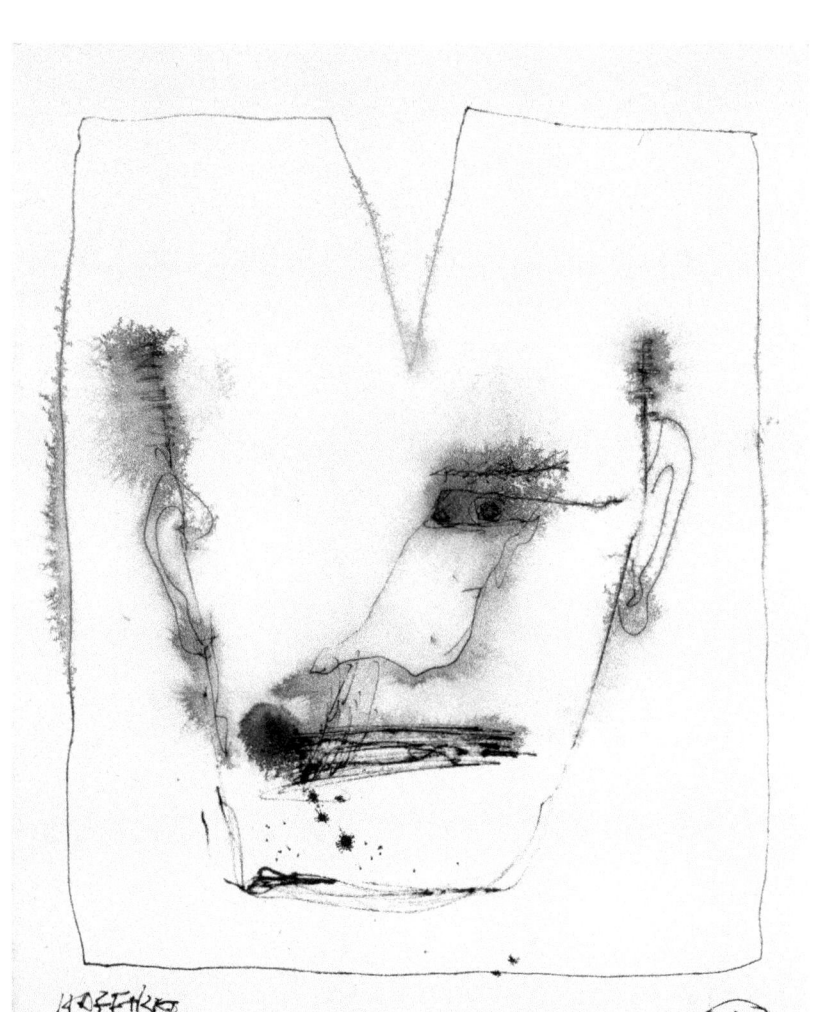

KOSSAKS

2023

MICHAEL BRODSKY

Michael Brodsky is the author of fourteen published works of fiction. They include the novels *Detour* (1977, revised 2003) for which he received the Ernest Hemingway Foundation Citation from PEN, *Circuits* (1985), *Xman* (1987), *Dyad* (1989) and *Lurianics* (2013) and the collections *Project and Other Short Pieces* (1982), *X in Paris* (1988), *Southernmost and Other Stories* (1996) and *Limit Point* (2007).

Born in New York on August 2, 1948, he graduated from Columbia College, Columbia University, in 1969 and went on to attend Case Western Reserve University School of Medicine in Cleveland for two years before leaving to devote himself to literature. Apart from some teaching, he has worked for most of his life as a technical editor.

A number of his plays, including *Terrible Sunlight* (1980), *Dose Center* (1990) and *Six Scenes: A Barracks Brawl* (1994), were performed in the heyday of off-off Broadway innovation.

He is currently writing another novel, *The Bull by the Horns*, whose focus is the perils and triumphs of an accidental whistleblower.

MICHAEL HAFFTKA

Michael Hafftka is an internationally acclaimed visual artist. His work is in the permanent collections of The Metropolitan Museum of Art, Museum of Modern Art, San Francisco Museum of Modern Art, The British Museum, Carnegie Museum of Art, Museum of Fine Arts Houston, the National Gallery of Art, and various other museums around the world.

Hafftka's artistic career began in the 1980s with shows in Soho and on Madison Avenue in New York City. Several museums exhibited his work, among them the Museum of Modern Art, The Housatonic Museum, Yeshiva University Museum, and Chapman University.

Hafftka's work has been written about extensively by the late art historian and curator Professor Sam Hunter (Princeton University), by the late John Caldwell (*New York Times* critic and SFMOMA curator), and by Michael Brodsky.

Hafftka joined the crypto art world in 2021 and has become a leading artist in that community. http://hafftka.art/

ACKNOWLEDGMENTS

I would like to express my immense gratitude to the writers Dick Kalich, Mark Kerstetter and George Salis* for their deeply valued friendship and unstinting support (with just the right dollop of salutary provocation) and for setting an enduring example through their noble commitment to literature.

Michael Brodsky

---

*Publisher's note: I, too, would like to extend my profound thanks to George Salis for bringing this novel to my attention and introducing me to its author. Without him, this publication would not have been possible. — Rick Schober

Milton Keynes UK
Ingram Content Group UK Ltd.
UKHW052238240324
439966UK00013B/798